Frederic Barlow

The Complete English Dictionary

General Repository of the English Language

Frederic Barlow

The Complete English Dictionary
General Repository of the English Language

ISBN/EAN: 9783741176036

Manufactured in Europe, USA, Canada, Australia, Japa

Cover: Foto ©Andreas Hilbeck / pixelio.de

Manufactured and distributed by brebook publishing software
(www.brebook.com)

Frederic Barlow

The Complete English Dictionary

THE

Complete English Dictionary:

OR,

GENERAL REPOSITORY

OF THE

ENGLISH LANGUAGE.

CONTAINING

A COPIOUS EXPLANATION

OF ALL THE

WORDS in the ENGLISH LANGUAGE;

TOGETHER WITH

Their different SIGNIFICATIONS, viz.

I. The WORDS, and the various Senfes in which they are ufed.
II. The TRUE PRONUNCIATION pointed out by being properly accented.
III. INITIAL LETTERS placed to denote the Part of Speech to which each Word belongs.
IV. A geographical DESCRIPTION of the four Quarters of the World.
V. A more particular DESCRIPTION of the Counties, Cities, and principal Towns in England and Wales,
than has ever appeared in any Book of this Kind.
VI. As the LIVES of the ENGLISH POETS, and others, celebrated for their Learning and Genius, can no where be introduced with more Propriety than in a DICTIONARY of the ENGLISH LANGUAGE, we have enriched our Performance with the moft entertaining and authentic Memoirs of thofe illuftrious Men who have flourifhed in thefe Kingdoms.

To which will be prefixed,

A COMPLETE ENGLISH GRAMMAR.

By the Rev. FREDERICK BARLOW, M. A.
Vicar of BURTON.

Affifted by feveral other GENTLEMEN.

LONDON:

Printed for the AUTHOR,

And Sold by T. EVANS, at No. 54, in Pater-nofter-Row; F. BLYTH, at the Royal Exchange; Mr. JACKSON at Oxford; Meff. FLETCHER and HODSON, at Cambridge; Mr. WILSON, at Dublin; Mr. ETHERINGTON, at York; and all other Bookfellers, &c. in Great Britain and Ireland.

To the P U B L I C.

PHILOLOGY, or the Definition of Words, is a Study as necessary to the Native as the Foreigner. It is for the Honour of this Nation, that this Branch of Learning is more cultivated at present in our own Island than in any other Part of the Globe. The Sanction which it has received from the greatest Geniuses among us, furnishes us at once with a Vindication and an Encouragement: But the Purchase of those voluminous Works, which have already been published on this Subject, is too expensive for those who stand in the greatest Need of Information in this Branch of Literature; and there is at present no other Alternative, than the Choice of a large Folio, which costs several Pounds, or a small Volume in Octavo, of the Value of only Six Shillings. As the former, therefore, is too prolix, and the latter too concise, being a mere Abridgement, we imagined that a Medium between the two Extremes would, at once, contribute to the Improvement and Oeconomy of the Purchasers.

The Work now proposed will contain not only every Article necessary for understanding our Language, but will likewise comprehend the Biography or Lives of the most celebrated Persons who have flourished in these Kingdoms; and, to render it still more instructive, will contain a general geographical Description of the four Quarters of the World, and a particular Account of the Counties, Cities, and principal Towns of England and Wales. Though concise, it will at the same Time be full; and though less than the Folios on the same Subject, it will be so copious as to contain double the Matter of an Octavo Dictionary in one Volume.

As an additional Improvement, we shall have Recourse to the Art of Designing, and embellish this Work with Copperplates, equally necessary and ornamental.

Burton, Feb. 1, 1772.   F. BARLOW.

. That every Person may have an Opportunity of judging of the Execution of this Work, the First Number may be perused gratis, and returned if not approved.

THE

SUBSCRIBERS NAMES.

A.

AICKEN, Mr. James, Drury-lane theatre.
Alston, Mr. Bristol
Anderson, John, Exeter-court, Strand.
Ditto,———— ditto—————, Mortimer street, Cavendish square.
Annet, Edward, Sunbury.
Ashby, Mr. Sawly, Derbyshire.

B.

Barker, William.
Ballamy, Samuel, Clapton.
Barlow, Mr. Loughbro.
Beauchamp, Mr. Westminster.
Picket, Tho. Liverpool.
Bell, William.
Benson, J. Esq; Pontefract.
Bentley, John, Soho, near Birmingham.
Birchall, Mr. Robert, London.
Bishop, Mr. Samuel, Cursitor-street.
Blackwall, Mr. James, Windmill-street.
Bone, Mr. Henry, Bristol.
Booth, Mr. Smalley, Denbighshire.
Bowden, Richard, ditto.
Boys, Mr. Dorset.
Booth, Jesse, Lombard-Street.
Baintnal, Rev. Mr. Docfield, Derbyshire.
Brown, Mr. Bookseller, Ashborne, ditto.
Brown, C. master of the academy in Charles-street, Hatton-Garden.
Bullock, Mr. John, Brewer-street.
Burnet, James Luke, Staffordshire.
Burges, William, Nottingham.

C.

Charlett, Arthur, Esq.
Clark, Mr. Castlecary, Somersetshire.
Clark, Mrs. Ann Butler, Shepton Mallet, ditto.
————, Mr. J. A. Idol-lane.
————, William Jacob-street.
Clarkson, Mr. Mungo, Newport, Isle of Wight.
Clementson, Edward, Melton Mowbray, Licester.
Clifford, Mr. Pontefract.
Cook, Mr. schoolmaster, North-Cadbury, Somersetshire.
Cooke --- James, Birmingham.
Comly, Mr. Timothy.
Copeland, Bond, Norwich.
Cox, Mr. Daventry, Northamptonshire.
Cox, Mr. James, Wrington, Somersetshire.
Craven, Mr. George, Soho near Birmingham.
Crocker, Mr. A. schoolmaster, Ilminster, Somersetshire.
Crofts, Mr. Holbrook, Derbyshire.

D.

Davis, Mr. Langport, Somersetshire.

Daw

SUBSCRIBERS NAMES.

Dawglafs, Mr. Jofeph.
Dauglas, — John, Whitby, Yorkfhire.
Dunkly, Mr. Whilton, Northamptonfhire.

E.

Early, Mr. Thomas, Piccadilly.
Edwards, Mr. Barrow, Somerfetfhire.
Ellmore, ———, Fundenhall.
—— Everfhat, Dorfet.
Exom, Mr. Hathom.
Everard, ———, Gemmingham.

F.

Faillant, Mr. Peter.
Fairn, Mr. James.
Fenn, John, Efq; Drury-lane.
Fifher, Mr. Thomas, Cheapfide.
Flinders, John, Ilkefton.
Ford, --- So.
Fritchly, Mr.
Fry, Mr. North Cadbury, Somerfetfhire.
Fulcher, Mofes, Norwich.

G.

Galpin, Mr. Somerton, Somerfetfhire.
Gifford, Mr. James, Ruffel-court.
Gilborne, Winton Francis, Nottingham.
Gill, Mr. Chard, Somerfetfhire.
Gillbam, Mr. James, Walfal, Staffordfhire.
Godwin, Mr. Thomas.
Goff, ———, Norwich.
Goldhawk, Mr. John, Shipperton.
Gregfon, Mr. Chriftopher, Apothecary's-hall.
Griffiths, Mr. Lambeth.

H.

Hammond, Mr. School-mafter, Hofington, Somerfetfhire.
——Afbby, Northamptonfhire.
Hanvard, Luke, Norwich.
Harcourt, Edward, ditto.
Hard, William, Nottingham.
Harrifon, Mr. Lea Lane, Derbyfhire.
Harvey, Mr. Richard, ditto.
Harvey, Anthony, Bafsford.
Hawkins, Henry, Long-acre.
Hayes, Mr. Diegeworth.
Heardner, Mr. School-mafter, Mayfield, Suffex.
Heath, Mr. Job, White-crofs-ftreet.
Hill, --- Ifaac, Brewton, Somerfetfhire.
—— Thomas, Chandois-ftreet.
Hind, Mr. Thomas, David-ftreet, Berkley-fquare.
Hogben, ---Henry, Dodington, Kent.
Hullam, Mr. Doefield, Derbyfhire.
Houfon, ———, Norwich.

Hutchin

Houchin, John, Saxtingham.
Hutton, Samuel, Nottingham.

J.

Jeffry, Mr. Wells, Somersetshire.
Johnson, Mr. Alexander, Drury-lane Theatre.
Jones, Rev. Mr. Little Baddow, Essex.
———— Mr. William, Inner Temple.
Jukes, --- Tho. Soho, near Birmingham.

K.

Kates, Mr. Shepton-mallet, Somersetshire.

L.

Lavers, W. F.
Landeg, David, Esq;
Lees, James, Serjeant, Westminster.
Leggett, Mr. Abraham, Shipperton.
Lima, Mr. Manoel, London.

M.

Mackay, John, Serjeant, Exeter-court Strand.
Mc. Grigor, Alexander, Serjeant, ditto.
Mann, Mr. John.
Mariott; --- William, Olney, Buckingham.
Mather, ————, Soho, near Birmingham.
Metcalf, Mr.
Milligan, Mr. William.
Mitchell, Mr. Pool, Dorset.
Moore, Mr. John, Wells, Somersetshire.
Morice, John, A. M. Cheshunt, Herts.

N.

Nott, Mr. Randolph.

O.

Oldfield, Tho. Hinton, Burley, Guildford.
Osborne, Mr. Thomas, Denbigh.
Otway,————-Richard, Shipperton.
Overbury, ————, Bristol.

P.

Parish, Mr. William.
Parker, ——— John, gent. Roll's Buildings.
Partridge, Mr. Bristol.
Payne, Mr. Robert.
Peacock, ——— John Luke, Staffordshire.
Pease, Mr. Pontefract.
Penchard, ——— Geo. Sturminster, Menshall, Dorset.
Pidding, Mr. Daniel, Bristol.
Pitcher, Robert, Norwich.
Polglass, J. Esq; Hothfield.
Podmore, Thomas, Nottingham.
Pons, Mr. Theophilus, teacher of the French and English Languages,
   Rue St. Honore, au Roi. d'Espagne a Paris; 2 Copies.
Portch. Mr. William.

Proctor, ———, Norwich.

Q.

Quincey, Francis, Holt.

R.

Raives, Mr. jun. Sherbone, Dorset.
Readman, John, M. D.
Robinson, Mr. Edward, Daventry, Northamptonshire.
Routh, Mr. John, School-master, Whitby, Yorkshire.

S.

Salkeld, Mr. George, St. Pauls Church yard.
Saunders, ——— William, Shipperton.
Savery, John, Esq; Medbury, Devonshire.
Seniour, Mr. D. Sittingbourn.
Smith, Captain George, Acad. reg. Woolwich, inspector.
Smith, ———, Beccles.
Smith, Mr. Robert, Shipperton.
———, Thomas, Cleft Lewes.
———, Painter, at Derby.
———, Farrier, — ditto.
Smout, Mr. George.
Strickland, Mr. Thomas, Soho, near Birmingham.
Sutton, Mr. Bristol.
Swift, Mr. John, Great Queen-street, Lincoln's Inn-Fields.

T.

Tapp, William, Serjeant, Westminster.
Tappin, Mr. James.
Timms, Atkin, Nottingham.
Tirtchly, Mr. Shattle, Derbyshire.
Thompson, — William, Daventry, Northampton.
Thrall, Mr. Thomas, Long-Acre.
Turner, Mr. Godfrey, Breadsal, Derbyshire.
Tyson, --- Henry, Soho near Birmingham.

W.

Wainer, Mr. Loughborough, Leicestershire.
Walker, Rev. Mr. Bristol.
Waller, Mr. John.
Wansey, ---, Bristol.
Watson, Rev. Mr. Horsington, Somersetshire.
Weatherhead, Mr. Thomas.
Weston, Mr. Nathaniel, Bedford,
Williams, Mr. Daniel, St. Thomas, Southwark.
———, Serjeant, Westminster.
Williamson, Mr. Richard, Long-Acre.
Wild, Mr. John, Reading, Berks; 2 Books.
Wilson, --- Thomas, Gent. Temple.
Woollam, Mr. Gerrard-street, Soho.
Wootton, James, Esq; Long-lane, Southwark.
Wright, Mr. George, Sunbury.
Wyatt, Mr. Charles, Soho, near Birmingham.

Y.

A NEW AND CONCISE

GRAMMAR

ENGLISH TONGUE.

GRAMMAR is the art of rightly expressing our thoughts by words. It is divided into *particular* and *universal*, or *general grammar*. *General grammar*, explains the principles which are common to all languages. *Particular grammar*, implies those common principles to any particular language according to its established use and custom. *Grammar*, therefore, treats of sentences and the several parts of which they are compounded. Sentences consist of words, words of one or more syllables, syllables of one or more letters; and these compose the whole subject of grammar.

Grammar is properly divided into four parts; 1st, That which treats of letters called *orthography*, when confined to writing; and *orthoepy*, when applied to speech. 2dly, That part which relates to syllables, is called *prosody*. 3dly, That part which relates to words, their kinds, derivations, endings, changes, analogy; and is called *etymology*: and 4thly, That which treats of the right placing or joining of words together in a sentence, which is called *syntax*. A letter is the first principle, or least part of a word.

In English, there are twenty six letters, as

A, a; B, b; C, c; D, d; E, e; F, f; G, g; H, h; I, i; J, j; K, k; L, l; M, m; N, n; O, o; P, p; Q, q; R, r; S, s, s; T, t; U, u; V, v; W, w; X, x; Y, y; Z, z.

From the foregoing alphabet it appears, that among the small letters s has two forms, the long ſ being used in the beginning and middle of words, and the short s at the end.

The letters are divided into vowels, semivowels, consonants and diphthongs.

A vowel is a letter that may be sounded by itself.

A semivowel makes an imperfect sound by itself, such are l, m, n, r, s, ſ.

A consonant cannot be sounded without a vowel.

A diphthong is compounded of two vowels, pronounced with one impulse of the voice.

A triphthong is a sound composed of three vowels, as in *lieu*.

CHAP. I. Of the Vowels.

THE vowels are six, *viz.* a, e, i, o, u, y.

A, has three sounds; slender, open, and broad.

A *slender*, is found in most words, particularly in those which end with an *e* final, as in *face*, and in those which end in *tion*, as *gratior*.

A *open*, is used in *man*.

A *broad*, is pronounced as if followed by an *u*, or *w*, as in *all*, *fall*.

The *a* short approaches to the *a* open, as in *less*.

The *a* long, if followed by an *e* final, is always slender, as *cam*, *came*.

The *a* forms a diphthong only with *i* or *y*, and *u* or *w*, as in *gain*.

Au or *aw* has the sound of the German *a*, as in *claw*, *taught*.

B.

E, occurs more frequently in the English language than in any other.

Before a double confonant it is always fhort, as in *fell*, *dwell*.

At the end of words, it is generally mute, or not founded, unlefs in monofyllables that have no other vowel, as *the*, *me*; or in proper names, as in *Penelope*; or when ufed to foften the foregoing confonant, as in *fince*; or when it ferves to lengthen the preceding vowel, as *can*, lengthened into *cane*.

When the *e* comes before an *n*, or after an *r* or *l*, it has an obfcure found, as in *hearten*, *audible*, *maffacre*.

It forms a triphthong with *a* as in *near*; with *view*; and with *u*, as in *Heu*.

Before *a* it is generally founded like *e* long, as in *dean*; but in *great* it is dropped, and gives the *a* the fame found as in *grate*.

Ei is founded like *ee*, as in *deceive*.

Eu is founded like *u* long as in *Eulofia*.

E, a, u, are combined and founded like *u* long in *beauty*, and its derivatives.

Eo, is founded like *e* long in *people*; like *e* fhort in *leopard*; and like *o* fhort in *yeoman*.

I, is founded long before a confonant followed by an *e* final, as in *fire*; but is fhort in *fin*.

Before *r* or *u* it is generally fhort, as in *dirt*: it forms a diphthong only with *e*, as in *field*; but in *friend*, the *i* is dropped, and the found fhort. In the triphthongs it is founded like *u* open, as in *lieu*.

O, is long in words ending with an *e* mute, as in *bone*. It forms a diphthong with *a*, and has the found of *o* long, as in *moan*; as likewife with *e*, which is the only proper diphthong in the Englifh language, as in *foil*, *toil*; but in fome words it is mute, and ferves only to lengthen the found of the *i*, as in *foul*, pronounced *spile*; joined to another *o*, it forms a diphthong, as in *boot*. It forms a diphthong with *u* or *w*, as in *boar*, *power*; but it fome words has the found of *e* long; as in *foul*, *grow*; in *fow*, the verb, fignifying to fcatter feed, to diftinguifh it from *fow*, the fhe of a boar. *Ou* is likewife fometimes pronounced like *o* foft, as in *court*, and in *cough*; like *u* clofe, as in *could*; and like *u* open, as in *rough*, *tough*.

O, in the plural of *woman*, is pronounced like an *i* fhort, *women* being pronounced *wimen*.

O fhort, is founded like *u*, in *fon*, *tum*.

U, is long in the laft fyllable of words ending with an *e* mute, as in *ufe*, otherwife it is fhort, as in *but*, *cut*, *burft*. It is joined with *a, e, i, o*, but in fuch combinations has the force of *v* or *w*, as in *quaff*, *requeft*. Sometimes in *ui* the *i* lofes its found, as in *juice*; it is mute fometimes before *a; e, i*, and *y*, as in *buy*, *guard*, *gueft*, *guife*. In words that terminate with *ue*, the *u* is mute, as in *prorogue*,

Y, is borrowed from the Greek, and its name from the Saxons. As no English words end in *i*, when *i* would occur at the end of a word, it is ufed to fupply its place, as in *thy*; it is likewife ufed before an *i*, as *dying*. It forms a diphthong with *a, e, o*, and *u*, as in *may*, *they*, *deftroy*, *buy*.

CHAP. II.   Of the Confonants.

A Confonant is a letter that cannot be founded without adding a vowel before or after it, as *m*, which is founded *em* by prefixing a vowel before it; and *p* founded *pe*, by fubjoining a vowel after it.

The confonants are fubdivided into mutes, and femivowels.

A mute is a letter which makes no found without a vowel, fuch are *b, c, d, g, p, q, t*; all the other confonants are called femivowels.

A femivowel is a letter that makes an imperfect found without the addi-

tion

tion of a vowel, such are f, b, l, m, n, r, s, x, four of these are called liquids.

A liquid is a letter which loses part of its sound in another consonant joined with it, such are l, m, n, r.

B, has one varied sound, is used before all vowels, and before the consonants l and r, as in blaze, break. In the following words it is mute, debt, subtile, lamb, limb.

C, is sounded like s before e, i, and y, or before an apostrophe, denoting the absence of e, as in cement, city, cypher, grac'd for graced; but before a, o, u, l, or r, or at the ends of words, it is sounded hard like k, as in can, cost, cub, clash, crush, public. Joined to h, it has a like sound as sh, as in church; but in words derived from the Greek, it is sounded like k, as in chymist; but when arch is compounded with a word beginning with a consonant, it has the found of the English ch in church, as in arch-bishop. In words derived from the French, it is sounded like sh, as in machine.

D, has but one uniform sound, and is used before all the vowels, and the consonants r and w, as draw.

F, is pronounced before a liquid, as in flame, and has one unvariable sound, excepting that of is sometimes pronounced like ov.

G, has two sounds, that before a, o, u, being hard, as in game, but soft before e, i, y, or before an apostrophe, when it denotes the absence of e, as in gender, and judg'd for judged. At the end of a word it is always hard, as in dog. Its sound before e and i is sometimes hard, especially in words not derived from the Latin or French, as in give, get. For this reason it is soft in giant. In words ending with er it is hard, as in anger. When h is followed by u, or an h, at the beginning of a word, its sound is hard, as in guide, ghost, but when g is followed by h in the middle, and sometimes at the end of words, is silent; thus though it is pronounced tho'. Otherwise, it has the sound of f, as in tough.

H, is a note of aspiration, and shews, that the vowel following it must be pronounced with a strong emission of breath, as in hat, excepting in h it, herb, hostler, honour.

J. This consonant is sounded like a soft g.

K, has the sound of c hard, and where the c would be soft; as in kept, skirt, king; sceptic should likewise in English be written with a k, not a c, as skeptic.

L, is the same in English as in other languages. At the end of monosyllables it is doubled, as in kill, full; because these words were originally written killl, fall; but in compound words one of the l's is suppressed, as in skilful. In some words it is mute, as in calf.

M, has always the same sound.

N, has always the same invariable sound, and after m at the end of a word is mute; as in condemn.

P, has always the same sound; when followed by s, and between m and t, it is mute; as in damps, tempt.

When joined with h, in words derived from the Greek, it has the sound of f, as in philosophy, Philip.

Q, in English, as well as in other languages, is always followed by u, as in quarrel. But in words derived from the French, it retains the French sound, and is pronounced like k, as in conquer.

R, has the same rough snarling sound as in other languages. In words derived from the Greek, it is joined with h, especially in such as had the r affirmed, as in myrrh. Re, at the end of words derived from the Greek or French, is pronounced like er weak, as in theatre, metre.

S, has naturally a sharp hissing sound, as in fifter; when it ends a word,

it is founded like z y as in brr; unless in this, thus, us, yes; in those words
which are derived from the Latin, as surplus, and in adjectives which end in
us, and are derived from the French, as in gracious, religious; where we
should remark that the o is silent, those words being founded as if written
gracius, religius. S has the sound of s before sex, if a vowel goes before it,
as in infusion, but that of s sharp, if it follow a consonant; as in reversion.
Before a mute it has the sound of z, as in advise; before y at the end of
words, as in rosy, and in bosom. It is mute or not pronounced in isle, viscount.

T, is founded hard before a, e, i, o, u, and r, provided a vowel does not
follow i, in which case it has the sound of s, as in salvation; but when s
goes before it, it retains its hard sound, as in question. When joined with h,
it has two sounds, the one soft, as in all the pronouns, relative words and
conjunctions, in all words between two vowels, especially such as end is, ther,
as father, and between r and a vowel, as in further. In other words, it is
founded hard, as in the prepositions with, without, in the words think, thrive,
&c. and in the adjectives thick, thin. Where it is softened at the end of
a word, an e final should be added; as in breath, th is founded hard, but in
breathe, soft.

V, has a found much resembling an f soft; as in vain.

W, at the beginning of a syllable, resembles a v, as in water. It is used
before all the vowels except u. When w is used before the letter h, it is
really founded after it, as in when, which, what; which our Saxon ancestors even spelt in this manner, writing huen, huich: In where and wholesome, the w is silent.

X, begins no English word; but when used, has the sound of ks.

Y, is used as a consonant before a vowel or diphthong.

Z, begins no English word; when used it has the sound of s hard, as its
name expresses.

CHAP. III. Of Etymology.

ETYMOLOGY teaches the derivation of one word from another, and
the various modifications by which each word is diversified.

Words are either primitive or derivative. A primitive word is that which
is derived from no other in our language, as ball. A derivative is that which
comes from some other word in our language, as fisher, from fish.

Words are again divided into nine sorts, as Noun, Pronoun, Verb, Participle, Article, Adverb, Conjunction, Preposition, Interjection.

The first four, viz. noun, pronoun, verb, and participle, are declined;
but the last five, article, adverb, conjunction, preposition, and interjection,
are not declined.

Declension means the altering of the last syllable of a word.

An Article is a word placed before nouns, to shew and limit the extent of
their signification.

The English have but two articles, A and The, but an n is added to it before a vowel, excepting the y, w, and an h silent. A is used to point out
a single thing of the kind, in an indeterminate manner; but the determines
what particular thing is meant; thus, " this is a good book; i. e. one a-
mong the books that are good." Again, " this is the book; that is, this
particular book; from hence a is called the definite, and the the indefinite
article.

It it the nature of both the articles to limit or determine the thing spoken of. A determines it to a single thing of the kind; leaving it still uncertain which. The determines which it is, or of many, which they are.

A

A therefore can only be joined to substantives in the singular number; but *the* may be joined to plurals.

The definitive article *the* is sometimes used with adverbs of the comparative and superlative degree, to mark that degree the more strongly, as, " *the more* I examine it, *the more* I approve it." " I like this *the least* of any." In some few cases it is prefixed to the proper names of towns, ships, &c. as *the* Hague, *the* Britannia. *A* is used to express things not seen before, as, *a beggar is gone by*: this implies that we have not seen him before; but if he pass by the next day, we then say, " there goes *the* beggar," that is, the same we saw yesterday, or a beggar who was seen before.

The is used to express emphasis or excellence. When a substantive is without any article it is to be understood in its most unlimited sense; not one in general, or one in particular, but every individual that can be comprehended in the term, is to be understood; thus, " *man* is born to trouble;" that is, every one who partakes of the human nature, or all mankind.

A noun is a word made use of to convey the idea of any thing, or the quality belonging to it; and is therefore subdivided into substantive and adjective.

A noun substantive is the name of the thing itself, as a *man*.

A noun adjective is a word that expresses only the qualities or properties of a thing, as *good*.

Substantives are subdivided into proper, or common.

A noun substantive *common*, or appellative, is a word which stands for an universal, or a whole rank of beings of the same kind, as *man*, *bird*.

A noun substantive *proper*, is a word that is appropriated to some individual, and distinguishes it from others of the same kind; as *Anne*, is a name which belongs to a particular woman, and is used to distinguish her from others of the same sex or family.

[NUMBER. Substantives may likewise be considered as applied to one or more, which is called number, and distinguished into singular or plural.

The singular number is used when we speak but of *one* person or thing, as a *stick*.

The plural number is used when we speak of *more* than one person or thing, as *we, ye, they, boys, sticks*.

The plural number in English is generally formed by adding an *s* to the singular, as *stick* makes *sticks* in the plural. The plural number therefore has no more syllables than the singular; unless when the singular ends in *ce, ze, se*, or *ge*, and then it has a syllable more than the singular, thus *cage* makes *cages, maze* makes *mazes*.

When the singular ends in *ch, sh, ss*, or *x*, an *e* is put before the *s* in the plural, thus, *church, churches*, &c.

Words that end in *f* or *fe*, make the plural by changing *f* and *fe* into *ves*, thus, *calf, calves; wife, wives*.

But the following words *hoof, roof, grief*, &c. and generally speaking, words ending in *ff*, make the plural according to the general rule; f. i. by the addition of *s*; thus *muff* makes *muffs*, and *hoof* makes *hoofs*.

Nouns ending in *y* make their plural in *ies*, because they were formerly written with *ie* in the singular, thus, *frailty* makes *frailties* in the plural.

The following words form the plurals irregularly: *die, dice; mouse, mice; louse, lice; goose, geese; foot, feet; tooth, teeth; penny, pence; man, men*, and its compounds.

Some words form their plural in *en*, thus, *child* makes *children; ox, oxen; brother, brethren* and *brothers*. At present *brethren* is seldom used but by divines.

The following words are used in both numbers: *Sheep, hose, fish, deer, swine,* &c.

These words have no singular; as *ashes, bellows, bowels, breeches, entrails, lungs, scissars, shears, snuffers, tongs, thanks,* and *wages.*

These words have no plural number, viz. The proper names of *cities, towns, seas, rivers,* and *mountains*; the names of *virtues* and *vices*; specific names merely such; those of gold, silver, or copper; the names of herbs, excepting *nettle, poppy, lily, colewort, cabbage,* &c. 2dly, The names of several kinds of corn and pulse, as *wheat, rye, barley, darnel,* &c. except *bean,* which makes *beans;* and *pea; peas. Bread, wine, beer, ale, honey, oil, milk, butter,* want the plural: but when some of these stand for individuals, or several sorts, they then admit of a plural, as *wines, oils.*

A *specific name* is that which signifies a whole species or kind, and may be distinguished, both from its having no plural, and from its never being used in the singular with *a* before it; for we never say *a flesh, a gold.*

CHAP. IV. The English Nouns, with respect to Cases.

IN order to denote the different relations in which one word stands to another, the learned languages have made a change in their last syllables; but as we find no other change in English nouns, excepting in the genitive, we may say we have no other case; for excepting in the genitive, the respect which things bear to one another, is in our language expressed by means of certain words called prepositions, such are *of, to, for, from, with, by.*

In English the genitive is expressed by adding *'s* to the nominative; as "the *king's* prerogative; *Charles's* wain." When this would sound harshly, or that of the genitive of the singular and the plural is the same, it is best to express it by the preposition *of.*

The ablative is expressed in English by the preposition *with, from,* or *by;* as, "he cut him *with* a knife."

CHAP. V. Of Gender.

GENDER is the distinction of sex.

Sex is either male or female; inanimate things are *neuter,* and therefore said to be of the *neuter* gender.

The English have four ways of distinguishing the sex.

I. By different words. Batchelor, maid or virgin; boar, sow; boy, girl; brother, sister; king, queen; lad, lass; lord, lady; master, mistress, &c.

II. When both sexes are comprehended under one word, we add an adjective to the word to distinguish the sex. Thus the word *child,* being applied to both sexes, we add the words *male* or *female;* as a *male* child, a *female* child.

III. Sometimes we add another substantive to the word, as, a *man servant* for the *male* sex, a *maid servant* for the *female.* These words are applied only to rational creatures. To distinguish the sex of birds, we add the words *cock,* or *hen,* as a *cock sparrow,* a *hen sparrow.*

But the common words we make use of to distinguish the sex are *he* and *she;* when we speak of the *male* sex, we use the word *he,* as a *he bear;* when we speak of the female, we use *she,* as a *she bear;* but when we speak of a thing that is neither male or female, we use *it;* for example, speaking of *snow,* we do not say, *he,* or *she* melts, but *it* melts; and when we use a word which leaves the sex undetermined, we add *it* likewise. "Do not wake the *child, it* is asleep."

Some words which express inanimate things, are used figuratively, and

leaving

sending formerly for hieroglyphics to signify persons, are therefore spoken of as being of some sex: thus of the *sun*, we say, "*His* going forth is from the end of the heaven." Of the *moon*, "In borrowed majesty *she* walks abroad."

IV. We likewise distinguish the female sex in some nouns by adding *ess* to the male, or changing the termination into *ess*; as, abbot, abbess; actor, actress; adulterer, adultress; Jew, Jewess; lion, lioness; prince, princess, &c.

CHAP. VI. Of the Adjective.

THE English *adjective*, is entirely undeclined, being never varied on account of case, gender, or number, but added to substantives in all relations, without any change: thus we say, *a good* father, *a good* mother, *good* silver, *good* men.

The Comparison of Adjectives.

Comparison is the act of setting two or more things together in the mind, to find out their agreement or disagreement; but by grammatical comparison, we mean comparing two or more qualities, whereby we are able to affirm, that the one is *more*, or *less*, or possessed of any quality in the highest degree: so of three things, we, by comparing them together, find three degrees of softness, the one being *softer* than the first, and the third the *softest* of the three. Hence we have three degrees of comparison, viz. the *positive*, the *comparative* and the *superlative*.

The *positive* expresses the quality of a thing simply, without any comparison included, as *soft*.

The *comparative* heightens or lessens the sense of the positive; as, this wool is *softer*, or, she is a *fairer* woman.

The *superlative* heightens the sense of the positive in the highest, or diminishes it to the lowest degree; as, the *wisest* man, i.e. one who has not his equal in wisdom.

The *comparative* degree is formed or made by adding *er* to the positive; thus, to *fair* we add *er*, which makes *fairer*. But if the positive ends with an *e* final we add only *r*; thus, to *wise* we add only an *r*, which makes *wiser*.

The *superlative* is formed by adding *est* to the positive; thus to *fair* we add *est*, which makes *fairest*; but, in case the positive ends with an *e* mute, we then only add *st*: if the positive be *wise* we only add *st*, which forms the superlative *wisest*.

But such adjectives as are borrowed from the Latin, and such as end in *ain, al, ant, ent, ive, en, ant, ible, ly, lest, id, some, v, al, able, ing, ish, ed;* if they be words of more than one syllable, form their comparative by putting *more* before the positive, and their superlative by prefixing *most*; thus, the comparative of *certain*, is *more certain*, and the superlative *most certain*. *Able* and *handsome* are exceptions, making *abler, handsomer*, in the comparative, and *ablest, handsomest*, in the superlative.

Some adjectives likewise are compared by using *better* to express the comparative, and *best* to denote the superlative; thus *learned*, in the comparative, makes *better learned*, and in the superlative *best learned*.

Big, bad, and *fit,* double the last consonant in their comparative and superlative degrees, in order to retain the short sound of the positive, thus *big* makes *bigger, biggest*; *bad, badder, baddest*; and *fit* makes *fitter, fittest*. The comparison of the following adjectives are irregular.

Positive	Comparative	Superlative
Good	Better	Best
Bad		
Evil }	Worse	Worst
Ill }		
Little	Less	Least

The following words have not the comparative degree ; *middle, middle-most, very, chief,*

Some adjectives make their superlative by adding *most* ; thus, *fore* makes *former,* and *foremost.* From *neath,* obsolete, comes *neather,* and *neathermost ;* but *hind* has two superlatives, as *hind, hinder, hindermost,* and *hinmost ;* yet *hindmost* is not so proper as *hindermost. Late* has two comparatives as well as two superlatives, for from *late* comes *later,* and *latter ; latest* or *last.*

Most is sometimes added to a substantive when it implies comparison, as *topmost, southmost.*

CHAP. VII. Of the Pronouns.

AS too frequent repetition of the same words is disagreeable and inconvenient we make use of several words to supply them, which are therefore called pronouns.

A *pronoun* is a word used instead of a noun substantive ; thus, instead of my own name, I say, *I ;* instead of your name, I say, *you ;* and instead of another man or woman's name, I say, *he* or *she.*

As all discourse may be confined to these three heads ; 1ft, in speaking of ourselves ; 2dly, in speaking *to* another ; and 3dly, in speaking *of* another ; these three heads are therefore called by the name of *persons.* For

1ft, When I speak of myself, I use the word *I ;* and when several speak of themselves, they use the word *we ;* which words, *I* and *we,* are of the *first* person.

2dly, When we speak to another, we use the word *thou* or *you ;* but when we speak to more than one, we use the word *ye* or *you ;* and the words *thou* or *ye* are of the *second* person

3dly, In speaking of another of the male sex, we say *he ;* but if of the female sex we say *she ;* and should we speak of any thing that is neither *male* nor *female,* we say *it ;* and if we speak of more things than one, let them be of the male or female sex, or even of no sex, we always use *they.* The words *he, she, it,* and *they,* are of the *third* person. Hence the *first* person singular h *I ;* the *second* person *thou,* or *you ;* the *third* person, *he, she, it.* The first person plural is *we,* the second, *you,* or *ye,* the third, *they.*

When pronouns are declined, they are said to have a foregoing state and a following state.

The *foregoing state,* is that in which a word is used before a verb : and the *following state,* that in which it is used after the verb.

From these pronouns are derived others, called pronouns *possessive,* so called because they denote possession ; from *me* comes *my* and *mine ;* from *thee, thy* and *thine ;* from *us, our* and *ours ;* and from *you, your,* and *yours.* These pronouns are sometimes used to express the cause or author of a thing ; as, " This is *your* doing ;" *i. e.* you are the cause of this. Again, " This is " *my* book ;" that is, I am the owner of this book. These possessive pronouns have no cases.

The *personal pronouns* have the nature of substantives, and stand by themselves ; the rest have the nature of adjectives.

A TABLE

A TABLE of all the Pronouns in the several States, from Dr. Wallis.

| | | | The foregoing State. | The following State. | Their possessives to be used | |
					With a Substantive	Without a Substantive
1 Person	Sing.		I	Me	My	Mine
	Plural		We	Us	Our	Ours
2 persons	Sing.		Thou or you	Thee	Thy	Thine
	Plural		Ye or you	You	Your	Yours
3 Persons	Sing.	Male	He	Him	His	His
		Fem.	She	Her	Her	Hers
		Neu.	It	It	Its	Its
	Plur.		They	Them	Their	Theirs
The Interrogative	Of Persons		Who	Whom	Whose	Whose
	Of Things		What		Wereof.	

Who is an interrogative so called from its being used in asking a question; and is used only when we speak of persons.

This, that, and *which,* are adjectives, though commonly reckoned to be pronouns, for they are not put to supply the place of substantives, but are joined with them, as, "*This* man." "*That* book." And if they occur at any time without substantives, their substantives are then understood. *This* and *that* are called *demonstratives,* because they shew what particular person or thing you mean. *This* makes *these* in the plural, and *that* makes *those.* *Which* is called an interrogative, when used in asking a question, and a relative when it has relation to some substantive expressed or understood, as, "Here is the book, *which* (book) you lost." It is the same in both numbers, and is used only when we speak of things.

CHAP. VIII. Of Verbs.

A Verb is a word that signifies to *be,* to *do,* or to *suffer.* Such verbs as signify merely being, are *essential* verbs; those that signify doing or action, are *active* verbs; and those that signify suffering, are called verbs *passive.* Verbs that signify condition or habit, are called *neuter.* In English we have, strictly speaking, no passive verbs, but express such verbs by means of auxiliary words.

b　　　　　　　　　　　　A

As actions may be confidered as being paft, or prefent, Verbs have tenfes, by which thefe fenfes are expreffed. The Englifh indeed have but two tenfes or times, viz. the prefent and the preter time; the verb having other different endings only to expref them.

The *prefent tenfe*, or time which now is, is expreffed by the verb itfelf, as, *I burn.*

The *preter tenfe* or time, called the preterite, is commonly made by adding *ed* to the prefent tenfe, as *burned*: but if the prefent tenfe ends in *e*, it is made by adding *d*, as *love*, *loved*.

Some verbs whofe prefent tenfe end in *d* or *t*, have their preter and prefent the fame, as *read*, *lead*; but it is to be obferved, that in pronunciation we make a diftinction, the prefent being pronounced long, and the preter fhort; on which account feveral authors of note have chofen, for diftinction's fake, to write the preter as pronounced; amongft which is Bolingbroke, who writes the preters of *lead* and *read*, *led* and *red*.

As actions are to be affirmed of ourfelves, to others, or of others, verbs are faid to have perfons, which are diftinguifhed by prefixing the pronouns perfonal to them in Englifh, as

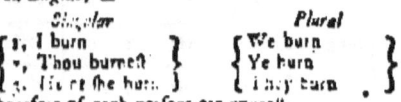

	Singular		*Plural*
1,	I burn		We burn
2,	Thou burneft		Ye burn
3,	He or fhe burn		They burn

the endings therefore of each perfons are expreft.

	Prefent tenfe fingular		*Preter tenfe fingular*
Perfons 1,	The verb		*ed*
2,	*eft*		*edft* or *dft* after *e* final
3,	*e b* or *s*		*ed* / *d*

And the Englifh differs from other languages with refpect to its tenfes, fo it does likewife with refpect to the *moods*.

CHAP. IX. Of Moods.

A Mood is a method made ufe of to exprefs the manner, poffibility, or neceffity of an action, together with the inclination of the agent. As the Englifh does not admit of a change in the end of its verbs, for this purpofe; therefore it is evident, that it has no moods. The manner in which we exprefs thefe circumftances of action, is by means of auxiliary words, and by the place of the nominative. To exprefs the *poffibility* of a thing, we ufe *can*; to convey the idea of *neceffity*, we ufe *muft*, or *ought*; to exprefs the *liberty* of the fpeaker, we ufe *may*; to denote the *inclination*, we ufe *will*, or *would*; and to fignify *command, permiffion, entreaty*, or *exhortation* or *doubt*, we place the fubftantive after the verb; as, fight *the Frentb*; do I underftand?"

CHAP. X. Of Participles.

A Participle is derived from a verb, and receives its name from *partaking* both of the nature of a verb and of an adjective; it partakes of the nature of a verb, becaufe it fignifies being, doing and fuffering; and partakes of the nature of an adjective, becaufe it will not make fenfe of itfelf; thus, in the fentence, "a *loving* child," the word *loving* is a participle; and fignifies action, as the verb *love* itfelf does; it partakes likewife of the nature of an adjective, becaufe when the word *loving* ftands by itfelf, it

requires

requires some other word to determine its sense, and when joined to the subjunctive *child*, makes a complete sentence.

There are two participles, one of which is *active*, and the other *passive*.

The *active* participle is made by adding *ing* to the verb, as *burn*, *burn-ing*; but if the verb ends in *e* mute, the *e* is omitted, as in *write*, *writing*; it is called the *active* participle, because it signifies *action*.

The *passive* participle is made by adding *ed*, *t*, or *n*, to the verb; as *burn*, *burned*; *lend*, *lent*; *beat*, *beaten*. This is called the passive participle, because when joined with the verb *to be*, it makes up the whole passive voice.

The auxiliary verbs are either perfect or defective.

CHAP. XI. Of the defective auxiliary VERBS.

A *Defective* auxiliary verb is that which is not used but in its own or the preter tense, has no participles, and admits of no helping verbs to be put before it: of this kind are *do*, *will*, *shall*, *may*, *can*, with their preter tenses *did*, *would*, *should*, *might*, *could*, or *must*.

When *do* is used as an auxiliary verb, it emphatically denotes the *present* time; and *did* the *preter*. Thus *I burn*, or *I burned*, is more emphatical or strong when we say *I do burn*, or *I did burn*. *Do* and *did* are formed thus;

	Singular	Plural
Persons	1 I do	We do
	2 Thou dost, or you do	Ye do, or you do.
	3 He doth, or does.	They do
Persons	1 I did	We did
	2 Thou didst, or you did	Ye did, or you did
	3 He did	They did

Shall or Will.

I shall, thou shalt, or you shall, he shall. Plural, *We shall, ye shall, or you shall, they shall.*

I will, thou wilt, or you will, he will. Plural *We will, ye or you will, they will.*

To distinguish *shall* from *will*, though they are both used to express something future, it will be necessary to observe, that in the first person *shall* expresses a future action; but *will* promises or threatens; thus *I shall proceed*, or *we shall proceed*, implies, that our proceeding is something future; but when we say *I will beat you*, or *I will pay you*, I promise or threaten beating or payment. Again, in the second or third persons, *shall* commands, promise, and threatens; but *will* barely foretells: thus when we say, *you shall go*, we command a person to go; when we say, *you shall have your money*, we promise to pay a person; and when we say, *he shall be hanged*, we threaten: but when we say, *he will be beaten, they will run away*, we only foretel something that may happen.

Shall, makes *should*, which is thus formed, *I should, thou should'st*, or *you should, he should.* Plural *We should, ye or you should, they should.*

Will, in the preter tense, makes *would*, and is declined thus, *I would, thou would'st* or *you would, he would.* Plural *We would, ye or you would, they would.*

In order to prevent impropriety, it should be observed, that though both *would* and *should* are used to denote what was, or had been to come, yet *would* is only used to intimate the will or intention of the doer; as, *I would write*, i. e. I am willing to write; but *I should*, denotes the bare futurity, or that the thing will be, and the propriety of doing it; as, *I should write*, i. e. it is proper for me to write.

Might is declined thus, *I might, thou might'st* or *you might, he might.* Plural *we might, ye or you might, they might.*

I

I may, thou mayst or you may, he may. We may, ye or you may, they may.

Can forms *could*, in the preter, and is thus declined; *I can, thou canst or you can, he can.* Plural, *We can, ye or you can, they can, I could, thou couldst, &c. We should.*

Must and *ought*, are thus declined; *I must, thou must, &c.* without any variation in the persons. *I ought, thou oughtst, or you ought, he ought, &c.*

Of the perfect helping or auxiliary Verbs.

The *perfect* helping verbs are *have, am,* or *be*: they are called *perfect* verbs, because they may be joined with other auxiliary verbs, and are used in most of the tenses. When *have* is used as an auxiliary, it denotes the time in which any past action was done, and is thus declined; *I have, thou hast, he hath.* Plural, *We have, ye have, they have.* Its perfect is *had,* and is declined after the following manner, *I had, thou hadst or you had, he had. Plural, We had, &c.* When *have* is present to another verb, it denotes that the action is just past; as, *I have* dined, *i. e.* the action of dining is just past. *Had,* denotes that an action was past before another which was past likewise; as, "When Peter came to my house, I *had* dined;" *i. e.* the action of dining was past, before that of Peter's arrival, though past likewise. *Had* is likewise used to signify the time past of an action not done, but intended to be done; as, "I *had* gone thither, but Peter prevented me;" *i. e.* the action of going thither was intended, and would have been past, had it not been for Peter's prevention. In this sense the second branch of the sentence begins with *but,* as in the example produced. When *shall* or *will* is added to *have,* it denotes the time that is not, but will be past; as "I *shall have* burned it, I *will have* transcribed it in an hour hence."

As the English have no verbs passive, this defect is supplied by adding *am* or *be,* to the participle passive: thus *love,* the participle passive, becomes a kind of verb passive when joined with *am,* as *I am loved.* But as *am* is a very irregular verb, it will not be unnecessary to add the manner in which it is declined in the present and preter tenses. In the present tense it is declined thus; singular, *I am, thou art, or you are, he is;* plural, *we are, &c.* or, *I be, thou be'st, he be;* plural, *we be, ye be, &c.* In the preter, we decline thus, *I was, thou wast, or you were, he was;* plural, *we were, ye were, or you were, &c.* or, *I were, thou wert, he were;* plural, *we were, ye were, they were.*

This verb makes *to be* in the infinitive, the active participle is *being;* and the passive participle *been.* The irregular verbs are so numerous, that a particular detail of them would take up too much room in this treatise; but as this omission is already supplied in the subsequent sheets, we may be excused for not producing them here.

Adverbs.

Adverbs are contractions, or clauses of sentences, added to verbs to denote the *manner,* and other circumstances of an action. They are distributed 1st, into those of Place, as *here, there.* 2dly Those of time, as *often, presently.* 3d'y, Those of *quality* and *manner,* which are derived from adjectives by adding *ly* to them; as *wisely, happily,* from the adjectives *wise,* and *happy.*

Prepositions.

A preposition, is so named because it is commonly put before the word to which it is applied, and serves both to connect words to one another, and to shew the relation between them; such are *of, with, from,* most of them originally denote place. Some of them are prefixed to words so as to become a part of them, as *a-bide, out-go, overcome;* the former which, &c. are call'd inseparable prepositions.

3   Con-

CONJUNTIONS.

The *conjunctions* are words which join sentences together, and shew the manner of their dependance on each other.

INTERJECTIONS

Are, as the name expresses, words *thrown in between the parts of a sentence*, without making any alteration in it, and denoting some emotion, or passion, of the mind.

SYNTAX.

Syntax treats of the order of words in a sentence, and the correspondence of one to another.

The subject of an *affirmation* in an affirmative sentence is *before* the verb, as, " *Alexander* conquered Darius." In an *interrogative* sentence, it is placed between the *verb* and its auxiliary, as " *Did Alexander* conquer?" The *object* of an affirmation is placed after the verb, as " Alexander conquered *Darius*."

The *adjective* is placed *before* the substantive, as, " a *good* man;" but yet it is placed *after*, when a verb comes between them, as, " the Lord is *great*;" and likewise, when the clause of a sentence depends upon the adjective, as, " Feed me with food *convenient* for me." The pronoun, adjective, or relative, is placed in the same manner as the adjective, *i. e. before* its antecedent.

The *adverb* is placed before the subject and the verb, as, " Alexander *entirely* ruined Darius;" or else between the *auxiliaries* of the verb and participle, as, " I have been *exceedingly* fatigued."

The adjective and verb must be in the same number as the substantives; as " *this* man I *love*; the sun *shines*."

When two substantives come before the verb, it must be in the plural, " Your youth and merit *have* been abased."

The *oblique* or *subsequent* state of the pronouns must be used after verbs transitive; " I love *her*; I wrote this for *him*."

A noun of *multitude*, which signifies *many*, may have a verb or pronoun either in the singular or plural numbers, as, " My *people is* foolish,"—" The assembly of the wicked *have* inclosed me."

If the *singulars* joined with a conjunction are of several persons, in making the plural pronoun agree with them, the *second* takes place of the *third*, and the first of either or both, as, " *You* and *I* won it at the hazard of *our* lives." —*You* and *he* had it between *you*.

The neuter pronoun [*it.*] is used to express the subject of any discourse or enquiry; the state of any thing or person; and the thing that is the cause of any event or effect, or any person considered as the cause, as, " 'Twas at the royal feast of Persia won.—It happened on a summer's holiday.—Who is *it* in the press that calls to me?—How is *it* with you?"

The verb *to do* has always a nominative case after it; as, " It was *I* that did it."

The adverbs *when, why, after,* &c. being left out, the participle is independent of the rest of the sentence, and is called in Latin the *ablative absolute*, but is in English the *nominative*, as, " The doors *being* shut, Jesus stood in the midst."

" God from the mount of Sinai, whose grey top
Shall tremble—*He* descending, shall, &c."

MILTON'S Par. Lost. xii. 227.

To before a verb is the sign of the *infinitive*; but some words have other verbs following them *without* this sign; as *bid, dare, make, feel, let,* and

some-

Sometimes *love*, as, "I *bade* him do it,—you. *dare* not *do* it,—I *saw* him *do* it,—I will make him *feel* it,—I *heard* him *say* it; I will *make* him *do* it." The North Britons seem not to have adverted to this rule in their compositions, in our language.

The infinitive mood is made absolute, or used independently of a sentence supplying the place of the conjunction with the subjunctive mood, as, "*to* confess the truth I was in the fault; that is, *that* I may confess the truth, &c.

The *infinitive mood* is sometimes used as a substantive to express the *action* which the verb expresses; thus the infinitive mood is substituted instead of a substantive in different cases; in the nominative, as, "*to win is* pleasant," in the subsequent or following case, as, "men *love* to win."

The *participle* with a *preposition* before still retaining its government is what the Latins call their gerund; as, "Felicity is to be obtained *by avoiding evil*."

The *participle*, with an *article* before it, and the *preposition* after it, becomes a substantive expressing the action which the verb implies, as, "These are the rules of logic, *by observing of* which, you may learn to reason well."

Or it may be expressed by the *participle* or gerund, as, "*by observing* which," not, "but *observing of* which," nor, "by *the* observing which."

The participle frequently becomes an adjective, when it is joined to a substantive merely to denote its quality, without respect of time, and as such it admits of comparison, as a *learned*, a *more*, or a *most* learned man.

Simple sentences are *explicative*, *interrogative*, or, *imperative*.

An explicative sentence is, when a thing is said to be, or not to be; to do, or not to do; to suffer, or not to suffer; in a direct manner. If the sentence be *negative*, the adverb *not* is placed *after* the auxiliary, or after the verb itself, if it have no auxiliary, as, "It did *not* touch him;" or, "It *touched* him *not*."

In an *interrogative* sentence, when a question is asked, the nominative case *follows* the principal verb, as, "Is it I? Did *Alexander* conquer the *Persians?*

In an *imperative* sentence, that is, when a thing is commanded, or permitted, the *nominative* case likewise follows the verb, as, "*Go, thou* traitor," or, "*Let us* be gone."

The English *adjective* having no variation of gender or number, cannot but agree with the substantive in those respects; yet as some of the pronouns have the plural number, they must agree in number with their substantives, as, "With respect to *these* civilities, *they* are an, &c."

In some cases the adjective becomes a substantive, and has another adjective joined to it, as, "the *chief good*."

Sometimes, on the contrary, the substantive becomes an *adjective*, or supplies the place of one, when joined with another substantive, as, "*sea-water*, *forest-tree*.

The *adverb* is placed *either before adjectives*, *after verbs*, and frequently *between* the auxiliary and the verb; as, "He made a *very* elegant harangue;" "He spake *unaffectedly*, and was *attentively* heard."

In English *two negatives* destroy each other, or are almost equal to an affirmative; as, "*Nor* did they *not* perceive."

Prepositions require the *adjective* or *following* case after them, as, "with *him*."

The *preposition* is frequently separated from the relative which it governs, and joined to the *verb* at the end of the sentence, or of some member of it, as, "Horace is an author *whom* I am much *delighted with*;" "The world is

is too well bred to shock authors with a truth *which* generally their book-sellers are the first that inform them *of*." However, the placing the preposition *before* the relative is more graceful, as well as more perspicuous, and agrees much better with the solemn and elevated stile.

The prepositions *to* and *for* are often understood, but more especially before the pronoun, as, " Give *me* the book ;" " Get *me* the money ;" i. e. " Give *to* me ;" " Get *for* me."

The prepositions *in* or *on* are often omitted before nouns expressing time, as, " *this* day fort'night, *next* month, i. e. on *this* day ; in next month, &c.

Two or more *simple* sentences joined together by one or more *connecting* words, form a compound sentence.

The *connecting* words are *relatives*, or *conjunctions*, the examples are these, 1. " Blessed is the man, *who* feareth the Lord." 2. " Life is short, *and* art is long."

The relative is the nominative case to the verb, when no other nominative comes *between* it and the verb : but when another nominative case comes between it and the verb, the relative is governed by some word in that sentence, as, " the God, *who* preserveth me, *whose* I am, and *whom* I serve."

Every relative has an *antecedent*, either *expressed* or understood, as, " *Who* steals my purse, steals trash ;" i. e. " *the man, who,* &c."

The relative is of the same person with the antecedent, and the verb like-wise, as, " *Who is this that cometh* from Edom, *this that is glorious* in his apparel ?"

Some *conjunctions* require the *indicative*, and some the *subjunctive* after them, while others have no influence at all upon the mood.

Hypothetical, conditional, conceffive, and exceptive conjunctions, generally require the subjunctive mood after them, as, *if, though, unless, whether, or* ; thus, " *If* thou *be* the Son of God :" " *Though* he *slay* me :" " *Unless* he *wash* his flesh :" " *Whether* it *were* I, or they."

That expressing *motive* or *end*, has the subjunctive, with *may, might, should*, after it.

When the qualities of things are compared, the latter noun is not governed by the conjunction *than*, or *as*, but agrees with the verb, or is governed by the verb, or preposition expressed or understood, as, " Thou art not as wise as *I* [am] :" " He is handsomer than [you think] *me*." If you complete the sentence, by supplying the part which is understood, in this manner, the case of the latter noun will be easily determined.

Interjections in English govern no cases, though they are usually followed with nouns in the nominative case, and verbs in the indicative mood ; yet neither the case nor mood is determined by them, but by the nature of the sentence : For though *me, thee, him, her*, and *us* are used after *them*, which are the dative cases in the Saxon, they are to be considered as such in these instances, and, as continuing such in the English, and as including in their very form the force of the prepositions *to* and *for*.

ADVER.

ADVERTISEMENT.

THE Editor begs leave to make his grateful Acknowledgments to the Public for the very favourable Reception this Dictionary has met with; and, as he could not comprize it within the proposed Limits, without departing from his Plan, and consequently abridging some Part of the Work, this Number, which is almost a DOUBLE One, is delivered at the Same Price as the other Numbers.

* As Mr. Barlow was unwilling to delay the Publication, by waiting for the remainder of the List of Subscribers, those Persons whose Names are not yet transmitted to the Publisher shall be inserted in the next Edition, if desired.

THE COMPLETE

ENGLISH DICTIONARY.

A, a Vowel, the first letter of the alphabet of all the known languages, excepting the Æthiopic, in which it is the thirteenth. The reason generally assigned for its priority, is, that it is the first sound pronounced by infants; needs no other motion to form it, but a bare opening of the lips, and is that which the dumb are soonest taught to pronounce. It is, indeed, so much the language of nature, that, upon all sudden and extraordinary occasions, we are naturally led to it, to express our admiration, joy, anguish, or aversion; and, where the passion is very strong, we frequently increase the force of the A, by adding an aspirate, as *ah!* In the English language it has three different sounds, which, in imitation of foreigners, may be stiled the *flender*, *open*, and *broad*.

A, set before nouns of the singular number, denotes one, as *a man;* that is, *one man;* or signifies something indefinite, as, *a man* may pass this way; that is, *any man.* Before a word beginning with a vowel, it is written *an;* as *an acorn, an owl.* The grammarians of the last age direct it likewise to be used before an *h;* which is observed by moderns before an *h* silent, as *an herb, an honest man;* but when the *h* is pronounced, or aspirated, we use *a,* as *a horse.*

A, when placed before a participle, denotes some action not yet finished, as I *am a walking.* In some cases it signifies *to*, "They go *a* begging to a bankrupt's door." *Dryd.* It has likewise a peculiar signification, denoting *each,* when we say, "They gain'd a thousand pounds *a* man."

A, in abbreviations, stands for *artium,* or *arts;* as A. B. bachelor of arts; *arms,* or *year;* as A. D. *anno Domini,* in the year of our Lord.

AA'RON, S. [אַהֲרֹן,] the brother of Moses, joined with him in his mission to Pharaoh, on account of his elocution; and af-

terwards, when the religious service of the Jews was founded by the Deity, was constituted their high-priest. The office was annexed to his family, and was to have descended in an hereditary succession.

AA'RON, S. the name of a saint, who suffered martyrdom under the Emperor Diocletian, in the year 303. He was of Caer-leon, the metropolis of Wales. What his family-name was, is unknown; it being customary with the Christian Britons of those days, at their baptism, to assume new names from the Greek, Latin, and Hebrew. All the particulars we have of his death, are, that he suffered the most cruel tortures, was buried, and had a church erected to his memory at Caer-leon, the remains of which bishop Goodwin says, " were visible not long since." His festival, in the Roman Martyrology, is on the first of July.

AARO'NICAL, Adj. belonging to Aaron. This term is used by divines, when treating of the difference between Aaron's priesthood and that of Christ.

AB, S. [אָב, *Father*] the eleventh month of the civil, and the fifth of the Jews ecclesiastic year. It answers to July, and consists of thirty days. Upon the first, they fall in commemoration of Aaron's death; on the ninth, because Solomon's temple was on that day burnt by the Chaldeans, and the second temple built by the Romans. They believe that the persons appointed to survey the land of Canaan, returned this day, and intimidated their brethren.

ABA'CA, S. a kind of plant or flax found in the Philippine islands. There are two sorts, the white and the grey. The white makes very fine linnen, but the grey is used only in cordage.

ABA'CTED, Part. [*abactus,* Lat.] any thing driven away by violence.

ABA'CTOR, S. [*abactor,* Lat.] one who drives away cattle in herds.

B   among

ABACUS, S. [Pinax, אבק, Heb. dust] among mathematicians, is used for a table covered with dust, on which they used to draw their schemes.

ABACUS, S. the uppermost member of the capital of a pillar, serving as a crowning both to the capital and the whole column. It was originally intended to represent a square tile laid over a basket. Its form varies in the different orders. In the Tuscan, Doric, and ancient Ionic, it is a flat square member, resembling the tile, its original. In the richer orders, it loses its native form. In the Corinthian, and Composite, its four sides are arched, or cut inward with some ornament, as a rose, or other flower, or a fish's tail in the middle of each arch. But architects will take greater liberties. In the Tuscan, where it is largest, and takes up one third of the height of the whole capital, it is sometimes filled the die of the capital. In the Doric, some place a cymatium over it; and in the Ionic, some make it a perfect ogee, and crown it with a filet. In proportion, as described by Vitruvius, is, that its diagonal from corner to corner, be twice its height. Scammozi uses this word for a concave moulding in the capital of the Tuscan pedestal.

ABADDON, S. [Abaddon, Gr.] an infernal angel, and one of the names of Satan.

ABAFT, Adv. [Abutan, Sax.] that part of the ship which is toward the stern, including all the space from thence to the mainmast. Thus "abaft the foremast," is behind it.

ABAISANCE, S. obeisance, an act of respect or reverence paid to a person, by a bow, &c.

To ABALIENATE, V. A. [abalieno, Lat.] to transfer to another.

ABALIENATION, S. [abalienatio, Lat.] a transferring one's right to another, also to lose cattle, slaves, lands, or possessions, by law, or due course of law.

To ABAND, V. A. See ABANDON.

To ABANDON, V. A. [abandonner, Fr.] To give up, resign, quit, desert, forsake, cast off.

ABANDONED, Part. Adj. [from abandon] given up, deserted, and wicked in the highest degree, as "an abandoned wretch;" one who is entirely immersed in wickedness, and arrived at the highest degree of depravity.

ABANDONER, S. [from abandon] the person who abandons, forsakes, &c.

ABANDONING, V. N. desertion, or forsaking.

ABANDUM, S. [barre, Sax.] any thing sequestered, proscribed, confiscated, or denounced to be forfeited.

ABAPTISTON, S. [Abaptiston, Gr.] from a, and baptiso] the perforating part of a surgeon's instrument called a trepan. It owes its name from its being contrived so, as to be kept from sinking into the brain, when the skull is cut through. This is done by

securing it with an edge round it, with wings on its sides; or making it of a conical shape, which is the common method.

ABAS, S. a weight used in Persia for weighing pearls. It is an eighth part lighter than the European carat.

To ABASE, V. A. [abaisser, Fr.] to humble, bring down, as "the proud shall be abased," to depress.

To ABASE, V. A. a sea term. To strike, take in, or lower the flag, in token of submission.

ABASED, Adj. [from abase] a term in heraldry, used for the wings of eagles, when the top looks downwards towards the point of the shield; or when they are shut; the natural bearing being spread, with their top pointing to the chief. A chevron, pole, or bend, &c. are abased when their points terminate in, or below the center of the shield; an ordinary is abased, when below its due situation.

ABASEMENT, S. [abaissement, Fr.] the state of being brought low; depression.

To ABASH, V. A. [verbassen, Du.] to affect with shame, or confusion; to dash. "they heard and were abashed, Milt. Par. Lost.

To ABATE, V. A. [abbatre, Fr. to beat down] to lessen or diminish. "The divine wisdom will abate the glory of kings." Davies. "To deject, or depress the mind; to lower or lessen the price of goods in buying or selling.

To ABATE, V. N. to grow less, "his passion abates, as the storm abates."

To ABATE, V. in common law is used both actively and neuterly. To abate a writ, is to defeat, or overthrow it, on account of some error. "A stranger abateth," that is steps into the possession of land between the former possessor and his surviving heir. In the neuter signification it is used thus: The writ of the demandant shall abate, that is, be frustrated, disabled, or overthrown.

ABATELEM, S. [Fr.] a prohibition of trading, issued against all French merchants, in the ports of the Levant, who refuse to pay their debts or stand to their bargains. 'Tis a sentence of their consul, which must be taken off, before they can sue any person themselves.

ABATEMENT, S. [from abate] the act of remitting or abating. The state of being abated. The sum or quantity taken away by abating; extenuation. "We cannot plead in abatement of our guilt." Att.

ABATEMENT, S. [in law] the act of the abator: as an abatement of the writ, is an exception, taken and made good, upon an action brought, in divers respects; either to the insufficiency of the matter, or uncertainty of the allegation.

ABATEMENT, S. [in heraldry] is something added to a coat of arms, to diminish its dignity, on account of some dishonourable quality

3

quality or action in the hearer; and is either by diminution or reversion, Abatement by diminution, is the blemishing any part by adding a mark or stain to the escutcheon. Abatement by reversion, is either by turning the whole escutcheon upside down, or adding another inverted. These marks must either be twenty or twenty, otherwise they become additions of honour.

ABATEMENT, *s.* [in commerce] the allowance given any trader in the price of goods, for advancing the money immediately for which he might have taken time.

ABATER, *s.* [from *abate*] the cause by which an abatement or diminution is effected, as "Abaters of acrimony." *Arbuthnot on Diet.*

ABATUDE, *s.* any thing diminished.

ABATURES, *s.* [hunting term] those sprigs of grass that are thrown down by a stag in his passage.

ABAWED, Part. [*abaubi*, Fr.] abashed, daunted, ashamed, Chron. now obsolete.

AB'BA, *s.* [אבא, Syr. father] it is made use of by St. Mark and St. Paul in their Greek, because the Syriac was then commonly known in the synagogues and assemblies of the Christians. At first it was a term of affection back in the Hebrew and Chaldee; but, at length, became a title of dignity and honour, which the Jewish doctors very much affected; in allusion to which it was that Jesus "forbad his disciples to call any man father upon earth."

AB'BACY, ABBATHY, *s.* [*abbatia*] the rights or privileges of an abbot.

ABBESS, *s.* [*abuesse*, Lat. *abess*, Fr.] the governess of a nunnery, or monastery of women, over which she exercises the same authority, as the abbot regular does over his monks; though on account of their sex, they are not allowed to perform the spiritual offices annexed to the priesthood; yet some have been allowed to communion a priest to act for them. F. Martene observes, that some have formerly confessed their nuns, and gave blessings; which Fleury confirms: but they abused the power so far, that it was necessary to check it and lay it aside. According to St. Basil they may be present at the confession of their nuns.

ABBEY, *s.* [*abbaie*, Lat. *abbaie*, Fr.] a monastery, or religious house, governed by an abbot, when inhabited by women, and by an abbot when occupied by men. Formerly in England, and at present abroad, great privileges were, and are granted them, such as being exempt from the visitation of the bishop of the diocese, and being a sanctuary, or asylum, for those who fled thither for protection from the law, even though their crimes were capital. Before the reformation, one third of the best benefices were appropriated to abbies; but being dissolved by Henry VIII. became lay fees; of these houses 190 were

dissolved whose revenues were between 200 l. and 35000 l. per annum, which according to Burnet, at a medium, amounted to 2,853,000 l. yearly.

ABBOT, *s.* [*abbod*, or *abbad*, Sax. from אב, Heb. father] the superior of an abbey, inhabited by the male sex. The name is as ancient as the institution of monks itself. They were at first laymen, and subject to the bishops and ordinary pastors; had no share in ecclesiastic affairs, and went on Sundays to the parish church, in the same manner as the rest of the people; but if too remote, had a priest sent to them to administer the sacrament. At last they were allowed to have a priest of their own body, who was generally the abbot himself, but his function was confined within the walls of his own monastery, and was still subject to his bishop. Originally men of great plainness and simplicity, they contented themselves with governing their own monasteries, but some of them having rendered themselves conspicuous for their learning. In the opposition they made to the heresies of those times, they were called from their obscurity, and placed by their bishops near the great altar. In this situation they lost their former simplicity, aimed independency, and notwithstanding they received a check from the council of Chalcedon, in process of time got their independency confirmed, and assumed the title of lord, with other badges of the episcopate, and particularly the mitre. Hence arose a new distinction of abbots mitred and not mitred; crosiered and not crosiered.

To ABBREVIATE, *V. A.* [*abbrevier*, Lat.] to shorten by omission of the less important parts, without loss of the substance; in this sense, it is the same as *abridge*. To shorten by contraction; thus, "abbreviate, or reducing many syllables to one." *Swift.*

ABBREVIATION, *s.* [from *abbreviate*] the act of abbreviating, or means used to abbreviate; a shortening of a word or passage, by dropping some of the letters, or substituting marks in their stead. Lawyers and physicians make use of them partly for speed, and partly for mystery, as, "aq. lac. fort." for "aqua lactis, fortis, strong milk water."

ABBREVIATOR, *s.* [*abbreviateur*, Fr.] one who abbreviates or abridges.

ABBREVIATURE, *s.* [from *abbreviate*] a mark used for the sake of shortening; a compendium, or abridgement, as, "an excellent abbreviature, of the whole duty of a christian." *Taylor's guide to devotion.*

To ABBROCH, *V. A.* [law term] to buy up, or engross any wares, the same as forestalling. *M. S. temp. Ed.* III.

ABBROCHMENT, *s.* [*abbrocamentum*, Lat.] the act of abbroaching.

ABBUTTALS, *s.* [*abbutum*, Lat. *abbuter*, Fr.] a law term. The buttings or boundings

of land, &c. shewing on what other lands, &c. they are bounded. The sides, on the breadth of land, are properly termed, lying or bordering; and the ends, in length, abutting, or bounding. *Cond.*

ABDELAVI, S. the Egyptian melon.

AB'DEST, S. a kind of washing used by Mahometans before prayer, entering the mosque, or reading the Koran.

To AB'DICATE, V. A. [abdico, Lat.] to renounce, resign, or voluntarily forsake an office. This sense of the word seems settled by the conference held at the Star Chamber at the revolution, and the decision of parliament.

ABDICA'TION, S. the act of abdicating, whereby a person in office renounces the same, before the legal time of service is expired. It is distinguished from resignation, as *abdication* signifies only the simple act of renouncing, or laying down an office; but *resignation* implies it to be done in favour of another. Thus Dioclesian and Charles V. are said to have *abdicated*; but Philip IV. of Spain to have resigned his crown, because he did it in favour of his successor.

ABDO'MEN, S. [abdomen, Lat.] the lower belly, which reaches from the thorax to the hips; and contains the stomach, guts, spleen, bladder, and intestines. It is subdivided in to three lesser cavities or regions: the upper part, called the epigastrium, commences from the diaphragm, and terminates two fingers breadth above the navel; the second, called the umbilical, begins where the former ends, and terminates two fingers breadth below the navel; the third, stiled the hypogastric, descends as low as the os pubis. The abdomen is lined internally with a thin, soft membrane, called the peritonæum, which surrounds all the viscera and keeps them in their proper places; but in case of its rupture, they fall down, and produce the disorders stiled hernias.

ABDO'MINAL, ABDO'MINOUS, Adj. [abdomen, Lat.] situated in the abdomen or belonging to it. Paunch-bellied, unwieldly.

To AB'DUCE, V. A. [abduco, Lat.] to draw, move from one place or position to another. Used only by physical or scientific writers.

ABDU'SENT, Adj. [abduco, Lat.] whose action is to pull back as the *abducent muscles*, whose office is to pull back the parts they are affixed to, in contradistinction to *adducent*, which signifies to draw close, thus, the adducent muscles of the fingers, are those which are made use of to thus the hand; but the *abductor*, those by which we open it.

ABDU'CTION, S. in logic, an argument wherein the major is evident, but the minor doubtful.

ABDU'CTION, S. in surgery, a species of fracture, wherein the ends of the bones re-

cede, and are at distance, from each other. *Harris. Barrow.*

ABDU'CTOR, [abductor, Lat.] in anatomy, is a name given to those muscles, which serve to draw back the several parts they are fixed to.

ABECEDA'RIAN, S. one who teaches the alphabet or the first rudiments of learning.

ABECE'DARY, Adj. belonging to, or inscribed with the letters of the alphabet, seldom used.

ABE'CHED, Part. [abecher, to feed, O. Fr.] fed or satisfied.

ABE'D, Adv. [from *a* contracted for *at* and *bed*] in bed.

To ABE'DGE, ABEG, V. N. to abide, to suffer, *Chauc.*

ABE'RFORD, or ABERFORTH, a town in the west-riding of Yorkshire, with a market on Wednesdays; and four fairs, on the first Wednesday in April, on the first Wednesday in May, on the first Wednesday in October, and on the Wednesday after St. Luke's day; which are all for horses, horned cattle, and sheep. It is 20 miles S. W. of York, and 180 N. N. W. of London. Lon. 16. 20. lat. 54. 20.

ABE'RFRAW, a town of North Wales, in the isle of Anglesey, which was a place of great account formerly, when the kings of North Wales had a palace here. It is now reduced to a small village, though it has four fairs, on March 7, Wednesday after Trinity Sunday, October 23, and Dec. 11, all for cattle. It is six miles N. W. of Newburgh. Lon. 13. 5. lat. 53. 7.

ABE'RGAVENNY, a town of Monmouthshire, which is well-built, and contains about 500 houses, with two parish churches, and an old castle. It has two markets on Tuesdays and Fridays; and three fairs, on May 14, for lean cattle and sheep; the first Tuesday after Trinity Sunday, for linnen and woollen cloth; and on September 25, for hogs, horses, and flannels. It is 16 miles W. of Monmouth, and 142 W. by N. of London. Long. 14. 30. lat. 51. 50.

ABER'RANCE, or ABER'RANCY, S. [aberro, Lat.] a deviation from the truth; whether an error, mistake, or false opinion. They affect no man any further than he deserts his reason, or complies with their *aberrancies.*" *Brown's Vul. Err.* h. iv. c. 3.

ABER'RANT, Part. [aberrans, Lat.] wandering or deviating from the right or known way.

ABERRA'TION, S. [aberratio, Lat.] a departing from the common track.

ABERRA'TION, S. in astronomy, a small apparent motion of the fixed stars, discovered by D. Bradley, owing to the progressive motion of light, and the sensible proportion, which the velocity thereof bears to the velocity of the annual motion of the earth. These

These small ecliptic motions of the stars occasion their declinations, and their distances from the poles of the world, to vary twenty minutes and a half on the one side or the other. Now this must proceed solely from the velocity of light, bearing a sensible proportion to the annual motion of the earth. Hence we may be able to compute the true velocity of light, and to demonstrate the motion of the earth, according to the Copernican hypothesis.

ABE'RRING, Part. [from *aberr*] deviating, or wandering from the truth. "*Aberring* several ways from the true and just compute." *Brown's Vulg. Err.* b. iv. c. 12.

ABE'SSED, Adj. [*abaisse*, Fr.] humbled, or cast down. *Now obsolete.*

To ABE'T, V. A. [*betan*, Sax. *betan*, O. E.] to support, or help. "*Abet*, that virgin's cause disconsolate." *Spenf. Fairy Q.* b. 1.

To ABE'TT, V. A. In Law, to aid, incite, advise, encourage, support, or set another on.

ABE'TMENT, S. [from *abet*] the act of abetting, or setting another on, either by command, advice, or assistance.

ABE'TTER, or ABE'TTOR, S. [from *abet*] one who encourages, supports, or stirs up. "Ought to sink into the minds of those who are their *abettors*." *Freehold.* No. 50.

ABE'TTOR S. [from *abet*] in law, one who instigates, encourages, or sets another on to the committing something criminal; or assists in the performance of it. "The *abettors* of murder, in some cases, are taken as principals, in others as accessaries; their presence or absence at the time of committing the fact, making the difference." 1 Inst. 475 Staundf. P. c. 105. These are *abettors* in felony, but none in treason; because the law esteems all those who are concerned in treason, as principals.

ABEY'ANCE, S. [*boyer*, Fr.] in law, a thing not in possession, but in expectation.

To AB'GREGATE, V. A. [from *ab*, and *grege*, Lat.] to separate from the flock. A word of no authority.

To ABHO'R, V. A. [*abhorreo*, Lat.] to reject with a strong and forcible aversion; to hate, or detest to great extremity. "A church of England man *abhors* the humours of the age." *Swift.*

ABHOR'RENCE, or ABHOR'RENCY, S. [from *abhor*] a passion of the mind, arising from the contemplation of any thing that appears entirely disagreeable, extremely vicious, and worthy of his greatest hatred.

ABHOR'RENT, Part. [from *abhor*] affected with abhorrence or aversion, "he would *abhorrent* turn." *Thompson's Summer*, 310. When used with *from* or *to*, but especially the former, it implies, a thing by no means compatible, or highly inconsistent with; as "so *abhorrent from* the vulgar, that they would as soon believe." *Granville's Seep. Scien.*

ABHO'RRER, S. one who *abhors*, or exercises the passion of *abhorrence*. "By the known *abhorrers* of epitcopacy." *Swift's Exam.* No. 22.

To ABI'DE, V. N. [*abide* or *abid*. Pret. from *abidon*. Sax.] to stay or remain in a place. "Let thy servant *abide*, instead of the lad." *Genef.* xliv. 33. To endure, or to support, as "they little know how dearly I *abide* that boast so vain." *Milt. Par. Lost.* To dislike *staying* with, or to have a great aversion to; "Thou canst not *abide* Tiridates." *Sidney*, b. II. When followed with by, it signifies to stand by, confide in, or rely upon; as, to *abide* by his testimony; to *abide* by his own skill, is to rely upon them; To *abide* by a man is to stand by, or support him. But these expressions, as Johnson observes, are somewhat low, and, if tolerable in conversation, should never be adopted in composition.

To ABI'DE, V. A. to wait for, expect, or await. "Where many skillful leeches him *abide*." *Fairy Q.* b. i. c. v. stan. 27. "Poor harmless lambs *abide* their enmity." *Shakf. Hen.* VI.

ABI'DER, S. [from *abide*] a person who lives or resides in a place.

ABI'DING, S. [from *abode*] a permanent state; continuance, residence. "Nothing in that place can consist or have *abiding*." *Raleigh's Hist. of the World.*

ABI'DING, Part. [from *abide*] continuing, dwelling, "Balaam saw Israel *abiding* in his tents." *Numb.* xxiv. 2. Fixed to any particular place, or settled for any space of time. "There were shepherds *abiding* in the field." *Luke* ii. 8. Making lasting impressions on the mind. "Ye have not his word *abiding* in you." *Joh.* v. 38.

AB'JECT, Adj. [*objectus*, Lat.] when spoken of persons; mean, low, and worthless; when applied to things and actions; contemptible, base, and despicable; when used of condition, miserable, forlorn, and wretched. "The lowest pitch of *abject* fortune." *Milt. Samps.*

AB'JECT, S. [*abjectus*, Lat.] a person, who, with respect to his circumstances is in the extremities of poverty; with respect to his reputation, in the greatest infamy; with respect to his principles, in the lowest abyss of baseness; and with respect to his expectations, void of hope, and abandoned to despair. "Yea the *abjects* gathered themselves against me." *Psalm*, xxxv. 15.

To AB'JECT, V. A. [*objicio*, Lat. to cast away] to put, or cast away; to reject with disdain, scorn, or contempt: A word seldom used.

ABJE'CTION, ABJECTNESS, S. [*objectio*, Lat.] a base, servile, mean disposition

tion of mind. "Servility and *abjectness* of humour is implicitly involved in the charge of lying." *Government of the tongue.*

AB'JECTLY, Adv. [from *abject* and *ly*] In a mean, base, servile, or despicable state.

ABI'LITY, [*habilité*, Fr.] in the singular number ; power requisite to the performance of any thing. "They gave after their ability." Ezra ii. 69. The plural, *Abilities*, generally signify the powers of the mind. "Wherever we find our *abilities* too weak for the performance," *Rogers's Sermons.*

ABINTES'TATE, [*ab*, and *intestatus*, Lat. leaves no will behind him] In civil law, a person who inherits the estate of one who died without a will, though he had a power of making one.

ABINGTON, AB'INGDON, or AB'EN-DON, S. [*alen*, Sax. an abbey ; and *dune* a mountain, or open plain] a small town on the Ouse in Berkshire, formerly called Sheovesham by the Anglo-Saxons. But Cilla, king of the West Saxons, building an abbey here in 675, it changed its name to Abbandun ; which it derived from the abbey, and its situation, (that is, according to the book of Abindon) upon the plain of an hill. Here William the Conqueror kept his court, anno 1084, and left his son Henry to be educated. It is a frontier rough and town incorporate, consisting of a mayor, two bailiffs, nine aldermen, and has a power of electing nineteen more. It is also a high-steward, recorder, and town-clerk ; sends one member to parliament ; has a charity-school, two alms-houses, and a free-school founded by Mr. Royse, in 1563. Its weekly markets are on Monday and Friday ; its fair, the first Monday in Lent, the 20th of June, the 19th of September, and the 11th of December. It gives the title of earl to a younger branch of the family of Bertie, dukes of Ancaster, which title was first conferred on James Bertie, lord Norfs, of Rycot, in the thirty-fourth year of King Charles I. It has a handsome market-house of Ashler-work, built on lofty pillars, with a large hall of free-stone above, in which the county assizes are held. The streets are well paved ; and the trade of the inhabitants consists chiefly in malt, of which they send vast quantities in barges to London, from whence it is distant by water 150 miles, and by land 54.

AB'ISH'ERING, AB'ISHER'SING, S. [*Fesci esomen*, Teut.] in ancient grants, and charters, is a liberty or freedom to be quit of americamens ; and also to have the forfeiture of others, within one's fee. *Rastal's Exp. of terms.*

ABISSI'NIA. See ABYSSINIA.

ABJURA'TION, S. [*abjuratio*, Lat.] in a general sense, is the act of denying, or renouncing a thing with an oath ; but more particularly, a solemn renunciation or renunciation of some person, doctrine, or thing. "All persons admitted into any office, must "take the test, which is an *abjuration* of "some doctrines of the church of Rome." *Ayliffe's Parergon.*

Oath of ABJURATION, taken by all that are matriculated in universities, admitted to scholarships, fellowships, holy orders, &c. Is renouncing upon oath any title or claim of the pretender, or any of his descendants to this crown, and denying ever to serve him in the capacity of a subject. In law, it signifies a sworn banishment for ever ; for anciently if a man had committed felony, and fled to some church or church yard, he could not be taken thence and tried ; but, on confession of his crime to the justice or c'roner, he was admitted to his oath of *abjuring* the kingdom. But, by stat. 21 Jac. I. all use of sanctuaries being taken away, this kind of abjuration ceased. *Stoundf. P. C.* lib. ii. cap. 40. 2 Instit. 629. *Stat. 21, Hen. VIII.*

To ABJURE, V. A. [*abjuro*, Fr. of *ab-juro*, Lat.] to quit or abandon, in allusion to the necessity they were under to quit the realm, who had taken the oath abovementioned ; to cast off, and to have no commerce with ; "To *abjure* for ever the society "of men." *Shak. Midsum. Night's Dream.* "no man that hath not *abjured* his reason." *Hale.*

To ABLAC'TATE, V. A. [*ablacto*, Lat.] to wean from the breast ; and, by metaphor, to leave off a thing. Seldom used.

ABLACTA'TION, S. in ancient gardening, a method of engrafting, wherein the cyon of one tree being united to the stock of another, is at last cut off, and as it were, weaned from its mother tree. In modern gardening, it is called inarching, or grafting by approach, which is practicable only, when the two trees are so near, that the cyon of one may be applied to the stock of another, without cutting off.

ABLAQUA'TION, S. [*ablaqueatio*, Lat. of *ab*, from and *laqus*, a ditch] in gardening, the digging away the mould, or opening the earth at the roots of trees, that the sun, air and rain may operate upon them, and thereby remove their soil and improve their pristine fecundity.

AB'LATIVE, Adj. [*ablativus*, Lat.] in Latin grammar, is the sixth and last case of nouns and participles. It is peculiar to the Latin, and from thence filled by some the Latin case. Priscian calls it the comparative case, because it is used in comparing, and follows an adjective of the comparative degree. It may properly be said to be only a supernumerary case, or a supplement to the other five ; and was not invented to express any relation of itself, but to be joined to some prepositions, as the others were not sufficient

fufficient to exprefs all the relations which things have to one another; hence arifes the grammatical maxim that every ablative is governed by a prepofition, either expreffed or underftood. In the plural number it is entirely wanting, becaufe the termination of the dative, and the ablative in that number is always the fame. This cafe is oppofed to the dative, becaufe that implies the action of giving, but the ablative that of taking away. In Englifh, French, &c. there is no mark to diftinguifh the ablative, and we only ufe the term in allufion to the Latin. Thus in this fentence; " he fpoke much of " the magnitude of the city." We fay the words, *of the magnitude*, are the ablative, and *of the city*, the genitive, becaufe they would be rendered by thofe two cafes, if we tranflated the fentence into Latin.

A'BLE, Adj. [*abal*, Sax.] indued with, or having power. " Ever learning, and " never *able* to come to the knowledge of " the truth." 2 *Tim.* iii. 7. Sufficient; " from a child thou haft known the holy " fcriptures, which are *able* to make thee wife." 2 *Tim.* iii. 15. By metaphor it fignifies great powers; arifing from knowledge, wealth, or intereft; " He was not afraid of " an *able* man, as Lewis the eleventh was." *Bacon's Hen.* VII.

To A'BLE. V. A. See ENABLE.

A'BLE-BO'DIED, Adj. ftrong in body.

To A'BLEGATE, V. A. [*ablego*, Lat.] to fend abroad upon an embaffy or other employment; to fend a perfon out of the way.

A'BLENESS, S. fufficient power or capacity to do a thing; ability of mind or body. See ABILITY.

A'BLEPSY, S. [*ablepfia*, Gr.] want of fight, natural blindnefs; inadvertence, unadvifednefs, or mifnefs. A word not in ufe.

To A'BLOCATE, V. A. [*abloco*, Lat.] to let out to hire; appropriated to one, who was hired himfelf, *Calvin's Lex.* Jur.

ABLOCA'TION, S. [from *abloco*] the act of letting out to hire.

A'BLUENT, Adj. [*abluo*, Lat.] that which wafhes clean, or has the power of cleanfing. Abluent medicines, are fuch as dilute, diffolve, and carry off, the acrimonious and ftimulating falts lodged in any part of the body; efpecially the ftomach and inteftines; fuch are ptifans, wheys, and juleps; but they are better known by the name to which we refer, i. e. ABSTERGENTS.

ABLUTION, S. [*ablutio*, Lat.] the act of cleanfing, " there is a natural analogy " between the *ablution* of the body and the " purification of the foul." *Taylor's Wor-* *thy Canton.* What is left after the act of wafhing; as " the pious train are " drench'd, and caft th' *ablutions* in the " main." *Pope's Iliad.*

ABLU'TION, S. a religious ceremony, ufed by the antient Romans, before they began to facrifice.

ABLU'TION, S. in pharmacy, the preparations which divers medicines undergo to cleanfe them from their impurities. In phyfic, it is the wafhing the external parts of the body by baths, or the internal by thin diluting fluids, as whey, &c. In chemiftry, the wafhing, or infufing certain medicines in water to frefhen them, and diffolve their falts.

ABNEGA'TION, S. [*abnegatio*, Lat.] a pofitive and abfolute denial of a thing.

ABNODA'TION, S. [*abnodatio*, Lat.] in gardening, the pruning or cutting away knots, knobs, or other excrefcencies from trees.

ABO'ARD, Adv. [from *a*, and *bord*, Sax.] a fea term, fignifying in a fhip, " he loudly called to them that were " *aboard*." *Fairy Queen.*

ABO'DE, V. N. [the preterperfect tenfe of *abide*] remained; ftayed; " *abode* with " him that day." *John* i. 39.

ABO'DE, S. [from *abide*] the act of ftaying, or continuing in any place. " Making a fhort *abode* in Sicily." *Dryden.* Joined to the word *make* it has always this fignification. It is ufed for the place wherein a perfon ftays, continues, remains or dwells. " I know thy *abode*," 2 *Kings*, xix. 27.

ABO'DEMENT. S. [from *abode*] a fecret impreffion on the mind, anticipation, omen, prefage, or prognoftication of fomething future; " Tufh I man, *abodements* " muft not frighten us now." *Shakfp.* *Hen.* VIII. Obfolete.

To ABOLISH, V. A. [*abolir*, Fr.] to deftroy; put an end to. " Invincible jea- " loufies and hate, which long-continued " peace hath fince *abolifhed*." Sir *John Hay-* *ward.* To annul, or annihilate. " More " deftroyed than they, we fhould be quite " *abolifhed*!" *Par. Loft*, b. II. 92.

ABOL'ISHABLE, Adv. that which can be abolifhed.

ABOL'ISHER, S. [*abolifh*] the thing or perfon that abolifhes.

ABOL'ISHING, Part. that which annuls, repeals, or cancels.

ABOL'ISHMENT, S. See ABOLISHING.

ABOLI'TION, [*abolitio*, Lat.] the act of abolifhing: now ufed inftead of *abolifhment.* " An apoplexy, is the *abolifhment* of all the " fenfes." *Arbuthnot.*

ABOLI'TION, S. in common law, the abrogating, or repealing any law, or ftatute. In civil law, the leave given by the prince or judge, to a criminal accufer to defift from further profecution.

ABOMA'SUS, ? S. [Lat.] the maw, ABOMA'SUM, $ or laft of the four fto- . machs,

machs in animals of the ruminating kind; being the place wherein the chyle is formed, and from whence the food descends immediately into the intestines.

ABOM'INABLE, Adj. [abominabilis, Lat.] that which raises in the mind horror, joined with aversion and detestation. "This "infernal pit, abominable, accursed." Par. Lost. b. x. In low and ludicrous language, it conveys only the idea of something superlative; as abominable unclean, i. e. superlatively so.

ABOM'INABLENESS, S. [abominable] the quality, which renders any thing abominable.

ABOM'INABLY, Adv. extremely, prodigiously, superlatively; in an ill sense, a word of low and familiar language.

To ABOM'INATE, V. A. [abominor, Lat.] to abhor, detest, or despise. "He "professed both to abominate and despise all "mystery." Gulliver.

ABOMINA'TION, S. [abominate] an object causing the greatest dislike, aversion, or detestation. "Every shepherd is an "abomination to the Ægyptians." Gen. xlvi. 34. "Whatsoever hath no fins, nor scales "in the waters, that shall be an abomination "to you." Levit. xi. 12. When used with the auxiliary verb to have, or rather, to have in, it signifies to reckon as foul; or to abominate. "You shall have their carcases in "abomination." Idem. xi. 11. As idols and idolatry are the objects of the divine hatred; they are therefore figuratively expressed by this word, as "When you shall see the "abomination of desolation." Matth. xxiv. 12, 15.

ABORIG'INES, S. the antient inhabitants of a country, whose original could not be traced; it is used in opposition to colonies.

ABOR'TION, S. [abortio, Lat.] the exclusion of a child from the womb, before the due time of delivery: In irrational animals, filled flinking or casting their young. If this should happen before the second month after conception, it is filled a false conception. Miscarriages are produced by causes immediately affecting the child, the membranes that involve it, the placenta, the funis umbilicalis, i. e. the navel-string, or the mother; with respect to the child, whatever is the occasion of its death, causes abortion likewise, sooner or later. A tenderness of the membranes which include the foetus, rendering them liable to ruptures upon every trivial occasion, often causes a miscarriage. There are frequent instances of a schirosity of the placenta, and a shortness of the umbilical cord, which have had the same effect. With respect to the mother, immoderate evacuations, sudden passions, frights, all distempers, either acute or chronical, too violent exercise, lifting a great weight, fullness of blood, stimulating

medicines, straining in order to speak loud, and a disagreeable smell, are frequent causes of abortion.

Abortion is very dangerous, where the time of pregnancy is so far advanced, that the foetus is large; where the cause is very violent, or the patient convulsed; where a large hæmorrhage precedes or ensues; or the foetus is putrified. But if neither of these symptoms occur, it is always more dangerous than a birth at the full period. And as there seems to be a very strict analogy between the fruits of animals and the seeds of plants; an instance from the vegetable tribe will be no small illustration, if not a confirmation of the assertion. "A walnut "drops spontaneously from its involucrum "or hull, when arrived at a state of maturity; but before it has arrived at that "state, cannot be separated without violence. Just so it is with respect to abortions."

ABOR'TION, S. is used for the foetus thus expelled, by the figure Metonymia, wherein the effect is put for the cause. "His wife miscarried, but as the abortion "proved only a female foetus." Life of Martin Scriblerus.

ABOR'TION, S. in gardening, is applied to such fruits as are produced too early, which commonly happens to those trees that are blasted by noxious winds.

ABOR'TIVE, Adj. [abortivus, Lat.] that which is brought forth before its time: "If ever he have a child, abortive be it." Shakesp. Rich. III. Any thing or design which miscarries, is frustrated, or comes to nothing. "This is the true cause why so "many passible conceptions prove abortive." South.

ABOR'TIVENESS, S. [from abortive] the state of abortion; want of success, disappointment.

ABOVE, Prep. [Bufan, Sax.] higher in place, or position; as, "Above the clouds, "it thy proud rostick found." Cowley. Used before nouns of time, it signifies more or longer than; as, "He fought above two "hours." Superiority, or higher in rank, power or excellence; "The Lord is above "all nations." Psalm cxiii. 4. "Cæfar "could not abide to have any above him." When used comparatively, it signifies preferable to; as, "There is no riches above a "found body; no joy above the joy of the "heart." Ecclus. xxx. 16.

ABOVE, Adv. It is used to denote a higher place; "To those above, men standing below, seem not so much lessened." Bacon. It is from hence used for the heavens, both in sacred and profane authors; "Trust the powers above." Pope's Iliad.

ABOVE-BOARD, [compound word] an expression borrowed from gamesters, who generally put their hands under the table in order to change their cards; and signifies, in

To open fight, plainly, honestly, without the least artifice, or diffimulation; "It is "the part of an honest man to deal above-"board," L'Estrange.

ABOVE-MENTIONED, Part. mentioned in a former part of a work or writing, "unfit for the utterance of the five "lines above-mentioned," Guard. No. 82.

To ABOUND, V. N. [abonder, Lat. abunder, Fr.] to have an exceeding great number, quantity or plenty of any thing. "A faithful man shall abound with bleſſings." Prov. xxviii. 2.

To ABOUND, V. N. when uſed without the particle, fignifies to increaſe prodigiouſly, "when iniquity ſhall abound." Matth. xxiv. 12. to be in great plenty, number, or exceſs.

ABOUT, Prep. [abutan, Sax.] applied to time or place, it fignifies, near, or within the compaſs of; as, "about night." "They "have ſet up a ſhop about the pſide." When put before words of meaſure, it has the ſame ſignification; "about four fingers long." The moſt ſimple acceptation is that of round, ſurrounding, or encircling, according to the Saxon, from whence it is derived; "Bind them about thy neck." Prov. ixi. 3. annexed to; or, appendant to a perſon, in the ſame manner as dreſs. "If you have "this about you." Milton. Concerning of, relating to.

ABOUT, Adv. In circumference, or compaſs. "Indeed, I am in the waiſt two yards about." Merry Wives of Windſor. From place to place; every where; "He went about doing good." Aſts. The longeſt way, in oppoſition to the ſhorteſt, or ſtraight, alluding to the circumference, and the diameter of a circle; "The ſure way (though moſt about) to make good." Boyle. When prefixed to verbs, it fignifies that the action or thing will ſoon happen; as, "about to fight;" "about to periſh."

To be ABOUT, V. N. to be employed or engaged in. "What is our great countrymen were about." Spect. No. 319.

ABOUT, Adj. [about, Fr.] a certain point, period, or ſtate, and is diverſified according to the verb to which it is joined. "Thus he has brought about his purpoſes." He has accompliſhed them. "Whether this will be brought about," by breaking his head." Spect. When joined with come, it fignifies, to be arrived at a certain ſtate or point. As, "The wind they long had wiſhed was come about." Dryd. Fables. When joined with go, it implies preparation, or deſign. "As, why go ye about to kill me." John vii. 19.

ABRACADABRA, [Abraxas, the name of a Syrian idol] a magical charm, invented by the elder Serenus Samonicus, who lived in the time of Severus and Caracalla, as a cure for the Semi-tertian.

ABRACALAN, a cabbaliſtic word, made uſe of by the Jews for the ſame purpoſe as the precedent.

To ABRADE, V. A. [abrado, Lat.] to rub off, to waſte or wear away by degrees. "Succeſſively abraded from them by a decurſion of waters." Halm's Origin.

ABRAHAM's BALM, S. in Botany, the hemp-tree, a ſpecies of willow.

ABRAHAM's BOSOM, is a term uſed in the ſcripture phraſeology, to denote a place of the greateſt felicity in the heavenly manſions.

ABRASION, S. [ſee ABRADE] the act of wearing away, or rubbing off. In Medicine, it fignifies the wearing away the natural mucus which covers the membranes, particularly thoſe of the ſtomach and inteſtines, by ſharp corroſive medicines or humours.

ABREAST, Adv. [breaſt, Sax.] in ſuch a poſition, that the breaſts may bear againſt the ſame line. "The riders rode abreaſt." Dryd. Ships are ſaid to fail three or four abreaſt, when they bear down by ſide of each other.

ABRIC, ALBRICK, S. among Chymiſts, ſulphur.

To ABRIDGE, V. A. [abreger, Fr.] to ſhorten in words, ſo as to preſerve the ſubſtance. "All theſe ſayings we will ſtudy to abridge in one volume." 2 Maccab. ii. 23. to diminiſh, leſſen, or cut ſhort. When followed by the particles from, or of, it denotes to deprive. "To be abridged from "ſuch a noble race," Merchant of Venice. "The city had many privileges, but is now abridged of moſt of them."

ABRIDGER, S. [from abridge] a ſhortener; a writer of compendiums, or abridgments.

ABRIDGMENT, S. [abregement, Fr.] the contraction of a large work into a leſs compaſs. "This one word is the abridgment of all volumes of ſcripture," Hooker, b. ii. §. 5. A leſſening, or diminution.

ABROACH, Adv. [ſee BROACH] running out, in alluſion to liquor that is broached, or tapped. "While every ſpout's abroach." Swift. To be ſet in ſuch a poſition, that the liquor contained may eaſily be drawn out. "The jars of gen'ious wine—he ſet abroach." Dryd. Virgil. To undertake. "What miſchiefs might be ſet abroach." Shakeſ. Hen. IV.

ABROAD, Adv. [from a, and brad, Sax.] without confinement; at large. "The lonely fox roams far abroad." Prior. In a foreign country. "The time I ſhould think fitteſt, for a young gentleman to be ſent abroad." Locke on Educat. In all directions. "An elm diſplays her duſky arms abroad," Dryd. Virg. From without, externally, in oppoſition to within. "More ſtates are overthrown through diſeaſes bred within

C

the

themselves, than thro' violence from *abroad*." *Hooker.*

To AB'ROGATE, V. A. [*abrogo*, Lat.] to deprive, to repeal, or annul. "Laws of that kind do *abrogate* themselves." *Hooker.*

ABROGA'TION, S. [*abrogatio.* Lat.] the act of repealing. "Demanded the *abroga tion* and repeal of those laws which were in force." *Clarendon*, b. viii.

To ABRO'OK, V. A. to bear or endure. "Ill can thy noble mind *abrook* the abject people." *Shakef. Hen. VII.*

ABRUPT, Adj. [*abruptus*, Lat.] craggy, broken. "Tumbling through rocks *ab rupt*." *Thomps.* Sudden, unexpected, without the customary preparatives. "To know the cause of your *abrupt* departure." *Shakef* Unconnected, when applied to writing; as, "The *abrupt* stile, which hath made many breaches." *Ben. Johnf. Difcov.*

ABRU'PTION, S. [*abruptio*, Lat. this word seldom occurs] a breaking off, separation.

ABRU'PTLY, Adv. hastily, unexpectedly, rudely, without the previous ceremonies required. "So lately found, and so *abruptly* gone." *Sidney*, b. ii.

ABRU'PTNESS, S. an hasty, unexpected, unceremonious manner, suddenness, or the state of unconnectedness, roughness, cragginefs.

A'BRUS, S. a kind of red phaseolus, or kidney-bean, growing in Egypt and the Indies.

ABS'CESS, S. [*abscessus*, Lat.] a critical difcharge of humours, which passes not off by the common conductories, but collects in larger quantities as to form a tumour or fuelling, and break or corrode the vessels, if not distended. The matter thus collected is sometimes included in a cystis or bag, and appears either curdy, or like honey, or tallow, and is termed an *ircvilded* tumour.

To ABS'CIND, V. A. [*abscindo*, Lat.] to cut off. Not often used.

ABSCI'SSA, ABSCI'SSE, S. [*abscissus*, Lat.] In Conics, a part of the diameter of a curve line, intercepted between the vertex of that diameter, and the point where any ordinate or semi-ordinate to that diameter falls, or that part of the axis to a curve-lined figure, that is cut off by an ordinate, and contained between the vertex and the ordinate.

ABSCIS'SION, S. [*abscissio*, Lat.] the act of cutting off. "Fabricius renders the *ab scission* of them difficult enough." *Wiseman's Surgery.* Seldom used.

To ABSCO'ND, V. N. [*abscondo*, Lat.] to keep one's self from the view of the public; to hide, applied especially to those who fly to escape the law.

ABSCO'NDER, S. [from *abscond*] the person who quits his residence, and hides himself to prevent his being discovered.

ABSCO'NDING, S. [from *abscond*] the act of avoiding the sight of mankind, or leaving one's dwelling for that purpose.

AB'SENCE, S. [*absence*, Fr. *absentia*, Lat.] distance which deprives a person both of the sight and converse of another, generally used in opposition to presence. "I mourn in *absence*, love's eternal night." *Dryd. Pal. and Arc.* Inattention to the present object, because a person in that state resembles one who is distant. "Reflecting on the little *absence*, or distractions of mankind." *Spect. No. 77.*

AB'SENT, Adj. [*absens*, Lat.] at a distance from; out of the sight and hearing of a person. "*Absent* from her sight." *Pope's Past.* Inattentive to, or regardless of something present, by employing one's thoughts on something else. "I distinguish a man that is *absent*, because he thinks on something else." *Spect. No. 77.*

To ABSE'NT, V. A. [See ABSENT] to withdraw, or decline the presence of a person or thing. "*Absent* thee from felicity a while." *Hamlet.*

ABSENTA'NEOUS, Adj. [*absentaneus*, Lat.] relating to absence.

ABSENTE'E, S. [*absent*] he that is absent from his station or country.

ABSE'NTER, S. one that does not attend; as, "An *absenter* from church."

ABSI'NTHIATED, Part. [See ABSIN'THIUM, Lat.] In Medicine, impregnated with wormwood; from

ABSIN'THIUM, S. [Wormwood, of *α-δinos*, *αψίνθιον*, unpleasant, from *α*, privative, and *ηδονε*, *ψύσθαι*, according to some, because delight] there are thirty-three species of this plant; but that used in Phyfic is the *Absinthium vulgare majus* of Bauhine, or common wormwood. The virtues of this herb, according to Boerhaeve, are immortal, as curing all dropsies not attended with a rupture of the viscera. An ounce of the juice, extracted from the green leaves, is of great service to persons labouring under a languor. A conserve made of the tender tops of the leaves is of excellent use where the stomach is clogged with phlegm, or unactive bile, providing the distemperature be not hot.

ABSO'LVATORY, Adj. [*absolutoire*, Fr.] that has relation to pardon or absolution.

To ABSO'LVE, V. A. [*absolvo*, Lat.] to clear or acquit; as, "He hopes and gives out, by the influence of his wealth, to be *absolved*." *Swift.* To free from an engagement or promise. "I am *absolved*." *Waller.* To pardon, in allusion to the absolution of a priest. "For God, not man, *absolves* our frailties here." *Pope's Holdfe.*

AB'SOLUTE, Adj. [*absolutus*, Lat.] perfect, without defect; complete. "The *words* of his mouth are *absolute*." "By sea he is an *absolute* master." *Shakesp. Anthon.* Without conditions, Independent, "God

in an *absolute* Being." Without restraint or limitation. " My crown is *absolute*." *Dryd.*

ABSOLU'TE NUMBER, in Algebraic Equations, is the known quantity which possesseth one side of an equation.

ABSOLU'TE EQUATION, in Astronomy, is the aggregate or amount of the excentric or optic equations.

AB'SOLUTENESS, S. completeness ; freedom from restrictions or limits. " The *absoluteness* and illimitedness of his commission." *Clarendon*, b. viii. When applied to the exercise of regal power, it signifies arbitrariness or despoticism. " Which made for his *absoluteness*, but not for his safety." *Bacon's Hen. VII.*

ABSOLUTELY, Adv. entirely, completely, perfectly. " *Absolutely* inconceivable." *Swift.* Without conditions or relation. " *Absolutely* considered, without a relation to our eyes." *Brerely.* Without any check, restraint, or limits. " *Absolutely* did reign." *Par. Lost.*

ABSOLU'TION, S. [*absolutio*, Lat.] in the Common Law, a full acquittal of a person by some final sentence ; a temporal discharge from further attendance upon a mesne process. In Ecclesiastical Law, a juridical act, whereby a priest pronounces pardon for sins.

AB'SOLUTORY, Adj. [*absolutorius*, Lat.] that which imparts pardon, forgiveness, or absolution. " Though an *absolutory* sentence should be pronounced." *Ayliffe.*

AB'SONANT, Part. [*absonans*, Lat.] of a harsh sound ; contrary to reason ; absurd ; foreign to the purpose.

AB'SONOUS, Adj. [*absonus*, Lat.] not agreeable to allusion, in the concords of music.

To ABSOR'B, V. A. [*absorbeo*, Lat.] to suck up " To *absorb* and extenuate the said singular parts." *Harvey.*

ABSOR'BENT, S. [*absorbens*, Lat.] in Physic, such medicines as dry up redundant humours, whether applied internally or externally. Such are the testaceous powders, chalk, &c. The term is likewise applied to the lacteals which *absorb* the chyle.

ABSOR'PT, Part. swallowed up. " The particular constitution of the earth, which made it obnoxious to be *absorpt* in water. *Burnet.*

ABSOR'PTION, S. the act of sucking up, or absorbing.

To ABSTA'IN, V. N. [*abstineo*, Lat.] to forbear, refrain from, or deny one's self any gratification. " To *abstain* from love's due rites." *Par. Lost.* " *Abstain* from all appearance of evil." 1 *Thes. v. 22.* With great elegance applied to inanimate things. " The doubtful billows scarce *abstain* from the tossed vessel." *Dryd. Virgil.*

ABSTE'MIOUS, Adj. [*abstemious*, Lat.] temperate in the enjoyment of sensual gra-

tifications. " As an *abstemious* hermit." It is likewise used substantively. " The instances of longevity are chiefly among the *abstemious*." Arbuth.

ABSTE'MIOUSLY, Adv. soberly, temperately.

ABSTE'MIOUSNESS, S. the quality of being temperate or abstemious

ABSTEN'SION, ABSTEN'TION, S. [*abstineo*, Lat.] the act of holding off or restraining.

To ABSTER'GE, V. A. [*abstergo*, Lat.] to wipe clean, to cleanse.

ABSTER'GENT, Part. [*abstergens*, Lat.] endued with a cleansing quality.

ABSTER'GENTS, S. in Medicine, a class of remedies, which abrade and clear away such mucous particles as they meet with in their passage, and, by that means, cleanse the parts from viscid or morbid adhesions, whether they be the matter of wounds, ulcers, &c. Their most usual name among modern practitioners, is that of *detergents*.

ABSTER'SION, S. [*abstersio*, Lat.] the act of cleansing. " The seventh cause is *abstersion*, which is a scowering off." *Bacon's Nat. Hist.*

ABSTER'SIVE, Adj. [*abstersivum*, Lat.] endued with the quality of cleansing. "There many a flower *abstersive* grew." *Swift.*

AB'STINENCE, S. [*abstinentia*, Lat.] in a general sense it signifies the refraining from any thing to which we have a propensity. In a more limited sense it signifies fasting, or the forbearance of necessary food. And in this acceptation it is distinguished from temperance, as that implies a moderate use of foods, but this is an entire avoiding of it for a time. *Abstinence* is certainly of great service to people of a sedentary life, to keep them from a multitude of diseases; and of great assistance to medicines in the cure of chronical or acute diseases. We shall produce one or two instances of its efficacy, from a thousand equally astonishing. The noble Venetian, Cornaro, after having tried all means that could be thought of for his recovery, was given over at forty, but was cured, and lived to an hundred, as himself assures us, by the mere diet of *abstinence*. In our own Island, as we are informed by Buchanan, one Laurence preserved himself to one hundred and forty; and Kentigern, afterwards called St Mungo, according to Spotswood, lived to one hundred and eighty-five, by the same means Nor should this be looked on as incredible, since most chronical diseases, the infirmities of old age, and the short lives of Englishmen, are, according to Cheyne, in his Essay on Health, owing to repletion, and may be cured by *abstinence*.

ABS'TINENCY, S. [*abstinentia*, Lat.] the same as *abstinence*. A word not in use at present.

AB'STINENT, Adj. [*abstinens*, Lat.]

temperate; modest, in opposition to rapacious, covetous, or luxurious.

ABSTORTED, Part. [*abstortus*, Lat.] plucked, torn, or wrested by violence.

To ABS'TRACT, V. A. [*abstraho*, Lat.] to take one thing from another. " Could we abstract from these perishing effects." *Decay of Piety* To separate. " The mind has a power to abstract its ideas." *Locke's Essay.* When applied to books or writings, it signifies the comprising their substance in fewer words and less compass. " Let us abstract them into brief compends." *Watts's Improvem.*

ABSTRACT, Adj. [*abstractus*, Lat.] separated from something else. " Considering things in themselves abstract from our opinions and other men's notions." *Locke's Essay.* Abstract terms signify the mode or quality of a being, without any regard to the subject in which it is; such as whiteness, roundness, life, death.

ABSTRACT Mathematics, are those branches employed about quantity without any restriction to any particular species of it.

ABSTRACT Numbers, are assemblages of units, considered in themselves, without being applied to any subject.

ABSTRACT, S. [from to abstract] a compendious view of a treatise, rather more superficial than an abridgment. " He could give a tolerable analysis and abstract of every treatise he read." *Watts's Imp.* It is applied figuratively to persons, " A man who is the abstract of all faults all men follow." *Shaksp.* Ant. and Cleop.

ABS'TRACT, S. In a particular sense signifies an idea formed in the mind, when we consider a mode or quantity separate from all the particular subjects in which they inhere.

ABSTRACTED, Part. [from abstract] separated; " abstracted from his own evil." *Milton.* Refined, or abstruse, [" Abstracted spiritual love" *Prior.*

ABSTRACTEDLY, Adv. [from abstract] in an abstract manner; distinct, or separate from contingent circumstances.

ABSTRAC'TION, S. [*abstractio*, Lat.] an operation or faculty of the mind, which distinguishes us from the brute creation, whereby we separate things naturally existing together, and form and consider ideas thus separated.

ABSTRAC'TION, S. implies the exercise of this faculty; the state of being abstracted, or inattentive to external objects; or absence of mind.

ABSTRAC'TION, S. in pharmacy, the drawing off, or exhaling a menstruum, from the subject it was designed to dissolve.

ABSTRAC'TITIOUS, S. in pharmacy, native spirit of vegetables.

ABSTRAC'TIVE, Adj. indued with the power of abstracting.

ABSTRA'CTLY, Adv. without reference to, or separate from any thing else. " Matter abstractly and absolutely considered." *Bentley.*

ABSTRU'SE, Adj. [*abstrusus*, Lat.] hidden or secret. " Th' eternal eye, whose sight discerns abstrusest thoughts." *Milton.* Not easily apprehended; difficult. " Since its so abstruse a subject, I may be pardoned, if I sometimes miss the mark." *Boyle.*

ABSTRU'SELY, Adv. in an obscure manner, opposite to plainly or obviously.

ABSTRUSE'NESS, S. [from abstruse] difficulty, obscurity; a relative term, implying, that the object is not easily to be comprehended by any particular person's understanding.

ABSU'RD, Adj. [*absurdus*, Lat.] defect of reason and judgment. " You had better take for business a man somewhat absurd, than over formal." *Bacon's Essay.* When applied to opinions or practices; contradictory, inconsistent; contrary to reason. " 'Tis phrase, absurd to call a villain great." *Pope's Essay on Man.*

ABSU'RDITY, S. [*absurdité*, Fr.] a contradiction to common sense; an inconsistence with reason; stupidity. " Look into their pretended truths; are they not so many wretched absurdities!" *Guard. No. 83.*

ABSU'RDNESS, S. [from absurd] injudiciousness, impropriety, faulty. See absurdity.

ABU'NDANCE, S. [*abundance*, Fr. *abundantia*, Lat.] in poetical writers, Plenty! " Crown'd abundance spreads my board!" *Crashaw.* Great number, " Abundance of people;" a great quantity, " What abundance of noble blood hath been shed!" *Raleigh's Essay.* Exuberance, overflowings, or luxuriance. " Th' abundance of an idle brain." *Fairy Q.*

ABU'NDANT, Adj. [*abundans*, Lat.] plentiful; " Good, the more communicated, more abundant grows." *Par. Lost, b. v.* Exuberant. " According to his abundant mercy, begot us to a lively hope." *1 Pet. i. 3.* Numerous, " Like some Indian province, wherein though mines and gems were more abundant than in other countries." *Boyle.* Joined with the particle in, it signifies overflowing, replete, or exuberant. " Abundant in goodness and truth." *Exod. xxxiv. 6.*

ABU'NDANT Numbers, are those whose aliquot, or even parts, when added together, exceed the number itself.

ABU'NDANTLY, Adv. [from abundant] in great numbers. " Let the waters bring forth abundantly." *Gen. i. 20.* Liberally. " God on thee abundantly his gifts hath also pour'd." *Par. Lost, b. viii.* Amply, more than sufficiently. " He abundantly confirms the other's testimony." *Dryden.*

To ABU'SE, V. A. [*abuser*, Lat. the fla-

this verb is pronounced like an *s*, the particle is formed by omitting the *e* final as *abuſing*) to make an ill uſe of ; " They that uſe this world, as not *abuſing* it." 1 Cor. vii. 31. To impoſe upon. " The world hath been much *abuſed* by the opinion of making gold." *Bacon's Nat. Hiſt.* To treat contemptuouſly and with *rudeneſs* ; " Laughed at them and *abuſed* them ſhamefully." 1 Mac. vii. 34. To ſeduce. " He perhaps, as he is very potent with ſuch ſpirits, *abuſes* me to damn me." *Hamlet.* To reproach, or treat with ill language.

ABU'SE, S. [from *abuſe, abuſus,* Lat.] the ill or improper uſe of any thing. " Another great *abuſe* of words, is Inconſtancy in the uſe of them." *Locke's Eſſay.* A vitious practice or bad cuſtom. " If *abuſes* be not remedied, they will certainly increaſe." *Swift.* Carnal knowledge, either with or without violence. " And through the deceit *abuſed* me." *Sidney.*

ABU'SER, S. [from *abuſe* and *uſer,* Goth. *ur uſer,* Sax.] the perſon who makes an ill uſe of any thing ; an impoſter, ſeducer, or raviſher ; one who makes uſe of reproachful language, or is guilty of rudeneſs towards another.

ABU'SIVE, Adj. [*abuſif,* Fr. *abuſivus,* Lat.] practiſing abuſe. " And wicked wit aroſe, thy moſt abuſive foe." *Pope's Miſcell.* Containing, or full of abuſe ; deceitful ; or ſeducing.

ABU'SIVELY, Adv. Improperly. In a reproachful, rude, and ill-behaved manner.

ABU'SIVENESS, S. [from *abuſe*] the uſe of reproachful language ; or the exerciſe of rude, and unmerited incivility. " Prophaneneſs, filthineſs, *abuſiveneſs.*" *Theob.*

To ABU'T, V. N. [*abutir,* Fr.] to border upon ; to end at ; to meet, or approach.

ABU'TILON, S. [Arab.] in Botany, the yellow mallows, called ſo by Linnæus. It has a ſingle annular complement, which is permanent, and divided into five parts at the top. The flower conſiſts of five petals joined at the baſe. In the center alſo many ſtamina, coaleſcing at the bottom to the ſtyle ; and forming a ſort of column, which reſts upon a round germen.

ABU'TMENTS, S. the parts of any ground, or buildings that approach, or border upon another.

A'BYSM, S. [*abiſme,* old Fr.] a deep place that has no bottom, whether by land or water. " Into the abyſm of hell." *Shak. Ant. and Cleop.*

ABY'SS, S. [*abyſſus,* Lat. *aʋʋſſος,* Gr.] a cavity without bottom. " The dark, unbottom'd, infinite abyſs." *Par. Loſt.* That in which any thing is loſt ; " In time's abyſs." *Dryd. Georg.*

The antient Hebrews, as well as the generality of the eaſtern nations, were of opi-

nion, that the *abyſs,* or ſea, encompaſſed the whole earth, on which it was founded ; that at the bottom of this *abyſs,* the Rephaim, or giants were confined for puniſhment, and the kings of Tyre, Babylon, and Egypt, ſuffered the torments of their guilt. Agreeable to this ſentiment St. John repreſents the devils and wicked men, as caſt down into the bottomleſs pit, an expreſſion which is a paraphraſe or explanation of the word *abyſs.* They likewiſe hold, that fountains and rivers owe their origin to this *abyſs,* by percolating through the pores of the earth, and that they return thither thro' paſſages of their own making. The Drs. Woodward and Nicholls, have illuſtrated and confirmed this hypotheſis in a very ingenious manner, as may be ſeen in the Natural Hiſtory of the former, and the vol. I. of the Conference publiſhed by the latter.

ABYSSINIA, a kingdom of Africa, bounded on the N. by that of Sennar, or Nubia ; on the E. partly by the Red Sea, and partly by Dancala ; on the W. by Gorham and Gingiro ; and on the S. by Alaba and Ommo /eidi. It was formerly of greater extent than it is at preſent, becauſe ſeveral provinces have revolted, and the Turks have made encroachments to the Eaſt. The land is fertile in many places, and the air is very hot, except in the rainy ſeaſon, and then it is very temperate. For four months in the year there are greater rains fall than perhaps in any other part of the world, which occaſion the ſwelling of the river Nile, that has its ſource in this country. It contains mines of all ſorts of metal except tin ; but the inhabitants make no great advantage thereof. The fields are watered by ſeveral ſtreams, except in the mountainous parts. The emperor, or king, is called Negus ; and he has been commonly taken for Preſter John. His authority is abſolute, and he often dwells with his whole court in tents. However, Abyſſinia is not without cities, as ſome pretend ; for Gondar is a large place, where he commonly reſides when he is not in the field. The inhabitants are black, or very near it ; but they are not as ugly as the Negroes. They make profeſſion of the Chriſtian religion ; but it has a great mixture of Judaiſm. The habit of perſons of quality is a ſilken veſt, with a ſort of ſcarf ; but the common people wear nothing but a pair of drawers.

ACACA'LIS, S. [from *acacalis,* the name of a nymph raviſhed by Apollo] in Botany, a ſhrub, bearing a papilionaceous flower and ſiliquous fruit ; which reſembles the plant *Aleppo, & wſtris, retuſiſolia ;* or Judas's Tree.

ACA'CIA, S. [*αϰαϰια,* Gr.] in botany, the Egyptian thorn, or binding bean-tree.

ACA'COS, Adj. [from *a* negative, and *ϰαϰος,* Gr. bad] a term applied, by medical writers,

writers, to diftempers which are not dangerous.

ACADE'MICAL, Adj. [from *academicus*, Lat.] belonging, or relating to an academy. " After the *academical* life." *Watton.*

ACADE'MIC, ACADE'MICK, Adj. [from *academicus*, Lat.] this word is wrote at prefent without a d at the end, though by older authors with a d] belonging to the academy.

ACADE'MIC, ACADE'MICK, S. it is fpelt either with or without a d at the end as is obferved in the preceding word] in a large fenfe fignifies, a member of a univerfity, or fchool, where languages and other branches of polite education are taught. " A young *academic*." *Watts's Improv.*

ACADEMI'CIAN, S. [*academicien*, Fr.] a member of an academy.

ACADE'MICS, ACADE'MICKS, S. [*academici*, Lat. from their frequenting the grove of *Academus*, which was afterwards turned into a fchool, and named from him *Academia*] They are diftinguifhed into the old and middle, the former of which had Plato for the founder and the latter Arcefilas; and, though confufed by writers, as being only fynonimes expreffive of the fame fentiments, yet the two fects feemed to differ widely; the old academy holding that all fubjects would admit of arguments pro and con; which they derived from the maxim of Socrates and their founder Plato that *he knew nothing*; but the new academies carried this farther, afferting, that " nothing can certainly be known;" building indeed upon the fame maxim as the other, but carrying it into the regions of fcepticifm.

ACADE'MY, S. [*academia*, Lat. *academeia*, Gr.] anciently, a fine villa or pleafure houfe, near Athens, belonging to one Academus, from whom it derived its name. During his time, gymnaftic fports were exercifed at it. It was afterwards adorned with fountains, trees, and walks, by Cimon, for the conveniency of philofophers, who met here to confer or difpute; Plato's difciples frequenting it, were from thence named academics, and all other learned focieties have fince affumed the name of academies.

ACADE'MY, S. is figuratively applied to fignify the fect of *academi* is explained above; who are by fome divided into three, and by others into five forts. 1. The antient academy, of which Plato was the founder. 2. The fecond academy founded by Arcefilas, who altered the fyftem of the former. 3. The new academy afcribed to Lacydes or Carneades. The 4th founded by Philo; and the 5th filled the Antiochim, from Antiochus, who tempered the antient academy with ftoicifm.

ACADE'MY, S. among moderns, is ufed for a place or feminary where the liberal arts and fciences are ufed to be taught, and in this fenfe applied to univerfities. " Our court fhall be a little *academy*." *Love's Loft Shift.*

ACADE'MY, S. in a confined fenfe, implies a regular fociety of learned perfons inftituted for the cultivation and improvement of any branch of literature. Moft nations of Europe have academies of this fort. England though it has not as many, can rival all other nations both in the antiquity and celebrity of thofe fhe has produced; the Royal Society being, for the extenfivenefs of its defign, the firft that was projected. And the fociety of antiquaries, fet on foot in the reigns of Queen Elizabeth and King James the firft, is prior to the French academy by thirty-nine years, and could from its firft inftitution in 1590, to 1814, reckon fuch refpectable names among its members, as muft at once claim the awe of foreigners, and extort their furprize to find how much our ifland had advanced in its progrefs in literature beyond any other.

ACADE'MY, S. in a particular fenfe, denotes a riding-fchool, where the other fciences of fencing, &c. are likewife taught. The place fet apart for riding, called the Manege, has generally a pillar in the center, and others placed in pairs at the fides. Blackfton obferves, in his firft lecture on the common law, that the Manege has been introduced into the univerfity of Oxford, by the bounty of one of the Englifh nobility.

ACAJOU, S. (the *rofe nut*) the fruit of a tree growing in the Antilles, and in many places of the continent of America. There are three fpecies of trees included under this name, of which the only one which bears fruit, is of a middling fize, with branches inclining downwards. Its leaves are broad, ftreaked with veins, and round at the end. The bloffoms grow in clufters, are of a very agreeable fmell when they firft open, of a white, but, afterwards of a carnation or purple colour. The fruit is in the form of an apple, fomewhat oblong, covered with a thin, fmooth fkin, of a lively red on the fide next the fun, on the contrary of a gold colour, and is crowned with an olive-colour creft. Its fmell is fweet and comforting; its fubftance abounding in fpungy filaments, which yield a juice, before the fruit is ripe of a tart ftyptic flavour, very good, for quenching thirft, and preventing fainting fits, when mixed with fugar; when the fruit is grown to maturity, it is then fweet, pleafant, and a bold force, fomewhat aftringent, and very dangerous fick.

ACALE'PHE, S. [*anaxeos*, Gr.] a nettle. Likewife a fifh, of eafy digeftion; a fea fowl; and a fea animal.

ACA'LYPHA, S. in botany three-feeded Mercury, ranged by Linnæus in his twentyfirft clafs, intitled Monœcia Monn Delphin, from

from its having male and female flowers in the same plant, and the stamina being united.

ACANA'CEOUS, Adj. [from *acanta*, Gr.] in botany, applied to all plants of the thistle kind, which have heads and are prickly.

ACA'NTHA, S. [*acantha*, Gr.] in its primitive signification, any thing that is sharp pointed, as a thorn, or the fins of a fish.

ACANTHA'BOLUS, S. [from *acantha*, Gr.] a chirurgical instrument, made use of to extract fish bones, or other bodies sticking in the æsophagus, or gullet.

ACA'NTHUS, S. [*acanthis*, Gr.] in botany signifies the *brancis ursina*, or Bear's Breech. This is ranked by Linnæus, in his fourteenth class, under the title of *didynamia angiospermia*, from the flowers having two long and two shorter stamina.

ACA'NTHUS, S. in architecture, the representation of the precedent plant on the capitals of pillars.

ACA'NTHUS, S. among the mythologists, a youth changed into the flower of his name.

ACA'PNON, S. [*acapnon*, Gr.] in medical writers signifies dry wood. Among botanists, the herb Marjoram.

ACAPA'LTI, S. a plant of New Spain of Mexico, which produces long pepper.

ACA'RNAR, or ACHE'RNER, S. in astronomy, a bright fixed star of the first magnitude in Eridanus.

ACA'RUS, S. an animalcule, or small creature bred in wax, which, according to Aristotle is the least object to be perceived by the unassisted sight. It likewise signifies a particular kind of vermin which lodge themselves under the cuticula, by some stiled handworms.

ACATALE'CTIC, Adj. [*acatalectos*, Gr.] in Greek or Latin poetry, a verse which is perfect with respect to the number of its feet, being complete without redundancy and full without defect.

ACATALE'PSIA, ACATALE'PSY, S. [*acatalepsia*, Gr.] the incomprehensibility of any doctrine arising either from the defect of the understanding or the nature of the object.

ACA'TERY, S. [from *acater*, Dutch, to provide food] an office in the king's household, which is a check between the clerks of the kitchen and the purveyor. The officers who belong to the *acatery*, are a serjeant, whose salary is 6 l. two joint clerks 120 l. and a yeoman of the salt stores.

ACATHA'RSIA, S. [*acatharsia*, Gr.] the filth which is not purged away in a diseased body. In surgery, it signifies, the fordes or impurities of wounds.

ACA'TIUM, S. [from *acatos*, Gr.] a kind of boat, or pinnance used by the ancients in merry affairs.

ACAU'LIS, ACAU'LOS, Adj. in botany, applied to plants, whose flower rests on the ground, without any visible stalk.

ACCAPI'TIUM, ACCAPITUM, S. in Law Books, the sum of money paid by a vassal to his lord, upon his admission to a feud.

ACCE'DAS AD CU'RIAM, [Lat. come to the court] in Law, a writ lying, where a man hath received, or apprehends false judgement, in a hundred-court, or court-baron; in order to remove the suit into any other, exempting the county court.

ACCE'DAS AD VICECO'MITEM, in Law, is a writ directed to the coroner, commanding him to deliver a writ to the sheriff, who suppresses a *pone* delivered. *Reg. Orig.* 83.

To ACCE'DE, V. A. [*accedo*, Lat.] to approach to; to agree, to come, or be added to. A term oftener made use of by political writers than any others; "France has acceded to the treaty between Sweden and Russia."

To ACCE'LERATE, V. A. [*accelero*, Lat.] the making a body, already in motion, to move on faster. "Accelerate the motion of the blood." *Arbuth. on Alim.* in a derivative sense, to hasten; "Accelerate his diligence in the most momentous enquiries." *Watts's Improvement.*

ACCE'LERATED MOTION, in Mechanics, is that which is continually increased; this being produced by a constant impulse, or power, which continues its action upon the body; if it cause an equal increase in equal times, the motion is said to be *uniformly accelerated.* Thus the motion of falling bodies is constantly accelerated, because gravity, every moment, adds a new impulse, which generates a new degree of velocity, and the velocity thus increasing, its motion must be increased likewise, or in other words it must move faster and faster every moment. Galileo, the restorer of reason in Italy, was the discoverer of this important truth, which is a natural consequence from Sir Isaac Newton's second law of nature or motion, viz. "The change of motion produced in any body, is always proportionable to the force whereby it is effected, and in the same direction wherein that force acts." As the height from which bodies can be let fall, is so small as not to alter gravity, it must therefore act upon them uniformly, during the whole time of their descent, and they must, consequently, acquire an equal degree of velocity, which will constantly increase in proportion to the time the body takes up in falling; and therefore, the space a body passes over in a uniform motion, is in a ratio compounded of the time and velocity, i. e. the velocity multiplied by the time is equal to the space passed over. Hence we may observe, that a body falls three times as far in the second portion of time, as it does in the first; five times as far in the third; seven times as far in the fourth, and so on, in a series of

odd numbers, as 1, 3, 5, 7, 9, 11, 13, 15, 17, &c.

When bodies are thrown perpendicularly upwards, their velocities decrease, as the times they ascend increase, because their gravity destroys an equal portion of their velocity every instant of their ascent. And the heights bodies rise to, when thrown perpendicularly upwards, are as the squares of the time spent, from their setting out, to the moment they cease to rise: i. e. if a body be thrown upwards, with such a degree of velocity as to continue rising twice as long as another, it will ascend four times as high; if thrice as long, nine times as high, &c. for the heights which bodies thrown up with different velocities arrive to, are to each other as the squares of those velocities.

ACCELERA'TING, Part. [from *accelerate*, the *e* final being dropt before *ing*, the participial ending, both in this word and in others, where it occurs, as *write*, *writing*] the hastening any event. "Inclin'd to the *accelerating* a battle." *Bacon's Hen.* VII.

ACCELERA'TION, S. [*acceleratio*, Lat.] the act of increasing the motion of the bodies; or the state of a body whose motion is increased.

ACCELERATION, in Physics, may be proved both *à priori*, and *à posteriori*. Nothing is more evident than that bodies fall with greater or less forces, in proportion to the height from whence they fall. A body let fall from the height of one yard, may make no impression at all in the ground; but if dropped from the top of the monument, would make a very great one. Some attribute this to the pressure of the air, which must increase in proportion to the increase of its column; but this hypothesis is overturned by the known laws of statics.

ACCELERA'TION, S. in antient Astronomy, is the difference between the solar revolution, and that of the primum mobile, computed at 3 minutes 56 seconds.

ACCELERA'TOR, or ACCELERATO'RES URI'NÆ, in Anatomy, two muscles, whose principal office is to expedite the discharge both of the seed and urine.

ACCENT, S. [*accent*, Fr. from *accentus*, Lat.] in Grammar, the marks made on syllables to regulate their pronunciation, and are divided into grave, acute, circumflex, long, or short. The grave is marked thus (`) over a vowel, and signifies that the voice is to be lowered; the acute indicates the contrary way, thus (´) and shews that the voice is to be raised; the circumflex, marked thus, (^) intimates that the voice is to be modulated in a manner resembling a quaver. The other accents seem to be appropriated to Prosody, of which that marked thus (-) and called the long accent, imports that the vowel over which it is placed is to be pronounced long, if not double its natural time; and the short

accent, marked thus, (˘) shews that the vowel is to be pronounced very quick.

ACCENT, S. language. "*Accents* yet unknown." *Shak-sp. Jul. Cæs.* Likewise the tone of the voice, or manner of speaking: "He that beguiled you in a plain *accent*, was a plain knave." *K Lear*.

The Hebrew accents, which were unknown to the antient Jews, are supposed to have been introduced about the sixth century by the Masorites, though originally invented by the Greeks. They are comprized under the two terms of tonic and euphonic accents. The former were used to denote the proper tone to be given to syllables, and are again divided into grammatical and musical; the latter to make the pronunciation more sweet and harmonious.

The Greek accents, are undoubtedly of modern invention, as is evident from inscriptions as well as manuscripts, none of which, till 770 years before Christ, have either accent, spirit, apostrophe, or iota. If it should be replied, that the reason why they do not appear on medals and inscriptions, was because they could not be conveniently placed, the argument still holds good with respect to the manuscripts, where they could have been placed conveniently enough.

ACCENT, S. in Music, is a certain modulation of sounds, used to express any passion, and is applied both to the voice and to instruments. Every bar is divided into accented and unaccented parts; of which the accented are the principal, intended to move and affect, and contain all the soul and expression of harmony. In common time, the first and third crotchets are the accented parts of the measure; but in triple time, the first and last; though the first is accented so strongly, that the accent of the last is scarce sensible.

To ACCE'NT, V. A. [*accentuo*, Lat.] to place or lay the stress of the voice on peculiar parts of words. "*Accenting* the words." *Locke on Education*, i. 177. The placing the marks of the accents in writing, or printing. It is used for speaking in general; to pronounce. To distinguish the verb from the substantive, in reading or converse, the dress of the voice is placed on the first syllable of the substantive, and on the last of the verb, thus, *ac'cent*, is the substantive, and to *accen't*, the verb.

ACCE'NTING, Verbal Noun, the act of toning or laying the stress properly on any word or syllable; also the marking the syllables, which are to be so pronounced, in writing.

ACCE'NTOR, S. [*accino*, Lat.] one who sings the treble, or highest part, in a choir.

To ACCE'NTUATE, V. A. [*accentuer*, Fr.] to place the proper accents on the vowels or syllables of any word.

ACCENTUA'TION, S. the act of placing

sing the proper stress of voice in speaking, or the marks of the accents on the syllables or vowels of any word.

To ACCEPT, V. A. [*accepto*, Lat. *accepter*, Fr.] to take a thing, offered by another, with kindness, or with approbation. " Charm by *accepting*, by submitting sway." *Pope.* It is sometimes used with the particle *of*, before personal pronouns, and signifies to make a reconciliation, or give a friendly reception.

ACCEPTABILITY, S. [*acceptabilitas*, Lat.] the quality which causes a thing or person to meet with a kind reception. " For the obtaining the grand *acceptability* of repentance." *Taylor's Worthy Com.*

ACCEPTABLE, Adj. [*acceptable*, Fr. *acceptabilis*, Lat. It is accented on the first syllable by most moderns, who have likewise the authority of Milton on their side : yet there are not a few, and among them men of great learning, who place the accent on the second syllable, chusing to pronounce it, *acceptable*.] It implies that which may meet to a favourable reception. " Using all honest arts to make themselves *acceptable* to the laity." *Swift.* Sometimes it implies merit, and that the thing be given is worthy to be received with approbation. " So fit, so *acceptable*, so divine." *Par. Lost,* b. iii.

ACCEPTABLENESS, S. the quality which renders a thing worthy of a reception or approbation.

ACCEPTABLY, Adv. It is used with the particle *to*, and implies such a manner as may cause desire or approbation. " They will find ways to express it *acceptably* to every one." *Locke's Educ.* i. 145. *Taylor's Guide.*

ACCEPTANCE, S. [*acceptance*, Fr.] the act of receiving, or the being received with approbation. " If he tells us his noble deeds, we must tell him our noble *acceptance* of them." *Shakesp. Coriol.* It sometimes denotes the sense or signification of a word, for which we generally substitute the word *acceptation*. " Under the common *acceptance* of it." *South.*

ACCEPTANCE of a donation, in Civil Law, is necessary to its validity.

ACCEPTANCE, S. in Common Law, is the tacit agreement to some act done by another before, which might have been avoided, if such agreement, or acceptance, had not been made. For example, if a husband and wife, seised of lands in right of the wife, join in making a lease or feoffment, reserving rent, and the husband dies; after which the widow receives, or *accepts* the rent; the lease or feoffment is confirmed by her *acceptance*, and it shall bar her from bringing a writ *cui in vita.* 1 *Inst.* 211.

ACCEPTANCE, S. in Commerce, is the subscribing or signing a bill of exchange, which makes the person debtor for the sum of its contents, and obliges him to discharge it at the time which it mentions. Accep-

tances may be divided into those which ought, and those which need not, be dated. The acceptances which need not to be dated, are those on bills payable at a day fixed, at usance, double usance, &c. On these the word accepted and the acceptor's name need only be written, thus, " Accepted, S. D." Though indeed it is not absolutely necessary to have bills of a fixed day accepted, yet it is an advantage to the bearer, because, by virtue of that acceptance, he has two securities instead of one ; that is, the acceptor and the drawer. If the person on whom such bill is drawn should make difficulties to accept it, the bearer has a right to have it protested, and to return it to the drawer. The acceptances which it is necessary to date, are those on bills drawn at so many days or months after sight, because the time does not begin to run till the day after the acceptance. These acceptances run thus, " Accepted, 7 August, 1759, Thomas Jones.". If the bearer of a bill consents to an acceptance at twenty days sight instead of eight days expressed in the bill, he may run the risk of the twelve days of prolongation, and in case the acceptor breaks within that time, the bill remains to his account, without any recourse against the drawer. And if a bill be drawn for three thousand pounds, and the bearer takes an acceptance for two thousand only, and receive no more, the remaining thousand will be at his own hazard. Yet if the bearer should have written orders from the drawer to have the bill accepted in either of the last mentioned forms, he will then have an undoubted right against the drawer for an indemnification. According to the custom of merchants, the desiring a person to leave his bill in order to be *accepted*, or desiring him to call on the morrow, &c. and it shall be accepted, amount to an acceptance, and oblige, as effectually, both by law and the custom of merchants, as if it were wrote on the bill and subscribed with the name of the party. Should a person promise conditionally to accept a bill, by desiring it to be left till the morrow, that he may look over his books, and accordingly the bill should be accepted, this will not amount to a complete acceptance, because the mention of looking over his books, implies that his having effects in his hands are the conditions of his acceptance ; as it was ruled by Lord Chief Justice Hale, at Guildhall, London.

ACCEPTATION, S. reception in general. " All are rewarded with like coldness of *acceptation*." *Sidney,* b. ii. Favourable reception, including approbation. The common sense, or meaning, generally affixed to a word.

ACCEPTER, S. [*accepteur*, Fr.] in Commerce, the person who accepts a bill by signing it, and thereby obliges himself to pay the contents, when due.

ACCEPTILATION,   S. [*acceptilatio*, Lat.]

D

Lat.] In Civil Law, an acquittance given by a creditor to a debtor, without receiving any part of the debt.

ACCE'SS, S. (*accessus*, Lat.) the way or means, by which any thing may be approached. " Here th' *access* a gloomy grove defends." *Dryd. Æn.*

ACCESS, S. [*acceffus*, Lat.] addition, enlargment, increase. " I, from the influence of thy looks, receive *access* in every virtue." *Par. Loft, b. ix.*

ACCESS, [*acces*, Fr.] In Medicine, the return of any periodical disease. " As the *accefs* of a gout ; the *accefs* of an ague, &c "

ACCESSARINESS, S. [from *accessary*] a state in which a person conduces to, or promotes any event, either good or bad.

ACCESSARY, S. [*accedo*, Lat.] In Common Law, one who is not a principal, but an accomplice, or partaker in any crime, either by advice, aid, or command. In Statute Law, one who abets, advises, or conceals, the committer or commission of felony. *Accessaries* are distinguished into *accessaries before*, or *accessaries after*, the fact ; an *accessary before* the fact, is one who procures another to do it, but is absent at the time of his commission. The *accessary after* the fact, is one who receives, assists, or harbours, a person, who he knows, has been guilty either of felony or murder. There can be no *accessary before* the fact in manslaughter, because it is done on a sudden and unpremeditated. There are no accessaries in the highest or lowest offences, but all the parties are deemed principals ; as in riots, forcible entries, &c. which are the lowest offences ; so likewise in high treason, which is the highest, there are no accessaries. A person who receives or harbours the accessary to a murder or felony, knowing him to be such, is the *accessary of an accessary.*

ACCESSARY, Adj. that which contributes to bring about any event or thing. " As for those things which are *accessary* hereunto, those things that so belong to the way of salvation." *Hooker.* In a law sense it implies guilt, and denotes a person to have been instrumental to the commission of something criminal.

ACCESSIBLE, Adj. [*accessible*, Fr.] that which may be approached, reached, or come to. It is used with the particle *to*, before the object. " As an island, we are *accessible* on every side." *Add. Freehold.* Applied to the understanding, it signifies something which it can attain. " Though *accessible*, in some measure to our senses." *Hale's Origin.*

ACCESSIBLE Height, in practical Geometry, is that which can be mechanically measured by the application of a measure to it ; whose base, or foot, may be approached to, and a distance measured, from thence, on the ground.

ACCESSION, S. [*acceffio*, Lat.] a coming to. " His Majesty's *accession* to the crown." *Com. Pray.* The addition or junction of. " *Accession* to a confederacy." The enlarging or increase of any thing by something added. " The included inch of air received some little *accefs* during the trial." *Boyle on Air.*

ACCESSION, S. in Physic, the beginning of a paroxysm.

ACCESSOR, S. [from *accedo*, Lat.] a comer to ; one who joins himself to any party.

ACCESSORILY, Adv. [from *accessory*] in the manner or form of a partaker, aider, abettor, or accessory.

The ACCESSORY NERVE, or ACCESSORIUS WILLISII, because named by that Doctor, called likewise *par accessorium* ; they belong to the eighth pair, arise by several filaments on each side of the medulla spinalis, or spinal marrow, about the beginning of the sixth pair of the neck. They gradually increase in their course upwards, by receiving several filaments from the posterior nervous plexus.

ACCIDENCE, S. [a corruption of the word accidents, from the Latin *accidentia*] the name of a compendious treatise, used by grammarians, to teach the various accidents, or properties, belonging to a language. That which is now commonly used in grammar-schools, was originally called Paul's Accidence, being composed by Dean Colet, the founder of that seminary, in 1509, and dedicated to W. Lilly, the first high master, in 1510. In 1513 the Dean added the construction of the eight parts of speech, which was first submitted to the correction of Lilly, and after that being sent to the famous Erasmus, the Dean's peculiar friend, was published with his alterations, anno 1515. So great was the reputation of these rudiments, that Cardinal Woolsey reprinted them with a prefatory discourse, and ordered them to be taught in the school he founded at Ipswich in 1528. But time and success, which are a greater recommendation than mere authority, have reflected the greatest eulogium upon these rudiments that any book can have. This being the first book made use of in education of grammar-schools, is used figuratively to signify the lowest degree of learning. " I do confess I do want eloquence—and never yet did learn my *accidence*." *Taylor.*

ACCIDENT, S. [*accidens*, Lat. from *accido*] an event or something which happens. " The flood and other *accidents* of time." *Ral.* Any thing which comes to pass by the operation of some unknown cause. Any thing done without the previous design or intention of the agent. " He was only instrumental of it, as the logicians say, by *accident*." *Swift.* Some unforeseen mischief or calamity. " What *accident*—hath rapt him from us ?" *Par. Reg. b. I.*

ACCIDENT, S. in Heraldry, is an additional

tional point or mark in a coat, which may be omitted or retained, without altering its essence.

ACCIDENT, S. In philosophy, something superadded to a subject, which may be separated from it without its destruction.

ACCIDENTAL, S. [accidentel, Fr.] In Logic, a property which may be separated from a subject without its destruction; used in contradistinction to such as are essential and inseparable. " Conceive as much as you can of the essentials of any subject, before you consider its accidentals." Watt's Logic.

ACCIDENTAL, Adj. not essential, or not necessary to the existence of a subject. That which happens without any previous design or intention of the agent. " Thy sin's not accidental, but a trade." Meas. for Meas. That which happens without the concurrence of any visible or perceptible cause. " Accidental in their production." Smith.

ACCIDENTAL POINT, in Perspective, a point in the horizontal line, where lines parallel to one another, though not perpendicular to the picture or representation, meet.

ACCIDENTALLY, Adv. in a manner which is not essential or necessary. " Other needful points, no less concerning the good of the commonwealth; though but accidentally depending upon the former." Spenser. By mere chance. " Although virtuous men do sometimes accidentally make their way to preferment." Swift. Without any previous design or intention.

ACCIDENTALNESS, S. the quality of being accidental.

ACCIPIENT, S. [accipiens, Lat.] a receiver; used, perhaps, instead of recipient.

ACCLAIM, S. [acclamo, Lat.] a shout of joyful applause. This word is seldom used at present. " With loud acclaims." Dryd. Fab.

ACCLAMATION, S. [acclamatio, Lat.] a shout testifying joy, esteem, and applause. " Who him received with joy, and acclamation loud." Par. Lost, b. vi. This tribute of gratitude to illustrious merit, has been paid by all ages and all countries, to their heroes and sovereigns, and though now confined to the theatre, or solemn entries of magistrates, had formerly an existence in the places of worship. The Hebrews, on this occasion, made use of the word Hosannah, the Greeks apud τυχη, or Good Luck. The Orientals to their monarchs, O King live for ever! The Romans at first, in such terms as they thought most suitable to the object; but under the Emperors they had a settled form, wherein they wished longer life, prosperity, and cried out Io Triumphe! The acclamations of the senate were more sober, expressing their unanimity, and the equity and justice of the tribute and subject of their applause. Among the moderns, the English acclamation is God save, or preserve, or long live, the King. The English, in their the-

atrical amusements, give theirs by clapping their hands, and crying out encore, a word borrowed from the French theatre, which implies a repetition of the admired speech.

ACCLIVIS, S. [acclivius, Lat.] In Anatomy, a muscle, filled likewise obliquus ascendens.

ACCLIVITY, S. [acclivitas, Lat.] the ascent of an hill; and, among Geometers, the slope of a line or plane, inclining to the horizon upwards. " Clamber up the acclivities." Ray on the Creat.

ACCLIVOUS, Adv. [acclivus, Lat.] rising with a slope.

To ACCLOY, V. A. [acclouer, Fr.] to stop up a passage. " With unseemly weeds the gentle wave accloys." Fairy Q. To be wearied or surfeited of a thing.

ACCOLA, S. [Lat.] a dweller in any particular place, who has removed from some other; used in opposition to incola, or native. Sometimes used to signify a borderer.

ACCOLENT, S. [accolens, Lat.] he who inhabits near, or a borderer on any place.

ACCOLADE, S. [accolade, Fr. from accoler, to take round the neck] a ceremony anciently used in dubbing a knight, which consisted in the King's laying both his hands round the knight's neck, and embracing him, as the word expresses. After this the Prince gave him a blow on the shoulder with a flat sword, and the ceremony was over.

ACCOMMODABLE, Adj. [accommodabilis, Lat.] that which may be fitted to another thing; that which may be reconciled to, is consistent with, or may be applied to. It is made use of with the particle to. " Such general rules as are accommodable to all this variety." Watt's Logic.

To ACCOMMODATE, V. A. [accommodo, Lat.] to supply with conveniencies, to entertain. " He accommodated his guests in the best manner." In the passive it is followed by the particle by, in the same sense. " Accommodated by the place." Shakesp. When followed by the particle to, it denotes to be reconciled to; to be made consistent with. " That could not be accommodated to the nature of things." Locke. In the active, when used with this particle to, it signifies to suit, to adapt. " That he might accommodate himself to the age." Dryd. on Dram. Poesy. To agree, or make up a difference.

ACCOMMODATE, Adj. [accommodatus, Lat.] convenient or proper. " Proper and accommodate to their present state and inclination." Tillotson.

ACCOMMODATELY, Adv. in a convenient, suitable, or fit manner.

ACCOMMODATION, S. [accommodatio, Lat.] In the plural it signifies entertainment, or the supply of such things as are necessary for the support of nature, either in a state of rest or action. When used with the particle

as, it denotes a suitable disposition of parts, or such. "The organization of the body with accommodation to its functions." Used without the particle, and with relation to disagreeing parties, it signifies an adjustment of their differences, reconciliation, or agreement. "There is very little prospect of an accommodation."

ACCOMMODATION, S. the application of one thing to another by analogy.

ACCOMPANIER, S. a companion. This word is seldom used.

To ACCOMPANY, V. A. [accompagner, Fr.] to go along with; "And there accompanied him into Asia, Sopater of Berea." Acts xx. 4. "To attend; that pain should accompany the perception of several ideas." Locke. To be connected or joined. "Folly is usually accompanied with perverseness." Swift.

ACCOMPANYMENT, S. [accompagnement, Fr.] something added to another for the sake of ornament, symmetry, &c. In music, the execution of a complete or regular harmony, on any musical instrument, commonly performed by the bass. In painting, those parts of a piece, which are added by way of ornament, and, like the episodes of an epic poem, have a relation to the chief figure. In heraldry, the belt, mantling, supporters, and other ornaments about the shield.

ACCOMPLICE, S. [complice, Fr. from complex, old Lat.] one who is concerned with another in the commission of any crime.

To ACCOMPLISH, V. A. [accomplir, Fr.] to perform, or fulfil. "Ye will surely accomplish your vows." Jerem. xliv. 25. "By new ways they think to accomplish wonders." Wotts. To satiate. "Now I will accomplish mine anger upon thee." Ezek. vii. 8. To expire. "The days of your dispersions are accomplished." Jerem. xxv. 34. To obtain. "The desire accomplished, is sweet to the soul." Prov. xiii. 19. To perfect, adorn, or furnish either the mind or body.

ACCOMPLISHED, Part. [from accompli] perfect, consummate, or complete, finished.

ACCOMPLISHER, S. the person who finishes, fulfils, completes; or communicates either external or internal embellishments.

ACCOMPLISHMENT, S. [from accomplish] in divinity, the existence of a person or thing, foretold. "The accomplishment of many of their predictions." Atterb. The completion, full performance, perfection, consummation. Both internal or personal embellishments which tend to make a person complete. "Thinking all other accomplishments unnecessary." Spect. No. 185. Finishing, or attainment.

ACCOMPT, S. [pronounced account accompte, old Fr. from adcomputare, Lat.] in its primary signification, all computations made arithmetically. In commerce, all the books in which merchants and other traders register their transactions with each other.

ACCOMPTANT, S. [pronounced accountant, from accomptant, Fr.] one who is not only well skilled in casting up all sorts of accounts, and can readily perform all arithmetical operations, but is likewise versed in book-keeping.

ACCOMPTANT-SHIP, S. [from accomptant] the qualification necessary for an accomptant. This comprehends not only a perfect skill in figures, but likewise a thorough knowledge of book-keeping, in all its branches. This qualification, though confined by precipitate inconsideration to the trader and merchant, is recommended by the great Mr. Locke, as an useful ornament to the gentleman, and the best means to enable him to support his figure, preserve his patrimony, and prevent profusion from committing devastations.

To ACCORD, V. A. [accorder, Ital.] to tune two or more instruments, so as they shall sound the same notes, when touched by the hand or bow. It is used with the particle to. "Her hands accorded the lute's music to her voice." In its secondary sense, it implies to harmonize. "The lights and shades whose well accorded strife." Pope.

To ACCORD, V. N. to be in union with, to agree, to correspond. "But my heart accordeth with my tongue." Shakesp. Hen. VI.

ACCORD, S. [accord, Fr.] in its primary signification, an unison, or the agreement in sound between two instruments, when turned alike, and struck at the same time. "The striking of the one would move the other, more than if it were another accord." Bacon's Nat. Hist. Harmony, agreement, or symmetry whether applied to the human fabrick or the arts of designing. "Beauty is nothing else but a just accord and mutual harmony of the members." Dryd. Dufresnoy. When joined with own, it implies something that is done spontaneously, or without any previous labour, art, or admonition. "That which groweth of its own accord of the harvest." Levit. xxv. 5. When joined with one, it implies unanimity. "They were all with one accord." Acts ii. 1.

ACCORDANCE, S. friendship "Pray, he may in long accordance bide with that great worth." Fairfax. Conformity, confidence, or agreement with. "By the accordance with that will." Hammond's Fundam.

ACCORDING, Part. sometimes followed by the particle as; conformably. "I have done according as thou badest me." Gen. xxvii. 19. In proportion to. "Let mercy be on us, according as we hope in thee." Psalm xxxiii. 22. Suitable, "Praise the Lord

Lord *according to his righteousness.*" Psal.
vii. 8. Agreeable.

ACCOR'DINGLY, Adv. of *qual.* In
manner conformable, or consistent with.
" To believe the doctrine, and to live *accordingly.*" Tillof. In the beginning of
a sentence it has a reference to that which
went before, and implies a deduction from
it, being synonimous to the words ; in that
respect ; or for that reason.

To ACCO'ST, V. A. [*accoster*, Fr.] to
go near a person and speak to him first ;
" With soothing words renew'd—Him thus
accosts." Par. Lost.

ACCO'STABLE, Adj. that may be spoken
with ; conversible, sociab'e ; of easy access.

ACCO'UNT, S. [See ACCOMPT] In its
primary signification, a calculation made by
figures. In its secondary, the amount, or
sum total of such a calculation. " Count
" ing one by one to find out the *account.*"
Eccles. vii. 27. A bill in writing, containing the articles for which a person is indebted to another, in single entry : but in
double, not only those particulars for which
another person credits you, but likewise
those for which you credit him. When
joined with the particle *of*, and the adjectives
great, some, &c. and their contraries, it
implies value, with respect to things ; and
figure with respect to persons. " Things of
smaller account have once set on work." Hooker.
" Only two men of *account*, and distinction."
Pope's Odyss. When joined with *find*, it denotes, advantage or profit. " People *find*
their *account* in buying goods," Pysitetus.
" I cannot yet comprehend how those persons find their *account* in any of these three."
Swift. When joined with *turn to*, it likewise
implies gain, &c. " As will *turn to account.*"
Spect. No. 509. When following the verb
put to, and either of the primitive or personal
pronouns, *my, your*, &c. it signifies the charging
of a person with it, and that he is responsible for, or must pay it. " If he oweth thee,
put that on *my account.*" Philem. 18.

ACCO'UNT, S. [*conte*, Fr.] generally
joined with *give*, and implies a circumstantial
description, or relation. " He gave an *account* of the battle." An explanation. " It
is easy to give an *account*, how it comes to
pass." Locke.

ACCO'UNT, or ACCOMPT, in Law, a
writ or action that lies against a person, who
on account of his office, whether that of
bailiff, or receiver to a nobleman or trader,
is to render an account to another, but refuses to do it. If a bailiff a writ of account
lies against him as such ; if a receiver, an
account may be had against him as such.

To ACCO'UNT, V. A. [See ACCOMPT]
to compute. In the passive it denotes to be
reckoned, to be esteemed. " We are *accounted* as sheep for the slaughter." Rom. viii.
36. To explain, by the assigning the causes

and reasons. " I know no other way to *account* for it." Swift. To estimate or to be
valued. " Silver was nothing *accounted of.*"
1 Kings x. 21. To be imputed. " It was *accounted to* him for righteousness." Gal. iii. 6.

ACCOU'NTABLE, Adj. obliged to assign
the reasons, or to explain the motives for
any proceeding.

ACCOU'NTANT, S. [See ACCOMP
TANT] a person skilled in figures and
versed in the art of book-keeping.

ACCOU'NTANT GENERAL, S. an officer belonging to the court of chancery, appointed by parliament to receive all money
lodged in court, and convey it to the bank
of England. His salary is paid out of the
interest, and no fees are taken in his office.
12 Geo. I. and 12 Geo. II. c. 24.

ACCOU'NT-BOOK, S. a book wherein
the transactions between traders are entered.
" By turning to my *account-book*, and seeing,
&c." Swift. Let. lxii.

ACCOU'NTING, S. [from *account*] the
settling, suing, or examining into a person's affairs.

ACCOU'NTING-HOUSE, compound S.
a place set a-part by merchants and other
traders, to transact their business, and keep
their books and vouchers in.

To ACCO'UPLE, [*accoupler*, Fr.] to accompany, to join or link together with.
Seldom used.

To ACCO'UTRE, V. A. [*accoutrer*, Fr.]
to dress, to furnish with all manner of necessaries ; applied to warlike preparations, to
equip. " In rags *accoutred* are they seen."
Dryd. Perf.

ACCOUTREMENT, S. [*accoutrement*,
Fr.] dress. " Putting on or off his different *accoutrements.*" Spect. No. 201. Equipage, furniture or habiliments of war. Ornaments. " Christianity is lost among
them in the trappings and *accoutrements* of
it." Tillof. Serm.

ACCRE'TION, S. [*accretio*, Lat.] the
increase, or growth of an organical or inorganical body by the accession of new parts ;
" Plants do nourish ; inanimate bodies do
not, they have an *accretion*, but no alimentation." Bacon's Nat. Hist.

To ACCRO'ACH, V. A. [*accrocher*, Fr.]
to encroach ; to draw away another's property. Law term in stat. 25. Ed. III. c. viii.

ACCRO'ACHMENT, S. the act of encroaching, or grasping the property of another.

To ACCRU'E, V. A. [from *accrue*, the
part. of *accroitre*, Fr. to grow to] to be
added to, as a natural production. " No alteration thereby *accruing* to the divine nature." Hooker. In a commercial sense, to
arise, or proceed from, in a good sense, as including the secondary idea of profit. " The
great profits which have *accrued* to the duke
of Florence." Addis.

ACCUBA'TION, S. [*accubo*, Lat.] the
posture

posture of lying down, practised by the ancients at their meals. "It will appear that *accubation*, or lying down at meals, was a posture used by very many nations." *Brown's Vulg. Errors.*

To ACCU'MULATE, V. A. [*accumulo*, Lat.] to heap up, or pile; to gather, or amass together in great quantities. Applied in its literal sense to material things, as, "To accumulate riches." In its figurative, to virtue, &c. "On horror's head, horrors accumulate." *Othello.*

ACCUMULA'TION, S. [*accumulatio*, Lat.] repeated acquisitions; an amassing. "Wonder at such an *accumulation* of benefits." *Wotton.* The state of a thing amassed. "Regular *accumulations* and gatherings." *Arbuth.*

ACCU'MULATIVE, Adj. that which increases; or that which is added to; additional; "If the injury meet not with meekness it then acquires an *accumulative* guilt." *Government of the Tongue.*

ACCURACY, S. [*accuratio*, Lat.] exactness, including the idea of industry. "Quote an authority with an insipid *accuracy*." *Dryden.* Justness, or nicety. "*Accuracy* of the calculations." *Arbuth.*

ACCU'RATE, Adj. [*accuratus*, Lat.] exact, just, including diligence and knowledge, when applied to persons; and excluding defect when spoken of things.

ACCU'RATELY, Adv. in a manner productive of exactness, and void of defect; nicely, exactly. "*Accurately* and harmoniously adjusted." *Bentley.*

ACCURATENESS, S. a process conducted with great care and productive of exactness or nicety. "With sufficient *accurateness*." *Newt.*

To ACCU'RSE, to consign, or devote to eternal misery.

ACCUR'SED, Part. devoted to destruction. "The city shall be *accursed*." *Josh. vi. 17.* Separated from the church of Christ and communion of saints; excommunicated. Execrable, including the idea of wickedness; doomed to everlasting misery. "The chief part of the misery of wicked men; and those *accursed* spirits, the devils." *Tillots.*

ACCUR'ST, Part. devoted to misery, including the secondary idea of wickedness, and alluding to the curse pronounced at the fall of our first parents.

"'Tis the most certain sign the world's *accurst*."
"That the best things corrupted are the worst." *Denh.*

ACCU'SABLE, Adj. that which is liable to be censured or blamed. "There will be a manifest defect and her improvision justly *accusable*." *Brown's Vulg. Errors.*

ACCUSA'TION, S. [*accusatio*, Lat.] the charging with some error or crime.

"Thus they in mutual *accusation* spent—
The fruitless hours." *Par. Lost.* In Law, a charge preferred against a person before a competent judge, in order to inflict some punishment on him for the guilt imputed to him. "No man can be imprisoned or condemned on any *accusation* without trial by his peers." *Magn. Chart. 9 H. III. stat. 25. and 28. Ed. III.*

ACCU'SATIVE, Part. [*accusativus*, Lat.] in grammar applied to the fourth case of nouns. As all verbs which affirm actions must have subjects to receive them, they most necessarily have some noun, or word after them to be the subject, or object of such actions; and in those languages which have cases, these nouns have a certain termination, which is called the *accusative.*

To ACCU'SE, V. A. [*accuso*, Lat. *accuser*, Fr.] to charge a person with a crime.

ACCU'SED, Part. charged with a crime. "When he was *accused*, he answered nothing." *Matt. xxvii. 12.*

ACCU'SEMENT, S. [from *accuse*] a charge brought against a person to prove him guilty of any crime. *Bailey* from *Chaucer.* Obsolete.

ACCU'SER, S. one who charges another with the commission of a crime. "Women, where are those, thine *accusers*?" *John viii. 10.*

ACCU'SING, Part. the bringing of a charge of guilt against a person, or the passing of censure upon a thing.

To ACCU'STOM, [*accoûtumer*, Fr.] to practise so often as to render habitual. To inure. "Ye that are *accustomed* to do evil." *Jerem. xiii. 23.* To make a constant use of.

ACCU'STOMABLE, Adj. [Sax. denoting power, or possibility] that which a person has practised for a continuance. "Diversified by *accustomable* residence." *Hales.*

ACCU'STOMABLY, Adv. usually; according to repeated practice. "The king's fines *accustomably* paid." *Bacon.*

ACCU'STOMARILY, Adv. in a manner agreeable to constant practice.

ACCU'STOMARY, Adj. usual, constantly practised.

ACCU'STOMED, Part. that which is frequently practised; or grown habitual. "It is an action *accustomed* with her." *Macbeth.*

A'CE, S. [from *as*, Fr. as Span. or *us*, Gr.] a single point, or speck on cards or dice. As an unit is the smallest number, it is figuratively used for the least quantity. "He will not bate an *ace* of absolute certainty." *Government of the Tongue.* The smallest distance. "I will not wag an *ace* farther." *Don Sebast.* "He was within an *ace* of ruin." But these latter expressions seem to be derived from *acies*, Lat. an edge.

ACE'TIAM, in Law a clause of a writ, where the action requires special bail, founded on the statute 23 Car. II. c. ii.

ACE'PHALOUS,

ACE'PHALOUS, Adj. something without a head. Naturalists apply this term to worms, which have been supposed formerly to have no head. Figuratively, those who have no superior, chief, or leader.

A'CER, S. [Lat. so called, because of the hardness of its wood] the maple tree. The timber of the common Maple is far superior to the Beech for all turnery ware; particularly dishes, cups, trenchers, and bowls; and when abounding with knots is highly esteemed by cabinet-makers for inlayings. It is in great request among instrument-makers, on account of the lightness of the wood, as it was formerly for tables, because of its whiteness.

ACE'RB, Adj. [acerbus, Lat.] that which had a compound taste of four and roughness, like that of unripe pears. All that fall under this denomination are astringent.

ACE'RBITY, S. [acerbitas, Lat.] the quality which communicates a taste compounded of sourness.

ACE'RIDES, S. [acerides] emplasters made without wax. A medical term.

ACE'SCENT, Part. [from acesco, Lat.] that which is liable to turn four. Sometimes used substantively. "Qualified with a sufficient quantity of acescents." Arbuth.

ACE'SIS, S. [akesis, Gr.] in Medicine, a remedy or cure.

ACETABULUM, S. in Anatomy a large cavity in a bone, which receives another, and, thus articulated is adapted to circular motion.

ACE'STA, S. [akestos] in Medicine, distempers that are curable.

ACETOSA, S. [Lat. four] forrel; which is derived from the Saxon sur, four. Linnæus confuses these plants with the Docks, including them under the same genus, which he stiles rumex.

ACETO'SE, Adj. [acetosus, Lat.] that which is four, or resembles vinegar in acidity.

ACETO'SITY, the quality which renders any thing four.

ACE'TOUS, Adj. [from acetum] that which is four. "An acetous spirit." Boyle.

ACE'TUM, S. [Lat. from aceo] vinegar. This liquor is the basis of the following.

ACE'TUM DISTILLATUM, [Lat.] in Chemistry, distilled vinegar, chiefly used in preparations for precipitation and dissolution, kept under the name of distilled vinegar.

ACE'TI SPIRITUS, spirit of vinegar, or distilled vinegar rectified. This is made by putting any quantity of distilled vinegar into a tall cucurbite, and drawing off half the quantity. That which rises will be light, limpid, watery, and less acid, whilst that which remains, after distillation, will be exceeding strong, sharp, and heavier than the former. From this process we learn the difference between rectification of wine and vinegar. In the former the first coming over, and the most volatile part is the best; in the latter, that which is more mixed and left behind. Hence vinegar is rendered stronger and more sharp by boiling; but wine being boiled, becomes weak, thick, turbid, and vapid.

ACE'TUM ROSA'TUM, [Lat.] vinegar of roses. It is used in the head-ach to bath the head and temples with.

ACE'TUM ALKALISA'TUM, alkalised vinegar, made of distilled vinegar, with the addition of some alkalised or volatile salt.

ACE'TUM PHILOSOPHORUM, a four kind of liquor, made by dissolving a little butter of antimony in a great deal of water.

ACHA'TES, S. [axates, Gr.] an agate, so called from a river in Sicily where it was first found.

A'CHE, S. [of ace, Sax. a pain, of ἄχος, ake, Gr.] a continual pain. "Fill all thy bones with ach-es, make thee roar." Shakesp. Temp. "Old ach-es throb, your hollow tooth will urge." Swift.

To A'CHE, V. N. to be affected with pain. "Our eyes will ake." Glanville's Scept.

ACHE'RNER, S. [Arab.] a star of the first magnitude in the southern extremity of the constellation Eridanus. Long. 10 deg. 31 min. of Pisces, lat. 59 deg. 18 min. S.

ACHI'A, S. [Ind.] a species of cane growing in the East-Indies, which is pickled green there, with strong vinegar, pepper, and other spices.

To ACHI'EVE, V. A. [pronounced achieve from achever, Fr.] to finish prosperously. "The greater part performed, achieve the less." Dryd. To gain or acquire. "Experience is by industry achiev'd." Shakesp.

ACHI'EVER, S. [pronounced achiever] he who acquires, or obtains. "A victory is twice itself, when the achiever brings home full numbers." Much-ado about Nothing.

ACHIEVE'MENT, [pronounced achievement, from achievement, Fr.] a great and hazardous exploit. The performance of an action. "Famous hard achievements still pursue." Fairy Q. An escutcheon, or coat of armour, originally granted for some great and heroic action. "With arms reversed, the achievements of the foe." Dryd.

ACHILLE'A, S. [Lat.] in Botany, Milfoil Yarrow, or Nose-bleed. It is a good vulnerary, is cooling, drying, and astringent, and of service in all kind of hæmorrhages, whether spitting or vomiting of blood, and of some efficacy in gonorrhœas.

ACHI'LLES, S. [αχιλλης, Gr.] the name of divers illustrious persons among the Greeks; but more particularly the son of Peleus and Thetis. He was born in Phthia in Sicily, and according to the poets, dipped by Thetis in the waters of Styx, while an in-

fant, to render him invulnerable; but that heel which she held him by, being untouched by the waters, her precaution lost its effect, and he received his death by a wound in that place. As another nostrum to make him immortal, she is reported to have anointed him with ambrosia. He was educated according to some by the centaur Chiron, but according to Homer by Phœnix.

ACHIL'LES, S. [Lat.] In the schools, a name given to the favourite arguments produced by each sect in favour of their respective systems.

ACHIL'LIS TENDO, [Lat. the tendon of Achilles] In Anatomy, a large tendon formed by the union of the four extensor muscles of the foot. It derives its name from the fatal wound given to Achilles, which is supposed to have been in this part.

ACHLYS, S. [from αχλυς, Gr.] in Physic, a disorder of the eyes.

ACINE, S. [axn, Gr.] In Medicine, used by Galen, 1. for a soft white mucilage swimming in the eye, very common in fevers. 2. A frothy matter with which the fauces are sometimes filled in an exulceration of the lungs. 3. Lint.

ACHOR, S. [achor, Lat.] In Physic, a small ulcer in the skin of the head, which is perforated by a great many holes, containing a viscid matter resembling ichor.

ACHORISTOS, Adj. [αχωριστος, Gr. of a privative, and χωρις χειρ. separate] Inseparable; in medicine, applied to those accidents, signs and symptoms, which always accompany each other.

ACHROI, S. [αχρως, Gr.] pale, through a deficiency of blood. Applied by old medical authors to those persons who have lost their natural colour.

ACHRYANTHIS, S. [αχρν, Gr.] In Botany. It grows near three feet high, with oblong pointed leaves, must be nursed on a hot-bed, and after it has acquired strength, may be transplanted into the full ground, where it will flower in July, and produce ripe seeds in September.

ACID, Adj. [acide, Fr. acidus, Lat.] that which raises the idea of sour, when applied to the organs of tasting. " Whose fruit is acid." Raion.

ACIDS, S. [acida, Lat. of αξυς, Gr.] in Chemistry and medicine, those substances which contain in them such qualities as affect the taste with a sensation of sourness, or have other qualities in common with them. The celebrated Boerhaave having proved by a great number of experiments, that all is the proper lium or food of fire, and an acid being essential to the composition of oil, we have another obvious characteristic, which will more justly discover acids in bodies, than either of those already mentioned; namely, that all bodies fall susceptible of flame, contain either

a manifest or latent acid; acids being the only bodies in nature, convertible into that species of fire, called flame. Vegetables flame so long as a black oil remains in them, but no longer; from whence it is evident, that this black oil contains an acid. Acids seem to be of the greatest use in the economy of the world, and universally diffused through every part of the terraqueous globe. In the bowels of the earth we meet them in almost every mine and mineral, but especially in those prodigious rocks of salt, which the luxury and industry of mankind have not been able to exhaust for ages. In the air it is universal; and it is remarkable that it abounds more therein, when the winds blow from the E. and N. than when the weather is serene. As these winds are remarkably cold, and as acid spirits, particularly nitre, increase the coldness of ice prodigiously, we have reason to assert, that the aerial acid is more concerned in the production of cold, than is commonly imagined. As acids are the great preservatives against putrefaction in the air, we shall find them no less so with respect to the sea. Was this vast body of water to putrify, in hot climates and in the warmer seasons, no animals could live in or near it. But this terrible catastrophe is prevented by the acid of the salt which is dissolved in sea water. Putrefaction being promoted by heat, it will follow, that the water in hot climates, would have a greater tendency to putrefy, and, consequently, that a greater degree of this salt is necessary to prevent it in hot climates than in cold. Accordingly it has been discovered, by an experiment made for that purpose, that the sea water increases in saltness, the nearer it approaches the line; and it has been proved likewise, that a pint of sea water in the Mediterranean contains an ounce of salt, but that the same quantity of water in the Baltic contains only half an ounce. Here let us admire the benevolence of the divine being, and while we see the characters of paternal wisdom so strongly impressed in every part of the volume of nature, be wrought to that rapturous acknowledgment of the Psalmist, in his poetical descant on the works of the creation contained in the cvii. Psalm.

ACIDITY, S. [from acid] the sensation of sharpness, excited by an acid on the organ of taste; sourness.

ACIDNESS, S. See ACIDITY.

ACIDULÆ, S. in Medicine, cold mineral waters, which contain a brisk spirit, in contradiction to thermæ, which are hot, being chalybeat, sulphureous, and aluminous.

To ACIDULATE, V. A. [aciduler, Fr.] to impregnate with acids; to turn sour by the infusion of an acid. " Watry liquors acidulated." Arbuth.

ACINIFORMIS, S. [from acinus, Lat. and forma, Lat.] applied, in anatomy, to

one

one of the coats of the eye, called *tunica uvea*, from its resembling a grape or berry.

AC'INOS, S. [*αxινος*, Gr.] In botany, Stone, or Wild Basil. Its species are two.

A'CINUS, S. [from *aan*, Gr.] In botany, those small grains growing in bunches, like grapes; as also the protuberances in the mulberry, strawberry, &c.

To ACKNOW'LEDGE, V. A. to confess. "*Acknowledge* thine iniquity." *Jer.* iii. 13. To approve, to own as a benefit. "But they his gifts *acknowledge'd* not." *Par. Lost*.

ACKNOW'LEDGING, Part. assuring to an opinion; including a belief of its truth. Retaining a grateful sense.

ACKNOW'LEDGING, S. the act of testifying a grateful sense of a benefit. Assent; owning, profession.

ACKNOW'LEDGMENT, S. assent; including a persuasion of the truth of any proposition. "*Acknowledgment* of the mystery of God." *Col.* ii. 1. Belief. The owning guilt, after the commission of a crime, or fault. A grateful sense of a benefit received.

ACME, S. [*axμη*, Gr.] the height or highest degree of any thing; usually applied by medical writers to denote the height of a distemper; which they divide into four stages. 1. *Arché*, the beginning. 2. *Anabasis*, the growth. 3. *Acme*, the height. And, 4. *Paracme*, or declension.

ACONITE, S. [*axoντon*, Gr.] in botany, Wolfsbane. Figuratively used for poison, in a general sense. "Despair, that *aconite* does prove." *Granville's Poems*. See ACONITUM.

ACON'TIAS, S. [*axoντιας*, Gr.] a comet, or meteor, with an oblong head, and a long slender tail, resembling a dart or arrow. Also a poisonous serpent in Sicily or Calabria.

A'COPIS, S [*axoπις*, Gr.] a precious stone, resembling glass, marked with spots of gold.

ACONI'TUM, S. [its etymology is dubious, but some derive it from a Greek privative, and *now*, dust, because it grows without earth] in botany Wolfsbane, or Monkshood. Every species of this plant are poisonous, they are extremely caustic and acrimonious, generally stopping delutition, and corroding the internal parts of those who eat them, producing mortal convulsions, inflammations, and mortifications.

A'CORI, S. [Lat.] the blue coral; It grows in the form of a tree upon a rocky bottom; is fished for upon, or about the Rio del Ré, or the King's River, on the coast of Africa, and is part of the merchandise for which the Dutch trade with the Camarones.

A'CORUS, S. [Lat.] in botany, the Sweet Rush. It is hot and dry, opening and attenuating, and esteemed, for removing obstructions of the liver and spleen, provoking

urine and the menses, and resisting putrefaction; it operates as cordial in the dropsy and scurvy, and provokes spitting in an asthma.

A'CORN, S. [*accern*, S x.] the fruit or seed born by the oak. "Nourished by the *acorn* he picked up under the oak." *Lecke*.

ACOU'STICS, S. [from *axove*,] Gr. the doctrine of sounds, or hearing. In medicine, remedies to cure any defects in hearing. In physics, those instruments which are made use of by people afflicted with partial deafness.

ACOU'STIC, Adj. [*axove*, Gr.] that which belongs to hearing. *Acoustic nerve*, in Anatomy, is the same as *auditory nerve*. See EAR.

To ACQUAINT, V. A. [*accoint r*, Fr.] generally followed by a personal pronoun, and the particle *with*. To inform. "He *acquaints* me that two or three men." *Tatler*. To be accustomed, or habituated to. "A man of sorrows and *acquainted with* grief." *Isai.* liii. 3. To know perfectly. "Art *acquainted with* all my ways." *Psal.* cxxxix. 3. To acquire a perfect and intimate knowledge of. "*Acquaint* yourselves with things antient and modern." *Watt's Logick*.

ACQUAI'NTANCE, S. [*accointance*, Fr.] followed by the particle *with*. Application productive of knowledge; "Nor was his *acquaintance* left with the poets." *Dryd.* Personal knowledge arising from familiarity. "Our admiration of a famous man lessens upon a near *acquaintance with* him. *Spect.* No. 256. An intimate friendship and alliance; "Would ye be admitted into an *acquaintance with* God." *Atterb.* A familiar and constant companion. "It was thou, mine equal and mine *acquaintance*." *Psalm.* xxxv. 13.

ACQUAI'NTED, Part. [from *acquaint*] that which is not uncommon, or unusual. "Thinly *acquainted* and familiar as us." *Shakesp. Hen.* IV. known by long study and contemplation. "Be well *acquainted with* God, and yourselves." *Watt's Log.*

ACQUE'ST, S. [from *acquest*, Fr. of *acquerir*,] by some spelt *acquist*, additional increase; acquisition. "New *acquests* are more burden than strength." *Bac. Hen* VII. "Signs of its new *acquests* and encroachments." *Woodw.* In Law, goods not held by inheritance, but obtained by purchase. In politics, something gained by conquest.

To ACQUIE'SCE, V. N. [*acquiescer*, Fr.] to yield to, comply with, be satisfied with. "*Acquiesce* in an airy ungrounded persuasion." *South.*

ACQUIE'SCENCE, S. [from *acquiescer*] a consent, submission or yielding to. "An entire *acquiescence* in all the bishops." *Clarend.* Approbation, excluding all repining; "A full satisfaction and *acquiescence* in the enjoyment." *Sect.* No. 256. Used with the particle

E

ticle

cicle in. In Commerce, the consent or agreement a person makes in follow the determination of an arbitrator; which when once given, can never be receded from.

ACQUI'RABLE, V. A. that which it is possible to attain; that which a thing can attain.

To ACQUI'RE, V. A. [acquiro, Lat.] to obtain by dint of application, or power, in opposition to what we receive from nature, or by inheritance. " Acquired an immense fortune." " Acquired too high a fame." Shakesp.

ACQUI'RED, Part. contracted by practice, in opposition to what is received from nature; " Natural wants, or acquired habits." Loc. Gained by labour, or obtained by power.

ACQUI'RER, S. he who obtains, attains, or gains.

ACQUI'REMENT, S. that which is gained by application or labour, generally applied to the ornaments of the mind. " These his acquirements, by sodality, were exceedingly enriched." Hayw. on Edw. VI.

ACQUISI'TION, S. [acquisitio, Lat.] the act of gaining, or obtaining. " By his own Industrious acquisition." Smith. The thing obtained. " An acquisition to some mighty monarchy." Swift.

ACQUI'SITIVE, Adj. [acquisitivus, Lat.] that which is acquired, in opposition to native.

ACQUI'ST, S. [from acquire, Lat.] gain, attainment, acquisition.

To ACQUI'T, V. A. [acquiter, Fr.] to deliver or free from. To be acquit from my continual smart." Spenc. To clear from an imputation of guilt, or neglect; to absolve in discharge. " He will not at all acquit the wicked," Nah. 1. 3. To discharge a duty. " Acquitted myself of the debt I owed the public." Dryd.

ACQUI'TMENT, S. [from acquit] the state of being cleared from any imputation or charge of guilt; or, the act of pronouncing such a discharge. " An acquitment, or discharge of a man upon some precedent accusation." Smith.

ACQUI'TTAL, S. [from acquit] the act of freeing a person from the suspicion or guilt of a crime. " The condemnation or acquittal of an accused person." Swift. Acquittance is two-fold, in law and in fact. Acquittance in fact, is when a person is not found guilty of the crime with which he is charged. Acquittance in Law, is when a person is tried as accessary with the principal, and he being cleared, the accessary is acquitted likewise in law.

ACQUI'TTANCE, S. [from acquit] a release or discharge from payment, debt, or any other thing we are obliged to perform. " Such shall find forbearance no acquittance." A receipt for money paid. " Produce ac-

quittances for such a sum." Shakesp.

ACRA'SIA, S. [aκρασια, Gr.] in Medicine, intemperance, or excess in eating, drinking, sleeping, or venery. Likewise the predominancy of one quality above another, either in mixtures, or the constitution of a human body.

A'CRE, S. [arr, or ærer, Sax. arr, Norman Fr. acter, aypæ, Gr.] a measure of land used all over England; containing in length forty perches, and in breadth four, be they more or less, and is always equal to 160 square perches, whatever be the figure of the land. As the perch differs in different counties, the acre must vary likewise. It is commonly 16 a-half feet; but in Stafford-shire 24.

A'CRE, S. a word used in the Mogul's dominions, instead of lack, to signify 100,000 rouples; the rouple is equal to the French crown of three livres, or thirty sols of Holland.

A'CRID, Adj. [arr, Lat.] a bitterness which leaves a hot and palatal sensation on the organs of taste. " Bitter and acrid differ only by the sharp particles of the first being involved in a greater quantity of oil." Arbuth.

ACRIFO'LIUM, S. [of arr and folium, Lat.] in Botany, a prickly leaf.

ACRIMO'NIOUS, Adj. abounding with corrosive, or sharp particles. " If gall cannot be rendered acrimonious." Harvey. Sharp and austere, applied to behaviour.

A'CRIMONY, S. [acrimonia, Fr. acrimonia, Lat.] a quality in bodies by which they corrode, destroy, or dissolve others; corrosiveness, asperity, sharpness. " Affects the organs with a sensation of acrimony or sharpness." Arbuth. Austerity of behaviour; severity, or bitterness of language.

A'CRITUDE, S. [acritudo, Lat.] a quality in a body which affects the taste with a sensation of rough, pungent, and hottish sour. " With its astringent and sweetish taste is joined some acritude." Grew.

ACKIVIO'LA, S. [from arr and viola,] in Botany, Indian cress.

ACROMA'TICAL, Adj. [of acromatus,] that which includes profound learning; that which contains the depths of science.

ACROA'TICS, S. [from acroamus, Gr.] a term applied to some abstruse lectures of Aristotle, to which only his most intimate friends were admitted. Dycke, Johnson.

ACRO'MION, S. [acromion, Gr.] the upper part of the scapula, or shoulder-blade, which receives the clavicula. In infancy it is a cartilage, ossifies gradually, and in one and twenty grows hard, like any common bone.

ACRO'NICAL, Adj. [from acro] in astronomy, the rising of a star when the sun sets, or the setting of a star when the sun rises.

ACRO'NICALLY

ACRONICALLY. Adv. that which rises or sets in an acronycal manner. "When he rises acronycally." Dryd.

To ACROSPIRE. V. N. [αχρος, Gr.] to shoot or sprout at the blade end. "Malt-ters are forbid to wet their malt, when on the floor, or permit it to acrospire." Stat. 6. Geo. I. c. 21.

ACROSPIRE, S. a shoot from the end of seeds, before they are sown. "Send forth their substance in an acrospire." Mort. Husb.

ACROSPIRED, Part. sending out shoots or sprouts; applied to seeds before they are sown.

ACROSS, Adv. [from a expletive, and cross from the Lat. crux, which implies one thing placed on another, so as to form an angle or rectangle] laid over a thing so as to cross it. "Across the strings." Bacon. "Across each other's shoulders." Addif. Folded over each other, "With arms across." Dryd.

ACROSTIC, S. [from αχρος] a poetical composition, the initial letters, or the letters which begin the verses, of which, when added together, form a particular name. This, as Mr. Addison observes, is a species of false wit.

ACROSTIC, Adj. [from acrostic] that which has the property of an acrostic. "Some province in acrostic land." Dryd.

ACROTERS, or ACROTERIA, S. [αχρωτηρια, Gr.] in architecture, small pedestals without bases, placed on pediments to support statues. Likewise the figures of stone or metal, placed on edifices, and sharp pinacles placed in rows, on flat buildings, with rails and ballustres.

To ACT, V. A. [ago, supine, actum, Lat.] to be active, to exert one's active powers, in opposition to inactivity. "He hangs between, in doubt to act or rest." Pope's Essay. To exercise its active powers, to perform its proper functions. "It is capable of being made to act with more or less difficulty." Smith. To perform the functions of life, to be excited to action. "Not out of love, but interest acts alone." Conq. of Granada. To perform, in allusion to the exhibitions of the theatre. "Act well your part, there all the honour lies." Essay on Man. To counterfeit. To exert action, or produce effects. "How body acts upon impassive mind." Garth. To perform a character in a play. "Garrick acts Benedict."

ACT, S. [acte, Fr. of actum, Lat.] something done; a deed. "The conscious wretch must all his acts reveal." Dryd. Some grand exploits, which bespeak a great exertion of powers. "Who can utter the mighty acts of the Lord?" Psal. calv. 4. Exercise of power, or exertion. "Your life is but one continued act of placing benefits on many." Dryd. In the attitude requisite for perform-

ing any action. "In act to shoot, a silver bow the bore." Dryd.

ACT, in Poetry, the division or principal part of a play, intended to give a respite both to the performers and the audience. The Romans were the authors of this invention, and Livius Andronicus the first person who introduced a regular piece, containing five acts, in the 263th year of Rome.

ACTS, in the plural, sometimes imply a narrative or history: As the acts of the apostles.

ACT of faith, in Spanish, Auto de fé, is a pompous procession of the Romish church, at Portugal especially, when the unhappy persons who have been convicted of heresy by the inquisition, are burnt alive.

ACTING, S. the playing or performing a character in a theatrical composition.

ACTING, Part. exerting the powers of action; personating or playing some part on a stage.

ACTED, Part. [from act] incited or stirred up to action. "Acted by malice, rather than candour." Performed on the stage. "Not acted these ten years."

ACTION, S. [actio, Lat.] the exerting or employing our active powers. "All out of work and cold for action." Shak. Hen. V. Something done. A deed. "By the Lord actions are weighed." Power, influence, agency, or operation. In Metaphysics, an immediate effect of what is stiled a self-moving power; or the exercise of an ability, which is being but to begin or determine a particular train of thought, or motion. In ethics, or morality, the voluntary motion of a reasonable creature. In painting, or sculpture, the posture, or attitude, expressive of the passion, the painter would convey to the mind of a spectator. In oratory, the accommodation, or conformity of the person, gesture, and voice of the orator to his subject. In epic poetry, either a real or imaginary, which is the subject of an epic or dramatic poem, its several properties are thus laid down by Mr. Addison: 1. That it be but one action, which is termed its unity: 2dly, That it be entire, which is stiled its integrity; and thirdly, that it be great, which is stiled its importance. In law, a legal demand of, or the form of a suit given by law for recovery of a person's right.

ACTION upon the case, in law, a general action given for redress of wrongs, done without violence, and not provided against by a law; So called because the whole cause or case is set forth in the writ. Action in the case for words, is where a person is injured in his reputation. Where any words are maliciously spoken of a person, for which, if true, he might be punished, action of the case will lie; to say of a person

E 2

fon that he is perjured, of a bishop, or member of parliament, that he is a papist, of an officer, that he is a jacobite, of a justice of the peace, he is a false justice: of a counsellor, he is no lawyer, or has disclosed secrets in a cause; of an attorney, that he is a knave in his profession, a maintainer of suits, or not worthy to be an attorney; of a doctor of physic, that he is an ass, fool, or empiric or mountebank; of a trader, that he is a bankrupt knave; of a merchant, that he is not able to pay his debts; of a man who is courting a woman, that he has the distemper, or of a woman, that she is with child by another person, so as either of them lose their marriage, is actionable. Though to call a man whoremaster, or a woman whore, except in London, by the custom of the city, is not actionable. *Cro. Jac.* 410. 2 *Sald.* 696.

ACTIONABLE, Adj. that which will subject a person to an action; punishable, blameable, culpable.

ACTIONARY, or ACTIONIST, S. [*actionaire*, Fr.] a proprietor of stock in a trading company.

ACTIVE, Adj. [*activus*, Lat.] that which can excite motion, in opposition to rest. " Moved by certain active principles, such as gravity." *Newton.* That which operates, or exerts power upon another, in opposition to passive. Practice, in opposition to theory. " In the active part they cannot Terror." *Denham.* Nimble, brisk, lively, vigorous, fond of action, in opposition to indolence. " Some with darn their active fineness try." *Dryd.* Active principles, in chymistry, are those which are supposed to act of themselves, without needing to be put into motion by others. In grammar, applied to verbs, are those which affirm action of the word going before them, or that a person or thing does something.

ACTIVELY, Adv. in a brisk, nimble, industrious manner. In grammar, so as to imply action.

ACTIVENESS, S. a quick and assiduous performance of business; nimbleness. Activity is more commonly used by modern writers.

ACTIVITY, S. propensity, readiness, nimbleness; a power of acting, operation, influence. " Salt put to ice, increaseth the activity of cold." *Bacon's Nat. Hist.* Continual exertion of our active powers in opposition to indolence.

ACTOR, S. [*actor*, Lat.] he that does or performs any thing; he that practises. " Young men may be learners, whilst men in age are actors." *Bacon.* He that performs a part on the stage; a player. " When a good actor doth his part present." *Denham.*

ACTRESS, S. [*actrice*, Fr.] a woman who performs on a stage. " And therefore that was an actress here." *Dryd.* A female,

who performs any thing. " Virgil, indeed, has admitted Fame as an actress in the Æneid." *Spell.*

ACTUAL, Adj. that which includes or implies action; " Besides her walking and other actual performances."—*Hooke.* That which is real, or existing. " Sin, there in power before—Once actual, now in body." *Par. Loft.* Exerting action, or active. " Contradict the danger of an actual fault.". *Dryd.*

ACTUALITY, S. [from actual] the power of exerting action; activity. Reality, or certainty. " The actuality of Christ's resurrection." *Fea.*

ACTUALLY, Adv. really; absolutely; in fact; " Where the historians were actually inspired." *Spell.* No. 483.

ACTUALNESS, S. a quality which denotes the reality of the operation, or existence of a thing.

ACTUARY, S. [*actuarius*, Lat.] in Law, the register or clerk, who compiles the minutes of the proceedings of a court.

ACTUATE, Part. [from *actus*, Lat.] to set in motion; to become active; to be wrought upon; to be animated; to be produced. " Grow actuate into a third and distinct perfection of practice." *Sanb.*

To ACTUATE, V. A. [from *actus*, Lat.] to exert, to excite to action. " Such in every man, who has not actuated the grace given him." *Dec. of Piety.* Influenced, or set in motion. " Mean and narrow minds are the least actuated by it." *Spell.* No. 255. To be put into motion; or to effect by being vigorously agitated.

ACULEATE, Adj. [*aculeatus*, Lat.] in Botany, that which ends in a sharp point; or is prickly.

ACUMEN, S. [Lat. of *acus*,] sharpness; applied either to material objects, or the faculties of the mind. " To signify genius, or natural acumen." *Dennial.*

ACUMINATED, Part. [from *acumen*] that which ends in a sharp point.

ACUTE, Part. [*acutus*, Lat.] sharppointed. Applied to persons of great sagacity, deep penetration, and sharpness of natural parts; used in opposition to dull and stupid. " The acute and ingenious author." *Locke.* Applied to the senses; to be rendered more quick in receiving impressions; or made more perfect. " Were our senses altered and made much quicker, and acuter." *Locke.* Acute, in geometry, that which terminates in a sharp point; acute angle, that which is less than ninety degrees; Acute angled triangle, is that which three angles are all acute. Acute-angular-section of a cone, the same as an ellipsis. Acute, in music, shrill, sharp or high, in respect of some other note; founds considered in these respects, constitute a tune, the foundation of harmony. Acute, in grammar, an accent, which raises or sharpens the

the voice. In phyfic, applied to violent defeafes, which terminates in a few days.

ACUTELY, Adv. In a fharp manner; ufed both in a primitive and fecondary fenfe, and applied both to perfons and things. With accuracy, fagacity, and precifion.

ACUTENESS, S. fharpnefs, fagacity, quicknefs of difcernment. Capacity of diftinguifhing, or receiving impreffions. Vehemence, productive of a quick or fpeedy crifis in a difeafe. "Refpecting rather the acutenefs of the difeafe." *Brown's Vulg. Err.* Shrillnefs, or fharpnefs, applied to found. "This acutenefs of found will fhew." *Boyle.*

ADACTED, Part [addactus, Lat.] driven by force.

A'DAGE, S. a maxim; or principle received and acknowledged as felf-evident. "Dar'ft thou apply that adage of the fchool?" *Dryd.* A proverbial faying. "As if contrary to the adage, fcience had no friend but ignorance." *Granville.*

ADA'GIO, Adj. [Ital.] flow, folemn, grave; in mufic, a flow movement, when repeated twice, as adagio, adagio, It implies a more flow motion than the former; it is fometimes abbreviated thus, adag°, ad°.

AD'AMANT, S. [adamas, Lat.] a ftone, fuppofed to be an impenetrable hardnefs. "Spears in pieces pofts of adamant." *Shal. Hen. V.* The diamond; "Among them the adamant of all other ftones." *Ray on Creat.* The loadftone.

ADAMANTEAN, Adj. [from adamant] hard and as impenetrable as adamant. "And frock of mail adamantean proof." *Milton.*

ADAMANTINE, Adj. [from adamant] made of adamant; "With adamantine columns." *Dryd.* Having the properties of adamant; hard, not to be broken. "In adamantine chains fhall death be bound." *Pope.*

A'DAM's-APPLE, S. [compound word, Adam pomum, Lat.] in anatomy, a prominence in the throat, in the middle of the cartilago fcutiformis.

To ADAPT, V. A. [adapto, Lat.] to fit or proportion one thing to another; "To your decays adapt my fight." *Swift.* To make one thing correfpond with another; to fuit. "A good poet, will adapt the very founds as well words as the things." *Pope.*

ADAPTA'TION, S. [from adapt] the adapting one thing to another; or the fitnefs, or fuitablenefs of one thing to another. "An adaptation or cramping of one unto the other." *Brown's Vulg. Err.*

ADAP'TION, S. [from adapt] the act of fitting; fuitablenefs. "Prudent adaption of thefe machines." *Cheyne.*

ADA'R, S. [Heb. mighty] the twelfth month of the Jewish ecclefiaftical, and the fixth of their civil year, containing twenty-nine days, anfwering fometimes to our

February, and fometimes entering into our March. As the lunar year of the Jews is one month too fhort, every third year they infert a thirteenth month, and name it Ve-adar, or fecond adar, which confifts of twenty-nine days.

ADA'TAIS, or ADA'TYS, S. a muflin, or cotton cloth, from Bengal in the Eaft-Indies; the piece is ten French ells long, and three quarters broad.

To ADCORPORATE, V. A. [adcorporo, Lat.] to join one body to another; to mix together; ufually written accorporate.

To ADD, V. A. [addo, Lat.] to increafe by fomething new; to enlarge; to aggrandize; "If to his works is add one grain of fenfe." *Dryd.* To perform the operation of joining one number, &c. to another. "He can repeat it and add it to the former." *Locke.*

A'DDABLE, Adj. that which is is in our power to add; that which may be added. "The firft number in every addition is called an addable number." *Cocker.*

A'DDER, S. [Atter, Attor, Sax.] a kind of a ferpent.

A'DDER-GRASS, S. in botany fo called, as Skinner imagines, becaufe adders lurk about it.

ADDERS-TONGUE, S. [ophioglossum, Lat.] is has no vifible flower; but his feeds are produced on a fpike, refembling an adder's tongue, whence it derives its name.

A'DDERS-WORT, in botany, an herb fo called on account of its virtue againft the bite of ferpents.

AD'DIBLE, Adj. that which it is poffible to add. "Addible numbers." *Locke.*

ADDIBI'LITY, S. [from add] the poffibility of being added. "The addibility of numbers." *Locke.*

AD'DICE, S. [pronounced adz from adefa, Sax. an ax] a fharp tool of the ax kind, whofe blade is fomewhat arching, and its edge afhyart the handle; ferving the purpofe both of a hammer and hatchet, one end being a driver, and the other a chopper. It is peculiar to the coopers.

To ADDICT, V. A. to devote, dedicate, or employ one's felf entirely. To abandon one's felf entirely to fomething bad. "Addicted himfelf to vice." *Johnfon.* Ufed with the particle to.

ADDICTEDNESS, S. propenfity, affiduity, attachment.

ADDIC'TIO, S. [addict, Lat.] a transferring goods to another by auction.

ADDISON, [JOSEPH,] Efq;——This very great ornament to the age he lived in, his own country in particular, and to the caufe of polite literature in general, was fon of the Rev. Dr. Lancelot Addifon, who afterwards became dean of Lichfield and Coventry, but at the time of this fon's birth

was rector of Mileston, near Ambrosbury, Wilts, at which place the subject of our present consideration receiv'd his vital breath, on the 1st day of May, 1672.—He was very early sent to school in Ambrosbury, being put under the care of the Rev. Mr. Naish, then master of that school; from thence, as soon as he had received the first rudiments of literature, he was removed to Salisbury school, taught by the Rev. Mr. Taylor, and after that to the Charter-House, where he was under the tuition of the learned Dr. Ellis.——Here he first contracted an intimacy with Mr. Steele, afterwards Sir Richard, which continued inviolable till his death.— At about fifteen years of age he was entered of Queen's college, Oxford, and in about two years afterwards, thro' the interest of Dr. Lancaster, Dean of Magdalen's, elected into that college, and admitted to the degrees of batchelor and master of arts.

While he was at the university, he was repeatedly solicited by his father and other friends to enter into holy orders, which, altho' from his extreme modesty and natural diffidence he would gladly have declined, yet, in compliance with his father's desires, he was once very near concluding on; when having, thro' Mr. Congreve's means, become a great favourite with that universal patron of poetry and the polite arts, the famous lord Halifax, that nobleman, who had frequently regretted that so few men of liberal education and great abilities applied themselves to affairs of public business, in which their country might reap the advantage of their talents, earnestly persuaded him to lay aside this design, and as an encouragement for him so to do, and an indulgence to an inclination for travel, which shewed itself in Mr. Addison, procured him an annual pension of 300l. from the crown, to enable him to make the tour of France and Italy.

On this tour then he set out at the latter end of the year 1699, did his country great honour by his extraordinary abilities, receiving in his turn every mark of esteem that could be shewn to a man of exalted genius, particularly from M. Boileau, the famous French poet, and the abbe Salvini, professor of the Greek tongue in the university of Florence, the former of whom declared that he first conceived an opinion of the English genius for poetry from Mr. Addison's Latin poems, printed in the Musae Anglicanae, and the latter translated into elegant Italian verse, his epistolary poem to lord Halifax, which is esteemed a master-piece in its kind.

In the year 1702, as he was about to return home, he was informed from his friends in England, by letter, that king William intended him the post of secretary to attend the army under prince Eugene in Italy.— This was an office that would have been ex-

tremely acceptable to Mr. Addison; but his majesty's death, which happened before he could get his appointment, put a stop to that, together with his pension.—This news came to him at Geneva; he therefore chose to make the tour of Germany in his way home, and at Vienna composed his Treatise on Medals, which however did not make its appearance till after his death.

A different set of ministers coming to the management of affairs in the beginning of queen Anne's reign, and consequently the interest of Mr. Addison's friends being considerably weakened, he continued unemployed and in obscurity till 1704, when an accident called him again into notice.

The amazing victory gained by the great duke of Marlborough at Blenheim, exciting a desire in the earl of Godolphin, then lord high treasurer, to have it celebrated in verse, lord Halifax, to whom that nobleman had communicated this his wish, recommended Mr. Addison to him, as the only person who was likely to execute such a task in a manner adequate to the subject; in which he succeeded so happily, that when the poem he wrote, viz. the campaign, was finished no further than to the celebrated simile of the angel, the lord high treasurer was so delighted with it, that he immediately presented the author with the place of one of the commissioners of appeals in the excise, in the room of Mr. Locke, who had been just promoted to the board of trade.

In the year 1705, he attended Lord Halifax to Hanover, and in the succeeding year was appointed under secretary to Sir Charles Hedges, then secretary of state; nor did he lose this post on the removal of Sir Charles, the Earl of Sunderland, who succeeded to that gentleman, willingly continuing Mr. Addison as his under Secretary.

In 1709, Lord Wharton being appointed lord lieutenant of Ireland, nominated our author secretary for that kingdom, the queen at the same time bestowing on him also the post of keeper of the records in Ireland. But when in the latter end of her majesty's reign the ministry was again changed, and Mr. Addison expected no farther employment, he gladly submitted to a retirement, in which he formed a design, which it is much to be regretted that he never had in his power to put in execution, viz. the compiling a dictionary to fix the standard of the English language upon the same kind of plan with the famous Dizionario della Crusca of the Italians. A work in no language so much wanted as in our own, and which from so masterly, so elegant and so correct a pen as this gentleman's, could not have fail'd being executed to the greatest degree of perfection. We have however the less reason to lament this loss, as the same design has since been carried on, and brought to a maturity that reflects

He taught us how to live; and, Oh! too high
    high
A price for Knowledge, taught us how to
    die.

and death of this great man, nothing more
remains in this place to be done, but to give
a list of his dramatic pieces, which were the
following three.

1. Cato. Trag.
2. The Drummer. Com.
3. Rosamond. Opera.

ADDI'TAMENT, S. [additamentum, Lat.]
a thing added. "Certain additaments that
contribute to its ornaments and use." Hale's
Orig.

ADDITI'TIOUS, Adj. a thing added
without authority. "Several additious books
and miracles." Univ. Hist. vol. x. 8vo. b.
xi. c. x.

ADDI'TION, S. [additio, Lat.] the adding one thing to another, to increase its
quantity, or dimensions. "By medical addition of heat, degrees." Brael. The thing
added, increase. "Addition to the power of
the commons." Swift. Interpolation, by
inserting something new, or spurious. "Additions to what Christ and his apostles have
designed." Hamm. Fundam. In arithmetic,
the second of the five principal rules. In
algebra it is expressed by this character +,
which is read plus, more or add. In law, a
title given to a man, besides his christian,
or surname, implying his state, degree,
age, occupation, or residence. "Bear the addition nobly ever." Shakesp. Coriolanus.

ADDI'TIONAL, Adj. [additionalis, Lat.]
that which is added. "The additional day."
Holder. That which increases. "An additional lustre." Spectat. Used of argument, a greater number, or more forcible
ones. "Afford us several additional proofs."
Atterb.

A'DDITORY, Adj. that which is added.

A'DDLE, Adj. [adl, or adel, Sax.] In its
primitive signification applied to eggs which
are corrupted under a hen, and produce nothing; in allusion to which it is used to signify a person of bad natural parts. "That
curdles eggs too fresh and addle." Hudib.
"But his brains grew addle." Dryd.

To A'DDLE, V. N. to corrupt, to make
rotten. "Such as are addled form." Brown.

ADDLE-PA'TED, adj. one of a dull,
stupid, and barren genius; silly. "Dull and
addle-pated." Dryd.

To ADDRE'SS, V. A. [addresser, Fr.] to
begin any action. "Addressed himself on
four to single fight." Dryd. To get ready;
to put into a state of immediate use. "Addressed his men to take the bank." Hayw.
To apply to by petition or speech. "Addressed the King." To direct one's speech
to. "To address the senate." Add. Cato.

ADDRE'SS, S. [addresse, Fr.] an application in order to persuade. "Venus had
heard the virgin's soft address." Prior. The
suit of a lover. "Made his addresses to me."
Spectat. No. 163. Behaviour. "A man of
polite address." Genteel carriage; quickness

of understanding, presence of mind, and readiness to make the best of every thing that
occurs. "The skill and address of a minister." Swift. An application to a superior.
"The humble address of the Lord Mayor,
&c." The direction of a letter. "I knew
who it came from as soon as I saw the address." "My address is, at ———."

ADDRE'SSER, S. the person who carries
address.

ADDU'CENT, Part. [adducens, Lat.]
that which draws to or close. In Anatomy
applied to those muscles which close, or draw
together, those parts to which they are affixed.

To ADDU'LCE, V. A. [from ad and dulcis, sweet; to sweeten; figurative, to soften,
to reconcile. "With many sugared words,
seek to addulce all matters." Bac. Hen. VII.

ADENO'GRAPHY, S. [from aden and
grapho, Gr.] a treatise which describes the
glands.

ADE'PT, S. [adeptus, Part. of adipiscor,
Lat.] one that is acquainted with all the secrets of his art.

ADE'PT, Part. [adeptus, Lat.] one who
has acquired a perfect knowledge of any
thing. "Such adept philosophers as we are
told of." Boyle.

A'DEQUATE, Adj. [adaequatus, Lat.] e-
qual, proportionate to. "Adequate and sufficient." Search. Full, perfect, sole, proper,
and entire. "Death seems to be the whole
adequate object of popular courage." Hamm.
Adequate ideas are those which perfectly represent their archetypes. But when we say
we have an adequate idea of any thing, it
must be understood only in a vulgar sense,
because scarce any ideas are so in a philosophic sense.

A'DEQUATELY, Adv. in a full, complete, and perfect manner; in its full extent, or true acceptation.

A'DEQUATENESS, S. equality, perfect
resemblance; justness of correspondence;
proportion.

ADFE'CTED, Adj. [affectus, Lat.] compounded of known and unknown parts. Ad-
fected equations in Algebra, where the unknown quantity is found in different powers,
thus $x^3 - px^2 + qx = a^2 b$, wherein
are three different powers of x, as x^3 x^2
and x.

To ADHE'RE, V. A. [adhaereo, Lat.] to
stick or join to, like any glutinous matter.
To hold together, join, or unite. "How
every thing adheres together." Shakesp. To
persist in, or remain firm to a person, or
opinion. "Adhere to the dictates of conscience." Boyle.

ADHE'RENCE, S. [from adhere] the
quality of sticking to; attachment; perseverance. "Their firm adherence to their religion." Spect. No. 495.

ADHE'RENCY, S. [from adherence] steadiness

finds of opinion, attachment, sticking to. "Vices have a native *adherency* of vexation." *Decay of Piety.*

ADHE'RENT, Part. [*adhærens*, Lat.] adhering or sticking to. "And stuck *adherent*." *Pope.* Query, Is this be not tautology? In Logic, something added or not essential. "Modes are *inherent*, or *adherent*; that is, proper and improper."

ADHE'RENT, S. [from *adhere*.] one firmly attached to any person, party, or opinion. "Their subjects and *adherents*." *Raleigh.*

ADHE'RER, S. one who is strongly attached to any person, party, or profession. "A firm *adherer* to the established church." *Swift.*

ADHE'SION, S. [*adhæsio*, Lat.] the act or state of sticking to. *Adherence* is used in the primary sense, and appropriated to persons; but *adhesion* in the secondary, and applied to matter. "More or less firm *adhesion* of the parts." *Locke.*

ADHE'SIVE, Adj. remaining close attached; sticking or keeping to. "*Adhesive* to the trial." *Thomson. Aut.*

ADJA'CENCY, S. [*adjacens*, Lat.] that which lies near; or bodies which border upon, and are near to. "The needle is not distracted by the vicinity of *adjacencies*." *Brown's Vulg. Err.*

ADJA'CENT, Part. [*adjacens*, Lat.] lying near, bordering, contiguous, or touching each other. "*Adjacent* to other mediums of, &c." *Newton.*

ADJA'CENT, [*adjacens*, Lat.] the context, or words immediately following or going before. "The words receiving a determinate sense from their companions and *adjacents*." *Locke.*

ADIA'PHOROUS, Adj. [*adiaphoros*, Gr.] indifferent or neutral.

ADJE'CTIVE, S. [*adjectivum*, Lat. *adjectif*, Fr.] a word which denotes the qualities of a subject: as, a wise minister; the word *wise* is an adjective, as denoting only the quality of the minister.

ADJE'CTIVELY, Adj. in Grammar, after the manner of a word signifying quality; or in the sense of an adjective.

ADIEU', S. [pronounced *addū*, of *à*, Fr. to, and *Dieu*, Fr. God: a form used at taking leave; In its original acceptation, a recommendation to the care and protection of the divine being, but commonly used only as a ceremony of parting. "While now I take a last *adieu*." *Prior.*

To ADJOIN, V. A. [*adjoindre*, Fr.] to join, to unite, to add, to stick together. "Should be as marks *adjoined*." *Watt's Log.*

To ADJOIN, V. N. [*adjoindre*, Fr.] to be contiguous to; to lie to near as to touch or join to. "Th' *adjoining* fane." *Dryd.*

ADJOINING, Part. lying close to, or immediately following. "That being understood, proceed to the next *adjoining*." *Locke.*

To ADJOURN, V. A. [pronounced *adjurn*, of *adjourner*, Fr.] to appoint a future day; to put off to another time; to defer to another time.

ADJOURNMENT, S. the deferring to another day; delay; procrastination. "We run out our lives in *adjournments* from time to time." *L'Estrange.*

ADIPO'SA, Adj. [of *adips*] In Anatomy, applied to a membrane betwixt the internal part of the fat, and the external surface of the muscles.

A'DIPOUS, Adj. [*adiposus*, Lat.] fat, greasy. Used only by old medical writers.

A'DIT, S. [*aditus*, Lat.] among Miners, an avenue, or passage, through which a mine is entered, and through which the ore or water is carried out. "*Adits*, pumps, and wheels." *Carew.*

ADITION, S. [*aditus*, Lat.] the act of going to a person.

To ADJUDGE, V. A. [*adjuger*, Fr.] to give to one of the contending parties in a suit at law. "Victory is *adjudged* to the opponent or defendant." *Locke.* To sentence, to condemn. "Thou art *adjudged* to the death." *Shakesp.* To resolve, to suppose.

ADJUDGED, Part. determined. "*Adjudged* cases."

ADJUDICATION, S. [*adjudicatio*, Lat.] the act of judging, or giving a judicial sentence.

To ADJU'DICATE, V. A. [*adjudico*, Lat.] to determine any claim at law; to give or assign.

A'DJUNCT, S. [*adjunctum*, Lat.] something united. "Learning is but an *adjunct* to ourself." *Shakesp.* One joined to another. "An *adjunct* of singular experience and trust." *Wotton.* Something added, not essentially belonging to a thing; a mode, which may be separated from its subject; as (smoothness in a bowl, learning in a man, motion in a body. *Adjuncts*, In Grammar and Rhetoric, are adjectives, or epithets, added to enlarge, or augment, the energy of a discourse.

ADJUNCTION, S. [*adjunctio*, Lat.] the act of joining together, or the state of a thing joined.

ADJUNCTIVE, Adj. [*adjunctivus*, Lat.] that which joins, or the thing joined.

ADJURA'TION, S. [*adjuratio*, Lat.] the form of an oath taken, or an oath administered, whereby a person lays under a necessity of speaking the truth without disguise.

To ADJU'RE, V. A. [*adjuro*, Lat.] to bind a person to perform or not perform a thing, under the penalty of a dreadful curse. "Joshua *adjured* them at that time, saying, Cursed, &c." *Josh. vi. 26.* To entreat earnestly and pathetically. "*Adjured* by all the bonds of civil duty." *Milt. Samps.* To swear by. "Ye lamps of heaven! inviolable

E

his powers! fatal fillets! ye facred altars! be all of you *adjured*." *Dryd.* To oblige a perfon to declare the truth upon oath.

To ADJU'ST, V. A. [*adjuſter*, Fr.] to make confiſtent, to regulate. " Faſter than the moſt viſionary projector can *adjuſt* his ſchemes." *Swift.* To ſettle, to reduce to a criterion. " *Adjuſt* their ſignification." *Locke.* To ſhew the conformity of one thing to another ; to render conformable ; to reconcile.

ADJU'STMENT, S. a juſt defcription, an explication of difficulties. " The further and clearer *adjuſtment* of this affair." *Woodw.* The ſuitableneſs of one part to another. " The various connexions and *adjuſtments* of each part." *Watts.*

A'DJUTANT, S. [*adjutans*, Lat.] a military helper, or aſſiſtant. An officer in the army, who aſſiſts a ſuperior, in diſtributing the pay, and over-ſeeing the puniſhment of the inferior men. The French uſe this term inſtead of an *aid du camp*.

ADJU'TANT-GE'NERAL, one who attends the general, aſſiſts in council, and carries the orders from one part to another.

A'DJUTOR, S. [*adjutor*, Lat.] a helper ; one who aſſiſts.

ADJUTO'RIUM, S. [Lat. *adjuvo*] in anatomy, the *humerus*, or ſhoulder-bone.

A'DJUTORY, Adj. [*adjutorius*, Lat.] that which affords aſſiſtance.

ADJU'TRIX, S. [Lat.] a female aſſiſtant.

AD LI'BITUM, [Lat. as you pleaſe,] a phraſe chiefly made uſe of by medical and muſic writers.

ADMEA'SUREMENT, S. (See MEASURE) the finding the dimenſions and quantity of a thing by a ſtandard or rule.

ADMENSURA'TION, S. [of *ad* to, and *menſura*, Lat.] the act of finding out the dimenſions by a ſtandard, rule, or meaſure.

To ADMI'NISTER, V. A. [*adminiſtro*, Lat.] to afford ; to give. " Let zephir's bland *administer* their tepid genial airs." *Phillips.* In politics, to conduct the affairs of government. " What e'er is beſt *adminiſtred* is beſt." *Pope.* In courts, to tender to a perſon to take his oath. " To *adminiſter* an oath." To perform the office of a miniſter or prieſt. " To *adminiſter* the ſacrament." In phyſic, to diſpenſe medicines, to preſcribe. " *Adminiſtring* phyſic." *Wiſeman's Voy.* To contribute to. " *Adminiſters* to the pleaſure" *Spect.* No. 477. In law, to take poſſeſſion of the goods and chattels of a perſon dying inteſtate.

To ADMI'NISTRATE, V. A. [*adminiſtro*, Lat.] to apply, or make uſe of. Seldom uſed.

ADMINISTRA'TION, S. [*adminiſtratio*, Lat.] the act of enforcing, applying, or paſſing ſentence according to the ſenſe of a law. " In the *adminiſtration* of his law."

Sbol. The duty of one of the chief officers of ſtate. " In the ſhort time of his *adminiſtration*." *Dryd.* The active or executive part of government. " The *adminiſtration* cannot be in too few hands." *Swift.* Diſpenſation. " By the univerſal *adminiſtration* of grace." *Sprat.* In law, the act of a perſon, who takes charge of the effects of one dying inteſtate, and is accountable for them.

ADMINISTRATIVE, Adj. that which aids, ſupports, or aſſiſts ; that by which any thing is diſcharged, executed, or performed.

ADMINISTRA'TOR, S. [*adminiſtrator*, Lat.] one who officiates as a miniſter in a church. " An occaſional or limited *adminiſtrator*." *Watts.* One that has the chief management of national affairs. He who has the goods of a man dying without will committed to his charge, and is accountable for them, when required by the ordinary.

ADMINISTRA'TORSHIP, S. the office, or duty of an adminiſtrator.

ADMINISTRATRIX, S. [Lat.] a female who adminiſters to a perſon dying inteſtate, committed to her charge.

A'DMIRABLE, Adj. [*admirabilis*, Lat.] deſerving admiration.

A'DMIRABLENESS, S. a quality including the idea of worth, excellence, and unexpected perfection.

A'DMIRABLY, Adv. in manner which excites an idea of perfection ; excellently. " *Admirably* well contrived." *Addiſ.*

A'DMIRAL, S. [*amiral*, Teut. *amiroil*, Dut. and *admiral*, Fr.] an officer, who has the chief command of a fleet. According to Du Cange, the Sicilians were the firſt, and the Genoeſe the next, who gave this name to the commander of their naval affairs ; and it is ſuppoſed that, Philip of France, introduced the name into Europe in 1284, and the firſt mention of this name among us was in the reign of Edward I. Lord high-*admiral*, is one inveſted with power to determine all crimes committed on the ſea and its coaſts. At preſent it is divided amongſt ſeveral perfons, who are ſtiled lords commiſſioners of the admiralty. Under the admiral is a rear-admiral, and a vice-admiral.

A'DMIRAL-SHIP, S. the office of an admiral.

A'DMIRALTY, S. [*amirauté*, Fr.] the office of the lords commiſſioners. It conſiſts at preſent of a firſt commiſſioner, who preſides at the board, and ſix others. All warrants for building, and providing ſhips with warlike ſtores are ſigned by them. They give directions to the navy and victualling officers, for preparing and victualling ſhips. *Admiralty-court*, is where the cauſes relating to maritime affairs are tried ;

a

trial; the chief is at Doctor's-Commons, London. All proceedings in this court run in the name of the lord-admiral, who has a deputy called judge of the admiralty, usually a doctor of civil law, two counsellors, advocates, proctors and a marshal. The judge is constituted by the king's patent, and holds his place, *quam diu se bene gesserit*; as long as he behaves himself well. This court is not esteemed a court of record, because it is governed by the civil law, and the judge is not authorised to take such recognizance, as a court of record may.

ADMIRA'TION, S. [*admiratio*, Lat.] a passion excited by very great excellence in any object. "There is a pleasure in *admiration*." *Tillotf.* Wonder; surprize; astonishment. "Your boldness I with *admiration* see." *Dryd.* In grammar, a point or mark, which denotes, that the sentence before it, implies wonder or admiration; marked thus (!)

To ADMI'RE, V. A. [*admiro*. Lat.] to regard with wonder, including esteem; and arising from the discovery of some unexpected excellence. "The philosophic passion truly *admires* and adores." *Glanville.* Sometimes used in a bad sense, to imply the passion of wonder excited by something extravagantly vicious.

ADMI'RED, Part. which occasions surprize, wonder, and astonishment. "Your most *admired* disorder." *Shak.*

ADMI'RER, S. one who feels the passion of admiration rising on beholding any thing surprisingly excellent. He who wonders, or regards with admiration. "Friends and *admirers* of each other." *Spect.* One who is captivated with the charms of a female; a lover.

ADMI'RINGLY, Adv. struck with admiration. "*Admiringly* and mournfully." *Shak.* With admiration. "We may further *admiringly* observe." *Boyle.*

ADMI'SSABLE, Adj. [*admitto*, Lat.] that may be admitted. "Supposing that this supposition was *admissible*." *Hale's Orig.*

ADMIS'SION, S. [*admissio*, Lat.] liberty or leave of entering. "For the *admission* of poor suitors." *Bacon's Hen.* VII. Access or liberty to enter. "A more intimate *admission* to himself." A power of entering, in opposition to resistance. "Free and easy *admission* to this heat." *Woodw.* The granting a proposition not clearly proved. In law, is when the bishop after examination, permits a priest to enter into a benefice to which he is presented, saying, *admitto te babilem.* If any person endeavour to be admitted not having episcopal ordination, he forfeits 100l. by stat. 14 Car. II. 1 init.

344.

To ADMIT, V. A. [*admitto*, Lat.] to grant free access to. "Does not one table Bavius still *admit*?" To permit or suffer.

"He *admitted*, for a fit clerk, a perfectly fit." *Clarend.* To grant or allow a supposition, as true. "*Admit* no fleet can hurt." *Fairfax.* To grant; to allow. "If you once *admit* of a latitude." *Dryd.*

ADMI'TTABLE, Adj. that which may be admitted or suffered.

ADMI'TTANCE, S. a permission to take and exercise any office. Introduction. Access. "'Tis gold, which buys *admittance*." *Shak.* Passage, power of entering. A prerogative or right of access. "Of excellent breeding, of great *admittance*." *Shak.* The acceding to, granting any position.

To ADMI'X, V. A. [*admisceo*, Lat.] to join to, mix, or mingle.

ADMI'XTION, S. the joining, blending, mixing, or incorporating one body or fluid with another.

ADMI'XTURE, S. the blending, mixing or mingling one thing with another.

To ADMO'NISH, V. A. [*admoneo*, Lat.] to exhort, persuade, or give advice. To reprove, to censure. "*Admonish* him as a brother." 2 Theffal. iii. 15. To give a hint, to warn. To remind of a fault. "He of their wicked ways shall them *admonish*." *Milt.*

ADMO'NISHER, S. one who reminds another of his duty, and reproves him for his faults, or errors.

ADMO'NISHMENT, S. a reproof for faults. "His *admonishment* receive." *Par. Loft.* "Thy grave *admonishments* prevail with me," *Shak. Hen.* V. now seldom used.

ADMO'NITION, S. [*admonitio*, Lat.] a hint of duty, advice. "*Admonition* concerning these, not unnecessary." *Hooker.* A reminding, or reproving a person for the neglect of duty. "They are written for our *admonition*." 1 Cor. x. 11. A state of reverential awe, and obedience. "Bring them up in the *admonition* of the Lord." *Ephef.* vi. 4.

ADMO'NITORY, Adj. [*admonitorius*, Lat.] that which excites us to the performance of our duty.

To ADMO'VE, V. A. [*admoveo*, Lat.] to go towards, to approach; or bring nearer.

ADNA'TA, Part. (from *adnascor*) in anatomy, applied to a coat of the eye, called *tunica adnata*; and likewise conjunctive or *albugineo*. It is called the white of the eye, and is formed by the tendons of the muscles which move it.

ADO', S. (from *a* expletive and *do*) trouble, difficulty. "With much ado he purity kept awake," *Dryd.* Bustle, noise, or tumult. "All this ado," *Locke.* A greater appearance or show of business than what is real, and is taken in a ludicrous sense. "I made no more ado, but took all. *Shak. Hen.* IV. "We'll keep no great ado." *Romeo and Juliet.*

ADO'CIO, a term used by some philosophers,

losophers, to denote the highest or superlative degree.

ADOLE'SCENCE, S. [adolescentia, Lat.] the state of a youth from his infancy, to his full growth; and lasting as long as the fibres continue to increase in dimension or firmness; generally computed to be between fifteen and twenty-five, or thirty years of age.

ADOLE'SCENCY, S. (See ADOLESCENCE) the state of youth between puberty and manhood. "In the last adolescency, and makes him twenty-five." Brown's Vulg. Err.

ADONIS, S. [of adon, Gr. and דָּן] in mythology, the son of Cynaras king of Cyprus, by incest; a favourite of Venus; he was so beautiful, that she carried him away by force, and forsook the celestial abodes to enjoy his company. But he being at last slain by an Erymanthean boar, the goddess was inconsolable for his loss; which was celebrated by an annual mourning; and the river Biblus becoming red, was generally esteemed as a proper time to begin the ceremony. Mr. Maundrel, in his travels, has given us a curious account of the manner of the mourning, and an explication of the rivers looking red, like blood, about that time. The moral of the fable is so obvious, that to explain it to those who know the consequences of illicit pleasures, would be giving an affront to their understandings. Adonis sacra, were the solemn ceremonies which were celebrated at Byblis, in the temple of Venus, in honour of Venus, and in memory of Adonis.

ADONIC, Adj. [from Adonis] a verse consisting only of a dactyle and spondee, and derives its name from being used in the dirges made to lament the loss of Adonis.

To ADOPT, V. A. [adopto, Lat.] to substitute another's child instead of one's own. "Yet I could some adopted heir provide." Dryd. To acquire, in opposition to what is inherent. "From the sollicitations of our natural or adopted desires." Locke. To rely or depend on, and make use as if our own. "He adopted the principles of the stoics."

ADOPTION, S. [adoptio, Lat.] the act of taking the child of another for our son, and giving him a right to all privileges which accompany that title; the ceremony consisted in purchasing the person that is to be adopted, of his parents, and in their assuming the names of the person who had conferred this favour upon them; in allusion to those three particulars it is that the Scripture says, "We might receive the adoption of sons." Gal. iv. 5. The state of an adopted person. "To remind us of our adoption." Rogers.

ADOPTIVE, Adj. [adoptivus, Lat.] that which is adapted. "So full power and interest is an adoptive son, as in a natural."

Bacon. "He who adopts. "An adopted son cannot cite his adoptive father." Ayliffe.

ADO'RABLE, Adj. [adorable, Fr.] that which is deserving of divine honour. "Says the adorable author of christianity." Cheyne.

ADO'RABLENESS, S. the quality of being worthy of divine honours.

ADO'RABLY, Adv. in such a manner as to be worthy of divine worship.

ADORA'TION, S. [adoratio, Lat.] the act of worshipping, including reverence, esteem, awe, and love. The external act of homage paid to God. "By way of external adoration." Homage paid to persons in high posts, or in high estimation. "What is thy toll, O adoration?" Shaksp. Hen. V.

To ADO'RE, V. A. [adoro, Lat.] to reverence, to honour. "The mountain nymphs and Themis they adore." Dryd. To pay a high degree of reverence and homage. "The people appear adoring their prince, and their prince adoring God." Tatler, No. 57. To love to a great extreme.

ADO'RER, S. one who pays divine honours or adorations to the Deity; one who has a great and reverential esteem. "He was so severe an adorer of truth." Clarend. A lover who almost idolizes the object of his flame. "I hear adorer too devoutly stand." Prior.

To ADORN, V. A. [adorno, Lat.] to deck or set off with dress; to ornament. "A gallery adorned with pictures." Cowley. To convey splendor or magnificence. "Thou shalt again be adorned with thy tabrets." Jer. xxxi. 6.

ADORNMENT, S. the advantage of ornament.

ADOWN, Adv. [adun, Sax.] from a higher to a lower situation; down. "Thrice did she sink adown." Fairy Queen. Used chiefly by poetical writers.

ADOWN, Prep. towards the ground, downwards, or down. "Adown her shoulders fell her length of hair." Dryd.

A'DRAGANTH, S. in Medicine, gum dragon.

ADRIFT, Adv. [drift, Isl.] driven by a torrent. "Trees adrift—Down the great river." Milton. At random, without restraint, or following the first impulse. "Frequent recollection will stop their minds from running adrift." Locke.

ADROIT', Adj. [Fr. adroit] active; dexterous; clever; cunning, or crafty. "An adroit flow fellow." Terras.

ADROIT'NESS, S. dexterity; readiness; activity; assiduity; cunning.

ADRY, Adj. thirsty; wanting to drink. "Drink the King's health when he was not adry." Spectat.

ADSCITI'TIOUS, Adj. [adscititius, Lat.] spurious; interpolated, and not genuine; borrowed, or counterfeit.

ADSTRICTION,

ADSTRICTION, S. [adstrictio, Lat.] the act of binding together; contracting into a lesser compass. Applied chiefly to medicine.

To ADVANCE, V. A. [avancer, Fr.] to come forward. "Her rosy steps in th' eastern clime advancing." Par. Lost. To raise to a higher post; to prefer; to exalt. "Ahasuerus advanced Haman." Esth. iii. 1. To adorn, to heighten. "As the calling dignifies the man, so the man much more advances his calling." Smith. To hasten the growth, when applied to vegetables. "This culture did rather retard than advance." Bacon. To propose or offer; to produce. "I dare not advance my opinion." Dryd. To pay the charges of an undertaking, before the time of reimbursement arrives; to give or lend a person money, &c. before he is capable of paying.

To ADVANCE, V. N. to move forward; to make a progress. "They who would advance in knowledge." Locke.

ADVANCE, S. [from advance] the act of approaching; liberties granted by a person in love to a suitor. "The indecent advances she made to detain him." Pope's Odyss. Gradation, gradual increase. "These gradual advances." Atterb. Rising to a higher degree. "For the advances, and perfecting of human nature." Locke.

ADVANCE FOSSE, or DITCH, in Fortification, a ditch drawn round the esplanade, to prevent a surprize from the besiegers. See FOSSE.

ADVANCEMENT, S. the act of advancing; progress. "It makes daily advancement." Swift. Promotion; preferment. "The quick advancement of her husband." Tatler, No. 33. Raising to a higher degree of perfection; improvement.

ADVANCER, S. one that promotes or advances. "Greater advancers of defamatory designs." Government of the Tongue.

ADVANTAGE, S. [avantage, Fr.] the better or superiority of a person. "The laity have some advantage over the clergy." Sprat. "Would have the advantage of us." Atterb. Superiority by stratagem or cunning. "Designing to take advantage, and prosecute him." Swift. A favourable opportunity. "Give me advantage of some brief discourse." Othello. A manner productive of great approbation or splendor. "True wit is nature to advantage dress'd." Pope. Self-interest, profit, or gain. "Thou saidst, What advantage will it be to thee?" Job xxxv. 3. A premium, or more than can be claimed by law. "You neither lend nor borrow upon advantage." Merch. of Venice. A favourable or additional circumstance?

To ADVANTAGE, V. A. [avantager, Fr.] to benefit, improve, or promote; to get or acquire profit. "What is a man ad-

vantaged, if he gain the whole world?" Luke ix. 25.

ADVANTAGED, Part. possessed of advantages or superior attainments.

ADVANTAGEOUS, Adj [advantageux, Fr.] conducing to profit. "Improved into a very advantageous opportunity." Hamm. Useful; serviceable. "Some advantageous act may be achiev'd." Milt.

ADVANTAGEOUSLY, Adv. conducing to convenience or advantage. "It was advantageously situated." Arbuth.

ADVANTAGEOUSNESS, a quality which conduces to profit or convenience.

To ADVENE, V. A. [advenio, Lat.] to become a part, including the idea of something superadded.

ADVENIENT, Part. that which is superadded; additional. "Extrinsically advenient." Glanv.

ADVENT, S. [adventus, Lat.] the space of four weeks, set apart by the church, to prepare for the approaching festival of Christmas.

ADVENTINE, Adj. [adventinus, Lat.] that which is acquired. "If the adventine heat be greatly predominant to the natural." Bac. Nat. Hist.

ADVENTITIOUS, Adj. [adventitius, Lat.] what is superadded, or acquired. "Tho' we may call the obvious colours natural, and the others adventitious." Boyle. Not of the same nature; additional, or increased. "Adventitious fires raised by high meats." Dryd.

ADVENTURE, S. [avanture, Fr.] an incident; a hazard. "Two flood upon their adventure." Harm. Without certain direction. "Blows flew at all adventures." Hayw. An attempt in which some risque is run. "Or, failing in the adventure, die." Dryd. An incident, or occurrence. "Humble adventurer." Tatler, No. 7. In Commerce, a parcel of goods, sent or carried by sea, at a person's own risque.

To ADVENTURE, V. N. to stand the chance, or risque; to endanger. "Adventured his life." Judg. ix. 17.

ADVENTURER, S. [avanturier, Fr.] one who exposes himself to hazard or danger; one who runs a great risque. "Our merchants shall no more adventurers be." Dryd. He who undertakes, either by himself or in companies, the settlement of colonies, or conquests of places. "The adventurers, and planters of New England." Postlethw. Dict.

ADVENTUROUS, Adj. [aventureux, Fr.] ready to expose himself to dangers. "Was never known a more adventurous knight." Dryd. Enterprising, full of hazard and difficulty. "Attempt a more adventurous song." Addis.

ADVENTUROUSLY, Adv. in a hazardous, difficult, and daring manner. "If he durst steal any thing adventurously." Shakesp. Hen. V.

G   ADVERB,

A'DVERB, S. [adverbium, Lat.] a word joined to a verb, adjective, or participle, to shew their manner, degree, or quantity. Thus, he walks slowly; the word slowly is an adverb joined to the verb walks, to shew the manner in which the action of walking is performed.

ADVE'RBIAL, Adj. [adverbialis] what is used in the manner of an adverb.

ADVE'RBIALLY, Adv. in the manner of an adverb. " I think alia was joined adverbially with trunk." Addison.

ADVE'RSARY, S. [adversaire, Fr.] one who opposes another. " Th'adversary of God and man." Milt. Antagonist. An enemy. " An adversary, on the contrary, makes a stricter search into us." Spectat. No 399.

ADVE'RSATIVE, Adj. [adversativus, Lat.] a word implying opposition or contrast.

A'DVERSE, Adj. [adversus, Lat.] contrary; opposite. " Twice by adverse winds—Drove back." Shakesp. Hen. VI. Acting in opposite directions. " Two polar winds blowing adverse." Milt. Contrary to the wish or desire. " Be try'd in humble state and things adverse." Par. Reg. Unsuccessful; calamitous; unfortunate. " Unhappy men, or adverse fate." Roscom.

ADVE'RSITY, S. [adversitas, Lat.] a state which is opposite to our wishes. " Let me embrace thee four adversities." Shakesp. A state wherein a person loses those conveniencies he before enjoyed; a state of affliction, misery, and misfortune. " Sweet are the uses of adversity." Shakesp.

ADVE'RSELY, or A'DVERSLY, Adv. unfortunately; unhappily; disagreeably. " If the drink you gave me touch my palate adversely." Shakesp.

To ADVE'RT, V. N. [adverto, Lat.] to regard, observe, or attend to. " To advert to more than one thing." Roy in Creat. To apply the mind to with attention.

ADVE'RTENCE, S. [from advert] attention; regard; consideration; reflection. " Allow but a faint advertence to his proposals." Decay of Piety.

ADVE'RTENCY, S. [from advert] attention; regard; consideration; observation. " Too much advertency is not your talent." Swift.

To ADVERTI'SE, V. A. [advertir, Old Fr.] to determine a thing in suspence. " The King his lord advertise—Whether our daughter were legitimate." Shakesp. Hen. VIII. To give notice or information. " They were to advertise the chief hero of the distresses." Dryd. To publish a thing stolen, lost, found, or wanted, now practised instead of crying it. For the utility of this practice, we need only appeal to the countenance it receives daily from the great officers of the state, the public trading companies of the nation, the most opulent mer-

chants of the kingdom, and the considerable revenue which accrues to the government from this one article.

ADVE'RTISEMENT, S. warning; instruction; advice. " My griefs are louder than advertisement." Shakesp. Intelligence or information. Publication, a notice of a thing in a news paper, or an article, containing the description of a thing lost, &c. offering a reward, &c.

ADVERTI'SER, S. he that conveys intelligence or information. The paper which contains intelligence.

ADVERTI'SING, Part. active in conveying intelligence, advice, or admonition. " Then advertising and holy to your business." Shakesp.

ADVI'CE, S. [advis or avis, Fr. This is distinguished from the verb by its spelling, being wrote with a s, but the verb with an f] opinion, or counsel. " By my advice—Let us impart." Hamlet. Instruction. " Without thy poor advice." Prior. Consultation or deliberation. " Taking advice with workmen." Bac. News or intelligence. " Advices from Switzerland import." Tatler, No. 6.

ADVI'SEABLE, Adj. that which is or may be proper to be advised; prudent. " Some judge it advisable for a man to account with his heart every day." South.

ADVI'SABLENESS, S. what renders a thing proper to be advised; fitness; propriety.

To ADVI'SE, V. A. [aviser, Fr.] to recommend. " I would advise all gentlemen to learn merchant's accounts." Locke. To give a person a hint of; to remind. " Such disfavure being on—As may advise him of his happy state." Parad. Lost. To inform, or give intelligence of an action transacted at a distance. " We are advised from Vienna." Tatler, No. 7.

To ADVI'SE, V. N. to consult; to consider; to examine; to give an opinion. " Advise if this be worth attempting." Par. Lost.

ADVI'SED, Part. prudently; after a due examination of the nature and consequences. " Let him rather be advised in his answer, than forward to tell faults." Bacon. Done with design; done on purpose.

ADVI'SEDLY, Adv. in a deliberate manner; with due consideration; prudently. " Cannot stay to consider advisedly." Ben. Ef. With any peculiar design; on purpose. " Advisedly undertaken." Suckling.

ADVI'SEDNESS, S. deliberation; caution; prudence. " To proceed with all just advisedness and adoration." Saunderson.

ADVI'SER, S. one who gives advice or counsel. " And with himself, his best adviser, talks." Wal. One who reminds a person. " To silence this impertinent adviser." Rogers.

ADULA'TION,

ADULATION, S. [adulatio, Lat.] the act of bestowing too much praise to a person; including too high a commendation of his virtues, and omitting his defects. "With titles blown from adulation." Shakesp. Hen V.

ADULATOR, S. a flatterer; a complimenter; one who praises too much the excellencies of another.

A'DULATORY, Adj. [adulatorius, Lat.] in a flattering or complimental manner.

ADULT, Part. [of adultus] grown up; arrived to maturity. "In their adult age, than in their minority." Decay of Piety.

ADULT, S. one who is between infancy and manhood. "Children, whose bones are more pliable and soft than those of adults." Shakesp.

ADULTNESS, S. the state between childhood and manhood. See ADOLESCENCE.

ADULTERANT, Part. [adulterans, Lat.] who is guilty of adultery; or debases by adulterate, or mixture.

To ADULTERATE, V. A. [adultero, Fr.] to violate the bed of a married person; to corrupt or debase. "To adulterate them with false-peace." To spoil by incorporating foreign words.

ADULTERATED, owing to the crime of adultery. "I am possess'd with an adulterate blot." Shakesp. Counterfeit. "The maker of adulterate wares." Dec. of Piety.

ADULTERATENESS, S. the quality of being adulterate, counterfeit.

ADULTERATION, S. [adulteratio, Lat.] the corrupting by a foreign mixture; or endeavouring to make things pass for more than their intrinsic value, by its resemblance to something better. "To make the compound pass for the rich simple metal, is an adulteration, or counterfeiting." Bac. Nat. Hist.

ADULTERER, S. [adulter, Lat.] the person guilty of lying with another's wife. "Whoremongers and adulterers God shall judge." Heb. xiii. 14.

ADULTERESS, S. a woman guilty of violating her husband's bed, by lying with another man. "The Spartan lady replied, when asked, What was the punishment for adulteress? There are no such things here." Govern. of the Tongue.

ADULTEROUS, Adj. guilty of the crime of adultery. "Such is the way of an adulterous woman." Prov. xxx. 20. Base, corrupted; idolatrous.

ADULTERY, S. [adulterium, Lat.] in its primary signification, the being false to the marriage bed. "Whoso committeth adultery lacketh understanding." Prov. vi. 32. Idolatry. "Committed adultery with stones and with stocks." Jerem. iii. 9.

To ADUMBRATE, V. A. [adumbro, Lat.] to shadow; to give a slight resemblance. "Heaven——is adumbrated by all

those excellencies which can endear." Dec. of Piety.

ADUMBRATION, S. [from adumbrate] the giving a slight representation or illustration; an imperfect resemblance, like that of a shadow. "At best a most confused adumbration." Glanville. A faint glimmering; a distant and confused likeness. "Some adumbration of the rational nature." Hale's Orig. In Heraldry, when any figure in a coat is so obscured, that nothing but the bare profile or outline is visible.

ADVOCATE, S. [advocatus, Lat.] one who has the pleading or management of a cause; one who vindicates or defends any tenet or action. "That cause seems commonly the better, that has the better advocate." Temple. "Advocate for folly." Pope. Lord Advocate, a great officer of State in Scotland, who gives his advice in all cases about making or executing laws, defends the King's rights and privileges in all public meetings, prosecutes all capital crimes before the justiciary; concurs in all pursuits wherein the King has interest; and is at liberty to plead all causes, unless when acting as an ordinary Lord of Sessions, in which case he can plead only the King's.

ADVOCATION, S. the office or business of an advocate.

ADVOLUTION, S. [advolutio, Lat.] the act of rolling to.

ADVOUTRY, S. [avoutrie, Fr.] adultery. "A marriage compounded between an advoutry and a rape." Bac.

ADVOWEE, S. [advoué, Fr.] one who has the right of advowson.

ADVOWSON, S. the right of presenting to a benefice.

To ADURE, V. N. [aduro, Lat.] to consume or destroy by fire, to burn up.

ADUST, Part. [adustus, Lat.] burnt up, scorched, rendered brittle by heat. "Such a heat as will not render the body adust." Bac. Capable of burning, scorching hot. "As the Lybian air adust." A habit of body which arises from a fermentation of choler and bile, and betoken heat or warmth of temper, cholerk. "The same adust complexion." Pope.

ADUSTED, Part. burnt, set on fire. "Concocted and adusted they reduc'd—To blackest grain." Mil. Lost. Warm or hot with respect to the humours of the body, or temper. "They are but spirits of adust choler." Howel.

ADUSTABLE, Adj. that may be burnt or scorched up.

ADUSTION, S. [from adust] the act of burning up, or drying. "The heat continuing its adustion." Harvey. The congregating the most subtile particles of the blood by heat, an inflammation about the brain and its membranes, accompanied with a hollow-

ness

nefs in the eyes, palenefs, and a drynefs of
the body.

ADZ, S. See ADDICE.

Æ, a dipthongue, in which the sound of
the *A* is obscure; though ufed by the Romans and Saxons, it feems now quite out of
ufe being changed for the fimple *e*, as in
equator, enigma, equinoctial and even in
knees.

ÆGILOPS, S. [αιγιλωψ, Gr.] a kind of
tumour or ulcer in the corner of the eye,
either with or without an inflammation.
When attended with an inflammation, it is fuppofed to be owing to an abundance of blood;
if without, from a vifcous pituitous humour
thrown on this part.

ÆGIS, S. [from αιγις, Gr.] in mytho-
gy, the name of the fhield or bucker of Jupiter, or Pallas. It has its name from Jupiter's covering his fhield with the fkin of the
goat amalthea, which he is faid to have fuck-
ed. This buckler he afterwards gave to Mi-
nerva, whofe fhield is ftill called by this name.

ÆGLOGUE, S. [from αιγος, Gr. and
λογος] a fpecies of poetry, wherein ruftics are
introduced as the actors. It now goes by
the denomination of a pastoral, or poem
wherein the perfons are fhepherds; from the
Lat. *paftor* a fheep herd.

ÆGYPTIACUM, [Lat. *Egyptian*] an
ointment, originally afcribed to Mefue, confifting of vinegar, verdigrease, and honey,
boiled to a confiftence. The fcum is called
Egyptian honey. It is an admirable detergent,
proper to keep down fungous excrefcences,
but fhould be lowered according to the circumftances of the cafe, for fear of it corroding too much.

ÆNIGMA, S. [αινιγμα, Gr.] fomething
put in, obfcure, and fometimes contradictory
terms, to exercife the fagacity of a perfon;
or an obfcure defcription of a thing, delivered in fuch terms as render the meaning not
intelligible at firft fight. The eaftern nations feem to have affected this fpecies of
writing very much; an example of it may
be found in Judg. xiv. 12. and its definition
by Bohours as being a witty, artful, abftrufe
defcription, may not be very improper. If it
be allowed to be, according to Mr. Addifon,
a fpecies of falfe wit, and rather the fport of
the underftanding, than the dictate of wifdom.

ÆOLUS, S. [from Æolus, the God of
wind] the name of a ventilator, or a machine
ufed to extract foul air out of a room.

ÆOLIPILE, S. [Author, Πυλαι, Gr.] an
hydraulic inftrument, which being filled with
water, and heated by fire, will afford a vapour, which iffues out with a prodigious violence and noife.

ÆON, S. [αιων, Gr.] duration.

ÆRA, S. in chronology, a certain fixed
point of time from which any computation
begins

ÆRARIUM, S. the public treafury of
the Roman ftate, refembling our bank, or
exchequer.

ÆRIAL, Adj. [*aerius*, Lat.] confifting
or partaking of air. "Vegetables abound
more with *aerial* particles." *Arbuth.* Produced by the air. "Aerial honey." *Dryd.*
Inhabiting the air. "Aerial animals." *Locke.*
Placed or fituated in the air; lofty; high.
"Aerial fpire." *Phillips.*

ÆRIAL PERSPECTIVE, the art of
conveying a proper diminution to the fhades
and light of colours, and fize of objects in
proportion to the diftance of the object. It
is founded on this principle, that the rays
emitted from an object to the eye, are weaker in proportion to the length of the column
of air through which they pafs.

ÆRIANS, S. [from *aerius*] a religious
fect in the fourth century, who were named
from Aerius their founder. Their tenets
refembled thofe of the Arians with refpect to
the Trinity; befides which they held that
prieft and *bifhop* were fynonimous terms, and
denoted but one order and dignity. Aerius
built his doctrine on fome paffages in St.
Paul's Epiftles, particularly upon that of 1 Tim. iv.
14. where the apoftle exhorts, "Not to neglect the gift he had received by the laying on
of the hands of the *prefbytery*." On which
he obferves, that there is no mention of bifhops; and that it is evident, that Timothy
was ordained by the prefbytery alone. To
this Epiphanius replies, Hær. 75, That the
word includes both bifhops and priefts, or the
whole affembly of ecclefiaftics.

ÆROLOGY, S. [ααρ and λογος, Gr.]
a difcourfe or effay on the properties of the
air.

ÆROMETRY, S. [from ααρ, αηρ, Gr. air,
and μετρεω, metreo, Gr. to meafure] the art
of meafuring air, including the laws of motion, gravitation, preffion, elafticity, rarefaction, condenfation, &c. Inftead of this
term modern writers fubftitute *Pneumatics.*

ÆROSCOPY, S. [ααρ and σκοπεω] the
act of obferving of the air.

ÆRY, S. See AIRIE.

ÆRUGINOUS, Adj. refembling or appertaining to the ruft of copper. It is by
fome defcribed as a green colour, and by
others as a brown.

ÆRUGOS, S. [Lat.] ruft, particularly
copper ruft; verdigrease.

ÆSTUM, in chemiftry, compofed of
thin plates of copper put into a crucible, with
alternate layers of fulphur and falt, and continued on a hot charcoal fire, till the fulphur is confumed. It is very deterfive, and
ufed for eating off proud flefh.

ÆSCHYNOMENOUS, Part. [αισχυνο-
μενος, Gr.] in botany, applied to thofe plants
that are called Senfitive.

ÆSTIVAL, Adj. [*aeftas*, Lat.] in geography relating to the fummer iflands.

ÆSTUARY,

AE'STUARY, S. [*aestuarium*, Lat.] In Geography, an arm of the sea, penetrating a great way into the land. In Pharmacy, a vapour bath.

AETHER, S. [*aether*, Gr.] in Physics, a thin matter, finer and rarer than air, beginning from the limits of our atmosphere, and expanded through all the regions of space. Sir Isaac Newton observes, that heat is communicated through a vacuum, almost as readily as through air; but as that could not be without some interjacent body, to act as a medium, this body must be subtile enough to penetrate the pores of glass, and may be supposed to penetrate those of all other bodies, and consequently to be diffused through all the parts of space. The existence of this aetherial medium being thus settled, the author proceeds to its properties inferring it to be more rare, fluid, active, and elastic, than air; and the cause of gravitation, of the elasticity of the air and the nervous fibres; of the emission, refraction, reflexion, and other phenomena of light; of sensation, muscular motion, &c. and that it is the *primum mobile*, or first source and spring of all physical action in the modern system.

AETHE'RIAL, Adj. [*aetherius*, Lat.] something that partakes of the nature of aether. Aetherial space, or region, is that in the heavens, where the pure unmixed aether is supposed to be found; and is used for heavenly. Aetherial oil, named likewise essential; is a fine subtile, essential oil, approaching to the nature of a spirit. The pure liquor, which rises next after the spirit, in distilling turpentine, is called the aetherial oil of turpentine.

AE'THIOPS-MINERAL, S. a preparation of quicksilver, and flour of brimstone, in equal quantities ground in a stone or iron mortar, till they become black, and no particles of quicksilver remain visible. It is prescribed as an ointment for the itch, and other cutaneous eruptions.

AETIO'LOGY, S. [*aitiologia*, Gr.] in medicine, a discourse or essay, explaining the causes of a disease. "The *aetiology* of the Hydrophobia," *Chamb.*

AE'TITES, S. [of *aeros*] an oval incrustated stone of a dark russet colour, hollow within, and including another stone, which when shook rattles. The virtues ascribed to it by Galen and Pliny, may be esteemed as vulgar errors, founded on superstition.

AETNA, S. [from *aetna*, or ΑΙΤΝΗ, a furnace] a remarkable burning mountain, the highest of any in Sicily. The inhabitants call it Mont Gibello, or by contraction, Mon-Gibell; i. e. the Mount of Mounts. Its ascent from Catanea is 30,000 paces, but on the side next Randazzo only 20,000; its circumference, at the bottom, is 100,000; it is of a circular form, and terminates in a peak somewhat resembling a sugar-loaf. The bottom is planted

with corn and sugar-cane, the middle with woods, olive-trees, and vines, and the top is covered with snow all the year. The amazing quantity of burning matter ejected, and the earthquakes attending its eruptions, have occasioned most terrible devastation and calamities. During that of 1693, fifteen or sixteen towns, eighteen estates, with men and cattle, besides villages and 93000 souls, were destroyed.

AFA'R, Adv. [of *a* expletive, and *far* of *feor*, or *feorran*, Sax.] at some distance. "In stronds afar remote." *Shakesp.* "Seeing a fig-tree afar off." Mat. xi. 13. Foreign or strange distance, in opposition to intimate friendship. "The promise is to all that is afar off." Acts ii. 39. "Preached peace to you which were afar off." Eph. ii. 17.

AFE'ARED, Part. to be under apprehensions at the prospect of some approaching evil, or calamity. Used with the particle *of* before the object. "He looks afeard of himself." *Peacham.* This word is now seldom used.

A'FER, S. [Lat.] the south west wind. "Notus and Afer, black, with thund'rous clouds." *Par. L.J.*

AFFADI'LITY, S. [*affabilité*, Fr.] a quality that includes modesty, good-nature, and condescension; applied generally to superiors. "Of a most flowing courtesy and affability to all men." *Clarend.*

A'FFABLE, Verbal Adj. [*affable*, Fr.] possessing complaisance, good-nature, and condescension. "He was affable and both well and fair spoken." *Bacon.* Applied to external appearance; favourable; inviting address. "With a serene and affable countenance." *Tatler.*

A'FFABLENESS, S. courteousness; polite, kind, civil, and complaisant behaviour. See Affability.

A'FFABLY, Adv. In an affable, civil, courteous manner.

AFFA'IR, S. [*affaire*, Fr.] something done, or that is to be done. Business, employment. "I was not born for great affairs." *Pope.* The transactions of a nation. "St. John's skill in state affairs." *Swift.* The circumstances of a person. "His affairs are in very bad order." Business. Intrigue. "He had a little affair with Mlle ———." This seems to be borrowed from the French, *il avoit une petite affaire.*

To AFFE'AR, V. N. [*affer*, Fr.] in law, to confirm, establish, and support. "His title is affeared." *Shakesp.*

AFFE'CT, S. [*affectus*, Lat.] See affection.

To AFFE'CT, V. A. [*afficio*, Fr. to produce or cause an effect, to cause, "Affect the earth with cold." *Milt.* To act upon. "Reciprocally affect each other." *Bentley.* To influence. "Those qualities relate to, and affect the actions of men." To excite, or stir up the passions. "Very much affected with the idea." To aim at, to endeavour after. To tend to. "The drift of every guild

fixed affords a round figure." *Newton's Opt.* To like or long for. " To tell us women what we moſt *affect.*" *Dryd.* To aſſume a character that is not real, or natural. " Spenſer, in *affecting* the auditors, with no language." *B. Johnſon.*

AFFECTA'TION, S. [*affectatio,* Lat.] an artful aſſuming of a character, or appearance, to which we have no claim. " An *affectation* to love the pleaſure of ſolitude." *Spect. No. 264.*

AFFE'CTED, Part. [*affectus*] that has the affections excited. To be fond of. Diſpoſed. " No marvel then if he were *ill affected.*" Aſſumed, and appearing unnatural. " Theſe and *affected* phantaſies." *Rom. and Juliet.* Full of affectation. " An *affected* woman." *Johnſ.*

AFFE'CTEDLY, Adv. affecting reality ; pretendedly. " You are neither naturally or *affected,* or ignorant." *Swift.*

AFFE'CTEDNESS, S. the quality of aſſuming falſe appearance, or character.

AFFE'CTION, S. [*affection,* Fr.] the ſtate of being affected, or influenced by any cauſe. " Cannot contain their urine for *affection.*" *Merch. of Ven.* Paſſions in general. " Zeal ought to be compoſed of the higheſt degrees of pious *affection.*" *Sprat.* Love, eſteem, regard, or good-will ; " Your *affection* towards any of theſe princely ſuitors." *Merch. of Ven.* Zeal ; an earneſt deſire of obtaining. " Set your *affections* on things above." *Col. iii. 2.* Affections of body, in phyſic, are certain modifications, occaſioned by motion ; they are divided into primary, or ſecondary ; the primary are ſuch as ariſe from the idea of matter, as quantity and figure ; or from that of form, as quality and power, or from both, as motion, place, and time. Secondary or derivative, affections are thoſe that ariſe from the primary, as diviſibility, continuity, &c. from quantity ; regularity, and its contrary, from figure, health, ſtrength, &c. from quality. In medicine, it implies a morbid ſtate of the body or ſome of its parts.

AFFE'CTIONATE, Adj. [*affectionné,* Fr.] zealous ; warm ; " In their love to God, and deſire to pleaſe him, men can never be too *affectionate.*" *Sprat.* Strongly inclined to. " Being *affectionate* of old to the war with France." *Bac. Hen. VII.* Fond, tender, endearing. " When we reflect on this *affectionate* care of Providence for our happineſs." *Rogers.*

AFFE'CTIONATELY, Adv. fondly, endearingly, benevolently.

AFFE'CTIONATENESS, S. the quality of exerciſing benevolent, kind, and ſocial paſſions.

AFFE'CTIONED, Adj. [from *affection*] full of affectation. See *affected.*

AFFE'CTIVE, Adj. that which excites diſagreeable or painful ſenſations.

AFFECTUO'SITY, S. paſſionateneſs.

To AFFE'RE, V. A. [*affer,* Fr.] in law, to confirm.

AFFETUO'SO, Adj. [Ital.] In Muſic, implies that the air ſhould be played ſlow, and ſo as to melt and touch with pity.

AFFI'ANCE, S. [*affiance,* Fr.] to confirm by plighting of faith ; betrothing. " *Affiance* made, my happineſs began." *Fairy Queen.* Figuratively, truſt, or confidence, reliance. " Ah! what's more dangerous than this fond *affiance.*" *Shakeſp. Hen. VI.* Firm truſt, and dependance. " Referring the event of things to God with an implicit *affiance.*" *Atterb.*

To AFFI'ANCE, V. A. [*affiancer,* Fr.] to engage to marry. " He was *affianced* long time before." *Fairy Q.* Confident, or ſecure.

AFFIDA'TION, or AFFI'DATURE, S. [*affido,* Lat.] mutual contract ; reciprocal oath of fidelity.

AFFIDA'VIT, S. a written oath, ſworn before an authoriſed perſon ; which contains the time, reſidence, and addition of the perſon who makes it ; and is admitted in evidence only on motions, if taken before a maſter of Chancery ; it is of no force in the King's Bench, or other court. 1 Liſtl. Abridg. 44. 46. Stat. 29 Char. II. c. 5. 21 Char. 1. B. R. 2 Liſtl. 41. Style 445. 2 Sal. 461. In a looſer ſenſe, declaration upon oath. " Count Rechteren ſhould have made *affidavit.*" Spect. No. 481.

AFFI'ED, Part. joined by contract, affianced ; engaged ; betrothed.

AFFILIA'TION, S. [*ad,* and *filius,* Lat.] adoption, of a ſon. Among the Gauliſh nobility, it was performed by the father's preſenting a battle-ax to his intended ſon.

AFFI'NED, Part. [*affinis,* Lat.] joined ; related to.

AFFI'NITY, S. [*affinité,* Fr.] relation by marriage ; not by blood. " *Affinity* to the tyrant." *Sidney.* Connexion, reſemblance to. " *Affinity* with the old Gallic." *Camden.*

To AFFI'RM, V. N. [*affirmo,* Lat.] to declare ; to aſſert ; to relate confidently. " Yet their own authors faithfully *affirm.*" *Shak. Hen. V.* To ratify, approve, eſtabliſh, or confirm a law, in oppoſition to repeal. " The houſe of peers has a power of judicature in ſome caſes, properly to examine, and then to *affirm.*" *Racon.* In this ſenſe we ſay. " To *affirm* the truth." *Johnſ. Dict.*

AFFI'RMABLE, Adj. [from *affirm* and *able,* Sax. power, or poſſibility] what may be affirmed, or aſſerted. " Applicable and *affirmable* of him when preſent." *Hale's Orig.*

AFFI'RMANCE, S. confirmation.

AFFI'RMANT, S. [*affirmans,* Lat.] one who affirms.

AFFIRMA'TION, S. [affirmatio, Lat.] confirmation. "Upon warrant of bloody affirmation." Shakesp. Assertion. "The affirmation on which his despair is founded. Confirmation. "Our statutes sometime are only the affirmation, or ratification of that, which by common law was held before." Hooker. In grammar, what is otherwise called a verb, because it expresses what we affirm of any subject. Thus "Charlotte endureth." Endureth is an affirmation, because it affirms the quality of endurance to be in Charlotte. The method by law allowed to Quakers as a pledge of their truth in judicial courts, instead of an oath, which they hold to be inconsistent with Christ's command; "Swear not at all." If they are guilty of a false affirmation, they are subject to the penalties of perjury: in criminal cases their affirmation is not taken as evidence.

AFFIRMATIVE, Adj. [from affirm] that which positively asserts a thing. "Many have believed the affirmative." Dryd. Positive; obstinate; dogmatical, or one that would affirm any thing. "Be not confident and affirmative in an uncertain matter. In logic, such propositions as affirm one thing to belong to another, and is as it were to unite them in thought and word; the predicate is taken in its whole comprehension, or every part is affirmed of the subject; as "A true Christian is an honest man." Here every part of honesty is affirmed of the true Christian. Affirmative in Algebra, applied to quantities, are those which express a real magnitude in opposition to those which are negative, or less than nothing. Affirmative sign in algebra, is what shews that the quantity it is prefixed to, is affirmative, and is marked thus +.

AFFIRMATIVELY, Adv. in a positive manner.

AFFIRMER, S. one who asserts or affirms; one who takes the affirmative side of a question, in a dispute. "If by the word virtue, the affirmer intends our whole duty." Watts.

To AFFI'X, V. A. [affixum, supine of affigo, Lat.] to be fixed to. "With names affixed to them." Locke. To connect, subjoin, establish. "Constantly affixed applause and disgrace." Rogers.

AFFLATION, S. [afflatum, supine of afflo, Lat.] the act of breathing upon any thing.

AFFLA'TUS, S. [Lat.] divine inspiration; in physic, a vapour, or blast, prejudicial to the health.

To AFFLI'CT, V. A. [affligo, Lat.] to use so as to occasion a deep sorrow. "They shall afflict them four hundred years." Gen. xv. 13. Followed by the personal pronoun, to practise the duties of sincere repentance. "That we might afflict ourselves before

God." Ezra viii. 21. To punish. "The Lord doth not afflict willingly." Lament. lib. 33. In the passive, to be in adversity or misery. "Is any one afflicted among you let him pray." Jam. v. 13. Sometimes used with as before the cause. "So afflicted at the loss of a fine boy." Spectat.

AFFLI'CTION, S. [afflictio, Lat.] what causes a sensation of pain; a disagreeable circumstance; a calamity. "All affliction is naturally grievous." Hooker. Misery, adversity, distress. "Some virtues are only seen in affliction." Spectat. No. 257.

AFFLI'CTIVE, Adj. that produces torment, misery, pain, concern, sorrow. "With all that was terrible and afflictive to human nature." South.

A'FFLUENCE, S. [affluence, Fr. affluentia, Lat.] in its primary sense, the flowing to any place; resort, or concourse, wealth, riches, plenty. "Let joy or ease, let affluence or content." Pope.

AFFLUENCY, S. See AFFLUENCE.

A'FFLUENT, Part. [affluent, Fr.] flowing. "The affluent flood." Harvey. Wealthy; plentiful; exuberant. "Loaded and blest with all the affluent store." Prior.

A'FFLUENTNESS, S. the quality of being wealthy.

A'FFLUX, S. [affluxus, Lat.] the act of flowing, or thing which flows. "It must be by new affluxes to London." Greaves.

To AFFO'RD, V. A. from fordian, or fordon, Teut. to yield, produce. "The soil affords grain." Supply, cause. "His ubiquity affordeth continual comfort." Brown's Vulg. Err. To be able to sell. "They may afford cheaper." Addis. To be rich enough to support a charge, or expence. "Wealth enough to afford that their sons may be good for nothing." Swift. Med. Educ.

To AFFO'REST, V. A. [afforestare, law Lat.] to convert ground into a forest.

AFFORESTA'TION, S. the act of converting grounds into forests. "Rich I. and Hen. II. made new afforestations." Hales's Com. Law.

AFFO'RESTING, S. [afforestatio] the turning lands into forests.

To AFFRANCHI'SE, V. A. [affranchir, Fr.] to make free.

AFFRA'ID, Part. [affrayé, Fr.] to be timorous, or fearful. It is usually spelt with a single f; though this is more consistent with analogy.

To AFFRA'Y, V. A. to terrify; to fright. "Or when the flying heavens he would affray." Fairy Queen.

AFFRA'Y, or AFFRA'YMENT, S. in an affright a skirmish, wherein a blow is given, or a weapon drawn. It differs from an assault, this being a public, but that a personal wrong.

AFFRIC-

AFFRI'CTION, S. [affrictio, Lat.] the act of rubbing one thing on another. "The affriction would quickly blacken them." Boyle. Friction is the word in use.

To AFFRIGHT, V. A. [from a expletive, and fright of frighten, Sax. to affect with fear or terror. "Thy name affrights me, in whose found is death." In the passive, used with at, to be intimidated, disheartened, and discouraged. "Thou shalt not be affrighted at them." Deut. vii. 21.

AFFRIGHT, S. [to affright] terror, fear, fright. "In fear and sad affright." Fairy Quen. The object which causes fear. "By sending these affrights." Johnf. Catel. This word is used chiefly among the poets.

AFFRI'GHTFUL, Adj. having such qualities as may cause fear. "All that is destructive or affrightful to human nature." Dec. of Piety.

To AFFRONT, V. A. of ad and frontem, Lat. to meet face to face, to confront. "We have sent for Hamlet hither—" That he may here —Affront Ophelia." Shakesp. Ham. To meet like an enemy. "And with their darkness durst affront his fight." Par. Loft. To injure, or abuse. "Dared to affront the wife of Aurelius." Addif.

AFFRONT, S. [affront, Fr. affronto, Ital.] an insult offered to the face; including the ideas of contempt and rudeness. "Doing affronts to his son." Bac. Rude behaviour, outrage. "Oft have they violated—The temple, of the law with foul affronts." Par. Reg. The offer of battle or attack, "Dreaded—on hostile ground, none daring my affront." Milt. Samson. This sense is very unusual, though agreeable to analogy.

AFFRONTER, S. one who offers the affront.

AFFRONTING, Part. which gives or causes an affront. "Among words, some are kind, others affronting." Watt's Log.

AFFRONTIVE, Adj. that which may affront or give offence.

AFFRONTIVENESS, S. a quality of giving affronts.

AFFUSION, S. [affusio, Lat.] the pouring one thing upon another. "The affusion of tincture of galls." Grew's Museum.

To AFFY, V. A [affier, Fr.] to bind by contract, to marry; to betroth, "For daring to affy a mighty lord." To fix a confidence in; "I do affy—In thy uprightness and integrity." Shakesp. Tit. and Andronicus.

AFIE'LD, Adv. to the field, "Afield I went amidst the morning dew." Gay.

AFLO'AT, Adv. [the diphthong is accented upon the a which is pronounced like a in rate, with an obscure, though scarce sensible sound of the e; from o, and flut from flotter, Fr. to swim on the surface of the water] swimming on the water; floating. "On such a full sea are we now afloat." Shakesp. Jul. Caes. Fluctuating. "Take my pas-

sion of the soul of a man, while it is predomination and afloat." Scrib.

AFO'OT, Adv. walking, standing. "Come afoot thither." Hamlet. In agitation; begun. "When thou seest this aff afoot." Ibid. On their march, applied to forces. "Albany's and Cornwall's powers—'Tis said they are afoot." Shakesp. Lear.

AFO'RE, Prep. nearer in place, not behind. "He stood afore her." Sooner applied to time, "I shall be there afore you." Shakesp. Lear.

AFO'RE, Adv. [from a and fore, Sax.] that which is past; prior or antecedent. "I wrote afore in few words." Ephef ill. 3. First, with respect to place or order. "Will you go on afore." Othello. In front, or in the forepart. "He rear'd high afore—His body monstrous." Fairy Queen.

AFO'RE-GOING, Part. that which precedes in order, or motion.

AFORE-HAND, Adv. previous; or before. Having the start, "afore-hand in all matters of power."

AFO'RE-MENTIONED, Part. something mentioned in a former part of a book or discourse.

AFO'RE-NAMED, Part. that has been in a former part of a work or discourse. "In all other aforenamed proportions." Peacham.

AFO'RE-SAID, Part. that which has been said or mentioned before. "The aforesaid experiment." Boyle.

AFO'RE-TIME, Adv. in times past, or those which have preceded the present. "Whatsoever was written aforetime." Rom. xv. 4.

AFRA'ID, Part. [from affrayer, Fr. and should therefore be written with a double f, as observed in affraid. The diphthongue is accented on the a, the sound of the e being very confused; and the word pronounced as if the i was dropped and written with an e final, thus afrade] to be affected with fear, dread or terror. "They were afraid to come nigh him." Exod. xxxiv. 30. Sometimes with of, and other times at before the object of terror. "Nor shalt thou be afraid of destruction." Job. v. 21. "They that dwell are afraid at thy tokens." Pfal. lxv. 8.

AFRE'SH, Adv. [from a and fresh, of fersch, Sax.] a new; once more; a second time.

AFRO'NT, Adv. [a front, Fr.] in the front; or in such a direction, that the face of one is directly opposite to that of another. "These four came all afront." Shakesp. Henry IV. See AFFRONT.

AFRICA, one of the four principal parts of the world, bounded on the N. by the Mediterranean sea; on the W. and S. by the ocean; on the E. by the Arabick gulph, and the isthmus of Suez. It is in the form of a pyramid, whose base from Tangier to the isthmus of Suez, is about 1000 miles. From the top of the pyramid, that is to say,

from

from the Cape of Good-Hope, to the moſt ſouthern part, is 3600 miles; and in the broadeſt part, that is, from Cape Verd to Cape Guarda-ful, it is 3500. The greateſt part of it is within the Torrid Zone, which renders the heat almoſt inſupportable in many places. However the ſoil in general are very fruitful, the fruits very excellent, and the plants extraordinary. The fleſh of the animals is in general very good; and there are more wild beaſts than in any other part of the world; ſuch as lions, tygers, leopards, panthers, rhinoceroſes, errons, and elephants. There are ſome animals that are found no where elſe; ſuch as the hippopotamus, or the ſea-horſe, whoſe teeth are ſo large that they ſerve inſtead of ivory, and are much better than the rhinoceros, with two horns on his noſe; and the moſt beautiful ſtriped wild aſs, which is eſteemed a fine preſent for the greateſt princes. As for the crocodiles, which were thought formerly to be peculiar to Africa, are now met with in other places, or at leaſt creatures ſo much like them, that it is hard to know the difference. Beſides theſe, they have oſtriches, camels, various ſorts of monkies, and many other animals not to be met with in Europe. There are ſeveral deſerts, particularly one of a large extent, which is almoſt without water; and whoſe ſands are ſo looſe, that, by means of a ſtrong wind, they will ſometimes bury whole caravans at a time. However, this is not quite without inhabitants, for there are wild Arabs, and other people, who rove from place to place, partly in ſearch of paſture, and partly to lie in wait for the rich caravans that travel from Barbary and Egypt, to Negroeland and Abyſſinia. There are many large rivers; but the principal are the Nile and the Niger. This laſt is thought by ſome to have its ſource near that of the Nile, and to run quite acroſs Africa, from E. to W. and to fall into the Atlantick ocean in ſeveral branches, of which the Senegal is the chief; but this is doubted by others, and not without reaſon. There are very high mountains in divers parts, particularly in Abyſſinia and Barbary; in which laſt country is Mount Atlas, that ſeparates Barbary from Biledulgerid, and runs from E. to W. Their religion is Mahometaniſm and Paganiſm, though there are Chriſtians in ſome parts, as in Abyſſinia and among the Portugueſe ſettlements. Africa is variouſly divided, according to different geographers; however, the beſt diſtinguiſh them by the names of Egypt, Barbary, Guinea, Congo, Cafferia, Abyſſinia, Nubia, and Nigritia, with the iſlands that ſurround it. See theſe articles. The Lon. is from 1 deg. to 71. The lat. from 1 to 35. S. and from 1 to 37. N.

AFTER, Prep. [from after, Sax. æfter or æftred, Goth.] Applied to time, it denotes ſomething had been done before. "After

the ſop Satan entered into him." Joke xiii. 27. When applied to place, behind, or following. When uſed with verb it implies purſuit. "After whom is the king come out." 1 Sam. xxiv. 14. Concerning, "Thou enquireſt after my iniquity." Job. x. 6. According to; in proportion to; "Give them after the work of their hands." Pſalm xxviii 4. Agreeable to, in imitation of. "Made after the ſame deſign." Addiſ.

AFTER, Adv. ſucceeding in time. "430 years after." Gal. iii. 17. Following in oppoſition to before. "Let him draw them after." Shakſp. Lear. †† As this word is uſed of time with reſpect to ſome action which preceded it, it cannot with any propriety be introduced, without the mention of ſomething as having gone before it. Thus, it would be very improper to ſay, I ſhall be happy after, but we ſay hereafter; and had we premiſed any circumſtance as preceding the date of future happineſs, the firſt expreſſion would have been highly proper; as, "tho' I was then very much afflicted, I was happy after." After is compounded with ſeveral words, wherein it is uſed in its primary ſignification, as may be perceived by thoſe which follow.

AFTER-AGES, S. ages which are to come. "What an opinion will after-ages entertain." Addiſ.

AFTER-BIRTH, S. in Midwifry, the coat, or membrane, wherein the fœtus is incloſed in the womb, called the ſecundine, and deriving its name from its coming away after the birth of the child. In brutes it is call'd the cleanſing.

AFTER-CLAP, S. ſome incident that happens after an affair is ſuppoſed to be ended. "For fear of after-claps." Spencer. It ſeems a low expreſſion.

AFTER-COST, S. expences incurred after the original bargain. "Leſt your after-coſt and labour prove unſucceſsful." Mortimer.

AFTER-DINNER, S. that ſpace of time which follows our ſecond meal, called dinner, and ſometimes uſed for afternoon. "An after-dinner's ſleep." Shakſp.

To AFTER-EYE, V. A. to follow with the eyes in keep in view.

AFTER-GAME, S. an expedient after the firſt attempt, has failed. "My firſt deſigns, my friends, have proved abortive—Still there remains an after-game to play." Addiſ. Cato.

AFTER-MATH, S. the after-graſs, or ſecond mows of graſs, cut in autumn.

AFTER-NOON, S. that ſpace from twelve at noon to the evening. "On dice and drink, and drabs, they ſpend the afternoon." Dryd. In the decline. "In the afternoon of her beſt days." Shak. Rich. III.

AFTER-PAINS, S. [never uſed in the ſingular] thoſe pains which are felt in the loins, groin, &c. after delivery, proceeding

from

ES, S. Seldom ufed in
ages; In time to cor

which are, 1ſt, The Antiquity, &c. of the High Court of Parliament. 2d, The Antiquities of Shires, of which he thinks Alfred was the author. 3d, The land Meaſures of England. 4th, The Authority and Office of Heralds. 5th, The Antiquity and Privileges of Inns of Courts, &c. 6th, The Diverſity of the Names of this Iſland. All theſe were publiſhed by Hearne; the manuſcripts he left behind him, were, A learned and elaborate Treatiſe of the Uſe of the Doomſday-Book, together with twenty-ſix more volumes of manuſcripts, he left to Sir Robert Cotton, in whoſe collection they are ſtill preſerved. After thus having ſpent his days in learned tranquility, he cauſed a monument to be erected for himſelf and his wife, in Weſtminſter-Abbey, in his life-time, where, after his death, which happened in 1615, he was interred.

AGARIC, S. [*agaricum*, Lat.] in Botany, an excreſcence growing in the ſhape of a muſhroom, upon the trunk and great branches of the oak and other trees, but the larch tree eſpecially. It is diſtinguiſhed into male, female, and ſpurious. The male, is of a yellowiſh colour, and pretty ſolid, is uſed in dying black, and one of the not colouring drugs which the French dyers are obliged to make uſe of in ſtriking that colour. The female is aſed in medicine, and ſhould be choſen white, large, light, brittle, and of a lively purenating ſcent. The ſpurious, or falſe, is the agaric of the oak, which is commonly reddiſh and very heavy. Modern practitioners have lately cried this up as a great ſtyptic, and recommended it for ſtopping the effuſion of blood, after amputation, in the larger blood-veſſels.

AGA'ST, Adv. [from *a* and *gaſt*, Sax.] with all the figns of a perſon who is terrified, ſhock'd, or amazed.

A'GATE, S. [*agate*, Fr.] a precious ſtone much harder than jaſper, and capable of receiving a better poliſh. Its colours are various, and in ſome of them repreſent ſuch figures as are very ſurpriſing. Agate, among the gold wire drawers, is the inſtrument they make uſe of in burniſhing.

A'GATY, Adj. [from *agate*] having or partaking of the nature of agate.

AGA'VE, S. [Lat.] in Botany, the common American aloe. This is the ninth genus of Linnæus, who has ſeparated it from the aloe, among which they were claſſed before. The opinion that it does not bloſſom till it is an hundred years old, is a great miſtake; becauſe, as that depends on the growth of the plant, in hot countries they flower in a few years; in cold ones they ſhoot up their ſtem ſlowly; and muſt be a longer time before they can bevel this beautiful viciſſitude.

AGA'ZED, Part. [from *agaze*] ſtruck with a ſudden terror or horror.

A'GE, S. [the *e* not pronounced, and ſerving only to lengthen the ſound of the *a*, and ſoften that of the *g*; from *age*, Fr.] a limited part of time, applied both to perſons and things. The number of years of which a perſon's life conſiſts; the period of his exiſtence. " The whole age of Jacob was 147 years." Gen. xlvii. 28. A race of men. " New heaven and earth ſhall to the ages riſe." Milton. The advanced part of a long life, where a perſon has ſeen a great number of years. " Nor men, the weak antiquea of age." Reſcom. The ſpace of 100 years. In Horſemanſhip, the method of diſtinguiſhing the horſe's age from his teeth, boots, coat, tail, and eyes. In Hunting, a hart diſcovered by the furniture of his head. In Aſtronomy, applied to the moon, the number of days elapſed ſince the laſt full moon, filled her quarter. In Chronology, a certain period of years, by ſome reduced to three portions; viz. the age of the law of nature, from Adam to Moſes; the age of the Jewiſh Law, from Moſes to Chriſt; and the age of grace from thence to the preſent glorious year 1771. Others divide this grand period into ſix ages; the 1ſt, from the creation to the deluge, contains 1656 years. 2d, From thence to Abraham's entering the promiſed land, 426 years. 3d, To the deliverance from Egypt, 430. 4th, To the foundation of Solomon's temple, 467. 5th, To the foundation of the temple in the Babyloniſh captivity, 424. And the 6th, From the Babyloniſh captivity to the birth of Chriſt, including 484 years. The Romans divided time into the following periods. 1, The obſcure and uncertain age. 2, The heroic, or fabulous age, terminating at the firſt Olympiad. 3, The hiſtorical, which began at the building of Rome. The poets divide the world into four ages; called the Golden, Silver, Brazen, and Iron Age: agreeable to this the Eaſt-Indians divide theirs in four ages likewiſe. The firſt, or Golden, which laſted 1,728000 years, was that in which their God Brahma was born, men were giants, their manners innocent, and their lives four hundred years, except from diſeaſes. Second, which laſted 12,96000, when their Rajas were born, vice crept into the world, men's lives were ſhortened to 300 years, and their ſtature diminiſhed in proportion. The third age continued 10,64000, when vice increaſed, and men lived only two hundred years. The laſt, is the preſent age, of which they hold that 4,827200 years are elapſed, and men's lives ſhortened to a fourth of their original duration. Age in Law, is that time of life at which a perſon is qualified to aſſume certain offices of ſociety, which

before

before he was, for want of years, incapable of. At the age of twenty-one a man or woman may contract and manage for themselves with respect to their estates. Where any persons marry, the man under fourteen, and the woman within twelve, they may at those ages disagree to the marriage. At fourteen a person may dispose of goods and personal estate (but not of lands) by will, and by law, be a witness. All under this age are not generally punishable for crimes, though they must answer damage for trespass. *3 Inst. 78. 171. 247. 2. 33. 21 Hawk. 634. Mod. Caf. 260.*

A'GED, Adj. having lived a long course, or series of years. "Very aged men." *Job. xv. 10.* To continue for many years; to practise long. "It is dangerous to be aged in any kind of course," *Shakesp.* That which has lasted many years; or decayed by length of time. "Of the aged oaks," *Stilingf.* This sense, though somewhat improper, may be allowed, when we consider the vegetable creation has been generally said to be induced with a principle stiled a vegetable soul; which is the cause of its increase.

A'GEDLY, Adv. in the manner of a person advanced in years.

AGEN, Adv. [agen, Sax.] a repetition; something by way of reply. "Thus her son reply'd agen." *Dryd.* This is the proper spelling, though now used only by poets. See AGAIN.

A'GENCY, S. the quality of acting; action; the state exerting action.

A'GENT, Part. [agens, Lat.] that which acts, opposed to patient, or passive.

A'GENT, S. [agens, Lat.] something indued with the power of action. In physic, that which has power to act on another, and to produce a change, or alteration. Natural agents are those which are determined by the great author of nature; to one sort of effects with an incapacity to perform any other, as fire to heat only, not to cool. These are subdivided, into univocal, or such as produce the effects of the same kind as the agents themselves; and, 2, into equivocal, whose effects are of a different kind. A free agent is, that which may perform or not perform any thing whose actions are caused by his own will, without any external necessity. If there were no free agents, there would be no creatures capable of gratitude or reasonable obedience to the Deity; no opportunity for him to display his wisdom, goodness and mercy in the government of them, nor any means of bringing them to the sublimest degree of intellectual happiness, viz. that which arises from morality. In Commerce, an agent is a person intrusted with transacting business for another. Also the person who manages the affairs of a prince at a foreign court, a sort of under-ambassador. Agent of the fact, is the same as a broker, who acts

between merchants, traders, bankers, and other persons in trade, to facilitate the traffic of money, and the negociation of bills of exchange.

A'GENT and PA'TIENT, in Law, is a person who gives something to himself, being both the doer of a thing, and the person to whom it is done.

To AGGLO'MERATE, V. A. [agglomero, Lat.] to gather up; to gather together.

To AGGLO'MERATE, V. N. to cluster together like balls. Figuratively, to stick together.

AGGLU'TINANTS, S. [agglutinans,] those substances which have a quality of gluing, or sticking things together. In physic, strengthening medicines, which recruit, and supply what is wasted in the animal actions; the things under this class are, isinglass, oil of beans, gum arabic, dragon's-blood, cassia, sage, vermicelli, pulse, comfrey, plantain, &c.

To AGGLU'TINATE, V. A. to make to another, as it were, to cause that part to stick to another. "Agglutinating to those parts," *Harvey.* Used with the particle *to.*

AGGLUTINA'TION, S. to join two things fast together; in medicine, the adhesion of a new substance, or giving a greater consistence to the animal fluids, to render them fitter for nourishment.

AGGLU'TINATIVE, Adj. that has the power of thickening the animal juices. That which has the quality of joining one thing to another. "Roll up the member with the agglutinative roller." *Wiseman.*

To AGGRA'NDIZE, V. A. [aggrandir, Fr.] to exalt, to raise, to prefer. "Only to aggrandize covetous churchmen." To enlarge, exalt, or ennoble, dignify. "To raise and aggrandize our conceptions." *Watt's Improvem.*

AGGRA'NDISEMENT, S. promotion to a high place in a state; the conferring power, honour, and riches on a person; it conveys the secondary idea of something selfish. "During his administration, we saw power not applied to the aggrandisement of a family, but to making his country the admiration and envy of all foreigners."

AGGRA'NDIZER, S. one who confers honour, power, and riches on another.

To AGGRA'TE, V. A. [of aggratare, Ital.] to ingratiate one's self; to gain the esteem of a person. "Each one sought his lady to aggrate," *Fairy Queen.*

To AG'GRAVATE, V. A. [aggravo, Lat.] to add to the weight of a thing. In its secondary sense; to add to the enormity. "Aggravating crimes encrease their fears." *Dryd.* To heighten, or render more painful.

AGGRAVA'TION, S. the making worse. Some circumstance to heighten guilt. "The aggravation superseded of committing against knowledge." *Hammond.*

AG'GRE-

A'GGREGATE, Adj. [*aggregatus*, Lat.] an assemblage or collection of various things into one mass.

A'GGREGATE, S. [*aggregatus*, Lat.] an assemblage or collection of several particulars. " An *aggregate* of mistaken phaenomena." *Glanv.* The total, or result of several things added together. " Compounded and constituted of the *aggregate* of them all." *Boyle.*

To A'GGREGATE, V. A. [*aggrego*, Lat.] to collect together several particulars or sums into one. " The *aggregated* soil." *Par. Lost.*

AGGREGA'TION, S. [*aggregatio*, Lat.] a whole or total made up of several parts. " These extraordinary *aggregations* of this fire." *Woodw.* In Arithmetic, the sum total; formed by the addition of several units together. " They are enlarged by their *aggregation* and being erroneous in single numbers." *Browne's Vulg. Errors.* In Physics, an assemblage of things that have no natural connection with each other, into one whole, as a mass of ruins. The joining, or enrolling.

To AGGRE'SS, V. A: to commit hostilities; to begin the attack; to cause or begin a quarrel.

AGGRE'SSION, S. [*aggressio*, Lat.] the act of beginning a quarrel or attack, either with respect to private persons or kingdoms. " A conspiracy of common enmity and *aggression*." *L'Estrange.*

AGGRE'SSOR, S. the person who begins hostilities. " The first *aggressors*." *Swift.*

AGGRIE'VANCE, S. [accented on the *e*, as if the *i* was dropt] what causes pain or uneasiness, including in it the secondary idea of Injury, or something undeserved.

To AGGRIE'VE, V. A. to say or do a thing which shall render a person uneasy. To offer an insult or injury, which shall occasion vexation. " *Aggrieved* with some practices of the pope's collectors." *Camd.* To suffer loss or damage, used in the passive, and with the particle *by*. " *Aggrieved* by the failing of his rents." In all these senses, the idea of grief is included, as flowing from the inconvenience to which they subject the person who endures them.

To AGROU'P, V. A. [*agroupare*, Ital.] to join or introduce variety of figures in one picture.

AGHA'ST, Adv. [*syndesmus*, Gr.] with all the fears of a person terrified by a ghost.

AGI'LD, Part. [*agild*, Sax.] free from penalty, or not liable to the customary fines and taxes.

A'GILE, Adj. [of *agile*, Fr.] active, swift, nimble. " Forward struck his *agile* heels." *Shakesp. Ilia. IV.* Applied to the mind, stout, vigorous, brisk. " Render it *agile*, witty, valiant, ligor." *Prior.*

A'GILENESS, S. the quality of performing with speed, or nimbleness.

AGI'LITY, S. [*agilitas*, Lat.] a capability of moving easily and without impediment. " Recover his former *agility* and vigour." *Watts.*

AGILLA'RIUS, S. [from *agellum*, a herd of cattle] in old law books, a hayward or keeper of cattle; who, on account of his office is exempt from all services to the lord. *Parch. Antiq.* 534.

A'GIO, S. in Commerce, the exchange or difference between bank and cash. It also signifies the profit arising from money advanced, and is the same as premium.

AGI'STER, S. in Common Law, officers appointed by patent, to take in and feed the cattle of strangers, and collect the money arising from thence, of which there are four in every forest, where the king hath any pawnage. *Manw. For. Laws,* &c.

AGI'STMENT, S. the feed of other people's cattle, at a certain rate per week.

AGI'STOR, S. See AGISTER.

A'GITABLE, Adj. [*agitabilis*, Lat.] that may be put into motion.

To A'GITATE, V. A. [*agito*, Lat.] to move by repeated actions. To put the particles of any liquor into motion, or fermentation. " The vessel was broken by *agitating* the liquor." To agitate, affect, or give motion to. " Informs each part and *agitates* the whole." *Blackmore.* To disturb. " The mind of man is *agitated* by various passions." To toss backward and forward, to discuss with great warmth. " Though this controversy be revived, and hotly *agitated* among the moderns." *Boyle.*

AGITA'TION, S. [*agitatio*, Lat.] the act of shaking or putting into a motion. Deliberate and careful examination, or discussion of a question. " Rather a logical *agitation* of the matter." *L'Estrange.* Disorder or perturbation of the mind. " His mother could no longer bear the *agitations* of so many passions." *Tatler,* No. 55. Consideration, deliberation, debate. " The project now in *agitation* for repealing the test." *Swift.*

AGITA'TOR, S. one who projects any scheme; occasions any disturbance or motion. One who manages the affairs of another. " The *agitators* of the army." This sense is very uncommon.

A'GLETS, S. [*aiguillette*, Fr.] a sharp point or tag. In Botany, the pendents hanging on the tips, or apices, of the chives, and stamina of flowers; as in the tulips, &c.

AGNA'TI, S. in the Roman Law, the male descendants from the same father, distinguished from *cognati*, who are the female descendants.

AGNA'TION, S. in the Civil Law, the relation between the male descendants from the same father.

AGNINA

AGNI'NA MEMBRANA, or PELLICU-
LA, S. the membrane, including the fœtus.

AGNI'TION, S. [agnitio, Lat.] an acknowledging or admitting.

To AGNI'ZE, V. A. [from agnosco,
Lat.] to own; to avow; to admit; to
acknowledge.

AGNO'MEN, S. [Lat. from ag for ad to,
and nomen, a name] an additional name to the
surname, on account of some peculiar action,
or circumstance.

AGNOMINA'TION, S. [agnominatio,
Lat.] the familiarity or allusion of one word
to another.

AGNOE'TÆ, S. [agnoetæ, agnoetai, Gr.
from agnoeo, agnoo, Gr. to be ignorant
of] in history, a sect of heretics, who held
that Christ, with respect to his human nature, was ignorant of some things, and
especially the day of judgment, founding
their opinion upon the celebrated text of
St. Mark xiii. 32. As the Arians have ap-
pealed to the same text for a confirmation of
their opinion, we may observe that neither
of these heresies can receive any sanction
from it; if we explain it as intimating that
the knowledge of the day of judgment does
not concern our Saviour, considered as the
Messiah, but as God.

A'GNUS-CASTUS, S. in Botany, called
likewise vitex. Its leaves are like those of
the olive, but longer; it is reported a preserver of chastity, on which account the
Athenian ladies used to lay on beds of it
during the feast of Ceres; but modern
practice seems to have entirely disclaimed the
use of it.

A'GNUS DEI, [Lat. the Lamb of God.]
a flat piece of white wax of an oval form,
stampt with the figure of the lamb, and
consecrated by the pope. They are now
forbid to be brought into England, by 13
Eliz. c. 2.

AGO', Adv. [from agon, Sax.] past.
"Sometime ago." Addis. "It happened
three years ago."

AGO'G, Adv. [agogo, Fr.] eager or
anxious for the possession of something;
longing; with the particle for before the
object. "See the herds of our servant
maids agog for husbands." Spect. To fix
one's fancy or affections on; with the particle on before the subject. "On which the
saints are all agog." Hudib. Used with the
verbs set and on, as may be collected from
the authorities produced.

AGO'NE, Adv. [agon, Sax.] past; formerly.

AGO'NISM, S. [agonisma, Gr.] a contention for superiority, or for a reward.

A'GONIST, S. a contender for a prize.

AGONI'STES, S. [agonistes, Gr.] one
who exhibited at the public games of Greece
and Rome, as a candidate for the prizes
awarded for superiority of strength, &c.

AGONI'STICAL, [from agonistes] relating to prize-fighting.

To AGONI'ZE, [agoniser, Fr.] to be tormented with sharp and excessive pain.

A'GONY, S. [agon] excessive pain, or
torture. When applied to the conflict,
which our blessed Redeemer experienced in
the garden, it comprehends not only the corporal anguish just mentioned, but the
greatest perturbation of mind likewise. "By
thine agony and bloody sweat; by thy cross
and passion; by thy precious death and
burial; by thy glorious resurrection and
ascension; and by the coming of the Holy
Ghost, good Lord deliver us!" Church Li-
tany.

A'GOUTY, S. a beast found in the Antilles, of the size of a rabbit; the hair of
its body is of a bright red, but its tail has
none. He has but two teeth in each jaw,
holds his food in his fore paws, and has a
remarkable cry. When angry, his hair
stands an end, and he strikes the earth with
his hind feet; when pursued he flies to a
hollow tree, which he will not quit till expelled by smoke.

To AGRA'CE, V. A. to grant favours
to; to confer benefits on; to inculcate or
inspire with graces by virtue of instruction.
"She graced, and that knight so much
agrac'd." Fairy Q.

AGRA'RIAN, Adj. [agrarius, Lat. of
ager, a field] in the Roman laws, a term
applied to such laws as relate to the division
and distribution of lands. Appropriated by
way of eminence to the law enacted by
Spurius Cassius, about the year 268, for an
equal division of the conquered lands to all
the citizens, and limiting the quantity of
ground to be possessed by each of them.

To AGREE', V. A. [agréer, Fr.] to be
in friendship, or in concord; the sentiments
of one person being the same as those of
another. "The more you agree together."
Pope. To engage to do a thing upon certain
conditions; to bargain. "When he had
agreed with the labourers for a penny." Matt.
xx. 13. To resemble. "Thou art a Gal-
ilean; and thy speech agreeth thereto."
Mark xiv. 70. To match, with regard to
colour. "Taketh one of the new, agreeth
not with the old." Luke v. 36. To tally
with; to be consistent with. "Their witness agreed not together." Mark xiv. 50, 59.
To make a difference, by consenting to
conditions proposed; in opposition to a further prosecution by law, followed by the
particle with. "Agree with thine adversary
quickly." Matth. v. 25. To yield one's
consent, to grant, or admit, with the particles to, or of, or upon. "Agreed to all reasonable conditions." Macriab. xi. 14.
"That is agreed on by all." Barnet. Applied to the effect which things have on
the organ of taste, and the human constitution.

tation, to cause no disagreeable sensation in the one, or occasion any uneasiness, or other disturbance in the other. "Dull food bread agreeing to every taste." *Wisd.* xvi, 20. "With such as it agree with," *&c.* It may be observed, that the repetition of the particle *with*, both at the beginning and the end of this sentence, is an impropriety, and what may be met with in most authors, owing to their inadvertence. To agree, secretly used, implies to put an end to a strife; to accommodate a difference; to reconcile. "The mighty rivals—Are now agreed." *Rowe.*

AGREE'ABLE, Adj. [*agreeable*, Fr.] suitable; conformable; consistent with; "The practice of all piety and virtue is agreeable to our reason," *Tillotf.* Pleasing; grateful; suitable; convenient. "Called to mind a thousand agreeable remarks." *Spect.* No. 241.

AGREE'ABLENESS, S. what renders a thing grateful to the taste, in opposition to nauseous. "Pleasant tastes depend not on the things themselves, but their agreeableness to this or that particular palate." *Locke.* That which renders a thing pleasing, implying a calm and lasting satisfaction. "It is very much an image of that author's writing, who has an agreeableness that charms us, without correctness," *Pope.* Likeness; affinity; resemblance. "The agreeableness between man and the other parts of the universe." *Grew.*

AGREE'ABLY, Adv. that is consistent with, or conformable to; used with the particle *to*. "Agreeably to that which is in the law." *Efd.* xviii. 12. In a manner that gives a pleasing satisfaction.

AGREED, Part. settled, or adjusted by mutual consent. "When they had got known and agreed names," *Locke.*

AGREE'INGNESS, S. suitableness; conformity to; resemblance of, and likeness to.

AGREE'MENT, S. [*agrément*, Fr.] friendship; alliance; concord. "What agreement hath the temple of God with Belial? 2 *Cor.* vi. 16. A contract, bargain, compact. "Your agreement with hell shall not stand." *Isai.* xxviii. 18. Resemblance; "Expansion and duration hath this further agreement." *Locke.* In Law, the joining together two or more minds, in any thing done, or to be done: This is divided into three kinds. 1st, An agreement already executed, as when money is paid for the thing agreed to. 2dly, An agreement after the act, where one does an act, and another agrees to it afterwards. And, 3dly, an agreement executory, when both parties are agreed that a thing shall be executed or performed in time to come. In case a party be forced into an agreement, he shall not be compelled to perform it, 1 *Salk.* 48. *Plowd.* 17. *2* *3.* *Terms de Ley,* 31. *Hob.* 99. *18*

Cor. L. 19 *Con.* 18. *a.* 1. *Lev.* 161. *Dyer.* 167. 1 *Inst.* 79. 5. *Repx.* 89. 1 *Lill.* 48.

AGREE'SES, S. [*agreffes,* Fr.] In Fortification, exactly the same as gabion. See OGRESSE.

AGRE'STIA, Adj. [Lat.] wild. In Botany, applied to plants which grow in the fields, and are not cultivated.

AG'RICULTURE, S. [from *agri*, Lat. a field, and *cultura*, Lat. tillage] the art of tilling the ground, so as to render it fruitful; whether manuring, fallowing, sowing, harrowing, reaping, mowing, &c. the management of the productions of different soils, and planting; together with the culture of forests, timber, &c. This art has been cultivated by the greatest men, with the most indefatigable assiduity. It took its rise among, and was perfected by the Chaldeans. It was practised and reduced into an art by the Greeks. The Carthaginians made it their favourite study; and at Rome it was an honourable employment: the highest encomiums that could be given a man, was, that he cultivated his own spot of ground well; the most illustrious senators applied themselves to it, and their dictators were taken from the plough. The Spaniards have a complete treatise on this subject, composed by J. Herra, at the command of cardinal Ximenes. The French writers have distinguished themselves on this subject, and as for our countrymen, let the productive quantities of corn, beef, wool, and hurds, our island produces, speak our praise, rather than the systems of those, whose genius has immortalized their names, by the pieces which we have on this subject. To conclude this article, is may be added, that agriculture, or husbandry, is the original source of most of our treasure, and the great fountain of all materials for commerce; and that the articles of commerce must consequently endear themselves to those who trade in them, and render agriculture still more amiable in their eyes. It will always be good policy, to ease the land, to promote trade; and to encourage the trading interest, in order to promote the same.

AGRIFO'LIUM, S. In Botany, the Holly Tree.

AGRIMO'NIA, S. [Lat.] In Botany, Agrimony. The flower cup is of one leaf, divided into five acute segments, and rests on the germen.

AGROUND, Adv. stranded; stuck fast upon shore; on the ground; hindered by the ground from passing further. "We don't not approach, we having been all of us aground." *Raleigh.* Meeting with some impediment or difficulty, which renders it impossible to proceed in an affair.

A'GUE, S. [from *aigu,* Fr.] a periodical fever, beginning with shivering, followed

by

by heat, and terminates in a sweat. When the cold fit is hardly discernable, and there is a return of the hot one only, it is called an intermitting fever. If the fit returns every day, it is called a quotidian; if every third day, a tertian; and if every fourth day, a quartan. It seizes the patient with a languor of the body, and a heavy pain in the head, back, loins, and legs; the hands and feet become cold, the whole body pale, the countenance and nails lived; this is succeeded by a horror and rigour; the tongue and lips tremble, the breathing is difficult, the pericordia uneasy, the pulse contracted, hard or unequal, after which the skin becomes moist, an unusual sweat succeeds, and the fit ends. This disorder is owing to an obstructed perspiration, or whatever else, by overloading the juices, produces a lentor, or want of due circulation in the blood. The shorter the intervals are between the fits, the sooner are they cured. Vernal agues, or those which are caught in the spring, disappear of themselves, at the approach of warmer weather; autumnal agues, at the approach of cold, are increased. The usual method of cure is by a vomit of Ipecacuanha, given an hour before the fit, as a preparation for administering the bark. As nothing can contribute more to increase its effects than the minuteness of its particles, it is recommended to the faculty to powder it as fine as possible. If the bark be good, six drachms taken in the interval of two fits, may stop a vernal ague, and an ounce an autumnal one: but though this quantity may remove the fit for the present, it is advisable to continue the medicine, even after it seems to have left the patient, for fear of a relapse. A circumstance that ought to be dreaded, and guarded against by a compliance with this advice.

A'GUED, Part. [from *ague*] being diseased with an ague; cold, shivering, trembling, alluding to the effects of this disorder. "With slight and agued fear." *Shak. Coriol.* This sense is seldom made use of by present writers.

A'GUE-FIT, S. the cold, shivering fit, which people have in the ague.

A'GUE-PROOF, Adj. able to resist the causes which produce agues, without contracting that disorder. "They told me I was every thing; 'tis a lie; I am not ague-proof." *Shak. K. Lear.*

To AGUI'SE, V. A. [accented on the i, and pronounced as if the u was entirely dropt, (soon *guise*, Fr. *guisa*, Ital.] to adorn, embellish, or set off.

A'GUISH, Adj. like, or resembling an ague. "Her aguish love now glows and burns." *Glanv.*

A'GUISHNESS, S. the quality of resembling an ague.

A'H! an Interjection. [*ach*, Teut.] to denote some sudden dislike. "Ah, sinful nation." *Isa.* L. 4. Sometimes it expresses contempt, and sarcastic reproach. "Ah! thou that destroyest the temple." *Matt.* xv: 29. Sometimes grief, and an appeal to the passion of pity and compassion. "Ah! Lord, wilt thou destroy the residue?" *Ezek.* ix. 8. Before *me*, it denotes sorrow arising from the contemplation of misery; and implies woe! "Ah me!" Before *that* it denotes wishing, and seems substituted instead of ob! "Ah that we lov'd ourselves but half so well." *Dryd.*

AHA', an Interjection, denoting joy at the calamities of others. When doubled, it implies a greater degree of transport mixed with contempt. "Let them be turned back that say, aha! aha!" *Psal.* lxx. 3.

AHEA'D, Adv. a sea term; beyond; before. "And now the speedy dolphin gets ahead." *Dryd.* To contract an inveterate habit. "They suffer them at first to run ahead."

AHEI'GHT, Adv. on high; a great distance above us.

AHOUA'I, S. In Botany, a plant which has flowers of one leaf, shaped like funnels, and divided into different segments at the top.

To AID, V. A. [pronounced as if the i was dropped, and written with *aa* or *a* final, as *and*, or *ade*, from *aider*, Fr.] to afford help or succour to; to deliver a person in distress, by giving him assistance. "Into the like he leapt, his lord to aid." To supply with, or support. "Aid them with victuals, weapons, money or ships." *Maccab.* viii. 26. To support a person, or thing, in a declining state; to give vigour to. "By the loud trumpet, which our courage aids." *Roscommon.*

AID, S. [from *aide*, Fr.] what contributes to render a thing more easy. Assistance. "The memory of things may receive considerable aid, if they are thrown into verse." *Watts's Improv.* Support given to a person, in danger from external violence, to enable him to repel it. "The ports of Ithaca, would arm in aid." *Pope's Odyss.* An assistant, or person, who, either by advice, or exertion of bodily strength, renders difficulties surmountable, distress more tolerable, and prosperity more transporting. "It is not good that man should be alone, let us make unto him an aid." *Wisd.* A subsidy, or money to support the necessities of the state. In Law, a petition made in a court, for calling in the help of another, interested in the cause, in order to his giving strength to the party in aid of him, and to avoid a prejudice accruing towards his own right, if not prevented.

AID-DE-CAMP, S. an officer, who receives and carries the orders of a general officer

...cer to the rest of the camp. *Aid-Major*, an adjutant; one who assists the major when present, and acts as his deputy when he is absent.

AI'DANCE, S. [from *aid*] assistance, help, aid.

AI'DER, S. one who assists, or helps, or aids.

AI'DLESS, Adj. deprived of, or requiring help, or assistance. Without aid, or assistance.

AI'GULETS, S. [*aiguin*, Fr.] tags at the end of fringes. " With golden *aguin* that glister'd bright."

To AIL, V. A. [from *egle*, Sax.] to disturb; to have a disagreeable sensation; to make uneasy. Sometimes before *me*, or other personal pronouns, it implies, the action of some unknown cause, occasioning irregularity, or disorder in behaviour and conduct. " What *ails me*, that I cannot lose thy thought." This word, including the idea of disorder in itself, is never joined to another which would limit its signification to any particular disorder. As we never say " *A fever ails him* ; but *something ails him*; nor, he *ails a fever*, but, he *ails something*.

AIL, S. [from *ail*,] a distemper; a disorder.

AI'LESBURY, the largest town in Buckinghamshire, with the title of an earldom, and a market on Saturdays, and three fairs, on Saturday before Palm-Sunday, June 14, and September 25, for cattle. It consists of several streets lying about the market-place, which is large, and in the middle of it is a very convenient hall, where the assizes are sometimes held. It sends two members to parliament; and is 16 miles S. E. of Buckingham, and 44 N. W. of London. Lon. 16. 55. lat. 51. 40.

AI'LING, Part. [from *ail*] one of a weak, puny constitution; subject to disorders.

AI'LMENT, S. [from *ail*] indisposition; disorder; illness. " Little *a knows oft* attend this fair." *Grave.*

To AIM, V. A. to put a weapon in such a position, as to hit the object; to throw a thing at an object, with an intention to hit it. *Dryd.* To endeavour to strike; used with the particle *at*. " *Aim'd* thou *at* princes." To direct the edge of satyr against a person. To have in view, and endeavour to obtain. " Swoln with applause, and *aiming* still at more." *Dryd.* To endanger. " It was evident that he *aimed* at his father's life."

AIM, S. the position of a weapon, intended to strike an object. " Soon bent his bow, uncertain of its *aim*." *Dryd.* The point or object which is intended to be hit. " The arrows fled not swifter towards the *aim*." *Shak. Hen. IV.* Endeavour; intention; purpose, or design. " With am-

biticus *aim*,—Against the throne and monarchy of God." *Par. Loft.* The end or object of a discourse. " The epistle has but one *aim*." *Locke.* Guess; prophecy. " With a near *aim*, of the main chance of things." *Shak. Hen. IV.*

AINSWORTH, (HENRY) an eminent Non-conformist minister, who flourished the latter end of the sixteenth and beginning of the seventeenth century. About the year 1590, he distinguished himself amongst the Brownists, which engaged him in such difficulties, that he was obliged to retire to Holland, and at Amsterdam erected a church, wherein he officiated, together with one Johnson. Having found a diamond of great value, he advertised it; and, when the owner, a Jew, demanded it, would not accept of any other acknowledgment, though very poor, but a conference with some of his rabbies, on the prophecies relating to the Messiah; the Jew having promised him this gratification, but being unable to perform the engagement, it is supposed he had him poisoned, in order to save his credit. His great skill in Hebrew, and his excellent commentaries on the scriptures, particularly on the Pentateuch, are in universal esteem. Moreri goes so far as to say, that the learned Lightfoot is not a little indebted to him; and his works were received with respect, even by his adversaries; insomuch, that it is not easy to produce any one oftener quoted, by the learned of all countries, than Dr. Ainsworth. He was certainly a person of profound learning, well versed in the scriptures, deeply read in rabbinical learning, of a strong understanding, quick penetration, and indefatigable diligence; it must be confessed, that the hastiness of his temper, his contempt of church government, and his proneness to dispute on trifles, were faults; but let the hand of charity always draw the veil over the defects of the great; and let us rather imitate their excellencies, than glory in scrutinising into their deficiencies.

AIR, S. [from *air*, Fr. *aer*, Lat. *aer*, Gr. or אֲוִיר, Heb.] that thin fluid body which surrounds our globe, forms the atmosphere, and is the cause of breathing. " If I were to tell what I mean by the word *air*." *Watts.* A portion of the element which encompasses us, considered as put into motion. " *Airs*, vernal *airs*." *Par. Loft.* A likeness very made of a thing. " Still you mov'd; you gave it *air* before me." *Dryd.* Posture; attitude; mien; behaviour. " Something wonderfully divine in the *airs* of this posture." *Addif.* Used after give, and the pronouns personal, without any other word following; to assume a character, or appearance of something superior to that which is real. " He gave himself *airs*." An affected and awkward manner of address. " Give them

themselves airs of kings." *Addis.* Appearance. "Communicated with the air of a force." In Philosophy, that thin elastic fluid in which we breathe, and which surrounds the globe to a great height, though scarcely to be perceived by us, yet absolutely necessary to our existence. If we examine the volume of creation, we shall find it the grand instrument of the Deity in most of his operations. It is this which puts every thing into motion, it lends activity to fire, growth to vegetables, improvement to chymistry, fluidity to water, health to animals; in a word, there is scarce any operation in nature, which happens without its assistance; there is no production of art that does not require its aid. If we run over the properties of air, we shall find them to be, 1st, fluidity, which is so inseparable from it, that no experiment, no change of temperature, can deprive it of it. As for its second property, weight or gravity, we need but put our hands on the receiver of an air-pump to be convinced of it; if its weight on that small portion of our fabric shall astonish us, how much do we be amazed when we consider what a vast weight is sustained by the whole! As it is found by experiment, that the compass of a foot square upon the superficies of our bodies sustains 2660 lb. the number of square feet upon our bodies, will give us the amount of the weight of air which is sustained; now as 15 feet square seems to be the true admeasurement of this superficies, he must sustain a weight equal to 39900 lb. for 2660 × 15 = 39900 lb. which is about 17 ton. Let us adore the divine wisdom, which shews itself in this configuration of our fabric, whereby we can sustain such a weight without being incommoded, and walk under a burthen, without difficulty, which at first thoughts might seem heavy enough to grind our very bones into powder. The third property of air is its elasticity, or its quality of returning again to its former dimensions, after being forced into a narrower compass, with a force proportionable to that by which it was compressed. To mention no other uses resulting from this property, 'tis to this that we owe our being able to support its gravity with so much ease. For it is demonstrable, that the elastic power which prevails in any particular portion of the air, without any other condensation than what is owing to the compressing air itself, can sustain the whole force of the incumbent atmosphere; and that a very small quantity, wherever confined, is able to produce the very same effects in a very large quantity in another place. Having thus run over the properties of the air, we might now consider what particles this heterogeneous fluid consists of; let it however suffice to say, that whatever fragrance exhales from flowers, or stenches arise from putrified bodies; whatever particles are

detached from minerals by heat, or animal bodies by perspiration; whatever vapours ascend from the waters, or exhalations from the earth; what fire forever electricity can disseminate, or the fermentation of ascending fumes of sulphur procure; are all to be found in this great support of our lives, and, under the direction of the Deity, the cause of all its blessings as well as the parent of most of its diseases. Air, in Music, a composition which is played alone; the melody and inflexion of a musical composition; thus we say, Handel's airs, &c. Airs in Horsemanship, the artificial or practised motions of a managed horse; such as the demi-air, demi-volt, curvet, &c.

To AIR, V. A. to expose to the air. "As the ants were airing their provisions." *L'Estrange.* To enjoy the air. "As I was here airing myself." *Addis.* To place before the fire. "Air the shirts." *Hudor.* To expose to the fire in order to warm, by setting the particles of fire into motion by heat. "Air this wine." To build nests. "If they were allowed to air naturally." *Carew. Serv. of Cornw.*

AIR-BLADDER, S. a bladder found among the entrails of fish, which enables them to rise or dive in the water. "The air-bladder in fishes seems necessary in swimming." *Carew.*

AIR-BUILT, Adj. built in the air; chimerical; having no foundation. "The air-built castle." *Dryden.*

AIR-DRAWN, Adj. formed by a condensation of the air; chimerical; imaginary.

AIRER, S. he that exposes a thing to the air; or holds a thing to the fire, in order to prevent the consequences of damp and stagnating air.

AIR-GUN, S. an instrument to shoot with by means of compressed air. It is composed of brass, and has two barrels, one of which is large, but the inward one, from whence the bullets are ejected, is small. The magazine air-gun was invented by L. Collot. By this contrivance ten bullets are lodged so near to the place of discharge, that they may be discharged successively. If the force of condensed air was equal to that of gunpowder, this instrument would answer the end of as many guns as it can contain bullets. In this machine, the bore of the syringe must not exceed half an inch diameter, because the pressure against every square inch is about 15 lb. and therefore every circular inch about 12. If the syringe be one inch in diameter, when one atmosphere is injected, there will be a resistance of 12 lb. against the piston, and when 10, a force of 120 to be surmounted; whereas 10 atmospheres act against the circular one-half inch piston, which is one fourth less, with only a force equal to 30 lb. or 40 atmospheres

spheres

spheres may be injected with such a syringe easily as to with one whose base is as big again; for the facility of working is inversely as the squares of the diameter of the syringe.

AI'RING, S. a short walk or ride, when we enjoy the fresh and open air, in opposition to the more confined within doors.

AI'R-HOLE, S. a hole to admit or let out air; a vent-hole.

AI'RINESS, S. open, or exposed to a free current of air; openness; briskness; levity; gaiety. "A certain talkativeness and airiness represented in their tongue." *Felton.*

AI'RLESS, Adj. not having a free current of air; having no communication with the external air.

AI'RLING, S. a youthful, light, gay, sprightly, thoughtless person.

AIR-PUMP, S. an instrument for extracting air; consisting of a glass receiver, wherein the objects are placed; two brass cylinders to extract the air with; a gage to determine the rarefaction of the air; a tube called the swan's neck, communicating with the receiver and the pistons; and a winch that gives motion to the whole. The first inventor of this machine was Otto Guericke, a burgo-master of Magdebourg, who performed his experiments at Ratisbon, in the year 1654; but this being very defective, Mr. Boyle, one of the family of the Orrery's, assisted by Dr. Hook, contrived another, which, as described by himself, had but one barrel. Papin afterwards invented one with two barrels; but that made by Hawksbee in 1709, surpassing any that preceded, is what is commonly used at present. For the sake of conveniency, a new machine of this kind has lately been invented, called a *portable Air-pump,* which may be removed from one place to another without any difficulty; its construction is indeed somewhat different from the former. It is by means of these instruments that we demonstrate a vacuum, the gravity and elasticity, the solidity and universal diffusation of air throughout all bodies; the cause of the ascent of water in pipes, and the suspension of mercury in tubes, and the necessity of this fluid for the support of life, the ill consequences of its stagnation, and other particulars equally useful, and subservient to the cause of grateful piety; by convincing us, that every particle of matter, whether of dense earth, or subtle air, bears the signature of divine wisdom, and that the whole walk of creation, and expanse of infinity, is full of his riches!

AI'R-SHAFT, S. In Mining, a passage made for the air by digging.

AI'RIE, S. See AIRY.

AI'RY, Adj. [*aërius,* Lat.] the subtile parts of bodies. "Emission of the thinner or more airy parts of bodies." Do high, a-

loft, or in that space of the system above the earth. "Through airy channels flow." *Addison.* Chimerical, having no foundation. "I hold ambition of so airy and light a quality, that it is but a shadow's shadow." *Shaksp. Hamlet.* Exposed to the weather, in opposition to warm, close, or confined. "The painters draw their nymphs in this airy habit." *Dryd.* Gay, sprightly, brisk, full of vivacity. "By this name of ladies he means all young persons, slender, finely shaped, airy, and delicate." *Dryd.* "Merry and airy at there." *Taylor.* Airy Triplicity, in Astrology, are the three signs, Gemini, Libra, and Aquarius.

AI'SLE, S. [*isle,* from *aîle,* Fr. a wing] the side walks of a church, parallel to the greater in the center called the *nef.* "The church is one huge *nef* with a double *aisle* to it." *Addison.* Johnson contends for its being wrote *aile,* agreeable to its derivation; but it may be observed, that their French words have formerly been spelt with an *s,* and tho' I pay great deference to Johnson, I cannot but reverence Addison.

AISTHETE'RIUM, S. [αἰσθητήριον, Gr.] the sensorium, or place wherein the soul is imagined to reside, and receive the notices of external objects by means of the organs of sensation. The Cartesians imagine it to be the pineal gland; but Willis the medulla oblongata in the corpora striata.

AI'T, or EYGHT, (a contraction of eylands, Belg.] a small island.

A'JUTAGE, S. [*ajutage,* Fr.] in Hydraulics, the spout of an artificial fountain, thro' which the water ascends. "If the ajutage be inclined, the water will ascend higher than when it is perpendicular."

To A'KE, V. N. [from *ace,* Sax. of αχθω, Gr.] to suffer a dull pain, in opposition to smart, which is an acute one and of a short continuance. "His limbs must ake, with daily toils oppress." *Prior.* This word is applied not only to bodily pain, but likewise to any uneasiness which affects the mind; and as it is derived rather from the Saxon than the Greek, is more properly spelt this way than ake, which is preferred by Johnson, i. e. ache.

AKI'N, Adv. being related by blood or descent. "I could wish, that being thy sister in nature, I were not afar off a to by fortune." *Sidney.* Resembling; having a near relation to. "From questions which may be akin to it." *Watts's Improvement.*

ALL, ATTLE, ADLE, contractions of the Saxon *æthel,* noble, are generally prefixed to compound names, and signify illustrious; but when borrowed from *al,* Sax. or *alle,* Gothic, they imply perfection, excellence, or fullness; *al,* Alfred, compounded of *al,* Sax. or *alle,* Goth. all, and *frithr,* i.e. or *fryth,* Sax. peace, signifies peace, ful. Almighty, from *ælmightig,* Sax. of *al,*

al, and *mighty*, powerfulness, implies perfect power, fullness of power, or power that performs any thing that is the proper object of that faculty, and is full without defect.

A'LA, S. [Lat. a wing] In Botany, the hollow of a stalk, or that hollow between the branch and leaf, from whence new shoots arise; likewise the foliaceous membranes running the whole length of the stem, from whence it is called *caulis alatus*, Lat. and *tige aïlée*, Fr. a winged stalk.

ALABA'STER, S. [from *alabaſtron*, Gr.] a stone that is softer than marble, but harder than plaister of Paris. It is of various colours, but the white is the most common; the horn and transparent of little value; and that of the colour of honey, with spots or veins, which is the most valued. The white is most commonly used for statues and vases, of which latter kind the antients seemed very fond, and generally made use of them to put their most costly perfumes in. This custom has, by the inadvertence of some criticks, been made use of to explain, or rather to obscure, the expression of St. Matt. xxvi. 7. and Mark xiv. 3. which is rendered an *alabaſter box*, *alabaſtron*, but is a general name for any box without handles, and may be easily reconciled to its being broke on that occasion; but according to our version cannot. Constantine has rendered the passage in our sense, and by that means cleared it of difficulties which the commentators have puzzled themselves with to no purpose.

ALABA'STER, Adj. something made of alabaster.

ALA'CK, Interj. It implies sorrow, grief, lamentation, or something which causes it.

ALA'CK-A-DAY, Interj. [how full of unhappiness is the day, from *alack* and *a day*] a sudden cry at any calamity, and signifies that the person is miserable.

ALA'CRIOUSLY, with great cheerfulness. "Epaminondas *alacriously* expired, in confidence that he left behind him a perpetual memory of the victories he had atchieved for his country." *Gov. com. of the Tongue.*

ALA'CRITY, S. [*alacritas*, Lat.] a chearful activeness, a willingness.

ALAMI'RE, S. in Music, the lowest note but one in the scale of music, and was invented by Guido Aretius.

A-LA-MO'DE, Adv. that is in the reigning taste or fashion.

A-LA-MO'DE, S. [Fr.] a thin, glossy, light, black silk, generally used for women's bowknets, hats, or hoods and men's hatbands and scarfs at funerals.

A'LAN, [WILLIAM] son of John Alan, born at Roſſal in Lancashire, in 1522. Educated at Oriel college, Oxford, where he was chosen fellow in 1550. In 1556 he was principal of St. Mary Hall; but on Queen

Elizabeth's accession to the crown, as he was a zealous papist, lost all hopes of preferment, and on that account retired to the English college at Louaine, of which he was the principal support. Joined to a majestic presence, he had an easy affable deportment, and, with the greatest severity of manners, a mildness in speech and behaviour, which attracted the affection of all he conversed with. He wrote a defence of purgatory, and prayers for the dead, in opposition to Bishop Jewel, wherein he endeavours to shew that a middle state is acknowledged by all protestants, and that the prayers for the dead were in use from the earliest ages of the church, which was answered by Dr. Fulke in 1580. The method Alan made use of to establish his point, was very proper to captivate the judgment; and his style, which was pure and flowing, made his performance still more dangerous and still more admired. His health decaying by too intense application, he came, even with the danger of his life, if we may be allowed the expression, in England for his recovery; but being too zealous in making proselytes, was discovered and obliged to go abroad again for safety. He was supposed to have been a great promoter of the invasion of these kingdoms by the Spanish armada; and in 1588 composed his piece, which consisted of two parts, the first explaining the Pope's bull against Queen Elizabeth, and the second exhorting the nobility and people of England to revolt in favour of the Spaniards. This book made a great noise, rendered him famous abroad and notorious at home; was, by moderate catholicks condemned, and by some ascribed to F. Parsons. In the last years of his life, he is said to have altered his sentiments with respect to government, to have lost his credit with the catholicks, and to have been poisoned by them on that account. As an English subject, he was a busy, enterprising, dangerous rebel; as a zealous papist, an active, learned, and industrious person; as an author, for matter, method, wit, learning, and diction, one of the most considerable writers of his age; as his most inveterate enemies have allowed. But we conclude with Pope on another occasion, "Oh grant an honest fame, or grant me none."

ALA'ND, Adv. [from *a* and *land*] on the land or shore; on the dry ground. "Moor'd aland." *Dryd.*

ALA'RIS, or ALIFO'RMIS, S. [from *ala* and *forma*, Lat.] in Anatomy, the innermost of the three veins in polite the elbow, which having an artery under it, and the middle one above, ought to be opened with great caution; the superius or outward one, named likewise humeral, may be opened without any danger.

ALA'RIS,

ALA'RM, S. [from *all*, Ital. and *arm*, Ital.] a military signal, by which men are now called to arms, but before the invention of drums and trumpets it was done by a loud cry or shout. It includes an idea of sudden danger; the notice of the approach of any sudden danger. "An *alarm* of fire." Tumult, or disturbance, causing fear, or terror. "Thy palace fill with insult and *alarms*." *Pope.*

To ALA'RM, V. A. to give the signal of arming, or preparing for any sudden danger; to excite fear or apprehension; to disturb. "When rage misguides me, or when fear *alarms*." *Tickell.*

ALA'RM BELL, S. a bell rung to give notice of the approach of an enemy, and to call to arms. "The *alarm bell* rings." *Dryd.*

ALA'RMING, Part. what occasions terror, fear, or apprehension of danger. "An *alarming* message." "An *alarming* pain."

ALA'RM-POST, S. the place appointed for the several companies of an army to repair to, in case of any sudden danger.

ALA'RUM, S. alarm. "Our alarm *alarums* chang'd to merry meetings." *Shaksp. Rich. III.* A clock, calculated to give notice of any particular time it is set to.

To ALA'RUM, V. A. See ALARM. "*Alarumed* by his sentinel the wolf." *Shak. Macbeth.*

ALA'S, Interj. [*helas*, Fr.] It implies lamentation, occasioned by some expected calamity; pity caused from the idea of another's distress. "*Ah!* poor Protheus." *Shaksp.* When applied to things, it is used with great elegance, and implies the relentings of humanity at the prospect of their approaching or present distress. "Stamp with thy foot, and say *alas!*" *Ezek. vi. 11.* When doubled, it implies such an increase of calamity as almost overpowers the mind. "*Alas, alas,* the great city Babylon!" *Rev. xviii. 10. Alas-the-day* is applied to time, and signifies its being very unfortunate, or productive of some mischief or distress. "*Alas-a-day,* you have ruined my poor mistress." *Cong. Old Batch. Alas-the-while* is used in the same sense. "For pale and wan he was; *alas the while!*" *Spenf. Paft.*

ALA'TE, Adv. not long past; lately; not long ago.

ALATE'RNUS, S. [called Evergreen] in Botany, the ever-green privet. There are four species; the first of which, according to Boerhaave, is deterfive, astringent, and cooling, of use in gargarisms for inflammations in the mouth, and quinsies.

ALATERNOE'IDES, S. [from *alaternus* and *eidos*] in Botany, a plant resembling the alaternus, excepting that it has three seeds joined together like spurge, but the alaternus has three seeds included together in one common capsula.

ALA'TI-PROCESSUS, S. in Anatomy, the processes of the *os sphenoides.*

ALA'Y, S. in Hunting, the adding several fresh dogs into the cry.

ALB, S. a vest worn by priests; a surplice.

ALBAN's, [St.] a town in Hertfordshire with the title of a dutchy, and two markets, on the Wednesdays and Saturdays, and three fairs, on March 25, June 17, and September 29, for horses, cows, and sheep. It is seated on the river Coln, and arose from the ruins of the ancient city Verulam, and receives its name from the monastery dedicated to St. Alban, a Romish martyr. The monastery is now used as a parish church, and in it were buried several persons of royal blood, particularly the famous duke Humphrey, whose body was discovered not many years since. It is 12 miles S. E. of Dunstable, and 24 N. W. of London. Lon. 17. 15. lat. 51. 40. It sends two members to parliament.

ALBA'RAZIN, ALBA'ZARIN, S. a kind of Spanish wool.

ALBE'IT, Adv. used to infer something; altho'; notwithstanding; granting. "The Lord hath said, *albeit* I have not spoken." *Ezek. xiii. 7.*

ALBE'RNUS, S. a sort of camblet which comes from the Levant.

ALBE'RTUS, S. a gold coin struck in Flanders during the administration of Albertus, Duke of Austria, weighing 4 dwts. 21 g 4ths carats fine, and though worth fourteen French livres, is received only for a mark at the mint of France.

ALBUGI'NEA, Adj. [Lat. from *albus*] in Anatomy, the outermost coat of the eye, which composes the white, called *adnata* and *conjunctiva.* Likewise the membrane immediately covering the testicles.

ALBUGI'NEOUS, Adj. [*alburgo*, Lat.] something belonging to or resembling that part of an egg which is called its white. "Giving vent first to an *albuginous*, then to a white concealed matter." *Wiseman's Surgery.*

ALBU'GO, S. [*albus*] in Anatomy, the white of the eye. Also a disorder of the eye.

ALBUM-GRÆ'CUM, dog's white dung, used with honey as a plaister, to deterge inflammations in the throat.

ALBU'MEN OVI, S. [Lat.] the white of an egg, used in medicine on account of its glutinous nature, mixed with bole ammoniac, to prevent any strained part from rising into a tumour, and to restore its tone or elasticity; likewise to consolidate fresh wounds and prevent too great an effusion of blood.

A'LBURN, Adj. a whitish brown, or a colour formed from a white and brown mixt together. See AUBURN.

ALCAHE'ST, S. [Arab.] an universal dissolvent;

diffolvent; a menftruum capable of diffolving any thing. Paracelfus and Helmont pretended that they had found out this fecret; but who could ever believe them?

ALCA'IC, Adj. in antient Poetry, a name given to feveral forts of verfes, the firft confifting of five feet, of which the firft is either a fpondee or iambic, the fecond an iambic, the third a long fyllable, the fourth a dactyl, and the fifth a dactyle or amphimacer. The fecond fpecies confifts of two dactyles and two trochees.

A'LCALI, or ALCALY. See ALKALY.

ALCALIZATION, S. See ALKALIZATION.

ALCA'NNA, S. [Arab. קנה] a drug ufed in dying, which is brought from the Levant. In powder it is green, but the tincture it makes differs according to the difference of the liquor in which it is fteeped; when foaked in water it is yellow; but when in vinegar, citron-juice, and allum-water, it is red. The oil extracted from the berries is of an agreeable fcent, and of ufe for foftening the nerves. The Levantines, whether Jews or Turks, make ufe of it as a cofmetic, or beautifier, to dye the nails of their fingers and their hair with.

A'LCHYMICAL, Adj. according to the procefs or method of alchymifts. "Made by projection or multiplication alchymical." Camden.

A'LCHYMIST, S. one who profeffes or ftudies alchymy.

A'LCHYMY, S. [of al and kemia, Egypt.] that part of chemiftry employed in curious refearches. Its chief objects have been, the making of gold; an univerfal medicine; an univerfal diffolvent; and an univerfal ferment, or a fubftance, which, being applied to any feed, will increafe its fecundity to infinity. Thefe vifionary attempts have indeed proved ferviceable to chemiftry, and been the accidental caufes of feveral noble difcoveries, though their authors have been looked on as fools by fome, and as madmen by others. The Alchymift of Ben Johnfon receives frefh beauties, when confidered as ridiculing this vain foible of his times; but otherwife is, at beft, an infipid performance, which can afford no pleafure to an audience, though graced by the action of a Garrick, whom modern critics juftly ftile the Rofcius of the Englifh ftage.

ALCMA'NIAN, Adj. a kind of lyric verfe, fo called from the inventor, Alcman.

A'LCOHOL, S. [from אל Arab. and כחל] in Chemiftry, the pureft fpirit of wine, rectified, by many diftillations, to its utmoft fubtility. Likewife a very fine powder.

ALCOHOLIZA'TION, S. the rectifying of fpirits, or of reducing any thing to a powder.

To ALCOHOLIZE, V. A. to rectify fpi-

rits by frequent diftillations, fo that, when fet on fire, they fhall confume away without leaving any moifture or dregs behind them; to reduce bodies to fuch a fine powder, that, when tried between the teeth, they fhall not appear any ways gritty.

A'LCORAN, S. [from אל Arab. and קראן] the volume of the Mohammedan law, compofed by Mahomet, affifted by Sergius a Jacobin, Sergius a Neftorian monk, and fome Jews. It is divided into four parts, called by the name of fome animal, as the Cow, the Emmet, the Spider, and the Fly. Though wrote by an illiterate perfon, it is extolled for the elegance of its ftyle, and urged to have been a divine compofition. It abounds in abfurdities and contradictions, which left they vindicate, by faying, that it was three and twenty years in compofing; and that the circumftances of things altering in that interval, the Deity himfelf repealed and altered feveral precepts, to fuit them with the nature of things. It was originally in loofe fheets, which Mahomet afferted he received fingly from God. To particularize its peculiar doctrines would carry us too far, though, perhaps, we may be a little more minute in the articles Mahomet, or Mahommedanifm. However, we muft add, that this book is held in fuch veneration by its profeffors, that it is death for a Chriftian or a Jew to touch it, and alfo to a Muffulman himfelf, if be handles it with unwafhen hands. Alwoa, among the Perfians, decotes a very high narrow fteeple, with two or three galleries running round it, where the priefts fay their prayers three times a day, going quite round the tower, that they may be heard by every part of their audience.

ALCO'VE, S. [alcoba, Span.] a recefs, or part of a room, feparated by an eftrade, in which is placed a bed of ftate, or feats to entertain company. "Deep in a rich alcove the prince was laid." Pope.

ALDBOROUGH, a fea-port town in Suffolk, with a market on Wednefdays and Saturdays, and two fairs, on March 1, and May 3, for toys. It is pleafantly feated in a dale, between a high hill to the weftward, and the fea to the eaft, with a river running S. W. and the old church ftands on a hill. It is 40 miles E. of Bury, and 88 N. E. of London. It fends two members to parliament, and is governed by a bailiff, twelve aldermen, and twenty-four common-council. It is a poor, ftraggling, long, dirty town, confifting of about 500 mean houfes, with the ftreets not paved, and here is no manufactory; a fmall fifhery is however carried on here. The harbour is tolerably good, but fmall; and there is here a fort of nine guns. The town was formerly much longer; but the fea has taken away whole ftreets, and gains upon it. Long. 18. o. lat 52. 50.

ALDBOROUGH, a town in the Weft-riding

rifing of Yorkshire, seated on the river Ouse, and it had a market, now disused. However, it sends two members to parliament, and is 15 miles N. W. of York, and 200 N. by W. of London. Lon. 16. 15. lat. 54. 15.

A'LDEBARAN, S. [Pers.] in Astronomy, a star of the first magnitude, in the eye of the constellation Taurus.

A'LESBURY, AY'LESBURY, or AI'LSBURY, S. [*aeghelburh*, from *aegle*, Sax. an eagle, and *buryh* or *berig*, Sax. a town] the largest and best borough town in Buckinghamshire, as early as the times of the Saxons, who took it by storm in 571. It was chiefly famous for St. Ædith, a native of it, who is reported to have performed several miracles. In the time of William the Conqueror it was a royal manor; who gave several yard lands, on condition that the owner should find litter, or *straw*, for his *bed*, whenever he came that way. Let the sons of voluptuousness attend to this circumstance; and admire the simplicity of former times! William of Ailesbury held it by this charter, with this addition, that he should likewise strew the King's chamber, and provide him three ells if be came in the winter; but if in summer, besides straw for the bed, he was to provide two green geese. This he was to repeat three times a year, if the King came thither so often. It has given the title of Earl to the noble family of the Bruces; Charles II. having conferred that title, in 1664, on Robert Bruce, earl of Elgin in Scotland, descended from the Kings of that country, to which their motto, *fuimus*, "we have been," seems strongly to allude. Round this town is a very famous vale for breeding and fattening sheep, for which this country is famous. The poorer sort are generally employed in making laces for edging; which though they may not equal, yet hinders, in a great measure, the importation of that commodity from France, and were to be hoped, that by due encouragement from the nobility, it might be entirely suppressed. It was made a town incorporate by Q. Mary in 1553; consisting of a bailiff, ten aldermen, and twelve capital burgesses: at present its chief officer is termed a constable. Its fairs are on the Saturday before Palm Sunday, the 14th of June, and on the 25th of September, for cattle. It sends two members to parliament, and is 34 computed, or 44 measured, miles N. W. of London.

A'LESHAM, S. [*aegisham*, Sax.] a market town in Norfolk, very much peopled by knitters of stockings. Its market is on Saturday; and its fairs, for lean cattle, ordinary horses, and chapmen or pedlars wares, on the 23d of March. It lies 119 miles N. of London.

A'LDER, S. [from *aelder*, Sax.] a tree whose leaves refemble those of the hazel, the male flowers of which are produced at remote distances from the fruit; which is squamose, and of a conical figure. There are three species. The wood is used by turners, and will endure long under ground, or in water.

A'LDERMAN, S. [from *aldorman*, Sax.] originally it implied a person, who, on account of his years and experience, was proper to preside over the affairs of a nation, and to assist a prince with his council. This term is now applied to the twenty-six persons, who preside over the twenty-six wards of the city of London; out of which the lord mayor is generally chosen by rotation. They are all qualified to act as justices of the peace. But they have not only the management of the civil, but likewise the military government of the city; are officers in its militia, and members of the artillery company. When we consider this better circumstance, and recollect, that the term signified the second order of dignity in the kingdom, and a person invested with rule, we may, though Johnson could not, see a great propriety in using it as, "An *alderman* of wit." *Dryd.*

A'LDERNY, an island in the British channel, separated from the coast of Normandy by a strait, called the Race of Alderny, which is a very dangerous passage, on account of the hidden rocks under it. It is a healthful island, and is fruitful in corn and pasture; but it has but one church. The inhabitants live together in a town of the same name, the island being but eight miles in circumference. Lon. 15. 10. lat. 49. 50.

A'LE, S. [*eala*, *eale*, or *aeleth*, Sax.] a common liquor, made of an infusion of malt and hops in boiling water; then fermented with yeast. It is distinguishable from beer in respect of its having a less quantity of hops and malt than beer has, in proportion to the same quantity of water. This article makes a principal branch of the revenues of the kingdom. It is distinguished into pale ale, which is made of pale malt, and brown ale, which is made of malt higher dried, and somewhat burnt in the kiln. In old dispensaries, we have a great number of medical compositions under the name of ales, which were so called, because their ingredients were steeped or infused in this liquor.

GILL-A'LE, S. [*gill*, Sax. ground-ivy, and *ale*] a liquor of ground-ivy leaves, steeped in ale; esteemed both abstersive and vulnerary, and good in the disorders of the breast, and obstructions in the viscera.

A'LE-CONNER, S. [from *ale* and *con*, of *connan*, Sax.] an officer of the city of London, to inspect the measures of public houses,

brewer. Four of them are chosen annually out of decayed citizens; but their office at present seems rather a fine-cure than a real employment.

A'LEGAR, S. [from *ale* and *eager* or *egar*, Run. four] In the county of Lincoln, the term given to four ale; by Londoners called *ale-vinegar*.

A'LEGER, Adj. [of *alegre*, Ital.] gay, sprightly, brisk, full of vivacity. "Make them strong and *a eger*." *Temple.*

A'LEHOOF, In Botany, the ground-ivy.

A'LE-HOUSE, S. [*ealehuse*, Sax.] a house where ale is sold. "Thee shall each ale-house, thee each gill-house mourn." *Pope's Dunciad.* This term has generally an idea of baseness or meanness affixed to it, "Triumph is become an ale-house guest." *Shakef. Rich. III.*

A'LE-HOUSE-KEEPER, S. one who keeps a house where ale or beer is sold; a publican. "You resemble perfectly the two ale-house-keepers in Holland." *Belinq b.*

ALE'MBEC, S. the upper part or head of a still, into which the vapours ascend.

A-LE'NGTH, Adv. lying at full length; along; stretched out.

ALE'RT, Adj. [*alerte*, Fr.] applied to military affairs, watchful, active, diligent, vigilant. Applied to common occurrences, brisk, pert, sharp, generally including the secondary idea of contempt. "I spy an alert young fellow, that cock'd his hat upon a friend." *Spect.* No. 401.

ALE'RTNESS, S. sprightliness, pertness, activity.

A'LE-TASTER, S. an officer to examine into the goodness and measures of ale and beer, within the jurisdiction of a leet or lordship.

A'LE-WIFE, S. a woman who keeps an ale house. "To beat and butcher an ale-wife." *Swift.* Seldom used, unless by the vulgar.

ALEXA'NDERS, S. [from *Alexandria*] In Botany, the Smyrnium. The flowers are produced in umbels, consisting of leaves placed orbicularly, and expanded in the form of a rose. The empalement becomes fruit almost globular, containing two seeds, sometimes shaded like a crescent, rough, streaked on one side, and plain on the other. These are two species, the first of which is ordered by the physicians for a medicinal use, and grows wild in most parts of England.

ALEXA'NDRINE, S. a kind of verse borrowed from the French, consisting among them of twelve or thirteen syllables in alternate couplets, and among us of twelve. They were formerly much used by our poets to clench their verses, and generally were the last of those ending in the same rhyme; but are now discarded for their want of harmony.

ALEXIPHA'RMIC, Adj. [*alexipharmakos*, Gr.] something that has the virtue of expelling poisons taken internally. Used substantively, it means remedies proper to expel that malignancy with which the animal spirits are affected in acute distempers, through the pores of the skin in the form of a sweat. The most efficacious remedies of this kind owe the virtue of their operation to the power they have of increasing the systole of the heart, and the elasticity of the arteries. This they effect, either by a subtile, acrid oil, an acrid, resinous, or fine mineral salt, and sulphur.

ALEXITE'RIAL, Adj. [from *alexetere*] that which expels poison or the malignant humours attending acute diseases.

ALEXITE'RICAL, or ALEXITE'RIC, Adj. [from *alexetere*] that which has the property of repelling poison or the malignant humours of fevers.

ALFANDI'GA, S. [Port.] the custom-house at Lisbon, where the duties of export and import are paid. We beg leave to observe, that all gold or silver lace, fringe, ribbons, and brocades are seized, because no person in Portugal is suffered to wear any gold or silver on his clothes or furniture in that kingdom. *Pointer.*

ALFORD, a town in Lincolnshire, with a market on Tuesdays for provisions and a little corn, and two fairs, on Whit-Tuesday and November 8, for cattle and sheep. It is seated on a small brook that runs through the town, and is a compact place. It is six miles from the sea, and 20 N. of Boston. Lon. 17. 30. lat. 53. 30.

ALGA'TES, Adv. by all means; on any terms. "For a space he must there algate dwell." *Fairy Queen.*

A'LGETRANE, S. a kind of pitch, found in the bay formed by the Cape of St. Helena on the isle La Plata.

A'LGEBRA, S. [*al* and *gebr*, Arab.] a branch of arithmetic, which takes the quantity sought as if granted; and, by means of quantities given, proceeds by consequence, till the quantity at first only supposed to be known, or some power of it, is found to be equal to some quantity or quantities known, and, consequently, itself known likewise. It is divided into numerical and literal; the numerical is that wherein the quantity sought is expressed by some letter or character, but all the given quantities by numbers. Literal or specious algebra, is that wherein the given or known quantities, as well as the unknown, are represented by letters of the alphabet. This is not like the numerical confined, but serves universally for the investigation of theorems, as well as the solution of problems either geometrical or arithmetical. The origin of this art is generally attributed to Diophantus.

ALGEBRA'IC,

ALGEBRA'IC, or ALGEBRA'ICAL, Adj. belonging to algebra.

ALGEBRA'IST, S. one acquainted with the operations of algebra. "No algebraist, or cipherer, can use more fubtile fuppofitions." *Grauut.*

A'LGENEL, S. In Aftronomy, a fixed ftar of the fecond magnitude, named Perfeus, on the left fide of the conftellation. Long. 27 deg. 46 min. 4 fec. of Taurus, and lat. 30 deg. 5 min. 20 fec. N.

A'LGEROTH, S. in Medicine, a preparation of antimony and fublimate, called *Mercurius Vitæ*, or Mercury of Life.

A'LGID, Adj. [*algidus*, Lat.] cold; chill. Want authority.

ALGI'DITY, A'LGIDNESS, S. that quality which renders a thing cold.

ALGI'FIC, Adj. [from *algidus*, Lat.] that which produces cold.

AUGOL, S. in Aftronomy, Medufa's head, a fixed ftar of the third magnitude in Perfeus. Long. 21 deg. 30 min. 41 fec. of Taurus. Lat. 22 deg. 23 min. 47 fec. N.

A'LIAS, Adv. [Lat.] otherwife; alfo; ufed to fpecify the different names by which a perfon has gone; as "Lowndes, *alias* Chapman, *alias* Lee."

ALIBA'NICS, S. a kind of cotton cloth, imported into Holland from the Eaft-Indies.

ALICO'NDE, B a tree in Lower Æthiopia, whofe fruit refembles the cocoa, but is not fit to eat. By beating the bark, they procure a kind of flax, which being fpun, will make a cloth very little inferior to that of hemp to the fight.

A'LIBLE, Adj. [*alibilis*, Lat.] that which nourifheth; or that may be nourifhed.

A'LIEN, Adj. [*aliénus*, Lat.] not of the fame kind. "Of *alien* trees." *Dryd.* Inconfiftent with; ufed with the particle *from.* "Not *alien* from their profeffion." *Boyle.* Eftranged from; at enmity with. "*Alien* from God and goodnefs." *Rogers.*

A'LIEN, S. [*aliénus*, Lat.] averfe to, or at enmity with. A foreigner, or one of another country, in oppofition to a citizen. "If it be proved againft an *alien.*" *March. of Venice.* Not of the fame profeffion, part, or fect. "Them only he holdeth for *aliens* and ftrangers." *Hooker.* In law, one born in a ftrange country, nor within the allegiance of the king, and is ufed in oppofition to a denizen, or natural fubject. One born out of the land, but within the limits of the king's obedience is no *alien*; thus thofe who are born in the Englifh plantations, are fubjects born, and likewife the children of aliens begotten and born here. A devife of lands by will to one that is an *alien* is void. See *Stat.* 23 Ed. III.

To A'LIEN, V. A. [*aliéner*, Fr.] to affign or transfer our property to another. "If the fon *now* thofe lands." To grow

averfe to, or diflike; ufed with the particle *from.* "The prince was totally *aliénated from* all thoughts." *Clarendon.*

A'LIENABLE, Adj. that which may be affigned or transferred to another.

To A'LIENATE, V. A. [from *aliénatum*] to transfer a thing to another. To become averfe to a thing. "If once their affections begin to be *aliénated.*" *Hooker.*

A'LIENATE, Adj. [*aliénatus*, Lat.] averfe to, or enemies to, ufed with the particle *from.* "Wholly *aliénate from* truth." *Tillof.*

ALIENA'TION, S. [*aliénatio*, Lat.] the act of affigning, transferring property. "Excluding all innovation and *aliénation* thereof unto ftrangers." *Spencer.* The ftate of *aliénation*; ufed with the particle *from.* Change of affection, from approbation to diflike. "The *aliénation* of his heart from the king." *Bac. Hen. VII.* Applied particularly to the mind, madnefs, want, or lofs of reafon. "*Aliénation* of mind." *Hooker.* Seldom ufed in its laft fenfe at prefent.

ALI'GEROUS, Adj. [*aliger*, Lat.] having wings.

To ALI'GHT, V. N. [from *alihtan*, Sax.] to defcend to a lower fituation. To get off an horfe. To fall upon from a higher place. "On our batter'd arms *alight.*" *Dryd.*

ALI'KE, Adv. equally. "All Reafons, and their change, all *pleafe alike.*" *Par. Loft.* Both, having difference or a diftinction. "Which claims *alike* the monarch and the flave." *Dryd.* Refembling. "*Alike* in place —But differing far in figure." *Pope.*

A'LIMENT, S. [*alimentum*, Lat. from *alo*, to nourifh] food, or that which fatisfies the calls of hunger. "By *aliment*, I underftand every thing which a human creature takes in common diet." *Arbuth.*

ALIME'NTAL, Adj. that which increafes the dimenfions of plants or animals, by being taken in food; that which nourifhes; or feeds. "Thefe weeds muft loofe their *alimental* fap." *Brown.*

ALIME'NTARINESS, S. the quality of affording nourifhment.

ALIME'NTARY, Adj. that which relates to aliment; that which nourifhes, or is eaten for diet. "Of *alimentary* roots fome are pulpy and very nutritious." *Arbuth.* "A vehicle to the *alimentary* particles." *Ray.* Alimentary powder, an invention of Mr. Boued, furgeon-major of a regiment in France. It is infipid to the tafte, but not difagreeable; and is fuppofed to be Turkey corn roafted, ground to powder, and mixed with a fmall quantity of fea falt, as fome chryftals of it have been difcovered; it does not appear to be compounded upon any animal fubftance; when prepared with hot water it makes a panada of the colour of gingerbread, fmells like toafted bread, and part-

ly like cummin feed; when prepared with cold water, it becomes four in a fhort time. An experiment of its virtues was firſt made on three ſoldiers at Lille, and afterwards on fix penſioners at the royal hoſpital of Invalids at Paris; fix ounces in ſomething leſs than a pint of water, were found ſufficient to ſuſtain any man a day, without eating or drinking any thing elſe. Though the fix Invalids had no more than this quantity per diem, or each day, for 15 days in October, 1754, yet they all continued hearty and well, though one of them was upwards of ſeventy, and the others young men. Aſimentary duct, in anatomy, according to Dr. Tyſon and others, that part of the body through which the food paffes, from its reception into the mouth, to its exit at the anus. Likewiſe in a more confined ſenſe, the ſame as the thoracic duct. See Ductus Alimentarius.

ALIMENTA'TION, S. the quality of affording nouriſhment.

ALIMO'NIOUS, Adj. [alimonia, Lat.] nouriſhing. "Digeſting the alimonious humours into fleſh." Harvey. Seldom uſed.

A'LIMONY, S. [from alimonia, Lat.] nouriſhment; but now generally appropriated to the law, wherein it implies that allowance which a married woman ſues for, upon any occaſional ſeparation, providing it be not for elopement or adultery; this was formerly recoverable only in the Spiritual Court, but may be ſued for now in Chancery; though indeed the former is moſt proper. 1 Inſt. 235. 11 Rep. 30.

A'LIPOW-MONTIS CETI, S. in Botany, a kind of white turberh, a very ſtrong purgative; which is found particularly near Cette, and from thence derives its name. Sometimes it is uſed inſtead of Sena, but as it is a much ſtronger purge, may be dangerous.

A'LIQUANT, Adj. [aliquantum, Lat.] in arithmetic, is that part of a number which will not divide it, without having a remainder. Or that which, being taken any number of times, will always be greater or leſs, than that of which it is an aliquant part.

A'LIQUOT, Adj. [aliquot, Lat.] in arithmetic or geometry, is ſuch a part of any quantity or number, as will exactly divide it without any thing remaining over. Thus 4 is the aliquot part of 8; 3 of 10; and 6 of 12. To find the aliquot parts of any number, divide the given number by its leaſt diviſor, and the quotient by its laſt diviſor, till you find a quotient no longer diviſible. Thus to find the aliquot parts of 60, divide that number by 2, its leaſt diviſor, and the quotient being 30, divide again by 2, which will be 15; this you are to divide by 3, and the next quotient will be 5; and as that is no longer diviſible without a

remainder, you have got the following parts 1, 2, 3, 4, 5, which are the aliquot parts of 60.

A'LISH, Adj. that which reſembles ale.

ALI'VE, Adj. [from a and live, of lifian, or leoſan, Sax.] having all the powers of action belonging to a living animal; a ſtate wherein the ſoul remains with the body, oppoſed to death. "Noah only remained alive." Gen. vii. 23. Chearful, ſprightly, gay, briſk, and full of ſpirits. Without diminution, or leſſening either with reſpect to power or activity. "The good affection of ſuch as inclined toward them might be kept alive." Hooker. In a popular ſenſe, it carries the force of a ſuperlative adjective, and adds a great and extraordinary emphaſis to the ſentence. "The proudeſt man alive." Clarend. This ſeems borrowed from the French de monde. In ſcripture language it implies a ſtate of religious purity, and vital union with the Deity, in oppoſition to wickedneſs, which is termed death. "Alive to God through Chriſt our Lord." Rom. vi. 11.

ALKALE'SCENT, Part. reſembling the qualities of an alkali.

A'LKALI, S. in medicine, by ſome writers defined to be that which will cauſe an efferveſcence when mingled with an acid; but Boerhaave ſhews, that too great a dependance on it may be productive of dangerous conſequences. See Alkali.

ALKALI'NE, Adj. having the qualities of alkali. "By diſſolving the fluids and keeping them from this alkaline ſtate." Arbuth.

To ALKA'LIZATE, V. A. [from alkali] to render alkaline by chemical proceſs; or to draw out the latent alkaline virtues of any thing.

ALKA'LIZATE, Adj. having the powers and qualities of a body which is drained of an alkali. "Other alkalizate ſalts." Boyle.

ALKALIZA'TION, S. in Chemiſtry, the act of mingling a fluid with an alkaline ſalt, to make it a better diſſolvent.

A'LKANET, S. [from alcanna and alkermes, Arab.] in botany, the Anchuſa, a plant of the Bugloſs kind, brought from the ſouth of France.

ALKEKE'NGE, S. in Medicine, a fruit or berry from a tree of the ſame name, the leaves of which are acid and bitter. The berries have a penetrating juice reſembling wine, or rather the juice of citrons; and is, on that account, recommended as a diuretic in burning fevers. Boerhaave ſays, that half an ounce of them bruiſed, and taken like tea or coffee, with ſugar, cleanſes the reins, corrects grumous blood, and is of ſervice in the yellow jaundice, ſtone, ſtrangury, gout, and dropſy.

A'LL,

A'LL, Adv. [See ALL, Adj.] entirely, wholly. "All ainan'd the priest let fall the book." Shakesp. Exclusive of any other. In antient writers, or those contemporary with Spenser, it is fignified, whilst, or just. "All as his straying flock he fed." Spens. Past.

A'LL, Adj. [al, æl, ealle, all, Sax.] The whole, or every one of the parts. "We are all one man's fons." Gen. xlii. 2. Every parcel, or every particle. "Take away dung till it be all gone." 1 Kings xiv. 10. Applied to time, the whole fpace or interval. "The God which fed me all my life long." Gen. xlviii 15. The whole extent. "There is none like him in all the earth." Exod. ix. 14. The major part. "For all feek their own, not the things which are Jesus Chrift's." Philip. ii. 21.

A'LL, S. the whole. "She cast in all, even all that fhe had." Mark xii. 44. This word is much ufed in compofition, and is borrowed from the Saxon æl, or alls, Goth. which are fo ufed, and imply excellence, fullnefs, perfection, or that which is in no refpect defective, as almighty, or almigty, that which is indued with perfect power, with fullnefs of power, or a power which is free from defect, and all-accomplifhed, among moderns, perfectly qualified.

A'LL-BEA'RING, Part. perfectly fruitful; producing all things.

A'LL-CHEA'RING, Part. imparting comfort to all; that which poffeffes the power of communicating mirth, gaiety, or fatisfaction to every one. "The all-chearing fun." Rom. and Julet.

A'LL-COMMA'NDING, Part. that which over-rules all; that which governs all. "The all-commanding image of bright gold." Raleigh.

A'LL-COMPOSING, Part. that has a power of compofing anxiety, or difturbance.

ALLANTO'IS, or ALLANTOEI'DES, S. [from ἀλλᾶς, Gr.] a thin membrane invefting the fœtus. It is probably the fame as that in animals, and ferves to convey the urine from the bladder, by the urachus, to the cavity formed by the amnios, till the time of delivery.

To ALLA'Y, V. A. [alloyer, Fr.] to mix one metul with another. In this fenfe fome fpell it allay, keeping more clofely to the French, from whence it is borrowed. To abate, or leffen. To quiet, pacify, or reduce to a calm. "If by your art you have put the wild waters in this roar, allay them." Shakesp. In this fenfe the word feems derived from a and lay, Sax. to reprefs, controul, or fubdue any violence.

ALLA'Y, or ALLO'Y, S. [allay, Fr.] a mixture of divers metals, or of divers parcels, of the fame metal of different fuenefs.

Minters never ftrike any gold or filver without alloy; brafs coin is made of an alloy of copper; jewellers, wire-drawers, and goldbeaters, are obliged to ufe an alloy in the gold they work; the brafs founders have their alloy of copper; the pewterers of red copper, regulus, antimony, &c. In England, the ftandard of gold coin is 22 carats of fine gold, and 2 carats of alloy in the lb. troy; the French and Spanifh are nearly the fame; the lb. weight is cut into fortyfour pieces and a half, each current for twenty-one fhillings. The ftandard filver is 11 oz. 2 dwts. and 18 dwts. of alloy of copper. The alloy in gold, being filver and copper, and in filver, copper alone. Alloy is ufed in a fecondary fenfe for fomething which leffens the properties of the thing with which it is mixed. "Dark colours eafily fuffer a fenfible alloy, by little feattering light." Newt. Optics. That which depreciates, or renders bafe, by diminution or leffening, in allufion to the mixing bafer metals with thofe of greater value, in order to alloy them. "The joy has no alloy of jealoufy." Rofcom.

ALLA'YER, S. the perfon or thing which is endued with a power of allaying, leffening, debafing, corrupting, or diminifhing. "Phlegm and pure blood are reputed allayers of acrimony." Harvey.

ALLA'YMENT, S. a diminifhing, or leffening. "The like allayment would I give my grief." Shak. Troil. and Cref.

ALL-CONQUERING, Part. having power to fubdue every thing.

ALL-DEVOU'RING, Part. that which devours or deftroys every thing.

ALLEGATION, S. [allego, Lat.] an affirmation; declaration, including the idea of fomething criminal. "To fwear falfe allegations." Shakesp. Hen. VI. An excufe pleaded in behalf or vindication of fome crime or fault. "Want of leifure, or any other idle allegation." Pope.

To ALLE'GE, V. A. [allego] to declare, affert, or affirm; to plead as an excufe. "If we forfake the ways of grace and goodnefs, we cannot allege any colour of ignorance, or want of inftruction." Sprat.

ALLEGEABLE, Adj. that may be charged, ufed with againft. "All that is allegeable againft X." Brown's Vulg. Err. Any thing that may be pleaded, followed by the words in and behalf. "There are many things allegeable in his behalf."

ALLE'GER, S. one that afferts any thing. "If we may believe it as confidently as the famous alleger of it." Boyle.

ALLE'GIANCE, S. [allegiance, Fr.] in Law, that natural, fworn, or legal obedience every fubject owes to his prince, and is an incident infeparable. "I did pluck allegiance from men's hearts." Shak. Hen. IV. Oath of allegiance is taken to the king, in quality

K 2

quality of a temporal prince, and is diffin-
guifhed from that of fupremacy, which is
taken to him as fupreme head of the church.

ALLE'GIANT, S. loyal; or confident
with that obedience a fubject owes his prince.
" Can nothing render but *allegiant* thanks."
Shak. Hen. VIII.

ALLEGO'RIC, Adj. fomething to be underftood figuratively, not literally. " What
kingdom – Real or *allegorick* I difcern not."
Par. Loft.

ALLEGO'RICAL, Adj. figurative, where
fomething elfe is meant, than what is expreffed; myftical; not literal. " Our Saviour faid, in an *allegorical* and myftical fenfe,
Except ye eat the flefh of the fon of man."
Bentley.

ALLEGO'RICALLY, Adv. figuratively,
not literally; after the manner of a compofition, formed entirely of figurative expreffions. " This place is to be underftood alle-
gorically." *Pope.*

ALLEGO'RICALNESS, S. of the quality
of concealing the fenfe under an allegory, or
continuation of rhetorical figures.

To ALLEGO'RIZE, V. A. to turn into
an allegory; to turn into an allegorical, or
myftical fenfe, oppofed to literal. " He
hath very wittily *allegorized* this tree."
Bad ipfe.

ALLEGORY, S. [αλληγορια., Gr.] a
figurative fpeech. Thus the Roman commonwealth is addreffed by Horace under the
picture of a fhip; our bleffed Lord calls himfelf the vine, and his difciples the branches;
and himfelf the good fhepherd, and his followers the fheep. This method of inftruction was peculiarly adopted by the eaftern
nations; and, if we pleafe, we may fay
that it did not want admirers in all, as the
fables of Æfop, the Ilias and Odyffes of
Homer, and the Eneis of Virgil, may be included under this fpecies of writing.

ALLE'GRO, S. in Mufic, one of the fix
diftinctions of time, expreffing the quickeft
motion, excepting prefto. If it be preceded
by *piu*, it muft be played in a flower or
graver manner than when *allegro* ftands
alone; if by *fia*, it muft then be fafteft of
all. To render this article a little plainer,
it will not be improper to add, that the
fix divifions of time are, grave, adagio,
largo, vivace, allegro, prefto.

ALLELU'JAH, S. [a corrupt fpelling,
inftead of *hallelujah*, of הללויה Heb. and
הלל a word, which, on account of its peculiar energy, is generally untranflated;
but fignifies, Praife ye the Lord. " A proper
preludium to thofe allelujahs he hopes eternally to fing." *Government of the Tongue.*
In Botany, the wood-forrel.

ALLEMA'NDA, or ALLEMAND, S.
[Ital.] in Mufic, a grave air, compofed in
common time, confifting of two parts, or
ftrains, each of which muft be played twice

over, in a grave manner, but at the fame
time wifh fo much fprightlinefs as to be diverting; Corelli feemed to have been peculiarly happy in this ftyle, and has given
abundance of fine examples of it in his compofition.

ALLE'RIONS, S. [Fr.] in heraldry,
eaglets, reprefented fpread, without beaks
or feet.

To ALLE'VIATE, V. A. [allevo, Lat.]
to lighten. In allufion to the diminifhing the
preffure of a heavy load. " Excellent remedies to *alleviate* thofe evils." *Bentley.* To
leffen, mitigate, or diminifh. " He *alleviates* his fault by an excufe."

A'LLEY, S. [allée, Fr.] in Gardening,
a ftrait walk, bounded on each fide with
trees or fhrubs. " All within were trees,
and *alleys* wide." *Fairy Q.* Counter-Alleys,
are fmall alleys by the fides of great ones.
A *Front-Alley*, is that which runs oppofite
to the front or face of a building. A
Tranfverfe Alley, is that which croffes the
former. A *Diagonal Alley*, is that which
cuts a fquare or parterre, from angle to
angle. A *Sloping Alley*, is that which is
neither parallel in point of fight, or level to
the ground of the front or tranfverfe alleys.
Alley in zig-zag, is that which, on account of
its defcent, has plat bands of turf to hinder
the gravel from being wafhed away. This
name is likewife applied to the path in a Labyrinth, which has a great many turnings and
windings, in order to conceal the place of
exit. The word is in towns applied to narrow paffages, to diftinguifh them from
ftreets. *Alley in Perfpective,* is that which is
larger at the entrance, than at the oppofite
extremity; in order to make it feem long.
Alley of Comparterent, is that which feparates
the fquares of a parterre.

ALL-FOURS, S. in Gaming, a well-
known play, wherein the whole a perfon
gains each deal, is limited to four, which
are the higheft, loweft, the knave of trumps,
and the game, or the greateft number to be
made from tens, and court cards; the latter
of which are reckoned four for on fee, three
for a king, two for a queen, and one for the
knave; and he who has every one of thofe
particulars, is faid to be *all-fours.*

ALL-HA'IL, Interj. a falutation or invo-
cation in acknowledgement of benefits.

ALL-HEAL, S. in Botany, a fpecies of
iron wort, deemed to be a very great vulnerary.

ALLI'ANCE, S. [alliance, Fr.] the union
of perfons or families by marriage. " A
bloody hymen fhall th' *alliance* join." *Shak.
Hen. VI.* In a political fenfe, the leagues
or treaties between different ftates; or the
ftate of kingdoms which are fo connected.
" Point out new *alliances* to Cato." *Addif.
Cato.*

ALLI,

ALLI'CIENCY, S. [from *allicio*, Lat.] the quality of drawing to; attraction. "The feigned central *alliciency*." *Glanv. Scep. Scient.*

To A'LLIGATE, V. A. to join or bind one thing to another; to unite.

ALLIGA'TION, S. the act of joining, uniting, or the ftate of things united, or joined together. In Arithmetic, the rule, wherein queftions are refolved relating to the mixtures of different commodities, with their value, effects, &c. when fo compounded. It is divided into mediate or alternate. Mediate is that which difcovers the mean rate of any limited quantity of a mixture, from the feveral quantities and prices of divers fimples given. *Alligation alternate*, difcovers what quantity of various fimples may be taken, to make up any affigned quantity of a mixture, worth a price propofed.

ALLI'SION, S. [*allifum* fupine of *allido*, Lat.] the action of beating or ftriking againft. "Severed from it by the boifterous *allifion* of the fea." *Woodw.*

ALL-JU'DGING, Part. that exercifes judgment without controul, or partiality.

A'LL-KNOWING, Part. one intimately acquainted with every thing that is the object of knowledge; or whofe knowledge is perfect.

A'LLIOTH, S. in Aftronomy, a ftar, in the tail of the great Bear, very ufeful in obfervations at fea.

ALLOCA'TION, S. [*alloco*, Lat.] the putting one thing to another. In Commerce, the allowance of an article to an account, and the puffing it as fuch. In the Exchequer -It is an allowance made upon an account; hence *allocatione facienda*, is a writ directed to the lord treafurer and barons of the Exchequer, on the complaint of fome accountant, ordering him to be allowed fuch fums as he has lawfully expended in the execution of his office.

ALLO'DIAL, Adj. [*allodium*, Lat.] in Law, that of which a perfon has an abfolute property, oppofed to feudal.

ALLO'DIUM, S. [derived, as all the words of feudal law muft be, from the language of the Germans, who were its founders, all, which in compofition fignifies perfection, and *lefne*, Teut. free, i. e. entirely free) a poffeffion which a man holds in his own right, without any dependance, charge, or homage to a fuperior lord. But as every perfon in England is obliged, either to do fervice, pay acknowledgement, or perform homage to the fupreme magiftrate, *nulla terra fine domino*, or there is no land without a lord, is a maxim in law.

ALLO'NGE, S. [*allonger*, Fr.] It is pronounced as of two words, and fpelt with an *n*, as *alonge*) in Fencing, a pafs, or pufh.

To ALLOO', V. A. [pronounced *halloo*, of *haller*, &c.] Teut. to fet a dog on, fo as to feize one of his own, or any other fpecies.

To ALLO'T, V. A. to diftribute; to affign a fhare; to grant. "Too fcrupulous in *allotting* them their due portion." *Tatler*, No. 91.

ALLO'TMENT, S. the parcel, fhare, lot, or part affigned to any one. "The *allotments* of God." *L'Eftrange.*

ALLO'TERY, S. that which is granted, or affigned on a divifion, diftribution, or lot. "The poor *allotery* my father left me." *Shak.*

To ALLO'W, V. N. [*allouer*, Fr.] to confefs, to yield, admit, grant, or affent to. "The pow'r of mufic all our hearts *allow*." *Pope.* To yield, fuffer, or permit. "Ready to *allow* the pope as little power here, as you pleafe." *Swift.* To confer an honour on a perfon, ufed with the particle *of*, and including the fecondary idea of condefcenfion in the perfon granting. "*Allowed of* God, to be put in truft with the Gofpel." *1 Theff.* 2. 4. To approve as juft, or confiftent with one's duty. "That which I do, I *allow* not." *Rom.* vii. 15. To give, to beftow, to pay as a debt. To give as a portion, or fhare; to grant without any obligation. "He *allowed* his fon the third part of his income." *John. Diff.* To make a conceffion, abatement, or to reftrain with a provifo, or caution. "*Allowing* ftill for the difference." *Addif.x.*

ALLO'WABLE, Adj. that may be granted, or permitted. "Freedom *allowable* among friends." *Boyle.* Without an error, or contradiction. "It is not *allowable*, what is obfervable in many pieces of Raphael." *Brown's Vulg. Err.* "That which ought to be fuffered. "Their purfuit of it, is not only *allowable*, but laudable." *Atterbury's Serm.*

ALLO'WABLENESS, S. the quality of a thing lawful, proper, and confiftent with the rules of reafon, law, and religion. "Their nature, ufe, and *allowablenefs* in matters of recreation." *Smith.*

ALLO'WANCE, S. the granting affent to any doctrine, opinion, or principle. "Without the notion and *allowance* of fpirits, our philofophy will be lame." *Locke.* Permiffion, licence, leave or confent. "Without the ftate's *allowance*." *Shak.* Liberty without reftraint. A fhare, portion, or divifion, granted, or fettled, applied to penfions, money, diet, circumftances, or the difpenfations of Providence. "Feed me with food of my *allowance*." *Prov.* xxx. 8. "Be content with your *allowance*." *Luke* III. 14. Conceffion, oppofed to rigour, or feverity. Reputation, fettled by univerfal confent. "Of very expert and approved *allowance*." *Shak. Othello.* In Commerce, thofe deductions granted at the Cuftom-houfe to goods rated by weight, and by dry, or liquid meafure,

fure. The deduction on goods rated by weight, are draught, which is made for each weight or scale; and tare, which is granted for casks, bags, and other packages. The allowance on goods rated by dry measure, is a number of ells on each piece or pack of foreign linens; goods rated by liquid measure, if entered, filled, and no more than seven or nine inches left in the pipe or hogshead, they are deemed outs, and no subsidy is paid; if more remains, the duty is only paid for the net wine contained in the cask, and an allowance made out of the duties for leakage: if entered unfilled, duty is paid for the full contents of the cask, and twelve per cent. allowed out of the duties for leakage. This last entrance generally turns out to the merchant's loss; but, in general, if any cask wants more than a tenth of being full, it is for his advantage to enter them filled, otherwise unfilled.

ALLOWED, Part. universally acknowledged, admitted, or established with respect to character.

ALLOY, S. (See ALLAY) baser metal, mixt with that of greater value; made use of to give the metal it is mixed with, a greater hardness. An abatement or lessening.

ALL-POWERFUL, Adj. a power capable of producing every thing that is consistent with infinite wisdom.

ALL-SAINTS-DAY, S. the day set apart by the church, to commemorate the exemplary lives and noble fortitude of all the saints and martyrs; added as a supplementary day to the rest of the festivals, that the human mind might be more strongly incited to exemplary piety, or pious martyrdoms; by considering the number of those which have preceded in those shining paths. The collect, epistle, and gospel, which the church of England uses on this occasion, seem extremely well adapted to this great end, and give us no small idea of the great abilities of the composers of its liturgy.

ALL-SEER, S. he that is present every where; he that sees every thing.

ALL-SEEING, Part. capable of seeing every thing; omniscient.

ALL-SOULS-DAY, S. a festival observed by papists, on the 2d of November, with a particular service relating to the souls in purgatory.

ALL-SUFFICIENT, Part. capable of doing every thing; absolutely perfect in himself. "He is every way perfect, and all-sufficient." Norris. Perfectly adapted to; applied to evidence, capable of producing confirmation, or conviction. "The testimonies of God are all-sufficient unto that end for which they were designed." Hooker.

ALLUBESCENCY, S. [allubescentia, Lat.] propensity, or willingness.

To ALLUDE, V. A. [alludo, Lat.] to have a distant hint, or allusion to a thing, without mentioning it. Used with the particles to and unto. "That artificial structure here alluded to." Burn. Theo.

ALLUM, S. [alumen, Lat. alun, Teut.] a fossil salt, or white mineral, separated from earth by washing it with water, which being impregnated with its salts, is after boiled and evaporated. There are three principal salts of this mineral, namely, that of Rome, or Civita Vecchia, that of England, called rock allum, white allum, or ice allum, and that of Liege and Mesiers; besides that which comes from the Levant. The allum of Civita Vecchia, is made of stones which are whitish, greyish, or blue, and are generally found under a plant called agrifolios. These are first baked or calcined by fire, after which, they are slacked, by flinging water on them, in the same manner as lime; after this, being placed in coppers filled with water, they are boiled over a very fierce fire, and skim'd of all the faeces which rise to the surface; this is poured into square wooden frames, of the form of a pyramid inverted, with a hole at the bottom, which is stopped. In these vessels the lye is left to settle for ten or twelve days, during which time, the salts shoot into chrystals; they then let out the water, wash the salts, and, having let them dry for two or three days, carry them into their warehouses. Italy produces the greatest quantity, and the best allum of any country. That of Rome or Civita Vecchia is reddish, because the earth from whence it is taken, is of that colour. In order to choose the best, take that which has but little dull, and is reddish both within and without, which may he knows only by breaking it; because the English, or that of Liege, is sometimes coloured, in order to pass for it. The allum of England, is in great pieces or lumps, clear and transparent like chrystal. It is made of a stone of a bluish colour, found in Yorkshire, urine, and sea-weed. The stone goes through the same process, as above described. After which, they pour in the lees of kelp; and, having drawn it into a settler or cooler, add urine to it; after the allum is washed or cleansed with water, as in the first process, mentioned above, it is put into a pan, where it boils a little; and then put into a large cask, where it stands for ten days, and is then fit for sale. The allum of Liege, or Mesiers, is of the same nature as the English, excepting that it is somewhat fatter. Allum of the Levant differs but little from those already mentioned. The large is the best, and the mine lies about three or four days journey from Smyrna. There is another sort brought from Constantinople, which is reckoned preferable

ſetable to it. Conſidered in a medical light, it is a ſtrong aſtringent, acid drier; its chryſtals have eight ſides, and when diſſolved, will coagulate milk. But its chief uſe is in dying, and colouring, as it renders the colours clear, bright, and laſting; and it not only fixes the colour in ſtuffs, but diſpoſes them to take, and adds life and delicacy to it. Thoſe who uſe the greateſt quantities of it are the cod-fiſhers, when they cure their fiſh upon the ſpot, before they ſhip them off. When judiciouſly applied, it is very proper to clarify liquors, that are foul, or muddy. Beſides the different ſorts of alum already mentioned, are the following: Burnt Alum, which is the Engliſh alum put over a fire in an iron veſſel to calcine, and render it whiter, lighter, and eaſier to powder; this is made uſe of by ſurgeons to eat off the fungous parts, or proud fleſh in wounds, and is ſucceſsfully ſprinkled on linen to abſorb the moiſtures which occaſion bad ſmells. The Saccharine Alum, derives its name from reſembling ſugar, and is made of ice-alum, roſe-water, and whites of eggs, boiled together to a conſiſtence. When cold, it becomes as hard as a ſtone, and is uſed in making paint for the ladies. Plume Alum, is a mineral ſtone, differing in nothing from the common alum, but from its parting into threads, reſembling the beard of a father, from whence it derives its name; theſe threads ſhine like ſilver, and are an inch and half, or two inches long. It comes from Milo, at the entrance of the Archipelago, and is very ſcarce. The Scaynale Alum, is a white tranſparent ſtone, reſembling rock chryſtal, which being calcined, grows white. Cariu Alum, is the ſame as ſalt of ſolder, called Sal Akali, of which there are five ſorts, moſtly uſed in medicine.

ALLU'MINOUS, Adj. [aluminus, Lat.] having the properties of alum.

ALLU'MY, Adj. [from allum] that which partakes of the qualities of allum. Bailey. Wants authority. See ALLUMINOUS.

To ALLU'MINATE, [allumer, Fr. allumo, Lat.] to give grace or light; to embelliſh in painting; to waſh prints with allum water, to keep the colours from ſinking or running. Bailey. In the firſt ſenſe it ſeems ſubſtituted for illuminate, by a miſtake of the author quoted; in the ſecond, it is very proper, but wants authority.

To ALLU'RE, [leurer, Fr.] to entice, attract, perſuade, or draw. To charm, or affect the mind with a ſenſation of joy or pleaſure.

ALLU'RE, S. [lodor, Belg.] an artificial bird, made uſe of by bird-catchers, to entice birds into their traps. Any thing that entices, or allures. In Commerce, a ſmall braſs coin, ſtruck in Sweden, worth four French ſols, or about two-pence farthing Engliſh.

ALLU'REMENT, S. temptation; enticement. "Adam, by his wife's allurement, fell." Par. Reg.

ALLU'RER, S. one who tempts, ſeduces, entices or inveigles.

ALLU'RINGLY, Adv. ſo as to entice, tempt, inveigle, invite or ſeduce.

ALLU'RINGNESS, S. a quality, whoſe charms engage the mind, as to engage in any action, good or bad.

ALLU'SION, S. [from ad ludere] ſomething ſaid with reference to a thing already known. A reference; hint, or implication. "Alluſions to cuſtoms not known." Burnet's Theory. In this ſenſe it is uſed with the particle to. In Rhetoric, a figure in which one word is ſubſtituted inſtead of another, on account of its reſembling it in ſound. Thus the emperor Tiberius Nero, from the fondneſs of drinking, was called Biberius, Mero, both which in Latin imply a Great Drinker. This is a very low ſpecies of wit, and has ſome reſemblance to a pun.

ALLU'SIVE, Adj. [from allufum] that comprehends a thing by implication; that which hints at ſomething, figurative, not plain. "The expreſſion in the other is figurative, or allufive." Rogers.

ALLU'SIVELY, Adv. in a manner wherein a reference is made to ſomething not expreſſed, but implied; figuratively, in oppoſition to plain or expreſs. "Thoſe eagles." Mat. xxiv. 28. by which allufively are noted the Roman armies, whoſe enſign was the eagle." Hammond.

ALLU'SIVENESS, S. the quality of expreſſing by implication, or by reference, oppoſed to directly, or plainly.

ALLU'VION, S. [alluvio, Lat.] a flowing, or ſwelling of waters near any lands. In Law, a ſmall and almoſt imperceptible Increaſe of waters made on lands lying near ſhore, or on the banks of large rivers.

A'LL-WISE, Adj. is endued with abſolute, perfect, or infinite wiſdom.

To ALL'Y, V. A. [from allier, Fr.] to join, or unite by kindred, friendſhip, or intereſt. "All theſe ſteps are allied to the inhabitants of the North." Spencer on Ireland. "Wants, frailties, paſſions, cloſer ſtill ally—The common intereſt." Pope. To reſemble, or be like, and in all theſe ſenſes uſed with the particle to. "They are indeed remotely allied to Virgil's ſenſe." Dryd.

ALL'Y, S. [allie, Fr.] one who is connected with another, owing to ſome contract; and is applied both to perſons and kingdoms. One united to another by friendſhip. "As an inferior and dependant ally." Temple.

ALMACA'NTAR, [from almacantar, Arab.] in Aſtronomy, a circle drawn parallel to the horizon. It is chiefly uſed in the plural, and ſignifies a ſeries of parallel circles drawn through the ſeveral degrees of the meridian.

A'LMA-

A'LMANACK, S. [from *almanach*, Fr.] a table or calendar wherein the days of the week, fasts, festivals, changes of the moon, eclipses, &c. are noted for the insuing year. The Almanack-makers formerly pretending to predict future events by the stars, Henr. III. of France made an edict in 1579, "That none of that tribe should for the future presume to publish predictions relating to the affairs of the state, or of private persons, in terms either express or covert." Several ingenious gentlemen have favoured us with perpetual Almanacks; or such as were not calculated for one, but a series of years; one of which may be seen in the Introduction to business, published by Hudson, an ingenious schoolmaster.

ALMA'NDIN, or ALMAND'INE, [*almandine*, Ital.] a precious stone, resembling the ruby, but fouler and lighter than the oriental. It is said by Pliny to come from Alabanda, a city of Caria, and is on that account called *Alabandin*.

ALMIG'HTINESS, S. an attribute of the Deity, wherein he is considered as able to perform every thing that is the object of power and wisdom; omnipotence. "The unicorn and elk live upon his provisions, and revere his power, and feel the force of his *almightiness*." *Taylor's Holy Living*.

ALMI'GHTY, Adj. possessed of perfect, absolute, or unlimited power; that which can do every thing that infinite wisdom can dictate, or infinite power can execute.

A'LMOND, S. [*amande*, Fr. *amandola*, Ital.] a fruit contained in a stone full of little cells, inclosed in a tough skin. They are divided into sweet and bitter, on account of their different tastes. The sweet are deemed nourishing; but must not be eat in too large quantities. The milky juice squeezed from them, when steeped in warm water and peeled, is good for consumptive and pleuritic persons. The oil which is drawn from them by expression is of great service in affections of the lungs, such as coughs, shortness of breath, sureness of the stomach, pleuritic pains, the stone, gravel, and all diseases of the kidnies and bladder, on account of its lubricating and softening the parts. There is an oil drawn from the bitter almonds by fire, which it is fit for no other use but to burn, or to be dropped into the ear to cure deafness. The almonds themselves are chiefly used for a cosmetic, and are esteemed a great beautifier. In the East Indies they serve instead of small money, especially where the cowries, or small shells, which come from Maldivia are not current. This fruit is so bitter that it is impossible to eat it.

AL'MONER, or ALM'NER, S. [*aumonier*, Fr.] one employed by a prince to distribute his alms.

A'LMONRY, S. the place, wherein the almoner distributes the alms to the poor.

ALMO'ST, Adv. [*al mest*, Belg.] applied to action, near doing it. "They be almost ready to stone me." *Exod.* xvii. 4. A considerable majority, nearly the whole. "Came almost the whole city together." *Acts* xiii. 44. Applied to time, very near the period mentioned.

ALMS, S. [never used but in the plural, of *alms* or *almess*, Sax.] money or other things given to the poor and distressed, including in it an idea of a tender sympathy in their afflictions.

A'LMS-BASKET, S. a basket carried about, in France and other foreign countries, to collect provisions, &c. alms for the convent. "The beggar's song that lived upon the *alms-basket*." *L'Est. Fables*.

A'LMS-DEED, S. deed of charity; or something done to relieve the distresses and want of others. "Dorcas full of *alms-deeds*." *Acts* ix. 36.

AL'MS-GIVER, S. one who is fond of relieving the necessities of the poor. "Yet was he a great *alms-giver* in secret." *Bac.*

ALMS-HOUSE, S. a house endowed for the lodging and support of the decayed and poor. "Behold you *alms-house* neat, but void of state." *Pope*.

ALMS-MAN, S. a man supported by charity; one who belongs to an alms house.

A'LNWICK, a thorough town of Northumberland, on the road to Berwick, with a market on Saturdays, and five fairs, on Palm-Sunday-eve, for shoes, hats, and pedlars ware; on May 12, for horned cattle, horses, and pedlars ware; the last Monday in July for horned cattle, horses, and woollen and linen cloth; on the first Tuesday in October, for horned cattle, horses, and pedlars ware; and on Saturday before Christmas, for shoes, hats, poultry, and linen cloth. It is a populous, well-built town, with a town-house, where the quarter-sessions and county-courts are held, and the members of parliament elected. It has three gates, which remain almost entire, and shew that it was formerly surrounded by a wall. It is defended by an old stately Gothic castle, the seat of his grace the duke of Northumberland, being lately repaired and beautified by the present duke. It is 33 miles N. of Newcastle, 29 S. of Berwick, and 310 N. by W. of London, Lon. 16. 15. lat. 55. 24.

A'LOES, S. [O'THN, Heb.] a tree, a plant, a medicinal juice, extracted from the plant. The wood grows in China, in the kingdom of Lao, and in Cochin China.

ALOE'TICAL, Adj. medicines composed of aloes. "Excited by *aloetical*, *aromadeum* and *acrimonious medicines*." *Wisen. Surg.*

ALOFT, Adv. [*lofter*, Dan.] in the air, on high; above. It is sometimes used as a preposition, and implies a higher situation. "The great luminary, *aloft the* vulgar constellations." *Par. Lost*.

ALO'NE,

ALO'NE, Adj. [from *al-een*, or *allem*, Belg.] fingle, having no companion. " It is not good for man to be *alone*." *Gen.* ii. 18. Having no affiftance. " Not able to perform it thyfelf *alone*." *Exod.* xviii. 13. Exclufively of all others; folely. " Who can forgive fins but God *alone*." *Luke* v. 21. After *let* it implies, not to difturb; to walk with patience the refult of an attempt without any intervening care, or indufly. " *Let* her *alone*; Why trouble you her? *Matt.* xiv. 6. " Lord *let* it *alone* this year alfo." *Luke* xiii. 8. Sometimes ufed ironically, as a prohibition to help a man, under a fuppofed perfuafion, that he dors not want affiftance. " *Let* him *alone*, let us fee whether Elias will come." *Matt.* xv. 36.

ALO'NG, Adv. [*ad longu*, Fr] at full length; proftrate. " Some rowl a mighty ftoar, fome laid *along*" *Dryd.* Motion meafured lengthwife. Ufed with *all*, for a continuance. Throughout; or from beginning to end, applied to writings. " Solomon, *all along* in his Proverbs." *Tillotf.* Joined to the particle *with*, it implies company; or together. " He to England fhall *along with* you." *Shakefp. Hamlet.* After *come* it implies attendance, and encouragement to proceed. " Come then my friend, my genius come *along*." *Pope.* Johnfon obferves, that this expreffion is borrowed from the French *allons*.

ALO'OF, Adv. at a diftance, which is within fight. " Our palace ftood *aloof* from ftreets." *Dryd.* When applied to perfons, it implies a diftance occafioned by caution and circumfpection. In a figurative fenfe, the art or cunning by which a perfon evades the anfwer or notice of a queftion propofed. " With a crafty madnefs keeps *aloof*." *Shak. Hamlet.* At a diftance, fo as not to appear as a principal, or party. " It is necefiary that the queen join, for if fhe ftand *aloof* there will be fufpicions," *Suckling.* Not connected with; having no relation or reference to. " Mingled with regards that ftand—*aloof from* the main point" *Shak. King Lear.* Among failors it implies, that the perfon at the helm, is to keep the fhip near the wind, when failing on the quarter wind.

ALOPE'CIA, S. a diftemper, wherein the greater part of the hair falls off.

ALO'SE, S. a fifh refembling the Sardine, which grows to the fize of a Salmon, called a Fifh of Paffage; Its ftomach and a bone found in its head, when reduced to powder, are good for the ftone and gravel, for abforbing acids, and ftrengthing the ftomach.

ALOU'CHI, S. a fweet fcented gum, which diftils from the tree that produces the white cinnamon.

ALO'UD, Adv. with an increafed ftrength of voice, fo as to be heard at a great diftance. With a great noife. " Thund'red this ice *aloud*." *Dryd.*

ALO'W, Adv. in a low place; very near the ground.

ALPA'GNA, S. an animal which the Peruvians ufe as a beaft of burthen, and make it carry too wt. Of its wool they make ftuffs, ropes, and bags; of his bones, tools for weavers; and of its excrement, fires, both for their chimneys and kitchens.

A'LPHA, S. [derived from the אַלֶף, Heb. to learn] the firft letter of the Greek alphabet, which being alfo their numerals, is ufed to fignify the firft in order of time, &c. as *rerga*, the laft letter in their alphabet, fignifies the laft; in allufion to this, Chrift fays, " I am *alpha* and *omega*."

A'LPHABET, S. [from αλφα and βετα, the two firft letters of the Greeks] a table of all the letters which compofe any language, and are marks to convey the fimple founds in forming words made ufe of. The number of the letters in the alphabet differs in moft of the languages we know of; the Englifh may have twenty-fix; the French twenty-three; the Hebrew, Syriac, Chaldaic, and Samaritan, twenty-two each; the Arabic twenty-eight; the Perfian thirty-one; the Turkifh thirty-three; the Georgian, thirty-fix; the Coptic thirty-two; the Mofcovians forty-three; the Greek twenty-four; the Latin twenty two; the Sclavonic twenty-feven; the Saxon twenty-four; the Gothic twenty-five; the Iflandic twenty-two; the Dutch twenty-fix; the Spanifh twenty-feven; the Italian twenty; the Ethiopic two hundred and two. The Chinefe were formerly fuppofed to have no alphabet, properly fpeaking, as having only hieroglyphics, which ftood for whole words, and amounted to 80,000; but an ingenious profeffor of the French academy, has lately demonftrated the Chinefe themfelves to have been a colony of the Egyptians, that they derived their language from that fertile fource of knowledge, which watered the whole world, and that their fuppofed characters, are not hieroglyphics, but combinations of letters, which he has refolved into their primitive elements, and fhewn to be the antient letters of the Egyptians, though very much altered by time, corrupted by ignorance, and obfcurated for want of tracing them fooner to their origin. Alphabet, in Commerce, is an index ufed by merchants and traders, having the twenty-four letters, in their natural order, affixed to different leaves, in which they fet down the firnames and chriftian names of thofe with whom they open accounts, with references to the folio, in which fuch accounts are opened.

ALPHABE'TIC, or ALPHABE'TICAL, Adj. placed or digefted in the fame order as in the alphabet.

ALPHABE'TICALLY, Adv. in the fame order as in the alphabet.

ALP'HERY,

A'LPHERY, [MIKEPHER] born in Ruffia, of the imperial line; but in the fourteenth century, his country being diftracted with inteſtine commotions, he was ſent to London, and conſigned to the care of Mr. Bidel, a merchant, who ſent him to Oxford. He went into orders, and had a ſmall living given him in Huntingdonſhire, rated at 10l. in the King's books. In this place he performed his duty with great chearfulneſs, and with ſo much content, that when invited to Ruſſia by ſome friends, who offered to run any riſks in recovering his rights, he refuſed them. In the year 1643, he felt the fury of the fanatics, who not only turned him out of his living, but when he had prepared himſelf a ſlender meal, in a hut he had erected within the church-yard, deprived him of it, and kicked out his fire. At the reſtoration he received his living, but being too old to diſcharge the duties of it himſelf, ſettled a curate in it, and ſoon after died at his ſon's houſe in Hammerſmith, in an advanced age. The ſingularity of a Ruſſian emperor's having been a country miniſter in England will afford ſuch a large field for reflection, that any hint of that kind might be branded with the name of officious prolixity.

A'LPISTLE or ALPIA, S. a kind of ſeed of an oval figure, of a pale yellow, inclining to a ſable colour, bright and glaſſy; made uſe of to feed birds with, when intended for breeding.

ALPHONSIN, S. in Surgery, an inſtrument to extract bullets, conſiſting of three branches, which are cloſed together by a ring that ſlides over them. Being introduced, thus cloſed, into the wound where the bullet lies, the ring is drawn back towards the handle, which opening the branches, they lay hold on the ball, and the ring being puſhed over them again, they graſp it ſo tight, that it is extracted without any difficulty. Bib. Anat. Med. i. i. 517.

ALPHONSI'NE, Adj. [from Alphonſo] in Aſtronomy, applied to the tables of Ptolemy's Almageſt, corrected by Alphonſo XII. King of Caſtile.

ALPHO'S, or A'LPHUS, S. [from αλφος, Gr.] in Medicine, a diſtemper in which the ſkin becomes rough and ſpotted.

AL'PINE, Adj. [alpinus, Lat.] what may be ſeen or met with on the Alps.

A'LPS, S. [Alpes, Lat.] a long chain of mountains, beginning at the mouth of the Varo, in Piedmont, and terminating near Aſſa, a river of Italy, on the Adriatic ſea, or gulph of Venice. Theſe mountains divide Italy from France, Switzerland and Germany; have but few paſſes, and thoſe of very difficult acceſs; and are, on that account, a great ſecurity to Piedmont from France. Hannibal, the famous Carthaginian, loſt moſt of his elephants in attempting the paſſage

and is reported to have made his way thro' ſome part of them, by making a road with boiling vinegar. The preſent King of Sardinia oppoſed the united forces of France and Spain, who had, with incredible conſtancy, made their way as far as Coni, and defeated them. The Swiſs look on the parts of theſe mountains which ſurround them, as a bulwark, and have by them been hitherto ſecured from any attacks, either from the Germans or French.

A'LQUIFOU, or ARQUIFOU, S. a kind of mineral lead, very heavy, eaſily reduced to powder, and hard to melt.

ALRA'MELECH, S. [אלרמלך Arab.] in Aſtronomy, the name of a ſtar of the firſt magnitude, called Arcturus.

ALRE'ADY, Adj. [pronounced as if the a was dropped, alreed, Belg.] the preſent time; now; in a time paſt; in oppoſition to future. "Which hath already been conſecrated." Hooker.

A'LSO, Conjunct. [alſwa, Sax.] uſed to denote, that what had been affirmed of one ſentence or perſon, holds good of the ſucceeding. "Thou alſo waſt one of them." Matt. xxvi. 73. In the ſame manner; likewiſe. "The ſon of man is Lord alſo of the ſabbath." Mark ii. 28. When at the end of a ſentence or period, it implies beſides. "Succourer of many and of myſelf alſo." Rom. xvi. 7. "God do ſo to me; and more alſo." 1 Sam. xiv. 44.

ALSTON-MORE, a town in Cumberland, with a market on Saturdays, and two fairs, on the laſt Thurſday in May, and the firſt Thurſday in September, for horned cattle, horſes, linen and woollen cloth. It is ſeated on a hill, at the bottom of which runs the river Tyne, with a ſtone bridge over it, and there is plenty of lead ore near it. It is 10 miles E. by S. of Carliſle, and 250 N. N. W. of London. Lon. 15. 15. lat. 54. 45.

A'LTAR, S. [altare, Lat.] a raiſed place whereon the antient ſacrifices were offered; that part of the church where the communion is received, or the table on which the vaſes and the elements of bread and wine are placed. Figuratively, Chriſt himſelf, to whom we bring all our offerings and ſervices. "We have an altar whereof they have no right." Heb. vii. 13.—xiii. 10. In Aſtronomy, a conſtellation of the ſouthern hemiſphere, conſiſting of ſeven ſtars.

A'LTARAGE, S. [altaragium, corrupt Lat.] in Civil Law, the offerings made on the altar, and the profits ariſing to the prieſt, including not only voluntary oblations, but likewiſe ſmall tythes. Terms de Ley, 39. 2 Cro. 516.

A'LTAR-CLOTH, S. the cloth which covers the communion-table. "Books, hanglings, and altar-cloths, which our Kings gave." Peacham.

To

To A'LTER, V. A. [alter, Lat.] to change, or make different; to vary, or differ in sense, applied to writings. "According to the Law, which altereth not." Dan. vi. 8. To corrupt the sense of an author, by erasing, adding, or changing. "Whosoever shall alter this word." Ezra vi. 11. Used neuterly, to change; to become different. "His countenance altered."

A'LTERABLE, Adj. [from alter and able, Sax.] that may be changed, or made to appear different.

A'LTERABLY, Adv. so as to admit of changes.

A'LTERANT, Part. [alterant, Fr.] having the power of producing changes. "Whether the body be aberrant or altered." Bac.

ALTERA'TION, S. [alteration, Fr.] the act of changing the form or tenor of a writing, the qualities of a body, the faculties of the mind, and making them different from what they were. "Alteration, though it be from worse to better, hath in it inconveniences, and those weighty ones." Hooker. The change itself, or the state of a thing changed.

A'LTERATIVE, Adj. having the power of making change. In Medicine, those remedies which produce a change in the humours of the body, and destroy some prevailing acrimony in the first passages and juices; or such as resolve concretions in the blood vessels, and dispose them to pass out of the body by perspiration or some other insensible evacuation.

To A'LTERCATE, V. N. [altercor, Lat.] to wrangle, contend, or dispute. Authorities for the use of this word are not obvious; but its propriety seems not to want them.

ALTERCA'TION, S. [altercatio, Lat. altercation, Fr.] a debate or dispute on any subject, including a warm defence of the contrary side of a question, but not amounting to a quarrel.

ALTE'RN, Adj. [alternus, Lat.] In Trigonometry, the base, so called, is either the sum or difference of the sides of an oblique triangle; if the true base is the sum, the altern base is the difference, but if the true base be the difference, the altern base is the sum of the sides.

ALTE'RN, S. [alternus, Lat.] that which succeeds; successive or alternately; that which follows by succession.

ALTE'RNACY, S. the succession of one action after another.

ALTE'RNATE, Adj. [alternus, Lat.] those things which succeed one another by turns; successive. "Did alternate passions fall and rise." Pope. In Geometry, applied to angles, it signifies the internal one, made by a line cutting two parallels, and lying on opposite sides of it. Alternate, in Heraldry, is applied to the situation of the quarters of a coat; thus, in quarterly, quartered, the first

and fourth are alternate. Alternate proportion, is when, of four proportional numbers, the antecedent of the former is compared to the antecedent of the latter, and the consequent of the former is compared to the consequent of the latter, as in the following proportion, A, B, C, D, wherein A and C are the two antecedents, and B, D, the two consequents; the alternate proportion is A, C; B, D, wherein the two antecedents A, C, and the two consequents B, D, are compared together.

ALTE'RNATE, S. [alternus, Lat.] what follows another in succession, or by turns; vicissitude.

ALTE'RNATELY, Adv. so that the thing which precedes shall follow that which comes after it. Thus when we say, that darkness follows light, and light darkness, they are said to follow each other alternately. "Toss'd alternately by hopes and fears." Dryd.

ALTE'RNATENESS, S. the quality whereby things sometimes go before, and sometimes follow each other.

ALTERNA'TION, S. succession, wherein that which preceded returns again. In Arithmetic, the different changes, alterations of place, or combinations that any proposed numbers are capable of; which is found by a continual multiplication of all the numbers beginning at unity, and ending with the last number of the things to be varied. Thus, if it be required to find how many changes can be rung on six bells, multiply the numbers 1, 2, 3, 4, 5, and 6, into each other, and the last product gives the number of changes, which are 720. In this manner, we find the number which can be rung on twelve bells is 4-9,001,600.

ALTE'RNATIVE, S. [from alternate, Lat.] a choice of two, whereby, if one be rejected, the other must be accepted. "A strange alternative!—Must ladies have a doctor or a dance?" Young.

ALTE'RNATIVELY, Adv. so that what goes before shall return again in succession; by turns; mutually; reciprocally.

ALTE'RNITY, S. a state wherein there is a continual succession, change, or vicissitude.

ALTHÆ'A, S. [from Althæa, Gr.] In Botany, the marshmallows. The syrup is often very much used in the gravel, to lubricate the passages, and render the passage of the stone more easy.

ALTHO'UGH, Adv. [pronounced as if it was written altho'] used to imply that a thing or conclusion may be allowed and maintained, notwithstanding something seemingly inconsistent had been allowed; notwithstanding; nevertheless.

ALTIM'ETRY, S. [altimetria, Gr.] the art of taking or measuring heights.

ALTI'SONANT, or ALTI'SONOUS, Adj.

L 2

Adj. [altisonus, Lat.] that which hath a lofty and pompous found.

A'LTITUDE, S. [altitudo, Lat.] height, or diftance from the ground, meafured upward. " Ten mafts attached, make not the altitude." Shakefp. Lear. Superiority, dignity, or height of excellence. " Your altitude offends the eyes—Of thofe who want the pow'r to rife." Swift. The higheft pitch of perfection. " Even to the altitude of his virtue." Shakefp. Coriol. In Geometry, the height above the ground, or the horizon. Altitude of the eye, in Perfpective, a right line, let fall perpendicular to the geometrical plane. Altitude of a figure, is the length of a perpendicular line let fall from the top to the bottom. Altitude, in Aftronomy, or the height of any object above the horizon, is divided into real or apparent. Apparent altitude is the arch of a vertical circle, intercepted between the fenfible horizon and the center of an object: Real or true altitude is the arch of a vertical circle, intercepted between the center of an object and the rational horizon. Meridian Altitude of the fun, &c. is an arch of the meridian, intercepted between the horizon and the center of an object. Altitude of the pole, is the height of the pole above the horizon. Altitude of the equinoctial, is its elevation above the horizon. Altitude of the nonagefimal degree, is its height, counted from the place where it rifes. Parallax of Altitude, is an arch of a vertical circle, intercepted between the true and obferved place of a ftar or other object. Azimuth of motion, is the meafure of any motion, computed according to the line of direction of the moving force.

ALTI'VOLANT, Part. [altivolans, Lat.] flying high.

A'LTO-RELIEVO, S. See RELIEVO.

ALTOGE'THER, Adv. [alt, Goth. and togædre, Sax.] entirely, abfolutely, without any exception. " Man, at his beft ftate, is altogether vanity." Pfalm xxxix. 5. In all refpects. " I was altogether fuch a one as thyfelf." Pfalm xxl. Perfectly, when concluding a fentence. " The judgments of the Lord are righteous altogether." Pfalm xix. 9. In company, without feparating. In a body. " Join you with me—And altogether with the duke of Suffolk,—We'll quickly hoife." Shakefp. Hen. VI.

ALTON, a town in Hampfhire, with a market on Saturdays, and a fair on December 29, for cattle and toys. It is feated on the river Wey, and the market is large, for cattle and provifions. It is 23 miles E. N. E. of Southampton, and 50 W. S W. of London. Lon. 6 52. lat. 51. 5. It is governed by a conftable, and is a fmall town, confifting of about 350 houfes, indifferently built, chiefly laid out in one pretty broad ftreet, only a part of which is paved. It has one church, a prefbyterian and a qua-

ker's meeting, with a famous free-fchool. It has a large manufacture of plain and figured barragons, ribbed druggets, and ferge de Nifmes; and round the town is a large plantation of hops.

A'LUDEL, N. [from a privative, and lutum; in chemiftry, a range of earthen pots without bottoms, fixed into each other without luting; the lower is a pot which contains the matter to be fublimated, and the uppermoft is a head which retains the flowers that rife.

ALVE'ARIUM, S. the cavity of the outer ear, wherein the wax is lodged.

ALVE'OLI, S. [Lat. a diminutive of alveus, Lat.] the fockets in the jaw-bone, which contain the teeth.

A'LUM, S. [alumen, Lat.] a mineral falt, of an acid tafte, accompanied with a confiderable degree of aftringency. See ALLUM.

A'LUM-STONE, S. a ftone of a corrofive nature, frequently ufed to confume the fungous excrefcencies, or proud flefh, of wounds. " Touching it with vitriol and alum-ftones." Wifeman's Surgery.

ALU'MINOUS, Adj. [aluminis, Lat.] refembling alum in its properties, or confifting of alum. " Of a vitriolic or aluminous nature." Wifeman's Surgery.

A'LWAYS, Adv. [alwæge, Sax.] without ceafing or intermiffion; continually; ever; frequently, fo as not to flip or omit any opportunity. " Cornelius prayed to God always." Acts x. 2. Conftantly. " Mephibofheth, thy mafter's fon, fhall eat bread always at my table." 2 Sam. ix. 10. Perpetually, applied to time; and every where, applied to place. " Lo! I am with you always, even to the end of the world." Matt. xxviii. 20.

A. M. an abbreviation for anno mundi, or the year of the world; and for artium magifter, or mafter of arts.

AM, Ver. Subf. [of eom, eam, and am, Sax.] when ufed fingly, it implies exiftence. " I fay unto you, that before Abraham was I am." John viii. 58. Applied to place, it fignifies prefence. " Where I am, there fhall my fervants be." John xii. 26. Affirmation. " Jefus faid, I am the bread of life." John vi. 35. When repeated, it implies felf and independent exiftence. " I am that I am." Exodus iii. 14. Thofe that are ftruck with the fingularity of the expreffion, will find their curiofity abundantly paid in the perufal of Bifhop Beveridge's difcourfe on this text.

AMABI'LITY, S. [amabilis, Lat.] that quality by which an object appears worthy of love. " No rule can make amability, our minds and apprehenfions make that." Taylor.

AMADE'TÆO, S. In gardening, a kind of pear, fo called from its delicious flavour.

flavour, according to Sir John Evelyn, in his *Hortullanus Gallicus.*

AMADOW, S. [Teut.] a kind of black match, or touchwood, which comes from Germany, made of a spongey excrescence growing on old trees, such as oak and fir. It is first boiled in common water, afterwards dried and well beaten; put into a strong lye of salt-petre, and then dried in an oven. The French druggists sell it wholesale.

AMAIN, Adv. [from *a* and *mægen*, Sax.] with all one's force, power, or strength. "We fled amain." *Milton.* Applied to the voice, as loud as possible. In sea affairs, a call to an enemy to surrender or to strike; from the French *à main;* or, when used to lower or let fall their sails implies the same as, All hands aloft to, &c.

AMALGAM, or AMA'LGAMA, S. [from αμα, Gr. and μαλιμ, Gr.] In Chemistry, a substance produced by incorporating quicksilver with a metal. The process with lead is performed by putting equal quantities of lead and quicksilver together in an iron vessel, melting them together over a fire, stirring them with an iron rod all the while, and, when cold, rubbing the mass in a mortar, which will unite with any additional quantity of quicksilver in the same manner, or as easily as salt does with water. The amalgame of tin, silver and gold, is formed by a method almost similar.

To AMA'LGAMATE, to incorporate metals with quicksilver. The minters, refiners, and silversmiths used this term to signify the operation performed by the mill, wherein they put their sweeps to clear them from filth and dirt; whereby the mercury which is put into the rub attracts the imperceptible particles of silver or gold mixed with filth, and forms them into a paste.

AMALGAMA'TION, S. the incorporating quicksilver with other metals.

AMANDA'TION, S. [*amandatum,* supine of *amando,* Lat.] the sending a person on a message, or any other employ.

AMANUE'NSIS, S. [Lat. from *a, minus,* Lat. and *ensis,* Lat.] one who writes down what is dictated by another; likewise a copier of writings.

AMARA'NTH, S. [*amaranthus,*] in Botany, amaranth, or flower-gentle. It has male and female flowers in the same plant. The male flower has either three or five flamina of the same length with the empalement, and crowned with oblong summits. The female flowers have an oval germen supporting three short styles shaped like awls and crowned with simple stigma. The empalement becomes an oval coloured seed-vessel, with one cell including a single globular seed. Linnæus ranges these plants in the fifth division of his twenty-fifth class, intitled, *Monœcia Pentandria,* from their having male and female flowers on the

same plant, and the former having five stamina; but, Mr. Ray, among the class of apetalous flowers, because they have no petals. There are fourteen species; the first whereof, when full blown, is certainly very beautiful, and no small ornament to the flower garden. In Poetry, is it used for an imaginary flower, which never fades. "Immortal amaranth!" *Par. Loss.* In dyeing, a colour which inclines to purple, so called from its resembling that of the flower just described.

AMARANTHINE, Adj. [from *amaranth* and *en,* Sax. denoting the material of which any thing is composed] composed of amaranth. "Amaranthine bow'rs." *Pope.*

AMARI'TUDE, S. [*amaritudo*] bitterness. "What amaritude or acrimony is apprehended in choler." *Harvey.*

AMA'SMENT, S. [from *amass*] a collection or heap; an accumulation; it includes in its secondary idea, a great deal of industry, but little judgement. "An amasment of imaginary conceptions." *Glanv. Sept. Scient.*

To AMA'SS, V. A. [*amasser,* Fr.] to gather or heap together. "To amass riches." *Atterb.* To lay up, or store in the memory, with great assiduity. "All that we thus amass together in our thoughts." *Locke.* To collect together in great quantities, including the idea of indifferent additions. "The life of Homer has been written by amassing of all the traditions and hints the writer could meet with." *Pope.* The use of the particle *of* in this quotation seems improper.

AMA'TORY, S. [*amatorius,* Lat.] In anatomy, a term applied to the obliques superior, and inferior, from their drawing the eye side-ways.

AMA'TORY, Adj. [*amatorius,* Lat.] that which excites love, "Whether by force, or amatory potions." *Brahsm.*

AMAURO'SIS, S. [Gr. αμαυρωσις,] In Medicine, a dimness of sight.

To AMA'ZE, V. A. [from *mæsan,* Belg. to wander, in allusion to the perplexity of a person in a labyrinth; or *mase,* Sax. a whirlpool, which a person in vain strives to extricate himself from] to astonish, from the excellence, perfection, greatness, or extraordinary qualities. "All that heard Paul, were amazed." *Afts* ix. 21. "Your courage, truth, your innocence and love, amaze and charm mankind." *Smith's Phædr. and Hipp.* To be confused or perplexed "If he be not amazed, he will be mocked; if he be not amazed, he will every way be mocked." *Shakss.*

AMA'ZE, S. astonishment, or perplexity, caused by an unexpected object. "Casting back his eyes with dire amaze." *Dryd.* "Fills all her jealous monarchs with amaze." *Milt.*

AMA'ZEDLY, Adv. expressive of astonishment, on the appearance of something unexpected

unexpected. " I speak *amazedly*." *Shak. sp.* " Why stands Macbeth thus *amazedly* ?" *Shakesp. Macbeth.*

AMA'ZEDNESS, S. the situation or state of the mind when affected with surprize, astonishment, confusion or perplexity. " At ter a little *amazedness* we were all commanded out of the chamber." *Shakesp. West. Tale.*

AMA'ZEMENT, S. the effect or state which on the mind, arising from some quality, which we could not suspect it to have possessed; confusion; perplexity. " Adding new fear to his first *amazement*." *Fairy Q.* " His impression left us still or as it with. *Milt.* Admiration, an extraordinary good opinion; surprize. " With *amazement* we shall read your story." *Waller.* " Filled with wonder and *amazement*." *Acts* iii. 10.

AMA'ZING, Past. causing surprize, astonishment; or admiration, on the discovery of some unexpected quality. " It is indeed *amazing* to see the present desolation of Italy." *Addison.*

AMA'ZINGLY, Adv. in such a manner as to excite astonishment, wonder or admiration, from some latent and unexpected quality, excellence or defect; prodigiously; surprizingly. " If we retire to the world of spirits, our knowledge of them must be *amazingly* imperfect." *Watts's Logic.*

AMA'ZON, S. (from a Gr. and prefix.) one of those women who composed the nation so called. They are said to have composed a nation of themselves, exclusive of males, and to have derived their name from their cutting off one of their breasts, that it might not hinder or impede the exercise of their arms. This term has often by modern writers been used to signify a bold daring woman, whom the delivery of her sex does not hinder from engaging in the most hazardous attempts. " Stay, stay, thy hands, thou art an *amazon*." *Shakesp. Hen. VI.* The last and present war with France has furnished us with several instances of females, who have undergone the fatigue of a campaign with alacrity, and run the hazards of a battle, with the greatest intrepidity. This term is likewise given to a celebrated river, called likewise the Maragnon, in America. It received its first name, the river of the Amazons, from the usual custom of the women attending their husbands to war, either to animate them by their words, or assist them by their presence; as was common in the early ages not only among the Gauls, but likewise among ourselves in England. This famous river begins at the foot of the Cordilleras, and falls into the Atlantic ocean; from the spring head to its mouth it runs eight or nine hundred leagues in a direct line, but allowing for its winding it cannot be less than 11 or 1200 leagues, or about 3000 English miles. The rivers it receives in its way are very numerous, some of which join

it after a course of 5 or 600 leagues, and are not inferior to the Danumbe or the Nile.

AMBA'GES, S. [Lat. from *ampo*, *ampli.* Gr. about, and *ago* to lead] a tedious round about way of expressing; a method of relating any subject, when in the narrative is not conducted directly to the point; but, by the insertion of several circumstances, which have not an immediate relation to it, the mind of the hearer is kept in suspence, and the information intended is delayed; this sometimes is owing to art, and at other times to ignorance. " Without *ambages* and circumlocutions" *Locke.* The last word in in this quotation conveys the same idea, and is used to explain the term to which it is subjoined.

AMBASSA'DE, S. [*ambassade*, Fr.] the office of a person, commissioned to negotiate the affairs of a state, in foreign parts. " When you disgrac'd me in my *ambassade*." *Shakesp. Hen. VI.*

AMBA'SSADOR, S. [*ambassadeur*, Fr. *embassador*, Span. some go so far as to derive it from the Heb. שגר *sagher*, to tell, and מלאך *malabre*, a messenger, others from *ambact*, Teut. a government; all which derivations, excepting the Spanish, authorise our writing it ambassador, with an a] a person sent by a prince or state, into that of a foreign one as their representative, to transact such affairs as concern the public. Their persons have always been esteemed inviolable; and, by the Civil Law, their moveables, cannot be seized on, either as a pledge, payment of debt, by order of execution or judgment, or by leave of the state, wherein they reside. An ambassador is distinguished from an envoy or agent, by the greatness of his power, and the superiority of his dignity. In a secondary sense, it implies any person sent on a message even by a private person; a messenger. " I come, without a pledge, my own *ambassador*." *Dryd.*

AMBA'SSADRESS, S. [*ambassadrice*, Fr.] the lady of an ambassador; in a secondary sense, a woman sent on a message. " Well, my *ambassadress*." *Rowe's Peni.*

AMBA'SSAGE, S. [*ambassage*, Fr.] the employ, or office of an ambassador. " The formal part of their *ambassage*." *Bac. Hen. VII.*

A'MBE, S. in Surgery, the name of an instrument made use of for reducing dislocated bones. It has received great improvements from several eminent practitioners; particularly, Mr. Le Cat and Mr. Freake, our own countryman, who not only made some additions to it, has likewise rendered it portable.

A'MBER, S. [*ambre*, Fr. *ambra*, Ital. but as it was chiefly found, at first, on the coast of Prussia, Skinner thinks it best to derive it from the language of the *natives*, and imagines it to be from *ava-burn*, Belg. to burn;

3   *burn*;

bers; in confirmation of which we find that the people on the coast of the Baltic, called it by the name of *amber-strias* by contraction, *bern-strea*, a combustible stone) a kind of a gum, or rosin, found in the Baltic, on the coast of Prussia. It has been held by some to be a kind of fossil pitch, the veins of which are at the bottom of the sea; but, as flies, ants, and other insects have been found buried in pieces of the yellow sort, it must certainly be a land production; to solve the difficulty arising from the appearance of these animal bodies, others affert that it is a gum or rosin, exuding in a fluid state from fir or pine trees, which then admitted those bodies, and that it hardens by time; but to this it is objected, that it has been dug out of the earth, and that there are several mines of it wrought in Prussia, in Stolpon and Dantzick: To enquire farther into its nature would be guilty of scepticism; the disposition of the strata of the place where it is found, the first of which is ligneous, the second vitriolic, the last sand, at the bottom of which the amber is met with in small pieces of a globular form, and full of insects, show that at it's first growth it was liquid; and that it is a concretion of oil, like petroleum or naptha, which it resembles both in smell and quality; fossil woods and coal will, by distillation, yield an oil very much like petroleum, or the oil of amber, and shows it to be formed from ligneous strata, by a process somewhat similar. The physical qualities of this substance, have recommended it in fumigation to remove defluxions, and in powder as an alterative, absorbent, sweetener, astringent, lithontriptic, diuretic, &c. The spirit is used externally in rhumatic pains and aches; and internally, in giddiness, &c. The oil, according to Boerhaave, when used externally, is very serviceable in restoring contracted, weak and torpid limbs. Mixed with oil of bitter almonds and dropt into the ear, it is almost an infallible cure for deafness occasioned by colds, or hardness of the wax.

A'MBER, Adj. made or consisting of amber. " *Amber*, bracelets, beads, and all his knavery." *Shakesp.* Of a yellow colour, and transparent. " All your clear *amber* drink is flat." *Bac.*

A'MBERGRIS, S. a fragrant drug, of a suety substance, not ponderous, of an ash-colour, variegated like marble, and melts like wax. The naturalists seem as much divided in their sentiments on the origin of this substance, as in that of the article preceding. Some have afferted it to be the dung of some oriental bird, others a kind of honey; moderns, have thought it the refin of a tree to us as yet unknown, or an animal concrete formed in balls in the body of the sperma ceti whale; but chemistry has shewn that this substance does not admit of solution

in aqueous menstruums, which all animal dungs and honey do; that this is not easily dissolved by rectified and phlogistic spirit of wine, though all resinous and vegetable substances are; and that ambergris does not produce one animal principal, when chemically analysed; hence it is probable that it is a species of bitumen produced from the earth, and washed from its bowels by the violence of the waves, for it is found floating in great quantities near the island of Madagascar, whose subterranean parts are imagined to be pregnant with that kind of bitumen. It is used by confectioners and perfumers, in order to scent their commodities, and is recommended by physicians as proper to raise the spirits and accelerate their motions. A solution of this drug is reckoned of great efficacy in strengthening the nerves, and is preferred to any other medicine in distempers, owing to a decay of the nervous system.

A'MBER-SEED, S. called likewise musk-feed; is produced from a plant, both in the Antilles and in Egypt.

A'MBER-TREE, S. by Botanists, filled *fratex Africanus antram spirans*. Its principal beauty is its small ever-green leaves, which if rubbed between the hands, emit a fragrance resembling amber.

AMBIDE'XTER, S. [from *ambi*, Lat. and *dexter*,] one who can use both hands equally; one who is a great temporizer, and would occasionally engage in parties diametrically opposite.

AMBIDEXTE'RITY, S. [from *ambidexter*] the being able to use both hands equally. In a secondary sense, double dealing; or espousing, occasionally, the interest of opposite parties.

AMBIDE'XTROUS, Adj. one who can make use of either hand. " *Ambidextrous*, and left hand men." *Brown's Vulg. Err.* In a secondary sense, adopting the sentiments, or espousing the interests of contrary parties. " All false shuffling and *ambidextrous* dealing." *L'Estrange.*

AMBIDE'XTROUSNESS, S. the quality of being able to use either hand; double-dealing; temporizing.

AM'BIENT, Part. [from *ambiens*, Lat.] that which covers or surrounds every part. " The *ambient* air wide interfus'd." *Par. Lost.*

AMBI'GENAL, Adj. [from *ambi* of *ampi*, Gr. and *genus*, Gr.] in Mathematics, a name applied by Sir Isaac Newton, to one of the triple hyperbolas of the second order.

AMBIGU', S. [Fr. from *ambiguus*, Lat.] an entertainment wherein the dishes are set on table without any regard to order. " Then compose an *ambigu*." *King's Art of Cool.*

AMBIGUITY, S. [from *ambiguus*, Lat.] the quality of a word, or expression, received

in different senses, and rendering it difficult to determine in which an author uses it; words whose signification are doubtful or uncertain; the uncertainty or doubtfulness of an expression. "With ambiguities they often entangle themselves." *Hooker.*

AMBI'GUOUS, Adj. [*ambiguus*, Lat.] having more senses than one. Applied to persons, those who make use of equivocation, or words which have double and uncertain meaning, including the secondary idea of a design to deceive. "Th' ambiguous God." *Dryd.*

AMBI'GUOUSLY, Adj. In such a manner, that a person's meaning, being uttered in equivocal terms, or words having two senses, is not easily discovered.

AMBI'GUOUSNESS, S. the quality which makes the signification of a word uncertain, and fills the mind with doubt to determine its precise idea, or meaning.

AMBI'T, S. [*ambitus*, Lat.] the circumference, circuit, or measure of the external part of any thing. "In measuring by the ambit, it is long or round about a foot." &c. *Grew.*

AMBI'TION, S. [*ambitio*, Lat.] the wish or desire of attaining something better. Applied to kings, it signifies a desire of more power, or more extensive empire; applied to private persons, a desire of greater posts, or preferment. "So high advancements have finished his ambition." *Sidn.* The desire of any thing noble, or excellent. "Urge them while their souls are capable of this ambition." Used with to before a verb, and *if* before a noun. "I had a very early ambition to recommend myself." *Addis.* "These was an ambition of wit." *Pope.*

AMBI'TIOUS, Adj. [*ambitiosus*, Lat.] desirous, and longing after a greater degree of power, an advancement in honour, or a more extensive dominion. Used with the particle of before the object. "Trajan, a prince ambitious of glory." *Arbuth.* Proud, lofty, aspiring; elegantly applied to inanimate things. "I have seen, th' ambitious ocean swell." *Shakesp. J. Cæs.*

AMBI'TIOUSLY, Adj. In such a manner as to shew a desire of thirst after greater dignity, power, riches, dominion, or preferment. "Each ambitiously would claim the hen." *Dryd.*

AMBI'TIOUSNESS, S. the desire of a greater degree of honour, power, &c.

To A'MBLE, V. N. [*ambler*, Fr.] to move on an amble. "To amble when the world is upon the hardest trot." *Dryd.* Figuratively, to move on with a gentle motion, in opposition to the jolts or shakes of a hard trot. "Him time ambles withal." *L'Estr.* To move with an uncouth, unaffected, or unnatural motion. To move by direction, in allusion to an horse in training.

"She'll make him amble on a gossip's message." *Roxe's Jane Shore.* "Before a wanton ambling nymph." *Shakesp. Rich. III.*

A'MBLE, S. a pace wherein the two feet of a horse on the same side move at the same time.

A'MBLER, S. a horse, that has been taught to amble or pace.

AMBLI'GONIUM, S. [Lat. from *ambligonios*, Gr. and *gonia*,] in geometry, an obtuse angled triangle.

AMBLO'SIS, S. [*amblosis*, Gr.] in Medicine, a miscarriage. See ABORTION, which is now most commonly used.

AMBLY'OPY, S. [from *amblyopia*, Gr.] in Medicine, used by Hippocrates, to signify that dimness of sight.

AMBRO'SIA, S. [*ambrosia*, Gr.] the imaginary food of the heathen deities, which rendered them immortal. Applied also to any delicious fruit, by way of hyperbole, and signifying that it would communicate immortality.

AMBRO'SIAL, Adj. [*ambrosius*, Lat.] heavenly, delicious, beyond the relation of mortals. "Ambrosial fragrance filled all heaven." *Par. Lost.* "Ambrosial honey, and ambrosial dews." *Dryd.*

AMBRO'SIUS, S. [AURELIANUS] a celebrated general, and king of the antient Britons; educated at the court of Alcluan, king of Armorica, who sent him, at their request, with ten thousand men, to assist them against the Saxons; and his success being very great, they afterwards chose him for their king. Geoffry of Monmouth pretends, without sufficient grounds, that he built Stone-henge, in memory of three hundred lords massacred by Hengist. He distinguished himself by his valour, in several encounters with the Saxons. After their defeat, he regulated the affairs of the church, and is supposed to have died in a battle, which he lost, against one of the Saxon generals in 508. He is celebrated for his modesty, both by Gildas and Bede, and is said by Geoffry of Monmouth to have been a person of great bravery and courage, of remarkable piety, immense liberality, discreet temperance, and famous for his aversion to lying; a good soldier, and every way fit for a general.

A'MBS-ACE, S. [*ambes as*, Span. *ambes as*, Fr.] a throw on dice, in which two aces are flung, esteemed a very bad chance. "I had rather be in his choice, than throw ambs ace for my life." *Shakesp.*

A'MBULATION, S. [from *ambulatio*, Lat.] the act of walking. "More offensive lassitudes than from ambulation." *Brown's Vulg. Err.*

A'MBULATORY, Adj. [from *ambulatorius*,] that which moves by walking. "The gradient or ambulatory are such, as require some bulk or bottom, to uphold them in their

their motions." *Wilk. Math. Mag.* Translucos, or that which falls out during a walk. " Of whom his majefty had an *ambulatory* view." *Watts.* Moveable, or fixed to no peculiar place. " An *ambulatory* court." *Johnfon's Dict.*

AMBUSCA'DE, [*embufcade*, Fr.] a place of concealment, in order to furprize an enemy. " Rous'd the Grecians from their *ambufcade*." *Dryd.* Applied elegantly to luxurious foods. " Innumerable diftempers lie in *ambufcade* among the difhes." *Spell. No. 18.*

AMBUSCA'DO, S. [*embofcada*, Span.] a private hiding place to furprize an enemy. " Of breaches, *ambufcadoes*, Spanifh blades." *Shakefp. Rom. and Jul.*

A'MBUSH, S. [*embufche*, Fr.] a place of concealment for foldiers to furprize an enemy. " Hold in clofe *ambufh*, hufe in open field." *Dryd.* The act of furprifing, by coming from a concealed or fecret poft. " Fears no affault or fiege—Or *ambufh* from the deep." *Par. Loft.* A fnare laid. " Once did I lay an *ambufh* for your life." *Shakefp. Rich. III.*

A'MBUSHED, Adj. laying in wait to furprize. " Swarming bands of *ambufh'd* men." *Dryd.*

AMBU'SHMENT, S. a concealment in order to furprize. *Ambufcade* is the word now in ufe, though this feems more fuitable to the genius and idiom of our language.

AMBU'STION, S. [*ambuftio*, Lat.] in Medicine, the effect which fire, or bodies heated by it, have on the flefh; when caufed by fire immediately termed a burn; when by boiling liquids, a fcald.

A'MEL, S. [*emaille*, Fr.] a liquid matter which bodies are covered with by the enamellers. " This white *amel* is the bafis of all the fine concretes." *Boyle.* See ENAMEL.

AME'N, Adv. [אמן Heb.] at the end of a fentence, it implies an affirmation, or a wifh. " I am alive for ever more. *Amen.*" *Rev. i. 18.* " The people faid, *amen.*" *1 Chron. xvi. 36.* Applied to Chrift, it implies the Truth, or he who has accomplifhed and verified not only all that the prophets have foretold concerning him, but likewife all that he has himfelf predicted. " Write all thefe things faith the *Amen.*" *Rev. iii. 14.*

AME'NABLE, Adj [*amenable*, Fr.] refponfible, or fubject to examination. Alfo tractable, or eafily governed, and is commonly applied to a woman, fuppofed governable by her hufband.

To AME'ND, V. [*amender*, Fr.] to alter for the better. To correct. To reform. " *Amend* your ways and your doings." *Jerem. xxvi. 13.* Ufed neuterly and applied to both, to grow from a more infirm ftate to a better; to recover. " The hour when he began to *amend.*" *John iv. 52.* Applied to fortune, or a perfon's circumftance, to grow

better. " As my fortune either *amends*, or impairs." *Sidney.* This word and *improve*, are very far from being fynonimous, tho' they are often ufed promifcuoufly; for *amend* carries with it the fecundary idea of fome preceding defect, or fault; but *improve*, though it implies the advancing to a greater degree of perfection, does not imply that the precedent ftate was culpable; for a perfon may be virtuous and ftill *improve* in virtue.

AME'NDABLE, Adj. that may be amended or corrected. " 'Tis then a plea of record, and not *amendable*." *4 Geo. II. 2.*

AME'NDE, S. [Fr. *amende*,] a fine by way of compenfation. *Amende honourable*, is punifhment in France, inflicted on capital offenders, confifting in ftripping the malefactor to his fhirt, and leading him with a rope round his neck into court, to beg pardon of his king, court, and country; fometimes death on the galleys are annexed to it. In allufion to this cuftom the phrafe is fometimes ufed, where a perfon is condemned to make a recantation in a public court, or to the perfon he has injured.

AME'NDMENT, S. [*amendement*, Fr] an alteration for the better; a correction. " Some things in it have paffed your approbation and *amendment*." *Dryd.* Applied to the morals, a change from vice to virtue. " Bring forth fruits anfwerable to amendment of life." *Mat. iii. 8.* Applied to the conftitution, it fignifies a change from ficknefs towards health; a recovery. " Hearing your *amendment*." *Shakefp.*

AME'NDER, S. one who makes the changes in a thing for the better.

AME'NDS, S. [*amende*, Fr.] fome compenfation to make good a damage done. " He fhall make *amends* for the harm done." *Levit. v. 16.* Attonement, or fatisfaction.

AME'NITY, S. [*amenité*, Fr.] a fituation which affects the mind with pleafure.

To AME'RCE, V. A. [*amercier*, Norm] in Law, to inflict a pecuniary punifhment, or fine. Sometimes ufed with *in*. " They fhall *amerce* him in a hundred fhekels of filver." *Deut. xxii. 19.* Sometimes with *of*, the fign of the Genitive cafe, in conformity to the Greek verb, which, in the fentence above cited, governs that cafe; and if applied to place, fignifies to banifh. " For his fault *amerc'd—Of* heaven." *P. r. Loft.*

AME'RCER, S. one who fets the fine upon an offender.

AME'RCEMENT, or AME'RCIAMENT, S. in law, the fine impofed on an offender againft the king, or other lord, who is convicted and therefore ftands at the mercy of either. Thefe amercements differ from fines becaufe they are punifhments certain and determined by fome ftatute; but amerciaments, fuch as are impofed arbitrarily, and being in their nature a more merci-

ful

ful fine, if they be too grievous, may be mitigated, and a release sued by the ancient writ called *misericordia*, Kich. 78, 814.

AMERICA, one of the four parts of the world, and by much the largest. It is bounded on all sides by the ocean, as appears from the latest discoveries; it being formerly supposed to join to the North East part of Asia. It took its name from Americus Vespucius, a Florentine, who is said to have discovered that part of this country seated under the line; but several good authors have proved this to be a mistake. America was first discovered by Christopher Columbus, a Genoese, in 1491. Some call it a new world, and with a great deal of propriety; for not only the men, but the birds and beasts differ in some respects from those that were known before. It has likewise a great number of trees, shrubs, and plants, that grew no where else, before they were transplanted to other places. All the men except the Eskimaux, near Greenland, seem to have the same original; for they agree in every particular from the Straits of Magellan, in the S. to Hudson's Bay, in the N. Their skins, unless dawbed with grease or oil, are of a red copper colour, and they have no beards, or hair on any other part of their bodies, except the head, where it is black, strait, and coarse. Many are the conjectures about the peopling this vast continent, and are almost as various as the authors who wrote about it. However, we have not room to enter into a detail of these particulars, and therefore we shall only observe, that, when the original of the Negroes is settled, we may also be pretty certain from whence these people descended. America is so long, that it takes in not only all the Torrid, but also the temperate and Frigid Zones. It is hard to say how many different languages there are in America; there being such a vast number spoken by the different people in different parts; and as to their religion, there is no giving any tolerable account of it in general, though some of the most civilized among them seem to have worshipped the sun. The principal motive of the Spaniards in sending so many colonies here was the thirst of gold; and indeed they and the Portuguese are possessed of all their parts which it is found in greatest plenty; but I decline entering into farther particulars. In general, it is divided into N. and S. America, and the principal kingdoms in these are Mexico and Peru. But the Portuguese are in possession of Brasil in S. America, and the English are masters of most of the E. Coast in N. America. That part which belonged to the French is called Canada, and they also laid claim to all the country on the back of our settlements, from the river of St. Laurence to the gulph of Florida. But as Quebec was taken on October 18, 1759, the French were obliged by the

peace in 1763, to relinquish the rest; that is, all the country they call Louisiana, after Lewis XIV. Besides those already mentioned in South America, there are Paraguay within land, Chili, on the South Sea, and Terra Magellanick to the North of the Straits of Magellan, whose bounds are not certainly determined. The names of the English settlements are Georgia, Carolina, Virginia, Maryland, Pensilvania, New-York, New-Jersey, New-England, and Nova Scotia; besides several of the Caribbee islands, is what is commonly called the West-Indies.

AMERSHAM, a town of Buckinghamshire, with a market on Tuesdays, and two fairs, on Whitmonday, and September 19, for sheep. It consists of along street, lying in the road, and about the middle there is a cross one, and in the intersection stands the church. The town-hall, or market-house is a brick building, supported by arched pillars with a lanthorn and clock at the top, and free-stones at the corner. It sends two members to parliament, chosen by the lord's tenants of the borough, who pay scot and lot, and are about 130 in number. It is 31 miles S. W. of Buckingham, and 29 N. W. of London. Lon. 16. 55. lat. 51. 40.

AMSBURY, or AMBERSBURY, a town in Wiltshire, with a market on Fridays, and three fairs, on May 6, June 11, and November 13, for horses. It is a scattering place, and is six miles N. of Salisbury, and 80 W. of London. Lon. 15. 55. lat. 51. 20.

AMES-ACE, S. two aces thrown on a pair of dice. "To shun *ames-ace* that swept my stakes away." Dryd.

AMETHODICAL, Adj. that which is not reduced to proper order; irregular.

AMETHYST, S. (from *amethustos*, Gr.) a precious stone of a violet colour, approaching towards purple; it is sometimes found without any colour; and is hardly to be distinguished from a diamond, except by its weight and hardness. The German is of a violet colour; and Spanish, blackish, of a dark violet; almost white, or tinctured with yellow. The oriental are the best, and those of Silesia, or Bohemia, very little inferior to them. They are not very hard, are cut upon a leaden wheel, covered with emeril powder, soaked in water; and are engraved either in creux or relievo, by an engine called a drill, or a wheel turned round by the foot, which gives motion to some iron or brass instruments, against which the stone is held with one hand. In Heraldry, the purple colour in a nobleman's arms; which is termed *purpure* in a gentleman's, and in a sovereign's, *mercury*.

AMETHYSTINE, Adj. of a fine colour, resembling that of an amethyst.

AMIABLE, S. (*aimable*, Fr. *amabilis*, Lat.) that which is an object of affection. That which

which attracts the affection of love or delight. " Doth not only delight as profitable, but as amiable alſo." Hooker. That which has the appearance of courtſhip or love; that which can engage the affection of another. " To lay amiable ſiege to the affections of Ford's wife." Shakeſp.

A'MIABLE, or amicable numbers, in Arithmetic, are thoſe which are equal to the ſum of each others aliquot parts. Thus 184 and 220 are amiable numbers, becauſe the aliquot parts 1, 2, 4, 5, 10, 11, 20, 22, 44, 55, 110, of 220, are equal to all the aliquot parts, 1, 2, 4, 71, 142, of the number 284.

A'MIABLENESS, S. that which renders a perſon an object of delight, pleaſure, or love.

A'MIABLY, Adv. ſo as to gain eſteem or love.

AMIA'NTHUS, or AMIANTUS, S. [αμιαντ⊙, Gr.] in Natural Hiſtory, a foſſil ſtone, or mineral ſubſtance, of a whitiſh colour, conſiſting of ſmall filaments, which reſiſts the moſt intenſe fire; it is found in India, Tartary, Siberia, Egypt, the iſle of Angleſey in Wales, Scotland, and other parts. The antients wrought it into a kind of cloth, or bags, in which they wrapped the bodies of the dead that were deſigned to be burnt; they made a paper of it likewiſe, which, when put into the fire, loſt all its former characters, and was fit to be wrote on afreſh. It is manufactured by putting three or four filaments on a diſtaff, and twilling them with wool; after the cloth is made it is put into the fire, which will conſume the woolen threads, and leave only the amianthus remaining. Though it is a vulgar opinion, that it loſes nothing of its weight by fire; yet in two experiments made with a piece of the cloth before the Royal Society, it loſt above a drachm of its weight each time. And it is very remarkable, that when taken red hot from the fire, and laid on a piece of white paper, it will not burn it.

A'MICABLE, Adj. [of amicabilis, Lat.] applied to perſons, endowed with all the qualities, kindneſs, and ſocial benevolence, which can knit the tie of friendſhip; applied to things, that which is endued with ſuch virtues, as promote the benefit or good of the poſſeſſor. " Enter each mild each amiable gueſt." Pope. According to Johnſon, this is a relative term, and includes in its idea more than one perſon; as we ſay, they live amiably together; but ſeldom ſay, an amicable action, or an amicable man. Yet we may venture, with due deference, to ſay, that this ſtinction is more nice than ſolid, and that the latter expreſſions are, according to our opinion, not at all improper.

A'MICABLENESS, S. the quality is exerted in performing acts of kindneſs.

A'MICABLY, Adv. in ſuch a manner as is conſiſtent with affection, undiſſembled concord, and hearty love; friendly; in oppoſi-

tion to hatred, enmity, or diſlike. " Two lovely youths that amicably walkt." Philips.

AMI'D, or AMIDST, in the middle; applied to things placed in a ſtraight line, between or in the center; and ſometimes in a more looſe ſenſe, within. " Of the fruit of this fair tree, amidſt — The garden." Par. Loſt. Surrounded by, or within the circle made by a group of objects. Within the compaſs, or amongſt. " Though no real voice or ſound, — Amid their radiant orbs be found." Spectat. No 465.

AMIE'S TIES, S. cotton cloth, from the Eaſt-Indies.

A'MISS, Adv. [from a and mis, Fox. Iſl. and Cimb.] Wrong, improper, blameable. " It might not be amiſs to have ſome conſcience." Tillotſon. Contrary to a perſon's meaning; in an ill ſenſe. " She ſighed within, they conſtru'd all amiſs." Fairfax. To be found fault with, to be objected to. " Your kindred is not much amiſs." Dryd. Inconſiſtent with the dignity, character, or attributes, when applied to God, or that which ought not to be. " If any man ſpeak any thing amiſs againſt the God of Shadrach." Dan. iii. 20. Improperly; without the neceſſary preparations; without attending to the conſequences; without any reſpect to the nature of things. Uſed as a ſubſtantive, calamity; miſchance, or ſin. " Each toy ſeems prologue to ſome great amiſs." Haw'n. This ſignification is very unuſual.

A'MITY, S. [amitié, Fr.] a ſtate, harmony, or a mutual intercourſe between two or more perſons. Applied to nations; peace, wherein ſtates are employed in promoting the good of each other. " Great Britain was in league and amity with the whole world." Davis. Applied to a ſingle nation, agreement, mutual love, concord, in oppoſition to civil commotions, or diſcord. " Ties them in a league of inviolable amity." Hooker. Applied to private perſons, a mutual affection, for each other; friendſhip. " You have a noble and a true conceit of godlike amity." Shak. This word is very ſeldom uſed by modern writers.

A'MMI, S. [αμμι, Gr.] in Botany, Biſhop's Weed, an umbelliferous plant, the great umble of which conſiſts of many ſmaller ones, growing like ſo many rays. The ſeed of this name, which enters into the Venice Treacle, comes from Candia, and is of an aromatic ſcent and taſte, reſembling thyme. It is eſteemed aperient, hyſteric, carminative, cephalic; is thought to reſiſt poiſon, and to be an excellent remedy againſt the bite of ſerpents.

A'MMON, [Gr. from αμμ⊙, Gr.] one of the titles given to Jupiter, among the Scythians; by methologiſts imagined to be the hieroglyphic of the Sun, and that the horns which he is repreſented with, are its beams.

           AMMO'-

AMMO'NIAC, s. [ammoniacum, Lat.] a medicinal gum which distils from a ferulaceous plant, on the plains of Lybia.

AMMO'NIAC, SAL, a volatile salt, of which there are natural and artificial. The natural was found near the same place as the plant. It is supposed to be generated by the urine of camels, mixing with the common salt of the sands, and, fermented by the intense heat of the sun, forms this substance. M. Lemery says, that a salt of this kind has been taken from Mount Vesuvius, endued with all the properties of the former; such at cooling water forming an aqua regia, when mixed with nitre, &c. The artificial ammoniac is brought from Egypt, and is made from the soot of suits, or dung of animals fed with straw, sublimed in glass bottles shaped like bombs. According to Boerhaave, it preserves all animal substances from

"So amorous is nature of whatsoever the producers." Dryd. Figuratively, that which is the cause of love, or that which is used by lovers. "Not made to court an amorous looking glass." Shaksp. Rich. III. "With amorous airs my fancy entertain." Waller. Shakespear has used it with the particle on, before the object. "My brother is amorous on Hero." Shaksp. Much-Adoe, i. e. Has fixed his affections, or doats on. But this has met with no authority to recommend it.

A'MOROUSLY, Adv. In a fond or loving manner. "Well amorously to thee swim." Dorne.

A'MOROUSNESS, s. the quality of being easily susceptible of love; fondness. "I can perceive that Lindamour has wit, and am replevess enough." Boyle.

AMO'RT, Adv. [amorte, Fr.] immersed

far fo various a flate of exiftence; particularly in the heart, lungs, foramen, ovale, &c.

AMPHIBLE'TROIDES, S. [Gr. from αμφιβλητρον, Gr. and ειδος] in anatomy, a coat of the eve.

AMPHIBO'LOGY, S. [from αμφιβολος, Gr. and λογος] in rhetoric, an abufe of language, wherein words are fo placed, as to admit of a different fenfe, according to the different manner of combining them.

AMPHI'BOLOUS, S. [from αμφι, Gr. and βαλλω] toffed between two parties from one to the other; agitated by oppofite of different parties. "Never was there fuch an *amphibolous* quarrel." *Howell.*

AMPHI'BRACHYS, S. [Gr. from αμφι, βραχυς,] the name of a foot in Latin and Greek poetry, confifting of three fyllables, the firft and laft of which are fhort, and the middle long.

AMPHIDRO'MIA, S [Gr. from αμφι, Gr. and δρομος, Gr.] a feaft celebrated by the antients the fifth day after the birth of a child.

AMPHI'MACER, S. [Lat. from αμφι, on each fide; μακρος, Gr. long] a foot in Greek or Latin poetry, confifting of three fyllables, the firft and laft of which are long, and the middle fhort; this is the converfe of the amphibrachys; that, in the word *aminam*, the firft and laft fyllables *am* and *am* are long, and *m* fhort.

AMPIOPRO'STYLE, [from αμφι, προ and στυλος Gr.] in architecture, an ancient temple, which had four columns in front, and as many behind.

AMPHISBÆ'NA, S. [Gr. αμφισβαινα] a ferpent, fuppofed to have two heads. Don John d'Ulloa, in his voyage to Peru, gives an account of one of this fpecies, in thofe parts, whofe exiftence was ftrongly afferted by perfons of very great credit; but he is fo ingenuous as to add, that he never met with an occular evidence.

AMPHI'SCII, S. [from αμφισκιοι, Gr.] in geography the inhabitants of the torrid zone, whofe fhadows fall north in one part of the year, and fouth in the other, according to the fun's place in the ecliptic.

AMPHI'SMILA, S. [Gr. αμφι, and σμιλη] a diffecting knife.

AMPHITHE'ATRE, S. [αμφιθεατρον, Gr.] an antient building of an oval form, with feats one above another in the infide, for fpectators to fee the combat of gladiators, wild beafts, &c. They were of prodigious dimenfion, as may be gathered from that of Titus, which is fuppofed to have contained 85,000, and that of Verona, ftill fubfifting, which, at a moderate computation, would hold 23,000 perfons.

A'MPHORA, S. [Lat. from amphora, Gr.] In antiquity, a liquid meafure among the Romans, and contained feven gallons and a pint Englifh. Likewife a meafure now

made ufe of at Venice, containing fixteen quarts retail, and twelve wholefale.

AMPLE, Adj. [amplus, Lat.] wide, fpacious, large, great; full; without reftraint. "Land where, and when you pleafe with *ample* leave." *Dryd.* Large, liberal; oppofed to parfimonious. Applied to writing, full, minute, containing all the circumftances, in oppofition to an abridgment, or a fuperficial and defective account. "An *ample* narrative."

A'MPLENESS, S. that which denotes a thing large, extenfive, copious; fufficient, applied to power; numerous and expatious, applied to veffels, largenefs. "Any thing in proportion either to the *amplenefs* of the body you reprefent, or of the places you bear." *Swift.*

To A'MPLIATE, S. [amplio, Lat.] to enlarge, extend, to add to. "To add and *to amplify.*" *Brown's Vulg. Err.*

AMPLIATION, S. [from *ampliatio*, Lat] increafing by additional circumftances; an exaggeration, or enlargement. "Odious matters admit not of an *ampliation.*" *Ayliffe's Parerg.* Enlargement, diffufivenefs, or dwelling long upon a fubject. The obfcurity of the fubject—May plead excufe for any *ampliations* or repetitions." *Hudson.*

To AMPLI'FICATE, V. A. [*amplifico,* Lat.] to enlarge, to dwell upon.

AMPLIFICATION, S. [*amplification,* Fr.] increafe of dimenfions, it is generally ufed for a figure of rhetoric, which confifts in a heightening of a defcription, commendation, definition, or the blame of a thing by fuch an enumeration of particulars, as muft forcibly affect the paffions. This is performed either by an enumeration of things, or words. The amplification by things confifts in a feries of definitions of the fame things, of which kind is Cicero's defcription of hiftory; in a multitude of concurrent circumftances; a detail of caufes and effects; an enumeration of confequences; comparifons; fimilitudes; examples, contraft of epithets, and rational inference. Amplification by words, confifts in ufing metaphors, hyperboles, fynonimous, fplendid and magnificent terms; circumlocutions, repetitions and gradations. To illuftrate what has been faid, take the following example of an *amplification.* "It is pleafant and virtuous to be good, becaufe that as to excel many others; it is pleafant to grow better, becaufe that is to excel ourfelves; nay, it is pleafant, even to mortify and fubdue our lufts, becaufe that is victory; it is pleafant to command our appetites and paffions, and reftrain them within the bounds of reafon and religion, becaufe that is empire." In allufion to this ufe of the term, it fignifies a very minute, and circumftantial account, in oppofition to a fummary relation. "I fhall fuccinctly, without any *ampli-*

amplification of all, shew, &c." *Dryden.*
Heightening, or exaggerating circumstances.
" With *amplifications* above their nature."
Brown's Vulg. Err.

AMPLIFIER, S. one who enlarges,
heightens, or represents a thing, in such a
manner as to make a most vigorous impression upon the mind.

To AMPLIFY, V. A. [*amplifier*, Fr.]
to increase the dimensions, or number of
parts. " A way to *amplify* any thing, is to
break it." *Bacon.* To increase, or heighten.
To extend, or enlarge. To render compleat,
or encrease by additions, applied to writings.
Used neuterly, with the particle *on*, it signifies to expatiate, to treat fully, to enlarge
upon. " When you afflict you *amplify* on the
former branches of a discourse." To represent in a pompous, heightened, and hyperbolical manner.

AMPLITUDE, S. [*amplitude*, Fr. *amplitudo*, Lat.] compass, extent. " Within the
amplitude of heaven and earth." *Grave.*
Supple. Greatness, or largeness. Capacity.
Copiousness; abundance. " Always proportioning the *amplitude* of your matter, and
the fullness of your discourse to your great
design." *Watts's Log.* Amplitude, in astronomy, is an arch of the horizon, intercepted between the east and west part thereof,
and the center of the sun, star, or planet at
its rising or setting.

AMPTHILL, S. a considerable market
town in Bedfordshire, situated between two
hills. Here is a noble seat built by John
Cornwale, baron of Funhop, out of the
French spoils, in the reign of Henry VI.
but afterwards being confiscated to the
crown, was famous for the retirement of
queen Catherine, during the process of her
divorce. In a pleasant park near this place,
is a seat belonging to the earl of Ailesbury,
built by the countess of Pembroke, from a
model in Sir Philip Sidney's Arcadia. Ampthill has fairs for cattle on the 4th of May,
and the 11th of December, and is forty-three
miles north of London.

To AMPUTATE, V. A. [*amputo*, Lat.]
In Surgery, to cut off a limb. " Their
furgeons were too active in *amputating* those
fractured members." *Wiseman.*

AMPUTATION, S. [*amputatio*, Lat.]
in Surgery, the cutting off a limb. The
method of preparing the patient, and the
whole process of this operation, is minutely
described by Mr. Sharp, a gentleman, whose
fame is not circumscribed within the narrow
limits of this island, but diffused all over the
continent. In a secondary sense, this word
is applied to cutting off branches, or shoots
in Gardening; and striking out unnecessary
and superfluous passages in writings.

AMSTERDAM, S. the capital of the
United Provinces, situated in North Holland, one of the most beautiful and richest
cities in Europe for its size; its foundation
is laid upon large piles, driven into the
Morass, over which it stands, the stadt-house alone being supported by 13,000 of
them; it was owing to this circumstance
that few coasters were formerly to be seen
here; but experience having taught them
that their apprehensions were groundless,
there are as many to be seen here, as in any
other city of the Netherlands. It is about
one third as populous as London or Paris,
has about 26,000 houses within its walls,
and 240,000 inhabitants, excluding those in
the suburbs. It possesses half the East India
trade, carries on an immense commerce with
Spain, the Spanish West-Indies, the Levant,
Italy, Portugal, engrosses almost all the
Dutch trade to Norway, and countries situated on the Baltic; carries on a great correspondence by way of remittances to London, and is situated in Lat. 52 deg. 29 min.
N. Long. 4 deg. 50 min. E.

AMULET, S. [*amulette*, Fr.] a medicine hung round the neck, or elsewhere,
to prevent, or cure any disorder. This
practice is very much controverted, and
while sneered at by some, as idolatrous, insignificant, and impious, is, on the other
hand, patronized by several very great
names, if those of Boyle, Zwelfer, Bellial,
Wainwright and Keil, &c. may be reckoned
such. The former of these gentlemen assert
the efficacy of such a remedy, in curing
him of a bleeding at the nose, and Zwelfer
gives an instance of Helmont's touches of
toads, worn as amulets, having preserved
the chief physician to the states of Moravia,
and his domestics from the plague; and
Pelini, not to mention the other two, has
demonstrated the possibility of their efficacy
in his last propositions. But, we would not
be thought hereby to patronize the extravagancies, to which this practice is carried by
some, or to revive the touching or wearing
a piece of gold about the neck, for the cure
of the scrophula or king's evil.

AMURCA, S. [Lat. *lees*] a medicine
made of the dregs of pressed olives, boiled
to the consistency of honey.

To AMUSE, V. A. [*amuser*, Fr.] to employ a person's thoughts on some object.
" He *amused* his followers with idle promises." To entertain with something agreeable, but not diverting.

AMUSEMENT, S. an employment.
Any thing which engages the mind; an
entertainment. " No unpleasant *amusement*
to look on with safety." *Swift.*

AMUSER, S. one who engages the attention, by specious promises.

AMUSIVE, Adj. that engages the attention to something trifling.

AMY.

A'MY. S. [*ami*, Fr.] in Law, a third
kinswise, *parbrio ary*, the nearest friend,
or relation to an infant or orphan.

AN, *article*, [*an*, Sax. *ein*, Goth.] an
indefinite article before nouns of the singular
number, which begin with a vowel or *an*
A, when not founded. Applied to number,
it fignifies one, as hour. Applied to a
fingle thing, it fignifies any, or fome.
"*As* honest man's the noblest work of
God." *Pope*. When prefixed before a verb,
is implies a particular state, circumstance,
or condition. " He was afterward an hun-
gred". *Matt.* iv. 2. Sometimes ufed as a
contraction of *and* if's providing. " As
they will take it." *Shak. Lear.* Coming
before if, is ufed inftead of *and*. " *An if*
he live to be a man." *Shak. Mer. of Ven.*
Sometimes it implies like, and is then ufed
inftead of *as if*. " Hours *an'* it were any
nightingale." *Guard.* No. 121.

ANA, Adv. [*ava*, Gr.] a word ufed in
physical preference, to fignify equal quantities.

ANABA'PTISTS, S. [from *ava*, Gr.
and *βαπίζω*] a religious fect, who hold, that
perfons are not to be baptized before they
come to years of difcretion, and are able to
give an account of the principles of their
profeffion. The first founders of this fect
were disciples of Martin Luther, whofe
names were Nicholas Storch, Mark Stubner,
and Thomas Munzer ; they first broached
their principles in 1521. The characters of
the three, given by Bayle, are as follows :
Each of thefe principles exerted himfelf according to his peculiar talent: Storch, being
a perfon of no learning, boafted of infpira-
tion ; Stubner, who had both learning and
parts, ftruck into fubtile explications of
fcripture ; and Munzer, who was a man of
a fanguine conftitution, and undaunted courage, gave a full fcope to his paffions.
Munzer, carrying his zeal fo high as to
exhort the people to oppofe the magiftrates,
and force fovereigns to lay down their authority, was apprehended and beheaded in
1525. In Moravia, the fect made fuch a
progrefs, that John of Leyden, one of their
leaders, was attended by no lefs than 40,000,
committed feveral outrages, feized on Mun-
fter, and fuftained a fiege there in 1586,
when, the town being carried, he was taken
and beheaded. The first time they landed
in England, was in the reign of Q. Elizabeth, anno 1560, who iffued out a proclamation, ordering them to depart the kingdom immediately. They afterwards divided
into feveral fects, moft of which are now
extinct. They who at prefent fubfift in
thefe kingdoms, are free from the grofs
errors of their first founders, reckoned a
quiet, well-behaved, and innocent fociety,
have fome men of learning among their

teachers; and are fingular in nothing but
their practice of baptifing.

ANABA'SIS, S. [*avaβασις*, Gr.] in Phyfic, the augmentation, or ftate of a difeafe,
lever, or fit in its growth.

ANABIBAZON, S. [Arab.] in Aftronomy, the node of the moon, where the
paffes the ecliptic from N. to S.

ANDROCHISMOS, S. [from *ave*, Gr.]
and *ῥέω*, in Surgery, an operation performed upon the haw of the eyelids, when
offenfive to the eye.

ANACA'MPTIC, Adj. [from *anakampto*,
Gr.] that which is bent back again ; reclected.
Anacamptics, is a term applied to that part
of philofophy, which treats of the reflection
of the rays of light, called *Necalic, Ca-
toptrica*.

ANACATHA'RTIC, Adj. [from *ave*,
and *a katho*] in Medicine, a vomit.

ANACEFHALÆOSIS, S. [*anakephalæ-
osis*, Gr.] in Rhetoric, a recapitulation.

ANA'CHORET, or ANA'CHORITE,
S. [fometimes fully written ANCHORITE,
from *anachoreo*, Gr.] a monk, who retires,
with the permiffion of his fuperior, to fome
defert and unfrequented place, in order to
live a life of greater aufterity and folitude.
We read of this fpecies of religious, under
the name of hermits, feveral of which may
now be met with in the eaft, who chufe
the dens and caves of rocks for their man-
fions, ufe the hard ground for their beds,
eat the fpontaneous productions of the earth
for food, and make ufe of the ftreams of
fome river for their drink. But fay ye, who
thus cuts yourfelves off from human fociety, does not humanity conftitute the
very effence of our nature, are not the
focial affections implanted in our breafts to
teach us to mix with, not to fhun, the
company of our fellow creatures; is not
virtue propagated more by examples than
difcourfe ; is it not better illuftrated by
refifting, than avoiding, dangers ; and did
the founder of your religion leave the fick
to dwell among men, to countenance you
in your inconfiderate refolution of quitting
the fociety of rational creatures, to dwell
among brutes?

A'NACRONISM, S. [*ava*, Gr. and
χρόνος] in Chronology, a miftake in computing the time when an event happened ;
it very often implies, that the date of an
event is too early. " This leads me to the
defence of the famous *anachronifm*, in making Eneas and Dido cotemporaries." *Dryd.*

ANACREONTIC, Adj. written in the
tafte of Anacreon.

ANADIPLO'SIS, S. [*anadiplosis*, Gr.]
in Rhetoric, a figure, wherein the word,
which ends one fentence or verfe, begins
another, as in the following fentence. " If
children, then heirs, heirs of God." *Rom.*

vili. ℔. In Phyfic, a reduplication, or doubling of a fit in a femitertian ague; or a renewal of the cold fit, before the preceding is entirely ended.

ANAGO'GICAL, Adj. [from ανω, and αγω, Gr.] applied to fcripture, thofe parts which relate to the life to come; and tranfport the foul above all the allurements of this vain, tranfitory ftate.

A'NAGRAM, S. [of ανα, and γραμμα, Gr.] the tranfpofing of the letters of a name, fo as to compute fome other word or fentence; this in the days of Monkifh ignorance was a fpecies of wit very much in vogue, but expired, together with rebufes, acroftics, and other triflings of narrow minds, on the revival of learning.

ANAGRA'MMATISM, S. the act of forming an anagram.

ANAGRA'MMATIST, S. a maker of anagrams.

ANALE'CTA, S. [from ανα, Gr. and λεγω] a mifcellany.

ANALE'MMA, S. [Gr. αναλημμα,] an orthographic projection of the fphere on the plane of the meridian, by ftrait lines and ellipfes.

ANALE'PTIC, Adj. [αναληπτικ@, Gr.] in Phyfic, medicines to reftore the body when emaciated.

ANALO'GICAL, a term, which fignifies any particular idea is attributed to feveral others. That which has a refemblance in fome refpects, though different in others, "Placed the minerals between the inanimate and vegetable province, participating fomething analogical to either." Hales.

ANALO'GICALLY, Adv. in a manner wherein there is fome kind of refemblance to the thing compared.

ANA'LOGISM, S. [αναλογισμ@, Gr.] in Logic, an argument drawn from the caufe to the effect.

To ANA'LOGIZE, V. A. [from analogy] to form a kind of refemblance; to interpret a thing as if he had a reference to fomething elfe. They reprefent the object of the defire, which is analogized by attraction and gravitation. Cheyne.

ANA'LOGOUS, Adj. that which bears a refemblance to a thing, only in fome particulars. "There is fomething analogous in the exercise of the mind to that of the body." L'Eftrange. Ufed with the particle to before the thing compared.

ANA'LOGY, S. [from ανα and λογος, Gr.] a likenefs between things, with refpect to fome of their qualities, but a difference in others. "Although not in all things, every where the fame, yet for the moft part retaining the fame analogy." Hooker. Ufed with the particles to, with, between or between, before the thing compared. "By analogy with all other liquors." Burnet. Theory. "If the body politic have no

analogy to the natural." Dryd. There was fome analogy between the cuftoms. Dryd. In Grammar, it implies the agreement which feveral words have to each other, with refpect to their mode, or meaning, though they differ in others, fuch as time and circumftance. "As the words grieve and grieved; which agree together with refpect to the uneafy fenfation caufed by fome object; but differ with refpect to time, as grieve implies the prefent time, and grieved a time paft, or elapfed. In Mathematics, it implies a refemblance of ratio's.

ANALY'SIS, S. [αναλυσις, Gr.] a feparation, folution, of a body into the parts of which it confifts. In Philofophy, the confidering the different parts of a thing feparately. The refolving any thing, into its conftituent parts. "We cannot know any thing of nature but by an analyfis of its true folidal caufes." Glanv. Scep. In Mathematics, it implies the difcovering of the truth or falfehood of a propofition by fuppofing it true, and examining its, confequences, till we arrive to fome evident truths, or impoffibility, the neceffary confequence of the firft propofition, and conclude from thence the truth or impoffibility of that propofition, which may afterwards be demonftrated by refuming the reafons, whereby it was difcovered. Analyfis in chemiftry, is the refolution of any fubftance into its firft principles, to difcover what it confifts of. Thefe principles have given grounds for great alteration, which the reader may find managed with accuracy and precifion, by Mr. Boyle, in his fceptical Chymift, and by Dr. Shaw, a man univerfally applauded for his knowledge of every branch of the medical art.

ANALY'TICAL, Adj. that which refolves things into their firft principles. "The inaccuratenefs of the analytical experiments fo called." Boyle. That which confiders and feparates a thing into all the parts, of which it is compounded.

ANALY'TICALLY, Adv. in fuch a manner as to refolve a fubftance in to its firft principles.

ANALY'TIC, Adj. [αναλυτικος, Gr.] the refolving a thing in its primacy, or conftituent parts; the arguing on the principles or conceffions of an opponent, till he is reduced to a dilemma, "He was in logic a great critic,—Profoundly fkill'd in analytics." Hudib. "The analytic method takes the whole compound as it finds it, and leads us to the knowledge of it, by refolving it into its firft principles or parts, and is therefore called refolution." Watts.

To ANALY'ZE, V. A. [αναλυω, Gr.] to refolve into its firft principles. To trace a thing into its firft principles, or motives. "To analyze the immortality of any action in its laft principles." Norris. To re-

folve

folve a proposition into its object, subject, predicate, argument, &c. " This last is what is meant in the logical schools, when they talk of *analysing* a text of scripture." *Watts's Logic.*

ANALYZER, S. that which reduces a thing into its first principles. " Whether the fire be a true and univerfal *analyzer* of mixt bodies." *Boyle.*

ANAMORPHOSIS, S. [from ανα, Gr. and μορφωσις,] in Perfpective, the defcribing a figure, which in one point of view, fhall appear to be deformed, but in another, regular.

ANA'NAS, S. in Botany, the pine-apple. As for the fruit itfelf, nothing can be more magnificent, than the colours with which it is embellifhed. Its fcales are green, bordered with a carnation colour; its ground is yellow, and from each fcale arifes a purple flower, which falls off as the fruit ripens, and on the top is a crown. The pulp of the fruit is agreeable to the fight, and of fo exquifite a tafte, that, in order to conceive any idea of it, we muft blend in our imagination, that of the peach, the ftrawberry, mufcadine grape, and rennet-apple.

ANA'PHORA, S. [Gr. αναφορα] a figure in Rhetoric, in which feveral fentences begin with the fame word.

ANAPLERO'TIC, S. [αναπληρος, Gr.] in Medicine, that which fills up any wound with flefh.

AN'ARCH, S. the author, or promoter of confufion; a rebel.

ANA'RCHICAL, Adj. not fubject to rule, or laws; rebellious; feditious.

A'NARCHY, S. [αναρχια, Gr.] a ftate wherein people are without the enforcement of laws, and will not fubmit to them; rebellion; fedition; and confufion. " Arbitrary power is but the firft natural ftep from *anarchy*, or a favage life." *Swift.*

ANASA'RCA, S. [from ανα Gr. and σαρξ,] in Phyfic, a kind of univerfal dropfy. At the beginning, the legs fwell, efpecially towards night, when they pit remarkably; the urine is pale, the appetite decays, and at laft the fwelling rifes higher, and appears in the thighs, belly, breaft and arms. " When the lymph ftagnates, or is extravafated under the fkin, it is called an *anafarca.*" *Arbuth.*

ANASA'RCOUS, Adj. having the properties of an anafarc. " A gentlewoman laboured of an afcites, with an *anafarcous* fwelling." *Wifem.*

ANASTOMA'TIC, that which opens the veffels, or removes obftructions.

ANASTOMO'SIS, S. [Gr. ανα, and στομα] in Anatomy, the action of the mouths of two veffels, whereby they communicate with each other the infenfations, or joining of the nerves.

ANA'STROPHE, S. [from ανα, and στρεφω, Gr.] in Rhetoric, difpofition, or

No. III.

placing of words, not agreeable to the grammatical conftruction.

ANA'THEMA, S. [from ανα, and τιθημι,] among the Jews it fignified, firft, fomething dedicated to the fervice of God; fecondly, fomething devoted to deftruction; thirdly, one who was the object of univerfal averfion; and fourthly, one who was banifhed from the fynagogue. From hence we may be able to determine the precife meaning of St. Paul, when he wifhes himfelf to be the *anathema* for his brethren, Rom. ix. 3. It is certain that he muft exprefs a readinefs to undergo fome eminent calamity, but to fuppofe that he would wifh himfelf *accurfed*, as fome imagine, is to brand him with a degree of impiety inconfiftent with his character; to fuppofe him to mean only a bare feparation from the church, though indeed a heavy calamity, feems not confiftent to that degree of ardour he exprefles for the converfion of his nation: It remains then, that his meaning muft include, that he was not only ready to be cut off from the fociety of Chriftians, as an acknowledged member of their community, but likewife was willing to become the object of publc fcorn derifion, and averfion, to bear all outrage, calamities, and tortures, and to lay down his life for the converfion of his country. The term implies not only the curfe of excommunication, but alfo, the perfon excommunicated.

ANATHEMA'TICAL, Adj. that which is in the form of an anathema or curfe.

To ANATHE'MATIZE, V. A. to pronounce excommunication againft any perfon, whereby he is deprived of all the privileges of fociety. " They were therefore to be *anathematized* after this manner." *Ham. Fund.*

ANATOCISM, S. [anatocifmus, Lat.] a fpecies of ufury wherein the lenders exact compound intereft of the borrower.

ANATO'MICAL, Adj. that which is ufed in Anatomy. " It has the ufe of an *anatomical* knife." *Watts's Log.* That which is difcovered by anatomy, or in the diffection of a body. " There is a natural involuntary diftortion of the mufcles, which is the *anatomical* caufe of laughter." *Swift.*

ANA'TOMIST, S. [anatomifte, Fr.] a perfon who diffects bodies, or plants; dividing every one of the parts from each other; enquiring into the wonder of their ftructure, drawing from thence fuch lights, as muft contribute to the knowledge both of the caufe and feat of difeafes, the various methods of rectifying the morbid parts in their former foundnefs; and difcovering the finger of divine wifdom vifibly imprefled on a ftructure confifting of fuch a variety of parts, harmonizing with each other, and univerfally promoting the good of the whole.

To ANA'TOMISE, V. A. [from ανα, Gr. and τεμνω] to diffect or feparate every

N   part

part of the body; to discover all the properties of a thing; to lay open the secret motives or disposition of a person's mind.

ANA'TOMY, S. [ἀνατομια, Gr.] the
dissecting the parts of an animal or vegetable body, to discover the different uses of its
several parts. It is divided into human and
comparative: the comparative considers
brutes and vegetables, in order to illustrate
the human fabric; the human is that which
is employed in separating and considering the
parts of a human body. After a long disuse, this art revived in the sixteenth century;
prior to which, the dissection of a human
body was looked upon as sacrilege; and so
late as the time of the emperor Charles V,
an assembly of divines was convened, to determine whether it was consistent with the
dictates of conscience, to dissect a human
body; and to this very day it is forbidden in
Muscovy. But what advantages, with respect to the improvement of physic, not to
mention the consequences of such an improvement, the mitigation of pain, the eradication of disorders, and the prolonging of
human life, does this injunction preclude.
In a secondary sense, this word implies the
art itself. "According to the knowledge
which is communicated to us by anatomy."
Boyd. The dividing or separating the parts
of any thing, applied both to mental and
external operations. "A way to amplify
any thing is to break it, and to make an anatomy of its several parts." Bacon. The bones
or body which has been robbed of its integu-
ments of flesh, &c. "Rouse from sleep
this fell anatomy." Shakesp. K. John.

A'NATRON, S. a native salt extracted
from the waters of the Nile. The artificial
Anatron is composed of ten parts of salt-
petre, four of quick-lime, three of common
salt, two or three allum, and two of vitriol,
dissolved in wine, boiled, strained, and evaporated to the consistence of a salt. This is
used to purify metals.

A'NCESTOR, S. [ancestre, Fr.] the person from whom one is descended. "Cham
was the paternal ancestor of Ninus." Raleigh.

A'NCESTRAL, Adv. that may be claimed
in right of our ancestors.

A'NCESTRY, S. those from whom a
person is descended; family; lineage; progenitors; pedigree. "Say, from what
sceptred ancestry ye claim." Pope. Descent;
or birth.

A'NCHENTRY, S. applied to a family,
or descent, antiquity: in a secondary sense,
dignity, pomp, and solemnity. "A measure full of state and ancientry." Shakesp.

ANCHI'LOPS, S. [from αγαι and ωψ]
in Surgery, a swelling at the innermost corner of the eye.

A'NCHOR, S. [ancora; Lat. from ἀγ-
κυρα, Gr.] an instrument formed of an heavy

strong piece of iron, &c. It consists of a
ring, to which the cable is fastened; the
beam or shank, which is the longest part of
the anchor; the arm, which runs into the
ground; the flouke, fluke, or palm, the
broad parts ending in a point, with barbs
resembling the head of an arrow which fastens it into the ground; and the stock, which
is a piece of wood fastened to the beam, near
the ring, which guides the fluke in its descent, so as it may fall right, and fix in the
ground. There are several sorts on board a
ship, which are called by different names;
the first and largest is called the sheet anchor, and never used but in violent storms;
the second the bowers, which are less, and
used when the vessel rides in a road or harbour, and are named the first and second, or
best and small bower; the third, when a
vessel is to be brought up and down the river by winds, though the tide be contrary,
which is a small anchor, called the redge, or
ridge anchor, by means of which they wind
her head about when she approaches too near
to shore; the fourth, the stream anchor, is
a small one, made fast to the stream cable,
by means of which the ship rides in gentle
streams and fair weather; the fifth, the
grapnell, is a small anchor for a ship or
boat. The dimensions of anchors, with respect to the length of the beam and their
weight, should be in proportion to the
breadth of the ship within; but as the tables calculated for this purpose, would swell
this work beyond its destined limits, we refer those who are desirous of farther information, to Bernouille's discourse on this
subject, which carried the prize at the academy of sciences. It is used with the following verbs, to drop or cast, which imply
the letting down, and to weigh, which signifies the pulling up the anchor. Figuratively,
Any thing which keeps from motion or
fluctuation. Shakespeare seems to have substituted this word instead of uncouthe. "An
anchor's cheer." Hamlet.

To A'NCHOR, V. N. to be secured or
stopped; to be kept from driving. "Near
Calais the Spaniards anchored." Bacon. Figuratively, to fasten; to stop. Anchor-holds.
The fastness or security procured by an anchor; a security against any calamity. Anchor-smith is a maker or forger of anchors.
"From the anchor-smith to the watch-
maker." Moxon.

A'NCHORAGE, S. the power or effect
which an anchor has to keep a ship from
driving; the duty paid for anchoring.

A'NCHORET, or A'NCHORITE, S.
one who retires into unfrequented places, to
practise austerities.

ANCHO'VY, S. [anchoie, Fr. anchova,
Span.] a small fish, used for sauce. They
should be chosen with round backs, small,
white

white on the red fide, and white within, becaufe the large and flat are feldom any thing
elfe but fardines.

A'NCIENT, Adj. [*ancien*, Fr.] having
endured for fome time ; that which has been
fome time ago ; applied to the Deity, it denotes exiftence before any other being ; paft,
or former. "We fhall begin our *ancient*
bickeringe." *Shakefp. Hen.* VI. Ufed as a
fubftantive, it implies one who lived at fome
time diftant from the prefent period, oppofed to modern. "Though the *ancients*
thus their rules invade." *Pope.* The fig-
ur ftreamer of a fhip ; formerly that of a
regiment, and from thence the bearer of it.
In which fenfe, Piftol is called *ancient* Piftol.

A'NCIENTLY, Adv. in times long paft,
or before the prefent inftant. "Which, with
the territory about it, *anciently* pertained to
this crown." *Sidney.*

A'NCIENTNESS, S. length of time ;
antiquity. "They were called Saturnian
from their *ancikerufs*." *Dryd.*

A'NCIENTRY, S. a long pedigree ; a
family which has been noted for a long courfe
of years.

AND, Conjunct. [from *and*, Sax. *ende*,
Belg.] a particle, by which words or fentences are joined. "To make difcoveries in
human life, *and* to fettle the proper diftinctions." *Tatler.* Before it, it fignifies tho'.
"They will fet a houfe on fire, *and* it were
but to roaft this egg." *Sac.* Moderns drop
the *and*, and ufe the particle *if* by itfelf.

ANDIRONS, S. [a corruption of *band-
irons*, that is fuch as may be eafily moved by
the hands] irons at each end of a grate, in
which a fpit turns ; or irons on which wood
is laid to burn.

ANDOVER, a market town in Hamp-
fhire, with a market on Saturdays, and three
fairs, on Midlent Saturday, for cheefe, horfes
and leather ; on May 12, for leather and
millinery goods ; and on November 16, for
fheep, horfes, leather, and cheefe. It is a
large town, which fends two members to
parliament, and is a great thoroughfare on
the weftern road. It is 10 miles N. by W.
of Winchefter, and 62 W. by S. of London. Lon. 18. 5. Lat. 51. 20. Near this
town is held an annual fair, on October 10,
called Weyhill, for fheep, leather, hops,
and cheefe. It is one of the largeft in all
England, and has booths fet up, wherein all
kinds of goods are fold.

ANDRO'GYNAL, Adj. [from *andro*]
that which partakes of both fexes, male and
female ; that which has the properties of an
hermaphrodite.

ANDRO'GYNUS, S. a perfon who unites
both the male and female fex in his ftructure.
An hermaphrodite.

ANE'CDOTE, S. [*anekdon*, Gr.] a piece
of fecret hiftory.

ANEMO'GRAPHY, S. [from *anemos*,
Gr. and *grapho*] a defcription of the winds.

ANEMOMETER, S. [from *anemos*,
Gr. and *metreo*] an inftrument to meafure
the force of the wind.

ANEMONE, S. [from *anemone*, Gr.]
in Botany, the windflower. It is ufed medi-
ally externally in medicine, in cerufines and
collyriums, for filters in the eyes.

ANEMO'SCOPE, S. [from *anemos*, Gr.
and *scopeo*] an inftrument which foretels
the changes of the wind.

ANE'NT, Prep. [from a redundant, and
ewen, Sax. near] concerning, about, or
touching. "He faid nothing *anent* this particular." Near ; oppofite to.

ANEURISM, S. [from *aneurysma*, Gr.]
in Surgery, a tumour caufed by the weaknefs
of an artery.

ANEW, Adv. [from *ane* or *new*,
Belg.] again ; once more ; a fecond time.
"He who begins late, is obliged to form
anew the whole difpofition of his foul."
Rogers.

ANFRACTUOSE, or ANFRA'CTU-
OUS, Adj. [from *anfractus*, Lat.] full of
winding paffages, like a maze or labyrinth.
Peculiar to medical or anatomical writers.

A'NGEL, S. [*angelos*, Lat. *aggelos*, Gr.]
a relative term, a perfon fent or commiffioned by another. In its primitive fenfe,
being a denomination of office, not of nature, it is applied to priefts, *Malach.* ii. 7.
To John Baptift, *Matth.* xi. 10. And to
Chrift himfelf, *Ifai.* lx. 6, *Gen.* xlviii. 6.
Exod. xxiii. 10. *Dan.* iii. 13. *Rev.* xli. 7. A
fpecies of incorporeal beings fuperior to mankind, and of different degrees of dignity,
power, and perfection. A gold coin, having the figure of an angel upon it. Figuratively, a perfon of great beauty. Ufed as
an adjective, it implies fomething more than
human ; one of the order of angels. "Virgins vifited by *angel* powers."

ANGE'LIC, Adj. refembling or partaking of the nature of angels.

ANGE'LICA, S. in Botany, the greateft
of the umbelliferous plants. It is ftomachic, cordial, and alexipharmic.

ANGE'LICAL, refembling angels ; that
which partakes of the properties of angels.
"*Angelical* contentment." *Wilkins.*

ANGE'LICK, Adj. See ANGELIC.

ANGELOT, a fort of fmall cheefe made
in Normandy. Alfo a mufical inftrument
refembling a lute.

ANGER, S. [from *anger*, Sax.] a paf-
fionate defire of thwarting the happinefs of
another. Figuratively, the pain or fmart of
a fore or wound, in allufion to the forenefs
and the reddening countenances of thofe who
are affected with this paffion. "The greateft *anger* and foreneft ftill continued." *Temple.*

To AN'GER, V. A. to offend a person, to provoke him.

AN'GERLY, Adv. like a person who resents an injury. "You look *angerly*." *Shakesp.* Instead of this word we use *angrily* at present.

ANGI'NA, S. [from *ango*, Lat.] a quinsey. See QUINSEY.

ANGIO'GRAPHY, S. [from *aggeion*, Gr. and *graphō*] a description of the vessels of the human body.

ANGIO'LOGY, S. [from *aggeion*, Gr. and *logos*] a discourse of the vessels of the human body.

AN'GLE, S. [*angulus*, Lat.] the meeting of two lines in a point, which incline to each other.

AN'GLE, S. [from *angel*, Sax.] an instrument to catch fish with. "His *angle* trembling in his hand."

To AN'GLE, V. N. to fish with a line; to entice by some allurements. "The hearts of all that he fhd *angle* for." *Shakesp.*

AN'GLE-ROD, [*angelroede*, Belg. *angel*, Port. *anroed*, Span.] the rod to which the line is fastened in angling. "Used for *angleroade*." *Bac.*

AN'GLER, S. one who angles. "Like a patient *angler*."

ANGLESEY, [the Ifle of] is the most western county of North Wales. It is 24 miles in length, 14 in breadth, and sends one member to parliament. It is separated from the continent by the river Meni, which divides it from Carnarvonfhire, and on every other fide. It is furrounded by the fea. It is a fertile spot, and abounds in corn, cattle, fith, fib and fowls, with very good millftones and grindftones. The chief town is Beaumaris. Near Kemlyn Harbour there is a quarry of ftone, called Afbeftos, which is a beautiful marble out of which may be got the Linum Afbeftinum, called here St Jermander's Wool. It is a ftone nor like flax, and will bear a common fire. And not far from this there is a yellow fulphureous copper ore, which has never been worked. At Llhbiadrig, about three miles eaftward from hence, there is a great body or vein of ftony oker, of various colours, as red, yellow, blue, and an extremely fine white clay, of the Cimolia kind. Thefe might be of great fervice to painters, potters, and ftone-cutters.

AN'GLICISM, S. a manner of expreffion peculiar to the Englifh.

AN'GRED, Part. provoked, enraged.

AN'GRILY, Adj. fo as to exprefs refentment.

AN'GRY, Adj. highly difpleafed or enraged. "Whofoever is *angry* with his brother." *Matt* v. 22. "Be provoked." "An *angry* man ftirreth up ftrife." *Prov.* xxix. 22. That which hath the appearance, marks,

or figns of anger. "An *angry* countenance." *Prov.* xxv. 23. Applied to wounds; inflamed, painful, or fore.

AN'GUISH, S. [*angoiffe*, Fr.] exceffive pain; immoderate forrow, anxiety and torture. "Tribulation and *anguifh* upon every foul of man." *Rom.* ii. 9.

AN'GUISHED, Adj. afflicted with great anxiety, torture, and forrow.

AN'GULAR, Adj. [*angular*, Lat.] having corners or angles.

ANGULA'RITY, S. the quality of having angles.

AN'GULARLY, Adv. like an angle.

AN'GULATED, Adj. [*angulus*, Lat.] having angles or corners.

AN'GULOUS, Adj. [from *angulus*] having corners or angles.

ANGU'ST, A. [*anguftus*, Lat.] narrow, confined.

ANGUSTA'TION, S. [*anguftus*, Lat.] the act of leffening the diftance between two appetite objects.

ANHE'LITUS, S. [from *anhelo*, Lat.] a quicknefs of breathing, occafioned by running, or afcending any fteep place.

ANI'GHTS, Adv. during the night; every night.

A'NIL, S. in Botany, the indigo plant. Linnæus ranges it in his feventeenth clafs, for tufe the flowers have ten ftamina in the two bodies.

ANI'LITY, S. [*anilitas*, Lat.] old age, confider. ! only as it refpects a woman.

A'NIMA MU'NDI, S. a pure etherial fubftance or fpirit, according to Plato and other ancient philofophers, diffufed through the mafs of the world, informing, actuating, and uniting its feveral parts into one great body or animal. Chriftians object to this opinion, that it confounds the Maker with his work, and takes away the ftrongeft barrier againft vice, the poffibility of a ftate of future rewards and punifhments. But thofe who choofe to fee this doctrine cleared of its abfurdities, and embellifhed with all the charms of harmony and eloquence, muft have recourfe to the Effay on Man, by Pope.

ANIMADVE'RSION, S. [*animadverfio*, Lat.] a remarking of a fault, with anger, feverity, or reproach; punifhment, cenfure, or the execution of the Laws; ufed with an or upon before the object. "Handled by priphlets on both fides, without the leaft *animadverfion* upon the authors." *Swift.*

ANIMADVE'RSIVE, Adj. [from *animadverfivum*, Lat.] having power to make the mind attend to any particular object; that which has the power of judging.

To ANIMADVE'RT, V. N. [*animadverto*, Lat.] to cenfure, to blame. "I fhould not *animadvert* on him." *Dryd.* To take notice of a fault, fo as to punifh it. "If the

the author of the universe *animadverts* upon him here below." *Grew's Cosmol.* Used with the particles *on* or *upon*.

ANIMADVERTER, S. one who inflicts punishment, or passes censure.

ANIMAL, S. [*animal*, Lat.] a being, consisting of a body and soul. In a secondary sense, it is used as a person beneath our notice, a mean, despicable, or contemptible creature. "A despicable *animal*." *Johnson.* We would ask, whether the idea of contempt is conveyed by the word *despicable* or the word *animal*? If by the former, Mr. Johnson's observation is too nice; If by the latter, what need is there for joining the word despicable to it. *Animal*, used as an adjective, implies something relating to animals. *Animal secretion*, is the act whereby the juices of the body are separated and selected from the common mass of the blood. *Animal spirits*, are a fine subtile juice, supposed to be the great instrument of muscular motion and sensation; but its existence is so much controverted, that it affords the candidates in physic, at our universities, no barren subject for the exercises which they perform for their degrees.

ANIMALCULE, S. [*animalculum*, Lat.] a very small animal, generally applied to such as cannot be discerned by the naked eye.

ANIMALITY, S. [*animal*, Lat.] that which has the property of an animal.

To ANIMATE, V. A. [*animo*, Lat.] to give life to; to quicken; to join, or unite, a soul to a body. "Men must have been *animated* by a higher power." Figuratively, to enliven, to make vocal, to inspire with the charms of sound. "None can *animate* the lyre." *Dryd.* To communicate bravery to; to encourage, hearten, or excite. "The more to *animate* the people." *Knolles.*

ANIMATE, Adj. [*animatus*, Lat.] Indued with a soul; that which has life.

ANIMATED, Part. vigorous; spirited; bold.

ANIMATION, S. the act of bringing into existence. "Plants are the first produced, which is the world of *animation*." *Bac.* The state wherein the soul and body are united; the enjoyment of life.

ANIMATIVE, Adj. having the power of communicating life; enlivening; encouraging; making vigorous.

ANIMATOR, S. [from *animator*, Lat.] that which enlivens. "They best unite to the t *animator*." *Brown's Vulg. Errors.*

ANIMOSE, Adj. [*animosus*, Lat.] violent; courageous; vehement.

ANIMOSITY, S. [*animositas*, Lat.] a disposition wherein a person is inclined to hinder the success, or disturb the tranquility of another.

ANISE, S. [*anisum*, Lat.] in Botany, a species of opium or parsley, of an aromatic scent and taste, reputed an aromatic.

ANKER, S. [*anker*, Belg.] a liquid measure of Amsterdam, containing about sixty-four pints of Paris, or thirty-two gallons English measure.

ANKLE, S. the joint which unites the leg to the foot. Ankle-bone, the protuberant bone of the ankle.

ANNALIST, S. one who writes annals.

ANNALS, S. [from *annales*, Lat.] a narrative, wherein the transactions are digested into periods, consisting each of one year.

ANNATES, or ANNATS, S. in Law, the first-fruits.

To ANNEAL, V. A. [pronounced as if written with n, from *en-arlen*, Sax.] to heat glass to make it retain the colours laid on it; to heat glass after it is blown, to prevent its breaking; to heat any thing so as to give it its temper.

To ANNEX, V. A. [*annexum*, Lat.] to join, or subjoin. "He *annexed* a codicil." To connect; to unite with; to belong to. "The authority which is *annexed* to your office." *Dryd.* Used as a substantive; properties or attributes. "Assumed the *annexes* of divinity." *Brown's Vulg. Err.*

ANNEXATION, S. conjunction; coalition; union. "These *annexations* of benefices." *Ayliff.*

ANNEXION, S. the adding of something as a supplement or aid; addition.

ANNEXMENT, S. something joined to another.

To ANNIHILATE, V. A. [*annihilo*, Lat.] to reduce to nothing; to put a period to; to extinguish; to destroy. "To *annihilate* the friendship of puny minds." *Swift.* To destroy all the properties of a thing. "The flood that hath altered, deformed, or rather *annihilated* this place. Applied to the different forms of government; to annul, to take away, extirpate, or put an end to.

ANNIHILATION, S. the act by which the existence of a thing is destroyed. Applied to the funds, or other national securities; the loss of so much of the principal.

ANNI NUBILES, [Lat.] in Law, that age wherein a female becomes marriageable, which, according to law, is at twelve years of age.

ANNIVERSARY, S. [*anniversarius*, Lat.] the return of any remarkable day in the calendar; some public rejoicing in honour of the anniversary day. In the Romish church, it signifies an office, which is not only to be said once a year, but every day, for the soul of the deceased.

ANNIVERSARY, Adj. [*anniversarius*, Lat.] that which happens once in the year; annual or yearly.

ANNO DOMINI, [Lat.] expressed by abbreviature, A. D. 1772, i.e. in the year of our Lord one thousand seven hundred and seventy-two.

ANNO-

ANNOTA'TION, S. [annotatio, Lat.] an explanation of the difficult passages of an author by way of notes.

ANNOTA'TOR, S. [Lat.] one who explains the difficult passages of another; a commentator. "I have not that respect for the annotators, which they generally meet with." Felton.

To ANNOU'NCE, V. A. [annoncer, Fr.] to proclaim; to give notice; to pronounce; to sentence in a judicial sense; to condemn. "Announce—Of life or death." Prior.

To ANNO'Y, V. A. [annoyer, Fr.] to disturb, vex, or make a person uneasy; to spoil; to diminish. "Nor vile jealousy—His dear delights were able to annoy." Fairy Q. "To be a nuisance to; to corrupt; to make unwholesome. "Where houses thick, and sewers, annoy the air." Milton. To disturb, or provoke. "Let them alone, and annoy them not." Ray

ANNO'Y, S. an attack; trouble; the things we fear bring less annoy—Than war." Dennis. Misfortune. "After pall annoy—To take the good vicissitude of joy." Dryd.

ANNO'YANCE, S. that which occasions trouble, dislike, injury, or hurt. "Rooks and magpies are great annoyances." Mortimer.

ANNO'YER, S. one who causes any annoyance.

ANNUAL, Adj. [annual, Fr.] for the duration of a year. "A thousand pounds a year, annual support." Shakesp. That which lasts only one year. "The roots of plants that are annual." Bac.

ANNUALLY, Adv. yearly.

ANNU'ITANT, S. [annus, Lat.] one who receives an annuity.

ANNU'ITY, S. [annuité, Fr.] a yearly revenue; a yearly allowance.

To ANNUL, V. A. [from nullus, Lat.] to abrogate; to abolish; made imperceptible, or as if annihilated. "And all her various objects of delight—Annull'd." Milton. Corruption.

ANNULAR, Adj. [from annulus, Lat.] resembling a ring. "Tied them to the bones by annular ligaments." Cheyne.

ANNULARY, Adj. [from annulus, Lat.] in the form of rings.

ANNULET, S. [a diminutive for annulus, Lat.] a small ring. In Heraldry, used for a mark that the person is the fifth brother; sometimes, indeed, a part of the coat of several families, reputed a mark of dignity. In Architecture, the small square number in the Doric capital, under the quarter round. Likewise a flat moulding, common to the other parts of the column.

ANNULLING, Part. Noun, the revoking or repealing of an act, &c.

To ANNUMERATE, V. A. [annumero, Lat.] to reckon a person or thing as belonging to a list, or being one of a number.

To ANNUNCIATE, V. A. [annuncio, Lat.] to inform a person of some particular he is a stranger to; to bring a message to a person; to discover a piece of news. Wants both authority and use to establish it.

ANNUNCIA'TION-DAY, S. the day celebrated in commemoration of the angel's visitation of the blessed Virgin, on the 25th of March.

ANODYNE, S. [from a, Gr. and oδυνη,] a remedy which abates pain.

To ANOINT, V. A. [pronounced as if the e was dropped, and an e final was at the end, in order to lengthen the sound of the i, from oint, oindre, Fr. to rub with some thing greasy. "Thou shalt not anoint thyself with oil." Deut. xxviii. To consecrate, in allusion to the method of pouring oil on the heads of such, as were dedicated to the discharge of some important post. "In his anointed flesh." Shakesp. Lear.

ANOINTER, S. one who anoints.

ANO'LIS, S. an American animal like a lizard.

ANOMALISM, S. that which is inconsistent with the common rules; irregularity.

ANOMALISTICAL, irregular. Anomalistical year, in Astronomy, the space of time wherein the earth passes through her orbit.

ANOMALOUS, Adj. [anomalos, Gr.] in grammar, those words that are not consistent with the rules of declining, &c. In Astronomy, that which seemingly deviates from its regular motion. Applied to irregularity of any kind; in a political sense, seditious. "There will arise anomalous disturbances, not only in civil and artificial, but also in military officers. Brown's Vulg. Err.

ANOMALOUSLY, Adv. inconsistently, irregularly, uncommonly.

ANOMALY, S. [anomalie, Fr.] a deviation from established rules and laws. "Most of these anomalies in writing might be avoided." Holder. In Astronomy, applied to a planet, is that whereby it differs from the aphelion, or apogee; This is distinguished into mean, eccentric and true; mean anomaly, is the distance of a planet's mean motion from the apogee, or in modern astronomy, the time wherein it moves from its aphelion, to the mean place or point of its orbit. Eccentric anomaly, is an arch of an eccentric circle, included between the aphelion, and a right line drawn through the center of the planet, perpendicular to the line of the apsides. Among the moderns it is implied an arch of the auxilar, terminated by a line of the apsides, and the line of mean motion of the center.

ANOMY, S. [from a, Gr. and νομος, Gr.] a breach of law, violation, or transgression.

ANON, Adj. [from a and non, Belg.] soon,

foon, prefently; quickly. When applied to vicissitude, revolution, or change of action; it fignifies then, afterwards, or fometimes.

ANONYMOUS, Adj. [from a, Gr. and onyma, Gr.] not having yet received a name. " Another anonymous infect of the waters." Ray. Applied to books, that which is with- out a name.

ANONYMOUSLY, Adv. fo as to be without a name. " The edition is to come out anonymoufly." Swift.

ANOREXY, S. [anorexia, Gr.] a want of appetite; ufed by medical writers, but not very common.

ANOTHER, pronoun, [from an, Sax. and other, Sax.] not like that which is men- tioned; different. " Another Jefus, another fpirit, another Gofpel." 2 Cor. xi. 4. One more; an addition; befides; " Have ye an- other brother." Gen. xliii. 7. Applied to identity, not the fame. " Then faid he to another, how much oweft thou?" Luke xvi 7. Any other, oppofed to one's felf. " Let another praife thee, and not thy own mouth." Prov. xxvii. 2. Joined with one, it implies a thing mutually performed; fomething re- ciprocal.

ANSPESSADES, or LANSPESSADES, S. [from lanciafprezzata, Ital.] a kind of infer- ior officers of foot, between the corporal and common centinel.

To ANSWER, V. A. [anfwerion, Sax.] to give that information, or fatisfaction, re- quired by a queftion. To reply to an ob- jection. " If it be faid, &c. I anfwer It is not neceffary." Boyle. To affign reafons; to be accountable for; with the particle for before a thing, and to before the perfon. " Our author muft anfwer for it." Brown's Vulg. Err. " Let thofe anfwer either to God or man." Temple. To equal, or fatis- fy any claim or debt; to pay. " Who ftu- dies day and night—To anfwer all the debt he owes." Shakfp. Hen. IV. To act upon again; mutually, or reciprocally to act up- on. " Do the ftrings anfwer to thy noble hand !" Dryd. To bear a proportion; to be proportionate to. " Anfwered the bulk of fo prodigious a perfon." Gulliv. Trav. To fuit, or promote. " The moft deferv- ing object, and the moft likely to anfwer the ends of our charity." Atterb. Among the Jews, it fignifies the obviating any ob- jection which is not expreffed; and fome- times is a mere expletive, or at moft, ferves to introduce a narrative. " The king an- fwered and faid to Daniel." Dan. ll. 26. Peter anfwered and faid to her." Aſts v. 8. To vindicate, or be received as a wit- nefs, teftimony or voucher in a perfon's be- half. " So fhall my righteoufnefs anfwer for me." Gen. xxx. 33. Applied to God, it fignifies his hearing, or fhewing that he has heard a requeft, by granting it. " The

Lord anfwered me, and fet me in a large place." Pfal. cxviii.

ANSWER, S. [anfwara, Sax.] a reply to a queftion; a folution of any objection. " Jefus gave him no anfwer." John x. 9. " Be ready to give an anfwer to every man." 1 Pet. 3. 15.

ANSWERABLE, Adj. that which will admit of an anfwer or reply. Obliged to give reafons for, or give an account of. Anfwera- ble to God only." Swift. That which matches or fuits; applied to colour, or the fabric of moveables. " Anfwerable to the hangings of the court." Exd. xxxviii. 18. Wor- thy of, fit, or fuitable. " Bring forth fruit anfwerable, to amendment." Matt. iii. 8. That which can fatisfy, or is equal to. " Means anfwerable unto other men's de- fires." Reforb. Ufed with the particle to.

ANSWERABLY, Adv. proportionably; in a manner fuitably with the particle to. " If free from iflands, they are anfwerably deeper." Brerew.

ANSWERER, S. one who anfwers, folves, obviates, or clears up the objections of an adverfary.

ANT, S. [from emt, a contraction of emmit, Sax.] fmall infects called alfo pif- mires, who herd together on hillocks, re- markable for their induftry, tendernefs, and economy. " Go to the ant thou flug- gard." Prov. v. 6. The common opinion of their hoarding up their provifions for the winter, though afferted in fcripture and con- firmed from Horace, is denied by Swammer- dam, Raumur, and other modern naturalifts; but thofe who are willing to entertain them- felves with this curious republic, will meet abundant fatisfaction from Swammerdam's Book of Nature, the Spectacle de la Nature, and the Guardian.

ANTA, S. [from ante, Lat.] In Archi- tecture, a pilafter at the corners of the walls of temples.

ANTAGONIST, S. [from ant, Gr. and agon, Gr.] one who contends with ano- ther. Applied to writers, he who oppofes the opinion, or fentiments of another. " Our antagonifts in thefe controverfies." Hooker. An oppofite. " The two extremes, and antagonifts of the fpecies." Guard. No. 108. In Anatomy, that which is fituated oppofite to, and counteracts another; thus the flexor, or the mufcle which bends, and the extenfor, or mufcle, which extends a limb, are called Antagonifts.

To ANTAGONIZE, V. A. [of ant, Gr. and agonizo, Gr.] to ftrive againft another.

ANTANACLASIS, S. [of antanaclafis, Gr.] in Rhetoric, a figure wherein a word is repeated in a different fenfe. " As let the dead bury their dead; the word dead, in the firft place, fignifying thofe who are immerfed in voluptuoufnefs, and in ways fenfible ci- ther

ther to the calls of grace, or their own danger; and in the second, one whose soul is separated from his body. It is likewise the returning of the same sentence, after the intervention of several others.

ANTANA'GOGE, S. [from αντι, Gr. αντι'ω] in Rhetoric, a figure, wherein, being unable to deny the crimes with which we are charged, we endeavour to load him with the same, or others.

ANTAPODO'SIS, S. [from αντι, Gr. απο- and δοσις, Gr.] a retreat or returning. In Rhetoric, a figure containing the counterpart of a simile. " Thus, as the husbandman weeds his ground, so should we weed and clear our minds;" the words in Italics are the Antapodosis.

ANTA'RES, S. in Astronomy, a star of the first magnitude in the constellation Scorpio.

ANTA'RCTIC, Adj. [from αντι, Gr. and αρκτος] opposite to the arctic, applied to Astronomy to the southern pole, and circle. The antarctic pole, is the south pole. The antarctic circle, is one of the lesser circles of the sphere, parallel to the equator and 23 deg. 30 min. distant from the south pole. The antarctic pole, in Geography is the southern extremity of the earth's axis.

To ANTECEDE, V. A [from ante and cedo, Lat.] to precede, or go before another in time, very seldom applied to place. " The fabric of the world did not long antecede its motion."

ANTECEDA'NEOUS, Adj. that which is before another.

ANTECE'DENCE, S. priority of existence; existence before. " Antecedence of their coalitimation preceding the existence." Hale's Orig.

ANTECE'DENT, Adj. [antecedens, Lat.] prior; former; before; or existing before. Used with the particle to. " Existence must be antecedent to merit." Collier. Used substantively, it implies the thing which must have gone before. " It is indeed the necessary antecedent." Smith. In grammar, the noun, which in the order of construction goes before a relative. In Logic, the first part of an enthymeme, or syllogism, consisting of two propositions only.

ANTECE'DENTLY, Adv. previously; prior to. " Consider him antecedently to his creation." Smith.

ANTECE'SSOR, S. [Lat. from antecedo] one who precedes, in the order of time.

ANTE-CHA'MBER, S. a chamber leading to a chief apartment.

ANTE-CU'RSOR, S. [Lat. from antecurro, Lat.] one who runs before; a harbinger; by divines applied to John the Baptist.

To A'NTEDATE, V. A. [from ante, and datum,] to place before its real period. To enjoy a thing in imagination before it exists. " Antedate the bliss above." Pope.

ANTEDILU'VIAN, Adv. [from anti, and diluvium,] that which existed before the flood. " All the stone and marble of the antediluvian earth." Woodw. That which relates or belongs to things before the flood. " Antediluvian chronology." Brown's Vulg. Err. Used substantively for those who lived before the flood.

A'NTELOPE, S. [from αντι, Gr. and λωψ,] in natural history, a sort of goat with wreathed horns.

ANTEMERI'DIAN, Adj. [from ante, and meridies, before noon.

ANTEMU'NDANE, Adj. [from ante, and mundanus] before the creation of the world.

A'NTEPAST, S. [from ante, and pastum] a foretaste, or earnest, of something future. " Antepast, to excite our guilt." Decay of Piety.

ANTEPENU'LT, or ANTEPENU'LTIMA, S. [Lat. from ante, penus, and ultimus,] in grammar the last syllable but two.

ANTEPI'LEPTIC, Adj. [from αντι, Gr. επιληψις, Gr. a convulsion fit] in Medicine, remedies against convulsions.

ANTEPRE'DICAMENT, S. [antepredicamenta, Lat.] in Logic, something requisite to be known in order to render the knowledge of the predicaments more easy.

ANTERIO'RITY, S. [anterior, Lat.] the state of being before another.

ANTE'RIOR, Adj. [Lat.] before another with regard to time or place.

A'NTES, S. [from ante, Lat.] in Architecture, pillars supporting the front of a building.

ANTESTA'TURE, S. [antestis, Lat.] in Fortification, an intrenchment of palisadoes or sacks of earth, thrown up in order to dispute the remainder of a piece of ground.

A'NTESTOMACH, S. a cavity which leads to the stomach; the crop in birds.

ANTHE'LIX, S. [from αντι Gr. and ελιξ, Gr.] the inward protuberance of the outward ear.

ANTHELMI'NTHIC, Adj. [from αντι and ελμινθος, Gr.] in Medicine, that which kills worms; " Anthelminthicks, or contrary to worms." Arbuth.

A'NTHEM, S. [anthema, Ital. antiphona, from αντι, Gr. opposite or reciprocal, and υμνος, a hymn or song. Johnson contends for its being spelt anthymn, as derived from the Greek; but as we may plainly see that it is borrowed from the Italian, there is no need of any alteration) a hymn performed in two parts by the opposite members of a choir.

ANTHE'RÆ, S. [Lat.] in Botany, the summits, tufts, knots, or little heads in the middle flowers, on the tops of the stamina.

ANTHO'LOGY, S. [from ανθος, Gr. and λογος, Gr.] a discourse of flowers.

ANTHRA-

ANTHRACOSIS, S. In Medicine, a disease in the bulb of the eye, or eyelids.

ANTHROPOLOGY, S. [from ἄνθρωπος, Gr. and λόγος, Gr.] a treatise upon man, considered as in a state of health, including the consideration both of the body and foul, with the laws of their motion. In Divinity, the applying the parts of a human body to God, such as eyes, ears, &c.

ANTHROPOMORPHITES, S. [from ἄνθρωπος, and μορφη, Gr.] one who attributes the shape of man to God. Applied to a sect, who took all the figurative and analogical expressions, of hands, eyes, ears, &c. applied to God, in a litteral sense; grounding their opinion on the scripture expressions. "That God made man after his own image."

ANTHROPHAGINEAN, Adj. in a terrifying, terrible, or savage manner.

ANTROPOPHAGY, S. the custom of eating of human flesh.

ANTHYPOPHORA, S. [Gr.] in Rhetoric, a figure, whereby objections are obviated, and answered.

ANTI, [Gr.] a particle, which signifies contrary or opposite.

ANTIACID, Adj. of a nature contrary to acid, an alkali.

ANTI-ARTHRITICS, S. [Gr.] remedies against the gout.

ANTI-BACCHIUS, S. [root and Bacchius] in antient poetry, a foot consisting of three syllables, the two first of which are long, and the third short.

ANTI-CHAMBER, S. See ANTE-CHAMBER.

ANTICHRESIS, S. See MORTGAGE.

ANTICHRIST, S. one who opposes the doctrine and mission of Christ. In a more confined sense, a tyrant, who at the latter end of the world is to make himself very conspicuous in his opposition to Christianity. In the opinion of the papists, but the protestants assert, that anti-christ is already come; that he is the pope; and the council of Gap, carried things so far in 1603, as to insert it as an article in their creed, that the pope was Anti-christ. No one, who would satisfy himself in this point, will repent his trouble in reading what Dr. Newton has said on this head in his Discourses on scripture Prophecies.

ANTI-CHRISTIAN, Adj. contrary, or opposite to Christianity.

ANTI-CHRISTIANISM, S. any doctrine contrary to Christianity.

ANTI-CHRONISM, S. [from ἀντι, Gr. and χρόνος, Gr.] that which is contrary to the order of time.

To ANTICIPATE, V. A. [from ante and capio, Lat.] to be beforehand with another. To do or enjoy a thing before its natural period. To render the application or advice of another useless, by giving it before him.

No. III.

ANTICIPATION, S. the doing a thing before its due period. Enjoyment in imagination, before its real existence; a fore taste; an implanted or innate opinion, supposed to be in the mind, before it is capable of discovering the reasons on which it is founded.

ANTIC, S. [a Fantique, Fr.] one who plays tricks; and makes use of odd and uncommon gestures; a Merry Andrew; a Buffoon.

To ANTICK, V. A. to make ridiculous, or despicable, in allusion to the gesticulations of buffoons and antic dancers.

ANTICKLY, Adv. with odd gesticulations and ridiculous grimaces.

ANTICLIMAX, S. [from anti, and κλιμαξ, Gr.] in Rhetoric, a figure, wherein the last sentence is weaker in its signification than the first.

ANTICOR, S. [from anti, and cor] in Farriery, a swelling in a horse's breast opposite to his heart.

ANTICOURTIER, S. one who opposes the court.

ANTIDOTAL, Adj. having the quality of preventing the effects of contagion, or poison.

ANTIDOTE, S. [antidotus, Lat.] a medicine to expel poison and to guard from contagion.

ANTILOGARITHM, S. the complement of a logarithm, or its difference from one of 90 degrees.

ANTILOGY, S. [Gr. of anti and λόγος] contradiction, applied to those passages of an author, wherein there seems to be, or really is, a manifest contradiction.

ANTIPLOQUIST, S. [from anti, and loquor, Lat.] one who speaks against the sentiments of another; a contradicter.

ANTI-MONARCHICAL, Adj. [from anti and μοναρχία] contrary to monarchy, or government by one person.

ANTIMONIAL, Adj. consisting of antimony.

ANTIMONY, S. [the stibium of the ancients, and στιμμι of the Greeks. It is supposed to have owed its present name to the following incident: Basil Valentine, a monk, observing it purge some hogs he had thrown it to; and fattening them afterwards, he prescribed a like dose to his brother monks; but they all dying, the medicine was called from thence antimoine, in French, from anti against, and moine, Fr. a monk.] It is a mineral substance, possessing all the properties of a metal, excepting malleability and ductility; is found in most mines, but especially those of silver and lead; and is distinguished into two sorts, crude and prepared. Crude antimony implies, that it is in the same state as it comes from the mines: Prepared antimony is that which is purified by chemistry. As the operations are violent and precari-

tions, it should be trusted only in the hands of discretion; though indeed it enters into most of the nostrums of empirics. It is not confined to medicine, but employed in casting of cannon-balls, and bells, in metalline specula, and types for printing, in melting of iron, and in refining gold, because when melted with the latter, it turns all other metals, not even silver excepted, into dross.

ANTINEPHRITICS, [from *antn* and *nephritis*,] remedies in diseases of the reins and kidneys.

ANT.NOMIANS, [from *anti* and *nomos*, Gr.] - sect who look upon the performance of moral duties as useless and insignificant.

ANTI-PARALYTIC, Adj. [from *anti*, Gr. and *paralusis*] remedies for the palsy.

ANTIPATHETICAL, having an aversion to a thing; " *Antipathetical* to all venomous creatures." *Howell.*

ANTIPATHY, S. [from *antipathie*, Fr.] a fixed aversion to any object; which operates so strongly, as not to be controuled; used with the particles against, to, and formerly with *t.* "A mortal *antipathy* against standing armies." *Swift.* " The strong *antipathy* of good to bad." *Pope.*

ANTIPERISTASIS, S. [from *anti* and *peristasis*] the action of two contrary qualities.

ANTIPESTILENTIAL, Adj. In Physic, that which prevents or removes the effects of the plague.

ANTIPHRASIS, S. [from *anti* Gr. and *phrasis*. Gr.] in Rhetoric, an ironical kind of expression, wherein we deny a thing to be what we ought to affirm it to be; as when we say, " The thing did not displease me," instead of, " The thing did not please me."

ANTIPODAL, Adj. the being *antipodes* with respect to their situation.

ANTIPODES, S. [from *anti* and *podes*] those who live on the opposite side of the globe, with their feet directly opposite to ours. The summer, winter, day, and night of the one, are contrary to those of the other; that is, when it is summer with the one, it is winter with the other, &c.

ANTIQUARY, S. [*antiquarius*, Lat.] one who applies himself to the study of antiquities. It is used as an adjective by Shakespeare, to imply old, antient, or former, alluding to the studies and researches of antiquaries. " Instructed by the *antiquary* times." *Troil. and Cress.* This is a very unusual, if not an improper acceptation.

To ANTIQUATE, V. A. [*antiquo*, Lat.] to render useless. " Without defending his *antiquated* words." *Dryd.*

ANTIQUE, Adj. [*antique*, Fr. pronounced like the French, *anteek*] that which is not in vogue. " The old and *antique* song." *Shaksp.* That which is really old. " Being true *antique*." *Prior.* Old fashioned. " Arrayed in *antique* robe." *Fairy Queen.*

Antic, wild, old; out of the fashion, uncouth, and ridiculous for its antiquity, " Not *antient* but *antique*." *Denn.* Used substantively for a relick of the antients. " Both very choice *antiques*." *Swift's Will.*

ANTIQUITY, S. [from *antiquitas*, Lat.] that period which has long preceded the present. The relicks or productions of antient times. " To extinguish all heathen antiquities." *Bacon.* " A long period of existence; long life; or old age.

ANTISCII, S. [from *anti*, Gr. and *scia*, Gr.] in Geography, those who reside on different sides of the equator.

ANTISCORBUTICAL, ANTISCOR-BUTIC, Adj. remedies against the scurvy.

ANTISPASIS, S. [from *anti*, Gr. and *spao*,] the drawing of humour from one part into another.

ANTISPASMODIC, Adj. [from *anti*, Gr. and *spasmos*,] remedies against the cramp, or any contractions of the muscles.

ANTISPASTIC, Adj. remedies which cause a removal of the humours.

ANTISPLENETIC, Adj. remedies against the spleen.

ANTISTROPHE, S. [from *anti*, Gr. and *strophe*,] a dance among the antients, wherein they used to turn sometimes to the right, and sometimes to the left; in allusion to which one part of a lyric ode is called by the same name; because the person, who repeated it, used at that time to change his position; it is generally an eccho of the strophe. In Grammar, a figure, wherein two terms that depend on each other are mutually converted.

ANTISTRUMATIC, Adj. [from *anti*, and *struma*] in Medicine, remedies against a scrophulous humour.

ANTITHESIS, S. [Gr. in the plural *antitheses*, from *anti*, Gr. and *tithemi*,] in Rhetoric, a figure wherein opposite qualities are compared with each other, to illustrate, amplify, and adorn the speech of an orator, or piece of any author. In the use of it great care should be taken not to carry it to excess, like Seneca, whose writings are, in some parts, a mere play upon words.

ANTITYPE, S. a thing that is formed according to a model, or pattern; a general similitude, or resemblance. That which has been previously represented by some type, as the death of Christ for the sins of the world by the sacrifice of the paschal lamb; the lamb being the type or hieroglyphic representation of Christ's death, and his crucifixion, the complexion, substance, safety, or antitype, shadowed out by it. See TYPE.

ANTITYPICAL, Adj. answering to some type; comfortable to some model or pattern; bears a resemblance in its circumstances to something which preceded, and is to be explained on the footing of an antitype.

ANTIVENEREAL, Adj. remedies against venereal injuries.

ANTLER, S. [andauiller,] the first pearls growing about the bur of a deer's horns.

ANTÆCI, S. [has no singular, from ανω, Gr. and αικια,] in Geography, those who live under the same semicircle of the meridian, but in different parallels, the one being as far distant from the equator S. as the others are N. their longitude is the same, as are likewise their noon, midnight, and all their days; but their seasons are contrary, it being summer with the one, when it is spring with the other, &c. The inhabitants of Felixstowe are the Antæci to those of the Cape of Good-Hope.

ANTONOMASIA, S. [from αντι, Gr. and ονομα, Gr.] in Rhetoric, a figure wherein the name of some dignity, office, profession, or science is put for a person's proper name.

ANTRA, S. [antre, Fr.] a cavern; a hole in a rock; a cave; a den. "Of antres vast." Shakesp.

ANVIL, S. [anfilt, anfilt, or anfilte, Sax.] a large mass of iron, whereon handicrafts lay their work to forge. They are either forged or cast; but the former are best; providing the upper part is steel. In a secondary sense it implies any thing subject to blows. "The anvil of my sword." Shakesp. It also implies that a thing is in agitation, is in readiness, or under consideration.

ANUS, S. [Lat.] in Anatomy the orifice of the intestines, through which the excrements are discharged. Also a small hole in the third ventricle of the brain. In Botany, the back opening, of a flower which has but one petal.

ANXIETY, S. [anxietas, Lat.] an uneasiness of the mind, apprehending the consequences of some future event. Among Physicians, it signifies an uneasiness occasioned by the violence of a disorder.

ANXIOUS, Adj. [from anxius, Lat.] uneasy on account of the consequences of some event. Very solicitous to find out the sense of an author; and bearing with an equal temper of mind, the impressions of any present evil; used with the particle of in the latter, and with for or about in the former sense.

ANY, Adj. [of ani, ænig, Sax.] either of the parts of which a thing is composed. "Any time; these four hours." Shakesp. Every one; applied to a whole collective body. "Any one who sees it will own." Pope. Applied by way of distinction to the members of a company; of a single one; in preference to all the rest; used with the particle of. "Affection towards any of them." Shakesp.

AORTA, S. [ανω, Gr.] the great artery arising immediately out of the left ventricle of the heart.

APACE, Adv. hastily; quickly; speedily; applied to quantity, in great numbers; and applied to the transition from one state to another, in haste, with speed.

APART, Adv. [apart, Fr.] separate, at a distance. "In a way apart from the multitude." Raleigh. Aside, or for a particular use, "Set apart for God." Prior. Separately, opposed to together, distinctly. "Afterwards nameth them apart." Raleigh. After the verb put it implies retirement, or quitting a former place. "Put apart your attendants." Shakesp. At the end of a sentence after the word compliment, &c. it implies abstaining from, or laying aside, "Compliments apart."

APARTMENT, S. [apartment, Fr.] part of a house; a room.

APATHY, S. [from α Gr. and παθος,] a freedom from passion, insensibility.

APE, S. [apa, Ifl. aep, Belg.] an animal resembling the human form; the toes of their feet, are as long as their fingers; their hair is red inclining to a green; they live on the tops of trees; have pockets on each side their jaws, which serve them as store-places. They are remarkable for mimicking the actions of human creatures; hence the word is used for one who affectedly imitates another.

To APE, V.A. to mimick or imitate, in allusion to the characteristic of the ape mentioned above.

APER, S. an imitator; a mimic.

APERIENT, Part. [aperiens, that which gently purges.

APERTION, S. [apertio, Lat.] an opening; a passage; a gap; an aperture.

APERTNESS, S. [from apertus, Lat.] openness. "The apertness and vigour of pronouncing." Holder.

APERTURE, S. [apertus, Lat.] the act of opening. An open place; a gap; a passage. The unravelling a difficult point, or laying it open to the consideration of others, explanation, or enlargement.

APETALOUS, Adj. [from α, Gr. and πεταλον,] in Botany, without petals, or flower leaves.

APEX, S. [Lat.] the summit of any thing. In Geometry, the angular point of a cone, or any like figure.

APHÆRESIS, S. [αφαιρεσις, Gr.] in Rhetoric, a figure, wherein a word or syllable is taken away from the beginning of a word.

APHELION, S. in Astronomy, that point of a planet's orbit, in which it is at his greatest distance from the sun.

APHILANTROPY, S. [from α, Gr. and φιλανθρωπια,] want of benevolence, inhumanity.

APHONIA, S. [from α Gr. and φωνη, Gr.] loss of speech.

APHORISM, S. [from αφορισμος, Gr.] a maxim in any science; a sentence comprehending a concise account of all the properties of a thing.

APHORISTICAL, Adj. composed in sentences

fentences unconnected, but containing important remarks.

APHRODYSIAC, APHRODISI'ACAL, Adj. [from αφροδιτη,] relating to the venereal difeafe.

A'PHRONITRE, S. [from αφρος, Gr. and νιτρον,] in Natural Hiftory, a kind of natural faltpetre gathering like froth on old walls, now called falt-petre of the rock.

APHTHÆ, S. [αφθαι, Gr.] ulcers in the mouth, palate, and gums, &c. attended with an inflammation and difficulty of fwallowing; when white or red, they are eafily cured; when livid or black they fometimes prove mortal.

A'PIARY, S. [apiarium, from apis, a bee] a place where bees are kept.

A'PICES, S. [the plural of apex, Lat.] in Botany, little knobs growing on the tops of the ftamina, or chieves of flowers, which have been difcovered by the microfcope to be a kind of feed veffels, containing fmall globular or oval particles, which are a kind of male fperm or feed, and falling down into the flower, impregnate, fecundate, and ripen the feed.

API'ECE, Adv. [pronounced as if written apiece,] each or feparately taken. "A fitthing a-piece." Swift.

APIS, S. an ox or bull worfhipped by the Egyptians under that name. Its whole body was to be black, except a white fquare fpot on its forehead, &c. When a calf was found with thefe marks, it was carried to the temple of Ofiris, where it was worfhipped, as the reprefentative of that deity, while living; and when dead, buried, with great folemnity. So far could the bare light of nature go, in a land which was the mother of arts and the fources of all the fciences: Let infidels blufh, at their boafts of unaffifted reafon, when they read this article, and when they compare the great truths revealed in the Mofaic and Chriftian difpenfations generoufly acknowledge the fource from whence they muft derive their moft fublime ideas, and be profelytes to that Saviour, who lived to teach and fet them an example, and died to redeem and fave them!

A'PISH, Adj. mimicking, or imitative. Affected, foppifh, filly, infignificant, empty, fpecious. "Apifh fophiftry." Glan. "Wanton, playful, and mimicking at the fame time. "Apifh folly." Prior.

A'PISHLY, Adv. after the manner of an ape; full of mimickry, and affected imitation.

APLU'STRE, S. [Lat.] an ancient enfign ufed by fhips. "The other has an apluftre."

APOCALYPSE, S [from αποκαλυψις, Gr.] a revelation, or the difcovery of fomething by the Deity, before unknown to mankind. Applied peculiarly to fignify the book of Revelation, written by St. John. Thofe who are defirous to fee his myfteries explained

with modefty, and treated with profound learning, will meet with no fmall fatisfaction from Dr. Newton's difcourfes on Prophecy, wherein he has given us fuch a comment as—but I fay no more, left I fhould injure the performance, for want of giving it due praife.

APOCALYP'TICAL, Adj. containing the revelation of any thing myfterious.

APO'COPE, S. [from απο, Gr. and κοπτω,] in Grammar, a figure wherein the laft letter or fyllable of a word is cut off.

APO'CRYPHA, S. [from απο, Gr. and κρυπτω,] fomething not known; applied to books it denotes that their authors are not certainly known; and their genuinenefs uncertain. Divines ufe the word in this fenfe when fpeaking of thofe books which the Jews did not receive in their canon of infpired writing, and the church of England, though fhe allows them to be read to her congregations, yet denies them to be of any authority in eftablifhing any doctrine.

APO'CRYPHAL, Adj. of doubtful authority; not inferted in the fcripture canon.

APO'CRYPHALLY, Adv. in a manner which is in want of authority, or has not the marks of authenticity.

APODIC'TICAL, Adj. [from αποδεικτικος, Gr.] demonftrative, plain, and convincing.

APOLLINA'RIANS, S. [from Apollinaris, their founder; a fect which arofe in the fourth century, who denied, that Chrift affumed true flefh, or a rational foul, but that his divinity was inftead of the latter, and that his flefh exifted with the fun from all eternity, was fent down from heaven, and conveyed through the virgin, as through a channel; that there were two fons, one born of God, and the other of Mary; that the God was crucified; that Chrift has now no body; and that the fouls of men are propagated by other fouls, in the fame manner as bodies are by other bodies. How fruitful is error, and when the imagination is taken for a guide inftead of reafon affifted by revelation, what a defpicable light muft men appear in to thofe exalted beings, who can fee remote truths by intuition!

APOLLO, S. [Lat.] in Mythology, the fon of Jupiter and Latona, who was born at Delos; to whom they attributed the art of divination, and the patronage of phyfic, and is the fun. The fable of his feeding Admetus's fheep, denotes that all creatures are fuftained by his genial warmth; and his killing the Cyclops for forging Jupiter's thunderbolts, his difperfing thofe peftilential vapours which are fatal to mankind. He is called the Sun in heaven, Bacchus on earth, and Apollo in the infernal regions, and reprefented with an harp in order to fhew the harmony of your fyftem, with a bachler, to denote his defending the earth, and with arrows, to fignify his power of life and death.

APOLOGE'TICAL, Adj. [from απολογεομαι,
pro.

pos, that which is faid, or written in defence of any thing.

APOLOGE'TICALLY, Adv. after the manner of an anfwer, defence, or apology.

APO'LOGIST, S. one who vindicates the faultinels of another; one who extenuates the faults of another.

To APO'LOGIZE, V. A. to plead in favour; to defend, or excufe.

APO'LOGUE, S. [from απι and λογος, Gr.] a ftory, or fiction, formed to convey fome moral truth to the mind, under the images of brutes; a fable: it is diftinguifhed from parable, becaufe that might have happened, but this could not; and the actors in that are rational beings; but thofe of the apologue are irrational.

APO'LOGY, S. [from απολογια, Gr.] a juridical word, implying a difcourfe made by a defendant, to clear himfelf from a charge brought againft him. Hence the defence of an opinion from the objections it is charged with, is general'y called by the fame name. At prefent the term is ufed to imply rather an excufe than a vindication; and an extenuation of a fault, rather than a proof of innocence; being more commonly appropriated to the common concerns of men in their private characters, than to the proceedings at the bar.

APOMECO'METRY, S. [from απο and μετρεω, Gr. and μετρον,] the art of meafuring to know how far things are at a diftance are from us.

APONEURO'SIS, S. [of απο and νευρον, Gr.] in Anatomy, the expanfion, or fpreading of a nerve.

APO'PHASIS, S. [from αποφασις, Gr.] in Rhetoric, a figure wherein the orator feems to wave, what he ironically mentions.

A'POPHLEGMA'TIC, S. [of απο and φλεγμα, Gr. phlegm] remedies to clear away fuperfluous phlegm, and ferous humours.

APOPHLE'GMATISM, S. [See Apophlegmatic] a Medicine intended to difcharge phlegm.

A'POPHTHEGM, S. [from αποφθεγμα,] a fentence which contains fome important truth, moral or divine.

APO'PHYGE, S. [from αποφυγη, Gr.] in Architecture, a ring of a column or pillar, whence it begins to fpring; originally nothing but the ring at the bafe of wooden pillars, to keep them from fplitting; but afterwards imitated in ftone-work.

APO'PHYSIS, S. [from αποφυσις, Gr] in Anatomy, the prominent parts of a bone.

APOPLE'CTIC, or APOPLE'CTICAL, Adj. of the nature of an apoplexy.

A'POPLEX, S. See A'POPLEXY.

APOPLE'XED, Adj. affected with an apoplexy.

A'POPLEXY, S. [αποπληξια, Gr.] a difeafe that fuddenly deprives a perfon of his fenfes, attended with a fufpenfion of the principal faculties of the foul. Caufed generally

by repletion; the head's being naturally large, and the neck fhort; the perfon's being corpulent, and redundant in pituitous humours. The indications of cure are an attenuation of the vifcidity of the humours, or derivation and revulfion of them, by all manner of evacuations.

APO'RIA, S. [from απορια, Gr.] in Rhetoric, a figure wherein the fpeaker expreffes himfelf in doubt where to begin.

APOSIO'PESIS, S. [from απο, Gr. and σιωπαω, Gr.] in Rhetoric, a figure wherein the fpeaker, through fome vehement affection leaves his period unfinifhed; but in fuch a manner as the fenfe may be eafily fupplied by the audience, as "The talents of a Pitt—but he needs no encomium."

APO'STASY, S. [of απο, and στασις, Gr.] the renouncing a religion; ufed always in a bad fenfe, and joined with the particle from.

APOSTATE, S. [from apostata, Lat.] one who has renounced the religion he formerly profeffed; ufed in a bad fenfe, with the particle from.

APOSTA'TICAL, S. after the manner of an apoftate.

To APO'STATIZE, S. [from apoftate] to renounce one's religion; to change one's religion for a worfe.

To APO'STEMATE, V. A. to turn to an apoftem; to form an abfcefs.

APOSTEMA'TION, S. the forming an abfcefs; the collection or gathering of corrupt matter, fo as to caufe a humour and fuelling in the part.

APO'STEME, or APO'STUME, S. [αποστημα, Gr.] a hollow fwelling filled with corrupt matter: an abfcefs.

APO'STLE, S. [apoftolus, of αποστολος, Gr.] one who was a difciple of Chrift on earth, and commiffioned by him, after his refurrection, to preach the Gofpel to the world. One of the ordinary travelling minifters, who went into different parts to preach the Gofpel, Rom. xvi. 7. One who is fent to collect alms and contributions; Rpophrodinus, your meffenger or apoftle, σποστολος, Gr. Philip. ii. 25. He who firft planted the Gofpel in any place. Applied to Chrift himfelf, as being fent from heaven to affume our nature, and invefted with authority to execute his prophetic, prieftly, and kingly offices. "Confider the Apoftle and high-prieft of our profeffion Jefus Chrift, Heb. iii. 1.

APO'STLESHIP, S. the office of an apoftle.

APOSTO'LIC, or APOSTO'LICAL, Adj. that which was authorized by the apoftles.

APOSTO'LICALLY, Adj. in the manner of an apoftle.

APO'STROPHE, S. [of απο, Gr. and στρεφω,] in Rhetoric, a breaking off from the thread of one's difcourfe, when applied to inanimate

inanimate things, it is reckoned a very great beauty; Adam's morning-hymn in Milton, is the most charming *apostrophe* that ever entered the heart of man. In Grammar, the contraction of a word by the placing a comma over that part which is dropped, as in the word *lov'ring*.

To APO'STROPHIZE, V. A. to interrupt the thread of discourse.

APO'THECARY, S. (from απο-θηκη, Gr.) one who prepares medicines according to the prescriptions of the college, and visits patients. The practice is genteel, and its members very numerous in London; till the year 1617 they were incorporated with the Grocers; but are now distinct, and have a hall in Blackfriars, where are two very fine laboratories, which supply the surgeons chests with medicines, for the use of the navy. If we consider there are near 1000 of this profession in London, how must we be surprised to find that, in Denmark, only two are allowed in the city of Copenhagen, and but one in any other considerable town.

A'POTHEGM, S. (a vitious spelling.) See APOPTHEGM.

APOTHEO'SIS, S. (απο, Gr. and θεος,) an heathen ceremony, whereby any great man was placed among the Gods; after which they paid him adoration, and swore by his name, with as much reverence as by those of any other deity. The ceremony, as described by Herodian, may be seen in Kennet's Roman Antiquities.

APO'TOME, S. (of απο, and τεμνω,) in Mathematics, the difference between a rational line and one only commensurable in power to the whole line. Euclid has handled this subject very copiously in his tenth book of Elem. In Music, the remaining part of an entire tone.

A PO'ZEM, S. (from απο-ζεω,) a medicine made by boiling roots, plants, &c. in water; called also a decoction.

To APPA'L, V. A. (*appalir*, Fr.) to give terror; to affright; to dishearten.

APPA'LMENT, S. (sudden affright, or terror.

APPARA'TUS, S. (Lat.) a collection of instruments proper to accomplish any design; the instruments used in philosophical experiments; the bandages, &c. of a surgeon; the furniture of a house, &c.

APPA'REL, S. (*appareil*, Fr.) cloathing; dress.

To APPA'REL, V. A. to cloth; dress; to adorn, or imbellish.

APPA'RENT, Part. (*apparent*, Fr.) plain, indubitable, seeming in opposition to real; visible, manifest, or known, and applied to the successor of the crown, certain, opposed to presumptive. Shakespear uses it substantively, in the last sense. " I'll draw it as *apparent* to the crown." Hen. VI. Apparent diameter in Astronomy, is the angle under

which we see the sun, moon, and stars. *Apparent magnitude*, is that which appears to the eye, and is measured by the quantity of the optic angle.

APPA'RENTLY, Adv. plainly, evidently; manifestly; seemingly.

APPARI'TION, S. (*apparition*, Lat.) a visible object; a spectre; a ghost. In Astronomy, a star's becoming visible, which before was below the horizon. The *circle of perpetual apparition* is that which is described about the pole as a centre, and touches the north part of the horizon in N. lat. and the S. in S. lat. all stars within which never set, but are always visible above the horizon.

APPA'RITORS, S. (from *appareo*, Lat.) persons ready at hand to execute the orders of the magistrate; those who cite persons to appear in ecclesiastical courts; the beadle who carries the mace before the masters, &c. in our universities.

To APPE'ACH. [See IMPEACH] to accuse; to inform against a person.

To APPE'AL, V. A. (*appello*, Lat.) to transfer a dispute from one to another, with the particle *from* before the person from whom. It is removed, and *to* before the person who is to be judge in his stead; to apply one's self to others for their opinions; or to cite as witness. To impeach, or charge a person with guilt, in allusion to an appeal in law. " *Appeal* each other of high treason." Shakesp.

APPE'AL, S. (pronounced as if the *a* was dropped and another *e* inserted in its room, as *appeel*,) the removal of a cause from an inferior to a superior court; used with the particle *to*. It generally means the accusation of a murderer by a person who had interest in the party killed. This is done either by bill or writ. The heir male is to bring an appeal for the death of his ancestor, and the husband for his wife; but it must be commenced within a year and a day after the death of the person murdered, and in the county where done. Figuratively, a summons to answer to a charge; an application or address. " A kind of *appeal* to the Deity." Bacon.

APPE'ALANT, S. (*appellant* is the word now in use,) one that brings an appeal.

APPE'ALER, S. one who appeals.

To APPE'AR, V. N. (*appareo*, Lat.) to become visible to the eye, with *in* before the place of the object. To be in the presence of another, so as to be seen by him, to be conspicuous; or attract observation. To answer a summons; to seem, to resemble. To be made manifest by proof and evidence. To be evident. " As will *appear* by what follows." Arbuthnot.

APPEA'RANCE, S. an object of sight; The thing seen. A phænomenon. Semblance, or show; the outside. The coming into a place. Personal attendance at a court;

of juſtice. Circumſtances which favour any opinion. Perſonal charms, probability, reſemblance, or likelihood.

APPEASEABLE, Adj. that which is reconcileable.

To APPEASE, V. A. [appaiſer, Fr.] to bring an angry perſon to an even temper; to pacify; to allay; to quiet any noiſe, outrage, or violence.

APPEASEMENT, S. reconciliation; a ſtate of peace and calmneſs, after the turbulent emotions of paſſion and reſentment.

APPEASER, S. [See APPEASE] one who brings about a reconciliation between parties that were vehemently offended with each other.

APPELLANT, S. [from appellan, Lat.] one who brings an appeal; one who appeals from a lower to a higher court.

APPELLATE, S. [from appellatum, Lat.] one againſt whom an appeal is brought.

APPELLATION, S. [appellatio, Lat.] the name, dignity, or title, by which men are diſtinguiſhed.

APPELLATIVE, S. [appellativum, Lat.] words which ſtand for univerſal ideas, or a whole rank of beings, whether general or ſpecial.

APPELLATORY, Adj. containing an appeal.

APPELLEE, S. a perſon againſt whom an appeal is brought.

APPENAGE, or APPANAGE, S. [apanagium, Lat. of panis, Lat. bread.] the fortune of a king's younger ſons, which in England depends entirely on his majeſty's pleaſure.

To APPEND, V. A. [from ad and pendeo,] uſed with the particle to; to hang one on another; to join ſomething as an additional part.

APPENDAGE, S. [Fr.] hanging on ſomething elſe; belonging or annexed to; accompanying in Law, any thing belonging to another, as neceſſary to its principal, or like an adjunct to his ſubject among the logicians. Uſed ſubſtantively for ſomething which belongs to another, not as a neceſſary, but a caſual, and adventitious part.

To APPENDICATE, V. A. [from appendo, Lat.] to annex or add one thing to another.

APPENDIX, ſomething added to another. Applied to action, concurrent circumſtances. Applied to books, a kind of ſupplement, or an addition to ſupply ſome omiſſions, and render them compleat; ſometimes added to the book, and ſometimes publiſhed by itſelf.

To APPERTAIN, V. N. [appartenir, Fr.] to belong to, as a right. To relate, or be confined to.

APPERTAINMENT, S. that which relates to any rank or dignity.

APPERTENANCIES, S. [appurtenance, Fr.] that which belongs or relates to a thing; the qualities, or properties of a thing.

APPERTINENT, Adj. [from ad and pertineo, Lat.] that which has a relation to.

APPETENCE, or APPETENCY, S. [appetentia, Lat.] ſenſual, carnal deſire; luſt.

APPETIBILITY, S. the quality which renders a thing the object of deſire.

APPETITE, S. [from appetire, Fr.] a propenſity to ſome object on account of the good it is imagined to poſſeſs. A violent longing after any thing, uſed with the particles of or to, before the object of deſire. "Immoderate appetite of power." Clarend. "An appetite to praiſe." Government of the Tongue. This laſt is not very proper. In Medicine, a natural, periodical deſire to eat or drink.

APPETITION, S. [appetitio, Lat.] a longing deſire. "Appetition or faſtening our affections on him." Hammond.

To APPLAUD, V. A. [applaudo, Lat.] to ſhew approbation by clapping of hands; to praiſe; to commend.

APPLAUDER, S. one who highly commends and praiſes the merits of another.

APPLAUSE, S. [applauſus, Lat.] praiſe beſtowed on merit, by teſtimonies of approbation and rapture.

APPLE, [apl, apple, alp, Sax.] the fruit of the apple tree. Apple of the eye. See PUPIL.

APPLEBY, the county town of Weſtmoreland, with a good corn-market on Mondays, and three fairs, on Whitſun Eve, for horned cattle; on Whitmonday, for linencloth, and merchandize; and on Auguſt 10, for horſes, ſheep, and linen-cloth. It is gone greatly to decay from what it was, in being only one broad ſtreet of mean houſes; however, it ſtill keeps the aſſizes and ſeſſions, and at the upper part is the caſtle. The church ſtands at the lower end of the town, and has lately been repaired; and they have likewiſe erected a town-houſe. It is ten miles E. by S. of Penrith, and 280 N. N. W. of London. Lon. 14. 5. lat. 54. 30. It is ſeated on the river Eden, by which it is almoſt ſurrounded, and ſends two members to parliament.

APPLE-TREE, S. [appl-tre, or appletreow, Sax. afalla, a fallenbre; Brit. Juſtin. Ruſt. Sciav. Boham. taking its name from the fruit it bears, as all trees do; not as a late author conjectures, apple-tree, becauſe Apples were one of the fruits dedicated to that deity.] In Gardening, a tree whoſe fruit is round, generally hollowed about the foot-ſtalk, with cells including the ſeed, ſeparated by cartilaginous partitions. Its fruit has various names, and are diſtinguiſhed

guished gener^{...}y into those that are fit for
the defert, the kitchen, and the cyder-prefs.

A'PLE-WOMAN, S. [a compound
word] a woman who fells apples.

APPLIANCE, S. See APPLICATION.

APPLICABILITY, S. the quality which
renders a thing fit to be applied.

APPLICABLE, Adj. [from *applies*, Lat.]
that which is agreeable, fuitable, or may be
allotment of a thing.

APPLICABLY, Adv. fo as to fuit,
agree with, or be conformable to any thing.

APPLICATION, S. [*applicatio*, Lat.]
the act of applying one thing to another.
Intenfenefs of thought or ftudy. The employment of a means to produce a particular
end. The defire, fuit, or requeft of a perfon. Attention to any particular affair,
with the particle *to*. The drawing inferences
from the comparifon of one thing to another. In Divinity, the act whereby Chrift
makes over and transfers to us the effects of
his holy life and death.

APPLICATIVE, Adj. that which makes
the application.

APPLICATORY, Adj. exerting the
act of applying.

To APPLY, V. A. [*applier*, obfolete,
appliquer, Fr. *applico*, Lat.] to put to a
thing. To lay remedies on a wound. To
ufe as relating or conformable to. To employ, to put to a certain ufe. To ufe as a
means. To fix the attention on any object;
to ftudy; ufed with the particle *to*. To have
recourfe to; to work upon; to ply. To
addrefs as a petitioner.

To APPOINT. V. A. [*appointer*, Fr.]
to fix the time of fome thing future. To
fettle by bargain. To decree.

APPOINTER, S. he who appoints.

APPOINTMENT, S. [*appointment*, Fr.]
a thing fettled between parties. An agreement to perform fomething future. Applied
to the Deity, a decree, eftablifhment, direction, or order. Applied to warlike habiliments, accoutrement. Applied to the amount
of a penfion, ftipend, falary, or wages.

To APPORTION, V. A. [from *portio*,
Lat.] to divide into fhares, or lots.

APPORTIONMENT, S. the dividing
into fhares or portions.

To APPOSE, V. A. [for *oppofe*] to embarrafs, to puzzle. For this we now ufe the
word *pofe*, which is a contraction of this
word, not as Johnfon conjectures, of *puzzle*.

APPOSITE, Adj. [from *appofitus*, Lat.]
proper, fuitable, well adapted to the purpofe,
feafonable, or conformable; applied to opinions or fentiments, proper, reafonable, or
agreeable.

APPOSITELY, Adv. fitly, fuitably; in
a manner confiftent with the greateft propriety.

APPOSITENESS, S. fitnefs; fuitablenefs; conformity.

APPOSITION, S. [from *appofitio*, Lat.]
the addition of fomething new.

To APPRAISE, V. A. [*appraifer*, Fr.]
to rate, value, or fet a price on goods.

APPRAISER, S. [*appreciateur*, Fr.] one
who values goods, who is fworn to do juftice
between the parties, and is therefore termed
a fworn appraifer, and is obliged to take the
goods at the price he values them at, if no
other will purchafe them at that rate.

To APPREHEND, V. A. [from *appre-
hendo*, Lat.] to lay hold on; to feize a
perfon, in order to bring him to juftice; to
think on with anxiety or terror. To have
an imperfect or inadequate idea of a thing,
in oppofition to comprehend.

APPREHENDER, S. one who feizes a
malefactor, to bring him to juftice; a con-
ceiver; a thinker.

APPREHENSIBLE, Adj. [from *appre-
henfibilis*, Lat.] what may be apprehended
or conceived.

APPREHENSION, S. [*apprehenfio*, Lat.]
the mere contemplation of things. The bare
perception of ideas in the mind, without
comprehending them, or making why deductions from them: in a more loofe fenfe,
opinion, or fentiment. Fear, or anxiety.
Sufpicion of fomething future. The feizing
of a malefactor, to bring him to juftice.

APPREHENSIVE, Adj. quick to conceive; fearful; fufpicious.

APPRENTICE, S. [*apprenti*, Fr. from
apprendre] a youth bound to a perfon for a
certain number of years, to learn his trade
or profeffion.

To APPRENTICE, V. A. to bind a
youth to one who is to teach him his trade,
&c.

APPRENTICESHIP, S. the time for
which a perfon is bound, in order to learn
a trade. Or the duty of an apprentice.

To APPRIZE, V. A. [*appris*, Fr.] to
give information, or notice.

To APPROACH, V. N. [*approcher*, Fr.]
to fhorten the diftance between objects; to
draw nearer; to be nearer its completion;
to be meant; to come near; to refemble.
Ufed actively, with the particle *to*; to bring
nearer to.

APPROACH, S. the act of coming nearer;
accefs. In Fortification, ufed in the plural,
works thrown up by befiegers in order to
advance nearer to the place befieged. In
Mathematics, the curve of equable *approach*,
is that wherein a body, defcending by the
fole power of gravity, fhall approach the
earth equally in equal times.

APPROACHER, S. the perfon who
comes, or advances towards a diftant object.

APPROBATION, S. [*approbatio*, Lat.]
the act of approving, liking, or efteeming
any thing.

APPROOF, S. [from *approve*; thus *proof*
is derived from *prove*] the act of affenting

Vo₂

to, or confirming any opinion from a persuation of its truth, or consistency with reason.

To APPRO'PERATE, V. A. [appropero, Lat.] to quicken a thing, with respect to motion; to hasten action.

To APPROPI'NQUATE, V. N. [from appropinquo, Lat.] to lessen the distance between any object; to draw nearer to; to approach.

To APPROPI'NQUE, V. N. See APPROPINQUATE.

APPRO'PRIABLE, Adj. any thing that may be peculiarly applied to.

To APPRO'PRIATE, V. A. [approprier, Fr.] to dedicate, or set apart to a particular use. To claim right to. To confine to a particular sense. In Law, to annex as a property.

APPRO'PRIATE, Adj. peculiar; consigned; restrained, or limitted.

APPROPRIA'TION, S. the application of things to some particular use. The claiming as belonging to one's self. In Law, the annexing a benefice to the perpetual use of some religious house; in order to the making of which the king's licence in chancery, and the consent of the diocesan, patron, and incumbent are necessary.

APPROPRIATOR, S. a person possessed of an appropriated benefice.

APPROV'ABLE, Adj. that which appears worthy of approbation.

APPRO'VAL, S. the acknowledgment of the merits, or good qualities of an object, after sufficient examination. Approbation.

APPRO'VANCE, S. See APPROVAL.

To APPRO'VE, V. A. [approver, Fr.] to be pleased or delighted with; sometimes used with the particle of. To ratify, or establish by sufficient reasons. To experience; to prove, or be convinced of from experience. "'Tis the curse of love, and still approved." Dryd. To make worthy of approbation, with the particle to. "To approve himself to God." Rogers.

APPROVEMENT, S. See APPROBATION.

APPRO'VER, S. one who approves; one who makes trial of. In common Law, one who having confessed himself to be guilty of felony, accuseth another as guilty of the same; and is obliged to prove his charge.

APPRO'XIMATE, Adj. approaching near to.

APPROXIMA'TION, S. the approaching nearer to any thing. In Arithmetic, a continual approach to a root or quantity sought.

A'PRIL, S. [aprilis, Lat.] the fourth calendar month in the year. It was called Eostur-monath by the Saxons, from their goddess Easter, to whom they sacrificed in this month; and from thence we call the paschal feast, Easter, at this day.

No. III.

APRON, S. [from aforan for foran, Sax.] a part of dress which hangs from the middle downwards, worn by men to keep their cloaths clean; by the women for ornament. Apron of a goose, is the fat skin which covers the belly. In Gunnery, a piece of lead to cover the touch hole of a great gun.

A'PRONED, Adj. a person who wears an apron.

A'PSIS, S. [aψις, Gr.] the part of the church wherein the clergy sat, and the altar was placed; more particularly the bishop's seat or throne. The case wherein relics were preserved. In Astronomy, the highest or lowest point of a planet's orbit.

A'PT, Adj. [from aptus, Lat. compared at present by more for the comparative, and most for the superlative, but formerly by adding er to the positive, for the comparative degree, and est for the superlative] fit, proper, suitable. That which has an inclination to, applied to persons; ready or quick, applied to the understanding.

To A'PTATE, V. A. [optatum, supine of apto, Lat.] to fit. "To aptate a planet, is to strengthen it in position of house, &c. to bring about the desired end." Bailey.

A'PTITUDE, S. [Fr.] fitness, suitableness. Tendency, propensity, applied to bodies; disposition, or byass, applied to the mind.

A'PTLY, Adv. in a manner proper to produce its end; with great propriety; justly; readily, or quickly.

A'PTNESS, S. suitableness; tendency; disposition, or inclination; quickness.

A'PUS, S. [Lat.] the bird of paradise, a constellation in the S. hemisphere.

A'QUA, S. [Lat.] water. Aqua Fortis, or strong corrosive liquor, is made by distilling purified nitre with calcined vitriol; or rectified oil of vitriol in a strong heat. It is supposed to have been invented about the year 1300. It is used by refiners in separating silver from gold and copper, by working goldsmiths; by the workers in Mosaic; for flashing and colouring their works; by dyers, in heightening their colours, particularly scarlet; by other artists, for colouring bone and ivory; by book-binders, to marble the covers of their books; by engravers, in etching copper-plates; and by diamond cutters, to separate their diamonds from metalline powder. Aqua-marina, a precious stone, which takes its name from its sea-green colour; is supposed to be the bery', and the sixth stone in the breast-plate of the Jewish high-priest. Aqua-regia, a strong corrosive spirit, which dissolves gold, made of spirit of nitre, and spirit of sea-salt.

AQUA'TIC, [aquaticus, Lat.] that which lives in the water; applied to plants, that which grows in the water.

A'QUA-

A'QUATILE, Adj. [aquatis] that which lives or grows in the water.

A'QUEDUCT, or A'QUÆDUCT, S. [aqua, Lat. and ductus, Lat.] a channel to convey water from one place to another. The Romans had some aqueducts which extended one hundred miles: there were nine that emitted themselves through 13,594 pipes of an inch diameter, and the city is supposed to receive in an hour's time, 500,000 hogsheads of water. That of Lewis XIV. near Maintenon, which carries the R. Eure to Versailles, is 7000 fathoms long, 2560 high, and, has 242 arcades. Yet though our New River is not conducted with so much parade, it is infinitely more useful, and considered as the project and performance of a private person, is at once stupendous, and worthy of the highest approbation. In Anatomy, this term is applied to a long canal in the Os petrosum.

AQUA'RIUS, S. [from aqua, Lat.] In Astronomy, one of the twelve signs in the ecliptic, which derives its name from the supposed quantity of rain which falls while the sun is in it.

A'QUEOUS, Adj. [from aqua, Lat.] watery; composed of water.

A'QUILINE, Adj. [from aquila, Lat.] resembling an eagle; applied to the nose, hooked like an eagle's beak.

AQU'OSE, S. [from aquosus, Lat.] watry, abounding with water. Aquose ducts, those in the Sclerotics, whereby the aqueous humour is supposed to be conveyed into the membranes which inclose it; discovered by Dr. Nuck, but not generally acknowledged.

AQU'OSITY, S. [from aquosus] waterishness.

AR'ADIA, a country of Asia, which is a peninsula, bounded on the W. by the Red Sea, on the N. E. by the river Euphrates, and the Persian gulph, on the S. by the ocean, and on the N. by Syria, and the desart of Dyrbekar. It is divided into three parts, Arabia Petrea, Deserta, and Felix, or the Happy. Arabia Petrea is the smallest of the three, and towards the N. is full of mountains, with few inhabitants, on account of its barrenness. It had its name from the town Petrea, its ancient capital, now destroyed. It differs little from Arabia Deserta, which is so called from the nature of the soil, that is generally a barren sand. However, there are great flocks of sheep, and herds of cattle near the Euphrates, where the land is good. In the desart there are great numbers of ostriches, and there is a fine breed of camels in several places. Arabia Felix is so called, on account of its fertility, with regard to the rest. Some give it the name of Yemen, but improperly; for it is a kingdom on the S. coast, whose capital is Sanaa. The Arabs in the desart live wandering

lives, removing from place to place, partly for the sake of pasture, and partly to lie in wait for the caravans, which they often rob. There are caravans which travel over part of this desart from Bussorah to Aleppo, and from Egypt to Mecca, in order to visit Mahomet's tomb. Arabia Felix produces frankincense, myrrh, balm of Gilead, gum-arabick, and more especially coffee, of which they export prodigious quantities. The Arabs that live in the desart have no houses, but tents. The famous Mahomet was a native of this country, and his followers soon after his death, conquered a great part of Asia, Africa, and Europe, establishing their religion wherever they came. Lon. from 52. to 77. Lat. 12. to 34.

A'RABIC, S. [from Arabic] the language of the Arabians, a branch of the Hebrew.

This word is likewise applied to a gum, which distils from a thorny plant in these parts.

A'RABIC, Adj. relating to, or used in Arabia. Arabic characters, are the figures we make use of in Arithmetic.

AR'ABLE, Adj. [from aro, Lat.] proper for ploughing; and to produce corn.

A'RAC, or A'RRAC, S. [pronounced rack] a spirituous liquor, made by the Chinese from cocoa, rice, or sugar. There are two sorts imported into England, viz. the Goa and Batavia. The Goa is distinguished into single, double, and treble distilled, the double distilled is that which is sent abroad, but though weak in comparison to that of Batavia, is preferred before it, on account of its method of distilling, which is in earthen vessels, but that of Batavia in copper.

ARACHNOI'DES, S. [from αραχνη] In Anatomy, a fine slender tunic, encompassing the chrystalline humour of the eye. Its use is to retain the chrystalline humour in its proper place; to separate the chrystalline from the aqueous humour; and to prevent its being continually moistened therewith.

ARÆOMETER, S. [from αραιος, Gr. and μετρεω, Gr.] in Hydrostatics, an instrument to discover the weight of fluids.

ARÆOTICS, S. [from αραιος, Gr.] medicines which thin the blood.

ARA'NEOUS, Adj. [from aranea, Lat.] resembling a cobweb. Araneus urinæ, contains something like a spider's web, with a fineness at top, and indicates a colliquation.

ARA'TION, S. [aratio, Lat.] the act of plowing.

A'RATORY, Adj. [from aro] relating to plowing.

A'RBALET, or A'RBALIST, S. [from arcus, Lat. and ballista] a cross-bow made with steel, set in a shaft of wood, with a string and trigger; bent with a piece of iron, fitted for that purpose, and used to throw bullets, large arrows, darts, &c.

A'R-

A'RBITER, S. [Lat.] a person chosen between parties, to decide the subject of their disagreement. One invested with a power to decide any difference.

ARBI'TRADLE, Adj. [arbiter, Lat.] arbitrary, voluntary; determined by the will.

ARBI'TRAMENT, S. [from arbiter, Lat.] choice; determination.

ARBITRA'RILY, Adv. In a despotic, tyrannical, or absolute manner.

ARBITRA'RINESS, S. or despoticalness. The prescribing rules, or enacting laws, without assigning any reason for so doing. Tyranny.

ARBITRA'RIOUS, Adj. [from arbitrarius, Lat.] depending solely on the will; precarious.

A'RBITRARY, Adj. [arbitrarius, Lat.] not restrained or limited; capricious, positive, despotic.

To A'RBITRATE, V. A. [arbitror, Lat.] to decide or determine. To judge of. To pronounce sentence.

ARBITRATION, S. [from arbiter, Lat.] the determination of a suit by a judge, mutually chosen by the parties at difference.

ARBITRATOR, S. [from arbitratio] one chosen to determine a difference between contending parties. He that has uncontroulable power. "Heaven's high Arbitrator sits secure." Par. Lost. He that determines, decides, or puts an end to any affair; a determiner. In Law, the difference between an arbiter and an arbitrator consists in the former's being obliged to proceed according to law, and the other's deciding only upon the principles of equity.

ARBI'TREMENT, S. [from arbitror, Lat.] a decision, pronounced by an umpire. A compromise. "As if they would make an arbitrement between God and man." Bacon.

AR'BOR, [Lat.] in Botany, a tree.

A'RBOR PHILOSO'PHICA, or the philosophical tree, in Chemistry, that which is formed from metalline chrystallisations which resemble a tree. Arbor Martis, or the Steel Tree, that which is formed from a dissolution of iron-filings in spirits of nitre. Arbor Porphyriana, or Porphyry's Tree, in Logic, is a scale of Beings, consisting of three sorts, as follows:

                SUBSTANCE
    Thinking   Extended
                BODY
    Inanimate   Animate
                ANIMAL
        Irrational   Rational
                MAN
        This   That
            P I T T.

AR'BOR VITÆ, or the Tree of Life, in Botany, so called from its continual verdure.

It is a native of Canada, a warm plant, good in a chlorosis; braised with honey, dissolves tumours: its oil is recommended as a stimulator and opener in the gout, and is of great service in cleansing beds from vermin.

AR'BORARY, Adj. [Arborarius, Lat.] that which belongs to a tree.

AR'BORET, S. [a diminutive of arbor, Lat.] a small tree, or shrub.

ARBO'REOUS, Adj. [arboreus, Lat.] belonging to trees. In Botany, a fungus or moss growing on trees.

AR'BORIST, [S. arboriste, Fr.] one who applies himself to study the nature and cultivation of trees.

AR'BOROUS, Adj. [from arbor, Lat.] formed of, or relating to trees.

AR'BOUR, S. [of arbor, Lat.] a shady bower, formed of the branches of trees, and contrived so as to admit the air, and keep off the sun and rain; formerly in great vogue; but, at present grown into disuse.

AR'BUTE, S. [arbutum, Lat.] in Botany, the straw-berry tree, which grows common in Ireland.

A'RC, S. [arcus, Lat.] a part of a circle, not exceeding a semi-circle. An arch.

ARCA'DE, S. [Fr.] an arch, or walk, containing several arches united together.

ARCA'NUM, [Lat. in the plural arcana] a secret.

ARCH, S. [arcus, Lat.] the sky. In Mathematics, part of any curve line, whether it be elliptic, circle, &c. Arch of a circle is a part of the circumference less than a semi-circle. Arch, in architecture, is a vault, or concave building, bent in the form of an arch of a curve, and is divided into circular. Alberti would have the arch in building never less than a semi-circle, with the addition of one-seventh of half its diameter; and Sir Henry Wotton has, by a chain of theorems, shewn it to be both the strongest, securest, and most beautiful. Arch of a bridge is the vaulted interval between its piers. Without interesting ourselves in the warmth of a dispute, we must observe, that arches, which are portions of a circle, are not so strong as those of the catenaria, because other arches sustain themselves only by the catenaria contained in their thickness; so that were they made thin, they must tumble of course; but the catenaria, though infinitely slender, must stand; because no one part of it tends downwards more than another. A triumphal arch in a gate built with stone, &c. and richly ornamented with trophies, &c.

A'RCH, S. [from αρχ⊖, Gr.] a chief. "My worthy arch and patron." K. Lear.

To A'RCH, V. A. [arcus, Lat.] to build, or to cover with arches.

P 2   ARCH,

A'RCH, A'. [from αρχ⊙, Gr.] chief, principal; used to express something of the first rank or order, as arch-bishop; but something superlative or, ill'd to quality, as in arch-dunce. It also implies a person ended with a great deal of low cunning. "An arch lad."

ARCH-ANGEL, S [from αρχ⊙, Gr. and αγγελ⊙, Gr.] one of the foremost order of angels. Also a plant named likewise Dead Nettle.

A'RCHANGE'LIC, Adj. relating, or belonging to archangels.

A'RCHBISHOP, S. [archbishop, Sax. of αρχ⊙, Gr. and επισκοπ⊙,] a chief bishop, or metropolitan prelate. In the East this title was not known till the year 320. According to Bede, the first establishment of this order in England was in the time of Lucius, the first Christian king, who erected three archbishopricks; namely, London, York, and Landaff, then called Kaer-Leion; the dignity continued in London 180 years, and was then translated to Canterbury. The archbishoprick of Caer-leon was first translated to St. David's, but, on account of the plague, was translated again to Doll in Bretagne. That of York continues to this day.

A'RCHBISHOPRIC, S the dignity, jurisdiction, or province of an archbishop. There are two in England, namely York and Canterbury, the prelates whereof are called primates, and after some altercation for superiority, that of Canterbury was called primate of all England, and that of York only primate of England. The archbishop of Canterbury had anciently jurisdiction over Ireland, as that of York had over Scotland. As for the former he was called the patriarch, pope of this new world, enjoyed marks of royalty, such as making knights and coining money, &c. is now the first peer of the realm, next to the royal family; has the power and probate of wills, grants licences and dispensations, and holds several courts. The archbishop of York has the same rights in his province, has precedence of all dukes not of the royal blood, and of all officers of state, excepting the lord high chancellor.

A'RCHDEACON, S. [archdiaconus, Lat.] a priest vested with jurisdiction over the clergy and is, next to the bishop.

A'RCHDEACONRY, S. the jurisdiction, or office of an archdeacon.

A'RCHDEACONSHIP, S. the office of an archdeacon.

A'RCHDUKE, S. [archidux, Lat.] a duke vested with greater privilege than others.

A'RCHDUTCHESS, S. the title of the sister or daughter of an archduke.

A'RCH, S. [from αρχη, Gr.] in Medicine, the beginning or first attack of a disease.

A'RCHED, Part. crooked, in the form of an arch. In horsemanship, arched legs, are an imperfection of a horse, whose legs are bent forwards, so as to make on the whole a kind of an arch or bow, when he stands in his natural position.

A'RCHER, S. [archer, Fr.] one who shoots with a bow; or uses a bow in battle. Though now laid aside in Christendom, yet they are still kept up in Turkey.

A'RCHERY, S. the art of shooting with a bow. Our ancestors were famous for being the best archers in Europe, and most of our victories in France were the purchase of the long bow; the statutes made in 13 Henry VIII. relative to this exercise, are worth perusal, and would afford noble hints towards rendering our militia invincible.

A'RCHES-COURT, S. the chief consistory of the archbishop of Canterbury, for debating spiritual causes. The judge of the court is called the dean of the arches.

A'RCHETYPE, S. [archetypon, Lat.] the original model, or pattern.

A'RCHETYPAL, Adj. original; a patent.

ARCHIEPI'SCOPAL, Adj. [from archiepiscopus] that which relates, or belongs to an archbishop.

ARCHIMEDES, a Greek, famous for his knowledge of mechanics, and inventor of several instruments and machines, which are the wonder even of this enlightened age. His studies, like those of our worthy countryman Dr. Hales, had no other object but the good of mankind, and were serviceable to his countrymen in particular; we need not mention his invention of a glass to burn the fleet of an enemy to the harbour; or the engines with which he annoyed the besiegers. But we must lament his fate, that notwithstanding Marcellus's charge was given to preserve him, he should be killed in his study, as he was busied in some useful project, by a common soldier. The spiral pump for raising water, is called Archimedes's screw.

A'RCHITECT, S. [architectus] a person skilled in building, who draws plans and conducts the work. Figuratively, any one who is the contriver of any design.

A'RCHITECTIVE, Adj. relating to building or architecture.

ARCHITECTO'RIC, Adj. [from αρχη, Gr. and τεκτων, Gr.] having the power and skill of an architect; or can produce any thing suitable to its nature and properties. The architectonic spirit is that plastic power, which produces animals from the ova of females; and resembles the Archeus of Chemists.

A'RCHITECTURE, S. [architectura, Lat.] the art of building. Architecture in perspective is that, wherein the members are of different measures, and diminish in proportion to their distance from the eye, in order to

make

make the work appear longer; of this kind is the celebrated ſtair-caſe of the Vatican, built by Bramino. Counterfeit architecture is that which has its fittings and projections painted on a plain ſurface, like the fronts of houſes in Italy, and the pavilions in Marly.

A'RCHITRAVE, S. [from *archi*, and *trabs*, Lat.] in architecture the loweſt member of the entablature. In timber building it is filled the maſter beam. In chimnies, the mantle piece; and over jambs of doors, or windows, hyperthyron.

ARCHIVAU'LT, S. [*archivolte*, Fr.] the inward contour of an arch; or a band adorned with mouldings running over the front of the arch ſtones.

A'RCHIVES, S. [from *archivos*, Lat.] places wherein records, or manuſcripts are preſerved. Alſo the records and manuſcripts themſelves.

ARCHPRE'LATE, S. one who is ſuperior to other prelates.

ARCH-THEASURER, S. the great treaſurer of the German empire. The right to this dignity was contelled between his late majeſty, as deſcended from Frederic V. elector palatine and the preſent elector.

A'RCHWISE, Adv. [Teut. a ſhape] in the manner or form of an arch.

ARCI'TENENT, Part. [*arcitenens*, Lat.] holding a bow.

ARCTA'TION, S. [from *arſto*, Lat.] ſtreightening; crowding or ſqueezing into a narrow compaſs.

A'RCTIC, Adj. [from *arctos*, northern;] lying near the north ſtar, called *arctus*. Arctic circle, a leſſer circle of the ſphere, parallel to the equinoctial, and 65 deg. 30 min. diſtant from it towards the North Pole.

ARCTU'RUS, S. [from *arctos* and *ura*,] a fixed ſtar of the firſt magnitude in the conſtellation Bootes.

A'RCUATE, Adj. [from *arcuatus*, Lat.] in the form of an arch.

ARCUA'TION, S. [from *arcus*, Lat.] the act of bending; the ſtate of being bent. In ſurgery, a bending of the bones, which appears in the caſe of the rickets. In Gardening, the method of raiſing trees by layers.

A'RCUATURE, S. [from *arcus*, Lat.] the bending of an arch.

ARCUBA'LISTER, S. [from *arcus* and *baliſta*] one who ſhoots with the croſs-bow. "A very good arcubaliſter." *Camden.*

A'RDENCY, S. applied to the affections, warmth; activity, vehemence.

A'RDENT, Adj. [*ardens*, Part. Lat.] hot, burning, inflaming; fierce, vehement, violent, paſſionate, inflamed.

A'RDENTLY, Adv. warmly, vehemently, paſſionately.

A'RDOR, S. [from *ardor*, Fr.] heat,

warmth, intenſeneſs, violence of affection. Uſed by Milton for a ſeraph; which in the original implies a flaming or burning ſubſtance. "From among thouſand celeſtial *ardures*." Par. Loſt. b. v. Yet this ſenſe is adopted by no other author.

ARDU'ITY, S. [*arduus*, Lat.] difficulty.

A'RDUOUS, Adj. [*arduus*, Lat.] lofty and difficult to aſcend. Something important, ſublime, and difficult to comprehend.

A'RE, the third perſon plural of the verb *am*, uſed when we ſpeak of two or more perſons. *Are* is alſo in muſic applied by Guido Rhemi to the loweſt note in his ſcale, or gamut.

A'REA, S. [Lat.] the ſurface between any lines or limits. Any ſurface, as the floor of a room, or the vacant part or ſtage. In Geometry, the ſpace contained within the lines bounding it. In phyſic, it is a ſpecies of the Alopecia.

To ARE'AD, V. A. [from *aredan*, Sax.] to adviſe. "Mark what I aread thee now." *Milt.* Now obſolete.

AREFA'CTION, S. [*arefacio*, Lat.] the act of making dry.

ARENA'CEOUS, Adj. [from *arena*, Lat.] conſiſting of ſand, ſandy.

ARENO'SE, Adj. [from *arena*, Lat.] ſandy, conſiſting of ſand

ARE'OLA, S. [Lat.] in Anatomy, the coloured circle ſurrounding the nipple.

AREO'PAGUS, S. [from *aris*, and *pagos*] a tribunal belonging to Athens, remarkable for the integrity of the deciſions, who ſat in the open air, in the night time, and at firſt took cognizance of civil cauſes; but afterwards judged thoſe who were guilty of oppoſing the eſtabliſhed religion of the country, or introducing new rites without authority. It was before this tribunal that St. Paul was brought, when he made a ſpeech in his own vindication, that contains in it all the beauties of antient oratory.

ARETO'LOGY, S. [from *aretos*, and *logos*, ethics, moral philoſophy.

A'RGENT, Adj. [from *argentum*, Lat.] reſembling ſilver, ſilvered; in Heraldry the white colour in arms.

A'RGENTATION, S. [from *argentum*,] the covering any thing with a thin or thick plate of ſilver; ſilvering.

A'RGENTINE, Adj. [from *argentum*, Lat.] ſounding like ſilver.

ARGILLA'CEOUS, Adj. [of *argilla*, Lat.] of the nature of clay.

ARGI'LLOUS, Adj. conſiſting of, or relating to clay; of the nature of clay.

A'RGO, S. [Gr.] a ſouthern conſtellation of fixed ſtars.

To A'RGUE, V. N. [*arguo*, Lat.] to evince the truth or falſhood of any thing by proofs. To perſuade; to bring reaſons for or againſt; to prove any thing by reaſon; to plead; to debate. "To argue a caſe.

To

To infer, in allusion to the deductions of reason. " So many laws, argu: fo many fins." Par Loll. To charge or prove by rational consequence; to be accused, or proved guilty, with the particle of. " Which can be truly accused of obscenity." Dryd. This latter sense alludes to the arguings of council at the bar.

A'RGUER, S. [from argue,] one who argues. A reasoner; a disputer.

A'RGUMENT, S. [from argumentum, Lat.] a proposition, which evinces the truth of any proposition; a reason brought to prove, or disprove any thing. The subject of any discourse or writing. A concise view of the heads of any discourse. A debate, or suit; a controversy. Sometimes used with the particle to before the thing to be proved; but most commonly, if not properly, with for. In Rhetoric, a probable reason alledged to gain belief. In Astronomy, an arch, by which we seek another proportional to the first.

ARGUME'NTAL, Adj. relating or belonging to argument; reasoning.

ARGUMENTATION, S. the evincing the truth or falsehood of any proposition. The act or effect of reasoning; defined by logicians, that operation of the mind, by which we infer one proposition from two or more premised; or the drawing a conclusion, before unknown, or doubtful, from some proposition more known and evident.

ARGUME'NTATIVE, Adj. consisting of argument, containing reasons.

A'RIA, S. [Ital.] in Musc, an air, a song, a tune.

A'RIANISM, S. the principles of the Arians.

A'RIAN, Adj. belonging to, or maintained by Arius. Used substantively for one of the sect of Arius, a presbyter, in 320, who held, that Christ, though the word, was inferior to the father, with respect to his deity; different from him with respect to his essence; not eternal, but created before all other things, out of nothing, or nonentities; that he had nothing of man in him but the flesh, with which the word was joined; and that the Holy Ghost was not man, but a creature.

ARI'DITY, S. [ariditas, Lat.] want of moisture; want of ardency in devotion.

A'RIES, S. [Lat.] in Astronomy, a constellation of fixed stars, the first of the twelve signs, in the zodiac which the sun enters; represented by the ram, because it is then the teeming time for that kind of animal. Likewise the name of a battering engine used by the antients, so called, from its having a ram's head on one end, or from its motion, which resembles that of a ram when fighting.

To A'RIETATE, V. N. [arieto, Lat.] to butt with the head like a ram.

ARIETA'TION, S. [from aries, Lat.] the act of butting or battering like a ram.

ARIE'TTA, S. [Ital. a diminutive of aria, Ital.] in Music, a short song or tune.

ARI'GHT, Adv. truly, justly, consistent with law; properly.

ARIOLA'TION, S. See HARIOLATION.

ARIO'SO, S. [Ital.] in Music, the movement of a common air, song, or tune.

To ARI'SE, V. N. [its Pret. arose, Part. arisen, from arisan, Sax.] to ascend, move upwards; to get up, as from sleep; to change the posture from sitting to standing; to become visible, in allusion to the appearance of corn above the ground; to come out of the grave; to flow or proceed from; to be born; to attack as an enemy; with the particle against.

ARISTA'RCHUS, S. [from αριστος, and αρχω,] a famous grammarian, born in Samothracia, who flourished in the 156th olymp. was tutor to the son of Ptolemy Philometor; famous for criticism, and his revisal of Homer's works, which he is reported to have divided into books, in the manner we have them at present; his exactness was great, but his decisions too magisterial with respect to the genuineness of the verses. Hence it is, that Horace and Cicero use his name to imply a severe critic in general; but moderns, dropping the idea of his positiveness, apply it commonly, but improperly, to denote an exact one.

ARISTO'CRACY, S. [from αριστος and κρατος,] a form of government in which the supreme power is lodged in the nobility.

ARISTOCRA'TICAL, Adj. a government administered only by nobles.

ARISTOLO'CHIA, S. [Lat from αριστος and λοχος,] in Botany, birthwort; of which there are three species; its English name is derived from its being of service to facilitate delivery; it is a very good vulnerary and alexipharmic.

ARITHME'TICAL, Adj. is performed by numbers; or agreeable to some rule in arithmetic.

ARITHME'TICALLY, Adv. performed according to some rule of arithmetic.

ARITHME'TIC, S. [from αριθμος, Gr.] in the art of numbering, calculating, or computing with exactness.

A'RK, S. [from arce, Lat.] a chest, or coffer, applied in Scripture to the vehicle in which Moses was exposed in the Nile. But more particularly the vessel built by Noah, to preserve himself, family, and the whole race of terrestrial and aerial animals, from the flood.

A'RM, S. [earm, arm, Sax.] the limb, which reaches from the shoulder to the hand; but more properly beginning at the shoulder, and ending at the elbow. The branch of a

from

tree. In Statics, that part of a beam which reaches from the center, where it is hung, to the end. In Geography, a branch of the sea, which runs into the land.

A'RM-PIT, or ARM-HO'LE, S. [*arm-hul*, Belg.] that cavity, or hole of the arm, which, at its extremity, is opposite to the shoulder.

To A'RM, V. A. [*arma*, Lat.] to furnish with weapons. In the manege, applied to a horse, to defend himself by pressing down his head, and bending his neck, so as to rest the branches of the bridle upon his neck, in order to withstand the effects of the bit. To *arm with the lips*, is said of a horse when he covers the bars with his lips, and deadens the pressure of the bit.

To A'RM, V. N. to take arms; to be provided against an enemy, or casualty.

ARMA'DA, S. [Span.] a fleet of men of war, applied particularly to that great one fitted out by the Spaniards, with an intention to conquer this island in 1588.

ARMADI'LLO, S. [Span.] a four-footed animal, of the Brazils, as large as a cat, covered with hard scales like armour, and feeds on roots, sugar-canes, and poultry.

A'RMAMENT, S. [*armamentum*, Lat.] great provisions of military stores; also an army, but most commonly applied to a fleet of men of war.

ARMAME'NTARY, S. a magazine of military stores; an arsenal.

A'RMATURE, S. [*armatura*, Lat.] military dress to defend the body from an attack; any thing to defend the body from external injuries.

A'RMED, Adj. in Heraldry, applied to beasts and birds of prey, when their teeth, horns, feet, beak, talons, or tusks, &c. are of a different colour; as, " A falcon *armed*."

ARME'NIAN, Adj. [belonging to, dwelling, or growing in Armenia. *Armenian bole*, in Pharmacy, an earthy substance of a pale yellowish, or scarlet colour, pinguious, heavy, easily broken, and dug out of the mines in Turkey. *Armenian stone* is a mineral earth, or stone, of a blue colour, spotted with green, black, or yellow, brought from Tyrol and Germany, and made use of in Mosaic work.

A'RM GAUNT, Adj. slender or starved. " An *armgaunt* steed." *Shakesp.*

A'RMIGER, S. [Lat.] an esquire, one that bears arms.

ARMI'GEROUS, Adj. [from *armiger*, Lat.] bearing arms.

ARMI'LLARY, Adj. [from *armilla*, Lat.] circular. *Armillary sphere*, is composed of several brass circles which represent those of the horizon, meridian, ecliptic, &c.

ARMI'NIANS, S. [from *Arminius*] the followers of Arminius, a famous minister at Amsterdam; who in the 16th century, se-

parated from the Calvinists, holding that predestination was conditional; that Christ both not only redeemed all, but that there is an universal grace given to all mankind; that grace is not an irresistible principle; that man is a free agent; that with respect to perseverance, a man may, after justification, fall into new crimes. To these principles of their founder they added, that the belief of the Trinity was not necessary to salvation, that there is not one passage in scripture, which commands us to worship the Holy Ghost; and are very great advocates for a general toleration.

ARMI'POTENCE, S. [from *arma*, Lat. and *potentia*, Lat.] power in war.

ARMI'POTENT, Adj. [*armipotens*] powerful, or strong in arms, or at war.

AR'MISTICE, S. [*armistium*, Lat. and *sisto*, Lat.] a short truce, or a cessation from arms.

A'RMLET, S. a small arm of the sea; a bracelet worn on the arm.

AR'MORER, S. [*armurier*, Fr.] one who makes or sells armour. One who dresses another in armour. The armourers company, in London, were formerly called brothers and sisters of the fraternity, or Guild of St. George, of the mystery of the Armourers of London. Their hall is in Coleman-street, and their arms as confirmed by patent of the 3d and 4th of Philip and Mary, 1556, are argent on a chevron gules; a gauntlet between four swords in saltier, on a chief sable; a buckler argent charged with a cross gules between two helmets of the first; their crest is a man demi-armed at all points, surmounting a torce and a helmet; their motto, " Make all sure." They are incorporated with the Braziers.

ARMO'RIAL, Adj. [from *armure*,] belonging to the coat or escutcheon of a family.

A'RMORIST, S. [from *armure*,] a person skilled in heraldry.

A'RMORY, S. [*armoire*, Fr.] a place where arms are kept. Arms. An escutcheon, or family coat.

AR'MS, S. offensive or defensive weapons. Figuratively, a state of hostility between two nations; war. In Heraldry, the badges of distinction, escutcheons, or other marks of honour. In birds or beasts of prey, those parts which they make use of in attacking others, or defending themselves.

A'RMY, S. [*armée*, Fr.] a collection of armed men, under their commanders.

AROMA'TICAL, Adj. [from *aromaticus*, Lat.] composed of spices; spicey; fragrant; strong scented.

AROMA'TIC, Adj. [from *aroma*, Lat.]
See AROMATIC.

AROMA'TICS, S. spices, or any fragrant, or high-tasted body. In Medicine, they are used to strengthen the stomach in cold cachectic habits;

habke; and, after the carrying off the watery in a dropfy, to fortify the fprings, and hinder them from filling again. As they are very good to prevent putrefaction, we cannot but admire the goodnefs of Providence, in having given them fo lavithly to warm countries, which are moft liable to diforders of that kind.

To AROMATIZE, V. A. [from *aroma*, Lat.] to fcent with fpices; to make any thing agreeable.

AROSE, the perfect of Arife.

AROUND, Adv. [*à la ronde*, Fr. *ronds*, Dan.] in a circular manner. On all fides, in allufion to the circumference of a circle furrounding its center. Ufed as a prepofition; encircling, encompaffing; round about. "Around his brows." *Dryd.*

A'RPENT, is the fame as *acre*. See ACRE.

A'ROUSE, V. A. to wake from fleep; to excite to action; to raife up from a ftate of dejection; to ftimulate.

A'RQUEBUSE, S. [fpelt improperly *harquebuse*, or *arquebuse*, Fr. *archbogio*, Ital.] a hand gun, carabine, fufee, or caliver.

ARRACK, S. See ARRAC.

To ARRAIGN, S. [*arranger*, Fr.] in Law, to fet a thing in order, to fit it for a trial; to indict, to accufe; to charge with crimes, applied to perfons. Ufed with the particle *for* before the crime. "Arraign you for want of knowledge." *Dryd.*

ARRAIGNMENT, S. the act of trying upon an indictment; accufation; or charge.

To ARRANGE, V. A. [*arranger*, Fr.] to difpofe, or put in regular order.

ARRANGEMENT, S. the act of putting things into order.

ARRANT, Adj. [as it carries with it the idea of fomething remarkable, is feldom derived from *ar*, Sax. remarkable, or one that has pre-eminence over others; not as Johnfon imagines from *errant*, Fr. which fignifying a vagabond, and being at firft ufed in that fenfe with the word *rogue*, loft its fignification, and was at laft made ufe of to convey the idea of fomething bad] notorious; infamous; vile.

ARRANTLY, Adv. notoriously, infamoufly, or fhamefully.

ARRAY, S. [fee the verb] the order of army drawn up to give battle; drefs.

To ARRAY, V. A. [from *array*, Fr.] to place an army in proper order. To deck, embellifh, or adorn with drefs; alfo with the particle *with*. In Law to rank or place a jury in proper order.

ARREAR, S. [from *arriere*, Fr.] what remains unpaid. That which has been due fome time, and is not difcharged.

ARREARAGE, S. the remainder of a fum of money remaining in the hands of an accountant fince his laft balance; in a more loofe fenfe, any money not paid when due.

ARREST, S. [from *arrest*, Fr.] in Law, the feizing a perfon, thereby depriving him of his liberty; either for debt, or any offence againft the Law. A ftopping from proceeding in an undertaking, ftoppage, or depriving a thing of its motion. "The ftop and *arreft* of the air." *Bac.* A fenfe feldom to be met with at prefent.

To ARREST, V. A. [from *arrester*, Fr.] to apprehend by virtue of a writ; to feize by law; to ftop, withhold, or bind.

ARRESTANDIS *bonis ne diffipentur*, in Law, a writ which lies for one whofe cattle or goods are taken by another, to prevent him from making away with them during the fuit.

ARRET, S. [Fr. *arret*] the decifion of a fovereign court, refembling our acts of parliament.

ARRESTO *facto fuper bona mercatorum alienigenarum*, in Law, a writ which lies for a denizen againft the goods of ftrangers in this kingdom, for goods taken from him in their country, after he fhall have been denied reftitution there.

ARRIERE, S. [ufed in French to imply a thing behind another, oppofed to *before*] the laft part of an army, or that which marches behind; for which we now ufe the word *rear*.

ARRIVAL, S. [from *arrive*] the coming to or arriving at any place, the attainment of any defign.

To ARRIVE, V. A. [from *arriver*, Fr.] to come to any place. Figuratively, to attain, or come to. Ufed with the particle *at*, before the perfon; to befall, to happen to. "To whom this glorious death *arrives*." *Milton*. This is an unufual, if not improper, acceptation.

AR'ROGANCE, or ARROGANCY, S. [from *arrogantia*, Lat.] the affuming more honour or merit, than is really our due.

ARROGANT, Part. [from *arrogans*, Part.] felf-conceited; haughty; affuming.

ARROGANTLY, Adj. felf-conceited, or haughty manner.

To ARROGATE, V. A. [from *arrogatum*, Lat.] to claim a thing or quality, which does not belong to us. Ufed with the particle *to* or *upon*, before the perfonal pronouns. "*arrogated* to herfelf." *Tillof.* "*Arrogated* unto themfelves." *Ralegh*.

ARRONDIE', Adj. [Fr. *arrondir*, in Heraldry,] the making things appear in relief by proper fhades. A crofs *arrondie*, according to Harris, is one compofed of the fection of a circle, which, in the fame arm, lay the fame way: fo that all the arms are of an equal thicknefs, and terminate at the end of an efcutcheon like a plain crofs.

ARROW, S. [*arwe*, Sax. *jara*, Span.] a flender piece of wood pointed, barbed, and fhot from a bow. *Arrow-Smith*, the perfon who fixed the plates or fteel to the heads of arrows.

ARSE,

ARSE, S. [Ærs, Sax. aers, ters, Belg.] the posteriors. Figuratively, the hind part of any thing; as, "The cart's arse."

AR'SENAL, S. [arsenal, Fr. arsenale, Ital.] a magazine, or place wherein warlike stores are kept.

AR'SENIC, S. [apsenic, Gr.] In Natural History, a ponderous, volatile, mineral substance, which gives whiteness to metals by infusion, but destroys their malleability; is extremely corrosive, caustic, and a strong poison. A single grain will turn one pound of copper to a beautiful seeming silver.

ARSE'NICAL, Adj. having the properties of arsenic.

ART, S. [art, Fr. of ars, Lat.] a metaphysical term, implying a collection of certain rules by which any thing may be performed; distinguished from science by its object; if the object be attained by the application of rules, or require practice, then it is an art; but if contemplated only with respect to its different appearances, the collection of observation relative thereto is a science. But these terms being used promiscuously by authors, the word art is sometimes used for something acquired, in opposition to that which is implanted by nature. A trade; cunning; artfulness; speculation. The liberal arts consist in the application, or exercise of the mind; the mechanic, those which consist in the exercise of the body, or hand. Art and part, in Law, used by the Scotch to signify the adviser and accomplice in a crime; or one who both contrived and acted a part in it.

ARTE'RIAL, Adj. that which belongs to an artery. The arterial blood is reckoned hotter, redder, and more spirituous than that of the veins.

ARTERIO'TOMY, S. [αρτηριοτομια, Gr.] In Surgery, the opening an artery, with a lancet, in order to draw blood from thence. Performed only in the temporary arteries, &c. on extraordinary cases. The most dangerous hæmorrhages proceed from wounding the arteries.

AR'TERY, S. [arteria, Lat.] a membranous, elastic, conical tube, without valves, destined to receive the blood from the heart, and to distribute it to the lungs, and other parts of the body; that which has its origin from the right ventricle of the heart, is called the pulmonary artery, and that which rises from the left the aorta. Providence has displayed its wisdom in the formation and disposition of these tubes, by covering them from external injuries, since the least of them cou'd not be wounded without danger; nor the largest without inevitable death.

AR'TFUL, Adj. according to the rules of art, artificial, opposed to natural. Full of cunning or craft.

AR'TFULLY, Adv. so as to shew a great

deal of cunning, or skill. Seldom used in a good sense.

AR'TFULNESS, S. the quality of attaining an end by cunning. Seldom used in a good sense.

ARTHRITIC, or ARTHRITICAL, Adj. [from arthritis,] gouty. That which has something like joints.

ARTHRITIS, S. [from αρθρον, Gr.] a disease which affects the joints; the gout.

AR'TICHOKE, S. [artichaut, Fr. articiocco, Span. choot, Teut.] In Botany, the cinara. Linnæus ranges them in the 19th sect. of his 19th class. There are three species. The fruit is like the cone of a pine-tree. For JERUSALEM ARTICHOKE, See SUN-FLOWER.

AR'TIC, Adj. spelt by some authors instead of Arctic, which see.

AR'TICLE, S. [of articulus, Lat.] In grammar, a word placed before a substantive to distinguish its signification. In English, we use two sorts, the definite and indefinite. A is the indefinite, and the the definite. We use them before a substantive, but not before adjectives, unless they are followed by a substantive, as a bad minister. They are never placed before pronouns, unless they include a substantive in them. Article likewise implies the heads of a discourse. In commerce, a single transaction, thing, or parcel in an account. Applied to time, a moment, an instant. "In that article of time," Clarend.

To AR'TICLE, V. N. to make conditions; to stipulate; to draw up or reduce into different heads. To bind or oblige a person to serve under certain conditions. "He articled him for seven years."

ARTIC'ULAR, Adj. [from articulus, Lat.] a disease affecting the joints.

ARTIC'ULATE, Adj. [from articulus, Lat.] that may be bent without being pulled asunder. Applied to the voice, it implies, that its sounds are distinct, and varied, but connected together so as to form words; an articulate pronunciation is that wherein the syllables and words are pronounced distinctly. Used by Bacon, to imply a discourse branched out into different articles, or minute; "Instructions extreme curious and articulate."

To ARTIC'ULATE, V. A. [articuler, Fr.] to pronounce in a distinct manner. To draw up articles, or to make terms.

ARTIC'ULATELY, Adv. distinctly.

ARTICULA'TION, S. In Anatomy, the juncture of two bones, so that they may be bent without being pulled asunder. Applied to the voice, the modulations and variations, which are so connected as to form syllables or words.

AR'TIFICE, S. [artifice, Fr.] an indirect method of attaining one's end, including

the idea of a futile contrivance ; a pretence,
stratagem, or fraud, in order to insure success in any undertaking ; opposed to open
integrity, and undisguised honesty.

ARTIFICIAL, Adj. [*artificial*, Fr.]
made by art. Something counterfeit opposed to real or genuine. That which displays
art. *Artificial lines* are drawn upon a sector,
or scale to represent lines and tangents.

ARTIFICIALLY, Adv. artfully, cunningly craftily. Performed by art, in opposition to natural.

ARTILLERY, S. [*artillerie*, Fr.] such
heavy engines of war, such as cannon, &c.
any weapons used in battle. " Jonathan
gave his *artillery* to the lad." 1 *Sam.* xx. 40.

ARTISAN, S. [Fr.] A low mechanic,
a manufacturer, or tradesman. Formerly applied to the practitioners in any art.

ARTIST, S. [Fr.] a person who excels in those arts which require good natural
parts. One who is capable of performing
an undertaking which requires judgment ;
opposed to a novice.

ARTLESLY, Adv. In a simple, innocent, and undisguising manner ; without any
embellishment ; naturally.

ARTLESS, Adj. without art, design, or
cunning.

ARUNDEL, a town in Suffex, with the
title of an earldom ; it has a good market on
Thursdays, and a small one on Saturdays.
The fairs are on May 14, Aug. 21, and
Dec. 15, for cattle; and on Dec. 17, for
pedlars ware. It is seated on the side of a
hill on the river Arun, over which is a
wooden bridge, where small ships may ride.
The ancient castle is seated on the summit
of the hill, and is said to be a mile in compass. It is eight miles E. of Chichester, and
55 S. W. by S. of London ; governed by
a mayor and 12 gestes, and sends two members to parliament, has two streets paved
with stones; about two hundred houses, and
eight hundred inhabitants. Long. 0. 25.
W. Lat. 50. 45. N.

AS, Conjunct. [*als*, Teut.] In the same
manner; when it answers *so*, or *such*, it
is used for *that*. Referring to the present
time, it implies something already done.
" Whistled *as* he went for want of thought."
Dryd. Since, or because; according to.
" *As* they please." *Boyle.* Answering *so*, it
implies condition, or the same manner.
Before *how*, it implies manner, or *how* ? in
what manner. Before *yet*, it implies till,
" *as yet*," i. e. till this time. Before *for*, with
respect to. Before *if*, supposing. Before
to with respect or regard to. Before *though*,
granting it to be real. *As will as*, no less
than with ; likewise, or besides. " Some
peculiarity *as well as* his face." *Locke.*
Likewise a Roman weight, the same with
their libra or lb.

ASBESTINE, Adj. [from *asbestus*] something incombustible not to be destroyed by
fire.

ASBESTOS, S. [from a Gr. *ασβεστος*,]
in Natural History, a stone not to be consumed in fire. See AMEANTHUS.

ASCARIDES, S. [Gr. from *ασκαριζω*,]
small, white, round, and short worms, which
decrease at each extremity, and resemble
needles, both with respect to their shape
and size, found glued together in the
intestinum rectum of infants, and derive
their name from their being always in motion. The best method of expelling them is
by clysters of gentian, cammomile, &c.

To ASCEND, V. N. [*ascendo*, Lat.] to
rise upwards ; figuratively to advance in
knowledge. In genealogy, to trace a pedigree backwards. Used in all these senses with
the particles *to*, *into* or *unto*. Used actively,
for climbing up any eminence.

ASCENDABLE, Adj. that may be ascended.

ASCENDANT, S. [from *ascendant*, Fr.]
superiority, or influence. In Astrology, the
horoscope, or degree of the ecliptic, which
rises above the horizon at a person's birth ;
called likewise the first house, and supposed to influence the whole series of a
person's actions. Figuratively, the greatest
height or perfection. In genealogy ancestors, or those nearest the root of a pedigree.
Used adjectively for something influencing
another.

ASCENDENCY, S. a bias ; influence or
superiority.

ASCENDING, Part. [from *ascendens*,
Lat.] going upwards. In Astronomy, those
degrees, or stars, above the horizon.

ASCENSION, S. [from *ascensio*, Lat.]
a motion upwards. In Divinity the miraculous ascent of our Saviour, when he went to
heaven, in the sight of his apostles ; which
is commemorated by the church ten days before Whit-Sunday, and called *Holy Thursday*.
Ascension, in Astronomy, is either *right* or *oblique*. *Right Ascension* is a degree of the equinoctial, counted from the beginning of
Aries, which rises with the sun or star in a
right sphere. *Oblique Ascension*, is a portion
of the equator, contained between the first
point of Aries, and that point of the equator which rises with the star in an oblique
sphere.

ASCENSIVE, Adj. [from *ascensus*, Lat.]
being in motion upwards.

ASCENT, S. [from *ascensus*, Lat.] motion upwards, a high place or eminence. In
Logic, a kind of argument, wherein we rise
from particulars to universals, by enumerating all the particulars which the universal
term contains.

To ASCERTAIN, V. A. [*acertener*, Fr.]
to determine. To take away all doubt ; to
establish

flablish. Sometimes used with the particle *of*.

ASCERTAINMENT, S. the determining a doubtful expression. A settled rule or standard.

ASCETIC, Adj. [*ασκητικος*, Gr.] employed entirely in exercises of devotion and mortification.

ASCETIC, S. [from *ασκεω*, Gr.] one who practises a great degree of austerity and mortification. Applied to the Essenes, among the Jews, and among the Christians, those of an exemplary life: not as Bingham observes, to monks who dwelt in deserts, but to persons of all denominations, who lived in towns or cities.

ASCHA'RIOUNS, or ASCHA'RIENS, S. the followers of *Al-hari*, one of the most celebrated doctors of the Mussulmen, who maintain, that God is the universal agent, and the cause of all the actions of mankind, who are notwithstanding free to choose such as they please. So that mankind are answerable for what is entirely independent of them, with respect to his production, but entirely dependent on them, with respect to its choice or volition.

ASCII, S. [from *a* Gr. and *σκια*] in Geography, those inhabitants of the torrid zone, who have no shadow at certain times of the year, because the sun shines perpendicularly on their heads.

ASCITES, S. [from *ασκος*, Gr.] in Medicine, a kind of dropsy.

ASCITIC, Adj. [from *ascitis*] dropsical.

ASCITITIOUS, Adj. [from *ascititus*, Lat.] counterfeit, spurious, opposed to genuine. That which is added to, or not inherent, opposed to essential.

ASCRIBABLE, Adj. deducible from, or imputable to.

To ASCRIBE, V. A. [from *ascribo*, Lat.] to deduce from; to attribute to. Used with the particle *to*.

ASH, S. [from *æfc*, *æsc*, Sax.] in Botany, the fraxinus. Its male flowers have no petals, and the germen has one seed like a bird's tongue. *Ash-coloured* is between brown and grey, resembling the bark of the ash.

ASHAMED, Adj. conscious of having done something which may be found fault with. Used with the particle *of* before the object. See SHAME.

ASHBORN, a town in Derbyshire, with a market on Saturdays, and seven fairs; on February 13, for horses of all sorts and horned cattle; on April 3, May 21, and July 5, for horses, horned cattle, and wool; on August 16, for horses and horned cattle; on October 20, and November 19, for coarse heavy horses and horned cattle. It is seated between the rivers Dove and Compton, over which there is a stone bridge, in a rich soil, and is a pretty large town, though not so flourishing as formerly. It is 10 miles N. E.

of Uttoxeter, and 133 N. N. W. of London. Lon. 1°. 55. lat. 53. 0.

ASHBURTON, a town in Devonshire, with a market on Tuesdays for wool and yarn only, and on Saturdays for provisions of all sorts. The fairs are on the first Thursday in March, the first Thursday in June, August 10, and November 11, principally for horned cattle. It sends two members to parliament, and is one of the four stannary towns. It is seated among the hills, which are remarkable for tin and copper; and has a very handsome church; as also a chapel, which is turned into a school. It stands near the river Dart, 19 miles S. W. of Exeter, 25 N. E. of Plymouth, and 192 W. by S. of London. Lon. 13. 20. lat. 50. 30.

ASHBY DE LA ZOUCH, a town in Leicestershire, with a plentiful market on Saturdays; and four fairs, on Easter-Tuesday and Whit-Tuesday for horses, cows, and sheep; on St. Bartholomew and St. Simon and Jude for horses and cows. It had a castle with a very high tower, a great part of which is still standing. It has also a good free-school, and is 13 miles S. of Derby, 19 N. of Coventry, and 98 N. N. W. of London. Lon. 16. 20. lat. 52. 40.

ASHEN, Adj. made or consisting of ash, or ash-wood.

ASHES, S. [it has no singular. *Asse*, *asce*, *ascan*, or *asca*, Sax.] that substance which things are reduced to by burning. The corpse of a dead person, alluding to the ancient custom of burning the dead. *Ash-Wednesday*, *Asch Wænsdag*, the first day of Lent, so called from the custom of the ancient Christians of sprinkling ashes on their heads on that day.

ASHORE, Adv. to the shore or land; on land.

ASHY, Adj. resembling the ash in colour, of a whitish grey.

ASIA, one of the four great parts of the world, and the second in order. It is bounded on the N. by the Frozen Sea, on the E. by the Eastern Ocean, which is part of the South Sea, on the S. by the Indian Sea, and on the W. by Europe and Africa. It is of larger extent than any of the three parts in our continent, and is generally said that the first man was created here; though many are of a different opinion, arising from the uncertainty where the garden of Eden was placed. But, be that as it will, arts and sciences were early cultivated here; though they are thought to come originally from Egypt: but all the considerable religions now known had their first beginning in Asia; and there are still a great number of people who maintain their ancient tenets, which, according to them, are a hundred thousand years old. They have one sort of religion in China, and another in India, whose priests

are the Brachmans; not to mention the Jews, Christians, and Mahometans, whose beginnings are sufficiently known to all the world. This was the seat of several ancient empires or monarchies; such as that of the Assyrians, Medes, Persians, and Greeks. It is 4740 miles in length from the Dardanels on the W. to the eastern shore of Tartary; and 4380 in breadth from the most southern part of Malacca, to the most northern cape of Nova Zembla. It may be divided into 30 great parts, namely, Turkey in Asia, Arabia, Persia, the Mogul's Empire, with the two Peninsulas of India, Thibet, China, and Corea, Great and Little Bucharia, with Carazm, Little and Great Tartary, Siberia, and the Islands. The governments of Asia are generally monarchical; and Turkey, Persia, the Mugul's Empire, Thibet, and China, are subject to single monarchs; but the rest is divided among several sovereigns; insomuch that there are reckoned seven emperors, and 30 kings, besides petty princes, and the rajas of India, which are very numerous. With regard to the extent of their religions, the Christian is but small in respect of the Mahometan, which comprehends one third of Asia; and the Pagan is about twice as much extended as the Mahometan. Besides these, some pretend there is the natural religion, which has about as many followers as the Christian. The languages are so many and so various, that it is impossible to enumerate them; but the chief are the Turkish, the Grecian, the Arabick, the Chinese, the Persian, and the Old Indian. In short, every country and island has almost a distinct language. Besides the animals we have in Europe, there are lions, leopards, tigers, camels, elephants, rhinoceroses, and many others. There are several great lakes; but the principal are the Caspian Sea, which is about 2000 miles in circumference, and the Lake Aral, which is about half as much, and has not been long known to the Europeans. As for the rivers, I shall not mention them here, but refer to their proper places.

ASIDE, Adv. that which is not straight or perpendicular; out of its true direction; not towards; from the company.

ASININE, Adj. (from *asinus*; Lat.) partaking of the nature of an ass.

To **ASK**, V. A. (*ascian, or acsian*; Sax: from hence we may see, that the London pronunciation *aks*, instead of *ask*, is a remain of the Saxon, and not so great an impropriety as appears at first sight) to desire a thing, sometimes with the particle *for*; to demand; to put a question; to enquire, with the particle *after*; to require.

ASKANCE, ASKAUNT, Adv. (from *a* and *skaunt*, of *scance*, Fr.) with the pupils of each eye turned to each corner of the eye-lid; obliquely; sideways; with a leer.

ASKER, S. one who makes a request, or proposes a question.

ASKEW, Adv. (from *scheef*, Belg. *schew*) aside, opposed to a direct look; oblique.

ASLANT, Adv. on one side, obliquely; implying a deviation from a straight or perpendicular situation.

ASLEEP, Adv. in that state wherein the senses are closed, the eyes shut, and a person enjoys that rest from animal labour called sleep.

ASLOPE, Adv. (from *a* and *slop*, Belg.) declining, obliquely; opposed to level or horizontal.

ASP, or **ASPIC**, S. (*aspis*, Lat.) a kind of serpent, whose poison is mortal in three hours after the bite.

ASPALATHUS, S. in Botany, a plant called the Rose of Jerusalem, or Our Lady's Rose. Liber is the wood of a small thorny tree, which grows on the banks of the Danube and Nissro in Rhodes: the best sort is heavy, red, or purple next to the bark, is fragrant to the smell, and bitter to the taste. It affords an essential oil, so much like that of rushes, that one might be taken for the other.

ASPARAGUS, S. [Lat. viliously pronounced *sparrow-grass*] in Botany, its flower is composed of six leaves, being male and hermaphrodite, sometimes in different and at other times in the same plant. From the center grows an erect stile, which becomes a berry with three cells, including one or two seeds. It is aperient, diuretic, good in the gravel and stranguary, and makes the urine very fœtid or rank.

ASPECT, S. (*aspectus*; Lat.) the face; a cast of the countenance; look or appearance. The front of a building. The different lights in which things may be viewed. In Astrology, the situation of stars or planets with respect to each other; or, according to Kepler, an angle formed by the rays of two planets meeting on the earth, able to excite some natural power or influence.

To **ASPECT**, V. A. (*aspicio*, Lat.) to look upon, gaze, or behold.

ASPECTABLE, Adj. (*aspectabilis*, Lat.) that which may be seen; that which is the object of sight; visible.

ASPECTION, S. (from *aspectus*, *supine* of *aspicio*, Lat.) the act of viewing or beholding. "On *aspection* of the picture of Andromeda." Bishop's Vulg. Err.

ASPEN, or **ASP**, S. (*esp*, or *espe*, Sax: *asp*; Dan.) a kind of poplar, whose leaves are always trembling.

ASPER, Adj. [Lat.] rough or rugged. In Commerce, a small silver coin, struck and current in the grand Seignior's dominions, of about 120 of them are worth 3½ d. English. *Pollux.*

ASPERA ARTERIA, in Anatomy, the trachea or wind-pipe, situated in the fore

and lower part of the neck. It is made up of segments of a circle, or cartilaginous hoops, disposed so as to form a canal open to the back, which consists of a glandular membrane; and is in breadth the 24th part of an inch.

To A'SPERATE, V. A. [aspero, Lat.] to roughen; to make rough.

ASPERIFO'LIOUS, Adj. [from asper, Lat. and folium]. in Botany, applied to those plants whose leaves are rough and placed alternately; having, according to Ray, a monopetalous flower, divided into five parts, and succeeded by four seeds: such are the bugloss, borra, &c.

ASPE'RITY, S. [asperitas, Lat.] unevenness or roughness; moroseness.

A'SPEROUS, Adj. [asper, Lat.] rough, rugged or uneven, opposed to smooth. "Black and white, the most asperous and unequal of colours." Boyle.

To ASPER'SE, V. A. [aspergo, Lat.] to lay any thing against the character of another; to slander; to calumniate.

ASPER'SION, S. [aspersio, Lat.] the action of sprinkling; applied, in Divinity, to the mode of baptism commonly practised; likewise, in Popish countries, appropriated to the method of sprinkling with holy water. Unmerited calumny, or slander.

ASPHA'LTIC, Adj. [from asphaltos] of the nature of asphaltos, bituminous, or pitchy.

ASPHAL'TOS, S. [Gr. asphaltos] In Natural History, a solid, heavy, brittle, brown, and even blackish, shining, resinous, inflammable, and pitchy substance, found chiefly on the surface of the Dead Sea, on which Sodom and the other cities were situated, mentioned Gen. xiv. 17, 18. Used by the Tartars to pitch their ships with, and by the antients in embalming their dead.

ASPHAL'TUM, S. [see ASPHALTOS] In Natural History, a bituminous stone found near the antient Babylon, and lately discovered at Neufchatel in Switzerland, by M. de la Sablonniere.

ASPHO'DEL, S. [filio-asphodelus, Lat.] In Botany, the day lilly. Linnæus ranges it in his sixth class, because the flower has six stamina and one stile. There are six species; and were by the antients planted near burying-places, to supply the uses of the deceased with nurture.

To A'SPIRATE, V. A. [aspiro, Lat.] to lay a stress of voice upon any syllable; to be pronounced with vehemence or a full breath.

A'SPIRATE, Adj. [from aspiratus, Lat.] pronounced with roughness, stress, or vehemence of voice.

ASPIRA'TION, S. [from aspiratio, Lat.] a fighting for; a longing after; an ardent desire. In Grammar, the pronouncing any word strongly or in full breath.

To ASPIRE, V. N. [from aspiro, Lat.]

to endeavour after something above our present circumstances or situation. Used with after.

ASQUI'NT, Adv. a position of the eyes, wherein they do not seem to look the same way. Obliquely, opposed to directly.

ASS, S. [erron. œs, Arm. asil, Teut. esne, Ital.] a domestic animal, remarkable for sluggishness, hardiness, patience, coarseness of diet, and long life. There are a wild sort in Persia, which are remarkable for their activity as the tame are for their sluggishness; but, what is very surprising, they are no sooner loaded, but they become like the dullest of the species. The asses of the east are by no means to be compared with ours, since their hair is abundantly softer, and their whole make bespeaks something superior. Hence it was, that formerly kings and princes used to ride on them; and our Saviour made his triumphant entry into Jerusalem on one of that species. Figuratively, a person of a mean, abject spirit; or sluggish, ignorant, and dull.

ASSA, S. In Pharmacy, divided into assa dulcis, or benzoin, and assa fœtida; a gum or resin, of a brownish colour, and a very offensive smell; from whence it receives both the name assa, and likewise that of devil's dung. It is the product of an umbelliferous plant which grows in the east, in the parts bordering on the Persian gulph, flowing either naturally or by incision from its root. Those who would be better acquainted with this plant, may have recourse to Kempfer's Voyages into Persia. It is of great efficacy in nervous and uterine disorders, epilepsies, &c. and much used by the oriental nations in their sauces.

To ASSA'IL, V. A. [from assaillir, Fr.] to attack, or fall upon an enemy. Figuratively, to attack with words or arguments.

ASSA'ILABLE, Adj. that which may be attacked.

ASSA'ILANT, S. [assaillant, Fr.] one who makes an attack, opposed to one who defends.

ASSA'ILANT, Adj. the using acts of violence; attacking.

ASSA'ILER, S. one who attacks another.

ASSAPA'NIC, S. In Natural History, the flying squirrel, a Virginian animal, which, though without wings, by means of stretching its legs and distending its skin, is said to fly the space of half a mile. 'Tis pity we have not a more minute description of it, in order to discover the mechanism it makes use of on these occasions. Dict.

ASSA'SSIN, S. [from assa, Arab.] one who lays in wait for another; a person who murders another.

To ASSA'SSINATE, V. A. [from assassiner] to murder treacherously or for hire; to way-lay.

4   A 5

ASSASSINATION, S. the act of murdering.

ASSASSINA'TOR, S. See ASSASSIN.

ASSAULT, S. (*affault*, Fr.) in War, a general and furious attack of a camp, or fortified place, the affailants being all the time without any cover or shelter. A Christian governor is obliged to sustain three affaults before he surrenders; and a Turk is forbid by his religion to capitulate for a place which has a mosque in it. This has lately been stiled a *coup de main*. See *Mordaunt's Trial*. Figuratively, an invasion or attack, applied to properties or opinions. In Law, a violent injury offered, by a blow, or a terrifying speech. *Lamb. Iren.* b. I. c. 3. 25 *Edw.* III. c. 24.

To ASSAULT, V. A. in War, to make a furious attack, without any cover, on a fortified place. To offer violence to; to attack.

ASSAU'LTER, S. one who affaults another.

ASSA'Y, S. (from *effay*, Fr. hence ancient writers borrowed the word *affay*, spelling it according to its pronunciation, and later authors *effay*, according to the original; but they are now used in different senses, and may be esteemed different words) examination, trial, attack. *Affay* of weights and measures, is the examination of them by the clerks of markets.

To ASSA'Y, V. A. (from *effayer*, Fr.) to put to trial; to try. To apply, in allusion to the application of the touch-stone in affaying metals.

ASSA'YER, S. one who tries metals, to determine how much they are above, or below standard.

ASSA'YING, S. the art of separating metals, sulphur, &c. from each other, to determine the quantity of each before the trial, and the advantage accruing from extraction. This is performed by reducing the ore into a fine powder, and melting it with lead in a crucible, after which it is put upon a test, where it is worked with a proper degree of heat, till the lead is either evaporated or vitrified, and leaves the silver in the form of a bead on the test; this is called cupelling. There is another method called quartation, which is performed by the infusion of aqua fortis into the mixed mass of ore and lead, instead of placing it on the test.

ASSEMBLAGE, S. (Fr.) the collecting a great number of things together, so as to form a whole; it differs from *affembly*, as that is used of persons, and this of things.

To ASSE'MBLE, V. A. (of *affembler*, Fr.) to unite several things or persons together. To bring several things together. Used with the preposition *together*. To join the different parts of a work together.

ASSE'MBLY, S. (from *affemblée*, Fr.) a collection or company of several persons, to enjoy the pleasure of conversation, news, cards, &c.

ASSE'NT, S. (from *affenfus*, Lat.) that act of the mind whereby it acknowledges any proposition to be true or false; agreement or consent.

To ASSE'NT, V. N. (from *affentire*, Lat.) to receive or admit a thing as true. Sometimes used actively, with the particle *unto*.

ASSENTA'TION, S. (*affentatio*, Lat.) the profession of one's opinion being the same as another, merely through compliment. Flattery, and includes the secondary idea of something base and mean.

To ASSE'RT, V. A. (from *affero*, Lat.) to affirm as true; to claim as one's due; to defend by words and actions.

ASSE'RTION, S. (from *affert*) affirmation; a proposition delivered in positive terms.

ASSE'RTIVE, Adj. (from *affert*) positive; obstinate; dogmatical; affirmative.

ASSE'RTOR, S. one who affirms. A maintainer, or supporter.

To ASSE'SS, V. A. (of *affeffare*, Ital.) to tax, or fine a person.

ASSE'SSMENT, S. (from *affefs*) the sum, or fine levied. The act of levying a fine.

ASSE'SSOR, S. one who settles a fine. In the imperial chamber, a counsellor who has a fallary annexed to his place, of which there are forty-one.

A'SSETS, S. (used only in the plural, from *affez*, Fr.) the goods of a deceased person, which are to be appropriated to the payment of his debts.

To ASSE'VER, or ASSE'VERATE, (*affevero*, Lat.) to affirm, or deny with oaths, imprecations, execrations, or curses.

ASSEVERA'TION, S. (*affeveratio*, Lat.) the act of attesting a thing by an oath, or imprecations.

ASSIDU'ITY, S. (*affiduité*, Fr. *affiduitas*, Lat.) a constant attention or application to study, or business; diligence.

ASSI'DUOUS, Adj. (*affiduous*, Lat.) unwearied; incessant; attentive.

ASSI'DUOUSLY, Adv. attentively, incessantly.

ASSIE'NTO, S. a contract made between this nation and Spain, for supplying their plantations with negroes. This is now carried on by a company of British merchants, and our captures of Senegal and Goree must tend not only to render this trade more advantageous in particular; but as it may force even the French to contract with us for the supply of their sugar colonies, will highly redound to illustrate the character of Mr. T. Cummings, the projector of that expedition.

To

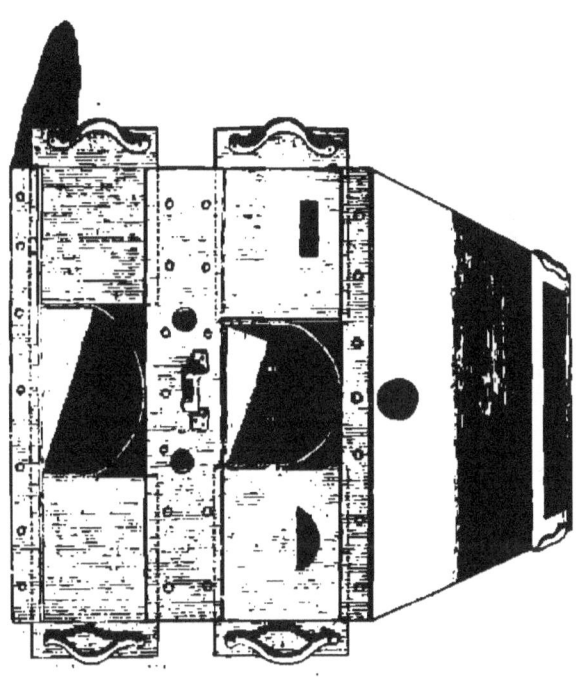

To ASSI'GN, V. A. [from *affigno*, Lat.] to diftribute; allot; appoint; determine, or fix. To produce; to make a perfon one's deputy; to transfer property to another. To prove, fhew, or demonftrate.

ASSI'GNABLE, Adj. that which may be fettled, fixed, marked out, or transferred.

ASSIGNA'TION, S. [from *affignation*, Fr.] the transferring property to another. In Commerce, an order to certain perfons to pay a debt to another, whofe name is mentioned. Generally ufed in amours, for an appointment made for meeting.

ASSIGNE'E, S. [*affigné*, Fr.] one appointed by another to perform any bufinefs. Commonly applied to thofe who are entrufted with the eftate of a bankrupt.

ASSI'GNMENT, S. the fetting any thing apart; an appropriation; an alienation.

To ASSIMI'LATE, V. A. [*affimilo*, Lat.] to convert to the fame nature; to bring to a refemblance.

ASSIMILA'TION, S. the action by which things are rendered like each other. In Phyfics, that action or motion by which a body transforms, or converts others into a nature, or fubftance, the fame as their own. Such are the converfion of all and fpirits into flame; that of earth and water into the fubftance of vegetables; and that of aliment into the bodies of animals; a refemblance, or effential likenefs. Ufed with the particle *with*. "*Affimilation with God*." *Decay of Piety.*

To ASSI'MULATE, V. A. [*affimulo*, Lat.] to counterfeit; to feign.

ASSIMULA'TION, S. [*affimulatio*, Lat.] a counterfeit, or fpecious refemblance.

To ASSI'ST, V. A. [*affifter*, Fr.] to relieve; to help; its motive is commiferation, and its object the neceffitous. But authors, who do not attend to this precifion, ufed the word either for *fuccour* or aid.

ASSI'STANCE, S. [*affiftance*, Fr.] the act of helping; help, aid.

ASSI'STANT, Adj. [from *affift*] fupplying the defects of another. An *affiftant furgeon*, or *phyfician*, is one who is called by another to help him in manual operations or advice.

ASSI'STANT, S. [from *affift*] one who helps or affifts another. In Law, one who partakes with another in the commiffion of a crime, as an accomplice, but not as a principal. One who is named to help a principal officer in the exercife of his duty or functions. An *affiftant* to a bifhop, or rector, is one who partakes with him in adminiftering the facrament, and in the difcharge of church offices. An attendant, is an improper ufe of the word.

ASSI'SE, S. [*affife*, Fr. a feating] In Law, a place wherein a judge and jury affemble for the trial of caufes; they are either general or particular. The term is likewife applied to fignify the whole procefs of a writ; a flatute for regulating the weight of bread; and the bread itfelf, as prefcribed by the ftatute. This excellent regulation was made 51 Hen. III. and that of the circuits of judges in the time of Hen. II.

To ASSI'ZE, V. A. to fix the price, or weight of a commodity.

ASSI'ZER, or ASSI'SER, S. an officer who infpects weights and meafures.

ASSO'CIABLE, Adj. [from *affociabilis*, Lat.] that which may be united to fomething elfe.

To ASSO'CIATE, V. A. [*affocier*, Fr. of *affocio*, Lat.] to join; to make one of a company. To join infeparably, applied to ideas. Ufed in all thefe fenfes with the particle *with*.

ASSO'CIATE, Adj. [from *affociatus*, Lat.] confederated; joined; making part of a fociety.

ASSO'CIATE, S. one who is joined to another as a companion, partner, or confederate.

ASSOCIA'TION, S. union; fociety. The act of forming a company or fociety. A contract or treaty, between two or more, for the better carrying on any defign. In Phyfics, combination, or union. In Metaphyfics, the connexion of two or more ideas in the mind, which conftantly follow each other in fuch a manner, that one can fcarce be excited without the other. It is thus that children think of fpirits in the dark; and the common obfervation, that "a burnt child dreads the fire," is founded on this habit.

ASSONANCE, S. [*affonance*, Fr.] in Poetry, is where the words of a fentence have the fame found, but are not properly a rhime.

ASSO'RTMENT, S. [*affortiment*, Fr.] in Trade, a ftock of goods of various forts. In Painting, the proportion and harmony between the feveral parts. A collection of fuch things as agree in fize and colour.

To ASSUA'GE, V. A. [from *fuavis*, *adfuadeo*, or *affuavior*, Lat.] to cool, or leffen; to calm; to pacify, or appeafe; to eafe, applied to pain. It generally implies the leffening the violence of fomething furious. To abate, or grow lefs.

ASSUA'GEMENT, S. [from *affuage*] that which leffens or abates the violence of any thing.

ASSUA'GER, one who pacifies, appeafes, or cools.

ASSUA'SIVE, Adj. [*affuadeo*, Lat.] that affuages, mitigates, or pacifies.

ASSUEFA'CTION, S. [from *affuefactus*, fup. of *affuefacio*, Lat.] the conftant ufe of a thing; habit.

A3-

ASSUETUDE, S. [from assuetudo, Lat.] the being accustomed to a thing. Custom.

To ASSUME, V. A. [from assumo, Lat.] to take. To represent a character; to arrogate, or claim what is not one's due; to suppose or look upon a thing as evident, without proof; to take up, applied to the use of an expression; to appropriate, to apply to one's self.

ASSUMER, S. a vain, arrogant person.

ASSUMING, Part. proud; arrogant.

ASSUMPSIT, V. A. [Lat. third person singular of the preter of assumo, Lat.] in Law, a voluntary and verbal promise to perform, or pay a thing to another. If a person does not pay for goods sold him, an indebitatus assumpsit lies against him.

ASSUMPTION, S. [from assumptio, Lat.] appropriating any thing to one's self. The supposing a thing true, without proof. The thing supposed, a postulate, or postulatum. The assumption of the Virgin Mary is celebrated on the 15th of August. In Logic, the minor, or second proposition in a categorical syllogism.

ASSUMPTIVE, Adj. [from assumptivus, Lat.] which a person may appropriate to himself. In Heraldry, assumptive arms are what a person may use as his own. He who takes a prince prisoner, may use or assume his arms or escutcheon as his own.

ASSURANCE, S. [assurance, Fr.] a certain expectation. Confidence; trust, or security. Conviction. In Commerce, a contract to make good the damages to be sustained by another in a voyage. See also INSURANCE.

To ASSURE, V. A. [assurer, Fr.] to declare positively. To make a person confident, by removing the causes of doubt or fear. To be betrothed. To assure, differs from affirming, only in the tone of the voice, and implies a total exemption from doubt.

ASSUREDLY, Adv. certainly; undoubtedly; positively.

ASSURER, S. [assurer, Fr.] In Commerce, one who indemnifies another against hazards at sea, &c.

ASTERISK, S. [from asteriscus, Gr.] a character used to render particular passages in an author conspicuous, or to refer to some note in the margin, marked thus *.

ASTHMA, S. [Gr. from aō, Gr. to breath] In Medicine, a difficulty of breathing, arising from a disorder in the lungs. The general indication of cure is bleeding, dispersing the collected matter, and keeping up a constant perspiration.

ASTMATIC, or ASTMATICAL, Adj. affected with an asthma.

ASTERN, a sea term, In the hinder part of a ship; or any thing situated behind the ship.

To ASTONISH, V. A. [etonner, Fr.] to occasion surprise, or wonder. To amaze.

ASTONISHMENT, S. [from etonnement, Fr.] a surprize; amazement; distinguished from admiration, both by the degree, and the nature of the object. "Astonishment is beyond bare admiration." South.

ASTRADDLE, Adv. See ASTRIDE.

ASTRAGAL, S. [astragalos, Gr.] in Anatomy, a bone of the tarsus, with a convex eminence, commonly called the ankle bone. In Architecture, a little round member, in the form of a ring or bracelet, serving as an ornament to the tops and bottoms of columns. In Gunnery, the little moulding on a piece of ordnance.

ASTRAL, Adj. [from astrum, Lat.] that which belongs, or relates to the stars. Astral year, is the time the earth takes to make its revolution round the sun. See SIDERIAL, and YEAR.

ASTRAY, Adv. wandering or deviating from the right path. Figuratively, wrong, or in an error, opposed to truth.

To ASTRICT, V. A. [of astrictum, Lat.] to lessen the distance between objects; to make the parts of a thing come nearer to each other.

ASTRICTION, S. [astrictio, Lat.] the act of making the parts of a thing approach nearer to each other.

ASTRICTIVE, Adj. [from astrictus] that which has a styptic, or binding quality.

ASTRICTORY, Adj. [from astrictorius, Lat.] having an astringent or binding quality.

ASTRIDE, Adj. [from a and stride] a posture wherein each of the legs is placed at a distance from another; open or wide, applied to the legs.

ASTRIFEROUS, Adj. [from astrifer, Lat.] bearing, exhibiting of, or having stars.

ASTRIGEROUS, Adj [from astrum, and gero, Lat.] bearing, or adorned with stars.

To ASTRINGE, V. A. [from astringo] to press together; to force the parts closer.

ASTRINGENT, Part. [astringens, Lat.] that which contracts the dimension of the vessels, and thickens the fluids so that they cannot pass so fast by way of excrement; when used internally, opposed to laxative; when externally, opposed to styptic.

ASTROITES, S. [Gr.] In Natural History, a kind of stone found at Shuckburgh in Warwickshire, and at Torque in Normandy, which derives its name from its resembling a star, it consists of several thin pentagonal joints set over each other, so as to form a kind of pentagonal column, of which colour, unless foiled by accident. They have been successively classed among petrifactions, fossils, the animal tribe, and lately by M. Peyssonel, among the vegetable.

ASTROLABE, S. [from astron, Gr. and lambano, Arab.] a planisphere or stereographic projection of the sphere upon the plane of one of the great circles.

ASTROLOGER, S. [from astrologus, Lat.] one who predicts future events from the

the supposed influences of the stars. Formerly used for ASTRONOMER.

ASTROLO'GIC, or ASTROLO'GICAL, Adj. relating to the principles of astrology.

ASTROLO'GICALLY, Adv. agreeable to the principles of astrology.

To ASTRO'LOGIZE, V. A. [from *astrology*] to study astrology; to solve, predict or foretell.

ASTRO'LOGY, S. [Lat. *astrologia*] the art of foretelling future events from the aspects, or positions of the stars. It is divided into natural and judicial; natural astrology is the art of predicting natural events, as changes of weather, winds, tempests, storms, thunder, earthquakes, &c. Judicial astrology, is that which pretends to foretell moral events, or such as depend on the free-will and agency of man, as if the stars had some influence on it, and directed it. It had its rise in Chaldea; from whence it spread to Egypt and Greece: as for ourselves and the French, we seem to have borrowed it from the Arabians.

ASTRO'NOMER, S. [from *aster* and *nomos*, Gr.] one who applies himself to the study of astronomy.

ASTRONO'MICAL, Adj. founded upon the principles of astronomy.

ASTRO'NOMY, S. [*astronomie*, Fr. *astronomia*, Lat.] properly speaking, a branch of mixt mathematics, acquainting us with the celestial bodies, their magnitudes, motions, revolutions, eclipses, &c. In a lower sense, the knowledge of the universe, and the primary laws of nature, in which respect it is a branch of physics, or natural philosophy.

ASTRO-THEO'LOGY, S. [from *astrum*, Lat. and *theologia*, Lat.] the proofs of a Deity drawn from an astronomical view of the heavens; the sublime arguments, which this topic affords to the divine, are treated of in so elegant a manner by Dr. Derham, in his Astro-theology, and in the Christian Magazine, just published, that it must be a great loss to an ingenious mind not to have known them.

ASLU'NDER, Adv. [from *asundran*, or *asundron*, Sax.] at a distance from each other; apart; separate.

ASY'LUM, S. [Lat. from a Gr. and *sulaō*, Gr.] a place of refuge, which sheltered a criminal, and secured him from the hands of an officer of justice. The Asylum, a house situated on the Surry side of Westminster-bridge, for the benefit of orphans, and other deserted girls of the poor, within the bills of mortality; who are maintained by voluntary contributions, and qualified for service. The design of this institution was to prevent their falling into the hands of procuresses, or turning prostitutes by necessity. Sir John Fielding was the projector in 1758.

ASY'MMETRY, S. [from a Gr. and *summetria*,] a defect of proportion, or harmony.

ASY'MPTOTE, S. a right line, which being continued indefinitely, continually approaches to a curve.

ASSYMPTO'TICAL, Adj. belonging to, or relating to the properties of, an asymptote.

ASYN'DETON, S. [from a Gr. and *sundeō*,] in Grammar, a figure wherein several sentences meet without any conjunction.

AT, Prep [*at*, Sax. *at*, Goth.] close to; In it. Before a word implying time it denotes the very instant in which a thing was done. Used instead of *with* it implies on account of. " *At* this news he dies." Shakesp. Before a personal pronoun, it implies an act of enmity. " He longs to be *at* him, *i. e.* to attack him." After *to* it implies intention, or employment. " She knew what he would be *at*." Hud. Used with command, It implies subject or obedience *at my command*." Sometimes it signifies; as, " *At* our hands." Pope.

A'TABAL, S. a kind of drum or tambour, made use of by the Moors.

ATE, the Preter of *eat*; thus *eat* is the preter of *to eat*, Id. I eat, and *frat*, the Pret. of *freten*, Goth. to eat with.

ATHA'NOR, S. [from יתן, Heb. an oven or furnace,] in Chemistry, a large immoveable furnace, made of earth or brick.

A'THEISM, S. [*atheisme*, Fr.] the opinion of those who deny the existence of a God.

A'THEIST, S. [of a Gr. and *theos*, Gr.] a person who denies the existence of a God. The advocates of this horrible opinion are divided either into such as deny the existence of a Deity, such as affect to doubt on this article, or such as deny the principal attributes of the divine nature, and suppose the Deity is a being without intelligence, and acting by necessity; or, properly speaking, a being that never acts, and is always passive. The sources of this opinion is generally vice, and a dread of future punishment. Ignorance, or want of stupidity; for according to lord Bacon, " Though a smattering in philosophy may lead a man into atheism, a deep draught will certainly bring him back again to the belief of a God and providence." Used adjectively, it implies something that partakes of the principles of an atheist.

ATHEI'STICAL, Adj. impious; after the manner of an atheist.

ATHEI'STICALLY, Adv. like an atheist.

ATHENS, a town of Greece, greatly celebrated for the learned men it has produced, it having been the principal academy of the Roman empire. It is now called Athina, and is an archbishop's see: though at present it is inconsiderable to what it was formerly. It contains about 15000 inhabitants, who are chiefly Christians of the Greek church

church, and they speak a corrupt sort of Greek. It has undergone various revolutions, and was taken by the Venetians in 1464, and, in 1687, but they were obliged to abandon it, and it is now under the dominion of the Turks. The citadel formerly called Acropolis, is built on a craggy rock, and has no entrance but on the W. side, and there are several magnificent ruins which sufficiently testify its former grandeur. It is the capital of Livadia, and it is situated on the Gulph Engia, 100 miles N. E. of Mistra, or Lacedæmon, 143 S. by E. of Laissa, and 320 S. by W. of Constantinople. Long. 41. 55. lat. 38. 5.

A'THEOUS, S. [from ἀθεος, Gr.] atheistical.

ATHI'RST, Adv. wanting drink, thirsty.

ATHERTON, a town of Warwickshire, with a market on Tuesdays, and four fairs; on April 7, for horses, cows, and sheep; on July 18 for pleasure; on September 19 for horses, cows, and considerable quantities of cheese; and on December 4 for horses and fat horned cattle. It is seated on the river Ankas, and is indifferently large and well built. It is three miles S. of Stratford upon Avon, 18 S. by W. of Coventry, and 104 N. of London. Lon. 16. 5. lat. 52. 40.

ATHLE'TIC, Adj. [from athleta, Lat.] strong, vigorous, active; robust.

ATHWART, Prep. across. Through. "Athwart the terrors." Addis. Cato. Full of vexation; aslide, or wrong.

ATLA'NTIC, S. that part of the sea or ocean which lies between Africa and America.

A'TLAS, S. [Lat.] a collection of maps, alluding to the fable of Atlas's bearing the world on his shoulders. In Anatomy, the first vertebra of the neck. In Architecture, those statues of men, used instead of columns or pilasters to support any member of architecture.

A'TMOSPHERE, S. [from ατμος, Gr. and σφαιρα, Gr.] that thin elastic fluid with which the earth is covered to a particular height; some persons confine the term only to that part of the air which is nearest the earth, receives its vapours and exhalations, and refracts the rays of light. It is not only absolutely fitted for the nourishment and refreshment of animals, the growth of vegetables, the production and propagation of fossils, but contributes to make the earth habitable, paints all the flowery creation with colours, gives us the all cheering rays of light; and not only contributes to shorten the tediousness of winter, but to open to us the volume of creation, which we could not read without its assistance, nor understand without its ornament. See the article AIR.

A'TMOSPHERICAL, Adj. belonging to the atmosphere.

A'TOM, S. [from atomus, Lat.] In Physics, a particle of matter so minute as to be

indivisible. Any thing extremely minute, or small.

ATO'MICAL, Adj. relating to atoms.

A'TOMY, S. See ATOM.

To ATO'NE, V. N. to agree. "He and Aufidius can no more atone, &c." Shakesp. to make satisfaction; to compensate; alluding to expiatory sacrifices. Used actively, to expiate; to make a recompence; followed by the particle with before the subject. "Each atones his guilty love with life." Pope.

A'TONEMENT, S. recompence, reconciliation, agreement. The uniting persons at variance with each other. In Divinity, the reconciling a person to God, by substituting the punishment of another in his stead. "Whose blood was brought in to make an atonement." Lev. xvi. 27. Ransom: "I have found an atonement." Job xxxiii. 24.

A'TOP, Adv. on the highest or uppermost part of a thing.

ATRABILA'RIOUS, Adj. [atrabilaire, Fr.] affected with melancholy.

A'TRA-BI'LIS, S. In Medicine, a state wherein the blood is deprived of its finer and more volatile parts, and rendered gross, black, unctuous, and earthy. Figuratively, the effects of such a habit.

ATRAME'NTEL, Adj. [from atramentum, Lat.] that which blackens.

ATRAME'NTOUS, Adj. black, that which has the quality of ink.

ATRO'CIOUS, Adj. [from atrox] that which is extremely, enormously or flagrantly wicked.

ATRO'CIOUSNESS, S. that which is extremely, obstinately, and enormously criminal.

ATRO'CITY, S. [from atrocitas, Lat.] that which heightens the enormity of the crime.

A'TROPHY, S. [from a, Gr. and τροφη, Gr.] in Physic, an universal consumption, proceeding from the whole habit of the body. See the article CONSUMPTION.

To ATTA'CH, V. A. [attacher, Fr.] In Law, to seize either body or goods. To have an affection, or inclination towards a thing, together with a fear of losing it.

ATTA'CHMENT, S. [attachment, Fr.] disposition of the soul towards an object which is dear to it, and which we are afraid of losing; such as our friends, or duties; and is generally used in a good sense. In Law, the apprehending a person or thing. Foreign attachment, is the seizing the goods or money of a person, which are in the hands of another, to discharge a debt he owes to a third person.

To ATTA'CK, V. A. [attaquer, Fr.] to set upon, invade, or abuse, to treat any one as an enemy, either by actions or words.

ATTA'CK, S. [attaque, Fr.] in war, an attempt.

attempt to conquer. A *falſe attack* is made only to divert the intention of the enemy. Figuratively, any hoſtile attempt.

ATTACKER, S. the perſon who attacks.

To ATTAIN, V. A. [*attindre*, Fr.] to procure, or obtain; to come to, applied to place; to reach, applied to improvements in knowledge. Uſed actively it implies to arrive at, or acquire; applied to ſtate, manner, or circumſtance; with the particle *to*. " *Attains* to the higheſt degree." *Arbuthnot.*

ATTAINABLE, Adj. that may be obtained, or acquired.

ATTAINDER, S. [*attaindre*, Fr.] in Law, is where a perſon is condemned of treaſon by trials or by parliament on a bill brought into the houſe.

ATTAINMENT, S. the act or power of attaining.

To ATTAINT, V. A. [*attaindre*, Fr.] to paſs ſentence for felony, or treaſon, whereby a perſon forfeits all his lands, his blood is corrupted, and his children rendered baſe. To debaſe, corrupt.

ATTAINT, S. a blot or ſtain, alluding to the conſequences of an attainder.

To ATTEMPER, V. A. [*attempero*, Lat.] to render leſs rigorous; to render ſupportable, applied to heat; to leſſen any quality by the mixture of another; to ſuit, adapt, or fit. Uſed with the particle *to*.

To ATTEMPERATE, V. A. [*attempero*, Lat.] to render agreeable or ſuitable to. Uſed with the particle *to*.

To ATTEMPT, V. A. [*attenter*, Fr.] to try, or endeavour.

ATTEMPT, S. an undertaking, a trial to do a thing.

ATTEMPTABLE, Adj. that may be attempted.

ATTEMPTER, S. the perſon who endeavours, tries, or attempts.

To ATTEND, V. A. [*attendre*, Fr.] to fix or apply the mind to an object; to liſten, to hearken, to wait upon; to accompany; to follow; to expect; to be intended for; to ſtay for.

ATTENDANCE, S. [*attendance*, Fr.] the act of attending; ſervice; a ſervant, generally applied to thoſe who wait on nobles and princes; application. " Give *attendance* to reading." 1 Tim. iv. 13.

ATTENDANT, Adj. [*attendant*, Fr.] waiting on another perſon as an inferior.

ATTENDANT, S. [ſee the adjective] one who attends another; a ſervant; that which is inſeparably united. In Law, one who owes ſervice to, or is dependant on another. Thus a widow, holding land of a guardian, is *attendant* on him. *Terms de ley*, 63.

ATTENDER, S. a companion or aſſociate.

ATTENT, Adj. [*attentus*, Lat.] liſtening to; intent.

ATTENTION, S. [Fr.] in Logic, an operation of the mind, and engages it to conſider it in ſuch a manner as to acquire a diſtinct idea thereof, as it were, all other Ideas which offer themſelves to the mind. Applied to the hearing, it ſignifies the ſtretching the drum of the ear in ſuch a manner, as to make it ſuſceptible of the loweſt ſounds.

ATTENTIVELY, Adv. ſo as to conſider or liſten to one particular object.

ATTENUANT, Part. [*attenuans*, Lat.] that which thins or dilutes. Uſed ſubſtantively, for thoſe remedies which rarify the fluids, divide, or thin, the conſiſtence of the humours, by breaking, or deſtroying, the ſtrong coheſion of their original particles; by acting on the viſcoſity of the fluids contained in the ventricle and inteſtines; by exerting their power partly in making the blood thin, or acting on the ſolids by irritating and increaſing their vibrations, whilſt others exert their powers only on the fluids.

ATTENUATION, S. [Fr.] applied to fluids it is the act of rendering them more liquid and thinner; or, according to Chauvin, the dividing and ſeparating the particles which before compoſed a ſolid maſs; in which ſenſe it is by chemiſts uſed for pulveriſing.

To ATTEST, V. A. [*atteſtor*, Lat.] to prove the truth of a thing.

ATTESTATION, S. [*atteſtatio*, Fr.] evidence or proof.

ATTIC, Adj. [from *attica*, Lat.] in Architecture, a kind of ſhorter ſtory over another, wherein no roof is to be ſeen. It alſo implies a brilliant kind of wit, and an elegance of ſtyle peculiar to the people of Attica.

To ATTIRE, V. A. [*attirer*, or *attourner*, Fr. *aierra*, or *aeira*, Teut.] to adorn with clothes; to embelliſh; to ornament.

ATTIRE, S. [*aierd*, Teut.] clothes or dreſs to adorn a perſon. In Hunting, the head or horns of a deer. In Botany, the third part or diviſion of a plant, including its generative parts, and divided into feminiform and floral; the feminiform conſiſts of the chives and apices, and the floral attire of thrums or fulls.

ATTIRER, S. one who attires another.

ATTITUDE, S. [Fr. of *attitudine*, Ital.] the poſture of a figure; the poſture of an actor to expreſs the ſentiments of the poet.

ATTOLLENT, Adj. [*attollens*, Lat.] that raiſes or lifts up.

ATTORNEY, S. [*attournatus*, Low Lat. from *ad* and *tour*, Fr.] a perſon appointed to do ſomething for another. *Attorney at law*, one retained to manage a ſuit or action.

Attorney

R 2

Attorney of the dutchy of Lancaster, is the second officer in that court, on account of his skill placed as an assessor to the chancellor. *Attorney General*, is a great officer, created by letters patent, to exhibit informations and prosecute for the crown.

ATTO'RNEMENT, or **ATTOURNMENT**, S. [*attornement*, Fr.] the agreement of a tenant of life to transfer property to another.

To **ATTRA'CT**, V. A. [of *attractum*] to allure or invite; to draw.

ATTRA'CTICAL, Adj. [from *attract*] having the power of attracting.

ATTRA'CTION, S. [from *attraction*, Fr.] in Mechanics, the art of a moving power, by which a thing is drawn towards it. In the Newtonian system, it is an indefinite principle, implying only a tendency of approaching. It is divided into the attraction of gravity, or the attraction of cohesion; the attraction of gravity is that by which all bodies tend toward the center; from hence proceed almost all the motions and changes in the system; it is by this principle that light bodies ascend, the vapours ascend, and the rain falls, the waves roll, the air presses, and the sea is swelled or decreased by the vicissitude of its flux or reflux. The attraction of cohesion unites the insensible particles together, and causes the roundness we see in drops of water or quicksilver. Also the power of alluring or enticing.

ATTRA'CTIVE, Adj. [*attractif*, Fr.] drawing, inviting, alluring, engaging.

ATTRA'CTIVE, S. that which draws or engages the affections.

ATTRA'CTIVELY, Adv. in a manner that draws or allures.

ATTRA'CTOR, S. that which draws to itself.

ATTRI'BUTABLE, Adj. that may be ascribed or imputed to a thing or person.

To **ATTRI'BUTE**, V. A. [of *attributum*, Lat.] to ascribe; to impute or charge.

A'TTRIBUTE, S. [*attribut*, Fr.] a property of a thing, flowing from its essence. In Divinity, the qualities or perfections of the Deity, divided into communicable or incommunicable; the communicable consist of his moral attributes, and the incommunicable such as belong to him and distinguish him as God. *Attributes*, in Painting and Sculpture, are those symbols which are added to any picture or statue, to express the office or dignity of the chief figure.

ATTRI'TE, Adj. [*attritus*, Lat.] worn off by rubbing two things together.

ATTRI'TION, S. [Fr. of *attritio*, Lat.] the action of rubbing two bodies together, so as to rob off some particles on their surfaces. Likewise the rubbing of two bodies together, which, though it does not wear away any particles of their surfaces, puts the fluids they contain into motion: thus the

sensations of hunger and pain are caused by the attrition of the organs which are formed for that purpose. In Divinity, an imperfect sorrow, or a sorrow and detestation of sin, arising from the idea of its baseness, and the fear of hell torments; which divines reckon insufficient to justify or excuse a sinner, unless it includes in it the love of God as the source of all justice.

To **ATTU'NE**, V. A. to put into tune; to make the voice or any instrument accord together. Used with the particle *to*.

To **AVAI'L**, V. N. [*avaler*, Ital. *valeo*, Fr.] used with the particle *of*, to turn to one's own use, benefit, profit, or advantage. Without the particle, to promote, procure, or succeed. "What means might best his safe return avail." *Pope*. It may be doubted whether this is not an improper use of the word. Used neuterly, i. e. without a substantive after it, it implies to signify, to be of use or advantage. "It avails nothing to have been encouraged." *Pope*.

AVAI'L, S. Profit, or advantage.

AVA'ILABLE, Adj. suitable or efficacious; powerful or proper.

AVA'NT-GUARD, S. [*avant-guarde*, Fr.] the first division of an army in battle array.

A'VARICE, S. [Fr. from *avaritia*, Lat.] an immoderate desire after riches, attended with excessive precaution against the instability of fortune, making a person deprive himself of the comforts of life, for fear of diminishing his riches.

AVARI'CIOUS, Adj. partaking of the nature of avarice.

AVA'ST, Adv. hold, stop, be quiet.

AVAU'NT, Adv. [*avant*, Fr.] a word implying abhorrence; begone! out of my sight! away!

AU'BURN, Adj. [*aubour*, Fr. black] brownish, sandy; nut-brown.

AU'CTION, S. [Fr. of *auctio*, Lat.] a kind of sale, wherein goods are sold to the highest bidder. Also the goods to be disposed of at such a sale.

AUDA'CIOUS, Adj. [*audace*, Fr.] bold, daringly impudent.

AUDA'CIOUSLY, Adv. in a daring, impudent manner.

AUDA'CITY, S. [of *audax*, Lat.] boldness; impudence.

AU'DIBLE, Adj. [from *audibilis*, Lat.] that is the object of hearing; that may be heard.

AU'DIBLENESS, S. that which renders a thing the object of hearing.

AU'DIENCE, S. [of *audio*, Lat.] attention given to a person that is speaking. In law, the presence of a judge, at a court to hear causes. The admission of ambassadors or public ministers to a king. In Canon Law a court belonging to the archbishop of Canterbury, so called from his bearing con-

ſes there perſonally. Perſons aſſembled to bear a public ſpeaker, or ſpeakers.

AUDIT, S. [from *audit*, Lat.] the examining the accounts of a perſon, by perſons publickly appointed for that purpoſe.

To AUDIT, V. A. [from *audio*, Lat.] to examine and ſettle an account.

AUDITOR, S. [*auditor*, Lat.] one who hears, one who examines either public or private accounts.

AUDITORY, Adj. [*auditorius*, Lat.] that which is conducive to hearing. In Anatomy, the *auditory* nerves are a pair of nerves ariſing from the medulla oblongata, and diſtributed the one to the ear, and the other to the eye, &c. How doth wiſdom appear in every part of our frame! It is owing to this contrivance, that when animals hear any unconth ſound they erect their ears, open their eyes, to be on the watch, are ready with their mouths to call out, and generally ſhriek. It is owing to this conſtruction that the voice correſponds with the hearing, and that people, who are otherwiſe dull of hearing, can perceive ſounds plainly, when communicated by the mouth; as any one may try by putting's watch in his mouth, or holding it between his teeth.

AUDITORY, S. [*auditorium*, Lat.] a place where perſons aſſemble to hear; a collection of perſons aſſembled to hear. The place in antient churches where the hearers uſed to ſtand during ſermon, which they durſt not leave under pain of excommunication. Called at preſent the *Nave*.

AUDITRESS, S. [from *audio*, Lat.] a female who attends public lectures.

To AVEL, V. A. [*avello*, Lat.] to tear off by force. "Theſe parts *avelled*." *Brown*.

AVE MARY, [from *ave Maria*, hail Mary,] a prayer uſed by the Romiſh church, beginning with thoſe words. Likewiſe the ſmall beads in the chaplet or roſary, ſo called from their ſaying *ave*, when counting them, to diſtinguiſh them from the greater, at which they ſay the *Pater noſter*, or Lord's prayer.

AVENA, S. [Lat.] In Botany, oats. This is a very profitable grain, very much liked by horſes, and, on account of its opening nature, very wholeſome food, but ſhould not be given them after houſing, till they have ſweat in the mow. Its meal makes tolerable bread, uſed in the North. In the South it is eſteemed in pottage, and in other places they make ale with the grain. See *Oats*.

To AVENGE, V. A. [from *a* and *venger*, Fr.] to puniſh in proportion to the crime committed.

AVENGEMENT, S. [from *avenge*] the act of puniſhing for crimes. Sometimes, but improperly, uſed for revenge.

AVENGER, S. one who puniſhes for crimes.

AVENUE, S. [*avenir*, Fr.] a paſſage by which any place may be approached. In gardening, walks of trees leading to a houſe, formerly planted in ſtraight lines the whole breadth of the houſe, or twelve or fourteen feet wider. Miller is very much againſt this practice, and propoſes making them ſerpentine, or planting trees in clumps, or platoons, at about 300 feet diſtance from each other, as a very great improvement. In Perſpective, it is a paſſage, which is narrower at the end then at the beginning. In Fortification, the opening, or communications, between a fort and baſtion.

To AVER, V. A. [*avouer*, Fr.] to affirm, declare, or aſſert a thing to be true.

AVERAGE, S. [*overegium*, Lat.] in Law, a due or ſervice which a tenant owed his lord, by his beaſt or carriage. In ſea commerce, the misfortune which happens to a ſhip or cargo. The ſimple average are the extraordinary expences for the ſhip or merchandize alone, which are to be borne by the thing that ſuffered the damage. The larger or common average are the damages ſuſtained for the common good of the merchandize or veſſels. Such are the things given to pirates for the ranſom of the ſhip or cargo, or the commodities flung overboard to lighten a ſhip in a ſtorm, &c. all which are to be borne proportionably by the loaders or freighters: the ſmall averages are thoſe incurred by entering into, or coming out of harbour, one third of which muſt be borne by the ſhip, and two-thirds by the cargo. An allowance given the maſter for his care of the goods above the freight. Alſo a medium, or mean proportion fixed between two different numbers.

AVERMENT, in Law, the eſtabliſhment of a thing by evidence.

AVERRUNCATION, S. [from *averrunco*] the act of pulling a thing up by the roots; extirpation.

AVERSATION, S. [of *averſus*, Lat.] a term alluding to the motion of a perſon who deteſts any thing, which is that of turning away from it; uſed with the particle *from*, it implies abhorrence, extreme diſlike or detestation: with the particle *to*, or *towards*, a natural antipathy, or averſion.

AVERSE, Adj. [*averſus*, Lat.] hoſtile, or angry with, alluding to the turning away from thoſe who have diſpleaſed us. Unwilling, abhorring, uſed properly with the particle *from*, but improperly, though commonly, with the particle *to*.

AVERSELY, Adv. unwillingly. Backwards, oppoſed to forwards. "It is emitted *averſely* or backwards by both ſexes." *Brown's Vulg. Errors*.

AVERSION, S. [from *averſo*, Lat.] diſlike ariſing from the diſagreeableneſs of an objects,

object, in allusion to a person's turning away from that which raises any disagreeable idea; the curse of dislike. Used by former writers with the particle *from*; but by later with the particle *to*, and sometimes *towards*. "They had an inward *aversion from* it." *Clarend.* "His *aversion towards* the house of York." Sometimes with the particle *for*. "A state *for* which they have so great an *aversion*." *Addison.*

To AVE'RT, V. A. [*averto*, Lat.] to turn aside, or keep off, applied to calamities.

AUF, S. a person void of common sense. A fool.

AU'GER, S. [*nauger*, Sax.] in mechanics, an instrument used to bore holes with; consisting of a handle and bit.

AU'GHT, *pron.* [from *auht* or *euht*, Sax.] any thing; as *far as*.

To AU'GMENT, V. A. [*augmentet*, Fr.] to encrease the value or dimension of a thing.

AU'GMENT, S. [Fr.] Increase, applied to dimension. In Grammar, used by the Greek grammarians, for the addition of letters, or the increase of quantity in verbs, and is either syllabic or temporal; syllabic when it increases the number of syllables, and temporal when it increases the time of pronunciation, or changes a short vowel for a long one.

AUGMENTA'TION, S. [Fr.] the action of adding or joining. The state of being increased. In Heraldry, additions made to an escutcheon. As the arms of Ulster, which are worn by all baronets in England. Applied to an act made in the year 1714, for encreasing the value of livings not exceeding 50l. per annum; now as these amount to 5597, and the number of augmentations to 1868, if 53 augmentations should be made annually by Q. Ann's bounty, 339 years would elapse before all the livings proposed to be augmented would exceed 50 l. per ann. and should the bounty be increased one half by benefactions, 216 years would elapse before the least would be worth 50l. per annum.

AU'GRE, S. See AUGER.

AU'GUR, S. [Lat. from *avium gestu*, the motions of birds] one who pretended to foretell the success of any undertaking by the flight of birds.

To AU'GUR, V. N: to foretell; guess; presage. Seldom used.

AUGURA'TION, S. [from *augur*] the determining future events, in the manner of augurs.

To AU'GURIZE, V. N. to foretell future events, by the flight of birds, &c. in the manner of augurs.

AU'GUROUS, Adj. presaging; foretelling.

AU'GURY, S. [*auguria*, Lat.] the act of predicting future events, by the flight or calling of birds. Figuratively, the rules observed by augurs; an omen, or prediction.

AUGU'ST, Adj. [*augustus*, Lat.] that which deserves or may claim reverence.

AUGU'ST, S. [from *Augustus*] the eighth month of the year, called by the Romans *Sextilis*, but named *August* from Augustus Cæsar. It was represented by the ancients under the figure of a young man crowned with a garland of wheat, a sickle of fruit on one of his arms, a scale in his hand, and bearing a victim.

AUGU'STAN, Adj. [from *Augusta*, Lat.] the Augustan confession; the articles of faith drawn up between Melancthon and Luther, in 1530, and presented by the latter to the emperor Charles V. at the diet held in Augsbourg.

AUGU'STNESS, S. that which renders a person an object of reverence, and awe.

A'VIARY, S. [from *avis*, Lat.] a place inclosed for keeping birds; figuratively, the collection of birds confined in such a place.

AUKLAND BISHOPS, a town in the bishoprick of Durham, with a market on Thursdays, and three fairs on Holy Thursday, June 21, and on the Thursday before Old Michaelmas day, for cattle and sheep. It is pleasantly seated on the side of a hill, and is noted for its castle, beautifully repaired about 100 years ago, for its chapel, whose architecture is very curious, and for its bridge. It is eight miles S. by W. of Durham, and 254 N. N. W. of London. Lon. 16. 33. lat. 54. 44.

AU'KWARD, Adv. See AWKWARD.

AULCESTER, a town of Warwickshire, with a market on Tuesdays, and three fairs on Tuesday before April 5, May 18, and October 17, for horses and sheep. It was formerly more considerable than it is at present, and is 14 miles W. S. W. of Warwick, 7 miles W. of Stratford upon Avon, and 81 N. W. of London. Lon. 15. 43. lat. 52. 13.

AU'LD, Adj. [*ald*, Sax] old. Now obsolete among the English, but still in use among the Scotch.

AU'LIC, Adj. [*aulicus*, Lat. of *aula*, a court] belonging to the court." In History, applied to the highest court of the empire of Germany.

AU'LNE, S. [Fr.] the French ell, consisting of six quarters English.

AU'NT, S. [from *tante*, Fr.] a female who is a sister to a person's father or mother.

To A'VOCATE, V. A. [from *avocatum*, Lat.] to call a person from what he is engaged in; generally implying the being called away from something important to something less so.

AVOCA'TION, S. [from *avocatio*, Lat.] the diverting a person's attention. That which interrupts a person in prosecuting a peculiar employment.

To AVOI'D, V. A. [from *vuider*, Fr.] to forbear, shun, quit, or leave, to escape; to free from. " Prevent and *avoid* putrefaction." *Bac.* Used anciently, with the particles *out of*, to escape by quieting, or to leave empty. " David *avoided out of* his presence." 2 Sam. xvii. 11.

AVOI'DABLE, Adj. the possibility of escaping the effects of a thing; that which may be escaped, or shunned.

AVOI'DANCE, S. the act avoiding the effects of any cause. The act of emptying, or carrying off.

AVOI'DER, S. one who shuns, escapes, or carries away.

AVOIRDUPOI'S, S. [from *avoir*, to have, and *du poids*, Fr. weight; a kind of weight, borrowed from the Romans, a pound of which contains 16 oz. bearing the same proportion to a lb. troy, as 17 to 16.

AVOLA'TION, S. [from *avola*, Lat. to fly away] the flying away; flight, or escape. Used only by scientific authors.

To AVOU'CH, V. A. [*avouer*, Fr.] to prove by vouchers; to justify, or vindicate. *Vouch* is in use, at present, in its stead.

AVOU'CHABLE, Adj. what may be proved by evidence or vouchers.

AVOU'CHER, S. he that proves by proper vouchers, or evidence.

To AVO'W, V. A. [from *avouer*, Fr.] to profess openly, to assert.

AVO'WARDE, Adj. that which may be publickly owned or asserted.

AVO'WAL, S. a public confession, or assertion.

AVO'WEDLY, Adv. professedly; publickly, openly.

AVOWE'E, S. [*avoué*, Fr.] the person to whom the right of advowson belongs.

AVO'WER, S. one who openly professes, asserts, or declares.

AURE'LIA, S. [from *aurum*, gold] in Natural History, the second change of a caterpillar towards a moth or fly. Under this state it has all the members or parts which appear in the future butterfly, according to Swammerdam's curious description in his book of nature; than which a more minute or more elegant, has not appeared.

AURE'LIAN, S. [from *aurelia*] one who applies himself to study the various changes of insects.

AU'RICLE, S. [*auricula*, Lat.] in Anatomy, that part the ear which is prominent from the head. Likewise two appendages, or caps, to the ventricles of the heart, so called from their resembling those of the ear.

AURI'CULAR, Adj. [from *auricula*, Lat. the ear] belonging to the ear. Secret or private. *Auricular* confession, is the private confession a person makes of his sins, to a priest.

AURI'CULARLY, Adv. in a secret manner.

AURI'FEROUS, Adj [*aurifer*, Lat.] that which produces gold.

AURO'RA, S. [Lat.] in geography, that faint dawn which appears in the E. when the sun is within 18 deg. of the horizon. In mythology, the goddess who presides over day break, the daughter of Hyperion and Thea.

AU'RUM FU'LMINANS, in chemistry, a dissolution of gold in *aqua regia*, afterwards precipitated with oil of Tartar, which, on the least addition of heat, goes off like the explosion of a pistol. *Aurum potabile*, is a dissolution of gold which makes it drinkable, formerly in great request among the faculty, but at present grown into disuse.

AUSCULTA'TION, S. [from *ausculto*, Lat.] the art of listening, or hearkening.

AU'SPICE, S. [*auspicium*, Lat.] the art of divination. A prosperous event, or the favour of a luckly person.

AUSPI'CIOUS, Adj. favourable, fortunate, kind, propitious.

AUSPI'CIAL, Adj. relating to the auspices.

AUSPI'CIOUSLY, Adv. favourably, fortunately.

AU'STERE, Adj. [*austerus*, Lat.] rigid, rough, four, astringent.

AUSTERE'LY, Adv. in a rigid, mortified manner.

AUSTE'RITY, S. [from *austere*] rigid severity and mortification, moroseness: severity or harshness of discipline.

AU'STRAL, Adj. [*australis*, Lat.] towards the South.

AUTHE'NTIC, or AUTHE'NTICAL, Adj. [*authenticus*, Lat.] a thing of established authority. That which is attended with proofs, and attested by persons of credit.

AUTHE'NTICALLY, Adv. so as to procure credit.

AUTHE'NTICALNESS, S. [from *authentical* and *ness*, or *ness*, Sax. implying an abstract quality] that quality which recommends a thing to a person's credit.

To AUTHE'NTICATE, V. A. [*authentiquer*, Fr.] to establish a thing by proofs of its genuineness.

AUTHENTI'CITY, S. the genuineness of a thing.

AUTHE'NTICLY, Adv. genuinely.

A'UTHOR, S. [*auteur*, Fr. *auctor*, Lat.] one who creates or produces any thing; the original inventor or discoverer of any thing; one who writes upon any subject.

AUTHO'RITATIVE, Adj. that which has an influence over another; that which commands or obliges.

AUTHO'RITATIVELY, Adv. so as to bespeak proper authority or licence.

AUTHO'RITATIVENESS, S. that quality which shews a person to have authority for the doing any thing.

AU-

AUTHO'RITY, S. [*autorité*, Fr.] that which leaves a person the liberty of choice, arising from superiority; supposes merit in the person invested with it; is communicated by the laws; is relative to right; includes the secondary idea of respect; and is applied to God with respect to his creatures, and to parents with respect to their children.

To AU'THORIZE, V. A. [*autoriser*, Fr.] to give a person licence; to encourage; to justify; to give credit.

AUTO'CRASY, S. [from *autos*, Gr. and *kratos*, Gr.] absolute and independent power.

AUTO DA FE'E, S. [Span. an act of faith] a solemn day assigned by the Inquisition for the punishment of heretics.

AUTOGRA'PHICAL, Adj. [of *autos*, Gr. and *grapho*, Gr.] written by a person's own hand.

AUTO'GRAPHY, S. a person's own hand-writing; an original.

AUTOMA'TICAL, Adj. [from *automaton*] that which is endued with a power to move itself.

AUTO'MATON, S. [from *autos*, Gr. and *mao*, Gr.] in Mechanics, a machine or engine which has the principle of motion in itself. The person who plays on a flute; the duck which eats, drinks, and digests; the image which plays on the tambour and pipe, constructed by M. Vaucanson, deserve to be mentioned as great curiosities.

AUTO'MATOUS, Adj. having the power of motion in itself.

A'UTOPSY, S. [from *autos*, Gr. and *optomai*] the seeing a thing with one's own eyes. Applied by the antients to the communications which the soul had with the gods in the Eleusinian mysteries, which are learnedly handled by Dr. Warburton, the present bishop of Gloucester, in his Divine Legation of Moses.

AUTO'PTICAL, Adj. seen by a person's own eyes.

AUTO'PTICALLY, Adv. so as a person may be an eye-witness.

AUTUMN, S. [*autumnus*, Lat.] in Astronomy, the third season of the year, commencing at the equinox and ending at the winter solstice; including August, September, and October.

AUTU'MNAL, Adj. [*autumnal*, Fr.] belonging to autumn; produced in autumn. In Astronomy, the *autumnal* point is that point of the equinoctial line, from whence the sun begins to descend towards the south. The *autumnal signs* are Libra, Scorpio, and Sagittarius.

AVU'LSION, S. [*avulsio*, Lat.] the act of pulling asunder two things already united.

AUXE'SIS, S. [Lat. from *auxo*, Lat.] in Rhetoric, a kind of amplification, whereby the sense is increased.

AUXI'LIAR, or AUXI'LIARY, S. [*auxiliare*, Fr. from *auxiliaris*, Lat.] one who assists another. Sometimes applied to things.

AUXI'LIAR, or AUXI'LIARY, Adj. [*auxiliaris*, Lat.] affording help or assistance. In Grammar, applied to verbs prefixed to others, and help to conjugate certain tenses. In French they make use of *avoir* and *être*; in Spanish *soy*; in Italian *ho* and *sono*; and in English *be* and *have*; the former of which is borrowed from the Sax. *am*, and *be*, Goth.

AUXILIA'TION, S. [from *auxiliatio*, Lat.] the act of affording help.

To AWAI'T, V. N. to expect a thing future; to be designed for.

To AWA'KE, V. A. [from *awaecian*, or *weccian*, Sax.] to raise from sleep; to reduce a thing in a dormant state into action; to cease to sleep.

AWA'KE, Part. one that is risen from sleep.

To AWA'KEN, V. A. See AWAKE.

To AWA'RD, V. A. [from *a* and *ward*, Sax.] to pass sentence or judgment as an arbitrator; to give one's opinion.

AWA'RD, S. the opinion of a person chosen to determine a difference between contending parties.

AWA'RE, Adj. cautious, or upon one's guard; watchful.

To AWA'RE, V. N. [see the adjective] to be cautious; to be on one's guard.

AWA'Y, Adj. [*aweg*, Sax. *wech*, Belg.] absent, or out of sight. At the beginning of a sentence, it has the force of a verb in the imperative mood, and signifies leave this place. "*Away*, old man." *Shak.* To remove, abandon, or quit. "*Away with your sheep-hooks.*" *Dryd.*

AWE, S. [from *ew*, Arm. *aga*, Brit.] respect mixed with terror, including the idea of superiority.

To A'WE, V. A. [from the noun] to influence by authority, splendor, dignity, or age.

AW'FUL, Adj. that which causes respect or awe.

A'WFULLY, Adv. in such a manner as to command respect and awe.

A'WFULNESS, S. that quality which strikes respect and awe.

AWHI'LE, Adv. [from *a* and *while*, as Johnson observes, improperly called an adverb, being nothing else but the word *while*, and its article *a*] space or interval of time; sometime.

AW'KWARD, Adj. [from *award*, Sax.] perverse; clumsy; unhandy; clownish; opposed to genteel or elegant.

A'WKWARDLY, Adv. clumsily.

A'WK.

A'WKWARDNESS, S. that quality which denotes a person to be clownish, clumsy, unexperienced, and unhandy

AW'L, S. [æl, ale, Sax.] a sharp pointed instrument used by shoemakers.

AW'NING, S. [from aulne, Fr. an ell] a sail or tarpaulin, over any part of the ship, &c.

AWO'KE, the preter of awake.

AWRY', Adv. out of a straight line; on one side; uneven; erroneously.

A'X, or A'XE, S. [from acse, Sax. axt, Dan.] an instrument to hew wood.

AXBRIDGE, a town in Somersetshire, with a market on Thursdays, and two fairs, on March 25, and June 11, for cattle, sheep, cheese, and toys. It is seated under Mendip hills, which are rich in lead mines, and proper for feeding cattle. It is a mayor town, consisting of one principal street, which is long but narrow. It is 10 miles W. W. of Wells, and 130 W. of London. Ldn. 14 35. lat. 51. 30.

AXI'LLA, S. [Lat. a diminutive of axis] the hollow under the arm, called also the arm-pit.

AXI'LLARY, Adj. [see AXILLA] belonging to the cavity under the arm.

AXMINSTER, a town of Devonshire, with a market on Saturdays, and three fairs, on April 25, Wednesday after June 24, and the first Wednesday after September 29, all for cattle. It is seated on the river Ax, near the edge of the county, in the great road from London to Exeter, and was a place of some note in the time of the Saxons. This town has a portreve; but has no constable, nor any other officer. It has one church, and about 200 houses; but the streets, tho' paved, are somewhat narrow. Here is a small manufactory of broad and narrow cloths; also some carpets are made here in the Turky manner. It is 25 miles E. by N. of Exeter, 43 W. by S. of Salisbury, and 146 on the same point from London. Lon. 14. 20. lat. 50. 40.

A'XIOM, S. [Gr. αξιωμα] a proposition whose truth is so clear, that it cannot admit of proof by any thing more clear, plain, or evident. A proposition wherein the agreement or disagreement of its ideas are immediately perceived and self-evident.

A'XIS, S. [Lat.] a line drawn through the center of a body, about which it turns. Axis in peritrochio, is one of the five mechanical powers used to raise weights.

A'XLE, or A'XLE-TREE, S. [from acse, Sax. and arow, Sax.] a piece of wood, &c. passing through the center of a wheel, on which it turns.

A'Y, Adv. [from ja, Sax. or gab, Goth.] used to affirm the truth of a thing.

A'YE, Adv. [ay; and. æa, Sax.] always; time without end; for ever; to all eternity.

N°. IV.

ATEL, S. [æyeul] in Law, that which a person succeeds to in right of his grandfather; or a writ which lies where a grandfather was seised of a demesne on the day of his death, but a stranger enters the same day and dispossesses the heir.

A'ZIMUTH, S. [Arab.] in Astronomy, an arch of the horizon, intercepted between the meridian of a place and any given vertical line, in which the sun or a star is found. Magnetical azimuth, is an arch of the horizon, intercepted between the sun's azimuth circle and the magnetical meridian. Azimuth compass, is an instrument used at sea, to find the sun's magnetical azimuth.

AZU'RE, S. [azur, Fr. azurro, Ital. azul, Span. lazur, Arab. from lazuli, blue stone] the blue colour of the sky. In Heraldry, the name given to the blue colour in an escutcheon.

A'ZURE, Adj. that which is of a sky-blue.

A'ZYGOS, S. in Anatomy, a vein which empties itself into the cava, and is situated on the right side of the thorax.

AZYMITES, S. [from azymos] those who communicate with unleavened bread, or bread without ferment, as in the Romish church; but the Greeks make use of fermented.

AZY'MUS, S. [from a, Gr. and ζυμη] bread without ferment or leaven.

B.

B, is the second letter of the English alphabet, and the first consonant; it is the first letter in the ancient Irish, and Abyssinian; it is the ninth in the Ethiopic, and the fixteenth in the Armenian. It is called a labial, from the method of pronouncing it, which is by pressing the whole length of the lips together, and forcing them open again by a strong breath. It is used as an abbreviature for Bachelor, B. A. for Bachelor of Arts, or B. Bishop, as B. Sherlock, Bishop Sherlock, the late exemplary and pious Bishop of London.

To BA'A, V. N. to bleat, or make a noise like a sheep.

To BA'BBLE, V. N. [babble, Fr.] to prate like a child; to reveal secrets.

BA'BBLE, S. [babil, Fr. babel, or babel, Belg.] foolish prating.

BA'BBLER, S. one who talks much without proper ideas of the words he makes use of.

BA'BE, S. [baban, Brit.] a young child, an infant.

BA'BERY, S. toys, or trinkets, to please or divert infants.

BA'BISH, Adj. [from babe and ish of ish, Sax. which, when added to a substantive, signifies likeness] resembling the choice of a very young child. Childish.

S   BABOON,

BABO'ON, S. [*baboin*, Fr.] In natural hiſtory, one of the ſpecies of monkeys.

BA'BY, S. a young child. Likewiſe, when uſ'd with the word *jointed*, a painted image, reſembling a human form, which children divert themſelves with. A doll.

BABYLON, once a famous city in Aſia, and perhaps at that time the largeſt in the world. It is now ſo ruined that the place where 'it ſtood cannot be diſcovered with any certainty. However, we are ſure that it was ſeated on the river Euphrates; and as ſome think over againſt Bagdad, on the Tygris. This laſt place is, by many travellers, falſely called Babylon. This was alſo the name of a city in Egypt, ſuppoſed to ſtand near the place where Cairo ſtands now. What authors tell us concerning the bigneſs of Old Babylon is almoſt incredible; for they affirm it was 366 ſtadia in circumference, which is about 50 of our ſtatute mil'; however, it was not full of houſes; for within the walls, there were not only gardens and orchards, but cultivated fields. It was divided by the Euphrates into two equal parts, that communicated by a ſtone brid‚e 625 feet in length, and 30 broad. The tower of Babel within this city was built in a ſquare form, and was 460 cubits high; and the circumference at the bottom was 4 or 5000. The hanging gardens at Babylon, were ſuch a prodigious work that they paſſed for one of the ſeven wonders of the world. There were four of them that contained each four acres of land, and they were ſupported by vaſt columns at the top of a palace that was 2,500 paces in circumference, and they were diſpoſed in the form of an amphitheatre. The walls of Babylon were alſo ſo aſtoniſhing, that theſe alſo paſſed for one of the ſeven wonders; and they were built of bricks, and inſtead of mortar they made uſe of bitumen; the circumference was 50 miles as above, and they were 200 feet high, and 50 thick, according to ſome. There was alſo a temple conſecrated to Belus, whoſe magnificence correſponded with the grandeur of the city, which was the capital of the Aſſyrian empire, and afterwards of the kingdom of Babylon, founded by Nabonaſſer.

BACCHANA'LIAN, S. a perſon who attended the feaſt of Bacchus. A riotous drunken perſon.

BACCHANALS, S. See BACCHANALIA.

BA'CCHUS, [from *Barchus*] in ancient Poetry, a foot conſiſting of three ſyllables, the firſt ſhort, and the two laſt long; and derives its name from being uſed in the hymns compoſed in honour of Bacchus.

BACCIFEROUS, Adj. [*baccifer*, Lat. from *bacca*, a berry, and *fero*, to bear] in Botany, ſuch vegetables as bear berries; ſuch as the briony, lilly of the valley, &c.

BACCI'VOROUS, Adj. [from *bacca*, Lat. and *voro*, Lat.] feeding on berries.

BA'CHELOR, S. [*baccalaureus*, Lat.] a man who has never been married; oppoſed both to a huſband, and widower. One who takes the firſt degree in any profeſſion.

BA'CHELORSHIP, S. the ſtate of an unmarried man. The ſtate, dignity, or office of a bachelor, at an univerſity.

BACK, S. [*bac*, *bæc*, Sax.] in Anatomy, the hind part of the human ſtructure, extending from the neck to the thighs; that part oppoſite to the palms of the hands. The hind part, or that which is not in ſight. Applied to any edge tool, the thickeſt part, oppoſed to the edge. A large ſquare trough, uſed by brewers to hold liquor in. Figuratively, one who will ſecond another in an attempt. To *turn one's back* on an enemy, is to run away from him, and implies cowardice, being oppoſed to the phraſe to *face* an enemy. To *turn one's back on a friend*, or *petitioner*, implies diſdain, or contempt.

BA'CK, Adv. applied to motion, from whence a perſon came. Applied to action, and uſed with the verb *go*, to retreat, oppoſed to progreſſion, or advance. Applied to time, that which is paſt. After *long*, applied to the increaſe of plants, to ſtop or hinder the growth. Again; a ſecond time.

To BACK, V. A. to mount, or break a horſe for the ſaddle; to make him go backwards by pulling the reins. To ſecond, ſupport, or abet.

To BA'CKBITE, V. A. to ſpeak againſt, or defame a perſon in his abſence.

BA'CKBITER, S. one who cenſures, or vilifies a perſon in his abſence.

BA'CK-DOOR, S. a paſſage out of a houſe behind; a private paſſage.

BA'CKED, Part. having a back. Forced to go backwards; ſupported.

BACK-GA'MMON, S. [from *bach*, Brit. and *gammon*, Brit.] a game played with dice and men on a board, or table.

BACK-PIECE, S. a piece of armour made to cover the back.

BA'CKSIDE, S. the back, or hinder part of any thing. Applied to the poſteriors of a human creature; a yard, or ground behind a houſe.

To BA'CKSLIDE, V. N. to return to idolatry. To apoſtatize; to quit the true religion.

BA'CKSLIDER, S. one who quits, or departs from the true religion. An apoſtate.

BA'CKSTAFF, S. [from *back* and *ſtaff*, ſo called from the obſerver's turning his back towards the ſun in taking an obſervation.] in Navigation, an inſtrument for taking the ſun's altitude at ſea.

BA'CK-STAIRS, S. the back private ſtairs of a houſe.

BA'CK-STAYS, S. in ſhip-building, the ropes belonging to the main and fore-maſts.

BA'CK.

BACK-SWORD, S. a fword with one fharp edge. Ufed figuratively, for a cudgel. " He underftands backfword."

BA'CKWARD, or BA'CKWARDS, Adv. [from back, Sax. and weard, Sax.] the going from a perfon with the face towards him, the legs being moved toward the hind part. Towards the back, or behind. Upon the back. Ufed in oppofition to forwards, from a perfon, and towards him. Applied to the fuccefs of an undertaking, joined with the word go; it implies, not to profper or advance; to want fuccefs. Applied to time; that which is paft.

BA'CKWARD, Adv. unwilling; reluctant; flow.

BA'CKWARDLY, Adv. [from backward, and ly of lice, Sax. implying manner] applied to the motion whereby a perfon goes from another, with his face towards him. In a perverfe, unwilling manner. Reluctantly.

BA'CKWARDNESS, S. unwillingnefs, flownefs, reluctancy.

BA'CON, S. [from Baccun, Brit.] the flefh of a hog, falted and dried. To fave one's bacon, is a phrafe for preferving one's felf from mifchief, borrowed from the care of houfewifes in the country, to preferve their bacon, their only food, from the hands of plunderers.

BACON, (FRANCIS) vifcount St. Alban's, and high chancellor of England, in the reign of king James I. the glory and ornament of his age and nation, was the fon of fir Nicholas Bacon, lord keeper of the great feal, was born at York-houfe in the Strand, on the 22d of January, 1561. In his tender years his abilities were fo remarkably confpicuous, that queen Elizabeth, whofe peculiar felicity it was to make a right judgment of merit, was fo charmed with his folidity, and the gravity of his behaviour, that fhe would often call him her young lord keeper: He was educated at Trinity-college, Cambridge, and made fuch incredible progrefs in his ftudies, that before he was fixteen, he had not only run through the whole circle of the liberal arts as they were then taught, but began to perceive thofe imperfections in the reigning philofophy, which he afterwards fo effectually expofed, and thereby not only overturned that tyranny which prevented the progrefs of true knowledge, but laid the foundation of that free and ufeful philofophy, which has fince opened a way to fo many great and glorious difcoveries. On his leaving the univerfity, his father fent him to France, where, before he was nineteen years of age, he wrote a general view of the ftate of Europe; but fir Nicholas dying, he was obliged fuddenly to return to England, when he applied himfelf to the ftudy of the common law, at

Gray's-inn, and, in 1588, was made one of the queen's counfel; but notwithftanding her majefty's early prepoffeffion in his favour he met with many obftacles to his preferment during her reign; for his enemies reprefented him as a man, who, by applying too much of his time in purfuit of other branches of knowledge, could not but neglect that of his profeffion; but his Maxims of Law and Hiftory of the Alienation Office, both of which works were written in this reign, though they were not publifhed till after his deceafe, fufficiently fhew the injuftice of thefe reprefentations; he alfo diftinguifhed himfelf during the latter part of the queen's reign, in the houfe of commons, where he fpoke often, and yet with fuch wifdom and eloquence, that his fentiments were generally approved by that auguft affembly. But notwithftanding the little regard paid by the court to his merit, he ferved the queen, as long as fhe lived, with zeal and fidelity, and after her deceafe, compofed a memorial on the happinefs of her reign, which did equal honour to her adminiftration, and the capacity of its author. Upon the acceffion of king James, he was foon raifed to confiderable honours; for on the 23d of July, 1607, he was introduced to the king at Whitehall, and received the honour of knighthood. In 1611, he was conftituted judge of the marfhal's court; in 1613, he was made attorney-general; in 1617, he was chofen lord keeper; and, in 1618, lord high chancellor of England; the fame year he was created baron of Verulam in the county of Hertford; and in January, 1621, was advanced to the dignity of vifcount St. Alban's; but he was foon after furprifed by a dreadful reverfe of fortune; for that very year complaints being made to the houfe of commons of his lordfhip's having received feveral bribes, thofe complaints were fent up to the houfe of lords, and new ones being daily made of a like nature, things foon grew too high to be got over. The king was extremely affected, and even fhed tears at the firft news of this affair; and the lord chancellor had all the friendfhip and protection afforded him that was either in the power of the marquis of Buckingham, or even in the king his mafter, who actually in hopes of foftening things a little, procured a recefs of parliament; but this method having a quite contrary effect, his lordfhip, inftead of entering into a long and formal defence, threw himfelf upon the mercy of the houfe, by an humble fubmiffion, which he drew up in writing, and prevailed upon the prince of Wales, afterwards king Charles I. to prefent to the houfe; and this confeffion and fubmiffion he afterwards explained and confirmed; on which he was fentenced to pay forty thoufand pounds, to be imprifoned

In the Tower during the king's pleasure, to be for ever incapable of any office or employment in the state, and never to sit in parliament, or come within the verge of the court. However, after a short confinement in the Tower, he was discharged, and afterwards received a full pardon from the king; yet the fault which thus tarnished the glory of this great man, is said to have principally proceeded from his indulgence to his servants, who made a corrupt use of it: however his failings hurt only his contemporaries, and were expiated by his sufferings; but his other virtues, his knowledge, and, above all, his zeal for mankind, will be felt while there are men, and while they have gratitude; the name of sir Francis Bacon, or lord Verulam, can never be mentioned but with admiration!

The honourable Mr. Walpole, speaking of this great man, calls him the Prophet of Arts, which Newton was afterwards to reveal; and adds, that his genius and his works will be universally admired as long as science exists.—" As long as ingratitude and adulation are despicable, so long shall we lament the depravity of this great man's heart.—Alas! that he who could command immortal fame, should have stooped to the little ambition of power."

His works, which are the glory of our nation, are collected together, and printed in four volumes folio; of these his Novum Organum is esteemed the capital. In short, the lord Verulam died at the earl of Arundel's house, at Highgate, on the 9th of April, 1626, and was privately buried in the chapel of St. Mary's church, within the precincts of Old Verulam, in the chancel of which church, sir Thomas Meautys, once his secretary, and afterwards clerk of the council, caused a neat monument of white marble to be erected, with his lordship's effigies sitting in a contemplative posture, under which is the following inscription:

FRANCISCUS BACON,
Baro de Verulam, Sancti Albani vicecomes,
Seu notioribus titulis,
Scientiarum Lumen, Facundiæ Lex,
Sic sedebat.
Qui postquam omnia naturalis sapientiæ,
Et civilis arcana evolvisset,
Naturæ decretum explevit,
Composita solvantur;
Anno Domini, M.DC.XXVI.
Ætatis LXVI.
Tanti viri
Mem.
THOMAS MEAUTYS,
Superstitis cultor,
Defuncti admirator,
H. P.

In English thus:

FRANCIS BACON,
Baron of Verulam, Viscount St. Alban's,
Or by more conspicuous titles,
Of Sciences the Light, of Eloquence the Law,
Sat thus.
Who after all natural wisdom
And secrets of civil life he had unfolded,
Nature's law fulfilled,
Let Compounds be dissolved;
In the year of our Lord, M.DC.XXVI.
Of his age, LXVI.
Of such a man
That the memory might remain,
THOMAS MEAUTYS,
Living, his attendant,
Dead, his admirer,
Placed this monument.

BACULOMETRY, S. [baculus, Lat. and μετρέω, Gr.] the art of measuring heights, by staves or rods.

BAD, Adj. [bad, Pers.] a relative term, that which lessens or destroys the happiness of ourselves or others; applied to moral agents, that which they voluntarily perform, in order to lessen or destroy their own happiness or that of others; one who habitually transgresses the laws of God; that which is performed contrary to any moral law; that which is prejudicial.

BAD, or **BADE**, is the preter tense of bid.

BADGE, S. [from bad, Sax.] a mark worn to denote a person's dignity, profession, trade, or rank.

To **BADGE**, V. A. [badian, Sax.] to set a mark; to stigmatize.

BADGER, S. [from bajulus, Lat.] In Law, one who is licensed to buy corn in one place and sell it in another.

BADGER, S. [bedour, Fr. or backer, Teut. from its biting terribly] In Natural History, a four-footed beast, resembling a hog and dog. It dwells in burrows, lives on insects, carrion, and fruit; stinks very much, and fattens by sleeping. Its skin is of the common peltry kind, and its hair is used in making brushes for limners and gilders. Badger-legged, with legs of an unequal length, resembling those of a badger, " Big-bellied, badger-legged." L'Estrange.

BADLY, Adv. inconsistent with a person's understakings; sickly; applied to the execution of any piece of design, not suitable to the ideas of taste or elegance.

BADNESS, S. transgressions against the laws; applied to things, it denotes that they are inconsistent with the good, ease, or pleasure of rational or irrational beings; applied to weather, a want of serenity, calmness, or sunshine; want of health, sickness.

BAETAS, S. [Span.] a species of woollen stuffs, not crossed, called vogessus by the French.

To BA'FFLE, V. A. [*baffler*, Fr.] to frustrate the intentions of another; applied to an army, it signifies the eluding the designs of an enemy, or rendering all their attempts abortive.

BA'FFLE, S. [from the verb] applied to literary contests or disputes; a dilemma, or the being reduced to such a streight as to be able to say nothing in one's own defence.

BA'FFLER, S. that which defeats, or renders any design abortive.

BA'G, S. [from *bagge*, Ill.] a receptacle made of linen, &c. in the shape of a long square when empty, and open only at one of its ends. Likewise a kind of ornament made of black silk, worn by gentlemen over the hind locks of their hair or perukes. In Natural History, the thin membrane or cystis, containing the poison of vipers; that which contains the honey in bees, &c.

To BA'G, V. A. to put into a bag. Used with a double g in all the examples which occur. "Bagg'd in a blue cloud." Dryd. Used neuterly, to swell so as to imitate or resemble a full bag.

BAGATE'LLE, S. [Fr.] a trifle; a toy; a bauble.

BA'GGAGE, S. [Fr. *bagin*, Ital.] the utensils of an army; a woman of bad character, a prostitute; so called from being left with the baggage of an army in an engagement, or carried in the baggage waggon on a march; derived from the French *bagasse*, or *bagatela*, Ital. a whore.

BA'GNIO, S. [pronounced as if the g was omitted, from *bagno*, Ital. a bath] a house for bathing, cupping, sweating, and swimming. But, with sorrow we speak it, sometimes set apart for such practices against modesty, as introduce one of the most odious diseases which can affect the human constitution.

BA'G-PIPE, S. in Music, a wind instrument much used in Scotland.

BAGUE'TTE, S. [Fr. a diminutive of *bague*, Fr.] In Architecture, a little round moulding, less than an astragal; when carved and enriched with pearls and foliage, Le Clerc says, it should be named a chaplet.

BA'IL, S. [from *bailler*, Fr.] the act of setting a person at liberty who is arrested or imprisoned for an act civil or criminal, under security taken for his appearance; also the person who gives such security. Bail is either common or special.

To BA'IL, V. A. to deliver a person from imprisonment, by being surety for his appearance; to admit to bail.

BA'ILABLE, Adj. that which the law permits to be bailed.

BA'ILIFF, S. [*baillif*, Fr. according to which we pronounce it in the singular, and name them *bailies* in the plural] in Law, an officer who executes writs, arrests or takes a

person into custody; one who manages a person's estates in the country.

BA'ILIWIC, S. [from *bailiff* and *wic*, Sax.] the jurisdiction of a bailiff, within his hundred.

To BA'IT, V. A. [*aton*, Sax. *beitan*, Teut.] to put something on a hook, &c. to catch fish or other animals; to refresh one's self on a journey; to attack; to set dogs upon. This latter sense seems to be borrowed from the French *battre*, to beat.

BA'IT, S. [*batan*, Teut.] a lure, made of or to catch fish, or other animals; an allurement or enticement; a refreshment on a journey.

BA'IZE, S. [*baey*, Belg. *bay*, Teut. *baiata*, Ital.] a coarse open woollen cloth.

To BA'KE, V. A. [*baked* the Pret. of *baked* Piet. of *ge bake*, Ill.] to dress any thing in an oven. Figuratively, to harden with heat. Used neuterly, for the making bread, and making it eatable by means of the heat of an oven. To be heated, or dressed in an oven. Baked meats, are such as are dressed in an oven; opposed to those that are cooked by a fire.

BA'KEN, Participle Preter of bake.

BA'KER, S. [*bakare*, Ill.] one who subsists by baking. This trade is very antient, and was a brotherhood in England before 1155, in the reign of Hen. II. The white bakers were incorporated in 1307 by Edw. II. and the brown in 1621, in Jam. II.'s time. Their hall is in Harp-lane, Thames-street, London; their court-day the 1st Monday of the month; their arms, gules, a balance between three garbs or, and a chief barry wavy of six argent and azure, the hand of justice glorified, issuing out of the clouds proper, holding the balance between two anchors of the second; the motto, "Praise God for all." The assize of bread is in the mayor and commonalty of London, by grant from Hen. IV.

BA'KEWELL, a town in Derbyshire, with a market on Mondays, and five fairs on Easter-Monday, Whit-Monday, August 15, Monday after October 10, and Monday after November 22, all for cattle and horses. It is seated on the river Wye among the hills, and the market is good for lead and other commodities. It is 20 miles N. W. of Derby, and 142 on the same point from London. It lies in a deep valley, and has a large church with a lofty spire. Lon. 15. 0. lat. 55. 15.

BA'LANCE, S. [*bilanx*, Lat.] in Mechanics, one of the six simple powers, used for finding the difference of weights in heavy bodies. Figuratively, the act of comparing two ideas in the mind. In Commerce, such a sum, or quantity, as will make both sides of an account equal, when added to the least. In a Political Sense, that pitch of gove

power which is necessary to keep between states, to prevent either from acquiring universal monarchy. In Watch or Clock-work, that part which regulates the beats. In Astronomy, the sign called Libra.

To BA'LANCE, V. A. [balancer, Fr.] to weigh in scales; to reduce; to bring two bodies to one equipoise in scales. In Mercantile Affairs, to make the creditor and debtor side of an account equal. Used neuterly, to be in a state of suspension, by the seeming equality of opposite motives, applied to the mind. "Why you should balance a moment about printing it." Atted. This phrase is borrowed literally from the French.

BA'LANCER, S. one who weighs or considers any thing.

BALA'NUS, S. [Lat. an acorn] In Anatomy, the glands of the penis.

BA'LASS, RUBY, S. [balai, Fr. an Indian word originally] a ruby of a crimson colour, with a purple cast.

BALCONY, S. [balcon, Fr. balcone, Ital.] a projecture beyond a building, generally before a window, supported by pillars, and surrounded by balustrades.

BALAZE'US, S. [Ind.] white cotton cloths manufactured in Surat.

BA'LD, Adj. [bal, Brit.] having lost its hair. Applied to trees, stripped of their leaves. Applied to style in writing, void of elegance.

BA'LDERDASH, S. [from balder, of bald, Sax. and dash, to mingle] any thing put together without judgment or discretion.

To BA'LDERDASH, V. A. to counterfeit a liquor, to adulterate.

BA'LDLY, Adv. without hairs; without leaves; without ornaments or elegance.

BA'LDNESS, S. the want or loss of hair; loss of leaves; want of ornament or elegance.

BALDOCK, a town in Hertfordshire, with a market on Thursdays, and five fairs, on Wednesday after February 4, the last Thursday in May, August 6, and December 11, all for cheese, household goods, and cattle. It is a long town, lying on the N. road, and is seated between the hills, in a chalky soil, fit for corn, and is chiefly of note for its trading in malt. It is 9 miles W. of Royston, 58 S. S. E. of Oakham, and 38 N. N. W. of London. Lon. 17. 20. lat. 51. 55.

BA'LE, S. [balle, Fr. bale, Teut.] a large quantity of goods, packed in cloth, corded round very tight, and garnished with straw or hay to keep them from damage or the injuries of weather.

BA'LE, S. [from balegve, Goth.] grief, misery, anguish, calamity.

To BA'LE, V. N. [emballer, Fr. embalare, Ital.] to pack goods in a bale.

BA'LEFUL, Adj. full of anguish, misery, mischief, grief; fatal, destructive.

BA'LEFULLY, Adv. in such manner as to produce sorrow, anguish, calamity, or sickness.

BA'LK, S. [balk, Belg. and Teut.] a beam; a rafter or pole over any building, used by bricklayers for the large poles with which they make their scaffolds.

BA'LK, S. [from vallivre, to pass over] in Husbandry, a ridge of land left unploughed between two furrows, or at the end of a field. Also the disappointment of a person's curiosity or expectation.

To BA'LK, V. A. to disappoint; to render a person's endeavours ineffectual; to frustrate; to miss; to omit, when the contrary is expected; to pile on a heap. "Three and twenty knights..balk'd in their own blood." Shak. Alluding to the balks of which scaffolds are made.

BA'LL, S. [bal, Belg. Teut. balle, Fr.] any thing of a round form. Ball and socket, in Mechanics, consists of a ball or sphere of brass, and is generally added to surveying instruments, to fix them in any position.

BA'LL, S. [hall, Fr. from baller] a place wherein people are assembled to dance.

BA'LLAD, S. [balade, Fr. ballata, Ital.] words set to music and sung. This was the primary signification of the word, as may be collected from the ancient version of Solomon's song; wherein it is stiled the Ballad of Ballads, which, according to the Hebrew idiom, implies the best Ballad. At present the word is confined to trifling pieces, set to music, and sung about the streets.

BA'LLAD-SINGER, S. a person who sings ballads.

BA'LLAST, S. [ballaston, Sax.] a quantity of stones, sand, &c. laid in a ship's hold, to make it draw more water, sail upright, and prevent its overfeating. Lead or corn sometimes serve for this purpose. Flat vessels require most ballast; and a ship is said to be in ballast when it has no other lading. Figuratively, what is used to keep any thing steady.

To BA'LLAST, V. A. [from the noun] to lade a ship with sand, &c. to keep her steady. Figuratively, to make the addition of something to keep a thing steady.

BA'LLETTE, S. a stage dance, mixed with dramatic characters, alluding to some actions in real life.

BA'LLIARDS, S. this is the most proper spelling, though seldom used. See BILLIARDS.

BALLO'N, or BALLO'ON, S. [ballon, Fr.] in Chemistry, a large, short-necked, round vessel, to receive the spirits which are drawn off by fire. In Architecture, a ball or globe on the top of a pillar, &c. by way of a crowning. A ball of pasteboard, filled with combustibles, which mounts to a great height, and bursts into stars.

BA'LLOT,

BA'LLOT, S. [*ballotte*, Fr. a diminutive, signifying a little ball] a little ball used at elections, &c. in giving votes. The sum of votes so collected. At present applied to the votes given at elections, by holding up of hands; sometimes by a ticket dropped into a receptacle for that purpose.

To BA'LLOT, V. N. [*balloter*, Fr.] to choose, by dropping a ball into a box. To elect, by dropping in a ticket. To elect by holding up the hand.

BALLOTA'TION, S. the act of electing by ballot.

BALLOTING, S. [from *ballot*] a method of electing a person into an office, by means of little balls of different colours, put privately into a box. At present we make use of tickets, with the candidates or the elector's name wrote in it; or else hold up hands.

BA'LM, S. [*balme*, Fr.] any fragrant ointment; figuratively, any thing that sooths or diminishes pain. In Botany, a species of mint. In Pharmacy, an oily resinous substance.

To BA'LM, V. A. to anoint; to ease or sooth pain.

BA'LMY, Adj. having the qualities of balm. That which sooths or mitigates pain. Fragrant, sweet-scented. "O *balmy* breath." *Shakespear's Othello.*

BALNEA'TION, S. [from *balneum*, Lat.] the act of bathing. "As is observable in *balnearions.*" *Brown.* Seldom used by later writers.

BA'LNEATORY, Adj. [*balneatorius*, Lat.] that which belongs to a bath.

BA'LSAM, S. [*balsamum*, Lat.] an oily, resinous, fragrant substance, oozing from incisions in certain plants. *Balsam or balm of Gilead*, issues from a tree, called balsamum, in Judea; its juice is at first liquid, and thickens afterwards. The *balm or balsam of Mecca*, is a dry white gum, which distils from a tree that grows between Medina and Mecca, resembling the turpentine tree; it is made use of both as a cosmetic, or beautifier, by the ladies, and as a medicine by the gentlemen of the faculty; taken inwardly, it is good for pains in the stomach and reins, weakness in the lungs, want of appetite, and the cholic; used externally, it is reckoned an infallible cure for wounds, which it heals in twenty-four hours. *Balsam of Peru, capaij, or capivi*, comes from Peru, Guiana, and the Levant, and is much used in gonorrheas, obstructions in the ureters, gravel, &c. *Balsam of Tolu*, drops by incision from trees which grow in Spain; is a liquid resin, which, as it grows old, resembles Flanders glue, both in consistency and colour.

BALSA'MIC, or BALSA'MICAL, Adj. having the virtues of balsam; having mild, restorative, and healing qualities.

BA'LUSTER, S. [from *balustre*, Fr.] in Architecture, a small column or pilaster.

BA'LUSTRADE, S. an assemblage of one or more rows of balusters, fixed on a terras, bridge, or building, by way of security, or separating one part from another.

BAMBO'O, S. [*bambou*, Ind.] in Natural History, a large kind of reed or cane, growing in the maritime parts of the East Indies. Each shoot is at the bottom as big as a man's thigh, decreasing gradually to the top, where it bears a blossom or flower. Its leaves are half a foot long, and their breadth towards the middle is an inch, or something more. The Indians build their houses, and make all their kitchen utensils with them, in which they discover great address and dexterity.

To BAMBO'OZLE, V. A. [from *bam*, Sax. and *bryster*] to trick or impose on a person; to confound.

BAMBO'OZLER, S. a cheat, a sharper, a tricker.

BAMPTON, a town in Devonshire, with a market on Saturdays, and two fairs, on Whit-Tuesday, and October 24, for cattle. It is seated in a bottom, surrounded with hills, and contains about 300 houses, with a large church. It is 14 miles N. N. E. of Exeter, 18 S. S. W. of Minehead, and 167 W. by S. of London. Lon. 13. 55. lat. 51. 5.

BA'N, S. [*ban*, Ind.] any thing publicly proclaimed, commanded, or forbidden. In Church Government, a proclamation of the intention of two parties to marry, which is done thrice in the church they each belong to, before the marriage ceremony can be performed. A curse or excommunication. The *ban* of the empire, is a public act or proclamation, whereby a person is suspended of all his rights as a member or elector.

To BA'N, V. A. [*bannen*, Belg.] to curse, to execrate.

BANBURY, a town of Oxfordshire, with a market on Thursdays, and seven fairs, on Thursday after January 17, for horses, cows, and sheep; on the first Thursday in Lent, for the same and fish; on Holy Thursday, June 13, and August 12, for horses, cows, and sheep; on Thursday after October 10, for hiring servants, hogs, and cheese; and on October 29, for cheese, hogs, and cattle. It is a large well-built mayor-town, containing several good inns, and its markets are well served with provisions. It is the second town for beauty in the county, and is seated on a flat on the river Charwell. The houses are generally built with stone, and the church is a large handsome structure. It has been long noted for its cakes and cheese, and is 17 miles W. N. W. of Buckingham, 20 E. S. E. of Stratford upon Avon, and 27 N. W. of London. It sends

one member to parliament. Lon. 16. 15.
lat. 52. 5.

BA'ND, S. [band, Ifl. bandi of bindan,
Goth.] that which keeps a person to a certain
place, without liberty of going further. Figuratively, what has the power of knitting
a close connexion between persons; a company of persons so united. That which is
bound round a person or thing; a piece of
linen neckcloth, consisting of two square
leaves hanging down from the chin to the
breast, worn by clergymen, &c. Bands, applied to a saddle, are two pieces of iron nailed upon the bows to keep them in their
proper situation.

To BA'ND, V. A. to unite together. To
cover, or bind with a fillet, or band.

BA'NDAGE, S. [Fr.] in Surgery, the applying bands or rollers; properly, a piece of
linen cloth or fillet, and should be made of
linen that is worn for fear of fretting the
part, or making it uneasy. Bandages are
either simple or compound; simple, when
made of one entire piece, and compound
when consisting of more.

BA'NDALEER, [from band of bindan,
Goth.] a large leathern belt worn over the
right shoulder, and hanging down under
the left arm.

BA'NDBOX, S. a box made of pasteboard, for keeping bands, ribbands, head-
dresses, &c.

BA'NDIT, S. [bandito, Ital.] an outlawed
robber. "No savage fierce, bandit, or
mountaineer." Milt.

BANDI'TTO, S. [Ital. the plural of ban-
ditti] a set of outlawed thieves on the continent, who live on the plunder of passengers.

BANDOLEERS, S. [bandouliers, Fr.]
small wooden cases, covered with leather,
containing a charge for a musket.

BA'NDROL, S. a silk flag, which hangs
on a trumpet.

To BA'NDY, V. A. to beat to and fro.
To give and take; to exchange, to contend.

BA'NDY, Adj. crooked. Thus bandy-
legged is applied to a person who has crooked
legs.

BANE, S. [bane, Ifl.] murder, that which
will destroy life; poison, ruin, destruction.

To BA'NE, V. A. [from the noun] to
destroy, kill, or poison.

BA'NEFUL, Adj. destructive to life;
poisonous.

BA'NEWORT, S. a poisonous plant; a
species of the nightshade.

To BANG, V. A. [bangen, Belg.] to
cudgel or strike; to use a person roughly.

BA'NG, S. a blow with a stick, or cudgel,
or the hand.

BANGOR, a town of Carnarvonshire, in
North Wales, with a bishop's see, on which
account it has the title of a city. It has a
market on Wednesdays, and three fairs on
April 5, June 25, and October 28, all for

cattle. It was so considerable in ancient
times, that it was called Bangor the Great,
and was defended by a strong castle. It is in
a low situation, and the principal buildings
are the cathedral, and the bishop's palace;
but it is now an inconsiderable place. It is
36 miles W. of St. Asaph, and 236 N. W.
of London. Lon. 13. 30. lat. 53. 20.

To BA'NISH, V. A. [from bannir, Fr.] to
make a person depart from his own country,
to drive from the mind; to expel. Used
with the particle from.

BA'NISHMENT, S. the state of a person
banished. In Law, a kind of civil death,
whereby a person is cut off from all benefits
arising from the country in which he was
born, obliged to quit it, and live in a foreign
country. This punishment is generally inflicted for crimes against the state, as in cases
of high treason. The punishment of capital crimes is sometimes converted into a banishment for life; and is then termed trans-
portation.

BA'NK, S. [banc, Sax. bank, Ifl.] a rising ground on each side of a river washed by
its waters, which it hinders from overflowing.
Earth cast up on one side of a trench between two armies.

BA'NK, S. [banc, Fr. banco, Ital.] a bench
where rowers sit in vessels. In commerce, a
repository, wherein persons agree to keep
their cash.

To BA'NK, V. A. to inclose with banks;
to place money in a bank.

BANK-BILL, S. a promissory note given
by the bank for money placed there.

BA'NKER, S. a private person entrusted with the cash of others, payable on demand. The great service of this body of
people to trade may easily be understood, if
we consider in the first place, that they are a
check on the bank, to prevent high interest
and exorbitant premiums; in the second
place, that they have contributed more than
once to support public credit, and even that
of the bank, when nothing else could have
done it; that during the recoining in the
time of K. Will. III. they made their payments, and maintained their credit even beyond the bank; and that the trader is at
less trouble, and can more expeditiously
draw his cash out of their hands, than out of
the bank; and that they are more ready and
less scrupulous to discount than the bank
is.

BA'NKER'S NOTE, S. a promissory
note given by a banker.

BA'NKRUPTCY, S. the state of a person
declared a bankrupt.

BA'NKRUPT, S. [banqueroute, Fr.] in
Law, one who living by buying and selling,
has got the goods of others in his hands and
concealeth himself from his creditors; or
otherwise commits an act of bankruptcy.

To BA'NKRUPT, V. A. to take out a
statute

ftatute of bankruptcy against a perfon; to lavifh the effects of another fo as to ruin him.

BA'NNER, S. [*banner*, Brit. *banner*, Fr.] a flag, or enfign ufed in an army.

BA'NNERET, S. [a diminutive of *banner*, *banner heiron*, I cut.] an order created by having the end of their enfign cut off by the king. They were fecond to none but knights of the garter. were reputed the next degree below the nobility; and were allowed to bear arms with fupporters. The laft perfon of the order was Sir John Smith, created after Edghill fight, for refcuing the ftandard of Charles I.

BA'NNIMUS, [low Lat. from *bannio*, to banifh] the form of expelling a fcholar from Oxford.

BA'NNIAN, S. a man's morning garment, made double breafted; it is longer than a coat, and without pocket-holes to the fkirts or plates at the fides, and refembles the drefs of the Banians in the Eaft Indies.

BA'NNACK, S. a cake made with oatmeal and peafe mixed with water; common in the north countries.

BA'NQUET, S. [*bancheto*, Ital.] a feaft or elegant entertainment.

To BA'NQUET, V. A. to entertain, or give a feaft; to regale.

BA'NQUETER, S. a perfon who lives fumptuoufly, or keeps a good table

BA'NQUET, or BA'NQUETTING-HOUSE, S. a houfe where grand publick feafts are given.

BA'NQUETTE, S. In Fortification, a fmall bank for foldiers to afcend to fire behind an entrenchment.

To BA'NTER, V. A. [*badiner*, Fr.] to make a perfon become an object of ridicule; to tell a perfon of his faults in a jocofe manner; to rally.

BA'NTER, [from the verb] a jeft; ridicule, or raillery.

BA'NTERER, S. one who ridicules, jokes, plays on another on account of fome fault.

BA'NTLING, S. [from *band*, Ital. a band, and *ling*, Sax. fwaddling clothes; Johnson derives it from *baien*, Scot. of *born*, Goth. a child] a little child; an infant in fwaddling clothes.

BA'PTISM, S. [*baptifma*, Lat. of *baptifmos*, Gr.] one of the facraments whereby people are initiated into the church, and made members of Chrift; children of God, and inheritors of the kingdom of heaven. Being a ceremony in ufe among the Jews, for the admiffion of profelytes into their religion, it was adapted by Chrift in his, and confifts of two parts; an outward and vifible fign, which is the wafhing with water, and is fignificative of the inward fpiritual grace, or death to fin, figured by the perfon's being buried or plunged under water, in its original fignification. The difpute, whether it fhould be adminiftered to infants, or fuch

No. IV.

only as are arrived to years of difcretion; whether it fhould be performed by fprinkling or immerfion, i. e. plunging. we fhall not engage in; but before we conclude this article, we muft obferve, that the Quakers entirely omit water-baptifm, holding that they are baptifed by the Holy Ghoft. In a fecondary fenfe, it fignifies the fufferings of Chrift, whereby the facrament of baptifm is applied for his entrance into his kingly office. "I have a *baptifm* to be baptifed with," *Luke*, xii. 50. *Matt.* xv. 22. In fea-language, the ceremony which the perfons or fhip are fubject to, the firft time they pafs the tropic, or line.

BAPTI'SMAL, Adj. [from *baptifm*] relating to, or done at, our baptifm.

BA'PTIST, S. [*baptifte*, Fr.] one who adminifters the facrament of baptifm; applied to St. John, our Saviour's fore-runner. One who holds that baptifm fhould be adminiftered only to adult perfons.

BA'PTISTERY, S. [*baptifterium*, Lat.] the place in a church where the baptifm is adminiftered; the font.

To BAPTI'ZE, V. A. [*baptizo*, Gr.] to perform baptifm; to chriften.

BA'R, S. [*barre*, Fr.] a piece of wood or iron to fecure any entrance from being forced. A rock, or fand bank, at the entrance of a harbour, to keep off fhips of burden. The part of a court of juftice where the criminal generally ftands. An inclofed place at a tavern, inn, coffee-houfe, &c. Any obftacle or impediment, in law. a peremptory exception againft a demand or plea brought by a defendant in an action. A bar to common intent, is an ordinary or general one, which difables the plea of the plaintiff. A bar fpecial, is that which is more than ordinary, falls out in the cafe in hand and on fome fpecial circumftance of the fact. A bar of gold or filver is a lump melted and caft into a mould, without having been wrought. Bar, in the manege, are the ridges or upper part of the gums without teeth, between the tufhes and grinders of a horfe, againft which the bit acts, and by means of which the beaft is governed. In Mufic, the ftraight ftrokes drawn perpendicularly acrofs the lines in a piece of mufic, in common time. they include the meafure of four crotchets; in triple time, three crotchets; and are ufed to regulate the beating or mufical meafure of time. In Heraldry, an ordinary refembling the *fefs*, differing from it in its narrownefs, and that it may be placed in any part of the fhield. *See bar*, two half bullets joined together by an iron-bar.

To BAR, V. A. to faften or fecure by a piece of iron, or wood. Figuratively, to exclude, except againft, hinder, or put a ftop to. In farriers, to bar a vein, is an operation performed upon the vein of the legs, or other parts of a horfe, by taking it out of the fkin,

T

fhin, tying it both above and below, and
: ftriking between the two ligatures.

BARALIPTON, S. In Logic, the firſt
in direct mood of barbara, or the firſt figure
of ſyllogiſms; and is when the two firſt
propoſitions are general, and the third or
concluſion is particular; the middle term being the ſubject in the firſt propoſition; and
the predicate or attribute of the ſecond; the
major term is the ſubject of the concluſion,
and the minor the attribute or predicate, as
thus:

Ba, Every animal is indued with ſenſe.
Ra, Every man is an animal.
Lip, Something indued with ſenſe is a
man.

BA'RB, S. [barbe, Lat. barba, Fr.] a
beard; any thing that grows in its place, or
reſembles it. The piece of wire at the end
of a fiſh-hook, which hinders it from being
extracted; the pieces of iron which run back
from the point of an arrow.

BARB, S. a horſe brought from Barbary,
remarkable for beauty, vigour, and ſtiffneſs,
for its never lying down, and for its ſtanding
ſtill, when the rider drops his bridle. They
have a long walk, ſtep ſhort on a full career,
are of a ſlender make, ſixteen hands high,
ſoon grow ripe, but never old, retain their
metal, as the duke of Newcaſtle obſerves, as
long as their lives, and are much prized for
ſtallions, fed in Barbary on camels milk,
will out-run oſtriches, and are commonly
ſold for 1000 ducats, or 100 camels.

BA'RBACAN, S. [Arab. barbacane, Fr.
barbacana, Span.] a long narrow canal, or
paſſage for water in walls, where buildings
are liable to be overflowed.

BA'RBARA, S. in Logic, a ſyllogiſm in
the firſt mood of the firſt figure, wherein all
the propoſitions are univerſal.

BARBA'RIAN, S. [barbarus, Lat.] in its
primary ſenſe, a foreigner; but in proceſs
of time it was uſed to denote a perſon void
of all the elegant embelliſhments of life,
and the ſocial affections of benevolence,
kindneſs, pity, and humanity.

BARBA'RIAN, Adj. rude; unpoliſhed;
cruel; ſavage; void of pity; void of compaſſion; void of humanity.

BA'RBARISM, S. [barbariſmus, Lat.] in
Grammar, inelegant language; uncultivated
ignorance; rudeneſs, want of politeneſs,
ſavageneſs; crudity.

BA'RBARITY, S. from barbarus, Lat.]
unpoliteneſs; ruſticity; applied to manners,
cruelty, ſavageneſs. Applied to language,
an improper expreſſion.

BA'RBAROUS, Adj. [from barbarus,
Lat.] ignorant, unacquainted with the polite arts and ſciences. Void of benevolence,
pity, or humanity; cruel; ſavage.

BAR'BAROUSLY, Adv. in a barbarous
manner.

BA'RBARY, a large country of Africa, in-

cluded between the Atlantic Ocean, the Mediterranean Sea, and Egypt, extending itſelf
along the ſea-ſhore on the ſide of the Mediterranean. However, ſome reckon that it
extends ſouthward as far as Negroland, but
very improperly. It includes the kingdoms
of Barca, Tripoly, Tunis, Algiers, Fez, and
Morocco; and is near 2000 miles in length,
and in ſome places 750 in breadth. It was
known to the antients by the name of Mauri-
tania, Numidia, Proper Africa, and Lybia.
It is the beſt country in all Africa, except
Egypt; and is fertile in corn, maize, wine,
and fruits; particularly, there are citrons,
oranges, figs, almonds, olives, dates, and
melons. Their chief trade conſiſts in the
ſale of their fruits, in the horſes called barbs,
Morocco-leather, oſtrich feathers, Indigo,
wax, tin, and coral. The reigning religion
is the Mahometan, and there are ſome Jews;
but no Chriſtians, except the ſlaves.

To BARBECUE, V. A. [Ind.] to dreſs
a hog whole, by ſplitting it to the back-
bone, and broiling it upon a grid-iron. A
Weſt-Indian diſh.

BARBECUE, S. a hog dreſſed whole.
See the verb.

BA'RBELS, S. [Fr. barbe, barbelle, Ital.]
a large, coarſe, river fiſh.

BA'RBER, S. [barbier, Fr. barbiere, Ital.]
one who ſhaves. The company of barbers
were formerly incorporated with the ſurgeons,
under the title of barber-ſurgeon, and were
originally but one trade; hence it is, that
we ſee them ſtill affecting the lower branch
of that art, and adorning their windows
with ſtumps of teeth, and profeſſing bleeding.

BA'RBER-MONGER, S. a fop, or one
whoſe hair is foppiſhly dreſſed. "Barber-
monger draw." Shakeſp.

BA'RBERY, S. in Botany, the piperidge-
buſh, which grows in hedges to eight or ten
feet, with white bark, the ſtalks armed with
thorns growing by threes, the leaves oval
and ſawed; the flower has a coloured empalement, compoſed of ſix concave leaves,
with two coloured nectariums, and ſix obtuſe
erect ſtamina; the germen is cylindrical,
without ſtile, and becomes an obtuſe berry,
with a punctum, and one cell incloſing two
ſeeds, at firſt green; but when ripe they
turn to a fine red.

BARD, S. [bardd, Brit.] among the
antient Britons, Danes, and Iriſh, a ſet of
men who uſed to ſing the exploits of heroes,
they were reverenced as perſons of extraordinary abilities, even by crowned heads, who
paid them the greateſt deference. The curious reader, who would be better acquainted
with them, may have recourſe to Warburton's
Antiquities, a book not leſs valuable than
ſcarce. Even in the preſent times, the word
implies a poet.

BA'RE, Adj. [bar, Sax. naked, from
abaran,

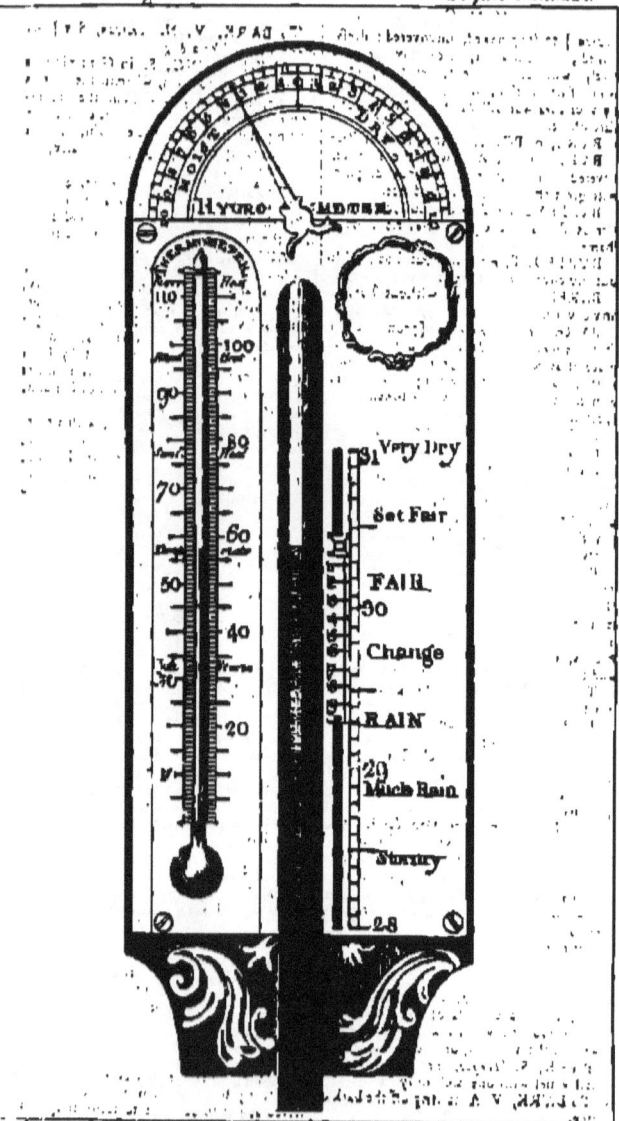

thereon,] to strip naked, un covered; devil; naked; without a hat, or cap, &c. Figuratively, without ornament, delicate; or in want of accessaries; alone, solitary. "Live by your *bare* words." Shelsp. Much worn, threadbare.

BA'RE, or BORE, S. the preter of *Bear*.

BA'REFACED, Adj. with the face uncovered. Figuratively, without disguise; with great effrontery, or impudence.

BAREFA'CEDLY, Adv. in such a manner as shews that a person has no sense of shame.

BA'REFOOT, Adj. without shoes, without any covering to his feet.

BAREFO'OTED, Adj. without shoes, or any covering to the feet.

BA'RE-HEADED, Adj. [pronounced as if the *a* was dropped, and *ed* supplied its place, thus, *bare-headed*, from *bare* and *head*] without a hat, any covering to the head. Among the English, this is a token of respect and politeness.

BA'RELY, Adv. without clothes; without any thing else, only.

BA'RENESS, S. nakedness, meanness with respect to the quality of clothing. Applied to foil, its want of fruitfulness; applied to circumstances, such as cannot supply the necessaries of life; indigence; poverty.

BA'RGAIN, S. [*bargen*, Brit. *bargyn*, Ital.] an agreement made between traders. The thing bought or sold. The conditions of sale. In law, *bargain and sale* is a deed or instrument, whereby the property of lands &c. is, for a valuable consideration, granted and transferred from one person to another.

To BA'RGAIN, V. A. to agree to terms for the sale of any thing.

BARGAINE'E, S. one who agrees to the condition of a bargain.

BA'RGE, S. [*bargie*, Belg.] a large flatbottomed vessel; likewise a large pleasure-boat, built with a room to contain several persons.

BARK, S. [from *barck*, Dan. *barck*, Teut.] In Botany, the outside covering of a tree. It is composed of woody cells, and vesicles filled with a juice, resembling the chyle of animals; the vesicles run horizontal, and the woody cells appear through a microscope, like so many barrels joined together in different numbers; the necessity of this covering, soon appears from a tree's decaying when stripped of it. In the East-Indies, they spin it like hemp, after steeping it in water, and weave stuffs of it called pinasses and blumbores; when filk is mixed with it, they call them nillaes, or cherquemollis.

BA'RK, S. [*barque*, Fr. *barca*, Ital.] a small vessel with one deck only.

To BA'RK, V. A. to strip off the bark of a tree.

To BA'RK, V. N. [*beorcan*, Sax.] to make a noise like a dog.

BARK-BINDING, S. in Gardening, a disease incident to trees, wherein the bark is so close, that the vegetation, and the circulation of the sap is hindered; this is cured by cutting the bark along the grain, and in apple-trees by cutting it perpendicularly, or strait down.

BA'RKER, S. one who makes a noise made by a dog. Applied to a person who takes the bark off trees. It is derived from *bark* the external rind or covering of a tree.

BARKHAMSTEAD, a town in Hertfordshire, with a market on Mondays, chiefly for malt, and three fairs on Shrove-Monday, and Whit-Monday, for cattle; and on St. James's-day, for cheese. It had formerly a strong castle built by the Normans, and has now a good free-school, founded by John Incent, dean of St. Paul's. It is 11 miles W. of St. Alban's, and 28 N. W. of London. Lon. 16. 55. lat. 51. 40.

BARKING, a town of Essex, with a market on Saturday, and one fair on October 22, for horses. It is seated on the river Roding, not far from the Thames, in an unwholesome air. It has been chiefly noted for a large monastery, now in ruins, there being nothing left standing but a small part of the walls, and a gate-house. It is eight miles E. of London. Lon. 17. 43. lat. 51. 30.

BA'RKY, Adj. having the properties of bark.

BA'RLEY, S. the grain from whence beer is extracted.

BA'RLEY-CORN, S. a grain of barley; the third part of an inch.

BA'RLEY-MOW, S. a heap of barley formed into a rick or stack.

BA'RM, S. [from *farm*, *beorm*, *breme* Sax.] what is put into drink to make it work, or into bread to make it light; called also yeast.

BA'RMY, Adj. well fermented or worked with yeast. " *Barmy* beer." Dryd.

BARN, S. [of *bern*, Sax.] a kind of house wherein any grain, &c. is put.

BA'RNACLE, S. in Natural History, the solan, or Scotch goose, so called from its having been supposed, in the days of unlettered ignorance, to have grown on trees. In Farriery, an instrument which is fastened to a horse's nose, when he is restiff.

BARO'METER, S. [from βαρος, and μετρεω,] an instrument to measure the weight of a column of air, to discover the heights of hills, &c. which consists of a tube filled with quicksilver. The form of these instruments are various, in order to obviate the inconveniencies attending their structure; but none has yet been so contrived as not to be liable to some irregularities.

T 2   ties.

tie, either from friction, attrition, or gravitating, which would render the experiments made by them less subject to error, or requiring allowances.

BAROMETRICAL, Adj. relating to, or concerning the barometer.

BARON, S. [from the bar, Teut. Celt.] a town which anciently included all the greater nobility. It is now a degree of nobility, next below that of a viscount. They have the following immunities and privileges; in criminal causes they are judged by their peers only, are not put on oath, but deliver the truth upon honour; are not impannelled on a jury, not liable to the writ *supplicavit capias* &c. they had no barons till Charles II. gave them a gold one with his peers. The two archbishops and all the bishops of England are parliamentary barons, and enjoy all the privileges of the others, excepting that they are not judged by their peers, for being not to be prehending in sanguinary causes, in such cases they are judged as to life by a jury of twelve. *Barons* of the Exchequer, are four judges, who determine causes, between the king and his subjects, in all things relating to the revenue and the Exchequer. *Barons* of the Cinque ports, are members elected, two for each, to represent them in the house of commons. *Baron* and *femme*, in Law, are husband and wife. *Baron* and femme, in Heraldry, is when the coats of arms of a man and his wife are borne per pale in the same escutcheon, the man's being on the dexter, or right, and the woman's on the sinister or the left side; but if the woman be an heiress, her coat must be borne on an escutcheon, or escutcheon of pretence. A *baron* of beef, is when two sirloins are not divided, but joined together by the back-bone.

BARONAGE, S. [*baronagium*,] the body of barons. The dignity, or lands of a baron.

BARONESS, S. [*baronessa*, Ital. *baronissa*, Lat.] the wife of a baron.

BARONET, S. [from *baron* and a diminutive termination] the lowest degree of honour that is hereditary, being next below a baron. It was founded by James I. A.D. 1611; who allowed them to charge their coat with the arms of Ulster. The title of *sir* is peculiarly granted them; though not dubbed knights they may claim it, and their patent is hereditary, being made out to them and the heirs male lawfully begotten of their bodies for ever.

BARONY, S. [*baronie*] the lordship, or fee of a baron, whether spiritual or temporal. According to Sir William Temple, they were the large share of the lands of conquered countries, granted by the Goths and other northern invaders to their generals and commanders.

BAROSCOPE, S. [from βαρὸς, and

σκοπέω, to search into] an instrument to show the alteration of the atmosphere. See BAROMETER.

BARRACAN, S. [Fr. *barracan*, Fr.] a kind of stuff resembling camblet.

BARRACK, S. [*barracca*, Span.] small huts erected by the Spanish fishermen. Also buildings raised to lodge soldiers in.

BARRATRY, S. [*barraterie*, Fr.] in Common Law, the moving or maintaining of suits in disturbance of the peace; made the taking and detaining houses, land, &c. by false pretences. In a Marine sense, applied to the masters or crew of a ship, which cheat the owners or insurers, by running away with, deserting, or sinking her, or embezzling the cargo.

BARREL, S. [*baril*, Brit. *barril*, Span.] an oblong vessel made of wood of a cylindrical form, and used as a liquid or dry measure. The barrel contains in wine measure 31 gallons and a half, beer measure 36 gallons, and ale measure 32. When applied to a certain quantity of weight, it differs according to the commodities it contains; a barrel of Essex butter weighing 106lb and of Suffolk 256. The barrel of herrings should contain 32 gallons wine measure, each 1000 herring. The barrel of salmon 42 gallons, the barrel of eels 42 gallons, and that of soap 256lb. Applied to a gun, that long cylindrical tube made of metal, through which it is charged. In Anatomy, a large cavity behind the tympanum.

To BARREL, V.A. [from the noun] to put into a barrel. Sometimes used with the particle up.

BARREN, Adj. [*bere*, Sax. *baer*, Teut.] applied to animals or soils, not able to produce; applied to genius, not able to produce any thing new; stupid.

BARRENLY, Adv. in such a manner as to produce nothing; in an unfruitful manner.

BARRICADE, [*barricade*, Fr.] any defence in the military art. Figuratively, any thing which obstructs or hinders.

To BARRICADE, V.A. to stop up a passage. To hinder the advance of any thing.

BARRICADO, S. [*barricado*, Span. for BARRICADE] in Fortification, a defence made with stakes shod with iron, &c. erected in passages or breaches.

To BARRICADO, V.A. to block up any avenue or passage; to hinder by putting obstacles and impediments in the way.

BARRIER, S. [*barrière*, Fr. *barriera*, Ital.] sometimes pronounced on the second, and more generally, though more properly, on the first syllable; that which keeps an enemy from entering into any country; a fence made at a passage to stop up an entry, of great stakes four or five feet high, placed at eight or

ten feet distance, with overthwart rafters; in order to hinder either horse or foot from facing an entrance; and in the middle is a bar of wood; moving at pleasure. Likewise, an exercise of men armed with short swords, and fighting together within an inclosure, to separate them from the spectators. Figuratively, an obstruction, impediment, or hindrance. A boundary, or limit.

BA'RRISTER, S. one who is qualified to plead the causes of clients in a court of justice. They were formerly obliged to study eight years, but now only seven, if not five, before they are called.

BARROW, S. (from *barrow*, Sax.) any carriage fit to be moved by the hand; a *hand-barrow*, is a frame on which things are carried by handles at its extremities, between two men: a *wheel-barrow*, is that with one wheel at the head, by which it moves when pushed forward by the handles.

To BA'RTER, V. A. (*barater*, Fr. *barattare*, Ital.) to exchange; the original method of carrying on all trade and commerce, till the invention of money. When used with the particle *away*, it implies, that the exchange is made to great disadvantage, or attended with loss. Sometimes used neuterly.

BA'RTER, S. in Commerce, the exchanging one ware for another; the original method of commerce, before the invention of money.

BA'RTERER, S. he that exchanges one commodity for another.

BARTON, a town in Lincolnshire, with a market on Saturdays, and one fair on June 11, for sheep. It is seated on the river Humber, where there is a considerable ferry to pass over into Yorkshire, which is of considerable advantage to the town, which is a large straggling place. It is 35 miles N. of Lincoln, 36 S. E. of York, and 165 N. of London. Lon. 17. 20. lat. 53. 40.

BA'SE, Adj. (from *bas*, Fr. *basso*, Ital.) proceeding from a mean, abject, and sordid disposition: applied to rank, low, and void of dignity: descended from mean parents, or begotten of parents who were never married: applied to metals, counterfeit, or adulterated. In Architecture, the lower part of a column or pedestal. The *Tuscan base* consists only of a single tore besides the plinth. The *Ionic base* has a large tore over two slender scotias, separated by two astragals. The *Corinthian base* has two tores, two scotias, and two astragals. The *composite base* has an astragal less than the Corinthian. *Base*, in Fortification, is an imaginary line drawn from the flanked angle of a bastion to that which is opposite to it. *Base of a triangle*, is properly that side parallel to the horizon. *Base ten*, is a tenure in fee at the will of a lord. *Base viol of a*

common, is the great one next behind the touch hole. *Base*, in Music, the large string of a musical instrument. See BASS.

BA'SENESS, S. the being void of generosity, magnanimity, or nobleness of soul, and proceeds from a narrowness, or meanness of spirit, including the idea of treachery, and an entire want of shame. Applied to metals, their want of the standard value. Applied to birth, dishonourable, mean. Applied to sound, low, grave.

To BA'SH, V. N. (*verbaersen*, Belg. to strike with astonishment) to effect a person with shame. Obsolete.

BASHA'W, S. (*passha*, Turk.) a Turkish governor, who has but two horse-tails carried before him.

BA'SHFUL, Adj. a person who is soon put out of countenance; one who is timorous of having done amiss, from a consciousness of his own ignorance.

BA'SHFULLY, Adv. timorously, sheepishly.

BA'SHFULNESS, S. a timorousness, fear, or shame, arising from a consciousness of having done something amiss. It is distinguished from *modesty*, because it is founded in reason; but this in suspicion and ignorance: modesty likewise hinders a person from doing any thing unbecoming, but bashfulness hinders us from doing any thing graceful. The one keeps us from committing any thing inconsistent with virtue; but the other keeps us from doing even our duty, and exposes us more to the commission of vice, than a courageous performance of virtue.

BA'SIL, S. the sloping edge of a carpenter's tool. The skin of a sheep tanned. In Botany, a plant, named ocrymum.

To BA'SIL, V. A. to grind away the edge of a tool to a certain angle. Used with the particle *away*.

BASI'LICA, S. (from *βασιλικος*) in Anatomy, the middle vein, running the whole length of the arm.

BASI'LIC, or BASI'LICAL, Adj. something relating to the basilical vein.

BASI'LICON, S. (Gr. *βασιλικον*) an ointment called also tetrapharmacon, composed of rosin, wax, pitch, and oil of olives.

BA'SILISK, (*βασιλισκος*,) a serpent about three palms long, said to drive all others away by its hissing, and to kill by its very look; it is called likewise a cockatrice. In Gunnery, a species of cannon or ordnance. "Cannons and basilisks." Bac.

BA'SIN, S. (*bassin*, Fr. *bacino*, Ital.) a small vessel to hold liquors. A pond; a canal; a concave piece of metal, used by opticians to grind their convex glasses in. A round shell, or case of iron wherein hatters mould their hats. In Anatomy, a round cavity between the anterior ventricles of the brain, the pituitary glands, and the veins.

BA'SIS,

BA'SIS, S. [Lat.] the foundation, or that on which any thing is supported.

To BASK, V. A. [bakan, Sax.] to warm, by exposing to the sun, used with the particles in or with. To lie in a warm place.

BASKET, S. [basgawd, Brit.] a vessel made with twigs, &c. woven together. A *basket-woman*, is one who plies at markets with a basket, to be employed by persons who buy provisions there.

BA'SS, [*bass*, Ital.] in Music, the lowest of all the parts, and is a foundation to the others. That part of a concert, consisting of the deepest, and most solemn sounds. *Counter-bass* is the second, when there are several in the same concert. *Thorough-bass*, proceeds from the beginning to the end, and is the harmony made by basviols, theorbos, &c. playing both while the voices sing, and the instruments perform; and also filling the intervals when they stop. According to Brossard, it was invented in 1600, by Ludovico Viadana, an Italian, and is marked by figures over the notes when for organs, harpsichords, &c.

BA'SS, S. [from *bas*, Fr.] to knead on.

RA'SSO, S. [Ital. for BASS] in Music, sometimes extended to the bass universally, and at other times confined to that only which is sung.

BA'SSON, or BASSOON, S. a musical wind instrument, blown with a reed, with eleven holes stopped like those of a flute, dividing into two parts, and used for the bass in concerts with hautboys.

BASSO RELIEVO, S. [Ital.] in Sculpture, figures which do not project much beyond the ground, on which they are carved. According to Felibien; when figures appear, with almost their full relievo, it is called *mezzo relievo*; when they stand out one half *mezzo relievo*, and when they swell out less, *basso relievo*.

BA'SS-RELIEF, S. [from *bas*, Fr. or *basso*, Ital. low, and *relievo*, Ital. or *relief*, Fr. raised work] See BASSO RELIEVO.

BASS VI'OL, S. a musical stringed instrument, of the same form as the violin, but larger, struck with a bow. Its sound is more grave, sweet, and majestic than that of a violin, and of a much nobler effect in a concert.

BA'STARD, S. [from *bastard*, Brit. *bastarde*, Fr.] in Law, a person born of parents, who have not been married, and cannot inherit land as heir to his father. Any thing which degenerates from that which produces it, any thing spurious.

To BASTARDI'ZE, V. A. to prove a person not begotten in marriage; to get a bastard.

BA'STARDLY, Adv. like a bastard, degenerately, spuriously.

BA'STARDY, S. [from *bastard*] in Law, a state of birth, wherein a person is produced from persons not married.

To BASTE, V. A. [part. past *basted* or *baste*; *basean*, Arm.] to beat, &c. in Cookery, to moisten meat while roasting with butter. To stitch, or sew two selvedges together.

BASTINA'DE, or BASTINA'DO, S. [*bastonade*, Fr.] the beating with a stick or cudgel. The punishment among the Turks of beating the soles of the feet with a piece of wood.

To BASTINA'DE, or BASTINA'DO, V. A. [*bastonner*, Fr.] to beat with a stick or cudgel; to beat on the soles of the feet, like the Turks.

BA'STION, S. [Fr.] in Fortification, a large mass of earth faced with sods.

BA'STON, or BATTOON, S. in Heraldry, a kind of bend, only one third of the usual breadth of the bend, not reaching quite across the shield, a sign of bastardy, and should not be removed till the third generation.

BAT, S. [*bat*, or *batt*, Sax.] a kind of club, flat on one side towards the bottom, used in the game of cricket.

BAT, S. [from *bophat*, Arab.] an animal with the body of a mouse, and wings like a bird, consist of a membrane, which it extends in its flight; it produces and suckles its young like four-footed creatures, never grows tame, feeds on flies, insects, oily substances, such as candles, cheese, oil, &c. appears only in summer evenings. In Africa, they have tails as long as mice; at China, are as large as pullets, and are different eating; at Madagascar, they are said to be as large as foxes; and in Peru, are very dangerous on account of their getting into bed-chambers, and fastening on a person's legs, arms, &c. while sleeping, and bleeding him, unless prevented, to death.

BA'TCH, S. [*bac*, Sax.] the quantity of bread baked at once.

BA'TCHELOR, S. See BACHELOR.

BATE, V. A. [contracted from ABATE] to lessen, to lower the price. To abstain, or refrain from a thing. To except. "Bate but the last." Dryd. Neuterly, to grow less. To slacken or make slower, applied to motion, or passion. Used with the particle of, before the thing lessened.

BA'TH, S. [from *baðian*, Sax. to wash] a quantity of water collected into some convenient place for persons to wash in. They are divided into hot and cold. The *hot* bath is that whose waters are warm. The most celebrated of this kind in England are those near Wells, in Somersetshire, and owe their warmth to an admixture of sulphur, &c. and steel, with which they are impregnated. They produce a perspiration of 3 oz. in an hour, and are of great use in disorders of the head, palsy, diseases of the skin, scurvy, *&c.*

ftone, conftipations of the bowels, and moft chymical diforders. Cold bathing operates both by its coaftringing power, and its weight. It diffolves the blood; removes any vifcid matter; generates fpirits, fweats urine; and removes obftructions in the vifcera. To thefe we may add phyfical herbs, called aromas, when confifting of herbs boiled in fuch, when made of afhes, falt, &c. Vapour baths are thofe in which the body of the patient is not plunged, but only particular parts are expofed or held by the vapours which exhale from them. Knights of the Bath, are fo called from their being ufed to bathe before their creation; faid to have been inftituted by Richard II. extended by Henry IV. and revived by George I. his prefent majefty's noble grandfather and progenitor.

BATH, a town or city of Somerfetfhire, with the title of an earldom, and two markets on Wednefdays and Saturdays, and two fairs on February 3, and June 29, for cattle. It is famous for its hot baths, which draw every year a great number of polite company, partly for the fake of recovering their healths, and partly for diverfion. It is feated on the river Avon, over which there is a handfome ftone bridge, in a bottom, furrounded by fteep hills. Of late years it has been adorned with very handfome public and private buildings, and particularly a magnificent hofpital for the benefit of the poor, who are obliged to come thither for the fake of the waters. The fprings, or wells, are diftinguifhed by the names of the Crofs-bath, the Hot-bath, and the King's-bath. It is twelve miles E. N. E. of Briftol, 19 N. E. of Wells, and 108 W. of London. Long. 15. 5. lat. 51. 27.

BATTA'LIA, S. [from battaglia, Ital.] the drawing up an army in order of battle.

BATTA'LION, S. [bataillon, Fr.] a fmall body of infantry drawn up in order of battle.

BATTLE, a town in the county of Suffex, with a market on Thurfdays, and two fairs on Whitfun-Monday, and November 22, for cattle, and pedler's wares. It is feated in a dirty part of the county, and is famous for the decifive victory gained by William duke of Normandy, over Harold king of England, in 1066. It is eight miles N. of Haftings, 12 E. of Lewes, and 57 S. E. of London. Long. 18, 10. Lat. 50. 55.

BA'TTEN, S. a name given by workmen to a long, thin narrow piece of wood.

To BA'TTEN, V. A. [from batter, Teut.] to glue, or faiten; to grow fat; to live luxurioufly. Applied to land, to make fruitful.

To BATTER, V. A. [battre, Fr. to beat] to beat, or to beat down: to beat or wear out with blows or fervice.

BATTER, S. In cookery, a mixture of flour, eggs, and milk beaten together. It is called batter, on account of its being beaten.

BA'TTERY, S. one who batters; In fortification, a place where artillery is planted, to play upon the enemy. In Law, the beating any perfon unjuftly; the perfon fo injured has a right to indict the other party; but if the plaintiff made the firft affault, the defendant is difmiffed, and the plaintiff liable to be fined for his unjuft fuit.

BATTLE, S. [bataille, Fr.] an engagement between two armies. The fight of two individuals is improperly called a battle. A battle fuppofes a number on both fides. "In the battle's front." Chron's Leviath. Battle fometimes ftands for part, or a divifion of an army. But the word is ufed in this fenfe only by authors, whofe language is now become obfolete. However, the middle of an army goes univerfally by the name of the main body.

To BA'TTLE, V. A. [batailler, Fr.] to engage in battle, to contend.

BATTLE-ARRAY, S. arrangement, or proper difpofition of men to engage an enemy.

BA'TTLEDOOR, S. an inftrument to ftrike a fhuttle cock.

BA'TTLEMENTS, S. notches on the top of a tower, wall, parapet, &c. to look through.

BA'TTOLOGY, S. [βαττολογια, Gr.] a tedious circumlocution.

BA'TTON, S. a truncheon ftaff, borne by a marfhal as a mark of his dignity.

BAVARIA, a confiderable country of Germany, with a title of a dutchy. It is bounded on the N. by Bohemia, and the Upper Palatinate, on the E. by Auftria, the archbifhopric of Salifburg, and the bifhopric of Palfau, on the S. by the bifhopric of Brixen, and the Tyrol, and on the W. by the river Lech. It is about 125 miles in length from E. to W. and 37 in breadth from N. to S. The principal rivers are the Danube, the Ifon, the Ifer, and the Lech. The air is wholefome, and the foil fertile in wine, wheat, and good paftures; but the country is poor, becaufe it has little trade. It is divided into the upper and lower; and the duke is one of the electors fince the year 1623. We muft not confound the dutchy of Bavaria with the circle of that name, which is much more extenfive, comprehending, befides the former, the Upper Palatinate, the archbifhopric of Salifburg, the bifhopric of Freifingen, Paffau, and Ratifbon, and the dutchy of Newburg. It is bounded on the E. and S. by the circle of Auftria, and on the W. and N. by the circle of Franconia, Suabia, and Bohemia. The palatinate of Bavaria is part of Bavaria; and its capital is Amberg.

BAU'BLE, S. [from *baubella*] a plaything; a toy; a trifle.

BAW'D, S. [*boude*, Fr.] one who procures women for lewd purposes.

BAW'DILY, Adv. in an obscene, immodest manner.

BAW'DRY, S. [contracted from *bawdry*] the bringing persons together for immodest purposes. Applied to language, that which is obscene, and not fit for a modest person to hear.

BA'WDY, Adj. that which expresses unchaste ideas in plain terms.

BA'WDY-HOUSE, S. a place where strumpets and unchaste persons carry on their immodesty, and prostitution is practised.

To BA'WL, V. A. [*balo*, Lat.] to cry with a loud voice; a low term; and carries with it the idea of something mean and inelegant.

BA'Y, S. [*bay*, Fr.] applied to the colour, is that which inclines to red, and approaches near to a chesnut; horses of this kind have black manes, which distinguish them from sorrel.

BA'Y, S. [*baye*, Belg. *baia*, Ital.] in Geography, a part of the sea which runs into the land, and is broader in the middle than at the mouth.

BA'Y, S. [*baiare*, Ital. to bark, alluding to the barking of dogs at a stag in these circumstances] the state of one surrounded by enemies. In Botany, the *laurus*, a kind of evergreen, which formerly used to be formed into wreaths as a reward for poets, &c.

To BA'Y, V. N. [*aboy.r*, Fr.] to bark at; to surround.

BAY-SALT, S. salt made of sea water, exhaled by the heat of the sun, and derives its name from its colour.

BA'YONET, S. [*bayonette*, Fr.] a short dagger which goes over the muzzle of a musquet and fixes it on it.

BDE'LLIUM, S. a kind of aromatic gum, which drops from a tree resembling an olive; now brought from the Levant.

To BE, V. S [from *beon*, Sax.] an auxiliary verb by which we form the passive; sometimes used to affirm the state of a thing and at others the existence. To be reserved for a person future, in opposition to present. "Always to *be* blest." *Pope.*

BE'ACH, S. that part of the sea shore washed by its waves.

BE'ACHED, Adj. exposed to the waves.

BE'ACHY, Adv. abounding in beaches.

BE'ACON, S. [from *beacen*, or *beacn*, Sax.] a signal. Signals and marks erected to be seen at sea, for the security of vessels.

BE'ACONAGE, S. [from *beacon*] a tax for the maintenance of a beacon.

BE'AD, S. [*bead*, Sax.] small round pieces of glass, &c. moving on a string used by those of the Romish church to count their sins and prayers on. Likewise used as ornaments

round the necks of women. Figuratively, any thing of a round form. "*Beads* of sweat." *Shakesp.* In Architecture, a round moulding, carved to resemble a necklace.

BE'ADLE, [Belg. *bidelle*, Ital. *bidel*, Span.] in Law, a public crier, who cites people to appear; one whose office is to apprehend strollers, vagrants and petty offenders in a parish. At the university, one who walks before the masters in public processions. Squire beadles attend peculiarly on the vice chancellor.

BE'ADROLL, S. a catalogue of prayers for souls of the dead, which are generally counted on their *beads*.

BE'ADSMAN, S. one devoted to prayer; one who professes to pray for another.

BE'AGLE, S. [*bigle*, Fr.] an English hunting dog, of a smaller size, used in coursing hares.

BE'AK, S. [*bec*, Fr. *beck*] the bill of a bird. In Farriery, a little lhoe about an inch long turned up, and fastened to upon the fore part of the hoof. In Geography, a sharpe promontory, somewhat resembling the beak of a bird.

BE'AKED, Adj. sharp pointed.

BE'AL, S. [*bulla*, Ital.] a pimple, protuberance or any eruption in the skin.

To BE'AL, V. N. to ripen to come to a head. Seldom used.

BEA'LT, BEALTH, or BUILTH, a town of Brecknockshire, in South Wales, with a great market on Mondays for live cattle, and two lesser on Thursdays and Saturdays for provisions. There are also three fairs, on June 27, October 2, and December 6, for sheep, horned cattle, and horses. It is pleasantly seated on the river Wye, and consists of about 100 houses, whose inhabitants have a trade in stocking. It is 16 miles N. of Brecknock, 53 N. of Cardiff, and 91 S. of Chester. Lon. 3. 18. lat. 52. 4.

BEAMINSTER, or Bemifter, a town in Dorsetshire, with a market on Thursdays, and one fair on September 19, for horses, bullocks, sheep, and cheese. It is a pretty place, and is seated on the river Bert, and is four miles S. of Crookhorn, fifteen W. N. W. of Dorchester, and 133 W. by S. of London. Lon. 2. 50. lat. 52. 45.

BE'AM, S. [Sax. *beam*, Belg.] a large piece of timber, measuring more in length than thickness, supporting the principal rafters of the roof. There are generally two in a building, into which the girders of the garret floor, and if the building be of timber, the tenons of the posts are framed. Applied to a ballance, that piece of iron, &c. which supports the scales. The pole, or that piece of wood in a coach or chariot, which runs between the horses. Applied to a ship, the large main cross timbers, preventing the sides of a ship from
falling

falling together, and supporting the decks and orlops. Among weavers, a cylindrical piece of wood on which the threads of the warp are rolled, and enrol as the work advances; likewise the cylinder on which the stuff is rolled as it is weaved, placed on the fore part of the loom. A ray of light. The strait part or shank of an anchor, to which the hooks are fastened.

To BE'AM, V. N. [from *beam*, Sax.] to emit or dart rays of light or lustre.

BE'AMY, Adj. shining, radiant. Applied to deer, having horns.

BE'AN, S. [*bean*, *ban*, Sax.] in Botany, a kind of pulse. By the new husbandry, the produce of beans has exceeded the old, by more than ten bushels an acre.

To BEA'R, V. A. [pronounced as if the *e* was omitted, like the *a* in *dare*, the Preter is *bore* or *bare*, and the Part. Passive, *bore* or *born*, of *bæran*, Goth.] in its primary tense, to support, of carry a burden; to wear. Used with *up*, to support, sustain, or keep from falling. To endure; to permit, or suffer without resentment; to countenance, or encourage; to produce, or bring forth. Joined with *charge*, to defray or pay. "Somewhat that will *bear* your charges." *Pryd.* To behave, joined with *off*, to ward or defend from, or elude. "It cannot *bear off* a greater blow." *Hayes*. Likewise to carry away by violence, joined with *down*. "Justled, *bore down* one another." *Hayes*. Used with *hard*, to urge, press, or importune. "Cæsar doth *bear* me hard." *Shak*. Used with the particle *on*, to incite, stimulate, or sustain a person in an attempt. "Confidence then *bore* thee *on*." *Par. Lost*. Joined to *price*, to sell well, or at a certain value. Joined with *out*, to support, to maintain, to defend, to defend. Used neuterly, to endure the frowns of adversity; to suffer without complaint. To produce fruit, applied to vegetables. Used with *hit*, to behave or act. "*Bear hit*, a true friend." *Smel*. In Navigation, used with *in*, to fail towards. Used without the particle, to lay or be situated. Used with *upon* or *against*, to act or exert in action. Used with *up* and *against*, to oppose or struggle with.

BEA'R, S. a wild beast, with long shaggy hair, and hooked claws. In the winter they sleep, the male forty days, and the female four months, so as fierce to be wakened by blows, and though they fast all that while are fat. Their skins are used for housings, those of their young for muffs, and they are reckoned by the French a cure for the king's evil, rheumatism, and gout. In Astronomy, applied to two constellations in the N. hemisphere, called the *greater* and the *less*.

BEARALSTON, a town in Devonshire, that does not consist of 100 houses. It had a market on Thursday, which is now come

to nothing, and it has no fairs; but it sends two members to parliament. It is 10 miles N. of Plymouth, and 201 W. by S. of London. Lon. 4. 30. lat. 50. 25.

BE'ARD, S. [the *e* is pronounced long, as if the *a* was dropped, *beerd*, S.x.] the hair on a person's cheek, lips, and chin. Applied to vegetables, the prickles which grow on the ears of corn. In an arrow, it is the barb at the head. In a horse, that which bears the curb of the bridle. In Astronomy, the beard of a comet, is the rays emitted towards the part to which it moves. Used with the particle *to*, it signifies the face, and includes the idea of defiance. "Jeer'd —Their reverend persons to my *beard*." *Hud.*

To BE'ARD, V. A. to take one by the beard, including the idea of contempt; to oppose publicly.

BE'ARDED, Adj. a person who has a beard; applied to vegetables, that which has long ears; applied to instruments, that which is forked, jagged.

BE'ARDLESS, Adj. not having a beard. Figuratively, young, youthful.

BE'ARER, S. one who carries, or conveys a thing from one to another, peculiarly applied to a person who carries; one who wears, applied to dress; one who supports or sustains; that which produces or yields fruit, applied to vegetables. In Commerce, the person, who presents a bill for payment, and in whose favour, the last indorsement, if any, was made. In Heraldry, see SUP-PORTERS.

BEA'RING, S. the act of supporting or carrying a burden. In Geography and Navigation, the situation of a place, with regard to the points of the compass.

BE'AST, S. [pronounced as if the *a* was dropped, and the *e* doubled, *beste*, Fr.] an animal without reason, generally applied to those that are four-footed. Figuratively, one who acts inconsistent with the character of a rational creature; a term which carries with it the secondary idea of great detestation in the person using, and something inconsistent with humanity in him who causes it.

BE'ASTLINESS, S. that, which is unworthy of a man; indecency; nastiness.

BE'ASTLY, Adv. resembling a beast, either in its form, or flowing from a want of reason.

To BEAT, V. A. [*beten* and *beetan*, Sax.] to strike a person; to pound to powder; to forge; to subdue or vanquish. Used with the particle *down*, to depress; to lessen the price. Used with *head*, to apply one's thoughts. "Waste his time, and *beat* his head about the Latin Grammar," *Locke*. In this sense it is followed with *about*. Joined with *up*, and followed with *quarters*, to attack suddenly, to surprise or alarm. "By *beating up* his quarters." *Clarend.* Neuter-

ly, to move or throb, so as to affect the hand with a kind of stroke, applied to the pulse, or the heart.

BEAT, Part. Pass. violently attacked; struck; conquered.

BEAT, S. a stroke; a blow; the sound made by a drum; the throb of the pulse, or heart.

BEATEN, Part. Pass. [from beat] conquered; vanquished; often trod.

BEATEN, S. an instrument to strike blows; a pestle; one kind of punishing or striking. " The best school-master of our time was the greatest beater." Ascham.

BEATIFIC, or BEATIFICAL, Adj. [beatificus, Lat.] what renders a person completely happy; applied by divines to the joys of heaven.

BEATIFICATION, S. [from beatify] in the Romish church, an acknowledgment that a person is in heaven, but not allowed the honours of saints conferred by canonization. Applied, by demonstrators in electricity, to the glorious appearance a person makes in a dark room, when surrounded by a visible electrical atmosphere.

To BEATIFY, V. A. [from beatus, Lat.] to make completely happy; to bless; to acknowledge a person to be received in heaven, though not possessed of the dignity of a saint, 'a term used by the Romish clergy.

BEATING, S. punishment by blows.

BEATITUDE, S. [beatitudo, Lat.] in Divinity, a state of perfect happiness, applied to saints and angels in heaven. In the plural, applied to our Saviour's sermon on the mount, which begins with pronouncing blessedness or happiness to peculiar objects.

BEATS, S. in Clock-work, the strokes made by the spindle of the balance, or of the pads, in a royal pendulum.

BEAU, S. [Fr. pronounced bo] an effeminate man, who is passionately fond of dress, makes it his study and pride, to the neglect of improving the more noble part of him.

BEAVER, S. [pronounced as if the a was dropped and an e substituted in its stead, bievre, Fr.] an amphibious animal, about four feet long; its head resembles a mountain rat's, its snout is long, and its jaws furnished with ten large and sharp teeth, two of which are incisive and eight molar. The elegance of their building, the policy observed in their societies, and other curious particulars, may be seen in the Mem. of the Roy. Acad. of Sciences for 1704, the Spectacle de la Nature, &c. Figuratively, beaver is used for a hat.

BEAVERED, Adj. [from beaver] covered with or wearing a beaver hat.

BEAVISH, Adj. effeminately nice; foppish; tawdry.

BEAUMONT, [FRANCIS] and JOHN FLETCHER.

As these two gentlemen were, while living, the most inviolable friends and inseparable companions; as in their works also they were united, the Orestes and Pylades of the poetical world, it would be a kind of injury done to the manes of their friendship, should we here, after death, separate those names which before it were found for ever joined.—For this reason we shall, under this single article, deliver what we have been able to collect concerning both; yet, for the sake of order, it will be proper first to take some notice of those particulars which separately relate to each. First then, as his name stands at the head of this article, we will begin with

Mr. Francis Beaumont.—This gentleman was descended from a very ancient family of that name, seated at Grace-Dieu in Leicestershire. His grandfather, John Beaumont, had been master of the rolls, and his father, Francis Beaumont, one of the judges of the court of common pleas. Nor was his descent less honourable on the side of his mother, whose name was Anne, the daughter of George Pierrepoint, of Home Pierrepoint, in the county of Nottingham, Esq; and of the same family from which the present duke of Kingston derives his ancestry.

Our poet however appears to have been only a younger son, Jacob mentioning a brother of his by the title of Sir Henry Beaumont, though Cibber, in his Lives of the Poets, vol. i. p. 157. calls him Mr John Beaumont. He was born in the year 1585, and received his education at Cambridge, though in what college is a point which we have not been able to trace. He afterwards was entered a student in the Inner Temple. It is not however apparent that he made any great proficiency in the law, that being a study probably too dry and unentertaining to be attended to by a man of his fertile and sprightly genius. And indeed, we should scarcely be surprised to find that he had given no application to any study but poetry, nor attended on any court but that of the muses; but, on the contrary, our admiration might fix itself in the opposite extreme, and fill us with astonishment at the extreme assiduity of his genius and rapidity of his pen, when we look back on the voluminousness of his works, and then enquire into the time allowed him for them; works that might well have taken up a long life to have executed. For although, out of fifty-three plays, which are collected together as the labours of these united authors, Mr. Beaumont was concerned in much the greatest part of them, yet he did not live to complete his thirtieth year, the king of terrors summoning him away in the beginning

of March 1615, on the 9th day of which he was interred in the entrance of St. Benedict's chapel in Westminster abbey. He left behind him only one daughter, Mrs. Frances Beaumont, who must have then been an infant, as she died in Leicestershire since the year 1700. She had been possessed of several manuscript poems of her father's writing, but the curious Irish seas, which robbed the world of that invaluable treasure, the remaining part of Spencer's Fairy Queen, deprived it also of these poems, which were lost in her voyage from Ireland, in which kingdom she had resided for some time, in the family of the duke of Ormond.—Let us now proceed to our second author,

Mr. John Fletcher. This gentleman was not more intensly deserved than his poetical colleague. His father, the reverend Dr. Fletcher, having been first made bishop of Bristol by queen Elizabeth, and afterwards by the same monarch, in the year 1592, translated to the rich and honourable see of London. Our poet was born in 1576, and was, as well as his friend, educated at Cambridge, where he made a great proficiency in his studies, and was accounted a very good scholar. His natural vivacity of wit, for which he was remarkable, soon rendered him a devotee to the muses, and his close attention to their service and fortunate connection with a genius equal to his own, soon raised him to one of the highest places in the temple of poetical fame. As he was born near ten years before Mr. Beaumont, so did he also survive him by an equal number of years. The general calamity of a plague, which happened in the year 1625, involving him in its great destruction, he being at that time forty nine years of age.

During the joint lives of these two great poets, it appears that they wrote nothing separately excepting one little piece by each, which formed of two trivial a nature for either to require assistance in, viz. The Faithful Shepherd, a Pastoral, by Fletcher, and The Masque of Gray's-Inn Gentlemen, by Beaumont. Yet what share each had in the writing or designing of the pieces thus composed by them jointly, there is no possibility of determining. It is however generally allowed that Fletcher's peculiar talent was wit, and Beaumont's, though much the younger man, judgment. Nay, so extraordinary was the latter property in Mr. Beaumont, that it is recorded of the great Ben Johnson, who seems moreover to have had a sufficient degree of self-opinion of his own abilities, that he constantly, so long as this gentleman lived, submitted his own writings to his censure, and, as it is thought, availed himself of his judgment at least in the correcting, if not even in the conceiving all his plots.

It is probable therefore that the forming

the plots and contriving the conduct of the fable, the writing of the more serious and pathetic parts, and lopping the redundant branches of Fletcher's wit, whose luxuriance we are told, frequently stood in need of castigation, might be in general Beaumont's portion in the work, while Fletcher, whose conversation with the Beau monde which (indeed both of them from their births and stations in life had been ever accustomed to) added to the volatile and lively turn he possessed, rendered him perfectly master of dialogue and polite language, might execute the designs formed by the other, and raise the superstructure of those lively and spirited scenes which Beaumont had only laid the foundation of; and in this he was so successful, that though his wit and raillery were extremely keen and poignant, yet they were at the same time so perfectly genteel, that they used rather to please than disgust the very persons on whom they seemed to reflect.—Yet that Fletcher was not intirely excluded from a share in the conduct of the drama, may be gathered from a story related by Winstanley, viz. that our two bards having concerted the rough draught of a tragedy over a bottle of wine at a tavern, Fletcher said, he would undertake to kill the king, which words being over-heard by the waiter, who had not happened to have been witness to the context of their conversation, he lodged an information of treason against them. But on their explanation of it only to mean the destruction of a theatrical monarch, their loyalty moreover being unquestioned, the affair ended in a jest.

On the whole, the works of these authors have undoubtedly very great merit, and some of their pieces deservedly stand on the list of the present ornaments on the theatre. The plots are ingenious, interesting and well managed, the characters strongly marked, and the dialogue sprightly and natural, yet there in is the latter a coarseness which is not suitable to the politeness of the present age, and a fondness of repartee, which frequently runs into obscenity, and which we may suppose was the vice of that time; since even the delicate Shakespeare himself is not entirely free from it. But as these authors have more of that kind of wit than the last-mentioned writer, it is not to be wondered if their works were, in the licentious reign of Charles II, preferred to his. Now, however, to the honour of the present taste be it spoken, the tables are entirely turned, and while Shakespeare's immortal works are our constant and daily fare, those of Beaumont and Fletcher, though delicate in their kind, are only occasionally served up, and even then great pains is ever taken to clear them of that filth, which the bean gout of their contemporaries considered as their supremest relish, but which the more undepraved taste

of

of ours, has been justly taught to look on as what it really is, no more than a corrupted and unwholesome taint.

BEAUMARIS, a town of Anglesea, in North-Wales, with two markets, on Wednesdays and Saturdays, and four fairs, on Friday 13, Holy Thursday, September 19, and December 19, all for cattle. It stands on the Height Menay, and was fortified with a castle by Edward I. It is governed by a mayor, recorder, two baliffs, and twenty one common council men, and sends one member to parliament. Here the general and quarter-sessions are held, and the county goal is kept. It lies on the road from Chester to Holyhead, and was formerly a place of good trade, by means of its excellent harbour. Here is plenty of corn, butter, and cheese. It is 59 miles W. by N. of Chester, 27 E. of Holyhead, and 241 N. W. of London. Lon. 13. 15. lat. 53. 20.

BEAU'TEOUS, Adj. formed with elegance and symetry.

BEAU'TEOUSLY, Adv. so as to raise an idea of regular feature, sineness of shape, and elegance of complexion.

BEAU'TIFUL, Adj. having symmetry of parts necessary to convey the idea of beauty.

To BEAU'TIFY, V. A. [from beauty and fy, Lat.] to recommend any thing to the approbation of a person by heightening or increasing its charms. Applied to the endeavours of females to make their persons appear more agreeable by the advantage of dress. Used neuterly, to increase or advance in beauty.

BEAU'TY, S. [beauté, Fr.] that which raises delight and approbation in the beholder. Applied to Music, Morals, Painting, &c. implying an idea of excellence in the object capable of raising delight in the mind. A person blest with all that symmetry of features, beautiful contours of limbs, elegance of shape, and sweetness of complexion, that raise delight in the mind of a beholder, and extort approbation by its excellencies.

To BEAU'TY, V. A. to embellish, adorn, or make beautiful. "Beautify'd by plaist'ring art." Shakesp. Obsolete.

To BECA'LM, V. A. to reduce a storm to rest and quietness. ; To pacify turbulent passions. Though some have been so nice as to distinguish between calm and becalm, insinuating, that the former implies to stop motion, and the other to keep from motion, yet authors are so indeterminate in the use of these terms, that it would be impossible to understand them by such a key.

BECA'ME, the preter of become.

BECA'USE, Conj. used to imply a reason or cause. Used with of, it signifies the reason why a thing is, or is not, done.

BECCLES, a town in Suffolk, with a good market on Saturdays, and four fairs, on Holy-Thursday, June 29, and October 2, for petty chapmen ; as also, on July 15, for toys. It is a large town, with a handsome church, and a tall bulky steeple, seated on an eminence some distance from the church. Here the sessions for the liberty of Blithing, are commonly held. It is 15 miles S. W. of Yarmouth, 39 N. N. E. of Ipswich, and 107 N. E. of London.

To BECHA'NCE, V. N. to happen.

BE'CHICS, S. [βηχικα,] medicines to relieve a cough.

To BE'CK, V. A. [beacn, Sax.] to invite or call a person by a signal, or a nod.

BE'CK, S. (from the verb) external signs, generally made with the head, or hands.

To BECKEN, V. A. to make signs to a person to come to one.

To BE'COME, V. A. to grow ; to alter or change. Used with of, to happen. "What will become of me?" Dryd.

To BE'COME, V. A. to adorn, or grace. Applied to things, to suit, to be proper for, to agree, to be adapted.

BECO'MING, Part. suitable or proper. Sometimes used with the particle of, though seldom.

BECO'MINGLY, Adv. suiting the circumstances and rank of a person.

BED, S. [bed, Id. bedd, Sax.] a place for persons to sleep in or lly on. Figuratively, lodging, Marriage. In Gardening, a piece of made ground for raising plants ; the channel of any river. To be brought to bed of, to be delivered of, &c. To make a bed ; to lay the cloaths smooth, and make it fit to be laid on. Bed of a mortar, in Gunnery, a solid piece of oak hollowed in the middle to receive the breech, and half the trunnions. Applied to a gun, the thick plank lying immediately under the piece, and is, as it were, the body of the carriage.

To BED, V. A. [beddan, Teut.] to place in a bed ; to go to bed to, or with. To range, or lay things in order upon one another. Used with the particle with, to lie in the same bed with one another.

To BEDA'BBLE, S. to wet, so as to create uneasiness.

To BEDA'GGLE, to daub, or plash the bottom of a garment, by not holding it up ; and includes the idea of slovenry, or untidiness.

To BEDA'SH, V. A. [from be and dash] to scatter wet on a person by beating it with a stick, or casting a stone in it.

To BEDA'WB, V. A. to cover a thing with dirt. To apply or lay on paint in an ignorant manner.

To BEDA'ZZLE, V. A. to overpower the sight by too much lustre.

BED-CHAMBER, S. a room with a bed for sleeping in. Lords of the bedchamber are

ten

ten, of the first rank, who attend in their turns. The first of them is called the groom of the stole.

BED-CLO'ATHS, S. the blankets, quilt, coverlid, &c. on a bed.

To BEDE'CK, V. A. to set out or embellish a person with apparel.' To adorn; to grace.

To BE'DEW, V. A. to wet by sprinkling, alluding to the manner in which the dew moistens the earth.

BED-FELLOW, S. one who lies in bed with another.

BEDFORD, the county-town of Bedfordshire, with two markets on Tuesdays and Saturdays, and six fairs, on the first Tuesday in Lent, April 21, July 5, August 21, October 11, and December 19, for all sorts of cattle. Bedford is seated on the river Ouse, which divides it into two parts, which are united by a bridge with two gates, one at each end, to stop the passage occasionally. It has five churches, and formerly had a strong castle, whose site is now a very fine bowling-green. It is governed by a mayor, twelve aldermen, a recorder, two bailiffs, a town-clerk, and two serjeants at mace. The Tuesday-market is on the south side for cattle; and that on Saturday, on the north-side, for corn. It is 17 miles E. by N. of Buckingham, 52 E. N. E. of Oxford, 28 W. by S. of Cambridge, and 47 N. by W. of London. It has the title of a duchy, and sends two members to parliament. Lon. 17. 10. lat. 52. 6.

BEDFORDSHIRE is in the diocese of Lincoln, and is 24 miles long, and 16 broad. It contains 12,170 houses, 67,350 inhabitants, 116 parishes, 10 market-towns, and sends six members to parliament. It is a pleasant inland county, and is diversified with fruitful plains and rising hills, abounding in cattle, corn, and rich pastures; it is noted for barley, bone-lace, and a manufacture of straw.

To BEDI'GHT, V. A. to set off with clothes, dress, or other external ornaments.

To BEDI'M, V. A. to obscure by greater brightness.

BE'DING, S. [bedinge, Sax.] the bed-clothes which are on a bed stead.

BEDLAM, S. [formerly spelt Bethlehem, a religious house near Moor-gate, in London, now an hospital for mad people, בית־לחם, Heb. a house for the abode and cure of mad people. One who has lost his senses; a madman.

BE'DLAM, Adj. [from the noun] belonging to a mad-house.

BEDLAMI'TE, S. a mad person, a lunatic.

BED-MAKER, S. a person in the universities, who makes the beds, cleans the rooms, and runs of errands for the students.

BED-POST, S. the post which supports the tester or canopy.

To BEDRA'GGLE, V. A. to fill the lower part of a garment, by letting it drag in the dirt; a great sign of slutishness or slovenry.

To BEDRE'NCH, V. A. to wet or soak with a large quantity of some fluid.

BED-RI'D, Adj. confined to one's bed.

BED RI'DDEN, Adj. one who, being worn out by age, &c. and unable to quit his bed.

BE'DRITE, S. the marriage dues.

BEDU'NG, V. A. to cover or enrich with dung.

BEE, S. [beo, Sax. bi, Dan.] In natural history, a small insect well-known, remarkable for industry.

BE'ECH, S [bece, Sax.] a well-known tree. Also the sea-shore.

BE'ECHEN, Adj. [becens, Sax.] consisting of or belonging to beech.

BE'ER, S. [bere, Sax. bire, Germ.] a liquor made of malt and hops.

BE'EF, S. [boeuf, Fr.] the flesh of black cattle.

BE'EF-EATER, S. a yeoman of the king's guards.

BE'SOM, S. [besm, besma, Sax.] a household instrument. Also called a broom. It is used to sweep the dust off the floor.

BE'ET, S. [from beta, Lat.] a plant of which there are seven species.

BEE'TLE, S. [bytel, Sax.] an insect with four wings, the two outward being sheaths for the other; they are black, and abound in damp places. A great sledge. A wooden mallet.

To BEE'TLE, V. N. to jut out, project, or hang over.

BEE'TLE-HEADED, Adj. stupid, ignorant.

To BEFA'LL, V. N. to happen to a person.

To BEFI'T, V. A. to suit; to tally with; agree with.

To BEFO'OL, V. A. to delude; to deride; to play upon a person.

BEFO'RE, Prep. [beforan, Sax.] in the front, or fore-part.

BEFO'RE, Adv. earlier in time, prior to.

BEFO'RE-TIME, Adv. in ancient times, of old.

To BEFO'RTUNE, V. N. to happen to. Generally taken in good sense.

To BEFO'UL, V. A. to daub, smear, or soil.

To BEFRIE'ND, V. A. to do an act of kindness; to confer a favour.

To BEFRI'NGE, V. A. [a compound of be and fringe] to adorn or embellish with fringes.

To BEG, V. N. [beggeren, Teut.] to pray, request, intreat, petition, or crave charity, or assistance.

To BEGE'T, V. A. to generate, or bring forth, to produce.

BEGE'TTER, S. he that generates, or causes a woman to conceive a child.

BE'GGAR, S. one that begs or lives upon charity.

To BE'GGAR, V. A. (from the noun) to reduce a person from plenty and opulence to want.

BE'GGARLINESS, S. meanness; wretchedness; penury.

BE'GGARLY, Adj. indigent, mean.

BE'GGARLY, Adv. in a poor mean shiftt manner.

BE'GGARY, S. extreme poverty, wretchedness.

To BEGI'N, V. A. (began, pret. begun) to commence, to enter upon a thing.

BEGI'NNER, S. he that first begins the original.

BEGI'RT, Part. tied, or bound round.

To BEGUI'LE, V. A. (begeilan, Sax.) to impose upon, deceive, seduce.

BEGU'N, Part. Pass. of begin.

BEHA'LF, S. interest, side, party, favour.

To BEHA'VE, V. A. (behaeven, Lat.) to act, conduct, or carry one's self.

BEHA'VIOUR, S. conduct; deportment; manner.

To BEHE'AD, V. A. to cut off a person's head.

BEHE'LD, Part. Pass. from behold.

BEHE'ST, S. the positive and absolute commands of a superior; such as the orders of a parent, a king, and of the Deity.

BEHI'ND, Prep. (of be and hindan, Sax.) after; backwards. Opposed to forwards. Following, in opposition to before. Remaining, after a person's departure, or death. Applied to motion, at a distance from that which moves or goes before. Used comparatively, it implies great inferiority. Used adverbially, something not yet discovered, or perceived by the mind. "There is no evidence behind." Locke.

BEHI'ND-HAND, Adv. being in debt. Used with the particle with, not so eager as others in undertaking a thing, but after them some time. Used as an adjective in this sense by Shakespeare, "my behind-hand slackness."

BE'HN, S. in pharmacy; the name of two roots, from which excellent cordials and restoratives are made. They are most plenty in the Levant, and chiefly about Mount Lebanon.

BEHN, [Mrs. APHARA, or APHRA.] Some kind of a dispute has arisen in regard to this lady's christian name, in consequence of Langbaine's having attributed that of Astraea to her as a real name, which was indeed no more than a poetical one, by which she was known and addressed by her contemporaries. She was a gentlewoman by birth, being descended from a very good family, whose residence was in the city of Canterbury. She was born some time in Charles I's reign, but in what year, is uncertain. Her father's name was Johnson, who, through the interest of the lord Willoughby, to whom he was related, being appointed lieutenant-general of Surinam, and six and thirty islands, undertook a journey to the West-indies, taking with him his whole family, among whom was our poetess, at that time very young. Mr. Johnson died in the voyage, but his family reaching Surinam, settled there for some years.

'Here it was that she learned the history of, and acquired a personal intimacy with, the American prince Oroonoko, and his beloved Imoinda, whose adventures she herself so pathetically related in her celebrated novel of that name, and which Mr. Southerne afterwards made such an admirable use of in making it the ground-work of one of the best tragedies in the English language. Her intimacy with this prince, and the interest she took in his concerns, added to her own youth and beauty, afforded an opportunity to the ill-natured and censorious to accuse her of a nearer connection with him than that of friendship. This, however, a lady of her acquaintance, who has prefixed some memoirs of her life to an edition of her novels, takes great pains, and I think very much to the purpose, to acquit her of.

On her return to London, she became the wife of one Mr. Behn, a merchant, residing in that city, but of Dutch extraction. How long he lived after their marriage, is not very apparent, probably not very long; for her wit and abilities having brought her into high estimation at court, king Charles II. fix'd on her as a proper person to transact some affairs of importance abroad during the course of the Dutch war. To this purpose she went over to Antwerp, where, by her intrigues and gallantries, she so far crept into the secrets of state, as to answer the ends proposed by sending her over. Nay, in the latter end of 1666, she, by means of the influence she had over one Vander Albert, a Dutchman of eminence, whose heart was warmly attached to her, she wormed out of him the design formed by De Ruyter, in conjunction with the family of the De Wits, of sailing up the Thames, and burning the English ships in their harbours, which they afterwards put in execution at Rochester. This she immediately communicated to the English court, but though the event proved her intelligence to be well grounded, yet it was at that time only laughed at; which together, probably, with no great inclination shewn to reward her for the pains she had been at, determined her to drop all farther thoughts of political affairs, and, during the remainder of her stay

at Answer, to give herself up entirely to the gaiety and gallantries of the place. Vander Albert continued his addresses, and after having made some unsuccessful attempts to obtain the possession of her person on easier terms than matrimony, at length consented to make her his wife; but while he was preparing at Amsterdam for a journey to England with that intent, a fever carried him off, and left her free from any amorous engagements. She was also strongly solicited by a very old man, of the name of Van Bruin, at whose expence she diverted herself for a time, and then rejected him with that ridicule which his absurd addresses justly merited.

In her voyage back to England, she was very near being lost, the vessel she was in being driven on the coast by a storm, but happened to founder within sight of land, the passengers were, by the timely assistance of boats from the shore, all fortunately preserved.

From this period she devoted her life entirely to pleasure and the muses. Her works are extremely numerous, and all of them have a lively and amorous turn. It is no wonder then, that her wit should gain her the esteem of Mr. Dryden, Southerne, and other men of genius, as her beauty, of which in her younger part of life she possessed a great share, did the love of those of gallantry. Nor does she appear to have been any stranger to the delicate sensations of that passion, as appears from some of her letters to a gentleman, with whom she corresponded under the name of Lycida, and who seems not to have returned her flame with equal ardor, or received with that rapture her charms might well have been expected to command.

Her works, as I have before observed, were very numerous, consisting of plays, novels, poems, letters, &c.

As to the character her plays should maintain in the records of dramatic history, it will be difficult to determine, since their faults and perfections stand in strong opposition to each other. In all, even the most indifferent of her pieces, there are strong marks of genius and understanding. Her plots are full of business and ingenuity, and her dialogue sparkles with the dazzling lustre of genuine wit, which every where glitters among it. But then she has been accused, and that not without great justice, of interlarding her comedies with the most indecent scenes, and giving an indulgence in her wit to the most indelicate expressions. To this accusation she has herself made some reply, in the preface to the Lucky Chance; but the retorting the charge of prudery and preciseness on her accusers, is far from being a sufficient exculpation of herself. The bell, and perhaps the only true excuse that can

be made for it is, that although she might herself have as great an aversion as any one to loose scenes or too warm descriptions, yet, as she wrote for a livelihood, she was obliged to comply with the corrupt taste of the times. And, as she was a woman, and naturally, moreover, of an amorous complexion, and wrote in an age and to a court of gallantry and licentiousness, the latter circumstances, added to her necessities, compelled her to indulge her audience in their favourite depravity, and the former, assisted by a rapid flow of wit and vivacity, enabled her so to do; so that both together have given her plays the loose cast, which it is but too apparent they possess.

Her own private character we shall give in the words of one of her own female companions, who, in the memoirs before-mentioned, prefixed to her novels, spoke of her thus. " She was," says this lady, " of a generous humane disposition, something passionate, very serviceable to her friends in all that was in her power, and could sooner forgive an injury than do one. She had wit, humour, good-nature, and judgment: she was mistress of all the pleasing arts of conversation: she was a woman of sense, and consequently a lover of pleasure. For my part I knew her intimately, and never saw ought unbecoming the just modesty of our sex; though more gay and free, than the folly of the precise will allow."

After a life intermingled with numerous disappointments, which a woman of her sense and merit ought never to have met with, and in the close of a long indisposition, Mrs. Behn departed from this world, on the 16th of April 1689, and lies interred in the cloyster of Westminster abbey, under a blue marble stone, against the first pillar in the east ambulatory, with the following inscription:

MRS. APHRA BEHN,
Died April the 16th,
1689.
Here lies a proof that wit can never be
Defence enough against mortality.

Revived by Tho. Waine, in respect to so bright a genius.

To BEHOLD, V. A. [*beholden*, Sax.] to observe a person; to have a person in sight.

BEHO'LD, an interjection similar to that of *lo*.

BEHO'LDEN, Part. Indebted to; lying under an obligation to a person for favours conferred.

BEHO'LDER, S. one who sees or casts his eyes upon an object.

BEHO'OF, S. [from *behove*, *b-list*, Sax.] an obligation, the profit, or advantage which may accrue from a thing.

To BEHO'OVE, V. N. [from *behofab*, Sax.]

4

Sax) to be incumbent as a duty, to be fit and suitable. This term is sometimes used by modern authors; tho' it begins to grow antiquated.

BEING, the *participle* of the verb *to be*.

BEING, S. a term, signifying the exillence of a thing: thus we say, the Supreme *Being*; an infinite *Being*; a finite *Being*.

To BELABOUR, V. A. to strike; to beat a person severely.

To BELACE, V. A. in navigation, to fasten; to *lace a rope*. *Johnson*.

BELA'FED, Adj. benighted. Too late.

To BELAY, V. N. to lie in ambush, or in wait for.

To BELAY, V. A. [*beleggen*, Belg.] to mend a rope, by laying one end over another.

To BELCH, V. A. [*bealcan*, Sax.] to break wind upwards.

BELCH, S. the act of breaking wind upwards.

BELDAM, [from *belle dame*, Fr.] a name given irreverently to an old woman.

To BELEAGUER, V. A. [*beleggeren*, Belg.] to block up a place, or besiege.

BELEMNITES, [from *βέλος*,] in natural history, arrow-head or finger-stone, of a whitish colour. It is about the size of a finger, more or less round, of a pyramidal form, variable, of the nature of chalk, and a fossil.

To BELIE, V. A. [a compound of *be* and *lie*, *beleogan*, Sax. *beliegen*, Belg. and Teut.] to invent a falsehood; to feign; to charge with falshood; to calumniate, and to misrepresent; to accuse a person falsely; to represent under a feigned appearance. " A dragon's form *bely'd* the God." *Hastes*.

BELLAMITE, S. [*belle amie*, Fr.] a dear friend. The term is now obsolete.

BELLAMOUR, S. [*belle amour*, Fr.] a gallant. Obsolete.

BELL-FLOWER, S. [*bell* and *flower*, because it is shaped like a bell] a plant, by botanists called *campanula*. Its empalement has five acute parts; the flower is of one leaf, shaped like a bell; and in the bottom is a five cornered nectarium. There are thirteen species.

BELL-FOUNDER, S. a person who casts bells.

BELFRY, S. that part of the steeple of a church in which bells are rung, probably a corruption of the French word *beffroy* a steeple, or tower of a church.

BELL-GARD, S. [*belle regard*, Fr.] a soft glance; a kind of languishing look. Now obsolete.

BELIEF, S. [pronounced as if written *beleef*, *geloofe*, Sax.] to credit, the assent of the mind to, arguments used to persuade us to receive any proposition for truth, without certain knowledge that it is so: that which causes *belief*, is something not evidently joined to, or shewing the agreement or dif-

agreement of those ideas under consideration. Thus, in a general sense, it implies an assent of the mind to any proposition; in a restrained sense, an assent founded on the authority, &c. of a person asserting the truth of a thing. When the revelation of God is the object, it is called divine belief; when that of a man is the object, it is then *human belief*. The articles assented to by a person. The heads of a person's religion; the things believed.

To BELIEVE, V. A. [*gelasfan*, Sax.] to assent to a proposition merely on the credit or authority of the proposer. Opposed to *know*, which implies an assent built on irrefragable arguments, connected with, and flowing from the nature of the thing; wherein the connexion of each intermediate idea is visible and certain. To put a confidence in the veracity or truth of any one, " *Believe in* for ever." *Exod.* xix. 9. When used neuterly, to have a firm persuasion of a thing which is probable. Used with the particle *in*, it implies a strong assent to the truth of a proposition.

BELIEVER, S. a person who gives credit to a thing. One who assents to the truth of christianity, in opposition to one who refuses his assent, demands demonstrative proof, and is, on that account, stiled an *unbeliever*, or infidel.

BELIEVINGLY, Adv. after such a manner as shews that a person credits or assents to the truth of any proposition or doctrine.

BELIKE, Adv. perhaps; probably; made use of to shew that the sentence it is joined with is uncertain. Sometimes used as a mark of irony, or jeer.

BELL, S. [*bell*, Sax.] a machine, or vessel, ranked by musicians among the instruments of percussion; made of a compound metal of tin and copper, or pewter or copper. Its sound arises from a vibratory motion of its parts, like that of a musical chord; for the stroke of the clapper changing its circumference from a round to a spherical form, which by elasticity endeavouring to recover its former shape, undergoes alternate changes of figure, and by that means gives a tremulous motion to the air, in which sound consists. That of Nankin in China, weighs 50,000lb, double the weight of that at Erfurt, is 12 English feet high, and 7 1 half diameter, and 23 in circumference; and Le Comte says, that at Pekin, there are 7 other weighing 120,000 lb. each. The Turks have an aversion to bells, and prohibit christians the use of them in Constantinople. The cups of flowers, from their resembling a bell in their shape. *To bear the bell*, is to surpass others; alluding to the wether which wears a bell, and is followed by the flock; or to the first packhorse of a drove, who has bells on his collar.

To BELL, V. N. in botany, to grow in the shape or form of bells.

BELL

BELL FA'SHIONED, Adj. resembling a bell in its shape, being hollow, and small at one end, and increasing at the other.

BE'LLE, S. [from *belle* Fr.] a female who dresses elegantly, and has all the polite accomplishments that can adorn her.

BE'LLES LETTERS, S. those branches of education that adorn the mind, are of service to men as focial creatures, and accomplish them to shine in conversation, or to make a figure in the highest polls of government Languages, classical learning, geography, rhetoric, chronology, and history may be accounted the principal parts of learning under this term.

BELLI'GERANT, Part. [from *bellum*, Lat. war, and *gerens*, Lat. waging] a modern term, that which is at war; that which is engaged in war. " The *belligerant* powers," which is proper.

BELLI'GEROUS, Adj. engaged in, or relating to war.

BELLO'NA, S. in mythology, the fister of Mars and goddess of war.

To BE'LLOW, V. A. [*bellan*, Sax.] to make a loud noise; as that of a bull, the fea in a storm, or outcries of human creatures.

BE'LLOWS, S. [*belg*, Sax. it has no fingular.] an instrument, into which air is drawn, and expelled out of a metal tube called its nozzle. Their use in increasing the power of fire is well known. The reason affigned by the author of the Spectacle of Nature, from their driving away the aqueous particles of the coals, is indeed very pretty, but not sufficient to account for this phenomenon of itself; and perhaps not consistent with fact. This term is generally joined with *pair* when we would use it as a fingular noun, *a pair of bellows*; and in this sense, Dryden says, *a bellows*; by an ellipsis, without which he is guilty of a very great impropriety.

BE'LLY, S. [*belig*, Sax. *balg*, *bælch*, Belg.] that part of the body which contains the entrails, bowb to men and beasts. Used figuratively, for gluttony, or luxury in eating. The protuberant part in any vessel. The womb, entrails, or the middle of any hollow place.

To BE'LLY, V. N. to fwell; to protuberate; to be larger in one part than it is in another.

BE'LLY-ACHE, a pain in the belly, the cholic.

BE'LLY-FULL, S. a fufficiency of food, or as much as fatisfies the appetite.

BE'LLY-ROLL, S. in hufbandry, a roller, ufal to roll ground after it is ploughed.

BE'LL-MAN, S. in London, a fuperior kind of watchman, with a bell which he rings at certain places in his parish, before he repeats fome verses on the eves of a festival. In country towns, applied to the cryer, who bears a bell which he rings, to give notice to

No. IV.

the neighbourhood, before he makes his proclamation.

BE'LL-METAL, S. the metal out of which bells are made, consisting of 20 lb. of pewter, or 23 lb. of tin, to 100 wt. of copper.

To BE'LOCK, V. A. to join or fasten one thing into another, so as it cannot be easily feparated.

To BELONG, V. N. [*behoogen*, Belg.] to be the property of a person. To have relation to; to be dependd on. " To whom *belong*st thou." 1 Sam. xxx. 13. To be appropriated to; to have for its peculiar object. " The things that *belong* to the Lord." 1 Cor. vii. 32. Used in all these sentes with the particle *to*.

BELO'VED, Part. esteemed careful with the greatest warmth of affection. In Divinity, an object worthy of the greatest condidence on account of his fidelity, or the highest approbation on account of its merit, and of the warmest ardours of love, on account of the immensity of its benevolence, and the stupendousnets of his endearments. " This is my *beloved* son." Matt. iii. 17. and xvii. 5. Mar. i. 11. and ix. 7. Luke iii. 22.—ix. 35.

BELO'W, Prep. not so high as another object, inferior, unbecoming on account of its meannefs; unfit or degrading. " 'Tis much *below* me." Dryd. In a lower situation, near to the earth. On earth, when oppofed to heaven.

BELSWA'GGER, S. one who bluflers, noife, and puts on an air of importance. Johnson interprets it a whore-mafter.

BE'LT, S. [*belt*, or *belte*, Sax.] a girdle to fasten round a person's middle. In Farming, a distemper in sheep. In Astronomy, two bright marks like girdles furrounding the body of the planet jupiter, brighter than the rest of his disk, and varying both in their dimensions and situations.

BE'LWETHER, S. a sheep, which draws the rest after him by the sound of a bell hanging to his neck.

To BEMA'D, V. A. to deprive a person of the right use of his reafon; to make a person rave. " Bemadding, forrows." Shakesp.

To BEMI'RE, V. A. to daub, or fmear with dirt.

BEMI'RED, Part. covered with dirt or foil. Stuck in a dirty or boggy place, applied to a horfe.

To BEMO'AN, V. A. [*bemænan*, Sax.] to express grief or forrow for any calamity, including the idea of tears, and pity.

BEMO'ANER, S. one who pities and laments, at the difasters of another.

To BEMU'IL, V. A. [*souiller*, Fr.] to bedaub, to fall, to be rolled in the dirt.

To BEMO'NSTER, V. A. to make a thing hideous, horrible, or monftrous.

BEMU'SED, Adj. addicted to rhiming or poetry.

BE'NCH, S. [from *benc*, *benct*, Sax.] a feat

feat made of a long board. The feat where an judge, &c. fit; figuratively, the perfons fitting on it, &c. uſed.

To BENCH, V. A. to erect, or make bench. To feat or prefer a perſon to a feat on bench.

BENCHERS, S. [from bench] in Law, the ſenior barriſters of inns of court, intruſted with the government and direction of it. A perſon muſt have been a reader, and admitted to plead within the bar, before he acquires the honour of this title.

To BEND, V. A. [Prev. and Part. preter bended or bent, like the Ill. bende] to force from a ſtraight line to a curve. The object to which a motion is directed. Figuratively, to apply the mind to any particular ſubject. To be diſpoſed to. To make ſubmiſſive; to bring to terms. In Navigation, to faſten; " Bend the cable," is to faſten it to the ring of the anchor. Uſed neuterly, to looſen a ſtraight ſhape, by means of ſome weight or force. To hang, or jut over. " A cliff, whoſe high and bending head," Uſed with the particles or upon, to be ſtrongly inclined to or reſolved on. To bow the body, or knees in token of reſpect.

BEND, S. the part of a line, &c. which forms an angle. The crooked timbers which compoſe the ſides of a ſhip. In Heraldry, an ordinary or bearing, made by two lines drawn across a ſhield, from the upper part on the right to the lower on the left.

BENDABLE, Adj. that which may be bent, or make crooked.

BENDER, S. one who crooks any thing; that which forces a ſtraight to a crooked line. The circular piece of wood, which forms the top of a bow's hire.

BENDY, Adj. [bendé, Fr.] in Blaſonry, the dividing an eſcutcheon into an equal number of partitions; if they be odd, the field muſt firſt be named and then the number of bends.

BENEAPED, Adj. a ſea term, implying that a ſhip has not the depth of water ſufficient to ſet her a float.

BENEATH, Prep. [beneath, be-neban, Sax.] not ſo high as, or under, ſomething elſe. Applied to rank or dignity, inferior to. Applied to actions, not becoming; unworthy of a perſon. " Nothing beneath his high ſtation." Attrib. Uſed adverbially, or without a noun after it, in a lower place, or under, oppoſed to upon. Below, in Scripture, oppoſed to above. " In heaven above, or in the earth beneath." Exod. xx. 4.

BENEDICT, S. [Biſhop] a famous abbot in the 7th century, deſcended of a noble family among the Saxons, and flouriſhed under Oſui and Egfrid, kings of Northumberland. In his 24th year he abandoned all temporal views, in order to devote himſelf to religion; and by his frequent voyages did

not a little contribute to introduce the polite arts into this iſland. Architecture, painting, muſic, and other arts, received great improvements from thoſe artiſts he brought over with him from Rome and France; and what added no ſmall commendation to him, was, that all his embelliſhments were appropriated to the ſervice of the church. Chanting in choirs was introduced by him in 678. He founded two very confiderable monaſteries, lived an exemplary life, and enjoyed one quality ſeldom to be met with in a ſaint, a refined taſte joined to a remarkable auſterity.

BENEDICTINES, S. an order of Monks, who wear a black gown, with large wide ſleeves, and a capuche on their heads, and were in England named Black Friars. No religious order has been ſo remarkable for wealth, extent, and number of ſons; nor can any boaſt of a nobler liſt of members.

BENEDICTION, S. [from benedictio, Lat.] a devout prayer to the Deity to beſtow bleſſings on a perſon, generally applied to the bleſſing of a biſhop. Happineſs acquired by, or owing to a bleſſing. In the Romiſh church, the form of making a biſhop, called conſecration.

BENEFACTION, S. [of benefactum, ſupine of benefacio, Lat.] a good and benevolent action; a charitable gift.

BENEFACTOR, S. the perſon who confers a benefit; generally applied to thoſe who leave and endow alms-houſes, ſchools, and colleges. Sometimes to thoſe who in a public capacity contribute to the benefit and advantage of a nation.

BENEFACTRESS, S. a woman or female, who confers a benefit.

BENEFICE, S. [beneficium, Lat.] a church endowed with a reward or ſalary for the performance of divine ſervice, or the ſalary itſelf, given on that account.

BENEFICED, Adj. having, or poſſeſſing a church-living.

BENEFICENCE, S. [from beneficentia] a diſintereſted inclination to promote the welfare of another; diſtinguiſhed from charity as diſtreſs is the object of that; but all perſons may be the objects of this; it differs from benignity or humility, which is reſtrained to the diſpoſition of the mind, but this always includes action.

BENEFICENT, Part. [beneficus, Lat.] performing diſintereſted acts of kindneſs, and aſſiſtance.

BENEFICIAL, Adj. [from beneficium, Lat.] that which relieves, or is of ſervice.

BENEFICIALLY, Adv. in ſuch a manner as to relieve, or aſſiſt.

BENEFICIARY, Adj. holding any dignity, as tributary to another, Uſed ſubſtantively, it implies one who is in poſſeſſion of a church living, or benefice. " The bene-
ſiciary

fixtory is obliged to serve the parish churches."
Ayliffe.

BENEFIT, S. [from *bene*, and *fo*, Lat.] that which advantageth, or turns to the profit of another. An act of kindness, to assist another. Among players, all that is received at the theatre, which are applied to their own use. In Law, *benefit* of the clergy, was an antient liberty of the church, whereby any priest might on his petition, even in the case of murder, be delivered to his ordinary, in order to purge himself. It is at present confined to signify a person's being only burnt in the hand for felony.

To BENEFIT, V. A. to do something whereby another may receive advantage To promote, increase, or render better. "Far from *benefiting* trade." *Arbuth.* To improve; to reap advantage from.

BENEVOLENCE, S. [from *benevolentia*, Lat.] a disposition of mind, to do another all the good we can, without any views of interest; the good deed proceeding from this disposition.

BENEVOLENT, Part. [from *benevolens*, Lat.] inclined to do good, without any views of interest.

BENGAL, a country of Asia, in India, lying near the mouth of the river Ganges, bounded on the N. by the provinces of *Patna*, and *Jesuat*; on the E. by the kingdoms of Arracan, and Tipra; on the S. by the bay of Bengal, and the province of Orissa; and on the W. by the provinces of *Narvar* and *Malva*; being about 400 miles in length from E. to W. and 300 in breadth from N. to S. In this province, the English, Dutch, and French, have factories; and the principal of that of the English, is call d Calcutta, or Fort St. George. This country has the same advantage as Egypt, which is annually overflowed by the river Nile; for this is watered in the same manner by the Ganges. The inhabitants are chiefly Gentoows, whose women had a custom of burning themselves with their dead husbands; but this practice is now greatly restrained, by the authority of the Great Mogul. It is governed by a Nabob, one of whom lately took Fort St. George, and committed great cruelties among the people of the factory; but he has since been deposed, and killed, and there is now a friend to the English in his room. In general, Bengal is a fruitful, pleasant country, by some esteemed a sort of earthly paradise, and it lies very convenient for carrying on a trade with the parts round about it, and for purchasing their various commodities and manufactures.

BENJAMIN, S. (*benzoin*) In Pharmacy, a gum of a tree, abounding in Cochin China, resembling the almond. The gum is both in drops and lumps, the former of which is the true, of a yellow, or gold colour without, and white within, friable, without any taste,

and aromatic. The best comes from Sumatra. It is a great and powerful expectorant, and given in asthmas, intentions of the lungs, and inveterate coughs.

To BENIGHT, V. A. to be overtaken by darkness. To wander in the dark.

BENIGN, Adj. [from *benignus*] inclinable to do good. Kind, generous, or liberal. In Medicine, wholesome, gentle. "Salts of a *benign*, mild nature." *Arbuth.* Applied to a disease, when all the symptoms of it are favourable.

BENIGNITY, S. [*benignitas*, Lat.] a disposition to be kind, or humane to another.

BENIGNLY, Adv. In such a manner as to shew kindness, humanity, and condescension.

BENISON, S. [*benisson*, Fr.] a blessing. A rapture of joyful gratitude on account of some benefit received.

BENT, S. [from *bend*, Ifl.] that part which is forced from a straight line; that which forms an angle. The declivity, or slope of a hill. "On a *bent*, the temple stood." *Dryd.* After the word *full*, stretch applied to the purpose, in alluring to the stretching a bow; propensity or inclination, applied to the affections, with the particle *of* before the affection. Tendency, or the different appearances of an object.

To BENUM, V. A. [from *benyman*, Sax.] to destroy the sense of feeling, applied to the effect of cold upon the body; or the approach of death.

To BEPAINT, V. A. to cover with colours. Figuratively, to change the colour of the complexion. "Else would a maiden blush *bepaint* my cheek." *Shak.*

To BEPISS, V. A. to be unable to hold or retain one's urine.

To BEQUEATH, V. A. to leave, or give a person any thing by will.

BEQUEST, S. something left by will; a legacy.

To BEREAVE, V. N. [preter *bereaved*, or *bereft* from *bereafan*, Sax.] to take forcibly away. To spoil; to rob; to strip a person of his property.

BEREAVEMENT, S. the act of leaving a person destitute of any thing.

BEREFT, part. passive of *bereave*.

BERGAMOT, S. [*bergamotte*, Fr.] a fine juicy pear, of a globular form. An essence or perfume, drawn from the fruit of a lemon-tree ingrafted with the stock of a bergamot pear tree. The original inventor of this essence, acquired no small fortune from the secret. Likewise a kind of snuff, of a large grain.

BEROMOTE, S. [from *berg*, and *mot*, Sax.] a court held on a hill in Derbyshire, to decide the controversies between the miners.

            X 2   BERK-

BERKSHIRE, an English county, 39 miles in length, and 25 in breadth. It is bounded on the N. by Oxfordshire and Buckinghamshire, on the W. by Wiltshire, on the S. by Hampshire and Surrey, and on the E. by Middlesex and part of Buckinghamshire. It contains 140 parishes, 12 market-towns, and 16608 houses. The principal town is Reading. In general it is a fruitful country, and particularly in the vale of the White Horse; and it has the title of an earldom.

To BERHYME, V. A. to make a person the subject of a poem.

BERME, S. [Fr.] In Fortification, a piece of ground from 3 to 5 feet wide, left between the rampart and the moat.

BERMUDAS, S. [from Bermudas, a Spaniard, who discovered them in 1552, likewise named Summers islands, from Sir G. Summers, who took possession of them in 1609] a cluster of islands in the Atlantic Ocean; in lat. 32 deg. N. and long. 63, deg 48 min. W. St. George is the most considerable of them, where the number of English is computed at 10,000, besides slaves. The climate is temperate; their chief growth is in Indian wheat and tobacco, the bitter of which is very indifferent. Their cedars excel those of any other country, either for their fragrancy, durableness, or hardness; and are so abundant, that they build their vessels of them, which are reckoned the best sailors of any in all the West Indies. They have fish in great plenty, amongst which the fork-fishes are so numerous, that the inhabitants almost live entirely upon them.

To BEROB, V. A. to steal; to rob.

To BERRY, V. N. to produce berries.

BERTRAM, S. [pyrethrum, Lat.] in Botany, an herb, named also bastard pellitory.

BERWICK, a town on the borders of England and Scotland, which properly belongs to neither, with a market on Saturdays, and one fair, on Friday in Trinity-week, for black cattle and horses. It is a town and county of itself, and is a place of great strength; its wall hewn nude as its being defended with walls, a castle, and other fortifications. It is large, populous, and well built, and has a good trade in corn and salmon. It is seated on the river Tweed, over which there is a very handsome bridge of fixteen arches. It sends two members to parliament, and has the title of a dutchy. It is 347 miles N. of York, and E. S. E. of Edinburgh, and 339 N. by W. of London. Lon. 1, 5, gr. lat. 13, 4.

BERYL, S. [beryllus, Gr. beryon, Lat.] a precious transparent stone, like chrystal, found in the mines of the Indies. It inclines a little to a sea-green, and we from thence called aqua marine; to make it more sparkling and white, it must be cut feries-wise, as it receives no brightness from the polish. It is

and the fifth stone in the breast-plate of the Jewish high priest.

To BESCREEN, V. A. to conceal, or hide any thing.

To BESEECH, V. A. [bitten beseochen; I pray beseechen; from be and seech, Sax.] to intreat earnestly; to ask for as a great favour.

To BESEEM, V. N. [ziemen, Belg.] to suit. To beseem, to be worthy of.

To BESET, V. A. [preter I beset; I have beset, bisetan, Sax.] to surround, alluding to an enemy's surrounding a body of men. Used with hard, or sore, to oppress, perplex, or embarrass. To lay in wait, to endanger, to encompass.

To BESHUT, V. A. [beschutten, Belg.] to shut out; experiments.

To BESHREW, V. A. [from beshrew, Teut.] to wish any calamity to a person. "I beshrew the sloth." Dryd.

BESIDE, or BESIDES, Prep. [from be and side, Sax.] by, or at the side, or near. "Beside him hung his bow." Parad. Lost. Something more, over and above. "Great numbers; besides those whose names are in the Christian records." Addif. Before a reciprocal pronoun, it implies the loss of reason. "Thou art beside thyself." Acts. Something more than what has been mentioned; the rest; or that which has not been mentioned.

To BESIEGE, V. A. to surround, or attack a place, in order to conquer it.

BESIEGER, S. a person who besieges.

To BESMEAR, V. A. [of smearan, Sax.] to daub with any thing which alters the colour of a thing, to tarnish, or deprive of its lustre, applied to character. "Would not let ingratitude—so much besmear it." Shak.

To BESMOKE, V. A. to foul, or dry in smoke.

To BESMUT, V. A. [from be and smut, Sax.] to smear with any thing black, especially with smoke, soot, &c.

BESOM, S. [besm, bisem, Sax.] an instrument used by housewives to sweep their floors clean, by the Londoners generally called a broom.

To BESORT, V. A. to suit; to be fit, become; or agree with. "Such men as may besort your age." Shak.

To BESOT, V. A. to stupify with drunkenness. To be extremely in love with. "Besotted on that face and eyes." Dryd.

BESOUGHT, part. pass. of Beseech.

To BESPANGLE, V. A. to make a thing shine or glitter.

To BESPATTER, V. A. to cast small quantities of water. To tarnish the character of a person. "Whom never faction could bespatter." Swift.

To BESPAWL, V. A. to daub with spittle.

To

To BESPEAK, V. A. [pronounced as if written with ee, *bespeek*, preter, *I bespoke*, or *I bespake* ; I *boren bespoken*, or *bespoken* ; from *be*, *be*, and *speken*, Sax. to give orders for the making of a thing. To engage beforehand. " To *bespeal* his custom." Life of J. Bull. To discover before-hand. To address in discourse ; to speak to. " Thus the queen *bespoke*." Dryd. To declare, to show.

BESPEAKER, S. he that gives orders for the making of any thing ; he that bespeaks.

To BESPECKLE, V. A. to mark with spots.

To BESPEW, V. A. to vomit upon.

To BESPICE, V. A. to season with spices.

BESPOKE, irregular part. from *bespeak*.

To BESPOT, V. A. to mark with spots.

To BESPREAD, V. A. (pronounced *bespread*, as if this a was dropped ; from *be* and *spread*, of *spreden*, Sax.) to extend a thing to full length over another ; to cover with. Used with the particle *with*, before a thing *spread*, or used as a cover. " *Web* painted flowers *bespread*." Dryd.

To BESPRINKLE, V. A. to spirt water, so as to make it fall in drops.

To BESPUTTER, V. A. to wet by sputtering spittle in drops from between the lips.

BEST, Adj. (the superlative degree of *good*, the comparative *better*, from *god* or *ket*, *bettera*, *best*, Sax.) the highest degree of good, applied to persons or things ; the utmost exertion of power or ability. " Let such men do his *best*." Shak. Used with *at*, the highest degree of perfection. Joined with *make*, to carry a thing to the highest degree of perfection, or gain all the advantage from it that is possible. " Almatcher, In order to make the *best* of it." Addis. Used adverbially, for most. " Where it liketh him *best*." Deut. xxiii. 16.

To BESTAIN, V. N. to alter, or discharge the colour ; to mark with spots or stains.

To BESTEAD, V. A. [Preter. *I bested*, or *have bested*) to support, sustain, or help ; to treat, use, or furnish with conveniencies. " Hardly *bested*." Afcieb viii. 21.

BESTIAL, Adj. [from *bestia*, Lat.] having the nature of a beast ; having no regard for reason, delicacy, virtue, shame, or humanity, and carries with it an idea of the highest reproach.

BESTIALITY, S. that quality which is opposite to every principle of humanity, and includes the secondary idea of great baseness and the highest reproachfulness.

BESTIALLY, Adv. so as to resemble a beast, and below the dignity of humanity ; a term of severe reproach.

To BESTICK, V. A. to fix darts, or any pointed mark upon a subject ; to wound all over.

To BESTIR, V. A. to exert one's self vigorously, including the idea of inactivity

or rest before it. . Generally used with the reciprocal pronouns, *him*, *her*, *herself*, &c. " They must needs *bestir* themselves." Ray. But Shakespeare used it, before common nouns. " You have so *bestirred* your valour." This construction is never adopted by present writers of any note.

To BESTOW, V. A. [*bestowian*, Belg.] to give a person a thing, including the idea of a favour ; to give in marriage ; to lay out or spend, used with *for*. " Thou shalt *bestow* that money for whatsoever thy foul lusteth after." Deut. xiv. 26. To place ; to lay up in a place. " *Bestowed* them in the house." 2 Kings vi. 24.

BESTOWER, S. he that gives a thing, which could not be claimed as a right. He that confers a favour.

To BESTREW, V. A. [Part. *bestrewed* or *bestrown*) to scatter, or sprinkle over ; to cover with. Preter. *I bestrewed*, *I have bestrewed*, or *bestridden*.

To BESTRIDE, V. A. to stand over any thing, so as to have a leg on each side of it. As this posture is that of a person on horseback, it is put figuratively for a person riding. " He *bestrides* the lazy-pacing clouds." Shak. To stand over a thing in order to defend it. " He doth *bestride* a bleeding kind." Shak.

To BESTUD, V. A. to adorn with shining marks or studs.

BET, S. [from *wetten*, Teut.] the money deposited by the parties who lay a wager, to be given to the winner.

To BET, V. A. to lay a wager, or risque a sum of money on the success of a thing or undertaking.

BET, the old Preter of *bet*. Now obsolete.

To BETAKE, V. A. [Preter. *I betook*, Part Passive, *betaken*) to apply ; to have recourse to ; to take to, fly, go, or pass. " They both *betook* themselves, different ways." Par. Loft.

To BETEEM, V. A. to bestow or give ; to produce.

To BETHINK, V. A. [Preter. *I bethought*, from *be* and *thencan*, Sax.) to recollect one's self ; to suspend our thoughts, in order to examine some particular idea ; generally used with the reciprocal pronouns *my*, *himself*, &c. " I have *bethought* me of another fault." Shak.

BETHLEHEM, S. [from בֵּית, and לֶחֶם, Heb.] the name of a city in Judea, the birth-place of our Lord and Saviour Jesus Christ. Applied, according to its etymology, to an hospital. See BEDLAM.

BETHLEHEMITE, S. a bedlamite, a lunatic.

BETHOUGHT, [pronounced *bethawt*] the preter of *bethink*.

To BETHUMP, V. A. to strike, bang, or beat.

To BETIDE, V. A. [Preter. *it betided*, or

or befid, from tid, Sax.] to happen; to befall.

BETI'ME, or BETI'MES, Adv. early; in season; without delay; soon; in a short time, applied to convenience or duration. "Which rideth *betimes*." *Bacon*. Joined with *morn g*, early, and long after day-break. "They rose *betimes* in the morning." *Macn. iv. 5a.* Used with the particle *in*.

To BETO'KEN, V. A. to declare, to signify, to shew or discover.

BE'TONY, S. [*betonia*, Lat.] in Botany, a plant. Linnæus ranges it in the 11th class of his first sect. There are seven species. The common sort, growing with a white flower in the woods in England, is greatly esteemed as a vulnerary.

BETO'OK, Irregular Participle, from *betake*.

To BETO'SS, V. A. to be tossed, agitated, disturbed, or tormented.

To BETRA'Y, V. A. [*bedriegben*, Belg.] to deliver one to his enemies, though bound to the contrary, including the idea of treachery; to disclose a secret; to discover some failing. "Lest you *betray* your ignorance" *Watts*. Used with the particle *to*, to expose to; to make a person liable to fall into some inconveniencies, or subject to some failing. "To *betray* him to great errors." *K. Charles.* To discover as a relique, signal, or mark. "Nor a stone *betray*—I be place." *Addis.*

BETRA'YER, S. the person who betrays; one who discloses a secret. Applied to things, or abstract idea, with great elegance, and implies the frustrating or disappointing any design. "For the *betrayer* of all freemen." *Hooker.*

To BETRI'M, V. A. to adorn or embellish with dress.

To BETRO'TH, V. A. [*betrowen*, Belg.] to promise a person in marriage. In Law, to nominate to a bishoprick.

To BETRU'ST, V. A. to rely upon the fidelity of another. Used with the particle *to* before the person trusted, and *with* before the thing or person committed to the charge of another. "*Betrust* him with all the good." *Green.*

BE'TTER, Adj. [the comparative degree of *good*, of which *best* is the superlative, from *god* or *bon*, Sax.] that which exceeds the thing it is compared with. Used with the definite particle *the* and followed by *of*, something superior to; that which hath some advantages over the thing compared. "Altered *for the better*." Used substantively, a person superior to ourselves. "The courtesy of nations allows you my *better*." *Shak.*

BE'TTER, Adv. [the comparative of *well*] in a more complete, perfect, exact manner; more profitable.

To BE'TTER, V. A. [*betern*, Teut.] to

improve; to increase the value; to amend; to surpass; to excell.

BE'TTER, S. a person who risques a sum of money on the success or miscarriage of a thing or person; one who lays wagers.

BE'TTY, S. [from *betan*, Sax.] a strong wedge, like a chissel, used for breaking open doors. Also the name of a pint flask.

BETWEE'N, Prep. [*betweonum*, Sax.] in the middle, or having one of the two things mentioned on each side of us. Applied to time, the middle space. Applied in quantities, partaking of each. "Between black and white." Applied to things opposite to each other, it implies the idea of difference acquired by comparison. "Distinguish betwixt what require or what not." *Locke.* By themselves, privately. "That was done *between* them." *Greenwood. Between* is properly used when speaking of only two persons, but *among*, when more are included. Though it must be confessed that authors seldom attend to this distinction, and use the words promiscuously.

BETWI'XT, Prep. See BETWEEN.

BE'VEL, or BE'VIL, S. a kind of square, one or both legs of which are crooked; having moveable on a point or center, it may be set to any angle, and supply the deficiencies of the common square and mitre, by setting off an angle greater than 90, in which it exceeds the former, or less than 45 deg. in which it has the advantage of the latter. Bevil angle, is that which is not square, whether it be obtuse or acute.

To BE'VEL, or BE'VIL, V. A. to form a bevil angle.

BE'VERAGE, S. [*beveraggio*, Ital.] any thing drinkable. A kind of water cyder, made by putting the mare into the fat, and adding water, which stands on it 48 hours, is then pressed and stoned immediately. A treat on putting on, or first wearing a new suit of cloaths.

BE'VY, S. [from *beva*, Ital.] a flock, or number of birds. An assembly or company.

To BEWA'IL, V. A. to grieve for any calamity, including the idea of sorrow expressed by tears, and cries of misery.

To BEWA'RE, V. A. to act with caution so as to provide against any future misfortune. It has the particle *of*, before the thing which raises the suspicion or danger; and is used only in such forms of speech as would admit the word *be*; as, *be may beware, be him beware, be will beware*; but not in those wherein the auxiliary verbs occur, as we do not say, *I did beware, I love bewared, or bave bware.*

BEWDLEY, a town of Worcestershire, with a market on Saturdays; and three fairs, on May 4, for horned cattle, horses, cheese, linen and woollen cloth; on December 10, for hogs only; and on December 11, for horned cattle, horses, cheese, linen, and woollen

woollen cloth. It is pleasantly situated on the river Severn, and is a neat well-built town, enjoying a good trade for malt, leather, and caps. It is 14 miles N. of Worcester, 22 E. of Ludlow, and 122 N. W. of London. It sends one member to parliament. Lon. 15. 14. lat. 52. 25.

To BEWE'T, V. A. to render a thing moist or wet.

To BEWI'LDER, V. A. to lose in a place or wood; to puzzle and perplex with difficulties. "Lost and bewildered." Addif.

To BEWI'TCH, V. A. [of witce or wicca, Sax.] to subject to the power of diabolical charms. In its secondary sense, to operate so powerfully on the mind by personal or mental charms, as to be irresistible.

BEWI'TCHERY, S. suppposed to be an irresistible power, which persons dealing in magic had over others. In its secondary sense, an irresistible charm, either personal, mental, &c.

To BEWRA'Y, V. A. [bewregan, Sax.] to discover or make known a thing that is hid or secret.

BEWRA'YER, S. one who discovers a thing which should be concealed. A divulger of secrets, used in a bad sense, and including in it either the idea of folly or treachery.

BEYO'ND, Prep. [geond, beyond, begeondon, Sax.] applied to a place, that which is at the greatest distance from us. Farther than, . "Beyond the mountain." Across or over. "Beyond the sea." Deut. xxx. 13. Too great for, or out of the reach of: exceeding; above; superior. "Thy goodness beyond thought." Par. Loft. To go beyond, is to deceive or defraud by a greater degree of craft or cunning. "That no man go beyond or defraud." 1 Theff. iv. 6.

BE'ZEL, or BE'ZIL, S. that part of a ring in which the stone is set.

BE'ZOR, S. [from badzeher, Perf.] an antidote against poison: also a medicinal stone brought from the East or West-Indies, found in the stomach of an animal of the goat kind, and composed of several coats, like an onion. Oriental bezoar, comes particularly from the kingdom of Golconda and Cannanor, in the East-Indies; being found mixed with the dung of the peacan, a goat, and bears a very high price, though more valuable for its rareness than its real use. It is used in the epilepsy, swimmings in the head, palpitation of the heart; jaundice, cholic, and enters into one species of Gascoign's powder. The occidental bezoar, comes from the West Indies, and is formed in the stomachs of the guinaeous, jachos, vicunnas, and taragous; but that which comes from the last is the best.

BEZOA'RDIC, Adj. medicines compounded with bezoar.

BIA'NGULATED, or BIA'NGULOUS, Adj. [angulus, Lat.] having two angles or corners.

BI'AS, S. [biais, Fr.] the weight in one side of a bowl to regulate it in its course, and to turn it from a straight line. Figuratively, any influence, or propensity.

To BI'AS, V. A. to influence or persuade a person to any particular measure.

BI'B, S. [from bibo, Lat.] a piece of linen put under the chin of infants when feeding. Also a piece of linen pinned on the front of a woman's stay.

BIBA'CIOUS, Adj. [bibax, Lat.] greatly addicted to drinking.

BIBA'CITY, S. [bibacitas, Lat.] the quality of drinking too much, or to excess.

BI'BBER, S. [from bibo, Lat.] a person who drinks much, or to excess.

BI'BLE, S. [from Biblos, Gr. a book, called so by way of eminence] the volume which contains the great truths of religion and conduct revealed from heaven by God, comprehending the Old and New Testament. The translation of this sacred volume was begun, and some part of it was done even by king Alfred. Adelme translated the Psalms into Saxon, in 709; other parts were done by Edfrid, of Lichen, in 730; the whole by Bede, in 731. Freskin published the whole in English, in 1357. Tindal's was brought hither in 1534; revised and altered in 1538; published with a preface of Cranmer's in 1549. In 1551, another translation was published, which being revised by several bishops, was printed with their alterations in 1560. In 1607, a new translation was published by authority, which is that which is now used.

BIBLIO'GRAPHER, S. [from Biblos,] one who writes or copies books.

BI'BULOUS, Adj. [bibulus, Lat.] that which sucks, drains, or drinks any fluid.

BI'CEPS, S. Adj. [Lat.] in Anatomy, that which has two heads. Biceps humeri, is a muscle of the arm with two heads or beginnings. The biceps femoris, or tibiae, is a muscle of the leg with two heads, the uppermost and longest of which arises from the protuberance of the ischium; the lower from the linea aspera of the os femoris, below the termination of the gluteus maximus; its office being, not only to bend the thigh together with the sartorius, but likewise to turn the leg together with the foot and toes outward, when we sit with the knees bent.

BICI'PITAL, or BICI'PITOUS, Adj. [biceps, Lat.] having two heads.

To BI'CKER, V. N. [from bicra, Brit.] to skirmish, or quarrel. To tremble or quiver, or move backward and forwards. "The bickering flame." Par. Loft.

BI'CKERING, S. a quarrel, skirmish, or sudden attack; a misunderstanding. "They fell to such a bickering." Sidney.

BI'CKERN, S. the pointed iron at one end of an anvil.

BI'CORN,

BI'CORN, or BICORNOUS, Adj. [from *bis.* and *cornu,* Lat.] having two horns.

BICO'RPORAL, Adj. [from *bis* and *corpus,* Lat.] that which has two bodies.

To BI'D, V. A. [preter *I bid,* *bad,* *bade.* I have *bid,* or *bidden,* from *biddan,* Sax.] to ask, or invite a person as a guest. "Bid to the marriage." Matth. xxii. 9. To order or command. To offer, or propose, a sum for the purchase of a thing. To publish, or proclaim. "Our banns thrice *bid.*" Gay. Opposed to *forbid,* which sets aside a marriage. To utter, or denounce. "He *bids* defiance." Grew. To pray, according to the meaning of the Sax. from whence it is derived. ¶ Joel ii. 20.

BIDA'LE, S. an invitation of friends.

BI'DDEN, Part. Pass. [from *boeden,* Sax.] invited. Commanded, or compelled.

BI'DDER, S. one who offers a price or sum for any thing.

BIDDIFORD, a town in Devonshire, with a market on Tuesdays, and three fairs on February 14, July 18, and November 13, for cattle. It is commodiously seated on the river Torige, over which there is a large stone-bridge, with 24 piers, and so high, that a vessel of 60 tons may pass under it. It is a large well-inhabited place, and carries on a considerable trade. It is 16 miles S. by W. of Ilfracomb, 7 N. of Torrington, and 197 W. of London. Lon. 13. 10. lat. 51. 10.

BI'DDING, S. [from *bid*] command, order, or invitation.

To BI'DE, V. A. [*bidan,* *abidan,* Sax.] to endure, suffer, or permit. To dwell, remain, or continue.

BIDE'NTAL, Adj. [*bidens,* Lat.] having two teeth. That which has two prongs.

BI'DING, S. dwelling; constant stay, or residence.

BIE'NNIAL, Adj. [from *biennis,* Lat.] continuing for two years.

BIER, S. [*boer,* Sax. from *beran,* Sax. to bear, *bar,* Arm. *bar,* Perf.] a frame of wood, to convey dead persons to the grave.

BIE'STINGS, S. [from *byfing,* Sax.] In Farming, the first milk given by a cow after calving, being thick, taking very saltish, and unfit for the food of the human species.

BIFA'RIOUS, Adj. [*bifarius,* Lat.] that which may be understood two ways.

BI'FEROUS, Adj. [*bis,* Lat. and *fero,* Lat.] bearing, or producing fruit twice a year.

BI'FID, or BI'FIDATED, Adj. [*bifidus,* Lat.] in Botany, divided into two; split in two, opening with a cleft. Millar affects this term in his Gardener's Dictionary more than any other writer we know of.

BI'FOLD, Adj. [from *bis,* Lat. and *fold*] double; or consisting of two opposites.

BI'G, Adj. [*bugen,* *bygen,* Kull.] large, jagменt, swelling out. Joined to *with,* or

of, pregnant; with child. "Big with young." Bac. Swelling, or distended with grief. Proud; haughty.

BI'GAMIST, S. [from *bigamy*] one who has married twice, before his first wife is dead.

BI'GAMY, S. [from *bis,* Lat. and *gamos,* Gr.] the having of two wives at the same time; which is felony by the law.

BIG-BEL'LIED, Adj. swelling out, protuberant; with child; pregnant.

BI'GGIN, S. [from *beguin*] the under cap of an infant, which covers the hind part of his head.

BIGGLESWADE, a town in Bedfordshire, with a market on Wednesdays, and five fairs, on February 13, the Saturday in Easter-week, Whit-Monday, July 22, and October 28, for all sorts of cattle. It is seated on the river Ivel, over which it has a handsome stone-bridge. It is much more considerable than it was formerly, on account of the great northern road, which runs through it, and it has several commodious inns for travellers. It is 11 miles S. S. E. of St. Neot's, 46 N. N. W. of London, and 10. S. E. of Bedford, being one of the greatest barley markets in England. Lon. 17. 15. lat. 52. 5.

BI'GLY, Adv. haughtily; in a blustering manner; proudly.

BI'GNESS, S. largeness, bulk, dimensions, or extent.

BI'GOT, S. one who is strongly attached to any religion or opinion, notwithstanding the strongest reason urged to convince him by a contrary party. Used in a bad sense, and with the particle *to,* before the object.

BI'GOTED, Adj. [from *bigot*] obstinately prepossessed, in favour of any person, or opinion. Used with the particle *to.*

BI'GOTRY, S. obstinacy, or attachment to any party or opinion. Used with the particle *to.*

BI'LE, S. [from *bilis,* Lat.] in Anatomy, a yellow bitter liquor or fluid, separated from the blood in the liver, collected in the gall-bladder, and discharged into the lower end of the duodenum. Of the greatest consequence in preserving health, and remedying most inconveniences, that happen to the human constitution. By its saponaceous and sulphureous qualities, it sheaths the acids of the chyle, contributes not a little to the work of digestion, and the mixture of the internal fluids; being found in most, if not all animals, we may safely conclude, that the wise Architect of animal bodies has placed it therein, both for necessary and noble uses.

BI'LE, S. [from *bile,* Sax.] a red inflammatory swelling or tumour.

BI'LGE, S. [*bilge,* Sax. *bulgia,* Ital.] that part of a ship's bottom on which the rests, when a-ground. *Bilge water,* that which rests

refts on a fhip's bottom   Bilge-pump, is that which is applied to the fide of a fhip, to pump out the bilge-water.

To BI'LGE, V. N. a fea term, to damage the boards of a veffel againft a rock. To fpring a leak.

BI'LIARY, Adj. [from bile or bilis, Lat.] that which relates to, or conveys, the bile.

BILI'NGUOUS, Adj. [from bilinguis, Lat.] that which has two tongues; one who can fpeak two languages.

To BILK, V. A. [bilk, or bilken, bira, Teut.] to cheat; defraud, or contract a debt, without intending to pay it.

BILL, S. [bile, Sax.] the horny fubftance protuberating from the head of a bird, or fowl. A beak.

BILL, S. [bille, Sax.] an edged tool, with a hooked point, of the ax kind, fitted to a handle, and ufed to lop trees. If the handle be fhort, it is named a hand-bill; but if long, a hedge-bill.

BILL, [bills, Sax. biller, Fr.] In Trade, or Commerce, a written or printed account of goods delivered to, or work done. A writing wherein a perfon obliges himfelf to pay a fum of money to another at a certain time. Bill of credit, is that which is given to another, impowering him to take up money of his correfpondents in foreign countries. A Bill of entry, is an account of goods entered at the cuftom-houfe, either inwards or outwards. Bill of exchange, is a piece of paper drawn by a perfon on another in a different place, for money received by him at home. Bill of lading, is a memorandum or acknowledgement, under the hand of the mafter of a veffel, of his having received goods on board, together with a promife to deliver them, as configned. Bill of parcels, an account given of the feveral goods bought, and their prices. Bill of fale, is a folemn contract under feal, whereby a perfon transfers his goods to another. Bill in Law, is a fingle bond without a condition. In parliament, a writing containing fome propofals offered to the houfe to be paffed into a law. A defcription of fome curiofity, or commodity delivered by the perfons who fhow or fell it, called a hand bill. A bill of mortality, is an account of the number of perfons dying within certain limits and times. A bill of fare, an account of the difhes of an entertainment.

BI'LLA VERA, in Law, words indorfed by the grand jury on an indictment, fignifying that they find it probable, and worthy further confideration: whereupon the offender is faid to ftand indicted, and if it touches life, is refered to the petty jury, or jury of life and death.

To BILL, V. A. [from bill, Sax.] to join bills together. To carefs with great fondnefs, alluding to the manner of doves joining their bills together. Ufed neuterly, to

No. V.

publifh by a hand-bill, with about "A compofition he billed about." L'Eftrange.

BI'LLET, S. [Fr.] a fmall written paper. A ticket directing foldiers where to lodge. A fmall log of wood. In Heraldry, a bearing refembling a long fquare.

BI'LLIARDS, S. [it has no fingular, Billiards, Ital.] a game played on an oblong table, fixed exactly horizontal, with little ivory balls, which are driven by the oppofite parties into hazards, holes, or pockets, placed at the ends and fides of the table.

BI'LLOW, S. [from bhur, Ifl.] a large, high fwelling wave.

To BI'LLOW, V. N. to fwell or become tempeftuous.

BI'LLOWY, Adj. ftormy, tempeftuous, fwelling.

BI'N, S. [binne, Sax. benne, Belg.] a long fquare cheft of wood, wherein corn, &c. are put.

BI'NARY, Adj. [binus, Lat.] confifting of or confined to two. Binary Arithmetic, a method of computation propofed by M. Leibnitz, wherein inftead of the ten figures in common arithmetic, he makes ufe of only o and 1, and the cypher multiplies every thing by 2. Thus 1 is one, 10 two, 11 three, 100 four, a method that feems to have been ufed by the Chinefe 4000 years ago.

To BIND, V. A. [preter bound] to confine a perfon's limbs by bonds; to fenfound, encompafs, confine, faften together; to fix a bandage on; compel; to oblige by oath or bargain; in phyfic, to ftop a loofenefs, or make coftive. To bind a book, to few the fheets together, and place them in a cover. Ufed with the particle to, to make fubject or fubfervient to. "Thou art bound to vice." With the word over, to be obliged to appear at a court of juftice. To contract or join the parts together.

BI'NDER, S. [from bind] one who binds.

BI'NDING, S. that which is bound, or tied round any thing. A bandage.

BI'NOCLE, S. [from binus, Lat.] and oculus, Lat. a telefcope fitted with two tubes, fo that diftant objects may be feen by both the eyes.

BINO'MIAL, Adj. in Algebra, a root confifting only of two parts connected with this fign +. Thus x + y is a binomial confifting only of thofe two quantities.

BIO'GRAPHER, [from βίος, Gr. and γραφω,] one who writes or compiles the lives of particular perfons.

BI'PAROUS, Adj. [from binus and pario, Lat.] bringing forth, or producing two at a time.

BI'PARTITE, Adj. [from binus, and partitus, Lat.] having two parts correfponding with each other, divided into two.

Y   BIPA.

BIPARTITION, S. [from *bipartite*] the act of dividing into two.

BIPED, S. [*bipes*, Lat.] having two feet.

BIPEDAL, Adj [*bipedalis*, Lat.] having two feet.

BIPENNATED, Adj. [from *binæ pennæ*, Lat.] that which hath two wings.

BIPETALOUS, Adj. [from *bis* Lat. and *petalon*, Gr.] in Botany, that which hath two leaves, or petals.

BIQUADRATE, or BIQUADRATIC, [from *bis*, Lat. and *quadro*, Lat.] the next power above the cube, or the square of the cube root.

BIRCH, S. [*bire*, *birce*, *beorce*, Sax.] In Botany, *Betula*, hath male and female flowers at a distance from each other. Linnæus places it in the 4th sect. of his 21st class. There are four species. This tree is very fit for planting in a bad soil, and is very profitable. The broom is made use of by hoop-benders; those who make ox yokes, and instruments of husbandry, make use of the wood, which is very hard. The French use it for wooden shoes; and in other countries they work it into wheels. *Birch-broom*, a broom or besom made with the small twigs of the Birch-tree. See *Besom*.

BIRCHEN, Adj. [from *birch* and *en*, Sax.] made or consisting of birch.

BIRD, S [*bird*, *bridde*, Sax.] in natural history, a two-footed animal covered with feathers, and furnished with wings. If we consider the form of this animal, so well adapted for flight by the make of its body, the stiffness of its wings, the lightness of its clothing, and the thinness of its bones; if we consider the provision nature has made against the length of his aerial progress, by furnishing it with a pouch to contain its food called the crop, and with an oil to smear its wings with, to render them the better able to resist the air, and the moisture of the atmosphere, or water, we can scarce help admiring the art of divine wisdom, which shews itself so conspicuously in its make; but if we call in the microscope to our aid, a single feather, nay the very beards of a feather, will astonish us with beauties, and entertain us with the inexplicable elegancies.

To BIRD, V. A. [from the noun] to catch or snare birds.

BIRD-CAGE, a receptacle to keep birds in.

BIRD LIME, S. a glue made use of by bird-catchers, to take birds with; made of the bark of holly boiled for ten or twelve hours, which having stood in a moist place for a fortnight, is pounded into a tough paste, cleared in a running stream, fermented for four or five days, and incorporated with a third part of nut oil over a fire.

BIRDS-EYE, S. [*Eye*] In Botany, *Adonis*. Linnæus ranges it in the seventh division of his 13th class. There are three species.

BIRDS-FOOT, S. in Botany, *ornithopus*. The flowers are of gold colour, and the pods turn inward at the top like a bird's foot.

BIRMINGHAM, a very large town in Warwickshire, with a market on Thursdays, and two fairs, on the Thursday in Whitsun-week, and on October 10, for hardware, cattle, sheep and horses. It is no corporation, it being only governed by two constables and two bailiffs; and therefore free for any person to come and settle there; which has contributed greatly to the increase not only of the buildings, but the trade, which is the most flourishing of any in England for all sorts of iron-work, besides many other curious manufactures. The town stands on the side of a hill, forming nearly a half-moon. The lower part is filled with the work shops and warehouses of the manufacturers, and consists chiefly of old buildings. The upper part of the town contains a number of new and regular streets, and a handsome square, elegantly built. It has two churches; one in the lower part of the town, which is an ancient building, with a very tall spire; the other is a very grand modern structure, having a square stone tower with a cupola and turret above it; in this tower is a fine peal of ten bells, and a set of musical chimes, which play seven different tunes, one for each day in the week. It has also two chapels, and meeting houses for every denomination of dissenters The houses in this town amount to about six or seven thousand, and their number is continually increasing. It is 17 miles N. W. of Coventry, 48 S. E. of Shrewsbury, and 109 N. W. of London. Lon. 25. 55. lat. 52. 50.

BIRTH, S. [*beorth*, Sax. *birt*,] the act of bringing forth. The entrance of a person into the world; any production. In sea affairs, a proper place for a ship to ride in. A place separated by canvas, wherein the sailors mess, and put their chests.

BIRTH-DAY, S. the day on which a person is born; the day celebrated annually, on which a person was born.

BIRTH-NIGHT, S. the night on which a person is born. The night annually celebrated at court with great festivity and splendour, on account of the king's being born on that day or night.

BIRTH-PLACE, S. the place wherein a person is born.

BIRTH-RIGHT, S. acquired by birth.

BISCOTIN, S. [Fr.] a confection made of flour, marmalade, eggs, &c.

BISCUIT,

BI'SCUIT, S. [from *bis*, Lat. and *cuit*, Fr.] a kind of bread made of wheat flower, mixed with leaven and warm water, baked for long voyages. It will keep a whole year. Likewise a fine delicate pastry, or cake.

To BISECT, V. A. [from *bisus*, and *secare*, Lat.] to divide any line into two equal parts.

BI'SECTION, S. [from *bisect*] in geometry, the act of dividing into two equal parts.

BI'SHOP, S. [from *biscop*, or *bisop*, Sax.] a prelate consecrated for the spiritual government of the diocese, who collates to benefices, ordains priests and deacons, licences physicians, surgeons, and scho l-masters. The bishops are all peers of the realm, except the bishop of Suder and Mann. The bishops are barons in a three-fold sense; feudal, on account of the temporalities annexed to their bishoprics; by writ being summoned by writ to parliament; and lastly, by patent and creation. They have precedence of all other barons, and vote both as barons and bishops. Next to the two archbishops, the bishops of London, Durham, and Winchester, have always the precedence; and the others according to the priority of consecration.

BI'SHOPRIC, S. the diocese, which belongs to a bishop.

BISHOPS-CASTLE, a town in Shropshire, with a market on Fridays, and five fairs, on Friday before Good-Friday, the Friday after May-day, July 5, September 9, and November 1 5, for sheep, horned cattle, and horses. It is seated not far from the river Clun, and is a corporation, which sends two members to parliament, and the market is much frequented by the Welch. It is 21 miles W. of Worcester, 8 E. of Montgomery, and 150 N. W. by W. of London. Lon. 34. 35. lat. 52. 10.

BI'SK, S. [from *bisque*, Fr.] a basket. A soup, or broth, made of different sorts of flesh boiled.

BI'SKET, S. See BISCUIT.

BI'SMUTH, S. in natural history, a considerable heavy semi-metal, very susceptible of rust; and, though not sonorous itself, yet, when added to any other metal, makes them more sonorous, and at the same time more brittle.

BISSE'XTILE, S. [from *bis*, and *sextilis*, Lat.] a year, containing 366 days, which happens every four years, when a day is added to the month of February, to make up for the six hours which the sun spends in his course each year, beyond 365 days.

BISTOU'RY, S. [*bistouri*, Fr.] a surgeon's instrument, used in making incisions; of which there are three sorts. 1. That whose blade turns like that of a lancet; 2. The straight bistouri, with the blade fixed in the handle; and, 3. The crooked bistouri, shaped like a half-moon, with the edge in the inside.

BISU'LCOUS, Adj. [from *bisulcus*, Lat.] cleft in two parts, cloven footed.

BI'T, S. [from *mecal*, Sax.] the iron appurtenances of a bridle; but more particularly the bit-mouth.

BI'T, S. [from *bite*] A small piece; applied to a bit, a Spanish piece in the West Indies, worth 7 ½ d used in honor or work, a low phrase for a small degree of either.

BI'TCH, S. [*bicce*, *bic*, Sax.] the female of the dog, wolf, fox, and other kind. In low language used to signify a person of an unchaste disposition, or to convey the idea of one acting contrary to all the laws of reason and decency.

To BI'TE, V. A. [Preter *bit*, Part. Passive *bitten*, or *bit*, *bitan*] to wound, or pierce, with the teeth. To affect with pain, applied to cold. To make a person uneasy, applied to satire. To make the mouth smart, applied to sharp taste of some acid bodies. To deceive, to cheat or defraud.

BI'TE, S. [from the verb] to divide, seize, or wound, any thing with the teeth. In low and familiar language, a person who deprives another of his property by false appearances. A sharper, a cheat, trick, or fraud.

BI'TER, S. one who bites. One that readily or quickly swallows a bait, applied to a fish. One who deceives, or defrauds another.

BI'TTEN, Part. Passive of *Bite*.

BI'TTER, Adj. [Sax. Belg. and Teut.] that which excites a hot pungent taste, like that of wormwood. Wretched, miserable, painful, unpleasing.

BI'TTERLY, Adv. having a bitter taste. In a sorrowful, painful, and severe manner. Used sometimes to express the superlative degree. " He wept *bitterly*."

BITTERN, S. [*butor*, Fr.] In natural history, a bird with a long bill and legs, which feed on fish. The liquor which runs from common salt, after it is taken out of the boiling pan, or that which remains after its chrystallization.

BI'TTERNESS, S. a kind of flavour or sensation, opposite to sweetness, which is caused by a mixture of an earthy matter with salt. Severity, authority; keenness; sharpness, or extremity; sorrow, trouble, distress, vexation.

BI'TTER, S. in sea language, any turn of the cable round the bitts, so that it may be let out gradually or by degrees.

BI'TUMEN, S. in natural history, a fat tenacious inflammable mineral substance, or a fossil body which easily takes fire.

BITU'MINOUS, Adj. [from *bitumen*] having the qualities of bitumen.

BIVALVE, Adj. [from *bini* and *valvæ* Lat.] in natural history, applied to fish having two shells, such as oysters; and in botany to plants whose seed pods open their whole length, to discharge their seeds, as peas or beans.

BIVA'LVULAR, Adj. having two shells.

BIVE'NTER, S. a muscle between the whole base of the jaw and the throat.

To BLAB, V. A. [*blabberen*, or *blapperen*, Teut.] to reveal a secret. To discover or speak. "That delightful engine of her thoughts that *blabbed* them with such pleasing eloquence." *Shak.* This is neither an improper use of the word, and should not be retained. Used neuterly to talk, tattle, or make discoveries by inconsiderate tattling.

BLAB, S. a tell-tale; one who discovers secrets.

BLA'BBER, S. one who discovers a secret.

BLACK, S. [*black*, Sax. *black* ink, Teut.] want of light, and colour. Dyers *black* for stuffs of a high price, is composed of indigo, woad, boiled with allum, tartar, or allom of lime or wine, maddered with common madder, and given with gall-nuts of Aleppo, copperas and Ibumae. The best black cloth should first be dyed blue. It being observed that the black dye of English woollen cloth is less beautiful than that of France or Holland; it is supposed that this is owing to the overpressing; since every addition to the gloss is a proportionable diminution of the colour. The Holland cloths are so entirely free from gloss as to take no stain from water, even on the first day's wearing; and the black is so much more perfect that, while the cloth continues in tolerable order, it cannot be distinguished at a distance from velvet. *Ivory black* is ivory burnt between two crucibles, and ground with water, used by painters and jewellers, to blacken the bottom ground of the collets or bezels in which they set diamonds; *Spanish black*, is burnt cork. *Lamp or Lamb-black*, is the footy smoak or soot of rosin, mixed with oil of wall-nuts or linseeds and turpentine boiled together, it is used by printers for the ink they print with. To look black, implies sullenness, and is a sign of displeasure. "Looked black upon me." *Shak.* Applied to moral action, excessively wicked.

To BLACK, V. A. to make black.

BLACK, Adj. that is of a black colour.

BLA'CKAMOOR, one whose complexion is black.

BLA'CKBERRY, S. in botany, a species of the Bramble.

BLACK-BIRD, S. in natural history, a bird so called from the colour of its feathers. Its bill is yellow, and its song resembles a man's whistling.

BLACK-BROWED, Adj. having black eye-brows; dark, gloomy, dismal.

BLACK-CATTLE, S. a term including oxen, bulls, or cows.

To BLA'CKEN, V. A. to make a thing black, to darken. "the cloud *blackened* the face of the whole Heaven." *Smith.* To fully a person's character.

BLA'CK-GUA'RD, S. in low language used to convey the idea of a person of mean circumstances, and base principles.

BLA'CKISH, Adj. inclining or approaching to a black colour; somewhat black.

BLA'CKNESS, S. want of light, or darkness.

BLACK-ROD, S. a rod of a black colour, on the top of which is a golden lyon, carried by the gentleman usher of the black rod, before the king at the feast of St. George, at Windsor; he has likewise the keeping of the Chapter-house, when a chapter is fitting; is of the king's chamber, and attends the house of peers, while the parliament is fitting.

BLA'CKSMITH, S. one who forges works in iron.

BLACK-SEA, formerly called the Euxine Sea, lies between Europe and Asia, bounded on the N. by Tartary; on the E. by Mingrelia, Circassia, and Georgia; on the S. by Natolia, and on the W. by Romania, Bulgaria, and Bessarabia. It lies between Lon. 50. and 61. and from lat. 41. to 46. being entirely surrounded by the Turkish dominions, who have the sole navigation of it. The Russians once made an attempt to trade upon this sea; but by late treaties they were obliged to give up all their fortresses they had upon it, and consequently to abandon the navigation.

BLAD'DER, S. [*bladr*, Sax. *bladder*, and *bladder*, Belg.] in anatomy, a thin dilatable, membranous body, which serves as the receptacle of the urine after its secretion from the blood in the kidneys. Its figure, in quadrupeds, resembles a pear, with the broadest part upwards; but in human bodies is nearly that of a short oval; when empty it is rounder above than below, and when full, broader below than above. It has three coats; the first is a muscular one, and consists of long internal fibres; the second nervous, and resembling that of the stomach; the third or internal coat, is composed of glands, continually discharging a muxilaginous serum, which moistens the inner surface of the bladder, and defends it from the acrimony of the urine. Around its neck goes a small muscle, called sphincter vesicæ, which contracts the orifice of the bladder, and prevents the urine from dropping out involuntarily, or till it thrusts open the passage, by the contraction of the second coat of the

bladder,

bladder, called the *detrusor urinæ*, or that which thrust out the urine. It likewise signifies a pustule or blister.

BLA'DE, S. [from *blæd, bled, Sax.*] In botany, the spire or leaf of grass; the green shoots of corn, which rise from the seed. Hence the thin piece of metal, beaten with a hammer or craft, and more particularly that part of a sword or knife, is called a blade, from the former's resembling a blade of grass. A bold, enterprizing person.

BLA'DE or BLA'DE-BONE, S. In anatomy, the scapula, or scapular-bone, of a flat and triangular form.

To BLA'DE, V. A. to fit a blade to a handle.

BLA'DED, Adj. having leaves, or blades.

BLAIN, S. [*blegene, Sax.*] a pustule or blister.

BLA'MABLE, Adj. that which deserves censure.

BLA'MABLY, Adv. and deserving censure or blame.

To BLA'ME, V. A. [*blâmer, Fr.*] to charge a person with having done a fault, or something wrong, applied to things, to accuse of defect. Usually joined with the particle *for*; "The reader must not *blame me for* making use." *Locke*. Improperly used with *of*. "Erroneous he blamed *of*." *Knolly*.

BLA'ME, S. the charging with faults. That which merits censure.

BLA'MEFUL, Adj. that which highly deserves censure.

BLA'MELESS, Adj. that which deserves no censure or blame;

BLA'MELESSLY, Adv. in such manner as not to merit censure.

BLA'MER, S. the person who censures, or blames.

BLA'MEWORTHY, Adj. that is deserving censure or blame.

To BLA'NCH, V. A. [*blanchir, Fr.*] to whiten a thing; to peel applied to the peeling almonds, which discovers their kernel of a white colour. Used neuterly, to evade. "Books will speak plain when counsellors *blanch.*" *Bacon.*

BLA'NCHING, S. the art, or method of making any thing white.

BLA'ND, Adj. [*blandus, Lat.*] soothing, mild, applied to language; soft, temperate, applied to the weather.

BLA'NDISHMENT, S. [from *blandish*] an insinuating address, by which a person attracts the esteem of another. Soft, mild and kind expressions by which a person steals into the favour of another. A behaviour or treatment by which a person endeavours to gain the affections of another.

BLA'NK, Adj. [*blanc, Fr.*] whitish or pale. That which is not written on; confused; dejected. Applied to verse, that which is without rhime; in its original use

implying defect, as *blank* paper implies a want of writing.

BLA'NK, S. a space, which has no writing on it, but it is left so in order to be filled up. In Lotteries, a ticket which has no prize drawn against it; the mark which an arrow or piece is aimed at.

BLA'NKET, S. [*blanchette, Fr.*] a stuff made of wool, in the loom like cloath, but crossed like serge, worked with blue or red wool at each end, and with a crown or other ornament at each corner, used for beds, being placed both above the upper, and beneath the under sheet to procure warmth. The Whitney blankets are, and have long been, in the greatest repute in England.

To BLA'NKET, S. to wrap in a blanket. "I'll *blanket* my loins." *Shak. Lear.*

BLA'NKETING, S. the tossing a person in a blanket, which is done by several people holding the extremities, and is intended as a chastisement for some misdemeanours or crime.

BLA'NKLY, Adj. so as to shew confusion, or disappointment. With whiteness; with paleness.

To BLA'SPHEME, V. N. [*blasphême, Lat.*] to speak ill of God or things relating to his service. In Law, an indignity, or injury offered to the Almighty, by denying what is his due, or attributing to him what is not agreeable to his nature, *Linden. cap. 1.* Those who deny the being and providence of God, are contumelious reproachers of Jesus Christ, or by writing or speaking shall deny any of the persons in the Trinity, are punishable by fine, and rendered incapable of any office. *1 Howel. P. C. 97. 9 and 10 Will III. c. 32.*

BLASPHE'MER, S. one who speaks things of the Deity inconsistent with his nature, or the reverence he owes him as a creature; one who utters disrespectful, or irreverent things of any person in the holy Trinity.

BLA'SPHEMOUS, Adj. [from *blasphème*. Usually pronounced with the accent on the first syllable, but used by Milton and old authors, with it on the second] disrespectful or irreverent with respect to God and heavenly things. "*Blasphemous* words the speaker vain do prove." *Sidney.*

BLA'SPHEMOUSLY, Adv. in such a manner as to speak ill of God and heavenly things.

BLA'SPHEMY, S. an offering some indignity to God; his holy writ, or the doctrines revelation, either by speaking or writing any thing ill of them, or ascribing any thing ill to them inconsistent with their natures and the reverence we owe them.

BLA'ST, [*blast, Sax.*] a puff, or current of wind. The sound made of a trumpet or other wind instrument. A warm air, which withers.

withers trees, or causes a pestilence. The plague or pestilence. " By the blast of God they perish." Job iv. 9. This sense is derived from Blasa, Sax. bjða or blast l'ol. and aleypa, Rull.

To BLA'ST, V. A. [blastan, Sax.] to infect with some sudden infection, by means of the air. To make a thing to wither. To ruin a person's character by false rumours. To render an enterprize abortive. " His enterprize was blasted." Arbuth. To deafen or assist the ear with a very loud noise applied to wind instruments. " Trumpeters. — blast you the city's ears." Shakesp.

BLA'STING, S. the blowing up the vein of a mine by gun-powder.

BLA'STMENT, that which withers, kills, or renders a thing abortive.

BLA'TTA-BYZANTIA, S Lat. in Natural History, a testaceous body so called from its coming from Byzantium or Constantinople, and is the operculum or upper part of a turbinated shell of a fish, which yields a purple dye, shaped like the claw, or talon of a wild animal, very thin, of a brown colour, easy to burn, and of a disagreeable smell when burnt. It has a cordial medicine.

BLA'TANT, Adj. [blatiant, Fr.] bellowing, like a calf, " the blatant beast." Dryd.

BLA'ZE, S. [blase, Sax. blæst, H.f. Schav.] a light of a flame, figuratively, a spreading abroad, or extending a report, in allusion to the diffusion of light, which is made by a body in flames. A white mark on a horse's forehead.

To BLA'ZE, V. to shine, or give light, to make a thing universally known by report.

BLA'ZER, S. one who spreads abroad any report or rumour. Not in use, though no other word seems to have been substituted in its stead.

To BLA'ZON, V. A. [blasonner, Fr.] in Heraldry, to name all the parts of a coat, in their proper terms. Figuratively, to let out, deck or adorn. To discover to advantage; to display. " How thyself thou blazonest—in these two princely boys!" Shakesp. To celebrate. To spread abroad, to make universally known.

BLA'ZON, S. [from the verb] in Heraldry, the art of properly expressing the several parts of a coat of arms. This is done by beginning with the metal of the field, then naming the manner of its divisions, its charge, and if many things are born on it, by naming that first which is born in the chief. Names repetition of words must be made use of; all persons, beneath the degree of a noble, must have their coats blazoned by metals and colour, nobles by precious stones, and kings and princes by planets; blazon is used figuratively for making any thing public; or a pompous display of any quality.

To BLE'ACH, V. A. [blecan, Sax.] to whiten by exposing to the air and sun. To grow white, in the sun, or open air.

BLEACHING, S. the art of making a thing white, which is not so before. Bleaching silk is performed by boiling it in river water, in which good London or Genoa soap has been dissolved, beating it, washing it in cold water, wringing it slightly, putting it a second time into water mixed with soap and a little indigo, wringing it hard, and suspending it in the air over the fumes of burning sulphur. Woollen stuffs are bleached with water and soap, with the vapour of sulphur or brimstone; and with chalk, indigo and the vapour of sulphur. The method of bleaching linen as practised at St. Quintin, is as follows; the linens when taken from the loom are steeped in clear water a whole day, being cleared of their filth, they are thrown into a bucking tub filled with cold lye made of wood-ashes and water; taken out of this lye, they are washed in clear water, spread in meadows, where they are watered now and then by scoops. After lying thus some time, they are watered, with a fresh lye, of a different composition, poured on hot; then spread in the meadow again, and the operation repeated till they are come to their proper whiteness. Being then placed in a gentle lye to recover their softness, they are washed in clear water, rubbed with black soap, washed well, and soaked in skimmed milk; being washed again, they are dipped into water, in which starch or smalt has been steeped; after this they are fastened to poles stuck in the ground, and when three parts dry are taken from the poles and beaten with wooden mallets, to beat down the grain and make it look more beautiful; after which they are folded in squares and pressed. If it be considered what importance the linen manufactories are of to this nation, we shall be rather commended than blamed for dwelling so long on this article; and before we conclude we cannot help saying that the perfection to which the Irish and Scotch have arrived to in this article, bids fair to establish the character of our linens above what the most sanguine persons could have promised at its first attempts, and if prosecuted with the same ardour must soon render us in this branch of manufacture equal to the Dutch or any nation, that has hitherto been thought inimitable, or at least not to be equalled.

BLE'AK, Adj. [from bleac, or blæc, Sax.] cold, sharp, chill.

BLE'AK, S. [from bleac, Sax.] in Natural History, a small river or fresh water fish.

BLEA'KNESS, S. extreme coldness, applied to the air.

BLE'AKY, Adv. cold, sharp or chilly, owing to the wind.

BLE'AR,

BLEAR, Adj. [blear, Belg.] dim or fore with rheum ; that which caufes diminiſh of the fight.

To BLEAR, V. A. to occaſion dimnefs ; to make the eyes fore with rheum.

BLEAREDNESS, S. foreneſs, or dimnefs of fight, occaſioned by a deſtruction of rheum.

To BLEAT, V. A. [blætan, Sax.] to make a noife like a ſheep.

BLEAT, S. [from the verb] the cry or noiſe of a ſheep.

BLED, Part. from BLEED.

To BLEED, V. N. to lofe blood by a wound, &c. To die by bleeding, " The lamb thy riot dooms to bleed to day." Pope. To extract blood ; to let blood.

To BLEMISH, V. A. to fpot, ſtain, or any other ways deprive a thing of it beauty, value, or perfection. To defame.

BLEMISH, S. [from the verb] applied to charms, any thing that diminiſhes their perfection. Applied to goods ; a defect in the making, or owing to fome accident. A reproach, difgrace, or defect.

To BLEND, V. A. [blendan, Sax.] to mix things together imperfectly, applied to the mixing of colours ; " but blended not united." Boyle.

BLENHEIM, a village of Germany, in Suabia, rendered memorable for the victory over the French and Bavarians, obtained by the Allies, under the command of the Duke of Marlborough and Prince Eugene. In memory of this battle, the fine palace of Blenheim was built, near Woodſtock, at the charge of the government. It happened in Auguſt 1704. It is ſeated on the W. fide of the Danube, 3 miles N. E. of Hochſted, 27 N. E. of Ulm, and 25 N. W. of Auſburg. Long. 20. 0. lat. 48. 40.

To BLESS, V. A. [præter, I bleſſed or bleſt, from blefian, Sax.] to wiſh happineſs or ſucceſs to a perſon. To praife God for happineſs received, to confer every thing that can make a perſon happy, applied to the Deity.

BLESSED, Part. Paff. of BLESS ; bleſſader ; bleſſed and bleſſed, ſil.

BLESSEDLY, Adv. ſo as to communicate the greateſt happineſs.

BLESSEDNESS, S. that which renders a perſon happy. The ſtate of felicity in heaven. The divine favour.

BLESSER, S. he that prays or confers wiſhes, the happineſs of another.

BLESSING, S. a prayer wherein happineſs is requeſted. Figuratively, the divine favour, including its actual interpoſition in behalf of a perſon either by granting his prayers, or profpering his undertakings. Any means or cauſe of happineſs ; any great advantage, or benefit. " A juſt and wife religſtrar is a bleſſing." Atterb. The preſents of one friend to another, ſo called in Scripture

on account of their being marks of a mind diſpoſed to implore the greateſt bleſſings for another ; " Receive my preſent ; Take, I pray thee, my bleſſing." Gen. xxxiii. 10.

BLEST, Part. from BLESS.

BLEW, the pret. of BLOW.

BLIGHT, S. [from blight, Teut.] in Botany, a diſeaſe incident to plants, or trees ; the caufes of which have been varioufly afſigned by different authors. But as they are univerfally acknowledged to proceed from continued dry eaſterly winds, may they not fiſt ſtop the perſpiration of the bloſſoms and then thoſe of the leaves ; and may not their perſpiring matter, thus rendered thick and glutinous, become a proper nutriment to the ſmall inſects always found praying on them ? not that theſe inſects are the firſt caufe of blights, as Mr. Bradley contends, though it muſt be confeſſed, that whenever they meet with proper nutriment, they multiply exceedingly ; and are inſtrumental in promoting this diſtemper. Blights are likewife cauſed by ſharp and hoary froſt in the night, which ſtarve the tender parts of the bloſſoms, and being ſucceeded by a hot ſun-ſhine in the day time, a ſcalding heat is acquired by the globules of moiſture, not yet dried by the ſun, which ſcorches the tender flowers. Sometimes indeed they are owing to nothing but a weaknefs in the trees themſelves, proceeding either from want of nouriſhment, from ſome ill qualities in the ſoil where they grow, ſome bad quality in the ſtock, ſome inbred diſtempper of the buds or eyes, imbibed from the mother tree, or miſmanagement in pruning. For the blight of corn, ſee SMUT. Figuratively, any thing which makes an undertaking miſcarry ; or diſappoints a perſon's expectations.

To BLIGHT, V. A. to render a tree barren ; to wither, to blaſt, deſtroy, or kill. " blight the tender buds of joy." Lyttel.

BLIND, Adj. [blind, Sax. Dan.] deprived of fight, ignorant. " All authors to their own defects are blind." Dryd. Sometimes with of, " Blind of the future." Dryd. Dark, not eafily to be feen. In Chymiſtry, blind veffels, are ſuch as have no opening but on one ſide.

To BLIND, V. A. to deprive one of fight; to prevent a perſon from ſeeing, by placing fomething between his eyes and the object, or by tying ſomething over his eyes. To darken ; to render a thing obſcure and not eafily comprehended.

BLIND, ſomething to intercept the light; a piece of canvas painted or unpainted placed in a window, to hinder a paſſenger from ſeeing into a room. Figuratively, fomething to divert the eye or mind from attending to the defign of a perſon.

To BLINDFOLD, V. A. to hinder one from ſeeing by tying ſomething before his eyes.

BLINDFOLD, Adv. with the eyes covered

vered, or that. Without confideration; Implicitly. "Be no longer led *blindfold.*" *Freehold.*

BLI'NDLY, Adv. without fight. Hardly to be perceived, oppofed to plain, or legibly. Implicitly. Without any direction, judgment, or wifdom. "*Blindly gathered into this goodly bill.*" *Dryd.*

BLI'NDMAN'S-BUFF, S. a play wherein a perfon endeavours to catch fome of the company, after his eyes are covered.

BLI'NDNESS, S. lofs of fight. Figuratively, ignorance or want of knowledge.

BLI'NDSIDE, S. the foibles or weaknefs of a perfon.

To BLINK, V. N. [*blinken*, Dan.] to wink with one eye; to fee obfcurely with one eye.

BLI'NKARD, S. [from *blind* and *ard*, Belg.] one who has bad eyes. Figuratively, one who difcerns but very imperfectly.

BLISS, S. [*bliffe*, Sax.] joy. A ftate of happinefs, or felicity.

BLI'SSFUL, Adj. [from *blifs* and *full*, of *fullen*, Sax. to fill] abounding with joy; pofleffed of the higheft degree of happinefs, or blifs.

BLI'SSFULLY, Adv. fo as to fhow the greateft figns of joy and happinefs.

BLI'STER, S. [*blyfter*, Belg.] a fwelling of the fkin, generally filled with a watery fluid; fcalding, &c. alfo a medicine which draws the humours to a particular part.

To BLI'STER, V. N. to rife in blifters; to raife blifters by burning. To apply a phifter to raife a blifter.

BLI'THE, Adj. [*blithe*, Sax.] gay, airy, joyous, fprightly, jocund.

BLI'THLY, Adv. in a joyoufly, airily, gaily manner.

BLI'THNESS, S. the ftate of joyful alacrity and fprightlinefs, owing to the poffeffion of fome good.

BLI'THSOME, Adj. gay, airy, fprightly, chearful.

To BLO'AT, V. A. [from *blawan*, Sax.] to fwell with wind; to difcover pride by the looks or gefture. To look as if fwelled by wind; generally applied to a perfon's growing lufty, but appearing at the fame time unfound.

BLO'ATEDNESS, S. the being puffed up with fat, or fwelled with wind.

BLO'BBER-LIP, S. a thick lip.

BLO'B-LIPPED, or BLO'BBER-LIPPED, Adj. having thick lips.

BLOCK, S. [*block*, Belg.] a heavy piece of timber. Any waffy body. A piece of wood in the fhape of a head, ufed by barbers. A piece of wood ufed by hatters to drefs their hats on. The wood on which ftate criminals are beheaded. Figuratively, an obftruction, or impediment. "No crime is *block* enough in our way." *Decay of Piety.* A perfon of dull parts, or apprehenfion.

To BLO'CK, V. A. [*bloquer*, Fr.] to ftop up a paffage. To enclofe a town to prevent any one from going into, or coming out of it.

BLOCKHOUSE, S. [*blockhuys*, Belg.] a fortrefs built to fecure a paffage.

BLO'CKA'DE, S. [from *blockeyn*, Teut.] a fortrefs or bulwark; a kind of fiege, wherein all paffages and avenues are feized and fhut up, fo as the befieged are reduced to the neceffity of furrendering or ftarving.

To BLOCKA'DE, V. A. to block up all the avenues to a place, fo as to prevent the enemy from receiving any fupplies of men, or provifions.

BLO'CK-HEAD, S. a perfon of a dull apprehenfion, and great ftupidity.

BLOCKHEA'DED, Adj. remarkably ftupid, dull, and incapable of improvement.

BLO'CKISHNESS, S. want of capacity, dullnefs of apprehenfion; ftupidity.

BLO'CKTIN, S. that which is pure and unwrought.

BLO'MARY, S. [from *bloma*, Sax] the firft forge in an iron work, through which the metal paffes after it has been firft melted from the mine.

BLOOD, S. [pronounced as if written *bludd*, *blud*, Sax.] a red fluid, circulating through every part of an animal body. That part which concretes into a mafs, is called the *craw*, and that which fuftains it and preferves its fluidity the *ferum*. *Blood* is ufed figuratively, for kindred, defcent, life. A perfon of a warm or fanguine temper; a rake, or one who indulges himfelf in the commiffion of irregularities.

To BLOOD, V. A. to ftain with blood; to let blood. Figuratively, to heat or exafperate, ufed with the particle *again/t*. "Much *blooded* one againft another." *Bacon.*

BLOOD-HOUND, S. a hound that follows by the fcent, felaes with great fierenefs, and will not quit the track of the perfon he purfues.

BLOO'DILY, Adv. cruelly, favagely; given to murder or bloodfhed.

BLOO'DLESS, Adj. having no blood; dead pale.

BLOOD-SHED, S. murder; flaughter.

BLOO'DSHEDDER, S. one who murders another, by giving him a wound which may make him bleed to death.

BLOO'DSHOT, or BLOO'DSHOTTEN, Adj. a diftemper in the eyes, wherein the blood-veffels appear of a bloody-colour.

BLOO'DSTONE, S. [*blood-ftein*, Dan.] in Natural Hiftory, a mineral of a green colour, fpotted with a bright blood-red: It is ufed in medicine as a ftyptic, or to ftop blood, and by goldfmiths and gilders to polifh their works.

BLOO'DY, Adj. ftained with blood Cruel; murderous; favage.

BLOODY,

BLOO'DY-FLUX, S. See DYSEN-
TERY.

BLOO'DY-MINDED, Adj. cruel; favage; murderous.

BLOOM, S. [*bloma*, Goth.] In Botany,
the flower on fruit-trees and plants, which
precedes their fruit. The fine blue fubftance
on plumbs, &c. Figur-atively, a flourifhing
ftate. In iron work, a piece of iron wrought
into a mafs two feet fquare.

To BLOOM, V. N. to produce bloffoms
of flowers. To flourifh.

BLOO'MY, Adj. full of bloffoms or
flowers. In a ftate of vigour, or perfection; flourifhing.

BLOSSOMS, S. [from *blofm, blofma*, Sax.]
in Botany, the flower which afterwards becomes fruit on trees or plants.

To BLOSSOM, V. N. to put forth
flowers or bloffoms. To yield, or he covered with flowers, which afterwards turn to
fruit.

To BLOT, V. A. [*Harris, Brit.*] to drop
ink on a paper or other fubftance. To efface any word with ink; ufed with *out*. To
render a thing invifible; to ftain, fully, or
difgrace. "It *blots* thy beauty." Shakefp.

BLOT, S. a fpot of ink dropped on paper. A dafh of the pen on a word to efface
it. Figuratively, a ftain. "A *blot* of
honour." Temple. Ufed at backgammon,
when a fingle man lies open to be taken up;
hence to *hit a blot*. "Too great a mafter, to
make a *blot* which may eafily be *hit*." Dryd.

BLOTCH, S. a fore, puftule, or eruption
on the fkin.

To BLOTE, V. A. [*blofen*, Belg.] to
fmoke or dry with fmoke.

BLOW, S. [*blewe*, Belg.] a ftroke given
with the fift, &c. a fingle attempt, a fudden
event, at once. "They lofe the province
at a *blow*." Dryd. The act of laying or de-
pofiting eggs in flefh, applied to flies.

To BLOW, V. N. [Pret. *blew*,] to
move, applied to the wind. To breathe
upon. To found by means of wind. "Let
the praifing organ *blow*." Dryd. To found
a mufical wind-inftrument. Ufed with *up*,
to mount into the air, applied to the effect
of gun-powder. "Some of the enemy's
magazines *blew up*." Tatler, No. 59. To
move by the force of wind. To increafe its
fire with a pair of bellows. To breathe upon. To form into fhape by means of the
breath, applied both to bubbles and glafs
works. Ufed with *up*, to fwell with the
wind. Figuratively, to grow vain, or proud;
to raife into the air, or deftroy, applied to
gun-powder. Ufed with *out* to extinguifh by
the breath. To cover with eggs, and corrupt applied to flies which depofite their eggs
in flefh that begins to putrify. "Let water-
flies *blow* me into abhorring." Shakefp. To
be *blown upon*; become common; to be ftale.

No. V.

To BLOW, V. N. [*blowan*, Sax.] In Botany, to bloffom, to flourifh.

BLOWTH, S. ready to blow or bloffom.
Figuratively, an imperfect ftate, capable of
improvement. "In the *blowth* and bud."
Raleigh.

BLOWZE, S. a female of a healthy countenance, or one whofe hair hangs negligently.

BLOWZY, Adj. having a ruddy face, or
the hair difordered.

BLUBBER, S. that part of a whale,
which contains the oil.

To BLUBBER, V. N. [*barbulare*, Ital.]
to weep fo as to make the cheeks fwell; to
fwell the cheeks with weeping.

BLUBBERED, Part. fwelled, big, or
large; generally applied to the lips.

BLUDGEON, S. a fhort thick ftick, ufed
as an offenfive weapon.

BLUE, Adj. [formerly fpelt *blew*, from
bleo, Sax.] of a blue colour; and as a fubftantive one of the primitive colours of the
rays of light, and among dyers for one of the
five fimple colours, of which they form the
others. It is made of woad, fmall woad, or
vouade, and indigo. The common woad is
the beft and moft neceffary for dying; the
vouade is inferior both in quality, fubftance,
and ftrength; the indigo gives a falfe colour,
but may be ufed in the proportion of fix
pound to each large bale of woad. Blue is
made more lively and bright, if the ftuff is
dipped, after dying, into luke-warm water,
or by fulling it with melted foap, and wafhing it afterwards. Painters blue is made differently, according to the different kinds of
painting it is defigned for. In limning,
fiefco, and miniature, ultramarine, blue
afhes, and fmalt are ufed; but, in oil, blue
bice, verditer, lapis, armenius, fmalt, and
litmoufe. Turnfole blue is made by boiling
four ounces of turnfole in three pints of
water for an hour; this is made ufe of in
painting on wood. Pruffian blue is made by
calcining tartar and ox blood together, boiling them afterwards in water, and mixing
with Englifh vitriol, crude allum, and fpirits
of falt. To *look blue* upon a perfon, is to behold him with an unfavourable countenance.

To BLUE, V. A. to make of blue, to
give linen a bluifh caft, by dipping them
into cold water.

BLUE-BOTTLE, S. in Botany, a flower
fhaped like a bell, of a blue colour. In Natural Hiftory, a large fly with a fhining blue
body.

BLUELY, Adv. like a blue colour, fomewhat blue, bluifh.

BLUENESS, S. that quality which denominates a thing blue. The bluenefs of the
fkies, is owing according to Sir Ifaac Newton, to the particles of the clouds being at
firft

first of such a bigness as to reflect the azure rays, before they can constitute clouds of any other colour. This being the first colour they can reflect, must likewise be that of the finest and most transparent skin, whose vapours are not gross enough to reflect any other colour. De la Hire, after observing that any black body, viewed through a white one, gives the idea or sensation of blue, says that the blueness of the sky is owing to its immense depth, which is devoid of light, being seen through clouds or air illuminated and whitened by the sun; the veins appear blue, because the blood therein being in a state of obscurity, must appear black and being seen through the membrane of the vein or white skin, will produce the perception of blueness.

BLUFF, Adj. big, swelling, surley.

BLU'ISH, Adj. somewhat blue.

BLU'ISHNESS, S. a small degree of blue.

To BLUNDER, V. N. [blunder, IS.] to be guilty of a gross mistake. To go about in a confused manner. "Blunders round about a meaning," Pope.

BLU'NDER, S. a gross or stupid mistake.

BLU'NDERBUSS, S. [from donderbusse, Belg.] a gun or fusil, that may be charged with several bullets. A person guilty of gross and ridiculous mistakes.

BLU'NDERER, S. one who cannot distinguish one thing from another; one who blunders.

BLU'NT, Adj. that which will not pierce, or cut, on account of its thickness, opposed to sharp; void of ceremony or politeness. Not easily penetrated.

To BLUNT, V. A. to spoil the edge or point of any weapon, so as to hinder it from piercing, or cutting. Figuratively, to lessen the violence of any passion.

BLU'NTLY, Adv. not able to pierce or cut; without ceremony, politeness, or elegance.

BLU'NTNESS, S. want of edge, or point. Plainness; abruptness, want of politeness.

BLU'R, S. [burra, Span.] a blot or stain. a defect.

To BLUR, V. A. to efface, to erase, to stain.

To BLU'SH, V. N. [blysen, Belg.] to redden in the face at being charged with any thing which excites shame. Figuratively, to bear the colour of a blush. Used with at before the cause. "blush at your vices," Calamy.

BLU'SH, S. a redness of the cheeks, generally occasioned by the sight of some unchaste object. This is owing to the same nerve's being extended to different parts of the body. For the fifth pair being branched from the brain to the eye, ear, muscles of

the lip, cheek, palate, tongue, and nose, when a thing is heard or seen which affects the cheeks with blushes, at the same time as it affects the eye and ear, it drives the blood into their minute vessels. Figuratively, any red colour; "the rosen blush so rare." Crashaw.

BLU'SHY, Adj. resembling a blush, "a blushy colour." Harvey.

To BLU'STER, V. N. to roar; applied to the wind. Figuratively, to bully, hector, or swagger.

BLU'STER, S. the roaring noise occasioned by the wind. Figuratively, the noisy turbulence of anger, or vanity.

BLU'STERER, S. a bully; a vain boaster.

BLU'STROUS, Adj. applied to the wind making a great noise. Applied to persons, assuming the airs of their superiors.

BO, interj. a word used to excite terror.

BOAR, S. [formerly spelt barr, bar, or bare, Sax.] the male hog, or swine.

BOA'RD, S. [bord, Sax.] a piece of thin timber, for the use of building. A table, "may Ceres bless thy board." Prior. A table, round which a council sits, the council board; the board of works. Entertainment, diet, or food. The deck, or floor of a ship. Used with on.

To BOA'RD, V. A. to enter a ship forcibly. To make the first attempt; to cover with boards.

To BOA'RD, V. N. [from borda, Brit.] to lodge and diet at a house.

BOA'RD-WAGES, S. money allowed servants for victuals.

BOA'RDER, S. one who diets at another's table, at a settled rate. A scholar that lives in the master's house.

BOA'RDING-SCHOOL, S. a school where the scholars live with, and are boarded or found in victuals by the master.

BOA'RISH, S. of the nature of a boar. Fierce, cruel, savage, brutish.

BOA'RISHNESS, S. want of delicacy, and humanity.

To BOA'ST, V. N. [bost, Brit.] to display one's abilities in an assuming manner. Used properly with of, and sometimes with the particle in. When used with against, it implies to set one's self exceedingly, or with great vanity, in opposition to another. "You have boasted against me." Ezek. xxxv. 13. Used actively, to display with great pride and ostentation; to magnify, exalt; or be proud of.

BOA'ST, S. what a person is proud of. A vain conceited display.

BOA'STER, S. one who makes a pompous display of his advantages.

BOA'STFUL, Adj. inclined to brag; ostentations.

BOAST-

BO'ASTINGLY, Adv. In such a manner as to display vain conceit.

BO'AT, S. [*bat*, *bate*, Sax.] a small open vessel, commonly wrought or moved by oars. When rowed by one man, called a sculler; when by two, named oars.

BO'ATSWAIN, S. an officer in a ship, who has charge of all her rigging, the long boat, and her furniture, stowing her by himself; calls out the several gangs to their watches, and other offices, and punishes all offenders, that are sentenced to receive punishment.

To BOB, V. N. applied to a thing which being suspended by a string, plays backwards and forwards; to play or swing against a thing, "*bobing* at their ears." Dryd. To give a person a hunch or push with the elbow.

BOB, S. a jewel which hangs from the ear. A blow, or push with the elbow.

BOB, S. a short peruke.

BO'BBIN, S. [*bobine*, Fr.] a small piece of wood in the form of a cylinder, with a little border jutting out at each end, to wind thread, worsted, silk, &c. upon. The small reed put in the hollow of a shuttle. Likewise a round white tape, used by the ladies.

BO'BCHERRY, S. a game among children, wherein a cherry is suspended by a string, which they endeavour to bite.

BO'BWIG, S. See BOB, substantive.

BO'CASINE, S. [Fr.] a kind of gummed linen cloth; buckram.

BOCARDO, in Logic, the fifth mode of the first figure of syllogisms.

BO'CKLAND, in old Law, that which was held by charter and not alienable; the same as freehold.

To BODE, V. A. [*bodian*, Sax.] to expect; to portend, used both in a good and bad sense. Used neuterly to foreshew, with the particle to before the person whom it must befall.

BO'DEMENT, S. signs foreshewing some future event. "portents, omen, or prognostic."

BO'DICE, S. stays, or a kind of waistcoat laced before, worn by country people.

BO'DILESS, Adj. without a body. Incorporeal; immaterial.

BO'DILY, Adj. that which consists of matter. That which belongs to the body; real.

BO'DKIN, S. [Brit. *bodkin*, Teut.] an instrument with a sharp point to make holes with. An instrument formed, like a needle with a long eye, used by females to run a ribbon or string in any parts of their dress.

BODY, [*bodige*, Sax.] a solid, extended, palpable substance, capable of any sort of motion, or any kind of forms, composed of particles infinitely hard, so as never to wear or break into pieces. In Anatomy, that part of an animal composed of bones, muscles, nerves, canals, juices, which are displayed with no small degree of eloquence, by Derham in his Physico Theology. A person, a human being. The real existence of a thing in opposition to an image, representation or type. "But the *body* is of Christ." Coloss. A collection of persons united; *a body of men*. Applied to a coach, among joiners, the cage or wooden frame, afterwards covered with leather, &c. on the out-side, and lined and stuffed within. Applied to dress, that which covers the body. "The *body* of a coat or gown." The materials which compose a manufacture. Applied to liquors, strength. "Brandy of a good *body*." Substance. The main or chief part of a thing. "The *body* of a church." A perfect system which contains all the branches of a science. "A *body* of surgery." "A *body* of husbandry."

BODY CLOATHS, S. the cloaths which cover a horse's body, when dieted, &c.

To BODY, V. A. to produce, or bring into being. "Imagination *bodies* forth the forms of things unknown." Shak.

BOG, [from *bog*, Irish] a moist rotten spot of earth, which sinks and gives way to the weight of the body. A marsh or morass.

To BO'GGLE, V. N. [*bogil*, Belg.] to start, or fly back at a disagreeable object; to hesitate, to doubt, to dissemble.

BO'GGLER, S. a person who doubts, or hesitates; a timorous person.

BOG-HOUSE, S. a necessary-house.

BO'GGY, Adj. consisting of, or abounding in bogs.

BO'HEA, [*wuvi bui*, Chin.] a tea which comes from China, and is the second gathering; for all tea grow on the same plant, and differ only according to the season of gathering, and the method of drying. Where perspiration is too great, the force of the vessels too strong, the circulation of the blood too rapid; in spitting blood, either from the tenderness of the vessels of the lungs, sharpness, or velocity of the humours; in abscesses of the lungs and hectic coughs; in obstructions from the fulness of the humours; and in inflammations of the side, from a fullness of the vessels, bohea tea is very serviceable, and where it agrees with a person, excels all other vegetables for preventing sleepiness or dulness, for taking off weariness or fatigue; for raising the spirits, corroborating the memory, and other such uses; which depend on a due temperature of the brain, if used chiefly in an afternoon, drank moderately, and not too hot, as is the general custom.

BOHEMIA, a kingdom of Europe, bounded on the N. by Misnia, and Lusacia, on the E. by Silesia and Moravia, on the S. by Austria, and the W. by Bavaria. Some place Silesia and Moravia in this kingdom; bu

but about this geographers diff r; and some will have it only to consist of Proper Bohe mid and Moravia; but this is a distinction of no consequence. It is about 200 miles in length, and 150 in breadth, and is very fertile in corn, saffron, hops, and pastures. In the mountains there are mines of gold and silver, and in some places they find diamonds, granates, copper, and lead. The Roman Catholic religion is the principal, though there are many Protestants. The chief rivers are only the Muldau, the Elbe, and the Oder. Their language is the Sclavonian, with a mixture of the German. The capital town, or city, is Prague. It is subject to the house of Austria.

To BO'IL, V. N. [*bouiller*, Fr.] to be greatly agitated with heat; to be set into a violent motion by fire, and so to be able to scald any thing, applied to water. Figuratively, hot; to be placed in boiling water; to dress victuals by boiling. To *boil over*, applied to fluids, to have its contents to rarefied by heat, as to run over the sides of a vessel not large enough to contain it in that state.

To BO'IL, V. A. to dress victuals, in boiled water.

BO'IL, S. See BILE.

BO'ILARY, S. a place where salt is boiled, at the salt-works.

BO'ILER, S. one who boils. A vessel in which a thing is boiled.

BO'ILING, S. the particles of fuel passing the pores of the vessel, mix with the liquid; and meeting with a resistance there sufficient to destroy their motion, they communicate it to the water; hence arises a small intestine motion in the particles of that fluid, but the first cause still continuing, that motion is increased till the agitation of the water becomes sensible. The particles of air dilated and expanded thus by heat, moving upwards, will meet and coalesce in their ascent, by which means great quantities of water will rise and fall alternately, or, in other words, the water will boil; but the heat continuing and the rarefaction increasing, the water will now be too much for the vessel to contain, and will consequently swell over its sides, which the vulgar call boiling over. It is necessary to be added, that when water boils it cannot be rendered hotter by any degree of fire whatever; for as the heat of boiling water is in proportion to the pressure of the atmosphere upon its surface, while that pressure remains the same, the heat will be the same likewise.

BO'ISTEROUS, S. [*byster*, Pol.] violent, furious, stormy; roaring, applied to the wind; warm, hot, outrageous, applied to persons; violent, applied to heat. "The heat becomes too powerful and *boisterous*." *Woodw.*

BO'ISTEROUSLY, Adv. in a violent furious manner.

BO'LARY, Adj. [from *bole*] partaking of the quality of bole or clay.

BO'LD, Adj. [*bald*, Sax.] daring, brave, courageous, fearless; applied to work of art, executed with great spirit and freedom; swelling or standing out to the sight, applied to painting and sculpture. Imprudent, rude, applied to the behaviour. To *make bold*, to be free.

To BO'LDEN, V. A. to grow bold; to make bold.

BO'LD-FACED, Adj. impudent.

BO'LDLY, Adv. in a manner free from fear or timorousness. Confidently; impudently.

BO'LDNESS, S. a readiness or alacrity to prosecute a design, notwithstanding its difficulties, applied to action; courage, intrepidity, undauntedness. An execution performed with great freedom and spirit, opposed to a scrupulous exactness; a reason for undertaking a bold action. "Having therefore *boldness* to enter, &c." *Heb.* x. 19. The power to speak or do what we intend, before others, without fear or disorder. Impudence, rudeness.

BO'LE, S. [*bolus*, Lat.] In Natural History, a ponderous different coloured earth and some mark, but less fat than clay, somewhat soluble in the mouth, of a rough taste, and stains when handled. *Armenian bole*, is a ponderous fat earth, of an astringent taste, found in Armenia. By Galen, recommended in dysenteries, or other fluxes, in spitting of blood, and ulcers of the lungs. Outwardly applied, it is drying, styptic, and astringent, and therefore proper to stop blood flowing from fresh wounds.

BO'LIS, S. [Lat.] in Natural History, a great fiery ball, swiftly hurried through the air.

BO'LSTER, S. [*bolster*, Sax.] a long ticking sack filled with feathers, flocks, &c. Used to support a person's head in bed. A pad to hide some deformity. In Surgery, a piece of linen doubled, laid upon a wound.

To BO'LSTER, V. A. to raise a person's head with a bolster. In Surgery, to keep the lips of a wound close, by a compress. Figuratively, to support or maintain. "To *bolster error*." *Hooker.*

BO'LT, S. [*bolt*, Brit. *boult*, Belg.] a dart shot from a cross-bow. Lightning; a thunder-bolt. Used with *upright* is straight or upright as to straw. "I stood best upright." *Spen.* No. 90. A short piece of iron made to fasten doors. Irons made use of to secure a felon. "Lay *bolts* enough upon him." *Shakesp.* An obstacle, impediment.

To BO'LT, V. A. to fasten or secure with a bolt, to speak without hesitation. "When vice can *bolt* her arguments." *Milton.* To confine or restrain, used with the particle

particle up, "Shackles accident, and *boils up* change." *Sharp.* To separate the fine from coarse parts of any thing with a sieve. Figuratively, to separate truth from falshood, by rigorous examination; used with the particle *out*. "Time and nature will *bolt out* the truth." *L'Estrange.* To clear from impurities, to purify or cleanse. "The fanned flow, that's *bolted* by the northern blast." *Shakespeare.*

To BOLT, V. N. to spring out suddenly, to shut out, To come in a hurry.

BO'LT-ROPE, S. the rope on which the fail of a ship is fastened.

BO'LTER, S. a sieve made use of to separate flour from bran.

BO'LTSPRIT, S. See BOWSPRIT.

BO'LUS, S. [Lat.] a medicine made into a soft mass, about the size of a nutmeg.

BO'MB, S. [*bombus*, Lat.] in Gunnery, a hollow ball of cast iron, furnished with a vent for a fusee or wooden tube, replete with combustible matter, to be thrown out of a mortar-piece. When the fuse is set on fire, it burns till it reaches the gunpowder, which goes off and bursts the shell to pieces with incredible violence. The largest are about 17 inches in diameter, two inches thick, carry 48 lb. of powder, and weigh about 490 lb. Their invention is of late date, since the first mention of them is in 1588, at the siege of Watchendonk in Guelderland.

To BO'MB, V. A. to attack with bombs. To bombard.

BO'MBARD, S. [*bombarda*, Lat.] a piece of artillery, exceeding short and thick, with a very large mouth, called by some a basilic.

To BOMBARD, V. A. to fling bombs. To attack with bombs.

BOMBARDIE'R, S. the person who drives the fusee, fixes the shell, points, loads, and fires the mortar. The engineer, who fires or directs the throwing of bombs out of the mortars.

BOMBA'RDMENT, S. an attack by throwing bombs.

BOM'BASIN, S. [Fr. pronounced *bombazeen*, from *bombicinus*, Lat.] a slight silken manufacture.

BOMBA'ST, S. [probably derived from *Bombasius*, one of the names of Paracelsus, who was remarkable for his vanity and unintelligible jargon] high, pompous and swelling expressions without any important sense.

BO'MBAST, Adj. pompous, sonorous, but conveying mean ideas.

BO'MB-KETCH, or BO'MB-VESSEL, a small vessel stoutly built, to bear the shock of a mortar at fea, when bombs are to be thrown from it into a town. They have sometimes three masts, and square fails, sometimes ketch fashion, with one and a mizen.

BO'MBARDA, S. a girl of the town; a prostitute.

BON CHRE'TIEN, S. [Fr. good christian] a pear so called.

BOND, S. [*bond*, *bonda*, Sax.] any thing which confines or binds cords, or chains. Union, joining, or connexion. Captivity, imprisonment, loss of liberty; obligation. A tye, applied to alliance. In law, a deed by which a person obliges himself to perform certain acts.

BO'NDAGE, S. flavery; captivity.

BOND-MAID, S. a female slave.

BOND-MAN, S. a man slave.

BOND-SERVANT, S. one who is under bond to serve his master.

BOND-SERVICE, S. flavery.

BOND-SLAVE, S. a person confined to flavery.

BOND'S-MAN, S. a slave, a person who has given his hand, as security for another.

BOND'S-WOMAN, S. a woman slave or who has given her bond.

BONE, S. [*ban*, Sax. *bein*, Teut.] in Anatomy, a white, hard, brittle substance, supporting and strengthening the body; defending some of the more essential parts, giving shape to the human fabric and assisting it in its motion. The wisdom and benevolence of providence is very conspicuous in their formation; they are bigger in their extremities than in the middle, that their articulations might be the stronger and less subject to luxation; and that the middle of the bone should be strong enough to support its destined weight and resist accidents, the fibres are in that part more closely compacted together; to which we may add, the hollowness of the bone itself, which renders it not so easily broken, as if solid and of a smaller size; for if two bones of equal length, and of an equal number of fibres, the strength of the one to the strength of the other, will be as their diameter. To this must be added, the oily matter, found in the cellular substance of the bone, and the marrow included in its cavity, which prevents its growing dry, and by that means becoming brittle: it lubricates the articulations of the bones, hinders their ends from being worn, on over-heated by motion, moistens the ligaments by which they are tied to each other, and renders their motion easy. The number of bones in a human fabric are reckoned to be 245, exclusive of the *Offa fesamoidea*, which amount to 48 more. To expatiate on the use contrivance of their various connexions and other particulars relating to their texture, uses and articulations, does not suit the intended compass of this work, but whoever would at the same time acquaint himself with their wonders, and be led to acknowledge the benevolence of Providence, will find no small improvement, and pleasure in the perusal of Cheselden's Osteology. *L'Estrange.* To *make no bones*, is to make no scruple. *To give a person a bone to* pick,

pick,

pet, a low phrase, for laying an obstacle in his way; A bone of contention; a cause of strife, alluding to setting dogs a fighting, by flinging a bone between them.

To BO'NE, V. A. to take the bones from the flesh.

BONE-LACE, S. a cheap sort of flaxen lace.

BONELESS, Adj. having no bones.

BONESETTER, S. one who sets broken, or dislocated bones.

BO'NNET, S. [bonet, Fr.] a cap; or outward covering made of silk, worn instead of a hat by the ladies. In Fortification, a small work, or little ravelin, without a ditch. Bonnet a prêtre, or a priest's cap, an outwork with three salient angles and two inwards, differing from a tenaille, from its sides growing narrower at the gorge, instead of being parallel, and opening at the front or head, like a pair of arrands, or swallow's tail. Among Sailors, small sails set on the courses, or fastened to the bottom of the mizzen, mainsail, or foresail of a ship.

BO'NNILY, Adv. gayly, handsomely.

BONNY, Adj. gay, chearful, handsome, sprightly.

BONUM MAGNUM, S. a species of pear.

BONY, Adj. consisting of bone. Abounding in bone.

BOOBY, S. [from bobo, Span.] a dull, heavy, stupid fellow.

BOOK, S. [from boc, Sax. buch, Teut.] a composition of some person, of a length sufficient to make a volume. A collection of papers sewed, or bound intended to be wrote on. The division of an author's subject. Used with the particle in, and the personal pronouns his or my, to be much esteemed by a person, "I was so much in his books, that, &c." Addif. Without book, by the mere strength of memory, by the strength of a person's natural parts, without having committed his thoughts to writing.

To BOOK, V. A. to write any thing in a book.

BOOK-BINDER, S. one who binds books.

BOOKFUL, Adj. one who has gathered opinions from books, without having digested what he has read.

BOOKISH, Adj. fond of books, or reading, pedantic.

BOOKISHNESS, S. a great fondness for books.

BOOK-KEEPER, S. a person employed in a compting-house, to register the transactions daily carried on, and to methodize them.

BOOK-KEEPING, S. the art of keeping accounts, or registering a person's transactions in such a manner, that he may at any time know the true state of the whole or any

part of his affairs with clearness and expedition.

BOOK-LEARNED, Adj. conversant in books; one that reads much, but has no parts or invention.

BOOK-LEARNING, S. improvement acquired from books.

BOOKSELLER, S. one whose business it is to sell books.

BOOK-WORM, S. a mite or worm which preys upon books. Figuratively, one who applies himself too intensely to study.

BOOM, S. [from, Sax. buan, Belg.] a long pole used to spread out the clew of the studding sail, main sail, or foresail. A bar of timber laid a-cross a harbour, to secure its entrance.

BOON, S. [from bene, Sax.] a gift, present, or favour.

BOON, Adj. [bon, Fr.] merry; gay; brisk.

BOOR, S. [boer, Belg.] an unpolished countryman, a clown.

BOORISH, Adj [bowrisch, Teut.] unpolished; rude; clownish.

BOORISHLY, Adv. unpolitely, rudely.

BOORISHNESS, S. a quality inconsistent with good manners or politeness. Clownishness.

To BOOT, V. A. [boten, Belg.] to be of advantage. To profit. To enrich, or accumulate.

BOOT, S. [bote, bote, Sax.] gain, profit, advantage. To boot, implies besides, over and above.

BOOT, S. [botes, Arm.] a leather covering for the legs and feet, used by those who ride on horseback. A leathern receptacle under a coach-box, used for carrying parcels, &c.

To BOOT, V. A. to put on boots.

BOOTED, Part. having boots on the legs. In boots.

BOOTCATCHER, S. one who pulls off the boots at an inn.

BOOTES, S. [Lat.] In Astronomy, the name of a northern constellation of fixed stars, consisting of 551 one of which is of the first magnitude.

BOOTH, S. [buth, Brit. bode, Sax.] a temporary house built of boards, or boughs.

BOOTLESS, Adj. unavailing; unsuccessful; unprofitable. "I have sent him bootless home" Shak.

BOOT-TREE, S. an instrument which is drove in by main force, in order to stretch or widen a boot.

BOOTY, S. [bote, buit, Belg.] plunder, pillage, spoils. Things acquired by robbery, or plunder. To play booty, is to play unfairly.

BOPEEP, S. the act of thrusting the head in sight, and drawing it back again instantaneously.

BOR-

BORABLE, Adj. that which may be bored.

BO'RACE, S. [*borago*, Lat.] in Botany, its impalement is permanent, and divided into five parts. Its flowers are used in medicinal cordials, and the herb for cool tankards in the summer.

BO'RAX, S. [Lat.] a salt prepared from the evaporation of water which runs from the copper mines in the East-Indies. Likewise an artificial salt made of sal ammoniac, nitre, calcined tartar, sea salt, and alum dissolved in wine. The native borax called by the Arabians, rincar, or tincal, which signifies a nitre fit for soldering gold, is used, for soldering and fluxing metals, and promoting the fusing of such, as it would be very difficult to melt without it. In Medicine, it is used as an emenagogue, stimulant, and diuretic, in a suppression of the menses, and to promote delivery; is usually joined with myrrh and saffron, and its dose is from 5 to 15 grains. It is used as a cosmetic, or beautifier; and if not so dear, would recommend itself to the dyers to give a gloss to their colours.

BO'RDER, S. [*bord*, Sax.] the extremities, or edge. The confines of a country. The outer part of a garment. A strip of flowers at the edge of a flower bed, &c. in a garden. In Heraldry, an addition on the limb of a shield. It is accounted, as a signal of protection, favour, or reward; and is bestowed by kings on such as they regard or esteem. In Printing, an ornament of flowers, &c. round the edges of a composition.

To BO'RDER, V. N. to live near to the extremities of a country. To be near. To approach. "All wit which *borders upon* prophaneness." *Tillotf.* Used with the particle *upon*. Used actively, to set a narrow ornament at the edges of a thing.

To BO'RE, [*borian*, Sax.] to make a hole by a sharp pointed instrument; To push forwards with violence. In Farriery, to carry the nose near the ground, applied to an horse.

BO'RE, S. the hole made by boring; the instrument used in boring; the dimensions of a hole or cavity.

BO'RE, the preter of *bear*.

BO'REAL, S. towards the north.

BO'REAS, S. [Lat. supposed to be derived from *bor*, Celt. the morning, because people situated in that part receive their light from thence] the north wind.

BO'REE, S. [Fr.] a dance comprised of three steps joined together by two motions, and begins with a crochet rising.

BO'RER, S. a gimlet, or piercer; the person who bores.

BO'RN, past passive of *bear*.

To be BO'RN, V. N. to come or be brought into the world; to be designed by

birth, used with the particles *to* and *for*. "He was *born to* empire." And with the particle *of* before the mother. "*Born of* the Virgin Mary." *Creed.*

BO'ROUGH, S. of [*borhoe*, *borhg*, *burb*, *burg*, Sax.] a town or corporation, which sends members to parliament. The whole number of boroughs amounts to 149. *Royal boroughs*, are corporations in Scotland, made for the advantage of trade, having commissioners to represent them in parliament. *Borough-English*, in Law, a customary descent of lands and tenements, whereby estates descend not to the eldest, but to the youngest son, or if the owner have no son, to his younger brother. *Littleton* says, the reason of this custom is founded in a presumption, that the youngest is least able to provide for himself. *Kitch.* 102. *Dyer*, 179. *Head-borough*, is the president, or chairman of a hundred. In parishes, a kind of head-constable, having others for his assistants.

BOROUGHBRIDGE, a town in the N. Riding of Yorkshire, with a market on Saturdays, and three fairs, on April 27, for horned cattle and sheep, on June 22, for horses, horned cattle, sheep, and hard-ware, and on October 23, for horned cattle and sheep. It is seated on the S. side of the river Youre, over which there is a handsome stone bridge. The town is not large, but commodious; and sends two members to parliament. It is 17 miles N. of York, 53 S. of Durham, and 200 N. by W. of London. Lon. 16. 30. Lat. 54. 10.

To BO'RROW, V. A. [*borgian*, Sax.] the taking things of another on condition of returning them again. Figuratively, to take that which belongs to another. To assume a property that you have not. "In *borrow'd* shapes." *Shak.*

BO'RROW, S. the state of a thing borrowed; the thing taken of another to be returned again.

BO'RROWER, S. he that takes of another, on condition of returning it. He that uses what is another's, as if it were his own. He that adopts the sentiments of another, without acknowledging that they are so.

BO'SCAGE, S. [Fr.] a grove, or thicket. In Painting, a picture or landskip, representing woods. In Law, mast, or such sustenance as trees afford cattle.

BO'SKY, S. [*boscque*, Fr.] abounding with wood, woody.

BO'SPHORUS, S. [from *bora*, Gr. and *mph*] a narrow streight or arm of the sea, which it might be supposed an ox could swim over; at present confined to that of Thrace, called the streights of Constantinople; and the Cimmerian or Scythian Bosphorus.

BO'SQUETS, S. [from *boschetto*, Ital.] small grove, or compartiment, formed of trees, shrubs, or tall growing plants, planted

in quarters. When formed of trees, whose verdure is of different degrees, surrounded with hedges of lime, elm or hornbeam, which do not intercept the sight of the trees, and interspersed with some of the largest growing flowers, they have a very good effect; but are proper only for spacious gardens, and are both expensive in their first making, and in their keeping afterwards.

BO'SOM, S. [*bofme*, *bojm*, Sax.] the breast; the embrace of the arms; bubbling any thing to the breast. The middle of any inclosure. "The *bofom* of the wood." The warmest and most tender affections. In Composition, it implies any thing near or dear to a person; thus *bofom-friends*, *bofom secret*.

To BO'SOM, V. A. to inclose. in the bosom. To keep secret.

BO'SS, S. [*bosse*, Fr.] an ornament raised above the other work; a shining prominence. The prominent part. A thick body.

BO'SSAGE, S. in Architecture, a projecting stone laid rough in a building.

BOSTON, a town of Lincolnshire, with two markets, on Wednesdays and Saturdays, and three fairs, on May 4, for sheep, another on August 11, called Tunn-Fair, and on December 11, for horses. It is commodiously seated on both sides the river Witham, over which it has a handsome, high, wooden-bridge; and, being not far from its influx into the sea, enjoys a good trade. It is a large handsome town, with a spacious market-place; as also a high steeple, which some pretend is the best built tower in the world; and it serves as a land-mark for sailors. It is 37 miles S. E. of Lincoln, 49 N. by N. E. of Peterborough, and 114 N. from London. Lon. 17. 30. lat. 53. 3.

BOSTON, the capital town of New-England, in North-America, seated on a peninsula at the bottom of a fine bay, covered by small islands and rocks, and defended by a castle and platforms of guns, which render the approach of an enemy very difficult. It lies in the form of a crescent about the harbour; and the country beyond rising gradually, affords a delightful prospect. There is but one safe channel to approach the harbour, and that is so narrow, that three ships can scarce sail a-breast; but within the harbour, there is room for 500 sail to lie at anchor. At the bottom of the bay, there is a pier, near 2000 feet in length, which ships of the greatest burthen may come up close to; and, on the N. side, there are warehouses for the merchants. The streets are handsome, and the chief runs from the pier to the town-house. There are 10 churches of all denominations, of which 6 belong to the independents. At each end of the town there is a battery of eight guns; and, about a league from it, there is a beautiful strong castle, with a large garrison in time of war. The number of inhabitants are reckoned to be about 14,000;

and it is one of the most flourishing towns in North-America. Lon. 3. 6. 0. lat. 42. 24.

BOSWORTH, a town in Leicestershire, with a market on Wednesdays, and two fairs, on May 8, for horses, cows, and sheep, and on July 10, for horses and cows. It is seated on a pretty high hill, in a country fertile in corn and grass. It is noted for a bloody battle fought here between Richard III. and Henry earl of Richmond, afterwards Henry VII. wherein King Richard lost his life and crown. It is 13 miles S. W. of Leicester, and 104 N. N. W. of London. Lon. 16. 10. lat. 52. 45.

BOTA'NIC, BOTA'NICAL, adj. [*botanicus*, Gr.] relating to herbs; skilled in herbs.

BO'TANIST, one skilled in the nature of plants, and their culture. The most famous of our nation are Dr. Hales; Dr. Hill; Bradley and Miller; Though Linnæus, a foreigner, seems to be more universally known and followed.

BOTA'NOLOGY, S. [*botanologia*, Gr.] a discourse or treatise on plants.

BO'TANY, S. [from *botane*, Gr.] the science of herbs and plants. This study was very little cultivated till Bauhine arose in the 16th century and both reduced it to method, and increased the number of its objects. Our countryman Mr. Ray, did not a little contribute to the perfection of this science, and is looked on by foreigners with veneration even to this day. Tournefort is not wanting in his claim for our esteem, it must be owned his pains and assiduity were very great, but if we at present consider the beautiful order into which vegetables are now reduced, and the precision with which their several classes are ordered by the care of Linnæus, Miller, &c. we must own ourselves much obliged to moderns for that accuracy, which the ancients were strangers to.

BOT'ARGO, S. [*botargo*, Span.] a kind of sausage made with the roes and blood of the mullet fish. It is eat with olive oil and lemon juice, cut into slices, like the country, is reckoned an elegant dish, and much in vogue in catholic countries, during Lent.

BO'TCH, S. [*dos*, Fr. *beune*, Ital.] a swelling, which afterwards exsuills, and causes a disagreeable idea. Figuratively, work clumsily finished. Something added, in a clumsy manner.

To BO'TCH, V. A. [*botsen*, Dan.] to mend or patch in a clumsy manner. To join things, which do not agree with each other. To mark with patches, scabs.

BO'TCHER, S. one who mends in a clumsy manner; a person who performs any thing in a clumsy manner.

BO'TCHY, adj. marked with botches, sores.

BOTH, Adj. [*bustu*, Ill. *bam*, *batwa*, Sax.] two persons or things, it unites them into

4

into one collective idea, which implies the two.

BOTS, S. [from *bitan*, Sax.] a species of small worms breeding in horses.

BO'TTLE, S. [*bouteille*, Fr.] a vessel with a narrow mouth to contain liquor. Figuratively a quart. A bundle of grass or hay.

To BOTTLE, V. A. to put liquor into bottles. "A hogshead of wine is to be *bottled off*." *Swift.*

BOTTLE-FLOWER, S. [in botany] the *cyanus*, or *centaurea*, a compound flower. There are twenty species. That which is used by the colliers, grows on the mountains of Italy and Spain, the root of which was reckoned to be binding, good for all kind of fluxes, and of great use to heal wounds; but is seldom prescribed at present.

BOTTLE-NOSED, Adj. one who has a large nose, especially towards the end.

BOTTLE-SCREW, S. a spiral wire to pull a cork out of a bottle.

BO'TTOM, S. [*botm*, Sax.] the lowest part of a thing. The bed of earth, or gravel over which the water glides. A valley, a dale; foundation. To be at the *bottom*, to be concerned in, to be privy to. "He was at the bottom of many excellent counsels." *Addis.* To venture in one *bottom*, to run a risque together. The *bottom* of a lane or street, is the lowest part. The *bottom* of beer, the dregs. Applied to thread, a ball, or bundle.

To BO'TTOM, V. A. [from the noun] to build upon as a foundation; to wind thread into a ball. Used neuterly, to be built on; or supported by.

BOTTOMED, Adj. having a bottom. "Flat-*bottomed* boats." *Bacon.*

BOTTOMLESS, Adj. having no bottom; exceeding deep. Figuratively, boundless, insatiable. "Then be my passions bottomless." *Shak.*

BOTTOMRY, S. in trade, the borrowing money upon the security of the keel or bottom of a ship. Likewise the lending money, for which the lender is to be paid a larger sum at the return of the ship, standing to the hazard of her voyage, in consideration of which though the interest demanded be 20, 30, or 40 per cent. and upwards, it is not esteemed usury.

BOU'D, S. an insect which breeds in malt, called also a weevil.

BOUGH, S. [from *bog, boga*, and *bah*, Sax.] an arm or large shoot of a tree, larger than a branch.

BOUGHT, preter of *buy*.

BOUILL'ZE, or BOUILL'ON, S. [Fr.] any thing made from boiled meat; broth, or soup.

To BOULT, See BOLT.

No. V.

To BOU'NCE, V. N. [formed from its sound] to strike with such force as to rebound back, making a noise at the same time; to spring with force, like beer out of a bottle. Bully, or hector.

BOU'NCE, S. a violent, and sudden stroke or blow; a sudden crack or noise; a threat or boast.

BOU'NCER, S. one who is vociferous in his own praise. A bully, a boaster.

BOUND, S. [from *bind*, *borne*, Fr.] a restraint, a leap, or spring; the flying back of any thing which is struck against another.

To BOU'ND, V. N. [*bondir*, Fr.] to spring or move on by leaps; to fly back when struck against a thing. Used actively, to make a thing leap, or move by fits, from the earth.

BOU'ND, part. of BIND.

BOU'ND, Adj. [*obondre*, Sax.] destined to a certain place.

BOU'NDARY, S. the extremities, confines, or limits of a thing, or country.

BOU'NDEN, part. passive of BIND.

BOU'NDLESS, Adj. unlimited; confined by no power: insatiable.

BOU'NTEOUS, Adj. liberal, generous, kind.

BOU'NTEOUSLY, Adv. in a liberal generous manner.

BOU'NTEOUSNESS, S. the quality of conferring benefits from a principle of kindness.

BOU'NTIFUL, Adv. conferring favours from an internal principal of kindness; generous; very much abounding in valuable products. "As *bountiful* as mines of India." *Shak.* Used with *of* before the thing giving, and *to* before the person receiving. "Of which he is so *bountiful* to his kingdom." *Dryden.*

BOU'NTIFULLY, Adv. in such a manner as to confer favours from a principle of kindness. Applied to things plentifully producing what is of service.

BOU'NTIFULNESS, S. a great propensity to conferring benefits. A constant and unrestrained distribution of favours to an inferior. Generosity, munificence.

BOU'NTY, S. [from *bonté*, Fr.] the conferring or bestowing benefits, distinguished from charity, because exercised towards objects not entirely necessitous.

To BOU'RGEON, V. N. [from *bourgeonner*, Fr.] to sprout, to shoot; to produce buds.

BOU'RN, S. [from *borne*, Fr.] the extremities, bounds, or limits of a place or country.

BOURN, S. [from *burn*, Sax.] a brook or torrent.

BOURN, a town of Lincolnshire, with a market on Saturdays, and three fairs, on

A 2   March

March 7, May 6, and October 29, for horses and horned cattle. It is seated near a spring called Burdwell head, from which proceeds a river that runs through the town. It is a pretty large place, and has a good market for corn and provisions. It is noted for the coronation of King Edmond. It is 17 miles N. of Peterborough, 35 S. of Lincoln, and 93 N. of London. Lon. 17. 15. lat. 52. 40.

To BOUSE, V. N. [byysen, Belg.] to drink immoderately; to get intoxicated; to tope.

HOU'SY, Adj. intoxicated with liquor.

BOU'T, S. [botta, Ital.] a turn at once. Once. "This bout." This once.

BOU'TANT, Adj. [butter, Fr.] in Architecture, a pillar boutant is a large chain or pile of stone, made to support a vault, terrace, or wall.

BOU'TEFEU, S. [Fr.] one who is the author of quarrels, or contentions. An incendiary.

BOU'TISALE, S. [from bouty and sale] a sale wherein things are disposed of for less than their value, alluding to the sale of plunder or bounty, which seldom fetches its due value. "The great bountisale of colleges." Hayw.

To BOW, V. A. [bugan, Sax.] to bend the body in token of respect. To overpower with sorrow, to press, or crush. To bend, or be bent. To make a bow; to stoop. "Bowed down upon their knees." Judg. vii. 6. to stoop under the pressure of affliction. "They stoop, they bow down together."

BOW, S. a stooping of the head and body by way of ceremony.

BOW, S. [bava, Brit. boga, Sax.] a warlike instrument, the extremities of which are tied by a string, which being drawn towards the body of a person, bends the wood, and by its elasticity, forces an arrow placed on a string, with great violence, to a great distance. A long narrow piece of wood furnished with hair, and used in playing on stringed instruments. The loop of a ribband tied in a knot. Applied to a ship, that part which begins at the loof and ends at the sternmost parts of the forecastle. The piece of ordnance lying in this place, is called the bow-piece, and the anchors, which hang here, are called her great and little bowers.

BO'W-BEARER, S. one who carries a bow. In law, an under officer of a forest.

To BO'WEL, V. A. to pierce the bowels; to penetrate deep. "To the bowel'd cavern darting deep" Thomson.

BO'WELS, S. [from boyaux, Fr.] the intestines within the body; the guts. The inner part of any thing. "The bowels of the mountain," Addis. Tenderness, pity, humanity, or compassion.

BO'WER, S. an arbour formed of the branches of green trees, arched at the top. The anchor of a ship.

To BO'WER, V. A. to make or include in a bower. Figuratively to inclose.

BO'WERY, Adj. full of bowers; shady, resembling a bower.

BOWL, S. [from bwelin, Brit.] a drinking vessel, rather wide than deep, shaped like a tea cup, but of greater dimensions. The hollow part of any thing which holds liquor. "The bowl of a spoon." Swift.

BO'WL, S. [bol, Belg. boule, Fr.] a round piece of wood, to be rolled along the ground.

To BOW'L, V. A. to roll a bowl along; to roll a bowl at any mark; to knock down with a bowl.

BO'W-LEGGED, Adj. having crooked legs, which resemble a bow when bent.

BO'WLER, S. He that bowls or plays at bowls.

BO'WLINE, or BOWLING, S. a rope fastened to the middle part of the outside of a sail, by two or three ropes, like a crow foot, called the bowling bridle.

BO'WLING-GREEN, S. a piece of ground of a true horizontal surface, kept for playing at bowls.

BO'WMAN, S. a person who shoots with a bow.

To BOW'SSEN, V. A. [from byssen, Belg.] to plunge into water; to drench. "Bowssened again." Carew.

BO'WYER, S. one who shoots with a bow; one who makes bows.

BO'W-STRING, S. the string by which a bow is bent.

BO'W-SPRIT, or BOLT-SPRIT, [from bolt and sprit, Belg.] a mast at the prow of a vessel, resting slopeways on the head of the main stern, fastened by the forestay and to the partners of the foremast; serving to carry the sprit, and sprit-top-sail and jackstaff.

B'OX, S. [box, buxtreow, Sax.] its leaves are plinnated and ever green. Linnæus ranges it in the fourth section of his 21st. class. There are three species. Its wood is yellowish, hard, solid, even, very heavy, and takes a good polish. The best is used in sculpture, wind and string instruments of music, such as flutes, violins, &c. that of an inferior quality serves for smaller works, such as balls, tops, handles, combs, &c.

BOX, S. [boxb, Teut. box, Sax.] a case to hold any thing. The case of a mariner's compass. The inner case of a watch. The first story of seats in a play-house formed into small square rooms.

BOX, S. [bod, Brit.] a blow or stroke on the face with the hand.

To BOX, V. A. to fight with the fists. To strike with the hand.

BO'XEN, Adj. made of box; of a box colour.

BO'XER, S. one who fights with his fist.

BOY,

BOY, S. [from _boke_ or _babe_, Teut from בֹ _bob_, Heb.] one of the male sex till they are fifteen years old; a person who wants the sedateness and discretion of manhood.

BOY'AR, or BOIAR, S. [Ruff.] a name of dignity applied, in Ruffia, to the lords of the Czar's court, who are thirty in number, compose his council of state, are obliged to reside at Moscow, or follow the prince when he goes to any other place; they attend his levee every day, striking their foreheads as a mark of their respect and loyalty; when they ride on horse-back, they carry a battle-drum before them on which they strike, with the butt end of their whip, to give notice of their approach, that people may make way for them; and act both as counsellors of state, and judges in private affairs. Likewise the title of the nobility of Transilvania, who are descendants of the Vaivods.

BOY'HOOD, S. the state extending from infancy to youth, or till a person is fifteen years old.

BO'YISH, S. like a boy. Childish, trifling, poetile.

BO'YISHLY, Adv. in a childish, trifling manner.

BO'YISHNESS, S. want of thought or sedateness, childishness, trifling.

BO'YISM, S. that which becomes a boy only; a term of reproach.

To BRA'BBLE, V. N. to contest a thing. To quarrel, to clamour.

BRA'BBLER, S. a clamorous, quarrelsome fellow.

To BRACE, V. A. [embrasser, Fr.] to tie, or wind tight round a thing. To strain or stretch.

BRACE, S. a bandage; that which keeps the parts of a thing close together, that which keeps a thing stretched. In Printing a crooked line, marked thus } and used by poetical writers at the end of a triplet, the state of a thing that is stretched. "When it has lost its _brace_, or tension." _Hester_. In Architecture, a piece of timber used to keep a building steady. In sea affairs, ropes fastened to the yard arms of a ship. Applied to a coach, the thick thongs of leather on which the body of the coach hangs.

BRA'CE, S. in hunting, two, or a pair.

BRA'CELET, S. [a diminutive of _bras_, or _bras_, Fr.] an ornament worn round the wrist. The African nations wear them on their legs just above the ancle, and on the fleshy part of their arms above the elbow, and are so passionately fond of them that they will barter their richest merchandize, nay, even their parents, wives, and children for them. A piece of defensive armour for the arm. Among gilders, a piece of leather filled with stuff, worn by them on the wrist of the left arm, that they may not hurt themselves

silver by leaning on the vice, in order to polish or burnish their work.

BRA'CER, S. that which braces, or makes tight. A bandage.

BRA'CHIAL, Adj. [from brachium, Lat.] that which belongs to the arm.

BRA'CHIÆUS, S. [from brachium, Lat.] an arm] in Anatomy, the name given to two muscles of the arm, the one the external, and the other internal.

BRA'CHMANS, S. [perhaps from בָּרַךְ, to fly] Indian philosophers, who lived a very good life in woods, slept on hides, abstained from the flesh of animals, and believed the doctrine of the transmigration of the soul. They spent the greatest part their time in praying and singing anthems; began their care of their pupils so early, that they fear some persons to the mother as soon as they knew she was with child, who attended her during her pregnancy, giving her noble lectures during that dangerous state, and when she was delivered carried the child with them. They considered life as a state of conception, and death as a birth to a happy life, for those who had regulated their lives according to the dictates of true philosophy. They esteemed the accidents of human life indifferent, because one person is generally pleased with what another dislikes, and the same person is of different sentiments with respect to the same things in different periods of his life. In Physics, they held that the world had a beginning and would have an end, that it was round, and that the Deity made and pervades it every where, that it was made out of water, and that the stars and heavens were formed out of a quintessence, or peculiar element.

BRA'CHYGRAPHY, S. [from βραχύς, Gr. short, and γράφω, Gr. to write] the art of writing a thing by characters in a shorter time and compass, than by letters.

BRACK, S. [from break] a breach, a broken, or ruinous part. "The place was but weak, and the breaks fair." Heywood. Obsolete.

BRA'CKET, S. [braccio, Ital.] a piece of wood fixed against a wainscot or wall, to support something.

BRA'CKISH, Adj. [from brack, Belg.] saltish, that which is somewhat salt.

BRA'CKISHNESS, S. the saltness which is found on tasting sea water.

BRAD, S. a kind of nails, without a spreading head like other nails, pretty thick towards the upper end, that the top may be driven into the board they fasten.

To BRAG, V. N. [se vanter, Belg.] to display an advantage with great vanity; to boast. Used with of before the thing boasted of. "Brags of his impudence; but learns to mend."

BRAG, S. proud display of any advantage. Figuratively, the thing itself which causes

A a 2

causes boasting; glory. " Beauty is nature's *brag*, and must be shewn," *Milton*.

BRA'GGADOCHIO, S. a person who
vainly sets forth his own good qualities more
they deserve.

BRA'GGART, S. [*bragger*, Teut.] one
who boasts of his own abilities too much.

BRA'GGART, Adj. proud, conceited,
vain.

BRA'GGER, S. one who properly displays his pretended abilities.

BRA'GLESS, Adj. without boasting;
without being boasted of.

To BRA'ID, V. A. [*bregden*, Belg.] to
weave or plait together.

BRA'ID, S. [from the verb] a lock of
hair, any thing collected by plaiting. A
small narrow lace used for womans shoes, &c.

BRA'ILS, S. small ropes used in furling
the sails across. They are reeved through
blocks, which are seized on either side the
clue, come down before the sails of the ship,
are fastened at the skirts of the sail to the
creagles, and serve, when the sail is furled a-
cross, to haul up its bunt, that it may more
easily be taken up or let fall. To *hale up the
brails*, or *trail up the sail*, implies that the
sail is to be haled up, in order to be furled,
or bound close to the yard.

BRA'IN, S. [*bragen*, Sax. *breyne*, Belg.] In
anatomy the large soft whitish substance, in
the inside of the cranium or skull; wherein
all the organs of sense terminate, and wherein
the soul is said to reside. It is divided into
the cerebrum, cerebellum, medulla, oblongata, or medulla spinalis. The cerebrum or
brain properly so called, is a kind of medol-
lary mass of a moderate consistence, and of
a greyish colour on the outward surface, filling all the superiour portions of the cranium.
Its substance is of two kinds, distinguished by
two different colours; the softest being of
a grey, or ash colour, and lying principally
on the outer part of the cerebrum like a cortex, or bark, has been named the cortical
substance. The other which is more solid
and white, occupies the inner part, and is
called substantia medularis, or substantia alba.
The brain being supposed to secrete the subtile fluid which supplies the nerves, and being the elaboratory where the animal spirits
are formed, its bulk seems to be necessarily
large, as these processes require a great number of glands to carry them on. Hence we
may be able to assign a reason why the brain
is much larger in men than in any other animals, and why it is generally biggest in such
other animals as shew the greatest degree of
sagacity, such as monkies, &c. For a considerable stock of animal spirits being required in cogitation, memory, &c. where they
fail these powers must fail likewise, and
they must fail, if there be not a quantity of
brain sufficient to supply them. Accordingly anatomists have observed that in fools the

brain is smaller than in men of sense, and
account for it, by supposing it the cause of
folly, a sufficient stock of spirits being wanted to reason strongly; or from the œconomy of nature, which proportions the stock of
spirits according to the expence required.
Dr. Brown, having doubted of this truth,
and imagined that such creatures as have
large skulls and small bodies, might overthrow the common opinion, ingeniously
owns, that, on making the experiment, he
was undeceived and obliged to subscribe to
the opinion of those who hold that men have a
larger or bigger brain than any other creature.
Brain is used figuratively for the understanding.

To BRA'IN, V. A. to knock or dash the
brains out.

BRA'INLESS, Adj. having no brain.
Figuratively, silly, foolish, thoughtless.

BRA'IN-PAN, S. the skull.

BRA'INSICK, Adj. disordered in the
brain. Giddy, thoughtless, mad.

BRA'INSICKNESS, Adv. obstinacy, folly, giddiness, madness.

BRA'IT, S. among jewellers a rough diamond.

BRA'KE, S. a thicket of brambles or
thorns.

BRA'KE, S. [*braecke*, Belg.] a wooden
mallet. The handle of a ship's pomp. A
baker's kneading trough. A sharp snaffel
for horses.

BRA'KY, Adj. abounding in brakes, or
thorns.

BRA'MBLE, S. [*bræmbkl*, *brimbel*, *bræm-
ble*, Sax.] In botany, the *rubus*, Lat. or *ronce*,
Fr. There are ten species. In a popular
sense, the word is applied to any rough
prickly shrub.

BRA'MINS, S. [from *brahma*, the name
of the prophet whom they acknowledge] a
sect among the Chinese. Those of Bengal
live a very austere life, going bare headed
and bare footed in burning sand, and live only upon herbs. Those of Indostan, pretend
that their sacred books were given by God,
to their prophet Brahma. They believe the
transmigration of souls; and say that, at
the production of the world, all things came
out of the bosom of God, and that the world
will perish by all things returning to their
first original. This opinion they explain in
the following manner; a very large spider
was the first cause of all things, which spun
this wonderful web of creation out of his
own bowels, and sitting at the head of it,
feels, perceives, and regulates the motion of
every part. But when he has sufficiently diverted himself in adorning and contemplating his work, he contracts the threads he
had spun, again in his own entrails, and
thus resorbs every thing into himself, and
annihilates the whole creation. Those of
Siam, believe that the first men were larger
than the present, living many ages without
sick-

ficknefs, that our earth fhall be deftroyed by fire, and that another fhall proceed from its afhes, which fhall have no fea, and be bleffed with an eternal fpring. The Bachmians of Coromandel believe a plurality of worlds, and that they are fucceffively deftroyed and renewed at certain periods. They have all fuch a veneration for cows, that they think themfelves extremely happy if they can die with the tail of one in their hands.

BRAN, S. (from *bran*, Dict. *bren*, Fr.) the fkin or hufk of corn, feparated after grinding, from the flour, by means of a fieve, or bolting mill. The ftarch-makers make ufe of wheat bran to make ftarch, which is nothing but the fettling at the bottom of the veffels in which they foak bran.

BRANCH, S. [*branche*, F.] in Botany, the arm of a tree which fprouts from the trunk and ferves to form the head thereof. The branches of trees almoft always fhoot from the trunk in an angle of 45 degrees; and as the whole fpreading is confined within an angle of 90 degrees, that fpace could not be filled up any other way, than by forming all the interfections, which the fhoots and branches make, in an angle of 45 degrees eafy. A manifeft proof this, of a fuperintending wifdom in the creation, and a demonftration of an intelligent being the creator of all things! Figuratively, any detached part from a whole; a fection or fubdivifion. Any part which is joined to another, like a branch to a tree. "The *branches* of a candleftick," fometimes the collection of branches, applied to the chandeliers of churches, or public places. A fmall ftream running into, or from a river. A part of a pedigree or family. (The antlers or fhoots of a ftag's horns. In Horfemanfhip, two crooked pieces of iron, belonging to a bridle, fupporting the mouth-bit, the chain and the curb, and faftened to the head-ftall at one end, and to the reins at the other. In Architecture, the reins or arches of Gothic vaults travering from one angle to another.

To BRANCH, V. A. to divide like branches; to fhoot in branches. To feparate a fubject into feveral parts, ufed with the particle out. "*Branch* out into further diftinctions." *Locke.* To fpeak largely; to expatiate. "I have known a woman *branch* out into a long differtation upon the cafing of a petticoat." *Spect.* No. 247. To have horns fhooting out into antlers.

BRANCHINESS, S. fulnefs or abundance of branches.

BRANCHLESS, Adj. without fhoots or boughs, unfruitful or barren.

BRANCHY, Adj. full of branches, extending, fpreading. "The unwieldy loppings of a *branchy* tree." *Watts.*

BRAND, S. (*brand*, Sax.) a ftick lighted at one end. Figuratively, a thunderbolt.

"The Sire Omnipotent prepares the *brand*." Garth. A mark on the hand of a criminal by a burning iron.

To BRAND, V. A. [*brenbra*, Belg.] to mark with a burning iron; to charge as infamous; to ftigmatize.

To BRANDISH, V. A. (*brander*, Fr. *brandire*, Ital.) to wave or flourifh a weapon. Figuratively, to make a parade, or flourifh with; alluding to fencers flourifhing their weapons as a prelude to an engagement. "*Brandifhing* fyllogifms."

BRANDLING, S. [from *brandlire*, Fr. and Eng] the dew worm, called likewife the lob worm.

BRANDY, S. [*brandvin*, Fr. *brandewyn*, Belg.] in Diftillation, a proof fpirit, obtained from real wines, or fermented juices of grapes. When rectified to fpirits of wine, they are ufed by dyers, and efteemed one of their not-colouring drugs. The Nants brandy is the moft efteemed, becaufe it has a better tafte, is finer and ftronger, and will bear proof the longeft. It fhould be drunk very moderately, and rather as a medicine than a drink. When the ftomach is raw, weak, and lax, a moderate dram may raife a gentle tenfion, and by rarifying the vifcid phlegm make its coats play with new vigour. In flatulencies, a faintnefs or languor from a wafte or diffipation of the animal fpirits; in dropfies; and when the ftomach is weakened by too large a meal of tenacious food, it is of very great fervice; but all thefe good effects will not counterballance the mifchiefs done by the indifcreet, or immoderate ufe of this fpirit. For as it rarifies the blood at firft, the more thin and fpirituous parts exhale the fooner, and carry off with them fome of the fineft ferum, on which the blood beermies, afterwards, thicker, and the folids more dry and ftiff. From hence we might be excufed, for fuppofing that the world had been happier, if men had never known the tafte of brandy, or had contented themfelves with water, or good table-beer.

BRANGLE, S. [*brangen*, Teut.] wrangle, fquabble, contention.

To BRANGLE, V. N. to wrangle or quarrel about trifles.

BRANNY, Adj. the bran; confifting of bran; having the appearance of bran.

BRASIL, or **BRAZIL,** S. (pronounced *Brazeel*) a heavy, dry, hard wood, fo called becaufe it is fuppofed to have come originally from Brafil in S. America. The tree grows commonly in dry and barren places, among rocks; becomes very thick and tall, the branches are long and large, the leaves fmall, of a fine bright green, refembling thofe of box, but fomewhat longer. Its trunk is generally crooked like that of hawthorn. The bark is fo prodigioufly thick, that the tree which is fo big round as a man's body, when it is on, will fcarce exceed the dimenfions of his

his leg, when it is taken off. The wood is
used by turners and takes a good polish: its
chief use is in dying, where it serves for a
red; but as the colour it yields is spurious,
the French dyers are prohibited making use
of it in dying commodities of any value. So
indefatigable are they in extending and supporting the credit of their trade.

BRASS, S. (*bræs*, Sax.) a factitious, yellow
metal made of copper melted with lapis calaminaris. The calamine is first calcined and
ground to powder, then mixed with charcoal dust, and to 7lb. of this mixture is added five of copper, which being placed in a
wind furnace 11 or 12 hours, the copper im-
bibes about one third of its weight of the calamine, and is converted into brass. It is
somewhat strange that the calamine, though
no metallic body, should mix so with the copper as not only to increase its weight, but
likewise to follow it under the hammer. But
it should be known, that the change made in
copper by the calamine is owing to the zink
it contains, of which it is only an ore; for
zink, when separated from the calamine, will
have the same effect. Brass must be hammered or forged rather hot, because it breaks
when hammered cold, after a second melting
it loses its malleability entirely, but this is
recovered by adding eight or ten pound of
old copper to a cwt. some indeed put lead,
but this is rather from a principle of saving,
than a regard to service. The brass used for
great guns, as Mr. Chandler observes, should
not be made of pure copper and calamine is
only, but should be mixed with coarser metals,
such as lead, and pot metal, to make it run
closer. For the finest statues of brass the
proportion is one half copper and one half
brass. For bells they put 20 or 24lb. of tin
to the same weight of copper, to which they
add two pounds of antimony to render the
sound more soft, and 3 or 4lb. for kitchen
furniture. Corinthian brass, so famous in
antiquity, was formed from the melting of
silver, copper, and gold into one mass in the
conflagration of the city of Corinth by L.
Mummius, about 146 years before Christ. A
curious watch of this metal which formerly
belonged to king Charles the First, is now in
the archives of Jesus' college library at Oxford. brass is used figuratively for impudence.

BRAT, S. (*bratt*, Sax.) a child; an infant; products or effects. "The brats and
obimrings of the contrary fiction. *Stith.*

BRAVADO, S. (from *bravada*, Span.)
a proud boast or challenge.

BRAVE, Adj. not terrified with dangers
or difficulties. Willing to attempt any dangerous enterprize.

BRAVE, S. (*brave*, Fr. *bravo*, Ital.) a
person who is bold to excess.

To BRAVE, V. A. to undertake a thing
fearless of danger. To defy; contemptuously to provoke a person to resentment; to bid

defiance to. "Like a rock unmov'd, a rock
that braves—the raging tempest." *Dryd.* To
firm unaffected with or insensible of.

BRAVELY, Adj. in such a manner as
not to be terrified by difficulties or daunted by dangers. Intrepidly; courageously.
"Who bravely twice renewed the fight."

BRAVERY, S. a disposition of mind,
which enables a person to accomplish his designs, notwithstanding any difficulties or
dangers. Boasting; or boldness.

BRAVO, S. (Ital.) one who assassinates
another for hire.

To BRAWL, V. N. (*brallen*, Belg. or
brauler, Fr.) to quarrel about trifles. To
make a noise.

BRAWL, S. a noisy quarrel, scurrility.

BRAWLER, S. a person who is quarrelsome and noisy.

BRAWN, S. (from *bar*, a boar, and *raa*
from *ranen*) the muscular parts of the body. "The brawn of the arm." *Prethus.*
vigour or strength. "Brawn without brain
is thine." *Dryd.* The flesh of a boar sou-
sed. A boar.

BRAWNER, S. a boar designed for
brawn.

BRAWNINESS, S. strength arising from
the muscles.

BRAWNY, S. strong, robust, sinewy, of
great strength.

To BRAY, V. A. (from *bracan*, Sax.
brayer, Fr.) to beat into pieces, or powder by
a pestle.

To BRAY, V. N. (*braire*, or *braire*, Fr.)
to make a disagreeable noise like an ass.

BRAY, S. (from the verb) the noise of
an ass. A terrible or disagreeable sound.
"The horrid resounding trumpet's dismal
bray." *Shak.*

BRAYER, S. a person who makes the
noise of an ass. In Printing, an instrument
to temper the ink.

To BRAZE, V. A. (from *brass*) the
soldering two pieces of metal together by
melting thin pieces of brass, brass and tin,
brass and silver, or borax and rosin between
them. Figuratively, to be hardened in impudence.

BRAZEN, Adj. made of brass. Caused
by brazen instruments; "with brazen din
blast you the city's ear." *Shak.* Impudent;
daring.

To BRAZEN, V. N. to deny a thing
with great impudence. To behave with unconcern. To bully. "He would brazen it
out." *Arbuth.*

BRAZEN-FACE, S. one who has no
sense of shame. One who never blushes, or
changes countenance at the charge or under-
going of any crime. An impudent fellow.
"Well said brazen-face." *Shak.*

BRAZEN-FACED, Adj. void of any sense
of shame; impudent.

BRA-

BRA'ZENNESS, S. the quality of appearing like brass. Undaunted impudence.

BRA'ZIER, S. one who makes, or deals in brass ware.

BRAZI'L, S. [pronounced *Brezeel*] in Geography, a territory in South-America belonging to the Portuguese, bounded on the E. by the Atlantic Ocean, on the W. by the land of Amazons, on the N. by the Terra Firma, and on the S. by Paraguay and part of the same ocean. If we take its breadth from E. to N. from St. Augustin under the 35th deg. of W. longitude to the 5th, where its boundaries are commonly fixed, it may be compared at somewhat more than 300 leagues, or 900 miles; its length from Cape Aquara to that of St. Vincent is 1410 miles, and if allowance be made for the windings of the coast, upwards of 2000. Its riches consist chiefly in diamonds, which are so large and beautiful, that the king of Portugal has prohibited the digging for them, to prevent the fall of the price of so valuable a commodity. Since the Portuguese have carried on their own trade to these parts, the king's revenue has been so advanced, that it does not amount to less than two millions sterling annually in gold; but if the return of gold is so enlarged, that of exports to these parts have increased in proportion; and the number of shipping which formerly was no more than 12, is now enlarged to three fleets, which set out at three different times of the year. Among their imports, one article consists of the woollen cloths of Great-Britain, and it were to be wished that the manufacturers of that commodity would both from the goodness of its fabrick, and the beauty of its colour, endeavour to render it impossible for any nation to deprive them of that branch of trade. The advantages of the Portugal trade, by means of their Brazil colonies, has improved their shipping, increased the number of their seamen, and added, not a little, to the credit of their whole country. May our mother-country from this hint learn the utility of her colonies, cherish and protect them, as essential to her own subsistence, and renal every danger which shall threaten them with ruin, or every misconduct, which shall tend to stagnate their trade, or subject them to the least encroachment from neighbouring rivals!

BRA'ZING, S. the act of soldering two pieces of iron together, by means of thin plates of brass melted between them. When two pieces of broken saw are to be joined, they are covered with powdered borax wetted with water and mixed with brass powder. The nicest brazing is performed by a solder made either of brass and a tenth part of fine tin, or of one third brass and two thirds silver mixed with borax and rozin.

BREACH, S. [*breche*, Fr.] the dividing, the union between the parts of a thing. In Fortification, a hole, a gap, or aperture made in any part of the works of a town, either by cannon or mines. Figuratively, a defect. The violating any law; or obligation. Quarrel, discord.

BREAD, S. [pronounced *bred, bread,* Sax.] a baked mass of dough made from the flour of wheat or other grain, and a constant part of food. The many abuses which have crept into the composition of so necessary an article to our subsistence, some time ago made so great a noise, that it seemed not unworthy the cognizance of a British parliament; who not only decreed penalties against such as should, for the future, mix it with any of the ingredients prohibited; but likewise settled its assize, that the poor should not be deprived by extortion of a sufficient quantity for their hard-earned money. Figuratively, any kind of food necessary for the support of life. "Give us this day our daily *bread* ?" . . . . *To eat a person's bread,* is sometimes used as a phrase to imply, that he has been admitted to the most intimate civilities of friendship. "who having *eaten* of our *bread,* have lift up themselves against us." *King Charles.*

BREA'DTH, S. the measures of any thing from side to side. *Within an hair's breadth,* a phrase denoting extreme nearness applied to situation, and a narrow escape from danger.

To BREAK, V. A. [pronounced *brake,* preter, I *broke* or *brake,* participle passive, *broke* or *broken,* from *brecan,* Sax.] to divide or separate the parts of a thing by force. To burst by violence. Used with the word *down,* to destroy or demolish. "When God breaketh *down,* none can build up." *Barn. Theor.* To pierce or penetrate, applied to light. "A dim, winking lamp which feebly *brake*—the gloomy vapours." In Horsemanship to tame, to *break* a horse, applied figuratively to the human species. "To *break* our fierce barbarians into men." *Addiss.* To make a bankrupt. "*Breaks* the merchant." *Swift.* To unbind so as to make the blood appear. "She'll sooner *break* your head." *Dryd.* Applied to promise, oaths, or duty, to violate, to disregard. "I never more will *break* an oath." *Shak.* To intercept, prevent, or hinder the effect of. To interrupt. "His voice *broke* with sighs." *Spect.* N°. 164. To separate, joined to *company.* "They were forced to *break* company." *Atter.* Used with and, to discover our sentiments; how to *break* my mind." *Dryd.* Used with *fast.* To eat the first meal, in the day, "So *break* your fast." With *off* to stop, hinder or prevent. "To *break off* all his commerce with the tongue." *Addis.* Used with *up* to dig, applied to the ground; To disband, applied to an army. "Solimen, returning to Constantinople, *broke up* his army." *Knolles.* Used with *wind,* to discharge wind from the intestines.

To BREAK, V. N. to burst; to open a tumour so as to discharge matter; to dawn. "As soon as the day *breaks.*" *Spect.* No. 465.

265. To become unable to satisfy one's debts, to become a bankrupt. "He that puts all upon adventures doth oftentimes *break*." *Locke*. To decay in health and strength. "The dean begins to *break*." *Swift*. To burst from. To force a passage. "To *break through*." When followed with the particles *of* and *about*, to explain, discover, or to talk with a person. "I am to *break with thee* of some affairs." *Shak*. To fly, or separate from with violence, used with the particle *from*. To enter abruptly. To intervene, without regard to the ceremonies of polite behaviour. "*Breaks in* upon conversation." *Addis*. Joined with *loose*, to disengage from any obstacle, or tye. To desist from an undertaking; to quit a habit; to desist suddenly, with the particle *off*. "Do not peremptorily *break off*." *Bacon*. To rage, or make its appearance, applied to a distemper. "A violent fever *broke out*." To have pimples or other cutaneous eruptions in the body. To separate, or cease from business, used with the particle *up*. "What we obtain by conversation is oftentimes lost, as soon as the company *breaks up*." *Watts*. To quit a friend, to refrain from the company, or cease having any intercourse with a person who has been a friend. "Whosoever *breaks with his friend* upon such terms." *South*.

BREAK, S. in the morning, when the rays of light *break* the gloom of darkness, it implies the dawn. "From *break* of day until noon." *Knolles*. A pause or interruption. In printing, or writing, a line drawn between words, signifying that the sense is suspended.

BREAKER, S. he who divides a thing by force. A wave broken by rocks, or banks.

To BREAKFAST, V. N. to eat, after having abstained some time, generally applied to the first meal in the day.

BREAKFAST, S. the first meal in the day. Any thing to eat after a long want of food.

BREAM, S. [pronounced *brem*, from *breme*, Fr.] in natural history, a large fish, delighting in rivers, or ponds, very broad, with a forked tail, and scales of a golden colour. It has large eyes, a narrow sucking mouth, two sets of teeth, and a losing bone to help its grinders. The male but two large melts, and the female two large bags of spawn.

BREAST, S. [pronounced and formerly wrote *brest*, of *breost*, Sax.] in anatomy, two prominences, situated in the anterior and towards the lateral parts of the thorax. In women they are more conspicuous than men, being in the latter rather ornaments, than necessary appendages. In children of both sexes they are commonly no more than verruca, of a reddish colour, called papillæ, or nipples, surrounded by a broad circle, more or less brownish, called areola. When females are arrived to the age of puberty, a third part is added which make them of a glo-

bular form, and is termed *mamma*. It increases with age, and in pregnant women or those that give suck is largest; but in old age grown flabby. Its substance is partly glandular, partly made up of fat. In virgins the tubes which compose the glands, like sphincter muscles, contract so closely, that no part of the blood can enter them; but when the womb swells with the fœtus, and compresses the descending trunk of the great artery, it then flows in greater quantity and greater violence, so as to be able to form itself a passage into the glands, which on account of their narrowness admit only of a thin water; increasing however with the dimensions of the womb, they receive a thicker serum, and after the birth run with a thick milk, because the blood which before nourished the fœtus, &c. beginning then to stop, gives a greater dilation to the mammillary glands. 'Tis from this constitution of the arteries mentioned above, that the pain is owing, which women feel, when the draught comes in, at their first giving suck; but when this obstruction is removed by frequent and habitual draughts, we find that the pain is complained of no more, and the parental office is performed with no sensation, but those of affection and joy. In beasts the word is applied to that part which extends from the neck to the fore legs. Figuratively, the heart, bosom, conscience, or soul. "The law of man was written in his *breast*." *Dryd*. Affection, love, regard.

To BREAST, V. A. to meet; to struggle against. "*Breasting* the lofty surge." *Shak*.

BREAST-BONE, S. in anatomy, the bone, called the sternum.

BREAST-HIGH, Adj. up to the breasts; "*Breast-high* in mud." *Dryd*.

BREAST-KNOT, S. a bunch of ribbands worn by females, near their breasts.

BREAST-PLATE, S. armour worn on the breast. "What stronger *breast-plate* than a heart untainted!" *Shak*.

BREAST-WORK, S. works thrown up as high as the breast, in a fortified place.

BREATH, S. [pronounced *brith*, *braðe*, Sax.] the air which proceeds from the mouth, in the action of respiration, also life. "No man has more contempt than I of *breath*." *Dryd*. A respite or pause. A breeze or gentle current of wind or air. "Not a *breath* of wind." *Addis*.

BREATHABLE, Adj. [pronounced *breathable*, from *breathe*, and *able*, of *abel*, Sax. possibility or power] that which may be breathed; or that which is fit to be breathed. "*Breathable* air."

To BREATHE, V. N. [pronounced *breathe*] to draw in and expel the air at the mouth, by the action of the lungs. To live.

To BREATHE, V. A. to fill with, or discharge the lungs of air; to act upon by breathing.

breathing to animals. "He *breathed into* us the breath of life." *Decay of Piety.* To found by the breath, applied to wind instruments. "To *breathe* the flute." *Prior.* To send up in vapours. "His altar *breathed* ambrosial odours." *Par. Lost.* To open by a lancet. "To *breathe* a vein."

BRE'ATHER, S. a person who is alive. One who utters or speaks, "Scandal confounds the *breather*." *Shak.* He that causes or animates by his breath.

BRE'ATHING, S. the action of drawing breath; alive. A sigh of devotion; a secret prayer; an aspiration. "To high heav'n his pious *breathing* turn'd." *Prior.* Breathing place, vents, or chinks, that let in fresh air. "The warmth distends the chinks and makes new *breathings*." *Dryd.*

BRE'ATHLESS, Adj. unable to *breathe* from fatigue, or hurry. Dead; "The *breathless* corpse."

BRE'D, the participle of BREED.

BRE'DE, S. [see BRAID] a border of needle-work resembling flowers, &c. "Curious *brede* of needlework." *Addis.*

BRE'ECH, S. [pronounced *britch*, from *braccas*, to break, on account of the fissure in that part of the body] the back and lower part of the body. *Tully*, and after him the ingenious Mr. Derham, have taken notice of the art which appears in thus situating this sink of the body, that it might not offend. Figuratively, the breeches. "You might still have worn the petticoat—and ne'er have stolen the *breech* from Lancaster." *Dryd.* Applied to a piece of cannon, the hinder part, or that part behind the touch hole.

BRE'ECHES, S. [pronounced *britches*, from *brac*, *bracca*, *Sax.*] that part of a man's dress, which covers his thighs. To wear the *breeches*, implies that a woman usurps authority over her husband.

BRE'CON, or BRECKNOCK, a town of S. Wales, and capital of Brecknockshire. It is called by the Welch, Aber-Hodney, and is seated at the confluence of the rivers Hodney and Uſk. It is an ancient place, as appears by the Roman coins that have been often dug up here. It is a large town, containing three churches, one of which is collegiate, and stands at the W. end. The houses are well built, and it formerly had a wall, with three gates, and a stately castle. The assizes are kept here, and it has a good trade in cloathing. The market is on Saturdays, which is well supplied with corn, cattle, and provisions; and it has four fairs, on May 4, July 5, September 20, and November 17, for leather, hogs, cattle, and all sorts of commodities. It sends one member to parliament, and is 34 miles N. W. by W. of Monmouth, 14 S. E. by E. of Lhobeder, and 163 W. by N. of London. Lon. 14. 10. lat. 52. 0.

No. V.

BRECKNOCKSHIRE, a county of S. Wales, 39 miles in length, and 27 in breadth. It is full of mountains, some of which are exceeding high, particularly Monuchdenny-hill, not far from Brecknock. However, there are large fertile plains and valleys, which yield plenty of corn, and feed great numbers of cattle. It has 45,934 houses, 61 parishes, and 4 market towns, and there were formerly 9 castles. It is bounded on the E. by the counties of Hereford and Monmouth, on the S. by Glamorganshire, on the W. by Carmarthen and Cardiganshire, and on the N. by Radnorshire.

To BRE'ED, V. A. [preter. I bred, or have bred, from *bredan*, *Sax.*] to bring forth, or generate. To educate; nourish, or rear; to cause "Intemperance and lust *breed* infirmities." *Tillot.* To eat, applied to the teeth. "Children *breed* their teeth." To keep animals for procreating. "He *breeds* a great number of canary birds." "He *breeds* horses."

To BRE'ED, V. N. to conceive, to be pregnant. "Lucina, it seems, was *breeding*." *Spect.* No 431. To increase by propagation. "Flies *breed* in putrefied carcases." *Bentl.* To increase a breed.

BRE'ED, S. a species of animals; a cast; or kind. Offspring. What is produced at one hatching. "A hundred at a *breed*." *Grew.*

BRE'EDER, S. that which produces any thing. That which educates, or brings up. A person who is not barren; one who is very prolific; one who raises a breed.

BRE'EDING, S. education, instruction; polite behaviour. The method of rearing a child.

BRE'ESE, S. [*briosa*, *Sax.*] a stinging fly, called also the gad-fly.

BRE'EZE, S. [*breeze*, *Ital.*] a gentle, cooling, breath of wind. In Navigation, a shifting wind blowing from the sea and land alternately. In brick-making, small ashes and cinders formerly made use of instead of coals, for burning bricks, but now prohibited by 12 Geo. I. c. 35.

BRE'EZY, Adj. refreshed or cooled by breezes.

BRE'HON, S. [Irish] a person among the Irish who decides, or determines a contest between opposite parties. "In the case of murder, the *brehon*, that is, their judge, will compound between the murderer, &c." *Spenser.*

BRESLAW, a large, rich, and populous town of Germany, and capital of Silesia, with a bishop's see, an university, and the title of a principality. It is seated at the confluence of the rivers Oder and Ola, which last runs through several of the streets, and is of great use to those whose business wants water. All the houses are built with stone, and it is surrounded with good walls, then g-

B b   thened

thesed with ramparts and other works. There are two islands near it, formed by the river Oder; in one of which is a church, whose tower was burnt by lightning in 1730: in the other, called Thum, is the cathedral church. The bishop's palace, and the canon houses, built not long since, are near the cathedral. The royal palace was obtained by the Jesuits, where they founded an university in 1702. The two principal churches belong to the Protestants; near one of which there is a college, and a handsome library. It was taken by the king of Prussia in 1741, and retaken by the Austrians in 1757; but they did not keep it long, for the king of Prussia became master of it again the same year. It is 40 miles N. of Glatz, 112 N. E. of Prague, 135 N. W. of Cracow, and 165 N. of Vienna. Lon. 34. 40. lat. 51. 4.

BREST-SUMMERS, or **BRESSU-MERS,** S. In timber buildings, pieces into which the girders are framed.

BRET, S. [*brett*, Teut.] a round flat fish, of the turbot kind.

BRETHREN, S. the plural of *brother*, borrowed from the oblique cases of *brother*, Sax. which makes *brether*, or of the Gothic *brothar*, which makes *brothrahans*, or *brothrans* in the plural.

BREVE, S. in Music, a long note equivalent to two measures, minims, semibreves, or bars.

BREVIARY, S. [*breviaire*, Fr. of *brevis*, Lat. short.] In Divinity, a church-book, containing the office of the breviary, the prayers and other parts of the service, with its variations on particular days and hours. The office or service made use of in the Roman church either by day or night. An abridgment or compendium, "Caesonius has given us an abridgment, or *breviary* thereof." *Ayliff.*

BREVIAT, S. [from *brevis*] a short compendium, or abridgment.

BREVIER, S. (pronounced bre-ve-ire) In Printing, a particular letter, which is the smallest of any excepting the nonpareil, and was probably so named either from its being used in printing breviaries, or else, because it can contain a greater quantity in a *shorter* space than any other type besides the nonpareil. This book is printed in *brevier.*

BREVITY, S. [*brevitas*, Lat.] conciseness, shortness.

To **BREW,** V. A. [*brui*, Brit.] to make beer or ale. Figuratively, to make any liquor by boiling different ingredients. To form, make or prepare by mixing different things together. To contrive; to plot or devise.

BREWER, S. one who makes beer and sells it.

BREW-HOUSE, S. a house wherein beer or ale is made.

BREWING, S. the method of making beer. The quantity of liquor produced by brewing. "A *brewing* of new beer." *Bacon.*

BREWIS, S. a piece of bread boiled in a pot with meat.

BRIAR, S. See BRIER.

BRIBE, S. [*bribe*, Fr. a piece of bread given to a beggar] a reward given to a person to engage him to determine contrary to the merits of a cause. Something given to stifle evidence; something given to an elector for a vote.

BRIBERY, S. the act of giving a person money to engage him to vote or act on any particular side.

BRICK, S. [*bricke*, *bricke*, Belg.] a fat reddish or white earth formed in molds of various sizes, first dried, and afterwards burnt in a kiln. Not to mention all the variety of bricks, which would swell this article to an immoderate length, we think it no ways trifling to take notice of a new kind of bricks mentioned by Barbaro in his comment on Vitruvius, of a triangular form, every side a foot long, and only an inch and an half thick, which he observes could have many advantages above any others; as being more commodious in the management, of less expence, and of better or faster shew; adding both beauty and strength to the mural angles, and falling very gracefully into indented work. Sir H. Wotton wondered they had never been brought into use, when recommended by so great an authority. Mr. Mylne in his plan for the building a new bridge at Blackfriars seems not only to have adopted this hint, but likewise to have improved it in placing joggles or cubical stones in the joints of the arches; by which invention he has taken away the lateral pressure of the stones against the abutments, and given the elliptical arch such a degree of strength, as it never could boast of before. Oil of brick is olive oil imbibed by heated bricks, pounded afterwards, and distilled in a retort.

To **BRICK,** V. A. to lay, case, or build with bricks.

BRICK-BAT, S. a piece of a brick.

BRICK-DUST, S. the powder of bricks made by rubbing them on each other, or pounding them.

BRICK-EARTH, S. earth used in making bricks.

BRICK-KILN, S. a place to burn bricks in.

BRICKLAYER, S. one who builds with or uses bricks.

BRICK-MAKER, one who subsists by making bricks.

BRIDAL, Adj. [from *bride*] belonging to a wedding.

BRIDE, S. [*brid* or *bryd*, Sax.] a name given to a woman on the day of her marriage.

ringe, and for some time after the wedding day is over.

BRI'DAL, S. the wedding day; the wedding feast.

BRI'DE-CAKE, S. a cake to entertain the guests at a wedding.

BRI'DEGROOM, S. a new married man, a man on his wedding-day.

BRI'DEMEN, S. the male attendants, as the bride-maids were the female attendants of a wedding.

BRI'DEWELL, S. [St. Bridgid's well, a medicinal water] a house of correction near Fleet-ditch, London, built by Henry VIII. for the reception of the emperor Charles V. any place where vagrants and strumpets are obliged to beat hemp.

BRI'DGE, S. [brigg, brigge, Sax. brugge, Teut.] a building of stone or timber, consisting of arches, intended for the passage of men or carriages over a river. In examining the perfection of a bridge we should first consider the easiness of its passage for carriages and men over, and for boats under it. The word bridge is used figuratively for the upper part of the nose, and in the musical instruments for a piece of wood which supports the strings. Hanging bridges are not supported either by posts or pillars, being sustained only by the two extremities. A draw-bridge, is made fast only at one end with hinges, so that the other may be lifted by chains fixed to it. A flying-bridge is made of pontoons, leather boats, casks, &c. covered with planks for the passage of an army.

To BRI'DGE, V. A. to make or erect a bridge over any river.

BRIDGNORTH, a town in Shropshire, with a market on Saturdays, and four fairs, on Thursday before Shrove-tide, for horned cattle, sheep, hogs, cheese, wick yarn, linen and woollen cloth, on June 30, for the same, and a large quantity of sheeps wool, on August 2, for the same and lambs wool, and on October 29, for horned cattle, horses, sheep, salt, butter, and cheese. It is a corporation-town, governed by 14 aldermen, 48 common-council, and consists of about 500 houses. It is seated on the river Severn, which divides it in two, but is joined together by a handsome stone-bridge. They are called the Upper and the Lower Town. The streets are broad and paved, and it has two parish-churches. It was formerly fortified with walls, and had a stately castle, seated on a rock, now in ruins. It sends two members to parliament; and is 26 miles N. W. of Birmingham, 21 S. E. of Shrewsbury, and 136 N. W. of London. Lon. 15; 5. lat. 52. 40.

BRIDGEWATER, a town of Somersetshire, with two markets, on Thursdays and Saturdays, and four fairs, on the second Thursday in Lent, June 24, September 21, and December 29, for cattle, and all sorts of goods. It is seated on the river Parret, over which there is a stone bridge, and near it ships of 100 tons burthen may ride. It is a large well frequented place, with the title of a dutchy, and sends two members to parliament. There are in it several large inns, and the market is well supplied with corn and provisions. It is 8 miles S. of Bristol Channel, 18 S. W. of Wells, 36 S. S. W. of Bristol, and 143 W. by S. of London. Lon 14. 55. lat. 51. 15.

BRI'DLE, S. [bridel, brill, Sax.] the bit, throat-band, reins, &c. which are fastened on a horse's head to manage and govern him. A restraint, curb, or check.

To BRI'DLE, V. A. [bridlian, Sax.] to put on a bridle, to manage a horse by means of a bridle; to check; restrain; or keep within bounds. To hold up the head affectedly.

BRIEF, Adj. [bref, Fr.] short, concise, not diffusive, or verbose. " The brief stile is that which expresseth much in little." B. Johnson.

BRI'EF, S. [pronounced breef, bref, Ш.] a short account or description. In Law, a writ whereby a person is summoned to answer to any action. An abridgment of a client's case, for the instruction of council on a trial. In Canon Law, letters patent, generally read in churches, giving a licence for making a collection all over the kingdom, for any publick or private loss.

BRIE'FLY, Adv. shortly, in few words, concisely.

BRIEFNESS, S. conciseness, shortness.

BRIER, S. [brær, Sax.] in Botany, a kind of prickly tree, distinguished into sweet or wild; and is a species of the rose.

BRI'ERY, Adj. full of or consisting of briers, or thorns.

BRIGA'DE, S. [brigade, Fr. brigata, Ital.] in the military art, a part or division of an army, under the command of a brigadier. A brigade of an army is a body of horse of ten or thirteen squadrons. A brigade of a troop is a third part of it, when consisting of 50 soldiers; but only a sixth, when it consists of too.

BRI'GADIER-GENERAL, S. [pronounced brigadeer] an officer commanding a brigade; and ranking next below a major-general.

BRI'GAND, S. [Fr.] a robber; one who belongs to a gang of robbers.

BRI'GANDINE, S. [from brigand, Fr.] a kind of antient defensive armour, like scales. A coat of mail.

BRI'GANTINE, S. [brigantin, Fr.] a small light, flat, open vessel, going both with sails and oars.

BRI'GHT, Adj. [beorht, Sax.] shining, splendid, glittering. Figuratively, strong, or clear. " Brighter evidence." Watts.

Noble,

Noble, shining, illustrious. Applied to sagacity, quick, penetrating. "A bright fellow."

To BRIGHTEN, V. A. to make a thing shine, which was dull. Figuratively, to disperse, alluding to the sun-beams dispelling any clouds or mist by their warmth, or to the light's dispersing darkness at break of day. "Brighten up my sorrow." Philips. To make fair or conspicuous, to heighten, to shine again after being obscured.

BRIGHTHELMSTONE, a sea-port town of Sussex, with a market on Thursdays, and two fairs, on Holy-Thursday and September 4, for pedlar's ware. It is an indifferent large and populous town, but ill-built. It is now a fashionable place for bathing. It has a pretty good harbour, and is 9 miles W. by N. of Seahaven, 7 E. of New-Shoreham, and 56 S. of London. Lon. 17. 25. lat. 50. 50. It was at this place king Charles II. embarked for France in 1651, after the battle of Worcester.

BRIGHTLY, Adv. with splendour, with lustre and brightness.

BRIGHTNESS, S. lustre, splendour, goodness, sagacity, perfections that attract notice. "The brightness of his parts." Prior.

BRILLIANCY, S. [from brilliant, Fr.] lustre, or splendour.

BRILLIANT, Adj. [brilliant, Fr.] sparkling, shining, witty.

BRILLIANT, S. [from briller, Fr.] a diamond quite flat underneath, and cut on his upper part in triangular faces.

BRILLIANTNESS, S. See BRILLIANCY.

BRIM, S. [brymme, Sax.] the edge of a thing; that part of a hat which is cocked or turned upwards; the top of a bank washed by a river.

To BRIM, V. A. to fill full, or up to the brim; to be full to the top.

BRIMFUL, Adj. full to the top; ready to run over. "Brimful of tears." Addis.

BRIMMER, S. a vessel, glass, or bowl filled up to the brim.

BRIMMING, Adj. filled to the top. "The brimming glasses." Philips.

BRIMSTONE, S. [of brynne-stone, from brynne, fire, and stone a stone.] in Natural History, a fat unctuous mineral, yellow, dry, solid, and friable.

BRIMSTONY, Adj. consisting of, abounding in brimstone.

BRINDED, Part. [brim, Fr.] streaked, marked with streaks, tabby. "The brinded cat."

BRINDLE, S. having streaks upon the skin of a beast, of a different or darker colour.

BRINDLED, Part. marked with streaks.

BRINE, S. [sea brine, Sax.] any salt liquor; sea-water; the sea; tears. "What a deal of brine hath wash'd thy sallow cheeks." Shak. The liquor of salted meat.

BRINE-PIT, S. a pit of salt water.

BRING, V. A. [Preter and Part. Passive, brought, from bringan, Sax.] to fetch a thing to another, to procure. To bring back, to make a person on his return, to recover, to recall; to bring about, accomplish; to bring, to clear from any charge; to bring over, to prevail on a person to alter his sentiments, to convert or seduce; to bring under, to subdue or vanquish; to bring up, to instruct, educate, to teach, to introduce a fashion.

BRINISH, Adj. resembling brine, saltish.

BRINISHNESS, S. the taste of salt water.

BRINY, Adj. tasting salt or like brine.

BRINK, S. brind, Dan. [brig, Belav. brigh, Epir.] the edge of a river, precipice, &c. Figuratively, the highest degree of danger. Upon the brink of ruin.

BRISK, Adj. [or brys, firm, vigorous, Brit.] lively, gay, airy, sprightly. Vigorous, full of activity and power. Sparkling, mantling, applied to liquors; bright, glaring.

BRISKET, S. that part of the breast of an animal, next to the ribs.

BRISKLY, Adv. in a brisk, lively, active, manner.

BRISKNESS, S. vivacity, liveliness, activity, gaiety.

BRISTLE, S. [bristl, Sax.] the strong hair which grows on the back of a boar, &c.

To BRISTLE, V. A. to raise the bristles upright, when enraged; applied to a hog. To grow angry; to bristle up, to advance to an enemy in order to attack him, or revenge an affront. To stand erect.

BRISTLY, Adj. encompassed with a substance like hairs. In Botany, "The bristly chesnut." Dryd. Thick set with bristles.

BRISTOL, S. a sea-port town, which is partly in Gloucestershire, and partly in Somersetshire, with a bishop's fee. It is now accounted the second town or city in England, both with regard to its magnitude, riches, and trade. It has 18 churches, besides its cathedral, and several meetings for protestant dissenters, among which the quakers are a large body. The most remarkable church, besides the cathedral, is St. Mary Radcliff, just without the walls, in the county of Somerset, which some think is the finest parish church in the kingdom. There was a bridge over the river Avon, with houses on each side, like those which London-bridge lately had. This bridge is entirely taken down. They have an exchange like that of London, which was opened in September 1743. The key is on the river Froome, a little above its confluence with the Avon, over which there is a drawbridge, for the admittance of ships that come up with the tide; and this leads to the college-green, where the cathedral stands. They have a prodigious trade; for it is reckoned they send 2000 ships yearly to several parts of the world. Here are no less than 15 glass-houses.

houses, they having plenty of coal from King's-wood and Mendip-hills. The hot-well is resorted to for the cure of several dis-eases, and is about a mile from the town, on the side of the river Avon. St. Vincent's rock, above this well, is noted for a sort of soft diamonds, called Bristol-stones. Besides this well, there is a cold spring, which gushes out of a rock on the side of the said river, that supplies the cold bath. There are seve-ral manufactures, particularly woollen stuff, carried on by the French refugees. From the College green there is a delightful pros-pect over the city and harbour, and in it stands a stately high cross of Gothic struc-ture, with the effigies of several of the kings of England around it. Near Queen's-square, which is adorned with rows of trees, and an equestrian statue of K. William III. stands the custom-house. The number of houses are computed at 13,000, and the inhabitants at 95,000. The walls have been demolished a long time ago; but there are several gates yet standing. They use sledges or slads, in-stead of carts, because the vaults of the com-mon shores will not admit them. It has two markets, on Wednesdays and Saturdays, and two fairs, on St. James's day, and Ja-nuary 25, which are very large; insomuch that there is a great resort to the former, not only from the neighbouring towns, but from London. The Londoners have shops at both fairs; during which time the neigh-bouring inns make 100 beds a-piece for their guests; and all sorts of goods are then bought and sold. It sends 2 members to parliament, and has the title of an earldom. It is 35 miles W. S. W. of Cirencester, 50 S. of Hereford, 105 S. of Shrewsbury, 145 S. of Chester, 70 N. E. of Exeter, 36 S. S. W. of Gloucester, 62 S. S. W. of Worcester, 68. W. by S. of Oxford, 12 W. N. W. of Bath, and 115 W. of London. Lon. 14. 55. lat. 51. 27.

BRIT, S. In natural history, a salt water fish.

To BRITE, or BRIGHT, V. N. in Husbandry, to grow too ripe, applied to bar-ley, wheat, or hops.

BRITISH, Adj. belonging to, or con-cerning Britain.

BRITTLE, Adj. [brittol, Sax.] that which crumbles to pieces without the least violence.

BRITTLENESS, S. that quality which renders a thing easy to break.

BRIZE, S. In natural history, the gad-fly. Obsolete.

BROACH, S. [broche, Fr.] a flake forced through a joint of meat by means of which it is turned round, and its parts are successive-ly exposed to the action of the fire, in roast-ing. Also a musical instrument.

To BROACH, V. A. to pierce with a

spit; to force a spicket, or rack into a ves-sel; to tap; to open; to be the author of; to invent.

BROCHER, S. a spit to roast meat on; the first inventor, promulgator, author.

BROAD, Adv. [from brad, Sax.] wide, or the extent between the sides. Diffusive, clear, bright, intelligible. " Appears in the broadest light." D. of Piety. Gross, ob-scene.

BROAD CLOTH, S. a manufacture made of sheeps wool, the staple commodity of this nation, so called from its breadth, which is so great that it is weaved by two persons, who sit at each side and fling the shuttle to one another. The decay of this branch of foreign trade, owing to the French sup-planting us in markets abroad, and several nations setting up manufactories of their own, which were before supplied by us, should give us a timely alarm; the loss, the entire loss of this branch of commerce must involve the nation in such a scene of indi-gent misery, that no one can form any ade-quate idea of at this distance; and as the smuggling of our wool, the high price of our labour, and consequently the dearness of the commodity at foreign markets, are the seve-ral causes which give our rivals this advan-tage over us, it is hoped that the time will come, when the smuggling of wool will be prevented by more effectual methods than any that has yet been projected, and that the taxes, which are laid on the necessaries of life, will be transferred to its luxuries, which will at once enable the manufacturer to work for less, and the merchant to vend cheaper abroad.

BROAD-EYED, Adj. that which has a very large prospect in sight. " In despite of broad eyed watchful day." Shak.

BROADLY, Adv. in a broad or wide manner.

BROADNESS, S. obscene, immodest. " To palliate the broadness of the meaning." Dryd.

BROAD-SHOULDERED, S. of great width, between the shoulders.

BROAD-SIDE, S. the firing all the guns on one side of a ship into an enemy's ship. Figuratively, an attack. In Printing, a sheet of paper containing a large page, print-ed only on one side.

BROADSWORD, S. a sharp edged sword with a broad blade.

BROADWISE, Adv. according to the breadth.

BROCADE, S. [brocado, Span.] a stuff of gold, silver, or silk, raised, and embellish-ed with flowers, or other ornaments. Form-erly it signified only a stuff woven of gold or silver; from thence it was extended to silver or gold stuffs shot with silk, and at present is applied to any manufacture of silk adorned or

or embellished with flowers or ornaments of a colour different from the ground.

BROCADED, Part. woven with flowers of various colours. Dreſt or cloathed in brocade.

BRO'CAGE, S. [from *bryke*] money gained by promoting bargains. The trade of buying and ſelling ſecond hand things.

BRO'CCOLI, S. in Botany, a ſpecies of cabbage.

BRO'CKET, S. in Hunting, a red deer two years old.

To BROGUE, or BROGGLE, V. A. [*brocarie*, Fr.] to fiſh for eels by making the water muddy.

BRO'GUE, S. [*brog*, Ir.] a wooden ſhoe; a corrupt manner of pronouncing.

To BROIDER, V. A. to work flowers on ſilk, &c. with the needle.

BRO'IDERY, S. flowers wrought on ſilk, &c. by the needle.

BROIL, S. [*brouiller*, Fr.] a conteſt, quarrel, tumult, or war.

To BROIL, V. A. [*brusler*] to dreſs meat on the coals, or on a gridiron over a fire. Neuterly to ſweat by exerciſe. Uſed improperly for to *dure*, though the French, it muſt be confeſſed, literally ſignifies it.

To BRORE, V. N. [from *brucian*, Sax.] to buy and ſell for another by commiſſion.

BROKE, or BROKEN, the Particle Paſt of *break*.

BRO'KEN-HEARTED, Adj. diſpairing; dejected; diſconſolate.

BRO'KENLY, Adv. [from *broken* and *ly*, of *this*, implying manner] in an unconnected manner, by looſe ſentences.

BROKER, S. [formerly called *brogger*, i. e. a broken tradeſman, from *brec*, Sax. no other perſons being admitted by the 8th and 9th of William III] one who buys or ſells for another by commiſſion. This profeſſion is very neceſſary in commerce, both as it furniſhes the merchant with ſuch commodities as he wants, and gets the manufacturer a cuſtomer for his goods, which might otherwiſe lie upon his hands. By abuſe, the word is applied to thoſe who deal in ſecond-hand goods. Exchange-broker, is one who concludes bargains for others, relating to the remitting of money, or bills of exchange. Stock-brokers, are thoſe who buy or ſell, for others, ſhares in the joint ſtock of any public company. Pawn-brokers, are thoſe who lend money upon a pledge of goods.

BRO'KERAGE, S. what is given a broker for commiſſion, generally a certain ſum per cent.

BRO'MESGROVE, S. a town in Worceſterſhire, with a market on Tueſdays, and two fairs, on June 24, and October 21, for linen-cloth, cheeſe, and horſes. It is ſeated on the river Salwarp, and is a pretty good town, containing about 400 houſes. It drives

a conſiderable trade in cloathing, and has a good market for corn, cattle, and all ſorts of proviſions. It is 11 miles E. N. E. of Worceſter, 16 W. S. W. of Coventry, and 118 N. W. of London. Lon. 15. 30. Lat. 52. 26.

BRO'NCHIA, S. [Lat.] in Anatomy, the little tubes into which the wind-pipe is branched at its entrance into the lungs.

BRONCHO'CELE, S. [from *bronchos*.] in Surgery, a tumour on the inveſting membrane of the wind-pipe, ſometimes growing ſo large, as to extend itſelf from one jugular to the other, appearing like an hemiſphere.

BRO'NCHIAL, Adj. belonging to the throat.

BRONCHO'TOMY, S. [from *bronchos*, the throat, and *temno*, Gr. to cut] in Surgery, an operation by which an inciſion is made in the wind-pipe, to prevent ſuffocation in a quinſy. This is performed by making a longitudinal inciſion of three quarters of an inch long, through the ſkin between the third or fourth rings of the trachea, the wind-pipe is then cut through by a ſmall tranſverſe inciſion, and a ſilver tube, about half an inch long, is immediately introduced, and the wound healed like a ſimple one, by an external application.

BRONTO'LOGY, S. [from *bronte*, Gr. and *logos*] a diſcourſe on thunder.

BRONZE, S. [*bronze*, Fr.] a method of ſtatuaries to make their plaiſtered buſts appear as if compoſed of braſs. Of this there are two ſorts, the red braſs or bronze, and the yellow or gilt braſs. The latter is made only of copper filings, but with the red they mix ochre. In order to prevent its turning green, it muſt be dried with a chaffing diſh of coals, as ſoon as it is applied. The fineſt braſs colour is made of powdered braſs imported from Germany, mixed with a varniſh compoſed of 1lb. 4oz. of ſpirits of wine, 2 oz. of gumlac, and 2 oz. of gum ſandarac, powdered ſeparately, and afterwards diſſolved in the ſpirits, over a fire. Figures of plaiſter covered with this compoſition look as well as if they were of caſt braſs.

To BROOD, V. N. [*bredan*, Sax.] to hatch, or to be hatching; to ſit like a hen hatching her eggs. "Where *brooding* darkneſs ſpreads his jealous wings." *Milt.* To ſit near, and watch with great care and anxiety. "Brood o'er their precious ſtores." *Smith.* To prepare or make preparations. "Ever amongſt nations a *brooding* of a war." *Bacon.* Figuratively, to keep to memory by inceſſant anxiety. "You'll ſit and *brood* your ſorrows on a throne." *Dryd.*

BROOD, S. [*brod*, Sax.] a parcel of chickens or birds hatched at one time. Figuratively, offspring, children. Production.

Ufed with *to*, the act of hatching. " His melancholy fits on *bread*."

BROODY, Adj. inclining to hatch.

BROOK, S. [*broc*, Sax. *broek*, Belg.] a fmall and fhallow ftream of water.

To BROOK, V. A. [*brucan*, Sax.] to endure without refentment, to put up with, to permit or fuffer.

BROOKLIME, S. in Botany, a kind of water fpeedwell.

BROOM, S. [*brom*, Sax.] in Botany, the *geniſta*, Lat. *genet*, Fr. the empalement of the flower leaf is tubulous, and divided into two lips. Linnæus ranges it in the third fect. of his 17th clafs, and Tournefort in the firft fect. of his 22d. There are ten fpecies. Likewife an utenfil made with the twigs of the abovementioned plant, and ufed in fweeping.

BROOMY, Adj. full of, or confifting of broom.

BROTH, S. [*broth*, Sax.] a kind of foup, made by boiling meat in water.

BROTHEL, or BROTHEL-HOUSE, S. [*bordil*, Fr. *bordello*, Lat.] a houfe fet apart for the practice of vice and lewdnefs.

BROTHER, S. [*brethren* and *brothers* in the plural, from *brother*, Sax.] a term of relation between two male children from the fame father or mother, or both. Figuratively, a perfon united by friendship. One of the fame trade. A perfon refembling another in conduct, &c. " He that is flothful in his work, is *brother* to him that is a great wafter." *Prov.* xviii. 9. One of the fame fociety. *A brother mafon.*

BROTHER-HOOD, S. the ftate of a brother; the relationfhip of a brother; men incorporated together by the fame charter; men of the fame trade; men in the fame convent.

BROTHERLY, Adj. fuitable or belonging to a brother.

BROTHERLY, Adv. in the manner of a brother; affectionately.

BROUGHT, Participle Paffive of *bring*.

BROW, S. [*browe*, Sax. *brauw*, Belg.] the collection of hairs over the eye in human creatures, which not only tends very much to beautify the face, but likewife is of great fervice in keeping the fweat from defcending into and offending the eye. Figuratively, the look or air of the countenance. Applied to a hill, the extremity of its furface.

To BROWBEAT, V. A. to undervoter to awe by ftern, infolent, and haughty looks.

BROW-BOUND, Part. having the forehead or head encircled; crowned. " *Brow-bound* with oak." *Shak.* Not in ufe.

BROWSICK, Adj. dejected, forrowful, hanging the head. " Our *browſick* crew." *Sterling.*

BROWN, Adj. [*brun*, Sax.] fun-burnt, of a brown colour. Figuratively, dark or

gloomy. Ufed fubftantively, a dark or dufky colour.

BROWN-STUDY, S. a profound ftudy, fo called from the mind's being darkened, or rendered, by its intenfe application, inattentive to any thing which paffes without it. A reverie.

BROWNISH, Adj. fomewhat brown, inclining to brown.

To BROWSE, V. A. [*brouſer*, Fr.] to eat herbs, leaves, or grafs. To crop or feed, applied to cattle. Actively, to feed or eat. " *Browſing* upon the leaves." *L'Eſtrange.*

BROWSE, S. paffure, more properly leaves or fhrubs.

To BRUISE, V. A. [*pronounced bruze*, *bryſan*, Sax.] to crufh or hurt. To crufh by any weight, to beat in a mortar.

BRUISE, S. a hurt with fomething blunt and heavy, whereby the fkin is not broke.

BRUISE-WORT, S. in Botany, a plant ufed in bruifes.

BRUIT, S. [*bruit*, Fr.] a rumour, or noife. The general topic for converfation.

To BRUIT, V. A. to fpread abroad, to publifh, to divulge, to rumour.

BRUMAL, Adj. [*brumalis*, Lat.] belonging to the winter.

BRUMA, or BRAHMA, S. the idol of the Brachmans, who they fay, produced as many worlds as he has confiderable parts; the firft world, which is above the heavens, being formed of his brain; the fecond of his eyes; third, of his mouth, &c. In fome of his ftatues, or images, the firft world is marked on the top of his head, the fecond upon his right eye, the third upon his mouth, &c. They affert that there is a ftrong connection or relation between the worlds and the parts from whence they are formed; and that the different difpofitions of mankind are owing to the worlds from whence they are produced. Thus, they fay, wife men and great wits come from the firft world; prudent perfons from the fecond; great orators from the third, &c. We who enjoy the bleffed light of Revelation, may indeed fmile at thefe abfurdities; but how much fhould we have furpaffed them without this advantage.

BRUNETT, S. [*brunette*, Fr.] a female of a brown complexion.

BRUNSWICK, the dutchy of, is a country of Germany, bounded on the N. by the dutchy of Lunenberg, on the W. by the circle of Weftphalia, from which it is feparated by the river Wefer, on the S. by Heffe and the little territory of Peichfield, and on the E. by Thuringia, with the principalities of Anhalt and Halberftadt, and the dutchy of Magdeburg. The rivers are the Wefer, the Ocker, and the Lyne; and it is fertile in corn, but principally in paftures. It is divided into three principalities, Wolfembuttle, Grubenhagen, and Calenberg, which alfo

sif; comprehends the dutchy of Oettingen. The principality of Wolfembottle has its own Dukes; but the other two belong to the Elector of Hanover. The territories of the house of Brunswick are more extensive; the principal of which are the dutchies of Brunswick and Lunenburg, with the county of Danneburg, which is annexed thereto. The rest are the counties of Blanckenburg, Dieport, and Hoye, besides two or three smaller districts.

BRUNT, S [*brunt*, Belg.] the onset, or attack of an enemy. The force, violence, and stroke of a cannon. " An heavy *brunt* of cannon ball. *To bear the brunt*, is to sustain an attack. Figuratively, any difficulty, or cross accident.

BRUSH, S [*broffe*, Fr. Ital.] an instrument made of hair fastened to wood, used either for brushing, cleaning cloaths, or painting. Figuratively, a slight attack or skirmish; a shock or rough usage; used generally with the verb *give*. " They had not *given* us such a *brush*." *Hudib.*

To BRUSH, V. A. to rub off dust with a brush; to touch in one's passage; to *brush up*, to make a thing look well by a brush. Used neuterly to pass close to a person. " *Brush'd by.*" *Dryd.* To skim upon the surface, so as just to touch.

BRUSHER, S. a person who uses a brush.

BRUSHWOOD, S. [*bruciosh*, Ital.] small sticks or branches used for fire. Low, close, and shrubby thickets.

BRUSHY, Adj. rough or shaggy, resembling a brush.

To BRUSTLE, V. N. [*brastlian*, Sax.] to make a noise like the rustling of rich silks. Figuratively, to swagger, hector, or threaten.

BRUTAL, Adj. [from *brute*, *brutal*, Fr.] belonging to a beast, inhuman, cruel, savage, filthy.

BRUTALITY. S. [*brutalité*, Fr.] churlishness, savageness, cruelty, inhumanity.

BRUTALIZE, V. N. [*brutalizer*, Fr.] to grow morose, savage, or inhuman.

BRUTE, Adj. [*brutus*, Lat.] senseless, savage, inhuman; void of all the tender and social affections; rough; unpolished; uncivilized.

BRUTE, S. an animal without reason; a beast. As providence seems to have been profuse of its gifts to this species of beings, and in bodily qualities to have given them the advantage over ourselves, we have certainly a noble lesson taught us by nature, who by this means seems to invite us to cultivate that part which sets us above them, and at the same time shews how great a folly it must be in us to pride ourselves in such things, as are unworthy of our nature, and though they make us resemble the brute creation, at the same time shew us, that in those particulars they abundantly surpass us. Figuratively, applied to men as a term of the most contumelious reproach, and implying a person unworthy of the name of a man, void of humanity, and an enemy to reason.

BRUTISH, S. resembling a beast, rude, inhuman, ignorant.

BRUTISHLY, Adv. in the manner of a brute, or beast. Figuratively, without making use of reason, implicitly. " *Brutishly* to submit to any man's dictates." *K. Charles.* In a savage, cruel, inhuman manner.

BRUTISHNESS, S. savageness; insensibility; want of reason. See BRUTALITY, which is a better word.

BRYONY, or BRYONY, S.[*bryonia*, Lat.] in Botany, has male and female flowers on the same plant. Linnæus places it in the tenth section of his 21st class. Its juice is a powerful dissolvent and attenuant, though too rough in its operation; is given with success in epilepsies, asthmas, palsies, dropsies, and hysteric complaints, but should be corrected by the addition of cream of tartar, vinegar, or some of the aromatics.

BUBALE, S. [*bubble*, Belg. *bolla*, Dan.] a small bladder of water, or any fluid filled and expanded with air. Figuratively, something easily destroyed; a cheat. A cant word given to projects for raising money on imaginary grounds, wherein the subscribers were promised great advantages, but were disappointed of their hopes, and cheated of their money; the history of the years 1719, 1720, and 1721, afford us several remarkable instances of this sort both in England and France, among which were the South Sea, that ruined thousands in the former, and the Mississippi scheme, which was not less fatal to the latter.

To BUBBLE, V. N. to rise in bubbles; to make a gentle noise as it runs or flows, applied to waters. Actively, to cheat, or defraud by.

BUBBLER, S. one who cheats by promising extraordinary advantages for the loan of money.

BUBBY, S. a woman's breast, a low familiar term.

BUBO, [from *Bubon*, Gr.] in Surgery, a tumour attended with an inflammation in the groin, &c. When it affects no parts but the groin or arm-pit it is termed malignant; and mild when it rises spontaneously, or while the patient is in a good state of health, and free from any contagious disease, or makes its appearance at the end of some mild fever. A malignant bubo is owing to some contagious disease, or venereal taint. A mild bubo is occasioned by the stagnation of a glutinous and insipissated blood, differing from other inflammations only in its place. Venereal buboes are caused by the lymph's being rendered thick and viscid and consequently stagnating in the inguinal glands, i. e. the glands of the groin.

BUBO-

BUBONOCE'LE, S. [from βουβὼν, and κήλη,] in furgery, a tumour, or rupture, formed by the defcent of the inteftines, omentum, or both, into the tunica vaginalis or the fpermatic cord and fometimes even into the tunica vaginalis of the tefticle. The tunica vaginalis of the fpermatic cord, is the coat furrounding the fpermatic veffels down to the epidymis; the tunica vaginalis of the tefticle, is the bag which containsit.

BUCCALLS, S. [glandula, Lat.] In Anatomy, fmall glandules in the infide of the cheeks.

BUCCINA'TOR, S. [of buccina, Lat.] in anatomy, a mufcle on each fide the face, common to the lips and cheeks, forming the inner fubftance of the latter, made ufe of by trumpeters, when founding their inftrument; it ferves to draw the lips or mouth on one fide, contracts its cavity and thrufts forward the meat in chewing.

BU'CCINUM, S. [Lat.] a fea fhell of a fpiral fhape, like that of a fnail; the fifh whereof yields the purple colour. The firft of this fpecies, was difcovered by an Englifhman, in 1680, as appears from the literary journals.

BU'CK, S. [bucca, Brit. bucc, Sax.] the male of the fallow deer, rabbits, goats, hares, &c. A cant name for a club, or fociety, fo called from their ufe of hunting terms, and are fpurious fhoots of the freemafons.

BU'CKAS, S. [bewrbe, Teut. burota, Ital.] lye made of afhes for the wafhing linen.

To BU'CK, V. A. to copulate; when from buck fignifying lye, it implies to wafh clothes in lye.

BUCKINGHAM, the chief town of Buckinghamfhire, with a market on Saturdays, and eight fairs, on Monday-fevennight after Epiphany, March 7, May 6, Thurfday in Whitfun-week, July 10, September 4, October 2, and November 8, for cattle. It is feated in a low ground, on the river Oufe, by which it is almoft furrounded, and over it there are three handfome ftone-bridges. There was formerly a ftrong caftle in the middle of the town, which is now demolifhed. The town-hall is in the N. part of the town, and the church on the S. There is likewife a county-goal, built not many years fince. It is a corporation, fends two members to parliament, and had the title of a dutchy. The number of houfes are about 300; and it is 25 miles N. E. of Oxford, 55 W. S. W. of Cambridge, and 60 N. W. of London. Lon. 16. 35. lat. 51. 50.

DUCKINGHAMSHIRE, a county of England, bounded on the N. by Northamptonfhire, on the E. by Bedfordfhire, Hertfordfhire and Middlefex, on the W. by Oxfordfhire, and on the S. by Berkfhire, from which it is feparated by the river Thames. It is about 39 miles in length, and 18 in

breadth, containing 13,390 houfes, 231,340 inhabitants, 85 parifhes, and 15 market-towns, whereof fix fend members to parliament. The air is healthy, and the foil is rich, being moftly chalk or marle. The moft general manufacture is bone-lace, and there are alfo fome paper mills. The principal rivers, befides the Thames, are the Oufe and Cola; and the chief town is Buckingham.

BU'CKET, S. [loquet, Fr.] a wooden veffel refembling a pail, ufed to draw water out of a well; likewife a leathern veffel of the fame form, ufed in fires to ferve the engines with water.

BU'CKLE, S. [boucel, Brit. boucle, Fr.] an inftrument made of metal, to faften the ftraps of the fhoes, the harnefs of horfes, &c. A curled lock of hair.

To BU'CKLE, V. A. to faften with a buckle. Figuratively, to join in battle array, ufed with the particle with, "the avant guard were buckled unto them in the front." Chaucer. To marry, or join. "Is this an age to buckle with a bride." Dryd. To curl a wig; to curl hair.

To BU'CKLE, V. A. [buck'n, Teut.] to bend or bow under a weight, ufed with under. Figuratively, to bend ones inclinations, to apply, or attend to. "Go buckle to the law." Dryd.

BU'CKLER, S. [buckeld, Brit. bouclier, Fr.] a piece of defenfive armour, buckled to the arm, and ufed by the ancients to defend their bodies from the enemy; being found cumberfome, they were changed for the fhield, which is of lefs dimenfions. On medals, they either fignified public vows for the fafety of a prince; or that he was efteemed the protector of his people; hence the Romans called Fabius, the buckler of Rome.

BU'CKMAST, S. the fruit of a beech-tree.

BU'CKRAM, S. [bugram, Fr. buckrame, Ital.] a coarfe cloth gummed, calendered and dyed; ufed to ftiffen garments and to wrap up cloths, ferges, &c.

BU'CKTHORN, S. [from buck, Sax and thorn, Sax.] In Botany, a plant called rhamnus, Lat. and nuprun, Fr. It is ranged by Tournefort in the 11th fect. of his 2eth clafs, and by Linnæus in the firft fect. of his 5th. There are four fpecies. The berries of the common fort are ufed in medicine, in the fyrup of this name, which is efteemed no bad purge in the dropfy, jaundice, and other cutaneous eruptions; but, it has grown into difrepute from the mixtures of other berries; the beft ways of diftinguifhing the true and genuine from the heterogeneous mixture, is to obferve, that every berry contains four feeds, and that the juice, when rubbed on paper, will tinge it with a green colour.

colour. From the juice of the berry is likewise made a very fine green colour, called by the French, *ver de vessie*, which is very much esteemed by miniature-painters.

BU'COLIC, S. (from *boukolos*) pastoral poetry, supposed to have had its original in Sicily, and all the mirth and diversions of shepherds, to have been inspired by love, and owing to leisure.

BUD, S. [*botte*, Belg. *bouton*, Fr.] in botany, the small protuberances on the bark of a tree, which turn to shoots, &c. They are first formed in the pith, and are forced along certain channels till they meet the air at the tender bark, through which they since their way; like a seed they contain a whole plant, from which they differ in not having any lobes or ear leaves, and as they take root in the tree, where they meet with the proper juices to nourish, they do not seem to need them. Among gardeners it denotes the first tops of tender plants, and in husbandry, a second calf of the first year, being so named from the budding of its horns. Figuratively, the beginning, first appearance, tender and immature state of a thing. " Nip vice in the *bud*."

To BUD, V. N. to swell with little prominencies, applied to vegetables. To put forth shoots. 'To be in the bloom of youth. " Young *budding* virgin." *Shak*. Actively, in Gardening, to innoculate by inserting a bud into a tree.

To BUDGE, V. N. [*bouger*, Fr.] to move to another place, to quit a place.

BUDGE, Adj. stiff, surly, morose, formal. " Those *budge* doctors of the floic." *Milton*.

BUDGET, S. [*bougette*, Fr.] a small bag. Figuratively, the breast or bosom, " In whose bottom or *budget*, most of Perkins secrets were laid up." That which is contained in a *budget*, a store, or stock.

BUFF, S. [from *buffle*] the hide of a buffalo dressed in oil; any other skin dressed likewise.

BUFFALO, S. [Ital.] in Natural History, a wild animal, like an ox, its horns are very broad, thick, and black, its body thick, and its hide very hard, its hair is short and black, very thick on the head, which is very small in proportion to the rest of its body, its tail having scarcely any hair at all; it may be tamed, and in Italy is worked in the plough. Its horns are used by the turners to heads for chaplets and snuff-boxes, its hide is used in coats for soldiers, and its hair mixed with that of cows, is used for stuffing seats.

BUFFET, S. [*buffet*, or *buffet*, Ital.] a blow on the head with the fist. Indignity, perfecution, or hardship. " A man—that fortune's *buffets* and rewards hast taken." *Shak*.

BUFFET, S. [*buffet*, Fr.] a kind of closet, with an arch at the top, with shelves used to place china and plate in for ornament and use.

To BUFFET, V. N. [*buffeter*, Fr.] to strike on the head; to strike any thing with the hand. " *buffeting* the billows."

BUFFLE, S. [*buffle*, Fr.] See BUFFALO.

BUFFLE-HEADED, Adj. having a head like a *buffalo*. Dull, stupid.

BUFFOON, S. [*buffon*, Fr.] one who strives to entertain by low jests and antick postures. A merry-andrew, a jack-pudding.

BUFFOONERY, S. low jests, ridiculous pranks, or scurrilous mirth.

BUG, S. [from *bug*, Brit. *bugan*, Rusf.] an insect of a roundish flat form, a darkish red colour, which breeds in household stuff and beds. Likewise a flying insect like a beetle, and named a *May-Bug*, or *May-Fly*. " Yet let me flap this *bug* with gilded wings." *Pope*. Hence we may see the propriety of the poet's ascribing wings to this creature, and at the same time vindicate him from *Johnson's* criticism, in his Dictionary, who says that, " Wings are *erroneously* ascribed to it."

BUG, or BUGBEAR, S. an object of terrour; a spectre; a ghost; generally applied to frighten children.

BUGGY, Adj. abounding with bugs.

BUGLE, or BUGLE-HORN, S. [of *bugan*, Sax.] a hunting horn.

BUGLE, S. a shining bead, made of glass.

BUGLE, S. [*bugula*, Lat.] in Botany, a plant, with a short permanent empalement of one leaf, slightly cut into five parts. The common sort is greatly esteemed as vulnerary, and used both externally and internally.

To BUILD, V. A. [pronounced *bild*, the preter. I *built*, or have *built*, from *bilden*, Belg.] to raise houses, &c. To raise on any thing as a support or foundation. " Love *built* on beauty from as beauty dies." *Lansar*. Used with *on* or *upon*, to ground or establish an opinion; to depend on; to rest on, " A surer way than to *build* on the interpretations of an author." *Addf*.

BUILDER, S. one who raises houses, or builds.

BUILDING, S. a fabric or place erected for shelter for dwelling, or for security of magnificence. A regular building is square, having its opposite sides equal, and the parts disposed with symmetry. An irregular building is that whose plan is not contained within equal or parallel lines, and whose parts have no proportion to each other. An insulating building is that which stands by itself, being encompassed with streets or some open square, like St. Paul's Cathedral in London. An engaged building, is that which is encompassed

paſſed with others, having no front towards any public place, nor any communication but through a back paſſage. *Building* is uſed in its primary ſenſe, for the art and act of raiſing edifices. Figuratively, the body which is the habitation of the ſoul. "We know that if our earthly tabernacle be diſſolved we have a *building* of God." 2 *Cor.* v. 1. The church of Chriſt. "In whom all the *building* fitly framed." *Ephe.* ii. 21. The ſeveral parts or the elevation of an edifice. "To ſhew him the *building* of the temple." *Matt.* xxiv. 1.

BUL'B, S. [*bulbus*, Lat. of *Bolbos*, Gr.] in Botany, a thick root nearly round; of which there are two ſpecies. 1. The tunicated, or coated, conſiſting of many coats involving each other, as in the onion, which when cut in halves, plainly ſhews the coats involving each other. 2. The ſquamous, or ſcaly, conſiſting of ſeveral ſcales lying over each other, like tiles on a houſe, or ſcales on a fiſh, of this kind is the lilly. It is very remarkable that theſe roots are annually renewed or repaired out of the trunk or ſtalk itſelf; the baſis of the ſtalk continually and inſenſibly deſcending below the ſurface of the earth, is there changed into a root. Thus, the ſtalk of brown-wort ſinking down by degrees till it is below the mold, becomes the upper part of the root, and continuing ſtill to ſink, the next year, becomes the lower part, and the next after that rots away; a new addition being ſtill yearly made out of the ſtalk, as the elder parts rot away.

BULBA'CEOUS, Adj. the ſame as *bulbous*.

BU'LBOUS, Adj. reſembling or containing a bulb, having a round root.

To BU'LGE, V. N. [*bilge*, Sax.] to ſpring a leak, applied to a ſhip. To founder. To ſtick or jut out. "Timber that *bulges* from its bottom." *Moxon.*

BU'LFINCH, S. [*bogfinck*, Dan.] a ſong bird remarkable for its imitating the flagelet.

BU'LIMY, [*Boulimos* and *limos*, Gr.] in Medicine an enormous appetite, attended with faintings and coldneſs at the extreme parts. The philoſophical tranſactions mention a perſon in this diſorder, who would eat an ordinary ſhoulder of mutton at a meal, and would feed on ſow-thiſtle, &c. but was cured by throwing up ſeveral worms of the length and thickneſs of a tobacco pipe.

BU'LK, S. [*bulcke*, Belg.] ſize, dimenſions, number, the greateſt part. "The *bulk* of the people." *Freehold*, No 51. The whole ſpace in the hold of a ſhip for the ſtowage of goods; likewiſe the cargo. To *break bulk*, is to unload a part of the cargo.

BU'LK, S. [from *bielke*, Belg.] in Building, a part of a building projecting from the window.

BU'LKHEAD, S. partitions made with boards acroſs a ſhip.

BU'LKINESS, S. the greatneſs of ſize or dimenſions.

BU'LKY, Adj. of a large ſize, or ſtature.

BU'LL, S. [*bulle* or *bul*, Belg.] the male of black cattle. Figuratively, a loud, noiſy, furious or dangerous enemy. "Many *bulls* have encompaſſed me." *Pſalm.* xxii. 12. In Aſtronomy, one of the 12 ſigns of the Zodiac. A blunder.

BU'LL, S. [*bulla*, Fr. *bulla*, Lat.] In Eccleſiaſtic Hiſtory, an inſtrument made out at the Roman or Pope's chancery ſealed with lead, and of the ſame nature with the edicts of ſecular princes. The ſeal preſents on one ſide the heads of St. Peter and St. Paul, and on the other the name of the Pope and the year of his pontificate. The bulls, which are written in an old Roman Gothic character, have the ſeal ſuſpended by ſilken threads, if letters of grace and favour; but, if letters of juſtice or executory, by an hempen cord.

BU'LL-BAITING, S. the worrying a bull with dogs.

BU'LL-CALF, S. a male calf. A ſtupid fellow, uſed as a term of reproach.

BU'LL-DOG, S. a ſpecies of dogs of a ſtrong make, remarkable for never quitting his hold, whenever it has faſtened, and uſed in baiting bulls, which they ſeize by the noſe and pin to the ground: even among the Romans they were famous for their great ſtrength, as appears from Claudian's *magnique tauros fractturi colla Britanni*. "England's huge breed of ſtrength enough to break—the neck of *bulls*." Yet it muſt be obſerved that their qualities are local; and that they degenerate when tranſported to a foreign country.

BU'LLET, S. [*boulet*, Fr.] a leaden ball uſed to load guns with.

BU'LL-FINCH, S. in Natural Hiſtory, a ſmall bird, which has neither ſong nor whiſtle of its own, but famous for learning either by the mouth or flagelet.

BU'LL HEAD, S. figuratively, a ſtupid perſon. In Natural Hiſtory, a fiſh called likewiſe the miller's thumb. Its body is variegated with ſpots of white, black, and brown. When ſpawning, which is during the ſummer, their vents ſwell like a dug, and in winter they diſappear, like the ſwallows.

BU'LL-WEED, S. in Botany, a plant named likewiſe the *knapweed*.

BU'LLACE, S. in Botany, a ſour wild plumb, of a globular form and lemon colour.

BU'LLION, S. [*billon*, Fr.] gold and ſilver in the maſs; ſo named either when they are firſt ſmelted from the ore, or after they are refined and caſt into ingots, or bars. The opinion againſt reckoning gold and ſilver a commodity or merchandize, which ought to be carried out of the kingdom, ſeems grounded on want of experi-

cost and an absolute ignorance of the nature of trade. Even in countries where the mines of these metals are, the prohibition of their exportation, has proved a great obstruction to their commercial industry, and rendered that treasure useless. The retaining it in a nation without circulating out of it must be a national loss; as it is nothing but keeping a dead stock to that value, which is of no more use to the public than the like value of statues. It is of no other use at home, than making our payments, and when that end is answered, the plenty of gold or silver, will be rather a national loss, because it would naturally enhance the price of commodities to ourselves, thereby lessen the demand for them by foreign nations, and, in time, ruin trade and impoverish the people; for when we have greater plenty of money must we not give greater prices for labour, and the native commodities of wool; would not this oblige the manufacturer to encrease the price of his commodity; and would not all those nations, who think they pay enough at present, instead of complying with extraordinary demands, go to those markets, where they can buy cheaper? Besides, what must become of the interest of money? would it not fall in proportion to the increase of cash? and if so, how many must starve, who now live on the interest of the money they have in the funds? We are indeed arguing upon a supposition that never can be reduced to practice; for it is impossible to keep bullion at home; while we carry on trade there must be a balance against us somewhere or another, and that balance must always be paid in bullion; foreigners have large sums in our funds, and a lowering of the interest will make them draw them out, so that these means of making money plenty will always make it scarce. The only method to keep enough at home, will be to lessen our dealings with those nations where the balance of trade is against us, and then we shall find that the carrying bullion out of the kingdom will not only be the best means of lessening the fatal mischiefs, which would arise from enhancing the price of labour, but as it would be a means of introducing commodities into the kingdom, which may be sure of a market abroad, would be the best means of turning the balance of trade in our favour, and effecting what is intended by the clamours against the exportation of gold or silver. This is meant as an answer to some objections, which narrow minds have made to the exports of the English India company; and may serve to shew their futility and unreasonableness.

BULLITION, S. (from *bullio*, Lat.) the state of boiling.

BULLY, S. one who uses threatening expressions, and insolent behaviour, with great shew of courage, but is in fact a coward.

In Low Language one who attends a strumpet, and espouses her quarrels.

To BULLY, V. A. to behave with unkind insolence and assumed courage, in order to frighten a person.

BULLRUSH, S. a large rush, growing in the sea, rivers, and in moist places. These on the sea banks in Holland, are planted there in order to prevent the water from washing away the earth; they grow very high, are cut in the summer, and used by the inhabitants in making baskets; as they are prickly, and different from ours. Mr. Dryden may be defended from Johnson's criticism in applying the following epithet to their name. "The *heavy bulrush* next in order flood." At the same time it must be added that our own country would afford that gentleman sufficient conviction of his being in error.

BULWARK, [*bollwerck*, Belg. *boulevard*, Fr.] a fortification; a security or protection.

To BULWARK, V. A. to fortify, or strengthen. "No *bulwark'd* town." *Addis.* This verb is seldom used.

BUM, S. [*bomme*, Belg. *bom*, Fr.] the posteriors. Used in composition to convey the idea of reproach, as in the following word, *bum-bailiff*.

BUM-BAILIFF, S. a person employed to arrest a person.

BUMKIN, S. [*bunkin*, Belg.] one who has not had a polite education, but is gross in his conceptions, rude to his behaviour, and void of experience. A rustic, or clown.

BUMP, S. a swelling or tumour occasioned by a blow.

To BUMP, V. A. to kick or strike; to make a loud noise.

BUMPER, S. a cup or glass filled as full as it can hold.

BUMKIN, S. *See* BUMPKIN.

BUMPKINLY, Adv. clownish, or after the manner of a countryman, who is a stranger to politeness and address. "An air of *bumpkinly* romance." *Clarissa.* A new word coined by Richardson, and without proper authority.

BUNCH, S. [*bunge*, Ital.] any prominence, hard knob, or swelling. Many things of the same kind growing together; a cluster; several things collected or tied together. "*Bunch* of keys." *Locke.* Any thing collected together in a knot, so as one of the extremities may be at liberty and free from bondage. "A *bunch* of hairs discoloured diversly."

To BUNCH, V. A. to grow in knobs; to swell.

BUNCH-BACKED, Adj. hump-backed; crooked.

BUNCHINESS, S. the growing in knobs, or clusters.

BUNDLE, S. a parcel of goods, &c. tied or wrapped together.

To

To BU'NDLE, V. A. to tie several things together. Figuratively, to be collected together, to be comprehended or connected, applied to the ideas of the mind, and also with up or together. "Several things will not be *bundled up together*, under our terms or ways of speaking."

BU'NGAY, a town in Suffolk, with a market on Thursdays, and two fairs, on May 14, for horses and lean cattle, and on September 25, for hogs and petty chapmen. It is seated on a spot watered by the river Waveney, which separates it from Norfolk. It has two parish-churches, one of which is handsome, and between both, in the midst of the town, are the ruins of a famous nunnery. Here is also one dissenting meeting-house, and a grammar-school. The town contains about 600 houses, and the streets are pretty wide, and well paved. Here are likewise the remains of a castle supposed to be built by king John. About 60 years ago, almost every house was burnt to the ground, when the records belonging to the castle and convent were consumed. It is however now a good trading town; and the women are employed in knitting worsted stockings. The market is large for corn, which is brought out of Norfolk. It is 16 miles N. by E from Ipswich, 20 S. of Suffolk, and 101 N. E. of London. Lon. 16. o. lat. 52. 35.

BU'NG, S. [*bung*, Brit.] a stopple of wood, cork, &c. for the bung-hole of a cask.

To BU'NG, V. A. to stop a barrel at its largest hole.

BUNG-HOLE, S. a large round hole in a barrel.

To BU'NGLE, V. N. to perform in a clumsy, awkward manner; clumsy performance.

BU'NGLER, S. [*bungler*, Brit.] an ignorant workman, one who does a thing in a clumsy manner.

BU'NGLINGLY, Adv. in a clumsy or awkward manner.

BU'NN, S. [*bannide*, *buanch*, Span.] in Pastry, a small cake.

BU'NT, S. the middle part of a sail formed into a bag or pouch that it may contain more wind.

To BU'NT, V. N. to swell.

BU'NTER, S. (a cant word) a woman who picks up rags, used figuratively, to convey the idea of a dirty, filthy, mean creature; a prostitute.

BU'OY, S. (from *bucr*, *beis*, or *boye*, Fr.) a piece of wood, cork, &c. floating on the water, tied to a cable fastened to the bottom of the sea, to inform pilots and mariners where anchors are dropped in the harbours, where the wrecks of ships are sunk, together with shallow places, sand banks, and other impediments.

To BU'OY, V A. to raise up; to keep afloat. Used with the participle up. Figuratively, to keep any thing from sinking under oppression. To cause a thing to abound by

its specific likeness. Figuratively, to surmount all difficulties and impediments. "Rising merit will *buoy* up at last." *Pope*.

BUO'YANCY, S. that quality which prevents a thing from subsiding, sinking, or descending. "The winged tribes owe their flight and *buoyancy* to it." *Derham*.

BUO'YANT, Adj. light; that which will not sink; that which animates. "His vivid nerves so full of *buoyant* spirits." *Thomson*.

BUR, S. (*bourre*, Fr.) the head of a plant covered with prickles, which sticks wherever it is cast.

BU'RDEN, S. (spelt more properly *burthen*, of *byrt̄er*, Sax.) a load; figuratively, a difficulty, oppression, affliction, or uneasiness; the weight a ship can carry; a prophecy denouncing calamities and afflictions. "This *burden* concerning the prince." *Ezek.* xii. 10. The duties required by the gospel dispensation. "My *burden* is light," *Matt.* xi. 30. In music, the drone or bass of an organ, bagpipe, &c. the words repeated at the end of every stanza of a song are called the *burden* of a song: this sense is derived from *bourdar* of *bourdenner*, (Fr.) to hum.

To BU'RDEN, to load; to encumber, or put a person to expence. "I did not *burden* you." 2 *Cor.* xii. 16.

BU'RDENSOME, Ad. heavy; figuratively, applied to afflictions, or trouble.

BU'RDOCK, S. in Botany, a plant.

BUREAU, S.[Fr. pronounced *burô*] a chest of drawers, with the top sloping, and furnished with pidgeon holes.

BU'RGAMOT, S. [*bergamotte*, Fr.] a species of mellow juicy pear.

BOURGEOIS, S. [pronounced *boorjôi*, Fr.] a citizen or burgess. In Printing, a type somewhat larger than what this book is printed on.

BU'RGESS, S. [*bourgeois*, Fr.] an inhabitant of a borough or city; or a representative of a borough in parliament.

BU'RGH, S. [see BURROW] a corporate town or borrow.

BU'RCHER, S. [from *burg*, and *wer*, Sax.] one who has the right of a citizen, or a vote for a member of parliament.

BU'RGHER-SHIP, S. the dignity, or privilege of a burgher.

BU'RGLAR, S. [see BURGLARY] a person who is guilty of house-breaking.

BU'RGLARY, S. [*burg-brice*, Sax. housebreaking, from *burg* a house, and *brice*, Sax. breaking] in Law, a felonious entering a person's house in the night-time, with an intent to commit felony; if it is in the day-time, it is then called *house-breaking*, by way of distinction. This species of felony was never so much practised as at present.

BU'RGOMASTER, S. [from *burgir*, Belg. and *meister*, Belg.] the chief magistrate of the towns of Holland, Flanders, and Germany, similar to that of an alderman in London. In Amsterdam they
are

are elected by those who have been burgher-maſters themſelves, they diſpoſe of all offices, keep the key of the bank, which is never opened but when one or more of them is preſent; their ſalary is about 500 guilden per annum, they are attended by a numerous retinue of penſioners on all public occaſions, and all their feaſts, public entertainments, &c. are defrayed out of the common treaſury.

BU'RIAL, S. [from *bury*] the placing a dead body in the earth. Figuratively, the placing any thing in the earth, or under water. The burial ſervice, is an office performal at the grave and interment of one of its members. Its ſolemnity and gravity, the judicious arrangement of its ſeveral parts, and the propriety of thoſe portions of Scripture uſed on this occaſion, muſt convey a high idea of the abilities and piety of the compoſers, and when duly attended to in its performance, or delivered with that pathos and ſolemnity, which its awful periods require, muſt draw tears from the eyes, plant daggers in the heart, and like the ſound of the Archangel's trumpet, awaken the moſt obdurate ſinner to ſeriouſneſs.

BU'RIER, S. he that buries or lays a corpſe. Figuratively, that removes any thing out of ſight.

BU'RINE, S. [Fr.] an engraving tool; a graver.

BU'RLESQUE, S. [*burleſco*, Ital. *burlare*, Ital. to jeſt] a kind of poetry, wherein both perſons and things are repreſented in a ridiculous light; it ſeems to have been invented by *Berni* in Italian, and from Italy paſſed into France, where it became ſo much the reigning taſte, that in the year 1649, appeared a book, entitled the paſſion of our Saviour in burleſque verſe; we mention this irreverent title only to brand it with its proper degree of infamy and deteſtation. The beſt piece of Engliſh burleſque poetry, is *Butler's Hudibras*, and is like to continue ſo, unleſs ſome extraordinary genius ſhould tread in his footſteps, and cultivate a ſpecies of compoſition, which our beſt authors have read with rapture, but never had the hardineſs to rival.

To BURLE'SQUE, V. A. to turn any thing to ridicule; to repreſent a thing luſiſerouſly.

BU'RLY, Adj. tall or over-grown; of large dimenſions; high ſounding, ſwelling, or pompous.

To BU'RN, V. A. [*prenz*, I *burnt*, or I have *burnt*; *bernan*, by*ran*, Sax.] to conſume by fire; to cauſe a wound by fire; to be on fire, to kindle; figuratively, to ſhine as if in flames. "The barge, like a burniſh'd throne, *burnt* on the water." *Shak.* "To be violently inflamed by paſſion; to make the cheeks glow with heat." "That *burning* ſhame detains him from his Cordelia." *Shak.* To be hot, "Like a young hound upon a *burning* ſcent." *Dryden.*

BU'RN, S. a wound, injury, or hurt received from fire.

BU'RNING, S. the action of fire or ſome ſubſtance, whereby the minute parts are put into violent motion, and ſome of them aſſuming the nature of fire themſelves, fly off to their proper ſphere, while others either aſcend in vapours, or are reduced to aſhes; alſo flame, or fire.

BU'RNING-GLASS, S. a convex glaſs which collects the rays of the ſun into a point, where any combuſtible matter being placed is ſet on fire. The burning-glaſſes made of looking-glaſs, are much more powerful than thoſe made by lenſes or glaſſes, that tranſmit the rays of light through them. Mr. Villette's mirror condenſes rays 17,733 times, and conſequently burns with a heat 906 times greater than common fire; and that it may not ſeem ſtrange, that even this glaſs cannot condenſe the rays of the moon when in full, ſo as to produce any ſenſible heat, we ſhould recollect that the denſity of the moon's rays is to thoſe of the ſun as 300000 to 1, and therefore the burning-glaſs muſt condenſe the rays of the moon three millions of times to raiſe the liquor of the common thermometer, which is an effect 300 times greater than Villette's mirror can produce. After hinting that the Royal Society has a burning-glaſs, conſiſting of 7 concave glaſſes ſo placed, that their ſeveral foci meet in one phyſical point, which was preſented them by the great Sir Iſaac Newton, and vitrifies brick in a moment, and melts gold in half a minute; the poſſibility of Archimedes's ſetting the Roman fleet on fire by burning-glaſſes ſeems worthy of notice. Though Deſcartes has endeavoured to run it down as impracticable, the experiments of Mr. Buffon ſeems to prove it to be more than a bare probability, ſince by his polyedron of 6 feet broad, and as many high, conſiſting of 168 ſmall mirrors, or flat pieces of looking-glaſs, each 6 inches ſquare, he hath ſet fire to birch-wood at 150 feet diſtance, in March; at another time he has burnt wood at 200 feet, and melted tin and lead at the diſtance of 120 feet, and ſilver at that of 50.

To BU'RNISH, V. A. [*burnir*, Fr.] to poliſh ſo as to make a thing ſhine. Neuterly, to grow bright or gloſſy.

BU'RNISHER, S. one who burniſhes; an inſtrument uſed by poliſhers, made of the fineſt ſteel, poliſhed on a wheel till it is as bright as looking-glaſs, that which is uſed in burniſhing gold and ſilver is made round, ſometimes with one, and ſometimes with two handles; an engraver's burniſher is about 6 inches long, on one ſide in the ſhape of a heart with a long point, made round out very thick or ſharp, the other end is of iron, reſembling the head of a dart with three angles, ſharp on three ſides; it is likewiſe named a gruter. Bookbinders uſe a dog's tooth to burniſh the edges of their books, and gilders the ſame,

or elfe a wolf's tooth, blood-stone, tripoll, a piece of white wood, emery, &c.

BU'RNISHING, S. the polishing gold, silver, &c.

BU'RNT, Participle Paffive of burn.

BU'RR, S. [for BUR] the lobe of the ear; also a fweat-bread of meat.

BURR PUMP, S a pump by the fide of a fhip, with a ftaff 7 or 8 feet long, having a bur or knob of wood at the end, which is drawn up by a rope faftened to the middle, and is called likewife a bilge pemp.

BU'RREL, S. [bourre, Fr.] in Gardening, a fpecies of pear, called likewife the red butter pear, from its fmooth, delicious, foft pulp.

BU'RROCK, S. a fmall wear or dam in a river, where wheels are laid to catch fifh.

BU'RROW, BU'RG, BU'RGH, S. [from burg, or burig, Sax.] a corporate town, which fends members to parliament; also the holes made in the ground by rabbits.

To BU'RROW, [from bur, Sax.] to make holes in the ground like rabbits. Figuratively, to hide or bury like a rabbit in its burrow.

BU'RSAR, S. [burfarius, Lat.] an officer in a college, who keeps its accounts; a treafurer. In Scotland, a ftudent fent to the univerfities by each prefbytery, from whom they have a fmall annual allowance for four years, refembling the exhibitioners at Oxford.

BURSE, S. [bourfe, Fr. burfa, Lat.] an exchange, or place where merchants meet to tranfact bufinefs.

To BURST, V. N. [Preter. I burft, have burft, or berften, from burfton, Sax.] to fly afunder with violence; to break away; to free a paffage, with the particle out; to begin an action, including the idea of violence. Ufed with into, "She burft into tears." Applied to motion, to come in fuddenly. Ufed actively, to break, feparate, or difunite with fudden violence.

BURST, S. a feparation of a thing with violence; an explofion. Figuratively, any fudden and violent action.

BURST, or BURSTEN, [Participle of burft] in Surgery, applied to a perfon who has a rupture.

BU'RSTWORT, S. in Botany, the hernia. This genus is placed by Tournefort in the fecond fect. of his 15th clafs, and by Linnæus in the fecond fect. of his 5th.

To BURTHEN, V. A. } See BURDEN.
BU'RTHEN, S. }

BURTON UPON TRENT, a town of Staffordfhire, with a market on Thurfdays, and four fairs; on April 9, for horned cattle and horfes; on Holy Thurfday, for horned cattle; on July 16, for toys; and on October 29, which is confiderable for horfes and horned cattle. It had formerly a large

abbey, and over the river Trent it has now a famous bridge of free-ftone, about a quarter of a mile in length, fupported by thirty-feven arches. It confifts chiefly of one long ftreet, which runs from the place where the abbey ftood to the bridge, and it has a good market for corn and provifions. Burton ale is accounted the beft of any country ale brought to London. It is 12 miles N. E. of Litchfield, 12 S. W. of Derby, and 115 N. N. W. of London. Lon. 1 5. 59. lat. 52. 48.

BURY ST. EDMUND's, a town of Suffolk, with a market on Wednefdays, and two fairs; on September 21, which lafts three weeks, and on December 9, which continues three days, for horfes, bears, and cheefe. The fituation is exceeding pleafant, and the air is fuppofed to be the beft in England, for which reafon it is frequented by the better fort of people. It was formerly of great note for its abbey, which was faid to be the fineft and richeft of any in England, and ftood between the two churches, which are both very large, and feated in one church-yard. In St. Mary's, one of thefe churches, lies Mary Queen of France, who was married to Thomas Duke of Norfolk. It fends two members to parliament, and is governed by a recorder, 12 aldermen, and 24 common council. The ftreets, which are always clean, are pretty wide, and well paved; and it contains about 1000 houfes, which in general are well-built, and 7000 inhabitants. The town took its name from St. Edmund the King's being buried here, after being murdered in a wood, and his head fevered from his body. Befides the above churches, there are one Prefbyterian, one Independent, and one Quakers meeting. Here is a fpacious market-hall, a grammar-fchool, a fine fair-field, and a beautiful crofs. The market is very large for corn, fifh, and fowl. The affizes for the county are held here. It is 14 miles E. of Newmarket, 25 W. N. W. of Ipfwich, 43 N. of Chelmsford, and 75 N. N. E. of London. Lon. 18. 20. lat. 52. 20.

To BU'RY, V. A. [pronounced by the Londoners berry, from birian, byrigan, or byrigren, Sax.] to inter a corpfe in a grave; to inter with funeral rites; to cover with earth. Figuratively, to conceal or hide.

BU'RYING-PLACE, S. a church-yard; a burying-ground.

BUSH, S. [bofch, Belg.] a thick fhrub. The branch of a tree, hung before a door, to fhew that liquors are fold, "Good wine needs no bufh." Shak.

To BU'SH, to grow thick, to grow together.

BU'SHEL, S. [boiffeau, Fr. bufellus, Low Lat.] a dry meafure of eight gallons; a great quantity.

BU'SHINESS,

BUSHINESS, S. the growing in great
numbers near one another, like the branches
of a bush.

BUSHY, Adj. full of branches, but
short; thick of branches. Figuratively,
growing in great numbers. "A thick curly
beard." Addif. Abounding in bushes

BUSILESS, Adj. [pronounced bizziss,
from bufy and lefs, of —, Sax.] without
employ; at leisure; not engaged in any employment.

BUSILY, Adj. [pronounced bizily] in-
dustriously; in an odious inquisitive manner. "If too busily they should enquire."
Dryd. With an air of active importance
from a multiplicity of business.

BUSINESS, S. [pronounced bizness or
bizness, from bufy and n.ss, of ness, Sax.]
employment; a man's trade or profession,
affairs, or concerns. After more or made, a
person's whole study and peculiar employment. "Made it his business to lash the
faults of other writers." Addif. Joined
with love, a notion that may be assigned for
any measure or undertaking, a propriety.
"What bufefs had the tortoise among the
clouds." L'Estr. To do a man's business, is a
low and familiar phrase for killing or ruining him.

BUSK, S. [bufque, Fr.] a piece of steel,
&c. worn at the stomacher of a woman's
stays, to keep them in proper form.

BUSKIN, S. [bufcion, or brofeon, Belg.
Buzzectino, Ital.] a kind of half-boot worn
by the antients, laced or fastened before.
Its sole was so thick, that is made a person
considerably taller, was worn by the dramatic performer in tragedy, and distinguished
from the sock worn in comedy, which was
of a thinner sole, and consequently lower.
Figurat velp, tragedy. "Garrick is no less
admiral in the sock than in the buskin."

BUSS, S. [bus, Ir.] a salute with the
lips, attended with a smacking sound, and
familiar endearment; distinguished from a
kiss, which is a bare touch of the lips, and
given with a greater shew of ceremonious
fondness. Authors, without attending to
this distinction, use them promiscuously,
looking on buss as a low term to convey the
same idea as a kiss. In Fishery, a small veffel from 48 to 60 tons burthen, used in the
herring fishery, with two small sheds or ca-
bins at each end, that at the prow serving
for a kitchen; derived from buffe, Teut.

To BUSS, to salute with the lips. Figuratively, to touch. "Whose wanton toys do
bufs the clouds." Shak.

BUST, S. [bufto, Ital.] in Sculpture, the
figure of a person in relievo, containing the
head, shoulders and stomach, without the
arms.

BUSTARD, S. [bistarde, Fr. busriaco,
Ital.] a wild turkey, so called from its diffi-

culty in flying and raising itself from the
ground, on account of its weight.

To BUSTLE, V. N. [supposed by some
to be derived from bruit.ier, Sax. to make a
noise, but more probably from —— to
nimbly about a thing; to move quick for
—— on anything.

BUSTLE, S. a great hurry of a mess,
noise, tumult.

BUSTLER, S. a stirring, industrious mind.

BUSY, Adj. [pronounced bizzy of bysy, in
busien, Sax.] engaged. Actively, diligent,
officious, or meddling with things that do not
concern a person.

To BUSY, V. A [see the noun, participle
busied] to keep a person employed. To employ, used with the particles about and with.
"The idea it is busied about." Locke. "Bufy
giddy minds with foreign quarrels." Shak.

BUSY-BODY, S. a person full of officiousness, meddling with the concerns of other
people.

BUT, Conj. [buten, late, buton, Sax.]
when it breaks off the thread of a discourse,
it intimates a stop of the mind, signifies,
saveheit. "but to say no more." When
applied to limit the sense to what is expressed, it signifies only. "I saw but two women." Joined with did or had, it denotes un-
ly. "I'ld but men consider." Tillot. When
used to introduce the minor of a syllogism, it
only implies that the latter proposed
should be joined to the former; and may
be changed for now. "All animals have
sense, but a dog is an animal." After a
comparative noun it has the force of than.
"No sooner up, but he privately opened the
gate." Guard. No. 167. After the words
doubt, question, or other terms implying uncertainty, if proceeded by a negative, it implies that the excepted clause, which follows,
is an object of the highest assurance and confidence, and may be changed for then, which
is sometimes expressed with it. "There is
no doubt but the king of Spain will reform,
&c." Addif. "They made no account, but
that the navy, &c." Bacon. Joined with
an adverb or noun expressive of time, it
confines, limits, or restrains the action or
thing mentioned to the period expressed.

BUT, S. [but, Fr.] a limit or boundary. Seldom used.

BUT-END, S. the broad or blunt end.

BUTCHER, S. the u is pronounced long,
[boucher, Fr.] one who kills and sells the
flesh of cattle in a market, or his own
house. It is indeed strange that the act 4
Hen. VII. c. 3. "which forbids any butcher
to slay beasts within the walls of the city of
London, on pain of forfeiting 13d. or 8d.
for every cow or other beast," should be e-
vaded and never put in execution, though it
is plain that nothing could contribute more

to

to the cleanliness of the streets, the wholesomeness of the air, the preventing those accidents which are caused by over-driving black cattle in the streets, or, what is not less important, the removing from infant minds such scenes as tend to smother the tender glowings of humanity; and, by familiarising the sight to bloodshed, make the soul contract such habits of barbarity and cruelty, as discretion will not be able to root out, and reason at his greatest maturity, will find a hard task to restrain. Butcher is used figuratively, for one who is of a barbarous disposition. "Conquerors are but the butchers of mankind." Lucas.

To BU'TCHER, V. A. to flay or kill a beast. Figuratively, to murder in a barbarous and cruel manner.

BU'TCHERLINESS, S. a state or quality denoting a disposition void of every principle of humanity, and delighting in the most cruel murders.

BU'TCHERY, Adv. in a cruel, barbarous manner.

BU'TCHERY, S. the trade of a butcher. Figuratively, the commission of murder; cruelty, barbarity.

BU'TLER, S. [formerly spelt bottler, that is one who fills bottles, bouteillier, Fr.] a servant who has the care of liquors used in a family.

BU'TLERSHIP, S. the office of a butler.

BU'TT, S. [botte, byrte, Sax.] a vessel containing 126 gallons of wine, 108 of beer, and from 15 to 22 cwt. of currants.

BU'TT, S. [bout, Fr.] that which a person is to shoot at. Figuratively, the object to which any person's measures are aimed. One who is the object of ridicule to a company.

To BU'TT, V. A. [butin, Belg.] to give a blow with the head, applied to the method of attack used by a ram, and to that of any other animal, which attacks in the same manner.

BU'TTER, S. [butere, Sax.] a fat unctuous substance made from cream. Suffolk is famous for very good butter, and very bad cheese; of the former it produces great quantities, which have been exported to the colonies, and brought back again without any diminution of its goodness. This common and useful article is both nourishing and pectoral, opens the body, blunts the sharpness of corrosive poisons, is a dissolver and digester, good to ease pain, and removes inflammations. Yet it must be owned, that when used to excess, it relaxes and weakens the stomach, destroys the appetite, creates nauseousness, and heats much.

To BU'TTER, V. A. to spread upon any thing. In gaming, to increase the stakes at every throw.

No. VI.

BUTTER-BUR, S. in Botany, the petasites. This genus is ranged by Tournefort, in the 2d. section of his 12th class, and by Linnæus, in the 2d. section of his 19th.

BUTTER-FLOWER, S. in Botany, a yellow flower, with which the fields are covered in May, and deriving its name either from its resembling the colour, or its contributing to colouring butter in that month.

BUTTER-FLY, S. [butter-floge, Sax.] in natural history, a beautiful insect, produced from an egg, erucca-worm, caterpillar, and aurelia. The wonders of the different stages before it arrives to its maturity, and the profusion of splendour which appears in its structure, when arrived to the butter-fly state, would require too much room to expatiate on here, but may be treated of in the several articles which occur in this work relative thereto. But let it be allowed me to say, that those who would be acquainted with the different species, should consult the Spectacle of Nature, Swammerdam, Malpighi, and Derham's Physico Theology.

BUTTER-MILK, S. the whey separated from the cream in making butter.

BUTTER-WORT, S. in Botany, a plant called likewise the sanicle, deriving its name according to Skinner, from the fatness of its leaves.

BU'TTERY, Adj. having the qualities of butter.

BU'TTERY, S. a room where butter, cheese, or other provisions are kept.

BU'TTOCK, S. the broad, thick, fleshy part of animals joined to the hip. The buttock of a ship is her full breadth right astern, from the tuck upwards: when built broad or narrow at the transom, she is said to have a broad or narrow buttock.

BU'TTON, S. [bouton, Brit.] a small, flattish round ball made of metal, &c. sewed to the clothes to fasten any part of dress together. A knob or ball. In Botany, the round head of a plant; a bud. A brass knob of a lock serving to open or shut a door.

To BU'TTON, V. A. to sew buttons on a garment. To close or fasten with buttons. Figuratively, to include, cloath, or involve, with the particle up. "Whole heart is button'd up with steel." Shak.

BU'TTON-HOLE, S. the hole in a garment to receive the button in.

BU'TTRESS, S. [from abutoir, Fr.] a kind of buttment made archwise, or a mass of stone, or brick, serving to prop the sides of a building, or wall, &c. when it is very high, or has any considerable load to sustain on the other side, as a bank, &c.

To BU'TTRESS, V. A. to prop or support.

BU'TYROUS, Adj. [from butyrum, Lat.] like butter; fat, unctuous.

BUX'OM, Adj. [buxfum, Sax.] obedient, tractable, opposed to obstinate or resisting. Figuratively, void of resistance, yielding, giving away. " He with broad fails—winnow'd the buxom air." Par. Loss. Gay, lively, wanton, jolly.

BU'XOMLY, Adv. wantonly, gaily, or amorously.

BU'XOMNESS, S. the quality of being wanton, gay, or amorous.

To BU'Y, V. A. [pronounced by, preter I bought, or have bought, from bicgan, Sax.] to purchase a thing. Figuratively, to exchange one thing for another. " Pleasure with praise, and danger they would buy." Denm. To buy up, or purchase large quantities of any commodity. Used with off to escape by means of money; to bribe, or corrupt by bribery. " dissuade, or buy off confidence." South.

BUYER, S. [pronounced by-er] he that purchases.

To BUZZ, V. N. [bizzen, Teot.] to hum like bees, flies, &c. Figuratively, to whisper, or talk so as to make a noise like the humming of bees.

To BUZZ, V. A. to whisper; to divulge, publish, or spread a rumour.

BUZZ, S. the humming sound of bees, &c. A whisper.

BU'ZZARD, S. [busard, or buzart, Fr.] a kind of hawk. Figuratively, a blockhead, or dunce; generally used with the epithet blind.

BU'ZZER, S. a secret whisperer, or one who raises by false rumours.

BY, Prep. [big, bi, Sax.] after words signifying action, it implies the agent, cause, or means; after quantity it expresses the proportion; at the end of a sentence it implies imitation, or conformity; " A model to build others by." Asherb. After an adjective of the comparative degree, it denotes the difference, or proportion in which one thing exceeds another. " Shorter by the head." Applied to time, it signifies that a thing or action is limited to the period expressed. Applied to maxim or passage, it implies close, or by the side. Applied to place or situation, it denotes nearness. Joined to the pronouns himself, herself, &c. it signifies the exclusion; alone. After keep it signifies possession, or ready for use. " He keep some of the spirit by him." Boyle. Used adverbially, it signifies near. By and by; signifies shortly.

BY-DESIGN, S. a design not foreseen, or intended, but intervening by accident.

BY-END, S. private, or self interest.

BY-INTEREST, S. self or private interest opposed to that of the public.

BY-LAW, S. a law made by corporations, &c. In cases which are not provided for by the public laws.

BY-NAME, S. a name of reproach, a nick-name.

BY'-PAST, Adj. past, peculiar to the Scotch. " Three hundred years by-past." Chryst.

BY'-PATH, S. a private path.

BY'-ROAD, S. an unfrequented road, opposed to a public one.

BY'-STREET, S. an obscure street.

BY'-VIEW, S. a self-interested, private, or mercenary purpose.

BY'-WALK, S. a private walk, opposed to a main road.

BY'-WAY, S. a private and obscure way, which has no communications with, and cannot be seen from a public road.

BY'-WORD, S. [bi-word, Sax.] a saying, proverb, or term of reproach.

BYE or **BEE**, [from by, Isl. or bye, Sax.] imply a dwelling, place, or city, and are added to the names of persons, to signify that they lived or had seats in the places, to which these names are appropriated.

BY'ZANTINE, S. [from byzanium] a wedge of gold which the king offers on receiving the sacrament on Christmas-day.

C.

C, The third letter, supposed to have been borrowed from the Anglo-Saxon, C, which is the third letter of their alphabet, as well as ours, has the same sound, and in their small characters was written in the same form, as is as at present by ourselves. It is sounded by expressing the breath between the tongue, raised to the roof of the mouth near the palate, and the lips open. Before the vowels a, o, u, and all consonants, it is pronounced hard, as in copy, cot, &c. but before i, e, and y, it has a sound like the s, but somewhat more sharp, as in cit, cell, cyder; before an b, it has a peculiar sound, between the hardness of the t, and the softness of the s, as in chain, cheese; but in words derived from the French, it is sounded like an s, before b, as in chaise, which is pronounced shaise. Used as a figure, it stands for 100, and when double CC, 200. In Music, it stands for the highest part to a thorough bass.

CA'BAL, S. [cabaler, Fr.] a body of men united to disturb the administration of a state. An intrigue, or plot.

To CABAL, V. N. [cabaler, Fr.] to form plots, or engage in intrigues for subverting or changing an administration.

CABALA, S. [קבלה, Chald.] In its primary sense any sentiment, opinion, usage, or explication of Scripture, transmitted from father to son. The origin of the Cabala, among the Jews, is owing to a tradition, that at the time when Moses received the law from God at Mount Sinai, he received likewise the explication of the obscure passages, which on his coming down he communicated

to Aaron, his sons, and the 70 elders, but they being not committed to writing were handed down to future ages, only by tradition. Cabala, is likewise applied to the abuse of some text of Scripture, whereby certain visionaries pretend to discover some future event from the various combinations of words.

CA'BALIST, S. a sect among the Jews, which interpret Scripture according to the rules of the cabala. The Jews are divided into Karaites, who reject all tradition and the Talmud, retaining only the pure text of Scripture; and the Rabbinists or Talmudists, who likewise receive the talmud and traditionary exposition of Scripture. The first heretics among Christians struck into this by-path, and their descendants amongst the moderns, the Hutchinsonians, by treading in their steps, have almost made it a common road.

CABALI'STIC, CABALI'STICAL, Adj. something relating to, or founded upon the principle of the Caballists. Something mystical.

CABA'LLER, S. a person who enters into plots, to disturb and change the administration.

CABA'LLINE, Adj. [caballinus, Lat.] belonging to a horse.

CA'BARET, S. [Fr.] a place where wine is sold. "Passing by some cabaret." Brambal.

CA'BBAGE, S. [cabus, or chour cabus, Fr.] in Botany, the brasica, a kitchen plant with large fleshy and glaucous coloured leaves. Linnæus ranges it in the second sect. of his 15th class, joining the turnep, navew, and rocket to it; and its species are eight; the varieties of the first, being eleven, and those of the third sort, two. Also a cant word among taylors for remnants of cloth which they keep for themselves.

To CA'BBAGE, V.A. to defraud a person of part of his cloth, or to retain the superfluities of cloth from a customer.

CA'BIN, S. [caban, or chabin, Brit.] a little hut. On board ships, small cells, or apartments.

To CA'BIN, V. N. to live in a cabin. Figuratively, to live or lie in a small place. "And cabin in a cave." Shak. Used actively, to confine in a cabin. "But now I'm cabin'd, crib'd, confin'd." Shak.

CA'BINED, Adj. belonging to a cabin.

CA'BINET, S. [cabinet, Fr.] a kind of chest with several drawers for preserving curiosities, or keeping clothes. In Architecture, the most retired place in the best part of a building, set apart for writing, studying, or privacy. A room in which private consultations are held.

CA'BINET-MAKER, S. one who makes cabinets, and other wooden houshold furniture.

CA'BLE, S. [cabl, Brit. cable, Fr.] a thick, large, strong, three strand-rope, fastened to an anchor, to hold the ship when she rides; generally 120 fathoms in length; whence a cable's length is figuratively used for 120 fathoms. A cable is said to be well laid, when well wrought, or made; to be served or plaited, when bound with ropes, or clouts to prevent it from galling the hause; to be splired, when the several strands are interwoven, to join two pieces or ends together; to be coiled, when rolled up in a ring, the several rounds being called cable tire; to pay more cable, is to let more out; to pay cheap the cable, is to let or hand out apace; and to veer more cable, is to let more out. When two pieces of cable are spliced together, it is called a shot of the cable.

CA'BLED, Adj. resembling cables. Cabled flutes, in Architecture, are those which are filled up with pieces in the form of a cable. In Heraldry, a cabled cross, is that which is formed of the two ends of a ship's cable; sometimes, but improperly, a cross covered with rounds of rope, this being rather a cross corded.

CA'BOCHED, Adj. in Heraldry, the head of a beast cut off behind the ears; distinguished from couped, which is by an horizontal section.

CACAO, for CHOCOLATE-NUT.

CACHE'CTIC, or CACHECTICAL, Adj. [from cachexy] having an ill habit of body.

CA'CHEXY, S. [from κακος and εξις, Gr.] in Medicine, an universal bad disposition of body, proceeding from a defect of nourishment, which according to Boerhaave, is owing either to a depravation of the nutritious juices, a disorder in the vessels which convey them, or a defect in the animal œconomy, by which the nutritious juices are formed, circulated, and applied to the solids.

To CA'CK, V. N. [caco, Lat.] to unload the body by a discharge or stool.

To CA'CKLE, V. N. [kackelen, Belg.] in its primary sense to make a noise like a goose; applied likewise to that of a hen. To laugh heartily.

CA'CKLE, S. the noise of a goose or fowl.

CA'CKLER, S. a fowl that cackles. A tell-tale, a tatler.

CACHOCHY'MY, S. [from κακος and χυμος,] in Medicine, a corrupt state of the vital humours, especially of the mass of the blood, arising from external contagion, or a disorder of the secretions, or excretions.

CACOPHO'NY, S. [from κακος and φωνη, Gr.] in Grammar and Rhetoric, the meeting together of letters, &c. which form a harsh sound.

CADA'VEROUS, Adj. [cadaver, Lat.] a dead body; resembling a dead body.

CA'DDIS, S. a kind of tape. In Natural History, a kind of worm or grub.

CA'DE, Adj. [according to Skinner, from caedo, Fr. soft or delicate,] soft, tender, tame, delicate. In Husbandry, a cade lamb, is a houk-lamb.

CA'DE, S. [cadus, Lat.] a cask or barrel. In the book of rates, a certain number of fish; a cade of herrings, is a vessel containing 500, and a cade of sprats, 1000.

CA'DENCE, S. [cadence, Fr. of cadens, Lat.] in its primary sense, a fall, decline or descent. "Now was the sun in western cadence low." Par. Lost. In oratory and Poetry, the fall of the voice, the flow of verses or periods. The French verses which are composed of Alexandrines, and divided into equal parts or halves in the reading, fatigue and satiate the ear by the sameness of sound; but the English, which like the Latin can vary its cadence according to the variety of its subjects, is always new and always pleasing. Though indeed this holds good of those compositions that are written in rhime, yet in blank verse it is abundantly more conspicuous. In Musc, cadence, is a certain rest, either at the end of a song, or of some of its parts, into which it is divided as into members or periods. A perfect cadence is that which consists of two notes sung after each other, or by degrees, conjoined in each of the two parts; and an imperfect cadence is when the last measure is not in octave or unison, but a sixth, or a third. The chief cadence or close, is the key itself in which the bass always concludes, the next in dignity is the fifth above, and the next to that, the third. Cadence, in Dancing, is when the several steps answer the different measure of the music. In horsemanship, an equal measure, or proportion observed by a horse in all his motions, when thoroughly managed.

CADET, S. [Fr.] the younger brother. A volunteer who serves in expectation of being promoted to a commission.

CA'DEW, or CADEWORM, S. [of cadus, Lat. a cask, from the manner in which they house themselves,] in Natural History, a kind of worms, which in time change into butter-flies. The ingenuity they discover in collecting those material, which are fittest for their purpose, and glueing them together so, that they shall be heavier than water, when their food lies at the bottom, and lighter, when they must gather it from the surface; the structure of their cell which is so contrived, that they can transport it without difficulty, thrust their body out of it to reach what they want, or withdraw it within, to guard it against danger; must certainly make us astonished, and at a loss, what to determine with respect to the dignity of human reason, or how sufficiently to acknowledge

that wisdom, which appears in every part of the creation.

CA'DGER, S. a higgler.

CAE'CIAS, S. [Lat.] a north-wind.

CA'DMIA, S. a recrement of copper ore produced in furnaces, when that metal is separated from its ore, driven by the blast of the bellows against the sides or roofs of the furnaces, or collected in its chimneys.

CADU'CEUS, S. [Lat.] a scepter or wand, entwined with two serpents, carried by Mercury, as the ensign of his office.

CAE'CUM, S. [Lat. hid or blind] in Anatomy, one of the three portions of the larger intestines, in the form of a round short bag, whose bottom is turned upwards, and its mouth downwards.

CAE'STUS, S. [Lat. from caedo, Lat. to beat] a large gauntlet used in combats among the antients; they surrounded the hand, wrist, and arm, to guard them from blows.

CA'G, S. See KEG.

CA'GE, S. [cage, Fr.] an inclosure in which birds are kept. A place for wild beasts. A prison for people guilty of petty crimes, wherein strumpets, &c. are confined in the night-time.

To CA'GE, V. A. to confine in a cage.

To CA'JOLE, [cajoler, Fr.] to flatter, footh, wheedle, or coax.

CA'JOLER, S. a flatterer, or wheedler, one who pretends to comfort a person, but is all the while treating him with ridicule.

CAI'TIFF, S. [chetif, Fr. cattivo, Ital.] a slave. A mean despicable contemptible villain.

CA'KE, S. [caccu, Brit. JNJ, Arab.] a rich kind of baked bread. Figuratively, an ignorant person.

To CA'KE, V. A. to harden like dough when put into the oven.

CALAMA'NCO, S. a well-known woollen stuff.

CA'LAMINE, S. [lapis calaminaris, Lat.] a hard heavy mineral substance, generally found in loose masses, from the size of a walnut, to those of two or three pounds. That which is of Mendip-Hills, in Somersetshire, is the finest in all the world. It is used in making of brass, and in medicine is reckoned no bad ingredient in eye-waters, is esteemed as a good desiccative in weeping ulcers, and composes the plaister, which goes by the name of Turner's Cerate.

CA'LAMINT, S. [calamintha, Lat.] in Botany, a species of the melissa or baum, which grows naturally in the mountains of Tuscany. It is good in all diseases of the breast, arising from a tough phlegm. Externally, it is used as a discutient, aperient, and dissolvent.

CALA'MITOUS, Adj. [calamiteux, Lat.] involved in misfortunes or calamities. Wretched, unfortunate, unhappy. Fatal, noxious, unwholesome, applied to things.

CALA'MITY,

CALA'MITY, S. [*calamitas*, Lat.] a state of distress, misery, or wretchedness.

CA'LAMUS, S. [Lat. a reed] in Botany, a reed, or sweet scented wood, of a knotty root, reddish without, and white within, the leaves are narrow, the form the same as that of other reeds, and the scent perceived in entering the marshes where it grows. " Sweet Cinnamon, and sweet *Calamus*." *Exod.* iii. 10.

CALA'SH, S. [*calache*, Fr.] a light four-wheeled, uncovered carriage.

CALCEDO'NIUS, S. [Lat.] a precious stone of the agate kind, of a milky grey, clouded with blue or purple.

CALCINA'TION, S. [*calcines*, *calcination*; Fr.] the rendering a body reducible to powder by means of fire.

CALCINA'TORY, S. a vessel used in calcination.

To CALCI'NE, V. A. [*calciner*, Fr. from *cals*, Lat. lime] to burn in the fire to a substance, which a small force will crumble. To reduce to ashes. Figuratively, to consume or destroy. " Fiery heats that union have *calcined*," *Drab.* Used neuterly, to turn to a cinder.

CALCO'GRAPHY, S. [from χαλχος and γραφω, Gr.] the art of engraving on brass or copper.

To CA'LCULATE, V. A. [*calculer*, Fr.] to find out the amount by arithmetic: to compute. To contrive or adapt to a certain purpose.

CALCULA'TION, S. an operation in arithmetic. Figuratively a deduction of reason.

CALCULA'TOR, S. one who computes, or calculates.

CALCULA'TORY, Adj. relating to calculation, or computation.

CA'LCULE, S. [*calculus*, Lat.] computation; amount; calculation.

CALCULO'SE, CA'LCULOUS, Adj stony, gritty; being afflicted with the stone or gravel.

CA'LCULUS, S. [Lat.] in Medicine, the stone in the kidneys, ureters or bladder. As is evident that whenever any small disuble substance fixes in any part of the body, it is immediately clothed with a stony crust: So likewise when any concretion of the earthly part of the blood stops in the ureters and forms a grain of sand, it is continually increasing its substance by the addition of new incrustations, and forms a stone in the kidneys. If this concretion should discharge itself by the urine, in a calu or gritty substance, it is properly called the gravel, but when it coalesces a hard indissoluble substance, the stone. When the concretion is lodged in the bladder, it is termed lithiasis; but, when in the kidney, nephritis.

CA'LDRON, S. [pronounced *cauldron*, from *chauldron*, Fr.] a large vessel to heat water in; a pot.

CALE'CHE, S. See CALASH.

§

CALEFA'CTION, S. [from *cal-facio*, supine of *califacio*, Lat.] the act of making a thing hot; the state of a thing made hot.

CALEFA'CTIVE, Adj. that which can, or does, make any thing hot; heating.

CALEFAC'TORY, S. that has the power of heating.

To CA'LEFY, V. N. [*calefio*, Lat.] to grow hot; to be heated.

CA'LENDAR, S. [*calendarium*, Lat.] a table of the days, months, festivals, fasts, &c. happening in the year. Julius Cæsar, made the year consist of 365 days, and left the 6 hours to form a day, at the end of every 4th year, which was added to the month of February. This calendar was called the Julian and the old stile, in opposition to the new stile introduced by Gregory XIII. who finding the Julian gone too forward, cut off ten days from the calendar, and to remedy this defect for the future, left out one bissextile day every 100 years, making every four hundredth a leap year. By act of parliament, to remedy the inconveniences arising from the differences of stile, this kingdom adopted the Gregorian or new stile, by leaving out 11 days of the month of September in the year 1752. *Calendar*, is also the name of a machine or hot-press, made use of in pressing, smooth, or water silk, wool, or linen. It consists of two thick rollers of hard polished wood, placed crosswise between two very thick boards of hard wood, longer than broad; the undermost is fastened and supported by brick-work, and the upper moveable, though loaded with large stones weighing 20,000 lb. or more; this being fastened to a cable is moved backwards and forwards by means of a wheel, which is put in motion by men who walk in it. Some calendars are wrought by a horse, fastened to a wooden her. In Natural History, the word is applied to an insect which preys on corn.

To CA'LENDER, V. A. to dress any manufacture in a hot press.

CA'LENDER, S. one who dresses manufactures in a hot-press.

CA'LENDS, S. [from *Calenda*, Lat.] the first day of the month among the Romans; they were reckoned backwards: the 1st of February was called the calends of February, the 31st of January the second of the calends of February, and so on to the 13th, when the Ides commence.

CA'LENTURE, S. [*calv*, Lat.] in Medicine, an inflammatory fever, frequent at sea, attended with a delirium, wherein the patients imagine the sea to be green fields, and will drown themselves in it, if not prevented. This disorder is very frequent in hot climates, particularly in or near the Mediterranean, and seems to arise from a plethora and a viscidity of the juices.

CA'LF, S. in the plural *calves*, [*calf*, Sax.]

Sax.] the young of a cow. The English calves are far preferable to the French, being both stronger and larger. Their hides have likewise the same advantage, the French having tried in vain to rival us in this useful commodity. Figuratively, a facrifice, or something fubstituted instead of a facrifice. " So will we render the calves of our lips." Hof. xiv. 2. The swelling, flethy part of a man's leg. A dull, stupid, ignorant fellow.

CA'LIBER, [calibre, Fr.] in its primary fenfe, the extent or diameter of any round thing. An inftrument or rule, made of a piece of board notched or cut triangularly in the middle, ufed by carpenters and joiners to try whether their work be well fquared. Caliber compaffes, a pair of compaffes with the legs bent inwards, ufed to take the dimenfions of the bore of a cannon.

CA'LICE, S. [calix, Lat.] a cup: appropriated to the cups which the communicants drink out of at the facrament of the Lord's fupper.

CA'LICO, S. [from Calcut in India] a kind of linen manufacture imported by the Eaft-India company, fome of which are printed with the moft beautiful and lafting colours. Printed calicoes are prohibited to be worn, under penalty of 5l. to be paid to the informer. 7 Geo. I. c. 7.

CALI'DITY, S. [from calidus, Lat.] warmth, or heat.

CA'LIF, or CALIPH, S. [khalifah, Arab.] a title firft affumed by Abubeker the fucceffor of Mahomet, calling himfelf, khalifab refoul allah, the fucceffor of the meffenger of God, and born by thofe who fucceeded him. As they affume an abfolute power in affairs both temporal and civil, they feem very much to refemble the Pope in that refpect, who exercifes the fame power, and ftiles himfelf the fucceffor of St. Peter.

CALIGA'TION, S. [from caligo, Lat.] a want of light, which renders the fight of an object very imperfect; darknefs; dimnefs of fight.

CALI'GINOUS, Adj. [caliginofus, Lat.] dim, dark, gloomy.

CA'LIGRAPHY, S. [καλλιγραφια, Gr.] beautiful writing.

CA'LIPERS, S. See CALLIPERS.

CA'LIVER, S. See CALIBER.

CA'LIX, S. [Lat. a cup] in Botany, the outward greenifh cover, which encompaffes and defends the petals and other parts of a flower, ferving as a bafis and fupport to the whole.

To CA'LK, V. A. [calege, Fr.] to ftop the leaks of a fhip with oakum, tow, &c.

CA'LKER, S. one who ftops the leaks of a fhip.

CA'LKING, S. the act of ftopping the leaks or feams of a fhip with oakum or tow, which is afterwards covered with a mixture of tallow, pitch, and tar, as low as is drawn

water. Calking irons are made in the form of a chifel, fome of which are round, and others grooved, ufed to drive the oakum into the feams of a fhip.

To CA'LL, V. A. [pronounced caul, from kallen, Belg. calo, Gr.] to name a perfon; to fpeak or give notice to him by mentioning his name, ringing a bell, or other fignal, to come towards the perfon calling. Ufed with off, to make a perfon quit his prefent ftation, applied to animate things; to divert the mind, or turn the thoughts afide from the confideration of a fubject, applied to the understanding; ufed likewife with the particle away, in the fame fenfe. With up, it implies to bring back again, or revive. To call on and upon, to vifit, or go to a perfon's houfe. To call in, and followed by at, to enter a houfe or place on a journey or walk. Joined with account, it implies to examine or bring to account. To call names, to abufe a perfon by fome reproachful term or word. Joined to back, to revoke, retract, or not accomplish a thing intended, after fecond thoughts. To call in, applied to money, to collect or demand a fum lent; to refume a thing in another perfon's hands; to invite. To call on, to put a perfon in mind of a favour promifed, or to demand a thing promifed. To call over, to read a mufter-roll, or lift of names, with an audible voice. To call out, to challenge, and excite to combat. In Divinity, to call upon, to implore, to pray to in diftrefs, with confidence of affiftance. " Call upon me in the day of diftrefs " Pf. 115.

CA'LL, S. an addrefs by word of mouth. Figuratively, a miffion from God; a claim, or demand. " A perpetual call upon humanity." Spect. No. 181. Joined to within, not far off, within hearing. Figuratively, command or authority.

CA'LLING, S. the bufinefs a perfon profeffes; ftation; a clafs of people united by the fame principles, employment, or profeffion. In Divinity, admiffion into the church, or converfion, by an immediate impulfe from heaven.

CA'LLIPERS, S. See CALLIBER, of which this is a corruption.

CALLO'SITY, S. [callofité, Fr.] a hardnefs of the fkin, owing to hard labour or frequent rubbings, whereby it becomes infenfible. In Surgery, a kind of scale or knob, which joins the extremities of a broken bone, owing to the extravafation of the juices that run along the bone, which, gathering together in this place, dry, become a thick glue, and harden, fo as to leave no other fign of a fracture but the knob or inequality of the furface.

CA'LLOUS, Adj. hard, fwelling, infenfible. Figuratively, applied to the mind or confcience, infenfible to the dangerous confequences of vice, and unawed by threats of the Deity.

CA'LLOW,

CA'LLOW, Adj. unfledged; having no feathers.

CA'LM, Adj. [halme, Belg. calme, Fr.] undisturbed by winds, &c. Figuratively, undisturbed by boisterous passions. Free from any appeal to the passions, and entirely founded on cool reasonings, applied to compersions or argument. Used substantively for a freedom from tempests.

To CA'LM, V. A. to put an end to a storm; to sooth or pacify.

CA'LMLY, Adj. in a serene, cool manner, without any starts of passion, or turbulence of temper.

CA'LMNESS, S. [from calm and ness from nesse, Sax. implying an abstract quality] a state of quiet, free from the disturbance of the winds or rolling waves, applied to the sea and elements. Figuratively, a state of cool and sedate tranquility, unruffled by passion, and undisturbed by anxiety. Mildness.

CA'LOMEL, S. [kalos and melas, Gr.] in Chemistry, a name given to mercury, sublimated a fourth time or upwards, to make it gentle in its operations.

CALORI'FIC, Adj. [calorificus, Lat.] having the power of heating.

CALO'YERS, S. [kaloyeros, Gr.] monks of the Greek church, who live a very austere life, eat no flesh, keep four Lents, and never break their fasts till they have earned that meal by their labour. During Lent some of them eat but once in three days, and spend most of the night in acts of penitence and prayer.

CA'LTROPS, S. [caltroppe, Sax.] an instrument with four iron spikes disposed in such a manner, that one of them will always be upright, and three of them in the ground. They are used to annoy, and wound the horses feet of the cavalry. In Botany, a plant so called from its resembling the instrument just described.

To CA'LVE, V. A. to bring a calf, applied to a cow. Figuratively, to produce or bring forth. "The grassy clods now calv'd." Par. Lost.

To CALU'MNIATE, V. N. [from calumnior, Lat.] to accuse falsely; to reproach with crimes unjustly; in order to render odious. Used actively, to slander.

CALU'MNIATION, S. [from calumniatio] a false representation of a person's behaviour, in order to make him odious.

CALU'MNIATOR, S. [Lat.] one who slanders another, or charges him with false crimes or faults, with an intent to ruin his reputation.

CALU'MNIOUS, Adj. slanderous.

CA'LUMNY, S. [calumnia, Lat.] the falsely accusing of a person with crimes; slander.

CA'LX, S. [Lat.] in its primary sense, lime, or a sort of stone burnt in a kiln in order to make mortar. In Chemistry, a kind of ashes, or fine friable powder, which remains after a body has undergone the violence of fire for a long time.

CA'MBAYES, S. cottons made at Bengal, and imported by the East India company.

CA'MBRICK, S. [toile de Cambray, Fr.] a species of linen, very fine and white, at first manufactured at Cambray in France, from whence we formerly used to import it to the value of 200,000 l. per annum; but the government has interposed timely against so prejudicial a commerce, by several acts of parliament; and it were to be wished, that some of the nobility, who are the standards of fashion, would, by making our own cambricks become a sign of taste, second their endeavours, and keep such a quantity of cash in the kingdom to support our own poor.

CAMBRIDGE, the county-town of Cambridgeshire, with the title of a dutchy, and an university, which is one of the most ancient and flourishing in Europe, and is thought to have been founded during the Saxon heptarchy. The town consists of 14 parishes, and is governed by a mayor, recorder, a bailiff, and a town-clerk, 12 aldermen, and 24 common council; and the mayor, when he enters upon his office, takes an oath to maintain the privileges, liberties, and customs of the university, to which he is subservient. Its situation is low, and consequently the air is not so good as that of Oxford. It has a market on Wednesdays and Saturdays, and a very large fair, called Sturbitch, is held, about a mile from the town, on September 18, which lasts 14 days, and is famous for hops, leather, wool, cheese, and many other commodities; another fair is held on Midsummer-day, for horses, earthen ware, and wood, which holds 7 days. The town sends two members to parliament, and there are also two sent by the university. It consists of 16 colleges and halls, and about 1500 students. It has about 2500 middling houses, and the inhabitants are computed at 6000. The streets are generally narrow, tho' pretty well paved, yet lying low, make them very dirty. In the midst of the market-place is a very good conduit continually running, and a navigable river runs through the town from Lynn; but it is a dull place for trade. It is 80 miles E. N. E. of Oxford, 55 E. by N. of Buckingham, 28 on the same point from Bedford, 50 E. of Northampton, 31 E. S. E. of Coventry, 17 S. of Ely, and 52 N. by E of London. Lon. 17. 40. lat. 52. 15.

CAMBRIDGE SHIRE, an inland county of England, 47 miles in length, and 18 in breadth, and is bounded on the E. by Suffolk and Norfolk, on the S. by Essex and Hertfordshire, on the W. by Bedford and Huntingdon shires, and on the N. by Lincola

cole and part of Huntingdon shires. It contains 8 market-towns, 163 parishes, 27,000 houses, and about 140,600 inhabitants: and it sends 6 members to parliament. The principal river is the Ouse, which runs through the county from W. to E. The air and soil of the S. part is very good; but the N. fenny and aguish; and where there are large wares and moors full of fish. The capital town is Cambridge; besides which there is Ely, a bishop's see.

CA'ME, the preter of the verb *came*.

CA'MEL, S. [*camelus*, Lat.] a large four-footed animal, of which there are several species: one sort being large, able to carry burdens of a thousand pounds weight, having one hunch on his back; another sort has two hunches, like a natural saddle, and are used either for carrying burdens, or to ride on. In spring they cast their coats, and will continue 10 or 11 days, without eating or drinking. *The camel's going through the eye of a needle*, mentioned, Mat. x. 25. is a text much controverted, some thinking that the Greek word *gamilos*, should be translated a cable rope, which it signifies, as may be seen in Potter's antiquities of Greece, and is more conformable to the idea of the eye of a needle mentioned afterwards. To this some answer, that the phrase is highly proper according to the old translation, because there was a narrow place between two rocks in Judea, called the *eye of a needle*, through which it was impossible for so large a beast to pass: whether this assertion is established upon proper authority, I shall not determine, but conclude that either translation, as it communicates the idea of an insuperable difficulty, may be adopted.

CAME'LEON, S. in Natural History a little animal of the lizard kind, only its head is somewhat larger, and has 4 feet and a long flat tail, by either of which it can suspend itself; from the head to the last joint of the tail, its skin is rough like shagreen, which it can swell or contract at its pleasure. It has no neck, nor ears, but has two little apertures for nostrils. Its eyes are large and turn any way, to remedy the inconveniency of having no neck, and sometimes look in directions quite contrary. Its tongue is half as long as itself, round as far as the tip, which is hollow, on that account called a trunk, and used by it in catching flies, on which it subsists. Its changing its colour may be accounted from the power it has of contracting or swelling its skin.

CA'MELOT, CA'MBLET, or CA'M-LET, S. [from *camelot*, Fr.] a stuff made of goats hair, with wool or silk, or both. In some the warp is wool and silk twisted together, and the whoof hair. That of Brussels is reputed the best, and the English the next.

CA'MERA OBSCURA, S. [Lat. a dark chamber] in Optics, a machine for exhibiting the pictures of external objects in their proper colours, by means of a convex glass or scioptric ball, either in a portable box, or a darkned chamber.

CA'MERADE, S. [Fr. *camerade*, Span.] a very intimate friend and acquaintance. Now obsolete, or rather corrupted into the word *comrade*.

CA'MERATED, Adj. [*cameratus*, Lat.] arched or vaulted.

CA'MMOCK, S. [*cammoc*, Sax.] in Botany, the *anonis*, Lat. or *arrête, bœuf*, Fr. Linnæus ranges it in the 3d sect. of his 17th class, and Tournefort in the 24th sect. of his 10th. There are 10 species.

CA'MP, S. [*comp*, Sax. and Fr.] the place where an army rests, or dwells in tents or barracks. The Mogul's camp was said to be 20 English miles round, and composed of 800,000 men, 40,000 elephants; and what is more strange, to be pitched in 4 hours time.

To CA'MP, V. A. to fix tents in a field.

CAMPA'IGN, S. [*campaigne*, Fr.] the time during which an army keeps the field, without going into winter quarters. It might embarrass philologists at present to determine the extent of this term; when we find armies encamped during the whole winter; and keeping the field notwithstanding the inclemencies of the season. This word is used to signify a plain, or level country, but should be then wrote *champaign*, from *champagne*, Fr.

CAMPA'NIFORM, Adj. [from *campana*, Lat. a bell, and *forma*, a shape] in Botany, applied to flowers shaped like a bell.

CAMPE'STRAL, Adj. [*campestris*, Lat.] that which grows in fields, wild. " The *campestral* or wild beech." *Mort.*

CA'MPHIRE or CAMPHOR, S. [*caphur*, or *capur*, Arab. *camphora*, Lat.] a mixed substance, white, transparent, dry, brittle, of a strong and penetrating smell, easily evaporated in the air, when heated, and when in flames not easily extinguished, but burning even in water and in snow. There are two sorts, natural and fictitious; the natural is found in the island of Sumatra, between the wood and bark of a tree, and is preferable to the second sort, called the factitious *camphire*, or that of Japan. This is made of the root of the camphire-tree, which is cut into small pieces, boiled 48 hours, and received in covers like alembics, into which it ascends together with the steam. The camphire tree is a species of the *laurus*. Camphire is used as an anodyne, diuretic, and resister of putrefaction, in ulcerations of the kidneys, madness, and in hysteric complaints. Externally, in erysipelas, inflammations, and mixed with spirit of wine, as a fomentor for bruises.

CAM-

CA'MPHORATE, Adj. [from *camphora*, Lat.] that which is impregnated with camphire.

CA'MPION, S. In Botany the LYCHNIS.

CAN, S. [*canne*, Sax. *kanna*, Ital.] a drinking vessel made of wood in the form of a barrel; also any drinking vessel, not made of earth.

CAN, V. N. [*kennen*, Belg. *cch han*, Teut. *kand*, Dan.] to be able; to have power sufficient. Though taken as a sign of the potential mood, yet it differs very much from *may*, the proper auxiliary of that mood: *may* denoting right, lawfulness, or a permission to do a thing; but *can*, the power of the doer, or agent.

CANADA, or NEW FRANCE, a large country of N. America, which, according to the French, is bounded on the W. by the Ocean, on the S. by the Mississippi, on the E. by the English colonies, and on the N. by the river St. Lawrence and the territory of the Hudson's-Bay company. It was discovered by John and Sebastian Cabot, father and son, in 1497. This country in general is pretty good; but the winter continues for six months very severe. The land that is cleared of trees is very fertile, and the wheat that is sowed in May is reaped the latter end of August. Pulse in general, and especially pease, thrive very well, and are very good. The woods are full of wild vines, game, and animals peculiar to N. America; but the beaver is the most useful and curious of them all. The rivers and lakes are full of fish, and there are a great number of trees unknown to Europe. Canada turpentine is greatly esteemed for its balsamic qualities, and for the disorders of the breast and stomach. The original natives of this country speak four different languages, and may be divided into as many different tribes, viz. the Sioux, the Algonquiere, the Houronne, and that of the Eskimaux. Most of them live a wandering life, and maintain themselves by hunting. Their complexion is of red copper colour, like the rest of the Americans, with coarse hair, and no beards, except the Eskimaux, who are a hairy, cruel, savage nation. They are very fond of brandy, and, when they are drunk, they become almost mad. They all seem to worship the fun, and acknowledge tutelary gods as well as the First Being. Their wars are bloody, and at present they make use of fire-arms. The French inhabitants are about 50,000, who have a governor, and an intendant, and a bishop. Quebec is the capital town; which was taken by the English on the 18th of September in the year 1759; at the siege of which the brave General Wolfe lost his life, but not before he perceived that the English forces were victorious.

CANILLE, S. [Fr.] the lowest order of people; the dregs or scum of a people; a French term of contempt, adopted by some modern authors.

CANAL, S. [*canalis*, Lat.] a hollow place cut for the reception of water; any track of water made by art. In Anatomy, a passage through which any of the juices flow.

CANALES SEMICIRCULARES, [Lat.] in Anatomy, three canals in the labyrinth of the ear, opening into the orifice of the vestibulum, gradually increasing in their dimensions, that they may be adapted to all the variety of sounds, or tones.

CANALICULATED, Part. [from *canaliculus*, Lat.] formed in channels, or grooves.

To CANARY, V. A. implying a particular method of footing, used in jigs, or country dancing. "Jig off a tune at your tongue's end, *canary* to it with your feet." *Shak.*

CANARY-BIRD, S. a singing bird, formerly peculiar to the Canaries, of the linnet kind, a very loud note, and of great boldness.

To CANCEL, V. A. [*canceller*, Fr. *cancellare*, Ital.] to cross or deface a writing. Figuratively, to destroy a deed by turning off the seal, or name; to deface, obliterate, or destroy.

CANCELLATED, Part. marked with lines crossing each other. "*Cancellated*, with some resemblance to the scales of fishes" *Grew.* Seldom used.

CANCELLATION, S. an expunging, or annulling the power of an instrument, by two lines drawn in the form of a cross.

CANCER, S. [Lat. a crab] In Astronomy, a sign of the zodiac, into which the sun enters in June, and represented on globes by the figure of a crab. The stars in this constellation, according to Flamstead, are 51. The tropic of *Cancer*, is a smaller circle of the sphere, parallel to the equator, and passing through the beginning of the sign *cancer*. In Surgery, a roundish unequal, livid, hard tumour, generally seated in the glandulous part of the body, after some time, appearing with turgid veins shooting out from it, for which reason, according to some writers, is has received its name. The reason of its appearing on the breast, more than any other part, is that being full of glands, intermixed with lymphatics, the smallest compression, contusion, or puncture extravasates their contents, which growing acrimonious, by degrees form a *cancer*.

To CANCERATE, V. N. [from *cancer*] to grow cancerous.

CANCERATION, S. the growing cancerous.

CANCEROUS, Adj. having the virulence of, or tending to a *cancer*.

CANCRINE, Adj. [*cancer*, Lat.] belonging to, resembling, or having the properties of a crab.

CANDENT, Part. [*candens*, part of *candeo*, Lat. to heat] heated; in the highest degree of heat

heat next to that which fuses or calcines. "When totally *candent*." *Brown*.

CA'NDID, Adj. [*candidus*, Lat.] In its primary sense, but seldom used, white. "The *five, the very candid tooth*." Figuratively, ingenious, free from malice.

CANDIDA'TE, S. [*candidatus*, Lat.] one who seeks a thing, as an office; a competitor.

CA'NDIDLY, Adv. impartially; without prejudice, malice, or envy; fairly.

CA'NDLE, S. [*candela*, Lat.] a wick of common covered with wax, tallow, &c. of a cylindrical form, used to supply the want of day-light. Figuratively, light, or any thing which communicates light. "The *candle of the wicked shall be put out*." *Prov.* xxiv. 20.

CA'NDLE-LIGHT, S. the light afforded by a *candle*. Figuratively, night, opposed to day-light; candles. "I shall find him out by *candle-light*." *Swift*. Introduced as an improper expression.

CA'NDLEMAS, S. [*la chandeleuse*, Fr.] a feast of the church, celebrated on the second of February, in commemoration of the blessed virgin's purification, supposed to have been instituted by pope Vigilius, and to have received its name from the vast number of *candles* used in the procession, or consecrated for the use of the ensuing year.

CA'NDLE-WASTER, S. the person or thing which consumes *candles*. Figuratively, a prodigal or spendthrift.

CA'NDOUR, S. [*candor*, Lat.] a temper unsoured by envy, unruffled by malice, and unseduced by prejudice.

To CA'NDY, V. A. to melt and chrystallise sugar several times, to render it hard and transparent. Figuratively, to freeze, or be covered with a hard substance. "*Candied* with ice," *Shak*. To flatter: "Let the *candy'd* tongue lick absurd pomp." *Shak*. Neuterly, to grow hard, or be covered with flakes.

CANE, S. [*canna*, Span.] in Botany, a kind of reed growing in several joints, and of different dimensions. The Bamboo, which grows in the Indies, especially in Bengal, to a prodigious size, is wrought into bowls or other houshold utensils by the inhabitants. The walking cane is that which grows in the East-Indies, those which are without joints are by far the best, and most elastic. Hence the word signifies figuratively, a walking staff, a rod, and a dart, from the *inga de canas*, Span.

To CANE, V. A. to beat a person with a cane, or staff.

CANI'CULA, S. [Lat.] in Astronomy, the name of one of the stars, in the constellation of *canis major*, called also the dog-star.

CANI'CULAR, Ad. [*canicularis*, Lat.] of, concerning, or belonging to the dog-days.

CANINE, Adj. [*caninus*, Lat. from *canis*, a dog, resembling a dog.

CA'NISTER, S. [*canistrum*, Lat.] in the primary sense of a basket; also a small box of metal, wood, &c. to hold tea, &c.

CA'NKER, S. [*cancer*, Lat. *chancre*, Fr. wrote corruptly by authors in Natural History, a worm that preys on fruit, joined with the canker: a disease in trees, a spark in iron, which corrodes the metal like a caterpillar upon a flower. Figuratively, that which gradually destroys. In Botany, a wild and worthless sort of rose; a disease in trees, which makes the bark rot and fall off. Applied to brass, a kind of rust, or verdigrease which covers its surface.

To CA'NKER, V. N. to rust; to be corroded; to grow foul, or corrupt. Actively, to pollute, to eat or gnaw; to infect.

CANN, S. [*canne*, Sax. *kands*, Dan.] See CAN.

CA'NNIBAL, S. one who lives upon human flesh. Most of the American nations were included under this reproachful term by travellers; but for the dignity of human nature, most of their accounts have been groundless, and even among those who have given any countenance to the report, the custom has seemed rather the effects of provoked barbarity, than proceeding either from custom or familiar use.

CA'NNIBALLY, Adj. [from *cannibal* and *ly*, and *lice*, Sax. implying manner] after the manner or practice of *cannibals*, or those who are supposed to eat human flesh. "Had he been *cannibally* given."

CA'NNIPERS, S. See CALLIBERS.

CA'NNON, S. [*canon*, Fr. *cannone*, Ital.] a hollow, cylindrical instrument, used to shoot a ball by the force of gun-powder. This military engine is supposed to have been invented by J. Owen, an Englishman, and it is evident that the first which were ever seen in France, belonged to this nation, and were used in the battle of Cressy, 1346; and Mezeray asserts that the English by five or six pieces of *cannon* struck terror into the French, who had never seen such thundering machines before. In Painting, the largest size of types, used in the following word:

virtuous

To CANNONADE, V. A. to attack with *cannon*.

CANNONIER, S. [pronounced *cannineer*] one who discharges a cannon.

CA'NNOT, V. unable. "He cannot do it."

CANOE, S. [pronounced *canoo*] an Indian boat, made of the trunk of a tree, bored hol-

hollow ; or of the small sticks of a pliant wood, covered with seals skins; this last sort will hold only a single person, who sits in a round hole in the center. The canoes made of the trunk of one tree retain their name, when they will contain only three persons, but when they hold more than that number, those of the Americans, are called pirogues, and those of Guinea, cham.

CA'NON, S. [ϰανων, Gr.] a law or rule relating to the doctrine of a church, enacted by a general council. Applied to the Scripture, such books as are held to be really inspired, have been acknowledged as such by a general council, and inserted into the list of the Scriptures by primitive Christians; a law or rule. In surgery, an instrument used in sewing up wounds.

CA'NON, S. [chanoine, Fr.] one who possesses a prebend, or revenue for performance of divine service in a cathedral church.

CA'NON-BIT, S. that part of the bit, which is included in a horse's mouth.

CA'NONESS, S. [canoniffa, low Lat.] a woman, who enjoys a prebend, confined to maids, without being obliged to take the vows, or renounce the world.

CANO'NICAL, Adj. [canonicus, low Lat.] that which is established by the laws of the church. Applied to Books, those which are allowed to be divinely inspired. Applied to Hours, those which are preferred by the church for the celebration of any ceremony.

CANO'NICALLY, Adj. agreeable to the Laws of the church.

CA'NONIST, S. a professor of, or skilled in ecclesiastical law.

CANONIZA'TION, S. In the Romish church, a declaration of the pope, whereby after some solemnity, he enters a person into the list of the saints.

CA'NONRY, or CANONSHIP, S. office, or duty of a canon.

To CA'NONIZE, V. A. to enter in the list of saints; to make a saint

CA'NOPIED, Adj. covered with a canopy.

CA'NOPY, S. [from canopé, Fr. conopium, low Lat.] a cloth, curtain, or rich stuff hung either for state, or shelter over a person's head. Any thing which is extended over the head. "My footstool earth, my canopy the skies." Pope.

To CA'NOPY, V. A. to form a covering over the head.

CA'NOROUS, Adj. [canorus, Lat.] musical; tuneful.

CA'NT, S. [from cantus, Lat.] applied to language, a dialect used by vagabonds, to conceal their meaning; a whining tone of voice; a whining, formal pretention to goodness, attended with hypocrisy.

To CA'NT, V. N. [from the same] to make use of the jargon of vagabonds and thieves; to speak or read in a whining tone

of voice; to insinuate one's self into a person's good opinion by flattery.

CANTA'TA, S. [Ital.] in Music, a song consisting of recitatives, airs, and a variety of motions, generally for a single voice, with a thorough bass; sometimes for two or more voices, with other instruments. Mr. Hughes, the author of the Siege of Damascus, seems to have introduced this method of writing into England; and Mr. Stanley may be said to have contributed not a little, by his musical compositions, to have established it.

CA'NTER, S. one who endeavours to pass himself upon the world as a religious person, by a formal appearance of religion.

CANTERBURY, the capital town or city of the county of Kent, with an archbishop's see, founded by Augustine the monk. The cathedral is a large superb structure, and was once very famous for the shrine of Thomas Becket. Besides this it has 14 parish churches, and there are the remains of a great many Roman antiquities. Here is a castle much like that at Rochester, and the walls are of the same thickness; there are also walls round the town, with a deep ditch close underneath, and a great rampart of earth within. In general it is a large, populous, trading place, and has a good silk manufactory, which was introduced by the Walloons in the reign of Q. Elizabeth. It has two markets, on Wednesdays and Saturdays, and one fair, on September 19, for toys. It sends two members to parliament, and is seated on the river Stour, 15 miles N. W. by W. of Dover, 26 S. E. by E. of Rochester, and 56 on the same point from London. Lon. 19. 10. lat. 51. 18.

CA'NTERBURY GALLOP, S. in Horsemanship, the hard gallop of an ambling horse, commonly called a canter, and probably derived from the monks riding to Canterbury upon ambling horses.

CANTHA'RIDES, S. [Lat. the plural of cantharis] a beetle formed from an egg, which produces a worm, that is peculiar to the fig-tree, pine-tree, white-brier, and poplar, whose juices being very corrosive, or biting, are by Bacon supposed to be the causes of its corrosive or caustic quality. The parent insect is of the beetle kind, has hard and firm wings over thin and filmy ones, which it makes use of in flying. It is usually half an inch in length, and one-third in breadth; is of a fine shining beautiful colour; on the upper side of a bright green with a mixture of gold, and on the other of a brown; its head is small, furnished with two antennae or horns, of moderate length, very thin, and moveable with ease; its breast is flattish, its sides wrinkled, and covered with protuberancies; they are killed by the fumes of boiling vinegar, and afterwards dried. It is needless to mention their service in blisters, or the danger of too free a use of them, since experience has

E e 2   confirm-

enfirmed the former, and gives us too dreadful examples of the latter.

CAN'THUS, S. [Lat.] the corner of the eye formed by the meeting of the eye-lids; the inner or that next the nose, is called the greater, the outward and that next the temples, the less.

CA'NTICLE, S. [from *cantus*, Lat.] a song; used by divines in the plural, to signify Solomon's song.

CA'NTLE, S. [*kant*, Belg. a corner, *eschantillon*, Fr. a piece] a corner or angle projecting outwards; a piece with corners, "a monstrous cantle out." *Shak.*

CAN'TLET, S. a piece, a fragment. "Huge cantlets of his buckler." *Dryd.*

CA'NTO, S. [Ital.] a section, or book of a poem. In Music, a song.

CANTON, a large, populous, wealthy city and sea-port town of the province of Quantong in China. It is seated on the banks of one of the finest rivers in the empire, and it is deep enough for large vessels to come up to this place, where all the curiosities of China are brought. They have manufactures of their own, especially in silk stuffs, and the number of tradesmen is incredible. It yields a fine prospect going up the river, being almost surrounded with green fields mixed with pleasant groves and little hills one above another. It consists of three towns, divided by very high walls, and is about as large as Paris. The streets are long and strait, are paved with flag-stones, and adorned with several triumphal arches. There are also Bazars, or covered market-places, full of shops. The houses are only a ground floor, built with earth, or ornamented with bricks, and covered with tiles; however, the shops give it a very neat look. The better sort of people are carried about in chairs; but the common sort walk bare footed and bare-headed; and their goods are carried by porters, for they have no waggons. At the end of every street there is a barrier, which is shut up every evening, as well as the gates of the city; so that people are obliged to be at home early. The river is covered with barks, which have apartments in them for families, where many live and die. The number of inhabitants are computed at 1,000,000. Lon. 230. 5. lat. 25. 10.

CA'NTON, S. [*canton*, Fr.] a small part detached from the rest. A district, or part of a country governed by its own chief, or magistrates. In Heraldry, a square portion of an escutcheon, separated from the rest.

To CA'NTON, V. A. [from the noun] to divide into parts, parcels, or districts. "Canton'd out into petty states." *Addison.* "Canton'd out into parcels." *Swift.* To portion, to separate; to appropriate with the particle *out* followed by *to*. "they canton out to themselves a little province in the intellectual world."

To CANTON'IZE, V. A. to parcel out into small divisions.

CA'NVAS, S. [*canevas*, Fr.] clear unbleached cloth of hemp or flax, used for working tapestry by the needle; for blinds of windows; towels, &c. also a coarse cloth of hemp, for sails.

To CA'NVASS, V. A. [*canvasser*, Fr.] to enquire into, to examine; to debate, or dispute; or controvert. Used neuterly; to sollicit, or ask for their votes.

CA'NZONET, S. [*canzonetta*, Ital.] a short song.

CAP, S. [*cop*, Brit. *cappa*, Sax.] a clothing worn on the head, supposed to have been introduced in the year 1449, at the entry of Charles VII. into Rouen; and to have been only a retrenchment, or a part of the hood worn till that time. Being worn by cardinals, it is figuratively used for the office or dignity of a cardinal. The greatest, or chief of any sect, &c. In a ship, a square piece of timber put over the head of a mast with a round hole cut in it. Cap of maintainance, is one of the regalia carried at a coronation.

To CAP, V. A. to cover a thing. To pull off a cap. To pull off a cap in a compliment, or as a sign of respect and honour.

CAP-A-PIE, [Fr.] from head to foot, all over.

CAPABILITY, S. the being able to perform a thing.

CA'PABLE, Adj [Fr.] susceptible; fitted for; or adapted to. Used with the particle *of* before a noun.

CAPA'CIOUS, Adj. [*capax*, Lat.] capable of large dimensions; containing much; extensive.

CAPA'CIOUSNESS, S. the quality of containing or receiving many things.

To CAPA'CITATE, V. A. to render a person fit; to qualify a person for an undertaking. Used with the particle *for* before a noun.

CAPA'CITY, S. [*capacité*, Fr.] the dimensions of a thing, fitting it for the reception of other things. Applied to the mind, understanding; the inside, or hollow part of a vessel. A state, condition, or character.

CAPA'RISON, S. [*caparison*, Fr.] the cloathing of a horse of state, or sumpter horse.

To CAPA'RISON, V. A. to dress a horse for shew. Figuratively, to adorn a person with a splendid dress.

CAPE, S [*cape*, Fr. *capo*, Ital.] In Geography, a piece of land projecting into the sea; a head-land, or promontory. The neck-piece of a coat, when resting on the shoulders called a *falling-down* cape; but when set upright, a *stand-up* one, supposed to have derived its name from *caput*, Lat. a head, which the first sort covers, and seems to be borrowed from the hood or cowl of a monk.

CAPEL.

CA'PEL, (ROBERT) an eminent divine, born at Gloucester in the year 1586, descended of a good family in Herefordshire, and nearly related to the Capels lords of Essex. He was entered at Magdalen college Oxford, and as a divine, celebrated not only for his learning, his manner of preaching, his exemplary life, but likewise for the plainness with which he delivered the most obscure truths, the strength with which he asserted the peculiar doctrines of Protestants, and the humility with which he enjoyed the most eminent talents; so that his favourite expression, of another person might be properly applied to him. ", He was as learned a man as any in the world, as godly as learned, and as humble as godly." Being not under a necessity of taking the revenue of his benefice, he shewed such an example of generosity, as is scarce credible; to remit his dues, he thought might injure his successors, and therefore received them, but paid them to an indigent clergyman to enable him to support himself. His usual expression was, that, if God thought fit, a sudden death was better than a lingering one; and what he approved of he experienced, for on a Sunday, Sept. 21, 1656, after he had repeated his sermons at night to his family, according to his custom, read a chapter, said his prayers, and laid down in his bed, he expired before he had finished his ejaculations, and fled to heaven with the praises of God in his mouth. O envied death!

CAPE'LLA, S. [Lat.] a bright star of the first magnitude in the left shoulder of Auriga.

CA'PER, S. [capriole, Fr. capriola, Ital.] In Dancing, a spring in which the feet are moved across each other several times, before they reach the ground again.

CA'PER, S. [capparis, Lat.] a pickle and flower growing on the caper-bush, called caprier in French. Linnæus places it in the first sect. of his 13th class, and Tournefort in the 5th sect. of his 6th. The species are 10.

To CA'PER, V. A. To skip for joy; to dance with great activity.

CA'PERER, S. one who cuts capers in dancing. Sometimes used as a word of contempt to express a giddy, frolicksome, and thoughtless person.

CA'PIAS, S. [Lat. from capio, to take] In Law, a writ of two sorts, one before judgment, called capias ad respondendum. If a sheriff, on the first writ of distress, return that he has no effects in his jurisdiction; the other is a writ of execution after judgment.

CA'PILLARY, Adj. [capillus, hair, Lat.] resembling hairs. In Botany, applied to such plants as have no main stem, their leaves arising from their roots, and produce their seeds in little tufts on the back of their leaves. In Anatomy, applied to the minute arteries, which, in the brain, are not equal to one hair. In Physic, capillary tubes are those whose diameter is a half, one third, or quarter of a line, or the least that can be made: the ascent of water in these tubes has puzzled the philosophic world for some time; that of Dr. Jurin, who ascribes it to the attraction of the periphery of the concave surface of the tube, to which the water is contiguous and adheres, is liable to the least objections.

CA'PITAL, adj. [capitalis, Lat.] that which belongs to the head. " Needs must the serpent now his capital bruise expect." Par. Lost. Applied in crimes; criminal in the highest degree; chief or principal. Applied to letters or types, the larger sort. Capital stock; The fund of a trading company, or that sum of money which is contributed by the several parties to carry on their trade, &c.

CA'PITAL, S. among merchants, the sum brought in to make up the common stock. In Geography, the chief city of a kingdom, or residence of its monarch. In Architecture, the uppermost part of a column.

CA'PITALLY, Adv. so as to affect a person's life; capitally convicted, is applied to a person who is condemned to die. Applied to productions of art, in a high-finished excellent manner.

CAPITA'TION, S. [from caput, Lat. a head] a numbering by the heads. A sum of money imposed at so much per head.

CAPI'TULAR, S. [capitulum, Lat.] in its primary sense an act or law passed in a chapter; in its secondary, a chapter or member of a chapter.

To CAPI'TULATE, V. A. In its primary sense to draw articles; to set down the heads of a remonstrance; to make a head. In a secondary sense, to surrender a place upon certain stipulated conditions.

CAPITULA'TION, S. the surrender upon certain conditions. The terms agreed upon for the surrender of a place. Capitulations of the empire, are articles drawn up, before an election, by the electors, which the emperor ratifies before his coronation.

CA'POT, S. [Fr.] at the game of piquet when one party wins all the tricks.

To CA'POT, V. A. to win all the tricks at piquet.

CA'PREOLATE, Adj. [from capreolus, Lat.] in Botany, applied to such plants as twist and climb upon others by means of tendrils.

CAPRI'CE, S. [caprice, Fr.] a whimsey, freak, whim, or fantastic humour.

CAPRI'CIOUS, Adj. [capricieux, Fr.] a behaviour founded on mere whim and fancy; a sudden and frequent change of opinion.

CAPRI'CIOUSLY, Adv. in a whimsical fashi-

fanciful manner; or where a person's behaviour and fentiments are continually changing without any reasons for the alteration.

CAPRICIOUSNESS, S. the quality of
changing according to the flarts of fancy
without any regard to propriety.

CA'PRICORN, S. [*capricornus*, Lat.] in
aftronomy, the tenth fign of the zodiac.

CAP'SQUARES, S. ftrong plates of iron
over the trunnions of a gun.

CAP'STAN, S. [*cabeftan*, Fr.] a large
cylinder placed perpendicular on the deck of
a fhip, and turned by four levers which
crofs it, ferving by means of a cable, which
winds round it, to draw up heavy burdens. It is likewife ufed to tow a fhip,
and to weigh the anchors. The *main-capftan*,
is that which is placed behind the main-maft,
ftanding on the firft deck, and reaching four
or five feet above the fecond; the *jeer* or little *capftan*, ftands on the fecond deck, between the main-malt and the mizzen. To
launch out the capftan, is to flacken the cable
of it; *to pawl out the capftan*, is to keep it from
running back.

CA'PSULAR, Adj. [*capfula*, Lat.] hollow.

CAP'TAIN, S. [*capitaine*, Fr.] an officer
in an army. Captain of a company, is one
who commands a company under a colonel.
Captain lieutenant, is one who commands a
troop or company in the name of fome other
perfon who has the name, commiffion and
pay, but is excufed the fervice on account of
his rank. Lieutenant captain, is the captain's fecond, or he who commands the
company in the captain's abfence. Captain
general, is the commander in chief. Captain of a veffel whether of war, or in the
merchant's fervice, is the commander, or
mafter. Reformed captain, one who has his
commiffion fupprefled, and his company
difbanded, but yet is continued captain either
as fecond to another, or without any poft or
command at all.

CAP'TAIN-SHIP, S. authority, or rank
of a captain.

CAPTA'TION, S. [from *capto*, Lat.] a
flattering kind of addrefs ufed to gain the
good opinion of the vulgar. " Without
any of thofe dreffes, or popular *captations.*"
K. Charles.

CAP'TION, S. [from *capio*, to take] in
Law, is when a commiffion is executed, and
the commiffioners fubfcribe to a certificate,
declaring when and where the commiffion
was executed.

CAP'TIOUS, Adj. [*captieux*, Lat. *captieux*, Fr.] given to cavils, or objections.
Enfnaring.

CAP'TIOUSLY, Adv. in fuch a manner
as fhews a great inclination to raife objections.
In a fly, enfnaring, caviling, or infidious
manner.

CAP'TIOUSNESS, S. anger; peevifhnefs.

To **CAP'TIVATE,** Adj. [*captivorum*, fup-
pine of *captivo*, Lat. *captiver*, Fr.] to take
prifoner. Figuratively, to fubdue by the
power of fuperior excellence. To enflave,
ufed with the particle *to.*

CAP'TIVATION, S. the taking of a
perfon prifoner; the flate of a prifoner.

CAP'TIVE, S. [*captivus*, Lat. *captif*, Fr.]
a perfon taken prifoner in war, ufed with the
particle *to* before the perfon or thing fubdu-
ing. Figuratively, one fubdued by the beauty
of another.

CATIVE, S. [*captivus*, Lat.] confined;
imprifoned; fubdued.

CAP'TIVITY, S. [*captivité*, Fr. *captivi-
tas*, Lat.] a flate of fervitude, or imprifonment. Figuratively, the flate of the foul,
when the lufts are predominant. In Scripture the flate of a finful perfon, or one who
is in the power of fatan, either to tyrannize
over him or involve him in trouble. " The
Lord turned the *captivity* of Job." *Job.* xlii.
10. The power of fatia or the enflaving confequences of fin. " Thou haft led *captivity*
captive," *Pfal.* lxviii 18, is a beautiful phrafe
for the utter deftruction of every thing
which could enflave and fubdue the foul.

CAP'IOR, S. [from *captum*] one who
takes a prifoner, or prize.

CAP'TURE, S. [*capture*, Fr. *captura*,
Lat.] the taking of any prey. The thing
taken. In Law, the feizing for a debt, or
apprehending a criminal.

CAPU'CHINS, S. [pronounced *capufhens*]
monks of the order of St. Francis founded
by Matthew Bafchi who pretended to receive
feveral admonitions from heaven, literally,
or with the greateft flrictnefs to practife the
rules of St. Francis, and in 1529, having reduced the order to a complete form, was
elected general. They are cloathed with
brown or grey, are always bare-footed, never
go in a coach, and never fhave their beards.
Ufed in the fingular for a woman's cloak,
made in imitation of the drefs of the capuchins.

CAR, S. [*car*, Brit. *carru*, Belg. *carrus*,
Lat] a fmall carriage. Figuratively, ufed
by the poets for a chariot. Joined with the
word *northern*, ufed for Charles's-wain, or
the Bear, a conftellation. " Hyads and the
northern car." *Dryd.*

CA'RABINE, or **CA'RBINE,** S. [Fr.] a
fmall kind of fufee, about two feet long in
the barrel, furrowed within, carrying a ball
of 24 in the lb. and made ufe of by the light
horfe.

CARABINEER, S. a fort of light horfe.

CA'RAT, or **CA'RACT,** S. [*carat*, Fr.
from *caratta*, a weight.] a mark, that is
to fay, an ounce troy, divided into 24 equal
parts called *caracts*, and each caract into four
grains, is a weight by which the mint-mafters
difcover the finefs of gold. *Carat* weight is
the

the 24th part of an ounce; two troy grains making a carat grain. Carat is a weight used by jewellers, equal to four grains, but lighter than the mare-weight above; each of these grains are divided into half, one quarter, one eighth, and one fixteenth, &c. According to Tavernier, the Moguls famous diamond weighs 279 carats nine fixteenths

CA'RAVAN, S. [*caravane*, Fr.] a company of merchants travelling together in great numbers through deferts in the Eaft, for their mutual fafety and defence. Their beafts are moft commonly camels, and they are efcorted by an aga, with a body of janizaries.

CA'RAWAY, S. [*carvi*, Lat. from *caria*, the place where it originally grew] in Botany, the fpecies are two; the feed is ftomachic, diuretic and carminitive, one of the four hot feeds in the fhops: It diffolves flatulencies, promotes digeftion, and give eafe in the cholic, but being apt to irritate and heat too much, fhould be carefully avoided in inflammations.

CARBONA'DO, S. [*carbonada*, Span.] meat cut acrofs, or in fquares.

To CARBONA'DO, V. A. to cut acrofs, in cookery. To cut or hack.

CARBU'NCLE, S. [*carbunculus*, S.] a jewel of the ruby kind, of a rich blood-red colour. Figuratively, a large red pimple, breaking out upon any part of the face.

CARBU'NCLED, Adj. fet with carbuncles. Covered with pimples.

CARBU'NCULAR, Adj. refembling a carbuncle.

CARBUNCULA'TION, S. [*carbunculatio*, Lat.] in Botany, the blafting young buds of trees or plants, either with exceffive heat, or exceffive cold.

CA'RCASS, S. [*carquaffe*, Fr.] a dead body. The decayed parts of a thing. "The rotten carcafe of a boat." *Shakefp.* In Architecture, the fhell of a houfe, containing the partitions, floors, rafters, &c. or only the walls. In gunnery, a kind of bomb, of an oblong form, confifting of an iron fhell or cafe, with holes, but fometimes only of iron hoops, covered over with a pitched coarfe cloath, filled with combuftibles, and throws from a mortar.

CA'RCELAGE, S. [from *carcer*, Lat. a prifon] prifon fees, or garnifh.

CA'RCINOMA, S. [from *καρκινος* and *νεμω*.] an ulcer, called cancer. Alfo a diforder in the coat of the eye.

CARCINO'MATOUS, Adj. [from *carcinoma*] tending to a cancer.

CARD, S. [*carte*, Fr.] pieces of fine thin pafte-board, cut in oblong fquares of three inches and a half by two inches and a half, on which are painted feveral marks and figures, and ufed in feveral games. A court card is that which has the image of fome perfon painted on it: A pack of cards confifts of fifty-two cards. They are but of

late date, fince they feem to have been invented for the diverfion of Charles V. of France, and are made on the fame principles as the printing of illuminated or other letters, firft practifed at Haerlem. In Sea Affairs, the upper part of the mariner's compafs, whereon the names of the winds are marked.

CA'RD, S. [*kaerde*, Belg.] an inftrument compofed of iron wire, faftened by the feet in rows, to a fquare piece of wood of a foot long, ferving to comb, difentangle, and range wool or flax, in a proper order for fpinning.

To CA'RD, S. [from *kaerden*, Belg.] to comb wool, &c. to game; or play immoderately at cards.

CA'RDAMOM, S. [*cardamum*, Lat.] a medicinal feed, of which there are three fpecies, that commonly ufed in the fhops is the leaft, enters the Venice treacle, affifts digeftion. Strengthens the head and ftomach, and is diuretic.

CA'RDIAC, or CARDI'ACAL, Adj. [*cardiacus*, Lat. from *καρδια*, Gr. the heart] in Medicine, that which contributes to quicken the motion of the folids, thereby promoting the circulation of the blood, raifing the fpirits, giving prefent ftrength and cheerfulnefs, fo that the fenfations at the head, ftomach, and heart, are more lightfome and agreeable, than they were before.

CA'RDIFF, a town of South-Wales, in Glamorganfhire, with two markets on Wednefdays and Saturdays, and three fairs, on June 29, September 8, and November 30, for cattle. It is feated on the river Tave, over which there is a handfome bridge, and is a large, compact, well-built town, having a caftle, a wall, and four gates. It has a confiderable trade with Briftol; for veffels of fmall burden can come to the bridge. At prefent it has but one church, the water having deftroyed the other. The conftable of the caftle is the chief magiftrate, where they call mayor; befides him, there are two bailiffs, a recorder, 12 aldermen, 12 commoncouncilmen, a ferjeant at mace, and 8 conftables. It contains a parifhes, and about 300 houfes, formed into broad paved ftreets. Here the affizes and feffions for the county are held; and it fends one member to parliament. Near it are fome iron-works. It is 12 miles E. by N. of Cowbridge, 96 S. W. of Monmouth, and 163 W. of London. Lon. 14. 15. lat. 51. 30.

CA'RDINAL, Adj. [*cardinalis*, Lat. from *cardo*, Lat. a hinge] principal, chief, or moft confiderable. Cardinal points, are the four chief pol is of the horizon, *viz.* the North and South, Eaft and Weft, and cardinal winds are thofe which blow from either o thofe quarters. Cardinal numbers, are thofe integers or numbers from which the other are

are named and composed; thus one, two, three, are named cardinal numbers, to distinguish them from the ordinals, or such as express the order of things, viz. first, second, third, &c.

CARDINAL, S. one of the principal governors of the Romish church, by whom the pope is elected out of their own number, which contains six bishops, fifty priests, and fourteen deacons, who constitute the sacred colledge. They derive their name from their being as necessary, or useful to the apostolic see, as an axle or hinge on which the whole government of the church turns.

CARDIGAN, a principal town of Cardiganshire in South Wales, with a market on Saturdays, and four fairs, viz. on February 13, and April 5, for small horses and pedlar's ware; September 8, and November 19, for the same and cattle. It is pleasantly situated on the river Tivy, over which there is a handsome stone bridge with several arches. It is the shire town where the assizes are held, and the county goal kept. The shire-hall is well built; and it has but one church. It sends one member to parliament, and has the title of an earldom. It is 33 miles N. E. by E. of St. David's, 36 N. of Pembroke, and 198 W. N. W. of London. Long. 12. 55. lat. 50. 15.

CARDIGANSHIRE, a county in South Wales, 42 miles in length, and 20 in breadth, being upon the coast of the Irish sea, which bounds it on the west, Radnorshire is on the east, and Merionethshire on the north, and Carmarthenshire on the South. The air is more pleasant, and milder here than in other parts of Wales; and to the west and south there are plains fruitful in corn. It contains 3150 houses, 35380 inhabitants, 64 parishes, and 4 market-towns; and sends one member to parliament. There are several small rivers, which, rising in the mountains, fall into the sea, but the Tivy is the principal. It abounds with veins of lead and silver ore; a ton of which last will yield 70 or 80 ounces of silver. The mines have been worked several times to great advantage; and particularly Sir Hugh Middleton cleared £2000. a month for several years together, which enabled him to bring the New River water to London. Some private adventurers have attempted to work them, but have failed for want of a sufficient stock. An ancient British writer has affirmed there were beavers in this country; but he bestowed this name on otters, as some natural historians have done, for there are now plenty of these animals to be found near the river.

CARD-MAKER, S. a person who makes, paints, and sells cards, or one who makes the cards or combs made use of in preparing wool for spinning.

CARDUUS, S. [Lat.] a kind of thistle, used in medicine as a vomit.

CARE, S. [care or caru, Sax.] attention, concern or anxiety of mind. Caution previous to an undertaking with the word take; but protection, regard and support when followed with the particle of. "There is a God that takes care of us." Tillots. When applied to God it implies his providence over all his creatures.

To CARE, V. N. to be anxious, follicitous, or concerned. To be disposed, or inclined, with the particles for or to. To have a sympathy or affectionate regard for. "Not that he cared for the poor." John xii. 6.

To CAREEN, V. A. [carenin, Fr.] to lay a vessel on one side, in order to stop the leaks, or repair the other. To sail on the carren, is to lie on one side in sailing. The half careen, is when only half of the ship can be careened, from its not being possible to come at the bottom of the keel.

CAREER, S. [carière, Fr.] a course or race. Full speed, swift motion. A course of action not interrupted.

CAREFUL, Adj. [from careful, Sax.] abounding with great follicitude or anxiety.

CAREFULLY, Adj. cautiously, circumspectly, diligently.

CAREFULNESS, S. caution, diligence, application, vigilance.

CARELESSLY, Adj. without care; negligently.

CARELESS, Adj. without due attention, or application; without anxiety. "Wisely careless." Pope. Without thought, or premeditation.

To CARESS, V. A. [caresser, Fr.] to embrace with great affection. To treat with great civility.

CARESS, S. an embrace of great affection; an expression of great tenderness.

CARET, S. [caret, Lat. It wants] In Grammar, a mark implying some omission in writing, or printing, which should come in where this sign stands.

CARGO, S. [cargaison, Fr. or cargo, Ital.] the lading of a ship; wares on board a ship.

CARIES, S. [Lat.] In Medicine, the corruption of a bone, the rottenness of a bone.

CARIOSITY, S. [from caries] that quality of a bone, which wastes its substance.

CARIOUS, Adj. [from caries, Lat.] rotten, applied chiefly to bones.

CARK, S. [cearc, Sax.] an anxious care or apprehension arising from thoughts of some future event; For some time out of use, but now reviving.

CARLISLE, a town or city of Cumberland, of which it is its capital, with a market on Saturdays; and four fairs, viz. August 26, for horned cattle and linen; September 19, for horses and horned cattle; and on the first and second Saturdays after October 10, for Scotch horned cattle. It is a place of great antiquity, and is seated at the confluence of
several

everal rivers, which almost encompass it. The river Peterill being on the east, Cauda on the west, and Eden on the north, which soon after falls into the sea. It is surrounded with walls, and fortified with a castle, which stands on the west side of the town: the houses are well-built, and the cathedral church is a stately structure, with curious workmanship. It is a place of some trade in fustians, and sends two members to parliament. The gates are called Irish, English, and Scotch. It is 60 miles S. of Edinburgh, 70 N. of Lancaster, and 301 N. N. W. of London. Lon. 15. 5. lat. 54. 45. The Picts, or Roman wall, runs from hence to Newcastle, of which there are still some remains, and from which it is 60 miles distant to the W. and from Berwick upon Tweed 80 S. W. It was possessed by the rebels in 1745, and was retaken by the D. of Cumberland 24 days afterwards.

CA'RMAN, S. one who drives or keeps a cart.

CARMARTHEN, the capital town of Carmarthenshire in South Wales, with two markets on Wednesdays and Saturdays, and six fairs, viz. June 3, July 10, Aug. 12, Sept. 9, Oct. 9, and Nov. 14, all for cattle, horses, and pedlars ware. It is pleasantly seated on the banks of the river Towey, over which there is a large stone bridge, to which small vessels come up to unload their goods. It is a corporation, and the place where the assizes are held. It was once fortified with a wall and a strong castle, and is at present a considerable place, sending one member to parliament. It is 24 miles S. E. of Cardigan, 42 W. by N. of Brecknock, and 206 W. by N. of London. Lon. 13. 10. lat. 51. 50.

CARMARTHENSHIRE, a county of S. Wales, 48 miles in length, 25 in breadth, and bounded by Cardiganshire on the N. St. George's Channel on the S. Brecknock and Glamorganshires on the E. and Pembrokeshire on the W. It is fruitful in corn and grass, having many pleasant and rich meadows; and it has also wood, coal, and sea fish, especially salmon, which is exceeding good. The air is pretty mild and wholesome, it not being so mountainous as other counties. It contains 2765 houses, 16550 inhabitants, 145 parishes, 8 market-towns, and sends two members to parliament, one for the county, and one for the shire town. It is watered with several rivers and small streams.

CA'RMELITE, S. [Carmelite, Fr. of Carmel, the name of a mount] an order of friars; one of the four tribes of begging friars. This order is eminent for the devotion of its scapulary, its missions, and the great number of saints with which it has stocked the Romish church. The Barefooted Carmelites are a reform of the former, begun by St. Theresa in 1540; she began with the

nuns, whom she restored to the primitive austerity of the order; from them she applied herself to the friars, whom she likewise reformed, and, by persuading them to go without shoes, give rise to their name of barefooted. In Botany, Carmelite is a sort of pear.

CARMI'NATIVE, Adj. In Medicine, remedies which by their warmth attenuate and rarify the wind included in the intestines, and, by their irritations, invigorate their tonic undulations, so as to make them perspire, or explode either upwards or downwards with a noise.

CARMI'NE, S. a bright red colour, used mostly in miniature, and is the settling of the water into which cochineal, coram, and antour have been steeped. Some make it of the scum of Brazil or Fernambuca wood well beat in a mortar, and steeped in vinegar; but this is not to be compared to the former sort.

CA'RNAGE, S. [Fr. from carnis, genitive of caro, Lat. flesh] slaughter, havock, or heaps of dead bodies.

CA'RNAL, Adj. [carnal, Fr.] belonging to the fleshy part of a man; sensual; lustful; voluptuous.

CARNA'LITY, S. [from carnal] lust; wantonness; propensity to lust; unchaste pleasure; inability to raise ones ideas to abstract or spiritual things; grossness.

CA'RNALLY, Adv. in a gross, sensual manner; as if real flesh; in a sensible manner; really. "In the Sacrament we do not receive Christ carnally." Taylor.

CARNARVON, a town of Carnarvonshire in N. Wales, with a market on Saturdays, and four fairs, viz. on Feb. 25, May 16, Aug. 4, and Dec. 5, for cattle and pedlars ware. It is commodiously seated on the sea-shore, and has a prospect into the Isle of Anglesea. It is a place of great strength, as well by nature as art, being surrounded on all sides, except the E. with the sea and two rivers. It had a strong castle, which is now in ruins; and has only one parish church, but the houses and streets are tolerably handsome. It has the title of an earldom, and sends one member to parliament; is governed by the constable of the castle, who, by patent, is always mayor. It is 7 miles S. W. of Bangor, 18 S. W. of Aberconway, and 251 N. W. of London. Lon. 13. 10. lat. 53. 20.

CARNARVONSHIRE, a county of N. Wales, 30 miles in length, 13 in breadth, and bounded on the N. and W. by the sea, on the S. by Merionethshire, and on the E. by Denbighshire. The air is sharp and cold, it being full of high mountains, lakes, and rocks; however there are several fruitful bottoms and pleasant valleys, which feed sheep, cattle, and goats, and its rivers are full of fish. It contains 2765 houses, 16790 inhabitants, 68 parishes, and 6 market-towns.

The highest mountain is called Snowdon-hill, which is boggy on the top, and has two lakes full of fish. The sheep, which feed on the sides of it, yield the sweetest mutton in Wales. It sends two members to parliament, one for the county, and one for Carnarvon, which is the principal town.

CARNA'TION, S. [*carnadino*, Ital.] in Botany, a species of the clovegillyflower, consisting of two colours with streaks, which go quite through the leaves, and deriving its name from its resembling a flesh colour. In Painting, a lively red colour.

CARNE'LIAN, S. [improperly spelt *cornelian*] in Natural History, a precious stone, of which there are three species, a red, a yellow, and a white. It is found in England, but the finest sorts come from the East Indies, and are of a roundish form like common pebbles, between two or three inches diameter, of a fine, compact, close texture, of a smooth surface, and is extremely well adapted for seals, as it may be cut at a moderate price, will take a good polish, and separate easily from the wax.

CARNEOUS, Adv. [from *carneus*, Lat.] fleshy, or consisting of flesh. Used only by technical writers.

To CA'RNIFY, V. N. [from *carnis*, of *caro*, Lat. flesh, and *fio*, Lat. to become] to breed flesh, to convert or turn food into flesh. "I digest, I sanguify, I carnify." Hale. Not in use.

CA'RNIVAL, S. [*carnaval*, Fr.] a season of mirth and luxury celebrated by the Italians, lasting from Twelfth-day to Lent, and attended with every thing which pomp, ostentation, or festivity can furnish.

CARNI'VOROUS, Adv. [from *caro*, Lat. flesh, and *voro*, Lat. to devour] eating flesh, or that which lives on flesh. Whether man be a *carnivorous* animal, is a question that has embarrassed philosophers of no small eminence. Gassendus endeavours to prove the negative from the form of our teeth, which is not adapted to the comminuting flesh. Dr. Drake supports the argument by considering the nature of flesh, which, he says, is the hardest of digestion of any other food whatever, is denied persons in disorders, and disagreeable to infants till their palates are vitiated by custom. To the arguments already quoted, Dr. Wallis joins another, drawn from the resemblance of the intestines of mankind to those of animals which live on vegetable food, and from the similarity of their construction would conclude that their food should be similar. Yet experience and custom are more to be regarded than the specious arguments of sages.

CARNO'SITY, S. [*carnosité*, Fr.] in Surgery, a fleshy excrescence; proud flesh.

CA'RNOUS, Adj. [*caro*, Lat.] fleshy. In Botany, a soft substance like that of flesh in animals.

CA'ROL, S. [*cærolle*, Fr.] a song of joy or festivity, used among the country singers at Christmas; any kind of song.

To CA'ROL, V. A. [*carolare*, Ital.] to sing with great joy; to praise in songs.

CARO'TID, Adj. [*carotides*, Lat.] in Anatomy, two arteries on each side the neck, serving to convey the blood to the brain; arising near each other from the curvature of the aorta, the right immediately, the left most commonly from the trunk of the subclavia of the same side.

CARO'USAL, S. [from *carouse*, accented by Dryden, improperly, on the first syllable] a festival or holiday, celebrated with mirth and festivity.

To CAROU'SE, V. A. [from' *carousser*, Fr.] to drink freely; to drink a health.

CAROU'SE, S. a drinking match; a large draught; a merry meeting.

CAROU'SER, S. a toper, a sot.

CA'RP, S. [*carpe*, Fr.] a large fresh-water fish, remarkable for living out of water; for in Holland they hang them up, to fatten them, in a cellar or some cool place, in wet moss, with their heads out, and feed them with white bread soaked in milk, for many days; and this practice succeeds no less in England than there, as I have been informed by a Fellow of the Royal Society.

To CA'RP, V. N. [*carpo*, Lat.] to censure or blame. Used with the particle at.

CA'RPENTER, S. [*charpentier*, Fr.] one who performs the wood-work relative to houses, buildings, or ships.

CA'RPENTRY, S. the art of building either houses or ships with wood. In a house it includes the framing, flooring, roofing, the foundation, breast, doors, and windows. As houses were at first built only with wood, it must have been prior to masonry. This art is, by some travellers, reported to have arrived at the greatest perfection in the Maldivian islands, the works there being so well contrived, that they will hold tight and firm without either nails or pins, and cannot be taken asunder by any, but those who are employed in their construction.

CA'RPER, S. a person fond of finding fault; a caviller.

CA'RPET, S. [*tarpet*, Belg. *carpetta*, Ital.] a covering of stuff or other materials, wrought with the needle or in a loom, commonly spread over tables or laid on floors. From the former usage is derived the phrase of a *thing's being on the carpet*, to express its being in hand, in debate, or the subject of consideration and preparation. Figuratively, ground embellished with flowers, and of a smooth or level surface.

To CA'RPET, V. A. to spread with a carpet; to embellish with flowers and herbs. "Every where *carpeted* over with grass." Derham.

CA'RPING, Part. [from *carp*] fond of raising objections; censorious; captious.

CA'RPINGLY, Adv. captiously, censoriously.

CAR'RAT, S. See CARACT.

CA'RRAWAY, S. See CARAWAY.

CA'RRIAGE, S. [Fr.] a vehicle to convey persons or things. The act of conveying things from one place to another. The price paid for the conveying of goods, distinguished from that which is paid for conveyance of persons, and is termed *fare*. Figuratively, address, behaviour, conduct, or practices; proceedings, or the manner of transacting any affairs.

CA'RRIER, S. one who conveys a thing from one place to another. In Natural History, a species of pigeons, so called from their carrying letters, &c. tied to their necks, to the place where they were bred, be it at ever so great a distance.

CA'RRION, S. [*charogne*, Fr. *carogna*, Ital.] the flesh of a dead carcass, generally applied to dogs, horses, &c. Any putrified flesh. Figuratively, a gross, disagreeable person.

CA'RRION, Adj. [see the noun] relating to, or feeding on dead carcasses. "A prey for *carrion* kites and crows." *Shak.*

CA'RROT, S. [*carote*, Fr. *carota*, Ital.] in Botany, a well-known kitchen root, called the *daucus*; it has an umbelliferous flower, the principal umbel composed of rays; its involucrum having many leaves. It is ranged by Linnæus in the 2d sect. of his 5th class, and by Tournefort in the first sect. of his 7th. The species are seven.

CA'RROTINESS, S. resembling a carrot in colour, applied to the hair.

CA'RROTY, Adj. approaching to red, of the colour of a *carrot*.

To CA'RRY, V. A. [*charier*, Fr.] to remove a thing from one place to another. Used with the word *about*, and followed by a *personal* pronoun; to have with one, to carry in one's pocket. To accomplish, or attain. Used with the words *town*, &c. to gain or conquer after some resistance. To *carry it off*; to bear out, to outface, including the face of triumphant and unplanted impudence. Joined to the personal pronoun, *himself*, &c. To behave. To *carry away*, to impel, seduce, or urge by an irresistible violence. To bear, or have, joined to a noun, signifying likeness. "Something that *carries* an analogy to sense." *Hale.* To *carry up*, to raise, or continue a thing in one direction; to trace backwards. To *carry off*, to kill or put an end to a person's life. "If the change of the weather had not *carried* him *off*." *Temple.* To *carry on*, to prosecute, continue, or perform, in an undertaking.

CA'RT, S. [*cart*, Brit. *caretta*, Ital.] a carriage, with two wheels, drawn by horses, and used to convey goods from one place to another.

To CA'RT, V. A. to whip at a cart's tail. Neuterly, to use carts.

CA'RTEL, S. [Fr. *cartello*, Ital.] certain stipulations between persons at variance; applied to the conditions made by enemies for the mutual exchange of prisoners.

CA'RTER, S. one who drives a cart.

CA'RTILEGE, S. [*cartilago*, Lat.] a smooth, solid, elastic substance, softer than a bone. Its use is to prevent the bones from being wasted by continual friction; to join them together, and to contribute to the forming of the parts, as in the nose, ear, &c.

CARTILAGI'NEOUS, CARTILA'GI-NOUS, Adj. consisting of cartilages.

CARTO'ON, S. [*cartone*, Ital.] a drawing or sketch upon strong paper, to be calked through upon a wall, in order to be painted in fresco. A coloured design, or piece of painting intended as a copy for tapestry, &c. Of this kind are the celebrated *Cartoons* of Raphael lately at Hampton-court, which are now removed to the queen's palace.

CARTO'UCH, S. [Fr. from *cartouch*, or *gargousse*, Fr.] a case of wood, containing 48 musket-balls, and 6 or 8 balls of iron of a pound weight; being fired out of a hobit, or small mortar, for the defence of a pass. Likewise used for a cartridge.

CA'RTOUCH, S. [*cartoccio*, Ital.] in Architecture, an ornament representing a scroll of paper, usually in the form of a table, or flat member, with wavings, and having some inscription, device, or ornament of armory; they are sometimes drawn in maps, and filled with their titles.

CA'RTRAGE, or CARTRIDGE, S. [according to Skinner, from *cartouche*, Fr.] a charge of powder wrapped up in thick paper, for charging fire arms with expedition.

CA'RTRUT, S. the track, worn in a road by a cart wheel.

CA'RTULARY, S. [from *charta*, Lat.] a place where records are deposited.

To CA'RVE, V. A. [*ceorfan*, Sax. *kerven*, Belg.] to cut wood, stone, &c. into the forms of animals, vegetables, &c. In Cookery, to cut meat with address and expedition. Figuratively, to choose for one's self; to choose one's own lot. Used neuterly, to practice the profession of a sculptor or carver. In Cookery, to cut the meat at table, and help the rest of the company.

CA'RVER, S. one who forms statues, &c. In Cookery, one who performs the honour of the table, cuts the meat, and serves the rest of the company from the dishes. Figuratively, the disposer, master, or chooser of his own station, circumstance, or condition.

CA'RVING, S. the art of cutting images in wood, stone, or marble.

F f   CA'S

CA'SCADE, S. [cascade, Fr.] a fall of water. They are either natural, or artificial.

CA'SE, S. [caisse, Fr.] something made to cover a thing. A covering, sheath, or box. Hence, a case-knife, is one, that used to be carried in a sheath, but now applied to those knives which are used in cutting victuals at meals.

CA'SE, S. [casus, Lat. cas, Fr. caso, Ital.] the state of a person or thing. In Physic, the state of the body. In good case, fat or plump. Accident or contingent, applied to any future event. A question relating to particular persons or things. In Law, the representation of any fact. In case, implies provided; upon the supposition that, or if it should happen; a phrase frequently occurring in conversation, if not in books. Case, in Grammar, implies the various changes which nouns in Greek and Latin undergo in their several numbers. As the English expresses these terminations by particles prefixed to the nouns, but not by any alteration of their terminations, it is plain that it has no cases. Case, in Printing, is a narrow wooden box, divided into several compartments, containing each a number of types or letters of the same sort.

To CA'SE, V. A. to put in a case. Figuratively, to surround or inclose. " The casing air." Shak. To skin, or strip off the skin. " Some sport with the fox e'er we case him." L'Estrange. Neuterly, to represent an affair; to put cases. " Reasoning and casing upon the matter." L'Estran.

To CASE-HARDEN, V. A. to render iron hard and capable of resisting the file.

CA'SEMAN, S. in Printing, one who works at the case or sets the forms. A compositor.

CA'SEMENT, S. [casamento, Ital.] a window that opens upon hinges.

CA'SEWORM, S. in Natural History, the caddis, or cade-worm.

CA'SH, S. [caisse] in Commerce, ready money.

CA'SHEW-NUT, S. in Botany, a tree that grows in the West-Indies.

CASHIE'R, S. [pronounced casheer] a person who keeps the money, at a house or public office.

To CASHIE'R, V. A. [from casser, Fr.] to discard; to drive or expell on account of some misdemeanour; generally applied to those who belong to the army.

CASH-KEEPER, S. one who keeps the cash of another.

CA'SK, S. [casque, Fr.] a round hollow cycloidal vessel, used for keeping liquors, provisions or dry goods. A cask of sugar weighs from 8 to 11 cwt.; a cask of almonds 3 cwt. In Heraldry and Poetry, a piece of defensive armour used to cover or defend the head; a helmet.

CA'SKET, S. [a diminutive of cask, Eng.

or caisse, Fr.] a small box, or casket for jewels. Any thing which contains something of value. " Lock'd up within the casket of thy breast." Davies. A beautiful expression!

To CA'SKET, V. A. to put into a casket. " Casketed my treasure." Shak.

CASSAMUNA'IR, or CASSUMUNAIR, S. in Pharmacy, a root brought from the East-Indies. It is cardiac and sudorific; famous in nervous cases; given as a stomachic and carminative; and its dose in powder is from five to fifteen grains.

To CA'SSATE, V. A. [casser, Fr.] to destroy; render void; annul; or abrogate. " Supercedes and cassates, the best medium we have." Ray.

CA'SSIA, S. in Botany, a tree growing in the West-Indies, affording a clammy substance. Also a fragrant spice, supposed to be the bark of a tree resembling cinnamon. " All thy garments smell of myrrh, aloes and cassia." Psal. xlv. 1.

CA'SSOCK, S. [casaque, Fr.] a close long garment, worn by clergymen under their gowns.

To CA'ST, V. A. [preter and part. passive, cast, from kaster, Belg.] to throw at a distance, by the hand. To cast aside, to lay by as useless. " To cast down, to fling or throw from a high place. To cast anchor, to let down into the sea. In Law, to condemn, or get the better of an adversary. To cast up, in Arithmetic, to add up a sum to find its amount. To cast, in the Drama, to allot the parts of a play to particular persons. Cast an eye, to direct, glance, or look at. In Foundery, to make an image, &c. by pouring metal, &c. into a mould. Joined with light, to reflect, or impart. To cast away, to wreck, or shipwreck. To ruin, joined with the reciprocal pronouns, himself, &c. " To cast themselves away for ever." Hooker. To be cast down, to be disconsolate, or dejected. To cast off, to discard, or break acquaintance with, applied to persons; to reject, applied to rules, sentiments or laws; to free from, applied to any load or burthen; to refuse or withdraw, applied to subjection. To let loose, in hunting. " Cast off the dogs." To compute, calculate, or estimate. To be cast open, to be driven by violence of the wind or streets of weather. " Cast upon a certain island," Acts xxvii. 26. Used neuterly, with about and how to contrive; " Cast about how to draw, &c." Bac. In Foundery, to thicken into a particular form. In Carpentry, to warp, or grow out of shape. " Stuff is said to cast, or warp when it alters its flatness and straightness." Moxon.

CA'ST, S. the throwing a thing by the hands. The distance to which a thing may be thrown. A particular motion of the eye, generally

generally used as a softer expression for squinting. A throw at dice; figuratively, a venture, or resource. In Painting, a shade or tendency to any colour. Applied to the theatre, the distribution or allotting of the several parts of a play.

CA'ST-AWAY, S. a person in a multiplicity of misfortunes, and seemingly abandoned by Providence. One rejected by the Deity. Used adjectively, for something unemployed, useless, or lost for want of employment. "At our *cast-away* leisure." *Raleigh.*

CA'STED, the participle preter of *cast*, but improperly formed, and perhaps owing to a poetical licence, taken by *Shakespeare*, "with *casted* slough." *Hen. IV.*

CA'STER, S. one who throws. In Arithmetic, one who calculates; a founder; a fortune-teller.

To CA'STIGATE, V. A. [*castigatum*, supine of *castigo*, Lat.] to punish, or put to corporal pain for any fault. Figuratively, to correct, chastise, or restrain by punishment. "To *castigate* thy pride." *Shak.* Not used so frequently as *chastise*.

CASTIGA'TION, S. [*castigatio*, supine of *castigo*, Lat.] penance, discipline, or correction.

CA'STIGATORY, Adj. punishing, to make a person amend his faults.

CA'STING-NET, S. a fishing-net which is spread by throwing it in the water.

CA'STLE, S. [*castellum*, Lat.] a fortified place or edifice to defend a town or city from an enemy. *Castles in the air*, imply some chymerical project or expectation, which has no grounds in reason or the nature of things.

CA'STLING, S. the young of a brute animal which is cast before its time.

CA'STOR, S. a beaver, or hat made of the fur of a beaver.

To CA'STRATE, V. A. [*castro*, Lat.] to geld. Figuratively, to cut sentences out of any book; to mutilate.

CASTRA'TION, S. gelding, mutilation.

CA'STERIL, or CASTREL, a kind of hawk.

CA'SUAL, Adj. [*casus*, Lat. chance] something done without design; something happening unexpected; something which cannot be traced to its cause, or something whose cause is unknown.

CA'SUALLY, Adv. accidentally; without design; by chance.

CA'SUALTY, S. an event not intended, or expected; any accident which deprives a person of life.

CA'SUIST, S. [*casuiste*, Fr.] one who studies nice points in cases of conscience.

CASUI'STICAL, Adj. belonging to nice points, or cases of conscience.

CA'SUISTRY, S. the science employed about nice points in practical divinity, or ethics.

CA'T, S. [*catb*, Brit. *kate*, Belg. *chat*, Fr.] a domestic animal, which catches mice, and supposed to see in the dark, or with the least glimmerings of light. A piece of round wood cut considerably smaller at the ends than in the middle, used by children at a play thing.

CAT *in the pan*, a phrase used for a person's changing fide. *Cat o' nine tails*, a whip with nine lashes, used in punishing criminals for petty larceny offences.

CATACHRE'SIS, S. In Rhetoric, a figure, wherein the words are wrested from their primary signification, or when a word is improperly put instead of another, for want of a better; as the word *beautiful* is in the following sentence. "A voice *beautiful* to the ear." or the word *loss* in this "the *loss* of his pen." *Addis.*

CATACHRE'STICAL, Adj. improper; forced.

CATACLY'SM, S. [*cataclysme*, Gr.] a violent flowing of water. An inundation; generally used for the flood or general deluge, by learned authors; but should not be adopted as a common word.

CATACO'MBS, S. [from *cata*, Gr. and *cumbae*] subterraneous caverns for the burial of the dead.

CATALE'PSIS, S. [Gr. from *catalambano*] a disease wherein a person loses the use of all his senses, his limbs continuing flexible, and remaining in whatever position they are placed, and his eyes being open all the while.

CA'TALOGUE, S. [*catalogos*, Gr.] a list of things, wherein they are mentioned in separate lines or articles. The Britannic catalogue of stars composed by Flamstead, contains 2734 stars, and if it had been published by himself, would have been an everlasting glory to this nation.

CA'TAMITE, S. a person kept by the antient Romans and Italians, for the most infamous purposes.

CATAMOU'NTAIN, S. a fierce animal resembling a cat.

CATAPLA'SM, S. [from *cata*, Gr. and *plasso*, Gr.] a poultice, made of boiled herbs, &c. of the consistence of pap.

CA'TARACT, S. [from *catarractes*] a precipice in the middle of a river caused by a rock stopping its stream, from whence the water falls with great violence and noise. Among the most remarkable are those of the Nile and Danube, and that of Niagara, in America, of which our late conquests have supplied us with a very minute and accurate description. In Medicine, a total or partial loss of fight, from a little film or pellicle which swimming in the aqueous humour of the eye, gets before the pupil, and intercepts the rays of light.

CATA-

CATARRH, S. [from κατα, and ρεω] In Medicine, a defluxion of ferious matter from the head, &c. arising from a cold, or diminution of infenfible perspiration.

CATARRHAL, or CATARRHOUS, Adj. proceeding from a catarrh or cold.

CATASTROPHE, S. [Gr.] In Poetry, the change, or revolution in the last act of a play. It is either fimple or implex; fimple when there is no change in the ftate of the principal perfon, nor any difcovery, or unravelling, the plot being only a meer paffage from anxiety to repofe. The implex is, where the perfon undergoes a change of fortune, fometimes by means of a difcovery, and fometimes without. Figuratively, a dreadful event or accident.

CATCAL, S. a kind of whiftle, ufed at play-houfes, to fhow difapprobation of any dramatic performance.

To CATCH, V. A. [preter, I catched, or caught, I have catched, or have caught, from katfen, Belg.] to feize on fuddenly, with the hand. To purfue, or take what is running from one. To receive any thing falling. To receive a difeafe by infection; to contract. To feize fuddenly, to burn. " The fparks fhould catch his axle tree." Dryd. Applied to language, to enfnare a perfon in difcourfe, to feize fome unguarded expreffion in order to turn it to the difadvantage of the fpeaker. To captivate, or charm. " The foothing arts that catch the fair." To catch at, to endeavour to lay hold on, to make an offer to feize. " Saucy lictors will catch at us." Shak. Ufed neuterly, to be infectious, to fpread.

CATCH, S. the act of feizing, or taking any thing. A taint. Any thing which fastens by a fpring, or by entering into a loop. " The catch of a door." In Mufic, a fhort fong, and fet fo that the fingers fhall perform their feveral parts in quick fucceffions.

CATCHER, S. a perfon or thing that catches.

CATCH POLL, S. a word of contempt for a bailiff, or his followers.

CATECHETICAL, Adj. [from κατηχεω] confifting of queftions and anfwers.

CATECHETICALLY, Adv. by way of queftions and anfwers.

To CATECHISE, V. A. [from κατηχεω, catechifo, Gr. to inftruct by afking queftions] to afk a perfon queftions. To examine, to interrogate.

CATECHISER, S. one who teaches the catechifm. One who queftions, or examines.

CATECHISM, S. [from κατηχεω] the doctrines of Chriftianity, by way of queftion and anfwer.

CATECHIST, S. [κατηχιστης, Gr.] one who inftructs perfons in the principles of religion, by queftion and anfwer.

CATECHUMEN, S. [κατηχουμενος, Gr.] in the primitive church, a candidate for baptifm, having privately learnt the principles of Chriftianity.

CATEGORICAL, Adj. pofitive, in oppofition to hypothetical; abfolute; affirmative; adequate.

CATEGORICALLY, Adj. pofitively; expreffly; abfolutely.

CATEGORY, S. [κατηγορημα, Gr.] in Logic, an affemblage of all the beings ranged under one kind or genus; called in Latin, a predicament. According to Ariftotle, all our ideas may be divided into the ten following claffes, or categories, viz. Subftance, quantity, quality, relation, action, paffion, time, place, fituation or habit; fo that under fubftance or the firft are comprifed all fubftances, and under the nine others all accidents.

CATENARIAN, Adj. [from catena, Lat. a chain] relating to or refembling a chain.

To CATENATE, V. A. [from catena, Lat.] to chain, or faften with a chain.

CATENATION, S. [from catena, Lat.] the act of linking together. A connexion.

To CATER, V. N. to provide food or victuals; ufed with the particle for.

CATERER, S. a man who provides victual; a purveyor.

CATERESS, S. a woman who buys in provifions for a family.

CATERPILLER, S. in Natural Hiftory, a reptile, from whence butterflies or moths are produced, the numerous wonders to be found in this fpecies of animals, are well difplayed in Goedart's hiftory of infects; the Spectacle of Nature, Lewenhoek's dreams; and Swammerdam's book of nature.

To CATERWAUL, V. N. to make a noife refembling that of cats in their rutting time. To abandon one's felf to luft.

CATES, S. [keter, Belg.] nice and elegant food; nice cakes.

CATHARPINGS, S. fmall ropes in a fhip, running in little blocks from one fide of the fhrouds to the other, near the deck: ufed to force the main fhrouds tight, for the greater fecurity of the mafts, when the fhip rolls.

CATHARTIC, CATHARTICAL, Adj. [from καθαρτικος, of καθαιρω, Gr.] cleanfing, applied in Medicine to thofe medicines which cleanfe the body by ftool; but in a more general fenfe, to all medicines which cleanfe the body. Figuratively, any thing which cleanfes from crime or impurities. " Cathartics of the mind." Dec. of Piety.

CATHEDRAL, Adj. [from cathedra, Lat.] epifcopal, belonging to a cathedral, or metropolitan church. In familiar language, old, antique, folemn, or venerable.

CATHEDRAL, S. [from cathedra, Gr. a

feat) the chief church of a diocese, where divine service is sung, the bishop, prebends, and the rest of the chapter have seats; and where the bishop holds a court.

CATHERINE-PEAR, S. (pronounced *cattern-pear*) in Gardening, an early pear, with a remarkable red coat on that side which is near the Sun, the other side being yellow.

CATHETER, S. (Gr.) in Surgery, a hollow probe or instrument.

CATHETUS, S. in Geometry, a line falling perpendicularly on another line.

CATHOLIC, Adj. (*καθολικος*, Gr.) universal, true. *Roman Catholick*, is a title which the papists arrogate to themselves, to signify that all other religious professions are schisms or heresies. Catholic king, or majesty, is the title of the king of Spain, which was first borne by Ferdinand, and as Columbiere says, given him on account of his expulsion of the Moors.

CATHOLICON, S. a remedy for all disorders. Figuratively, an universal preservative.

CATLING, S. (*katt kin*, Teut.) in Surgery, a dismembering knife.

CATMINT, S. in Botany, the *nepeta*, or *mentis*, Lat. and *herbes aux chats*. It is ranged by Linnæus in the first sect of his 14th class.

CATOPTRICAL, Adj. relating to catoptrics.

CATOPTRICS, S. (plural from *καλoπτρω*, Gr. a looking glass) that part of optics which treats of the laws of light reflected from mirrors.

CAT-PIPE, S. the same as *catcal*, an instrument which affords a shrill, squeaking and disagreeable sound. "Some fongsters put them out of their road—are mere catpipes." L'E.tr.

CATS-EYE, S. among jewellers, a stone of the opal kind, but far inferior to it in beauty. It is naturally of a femicircular figure, and flat at bottom.

CATS-FOOT, S. in Botany, an herb, named also *ale-hof*, or ground-ivy.

CAT-STICK, S. a round stick, generally made of part of a broom-stick, used by boys to strike the little round piece of wood, called a *cat*. See CAT.

CATTLE, S (*katl-cyl*, Belg. Minshew derives it from *κατθεω*, or *κατθεσις*, Gr. to drive) four-fooved animals, distinguished into black *cattle*, such as horses, oxen, bulls, cows, and their young; and into small *cattle*, such as rams, ewes, lambs, goats, &c. Figuratively, persons; a word of reproach.

CAVALCADE, S. (from *cavalcade*, Fr. or *cavala*, Ital. a horse) a grand pompous procession on horse-back, or in coaches.

CAVALIER, S. (pronounced *cavaleer*, from *cavalier*, Fr.) a knight, gentleman, or soldier who rides; a horse-man. A reproachful term to those who adhered to king Charles, in the great rebellion.

CAVALIER, Adj. gay, war-like, brave, polite; also proud, haughty.

CAVALIERLY, Adv. bravely, politely, disdainfully.

CAVALRY, S. (*cavaliere*, Fr.) soldiers who fight and march on horse-back.

To CAVATE, V. A. (from *cavatum*, Lat.) to scoop, to bore. To make hollow.

CAUDLE, S. (*chaud-eau*, Fr. *chaudi-r*) a liquor used by women in their lying-in, being both diaphoretic and balsamic.

CAVE, S. (*cave*, Fr. *cavea*, Lat.) a hollow place made in a rock, or under ground. Figuratively, an hollow thing.

CAVEAT, S. (Lat. let him beware) in Law, a process in the spiritual court to stop the probate of a will, or the granting letters of administration.

CAVERN, S. (*caverna*, Lat.) a hollow place under ground.

CAVERNED, Adj. full of caverns, hollow, under-minded; dwelling in a cavern. "No *cavern'd* hermit." Pope.

CAVERNOUS, Adj. full of caverns.

CAUGHT, Participle preter of CATCH.

CAVIARE, CAVEARE, CAVIER, S. (*caviare*, Ital.) the hard roes of sturgeon salted, made into small cakes, and dried in the sun. They are eat with oil and lemon juice, are brought from Archangel, in Muscovy; and much used by those countries where Lent is observed with any strictness.

To CAVIL, V. N. (*caviller*, Fr.) to raise frivolous objections. Actively, to object to, to raise impertinent and frivolous objections against. "Then *cavil* the conditions." Par. Lost.

CAVIL, S. a groundless, impertinent, objection.

CAVILLATION. S. a disposition of raising groundless objections.

CAVILLER, S. a person who makes frivolous objections.

CAVILLING, V. N. now in use instead of CAVILLATION.

CAVILLINGLY, Adv. objecting in a frivolous manner.

CAVILLOUS, Adj. fond of starting groundless objections.

CAVITY, S. (*cavitas*, Lat.) hollowness, a hollow place.

CAUL, S. (*cawl*, Brit.) the hinder part of a woman's cap; the silk netting in the inside of a wig. Figuratively, a kind of net. In Anatomy, the omentum, or reticulum, a membrane in the abdomen, which covers a great part of the guts, contains them in their place, and keeps those parts warm. Also a membrane, on the head of some children, at their birth.

CAULIFEROUS, Adj. bearing a stalk.

CAULIFLOWER, s. (generally pronounced *collyflower*, from *caulis*, Lat. a stalk and *flower*) in Botany, a species of cabbage; this plant was brought from Cyprus, and
though

though not brought to such perfection as to be sold in markets till 1660, yet since 1700, they have been so improved, that we have not only enough for our own use, but export vast quantities of them to Holland, and supply most nations in Europe with the seed; even in France, though situated in a warmer climate, and priding itself in its botanical perfection, very rarely can raise any before Michaelmas, whereas we have them in May, June, and July, and far exceeding any nation in Europe, either in goodness or size.

To CAULK, V. A. See CALK.

CAUSABLE, Adj. that which may be effected by the operation of some cause.

CAUSAL, Adj. [causalis, Lat.] that which causes; relating to causes; implying or containing causes.

CAUSALITY, S. [causalitas, low Lat.] the operation of a cause.

CAUSATION, S. [from cause, low Lat.] the power of producing an effect.

CAUSATIVE, Adj. [from causa, Lat.] that which expresses a cause.

CAUSE, S. [cause, Fr. of causa, Lat.] that which produces any thing; a first cause is that which operates of itself; a second cause is that which derives its power from some other. Figuratively; the reason or motive for any undertaking. In a Law sense, the matter in dispute, or subject of a law-suit; a party or side in any dispute.

To CAUSE, V. A. to produce; to effect; to be the author of.

CAUSELESSLY, Adv. without foundation; unjustly.

CAUSELESS, Adj. derived from no cause; uncaused; without just grounds, or motives. " My fears are causeless." Denham.

CAUSER, S. that which produces.

CAUSEY, or CAUSEWAY, S. [the first spelling is proper, the second erroneous, from chaussée, Fr.] a massive collection of stone, flakes, &c. serving as a narrow path in wet or marshy places, or as a mole to retain the waters of a pond, or prevent a river from overflowing the lower grounds.

CAUSTIC, or CAUSTICAL, Adj. [from καιω, Gr. to burn] in Medicine, that which operates like fire.

CAUSTIC, S. a remedy which operates like fire, by destroying the part to which it is applied, and by rarifying the humours underneath, discharges the aqueous parts, and produces a kind of dry crust. It is used to eat off proud flesh, &c.

CAUTELOUS, Adj. [cauteleux, Fr.] wary, cautious, circumspect, including the weighing the consequences of a thing in one's mind; also cunning, treacherous.

CAUTELOUSLY, Adv. warily; cautiously; cunningly.

CAUTERIZATION, S. [from cautérise] the consuming flesh by hot irons, or caustic medicines.

To CAUTERIZE, V. A. [cautériser, Fr.]

in Surgery, to consume by the application of a cautery.

CAUTERY, S. [from καιω, Gr.] in Medicine, an application which destroys the texture of the parts by its violent activity, used to burn, sear, or eat through some solid part of the body.

CAUTION, S. [Fr. cautio, Lat.] a prudent manner of acting, wherein a person weighs the consequences of an undertaking; wariness; foresight. Provision made to prevent any particular event, or evil; warning.

CAUTIONARY, Adj. given as a security.

CAUTIOUS, Adj. [from cautus, Lat.] wary; opposed to rash, or thoughtless; watchful.

CAUTIOUSLY, Adv. warily.

CAUTIOUSNESS, S. the guarding against any bad consequence, or preventing any danger; a prudent, wary conduct; circumspection.

To CAW, V. N. to make a noise like a crow, &c.

To CEASE, V. N. [cesser, Fr.] to forbear or discontinue; to rest; to be extinct or fail; to put a stop or an end to.

CEASELESS, Adj. without intermission, pause, or respite; eternally.

CECUTIENCY, S. [cæcutientia, Lat.] a tendency to blindness, a dimness of sight, wherein a person can but just distinguish objects.

CEDAR, S. [cedrus, Lat.] in Botany, a tree, a native of mount Libanus, its wood is esteemed incorruptible, and was made use of by Solomon in building the temple; an oil is extracted from it which is reputed to be a great preserver of books and parchments, and is mentioned as indued with that quality by classic authors. It is an ever-green; prodigious thick, and resembles a pyramid.

CEDRINE, Adj. [cedrinus, Lat.] belonging to the cedar-tree.

To CEIL, V. A. [cælo, Lat.] to cover the inner roof of a building.

CEILING, S. [from cæl] the upper part of roof of a room, or a lay or covering of plaister over laths, nailed on the bottom of the joists, which bear the floor of an upper room.

To CELEBRATE, V. A. [celebro, Lat.] to make honourable mention of, including the idea of superior excellence and veneration; to praise or commend. To perform the solemn rites of any particular day.

CELEBRATION, S. [from celebratum, of celebro, Lat.] the performance of any rite; praise, fame, renown.

CELEBRIOUS, Adj. [celeber, Lat.] famed, renowned, celebrated.

CELEBRIOUSNESS, S. renown, fame.

CELEBRITY, S. [celebritas, Lat.] renown, fame.

CELERITY, [celeritas, Lat.] swiftness, opposed to slowness; velocity; rapidity.

CELERY, S. in Botany, a species of parsley, used in salads.

5   CELES-

CELESTIAL, Adj. [*cælestis*, Lat.] In the heavenly regions, applied to futuation; angelical.

CELESTIALLY, Adv. heavenly, angelically.

CELIBACY, S. [from *cælebs*, Lat.] the unmarried state.

CELIBATE, S. [from *cælibatus*, Lat.] a single life. See CELIBACY.

CELL, S. [*cella*, Lat. καλος, Gr. and חלל Heb.] a hollow place; a little apartment, wherein the ancient monks used to dwell; a small apartment in a prison. In Anatomy, little bags, bladders, or cavities wherein fluids are lodged. In Botany, the hollow places in the halks or pods of plants; the little divisions in beehives, in which the honey is stored; their hexagonal form gives us no inconsiderable idea of their prudence, or rather the wisdom of providence, because it is the only form in which they could have framed them to lose less room by interstices, or to have made them more capacious. The circle, triangle or square, could not have served their purpose so well, and their piecing on the only figure, which human prudence could have contrived for their benefit, shews them to be animated by a principle equal to that of human reason in this case, and reminds us that God is every where ordering all things by his wisdom, as well as sustaining them by his power.

CELLAR, S. [*cella*, Lat.] a place under ground for keeping stores.

CELLARAGE, S. cellar-room.

CELLULAR, Adj. [*cellula*, Lat.] abounding in little cells or cavities.

CEMENT, S. [*cæmentum*, Lat.] any glutinous substance used to stick things together. Bacon mentions a cement made of flour, whites of eggs, and stones powdered, which, he says, becomes as hard as marble. Among Chemists, the matter used for joining their veslels together. Figuratively, that which unites.

To CEMENT, V. A. to unite; to join.

To CEMENT, V. N. to join together in such a manner as not to be easily divided.

CEMENTATION, S. the act of joining by cement. Among Refiners, the art of purifying metals by a cement made of bricks, crocus martis, and verdris, alum, vitriol, salt, bloodstone, nitre, sulphur, sal ammoniac, sal gem, &c.

CEMETRY, S. [κοιμητηριον, Gr.] a church yard, or burying ground.

CENOBITICAL, Adj. [from *cænos*, and *βιος*, Gr.] living in community. "Cænobitical, and a monastical nuns." *Stillingfleet.*

CENSER, S. [*encensoir*, Fr.] the vessel in which incense is burnt.

CENSOR, S. [Lat.] a Roman magistrate employed to inspect and correct the people. Used by moderns to signify a person given to find fault and censure.

CENSORIAN, Adj. [from *censor*] relating to a censor.

CENSORIOUS, Adj. addicted to find fault with the actions or productions of others; a word of reproach including ill-natured severity to the person guilty of it. "Censorious of his neighbours." *Watts.*

CENSORIOUSLY, Adv. in a severe, censorious manner.

CENSORSHIP, S. the office of a *censor.*

CENSURABLE, Adj. deserving censure; blameable.

CENSURE, S. [*censura*, Lat.] the act of blaming; a reproof, or reprimand. In Ecclesiastical Government, a punishment inflicted on a person.

To CENSURE, V. A. to reprove a person publicly; to reprimand; blame; or find fault with; to condemn.

CENSURER, S. a person who is fond of censuring; one who is addicted to reproving others for their defects.

CENT, S. [an abbreviation of *centum*, Lat.] used to express the profit or loss arising from the sale of any commodity, the rate of commissions, &c. and signifies the proportion or sum lost, or gained, &c. in every 100, thus 5 per cent. loss, implies that the seller hath lost 5 pounds on every 100 pounds.

CENTAUR, S. [*centaurus*, Lat.] an imaginary being, represented by ancient poets, as composed partly of the human and partly of the brute species. In Astronomy, a constellation in the south hemisphere.

CENTISMAL, S. [*centesimus*, Lat.] the hundredth place in decimal arithmetic.

CENTIPEDE, S. [from *centum*, Lat.] a venomous insect, in the West-Indies, so called from its having a prodigious number of feet.

CENTLIVRE, Mrs. Susanna. This lady was daughter of one Mr. Freeman of Holbeach in Lincolnshire, who altho' he had been possessed of no inconsiderable estate, yet being a dissenter, and a zealous parliamentarian, was at the time of the restoration extremely persecuted, as were also the family of his wife, who was daughter of Mr. Markam, a gentleman of a good estate at Lynn Regis in Norfolk, but of the same political principles with Mr. Freeman, so that his estate was confiscated, and he himself compelled to fly to Ireland. How long he staid there I have not been able to trace, nor whether our authoress, who from a comparison of concurring circumstances, I imagine, must have been born about 1680, drew her first breath in that kingdom, or in England. These are particulars all her historians have been silent in regard to, yet I am apt to conjecture that she was born in Ireland, as I think it probable her mother might not return to her native country, till after the death of her husband, which happened when this girl was only three years old. Be this as it will, we find her left to the wide world by the death of her mother also, before she had completed her twelfth year. Whincop relates a romantic story of her in a very early period of her life, which although he seems mili-

ken in some parts of her history, (at least either he or Jacob must have been so) having made her father survive her mother, and even to have married again before his death, yet as he seems to have taken pains in collecting many circumstances of her life which are no where else related, I cannot think myself author-sed entirely to omit it. He tells us that after her father's death, finding herself very ill treated by her stepmother, she determined, though almost destitute of money and every other necessary, to go up to London to seek a better fortune than what she had hitherto experienced. That as she was proceeding on her journey on foot, she was met by a young gentleman from the university of Cambridge, (whose name, by the way he informs us of, and was no other than the afterwards well known Anthony Hammond, Esq) who was so extremely struck with her youth and beauty, and so affected with the distress which her circumstances naturally declared in her countenance, that he fell instantly in love with her, and enquiring into the particulars of her story, soon prevailed on her inexperienced innocence to seize on the protection he offered her, and go with him to Cambridge, where, equipping her in boy's cloaths, he introduced her to his intimates at college as a relation who was come down to see the university, and pass some time with him there; and that they continued this intercourse for some months, till at length, fired perhaps with possession, or perhaps afraid that the affair would be discovered at the university, he persuaded her to come to London, providing her however with a considerable sum of money, and a letter of recommendation to a gentlewoman of his acquaintance in town, sealing the whole with a promise, which however it does not appear he ever performed, of speedily following her to London, and there renewing their amorous intercourse. If this story is true, it must have happened when she was extremely young; Whincop, as well as the other writers acknowledging that she was married in her fifteenth year to a nephew of the late Sir Stephen Fox. But that gentleman not living with her above a twelve month, her wit and beauty soon procured her a second husband, whose name was Carrol, and who was an officer in the army, but he having the misfortune to be kill'd in a duel within about a year and half after their marriage, she became a second time a widow. This loss was a severe affliction to her, as she appears to have sincerely loved this gentleman. Partly perhaps to divert her melancholy, but chiefly it is probable for the sake of a support, she now applied to her pen, and became a votary to the muses, and it is under this name of Carrol that some of her earlier pieces were published. Her first attempt was in tragedy, in a play called the Perjured Hus-

band; yet her natural vivacity leading her afterwards more to comedy, we find but one more attempt in the buskin among eighteen dramatic pieces which she afterwards wrote.

Such an attachment she seems to have had to the theatre, that she even became herself a performer, though it is probable of no great merit, as she never rose above the station of a country actress. However, she was not long in this way of life, for in 1706, performing the part of Alexander the Great, in Lee's Rival Queens, at Windsor, where the court then was, she wounded the heart of one Mr. Joseph Centlivre, yeoman of the mouth, or in other words, principal cook to her majesty, who soon after married her, and after passing several years happily together, she died at his house in Spring-Garden, Charing-Cross, on the 1st of December, 1723, and was buried in the parish of St. Martin's in the Fields.

Thus did she at length happily close a life, which at its first setting out was overclouded with difficulty and misfortune. She for many years enjoyed the intimacy and esteem of the most eminent wits of the time, viz. Sir Richard Steele, Mr. Rowe, Budgell, Farquhar, Dr. Sewell, &c. and very few authors received more tokens of esteem and patronage from the Great; to which however the consideration of her sex, and the power of her beauty, of which she possessed a considerable share, might, in some degree, contribute.

Her disposition was good-natured, benevolent and friendly, and her conversation if not what could be called witty, was at least sprightly and entertaining. Her family had been warm party folks, and she seemed to inherit the same disposition from them, maintaining the strictest attachment to whig principles, even in the most dangerous times, and a most zealous regard for the illustrious house of Hanover. This party spirit, however, which breathes even in many of her dramatic pieces, procured her some friends and many enemies.

As a writer, it is no very easy thing to estimate her rank. It must be allowed that her plays do not abound with wit, and that the language of them is sometimes even poor, enervate, incorrect and puerile, but then her plots are busy and well conducted, and her characters in general natural and well marked. But as plot and character are undoubtedly the body and soul of comedy; and language and wit, at best, but the cloathing and external ornaments, it is certainly less excusable to shew a deficiency in the former, than in the latter. And the success of some of Mrs. Centlivre's plays plainly evince that the first will strike the minds of an audience more powerfully than the last, since her comedy of the Busy Body, which all the players had decried before its appearance, which Mr. Wilks

Wilks had even for a time abſolutely refuſed to play in, and which the audience came prejudiced againſt, rouſed their attention in deſpite of that prejudice, and forced a run of thirteen nights, while Mr. Congreve's Way of the World, which perhaps contains more true intrinſic wit, and unexceptionable accuracy of language than any dramatic piece ever written, brought on the ſtage with every advantage of recommendation, and when the author was in the height of reputation, could ſcarcely make its way at all. Nay, I have been confidently aſſured, that the very ſame great actor I mentioned juſt now, made uſe of this remarkable expreſſion with regard to her Bold Stroke for a Wife, viz. " that not only her play would be damn'd, but ſhe herſelf be damn'd for writing it." Yet we find it ſtill ſtanding on the liſt of acting plays, nor is it ever performed without meeting with the approbation of the audience, as do alſo her Buſy Body, Wonder, and Artifice.

That Mrs. Centlivre was very perfectly acquainted with life, and cloſely read the moods and manners of mankind, no one I think can doubt who reads her comedies ; but what appears to me the moſt extraordinary is, when we conſider her hiſtory, the diſadvantages ſhe muſt have labour'd under by being ſo early left to buſtle with the world, and that all the education ſhe could have had muſt have been owing to her own application and aſſiduity, when I ſay we conſider her as an abſolutely ſelf-cultivated genius. It is aſtoniſhing to find the traces of ſo much reading and learning as we meet with in many of her pieces, ſince for the drawing of the various characters ſhe has preſented us with, ſhe muſt have perfectly well underſtood the French, Dutch and Spaniſh languages, all the provincial dialects of her own, and ſomewhat even of the Latin, ſince all theſe ſhe occaſionally makes uſe of, and whenever ſhe does ſo, it is conſtantly with the utmoſt propriety and the greateſt accuracy. In a word, I cannot help giving it as my opinion, that if we do not allow her to be the very firſt of our female writers, ſhe has but one above her, and may juſtly be plac'd next to her predeceſſor in dramatic glory, the great Mrs. Behn. She wrote

1. Artifice. Comedy.
2. Baſſet Table. Com.
3. Beau's Duel. Com.
4. Bickerſtaff's Burying. F.
5. Bold Stroke for a Wife. C.
6. Buſy Body. Com.
7. Cruel Gift. Trag.
8. Gameſter. Com.
9. Gotham Election. Farce.
10. Love at a Venture. Com.
11. Love's Contrivances. Com.
12. Man's Bewitch'd. Com.
13. Marplot. Com.

14. Perjur'd Huſband. Trag.
15. Perplex'd Lovers. Com.
16. Platonic Lady. Com.
17. Stolen Heireſs. Com.
18. Wife well managed. Farce.
19. Wonder. Com.

CE'NTO, S. [Ital. and Lat. a cloak made of patches] in poetry, a piece wholly compoſed of verſes from other authors.

CENTRAL, Adj. [from centre] relating to, or placed in the centre, " Central earth." Pope. Dark at at the center. " Central night." Par. Loſt.

CE'NTRALLY, Adv. entirely ; perpendicularly ; relating to the centre of gravity. " Reſts centrally upon it." Dryd.

CE'NTRE, S. [centrum, Lat.] the point or middle of a line or plain, which divides it into two equal parts. Centre of a baſtion, is a point in the middle of the gorge. The centre of a battalion, is the middle of a battalion. The centre of a circle, is a point within it, from whence all lines drawn to the circumference are equal. Centre of gravity, is that point about which all the parts of a body balance each other. Centre of motion, is that point which remains at reſt, while all the other parts of a body move about it.

To CE'NTRE, V. A. to fix on ; to tend to ; to be collected together. " Thy joys are centred all on me alone." Prior. To meet, like rays in a centre.

CE'NTRIC, Adj. placed or ſituated in the centre central.

CENTRI'FUGAL, Adj. flying or receding from the centre.

CENTRI'PETAL, Adj. [from centrum, Lat. and peto, Lat.] tending towards the centre.

CE'NTRY, S. See SENTRY, or SENTINEL.

To CE'NTURIATE, V. A. [centurio, Lat.] to divide into hundreds.

CENTU'RION, S. [centurio, Lat.] a military officer who commanded an hundred men.

CE'NTURY, S. [centuria, Lat.] a hundred years, applied to time ; a hundred men applied to perſons.

CEPHA'LIC, Adj. [from κεφαλη, Gr. the head] remedies for diſorders in the head ; and are ſuch as attenuate the blood ſo, as to make it circulate through the capillary veſſels of the brain.

CERA'STES, S. [Gr. from κερας, Gr. a horn] a ſerpent ſuppoſed to have horns. " Ceraſtes horn'd." Par. Loſt.

CE'RATE, S. [from cera, Lat. wax] an ointment, made of oil, wax and other ingredients.

CE'RATED, Adj. [ceratus, Lat.] covered with wax.

CE'RECLOTH, S. a cloth ſpread with cerate or other ointment, or ſalve.

O g 2   CERE-

CEREMENTS, S. (from *cera*, Lat. wax) cloths dipped in melted wax, in which dead bodies were formerly wrapped.

CEREMONIAL, Adj. relating to a ceremony; consisting in mere external shew; formal. Used substantively, an external rite.

CEREMONIOUS, Adj. (from *ceremony*) consisting in external rites; superstitious; formal. Figuratively, awful. "O thou sacrifice, how *ceremonious*, solemn, and unearthly." *Shak.*

CEREMONIOUSLY, Adv. in a polite and civil manner, wherein a person shews more compliment than real friendship.

CEREMONY, S. (*ceremonia*, Lat.) an outward rite, or external form in religion. Polite address, or the manner used in order to shew civility in external behaviour.

CERTAIN, Adj. (*certus*, Lat.) resolved, determined; sure, clear, so as to admit no doubt.

CERTAINLY, Adv. without doubt, question, or scruple.

CERTAINTY, S. the state of being sure of a thing. A physical certainty, is that which depends on the evidence of sense; a mathematical certainty, is that which no man any ways doubts of, as that 100 is more than 1. A moral certainty, is that whose proof depends on clearness of testimony; and when these concur cannot be doubted of without obstinacy. Figuratively, an event which must necessarily happen.

CERTIFICATE, S. (*certifico*, low Lat.) a testimony in writing to certify any truth. Also any testimony.

To CERTIFY, V. A. (*certifier*, Fr.) to give certain notice of a thing. To attest.

CERTIORARI, S. (Lat.) a writ for the chancery or court of King's-bench, directed to an inferior court, to demand the records of a cause there depending; and is obtained on complaint that the party who seeks it, is not like to have a fair trial in the inferior court. *Finc. Nat. Brev. 242. 2. Lill. Abr. 257. 2. Holt's Hist. P. C. 225.*

CERTITUDE, S. (*certitude*, Lat.) freedom from doubt. See CERTAINTY.

CERVICAL, Adj. (from *cervicalis*, Lat.) situated in the neck; the cervical nerves, are so called from their being situated in the neck.

CERVIX, S. (Lat.) in Anatomy, the hinder part of the neck.

CERUMEN, S. (Lat.) ear-wax, at its first discharge from the glands it is fluid, but grows hard afterwards; the design of providence in securing this organ, both by the consistence, and bitterness of this excrement, from the inroads of insects, cannot be sufficiently admired and adored.

CERUSSE, S. (*cerussa*, Lat.) white-lead reduced to a powder, diluted with water on porphyry, and formed into a paste. As it is used by ladies as a beautifier, it will not be unreasonable to inform them, that it spoils the eye-fight, and if drawn in with the breath, causes incurable asthmas, and is a rank poison, if swallowed with the spittle; anticipates old age, and furrows with wrinkles "the human face divine." *Mills.*

CESARIAN, Adj. (from *Cæsar*) in Anatomy, the *cesarian* section, is the cutting a child from its mother's womb, either dead or alive. Those so delivered are called *cesars*, such were Julius Cæsar, Scipio Africanus, Manlius, and Edward VI.

To CESS, V. A. (of *assessus*, Ital.) to tax, to assess, to rate; or lay a rate upon.

CESS, S. (for *the word*) a tax; the act of levying rates, or taxing. Proportion, conception, bounds; compute, or the power of computing, or estimating. "The poor jade is wrong in the withers out of all *cess*." *Shak.*

CESSATION, S. (*cessatio*, Lat.) a pause, rest, or stop. Figuratively, a truce.

CESSIBLE, Adj. giving way to a stroke with ease, or without resistance.

CESSION, S. (Fr. *cessio*, Lat.) the act of yielding without resistance. In Common Law, an act whereby a person transfers his right to another. In Civil Law, a surrender of a person's effects to his creditors, to avoid imprisonment, a kind of bankruptcy. In Ecclesiastic Law, the doing of some act, or assuming some charge, whereby a person's benefice becomes vacant; such as the accepting of a second living when the first is rated at more than 8 l. in the king's books.

CESSIONARY, Adj. having delivered all his effects. See CESSION.

CESTUS, S. (Lat.) a girdle, which the poets ascribe to Venus.

CETACEOUS, Adj. (from *cete*, Lat. a whale) of the whale kind.

C FAUT, S. in Music, one of the notes in the gamut.

CHAD, S. a round kind of a fish.

To CHAFE, V. A. (*echauffer*, Fr.) to warm by rubbing; to make sore by friction. "Like an angry boar, *chafed* with sweat." *Shak.* To make angry; neuterly, to grow angry or fret.

CHAFE, S. (from the *verb*) anger, heat, or pevish warmth.

CHAFER, S. (*ceafor*, Sax. *keber*, Belg. *krafer*, Teut.) a yellow beetle, with two antennæ or horns, making a very loud buzzing noise when flying, and appearing generally in the month of May, whence they are sometimes called *May-bugs*.

CHAFF, S. (*ceaf*, Sax. *kaf*, Belg.) the husks of corn, which is separated from the flour by winnowing. Figuratively, any thing worthless.

To CHAFFER, V. N. (*kaufen*, Belg. to buy) to make a bargain. To haggle, to buy, to truck or exchange.

CHAFFERER, S. one who buys, or endea-

deavours to purchase a thing cheap ; a haggler.

CHAFFERY, S. buying, or selling. Traffic.

CHAFFINCH, S. according to *Phillips* a song bird so called from its delighting in chaff.

CHAFFY, Adj. consisting of chaff, like chaff. Light.

CHAFFING-DISH, S. an utensil to contain coals for warming; keeping any thing warm ; sometimes placed on tables, and fitted with a handle.

CHAGRIN, S. [pronounced *shagreen*, from *chagrine*, Fr.] unevenness of temper, ill-humour ; displeasure, peevishness.

To CHAGRIN, V. A. (*chagriner*, Fr.) to tease ; vex, or make uneasy.

CHAIN, S. [*chaine*, Fr.] a collection of round pieces of metal linked together. An ornament used round the neck by several magistrates. Iron links, with which beast or prisoners are secured. In Surveying, a series of iron links, used for measuring land. Figuratively, in the plural, a state of slavery. A series of things dependant on each other.

To CHAIN, V. A. [from the noun] to secure, or confine with a chain. To enslave. " Who *chained* his country." *Pope.* To unite in friendship. " In this vow do *chain* my soul with thine." *Shak.*

CHAIN-PUMP, S. a double pump used in large English vessels, which yields a great quantity of water.

CHAIN SHOT, S. two half bullets fastened together by a chain, used at sea.

CHAIN-WORK, S. work with open spaces, like the links of a chain ; and not unlike phillgree work. " Nets of chequer-work and wreaths of *chain-work*." 1 *Kings* vii. 17.

CHAIR, S. [*chair*, Fr.] a seat for one person, with a back to it. The seat of justice, or authority. A covered carriage born by two men ; a sedan. To *take the chair*, implies that a person presides at an assembly, or club.

CHAIRMAN, S. one who presides at an assembly or club. One who carries a chair, or sedan.

CHAISE, S. [Fr.] an open carriage on two wheels drawn by a single horse. Also a vehicle drawn by two horses.

CHALCOGRAPHY, S. [from χαλκος Gr. and γραφω] the art of engraving, writing on brass.

CHALDER ; CHALDRON, CHAUDRON, S. a dry measure for coals, containing 12 sacks. The chaldron should weigh 2000 lb. On board ship, 21 chaldrons are allowed to the score.

CHALICE, S. [Fr. *cale*, Sax. *kelb*, Teut.] formerly used for a cup, or drinking vessel, with a foot to it. " I'll have prepared him, —a *chalice* for the nonce." *Shak.* The vessel

used at the celebration of the Lord's Supper.

CHALICED, Adj. [from *chalice*] formed in the shape of a cup, or having a cup ; " On *chaliced* flow'rs." *Shak.*

CHALK, S. [pronounced *chawk*, *caulk*, Brit.] a white mark, for its purity, exceeding all other marble. It is of great service in the heart-burn, in the worms, and when after milk is apt to curdle on the stomach ; scraped into four beer, it blunts its acidities, and recovers it.

To CHALK, V. A. to rub or mark, with chalk ; to measure with chalk. To direct ; point out. " *Chalk'd out* a way for others." *Dryd.*

CHALKY, Adj. abounding with chalk ; white with chalk.

To CHALLENGE, V. A. (*challenger*, Fr.) to dare a person to fight. Figuratively, to dare a person to enter into a literary contest. To accuse. " Whom I may rather *challenge* for unkindness." *Shak.* To lay claim to as a right.

CHALLENGE, S. a provocation, or summons to fight. A claim of a thing, as a right. In Law, an exception against a person.

CHALLENGER, S. one who defies or provokes, another person to fight him. A claimant. In Law, one who objects to a juror.

CHALYBEATE, Adj. [from *chalybs*, Lat. steel] impregnated with steel.

CHAM, S. [Pers. mighty lord, Sclav.] the title of the sovereign princes in Tartary.

CHAMBER, S. [*chambre*, Brit. *chambre*, Fr.] any room between the ground floor, and garrets of a house. A retired room. An apartment, occupied as a public office or court of justice. Any cavity. A species of ordinance. " Cannons, demicannons, *chambers*." *Camden.*

To CHAMBER, V. N. to be wanton with woman.

CHAMBERER, S. [from *chamber* and *er*, implying an agent, from *wer*, Sax. a man] one that is addicted to women, and to intrigue.

CHAMBERLAIN, S. [*kammerling*, Teut. *chambellan*, Fr.] one who has the care of a chamber. The Lord great *chamberlain*, is the fixth officer of the crown, has the provision of every thing at the house of lords, disposes of the sword of state; dresses and undresses the king at his coronation, having for his fee, the king's-bed, all the furniture of his chamber, his night clothes, the silver bason in which he washes, and all the towels. Lord *chamberlain* of the houshold, has the oversight of all the officers belonging to the king's chambers, excepting the precinct of the bed-chamber. In great towns, a receiver of their rents and revenues. In London, the

the *chamberlain* has the cognizance of all disputes between masters and apprentices, and makes free, &c. Sir Stephen Theodore Janssen, the present *chamberlain* of London, is an ornament and an honour to human nature.

CHA'MBERLAINSHIP, S. the office and duty of a *chamberlain*.

CHA'MBER-MAID, S. a maid-servant, who attends and takes care of the chambers.

To CHA'MBLET, V. N. [*zambelat*, Arab. watered cloth] to be variegated; to appear like cloth or silk, watered by the calender. "Some have the veins more varied or *chamblited*." Bacon.

CHAME'LION, S. [χαμαιλεων, Gr.] See CHAMELEON, though this is the proper spelling.

CHA'MOMILE, S. [χαμαι, Gr. on the ground, and μηλον, Gr. a fruit] In Botany, a plant so called, from its trailing along the ground. Hoffman says, that the flowers of this simple are more beneficial and kind to the intestines, than those of any other plant, and prescribes them for clysters; but experience seems to have given it a greater recommendation than his pen; since nothing is more common than clysters of this sort.

To CHAMP, V. A. [*champoyer*, Fr.] to grind any thing hard with the teeth, so as to render it fit to swallow.

CHA'MPAIGN, S. [*compagne*, Fr.] a flat, open country.

CHA'MPARTY, or CHA'MPERTY, S. [from *champ*, Fr. lands and *partir*, Fr. to divide] in Law, a contract made either with the plaintiff or defendant, for giving part of the thing sued for, to the person who undertakes to bear the charges of a suit, provided he succeeds therein. 1 Inst. 368. Those who are guilty of it, are liable to imprisonment for three years, and a fine at the king's pleasure. 28 Edw. 1. c. 11.

CHA'MPIGNON, S. [Fr. pronounced *shampinion*] in Botany, a plant of a roundish form like a button, the upper part and stalk of which are very white, the under when opened of a livid flesh colour, but the fleshy part, when broken very white, when suffered to grow they will expand till the head becomes flat, or parallel to the horizon. The seeds of this vegetable were for some time unknown, till discovered by Dr. Fothergil, an eminent physician and naturalist.

CHA'MPION, S. [Fr. *campion*, Ital.] a person who undertakes a combat in behalf of another. The king's champion is an officer, who, while he is at dinner on his coronation day, challenges any to contest the king's right with him in combat; after which the king drinks to him, and sends him a gilt cup and cover full of wine, which he keeps as a fee.

CHA'NCE, S. [Fr.] a word which implies that an event was unexpected, or that the

cause of a thing is unknown. A future event; an unforeseen calamity or misfortune; a thing which was not intended; the manner of deciding things, whose direction is not reducible to any rules. "A *chance* at cards." No *chance*, is used to imply no probability of succeeding, or that the number of chances against a person is so many, that those for him are comparatively none.

To CHANCE, V. N. to happen unexpectedly.

CHA'NCE-MEDLEY, S. the killing of a person, without design.

CHA'NCEABLE, Adj. without design, accidental. "*Chanceable* coming in of Isabella" Sidney.

CHA'NCEL, S. [*chancel*, Norman Fr. the choir of a church] the eastern part of a church, from the altar to the rail that incloses it.

CHA'NCELLOR, S. [*chancelier*, Fr.] a word of various significations. The *lord high chancellor*, is the chief administrator of justice next the king, is invested with absolute power to mitigate the severity of the law in his decisions, has the disposure of all ecclesiastic benefices in the gift of the crown under 20 l. per ann. in the king's books, and takes place of all the nobility, excepting the royal family, and the archbishop of Canbury. *Chancellor of the Exchequer*, is an officer who takes care of the interest of the crown. *Chancellor of an University*, is the chief magistrate, who seals diplomas, letters of degrees, and defends the rights and privileges of the place. *Chancellor of the order of the Garter*, seals the commissions and mandates of the chapter, keeps the register and delivers transcripts of it under the seal of their order.

CHA'NCELLORSHIP, S. the office and duty of a chancellor.

CHA'NCERY, S. the highest court of judicature in this kingdom, except the parliament, whereof the lord chancellor is chief judge. Its jurisdiction is ordinary, or legal; and extraordinary or absolute. The ordinary court is that in which the lord chancellor observes the method of the common law; the extraordinary, that wherein he has an unlimited power, which he exercises in mitigating the rigour of the law, and giving remedy by bill and answer.

CHA'NCRE, S. [Fr. pronounced *shanker*] in Surgery, a tubercle which has its seat in the membranous humour that fills the vesicular texture. An ulcer usually arising from an inordinate use of women.

CHA'NCROUS, Adj. that has the qualities of a *chancre*.

CHANDELIER, S. [from *chandel*, Fr. a candle] a branch for holding candles.

CHA'NDLER, S. [*chandelier*, Fr.] a person who makes and sells candles.

To CHA'NGE, V. A. [*changer*, Fr.] to give

give one thing for another; to refign one thing for another; to give a perfon the value of money in other coin. To alter. Figuratively, to make a thing better or worfe. Applied to the moon, to increafe, or decreafe.

CHA'NGE, S. the act of giving any thing for another. Novelty; in ringing, the alteration of the order in which fets of bells are rung.

CH'ANGEABLE, Adj. that which may be changed; inconftant; fickle; applied to colour, that which appears different in different pofitions.

CH'ANGEABLENESS, S. want of confiftency, ficklenefs; what is liable to alteration.

CH'ANGEABLY, Adv. fo as to be fubject to alteration; inconftantly.

CH'ANGEFUL, Adj. altering upon flight grounds; fickle; inconftant.

CH'ANGELING, S. a child taken in room of another. A fool, natural, or ideot; one apt to alter his fentiments frequently.

CHA'NNEL, S. [canal Fr. canalis, Lat.] the hollow in which running waters flow; the arm of a fea, or a narrow river. Figuratively, a hollow place worn by any running ftream. "Scalding tears that wore a channel." Dryd. In architecture, the gutter or furrow of a pillar.

To CHA'NT, V. A. [chanter, Fr.] to fing; to celebrate in fongs or hymns; to found a chord with the voice to any mufical inftrument.

CHA'NT, S. [from the verb] a fong; a tune; a tune ufed in a cathedral.

CHANTER, S. [from chant and en of wor, Sax. a man] a finger in a cathedral; a fongfter.

CH'ANTRESS, S. a female finger.

CHA'NTRY, S. a chapel, endowed for priefts to fay the mafs in.

CHA'OS, S. [Gr.] the original confufed mafs of matter out of which all vifible things were made, called by Mofes, Tohu, Tabu, Heb. and which feems to have been believed by almoft all nations, as may be collected from Burnet's Archæologia Philofophica, and the notes in Le Clerc's edition of Grotius, on the truth of the Chriftian religion. Any confufed irregular mixture.

CHAO'TIC, Adj. refembling a chaos.

To CHAP, V. A. [kappen Belg.] to break into chinks by exceffive heat, applied to land; appear as if cut, applied to the effects of cold on the hands.

CHA'P, S. an opening or cleft in the ground, owing to exceffive drought.

CHA'P, S. [feldom ufed in the fingular, unlefs by anatomifts] the upper or under part of the mouth of a beaft.

CHA'PE, S. [chappe, Fr. chapa, Span.] the hook by which a fword is faftened to the fcabbard; the fteel ring by which a buckle is held to the ftrap.

CHA'PEL, S. [Fr. capella, Lat.] a little church; or fmall building, either adjoining to, or making part of a cathedral or church, or elfe built at a diftance from it, wherein divine fervice is performed; when at a diftance it is called a chapel of eafe. Likewife a name given to a printer's work-houfe, from that bufinefs being originally carried on in a chapel.

CHA'PELESS, Adj. nothing to faften it; no chape.

CHA'PELRY, S. the jurifdiction or limits of a chapel.

CHA'PLAIN, S. [capellanus, Lat.] one who performs divine fervice in a chapel; or is retained in the fervice, of fome noble perfonage to perform divine fervice, and inftruct the family in their duty to God. His majefty can retain as many as he pleafes, who have the power of holding as many benefices as he thinks proper to give them; an archbifhop may retain 8 chaplains, a duke or bifhop 6, a marquefs or earl 5, a vifcount 4, a baron 3, and a dutchefs, marchionefs, countefs and baronefs, being widows. 2; all which may purchafe a licence or difpenfation, and take two benefices with cure by 21 Hen. viii. c. 11.

CHA'PLAINSHIP, S. the office or revenue of a chaplain.

CHAPLESS, Adj. having no flefh.

CHAPLE'T, S. [chapelet, Fr.] a wreath of flowers to be worn round the head. In the romifh church a ftring of beads. In architecture, a little moulding, cut or carved in round beads.

CHAPMAN, S. [ceapman, Sax.] A buyer or feller.

CHA'PS, S. [plural of chap, ceaphes, Sax.] the mouth of a beaft of prey. Ufed vulgarly for the mouth of a human creature.

CHA'PT, or CHA'PPED, participle paff. of chap.

CHA'PTER, S. [chapitre, Fr. capitulum, Lat.] the divifion of a book; hence, to the end of the chapter, is a phrafe implying throughout; to the end. In Canon Law, a congregation of clergymen, under the dean, in a cathedral church.

CHA'R, S. in Natural Hiftory, a fifh, a kind of golden alpine trout, breeding in Winander mere, in Lancafhire, and other northern lakes.

CHA'R, S. [pronounced chair from care, Sax. care,] work done, by the day, by a woman.

To CHA'R, V. N. [pronounced chair] to do the occafional houfe work of a family.

CHA'RWOMAN, S. a woman, hired accidentally, or for old days, to clean a houfe or do other offices of a maid fervant.

CHA'RACTER, S. [Lat. χαρακτηρ, Gr.] a figure or mark to convey fome idea to the mind. A letter of the alphabet. The peculiarities of a perfon's hand-writing, diftinguifhing

guishing it from all others. An assemblage of virtues or vices, whereby one person is distinguished from another. Office, dignity or authority.

To CHA'RACTER, V. A. to engrave. " Thefe precepts or thy memory, fee thou *character*." Shakesp.

CHARACTERISTIC, CHARACTE-RI'STICAL, Adj. that which distinguishes from any thing of the same species.

CHARACTERI'STIC, S. a peculiar mark, or assemblage of qualities which distinguishes a person. In Grammar, the principal letter of a word which is preserved in most of its tenses and moods, derivatives, or compounds, serving to fix its etymology, or to ascertain its conjugation. Characteristic of a logarithm, is its index or exponent.

To CHARACTERISE, V. A. to describe a person or thing by the properties, which distinguish it from others. To mark with a peculiar stamp or form.

CHA'RCOAL, S. a kind of coal made of oak half burnt. That for powder mills is made of elder wood. The prodigious number of its pores deserves remark, there being according to microscopical observations, not less than 5,724,000 in a piece of an inch diameter. It is used generally in such works as require a strong clear fire; but as it foon destroys the elasticity of the air is very dangerous, very infidious, and destroys life gradually and imperceptibly.

To CHA'RGE, V. A. [*charger*, *tericter*, Ital.] to commit to a person's care, used with the particle *with*. To make a person debtor, to impute, or ascribe. To require as a duty, or impose as a task. To accuse. " His angels he charged with folly." Job iv. 18. To command peremptorily. To fill a space with inscriptions. " Charged with several parts of the Egyptian histories." Addis. Applied to fire-arms, to charge is to load.

CHA'RGE, S. a thing delivered to another's care. A command, precept or law. A commission, or post; accusation. Figuratively, the person entrusted to the care, protection, or custody of another. The exhortation of a judge to a jury. Expence or cost, generally used in the plural number. A quantity of money a person carries with him. " He had a great charge of money." In war, an attack, or onset. The quantity of powder, &c. with which fire-arms are loaded. In Heraldry, any figure or thing borne or represented in an efcutcheon, or coat of arms.

CHA'RGEABLE, Adj. requiring great sums of money; expensive; costly. Required of a person as a debt, duty or crime. " Some fault chargeable upon him." South. Liable to be blamed or accused, followed by with. " Chargeable with something warm." Spell. No 286.

CHA'RGEABLENESS, S. the quality of requiring much money to support it. Expensiveness, costliness.

CHA'RGEABLY, Adv. in a costly manner; at a great expence.

CHA'RGER, S. [*heber*, Belg.] a large dish.

CHA'RILY, Adv. in a deliberate, cautious manner, opposed to rashness.

CHA'RINESS, S. a deliberate and circumspect manner of proceeding; a nicety or delicacy. Scrupulousness

CHA'RIOT, S. [*char-rod*, Brit.] a covered four-wheeled carriage, having only back seats.

CHARIOTEE'R, S. a driver of a chariot.

CHA'RITABLE, Adj. [*charitable*, Fr.] inclinable to assist the afflicted and distressed with relief, do good even to enemies, and to pass the most favourable construction upon the words or actions of others.

CHA'RITABLY, Adv. in a kind, benevolent manner; without the least consciousness or malignity.

CHA'RITY, S. [*charité*, Fr. *charitas*, Lat.] a benevolent principle, exerting itself in acts of kindness and affection to all persons without respect to party or nation, and including in it not only a tender and affectionate regard for their interests, and a ready application of relief in their distresses, but a generous opinion of all their words and actions, putting the most favourable construction on both, even though the persons are our most inveterate enemies.

To CHA'RK, V. A. [*chiærigære*, Ital.] to burn to a coal, or cinder.

CHA'RLATAN, S. [Fr. *ciarlatano*, Ital. *ciarlare*, Ital. to trifle or prate,] a quack, a mountebank. " For charlatans can do no good," Hudib.

CHARLATA'NICAL, Adj. pretending to a knowledge of physic. Quackish.

CHA'RLATANRY, S. the practice of a quack. Figuratively, an endeavour to deceive by some pompous professions.

CHARLES'S WAIN, S. in Astronomy, seven remarkable stars in the constellation of Ursa Major, or the greater bear.

CHA'RM, [*charme*, Fr.] a kind of spell, supposed by the ignorant to have an irresistible influence; also any excellence which attracts or engages the affections.

To CHARM, V. A. to secure against evil by some spell. To influence by some excellence or pleasure.

CHA'RMER, S. a dealer in spells. One whose personal perfections attract admiration and love.

CHA'RMING, Part. [of charm] possessed of great perfections of person or mind, or other excellencies.

CHA'RMINGLY, Adv. in such a manner as to influence the mind irresistibly, and to
       convey

convey inexpressible pleasure.

CHA'RNAL-HOUSE, S. [charnier, Fr.] the place where the bones of the dead are deposited.

CHA'RT, S. [charta, Lat.] an hydrographical map, for the use of navigation. A plane chart is that in which the meridians are supposed parallel to each other, the parallels of latitude at equal distances, and the degrees of latitude and longitude every where equal. The globular chart invented by de la Hire, is a meridian projection, wherein the distance of the eye from the plane of the meridian is supposed equal to the sine of the angle of 45 degrees. This projection is the nearest of any to the nature of the globe.

CHA'RTER, S. [chartre, Fr.] in Law, a written evidence of things done between two parties. The king's charter, is where he makes a grant to any person or body politic; also the act of bestowing any privilege or right.

CHA'RTER-PARTY, S. [charta, or cartæ partie, Fr.] a deed indented, made between merchants and sea-faring-men, concerning their merchandise; settling the agreement in relation to fright between the merchant and commander, the latter of which is bound thereby to deliver the goods in good condition, at the place to which they are consigned; each party has a copy of the contract.

CHA'RTERED, Adj. invested with privileges by charter.

CHA'RY, Adj. [from cara, Sax. cautious, scrupulous.

To CHA'SE, V. A. [chasser, Fr.] to hunt. To pursue as an enemy. To drive from, or keep off; used with from. To render invisible, to drive from sight, applied to the stars; used with away. "Morn had chas'd away the flying stars." Dryd.

To CHA'SE METALS. See to EN-CHACE.

CHA'SE, S. hunting. The proper object of hunting. "A beast of chase." Dryd. pursuit; or the object of a person's actions. "Honour's the noblest chace." Grew. In Law, a large extent of woody ground, privileged for the reception of deer and game, somewhat less than a forest. Chase-guns, are those which are placed in the head or stern of a ship, the former of which are used when she is in pursuit of an enemy, and the latter when she is pursued herself.

CHA'SER, S. one who pursues, and endeavours to overtake.

CHA'SM, S. [χασμα, Gr.] a breach, a place unfilled, a vacant space.

CHA'STE, Adj. [chaste, Fr.] free from lust; free from any commerce with the other sex. True to the marriage bed; free from any obscenity.

To CHA'STEN, V. A. [chastier, Fr.] to correct or punish, to humble, or mortify.

No. VI.

"Chasten human pride." Prior.

To CHASTI'SE, V. A. to punish or afflict; to reduce to order or obedience.

CHASTI'SEMENT, S. correction, or punishment inflicted with a view of deterring a person from faults, any calamity.

CHA'STITY, S. [castité, Fr.] freedom from lust either in thought or deed. Free from immodest words.

CHASTI'SER, S. one who punishes.

CHA'STLY, Adv. in a manner consistent with the most rigorous modesty.

CHA'STNESS, S. freedom from incontinence, or any breach of modesty; abstinence from immodest expressions.

To CHA'T, V. N. [probably a contraction of the verb chatter] to talk on indifferent subjects, without any deep attention.

CHAT, S. trifling, and unimproving discourse. In Botany, the keys of trees. "Ash chats."

CHA'THAM, a town of Kent, adjoining to Rochester, and seated on the river Medway, it is the principal station of the royal navy; and the yards and magazines are furnished with all sorts of naval stores, as well as materials for building and rigging the largest men of war. The entrance into the river Medway is defended by Sherness and other forts; and, in the year 1757, by direction of the duke of Cumberland, several additional fortifications were begun at Chatham; so that now the ships are in no danger of an insult, either by land or water. It has a market on Saturdays, and two fairs, on May 15. and September 19, for horses, bullocks, and all sorts of commodities. It has a church, a chapel of ease, and a ship used as a church, for the sailors; it has likewise about 500 houses, mostly low, and built with brick; the streets are narrow and paved, and it contains about 5000 inhabitants. The principal employment of the labouring hands is ship-building in the king's yard, and private docks.

CHA'TTELS, S. [see CATTLE, bethyls, Belg.] any moveable possession. At present used only in law, for all things moveable and immoveable, which are divided into real and personal, of the latter sort are gold, silver, plate, jewels, furniture, cattle, &c. real, are such as concern the realty, lands and tenements, as a lease or rent for a term of years, interest in an advowson, statute merchants, &c.

To CHA'TTER, S. [caqueter, Fr.] to talk much, merrily in pastime. To make a noise by forcibly closing the teeth, from the effects of cold.

CHA'TTER, S. a noise like that of a pie. Impertinent talk.

CHA'TTERER, S. a person who spends his time in unimproving talk.

To CHAW, V. A. [kauwen, Belg. kewen, Teut.] to cut food into small pieces by the teeth

tenth. Figuratively, to endeavour to surmount a difficult point. " To see a jury *chew*, the prickles of unpalatable law." *Dryd.*

CHA'W, S. (perhaps a corruption of *jaw*) the mouth of a beast, or that part which he chaws with. " Put hooks into thy *chaws*." *Ezek* xxvii. 4.

CHE'AP, Adj. of small value, or worth; not dear.

To CHE'APEN, V. A. (*ceapan*, Sa.) ask the price of a commodity.

CHE'APLY, Adv. at a low price or rate; for less than it is worth.

CHE'APNESS, S. a relative term implying that a thing is purchased with little money.

CHE'AR, S. See CHEAR.

To CHE'AT, V. A. to deceive; to defraud, to impose upon.

CHE'AT, S. a fraud, an impostor. A person who imposes.

CHE'ATER, S. a tricker; an impostor.

To CHE'CK, V. A. (from *eschec*, Fr.) to stop a thing in motion, to chide, or reprove a person in such a manner as to make him decline the prosecution of a design. To compare the flourishing part of a draught or bill, with that which remains in the book from whence it was cut. To examine an account of another, by a private one kept by a person's self. To stop short by surprise; to interfere, to clash, to have a great restraint. " If love *check* once *with* business." *Bacon.* " It *checks* too strong upon me." *Dryd.*

CHE'CK, S. (*schach*, Teut.) a restraint, disappointment, repulse, reproof, a flight. A revolt. " Would not my wife *subjects take check* ?" *Shak.* A piece of paper with one end of it adorned with flourishes, which when cut out of a book, are generally divided to prevent forgery. A counter cypher to a bank bill. An account kept privately to examine that which is kept with a banker, or public office. A person who examines any account. Clerk of the check, has the management of the accounts relating to the pay of the yeomen of the guard, &c. A kind of linen with blue stripes crossing each other.

To CHE'CKER, or CHEQUER, V. A. (from *echets*, Fr. *chefs*) to vary with different colours. To variegate, to diversify.

CHE'CKER, CHE'CKER-WORK, S. any thing painted in squares, with different colours. Work whose colours change alternately, like those of the squares in a chess board.

CHE'EK, S. (*ceac*, *cheec*, *ceoca*, Sax.) the fleshy parts of each side of the face below the eye. Used by mechanics to express such parts of their works or tools as consist of two parts, parallel to and resembling each other. Cheek-tooth is the hinder tooth, or that which is situated behind the tusk or dog's tooth; the grinders. " The *cheek-tooth* of a great lion." *Joel* i. 6.

CHE'ER, S. (*chere*, Fr. an entertainment)

provisions for an entertainment; gaiety, or fullness of spirits, which rejoices the mind, and in a manner glitters on the face. Good *cheer* courage or fortitude of mind to sustain troubles without being dejected. " And they were all of *good cheer* " *Acts* xxvii. 36.

To CHE'ER, V. A. to animate, or incite. To raise the drooping hopes of one in a state of dejection. To make joyful, to gladden. " Hark ! a glad voice the lonely desert *cheers*.' *Pope.* To grow gay, or lively.

CHE'ERER, S. that which communicates joy.

CHE'ERFUL, Adj. abounding in gaiety, life, and spirits.

CHE'ERFULNESS, S. a disposition of mind undamped by dejection. Alacrity, vigour.

CHE'ERLESS, Adj. an absence of joy; or gaiety; sad, dejected, comfortless.

CHE'ERLY, Adv. in a gay, cheerful manner.

CRE'ERY, Adj. gay, joyful, chearful.

CHE'ESE, S. (*cyse*, Sax. *caws*, Brit. *caseus*, Lat.) a food made of milk, curdled by means of rennet. When new it loads the stomach, on account of its moisture and viscidity, but when of a tolerable age, will contribute to digest other food by the salts, with which it abounds. The art of making this necessary food, was, according to Pliny, introduced into this island by the Romans. The best reputed is that of Gloucestershire and Cheshire, tho' it must be noted that Cheddar cheese, is by all judges reckoned equal to Parmesan, and that the size of the cheeses made there is generally so great that a man can but just hand one of them to table. I myself have known one so large, that a young lady, of twelve years old, could fit within the hull of it, which had been scooped out, and had been intended as a present to lord Weymouth.

CHE'ESE-CAKE, S. in pastry, is made of soft curds, butter, and sugar.

CHE'ESE MONGER, S. one who deals in *cheese*; in London, the selling of butter, is likewise united to it as a branch of the same trade.

CHE'ESY, Adj. having the nature, qualities, form or taste of *cheese*.

CHELMSFORD, a town of Essex, with a good market on Fridays, and two fairs, viz. on May 17, and November 12, two days each, for cattle. It is seated on the road to Colchester between two rivers, over which there are bridges. It is a handsome, large, and well-frequented town, and takes its name from the river Chelmer. It is governed by a chief constable, has only one church, which is a very ancient and large Gothic structure, and three meeting-houses of the dissenters. The town consists of about 500 houses, which are, in general, pretty good; but the streets are paved only at the doors; however, the town lying on a small descent is always clean.

clean. There is here an excellent conduit, which contains several inscriptions, almost worn out by time; and it has such a supply of water, that it runs a hogshead and an half, and four gallons in a minute. Here the members for the county are chosen, and the affizes commonly held, as well as the four quarterly sessions. It is 43 miles S. of St. Edmond's-Bury, 27 S. E. by S. of Saffron-Walden, 23 N. E. of Gravesend, and 48 E. N. E. of London. Lon. 18. 5. lat. 51. 40.

CHE'MISTRY. See CHYMISTRY.

CHE'QUER, S. See CHECKER.

To CHE'RISH, V. A. [chérir, Fr.] to nourish a thing from an infant and infirm state, to one of strength and maturity; to help; to encourage; to protect.

CHERI'SHER, S. one who protects and encourages.

CHE'RRY, S. [cerise, Fr. cherogia, Ital.] In Gardening a fruit tree, with shining leaves its fruit grows on long pedicles, is roundish, or heart-shaped. It is supposed to have been first brought into Europe by Lucullus from Cerasus, a city of Pontus, in the year 680 of Rome, and about 120 years afterwards, i. e. A. D. 55, was introduced into this island. In Pharmacy, there is a simple water drawn from the stones of this fruit, which is reputed astringent.

CHE'RRY, Adj. resembling a cherry with regard to colour, red.

CHE'RUB, S. [כְּרוּב, Heb.] a celestial spirit, in the order of angels placed next to the seraphim.

CHERU'BIC, S. angelic, resembling a cherub.

CHERU'BIN, Adj. heavenly, angelical. "her cherubin look." Shak.

CHE'RVIL, S. [caerephyllum, Lat. from χαιρε, Gr.] In Botany, an umbelliferous plant, its principal umbel composed of several small ones called rays, has having itself no involucrum.

To CHE'RUP, V. N. [from chirp up] to make a noise by drawing in the air through the lips, after they are drawn into a kind of circle, to set a song bird a singing.

CHESHIRE, an English county-palatine, 50 miles in length, 33 in breadth, and is bounded on the E. by Staffordshire and Derbyshire, on the W. by Flintshire and Denbighshire, on the N. by Lancashire, and on the S. by Shropshire. It contains 14054 houses 164724 inhabitants, 13 market-towns, and 86 parishes. It sends 4 members to parliament, and the chief place is Chester. The principal rivers are the Dee, the Wever, and the Tame; but there are several small streams. The air and soil are very good, and the land is fitter for pasture than corn, for which reason they feed a great number of cattle; and from it we have very good cheese, well known over all the kingdom. Besides which there are very good salt-works, which

yield fine white salt; there are also mines of coal, and many meers and lakes.

CHESTER, the capital town or city of Cheshire, with two markets on Wednesdays and Saturdays, and three fairs, viz. on the last Thursday in February, for cattle; on July 5, and October 10, for cattle, Irish linen, cloves, hard-ware, hops, drapery, and Manchester goods. It is a place of great antiquity and is of a quadrangular, form; the walls are near 2 miles in circumference, and there are four gates, towards the four cardinal points. It has a strong castle, in which is the shire-hall, where all the causes belonging to the county-palatine are determined. By the bridge is a handsome water-house, and the principal streets are adorned with piazzas, under which are the tradesmens shops. It contains 10 parish churches besides the cathedral. It has almost a constant communication with Ireland; this and Holyhead being the principal places of taking shipping for Dublin. It is governed by a mayor, two sheriffs, 24 aldermen, sends two members to parliament, and is a bishop's see. It is a place of very considerable trade, and is 147 miles N. of Bristol, 40 N. W. of Shrewsbury, 39 W. S. W. of Manchester, 11 N. E. of Wrexham, and 182 N. W. of London. It gives title of earl to the Prince of Wales. Lon. 14. 33. lat 53. 18.

CHESS, S. [scheco, Fr. schaeck, Belg.] a game played with little round pieces of wood on a board divided into 64 squares. The antiquity of this game is so great, that it is not possible to trace its invention. Among the Chinese, it makes a considerable part of the education of their daughters, and seems to be as necessary a qualification as dancing among Europeans.

CHEST, S. [cyste, ceste, Sax.] a wooden box, greater than a trunk. The cavity of a human body from the neck to the belly, called the breast or stomach.

CHESTERFIELD, a town of Derbyshire, with a market on Saturdays, and seven fairs, viz. on Jan. 25, Feb. 28, April 3, May 4, and July 4, for cattle, horses, and pedlars ware; on Sept. 25, for cheese, onions, and pedlars ware; and on Nov. 25, for cattle, sheep, and pedlars ware. It is pleasantly seated on a hill, between two small rivers, and has the title of an earldom. It has a large handsome church, a free school, and several alms-houses. The sessions for the peace are held here for the N. part of the county. It is governed by a mayor, and the market is considerable for corn, lead, and country-commodities. The houses are, for the most part, built of rough stone, and covered with slate. It is 19 miles N. of Derby, 11 S. of Sheffield, and 127 N. W. of London.

CHE'SNUT, CHESNUT - TREE, S. [casten-beam, cyst-breem, Sax. chastaignier, Fr.] In Botany, has male and female flowers on the

H h 3

the same tree. It is ranged by Linnæus, in the 8th section of his 21st class. It should be propagated both on account of its beauty, shade, and timber, which is reckoned equal in value to the best oak, and in some cases superior to it; particularly in vessels for all kinds of liquor, which it gives the least taste to of any wood whatever, and when well seasoned will never shrink or increase in its bulk. It is very valuable for conveying water under ground, as it endures longer than elm or any other wood; on this account it is used for mill timber and water-works. Most of the old houses in London were built with this timber; it makes the best stakes and poles for pallisadoes or pediments, for wine props and hops; is proper for columns, tables, chests, chairs, bedsteads, and is much coveted both by the carpenter and joiner. Figuratively, applied to colour. Used adjectively, it signifies a brown, or that which is like the colour of the shell of a chesnut.

CHE'VALIER, S. a knight. In Heraldry, a horseman in compleat armour.

CHE'VAL DE FRISE, S. [pronounced shevâl de freeze, Fr.] In Fortification, a piece of timber traversed with wooden spikes pointed with iron.

CHE'VERIL, S. [chevereuil, Fr.] a kid. Figuratively, kid leather. Adjectively, stretching like kid leather. "Your soft cheveril conscience." Shak.

CHE'VRON, S. [Fr.] in Heraldry, one of the honorary ordinaries, representing two rafters of a house joined together, so as to form an angle.

To CHEW, [generally pronounced chaw, chewan, Sax.] to bite into small pieces between the teeth; to meditate or ruminate. "Chewing revenge." Prior.

CHICA'NE, S. [Fr.] the use of sophisms, distinctions, and subtleties, to prolong disputes and obscure the truth; artifice.

To CHICANE, V. A. [chicaner, Fr.] to prolong an affair or contest by artifice.

CHICA'NER, S. [chicaneur, Fr.] one who uses quirks or subtleties.

CHICA'NERY, S. [chicanerie, Fr.] artful prolonging any dispute by any artifice that can obscure the truth.

CHICHESTER, a town or city of Sussex, and capital of the county, with two markets on Wednesdays and Saturdays, and five fairs, viz. on April 23, Whit-Monday, and August 5, for horses and horned cattle; on October 10, for horned cattle, and on October 20, for horses and horned cattle. It is seated in a plain on the banks of the river Levant, which surrounds the S. and W. parts, and at a small distance falls into the sea. It is a bishop's see, and has a cathedral, with seven small churches built with flint-stone. It sends two members to parliament, and is governed by a mayor, a re-

corder, a deputy recorder, 14 aldermen, a bailiff, 27 commoners, and a portreeve. The buildings are very regular, and, the city being walled round, you may stand in the market-place, which is the centre, and see the four gates, which are all that belong to the city. It has some trade, but would have more if the harbour was not choaked up. It is 33 miles S. W. of Guilford, 29 S. E. of Winchester, and 63 S. W. of London. Lon. 16. 45. lat. 50. 50.

CHICK, or CHICKEN, S. [cicen, Sax. kiecken, Belg.] the young of a hen. The tender provision made for these animals in the egg, before they are hatched, by the white, and just as they are going to burst their confinement, by a part of the yolk's being inclosed in their belly, which serves them for nourishment till they are grown strong enough to pick meat, claims our wonder, and gives us such an instance of paternal care of the Deity, as must throw a new light on the tender title we address him by, when we call him, "Our Father which art in heaven." Chick is used figuratively, for a word of tenderness, implying that the person may, on account of his inability, claim our assistance. Sometimes it is used for a person void of experience. "Stella is no chicken." Swift.

CHICKEN-HARTED, Adj. timorous; cowardly; fearful.

CHICKEN-POX, S. a species of the small-pox, but the pustules are not so large, appear to the number of five or six, or twenty at most, on the face, very few on the body; the patient is very little indisposed either before, at, or after their appearance, and, if a grown person, scarce confined within doors by them.

CHICKLING, S. a young chicken.

CHICK-WEED, S. [cicen mete, Sax.] In Botany, a kind of weed much used by bird-breeders, and of service in breast swellings of the breast, occasioned by milk.

To CHIDE, V. A. [Preter. chide, Part. Pass. chid or chidden, cidan, Sax.] to reprove. Used with for. "Chide him for faults." Shak. To drive away by rebukes or reproof. "Chid me from the battle." Shak. To blame. "Fountains, o'er the pebbles, chid your flay." Dryd. To quarrel or be angry. "He does chide with you." Shak.

CHI'DER, S. one who is addicted to reproof.

CHIEF, Adj. [pronounced cheef, from chef, Fr.] the major part or greatest member. Main, applied to any end, or design. Extraordinary, applied by way of distinction or comparison. "Our chiefest courtier." Shak.

CHIEF, S. a commander. In chief, in Law, without any superiors. In Heraldry, the upper part of an escutcheon from side to side.

CHIEFLY,

CHIEFLY, Adv. generally, principally, commonly.

CHIEFTAIN, S. one who commands an army; the chief or head of a clan.

CHILBLAIN, S. (from *chill*, of *cale*, Sax. and *blein*, of *bleyn*, Belg.) small tumours on the fingers, toes, and heels, and when breaking out on the heels called kibes; arising from a contraction of the vessels wherein the blood circulates, by cold, which continuing, are, by the accession of fresh blood, greatly distended, and at length burst. Sharp recommends warm Hungary water, or spirits of wine camphorated, as a certain remedy, if applied before they break.

CHILD, S. [Plural, *children*, agreeable to the *Dutch-Cild*, Sax.] in its primary signification, an infant; the offspring of a person; the descendant of a man of any age. "The *children* of Ephraim." 2 *Cor.* xxv. 7. Figuratively, one who knows only the first rudiments of any doctrine. In the Old Testament, those who are worshippers of any being, and own his paternal power. "The *children* of Belial." 2 *Chron.* xiii. 7. In the New Testament, believers, or those who by adoption may call God their father, and transcribe his perfections into their lives. "Children of God." 1 *John* iii. 10. The produce or effect. "Child of integrity." *Shak.* Joined to *with*, it implies one that is pregnant or breeding. "Let wives *with* child." *Shak.*

To CHILD, V. N. to bring children. Figuratively, to be prolific or fruitful. "The *childing* autumn." *Shak.*

CHILD-BEARING, Participial Noun, pregnancy, breeding.

CHILD-BED, S. a lying-in.

CHILD-BIRTH, S. labour; travail; delivery.

CHILD-HOOD, S. [*cild-had*, Sax.] the interval between infancy and youth; adolescence.

CHILDISH, Adj. resembling a child, only becoming a child. "I put away *childish* things." 1 *Cor.* xiii. 11.

CHILDISHLY, Adv. in a trifling childish, indiscreet manner.

CHILDISHNESS, S. want of discretion, knowledge, or experience; in a good sense, artless simplicity, innocency.

CHILDLESS, Adj. having no children.

CHILDLIKE, Adj. that which is expected from a child.

CHILIFACTIVE, Adj. producing or forming chyle.

CHILIFACTORY, Adj. that which produces chyle.

CHILIFACTION, S. the act of turning or converting any food or substance into chyle.

CHILL, Adj. [*chill*, Belg.] that which stops circulation by its coldness. Figuratively, shivering; depressed, dejected or discouraged.

CHILL, S. a sensation of cold; coldness or chillness.

To CHILL, V. A. to reduce to a state of coldness. Figuratively, to stop or repress; to discourage, deject, blast, or destroy by cold.

CHILLINESS, S. cold; a sensation of shivering.

CHILLY, Adj. that which proceeds from or produces the sensation of cold. "A chilly sweet." *Fairfax.*

CHILLNESS, S. the quality of producing the sensation of cold or shivering.

CHIME, S. in Ringing, the sounding all the bells of a steeple, with all the variations in their order, that can produce music or an agreeable harmony. Figuratively, harmony of tempers, proportion, or other relations.

To CHIME, V. N. to be mutual; to answer each other; to wrest a thing to a particular purpose, or to put such a construction on a sentiment, as to make it agree with our own. "Any sect—will make all *chime* that way." To acquiesce in; to agree with. Applied to Poetry, to make the concluding syllables of two verses end with the same sound. Actively, to make an agreeable sound or harmony.

CHIMERA, S. [*chimæra*] a poetical fiction of a monster of the parts of different animals. Figuratively, a groundless imagination.

CHIMERICAL, Adj. imaginary, fantastic, not real.

CHIMERICALLY, Adj. in a wild, fantastic, vain manner, existing only in the imagination.

CHIMNEY, S. [*cheminée*, Fr.] the passage through which the smoke ascends in a house; the hearth or fire-place. As a remedy for smoky chimneys, it is advised to make the funnel narrower at bottom than at top, because the fire and internal air will then impell it with greater force and more ease; and, as it will be spread into a larger space when mounting, its gravity will be less, and its tendency to return into the room very little. *Chimney-corner*, is the fire-side, or, in country places, a seat at each end of the fire-grate used, in familiar language, as a place for idle and slothful persons. *Chimney-piece* is a composition of certain mouldings over the mantle-tree.

CHIN, S. [*cinus*, Sax.] that part of the face below the under-lip.

CHINA, the empire of, in Asia, is bounded on the E. by the ocean, on the N. by a great wall, above 1000 miles in length, which separates it from Tartary; on the W. by high mountains and deserts, and on the S. by the ocean, and the kingdoms of Tonquin, Cochin-China, and Laos. It is included between 112 and 151 degrees of Longitude, and between 21 and 55 of Latitude. Some pretend it is bounded without the great wall by the empire of Russia, but improperly; for that country has always been known by the name of Tartary, though it is now in
the

the Chinese dominions. It is about 2000 miles in length, from N. to S. and 1500 in breadth, from E. to W. and is divided into 16 provinces, which contains 155 towns of the first rank, 1312 of the second, besides 2357 fortified towns; in all which there may be about 50,000,000 of people. There are several large rivers, and where these are wanting, there are artificial canals, for the more ready communication and trading from one part to another; for they are all made navigable for large barks. It is generally a plain champaign country, and they scarce let an inch of ground remain unoccupied; for the hills are cut into several stages, or stories, from the bottom to the top, that the rain may water them all pretty equally, and render them more fruitful. Even the mountains are cultivated and covered with trees; and there are mines of iron, tin, copper, quick-silver, gold, and silver. There are corn and pulse of all sorts, especially rice; and there are a great number of simples, and several trees and fruits proper to the country, particularly one tree produces pease, very little different from those of Europe; another bears a kind of gum, which makes excellent varnish; and a third bears white berries, of the size of a hazel nut, whose pulp is nothing but a sort of tallow, of which they make candles; and a fourth, called the white-wax tree, produces white shining wax, of much greater value than the common bees-wax. The Bamboo cane grows to the height of an ordinary tree; and, though it is hollow within, yet the wood is very hard, and proper for many uses, such as pipes to convey water in, boxes, baskets, and for the making of paper, after it is reduced into a sort of past. It is now well known to all Europe, that this is the only country from whence all sorts of teas are imported. The complexion of the Chinese is a sort of tawney, and they have large foreheads, small eyes, short noses, large ears, long beards, and black hair, and those are thought to be most handsome who are most bulky. The women affect a great deal of modesty, and are remarkable for their little feet. There men endeavour to make as pompous an appearance as possible, when they go abroad; and yet their houses are but mean and low, consisting only of a ground-floor. They are addicted to all sorts of learning, particularly to arts and sciences; and they were the first inventors of printing, gun-powder, and the mariners compass, they all having been known here for a considerable number of years before the knowledge of them in any other part of the globe. The government of this empire is absolute, and the emperor has a privilege of naming his successor; but the chief mandarin has permission to remind him of his faults. He looks upon his subjects as his children, and pretends to govern them with a fatherly affection. There

is no country in the world where the inhabitants are so ceremonious as here; and yet, notwithstanding their seeming sincerity, they cheat as much in their dealings as in the most uncivilized countries. It is certain that their empire is a very ancient, and they themselves pretend it has existed many thousand years before our era of Noah's flood. However, it is generally allowed to have continued 4000 without interruption, though they have had twenty two different families on the throne. The last family now reigning, is that of the Tartars, who conquered China in 1640. Their religion is Paganism, and the sect of Fo is the principal.

CHIN-COUGH, S. [from *kichurt*, or *kich-boost*, Belg.] a violent dry cough, affecting children.

CHINE, S. [*esin*, Arm.] the part of the back, containing the spine or back bone. In Butchery, the back bones of a beast cut out so, as to contain some flesh, which is in great esteem with epicures.

To CHINE, V. A. to split along the back bone.

CHINK, S. [*cine*, Sax.] a narrow opening lengthwise.

To CHINK, V. A. to make pieces of any metal sound by shaking them together. To break in clefts, or gape.

CHINKY, Adj. full of narrow holes, or clifts.

CHINTS, S. a fine cloth made of cotton in the East Indies.

To CHIP, V. A. [from *couper*, or *chapler*, Fr.] to cut wood, &c. into small pieces.

CHIP, S. [*cyp*, Sax.] a small piece of wood, &c. separated from a larger, by a cutting tool.

CHIROGRAPHIST. S. one who delineates or describes the lines of a person's hands, and thence proceeds to foretell his fortune. " Let the *chirographist* behold his palms." *Martin Scrib.* Johnson imagines this to be an improper expression, and used instead of *chiromancer*, but the etymology and definition assigned above, seem to vindicate its propriety.

CHIROGRAPHY, S. [from χειρ, Gr. and γραφω] a person's hand-writing. Palmistry.

CHIROMANCER, S. [from χειρ, Gr. and μαντις] one who foretells future events by observing the lines of a person's hand.

CHIROMANCY, S. the art of foretelling by inspecting the lines of his hand. Palmistry.

To CHIRP, V. N. to make a noise like birds, which call to one another. To make gay, or cheerful. " He takes his *chirping* pint." *Pope.*

CHIRPER, S. a bird that chirps. A person that is cheerful, or merry.

CHIRURGEON, S. [corruptly pronounced surgeon, from χειρ, Gr. a hand, and *ipw*,

ργον, Gr. a work] one who cures such disorders, as require the operations of the hand.

CHIRURGERY, S. See CHIRURGEON. The art of curing wounds and various diseases, by external application. In the infancy of physic, this was the only branch that was practised; and after internal medicines were invented, we find them joined in the same person, and even the great Hippocrates, exercising both the office of physician and a surgeon.

CHIRU'RGIC, CHIRURGICAL, Adj. belonging to external or manual operation, or application in healing.

CHI'SEL, S. [*ciseau*, Fr. *cisello*, Ital.] a tool made of iron, used in carpentry, joining, masonry, sculpture, &c.

To CHI'SEL, V. A. to cut or work with a chisel.

CHI'T, S. [from *cito*, Ital.] a little child; a mere baby; a word expressive of contempt. A shoot, which sprouts from the end of barley or other grain. "Barley—will shew the *chit* or *sprit*." *Mortim.*

To CHIT, V. N. to sprout; to shoot at the end, applied to grain. "I have known barley *chit* in seven days." *Mortim.*

CHIT-CHAT, S. Idle and unimproving discourse. "A member of the *chit-chat* club." *Spect. No. 560.* Seldom used unless in conversation.

CHI'TTERLINGS, S. [from *schyterling*, Belg.] the guts or bowels. Likewise the border sewed on the bosom of a man's shirt; in this sense it is used in the singular number.

CHI'VALRY, S. [*chevalerie*, Fr. knighthood] knighthood, or military dignity. "Degrees and orders of *chivalry*." *Bacon.* This sense is obsolete. The qualification of a knight. The profession, or rules to be observed by a knight. An adventure, or exploit. In Law, a tenure of land by knights service, whereby the tenant is bound to perform some noble or military act to the lord.

CHIVES, S. [*cive*, *ceve*, Fr.] In Botany, the stamina which support the summits in the center of flowers.

CHLORO'SIS, S. [χλωρος, Gr.] In Medicine, a disorder incident to maids, wives, or widows, vulgarly called the green sickness, attended with a whitish, pale, or somewhat greenish colour; a full habit of body; a weakness of the legs, a difficulty of breathing; a swelling of the feet, an inactivity of mind, an oppression during sleep, a swelling of the eye-lids, and a slow and soft pulse.

CHO'COLATE, S. [Spanish] sometimes used for the nut of cacao-tree, which in botany, has an emplacement of five spear-shaped leaves. Chocolate, when applied to signify the cake from whence the liquor is made, is a composition of the nut, sugar, and vanilla. Its nutritive quality, when

diluted with water is great, and if used moderately, will not overload the stomach. The less aromatics are mixed with it the better, because they both render it hot and and lessen its nutritious quality.

CHOICE, S. [*choix*, Fr.] the preferring of a thing on reasonable motives. The thing chosen. That which merits a preference. A variety of things offered, to select from thence those which are best. *To make choice of*, is to prefer or select one or more things.

CHOICE, Adj. [comparative *choicer*, superlative *choicest*, *choice*, Fr.] that which ought to be preferred. In the superlative, the best. "My *choicest* hours of life are lost." Careful, frugal. "*choice* of his time." *Taylor.*

CHOICE-LESS, Adj. without a choice; not free. Under necessity.

CHOI'CENESS, S. that quality which gives a preference. Value, superior excellence.

CHOIR, S. [pronounced *quire*, *chorus*, Lat.] a band of singers. "The *choir* of angels." *Waller.* That part of a church where the choristers sit.

To CHO'KE, V. A. [*aceocan*, Sax.] to stop up the passage of the throat so as to prevent breathing. To kill, by stopping the breath. To intercept the motion of any thing; to smother. To hinder from growing; applied to vegetables, used with the particle *with*, "*Choked with corn*." *Luke* viii. 14.

CHO'KE-PEAR, S. In Gardening, a rough, harsh, unpalatable *pear*. Figuratively, a reproof, or check by which a person is put to silence. "Giving *choke-pears*." *Cleaveld.* A low expression.

CHO'KY, Adj. not easily swallowed, but apt to stick in the passage.

CHO'LER, S. [*cholera*, Lat. *colere*, Fr.] in Anatomy, the bile; used figuratively, for anger.

CHO'LERIC, or CHO'LERICK, Adj. angry, passionate.

To CHOOSE, V. A. [preter I *chose*, I have *chosen*, or *chose*, from *ceosan*, Sax. *choiser*, Fr.] to prefer, to give the preference to; to will; to select, or pick out of a number.

CHOOSER, S one who chooses or has the power of choosing. An elector.

To CHOP, V. A. [preter *chopt*, or I have *chopt*, *kappen*, Belg.] to cut with a cleaver, &c. by a sudden stroke. To eat quickly. Neuterly, to change. "The wind *chops about*." To *chop upon*, to meet with a thing suddenly, to appear as if cut. "*Chop* hands."

To CHOP, V. A. [*kopen*, Belg.] to exchange one thing for another. To be fickle in one's choice; to bandy; to perplex with nice distinction. "Leave off your *chopping* of Logic." *L'Estr.*

CHO'P, S. a piece cut off by a quick sudden blow. A piece of meat cut from off a joint.

a joint. A chink, cleft or hole. *Chop-houfe*, a kind of a cook's fhop, where meat is ready drefsed, fo called from their dealing, at firft, moftly in mutton *chops*, in fome places reforted to by people of no fmall fortune, and remarkable both for the elegance of the cookery, and the coftlinefs of the provifions.

CHOPPING, Adj. [from *chopping*] large, applied to infants. "A *chopping* boy." Clopping-bird, a thick bird of wood ufed by butchers.

CHO'PPY, Adj. [from *chop*] full of holes, or clefts; appearing as if cut, or *chops*.

CHOPS, S. [a corruption of CHAPS] the mouth of a beaft. Ufed alfo in contempt, for the mouth of a human creature. The mouth of any thing. As "the *chops* of the channel."

CHO'RAL, [from *chorus*, Lat.] belonging or relating to choir.

CHO'RD, S. [pronounced hard, as if the *h* was dropped; when it implies a ftring or rope, it is fpelt *cord*, but in its primitive fenfe the *h* is retained] the ftring of a mufical inftrument, by the vibration of which all founds are excited. In Geometry, a right line, terminating at each of its extremities in the circumference of a circle. In Anatomy, a fmall nerve extended over the drum of the ear.

CHO'RION, S. [Gr. from χοριον] In Anatomy, a thick, ftrong, whitifh membrane, which wraps the fœtus.

CHO'RISTER, S. [generally pronounced *quirifter*] one who fings in a choir, one who fings in a chorus, beautifully applied to birds. "The aerial *chorifters*." Ray.

CHORO'GRAPHER, S. [from χωρα, Gr. a region, and γραφω, Gr. to defcribe] a perfon that defcribes particular kingdoms, regions, or countries.

CHORO'GRAPHY, S. the art of defcribing countries.

CHO'RUS, S. [Lat.] feveral fingers joining in the fame tune. That part of a fong in which a whole company join. In antient drama, one or more perfons prefent on the ftage during a dramatic performance, ferving to introduce or prepare the audience for the introduction of any particular incident.

CHOUSE, the preter. of CHOSE.

CHO'SEN, the Participle paffive of CHOOSE.

To CHOUSE, V. A. to deprive a perfon of any thing by falfe pretences; ufed with *of*.

CHOUSE, S. a fit object for fraud; a bubble, a trick.

CHRIST, [*chriftus*, Lat. of χριϚος, Gr. anointed] one of the appellations given to our Lord and Saviour Jefus, fignifying the fame as *Meffiah*, and importing the validity of his claim to the high character he affumed

To CHRISTEN, V. A. [*criftnian*, Sax.] to initiate into the church by the facrament of baptifm. Figuratively, to give a name. "*Chriften* the fhip."

CHRI'STENDOM, S. [*criftendome*, Sax.] thofe parts wherein chriftianity is known and profeffed.

CHRI'STENING, S. [from *criften*, Sax.] the ceremony of baptifm, whereby perfons are entered and received as members of Chrift.

CHRI'STIAN, S. [*chriftianus*, Lat. χριϚιανος, Gr.] a perfon who profeffes the principles of his religion.

CHRI'STIAN, Adj. [*chriftianus*, Lat.] profeffing or exercifing the Chriftian religion. The *moft Chriftian* king is a title affumed by the king of France.

CHRI'STIAN-NAME, S. [from *criften* *name*, Sax.] that which is given a perfon at his baptifm. The quakers who do not baptize, have generally a meeting, in which the name is given to the infant, and inferted in a certificate.

CHRI'STIANISM, S. [*chriftianifmus*, Lat.] the peculiar doctrines of the Chriftian religion; thofe nations who profefs themfelves Chriftians.

CHRISTIA'NITY, S. [*chriftianité*, Fr.] the doctrines profeffed by Chriftians.

To CHRISTIANIZE, V. A. [from *criftian*, Sax.] to convert a perfon to the doctrines of Chriftianity.

CHRI'STMAS, S. [from *chrift* and *mefs*, of *mafs*, or *meffe*, Sax. a public fervice, or ceremony, the Lord's fupper, an offering] ufed in a fermon on Eafter-day 996, and in divers Saxon epiftles, before the doctrine of Tranfubftantiation was ever heard of] the day on which the nativity of our bleffed Saviour is celebrated. *Chriftmas-box*, a box in which money collected by fervants, at Chriftmas, is kept; alfo the collections made at Chriftmas.

CHRISTMAS-FLOWER, fee HELLEBORE.

CIROMA'TIC, Adj. [from *chroma*] In Painting, that paint which confift in colouring. In ancient Mufic, the fecond of the three kinds, confifting of femi-tones, varying and embellifhing the *diatonic*.

CHRO'NIC, CHRO'NICAL, S [from χρονος, Gr.] that which endures a long time. In Medicine, applied to thofe difeafes which from come to a crifis; they are owing to fome natural defect in the conftitution, or irregular manner of living; Dr. Cheyne imputes them moftly to repletion.

CHRO'NICLE, S. [*chronique*, Fr.] a regular and chronological account of tranfactions; a hiftory.

To CHRO'NICLE, V. A to infert in an hiftory; to record; to be rendered famous. "I expect to be *chronicled* in ditty." Cong.

CHRO'NICLER, S. an hiftorian; one who tranfmits any fact to pofterity, or preferves the memory of any tranfaction.

CHRO-

CHRO'NOGRAM, S. [from χρονος and γραμμα, Gr.] an inscription whose numeral letters compose some particular date: as in the capital letters in LaCLorVM in LaeVIa, make up the sum 1660.

CHRO'NOGRAM'MAST, S. one who composes chronograms.

CHRONO'LOGER, S. [from χρονος and λογος, Gr.] one who settles or adjusting the dates of former transactions.

CHRONOLO'GICAL, Adj. relating to chronology, the series of time, in which any transactions happened.

CHRONOLO'GICALLY, Adv. consistent with the rules of chronology, or the regular series of time.

CHRONO'LOGIST, S. [See CHRONOLOGER] one who from particular dates traces out and fixes the periods in which any remarkable transaction has happened.

CHRONO'LOGY, S. [See CHRONOLOGER] the art of tracing the times wherein any remarkable transaction is performed, or memorable events happened.

CHRONO'METER, S. [from χρονος, Gr. time, and μετρον, G. measure] an instrument to measure time.

CHRY'SALIS, S. [of χρυσος, Gr. gold from the general colour of its pellicle] in Natural History, a caterpillar, in its second state wherein it continues without eating, or any motion except in itself, till it bursts its pellicle, and changes into a moth or butter-fly; the curious anatomical observations which have been made by Swammerdam, on this dormant state of Insects, are well worth the perusal of the curious.

CHRY'SOLITE, [from χρυσος, Gr. and λιθος, Gr.] anciently a general term, given for all precious stones, that had a cast of gold or yellow in their composition. At present a precious stone of a greenish colour, with a cast of yellow.

CHU'B, S. [from cop, Sax.] in Natural History, a non spinous fish, or that which has no prickly fins, and only one in its back; it is full of small bones, and it in prime from Midway to Candlemas, but best in winter.

To CHUCK, V. N. [perhaps from the sound, or a corruption of chick. Chanfreter, Fr. to whisper] to make a noise like a hen calling her chickens.

To CHUCK, V. A. [choc, Fr.] to give a gentle stroke under the chin, so as to make the teeth touch each other, to endeavour to make money into a hole.

CHUCK, S. the noise of a hen. An expression of kindness or endearment, corrupted from chick. An endeavour to toss money into a hole in the ground. Chuck-farthing, a play wherein money is chucked or tossed into a hole.

To CHUCKLE, V. A. [schacken, Belg.] to call like a hen, to fondle, to grind.

CHUFF, S. [of, ofe, Sax.] a coarse, blunt, surly clown.

CHU'FFLY, Adv. in a surly morose manner. "John answered chuffly." Clar. Ta. Not used in any author of esteemed learning.

CHU'FFINESS, S. surliness, moroseness.

CHU'FFY, Adj. void of considerateness, good-nature, and politeness. Surly, morose.

CHU'MP, S. a large thick heavy piece of wood.

CHURCH, S. [cyric, circe, Sax.] the collective body of Christians. "The holy catholic church." A body of Christians, united by the same doctrines and making use of the mode of worship. Any number of persons professing Christianity, even in a private house. Figuratively, the religion of England as by law established, opposed to the modes of worship adhered to by dissenters. A place of worship. In Architecture, a large oblong building, consisting of a steeple, belfry, nave, choir, isles, pulpit, &c.

To CHURCH, V. A. to read the service, of returning thanks to God for a happy delivery, with the person who is recovered from childbed.

CHURCH-MAN, S. one who professes the religion by law established. A minister, or clergyman.

CHURCH-WARDEN, S. [cyricean-Ealder, Sax.] an officer elected yearly, in Easterweek, by the minister and parishioners of every parish, to look after the church, churchyard, &c. and likewise to observe the behaviour of the parishioner in such particulars, as appertain to the censure or jurisdiction of the ecclesiastical courts, he they are sworn into their office by the archdeacon, and, as of a kind of corporation, can sue or be sued for the church goods.

CHURCH-YARD, S. the ground belonging or adjoining to a church wherein the dead are interred.

CHU'RL, S. [ceorl, Brit.] a clown a morose ill-bred person. A niggardly, penurious, or miserly man.

CHU'RLISH, Adj. rude, ignorant, Ill-bred, surly, uncivil, selfish, avaricious. Figuratively, applied to things, harsh, not to be bent, stiff. "The metal will be hard, and churlish." Bacon.

CHU'RLISHLY, Adv. rudely, uncivilly, unkindly. "The olive did churlishly put over the son." L'Estrange.

CHU'RLISHNESS, S. the rude obstinate and surly behaviour of a clown.

CHURME, S. [cyrm, Sax.] a confused sound, murmur, or noise. "With the harms of a thousand saints." Bacon.

To CHURN, V. A. [cerne, Sax.] a vessel used to make cream into butter.

To CHURN, V. A. [kerren, Belg.] to turn a thing often in the mouth. "churn'd in his teeth." To make butter, by a continual motion.

To CHUSE, V. A. see CHOOSE.

CHYLA'CEOUS, Adj. consisting of or resembling chyle.

CHY'LE, S. [χυλος] in the animal economy, a milky liquor, extracted from dissolved aliments of every kind, and conveyed to the blood.

CHYLIFA'CTION, S. [from chylus, Lat. and factum] the converting the juice of aliments into chyle.

CHILYFA'CTIVE, Adj. endued with the quality of making chyle.

CHYLOUS, Adj. consisting, or partaking of the qualities of chyle.

CHY'MIC, or CHYMICAL, Adj. [chymicus, Lat.] made by or relating to chymistry. Perhaps more properly spelt chemic or chemical.

CHY'MICALLY, Adv. in a chymical manner.

CHY'MIST, S. [pronounced kimmist, see CHYMISTRY] a professor of chymistry.

CHY'MISTRY, S. [from χυμος, Gr. or χυ. Gr.] an art by which sensible bodies are so changed by means of fire, that their several powers and virtues are thereby discovered, and new bodies are composed by the mixture of different ingredients.

CIBA'RIOUS, Adj. [cibarius, Lat.] proper for, or partaking of the qualities of food; edible.

CI'CATRICE, CICATRIX, S. [Lat.] a little scar, remaining on the skin, after the healing of a wound. Figuratively, a mark or impression. " The cicatrice and capable impressure." Shak.

CICATRIZA'TION, S in Surgery, the act of healing a wound. The state of being skinned over.

To CICATRIZE, V. A. to heal and skin a wound over.

To CI'CULATE, V. A. [cicur, Lat.] to tame. Figuratively, to render or make mild or harmless. " So cicurated, and subdued." Brown.

CI'DER, S. [cidre, Fr. sidra, Ital.] a brisk, cool liquor prepared from the juice of apples made vinous by fermentation. Used with moderation it is good and wholesome, preferable to wine, because its spirits are less vehement, and detained by a viscous phlegm, which likewise contributes to render it cooling. That those who drink this liquor look more healthy, and are both more vigorous and sprightly, than those who drink wine, seems evident from the observation of Lord Bacon. " Of eight old people, says he, some were near, and others above 100; who during their whole lives, drank nothing but Cider, and were so vigorous, that they danced and jumped about like young men."

CI'DERKIN, S. the liquor made of the gross matter of the apples, after the cider is pressed out, by the addition of boiled water.

CTELING, see CEILING.

CILIA, S [Lat.] (in Anatomy, the passions of stiff hairs wherewith the eyes are guarded; their use is to keep out flies and motes, to break the impetuosity of the rays of light, and at the same time to leave space enough for the discernment of objects. They grow but to a certain length, need no cutting like the other hairs, and are sensible. Their points are bent with great art; those in the upper eyelids turning upwards, and those in the lower towards the earth, that nothing might obstruct our sight. And from hence we may learn how critical the great author of nature hath been, in forming even the least and most minute conveniencies, that belong to animal bodies.

CI'LIARY, Adj. [cilium, Lat.] in Anatomy, belonging or relating to the eyelids.

CILI'CEOUS, Adj. [cilicium, Lat.] made of hair. " A cilicious or sackcloth habit." Brown.

CI'METER, S. [cimeterra, Span.] a sort of a sword, used by the Turks, short, heavy, flat, and with but one edge.

CIN'CTURE, S. [from cinctura, Lat.] a girdle, or clothing worn round the body. An inclosure. In Architecture, a ring, list, or orlo, at the top and bottom of the shaft of a column.

CI'NDER, S. [cinder, Fr. sinder, Sax.] coals burnt till most of their sulphur is consumed, and reduced to a porous coke.

CI'NGLE, S. [cingulum, Lat.] a girt or belt for a horse.

CINNABAR, S. [cinnabaris, Lat.] a mineral substance; the ore out of which quicksilver is drawn, consisting partly of a sulphureous, and partly of a mercurial nature, and divided into native and factitious: the native is that which is just described; the factitious is made of flours of sulphur and quicksilver, first incorporated by fire and afterwards sublimated.

CINNAMON, S. [cinnamomum, Lat.] the bark of an aromatic growing in the island of Ceylon. It is an astringent in the prima viæ, or first passage, and in the remote seats of action, an aperient and alexipharmic. It strengthens the viscera, assists concoction, expels wind, and is a very pleasant cordial.

CI'NQUE-FOIL, S. [cinque, Fr. feuille, Fr.] a kind of five-leaved clover.

CI'NQUE-PORTS, S. [Fr. the five ports or havens; the following havens, viz. Dover, Sandwich, Rye, Hastings, Winchelsea, Romney, and Hithe; formerly applied only to five, which laying opposite to France, were thought by our monarchs to deserve more than ordinary care to prevent an invasion. On this account Cambden says, that William the Conqueror, appointed a warden, and king John granted them certain privileges, on condition of their supplying him with a fleet to invade France; they are all franchises,

chiefs, and the constable of Dover-castle, is lord-warden of all these cinque-ports.

CIN'QUE-SPOTTED, Adj. having five spots. " A mole cinque-spotted." *Shakesp.*

CI'ON, S. [*sion*, or *scion*, Fr.] in Botany, a young twig, or sprout of a tree.

CI'PHER, S. [*chifre*, *cifra*, Ital.] an arithmetical character marked thus (o), though of no value itself, in integers it encreases the value of figures when set on the right-hand. An affemblage of letters, confisting of the initials of a perfon's name, interwoven together. *A mere cypher*, a perfon of no importance, intereft, or importance.

To CI'PHER, V. N. to calculate or perform the operation of arithmetic.

CIR'CLE, S. [*circulus*, Lat. *circle*, Fr.] Figuratively, a curve line, which being continued, ends in the point from whence it begon, having all its parts equidiftant from a point in the middle called the center. The circumference of any round body. An affembly of people forming a kind of ring. A company. A series of things following one another alternately. " The *circling* years." Circles of the empire, are ten in number, which have a right to be prefent at the diets.

To CIR'CLE, V. A. to move round a thing. To furround, or encompafs; to conine. Actively, to move in a circle.

CIR'CLED, Part. that is in the form of a circle.

CIR'CLET, S. a circle; an orb.

CIR'CLING, Adj. furrounding like a circle.

CIR'CUIT, S. [*circuit*, Fr.] the moving round. A fpace inclosed with a circle. The circumference of any thing. The journies taken by the judges to hold affizes or administer juftice in thofe places that are diftant from London.

CIRCUI'TION, S. [*circuitio*, Lat.] the going round about. Circumlocution.

CIR'CULAR, Adj. [*circulaire*, Fr.] round, refembling a circle. Figuratively, fucceffion. Vulgar, mean, common. " Had Virgil been a circular poet." *Dennis*. Circular-letter, a letter addreffed to feveral perfons, who have the fame intereft or concern in fome common affair.

CIR'CULARLY, Adv. in the form or motion of a circle.

To CIR'CULATE, V. N. [from *circulo*, Lat.] to move in a circle; To be in ufe, fo as to be conftantly changing its owner, oppofed to be hoarded, applied to money. Actively, to put about, or hand from one to another, ufed of a cup or glafs in drinking. " Let the glafs circulate."

CIRCULA'TION, S. motion in a circle. A feries in which things preferve the fame order, and return the fame ftate. The circulation of the blood, was difcovered in England in 1628, by Harvey our country-

man, and may be evinced from all the blood's being evacuated on wounding one of the greater arteries. The circulation of the nervous juice is concluded from the fame principles as that of the blood.

CIRCUMA'MBIENCY, S. [*circum*, Lat. and *ambio*, Lat.] the act of encompaffing, furrounding, or inclofing.

CIRCUMA'MBIENT, Part. [*circumambiens*, Lat.] encircling; inclofing; furrounding, encompaffing.

To CIRCUMA'MBULATE, V. A. [from *circum*, Lat. and *ambulo*, Lat.] to walk round about.

To CIRCUMCI'SE, V. A. [from *circum*, Lat. and *fcindo*, Lat.] to cut off the forefkin. Figuratively, to reduce the mind to fuch a ftate as was typified by circumcifion, to renounce every pleafure and incentive inconfiftent with true religion, and to act as a perfon admitted into the kingdom of God.

CIRCUMCI'SION, S. [from *circumcifio*] the act of cutting off the forefkin. Figuratively, Judifm, or a Jew. " Cometh this bleffednefs on the *circumcifion* only." *Rom.* iv. 9. One who is of the fpiritual feed of Abraham, and poffeffes thofe qualifications fignified by circumcifion. " *Circumcifion* is that of the heart in the fpirit." *Rom.* ii. 29. " *Circumcifion* is the keeping of the Commandments." 1 *Cor.* vii. 19.

To CIRCUMDU'CT, V. A. [*circumductum*, Lat.] in Law, to fuperfede, nullify, or render of an effect.

CIRCUMFERENCE, S. [*circumferentia*, Lat.] the line furrounding any thing. The fpace inclofed in a circle. Any thing of a round form. " The broad *circumference* hung on his fhoulders like a moon." *Par. Loft.*

CIRCUMFERE'NTOR, S. [from *circumferor*, Lat.] an inftrument ufed by furveyors in taking angles.

CIR'CUMFLEX, S. [*circumflexus*, Lat.] an accent, marked thus (^) ufed to regulate the pronunciation.

CIR'CUMFLUENT, Part. inclofing any thing with water.

To CIRCUMFU'SE, V. A. [*circumfufus*, Lat.] to pour round; diffufe, or fpread.

To CIRCUMGYRATE, V. A. [from *circum*, and *gyrus*, Lat.] to roll round. " Veffels, curled, *circumgyrated* and complicated together." *Ray.*

CIRCUMJA'CENT, Part. [*circumjacens*, Lat.] bordering on every fide, contiguous.

CIRCUMINCE'SION, S. [from *circum*, Lat. and *inceffio*,] in theology, a term ufed by the fchoolmen, to exprefs the confubftantiality of the three divine perfons in the trinity. Damafcenus has made ufe of it in his explication of the text. " I am in my father, and my father in me." *John* xiv. 11.

CIRCUMLOCU'TION, S. [from *circum*, Lat.

I i 2

Lat. and *locaton*] a periphrasis; a round-about, or indirect way of expressing a person's sentiments in order to guard against disgust.

CIRCUMMU'RED, Adj. [from *ci cum*, Lat. and *murus*, Lat. a wall] encompassed, or surrounded with a wall. "*Circummured* with bricks." *Shak.*

CIRCUMNA'VIGABLE, Adj. [*circum navy*, Lat. to sail round] that which may be sailed round.

CIRCUMNAVIGA'TION, S. [*circum navigatum*, Lat.] the act of sailing round. "The *circumnavigation* of Africa." *Arbuth.*

CIRCUMPO'LAR, Adj. [from *circum*, Lat. and *polaris*] in Astronomy, those stars near the north pole, which move round it without setting.

CIRCUMROTA'TION, S. [from *circum*, and *roto*, Lat.] the act of whirling a thing round; the state of a thing whisked round.

To CIRCUMSCRI'BE, V. A. [*circumscribo*] to inclose in certain limits; to bound, limit, or restrain.

CIRCUMSCRIPTION, S. [*circumscriptio*, Lat.] limitation, restraint, boundary.

CIRCUMSCRIPTIVE, Adj. determining the shape or figure of a thing.

CIRCUMSPECT, Adj. [*circumspectum*, supine, of *circumspicio*, Lat.] cautious with respect to conduct; wary.

CIRCUMSPECTION, S. in its primary sense, the act of looking round about one. "With sly *circumspection*." *Par. L. fi.* Figuratively, a cautious, circumspect, or wary conduct.

CIRCUMSPECTIVE, Adj. [*circumspective*] in its primary sense, looking round about; wary.

CIRCUMSPECTLY, Adv. in a cautious, wary, discreet, and prudent manner.

CIRCUMSTANCE, S. [Lat.] a particular incident; an event. In the plural, the state or condition of a person, bad *circumstances*, signifying poverty, and good *circumstances*, riches.

To CIRCUMSTANCE, V. N. to be attended with peculiar incidents.

CIRCUMSTANT, Part. [*circumstans*, Lat.] standing round, or surrounding.

CIRCUMSTANTIAL, Adj. [*circumstantialis*, low Lat.] accidental; minute; containing every particular.

To CIRCUMVALLATE, V. A. [*circumvallatum*] to surround with fortifications.

CIRCUMVALLATION, S. [*circumvallatum*, Lat.] the art of entrenching or fortifying. In Fortification, a line or trench with a parapet, thrown up by besiegers, encompassing their camp to defend it.

To CIRCUMVENT, V. A. [*circumvenio*] to over-reach; to deceive, or impose upon.

CIRCUMVENTION, S. [*circumventio*,

Lat.] the imposing upon, or over-reaching a person.

CIRCUMVOLUTION, [*circumvolutum*, Lat.] the act of rolling a thing round; the thing rolled round.

CIRCUS, CIRQUE, S. [*circus*, Lat.] In Antiquity, a large building, furnished with rows of seats rising above each other, and used for the exhibiting shews to the people.

CIRENCESTER, a town of Gloucestershire, with two markets, on Mondays and Fridays, and three fairs, on Easter-Tuesday, July 18, and November 3, for cattle, sheep, horses, wool, oil, and leather. The market on Mondays is chiefly for corn, and on Fridays for wool, yarn, and provisions. It is seated on the river Churn, over which it has a bridge. It was a place of great account in the time of the Romans, being then 2 miles in circumference, and the ruins of the walls are yet to be seen. A great many Roman antiquities have been found here; and here the Roman roads meet and crossed each other. It had also a castle and an abbey, long since demolished. It is now a borough-town, and sends two members to parliament. It is 15 miles E, N. E. of Bristol, 18 S. E. of Gloucester, and 85 W. by N. of London. Long. 15. 35. lat. 51. 41.

CISSOID, S. an algebraical curve of the second order, invented by Diocles, an ancient Greek geometrician, in order to find two mean proportionals between two given right lines.

CIST, S. [*cista*, Lat. *ciste*, Sax.] a case, or covering; the coat of a tumour.

CISTED, Adj. [from *cist*] inclosed in a bag, case, or membrane.

CISTERN, S. [*cisterna*, Lat.] a leaden receptacle for water or rain, for family use; a large reservoir or repository of water.

CIT, S. [a contraction of *citizen*] one who resides in the city; generally used as a word of contempt.

CITADEL, S. [*citadelle*, Fr. *citadella*, Ital. a diminutive of *citta*, a city] a fort, or place fortified with four, five, or six bastions; built sometimes in the most eminent part of a city, and sometimes near it, in order to defend it against enemies.

CITAL, S. a reproof, or impeachment; a summons to appear in a court; a quotation.

CITATION, S. [from *citatum*, supine of *cito*, Lat.] in Law, a summons to appear before an ecclesiastical judge; the act of quoting an author's name, as espousing the sentiment a person would establish; the passage quoted from an author; a mention, detail, or enumeration. "A *citation* of such as may produce it in any other." *Harvey.*

CITATORY, Adj. having the power or nature of a citation.

To CITE, V. A. [*cito*, Lat.] to summons a person to appear in a court of justice; to enjoin, or call authoritatively on a person;

to quote. "That paffage which I cited before." Boy.

CI'TER, S. one who fummons another; one who quotes from an author.

CI'TESS, S. a female, or woman, who lives in a city. Us'd only by Dryden. "Cits and citeffes." Dryd.

CITIZEN, S. (citoyen, Fr.) In its primary fenfe, an inhabitant or dweller at any place; a perfon who is free of a city; one who carries on trade in a city. "When he fpeaks not like a citizen, you find him a foldier." Shak. Us'd by Shakefpear, as an adjective, to exprefs the milder virtues of peace, and that timoroufnefs a perfon is fubject to, who has never been converfant in camps. "Not fo citizen a wanton as to feem to die e'er fick." Cymbel.

CI'TRINE, Adj. (citrinus, Lat.) lemoncoloured; of a dark yellow. "The butterfly has its wings painted citrine and black."

CI'TRINE, S. (citrinus, Lat. citrine, Fr. and Ital.) a fpecies of chaftal of a beautiful yellow.

CI'TRON, S. (citrus, Lat.) a fruit, which comes from a hot country, and is in fmell, tafte, and fhape, fomewhat like a lemon, from which however it is diftinguifhed by its dimenfion, the fweetnefs of its pulp, the brifknefs of its fmell, and deepnefs of its colour.

CI'TY, S. (cité, Fr. civitas, Ital.) a large town inclofed with a wall. Alfo in Law, a town corporate, that hath a bifhop and a cathedral church; the inhabitants of a city; the heart or middle of a place, oppofed to the extremities. "The city and borough."

CI'TY, Adj. living in a city; refembling a citizen.

CI'VET, S. (civet, Fr. zibetto, Arab.) In Natural Hiftory, a little animal, a native of Peru and Guinea, not unlike our cat, excepting that its fnout is more pointed; its claws are lefs dangerous, and its cry is different. Ray thinks it rather of the fox or wolf kind. Under its tail is a bag, wherein the perfume of civet is formed, which is originally like greafe, or a kind of gum.

CI'VIC, Adj. (civicus, Lat.) relating to civil matters, oppofed to military.

CI'VIL, Adj. (civilis, Lat.) belonging to a city, or its government; polifhed, well regulated, oppofed to rude and barbarous. Civil war, is that which people of the fame nation wage with one another. Civil death, that which is inflicted by the laws. Civil power, or civil magiftrate, that which is exercifed on the principles of government, oppofed to military. Figuratively, polifhed, civilized, humane, well-bred, and complaifant; gentle; oppofed to wild, rude, and barbarous; beautifully applied to inanimate things. Civil law, implies the Roman law contained in the inftitutes, digefts, and code.

CIVI'LIAN, S. (civilis, Lat.) one who profeffes the civil law.

CIVI'LITY, S. the ftate of politenefs, oppofed to uncultivated barbarity; a polite addrefs; a kindnefs beftowed with politenefs.

To CI'VILIZE, V. A. to inftruct in fuch fciences as tend to reclaim man from favagenefs.

CI'VILLY, Adv. in a kind, good-natured and genteel manner, oppofed to rudenefs or brutality; in a genteel but not gaudy manner. "The chambers were furnifhed civilly." Bacon. This fenfe is now obfolete.

CLACK, S. (clac, Brit. clic, Fr.) any thing which makes a continued noife, fuch as that of a mill. Figuratively, inceffant tattle; the tongue. "He knows not when any clack will lie." Prior. From klatfche, Belg.

To CLACK, V. N. (criecian, Brit.) to let the tongue run apace, to talk much.

CLA'D, Part. Preter from clothe.

To CLAIM, V. A. (clamer, Fr.) to demand as a right, oppofed to afking as a favour.

CLA'IM, S. a demand, or right of demanding a thing, as a due. In Law, a title to, or demand of any thing in the poffeffion of another. This word is generally joined with the verb lay.

CLA'IMABLE, Adj. that which may be demanded or claimed.

CLA'IMANT, S. he that demands a thing as his property.

CLA'IMER, S. one who claims or demand s a thing as his property.

To CLAMBER, V. N. (klemen, Belg.) to afcend, or go up a fteep place with difficulty, fo as to be forced to ufe both the knees and hands.

To CLA'M, to clog with any glewifh matter.

CLA'MMINESS, S. viedity, ropinefs, thicknefs.

CLA'MMY, Adj. vifcous, ropy, glutinous.

CLA'MOROUS, Adj. fpeaking loud; turbulent; vociferous.

CLA'MOUR, S. (clamor, Lat.) a noife, or outcry; applied with no fmall elegance to inanimate things. "The loud Arno's buiftrous clamours." Addif.

To CLA'MOUR, V. N. to make a turbulent noife.

CLA'MP, S. (klampe, Belg.) a piece of wood added to another to ftrengthen it; a little piece of wood like a wheel, ufed in a mortice inftead of a pully.

To CLA'MP, V. A. to fit a board with the grain to another piece acrofs the grain; to prevent warping.

CLA'N, S. (klan, Scot.) a family, race, or tribe; ufed as a word of contempt.

CLA'NCULAR, Adj. (clancularius, Lat.) underhand, private, fecret, clandeftine.

CLANDE'STINE, Adj. (clandeftinus, Lat.) underhand; fecret; private.

CLANDE'STINELY, Adv. in a fecret

or

re private manner; always uſed in a bad ſenſe.

To CLANG, V. A. [*clango*, Lat.] to make a loud ſhrill noiſe reſembling that of a trumpet; or like ſwords beat together. Actively, to claſh or ſtrike together, ſo as to cauſe a noiſe.

CLANGOUR, S. [*clangor*, Lat.] a loud ſhrill ſound.

CLANGOUS, Adj. making a loud ſhrill noiſe.

CLANK, S. [from *clank*, perhaps a corruption from *clang*] a loud, ſhrill, or harſh noiſe.

To CLAP, V. A. [*clappen*, Sax.] to ſtrike together ſuddenly, ſo as to make a noiſe; to do any thing in a quick and unexpected manner; to applaud, commend, or praiſe a perſon by ſtriking the hands together; to infect with the venereal diſeaſe. Uſed with up, to do, perform, or finiſh any thing ſuddenly, or without much precaution; "A peace may be *clapped up* with that ſuddenneſs," *Howell*. Neuterly, to ſtrike with a quick or ſudden motion, "*clap* to the door." To ſtrike the hands together by way of applauſe.

CLAP, S. [*clap*, Brit. *Lapſ.* Teut.] a loud noiſe, made by the ſtriking two things together, or by exploſion applied to thunder; applauſe, or approbation, teſtified by ſtriking the hands together; the firſt ſtate of the venereal diſeaſe.

CLAPPER, S. one who applauds by ſtriking his hands together; the tongue which hangs in the inſide of a bell; a piece of wood in a mill for ſhaking the hopper. Figuratively, the tongue of a talkative perſon.

CLARENCIEUX, or CLARENCIEUX, S. the ſecond king of arms, ſo called from the duke of Clarence, ſon of Edward III. who firſt bore this office.

CLARE-OBSCURE, [*claro ſcuro*, Ital.] the lights and ſhades in a picture; the art of diſtributing the lights and ſhades to the beſt advantage; a deſign conſiſting only of two colours.

CLARET, S. [*vin clair*, Fr.] French wine of a clear, pale, red colour.

CLARIFICATION, the clearing from impurities the fining liquors.

To CLARIFY, V. A. [*clarifier*, Fr.] to fine or make any liquor clear. Figuratively, to free the underſtanding or mind from any impurities which might obſtruct its view of things.

CLARION, S. [*clairon*, Fr.] a trumpet with a ſhriller ſound than the common ſort. In Heraldry, a bearing thought by Guillim to be one of the ancient trumpets, but by others to be the rudder of a ſhip, or a reſt for a lance.

CLARITY, S. [*clarté*, Fr.] brightneſs, ſplendour, indigence.

To CLASH, V. N. [*kletzen*, Belg.] to make a noiſe, applied to two things ſtruck together. Figuratively, to act with oppoſite

views, uſed with the particle with; to contradict, oppoſe or diſagree. "*Claſhing* metaphors are put together." *Spect*. No. 595. Actively, to make a noiſe by ſtriking two things together.

CLASH, S. a noiſe made by colliſion; oppoſition of ſentiments or intereſts.

CLASP, S. [*gheſpe* or *cheſpe*, Belg.] a thin piece of metal curved at the extremities, uſed to faſten together the two corners of a book, the two fore parts of a garment, &c. Alſo an embrace.

CLASPER, S. in Botany, tendrils, ligaments, or threads, whereby ſhrubs and other plants lay hold on trees. Given by the wiſe Author of nature to ſuch plants whoſe branches being long, fragile, and ſlender, would fall by their own weight, or that of their fruit; in ſome plants they ſerve not only for ſupport, but likewiſe ſupply, as in the trunk roots of ivy, wherein they aſſiſt the root in conveying ſap to the branches; in the cucumber they ſerve for ſtabiliment, propagation, and ſhade.

CLASP-KNIFE, S. a knife which folds into the handle.

CLASS, S. [*claſſis*, Lat.] a collection of things ranged in order; a rank of order; in ſchools, a number of boys ſeated according to their attainments.

CLASSIC, CLASSICAL, Adj. [*claſſicus*, Lat.] in ancient literature, the authors of the Auguſtan age, who were of received note, and acknowledged abilities.

CLASSIC, S. an author of the firſt rank, and eſteemed a ſtandard for ſtyle, &c.

To CLATTER, V. N. [*clatrung*, *clodur*, Sax.] to make a noiſe by being ſtruck often together; alſo to make a noiſe by talking aloud, faſt, and firmly to the purpoſe. Actively, to ſtrike any thing ſo, as to make it ſound and rattle; to diſpute, or wrangle.

CLATTER, S. a rattling noiſe; a tumultuous noiſe.

CLAVATED, Part. [*clavatus*, Lat.] knobbed; or having plenty of knobs.

CLAVE, the preter of CLEAVE.

CLAVICLE, S. [*clavicula*, Lat.] in Anatomy, the collar bone, of which there are two ſituated between the ſcapula and ſternum.

CLAUSE, S. [*clauſula*, Lat.] a ſentence; a ſingle article.

CLAUSTRAL, Adj. [from *clauſtrum*, Belg.] belonging to a cloiſter. "Clauſtral priors." *Ayliffe*.

CLAW, S. [*clawu*, Sax.] the foot of a bird or beaſt, armed with a ſharp horny ſubſtance. Figuratively, the hand, eſpecially of a rapacious perſon; a term of reproach.

To CLAW, V. A. [*clawan*, Sax.] to ſcratch with the nails.

CLAWED, Adj. having claws, ſeized, or ſcratched with a claw.

CLAY, S. [*clæi*, Erſe. *kley*, Belg.] weighty, ſtiff

stiff and ductile earth, smooth to the touch, and easily dissolving in water.

To CLAY, V. A. to cover with clay; to manure with clay.

CLAY-COLD. Adj. [a compound word] as cold as clay, lifeless. "His clay-cold corpse." *Rowe*.

CLAYEY, Adj. confisting of clay.

CLAYISH, Adj. of the nature of clay; refembling clay.

CLEAN, Adj. [pronounced cleen, Sax.] free from dirt, pure. Free from wickedneſs, or impurity. Elegant, neat; oppoſed to unwieldy or encumbered. In a ſcripture ſenſe; free from any diſeaſe which rendered a perſon unfit for public attendance in places of worſhip, or the ſociety of others, applied to perſons; not fit to be eaten; or offered in ſacrifice, applied to beaſts. Entirely, perfectly, fully, or completely. "Domeſtic broils clean overthrown." *Shak*.

To CLEAN, V. A. to free from dirt, filth, or ſoil.

CLEANLY, Adj. free from dirt or filth. Figuratively, that which cleanſes or clears a thing from filth. Free from moral impurity; innocent, chaſte.

CLEANLY, Adv. in a clean, neat, decent manner.

CLEANNESS, S. [pronounced cleenneſs] neatneſs, freed from dirt or filth, applied to things or clothes. Elegance, exactneſs, and freedom from foreign mixture, or unchaſteneſs; applied to language. Freedom from guilt; or any immoral impurity, applied to actions.

To CLEANSE, V. A. [pronounced clenſe, clenſan, Sax.] to free from dirt or filth. To free from bad humours by medicine.

CLEANSER, S. in Medicine, that which removes any noxious humours from the body; a detergent.

CLEAR, Adj. [pronounced cleer, from cleer] tranſparent; that which may be ſeen through; free from filth, applied to ſtreams. Free from clouds, miſts or rain; applied to the weather. Without adulteration. Poſitive, plain, or free from any doubtful expreſſions. A releaſe; account is manifeſt, evident, or that which cannot be diſputed. Figuratively, void of guilt. Free from any undue bias, applied to the judgment. Free from deductions, applied to gain. Applied to perſons, judicious, or poſſeſſed of all the lights, which can ſecure from error; uſed in familiar converſation. Uſed adverbially, for entirely, totally, or quite. "Sin is clear off." *L'Eſtrange*.

To CLEAR, V. A. to remove any filth or obſtruction. Figuratively, to free from obſcurity, perplexity, or difficulty. To remove any charge of guilt. To cleanſe. To clarify or cleanſe from filth. To gain, without any deduction. To brighten, to

remove any thing which intercepts the light. To clear a ſhip, is to obtain permiſſion for ſailing or ſelling the cargo, by paying the cuſtoms.

CLEARANCE, S. a certificate that a ſhip has been cleared at the cuſtom-houſe.

CLEARER, S. that which removes any filth or obſtruction.

CLEARLY, Adj. free from darkneſs, obſcurity, or ambiguity. Plainly, oppoſed to confuſedly. Without any undue influence, "Deal clearly and impartially with yourſelves." *Tilloſ*. Without deduction or diminution applied to gains. Without evaſion, plainly.

CLEARNESS, S. tranſparency; freedom from dregs, or filth. Diſtinctneſs, plainneſs, freedom from obſcurity or ambiguity.

CLEAR-SIGHTED, Adj. [a compound word] judicious; penetrating; ſeeing into the conſequences of things.

To CLEAR-STARCH, V. A. to ſtarch linen in ſuch a manner, that it may appear tranſparent and clear.

To CLEAVE, V. A. [Preter. I clove, Part. cloven; cleaven, Sax.] uſed with the particle to, to ſtick, to adhere to, applied to things. Figuratively, to unite one's ſelf to a perſon; to attend, or accompany. "His grace doth cleave to the one." *Hooker*.

To CLEAVE, V. A. [Preter. I clove, clave, or cleft, Particip. cloven, or cleft, from cleofan Sax.] to divide a thing with a chopper, axe, &c. To divide, or ſeparate. Neuterly, to part aſunder. To ſuffer diviſion, or ſeparate.

CLEAVER, S. a large flat inſtrument of metal with a handle, uſed by butchers to ſeparate the joints of meat. One who chops or cleaves any thing.

CLEF, [from cliff. Fr.] in Muſic, a mark at the beginning of the lines of a piece of muſic which determines the name of each line, according to the ſcale.

CLEFT, Participle Paſſive, from cleave.

CLEFT, S. [kluſt, Teut.] a ſpace made by the ſeparation or diviſion of the parts of any thing. A crack.

CLEMENCY, S. [clementia, Lat. clemence, Fr.] willingneſs to forgive, unwillingneſs to puniſh, and tenderneſs in the inflicting puniſhment.

CLEMENT, Adj. [clemens, Lat.] tender and humane in executing or limiting puniſhment.

CLERGY, S. [clerus, Lat. cleros, Gr.] a body of men officiating in the public ſervice of the church.

CLERGYMAN, S. [from clergy and man] a perſon dedicated by ordination to the ſervice of the church. One in holy orders.

CLERICAL, Adj. [clericus, Lat.] belonging or relating to the clergy.

CLERK,

CLERK, S. [clerc, Fr. cleric, Sax.] in Law, a title given to the clergy. A writer in a public office. In Commerce, a person employed in a merchant's compting-house to transact the business that is performed by the pen. As this is an honourable employ, so likewise the qualifications required to discharge it properly are such as demand application, and deserves esteem. In the church service a layman, who pronounces the responses with an audible voice; gives out the singing psalms, &c.

CLERKSHIP, S. the office or employment of a clerk.

CLEVER, Adj. [its etymology is uncertain] dexterous, quick, skilful, well-pleasing, convenient, well. "'Twou'd found more clever." Pope. Well-made, handsome; any thing which a person likes, in low and familiar discourse; but should never make its way into books.

CLEVERLY, Adv. in an ingenious, skilful and proper manner.

CLEVERNESS, S. a proper, skilful, ingenious, and dexterous performance.

CLEW, S. [clywe, Sax.] a ball of thread. Any guide or direction, by means of which a person may be led to surmount any difficulty.

To CLICK, V. A. [cleken, Belg.] to make a sharp, and successive noise, like the beat of a watch.

CLIENT, S. [cliens, Lat.] in Law, one who employs a lawyer for advice, or to sue or defend.

CLIENTSHIP, S. the office or state of a client.

CLIFF, S. [clif, Sax.] a steep or craggy rock. In Music, improperly used for Clef.

CLIMACTER, S. [Gr. κλιμακτήρ] a certain period of life supposed to be attended with some great danger.

CLIMACTERIC, CLIMACTERICAL, Adj. [from κλιμαξ] containing a number of years. The climacteric year is a critical year in a person's life, wherein he is supposed to stand in great danger of death.

CLIMATE, S. [κλίμα, Gr. an inclination] in Geography, a space on the surface of the earth, measured from the equator to the polar circles. In a common or popular sense, any country differing from another, in respect of its seasons, the quality of the soil, or the manners of its inhabitants.

To CLIMATE, V. N. to inhabit. "Whilst you do climate here." Shak. Perhaps it has no other authority.

CLIMAX, S. [κλίμαξ, Gr. a ladder] in Rhetoric, a figure wherein the sense of a period increases every sentence, till it concludes.

To CLIMB, V. A. [Preter, and Participle Passive, climbed, from climban, Sax.] to ascend, including the idea of difficulty. To ascend,

by their specific levity, &c. applied to vapours. Actively, to mount, or ascend.

CLIMBER, S. one who ascends, any high or steep place.

CLIME, S. [from κλίμα Gr.] the same as Climate, generally used in poetry instead of Climate.

To CLINCH, V. A. [Preter clinched, and Participle Passive; from clyngan, Sax.] to shut the hand that fingers and thumb may reach over each other. To bend or turn the point of a nail, when driven through any thing. To confirm, settle, or establish, applied to argument.

CLINCH, S. a pun. In Navigation, that part of a cable which is fastened to the ring of an anchor.

CLINCHER, S. a cramp or hold-fast, made of iron bent, used to fasten planks.

To CLING, V. A. [Preter, I clung, or have clung, Part. clung, clyngan, Dan.] to stick close to or hang upon.

CLINGY, Adv. apt to stick, cling, or adhere to.

CLINIC, or CLINICAL, Adj. [from κλίνη, Gr. to lie down in a bed] those who keep their beds on account of any disorder. In Church Historians, applied to a person converted on his death-bed.

To CLINK, V. A. to strike metals together so as to make them found. Neuterly, to make a noise like the sound made by two pieces of metal struck together.

CLINK, S. a noise made by striking two pieces of metal together.

CLINQUANT, S. [Fr.] embroidery; gaudy dress; or tinsel finery.

To CLIP, V. A. [clippan, Sax.] to enfold in the arms; to hug. To cut with sheers, or scissors; to diminish, applied to coin. To cut short, not to pronounce fully, applied to language. "To clip the king's English." Confined or surrounded, used with the particle with. "Clips us with the sea." Shak.

CLIPPER, S. one that debases the coin, by filing, or otherwise diminishing its size.

CLIPPING, S. [see CLIP] that which is cut off from a thing.

CLOAK, S. [pronounced cloke] a loose outer garment without sleeves. Also, a pretext or pretence.

To CLOAK, V. A. to cover with a cloak. To conceal any design by some specious pretext.

CLOAK-BAG, S. a kind of portmanteau.

CLOCK, S. [cerk, Brit. from cloch, Brit.] a machine, going by a pendulum, serving to measure time, and shew the hour by striking on a bell. Hugens was the first person who brought the ingenious art of clock-making to any perfection, and the first pendulum clock made in England, was in the year 1622, by Fromantil, a Dutchman. What's o'clock, is a phrase, signifying what hour is it? It's so o'clock,

o'clock, implies, it is the fixth hour. Applied to stockings, clock fignifies the work with which the ankles were adorned, and as this was a means of making the female leg appear taperer than it otherwise does, it is wonderful this embellishment should now be laid afide.

CLO'D, [clud, Sax.] a lump of earth or clay; a turf; the ground; a dull, ignorant, stupid person.

To CLO'D, V. N. to unite into a mass; to curdle; also to pelt with clods.

CLO'DDY, Adj. consisting of little heaps or clods of earth.

To CLO'G, V. A. to overload; to burthen; to embarrass. Neuterly, to gather into a mass, used instead of clot. To be filled with any thing that may stop its operation.

CLO'G, S. any weight or thing which impedes or hinders; a restraint; an incumbrance, obstruction, or impediment. A composition of leather, worn by women over their shoes, to keep themselves clean or warm. A shoe. "In France—the middle fort make use of wooden clogs."

CLO'GGINESS, S. the being hindered from motion; obstruction; impediment.

CLO'GGY, Adj. that which stops up the passages or hinders motion.

CLOI'STER, S. [clis, Brit. clauster, Sax. cloistre, Fr.] a monastery for the religious of either sex. In a more limited sense, the principal part of a regular monastery, consisting of a square, built on each of its sides.

To CLOI'STER, V. A. to shut up or confine in a monastery.

CLOI'STERAL, Adj. solitary; retired; recluse; like a cloister.

CLOI'STERED, Part. solitary; inhabiting a cloister or a monastery or religious house. In Architecture, built round, or surrounded with a piazza or peristile.

CLOI'STRESS, S. a nun, or female inhabiting a religious house.

CLO'KE, S. See CLOAK.

To CLOSE, V. A. [clofa, Arm. clyfan, Sax.] to shut any thing; to conclude or finish. To confine, used with in. To join any thing broken. To close up, is to heal. Neuterly, to join two parts together, after being separated, used with upon. "The earth closed upon them." Figuratively, applied to creature, to agree to. To close in with, to join with a party. In Wrestling, to run up to a person and seize fast hold on him.

CLO'SE, S. any thing shut; a small inclosed field. Applied to time, the end of any period. "The close of night." Dryd. In Wrestling, a grapple or violent hug. A conclusion.

CLO'SE, Adj. so as nothing can come in or out. Stagnating, sultry, applied to the air. Having but few pores, applied to metals. "That very close metal." Lacke, Dense; concise; short. Applied to situation, contiguous or touching. Figuratively, applied to designs, to keep close, is to be secret or without discovery. Home; to the point. Retired, without going abroad. "Closely confined." Narrow.

CLOSE-BODIED, Adj. that which comes tight or close round the body.

CLOSE-HANDED, Adj. covetous; illiberal; ungenerous.

CLO'SELY, Adv. without vent or passage. Applied to pursuit, very near or without any great distance between. Literal. "I have translated closely."

CLO'SENESS, S. narrowness; want of air; denseness; compactness; without many pores; recluseness; solitude; reserve; avarice, or connection.

CLO'SER, S. a finisher; a concluder; a terminator.

CLO'SET, S. [from close] a small room for retirement. A shallow place, furnished with shelves, &c. for curiosities, &c.

To CLO'SET, V. A. [from the noun] to shut up, or conceal in a closet; to take into a closet, for the sake of privacy. "Lord Mansfield was closetted with the King."

CLO'SURE, S. the act of stopping up; confinement; conclusion; termination.

CLO'T, S. [lar, Belg.] a mass formed by thickening of fluids.

To CLOT, V. N. [Lieteren, Belg.] to grow into small masses; to gather into clods.

CLOTH, S. any thing woven for garments. The linen wherewith a table is covered at meals. The canvass on which pictures are painted. In the plural clothes, any thing with which a person is dressed to cover his nakedness, or embellish his person; wrote clothes, and pronounced clo's. Applied by way of eminence to woollen cloth, the great staple commodity, glory, and support of this nation; but as there is a manifest decay in the goodness of this manufacture of late years, it were to be wished that those at the helm would turn their thoughts to this article, and, by giving it all the national encouragement in their power, revive its character, and render it as reputable as they have the honour of the British arms.

CLO'THIER, S. one who carries on the manufactory of cloth. Camden observes in his Britannia, that most of the greatest scholars and eminent personages of this kingdom, have been descended from persons of this profession.

CLO'THING, S. dress, garments, or that which a person wears to cover and defend his body from the weather.

CLOT-POLL, S. a stupid person, a blockhead.

CLO'TTY, Adj. abounding with clots or lumps.

CLOUD, S. [clude, Belg. a spot] condensed vapours, suspended in the atmosphere. Clouds are the most considerable of all the meteors, as furnishing water and plenty to the earth, mitigating the excessive heats of the world zone, and screening it from the beams of the sun; collecting the rays of light by the numerous refractions they suffer in their passage thro' them, thereby prolonging the stay of light after the sun is descended below the horizon, and anticipating its coming some time before it has ascended above it; without their medium, the heavens would be one uniform sable substance, the rays of light would be scattered abroad in the immense regions of space without reaching our eyes, and the ravishing prospect of nature would become a large blot. Figuratively, the veins in precious stones. Any thing which obscures; a state of darkness; a crowd.

To CLOUD, V. A. to darken; to obscure; to be variegated or diversified with dark veins. Neuterly, to grow cloudy, dark, or overcast.

CLOUD-CAPT, Adj. covered by or touching the clouds. " The cloud-cape towers," Shak.

CLOUDILY, Adv. in a cloudy or dark manner. Figuratively, confusedly or obscurely.

CLOUDINESS, S. want of brightness or lustre; foulness, applied to diamonds or other precious stones.

CLOUDLESS, Adj. without clouds, clear, without spots.

CLOUDY, Adj. dark, obscured, or overcast with clouds. Figuratively, obscure, dark, imperfect, applied to ideas or notions. Sullen, gloomy, dejected, applied to the looks. Variegated with spots or veins, applied to marbles, agates, &c.

CLOVE, the Preter of cleave.

CLOVE, S. [clou, Fr. a nail, from its resembling the head of a nail] an aromatic fruit, growing on a tree twenty feet high, whose leaves resemble those of the bay tree, and a native of the Molucca islands, but has been extirpated thence by the Dutch, who have transplanted it to Ternate, in order to monopolize it entirely. The fruit is gathered when unripe, somewhat resembles a nail in figure, of a rough surface, dusky brown colour, and has on the top a round body of the size of a pepper-corn. It is used in foods, makes an ingredient in most family cordials. In Medicine, is esteemed carminative, good in all cephalic disorders arising from cold causes, in crudities, apoplexies, &c. and is a very good alexipharmic.

CLOVE-GILLY-FLOWER, S. in Botany, the dianthus or caryophillus. It is ranged by Linnæus, in the 2d section of his 20th class.

CLOVEN, Pret. from cleave.

CLOVEN-FOOTED, Adj. having the foot divided into two parts.

CLOVER, S. [from cleofer, Sax.] in Botany, a species of trefoil. To live in clover, is a phrase for living luxuriously, clover being reckoned a delicious food for cattle.

CLOVERED, Adj. covered with clover. " The clovered vale."

CLOUT, S. [clut, Sax.] a piece of cloth generally made double, serving to keep linens clean; a patch on a shoe or garment.

To CLOUT, V. A. to patch or mend clumsily.

CLOWN, S. [klunnegar, Ill. coarse or clumsy] a rustic or country fellow; one whose manners are unpolished.

CLOWNISH, Adj. like a clown; rude, awkward, ill-bred.

CLOWNISHLY, Adj. in a clumsy, coarse, clownish manner.

CLOWNISHNESS, S. unpolished rudeness; rustic simplicity; awkward address, like a clown.

To CLOY, V. A [encloüer, Fr.] to fill with too much food; to surfeit almost to loathing; to nail up guns.

CLOYLESS, Adj. that which will never satisfy or surfeit.

CLUB, S. [choppa, Brit.] a heavy, strong, thick stick. In Gaming, the name of one of the suits of cards, called in French trefle, from its resembling the trefoil leaf. The money every member is to pay at a drinking society. An assembly meeting at a public-house to pass the evening. Concurrence, contribution.

To CLUB, V. A. to contribute towards a public expence. To join and unite. To lend assistance. To pay one's proportion to a common expence.

To CLUCK, V. N. [cleccan, Brit.] to make a noise resembling that of a hen calling her chickens.

CLUMP, S. [klomp, Teut.] a shapeless thick piece of wood.

CLUMSILY, Adv. [implying manner] in an awkward, graceless manner.

CLUMSINESS, S. awkward, proceeding from want of breeding, parts, or experience; ungainliness.

CLUMSY, Adj. [from klumpsch, Belg.] awkward, unhandy, and without grace. Heavy, thick, and coarse, with respect to shape and appearance.

CLUNG, the Preter and Participle of cling.

CLUNG, Part. wasted away, shrunk.

CLUSTER, [cluder, cluster, Sax.] a bunch; growing close together and on one stalk; A number of insects together. Several people collected together.

To CLUSTER, V. N. to grow in bunches. To gather together in bodies, applied to bees. Actively, to collect into bunches.

To CLUTCH, V. A. [of uncertain etymology] to gripe or grasp ; to shut the hand close, so as to seize a thing.

CLUTCH, S. a gripe, grasp, or seizure, with the hand shut very close. In the plural, the talons of a bird or wild beast. Possession.

CLUTTER, S. a noise made about some trifling affair; a hurry or clamour.

To CLUTTER, V. N. to make a bustle about some trivial affair.

CLYSTER, S. [χγερη, Gr.] in Medicine, a decoction of various ingredients injected into the anus.

To COACERVATE, V. A. [coacervatus, Lat.] to heap up or together.

COACERVATION, S. the act of heaping together.

COACH, S. [coche, Fr. kocze, Bohh.] a carriage of pleasure and state, hung upon straps or springs, running on four wheels, and distinguished from a chariot, because it has two seats fronting each other. This carriage was originally intended for the country, and when first introduced into cities, there were but two even at Paris. The first courtier who set up this equipage, was John de Laval de Bois Dauphin, who could not travel on horseback on account of his enormous bulk. We find even in England, that as low as Queen Elizabeth's time, the nobility of both sexes attended her in processions on horseback; so that this vehicle seemed to be reserved for an age, when every petty tradesman scorned to preserve his health by the salutary exercise of walking, and chuse rather to entail debility on his posterity by aping nobility, and rivaling his superiors in the sum total of his expences.

COACH-BOX, S. the seat on which the person sits to drive a coach.

COACH-HIRE, S. money paid for the use of a hired coach.

To COACT, V. to act together or in concert.

COACTION, S. [coactus, Lat.] force, compulsion, obligation.

COADJUTANT, Part. [from con and adjutans, Lat.] helping or assisting a person in any action; cooperating. Substantively used for an accomplice; a cooperator.

COADJUTOR, S. [from con and adjutor, Lat.] an assistor, associate, or partner.

COADJUVANCY, S. [from con and adjuvans, Lat.] assistance, help, concurrence in any process or operation.

COAGMENTATION, S. [coagmentatio, Lat.] a joining, uniting, or heaping several particles together. The joining several syllables or words together, so as to form one word, or sentence. " Cementing and cogmentation of words." Johnson.

COAGULABLE, Adj. [from coagulo, Lat.] that which may thicken, curdle, or concrete.

To COAGULATE, V. A. [coagulo, Lat.] to make a thing curdle, or turn into clots ; to form concretions; to congeal.

COAGULATION, S. [coagulatio, Lat.] the act of turning into curds. Concretion; congelation. The state of a thing congealed, or curdled.

COAGULATIVE, Adj. having the power of causing congelations; curdling.

COAGULATION, S. that which causes condensations, or concretions. In Medicine, those substances which expel the most fluid parts of the humours, thereby thickening and incrassating them ; or else by imbibing some of the aqueous or fluid parts, these are called absorbents.

COAL, S. [col, Sax. kol, kohl.] a solid, dry, inflammable substance, found in large strata, of a black glossy hue, soft and friable and leaving when burnt, a great quantity of ashes. Used sometimes for charcoal.

COAL-BLACK, S. of the colour of coal; quite black.

To COALESCE, V. N. [pronounced coalēsse, from coalēsco, Lat.] to unite together, applied to the union of different particles : As when the particles of vapours run together, and form globules, and by that means cause rain.

COALESCENCE, S. [coalescens, Lat.] the act of coalescing or uniting of several particles.

COALITION, S. [coalitum, Lat.] the uniting of different particles, so as to compose one common mass.

COARCTATION, S. [coarctatio, Lat.] confinement, or restraint to a narrow space. The lessening any space. Restraint of liberty.

COARSE, Adj. [cors, Sax.] not refined, applied to metals. Rough, or having large threads, applied to cloth or silk. Rude, incivil, indelicate, applied to behaviour; not elegant, applied to language. Mean, vile, rough, and of no value, applied to the worth of any thing, or the manner in which it is wrought.

COARSELY, Adv. in a rude, rough, indecent or inelegant manner.

COARSENESS, S. want of purity, and refining; abounding in dross, applied to metals Consisting of large threads or wrought without any nicety, applied to manufactures. Want of elegance, or delicacy, applied to expressions. Want of politeness or breeding; clownishness, rudeness. A composition of mean and cheap materials ; that which may be bought at a low price, and is worth but little, applied to provisions.

COAST, S. [coste, Fr. costa, Ital.] land which is washed by the sea.

To COAST, V. N. to sail near a coast, or within sight of land. Actively, to sail by a place.

COASTER, S. one who makes a voyage from port to port, keeping within sight of the shore. One who sails near the shore.

CO'AT, S. [*cotte*, Fr. *cotta*, Ital.] the outward garment of a man. The lower part of a woman's dress fastened round the waste, and covering the legs. Any covering, or tegument. The hair or fur of a beast. In Heraldry, the escutcheon, &c. on which a person's arms are pourtrayed.

To COAX, V. A. to endeavour to persuade by flattery, to wheedle.

COAXER, S. one who endeavours to persuade by flattery; a wheedler.

To CO'BBLE, V. A. [*kobler*, Belg.] to mend any thing clumsily, applied generally to shoes. To do or make any thing in a coarse, unhandy, awkward, or rough manner.

COBBLER, S. a mender of shoes. Figuratively, a very clumsy bad workman.

CO'BIRONS, S. irons with a knobb at the upper end, used in country fire-places where wood is burned.

CO'BWEB, S. the web of a spider. The manner of spinning this toil, the geometrical proportion between its threads, their minuteness and slenderness, and the matter of which they are formed, are particulars worthy the consideration of a naturalist, and fill the curious mind with admiration. Figuratively, any snare or trap. Sometimes used for a restraint which may be easily removed.

COCHINE'AL, S. [*cochinilla*, Span. a wood-louse, from the similitude it bears to it] an insect found upon the opuntia, originally of a white colour, but turning red by means of the food it eats, and when dried affording a beautiful purple colour used by dyers.

CO'CHLEARY, Adj. [from *cochlea*, Lat.] made in the form of or resembling a screw.

CO'CHLEATED, Adj. [from *cochlea*, Lat.] twisted in form of a screw; turbinated.

COCK, S. [*coc*, Sax. *hrek*, Belg. *coq*, Fr.] the male of the species of domestic fowls, remarkable for its courage, pride and gallantry. Also the male of any birds. An instrument turning round a pivot, to shew the point from which the wind blows. An instrument used in drawing liquors from casks. The notch of an arrow. That part of the lock of a gun, which strikes the flint. Figuratively, a courageous person, or one who possesses great fund of spirit. In Marine Affairs, a small boat, called a cock-boat. A small heap of hay. The form in which the brims of a hat are placed. The stile or gnomen of a dial. The needle of a balance.

To COCK, V. A. to erect. "Cocks his ears." Gay. To mould the shape of a hat. To wear the hat with an air of smartness. To fix the cock of a gun ready for discharging. To place hay in small heaps. To look with an air of triumph and contempt, joined to the word *nose*. Neuterly, to strut, or look big. To train cocks for fighting.

COCKA'DE, S. a ribband formed in the shape of a rose, worn in a man's hat.

CO'CKATRICE, S. a serpent said to be formed from a cock's egg. Figuratively, a person of an insidious, venemous disposition.

To CO'CKER, V. A. [*coqueliner*, Fr.] to indulge too much; to fondle.

CO'CKER, S. one who keeps or trains cocks for fighting.

CO'CKEREL, S. [a diminutive noun from *cock*] a young cock.

CO'CKERMOUTH, a town of Cumberland, with a market on Mondays, and two fairs, the first Monday in May for horned cattle, and on October 10 for horses and horned cattle. The situation is low, between the rivers Derwent and Cocker, over which there are two stone bridges. It is between two hills, on one of which stands a handsome church, and on the other a stately castle. It is a borough-town, and sends two members to parliament. It is well inhabited, has good trade in coarse broad cloths, and has several handsome buildings. The market is the best for corn in the county, except Penrith. It is 44 miles S. E. by S. of Kendal, 25 S. W. by W. of Carlisle, and 287 N. N. W. of London. Lon. 14. 25. lat. 54. 75.

CO'CKET, S. [of uncertain etymology] a seal belonging to the custom-house. An instrument delivered to merchants as a certificate that they have paid the customs for their goods.

CO'CKLE, S. [*coquille*, Fr.] a small shell-fish.

To CO'CKLE, V. N. to contract into wrinkles by wet or rain.

CO'CKLED, Part. shelled; wrinkled by wet.

CO'CKNEY, S. [*pais de cocaigne*, in Boileau, is a country of dainties; one born in London, and as a word of contempt. Figuratively, any effeminate, luxurious, inexperienced person living in a city.

CO'CKPIT, S. a place wherein cocks generally fight.

CO'CKSURE, Adj. confident, certain, quite sure.

CO'CKSWAIN, S. [*cogfweine*, Sax.] the officer who has the command of the cockboat.

CO'COA, S. See CACAO, or CHOCO-LATE-NUT.

COD, or CODFISH, S. a sea-fish, caught in great plenty on the banks of Newfoundland.

COD, S. [*codde*, Sax.] in Botany, any husk in which seeds are lodged.

To COD, V. N. to inclose in a husk, or cod.

CO'DE, S. [from *codex*, Lat.] a book. A book of civil laws.

CO'DICIL, S. [a diminutive of *codex*, Lat.] a writing made as of a supplement to a will to supply something omitted.

4   T e

To CO'DLE, V. A. [of *coala*, Lat.] to parboil. To soften by hot water.

CO'DLING, S. an early kind of apple.

COE'FFICACY, S. [from *con*, Lat. and *efficacia*, Lat.] the united power of several things to produce an effect.

COEFFI'CIENCY, S. [from *con*, and *efficiens*, Lat.] the joint act of several things to produce any effect.

COEFFI'CIENT, Part. [*con* and *efficiens*, Lat.] that which acts jointly with another. Coefficient in Algebra, numbers or uneven quantities prefixed to letters, into which they are supposed to be multiplied. Thus, in 3 *a*, 2*a*; or *cxa*; 3 is the *coefficient* of 3*a*; *b*, of *ba*; and *c*, of *cxa*. In fluxions, applied to any generating term, is the quantity arising from the division of that term by the generated quantity.

COE'MPTION, S. [*comptio*, Lat.] the act of buying up or engrossing any commodity. "Monopolies and *coemptions* of wares." *Bac.*

COE'QUAL, Adj. [from *con* and *equalis*, Lat.] being in the same condition, and circumstance as another.

COEQUA'LITY, S. the state of two persons or things which are equal.

To COE'RCE, V. A. [*coerceo*, Lat.] to restrain by force, or punishments.

COE'RCIBLE, Adj. that which may be restrained.

COE'RCION, S. [from *coerceo*, Lat.] a check, or restraint.

COE'RCIVE, Adj. that which has the power of restraining. Forcible.

COESSE'NTIAL, Adj. [from *con* and *essentia*, Lat.] having or partaking of the same essence.

COESSENTIA'LITY, S. the partaking of the same essence with another.

COETA'NEOUS, Adj. [from *con* and *aetas*, age,] of the same age with another. Used with *to*, or *with*.

COETE'RNAL, Adj. [from *con* and *aeternus*, Lat.] equally eternal with another.

COETE'RNITY, S. [from *con* and *aeternitas*, Lat.] having an eternity of existence equal with another.

COE'VAL, Adj. [*coaevus*, Lat.] born at the same time; of the same age, followed by *with*, or *to*. "Coeval with eternity." *Pope.* "Coeval to mankind." *Hale.* Used substantively, for a person of the same age, or living at the same time as another. A contemporary.

COE'VOUS, Adj. [*coaevus*, Lat.] of the same age.

To COEXI'ST, V. N. [from *con* and *existo*, Lat.] to exist, at the same time or place; joined to the particle *with*.

COEXI'STENCE, S. having existence at the same time, or place with another; followed by *with*.

COEXI'STENT, Adj. having existence at

the same time with another. "Coexistent with the motions." *Locke.*

To COEXTE'ND, V. A. [from *con* and *extendo*, Lat.] to extend to the same space or duration.

COEXTE'NSION, S. the act of extending to the same space or duration with another, followed by *with*.

COFFEE, S. [*caoueb*, Turk. *caffé*, Fr.] the berry of a tree, propagated in most of our colonies, especially in Jamaica, where it is little inferior to the best Turkey. Its leaves resemble the common laurel. The liquor made from the berry roasted, was introduced into England, first by Mr. Daniel Edwards, a Turkey-merchant, in 1652, bringing with him one Pasquet, a Greek servant, to make *coffee* for him; who was the first person that ever set up a *coffee-house* in this kingdom.

CO'FFEE-HOUSE, S. a house where coffee is sold, and the daily and evening papers are taken in for the accommodation of customers.

CO'FFEE-MAN, S. one who keeps a coffee-house.

CO'FFER, S. [*coffre*, Sax.] a chest to keep money in. Figuratively, treasure. In Architecture, a small linking, or depressure between the modillions of the Corinthian cornice, generally filled up with a rose. In Fortification, a hollow lodgment, across a dry moat.

To CO'FFER, V. A. to put into chests or coffers. "Might *coffer* up." *Raw.*

CO'FFIN, S. [*cofin*, Fr. *cofana*, Ital. *kofe*, isl. a little house] the receptacle wherein a dead body is placed. In Pastry, a mould of paste for a pye. A round piece of paper with edges bent up perpendicularly, used by the apothecaries to drop their boluses in, to keep the outward paper clean. In Farriery, the whole hoof of a horse's foot above the coronet, including the coffin bone.

To CO'FFIN, V. A. to place, or put in a coffin.

To CO'G, V. A. [*cog*, Brit.] to perfuade, wheedle, or flatter. "I'll *cog* their hearts from them." *Shak.* To foist, used with *in.* "*Cogging* in the word." *Tilloj.* To obtrude falsehoods. To *cog* a die, is to secure it so, as to direct it in its fall.

CO'G, S. the tooth of a wheel by which it acts or operates upon another wheel.

To CO'G, V. A. to place *cogs* in a wheel.

CO'GENCY, S. [*cogens*, Lat.] the power of compelling; the power of enforcing or forcing assent, or obedience.

CO'GENT, Part. [*cogens*, Lat.] powerful, restless, forcible.

CO'GENTLY, Adv. forcibly extorting conviction and assent.

CO'GGER, S. a flatterer; a wheedler.

CO'GITABLE, Adj. [*cogitabilis*, Lat.] that which may be the subject of thought or meditation.

To

To CO'GITATE, V. N. [cogitatum, Lat.] to think; to meditate.

COGITATION. S. [cogitatio, Lat.] the act of thinking. Thought, intention, design. Meditation.

CO'GITATIVE, Adj. [cogitans, Lat.] given to thought, study, or reflection.

COGNATION. S. [cognatio, Lat.] relation; a partaking of the same nature.

COGNISE'E. S. in law, the person to whom a fine in lands is acknowledged.

CO'GNISOR. S. in Law, one that passes or acknowledges a fine in lands to another.

CO'GNIZABLE. Adj. [cognoissable, Fr.] proper for the consideration or inspection; subject to examination and notice.

CO'GNIZANCE, S. [pronounced connisance, from cognoissance, Fr.] the hearing of a matter judicially, used with the word of; the particular jurisdiction of a magistrate. A badge by which any person may be distinguished.

COGNO'MINAL, Adj. [cognomen, Lat.] having the same name. "His cognominal, or name-sake." Brown

COGNI'SCENCE, S. [from cognoscens, Prat.] knowledge; the state or act of knowing.

COGNO'SCIBLE, Adj. [cognosco, Lat.] that which may be known; that which is possible to be known.

To COHA'BIT, V. N. to dwell with another. To live together like man and wife.

COHA'BITANT, S. [con and habitans] one who dwells with another.

COHABITA'TION, S. [from con, Lat. and habito] the act of dwelling with another. The living together as man and wife.

COHE'IR, S. [coheres, Lat.] a man who enjoys an inheritance jointly with another.

COHE'IRESS, S. a female, who is entitled to an inheritance with another.

To COHE'RE, V. N. from [cohereo, Lat.] to stick together; to be connected; to depend on what has preceded, and connect with what follows. To suit, fit, agree, or be suited to.

COHE'RENCE, COHE'RENCY, S. [cohaerentia, Lat.] in physics, the state of bodies in which their parts are joined together. Relation, dependency, or the connection of the parts of a discourse with one another. Consistency.

COHE'RENT, Part. [cohaerens, Lat.] sticking together. Suitable, adapted to each other; consistent.

COHE'SION, S. [from cohaereo] the action whereby atoms are connected together, so as to form particles, and the particles are kept together, so as to form sensible masses. The secondary cause of this cohesion is acknowledged, by Sir Isaac Newton, to be unknown: who likewise informs us, that the different forms and properties of bodies, arise from the different cohesions. Figuratively, cohesion signifies the state of union, connection.

COHE'SIVE, Adj. having the power of sticking fast.

To COHO'BATE, V. A. to pour any distilled liquor upon its remaining matter, and distil it again.

COIF, S. [coife, Fr. cuffia, Span.] a headdress. A lady's cap. A serjeant's cap.

COI'FED, Adj. having or wearing a cap.

COI'FURE, S. [from coiffure, Fr.] a head dress. "I am highly pleased with your coifure." Spell. N°. 98.

To COIL, V. A. [cueillir, Fr.] to gather into a narrow compass. To coil a rope, is to wind it in a ring.

COIL, S. [culleren, Teut.] a tumult, noise, confusion, or bustle. A string or rope wound into a ring.

COIN, S. [coin, Fr. conio, Ital.] money or metal stamped with a lawful impression. Payment or compensation of any kind. As the rewards of merit do not consist so much in the intrinsic value, as their possibility of immortalizing the exploit, for which they are bestowed; and as medals are universally acknowledged the best comments on past actions, and the truest preservers of noble exploits, it were to be wished that monarchs would for the sake of encouraging either those who are eminent for their parts, or their warlike achievements, permit their citizens, and the circumstances for which they deserve immortality, to be stamped on a certain number of their annual coins, in order to transmit the names of heroes, to posterity, and to encourage others to tread in their steps.

To COIN, V. A. to stamp metals for money. To make, imitate, or forge any thing.

COI'NAGE, S. the stamping metals for money. The English coinage by adding the letters on the edge, contributes greatly to its perfection. This word is also used for coin or money. The charges or expence of coining. Forgery.

To COINCI'DE, V. N. [coincido, Lat.] to be consistent with. To concur, used with the particle with.

COI'NCIDENCE, S. concurrence, consistency, or uniting to effect the same purpose.

COI'NCIDENT, Adj. [coincidens, Lat.] concurring, consisting, and agreeing, to the support of any point.

COI'NER, S. a person who makes money. A maker of counterfeit money. An inventor.

CO'ISTRIL, S. a coward, a poltroon. "He's a coward and a coistril." Shak.

COIT, S. [kote, Belg.] a thing thrown at a mark. See QUOIT.

COI'TION, S. [from coitio, Lat.] the act of producing or propagating the species. The act of uniting two bodies together.

COL'ANDER, S. [pronounced cullender, from colander, Lat.] a sieve of hair, metal, &c. through which any mixture is strained.

COLA'TION, S. [from colatum, Lat.] the act

act of straining, or separating, any fluid from its dregs.

COLATURE, S. [*colatura*, Lat.] the act of separating the dregs of any fluid by straining it through a sieve.

COLCHESTER, S. a town of Essex, with a market on Saturdays, and four fairs, on Easter-Tuesday, for wholesale taylors, on June 24 for horses, on July 23 for cattle and hides, and on October 20 for cheese, butter, and toys. It is a place of great antiquity, and is pleasantly and commodiously seated on the S. side of the river Colne, which is navigable within a mile of the town, on the declivity of a hill, and extends from E. to W. It was surrounded by a wall which had six gates, and three posterns, besides nine watch-towers; but now these are, in a great measure, demolished. It had 16 parish churches, but now only 12 are used, these are not very large, and most of them were damaged in Cromwell's time. There are here also five meeting houses. The town consists of about 3000 dwelling-houses, most of them old built, with some few good brick ones; the streets are not very broad, though they are tolerably paved. The number of the inhabitants amount to about 5000. The town suffered greatly in the civil wars. There is a large manufactory of bays, for Spain and Portugal, and the town is famous for oysters and eringo-roots, and imports wine, brandy, coals, deals, &c. It was lately a corporation, but has lost its charter for some misdemeanour; however it still sends two members to parliament. Towards the E. are the ruins of an old castle, with a fence round it about two acres in circumference. It is 22 miles E. N. E. of Chelmsford.

COLD, Adj. [*cald*, Sax. *col*, Belg.] without warmth, having a sensation of cold, or shivering. That which is not volatile, or easily put into motion by heat. Figuratively, unaffected, indifferent. Not able to excite the passions. Reserved, chaste, temperate, not easily provoked to anger. Deliberate, calm, opposed to hasty. In Hunting, not scenting, or not affecting the scent.

COLD, that which is void of heat or motion. That which produces the sensation of cold. A disease occasioned by stopping perspiration.

COLDLY, Adv. without heat; with great indifference and unconcern.

COLDNESS, S. that quality which is opposite to heat. That quality which deprives a person of his natural warmth and heat. Want of kindness, love, or affection; coyness, chastity.

COLE, S. [*caul*, Sax.] a name for all kinds of cabbage.

COLESEED, S. in Botany, the rape, from whence the oil is drawn.

COLIC, S. [*colica*, Lat.] in Medicine, a severe pain in the lower venter. A bilious

colic, proceeds from bilious, sharp and stimulating humours, which irritate the bowels so as to cause continual gripes, attended with looseness; this is usually after a violent fit of anger, and relieved by laxatives and emollients. A flatulent colic is a pain in the bowels, which distends them prodigiously, is owing to dry faeces contained in the intestines, and managed with carminatives, and moderate openers. A nervous colic is from convulsive spasms, or contortions of the guts; this is remedial by brisk cathartics, joined with opiates and emollient diluters. The stone colic, proceeds, by consent of parts, from the irritation of the stone, or gravel in the bladder or kidneys, is treated by nephritics, oily diuretics, and greatly assisted by carminative and turpentine clysters.

COLIC, Adj. affecting the bowels.

COLLAPSION, S. the state of vessels closing of themselves. The act of closing together.

COLLAR, S. [*colare*, Lat. of *collum* Lat.] an ornament of metal worn by knights of several military orders, and having the badge of the order suspended at the bottom. That of the order of the garter consists of SS, with roses enamelled red, within a garter enamelled blue, and a George at the bottom. Also that part of the harness, which is round a horse's neck. The part of the dress which surrounds the neck. A collar of brawn, is a quantity of brawn rolled up.

To COLLAR, V. A. to seize by the collar. To collar brawn, is to roll it up and bind it tight.

COLLAR-BONE, S. the clavicle; one of the bones on each side of the neck.

To COLLATE, V. A. [*collatum*, Lat.] to compare one thing with another; applied to books, to compare and examine them. To place in benefice.

COLLATERAL, Adj. [from *con* and *lateris*] side to side, running parallel; mutual. In Geography, situated by the side of another; lying between the cardinal points. In genealogy, applied to relations of the same stock, but not in the same line of ascendants and descendants; such are uncles, aunts, nephews, cousins. Collateral descent, in Law, is what passes to brothers children. Collateral security, is an additional security.

COLLATERALLY, Adj. side by side, parallel. In an indirect manner, without design. Not in the same line of descendants.

COLLATION, S. [*colatio*, Lat.] the act of bestowing favours. The comparing one copy or thing with another. In canon Law, the bestowing of a benefice by a bishop. A public entertainment.

COLLATOR, S. one who compares copies or manuscripts. One who presents to a living or benefice.

COLLEAGUE, S. a partner or associate.

To

To COLLEAGUE, V. N. to unite or join with; followed by *with*.

To COLLE'CT, V. A. [*collectum*, Lat.] to gather several things together. To add into a sum. To retain the knowledge of from observation. To infer, or deduce from arguments; used with *from*.

COLLECT, S. [*collectum*, Lat.] a short comprehensive prayer.

COLLECTA'NEOUS, Adj. [*collectaneus*, Lat.] gathered or collected together.

COLLE'CTIBLE, Adj. that which may be deduced from any premises; used with *from*.

COLLE'CTION, S. [*collectio*, Lat.] the act of gathering several things together. An assemblage of things in the same place. A consequence, or deduction from some preceding argument or proposition.

COLLE'CTIVE, Adj. [*collectivus*, Lat. *collectif*, Fr.] gathered together; consisting of several parts forming a whole. In Grammar, a collective noun, is a noun which expresses a multitude, though used in the singular number; as an assembly, an army.

COLLE'CTIVELY, Adv. taken together, opposed to singly. In general; or generally.

COLLE'CTOR, S. [Lat.] one who collects or gathers scattered things together.

COLLEGE, S. [Fr. *collegium*] a collection of animals. "Thick as the *college* of the bees." Dryd. An unusual sense. A society of men dedicating themselves to the study of learning. A public place endowed with certain revenues, where the several branches of learning are taught; several colleges form an university. Not to mention any other colleges, that of the physicians in London deserves particular notice, and as the health and lives of his majesty's subjects are the sacred deposition entrusted to their care, it were to be wished, that the genuineness of drugs, and the qualities of medicinal compositions were inspected by them with a scrupulous exactness, that no ingredient should be omitted in any composition, because it would cost the apothecaries much in the purchase, or hinder their making a show in the quantity they sell by retail, when the only thing for which a medicine ought to be valued, is its quality.

COLLE'GIAL, Adj. relating to, or possessed by a college.

COLLE'GIAN, S. a member of a college.

COLLE'GIATE, Adj. consisting of colleges, regulated after the manner of a college. *Collegiate* church, is that which is endowed for a body corporate, consisting of a dean and secular priests, without a bishop.

COLLE'GIATE, S. a member of a college, or university.

COLLET, S. [Fr. from *collum*, Lat.] the neck. That part of a ring in which the stone or jewel is set.

To COLLI'DE, V. A [*collido*, Lat.] to strike, or beat, two things against each other.

COLLIER, S. a person who digs for coals. A dealer in coals; a vessel to convey coals by water.

COLLIFLOWER, S. See CAULIFLOWER.

COLLIGA'TION, S. [*colligatio*, Lat.] the binding things together. "The *colligation* of vessel.." Brown.

COLLI'QUATABLE, Adj. that which is easily dissolved.

COLLI'QUAMENT, S. the substance any thing is reduced to by dissolution, or melting.

COLLI'QUANT, Part. [*colliquans*, Lat.] having the power of melting.

To COLLIQUATE, V. A. [*colliquo*, Lat.] to melt, dissolve, or reduce a fluid by heat, &c.

COLLIQUA'TION, S. [from *colliquate*] the melting or dissolving any thing by heat.

COLLIQUA'TIVE, Adj. [from *colliquate*] melting or dissolvent. A *colliquative* fever, is attended with a diarrhœa, or profuse sweats, from too lax a habit of body.

COLLIQUEFA'CTION, S. [from *colliqueo*, and *faction*, the reducing different metals to one mass by melting.

COLLI'SION, S. [*collisio*, Lat.] the act of striking two things together.

To COLLOCATE, V. A. [*collocatum*, supine, of *colloco*, Lat.] to place; to station; to reside. "Wherein that virtue is chiefly *collocate*." Bac.

COLLOCA'TION, S. [*collocatio*, Lat.] the act of placing; disposition; residence.

COLLOCU'TION, S. [*collocutio*, Lat.] the talking with another. Conference.

To COLLO'GUE, V. A. to wheedle, flatter, or impose upon.

COLLOP, S. a piece or slice of any meat or animal.

COLLOQUY, S. [*colloquium*, Lat.] a conference, or conversation; wherein two or more are speaking together.

COLLU'CTANCY, S. [*colluctor*, Lat.] a tendency to resist, struggle with, or contest.

To COLLU'DE, V. N. [*colludo*, Lat.] to join in a fraud or imposition.

COLLU'SION, S. [*collusio*, Lat.] an agreement between two or more persons, to defraud or cheat another of his right.

COLLU'SIVE, Adj. fraudulently agreed upon between two or more persons, in order to cheat.

COLLU'SIVELY, Adv. contrived with a fraudulent design.

COLLU'SORY, Adj. carrying on a fraud by collusion.

To COLLY, to smut, or black with coal.

CO'LON, S. [from *colon*, Gr. a member] in Grammar, a point or stop marked thus (:) used

used to make a pause greater than that of the semicolon, and less than that of a period or full point; at present it is used in a period where the sense seems complete, but is lengthened by some supernumerary sentence, likewise in a very long period to give ease and respite to the breath, and a pause may be made at a colon, while a person may count three, without confusing or interrupting the sense of the rest of the period. In Anatomy, the greatest and widest of all the intestines, which is a continuation of the cæcum, begins under the right kidney near the haunch, and after several convolutions, terminates near the left kidney, to which it is joined, by a double incurvation like a Roman S.

COLONEL, S. [pronounced kurnel, Fr. colonello, Ital.] an officer in the army who commands a regiment. Lieutenant colonel, is the second officer of a regiment.

COLONELSHIP, S. the office or duty of a colonel.

To COLONISE, V. A. [from colony] to plant with inhabitants, brought from some other place; to plant with colonies.

COLONNADE, S. [colonna, Ital.] a series of pillars placed in a circle, and insulated with-inside. A polystile colonade, is that which is too immense for the eye to take in at a single view, such as that of the place of St. Peter, in Rome, consisting of 284 columns of the Doric order. Figuratively, any range of pillars.

COLONY, S. [colonia, Lat.] a body of people going from the mother country, to cultivate and settle some other place. Figuratively, the country settled in by a body of people from some other place. If we consider the sudden alteration made in the circumstances of this kingdom on the first planting of our colonies, the increase made in the marine, the number of souls with which it has peopled the metropolis; the reduction it has made in the interest of money; the several commodities, now furnished from thence, which we are obliged to buy at any rate from foreigners; and which we now export to foreign markets; if we consider the possibility of raising those commodities in our colonies, which, now being purchased from other estates, turn the balance of trade against us; if we consider how great a proportion of our exports are carried to these colonies, what a number of hands are employed at home in their manufacture, and consequently how much the value of lands are increased in this island by that means, I say if we consider these particulars only, it is to be hoped that the government will not lay any burthen, by new taxes on our colonies.

COLOQUINTIDA, S. [colobinthis, Lat.] the fruit of a plant in the Levant about the bigness of a large orange, of a golden colour, its inside is full of kernels which are taken out, before it is used. Both the pulp and

No. VII.

seed are intollerably bitter, on which account it is called bitter apple. As it is one of the most violent purgatives, it is seldom used in extemporaneous prescriptions, and therefore should be entirely laid aside by ignorant women, who sometimes rub their nipples with it, in order to wean their children.

COLORATE, Adj. [coloratus, Lat.] coloured; died; or stained.

COLORATION, S. [coloration of color, Lat.] the art of colouring or painting, colour or hue.

COLOUR, S. [color, Fr. colore, Lat.] the different sensations excited by the refracted rays of light. In a popular or general sense, the different hue in which any thing appears to the eye. The tints or hues produced by painting joined with true or false, description, representation, or appellation. In the plural, an ensign or flag. In Law, the probable plea of a defendant to an action brought, which in fact, is false.

To COLOUR, V. A. [color, Lat.] to mark, or die with some hue, tint, or colour. Figuratively, to palliate, or excuse; to assign some specious reason. Neuterly, to blush a word used only in conversation.

COLOURABLE, Adj. specious, plausible, probable.

COLOURABLY, Adv. in a specious manner.

COLOURED, Part. diversified with different hues or colours.

COLOURING, S. that branch of painting which teaches the laying of colours with propriety and beauty.

COLOURIST, S. a painter excellent in the manner in which he disposes his lights and shades.

COLOURLESS, Adj. void of colour, not any white, transparent.

COLT, S. [Sax.] a young horse that has never been broke. A raw unexperienced ignorant person.

To COLT, V. N. to frisk; riot; run about in a strange or behave in a wonton manner. Actively, to play tricks, or play the fool with a person.

COLTS-TOOTH, S. a superfluous tooth, in the mouth of a young horse; an inclination to wantonness, pleasure, or gaiety.

COLTER, S. [culter, Sax. kuter, Belg.] the sharp iron of a plough, which breaks up the ground.

COLTISH, Adj. like a colt; wanton.

COLUMBARY, S. [columborium, Lat.] a dove-cot; or pidgeon-house.

COLUMBINE, S. [columbine, Lat.] in Botany the aquilegia. It is ranged by Linnæus in the fifth division of his thirteenth class, and has four species.

COLUMBINE, S. [columbinus, Lat.] a pale violet dove colour. Also the chief female character in pantomime entertainments.

COLUMN, S. [columna, Lat.] in Architecture;

L l

texture, a round pillar to support or adorn a building; it should always be less at top than at bottom, decreasing in the proportion of a truncated cone or pyramid. In War, a deep file, or row of troops. In Printing, half a page, when the lines terminate in the middle of it, and begin again at the left hand margin.

CO'LUMNAR, CO'LUMNARIAN, Adj. formed in the shape, or resembling a column.

CO'LURES, S. [from *coluri*, Lat.] In Geography and Astronomy, two great circles imagined to intersect each other at right angles, in the poles of the world, one of which passes through aries, and libra; the other through cancer and capricorn.

CO'MA, S. [from *κωμα*, Gr.] a kind of lethargy, wherein a person has a violent propensity to sleep, whether it ensue or no.

CO'MART, S. a contract, or stipulation. "By the same comart and carriage of the articles." *Shak.*

CO'MATE, S. [from *cum* and *mate*, Lat.] a companion; a comrade. "My comates and brethren." *Shak.*

CO'MATOSE, Adj. lethargic, sleepy.

CO'MB, S. [the *b* is seldom pronounced, serving only to lengthen the pronunciation of the O from *comb*, Sax.] an instrument made of horn, box, &c. through which the hair is passed to cleanse or adjust it; there is a sort made of black lead used by the ladies to colour curraty hair, or to conceal those of a grey colour; which time has invidiously produced. Likewise an instrument made of iron wires through which flax, wool, or hemp is passed; the crest of a cock; the hollow places in a bee-hive, wherein the honey is stored, from *cumb*, Gr. a hollow place.

To CO'MB, V. A. [*comb*, North. Brit.] to pass a comb through the hair; to pass flax, &c. through a comb.

To CO'MBAT, V. N. [pronounced *cumbat*, from *combattre*, Fr.] to fight. Figuratively, to engage. "Love combated by pride."

CO'MBAT, S. [Fr.] a contest; a battle; a duel. Figuratively, to struggle. "The noble combat 'twixt joy and sorrow." *Shak.*

CO'MBATANT, S. [*combattant*, Fr.] one that fights with another; a stickler for any opinion; used with *for* before the thing defended.

COMBINA'TION, S. an union of private persons for some unjust or illegal purpose; union of qualities or bodies; mixture; association, applied to ideas. In Mathematics, the variation in which any number of things may be disposed.

To COMBI'NE, V. A. to join together in any purpose; to link together in affection or concord; neuterly, to join together, applied to things; to unite in one body; to unite in friendship.

CO'MBLESS, Adj. [from *comb* and *less*, of *leafe*, Sax. want, negation, absence] not having a comb, applied to a cock.

COMBU'STIBLE, Adj. that which may be burnt, or which soon catches fire.

COMBU'STIBLENESS, S. the quality of easily catching fire.

COMBU'STION, S. [from *combustion*, Lat.] the act of burning several things together; conflagration; destruction by fire. Figuratively, confusion, noise, commotion, bustle.

To COME, V. N. [pronounced *cum*, preter. I *came*, or *have come*, participle *come*, from *cuman*, Sax.] to move nearer to a thing or person; to approach, or advance towards, used with *from* before the place from whence the motion is made, and *to* before the thing or place where it ends or tends towards; *to come to*, is to arrive at, or attain; applied to knowledge. Used with *forth* and *from*, to proceed, or issue from; *to come about*, to happen, fall out, or chance to be, to change to any expected or wished for point, applied to the wind; *to come again*, to come a second time, to return; *to come after*, to follow, in scripture language, to become a disciple; or proselyte. "If any man will come after me." *Matt.* xvi. 24. Used with *at*, to reach to get within the reach of; *to come by*, to obtain, acquire; *to come in for*, to be easily enough to obtain a share of any thing; joined with *near*, to approach, to resemble; used with *of*, to proceed, or descend from; applied to effects, to be produced by, or flow from; *to come off*, to escape, general; joined with *well* or *safe*, to quit, or fall from, or leave. "His hat come off." *To come on*, to advance, to make a progress, to thrive, or grow, to advance to combat; *to come over*, to get the better of by artifice, to revolt, to rise, or descend into the worm, in distillation, to amount to, as the refuse of an arithmetical operation and proceeds; used with *to*, to agree, or consent; joined with the pronouns, *himself*, &c. to recover from a fright, &c. a faint; *to come to pass*, to happen, to fall out; used with *up*, to grow out of the ground, applied to vegetables, to become polite, or adopted by a majority, applied to fashions; joined to *with*, to overtake. "He came up with them at Exeter." *To come upon*, to invade, or attack; with *to* before it, something future.

CO'ME, interj. implies an exhortation to attention, dispatch, or courage.

CO'ME, Part. of the verb COME.

COME'DIAN, [*comedien*, Fr.] a performer on the stage; in a limited sense, one who appears in comedy; but in a more general sense, any actors. "His majesty's company of comedians."

CO'MEDY, S. [*comedie*, Fr. *comadia*, Lat.] a dramatic piece representing some entertaining transaction.

CO'MELINESS, S. grace, handsomeness, elegance of figure.

CO'MELY, Adj. handsome, graceful, applied to exciting reverence, suitable to a person's age, or condition; consistent with virtue.

CO'MELY,

CO'MELY, Adv. in a graceful, becoming, agreeable manner.

CO'MER, S. a visitor; a person who comes to, or settles in a place.

CO'MET, S. [cometa, or cometes, Lat.] in Astronomy, an opaque heavenly body, moving in its proper orbit, which is very excentric, having one of its foci in the center of the sun. It is distinguished not only by its orbit, but likewise by its appearance from the planets, as being bearded, tailed, and haired; bearded when eastward of the sun, and its light marches before; tailed when westward of the sun, and the train follows it; and haired when diametrically opposite to the sun, having the earth between it, and all its tail hid excepting a few scattered rays.

COME'TA'RIUM, S. [Lat.] a mathematical machine, representing the method of a comet's revolution. Mr. Martin has obliged the world with an instrument of this kind, which renders the doctrine of comets easy to the meanest capacity.

CO'METARY, COME'TIC, Adj. that which relates to a comet.

COMFIT, S. [confit, Fr.] a dry sweetmeat.

To COMFIT, V. A. to preserve with sugar.

CO'MFITURE, S. [from confit, or confiture] a sweet-meat.

To CO'MFORT, V. A. [pronounced cumfort, conforter, Fr.] to strengthen, excite, or enliven a person; to make a person cheerful.

CO'MFORT, S. support, assistance; consolation; that which causes a person to be cheerful.

CO'MFORTABLE, Adj. receiving relief to distress; having the power of lessening grief and distress.

CO'MFORTABLY, Adv. in a chearful, comfortable manner.

CO'MFORTER, S. one who lessens the degree of a person's sorrow. In Scripture, applied as a title to the Holy Ghost, wherein it signifies not only a comforter, but likewise an instructor, or adviser, as may be gathered not only from the context wherein he is mentioned as another comforter. John xiv. 16. but likewise from his office, which was to teach his disciples all things, v. 26, and chap. xv. 26. "To testify of Christ." and from the usual acceptation of the original word. "As in Isaiah." "ο μεν επι λογον μονον παρακλησιν." "Of men epi logon monon parakloumen." where the word parakaloumen, from whence the original word translated comforter is derived, signifies to exhort, persuade, or advise.

CO'MFORTLESS, Adj. without comfort, without any thing to allay the sensation of misfortunes.

CO'MIC, CO'MICAL, Adj. [comicus, Lat.] relating to comedy. Ridiculous or causing mirth from some gesture, raillery, &c.

CO'MICALLY, Adv. in such a manner as to raise mirth, after the manner of comedy.

CO'MICALNESS, S. that quality by which a thing appears odd, or ridiculous, and creates mirth.

CO'MING, S. the act of moving towards, Approach. Presence, or arrival. Joined with in, the products of a person's estate, pension, &c. "What are thy rents? What are thy comings in?" Shak.

CO'MING, Part. fond; forward; easily complying. Applied to time, something future.

CO'MMA, S. [κομμα, Gr.] in Grammar, a pause, or stop, marked thus, (.) used to distinguish such members of a discourse from each other wherein the sense is not compleat. In Music, the smallest of all the sensible intervals of tune. In Natural History, a very beautiful moth.

To COMMA'ND, V. A. [commander, Fr.] to order; to keep in subjection. To force or oblige a person to perform any thing. Applied to situation, to overlook, to be situated above any place, so as to be able to look into, or upon it. Neuterly, to possess power and authority sufficient to enforce any action.

COMMA'ND, S. authority or power; sway. Figuratively, the exercise of authority, or enforcing obedience.

COMMA'NDER, S. he that has authority over others, in a military sense, a leader, chief, or officer. A paving beetle, or rammer.

COMMA'NDMENT, S. [commandement, Fr.] an express order to do or abstain from any thing, including the idea of authority and obligation. Figuratively, the authority of commanding, or enforcing obedience. The Commandments are the precepts of the decalogue, so called by way of eminence, and containing the whole of our duty to God and man.

COMMA'NDRESS, S. a female who commands.

COMME'MORABLE, Adj. [commemoro, Lat.] deserving to be celebrated and kept in remembrance.

COMMEMORA'TION, S. the doing something to preserve the remembrance of a person or thing.

COMME'MORATIVE, Adj. tending to preserve the remembrance of any thing.

To COMME'NCE, V. N. [commencer, Fr.] to begin; to take its beginning. Actively, to begin a thing; in Law, "to commence a suit."

To COMME'ND, V. A. [commendo, Lat.] to praise; to praise any production on account of its good qualities or perfections. To deliver with full assurance of protection.

Used with *to*, " *To thee I do commend my* watchful soul." *Shak.* To defire to be mentioned in a respectful manner. " Commend me to your brother.

COMMEND, S. profession of esteem and respect. " I send to her my kind commends." *Shak.*

COMMENDABLE, Adj. worthy or deferving of praife.

COMMENDABLY, Adv. worthy of commendation.

COMMENDAM, S. [*commenda*, low Lat.] In Canons, a vacant benefice given to a perfon to supply till some other perfon is preented to it.

COMMENDATARY, S. one who holds a living in commendam.

COMMENDATION, S. praife. Recommendation. A meffage of kindnefs. Approbation.

COMMENDATORY, Adj. that which commends or engages notice.

COMMENDER, S. one who praifes, or commends another.

COMMENSALITY, S. [*commenfalis*, Lat.] the act of eating at the same table with another.

COMMENSURABILITY, S. [from *commenfurable*] the capability of being meafured

COMMENSURABLE, Adj. [from *con* and *menfura*, Lat.] in Geometry. having fome common allowed part; or that which may be meafured by fome common meafure.

To COMMENSURATE, V. A. to reduce to a common meafure.

COMMENSURATE, Part. equal, proportionate; as extenfive, ufed with *to*, or *with*.

COMMENSURATION, S. the meafuring a thing by fome common meafure. Proportion.

To COMMENT, V. N. [*commenter*, Lat.] to write note; to explain, or expound; ufed with *upon* before the thing explained.

COMMENT, S. [from the verb] notes or annotations. Expofition, explanation, remark.

COMMENTARY, S. [*commentarius*, Lat.] a critical explanation of the fenfe of an author. A memoir, or plain narrative of fome hiftorical tranfaction.

COMMENTATOR, S. one who writes remarks, notes, or explications.

COMMENTITIOUS, Adj. [*commentitius*, Lat.] invented, forged, fictitious; imagined purely to impofe upon.

COMMERCE, S. [*not* ufed in the plural; *commercium*, Lat.] the exchange, or the buying and felling merchandize both at home and abroad, in order to gain profit. If we confider it is owing to this that the number of our people, fhipping, colonies, and riches, the value of our landed eftates, the

strength of our ifland, and the refpectable figure it makes in the eye of all the world; we must acknowledge that thofe who fhall form any plan to render our trade more extenfive and profitable, deferve to be celebrated as true patriots, the ornament and bulwark of their country, and worthy immortal fame. Commerce is ufed figuratively, for intercourfe, or connection of any kind.

COMMERCIAL, Adj. relating to trade or commerce.

COMMERE, S. [Fr. pronounced *commair*] a common mother. " Stand a commere between their amities." *Shak.*

To COMMIGRATE, V. A. [from *con*, Lat. and *migro*, Lat.] to move with others from one country to another.

COMMIGRATION, S. [*commigrate*] the removal of feveral perfons from one country to another.

COMMINATION, S. [*comminatio*, Lat.] a threat, a declaration of punifhment, or vengeance. An office of the church; containing the threatnings denounced againft any breach of the divine laws and recited only on Afh-Wednefday.

COMMINATORY, Adj. imporing a punifhment for the breach or violation of it.

COMMINUTION, S. [*comminuo*, Lat.] the act of reducing into fmall particles, either by grinding, powdering, &c.

COMMISERABLE, Adj. [from *commifero*, Lat.] that which deferves pity and relief in diftrefs. Shewing pity and compaffion, by fympathizing with others in their afflictions.

To COMMISERATE, V. A. [*commiferatus*, Lat.] to pity, to fympathize with, and feel the misfortunes of others, as if they were our own, including the ideas of affiftance and relief.

COMMISERATION, S. [from *commiferatus*, Lat.] a tender, fympathizing, and affectionate regard for thofe in diftrefs, whereby a perfon feels their forrows, and endeavours to lighten their burthen.

COMMISSARY, S. an officer commiffioned occafionally, a delegate or deputy. In the army, a commiffary generaliter the mufters, is one who takes a view of the numbers or ftrength of every regiment, fees that the horfe be well mounted, and that the men be well clouthed, and accoutred. Commiffary general of provifion, furnifhes the army with food.

COMMISSION, S. [*commiffio*, Lat.] the act of employing another, to tranfact a thing for one's felf. An authority by which a perfon is entrufted with the care of tranfacting bufinefs for another. Figuratively, the fum allowed, or demanded for filling or buying, &c. for another. In Law, the warrant or patent for exercifing any jurifdiction, either ordinary or extraordinary. Charge, office, or employment. A commiffion of bank-

bankruptcy, is made out under the great feal, and directed to feveral perfons to act according to particular laws made in that cafe.

To COMMI'SSION, V. A. to authorize, empower, or appoint.

COMMI'SSIONER, S. one empowered to act in a particular quality by patent, or warrant.

COMMI'SSURE, S. [commiffura, Lat.] a joint; or a place where two parts of an animal body are joined together.

To COMMI'T, V. A [committo, Lat.] to intruft a perfon, ufed with to; to commit to memory, to learn by heart, to treafure any ideas in the mind, fo as to be able to recall them, when warranted. To fend a perfon to prifon. To perform, act, or perpetrate fome crime, or fault. Figuratively, to hurt, or lay as a depofite or a charge in any place.

COMMI'TMENT, S. the act of fending to prifon. The ftate of a perfon in prifon.

COMMI'TTEE, S. perfons to whom the confideration of an affair is referred.

COMMI'TTABLE, Adj. [from commit] liable to be committed. An object worthy of imprifonment.

To COMMI'X, V. A. [commixtus, Lat.] to mix, blend, or join feveral things together.

COMMI'XION, S. [commixum, Lat.] the act of joining feveral things together, more generally applied to the mixing of liquors together; that which is made by fuch a mixture.

COMMI'XTURE, S. the act of mingling feveral things together.

COMMO'DE, S. a woman's head drefs.

COMMO'DIOUS, Adj. [commodus, Lat. commode, Fr.] a relative term, implying the fuitablenefs of a thing to any particular purpofe. Convenient; feafonable; fpacious; well contrived. "A commodious room."

COMMO'DIOUSLY, Adv. conveniently. Enjoying the neceffaries and comforts of life, applied to condition. Suited to any particular end or view.

COMMODIOUSNESS, S. advantage, convenience.

COMMO'DITY, S. [commodité, Fr.] conveniency, profit, or advantage. Conveniency of time or place. In Commerce, merchandize, or that which is the object of trade.

COMMODO'RE, S. [commendador, Span.] in the Navy, a perfon commiffioned by an admiral to command a fquadron of fhips.

COMMON, Adj. [commun, Fr. communis, Lat.] belonging equally to more than one. Without a proprietor or poffeffor. Vulgar, mean, trifling; frequently feen, ufual, eafy to be had, or little value; intended for the ufes of every one; joined with the word woman, not confined to one perfon. In Grammar, applied to fuch verbs as fignify

both action and paffion; in Latin they generally end in or, as aspernor, I defpife, or am defpifed. Applied to nouns, thofe which fignify both fexes, as parens, fignifies both father and mother.

COMMON, S. a free open field for perfons to graze their cattle in.

In COMMON, S. an adverbial expreffion, implying equality; enjoined by feveral. Without diftinction, or difference, ufed with the particle with.

To COMMON, V. N. to enjoy a right of pafture in a common.

COMMONABLE, Adj. that which may become open and free, applied to ground.

COMMONAGE, S. [from common] In Law, the right of pafture in a common; of taking wood out of another perfon's grounds for houfe-bote, plough-bote, and hay-bote; of fifhing in another perfon's water, or of digging turf, in the ground of another. The joint right of ufing any thing equally with others.

COMMONALTY, S. [communauté, Fr.] the people of the lower rank. Figuratively, the bulk of mankind.

COMMONER, S. one of low rank, A perfon without titles. One who has a feat in the houfe of commons. In Law, one who has a joint right to pafture, &c. in an open field. In the univerfity, one who wears a fquare cap with a taffel when undergraduate. Applied to women, a lewd perfon.

COMMONLY, Adv. generally, frequently, ufually, according to repeated experience, oppofed to feldom or rarely.

COMMONNESS, S. frequency.

To COMMON-PLACE, V. A. to reduce to general heads.

COMMON-PLACE-BOOK, S. a book wherein things are recorded alphabetically, in order to affift a perfon's memory.

COMMON-PLEAS, S. the king's court, now held at Weftminfter, but was formerly moveable; it was erected at the time that Henry III. granted the great charter: all civil caufes, both real and perfonal, were formerly tried in it, and Fortefcue mentions it as the only court where real caufes were tried. In perfonal and mixed actions, it has a concurrent jurifdiction with the King's-Bench; but has no cognizance of the pleas of the crown; the chief judge is called Lord Chief Juftice of the Common Pleas, who is affifted by three other judges, who by a late regulation, are chofen for life, and confequently rendered more independant of their fovereign and the miniftry, than they formerly were.

COMMONS, S. the lower fort of people; the lower houfe of parliament, confifting of members chofen by the people, who act as their reprefentatives, pafs all money bills, are a check upon the other branches of the conftitution, and ought to be the great

great bulwark of English liberty and property. A portion of food usually eaten at one meal, so called at the universities, because it generally consists of a certain usual and common quantity.

COMMON-WEAL, or COMMON-WEALTH, S. in its primary sense, the common good. A form of government, in which the supreme power is lodged in the people. A republic; a democracy.

COMMORANT, Adj. [commorans, Lat.] residing, dwelling, or inhabiting in a place.

COMMOTION, S. [commotio, Lat.] to mutt, disturbance, sedition, disorder, or confusion. Figuratively, disorder of mind; perturbation. A violent motion or agitation. " The commotion of the sea."

To COMMUNE, V. A. [communico, Lat.] to converse; to talk together; to impart sentiments mutually in each other.

COMMUNICABLE, Adj. [Fr.] that which may be related or imparted to another.

To COMMUNICATE, V. A. [communico, Lat.] to impart to another; to confer or bestow a possession; to discover one's sentiments to another. In Theology, to receive the sacrament of the Lord's Supper. To be connected or joined. " The house communicates."

COMMUNICATION, S. [Lat. and Fr.] the act of discovering or revealing. A common token or passage from one place to another. The mutual intelligence between persons. A conversation, a conference.

COMMUNICATIVENESS, S. a readiness of imparting benefits or knowledge to others.

COMMUNION, S. [communis, Lat.] intercourse, fellowship, common possession. In Divinity, the common or public celebration of the Lord's Supper, or the public receiving that sacrament. A joining or adherence in the mode of worship established in any church.

COMMUNITY, S. [communitas, Lat.] a government; a body of people united together; common possession, or enjoyment; frequency or commonness. " Sick and blunted with community." Shak.

COMMUTABILITY, S. see COMMUTABLE] the quality of being capable of exchange.

COMMUTABLE, Adj. an alteration or change of disposition; a change of form or quality; the act of giving one thing in exchange for another; the act of substituting a pecuniary for a corporal punishment.

To COMMUTE, V. A. [commuto, Lat.] to exchange; to give one thing for another; to buy off or ransom.

COMMUTUAL, Adj. reciprocal; mutual.

COMPACT, S. [from con and pactum, Lat.] a bargain; a contract; an agreement.

To COMPACT, V. A. [compactus, Lat.] to unite together closely; to consolidate, or render solid by pressing the particles of a body close together, and thereby diminishing the number and dimensions of its parts; to league or enter into a bargain, joined to with.

COMPACT, Adj. [from the verb] close, dense, and heavy, not porous. Applied to stile, concise.

COMPACTEDNESS, firmness, hardness, density, owing to their having few and small pores.

COMPACTLY, Adv. in a close neat manner, applied to the joining two things together.

COMPACTURE, S. a joint or joining.

COMPANION, S. [compagnon, Fr. compagno, Ital.] one with whom a person frequently converses, or with whom he is generally seen; distinguished from a friend because not including the idea of affection, or mutual strife to exceed in benevolent offices.

COMPANIONABLE, Adj. agreeable, sociable.

COMPANIONABLY, Adv. in a sociable, agreeable manner.

COMPANY, S. [compagnie, Fr.] several persons assembled for conversation, or mutual entertainment. Several persons united to carry on one common design. A number or persons united or incorporated by some charter; a body corporate; a corporation. In War, a small body of infantry under one captain, the number of which is uncertain, but in the ordinary regiments consists of fifty centinels, three serjeants, three corporals; and in the guards it consists of eighty private men. To bear or keep company, is to go with a person, or to visit him often. Applied to females, to court, to be frequently with, in the quality of sweetheart.

To COMPANY, V. A. to go or walk with a person. To attend, to associate with.

COMPARABLE, Adj. worthy to be compared; equal to, or resembling. Containing qualities resembling those of another thing.

COMPARABLY, Adv. in a comparative manner.

COMPARATIVE, Adj. [comparatif, or comparative, Fr. comparativus, Lat.] that which results merely from a comparison with another, sometimes opposed to positive or absolute. In Grammar, the comparative degree, wherein two or more ideas are compared together, and the difference either in excess or diminution is expressed. In English, is formed by adding er to the positive, if it end in a consonant; but only an r, if it end with an e, as soft positive, softer the comparative, and this is borrowed from the Saxon, where the comparative ends in ir, rer, or, erre, r, re, re, thus rightwise, Sax. makes rightwiser, in the comparative; but words ending in ol, ch e, excepting able little, in ing, ip, est, est, ast, est, able, ed, id, some, excepting handsome

Azimuth Compass.

form, In *e*, *ive*, *col*, *en*, *ly*, *less*, *ry*, and
those which are derived from the Latin, ge-
n-rally make the comparative degree, by putting the word *more* before them; thus *general*
makes *more general* in the comparative; some
adjectives, indeed, are compared by prefixing the word *better* for the comparative,
especially the words *learned* and *natured*,
which forms borrowed from the French;
and the words *big*, *bot*, and *fit*, double the
last syllable of their positive; thus *big*,
makes *bigger*, &c. the reason for which
forms to be, to secure the same quick found
to the comparative, which is in the positive,
that they may not be founded *bear*, &c.
Those adjectives whose comparison is not
formed according to these rules, are called
irregular.

COMPA'RATIVELY, Adv. in a comparative manner. In a state of a comparison.

To COMPA'RE, V. A. [*comparo*, Lat.]
to bring two or more things together, to find
in what they agree or differ. To estimate
the qualities of a thing, by placing it near
another, and observing in what they differ
or agree. To liken. Figuratively, to equal.

COMPA'RE, S. [from the verb] likeness; estimate or judgment. The possibility
of being compared. *Beyond compare*, in
Milton, seems to mean beyond conception,
formed on the principles of analogy, or
similitude.

COMPA'RISON, S. [*comparaison*, Fr.]
the act of comparing, or judging of the
difference of two persons or things, by examining, or comparing them together. The
relation of two persons or things, considered
as opposed or set against each other, in order
to find wherein they agree or differ. The
state of a thing compared. *Comparison*, in
Rhetoric, is a figure not much unlike a
simile, but rather more sprightly, though
it is used promiscuously for it. In Grammar, the formation of an adjective, as *mild*,
milder, *mildest*.

To COMPA'RT, V. A. [*compartir*, Fr.]
to lay down a general plan, in all its different
parts, or divisions.

COMPA'RTIMENT, S. [Fr.] a design
composed of different figures. A division of
a picture, or design.

COMPARTI'TION, S. [from *compart*]
the act of laying down the several parts of
any plan. Also, the part of any plan.

COMPA'RTMENT, S. a division, or
separate part of a plan or design.

To CO'MPASS, V. A. [*composser*, Fr.]
to surround; to inclose. To walk round
any thing. To draw lines of circumvallation round a place. To grasp or inclose in
the arms. To obtain, attain, secure, or
have. In Law, to contrive, or do any
thing that tends towards a particular action.
" To *compass* the king's death."

COMPA'SS, S. [pronounced *compafs*] orbit, revolution, extent. Inclosure, *within
compafs*, without exaggerating, without hyperbole, without stretching. In Music, the
power of the voice, or of an instrument to
found any particular note. An instrument
consisting of a box, including a magnetical
needle, which points towards the north, used
by mariners. The invention of this instrument is claimed by the Neapolitans, Venetians, French, and English, but to whom it
ought to be ascribed, it is not easy to determine. In the plural, a mathematical instrument, consisting of two branches; used in
taking distances, drawing circles, and in working problems in the mathematics.

COMPPA'SSION, S. [Fr. from *cox* and
paffum, part of *pation*, Lat. to suffer] an humane disposition of mind which inclines us
to feel the miseries of others.

To COMPA'SSION, V. A. to pity, or
feel the forrows and distresses of another.

COMPA'SSIONATE, Adj. easily affected with forrow or pain, on beholding the
calamities of others.

To COMPA'SSIONATE, V. A. to pity
others; to be affected with grief, on seeing
the failings of another, and moved to make
allowance for them.

COMPA'SSIONATELY, Adv. in a pitying, tender, humane manner.

COMPA'TIBLE, Adj. [corrupted by a
vicious pronunciation from *compatible*, derived from *competo*, Lat.] confistent with; suitable to; becoming or agreeable to; used
with the particle *with*.

COMPA'TIBLENESS, S. the quality of
agreeing or fuiting with.

COMPA'TIBLY, Adv. fitly; fuitably
applicable to the fame fubject.

COMPE'ER, S. [*compere*, Fr.] an equal,
an affociate, a companion.

To COMPEER, V. A. [from the noun]
to be equal with. To match, to fuit.

To COMPE'L, V. A. [*compello*, Lat.] to
extort by force; to oblige.

COMPEL'LABLE, Adj. that which may
be compelled or forced.

COMPE'LLER, S. he that makes a perfon do or refrain from a thing by force.

COMPEND, S. [*compendium*, Lat.] an
abridgment of a difcourfe; a book containing the fubftance or chief heads of a fcience
in few words, and in a concife manner.

COMPE'NDIOUS, Adj. concife, brief,
applied to ftile; near or fhort, applied to
travelling.

COMPE'NDIOUSLY, Adv. in a fhort,
brief, or concife manner.

COMPE'NDIOSITY, S. fhortnefs or
brevity, applied to writings.

COMPE'NDIOUSNESS, S. brevity, or
fhortnefs.

COMPE'NDIUM, S. [Lat.] See COM-
PEND.

COM-

COMPEN'SABLE, Adj. [from *compenso*, Lat.] that which may be recompensed.

To COMPE'NSATE, V. A. [*compenso*, Lat.] to make amends for; to countervail; to counterbalance, to atone for.

COMPENSA'TION, S. [see COMPEN-SATE] amends; recompense; an equivalent.

COMPEN'SATIVE, Adj. that which can equal something else in worth. That which compensates.

To COMPE'NSE, V. A. [*recompense*, Lat.] to tare or be of equal weight in a scale. To counterbalance. To *compensate*, which is most in use.

CO'MPETENCE, CO'MPETENCY, S. [*competens*, Lat.] a sufficiency, without superfluity. Such a fortune as is amply sufficient to supply the necessaries of life. In Law, the power or capacity of a judge or court, for taking cognizance of an affair.

CO'MPETENT, Adj. [*competens*, Lat.] suitable, proportionable. Moderate; qualified or fit for; consistent with; applicable to; in Logic, to be predicated of.

CO'MPETENTLY, Adv. properly, sufficiently, without either excess or defect.

COMPE'TIBLE, Adj. [*compera*, Lat.] consistent with; agreeable or suitable to; joined to *with*.

COMPE'TIBLENESS, S. the quality of existing in or affirmed of a subject; consistence; suitableness.

COMPETI'TION, S. [from *cum*, Lat. and *petitio*, Lat.] the endeavouring to gain something in opposition to another; rivalry, contest, opposition; double claim, or the claim of more than one person to one thing, at the same time.

COMPE'TITOR, S. [from *cum* and *petitor*, Lat.] one who endeavours to gain a thing in opposition to another. A rival. Used with *for* before the thing claimed; but formerly with of "*Competitor of* the kingdom." *Knolles.* An enemy, or one of an adverse or opposite party. " More *competitors* flock to the enemy." *Shak.*

COMPILA'TION, S. [from *compilatio*, Lat.] a collection of various authors. An assemblage.

To COMPI'LE, V. A. [*compilo*, Lat.] to collect from various authors. Figuratively, to write, compose; to form from an assemblage of various incidents.

COMPI'LEMENT, S. the collecting several materials together. The act of piling together.

COMPI'LER, S. [from *compilo*, and *er* or *orr*, Sax. a man] a collector; one who collects from various authors.

COMPLA'CENCE, COMPLA'CENCY, S. [*complacens*, Lat.] a satisfaction arising on contemplating something, which, on account of its amiableness, produces joy. The cause of joy, of reciprocal pleasure and satisfaction.

A genteel address. Civility. Complaisance; politeness.

COMPLA'CENT, Adj. [*complacens*, Lat.] affable, kind; civil; polite, genteel.

To COMPLA'IN, V. N. [*se plaindre*, Fr.] to find fault with, including the ideas of grief and wrong. To charge a person with having been guilty of some fault or crime. " Wherefore doth a man complain; a man *for* the punishment of his fins." *Lament.* iii. 39. Actively, to weep, lament or bewail. " Is shame *complain*—the death of Richard." *Dryd.*

COMPLA'INT, S. [*complainte*, Fr.] a representation of injuries or pain, including the idea of dissatisfaction and wrong. Grief. The act of finding fault, the cause of complaining. A disease; a distemper.

COMPLAISA'NCE, S. [Fr.] a civil polite behaviour.

COMPLAISA'NT, Adj. [Fr.] civil, polite; endeavouring to please, by complying or yielding to a person's humours.

COMPLAISA'NTLY, Adv. in a civil, kind, polite manner.

COMPLE'AT, see COMPLETE.

CO'MPLEMENT, S. [*complementum*, Lat.] that completes any thing. A full, complete and requisite quantity or number. Accidents, or things, which are not necessary.

COMPLE'TE, Adj. [*completus*, Lat.] finished, perfect. Without defect, or imperfection. Ended, concluded.

To COMPLE'TE, V. A. to perfect, to finish. To answer fully. " *Completes* the nation's hopes." *Pope.*

COMPLE'TELY, Adv. perfect; fully; in a perfect or complete manner.

COMPLE'TENESS, S. perfection; that which is without defect.

COMPLE'TION, S. [*completus*, Lat.] accomplishment, conclusion. The greatest height, or perfect state.

CO'MPLEX, Adj. [Lat.] compounded, consisting of several parts.

CO'MPLEX, S. a collection, summary, or a collection of the whole or a thing, consisting of several parts. " The whole *complex* of all the blessings, &c." *Smith.*

COMPLE'XION, S. [*complexio*, Lat.] the colour of the external parts of the body, particularly the countenance. In Physic, the temperature, habit, or disposition of the body, arising from the predominancy of either of the four medical humours, blood, phlegm, bile, or colour.

COMPLE'XIONAL, Adj. depending on the temperature of the body.

COMPLE'XLY, in a compound manner, not simply.

COMPLE'XNESS, S. the state of being composed of several particulars.

COMPLE'XURE, S. the compounding one thing with others.

COMPLI'ANCE, S. [from *comply*] the allowing

allowing a thing demanded; the ready performance of a thing requested. Condescration, opposed to *stiffness*.

COMPLIANT, Part. [from *comply*] yielding to the touch. " The *compliant* boughs." *Par. Lost.* Yielding, condescending, opposed to *stiffness*.

To COMPLICATE, V. A. [*complicatus*, Lat.] to add one thing or action to another. To compose, a whole by the uniting of several things that are different from each other.

COMPLICATE, Adj. compounded of a variety of parts.

COMPLICATENESS, S. intricateness, difficulty.

COMPLICATION, S. the mixing or blending several things. A whole consisting of several things united. In Medicine, when two or more diseases affect a patient.

COMPLIER, S. a man of an easy temper; opposed to an *obstinate* person.

COMPLIMENT, S. [Fr.] a profession of great esteem, merely from ceremony and politeness, including the idea of preference and temporary or more apparent submission. A mere ceremonious expression, opposed to truth or sincerity.

To COMPLIMENT, V. A. to make use of respectful expressions from a bare principle of ceremony. To praise a thing or person contrary to one's real opinion.

COMPLIMENTAL, Adj. ceremonious.

COMPLIMENTALLY, Adv. in a mere ceremonious manner, opposed to *true* and *sincere*.

COMPLIMENTER, S. a person abounding in ceremony and compliments.

COMPLOT, S. [Fr.] a plot; a conspiracy or confederacy.

To COMPLOT, V. A. [*comploter*] to join together, to bring about any ill design.

COMPLOTTER, S. a conspirator; a confederate.

To COMPLY, V. N. [from *con* and *plier*, Fr.] to consent to any request, to yield to.

COMPONE, or COMPONED, Adj. [*componé*, Fr.] in Heraldry, composed of a row of angular parts, or chequers of two colours. Generally, a bordure, pale, or fess, composed of different colours, disposed alternately, and separated by fillets.

COMPONENT, Part. [*componens*, Genitive, of *componens*, Lat.] that which contributes to the forming of a compound body.

To COMFORT, V. N. [*comporter*, Fr.] to suit, to agree with, to act suitable to; used with the particle *with*. Actively, to bear, or tolerate. " That never can the present state *comport*." *Daniel.*

COMFORT, S. behaviour, conduct, deportment.

COMPORTMENT, S. behaviour, conduct or deportment.

No. VII.

To COMPOSE, V. A. [*composer*, Fr.] to form, or consist of, followed by *with*. To dispose, or put into a state proper but attaining any particular end. To join words together in a discourse. To contribute to the forming of a thing by being one of the particulars, or things of which it consists. To reduce to a state of calmness, rest and quiet. To make the mind fit for any undertaking, by freeing it from its disorder or perturbation. To reconcile. In Printing, to place letters or types in proper order. In Music to set any thing to tune.

COMPOSED, Part. calm, mild, serious, sedate, undisturbed.

COMPOSEDLY, Adv. [from *composed*, and *ly*, of *lice*, Sax. implying manner] in a calm, serious or sedate manner.

COMPOSEDNESS, S. sedateness, calmness, tranquility.

COMPOSER, S. an author or writer, one that sets words to music.

COMPOSITE, Adj. [Fr. from *compositus*, Lat.] In Architecture, the last of the five orders.

COMPOSITION, S. [from *compositio*, Lat.] the act of forming a whole from parts. The act of combining simple ideas together. The distribution of the several parts of a plan, design or picture. A work formed from several authors. The work or production of an author. Terms on which differences or quarrels are settled. In Music, the art of disposing notes so as to form tunes or airs, to be played on instruments, or sung by the voice. In Logic, a method of reasoning whereby we proceed from some general self-evident, truth, to other particular or single ones. In Pharmacy, the art of mixing several ingredients together to form a medicine. In Printing, the ranging several types or letters together in the composing-stick. In commerce, a contract between a debtor and his creditors, wherein they agree to accept a part of the debt for the whole.

COMPOSITIVE, Adj. formed of several qualities.

COMPOSITOR, S. [*compositeur*, Fr.] in Printing, the person who prepares the types, by arranging them properly therein for printing. A caseman.

COMPOST, S. [*compôt*, Lat.] in Agriculture, a mixture of different soils to make a manure for assisting the natural earth.

To COMPOST, V. A. to manure or enrich ground by a mixture of different soils.

COMPOSTURE, S. a compost or mixture of different soils.

COMPOSURE, S. composition, or a production, applied to writings. Arrangement, mixture or order. The form produced by the various combination of the particles of a body; frame; make; temperament. Sedateness,

M m   ness,

ness, freedom from any disturbance or perturbation. Adjustment, or reconciliation.

COMPOTATION, S. [from con and poto, Lat.] the act of drinking with another.

To COMPOUND, V. A. [from con, Lat.] to form by uniting several things together. To produce by being united. To reconcile, or put an end to a difference or quarrel by compliance with the demands of an adversary. To pay a part of a debt, for the whole. To bargain in the lump, to compound.

COMPOUND, Adj. [from the verb] produced from several ingredients. In Grammar, formed by joining two or more words. In Botany, applied to flowers, such as consist of many florets, semi-florets, or both. In Mechanics, applied to motion, that which is caused by several conspiring powers, moving in the same direction.

COMPOUNDABLE, Adj. that which may be asked.

COMPOUNDER, S. a reconciler; one who mingles, or mixes.

To COMPREHEND. V. A. [comprehendo Lat.] to comprise, include, or imply. To have an adequate, clear, and determinate idea of any thing.

COMPREHENSIBLE. Adj. [Fr.] that which we can attain an adequate or determinate idea of.

COMPREHENSIBLY, Adv. in a large extent or latitude.

COMPREHENSION, S. [Fr. comprehensio, Lat.] the act of comprising or containing. In Metaphysics, the knowledge or adequate idea of the essential modes or properties of a thing. A summary, compendium, or abstract. Capacity, or the power of the mind to admit several ideas at once.

COMPREHENSIVE. Adj. comprising much in a narrow compass; extensive.

COMPREHENSIVELY, Adv. in a comprehensive, or concise manner.

COMPREHENSIVENESS, S. the quality of including much in few words.

To COMPRESS, V. A. [compressus, supine of comprimo, Lat.] to bring into a narrower compass; to squeeze closer together; to embrace.

COMPRESSIBILITY, S. [from compressible] the capability of being reduced into a narrower compass.

COMPRESSIBLE, Adj. capable of being reduced into a smaller compass.

COMPRESSION, S. [compressio, Lat.] the act of bringing the particles of a thing nearer together by force. The act of pressing together.

COMPRESSURE, S. [from compress] the act or force of a thing pressing upon another.

To COMPRISE, V. A. [compris, part.] to contain, to include, to comprehend or contain.

COMPROBATION, S. [comprobatio, Lat.] a confirming by two or more persons.

COMPROMISE, S. [compromissum; Lat.] a compact or bargain, in which some concessions, or compliances are made on both sides.

To COMPROMISE, V. A. to settle a dispute by mutual concessions. To make a bargain, or contract, to bind to certain conditions. "Laban and himself were compromised." Strype

COMPROVINCIAL, Adj. [from con and provincial] belonging to the same province.

COMPTIBLE, Adj. ready to give an account; submissive; subject. "I am very comptible, even to the least sinister usage." Shakesp.

To COMPTROLL, V. A. [Johnson contends for this as the true spelling, and that the other is owing to a neglect of its derivation; though no modern authors or lexicons furply us with any other word than comptroller, Fr. for the verb, and comptrouleur, for the noun] See CONTROLL.

COMPULSATIVELY, Adv. in a violent manner; by compulsion, or restraint.

COMPULSATORY, Adj. compulsatoire, Lat.] having the power of forcing a person.

COMPULSION, S. [compulsio, Lat.] the act of forcing. A violence or force. The state of being compelled.

COMPULSIVE, Adj. [compulsif, Fr. compulsus, Lat.] having the power to force, forcible.

COMPULSIVELY, Adv. forcibly; by compulsion.

COMPULSIVENESS, S. the quality of obliging a person to do any act.

COMPULSORY, Adj. [compulsoire, Fr.] having the power of compounding or forcing.

COMPUNCTION, S. [Fr. compunction, Lat.] irritation. Sorrow, anxiety, contrition, or repentance, arising from a consciousness of guilt.

COMPUNCTIOUS. Adj. sorrowful. Repentant; full of remorse.

COMPUNCTIVE, Adj. [compunctim, Lat.] causing remorse or sorrow.

COMPURGATION, S. [compurgatio, Lat.] the justifying the veracity of one person by the testimony of others.

COMPURGATOR, S. [Lat.] one who by oath justifies another, or attests his innocence.

COMPUTABLE, Adj. capable of being computed or estimated.

COMPUTATION, S. the act of estimating the value of things. A calculation. An arithmetical process.

To COMPUTE, V. A. [computo, Lat.] to estimate; to reckon; to count, to calculate.

COMPUTER, S. one who computes. An accountant.

COMRADE, S. [camerade, Fr.] one who lives with another; this sense is somewhat obsolete; the most common acceptation is that of a person who is jointly concerned with another in an undertaking.

Ta

To CON, V. A. [connan, Sax.] In its primary state to know; in its secondary, to learn perfectly.

To CONCA'TENATE, V. A. [from con and catena, Lat.] to link together; to run or connect like the links of a chain.

CONCATENATION, S. a series of links; a connexion of things, which mutually depend on each other.

CONCA'VATION, S. the act of making a thing of a hollow, or concave form.

CONCA'VE, Adj. [concavus, Lat.] hollow, applied to the inner surface of a circular body, such as that of an egg-shell, a ball, &c. opposed to convex. Empty, without any thing to fill the cavity.

CONCA'VENESS, S. the state or quality of being hollow.

CONCA'VITY, S. the inner surface of a circular thing.

CONCA'VO-CO'NCAVE, Adj. hollow on both sides.

CONCA'VO-CONVEX, Adj. hollow or concave on one side, and convex or protuberant on the other.

CONCA'VOUS, Adj. hollow.

To CONCE'AL, V. A. [con and celo, Lat.] to hide from the sight or knowledge of others. To cover, to keep secret, opposed to discover.

CONCEA'LABLE, Adj. capable of being kept secret.

CONCEALEDNESS, S. the state of being hid from others.

CONCEA'LMENT, S. [from conceal] the act of hiding from others. The state of being kept secret. A place of retirement.

To CONCE'DE, V. A. [concedo, Lat.] to grant, or admit an opinion, as true.

CONCE'IT, S. [concept, Fr.] a conception, thought, or idea. Understanding. Strength of imagination, meer fancy, used in contempt. A pleasant thought. An high opinion of a person's judgment, which exposes him to ridicule.

To CONCE'IT, V. A. to fancy, imagine, conceive or think.

CONCE'ITED, Part. Proud of one's abilities; used with of before the object of conceit. "Conceited of their own wit." Bent.

CONCE'ITEDLY, Adv. in a scornful, proud, or whimsical manner.

CONCE'ITEDNESS, a high opinion of a person's own abilities; a word of reproach.

CONCE'ITLESS, Adj. stupid, void of understanding. Dull.

CONCE'IVABLE, Adj. that which may be understood or believed.

CONCE'IVABLY, Adv. in an intelligible manner so as to be apprehended.

To CONCE'IVE, V. A. [concevoir, Fr.] to be formed in the womb. To imagine. To think; to apprehend.

CONCE'IVER, S. one who apprehends, or conceives.

To CONCE'NTRATE, V. A. [from con and centrum, Lat.] to drive towards the center, or into a narrow compass. To condense.

CONCENTRA'TION, S. forcing into a narrow compass, or toward the center.

To CONCE'NTRE, V. N. [concentrer, Fr.] to tend towards the same center.

CONCE'NTRIC, CONCE'NTRICAL, Adj. having one common center.

CONCE'IVABLE, Adj. that may be understood. Intelligible.

CONCEP'TION, S. [conceptio, Lat.] the act of becoming pregnant. Notion, apprehension, idea. Sentiment; purpose.

CONCE'PTIOUS, Adj. [conceptum, Lat.] apt to conceive; fruitful.

To CONCE'RN, V. A. [concerner, Fr.] to relate to. To make uneasy, or sorrowful. To be of importance to. To be commissioned to act for another.

CONCE'RN, S. business; circumstance. Interest. Importance. Regard. Affection.

CONCE'RNING, prep. about; of, or relating to.

CONCE'RNMENT, S. the thing in which a person is interested. Importance. The engaging or taking part in an affair.

To CONCE'RT, V. A. [concerter, Fr.] to contrive or take measures; to bring or design to pass.

CONCE'RT, S. a communication of design. In Music, a performance of a number of musicians and singers.

CONCERTA'TION, S. [concertatio, Lat.] strife, contest, contention, quarrel.

CONCE'RTATIVE, Adj. [concertativus, Lat.] quarrelsome, contentious, wrangling.

CONCE'SSION, S. [concessio, Lat.] a yielding, including the idea of compliance. The thing yielded.

CONCE'SSIONARY, Adj. given by indulgence, purely to terminate a dispute.

CONCE'SSIVELY, Adv. by way of concession.

CONCH, [concha, Lat.] a shell; a sea-shell. "Adds Orient pearls, which from the conchs he drew." Dryd.

To CONCI'LIATE, V. A. [conciliare, supine os concilio, Lat.] to gain; to procure affection; to reconcile; to adjust.

CONCILIATION, S. [from conciliatum, Lat.] the act of procuring esteem or affection, or reconciling.

CONCILIA'TOR, S. [Lat.] one who settles variances between two parties. A reconciler.

CONCILIA'TORY, Adj. relating to reconciliation, or making peace between parties at variance.

CONCIN'NITY, S. [concinnitas, Lat.] decency, fitness, propriety.

CONCIN'NOUS, Adj. [concinnus, Lat.] comely, pleasant, agreeable. In Music, concinnous intervals, are such as are next to, and in combination with concords.

M m 2   CON-

CONCI'SE, Adj. [*concisus*, Lat. cut] short, brief, pertinent.

CONCI'SELY, Adv. [from *concise* and *ly*, implying manner] briefly, shortly, in a few words.

CONCI'SENESS, S. brevity, shortness, pertinence.

CONCLA'VE, S. [*conclave*, Lat.] in its primary sense, a private or inner apartment. An assembly of all the cardinals that are at Rome, for the election of a pope; the place where they assemble.

To CONCLU'DE, V. A. [*conclude*, Lat.] in its primary sense, to inclose or shut up; but now out of use. Figuratively, to include, or comprehend. To draw as a conclusion, or inference; to infer. To judge. To end, or finish, or complete. To acknowledge as a truth. "It is *concluded* that you are guilty."

CONCLU'DENT, Part. [*concludentis*, Lat.] decisive; consequential.

CONCLU'SIBLE, Adj. [*conclusus*, Lat.] happening as a consequence; to be inferred.

CONCLU'SION, S. [*conclusio*, Lat.] determination, or period to an affair. An opinion formed from experience. In Logic, the last part of an argument, or the consequence of something either assumed or proved before.

CONCLU'SIVE, Adj. [*conclusus*, Lat.] decisive; final.

CONCLU'SIVELY, Adv. in a determinate, peremptory manner.

CONCOAGULA'TION, S. a coagulation, or curdling.

To CON'COCT, V. A. [*concoctus*, Lat.] to digest in the stomach, so as to form into chyle. To purify.

CONCOC'TION, S. [from *concoctus*, Lat.] the change which the food undergoes in the stomach. Maturation.

CONCO'MITANCE, CONCOMITAN-CY, S. [*concomitans*, Lat.] united to; inseparable from; accompanying.

CONCO'MITANT, S. a companion. An attendant. An associate.

CONCO'MITANTLY, Adv. in the manner of an attendant, or companion.

To CONCO'MITATE, V. A. [*concomitatus*, Lat.] to attend on, or to be joined with another.

CON'CORD, S. [*concordia*, Lat.] the suitableness of one thing to another. Peace; union; a compact, or mutual agreement. In Grammar, that part wherein words are made to agree in number, person, and gender, &c. In Music, the relation of two founds, that are always agreeable to the ear, whether applied in succession or consonance.

CONCO'RDANCE, S. [*concordantia*, Lat.] an agreement. A dictionary to the Holy Scriptures; wherein all the words are ranged alphabetically, and their various places, where they occur, are referred to; than by Cruden

in English is a very accurate and elaborate work.

CONCO'RDANT, Part. [*concordantis*, Lat.] agreeing with; consistent with; in Music consisting of concords or harmonies, opposed to discordance.

To CONCORPORATE, V. A. [from *cum* and *corporis*] to unite, blend, or mix several things together.

CONCORPORA'TION, S. the mixing several things together. The state of several things joined together.

CONCOURSE, S. [from *cum* and *cursus*, Lat.] the assembling of several persons. A crowd. The point wherein two things meet together.

CONCREMENT, S. [from *concretus*, Lat.] a mass formed by concretion. A collection of matter.

CONCRE'SCENCE, S. [*concrescens*, Lat.] the quality of growing by the union of several particles.

To CONCRETE, V. A. to form from an union of several particles. To unite several masses. Neuterly, to coalesce, cohere, or join together.

CONCRE'TE, Adj. formed by the cohesion of several particles.

CON'CRETE, S. an assemblage or mixture. A mass composed of different particles.

CONCRE'TELY, Adv. so as to conclude the substance together with the quality; not abstractedly.

CONCRE'TENESS, S. curdling, congelation.

CONCRE'TION, S. the act whereby any thing soft becomes hard, or the particles of a fluid become fixed, so as not to yield to the touch. The uniting of several particles of bodies, so as to form one mass. Figuratively, the mass formed by a cohesion.

CONCRE'TIVE, Adj. having the power of uniting several particles together. That which has the power of turning a fluid into a solid. That which has the power of producing coagulation, or curdling.

CONCRE'TURE, S. a mass formed by the union or cohesion of several particles.

CONCU'BINAGE, S. [Fr. *concubinatus*, Lat.] the act of cohabiting with a woman, as a wife, without being married.

CON'CUBINE, [*concubina*, Lat. from *cum*, together, and *cumbo*, to lie] a woman who lives with a man, though not married to him. A kept mistress.

To CONCU'LCATE, V. A. [*conculcatus*, supine of *conculco*, Lat.] to trample under foot. Wants authority.

CONCU'PISCENCE, S. [*concupiscentia*, Lat.] an immoderate desire of women. Lechery; lust. Among divines, an irregular desire, or appetite after carnal things, and supposed to be inherent in our nature ever since the fall.

CON-

CONCU'PISCENT, Part. [concupiscens, Lat.] lecherous; lustful.

CONCUPISCEN'TIAL, Adj. having an immoderate desire either after women, or carnal things.

CONCUPI'SCIBLE, Adj. [concupiscibilis, Lat.] that which may be desired; that which excites, or creates desire.

To CONCU'R, V. N. [from concurro, Lat.] to meet together. To join in one design. To unite with; to be conjoined with; to assist in the effecting one common event.

CONCU'RRENCE, CONCU'RRENCY, S. union, conjunction, joined effort to promote any design. Agreement. In Law, a common claim.

CONCU'RRENT, Part. [concurrens, Lat.] promoting the same end or design.

CONCU'RRENT, S. that which assists, or contributes to the performance of any design.

CONCU'SSION, S. [concussio, Lat.] the act of putting into motion; shaking; agitation.

CONCU'SSIVE, Adj. [concussus, Lat.] having the power or quality of shaking.

To CONDE'MN, V. A. [condemno, Lat.] to pass sentence, used with to, before the punishment. To censure, blame, or find fault with; opposed to approve. To deem a person or thing worthy of blame, by comparing them with others.

CONDE'MNABLE, Adj. that which may be found-fault with, or is subject to condemnation.

CONDEMNA'TION, S. [condemnatio, Lat.] the act of pronouncing sentence against a person. Figuratively, the blaming a person. The state of a person on whom sentence has been passed.

CONDEM'NER, S. one who condemns, censures, or blames.

CONDE'NSABLE, Adj. capable of being more solid, or preffed into a smaller compass.

To CONDE'NSATE, V. A. [condenso, Lat.] to make more solid, by compression or force.

CONDE'NSATE, Adj. made thicker or more solid by compression.

CONDENSA'TION, S. [from condensatio] the act of bringing the parts of a thing closer, whereby the body is rendered more dense, compact, and heavy; this is by some distinguished from compression, which implies external force, and is by them restrained merely to the effects of cold; but by others, both these terms are used promiscuously.

To CONDE'NSE, V. A. [condenso, Lat.] to make any body more thick, compact, or heavy, by increasing the contact of its particles, which diminishes the fire of the pores of a body, and renders it, confequently, more solid. Neuterly, to grow

thick, applied to the effects of cold or heat. To become solid and weighty, by condensing to a smaller compass.

CONDE'NSE, Adj. [condensus, Lat.] compact.

CONDE'NSER, S. a pneumatic engine, by which an unusual quantity of air may be forced into a small space.

CONDE'NSITY, S. the state of a body, whose parts are fixed, consolidated, or compressed. Thickness, applied to confistence.

To CONDESCE'ND, V. N. [condescendre, Fr.] to lay aside the dignity of rank, to be on a level with inferiors. To behave with familiarity to inferiors. To stoop, yield, or comply.

CONDESCE'NDENCE, S. [condescendance, Fr.] an act of submission to inferiors. A granting some favour to a person, which he could not demand. Submission to some proposals, which implies a person's voluntary giving up his right, or foregoing something which he ought not to have agreed to.

CONDESCE'NDINGLY, Adv. so as to lay aside the claims of authority; or to yield up a right, from a principle of generosity.

CONDESCE'NSION, S. the behaviour of a superior, whereby he treats one of lower rank as his equal, grants him favours he cannot demand, and yields to his requests with so much kindness and good nature, as to gain his affections, and secure himself from the envy, which generally attends a high station.

CONDESCE'NSIVE, Adj. courteous; affable; civil.

CONDI'GN, Adj. [pronounced condine, from condignus, Lat.] suitable to, merited, deserved.

CONDI'GNNESS, S. proportion, suitableness to a person's crimes.

CONDI'GNLY, Adv. suitable to person's crimes. Deservedly.

CONDIMENT, S. [condimentum, Lat.] seasoning, sauce, an ingredient made use of by luxury to give food an agreeable taste. "They are for condiment, not nourishment." Bacon.

To CONDI'TE, V. A. [condio, Lat.] to pickle, to preserve or pickle.

CONDI'TION, S. [Fr. conditio, Lat.] a quality or property, which determines the nature of a thing. A moral quality or virtue. The circumstance of person or fortune. Rank. The terms of any contract, or agreement. Figuratively, a writing containing the terms of an agreement, or bargain.

To CONDI'TION, V. N. to make, or propose terms.

CONDI'TIONAL, Adj. to be performed on certain terms; not absolute, but subject to certain limitations. In Grammar, conditional conjunctions, are those which serve to make a proposition implying some restric-

tion

tion or limitation, which is requisite to its truth, and are *if*, *wlefs*, *provided that*, *in cafe of*, &c. A *conditional* proposition, is that which has two parts connected together by a *conditional* conjunction, the first part wherein the *condition* lies, is called the antecedent, and the other the consequent. Thus, "If there be no resurrection of the dead, Christ is not risen;" Is a *conditional* proposition, wherein, "If there be no resurrection, &c." is the antecedent, and, "Christ is not risen," is the consequent.

CONDI'TIONAL, S. the terms on which an action is to be done or forborn. "In respect of the *conditional*." *Boyle*.

CONDI'TIONALLY, Adv. on certain terms or limitations.

CONDI'TIONARY, Adj. stipulated, bargained. agreed.

To CONDI'TIONATE, V. A. to make *conditions* for; to perform on certain *conditions*.

CONDI'TIONATE, Adj. established on certain terms, or *conditions*.

CONDI'TIONED, part. [from *condition*] having particular qualities.

To CONDO'LE, V. N. [*condeo*, Lat.] to lament with others for any misfortune, or calamity; having *with* before the person for whom we grieve.

CONDO'LEMENT, S. grief, sorrow, lamentation. "To persevere in obstinate *condolement*." *Shak*.

CONDO'LENCE, S. a sympathizing grief, for the misfortunes of others, which expresses itself by lamenting with the distressed.

CONDO'LER, S. one who condoles, or expresses a complimentary concern for the sorrow of another.

To CONDU'CE, V. N. [*conduco*, Lat.] to promote an end by acting conjointly, followed by *to*; according to its primary sense, to conduct or accompany persons in their way. "He was sent to *conduce* hither the princess." *Hall*.

CONDU'CIBLE, Adj. [*conducibilis*, Lat.] having a power of promoting a design.

CONDU'CIVE, Adj. having a tendency, or power to promote any end.

CONDU'CIVENESS, S. the quality of contributing to the production of some end.

CONDUCT, S. [*conduit*, Fr.] management. Convoy or escorting with a guard. Behaviour, or a series of actions regulated by some standard.

To CONDU'CT, V. A. [*conduire*, Lat.] to attend a person, to shew him his way. Figuratively, to direct, lead, or guide, applied to the mind. To usher, or introduce, applied to ceremony. To manage.

CONDUCTI'TIOUS, Adj. [*conductitius*, Lat.] hired, employed, or serving for hire.

CONDU'CTOR, S. [Lat.] a guide. A leader. A manager. In Surgery, an instru-

ment used to guide the knife in cutting for the stone.

CONDU'CTRESS, S. a woman who directs, leads, or manages.

CONDUIT, S. [br. pronounced *cundit*] a canal used for the conveyance of water. An aqueduct.

CONE, S. [*conus*, Lat.] in Geometry, a solid body, whose base is a circle, and its uppermost part ending in a point; it resembles a sugar-loaf.

CONEY, S. See CONY.

To CONFA'BULATE, V. N. [*confabulatus*, Lat.] to talk easily, familiarly, and with cordialness together.

CONFABULA'TION, S. [*confabulatio*, Lat.] easy, familiar, cheerful conversation.

To CONFECT, V. A. [from *con* and *factum*, Lat.] to preserve fruit, &c. with sugar. This word seems now corrupted into Comfit.

CONFECT, S. a sweet-meat.

CONFE'CTION, S. the preserving fruit or vegetables by means of clarified sugar. A liquid or soft electuary.

CONFE'CTIONER, S. one who makes and sells sweet-meats.

CONFE'DERACY, S. [*confederation*, Fr.] a league, contract, or agreement, entered into by several states or persons. In law, the combination of two, or more persons, to injure or damage a third person.

To CONFE'DERATE, V. A. [*confederer*, Fr.] to unite in a league, to accomplish some design. Used with the particle *with*.

CONFE'DERATE, Adj. [*con* and *foedus*, Lat.] leagued, or united to accomplish some design.

CONFE'DERATE, S. [as the adjective] one who engages with another, to affift and defend each other. An ally.

CONFEDERA'TION, S. [Fr.] a league. An act whereby persons oblige themselves to affift each other. An alliance.

To CONFE'R, V. N. [*confero*, Lat.] to discourse with a person on some important subject. Actively, to compare the sentiments of one person or author, with those of another. To give a thing, to bestow a favour.

CONFERENCE, S. [*conference*, Fr.] the act of discoursing with another. A meeting appointed for the discussing of some one point in debate. Comparison.

CONFE'RRER, S. one that discourses with another. One that bestows a favour.

To CONFE'SS, V. A. [*confesser*, Fr.] to acknowledge the having done something amiss. Used with the particle *of*, before the crime. "*Confess* thee freely of thy crime." *Shak*. To disclose sins to a priest, to obtain absolution. To own the having committed a crime, with all its aggravating circumstances, to God, in order to ease the mind, and

become an object worthy of his pardon. To own, as a Master or Saviour, in Scripture. "Whosoever shall confess me before men." Matt. x. 32. To grant; to shew; to prove; to give testimony, or signal. To own, used as introductory to a sentence, in order to obviate any invidious remark. "I must confess I was most pleased." Addis. Neuterly, to perform the act of confession to a priest.

CONFESS'EDLY, Adv. avowedly; indisputably; certainly.

CONFES'SION, S. the acknowledgment of a crime. In the Romish church, an acknowledgment of sins in private to a priest, in order to obtain absolution. An act whereby we own our sins to God with all their blackening circumstances, in order to disburthen the mind, and render ourselves proper objects of his mercy and forgiveness. The general confession, is a prayer made use of by the church, containing an humble and penitent avowal of sin, drawn up in general terms, that every member of the congregation may join in it. It breathes so humble a sense of our own misery, so deep an idea of the enormity of sin, and contains so comprehensive a description of the duties of a penitent, that the piety and wisdom of the composers cannot be enough admired. A profession, an avowal, or an attestation of a truth, somewhat dubious before. "Who before Pontius Pilate, witnessed a good confession." 1 Tim. xi. 13.

CONFES'SIONAL, S. [Fr.] a little box, wherein the Romish priest takes the confession of a penitent.

CONFESSOR, S. [confesseur, Fr.] in the Romish church, a priest, authorised to receive the confession of penitents, and grant them absolution. The penitent who confesses his crimes either to God, or to a priest.

CONFEST, Adj. [a poetical word for confessed] generally known, acknowledged. Notorious.

CONFIDANT, S. [confident, Fr.] one intrusted with the secrets of another; generally applied to those, who are intrusted with the affairs of lovers.

To CONFIDE, V. N. [confido, Lat.] to trust in; to rely on.

CONFIDENCE, S. [confidentia, Lat.] a strong assurance of the fidelity and ability of another. A strong assurance of the efficacy of a person's own abilities, opposed to timidity; but when used in a bad sense, a vicious and assuming boldness, which renders a person both impudent and insupportable to others, and is opposed to modesty. Figuratively, the conscience of business, or ambitious integrity.

CONFIDENT, Part. [confidens, Lat.] convinced of a truth. Positive, secure of success; bold. Impudent, applied to behaviour.

CONFIDENTLY, Adv. in such a manner, as to discover no fear of a miscarriage

securely. Positively; without discovering the least doubt or fear.

CONFIGURATION, S. [Fr.] the order in which the particles of bodies are united together.

To CONFIGURE, S. [from con and figura, Lat.] to dispose, or form the particles of a body into any shape, by uniting them together in a particular manner.

CONFINE, S. a limit, border, edge, or utmost verge of a thing.

CONFINE, Adj. [confinis, Lat.] bordering upon. Touching; contiguous.

To CONFINE, V. N. to border upon; to touch, or be contiguous to. Used with on at present, but in Milton followed by with. "Confine with Heav'n." Par. Lost.

To CONFINE, V. A. [confiner, Fr.] to bound, limit, inclose, shut up, restrain, or imprison. To immure; to keep at home, without going abroad.

CONFINELESS, Adj. boundless; without limits; endless.

CONFINEMENT, S. the act of inclosing a person in prison. The state of a person in prison, or kept at home without liberty of going abroad; restraint.

CONFINER, S. a person who lives on the borders of a country. One who deprives another of his liberty.

CONFINITY, S. [confinitas, Lat.] nearness, neighbourhood; likeness, resemblance.

To CONFIRM, V. A. [confirmo, Lat.] to put beyond doubt by additional proofs. To settle a person in an office. To complete, to render perfect. To admit to the full privileges of a Christian by imposition of the hands of a bishop.

CONFIRMABLE, Adj. that which is capable of being made evident or confirmed.

CONFIRMATION, S. an additional proof to evince the truth of a thing or opinion beyond doubt, or contradiction. An ecclesiastic rite, whereby a person arrived to years of discretion, undertakes the performance of every part of the baptismal vow, made for him by his godfathers and godmother; this custom has been always practised in the church, and according to Hammond, is transferred from the very practice of the apostles.

CONFIRMATOR, S. [confirmo, Lat.] one who proves a thing beyond doubt or contradiction.

CONFIRMATORY, Adj. giving such additional proof, as may serve for the probability of any fact.

CONFIRMER, S. one who establishes a fact by new evidence.

CONFISCABLE, Adj. [from confiscatum, Lat.] liable to be seized on as a fine.

To CONFISCATE, V. A. [confiscatum, Lat.] to seize on private property, and convert it to the use of the chief magistrate, &c. by way of punishment.

CONFISCA'TION, S. [confiscatio, Lat.] the seizing of private property, for some crime.

CONFITURE, S. [Fr. from confiture] a sweet meat, or confection

To CONFIX, V. A. [configo fixine of —fix, Lat.] to fix or fasten down. "You ever be rivetted here." Shak.

CONFLAGRA'TION, S. [conflagratio, Lat.] a fire extending over a large space, and involving several things in its flames. Generally used for that fire which is expected to consume all things.

CONFLEXURE, S. [conflexus, Lat.] a bending together; a turning

To CONFLICT, V. N. [confictus, Lat.] to strive or struggle for victory.

CONFLICT, S. [confictus, Lat.] a combat, or fight between two, seldom used of a general battle. A contest. A struggle between opposite qualities. An agony, or pang, wherein nature seems to struggle.

CONFLUENCE, S. [confluentia, low Lat.] an union or joining of two or more streams. The act or condition of coming in great numbers. A concourse, or multitude gathered together.

CONFLUENT, Part. [confluens, Lat.] running one into another, mixing together. A confluent smallpox, is that species whereto the pustules run into each other.

CONFLUX, S. [confluxus, Lat.] the union of several streams. Figuratively, a crowd.

CONFORM, V. A. [conformo, Lat.] to reduce to the same form or manner. To render one's actions agreeable to any rule. To submit or yield. Used with to or with.

CONFORMABLE, adj. having the same form, resembling either in external or internal qualities. Agreeing with some standard or law. Compliant or submissive. Used sometimes with to, and sometimes with with.

CONFORMABLY, Adv. agreeably, consistent with. Suitably; with conformity. Used with to or with.

CONFORMA'TION, S. [Fr. conformatio, Lat.] the particular order of the parts of a body. The resemblance or agreement of actions to some particular standard.

CONFORMIST, one who complies with the mode of worship of the church of England, opposed to a Dissenter.

CONFORMITY, S. [from conform] likeness, resemblance; consistency. Compliance with the worship of the established church, used with to or with.

CONFORTA'TION, S. [conforto, low Lat.] strengthening. The increasing strength. "For no alteration and confortation." Bacon.

To CONFOUND, V. A. [confondre, Fr. confundo, Lat.] to mingle or mix things, so that their natures cannot be known. To substitute one word for another, which conveys different ideas. To puzzle or perplex. To amaze, confuse or astonish, to destroy.

CONFOUNDED, part. beaten in the highest degree; precipitous.

CONFOUNDEDLY, Adv. shamefully, hatefully, a low word, and seems generally made use of to convey an idea of great excess, or the superlative degree.

CONFOUNDER, S. one who perplexes, also those who confuse or destroy.

CONFRATERNITY, S. [confraternitas, Lat.] a botherhood or society united for some religious purpose.

CONFRICA'TION, S. [con and frico, Lat.] the act of rubbing one body against another. "A confrication of the hot vice the joy." Bacon.

To CONFRONT, V. A. [preconned confront, from confronter, Fr.] to stand opposite to. To oppose. In law, to oppose one evidence to another, in open court. To set in opposition. To contrast. To compare one thing with another.

CONFRONTA'TION, S. [Fr.] the act of opposing one evidence to another, or of bringing two witnesses face to face.

To CONFUSE, V. A. [confusus, Lat.] to put in disorder. To perplex by indistinct ideas. To render the mind unable to choose any proper method of action, either by hurry, or the commotion of passion.

CONFUSEDLY, Adv. indistinctly, mixed. Perplexed, or not clear; without any order. In obscure, or unintelligible terms, applied to language.

CONFUSEDNESS, S. want of distinctness or clearness with respect to ideas. Want of order, or regularity, applied to placing or arranging. Inability to reply.

CONFUSION, S. an irregular, careless mixture. Want of distinction and clearness, applied to ideas; or the joining two ideas in the mind which have no connexion. Astonishment; distraction of mind arising from the prospect of great and impending danger.

CONFUTABLE, Adj. that which may be confuted or shown to be false.

CONFUTA'TION, S. [confutatio, Lat.] the act proving the arguments of another to be false, or groundless.

To CONFUTE, V. A. [confuto, Lat.] to destroy the force of an argument. To show the proofs of an adversary to be groundless, or false.

CONGE', S. [Fr.] an action shewing respect or submission, consisting in bowing the body in men; and in women, in sinking with the knee bent, or making a courtesy. Leave, or the action of taking leave. Conge d'elire, Fr. i. e. leave of election, in common law, is the king's permission to a dean and chapter to choose a bishop.

To CONGEAL, V. A. [congelo, Lat.] to thicken a fluid by cold. Figuratively, to thicken any fluid; to grow thick.

CON-

CONGE'ALMENT, S. the clot, or which muſt formed in blood, &c. by cold.

CONGE'ALABLE, Adj. that which may be congealed.

CONGELA'TION, S. the act of freezing, or thickening a fluid body.

CONGE'NER, S. of the ſame kind or genus. Uſed with too great an air of pedantry by Miller. "The cherry tree has been often engrafted on the laurel, to which it is a congener."

CONGE'NEROUS, Adj. of the ſame genus or ſpecies.

CONGE'NIAL, Adj. (from con and genus, Lat.) partaking of the ſame genus, of the ſame nature, or kind.

CONGENIA'LITY, S. a partaking of the ſame genius, or diſpoſition.

CONGE'NIALNESS, S. a ſameneſs, likeneſs of diſpoſition.

CO'NGENITE, Adj. (congenitus, Lat.) implanted or born together with; connate.

CONGER, S. (congrus, Lat.) a large kind of eel, frequenting ſalt waters.

To CONGE'ST, V. A. (congeſtum, inplae, of congero, Lat.) to heap together.

To CONGLA'CIATE, V. N. (conglaciatus, Lat.) to turn or convert to ice.

CONGLACIA'TION, S. the converting into ice. Vitrifying, or turning into glaſs. "Chryſtal was a ſubject very unfit for proper conglaciation." Brown.

CONGLETON, a town of Cheſhire, with a market on Saturdays, and four fairs, on the Thurſday before Shrove-tide, May 10, July 5 and July 13, for cattle, and pedlars ware. It is ſeated on the river Dane, and is a large mayor-town, tho' it has nothing but a chapel of eaſe, the church being a ſtately ſtructure, and is two miles diſtant. Its manufactory is the making of leather-gloves, but the moſt conſiderable is ſilk, there being a large ſilk mill lately erected here by ſome Turkey merchants, which employs 700 hands. It is 7 miles S. of Macclesfield, 24 N. E. of Nantwich, and 157 N. W. of London. Lon. 15. 22. lat. 53. 7.

To CONGLOBATE, V. A. (conglobatus, Lat.) to make into the form of a globe.

CONGLO'BTE, Part. (conglobatus, Lat.) moulded into a ball. In Anatomy, a conglobate gland, is that, whoſe ſubſtance is not divided, but firm, intire, and continued.

CON'GLOBATELY, Adv. In a globular or round form.

CONGLOBA'TION, S. a round body; a collecting into a roundneſs.

To CONGLO'BE, V. A. (conglobo, Lat.) to gather into a firm round ball, or maſs.

To CONGLO'MERATE, V. A. (conglomeratum, Lat.) to gather ſeveral things into a round maſs, alluding to winding thread into a ball.

CONGLO'MERATE, Part. (conglomeratus, Lat.) gathered into a round ball. In Anatomy, a conglomerate gland, is that which

is compoſed of ſeveral conglobate glands, tied together, or wrapped up in one common membrane. Figuratively, twiſted, or collected together.

CONGLOMERA'TION, S. (from conglomerate, a collecting into a looſe round ball or maſs.

To CONGLU'TINATE, V. A. (conglutinatum) to glue, cement, or join by any viſcous, or glutinous ſubſtance. Neuterly, to ſtick or cohere together.

CONGLUTINA'TION, S. the act of ſticking together. The uniting the lips of wound.

CONGLU'TINATIVE, Adj. that has the power of ſticking together.

CONGLUTINA'TOR, S. that which makes things cohere or ſtick.

CONGO, a large country of Africa, between the equinoctial line and 18 degrees of S. latitude, containing the counties of Loango, Angola, and Benguela. It is bounded on the N. by the kingdom of Benin, by the inland parts of Africa on the E. by Matiman on the S. and by the Atlantic Ocean on the W. It is ſometimes called Lower Guiney; and the Portugueſe have a great many ſettlements on the coaſt, as well as in the inland country, which were firſt begun ſoon after the year 1484, at which time it was diſcovered. The heat is almoſt inſupportable, eſpecially in the ſummer months. They have many deſart places within land, in which are many wild beaſts; ſuch as elephants, tygers, leopards, monkeys, and monſtrous ſerpents; but, near the coaſt, the ſoil is more fertile; and there are fruits of many kinds, beſides palm-trees, from which they get wine and oil. The greateſt part of the inhabitants are negroes, going almoſt naked, worſhipping the ſun, moon, and ſtars, beſides animals of different kinds. But the Portugueſe have made a great number of converts, ſuch as they are. Congo, properly ſo called, is about 150 miles in length along the coaſt, and 370 in breadth. From March to September is called the winter ſeaſon, when it rains almoſt every day; and the ſummer is from October to March, and then the weather is always ſerene. The inhabitants are ſkilful in weaving cotton-cloths which ſerve them to hide their nakedneſs; and they trade in ſlaves, ivory, caſſia, and tamarinds. This country contains vaſt numbers of elephants, whoſe teeth are prodigiouſly large. Some pretend there are leopards here near 30 yards long, with a rattle at their tails; but this is a fable. The river Zaire is full of crocodiles, and ſea and river horſes. Some ſay there are gold mines here, but that the inhabitants do not know how to work them. Their current money is ſea-ſhells. The principal town is St. Salvadore. The trade is open to all European nations.

CONGRA'TULANT, Part. (congratulans) rejoicing or felicitating with another.

To CONGRA'TULATE, V. A. (from

ter and gratulaur, Lat.] to express joy on account of the good success of another; used sometimes with to, and sometimes with with before the person.

CONGRATULATION, S. the act of expressing joy on the success of another. The form in which joy is expressed for the success of another.

To CONGREE, V. N. [from con and gree, Fr.] to agree together. To join or unite. "Congreeing in a full and natural close." Shak.

To CON'GREGATE, V. A. [congrego, Lat.] to collect several things or persons together. Neuterly, to assemble, or meet together.

CON'GREGATE, Adj. collected together; forming one mass; compact. "Where the matter is most congregate." Bac.

CONGREGA'TION, S. a collection of several particles. In Divinity, an assembly of people met together for religious worship. An assembly of ecclesiastics, constituting a body.

CONGREGA'TIONAL, Adj. belonging to, or in the form of an assembly or congregation.

CON'GRESS, S. [congressus, Lat.] the act or force with which two bodies meet together; a shock, or conflict. An appointed meeting for the settling of affairs between nations.

CONGRES'SIVE, Adj. meeting together.

CONGREVE, WILLIAM, Esq; This gentleman was descended from the ancient family of the Congreves, of Congreve in Staffordshire, his father being second son to Richard Congreve, of that place. Some authors, and in particular Mr James Ware, contended for his having been born in Ireland, but as Jacob, who was particularly acquainted with him, and who in his preface acknowledges his obligations to Mr. Congreve for his communication of what related to himself, has absolutely contradicted that report, I shall on his authority, which I consider to be the same as Mr. Congreve's own, fix the spot of his nativity at a place called Bardsa, not far from Leeds in Yorkshire, being part of the estate of Sir John Lewis, his great-Uncle by his mother's side. It is certain, however, that he went over to that kingdom very young. For his father being only a younger brother, and provided for in the army by a commission on the Irish establishment, was compelled to undertake a journey thither in consequence of his command; which he afterwards parted with to accept of the management of a considerable estate belonging to the Burlington family, which fixed his residence there. However, though he suffered this son to receive his first tincture of letters in the great school at Kilkenny, and afterwards, to complete his classi-

cal learning under the direction of Dr. Ash, in the university of Dublin, yet being desirous that his studies should be directed to profit as well as improvement, he sent him over to England soon after the revolution, and placed him as a student in the Temple. The dry, plodding study of the law, however, was by no means suitable to the sprightly volatile genius of Mr. Congreve, and therefore, though he did not want approbation in those studies to which his genius led him, yet he did not even attempt to make any proficiency in a service which he was probably conscious he should make no figure in. Excellence and perfection were what, it is apparent, he laid down as his principle from the very first, to make it his aim the acquiring; for in the very earliest education of his genius, and a very early one indeed it was, viz. his novel, called Love and Duty Reconciled, written when he was not above seventeen years of age, he had not only endeavoured at, but indeed succeeded in, the presenting to the world not a mere novel according to taste and fashion then prevailing, but a piece which should point out, and be in itself a model of, what novels ought to be. And though this cannot itself be called with propriety a dramatic work, yet he has so strictly adhered to dramatic rules in the composition of it, that his arriving at so great a degree of perfection in the regular drama, in so short a time afterwards, is hardly to be wondered at. His first play was the Old Batchelor, and was the amusement of some leisure hours during a slow recovery from a fit of illness, soon after his return to England, and was in itself so perfect, that Mr. Dryden, on it's being shewn to him, declar'd he had never in his life seen such a first play; and that great poet having, in conjunction with Mr Southerne and Arthur Mainwaring, Esq; given it a slight revisal, Dr. Davenant, who was the manager of Drury Lane theatre, and was delighted both with the piece and it's author, brought it on the stage in 1693, where it met with such universal approbation, that Mr. Congreve, though he was but nineteen years of age at the time of his writing it, became now considered as a prop to the declining stage, and a rising genius in dramatic poetry.—The next year he produced the Double Dealer, which for what reason however, I know not, did not meet with so much success as the former.—The merit of his first play, however, had obtained him the favour and patronage of lord Hallifax, and some peculiar marks of distinction from queen Mary, on whose death, which happened in the close of this year, he wrote a very elegant elegiac pastoral.—In 1695, when Betterton opened the new house in Lincoln's-Inn-fields, Mr. Congreve joining with him, gave him his comedy of Love for Love, with which the company opened their campaign, and which

which met with such success, that they immediately offered the author a share in the management of the house, on condition of his furnishing them with one play yearly. —— This offer he accepted of; but whether through indolence, or that correctness which he looked on as necessary to his works, his Mourning Bride did not come out till 1697, nor his Way of the World till two years after that.—The indifferent success this last-mentioned play, though an exceeding good one, met from the public, complicated that disgust to the theatre, which a long contest with Jeremy Collier, who had attacked the immoralities of the English Stage, and more especially some of his pieces, had begun, and he determined never more to write for the stage —— This resolution he punctually kept, and Mr. Dennis's observation on that point will, I am afraid, be found but too true, when he said, "that Mr. Congreve quitted the stage early, and that Comedy left it with him." Yet, though he quitted dramatic writing, he did not lay down the pen entirely; but occasionally wrote many little pieces both in prose and verse, all of which stand on the records of literary fame.

It is very possible, however, that he might even sooner have given way to this disgust, had not the easiness of his circumstances rendered any subserviency to the opinions and caprice of the town absolutely unnecessary to him. For his abilities having very early in life raised him to the acquaintance of the earl of Halifax, who was then the Mæcenas of the age, that nobleman, desirous of raising so promising a genius above the necessity of too hasty productions, made him one of the commissioners for licensing hackney-coaches, or, according to Coxeter, a commission of the wine-licence. He soon after bestowed on him a place in the Pipe-Office, and not long after that gave him a post in the custom, worth six hundred pounds per ann.

In the year 1728, he was appointed secretary of Jamaica, so that, with all together, his income towards the latter part of his life was upwards of twelve hundred pounds a year. Thus raised above dependance, it is no wonder he would no longer render himself subject to the capricious censures of impotent critics. And had his poetical father, Mr. Dryden, ever been raised to the same circumstances, it is probable that his All for Love would not now have been esteemed the best of his dramatic pieces, nor would he have been compelled for a bare livelihood to the drudgery of producing four plays in a space of time scarce more than sufficient for screening the plot of one.

But return to Congreve. The greatest part of the last twenty years of his life were spent in ease and retirement, and he either did not, or affected not to give himself any trouble about reputation. Yet some

part of that conduct might proceed from a degree of pride. T. Cibber, in his lives of the poets, Vol. IV. p. 95, relates an anecdote of him, which I cannot properly omit here. "When the celebrated Voltaire, says he, was in England, he waited upon Congreve, and passed him some compliments as to the reputation and merit of his works. Congreve thanked him, but at the same time told that ingenious foreigner, he did not chuse to be considered as an author, but only as a private gentleman, and in that light expected to be visited. Voltaire answered, that if he had never been any thing but a private gentleman, in all probability he had never been troubled with that visit. And observes in his own account of the transaction, that he was not a little disgusted with so unfashionable a piece of vanity."

Towards the close of his life he was much afflicted with the gout, and making a tour to Bath, for the benefit of the waters, was unfortunately overturned in his chariot, by which it is supposed he got some inward bruise, as he ever after complained of a pain in his side, and on his return to London, continued gradually declining in his health, till the 19th of Jan. 1729, when he died, aged 57, at his house in Surry-Street, in the Strand, and on the 26th following was buried in Westminster-Abbey, the pall being supported by persons of the first distinction.

His dramatic pieces are seven in number, and their titles as follow:

1. Double Dealer.   C.
2. Judgement of Paris, Masq;
3. Love for Love.   C.
4. Mourning Bride.   T.
5. Old Batchelor.   C.
6. Semele.   Oratorio.
7. Way of the World.

To CONGRUE', V. A. [congruo, Lat.] to agree, to suit; to import.

CONGRUENCY, S. [congruentia, Lat.] agreement, suitableness, consistency.

CONGRUITY, S. fitness; suitableness. Consistency. In Geometry, applied to figures or lines, which correspond exactly when laid over each other. In the schools, a suitableness or relation between things, whereby we come at the knowledge of what may be expected from them.

CONGRUOUS, Adj. [congruus, Lat.] agreeable to, consistent with, or proportionate; used with to.

CONGRUOUSLY, Adj. consistently. Suitably.

CONIC, CONICAL, Adj. having the form of a cone. Conic section, in Geometry, is the curve line arising from the section of a cone by plane. Conics, or conic sections, that part of geometry which treats of cones.

CONICALLY, Adv. in form or shape of a cone.

To CONJECT, V. N. [conjectum, Lat. supine of conjicio, Lat.] to guess at a thing.

CONJEC'TOR, S. one that determines vaguely. A guesser.

CONJECTURABLE, Adj. that which may be guess'd.

CONJECTURAL, Adj. depending on uncertain principles, by mere guess, or conjecture.

CONJECTURA'LITY, S. that which is not deduced from certain principles. That which is inferrable only from guess.

CONJEC'TURALLY, Adv. by guess, by conjecture, opposed to the certain deduction or consequences of fixed principles.

CONJEC'TURE, S. [conjectura, Lat.] a guess; imperfect knowledge. Idea, or notion. "Now entertain conjecture of a time." Shakesp. This last sense is rather obsolete.

To CONJEC'TURE, V. A. [from the noun] to conclude or determine from uncertain or barely probable principles. To guess.

CONJEC'TURER, S. one who forms an opinion without proof. A guesser.

To CONJOIN, V. A. [pronounced conjoin, from conjordre, Fr.] to join or unite together. To join together in marriage. Neuterly, to league, or take part with another.

CONJOINT, Part. [pronounced conjoint, with thee i long] united; connected; associate. In Music, applied to two or more sounds heard at the same time. Conjoint degree, is applied to two notes immediately following each other in the order of the scale.

CONJOINTLY, Adj. together; in union.

CONJUGAL, Adj. [conjugalis, Lat.] belonging or relating to marriage.

CONJUGALLY, Adv. consistently with marriage; like married people.

To CONJUGATE, V. A. [conjugatus, Lat.] to unite; to pair in marriage. In Grammar, to decline verbs.

CONJUGATE, Adj. [conjugatus, Lat.] In grammar, greeing in derivation with other words, and resembling it in its meaning.

CONJUGATION, S. [conjugatio, Lat.] a couple or pair. The act of joining things together. Union. In Grammar, an orderly distribution of the tenses, persons, and moods of verbs. In Anatomy, a pair of nerves, serving to and performing the same office, or operating together.

CONJUNCT, Part. [conjunctus, Lat.] joined or one string with another; united.

CONJUNCTION, S. [from con Lat. and jungo] the joining of two bodies, armies or people. The uniting two things together. Figuratively, a league, or confederacy. In Astronomy, the meeting of the stars or planets in the same degree of the zodiac. Apparent conjunction, is when a right-line drawn through the centre of the two planets

does not pass through the centre of the earth, but through the eye. True conjunction is when that line, produced, passeth through the centre of the earth. In Grammar, a particle or word used to join the members of a period together, and signify the relation they have to each other; when the sentence consists of several members, the conjunction is generally placed between the two last; but when a vehement agitation or hurry of the mind is to be signified, the conjunction is to be omitted; and when an orator chuses to make the different circumstances of a thing seem more numerous and affect the mind more strongly, a conjunction placed between each member has a very good effect.

CONJUNC'TIVELY, Adv. in union, operating together.

CONJUNC'TIVENESS, S. the quality of uniting things.

CONJUNC'TLY, Adv. jointly; together.

CONJUNC'TURE, S. [conjoncture, Fr.] an union of several circumstances, or causes. A critical period of time. Connection of several things forming a whole. Consistency, or an union of qualities, which can exist at the same time. "What is can prevail to in a conjuncture with episcopacy." King Charles. Followed by with.

CONJURA'TION, S. magic words, charms, &c. which were supposed to have the power of raising the dead, and devils. A plot; a conspiracy.

To CONJU'RE, V. A. [conjuro, Lat.] to intreat a person earnestly. To bind persons together by a solemn oath, to form a conspiracy. "The third part of heav'n's sons conjur'd against the highest." Milt. To influence by the supposed power of magic. Neuterly, to practice magic; or deal in enchantments.

CONJU'RER, S. [pronounced conjurer,] an enchanter. An impostor, who pretends to have commerce with the world of spirits, and by that means to be able to foretell future events. Figuratively, and ironically a person of sagacity and deep penetration, generally used with a negative particle, "He is no conjurer."

CONJU'REMENT, S. in earnest, solemn, and an importunate entreaty. "Your earnest intreaties and fervent conjurements." Milt.

CONNATE, Adj. [from con and natus, Lat.] born with, innate. Born at the same time as another.

CONNA'TURAL, Adj. [from con and naturel, Lat.] consistent with nature. United with the being or born with. Of the same original or nature. "Mix with our connatural dust." Par. Lost.

CONNATURA'LITY, S. a resemblance of nature.

CONNATURA'LLY, Adv. born with or innate. "Connaturally to govern in the soul, antecedently to discursive ratiocination." Hale.

CON-

CONNA'TURALNESS, S. the quality of being born with, or being innate.

To CONNE'CT, V. A. [connecto, Lat.] to join together the members of a period, or the arguments of a discourse in such a manner, as they shall have a mutual dependance on each other.

CONNE'CTION, Adj. See CONNEXION.

CONNE'CTIVE, Adj. having the power of joining different things together.

CONNE'CTIVELY, Adv. jointly; in union; mutually depending on each other.

To CONNE'X, V. A. [connexum, Lat.] to join, link, or fasten together.

CONNE'XION, S. the act of fastening things together. Dependance, commerce, union, formed by interest. In writing, that which relates to the clause which precedes, and that which follows it. In the drama, the disposal of scenes of a play in such a manner, that the stage may never be left empty.

CONNE'XIVE, Adj. having the force of uniting together.

CONNI'VANCE, S. [see CONNIVE] in its primary sense, the act of winking; but not in use. Figuratively, the beholding any fault without taking notice of it, or punishing the committer: joined with at.

To CONNI'VE, V. A. [conniveo, Lat.] to wink. To pass by a fault without taking notice of it, or punishing the party, used with at.

CONNOISSEU'R, S. [Fr. from connoitre, Fr.] one who is acquainted with any object of knowledge or taste. A perfect judge, or critic. Sometimes applied to a pretended judge or critic, by way of irony.

To CO'NNOTATE, V. A. [from con and noto, Lat.] to imply, include, or infer something as a secondary idea, "God's foreseeing doth not connotate predetermining." Hammond.

To CONNO'TE, V. A. to imply, or infer.

CONNU'BIAL, Adj. [connubialis, Lat.] relating, or belonging to marriage.

CONO'ID, S. [from konos, Gr. and eidos, Gr.] In Geometry, a solid body like a cone, only it has an ellipsis instead of a perfect circle for its base.

CONO'IDES, S. [see CONOID] a gland in the third ventricle of the brain, called the pineal gland, supposed by Des Cartes to be the seat or residence of the soul.

CONO'IDICAL, Adj. resembling the form of a conoid.

CONQUASSA'TION, S. violent motion, or agitation.

To CO'NQUER, V. A. [conquerir, conquero, Lat.] to subdue, overcome; to surmount, to obtain the victory.

CO'NQUERABLE, Adj. that may be overcome, easily surmounted, applied to difficulties.

CO'NQUEROR, S. one who surmounts any difficulty; one who conquers by force of arms.

CO'NQUEST, S. [conquête, Fr.] the thing gained by victory; victory or success.

CONSANGUI'NEOUS, Adj. [consanguineus, Lat.] of the same blood; related by birth.

CONSANGUI'NITY, S. [consanguinitas, Lat.] relation by blood.

CO'NSCIENCE, S. [conscientia, Lat.] the faculty of judging of the nature of our actions, whether they be good or evil. The determination of the mind with respect to the nature of any action, after its commission. The knowledge of our own thoughts, or consciousness. Real sentiments, scruple or consciousness. "We must make a conscience in keeping the just laws." In ludicrous language, reason, used with it all. "Enough in all conscience."

CONSCIE'NTIOUS, Adj. [from conscientia, Lat.] scrupulous; acting according to the dictates of conscience; just.

CONSCIE'NTIOUSLY, Adv., agreeable to the dictates of conscience.

CONSCIE'NTIOUSNESS, S. exactness, or tenderness of conscience.

CO'NSCIONABLE, Adj. consistent with the dictates of conscience. Just.

CO'NSCIONABLENESS, S. equity; consistency with the dictates of conscience.

CO'NSCIONABLY, Adv. agreeable to the dictates of conscience. Justly. Reasonably.

CO'NSCIOUS, Adj. [conscius, Lat.] knowing from recollection. Bearing witness of, or sensible of from the dictates of conscience. Used with of, or to before the thing.

CO'NSCIOUSNESS, S. the perception of what passes in a man's own mind. An internal acknowledgment or sense of guilt.

CO'NSCRIPT, Part. [conscriptus, Lat.] written or registered.

CONSCRI'PTION, S. [conscriptio, Lat.] an enrolling or registering.

To CO'NSECRATE, V. A. [consecratum, supine of consecro, Lat.] to dedicate to divine uses. Used with to, to sanctify, or prescribe as pleasing to the Deity. Figuratively, to canonize.

CO'NSECRATE, Part. [consecratus, Lat.] set apart for the divine uses; sacred.

CONSE'CRATER, S. he who performs the rites by which a thing is consecrated.

CONSECRA'TION, S. the appropriating, or dedicating, any common or profane thing to religious uses, by means of certain ceremonies or rites. The benediction of the bread and wine in the sacrament. Among medallists, the apotheosis of an emperor, or his translation among the deities, and being deemed a god.

CONSE'CTARY, Adj. [consectarius, Lat.] following or happening as a consequence.

CON-

CONSECTARY, S. a proposition which follows some preceding definition.

CONSECUTION, S. [*consecutio*, Lat.] a chain or succession of consequences. In Astronomy, the month of consecution, is the space between one conjunction of the moon with the sun to another.

CONSECUTIVE, Adj. [*consecutif*, Fr.] uninterrupted succession. Following.

CONSECUTIVELY, Adv. after or following, as an effect, opposed to antecedently or causally.

CONSENT, S. [*consensus*, Lat.] compliance with a request. Agreement, according, or unity of sentiment. Harmony or agreement of parts. In Physic the perception one part enjoys together with another, by means of some fibres, nerves or muscles common to both.

To CONSENT, V. N. [*consentir*, Fr.] to agree in opinion. To promote the same end by action. To comply with a request, used with *unto*. To permit, used with *unto*.

CONSENTANEOUS, Adj. [*consentaneus*, Lat.] agreeable or suitable to; consistent with, used with *to* or *unto*.

CONSENTANEOUSY, Adv. consistent with, or suitable to. Used with *to*.

CONSENTIENT, Part. [*consentiens*, Lat.] universal unanimous, general; agreeing in opinion.

CONSEQUENCE, S. [Fr. *consequentia*, Lat.] that which follows from or is produced by any cause, or principle. Event, effect. The conclusion of an argument or syllogism, which follows from the agreement between the terms of the premises. That which will produce an effect. Used with adjectives signifying value, as *great*, *deep*, *little*, it implies importance, moment, or concern.

CONSEQUENT, Part. [Fr. *consequent*, Lat.] following or happening as an effect; used with *to*. Sometimes with *upon*.

CONSEQUENT, S. the proposition which contains the conclusion of an argument. An effect, or that which proceeds from the operation of any cause.

CONSEQUENTIAL, Adj. produced by assuming an air of consequence; a chain of causes and effects.

CONSEQUENTIALLY, Adv. deducing consequences. By consequence, eventually. So as the ideas may have a connection with or dependance on one another. In a regular series.

CONSEQUENTLY, Adv. by consequence; necessarily; from a necessary connexion of effects to their causes. In consequence.

CONSERVABLE, Adj. [*conservo*, Lat.] capable of being preserved.

CONSERVANCY, S. [*conservans*, Lat.] the courts held by the lord-mayor, for preservation of the fishery on the river Thames, are stiled courts of conservancy.

CONSERVATION, S. [*conservatio*, Lat.] the act of preserving or keeping.

CONSERVATIVE, Adj. [from *conservatus*, Lat.] having the power of keeping or saving from corruption or decay.

CONSERVATOR, S. [Lat.] one who preserves from corruption or decay. Conservator of the peace, was one who had an especial charge by virtue of his office, to see the king's peace kept. This office seems to have been abolished by the constituting justices of the peace; though it must be observed that the chamberlain of Chester, is still a conservator in that county, and petty-constables are, in common law, esteemed so likewise.

CONSERVATORY, S. [from *conservator*, Lat.] a place wherein any thing is kept in a manner suitable and proper.

CONSERVATORY, Adj. having the power of preserving.

CONSERVE, S. a preserved sweet-meat; a medicine in the form of an electuary. A place to keep and preserve vegetables in. "Set the pots into your conserve." Evelyn. This last is an unusual sense.

CONSESSION, S. [*consessio*, Lat.] a sitting together.

To CONSIDER, V. A. [*considero*, Lat. Fr.] to revolve in the mind; to meditate on; "I will consider thy testimonies," Psalms, cxix. 95. To view with attention. "When I consider the heavens." Psalms, viii 3. To remark; to call to mind; "Consider the ravens." Luke. all. 24. To take notice of and to pity. "Consider mine affliction." Psalms cxix. 153.

CONSIDERABLE, Adj. [from *consider*] worthy of notice or attention. Important; valuable; respectable. Large. "A considerable sum." Clarend.

CONSIDERABLENESS, S. importance; value; note; dignity.

CONSIDERABLY, Adj. in a degree deserving considerable notice. In a great degree.

CONSIDERANCE, S. [from *consider*] deliberation; or meditating on a thing. "After this cold considerance." Shak.

CONSIDERATE, Adj. [*consideratus*, Lat.] serious; given to consideration; prudent, opposed to rash or negligent. Having a respect or regard to. Pitying or moderate, opposed to rigorous.

CONSIDERATION, S. [*consideratio*, Lat.] the act of thinking on. Mature thought or deliberation. Meditation. Joined with *of*, worthy of notice. An equivalent. The motive or reason of action. In Law, the material cause of a contract, without which it is not obligatory.

CONSIDERER, S. one who thinks on any subject. A thinker.

To CONSIGN, V. A. [pronounced *consine* from *consigno*, Lat.] to transfer property to another, In Commerce, to send goods to another.

Figu.

Figuratively, to commit or entrust. "Consigned to writing." Adj. Neuterly, to yield, submit, or resign. "Confess to thee." Shak.

CONSIGNATION, S. [Fr.] the transferring property in Commerce, the sending goods to another. The act of signing "A direct seal a seat of pardon." Taylor.

CONSIGNMENT, S. [from consign] the act of transferring property. The writing by which property is transferred.

To CONSIST, V. N. [consisto, Lat. consister, Fr.] to subsist. To continue in the same state. To be comprised or contained, used with in. To be composed, used with of. To subsist or have being.

CONSISTENCE, CONSISTENCY, S. the degree of thickness or thinness, applied to fluids, substance. Uniformity, free from contradiction, or variety.

CONSISTENT, Part. [consistens, Lat.] not contradictory; reconcilable; agreeing; firm, or solid. Applied to the texture of things.

CONSISTENTLY, Adj. in a suitable manner. Agreeably; uniformly.

CONSISTORIAL, Adj. relating or belonging to some court where an ecclesiastic is judge.

CONSISTORY, S. [consistorium, low Lat.] a court consisting of ecclesiastics. The place where such a court is held. A court held at Rome; also any solemn assembly.

CONSOCIATE, S. [consociatus, Lat.] one who joins with another. An accomplice.

To CONSOCIATE, V. A. [consociatum, Lat.] to join things together. To cement. Followed by with. Neuterly, to unite or join with. "Consociating into the huge continent bodies of plants." Bentley. Used with into.

CONSOCIATION, S. alliance; connection; intimacy.

CONSOLABLE, Adj. that which admits comfort or consolation.

To CONSOLATE, V. A. [consolatus, Lat.] to assuage sorrow. To impart comfort or consolation. "To consolate thine ear." Shak.

CONSOLATION, S. [Fr. from consolatio, Lat.] that which alleviates grief or misery. Comfort. The consolation of Israel, Luke ii. 25. implies Christ; who was generally promised the Jews to comfort them under their greatest calamities; and being supposed by them to be a temporal prince, must have supplied them with a thought which rendered their suffering in bondage supportable, especially as they imagined that he should deliver them out of the hands of their enemies, and extend the dominion of the Jews to the uttermost parts of the earth; if this prospect afforded them comfort, how must it have been heightened, had they considered

our blessed Lord in this light, in which he is shewn in the New Testament?

CONSOLATOR, S. a comforter.

To CONSOLE, V. A. [consoler, Fr.] to cheer; to comfort. To diminish a person's grief or misery.

CONSOLER, S. that which consoles or administers comfort.

CONSOLIDANT, Part. [Fr.] in Surgery, having the property of closing wounds.

To CONSOLIDATE, V. A. [consolider, Fr., Lat.] to form into a compact or hard body. To harden. In Law, to unite two benefices into one; to join two funds into one. To join or unite two bills of parliament into one. Neuterly, to grow firm, hard, or solid.

CONSOLIDATION, S. [Fr.] the act of uniting into one mass. The act of uniting together.

CONSOLIDATIVE, Adj. that which has the power of closing or uniting.

CONSONANCE, CONSONANCY, S. [consonance, Fr.] in Music, the agreement of two sounds, produced at the same time, the one grave and the other acute, which mixing in the air occasion an accord agreeable to the ear; the fifth and octave seem to be the most pleasing consonances. Figuratively, consistence, or agreement of opinion, or sentiments. Friendship. "The consonancy of our youth." Shak. An uncommon sense, and not to be adopted.

CONSONANT, Adj. [Fr. consonans, Lat.] agreeable; consistent; reconcilable; followed by with or unto.

CONSONANT, S. [consonans, Fr.] in Grammar, a letter or character which cannot be perfectly sounded by itself.

CONSONANTLY, Adv. in a consistent suitable manner.

CONSONOUS, Adj. [consonus, Lat.] agreeing in sound; harmonious.

CONSOPIATION, S. [from consopio, Lat.] the act of laying asleep, or rendering insensible.

CONSORT, S. [consors, Lat. formerly accented on the latter syllable] a companion, generally applied to signify one joined in marriage to another. A melody formed by several instruments playing the same tune, corrupted from concert. "A consort of music." Ecclus. xxxii. 5. In consort, signifies united, or in conjunction.

To CONSORT, V. N. to unite or associate. Actively to join, or to marry; to mix.

CONSORTABLE, Adj. to be compared with. "Consortable to C. Brandon." Wotton.

CONSPECTUITY, [from conspectus, Lat.] sight, view, sense of seeing. "Your vision conspectuity." Shak. supposed by
join-

Johnfon to be peculiar to Shakefpear, and to be a corruption.

CONSPICUITY, S. [from *conspicuous*,] brightnefs, eafinefs to be feen. The plainnefs or evident of any truth.

CONSPI'CUOUS, Adj. [*conspicuus*, Lat.] eafy to be feen at a diftance. Figuratively, eminent, famous, celebrated. Eafily difcovered, manifeft, applied to truth.

CONSPI'CUOUSLY, Adv. eafily to be feen, or difcerned, remarkable for fome excellence : eminently.

CONSPI'RACY, S. [*conspiratio*, Lat. *conspiration*, Fr.] a private agreement between perfons to commit fome crime ; a plot. In Law, an agreement of two or more to indict one, or procure him to be indicted of felony.

CONSPI'RANT, Part. [*conspirans*, Lat.] joining with others in a plot.

CONSPIRA'TION, S. [*conspiratio*, Lat.] See CONSPIRACY.

CONSPIRA'TOR, S. [from *conspiro*, Lat.] one who has heartily engaged in a plot, or bad defign.

To CONSPI'RE, V. N. [*conspiro* Lat. *conspirer*, Fr.] to enter into agreement with others to carry on a plot, or bad defign. To tend mutually to one end ; ufed with *together*.

CONSPI'RER, S. See CONSPIRATOR.

CONSPI'RING, Part. tending mutually to produce or caufe one defign.

CON'STABLE, S. [pronounced *cunstable*, *connestable*, Fr.] the *magiftrate* of hundreds, were ordained by Edward I. to be chofen two out of every hundred for the prefervation of the peace. Thefe are called now, *high-conftables*, becaufe increafe of people and crimes have given occafion for officers of the like nature, in every town, called *petty conftables*. The *conftables* of the tower, of Dover-caftle, and of the caftle of Caernarvon, are properly governors of thofe caftles. To *over-run the conftable*, is to fpend more than a man can afford.

CON'STABLESHIP, S. the office and duty of a *conftable*.

CON'STANCY, S. [*constantia*, Lat. *constance*, Fr.] a ftate which admits of no change ; confiftency. Refolution ; fteadinefs. A firm, an inviolable attachment to a perfon, including an unalterable affection.

CON'STANT, Adj. [Fr. *constant*, Lat.] firm, ftrongly attached, affiduous, without intermiffion.

CONSTANTINOPLE, one of the largeft and moft celebrated cities of Europe, ftanding at the eaftern extremity of Romania, and capital of the Ottoman empire. It is feated on a fmall neck of land, which advances towards Natolia, from which it is feparated by a channel of a mile in breadth.

The fea of Marmora wafhes its walls on the S. and a gulph of the channel of Conftantinople does the fame on the N. It is delightfully fituated between the Black Sea and the Archipelago, from whence it is fupplied with all neceffaries. Conftantine the Great, being obliged to refide in the Eaft, chofe this place for his abode, and rebuilt it after the model of Rome. It was taken by the Turks in May 1453, who have kept poffeffion of it ever fince. The grand feignior's palace, called the feraglio, is feated on the fea-fide, and is furrounded with walls flanked with towers, and feparated from the city by canals. It is faid the harbour will eafily hold 1200 fhips. The number of houfes muft needs be prodigious, fince one fire has burnt down 50,000 in a day, without greatly changing the afpect of the city. However, in general, they are but mean, efpecially on the out-fide, where there are few or no windows, and the ftreets being narrow, gives them a melancholy look. They reckon that there are 3370 ftreets, fmall and great ; but they are feldom or never clean ; and the people are infefted with the plague almoft every year. The inhabitants are half Turks, two thirds of the other half Chriftians, and the reft Jews. Here are a great number of ancient monuments ftill remaining, and particularly the fuperb temple of Sophia, which is turned into a mofque, and far furpaffes all the reft. The ftreet called Adrianople, is the longeft and broadeft in the city, and the Bazars, or Bezeifteins, are the markets for felling all forts of merchandife. The old and the new are pretty near each other, and are large fquare buildings, covered with domes, and fupported by arches and pilafters. The new is the beft, and contains all forts of goods, which are there expofed to fale. The market for flaves, of both fexes, is not far off, and the Jews are the principal merchants, who bring them here to be fold. There are a great number of young girls brought from Hungary, Greece, Circaffia, Ruffia, Mingrelia, and Georgia, for the fervice of the Turks, who generally buy them for their feraglios. The Great Square, near the mofque of fultan Bajazet, is the place for public diverfions, where the jugglers and mountebanks play a great variety of tricks. The circumference of this city is by fome faid to be 15 miles, and by Mr. Tournefort 23 miles ; to which, if we add the fuburbs, it may be 34 miles in compafs. The fuburb called Pera is charmingly fituated, and is the place where the embaffadors of England, France, Venice, and Holland, refide. This city is built in the form of a triangle ; and as the ground rifes gradually, there is a view of the whole town from the fea. The public buildings, fuch as the palaces, the mofques, bagnios, and caravanferas for the entertain-

ment

ment of strangers, are many of them very magnificent. It is 112 miles S. of Adrianople, 700 S. E. of Vienna, 750 E. of Rome, 1100 S. E. of London, 1150 E. of Madrid, 1350 S. E. of Paris, and 1100 S. S. E. of Stockholm. Lon. 46. 15. lat. 41. 4.

CONSTANTLY, Adv. In an invariable, or unalterable manner. Perpetually.

To CONSTELLATE, V. N. [*conftello tut*, Lat.] to shine with a collected lustre. Actively, to unite the lustre of several bodies into one blaze or point.

CONSTELLATION, S. [Fr.] an assemblage of several stars which appear to be near one another. Figuratively, assemblage of several lustres, or excellencies.

CONSTERNATION, S. [Fr. from *confternatio*, Lat.] amazement, wonder, astonishment.

To CONSTIPATE, V. A. [*conftipatum*, Lat.] to crowd together, or into a narrow compass. To thicken any fluid body. To shut up or stop any passage. In Physic, to render costive.

CONSTIPATION, S. [from the verb the crowding into a narrow compass. The forcing the particles of a thing closer than they were before. The act of thickening, applied to fluids. Costiveness.

CONSTITUENT, Adj. [Fr. *constituent*, Lat.] essentially original, necessary to the existence of a thing; that of which any thing consists.

CONSTITUENT, S. [*constituent*, Fr.] the person or thing which constitutes to the formation of a thing, an elector. Also who makes the manner of describing any figure, or authorizes another to act for him. That which is necessary or essential.

To CONSTITUTE, V. A [*constituo*, Lat.] to give existence to a thing, to appoint. To make a thing to be what it is; applied to laws, to enact, pass, or establish. To depute.

CONSTITUTER, S. one who appoints another to act for him.

CONSTITUTION, S. [*constitutio*, Lat.] the act of establishing. The particular texture of the parts of a body. The habit or temperament of the body; temper of mind. An established form of government; that of this kingdom consisting of king, lords, and commons, counteracting and controlling the inconveniencies which would arise from either of the branches, when separate, is accurately displayed in *Montesquieu's L'Esprit de Loix*. A particular law enacted by a person in authority, whether civil or spiritual.

CONSTITUTIONAL, S. flowing from the particular habit of a person's body, or disposition of mind. Implanted in the very nature of a thing. Consistent with the form of government; legal.

To CONSTRAIN, V. A. [*contraindre*, Fr.] originally wrote *constraindre*, Fr.] to force, to violate, to ravish. To confine. " How

the limit stays the slender waste *constrain* ?" Gay.

CONSTRAINABLE, Adj. liable to force, or compulsion.

CONSTRAINER, S. one who forces or compels.

CONSTRAINT, S. compulsion or force, used to hinder a person from doing, what he is inclined to, or to force him to do what he is averse to. Confinement; reserve.

To CONSTRICT, V. A. [*constrictum*, Lat.] to contract, or bind close; to cramp.

CONSTRICTION, S. [*constrictio*, Lat.] drawing the parts close together. Contraction.

CONSTRICTOR, S. [Lat.] that which contracts. In Anatomy, applied to those muscles which close some of the tubes of the body.

To CONSTRINGE, V. A. [*constringo*, Lat.] to bind, or force closer together.

CONSTRINGENT, Part. [*constringens*, Lat.] having the quality of binding or closing.

To CONSTRUCT, V. A. [*constructum*, Lat.] to form from different materials. To build. To compile, or constitute; to render.

CONSTRUCTION, S. [Fr. of *constructio*, Lat.] the forming from an assemblage of different things. The form of a building; structure. In Grammar, the ranging the words of a sentence, so as to convey a complete meaning. Figuratively, the meaning, or interpretation of a word. Judgment, or manner of describing any figure, or problem in Geometry. In Algebra, the method of drawing a geometrical figure, whose properties shall express a given equation.

CONSTRUCTURE, S. an edifice; a building; a pile.

To CONSTRUE, V. A. [*construo*, Lat.] to place words in their proper grammatical order, and explain their meaning.

CONSTUPRATION, S. violation, defilement; the act of debauching.

CONSUBSTANTIAL, Adj. [from *con* and *substantia*, Lat.] of the same substance, or essence. Of the same kind or nature.

CONSUBSTANTIALITY, S. the existence of more than one in the same essence.

To CONSUBSTANTIATE, V. A. to unite in one substance or nature.

CONSUBSTANTIATION, S. the union of the body and blood of Christ with the bread, after consecration, according to the Lutherans.

CONSUL, S. [from *consulendo*, Lat.] the title of the chief magistrate at Rome, which were created on the expulsion of the Tarquins. At present a person commissioned to judge between merchants in foreign parts, take care of their interest, and protect their commerce.

CONSULAR, Adj. [consularis, Lat.] belonging to a consul.

CONSULATE, S. [consulatus, Lat.] the office of a consul. The time of his exercising the office of a consul.

CONSULSHIP, S. the office of a consul.

To CONSULT, V. N [consulto, Lat.] to deliberate with others. It has also before the person. Actively, to apply to for advice Figuratively, to plan, or contrive. To examine into the sentiments of an author.

CONSULTATION, S. [Fr. of consultatio, Lat.] the taking the advice of others. An assembly meeting together to give their opinions. In Medicine, applied to the calling in two or more persons to consider the distemper of a person. A council. Consultatio in Law, a writ whereby a cause removed by prohibition from a spiritual court, to the king's, is, on finding the suggestion false, returned to that court again.

CONSULTER, S. one who applies to another for advice or intelligence.

CONSUMABLE, Adj. that which may be altered, wasted, destroyed, or consumed.

To CONSUME, V. A. [consumo, Lat.] to waste. To diminish; to lessen. To destroy. Neuterly, to come to nothing, to grow less in substance.

CONSUMER, S. one who spends, wastes, consumes or destroys.

To CONSUMMATE, V. A. [consummer, Fr. consummatum, Lat] to perfect. To complete. To end

CONSUMMATE, Part. [consummatus, Lat.] perfect, complete; finished

CONSUMMATION, S. [Fr. consummatio, Lat.] completion or conclusion. The final determination of all things. The end of the world. Figuratively, death; an unusual sense!

CONSUMPTION, S. [Fr. of consumptio, Lat.] the consuming, wasting, or destroying. In Medicine, a decay occasioned by a preternatural decay of the body, by a gradual wasting of muscular flesh.

CONSUMPTIVE, Adj. having the quality of wasting. Affected with a consumption.

CONSUMPTIVENESS, S. a tendency, or inclination to a consumption.

CONTACT, S. [contactus, Lat.] the state of two bodies which touch each other.

CONTACTION, S [see CONTACT] the act of joining or touching.

CONTAGION, S. [contagio, Lat.] the communicating a disease to another. Pestilence, or that which affects with diseases, by unwholesome effluvia. Figuratively, the propagation of vice.

CONTAGIOUS, Adj. [contagieux, Fr.] Infectious; to be communicated to others.

CONTAGIOUSNESS, S. the propagating a disorder or vice to another.

To CONTAIN, V. A. [contineo, Lat.] to include within its sides; to comprise. Neuterly, to be chaste.

CONTAINABLE, Adj. possible to be included within certain bounds, or limits.

To CONTAMINATE, V. A. [contaminatum, Lat.] to defile; to pollute, to corrupt.

CONTAMINATE, Part. [contaminatus, Lat.] defiled, polluted.

CONTAMINATION, S. the act of polluting. The state of a thing polluted.

To CONTEMN, V. A. [contemno, Lat.] to despise; disregard, flight, or defy.

CONTEMNER, S. one who despises. A despiser; a scorner; it generally implies not only disregard, but likewise insult.

To CONTEMPER, V. A. [contempero, Lat.] to moderate, by mixture of some opposite quality.

CONTEMPERAMENT, S. temperature, or quality resembling another.

To CONTEMPERATE, V. A. to diminish any thing by the addition of its opposite quality.

CONTEMPERATION, S. the act of tempering, or moderating. The act of blending opposite humours.

To CONTEMPLATE, V. A. [contemplatus, Lat.] to consider with attention. To muse; think, or meditate.

CONTEMPLATION, S. intense thought on any subject. The employment of the thoughts about divine things. Study or speculation; opposed to action.

CONTEMPLATIVE, Adj. given to thought; studious. Having the power of considering or retaining any idea long in the mind, in order to discover its different properties, &c.

CONTEMPLATIVELY, Adv. thoughtfully; attentively; studiously.

CONTEMPLATOR, S. [Lat.] one employed in study. A meditator.

CONTEMPORARY, Adj. [contemporain, Fr.] born at the same time. Existing at the same time.

CONTEMPORARY, S. one who lives, or exists at the same time with another.

CONTEMPT, S. [contemptus, Lat.] the act of despising a thing. The state of being despised. Vileness.

CONTEMPTIBLE, Adj. worthy of scorn. Despised, unworthy of notice. Given to despise or contemn. "The man hath a contemptible spirit." Shak. This is an unusual acceptation.

CONTEMPTIBLENESS, S. that quality which renders a thing the object of contempt.

CONTEMPTIBLY, Adv. meanly; despicably.

CONTEMPTUOUS, Adj. using expressions of scorn and disdain.

CON-

CONTEMPTUOUSLY, Adv. in a manner which expresses a disdainful idea.

CONTEMPTUOUSNESS, S. the quality expressive of an insolent disdain.

To CONTEND, V. N. [contendo, Lat.] to strive or struggle with. To vie with; to support an opinion with positiveness; used with for, or about before the subject of contention, and with against or with before the person contending.

CONTENDENT, S. [contendens, Lat.] one who opposes the opinions of another. An adversary, opponent, or antagonist. "The contendents have been still made a prey." L'Estrange.

CONTENDER, S. an opponent, an opposer, an antagonist.

CONTENT, Adj. [contentus, Lat.] satisfied with one's lot. Submitting.

To CONTENT, V. A. to satisfy; to confine our desires to our possessions; or to give a person his demands.

CONTENT, S. a disposition of mind, whereby a person limits his desires to what he enjoys without murmuring at his lot. In the plural contents, that which is contained in any receptacle; the capacity of containing. The meaning of any writing. The things treated of by any author. "The table of contents."

CONTENTATION, S. satisfaction, content. "Contentation of the learned." Arbuth.

CONTENTED, Part. resigned to the dispensations of providence. Satisfied with one's present lot, without repining.

CONTENTION, S. an opposition of sentiments. A warm espousal of any doctrine in opposition to others. Emulation.

CONTENTIOUS, Adj. quarrelsome. Litigious.

CONTENTIOUSLY, Adv. quarrelsomely, contradictorily.

CONTENTIOUSNESS, S. proneness to contend or quarrel.

CONTENTLESS, Adj. dissatisfied with one's lot or condition.

CONTENTMENT, S. [contentement, Fr.] full satisfaction with our present lot, without desiring more. Pleasure, delight.

CONTERMINOUS, Adj. [conterminus, Lat.] bordering upon, followed by to. "Conterminous to the colonies." Hale.

To CONTEST, V. A. [contester, Fr.] to dispute; to oppose. To contend with a person for any right, or property. Neuterly, to strive, contend, or emulate, followed by with.

CONTEST, S. a dispute; a warm opposition. A difference; a controversy.

CONTESTABLE, Adj. that may be disputed, or controverted.

CONTESTABLENESS, S. the possibility of being contested, or controverted.

CONTESTATION, S. the act of opposing. Strife. Contradiction.

To CONTEX, V. A. [contexo, Lat.] to weave together; to interweave. To intermingle. "Quicksilver is contexed with the salts." Boyle.

CONTEXT, S. [contextus, Lat.] the general tenour. The parts which precede or follow a sentence.

CONTEXT, Part. woven close together; interwoven.

CONTEXTURE, S. [from contex] the peculiar arrangement, or disposition of things. The composition formed from an union of various separate parts. Constitution.

CONTIGUITY, S. a touching. A situation wherein two things touch.

CONTIGUOUS, Adj. [contiguus, Lat.] touching; bordering, applied to countries which join; generally used with to, and sometimes joined to with.

CONTIGUOUSLY, Adv. so as to touch, or join to another body.

CONTIGUOUSNESS, S. touching. Nearness.

CONTINENCE, CONTINENCY, S. [continence, Fr. continentia, Lat.] command over our thoughts and passions. Moderation in lawful pleasures. Chastity.

CONTINENT, Part. [continens, Lat.] chaste; moderate in the use of lawful pleasures.

CONTINENT, S. [continens, Lat.] in Geography, a large extent of land, containing several kingdoms not divided by the sea.

To CONTINGE, V. N. [contingo, Lat.] to touch; to reach; to happen; to befal.

CONTINGENCE, CONTINGENCY, S. [from contingent, Lat.] the being free to exist or not exist; what may happen, opposed to those which must necessarily happen.

CONTINGENT, Adj. [contingens, Lat.] not certainly happening. Casual.

CONTINGENT, S. something casual. A future event which may or may not happen. That which falls to a person's lot upon a division; thus the quantity of money and ammunition, or the number of men, the electors are obliged to furnish, in case of a war in Germany, are called their contingents.

CONTINGENTLY, Adv. in an uncertain, casual manner.

CONTINGENTNESS, S. the quality which denominates a future event to be uncertain.

CONTINUAL, Adj. [continuus, Lat.] incessant; without interruption; without intermission.

CONTINUALLY, Adv. without any pause or respite; incessantly.

CONTINUANCE, S. [from continue] an uninterrupted succession. Abode, or dwelling. Duration. Perseverance.

CONTINUATE, Adj. [continuatus, Lat.] intimately, or closely, uninterrupted, unbroken, or incessant.

CONTINUATION, S. an uninterrupted succession; perseverance.

CONTINUATIVE, S. an expression which denotes continuation, or duration.

CONTINUATOR, S. he that continues a succession without interruption; one who finishes a work which another has left imperfect.

To CONTINUE, V. N. [*continuer*, Fr.] to remain with a person. Joined to *with*; to last, to endure; to persevere in one uniform course of action; to unite without any thing intervening.

CONTINUEDLY, Adv. in a manner free from respite, pause, or cessation.

CONTINUER, S. one who perseveres or continues in any action.

CONTINUITY, S. [*continuitas*, Lat.] close union of the particles of a body, whereby they constitute one mass; texture or cohesion.

CONTINUOUS, Adj. [*continuus*, Lat.] joined together, or having no chasm or intervening space.

To CONTORT, V. A. [*contortum*, Lat.] to wrest, twist, or writhe.

CONTORTION, S. [from *contort*] the action of twisting; the state of a thing that is awry.

CONTOUR, S. In Painting, an outline which defines any figure.

CONTRA, Prep. [Lat.] used in Commerce, the credit side. In Composition it signifies contrary.

CONTRABAND, Adj. [*contrabando*, Ital.] illegal.

To CONTRACT, V. A. [*contractum*, Lat.] to draw together; to comprize; to make a bargain; to betroth, applied to a compact between a man and his intended wife; to acquire; to incur; to obtain; to shorten; to abridge. Neuterly, to shrink, or grow short.

CONTRACT, S. an agreement; a compact; the act of betrothing.

CONTRACTEDNESS, S. the quality which denotes a thing to be reduced; narrowness, smallness.

CONTRACTIBILITY, S. the possibility of being reduced, or shrunk.

CONTRACTIBLE, Adj. capable of being reduced.

CONTRACTIBLENESS, S. the quality of being reduced, by shrinking or contracting.

CONTRACTILE, Adj. having the power of contracting.

CONTRACTION, S. [*contractio*, Lat.] the act of shortening or lessening; the act of shrinking or decreasing; the state of a thing shrunk into a narrower compass. In Grammar, the reducing two syllables or vowels into one, as *I'or*, for *I have*. *Achilles* in Latin, pronounced *Achill*, instead of *Achillei*. An abbreviation; a thing or word abbreviated.

To CONTRADICT, V. A. [*contradictum*, Lat.] to oppose; to deny the assertion of another; to be opposite.

CONTRADICTER, S. one who opposes the sentiments of another; an opponent.

CONTRADICTION, S. the asserting the opinion of another to be false; opposition; inconsistency; contrariety; a species of direct opposition, wherein a thing is diametrically opposite to another, as "being, and not being."

CONTRADICTIOUS, Adj. inconsistent, or opposite; inclined to cavil.

CONTRADICTORILY, Adv. inconsistently; implying contradictions.

CONTRADICTORINESS, S. the highest degree of opposition; contradiction.

CONTRADICTORY, Adj. [*contradictorius*, low Lat.] opposite to, or inconsistent with, used with *to*. In Logic, applied to propositions, those which are in the most diametrical opposition, both the terms of one proposition being opposite to those of the other, and can never both be true, or both false at the same time.

CONTRADISTINCTION, S. the explanation, or the sense of a word, by producing one that has an opposite signification.

To CONTRADISTINGUISH, V. A. to distinguish or explain by contrast, or producing a contrary quality.

CONTRAFISSURE, S. In Surgery, a crack or fissure in the skull, in the part contrary to that wherein the blow was received.

CONTRAPOSITION, S. the placing opposite, or over against. In Logic, the same as *conversion*.

CONTRAREGULARITY, S. the opposing any rule; contrariety to rule. "Not so properly an irregularity, as a *contraregularity*." *Norris*.

CONTRARIANT, Adj. [from *contrarier*, Fr.] contradictory, opposite, irreconcilable.

CONTRARIES, S. [plural of *contrary*] in Logic, propositions which mutually destroy each other, and cannot both be true at the same time; or opposites, which are as remote from each other as possible, and mutually expel each other. Such are whiteness and blackness; cold and heat; good and bad, &c.

CONTRARIETY, S. [from *contrarietas*, low Lat.] opposition; inconsistency; a quality opposite to another.

CONTRARILY, Adv. in a manner opposite to, or irreconcilable with; in opposite directions.

CONTRARINESS, S. the quality of being opposed to, or inconsistent with.

CONTRARIOUS, Adj. [*contrarius*, Lat.] opposite, totally different.

CONTRARIOUSLY, Adv. oppositely; in contrary directions.

CONTRARIWISE, Adv. on the contrary; in a contrary, or opposite manner.

CONTRARY, Adj. [*contrarius*, Lat.] inconsistent; disagreeing; in an opposite direction;

rection; against, or unfavourable, applied to the wind.

CO'NTRARY, S. [contrarius, Lat.] a quality opposite to another; a proposition opposite to another, as necessity opposite on the opposite side; to die one by, an intention or purpose quite contrary; against, or in opposition.

CO'NTRAST, S. [contraste, Fr.] In Painting and Sculpture, difference between any two figures, by means whereof they cause a variety, and tend to set off each other.

To CO'NTRAST, V. A. in Painting, to place in a contrary attitude, &c. Figuratively, to set off one thing by coupling it with another.

CONTRAVALLA'TION, S. [from contra and valls, Lat.] in Fortification, a trench guarded by a parapet, without musket shot of the town.

To CONTRAVE'NE, V. A. [from contra and venio, Lat.] to oppose; to obstruct; to act contrary to a bargain or contract.

CONTRAVE'NTION, S. [from CONTRAVENE] an opposition to, or violation of any law.

CONTRI'BUTARY, Adj. paying a tribute to the same person; concurring to promote a design.

To CONTRI'BUTE, V. A. [contributum, Lat.] to pay or advance a portion of money towards carrying on a design. Neuterly, to bear a part in the promoting any design. Used with to before the motive or end for which the money or assistance is given.

CONTRIBU'TION, S. the paying a share of the expences required to carry on any undertaking; a sum of money collected from several persons.

CONTRI'BUTIVE, Adj. that which promotes or furthers any design.

CONTRI'BUTOR, S. [contributor, Lat.] one who bears a part; one who pays his share towards raising any sum.

CONTRI'BUTORY, Adj. promoting the same end; paying a share towards raising a fund.

CONTRISTA'TION, S. the making melancholy, or sad; the state of a person made sad; melancholy; sadness.

CO'NTRITE, Adj. [from contritus, Lat. of contero, Lat. to bruise] In its primary signification bruised, or much worn. In Divinity, sorrowful for sin from a love of God, opposed to attrite, which implies a sorrow for sin arising from a fear of the deity; the former is the spring of masculine and active piety and reformation, the other naturally productive of despair, superstition, or at best a negative righteousness.

CO'NTRITENESS, S. the quality which flows from the contrition of a penitent.

CONTRI'TION, S. [contritio, Lat.] the act of rubbing two things together, so as to wear off some parts of their surfaces. "The

breaking of their parts into less parts by contrition." Newton's Opt. In Divinity, that sorrow for sin which arises from the love of virtue and right behaviour.

CONTRI'VABLE, Adj. possible to be planned or contrived.

CONTRI'VANCE, S. the producing or planning any design, or scheme; a thing effected by a plot; a scheme, a plot, contrivance, a scheme, a plot, artifice.

To CONTRI'VE, V. A. [controuver, Fr.] to invent, plan, or project; to find, design, or scheme.

CONTRI'VER, S. an inventer; a projector; one who projects for accomplishing some design.

CONTRO'L, S. [controle, Fr.] the account kept as a check upon another. Figuratively, restraint, check, authority.

To CONTRO'L, V. A. [from the noun] to examine the accounts of another by a check kept for that purpose; figuratively, to restrain; to govern; to overpower.

CONTRO'LLABLE, Adj. liable to be controlled; subject to restraint.

CONTRO'LLER, S. one who examines public accounts by a check; one who has the power of over-ruling or restraining.

CONTRO'LLERSHIP, S. the office of a controller.

CONTRO'LMENT, S. the power of restraining the actions of another; opposition; resistance; sometimes confutation, but that sense seems now obsolete.

CONTROVE'RSIAL, Adj. relating to opposition of sentiments; that which may be disputed.

CO'NTROVERSY, S. [controversia, Lat.] an opposition of opinions or sentiments; a suit at law; a ground for quarrelling or finding fault; opposition, or struggling against the force of a thing. "The torrent roar'd—stemming it with hearts of controversy." Shak. A bold and unusual metaphor.

To CONTROVE'RT, V. A. [controverto, Lat.] to oppose the sentiments of another in writing.

CONTROVE'RTIBLE, Adj. that which may be opposed or disputed.

CONTROVE'RTIST, S. frequently engaged in disputes.

CONTUMA'CIOUS, Adj. [contumax] daringly, obstinate, implying a contempt of lawful authority. In Law, refusing to appear in court, when legally summoned, departing without leave, or disobeying its rules and sentence.

CONTUMA'CIOUSLY, Adv. so as to shew an insolent disobedience of lawful authority.

CO'NTUMACY, S. [contumacia, Lat.] disobedience; including insolence; and the highest degree of impudence. In Law, a wilful contempt and disobedience to any lawful summons, or sentence of a court.

3   CON-

CONTUME'LIOUS, Adj. [*contumeliosus*, Lat.] reproachful; full of sarcastic expressions. Figuratively, one who frequently uses reproachful language.

CONTU'MELIOUSLY, Adv. in a rude, reproachful manner, including disdain.

CON'TUMELY, S. [Lat.] language abounding with the bitterest expressions intended to render a person uneasy. Figuratively, infamy. "Eternal *contumely* attend that guilty title." *Addis.*

To CONTU'SE, V. A. [*contusum*, Lat.] to beat together; to bruise. In surgery, to hurt by a blow, so as to disfigure the skin, without breaking it.

CONTU'SION, S. [*contusio*, Lat.] the act of bruising. In medicine, a hurt occasioned by a fall, or blow which discolours the skin, without cutting it or making a wound.

CONVALE'SCENCE, S. [*convalescentia*, Lat.] a recovery of health.

CONVALE'SCENT, Part. [*convalescens*, Lat.] recovering from a disorder, to a state of health.

CONVE'NABLE, Adj. [Fr.] consistent with, agreeable to.

To CONVE'NE, V. A. [*convenir*, Fr.] to call or summons together. To assemble a number of persons. To summons to appear. Neuterly, to come or assemble together.

CONVE'NIENCE, CONVE'NIENCY, S. [*convenientia*, Lat.] suitableness, or fitness. Advantage, profit, ease, or freedom from any obstruction, or embarassment. That which may prove useful or convenient. Seasonableness.

CONVE'NIENT, Adj. [*conveniens*, Lat.] fit, suitable. Proper, necessary. Commodious. Seasonable, applied to time. Used with *to* or *for* before the following noun. "Food *convenient* for me." *Prov.* xxx. 8.

CONVE'NIENTLY, Adj. in such a manner as is suitable with a person's ease, interest, or advantage. Commodiously. In the best manner to promote any end. Properly.

CONVENT, S. [*conventus*, Lat.] an assembly of persons dedicating themselves wholly to the service of religion, and without any kind of commerce with the world. The place inhabited by the religious of either sex. It may be asked whether the Magdalen house is not founded on these principles; and may not give occasion to introducing convents of that sort into this kingdom?

CONVENTICLE, S. an assembly. Figuratively, a place of worship, generally applied by churchmen, to the meetings of non-conformists. A secret assembly.

CONVENTICLER, S. one who frequents private and unlawful assemblies. Used by way of reproach for a dissenter or a person who frequents meeting-houses.

CONVENTION, S. [*conventio*, Lat.] the coming together or union of the particles of a body. An assembly met to debate

on any point. A contract, or agreement for a certain time, used for a preliminary to a definitive treaty.

CONVENTIONAL, Adj. stipulated; or agreed to by contract.

CONVE'NTIONARY, Adj. acting according to agreement or contract.

CONVE'NTUAL, Adj. [*conventuel*, Fr.] to a convent.

CONVE'NTUAL, S. a monk, or one who resides in a convent.

To CONVE'RGE, V. N. [*convergo*, Lat.] to meet in a point, applied to the rays of light, or lines drawn from different surfaces.

CONVE'RGENT, Part. [*convergens*, Lat.] issuing from divers points, applied to the rays of light, or lines drawn from different points. *Converging* series. See SERIES.

CONVE'RSABLE, Adj. [written sometimes *conversible*, but improperly; *conversable*, Fr.] fit for conversation or company; affable; communicative; opposed to *morose* or *reserved*.

CONVE'RSABLENESS, S. the quality flowing from affability and good-nature, which fits a person for entertaining another with discourse.

CONVE'RSABLY, Adv. in such a manner as to engage others agreeably with discourse.

CONVE'RSANT, Part. [Fr. sometimes accented on the first syllable] used to, followed by *in*. "*Conversant* in books." Acquainted with; intimate, having intercourse with; used with *among*. Used with *about* it implies, employed or engaged.

CONVERSA'TION, S. [*conversatio*, Lat.] easy, familiar discourse with another. Intercourse. Behaviour, life, or moral conduct.

CONVE'RSATIVE, Adj. fit for or given to conversation.

To CONVE'RSE, V. N. [*converser*, Fr.] to live with, to accompany. Figuratively, to hold intercourse with; to be acquainted with. To be used to, followed by *with*. To discourse with another; and with *on* before the subject of conversation. "*Conversed* so often on that subject." *Dryd.* To have commerce with the other sex.

CON'VERSE, S. conversation. Figuratively, familiar acquaintance. In Geometry, the drawing a conclusion from something supposed.

CONVE'RSELY, Adv. in a contrary order; reciprocally.

CONVE'RSION, S. [*conversio*, Lat.] the change from one state to another. In Divinity, a change from wickedness to piety, or from a false to a true religion. In Logic, the change of the terms of a proposition, as in these sentences. "No virtue is vice; No vice is virtue." In Algebra, the reducing an equation to one common denominator.

CONVE'RSIVE, Adj. fit for conversation, or discourse; communicative,

To

To CONVE'RT, V. A. [_converto_, Lat.]
To change from a false religion to a
true one. To turn from a bad to a
good life. To turn towards any point.
" Crystal—will _convert_ the needle freely
placed." _Brown._ To change the terms of a
proposition so that the predicate shall become
the subject, and the subject the predicate, as
in the following. " All sin is a transgression of the law ; but every transgression of the
law is sin." _Hale._ To undergo or suffer a
change, used with _to_.

CO'NVERT, S. a person prevailed on to
change from a false to a true religion.

CONVE'RTER, S. one who persuades
another to change his religion.

CONVERTIBI'LITY, S. the possibility
of conversion.

CONVE'RTIBLE, Adj. that which may
be changed ; altered, or transmuted. Applied to terms or propositions, that which
may be used in stead of another.

CONVE'RTIBLY, Adv. so as to be in-
terchanged for the other, applied to words or
propositions.

CONVE'RTITE, S. [_converti_, Fr.] See
CONVERT.

CO'NVEX, Adj. [_convexus_, Lat.] swelling, protuberant, applied to the external
surface of a circular body. Used substantively, for _convexity_.

CONVE'XED, Part. bending outwardly
applied to the outward surface of any round
or spherical or round body.

CONVE'XEDLY, Adv. protuberant, or
in a convex form.

CONVE'XITY, S. the bending, or protuberance formed by the outward surface of
a round or globular form.

CONVE'XLY, Adv. in a convex form.

CONVE'XO-CONCAVE, Adj. hollow
or concave on one side, and protuberant or
convex on the other.

To CONVE'Y, V. A. [_convebo_, Lat.] to
remove. To transport ; used with _over_.
To _convey down_, to transmit by tradition.
To _convey to_, to transfer a right or property
to another. To transact with privacy. " I
will _convey_ the business." _Shakesp._ An unusual sense !

CONVE'YANCE, S. the act of moving a
thing to another place. The transferring of
property to another. The transmitting a
truth by tradition. A writing or instrument
by which property is transferred. A secret
private, clandestine, or juggling substitution
of one thing in the room of another.

CONVE'YANCER, S. a lawyer, conversant in drawing writings for transferring property.

CONVE'YER, S. one who carries or removes goods from another place.

To CONVI'CT, V. A. [_convictum_, supine
of _convinco_, Lat.] to prove guilty of some
crime.

CONVI'CT, Part. [_convictus_, Lat.] proved
guilty of a crime, or offence.

CONVI'CT, S. a person proved by a jury
to be guilty of a crime.

CONVI'CTION, S. the proof of guilt.
The act of proving a crime. Confutation,
consciousness of guilt.

CONVI'CTIVE, Adj. having the power
of convincing.

To CONVI'NCE, V. A. [_convinco_, Lat.]
to prove as to make a person acknowledge its
truth. To evince, manifest, or vindicate.
To prove guilty, or make a person own the
commission of a crime. " To _convince_ all
that are ungodly." _Jude_ 15. Used with _of_.
To overpower. " Their malady _convinces_ the
great essay of art." _Shakesp._

CONVI'NCEMENT, S. the same as
CONVICTION.

CONVI'NCIBLE, Adj. capable of being
convicted or proved guilty ; liable or easily
to be confuted.

CONVI'NCINGLY, Adv. in such a manner as to convince a person.

CONVI'NCINGNESS, S. the evidence of
any fact or truth.

To CONVI'VE, V. A. [_convivo_, Lat.] to
entertain several persons at a feast. Neuterly, to repast or feast one's self. " There
to the full _convive_ you." _Shakesp._

CONVI'VAL, CONVI'VIAL, Adj. [_con-
vivalis_, Lat.] relating or belonging to an entertainment of several persons.

CO'NUNDRUM, S. [a cant word] a low
jest, or quibble drawn from the double signification of words or things.

To CO'NVOCATE, V. A. [from _convo-
catum_, Lat.] to call together. To summons
several persons to meet.

CONVOCA'TION, S. [Fr. _convocatio_,
Lat. ; the act of calling several persons together. An assembly. An assembly of the
clergy, for consultation on matters ecclesiastical, during the sitting of parliament. Likewise an assembly at Oxford, consisting of the
vice-chancellor, &c. wherein the conferring
of degrees ; expulsion of members, and other
affairs relating to the university are transacted.

To CONVO'KE, V. A. [_convoco_, Lat.]
to call together several persons ; to summons.

To CONVO'LVE, V. A. [_convolvo_, Lat.]
to roll together ; to roll over each other.

CONVOLU'TED, Part. [_convolutus_, Lat.]
twisted, writhed, or rolled up.

CONVOLU'TION, S. [_convolutio_, Lat.]
the act of rolling things over one another.
The state of a thing rolled up.

To CONVO'Y, V. A. [_convoyer_, Fr.] to
protect ships by sea, or provisions, &c. by
land, from falling into the enemies hands.

CO'NVOY, S. [_convoi_, Fr.] ships attending
a fleet of merchants to protect them from an
enemy. A body of men used to guard provisions or ammunitions by land.

CO'NUSANCE, S. [_connoissance_, Fr.] notice,

tire, knowledge, or power of enquiring into an affair. So COGNIZANCE.

To CONVU'LSE, V.A. [*convulsus*, Lat.] to give an involuntary motion to any parts of the body.

CONVU'LSION, S. [*convulsio*, Lat.] in Medicine, an involuntary motion, or contraction of any part of the body. Figuratively, the breaking asunder the parts of a thing by a violent force. A tumult, or commotion, applied to affairs of the state.

CONVU'LSIVE, Adj [*convulsif*, Fr.] giving an involuntary motion. In Medicine, applied to those motions which are caused by convulsity.

CONY, S. [thee pronounced like *u* short, from *konin*, Belg.] in Natural History, an animal which burroughs and breeds in warrens, a rabit. A *cony-borough*, a hole made by a rabit in the ground to breed in.

To CO'O, V. N. to make a hoarse noise like a pigeon.

COO'K, S. [*coc*, Sax. *cog*, Brit.] one who professes to dress victuals. A *cook-maid*, is a female who dresses victuals. A *cook-room*, is an apartment in a ship, wherein provisions are dressed for the crew.

To COOK, V. A. [*coquo*, Lat.] to prepare or dress victuals. Figuratively, to prepare a thing for any particular purpose.

COO'KERY, S. the art of dressing or preparing victuals.

COO'L, Adj. [*koele*, Belg.] approaching to or somewhat cold. Figuratively, free from any violent passion. Not very fond; indifferent; unaffected with any passion or love.

To COO'L, V. A. [*koelen*, Belg.] to lessen heat. To moderate any passion. Neuterly, to become less hot; to become less eager.

COO'LER, S. that which has the power of lessening the degree of heat. A vessel used by brewers, to cool their sweet-wort in.

COO'LLY, Adj. between hot and cold. Figuratively, without heat or anger.

COO'LNESS, S. a middle state between heat and cold. Applied to the passions, freedom from any violent passion. Want of affectionate regard. Indifference.

CO'OM, S. [*suchin*, Fr. *cambus*, Lat.] the matter which works out of the wheels of carriages. A dry measure containing four bushels.

To CO'OP, S. [*kype*, Belg. *cupa*, Ital.] a vessel, for keeping liquor; an inclosure made with twigs to confine poultry in.

COO'P, V. A. to confine or shut up in a narrow compass; followed sometimes by *up* before the person or the thing confined, and used with *in* before the thing including.

CO'OPEE, S. [Fr.] the name of a particular step in dancing.

COO'PER, S. [*kuyper*, Belg.] one who

makes casks, or any vessel held together by hoops.

COO'PERAGE, S. the price paid for cooper's work.

To CO-O'PERATE, V. A. [from *cra* and *operatus*, Lat.] to labour with another to perfect or finish any work.

CO-O'PERATION, S. that act by which persons contribute to promote the same end.

CO-O'PERATOR, S. one who endeavours to promote the same end.

CO-O'RDINATE, Adj. [*co-ordinatus*, Lat.] of equal rank or degree.

CO-O'RDINATELY, Adv. in the same order, or rank.

CO-ORDINA'TION, S. the state of holding the same rank or degree. Applied to causes, it denotes an order or causes wherein several of the same kind, nature, and tendency, concur to the producing the same effect.

CO'OT, S. [*dort* or *meer-dort*, Belg. *raile*, Fr.] in Natural history, a small black water-fowl, chiefly in marshes and fens.

CO'T, S. [*cop*, Sax.] the top or head of any thing; or any thing rising to a head or point.

CO'PAL, S. [Span.] a resinous substance, pure, transparent, and of a fragrant smell.

COPA'RCENARY, S. in Law, joint succession.

COPA'RCENER, S. [*coparçonier*, Fr.] in Law, one who has an equal share of the inheritance of an ancestor, with another.

COPA'RCENY, S. an equal share with others of an inheritance.

COPA'RTNER, S. one who carries on business in conjunction with another. One equally concerned with another.

COPA'RTNERSHIP, S. a state wherein a person has an equal share, or is engaged in the same design with another.

COPA'YVA, S. [sometimes written *copivi*, *coptol*, *copaiva*, *copaiba*, *copayva*,] in Medicine, a gum from a tree in the Brasils, used in disorders of the urinary passages.

CO'PE, S. [*chappe*, Fr.] any thing which covers the head. Any thing spread over the head, as the skies; from *le chappe du ciel*, Fr. *la coppa del cielo*, Ital. An arch-work.

To COPE, V. A. to cover, "A large bridge—*cop'd* over head." *Addis.* To requite, or give as a recompence. "Three thousand ducats—we freely *cope* your courteous pains withal." *Shak.* To cope with, to contend with, to fight, or combat. Neuterly, to fight, oppose; struggle, or contend.

COPENHAGEN, a large, rich, and strong town or city of Denmark, with a famous university. There was a new palace built here in 1730, which is very magnificent; besides which, there are two others, in which the king sometimes resides. The citadel is a regular fort, defended by five good bastions, a double

ble ditch full of water, and several advanced works. The arsenal is furnished with naval stores sufficient to fit out a whole fleet. The exchange of the E. India company, their arsenal, the king's stables, the college, the house and provisions, the orphan-house, the opera-house, and the military school, are all superb structures. The royal library contains above 40,000 manuscripts and printed books, collected from all parts. The inhabitants are reckoned at about 60,000, without counting the soldiers and sailors. Before the terrible fire in 1728, there were above 6000 houses, of which 3785 were reduced to ashes, with a prodigious quantity of merchandizes of all sort. It is about five miles in circumference, and is seated on the eastern shore of the Isle of Zealand, upon a fine bay of the Baltic Sea, near the streight called the Sound. It is 300 miles S. W. of Stockholm, 450 N. W. of Vienna, 500 N. E. of London.

COPIER, S. one who transcribes or imitates any original. Sometimes used by way of reproach, for a person that is unable to produce any thing from the exercise of his own invention and understanding.

COPING, S. [coppo, Sax.] in Architecture, the upper tire of masonry, which covers a wall.

COPIOUS, Adj. [copia, Lat.] plentiful, abundant; redundant; not confined.

COPIOUSLY, Adv. plentifully; in great quantities; largely, in a diffusive manner.

COPIOUSNESS, S. plenty; abundance; Diffusiveness; exuberance; abundance of images, or a great flow of words, applied to writings, oratory.

COPPED, Part. [from cop] rising in a point at top.

COPPEL, S. [spelt likewise copel, cupel, cuple, and cuppel, from cuppe, Sax.] a vessel used by assayers and refiners, to try and refine their metals in.

COPPER, S. [koper, Belg. kuffer, Teut.] a hard metal of a reddish colour, heavier than iron or tin, but lighter than silver, lead, or gold, the hardest of all metals next to iron, and on that account mixed with silver and gold, to give them a proper degree of hardness, it is more liable to rust than any other metal, its ductility is very great and its divisibility prodigious. Copper, signifies also a large vessel or boiler fixed in brick work. A copper-plate, is a thin piece of polished copper, engraved with some figure or design. A copper-work, is a place where copper is wrought or manufactured.

COPPERAS, S. [coperoffa, Span.] a vitriolic substance. It is made use of in dying wool and hats black, in making ink, in tanning leather and in making oil of vitriol.

COPPER-SMITH, S. a person who deals in vessels made of copper.

COPPERY, Adj. containing copper; made of copper; tasting of copper.

COPPICE, S. [taillaux, Fr.] a small wood consisting of under wood or brushwood.

COPPLE-DUST, S. powder used in refining metals.

COPSE, S. [See Coppice, xevla, Gr.] underwood; short wood used for fuel. Brushwood.

To COPULATE, V. A. [copulatum, Lat.] to unite, or link together. Neuterly to come together, applied to the commerce between the sexes.

COPULATION, S. the embracing of the different sexes.

COPULATIVE, S. [copulativus, Lat.] a term of grammar, implying the joining of two or more sentences.

COPY, S. [copie, Fr. copia, Ital.] a writing from some other, and is wrote word for word from some original. An individual book or manuscript. A picture drawn from an original piece. A piece of writing for school-boys to write by. A copy-book, is a book of blank paper for school-boys to write in.

To COPY, V. A. to transcribe a writing. To imitate.

COPY-HOLD, S. in law, a tenure by which the tenant hath nothing to shew but the copy of the rolls made by the steward of the lord's court.

COPYHOLDER, S. a person admitted a tenant of any lands or tenements in a manor, by copy of court roll, according to the custom of the said manor.

To COQUET, V. A. to treat with an appearance of love, without any real affection. Neuterly, to act or pretend the lover.

COQUETRY, S. [coquetterie, Fr.] a desire of attracting the notice of the other sex. An affectation of love.

COQUETTE, [Fr. from coquuet, Fr. a prattler] a gay airy girl, who endeavours to attract the notice of the other sex, and to engage a number of suitors merely from a principle of vanity and without any inclination to marriage.

CORAL, S. [corallum, Lat.] a plant of a stony nature, growing in the water; whose external bark is of a fungous texture, of a yellowish or greenish colour, full of an acrid juice resembling milk, it covers every part of the plant, is easily seperated from it when moist, but adheres to it very firmly if suffered to dry. The whole coral plant grows to stones, without a root, or any ways penetrating them like other plants, taking the exact form of the solid it grows to, and covering it like a plate, whence several have conjectured that it is, in its original state, fluid. But as it is found to grow and take in nourishment like other plants, to produce flowers and seeds, or

or something analogous to them, it is certainly one of the vegetable kind. A coral, is applied to the toy which is hung pendant from the wasle of children, which consists of a piece of coral set in gold and silver, adorned with bells.

CO'RALLINE. Adj. [*coral線, Lat.*] consisting of or resembling coral.

CORALLOID, CORALLOIDA, Adj. [*coralloidea*] resembling a coral.

CO'RANT, S. [*courant, Fr.*] a dance consisting of a sprightly motion.

COR'BE, Adj. [*courbe, Fr.*] crooked, "The corbe shoulder it leans amiss." *Spens.*

CO'RD, S. [*cord, Brit. corde, Fr.*] a string made of hemp twilled. In Scripture, "The cords of the wicked." *Psal. cxxix. 4.* are the snares with which they intangle the weak and innocent. "To stretch a line or cord about a city" *Law. ii. 8.* is to demolish it, or to lay it level with the ground. The cords used in setting up tents, afford several metaphors, denoting either the stability or ruin of a place. A cord of wood, is a pile of wood of eight feet long, four high, and four broad.

To CO'RD, V. A. to bind things together with a cord.

CO'RDAGE, S. a quantity of cords. The ropes of a ship.

CO'RDED, Part. made of ropes, or cords. "A corded ladder." *Shak.* A corded silk, is that whose surface is not level, but rises in weals or stripes.

CORDELIER, S. a monk of the order of St. Francis, so called from the cord which they wear round their waste.

CO'RDIAL, S. [from *cordis, Lat.*] In medicine, a draught which increases the force of the heart, by bringing the serum of the blood into a condition proper for circulation and nutrition. Figuratively, any thing which occasions joy or gladness.

CO'RDIAL, Adj. reviving, strengthening. Applied to the affections, sincere, without hypocrisy.

CORDIA'LLITY, S. sincere affection. Sincerity.

CO'RDIALLY, Adv. free from hypocrisy, sincerely, affectionately.

CO'RDON, S. [Fr.] the ribbon worn by a knight of any order.

CORDWAI'NER, S. [*cordonnier, Fr.*] one who makes and sells shoes.

CO'RE, S. [*cœur, Fr. cor, Lat.*] the heart. The inner part of a thing. In a fruit, the part which contains the kernel. The part which contains the matter of a sore. Used by Bacon for a body or collection of people from *corps, Fr.* which is pronounced *cor.* "He was in a core of people." *Bacon. Hen. vi.*

CORF-CASTLE, S. a town of Dorsetshire, with a market on Thursdays, and two fairs, viz. on May 11, and October 19, for

hogs and toys. It is seated in a peninsula called Purbeck, on a river, and in a barren soil between two hills, on one of which stands the castle. It has one church, and 130 houses ; the streets are however bad, and not paved. It is governed by a mayor and aldermen, and sends two members to parliament. It is 18 miles S. by W. of Pool, to E. by N. or Weymouth, and 116 W. by S. of London. Lon. 15. 27. lat. 50. 33.

CORIA'NDER, S. [*coriandrum, Lat.*] a plant with a fibrous annual root. The germen is situated under the flower, and becomes a spherical fruit, divided into two parts, containing each an hemispherical concave seed, which is used in medicine, as a carminative and corrector to some cathartics.

CO'RINTH, S. [a famous city in Greece, wherein Christianity flourished, and was propagated by St. Paul, who wrote two epistles to its inhabitants, to guard them from some heresies, that were springing up amongst them] a small fruit commonly called a *currant.* "The chief riches of Zant consists in corinths." *Bacon.* The corinthian order, in Architecture, is one of the five orders, and is the most noble, rich, and delicate of them all.

CORK, S. [*cort, Belg. corcho, Span.*] in Botany, a species of oak, which is stripped of its bark every eight or ten years, and is so far from being injured thereby that it is preserved by that means to an hundred years or more. Of the bark are formed bungs for barrels, and stopples for bottles, which likewise go by the name of the tree, and are called corks.

CO'RKING-PIN, S. a large pin.

CO'RKY, Adj. resembling cork.

CORN, S. [*corn. Sax. Lat*vo, Goth.*] a plant, or grain, which produces bread. Grain unreaped. Grain in the ear. An horny substance growing on the toes. A single particle.

To CO'RN, V. A. to salt or sprinkle meat with salt.

CO'RNEOUS, Adj. [from *corneus, Lat.*] horny or resembling horn.

CO'RNER, S [*cornel, Brit.*] an angle formed by the meeting of two walls. Figuratively, a private place. The extremities, *Every corner.* implies the whole.

CO'RNER-WISE, Adv. from one corner to the other ; diagonally ; with the corner in front.

CO'RNET, S. [*cornette, Fr.*] a musical wind instrument, used by the ancients in war. An officer in the cavalry, who bears the colours in the troop, he is the third officer in the company. *Cornet,* in Farriery, is the lowest part of the pastern of a horse, runs round the coffin, and is distinguished by the hair which joins and covers the upper part of the hoof.

CO'RNETTER, S. a person who blows the cornet.

COR-

CORNICE, S. [corniche, Fr. cornice, Lat.] In Architecture, the uppermost member of the entablature of a column. Likewise all little projectures of masonry or joinery, as the cornice of a chimney.

CORNICLE, S. [a diminutive from corna, Lat.] a little horn. "On the long and shorter cornicle." Brown.

CORNICULATE, Adj. [from corna, Lat.] in Botany, applied to such plants, as after each flower, produce many horned pods called siliqua.

CORNIFIC, Adj. [from corna, Lat. and facio, Lat.] productive of horns.

CORNIGEROUS, Adj. horned; bearing horns.

CORNU-COPIÆ, S. [from cornu a horn, and copia, Lat. plenty] among the ancients a horn, out of which a plenty of every thing was supposed to grow. It is the characteristic of the goddess of plenty, and described in the form of a large horn, filled with flowers and fruits.

To CORNUTE, V. A. [cornutus, Lat.] to bestow horns; to cuckold.

CORNUTED, Part. [cornutus, Lat.] grafted with horns; horned; made a cuckold.

CORNUTO, S. a cuckold.

CORNWALL, an English county surrounded on all sides by the sea, except to the E. which joins to Devonshire, from which it is separated by the river Tamer. It is 75 miles in length, and 26 in breadth, but grows narrower gradually towards the land's end. It contains 27,620 houses, 165,660 inhabitants, 161 parishes, 27 market-towns, and sends 44 members to parliament. It is remarkable for the stannaries, where they get tin, and to these belong particular laws, immunities, and privileges. And there are particular places which have the coinage of tin, to which all the tin must be carried, to be stamped. The other commodities are, blue slate, corn, fruits, cattle, and a little silver. Sometimes a sort of diamonds have been found here, but not so hard as the true. This county was one of the places to which the ancient Britons retreated, whose language they retained for a considerable time, but is now almost extinct, unless at two or three parishes, at the land's end. The soil is generally hilly and rocky, covered with shallow earth, though there are many fruitful valleys, particularly near the sea, which they manure with sea-weeds, and sat sand. The air is pretty healthy, though they are much subject to high winds, and storms. It has the title of a dutchy, and the king's eldest son is duke of Cornwall.

CORNY, Adj. horny, hard like a horn. Producing corn.

COROLLARY, S. [corollarium, Lat.] an useful consequence drawn from something which is demonstrated. Something abounding, or a surplus, from the French. "Bring a corollary.—rather than want." Shak.

CORONAL, S. [from corona, Lat.] a crown, a garland. The top of the head. The coronal suture, in Anatomy is the first of the cranium, which reaches from one temple to the other, in young children it is open in the middle, and if closed too much, as is too generally the case, is subjects a person to the head-ach as long as he lives.

CORONARY, Adj. [coronarius, Lat.] relating to, or situated on the crown of the head.

CORONATION, S. the solemnity of crowning a king. Figuratively, the pomp or assembly present at the solemnity of the crowning of a king.

CORONER, S. [from crona, Lat.] a conservator of the peace in the county, where elected; in case of a violent death he is to make inquest together with 12 jurymen impanneled by him, to enter appeals for murder, pronounce judgements for outlawries, execute the king's writ, and what is remarkable, his office does not determine on the king's demise, as that of judges and all others which act by virtue of his commission.

CORONET, S. [coronetta, Ital.] a small inferior crown worn by the nobility; that of duke is adorned with strawberry leaves; that of a marquis with leaves and pearls placed interchangeably; that of an earl with the pearls raised above the leaves; that of a viscount is surrounded with pearls only; and that of a baron has only four pearls.

CORPORAL, S. [corrupted from caporal, Fr.] the lowest officer in the foot, who commands one of the divisions, places and relieves centinels, and keeps good order.

CORPORAL, Adj. [corporal, Fr.] relating to the body.

CORPORALITY, S. the quality of body, or matter.

CORPORALLY, Adv. in a sensible, a material, or bodily manner; bodily.

CORPORATE, Adj. [corporis, genitive of corpus] united into a body or community.

CORPORATENESS, S. the state of a body corporate.

CORPORATION, S. a body politic, authorized by the king's charter, to have a common seal, and to sue or be sued in their common capacity, as if an individual.

CORPORATURE, S. [corporis, Lat.] the state of a material being.

CORPOREAL, Adj. [corporeus, Lat.] consisting of matter or body, not spiritual.

CORPORIFICATION, S. [from corpus, Lat. and fio] the act of rendering a thing the object of the touch or other sense.

To CORPORIFY, V. A. to thicken or reduce into a body.

CORPS, CORPSE, S. [corps, Fr. from corpus, Lat. when applied to the human body every letter is pronounced; but when applied

to a body of forces, only as the body. A dead body, a carcase. A body or collection of soldiers.

CORPULENCE, CORPULENCY, S. [corpulentia, Lat.] the condition of a person over-loaded with flesh and fat.

CORPULENT, S. [corpulentus, Lat.] fleshy; fat.

CORPUSCULE, S. [corpusculum, Lat.] a small body; a particle of matter; an atom; a small fragment.

CORPUSCULAR, CORPUSCULARIAN, Adj. belonging to atoms, or the small particles of things.

To CORRADE, V. A. [corrado] to rub off; or wear away by rubbing.

CORRADIATION, S. [from cor and radius, Lat.] the conjunction of rays terminating in one point.

To CORRECT, V. A. [correctum, Lat.] to reprimand or punish a person for a fault. In Printing, to point out the faults of the compositor, that they may be amended before a sheet is worked off. To mend any error in writing. In Medicine, to counteract, the ill qualities of one ingredient by another. To give a person notice of his faults.

CORRECT, Adj. [correctus, Lat.] perfect; freed from errors or mistakes.

CORRECTION, S. punishment for crimes or faults. The amendment of an error in writing or printing. Something put into the place of that which was erroneous; an amendment. Reprehension, censure.

CORRECTIVE, Adj. having the power of altering or amending.

CORRECTIVE, S. that which has the power of altering or amending.

CORRECTLY, Adv. free from faults, on account of having undergone frequent amendments. Exactly.

CORRECTNESS, S. perfection arising from frequent alterations and amendments.

CORRECTOR, S. he who punishes for faults. In Printing, the person who alters the errors of the compositor in the proofs.

To CORRELATE, V. N. [from cor and relatus, Lat.] to have a reciprocal relation to each other, as father and son.

CORRELATE, S. a person that stands in an opposite relation, as father and son.

CORRELATIVE, Adj. [from cor, and relativus, Lat.] having a reciprocal relation, as father and son, husband and wife.

To CORRESPOND, V. N. [from cor and respondeo, Lat.] to answer; match; suit; to be proportionate or adequate. To keep up an acquaintance with another by letters, followed by with.

CORRESPONDENCE, CORRESPONDENCY, S. agreement; the matching of two things. An intercourse by letter. Friendship.

CORRESPONDENT, Adj. suiting; agreeing; answering.

CORRESPONDENT, S. one with whom

commerce is carried on, or intelligence kept by messages or letters.

CORRESPONSIVE, Adj. suitable to; answerable to.

CORRIGIBLE, Adj. [from corrigo, Lat.] that which may be mended. That which is the proper object of punishment. Corrective, or having the power of amending any fault.

CORRIVAL, S. a person who opposes another in his views of interest, power, wealth, or love.

CORROBORANT, Part. [corroborans, Lat.] having the power of giving strength.

To CORROBORATE, V. A. [from corroboratum] to confirm or establish. To strengthen.

CORROBORATION, S. the act of strengthening. Confirmation. The act of confirming.

CORROBORATIVE, Adj. having the power of increasing strength, or additional proof.

To CORRODE, V. A. to eat away by degrees. To prey upon. To consume.

CORRODENT, Part. [corrodens, Lat.] having the power of separating or reducing the particles of a body, applied to the effect of some menstruum, on fold bodies.

CORRODIBLE, Adj. That which may be consumed by some corroding liquor.

CORROSIBILITY, S. the possibility of being corroded.

CORROSIBLE, Adj. [from corrosus, Lat.] that which may be eaten, consumed, or separated by some liquor.

CORROSIBLENESS, S. the quality of being liable to be corroded.

CORROSION, S. the dissolution of the particles of a thing by an acid or saline liquor.

CORROSIVE, Adj. having the power of fretting or vexing.

CORROSIVE, S. that which has the power of eating or wasting away. That which has the power of fretting.

CORROSIVELY, S. Adv. in the manner of a corrosive. Having the quality of a corrosive.

CORRUGANT, Part. [corrugans, Lat.] having the power of contracting into wrinkles.

To CORRUGATE, V. A. [corrugatum, Lat.] to wrinkle, to furrow.

CORRUGATION, S. the act of contracting into wrinkles.

To CORRUPT, V. A. [corruptum, Lat.] to putrefy. Figuratively, to engage or prevail on a person to do something contrary to his conscience. To spoil, to vitiate, to grow rotten.

CORRUPT, Adj. [corruptus, Lat.] vicious, lost to piety, or morality; bribed by bribes; tainted; rotten.

CORRUPTER, S. that which putrifies.

One who seduces a person to vice. A seducer.

CORRUPTIBI'LITY, S. the possibility of being corrupted or putrified.

CORRU'PTIBLE, Adj. [corruptibilis, Lat.] that which may be putrified, destroyed, or rendered vitious.

CORRU'PTION, S. [corruptio, Lat.] rottenness, putrefaction. In Morality, a change from virtue to vice. In Politics, a state wherein persons are lost to the good of their country, and are bought by bribes. The means by which any person may be rendered vitious, or a thing may be made rotten. In Surgery, the matter contained in an ulcer.

CORRU'PTIVE, Adj. having the power of tainting, or making vitious.

CORRU'PTLESS, Adj. that which cannot be corrupted, or tainted.

CORRU'PTNESS, S. the quality of a corrupted body. Vice.

CO'RSAIR, S. [Fr. corsaro, Ital.] an armed vessel, which stops and plunders merchants vessels, especially those which are in the Mediterranean sea. A pirate.

CO'RSE, S. [corpse, Fr.] a poetical word for a dead body.

CO'RSELET, S. [Fr. corseletto, Ital.] a small armour for the fore part of the body.

CO'RTICAL, Adj. [from cortices, of cortex, Lat.] barky; belonging to the external part of any thing.

CO'RTICATED, Adj. [corticatus, Lat.] resembling the bark of a tree.

CO'RTICOSE, Adj. [corticosus, Lat.] abounding with bark.

CORU'SCANT, Part. [coruscans, part. of coruscc, Lat.] shining by flashes; flashing.

CORUSCA'TION, S. [coruscatio, Lat.] a quick, sudden flash. A glittering light.

CORYMBI'FEROUS, Adj. [from corymbus and fero, Lat. to bear] in Botany, applied to such plants as have a compound discous flower, without any down adhering to their seeds; they derive their name from their bearing their flowers in clusters, and spreading round in the form of an umbrella, as onions; of this kind is the corn marigold, &c. Mr. Ray distinguishes them into such as have a radiated flower, as the sun flower, &c. and such as have a naked flower, as the lavender, cotton and tansey.

COSME'TIC, Adj. [κοσμητικος, Gr.] having the power of improving the personal charms; beautifying. Used substantively for a beautifying wash.

CO'SMICAL, Adj. [κοσμικος, Gr.] relating to the world. In Astronomy, rising in the same degree of the ecliptic with the sun.

CO'SMICALLY, Adv. rising at the same time with the sun.

COSMO'GONY, S. [from κοσμος, Gr.

and γονη] the rise, origin, beginning, or creation of the world.

COSMO'GRAPHER, S. [from κοσμος, the world, and γραφευς, Gr. a describer] one who composes a description of all the parts of the world.

COSMO'GRAPHY, S. a description of the several parts of the world. It consists of geography and astronomy.

COSMOPO'LITAN, S. [from κοσμος, Gr. and πολιτης;] a citizen of the world. One who thinks himself at home in all companies, and in all countries.

CUSSACKS, a people inhabiting the confines of Poland, Russia, Tartary, and Turky. They are divided into several branches, the Kosakki-sa Parovi, the Kosakki-Donski, and the Kosakki-Jaiki. These last are the wildest of them all, though they dwell in large villages, along the banks of the river Yaik, near its fall into the Caspian sea. They live on husbandry, fishing, and their cattle, but rob their neighbours as often as they have opportunity. In the winter they keep at home, but in summer they rove in boats on the Caspian sea, with an intent to attack the vessels sailing thereon. Their religion is a mixture of Paganism, Mahometanism, and Christianity. Their only town is Yaikskoy. The banks of the rivers are exceeding fertile, and produce all the necessaries of life. Kosakki-sa-Parovi are the principal of the three branches, and dwell near the river Boristhenes or Nieper. These people are large and well made, have blue eyes, brown hair, and aquiline noses; the women are handsome, well shaped, and very complaisant to strangers. These are the people, who, joining with the Russian army, do so much mischief in the king of Prussia's dominions. The country which they now inhabit, is called Ukrain, and is one continued and exceeding fertile plain, which produces corn, pulse, tobacco, and honey. The pastures are so good, that their cattle are the largest in Europe. Their towns are all built of wood, after the manner of the Russians. Kosakki-Donski dwell on both sides of the river Don, and are much the same for size and shape as the former; these are under the protection of Russia, and profess the same religion. They live upon their cattle, husbandry, and robbing.

CO'ST, S. [kost, Belg.] the price, charge, expence. Figuratively, sumptuousness, luxury. Loss, detriment. In Law, that which is due to the attorney of the contrary party.

To CO'ST, V. N. [Preter and Participle Preter cost of costos, Ital.] to be purchased at a particular sum.

CO'STAL, Adj. [from costa, Lat.] belonging or relating to the ribs.

CO'STIVE, Adj. [constipatus, Lat. constipé, Fr.]

&c.] bound in the body ; going feldom to stool.

CO'STIVENESS, S. In Medicine, a preternatural detention of the excrements.

CO'STLINESS, S. fumptuoufnefs, expenfivenefs. The great fum paid for a thing.

CO'STLY, Adj. requiring a large fum for its purchafe. Expenfive ; rare ; valuable.

COT, S. [cote, Sax.] a fmall, low and mean houfe. A hut. Likewife an abridgment of congreon, one who loves effeminate compliments.

COTE'MPORARY, Adj. [from cum and tempus, Lat.] living at the fame time with another. See CONTEMPORARY.

COT QUEEN, S. [from cote, Sax. and queen, Sax.] Johnfon, without attending to its analogy or fignification, fuppofes it to be derived from requin, Fr. (a rogue, knave, or beggarly fellow) a perfon who officioufly concerns himfelf with woman's affairs Cot, its abbreviation, is only in ufe. See COT.

COTTAGE, S. [fee COT] a little mean building, houfe or hut.

COTTAGER, S. one who lives in a hut, or cottage.

COTTON, S. [cotton, Bris. cottone, Ital.] the down of the fruit of the cotton-tree. Cotton likewife fignifies a coarfe kind of cloth made of its threads, when fpun. The Manchefter velvet, which is made of this fubftance, both on account of its beauty and wear, recommends the growing of cotton very ftrongly.

COTTON, [Sir ROBERT] defcended from an antient family of that name, which flourifhed long before the reign of Edward III. they took their name from Cottin, in the county palatine of Chefter. This great man was born the 2ad of Jan. 1570, at Denton, near Conington, in Huntingdonfhire, he ftudied at Trinity college, Cambridge, and took his batchelor of arts degree in 1575. The noble collection of manufcripts for which this nation is abundantly indebted to him, was begun to be collected by him in the 18th year of his age. The affiduity with which he profecuted the ftudy of antiquities, the great dependance that all the great perfonages both in queen Elizabeth's, king James's, and king Charles's reign, had on his knowledge in this branch of literature, was great, and the many curious fubjects that were by them fubmitted to his decifion, muft give us a favourable and high idea of his abilities ; his generous defence of liberty in religion, as well as the ftate, muft attract him the admiration of all true Englifhmen ; and the noble collection of manufcripts relating to the hiftory and antiquities of this kingdom, which were afterwards increafed by his fon and grandfon, is a nobler maufoleum to his memory, than the pyramids of Egypt, are to its monarchs. To enumerate

the titles of his own writings, would require too much room in this place ; though it muft be acknowledged, that there is no hiftory of our nation extant, which does not owe all its value either to his writings, or his collections. When living, he was always ready to communicate, was careffed by all the learned and great, both at home and abroad ; was a member of the Society of Antiquaries, both at its firft inftitution, and revival, was looked on as an oracle in points of antiquity, and when he died, in 1631, left all the lovers of learning, in grief for a lofs which no perfon then living, could compenfate.

To COTTON, V. N. to rife with a nap. To cement ; to unite or join intereft with another. " It will not be eafy to cotton with another." Swift.

To COUCH, V. N. [coucher, Fr.] to lie down. To lie down, applied to beafts. To lie in wait or ambufh. To ftoop or fink down. Actively, to lay on a bed, to lay a thing in a bed or ftratum, or to fpread. " We couch malt about a foot thick." To bed, to hide in another body. To include ; to comprife, to urge by way of implication. " The great argument for a future ftate, is couched in the words I have read." Atterbury. In Surgery, to take off a film, which obftructs the fight.

COUCH, S. a long feat, on which people fit or lie down. Figuratively, a bed. A layer, or one thing fpread over another. " A couch, or bed of raw malt." Mortimer.

COUCHANT, Part. [Fr.] lying down ; fquatting. In Heraldry, applied to the pofture of a beaft lying with his belly on the ground.

COUCHER, S. one who couches ; an oculift.

COVE, S. [cuvernir, Fr.] a fmall creek or bay ; a fhelter, or cover.

COVENANT, S. [covenant, Fr.] an agreement between perfons for their performing certain conditions ; a writing, containing the ftipulated terms of a contract.

To COVENANT, V. N. to bargain, to agree, or ftipulate ; to agree with a perfon on certain conditions, ufed with for before the thing bargained for, and with before the perfon with whom the agreement is made.

COVENANTEE, S. in Law, one who is a party in a covenant.

COVENTRY, a town or city in Warwickfhire, which, with Litchfield, is a bifhop's fee. Its market is on Friday, and the fairs are, on May 2, for horfes, cows, and fheep, on Friday, in Trinity week, for flannels, linen, and woollen, and on the firft day they reprefent the lady Godiva on horfeback, and on November 2, for linen, woolen, and horfes. It is a city and county containing 19 villages and hamlets, and governed by a may-

dr, 2 bailiffs, sheriffs, 10 aldermen, and other officers. It holds pleas for all actions, has a goal for felons, as well as debtors, and sends two members to parliament. It comprehends 10 wards, 3 parish-churches, 2 of which have very lofty spires, and was surrounded with strong walls, which were demolished by the order of king Charles II in 1662. It has a grammar-school, with three masters, and exhibitions for both universities, and another free school for poor boys, besides several hospitals; as, one for ten old men, another for 20 blue-coat boys, a third for 8 married couples, and a fourth in West-orchard-street. In the market-place stood the stateliest cross in England, it being 66 feet high, and adorned with the statues of several kings, but it has been lately taken down. This town is of great extent, but the houses, being mostly very old, and chiefly built with wood and plaister, with stories projecting over each other, make but an indifferent appearance. It has a considerable manufacture in stuffs, particularly tammies, as also ribbands, and has the title of an earldom. It is 30 miles W. N. W. of Northampton, 58 N. E. of Gloucester, 11 N. E. of Warwick, 30 N. of Oxford, 37 S. of Derby, 26 N. W. of Lichfield, and 92 N. W. of London. Lon. 16. 9. lat. 52. 16.

COVENANTER, S. one who covenants with another. Applied, in the great rebellion, to those who took the solemn league or covenant.

COVENOUS, Adj. [from covin] in Law, fraudulent.

To COVER, V. A. [the e pronounced like a short u; from couvrir, Fr.] to spread with something; to conceal; to hide by specious pretexts; to obliterate; to conceal from human sight. "Charity shall cover a multitude of sins." 1 Peter iv. 8. To copulate, applied to horses; to wear a hat. "Covered in the presence of the king." Dryd.

COVER, S. that which is spread over something. Figuratively, concealment; or that which hides from view; a specious pretence. "The pretence of it is a handsome cover for imperfections." Collier.

COVER, S. shelter, a shelter from danger.

COVERING, S. dress, any thing spread over another person.

COVERLET, S. [couvrir and lit, Fr.] the uppermost bed-clothes.

COVERT, S. [couvert, Fr.] a shelter, a place of defence; a thicket.

COVERT, Adj. [couvert, Fr.] sheltered, secret, hidden, private, concealed by some specious appearance.

COVERTLY, Adj. close, private, or indirect manner.

COVERTNESS, S. the quality of being hidden, unperceived, or insidious.

COVERTURE, S. shelter, defence against

any danger; a specious pretext to conceal a bad design. In Law, the state of a married woman.

To COVET, V. A. [convoiter, Fr.] to desire earnestly; endeavour to acquire with great eagerness. "Covet earnestly the best gifts." 1 Cor. xii. 32. Neuterly, to have a strong and violent desire, followed by after. "Which while some, coveted after." 1 Tim. vi.

COVETABLE, Adj. that which is worthy to be desired.

COVETOUS, Adj. [convoiteux, Fr.] inordinately desirous of; eager after the acquiring money; avaricious. Desirous, fond, or eager to possess.

COVETOUSLY, Adv. in an avaricious manner.

COVETOUSNESS, S. the quality of being inordinately eager after gain.

COVEY, S. [the e pronounced like that in note, couvée, Fr.] a hatch; or an old bird with her young. A number or birds near one another.

COUGH, S. [pronounced coff, from kuch, Belg.] In Medicine, a convulsive motion of the diaphragm, &c. with a noise like that of an explosion, intended by nature to unburden the trachea of the serous humour with which its glands are overcharged.

To COUGH, V. N. [kuchen, Belg. hef, ill.] To make a noise in endeavouring to discharge the trachea or lymph of the lungs, with which it is over-charged, on account of the stoppage of perspiration. Actively, to eject or clear by coughing.

COUGHER, S. a person affected with a cough; one who coughs.

COVIN, COVINE, S. [couvoir, Fr.] an agreement between persons to cheat another.

COVING, S. [from cove or couvoir, Fr. to cover] in building, applied to those houses that project over the ground-plot.

COULD, [pronounced could,] the preterimperfect of can] was able, or capable to.

COULTER, S. [culter, Lat.] the sharp iron, which cuts the earth in a plough-share.

COUNCIL, S. [concilium, Lat. conseil, Fr.] an assembly met together to deliberate on any subject.

COUNSEL, S. [consilium, Lat. conseille, Fr.] advice given to a person. Consultation, or deliberation on measures proper for effecting any purpose. Examination or weighing the consequences of things. To keep counsel, secrecy, or concealing the measures agreed on at a council. Figuratively, a scheme, or plan formed with care and deliberation. In Law, a person who pleads at the bar, being an abbreviation of counsellor.

To COUNSEL, V. A. [conseiller, Fr.] to give advice, or inform a person of the most advantageous steps. To advise or direct.

COUNSELLOR,

COUNSELLOR, S. one who gives advice to another. A confidant. One whose business it is to advise in matters of state. In Law, a person who pleads at the bar.

To COUNT, V. A. [compter, Fr.] to number, tell, or reckon. To esteem in any particular light. Neuterly, to draw as a consequence from.

COUNT, S. [compte, Fr. comes, Lat.] a nobleman in rank between a duke and a baron.

COUNTABLE, Adj. that which may be counted or numbered.

COUNTENANCE, S. [contenance, Fr.] the form of the face. Figuratively, air, or look. Used with keep, a composure of the features and complexion wherein they undergo no change in countenance. Confidence or unchangeableness; out of countenance; bashfulness, blushing, or an appearance of conscious guilt and shame. Figuratively, protection, support. "Give countenance to piety and virtue." Atterb. Outward show, and appearance. "Unfold the evil here wrapt up in countenance." Shak.

To COUNTENANCE, V. A. to favour or protect. Figuratively, to act suitable to. To encourage; to appear in defence of.

COUNTENANCER, S. one who approves or encourages a person or design.

COUNTER, S. [contoir, Fr.] a false piece of money. The table or board on which goods are shown in a shop, or warehouse.

COUNTER, Adv. [contre, Fr. contra, Lat.] in opposition, contrary, used with to. In hunting, the wrong way, contrary, or a polite way.

To COUNTERACT, V. A. acting contrary to a thing.

To COUNTERBALLANCE, V. A. to ballance one thing against another. Figuratively, to have an opposite effect.

To COUNTERBUFF, V. N. to beat back a thing in motion. To strike or beat back.

COUNTERBUFF, S. a blow or stroke which makes a thing recoil.

COUNTERCHANGE, S. a mutual changing of things.

To COUNTERCHANGE, V. N. to give one thing for another.

COUNTERCHARM, S. a spell to destroy the effects of another.

To COUNTERCHARM, V. A. to counteract the effect of a charm.

To COUNTERCHECK, V. A. to stop by a sudden obstruction.

COUNTEREVIDENCE, S. a testimony opposite to a former one.

To COUNTERFEIT, V. A. [contrefait, from contrefaire, Fr.] to imitate with an intention to make the thing pass for an original. To resemble. Figuratively, to pretend to something really excellent.

COUNTERFEIT, S. copied from another, with an intention to be passed for an original. Forged; fictitious. Figuratively, an hypocrite.

COUNTERFEIT, S. an imposter. Something in imitation of another. A forger.

COUNTERFEITER, S. a forger; one who imitates a thing to pass it as an original.

COUNTERFEITLY, Adv. fictitiously; with dissimulation or hypocrisy.

COUNTERFESANCE, S. [contrefaisance, Fr.] the act of imitating with a bad intent. Forgery.

To COUNTERMAND, V. A. [contremander, Fr. contra, and mando, Lat.] to command something contrary to what has been ordered, to repeal an order. Figuratively, to oppose.

To COUNTERMARCH, V. A. to march in an opposite direction. To march back.

COUNTERMARCH, S. in War, a change of the wings and front of a battalion, whereby the men in the front come to be in the rear.

COUNTERMARK, S. a second or third mark put on a bale of goods belonging to two or more persons, that it may not be opened but in the presence of them all. The mark of the goldsmiths company on a piece of silver, added to that of the maker, to shew that it is standard. An artificial cavity or hollow made in the teeth of horses, that have outgrown their natural mark, to conceal their age, and make them appear younger than they are.

COUNTERMINE, S. in War, a subterraneous passage in search of the enemie's mine, to take out the powder, or any other ways frustrate its effects.

To COUNTERMINE, V. A. [from the noun] to dig a passage into an enemy's mine to take out the powder. Figuratively, to frustrate any design, or defeat by secret measures.

COUNTERPANE, S. [contrepoint, Fr.] a cloth or ornamental covering over a bed.

COUNTERPART, S. a part opposite to, or that answers another; a copy.

COUNTERPLEA, S. a reply to a plea, in order to oppose the plea of another.

To COUNTERPLOT, V. A. to play one plot against another, to hinder its effects.

COUNTERPLOT, S. a stratagem, plot, or artifice opposed to another.

To COUNTERPOISE, V. A. [from contre and poids, Fr. weight] to place one weight against another. To act against with equal weight. To act with equal power against any thing.

COUNTERPOISE, S. an equivalent, or thing of equal weight or worth with another. The state of being placed to destroy the effects, or counterbalance another weight or cause.

COUN.

COUNTERPOI'SON, S. a medicine by which the effects of poison are counteracted.

COU'NTERPRESSURE, S. an opposite force or preffure.

COUNTERSCARP, S. [*contreescarpe*, Fr.] in Fortification, that part of the ditch which is next the camp ; sometimes it is taken for the whole covert way, or glacis.

To COUN'TERSIGN, V. A. to sign an instrument signed before by a person of higher rank ; thus when a charter or patent is signed by the king, and afterwards by the secretary, the secretary is said to *countersign* it.

COUNTERTE'NOR, S. one of the middle parts of music, so called from its being opposite to the *tenor*.

To COUNTERVA'IL, S. [*contra* and *valeo*, Lat.] to be of equal force with another. Figuratively, to be equal to, to counterbalance.

COUNTERVA'IL, S. power, weight, or value sufficient to oppose any contrary effect, or objection. Figuratively, a compensation.

COUNTERVI'EW, S. opposition, in which two persons front each other. Figuratively, opposition, or a design which is contrary to that of another.

To COUNTERWO'RK, V. A. to endeavour to hinder another effect. To counteract.

COUNTESS, S. [*comtesse*, Fr.] the wife or lady of a count or earl.

COU'NTING-HOUSE, S. a place, apartment, or room where merchants and traders keep their accounts.

COU'NTLESS, Adj. innumerable, what cannot be numbered or counted.

COU'NTRY, S. [the *o* is dropped in the pronunciation, from *contrée*, Fr.] a tract of land under one governor. Those parts at a distance from cities or courts. The place of any person's birth.

COU'NTRY, Adj. rude, uncultivated, rustic. At a distance from the court. *Country-dance*, seems to be derived from the French, *contré*, which signifies that the partners stand opposite to each other ; but not from its being a manner of dancing peculiar to the country people.

COU'NTRYMAN, S. one born in the same place with another. Figuratively, one bred at a distance from cities or courts. A farmer, or husbandman.

COU'NTY, S. [*comté*, Fr.] a shire of the realm into which the kingdom is divided. An earldom. A count or earl. "The gallant, young and noble gentleman, the *county* Paris." *Shak*. Obsolete.

COUPE'E, S. [Fr.] a motion in dancing.

COU'PLE, S. [pronounced *cupple* of *couple*, Fr.] a chain which holds dogs together. Two. A pair. Figuratively, a man and woman joined in marriage.

No. VIII.

To COU'PLE, V. A. [*copulo*, Lat.] to chain dogs together. Figuratively, to join two things of the same kind together. To join a man and woman in marriage. It has *with* before the thing joined to another. Neuterly, to join in embraces.

COU'PLET, S. two verses which rhime together. Figuratively, a pair.

COU'RAGE, S. [Fr. pronounced *currege*] a manly bravery which enables a person to undergo any difficulties, and confront any dangers, arising from the sense of his duty.

COURA'GEOUS, Adj. [*courageux*, Fr.] resolutely bold, and ready to undertake any enterprise, though surrounded with difficulties.

COURA'GEOUSLY, Adv. resolutely opposing difficulties and dangers.

COUR'ANT, COURA'NTO, S. [*currante*, Fr.] a dance consisting of a nimble and quick motion. Any thing which is spread or published quickly.

COU'RIER, S. [from *currier*, Fr.] a messenger sent with dispatches from the state. An express.

COU'RSE, S. [the *o* is dropped and the *e* pronounced like that in *pure*] a race. Also the place where races are performed. A methodical procedure ; a series wherein the several parts comprise the whole of any science or system. " A *course* of philosophy, &c." Method of life, or train of action. Natural inclination ; take your own *course*. A series or consequence. In Cookery, a number of dishes placed at one time on a table. In Sea affairs, the tract in which a ship sails ; in the plural the sails by which the ship is enabled to keep on her course. *Words of course*, are those that are merely complimental.

To COU'RSE, V. A. to hunt, To pursue with dogs. To exercise in running or riding.

COU'RSER, S. a swift running horse.

COURT, S. [the *u* is dropped, and the *e* pronounced like *e* in *pure*, *cure*, Fr.] the place or palace where a prince resides. A hall wherein justice is administered. An open space or area before a house. A small place having an avenue which leads to it, and no passage at the other end. Figuratively, the retinue which attend on a prince. Any jurisdiction, military, civil, or ecclesiastical. To make *court* ; the art of pleasing or insinuating one's self into the favour of another.

To COURT, V. A. to woo, to strive to engage the affections of a woman. Figuratively, to solicit. To flatter. To endeavour to insinuate one's self into the favour of another.

COUR'TEOUS, Adj. [*courtois*, Fr.] affable, polite, full of respect, civil.

COUR'TEOUSLY, Adv. respectfully, civilly, complaisantly.

Q q   COUR'TE-

COURTEOUSNESS, S. civil, affable, and refpectful behaviour.

COURTESAN, COUR'TEZAN, S. [courtefanne, Fr.] an immodeft pueltude woman; a proftitute.

COUR'TESY, S. [courtoifie, Fr.] an affable and polite addrefs. An act of civility, or refpect. Figuratively, with women the bending the knees, and finking the body in ceremony. In Law, a tenure, purely by the favour of others. Courtefy of England, is a right which a perfon has to an inheritance, who marries an hetrefs, that has a child by him, even after both fhe and the child are dead.

To COUR'TESY, V. N. [pronounced curtfey] to fink the body by bending the knees; the method ufed by the fair fex, to fhew their civility.

COUR'TIER, S. one who frequents the court, or efpoufes the meafures of the court; one who endeavours to engage the affections of another.

COUR'TLIKE, Adj. elegant, polite, diffembling.

COUR'TLINESS, S. elegance of manners, civility, politenefs, diffimulation.

COUR'TLY, Adj. relating to the court. "Execute fome courtly ftrains." Pope. Elegantly, politely.

COUR'TSHIP, S. the act of endeavouring to gain the affections of a woman.

COU'SIN, S. [pronounced cuzin, coufin, Fr.] thofe who are born of two fifters, or two brothers; a title given by the king to a nobleman, efpecially thofe of the privy council.

COW, S. [cowe, or cu, Sax. koe, Belg.] the female of the black cattle, whofe milk is ufed for food, and for making butter or cheefe.

To COW, V. A. [contraction from coward] to deprefs, to keep in great fubjection, fo as to render a perfon timorous.

COWARD, S. [couard, Fr.] one who is timorous or afraid of oppofing danger; adjectively, timorous to a reproachful excefs.

COWARDICE, S. exceffive timoroufnefs, or fear.

COWARDLINESS, S. the quality of acting like a coward.

COWARDLY, in the manner of a coward.

COWARDSHIP, S. the qualities or character of a coward. "For his cowardfhip, aft Falftan." Shak.

COWISH, Adj. timorous, fearful, cowardly.

COWL, S. [cugle, Sax.] a veil worn by monks; a veffel or two in which water is carried on a pole between two.

COWSLIP, S. [cufloppe, Sax. fo called, according to fome, becaufe it refembles the breath of cows; but according to others, because its growing in pafture grounds makes it often meet a cow's lip) in Botany, a fmall yellowifh flower, a fpecies of the primrofe.

COXCOMP, S. [corrupted from cock's comb] the red dentellated, or fawed fubftance on the top of a cock's head; the top of the head. "She rapt them o' th' coxcomb with a ftick." Shak. An ignorant pretender to knowledge and politenefs.

COXCOMICAL, Adj. foppifh, conceited, vain. By Johnfon cenfured as a low word, and unworthy of ufe.

COY, Adj. [coi, Fr. from quietus, Lat.] modeft, referved; unwillingly fubmitting to the advances of a lover.

To COY, V. N. to behave with referve; to condefcend with reluctance.

COYLY, Adv. with referve; with modefty or unwillingnefs.

COYNESS, S. referve; unwillingnefs to admit the advances of a lover.

To COZIN, V. A. [pronounced cuzen, cofe, Scot.] cheat, trick, defraud, or impofe on.

COZENAGE, S. the act of impofing by falfe appearances; a fraud, impofture, or cheat.

COZENER, S. a perfon who cheats or defrauds another.

CRAB, S. [crabba, Sax. krabbe, Belg.] a roundifh, flat, fea fhell fifh; which every year lofe their fhell, and repair that lofs by means of a juice; alfo a wild, four, fmall apple, or the tree that bears it. Figuratively, a four, morofe perfon. In Aftronomy, one of the figns of the zodiac. See CANCER.

CRABBED, Adj. four, morofe, void of affability. Figuratively, difagreeable; applied to writings, not eafy to be underftood; difficult, or perplexing. "Whate'er the crabbedeft authour hath." Hudib. It is now compared by prefixing more for the comparative, and moft for the fuperlative.

CRABBEDLY, Adv. in a peevifh, morofe, and unfociable manner.

CRABBEDNESS, S. fournefs; crabbrnefs; morofenefs; and applied to writings, difficulty to be underftood.

CRAB'S-EYES, S. In Pharmacy and Natural Hiftory, whitifh bodies, from the fize of a pea to that of a horfe-bean, rounded on one fide and depreffed on the other, whereby they refemble the figure of an eye, and thence derive their name. They are found in two feparate bags on each fide of the ftomach of the craw-fifh, and are alkaline, abforbent, and in fome degree diuretic.

CRACK, S. [crac, Fr.] a fudden boafting, or feparation. Figuratively, the chafm made by a feparation of the parts of a body; the found made by a fudden and quick blow; a flaw; an immodeft woman; a boaft, or fomething

something beyond the truth; a boaster, or one that brags.

To CRA'CK, V. A. [kracken, Belg.] to break into chinks; to split; to make a flaw; to turn mad. Neuterly, to split, to open in chinks; to make a loud noise by a sudden blow; to boast, used with of.

CRACK-BRAINED, Adj. one who is disordered in his mind.

To CRA'CKLE, V. N. to make a low and continued noise.

CRA'DLE, S. [cradle, cradel, Sax.] a small moveable bedstead for children, and fitted with pieces of wood underneath, making the segment of a circle, by means of which it is rocked to and fro; figuratively, infancy. In surgery, a case in which a limb is laid, that has been lately set.

To CRA'DLE, V. A. to lay or rock in a cradle.

CRA'FT, S. [craft, Sax.] a trade or mechanic employ. Figuratively, the carrying on and perfecting any design without the knowledge of those whom it concerns. A kind of low cunning.

CRA'FTILY, Adv. in a cunning crafty manner.

CRA'FTINESS, S. cunning; or the practice of such artifices as may secure a person's designs, and hinder them from obstruction, even from those who are like to be injured by them.

CRA'FTSMAN, S. an artificer, manufacturer, tradesman, or mechanic.

CRA'FTY, Adj. cunning; full of art, whereby a person over reaches another.

CRA'G, S. [kraeghe, Belg.] a neck, or the small end of the neck. "A crag of mutton."

CRAG, S. [craig, Brit.] a rough steep rock. The rough rugged parts of a rock.

CRA'GGED, Adj. rugged, uneven.

CRA'GGEDNESS, S. the quality of abounding in ruggedness.

CRA'GGINESS, S. the state of being craggy.

CRA'GGY, Adj. uneven, broken, rugged, rough.

To CRA'M, V. A. to force more into a thing than it can conveniently contain; to fill with too much food; to thrust down by force, applied to feeding turkies, &c. to thrust in by force.

CRA'MP, S. [krampe, Dan. crampon, Fr.] in Medicine, a convulsive contraction of the muscules put of the body, attended with great pain. Figuratively, any restraint; a piece of iron bent at both ends, by which two bodies are held together.

To CRA'MP, V. A. to contract the musculous parts; to restrain, confine, or obstruct; to fasten together with cramping irons.

CRA'MP-FISH, S. in Natural History, the torpedo, a fish which benumbs the hands of those that touch it, and those that take it

with a line and fishing rod. This phænomenon, may be, perhaps, accounted for from the principles of electricity.

CRA'NE, S. [crane, Sax. gꞃan, Brit.] in Natural History, a bird with long feet, a long neck, and long beak, living chiefly on fish; an engine, with ropes and pulleys, to unload ships and carts; also an instrument to draw liquor out of bottles or casks.

CRA'NIUM, S. [Lat. from κρανιον, Gr.] in Anatomy, an assemblage of bones, which involve and include the cerebellum and brain, commonly called the skull. Its figure is round, by which means it is both liable to bear blows with less injury, and to contain the more in its inside. It advances out behind, is flatted on the two sides, which form the temples, which contributes to the enlarging both the sight and hearing.

CRA'NK, Adj. healthy, sprightly. In Sea Language, it is applied to a ship, which is said to be crank sided, when she cannot bear her sails, without danger of overfetting.

To CRA'NKLE, V. N. to run in and out; to run in meanders. "See how the river comes crankling in." Shak.

CRA'NKLES, S. an unequal surface; furrows occasioned by the windings of a stream.

CRA'NNIED, Adj. full of holes or chinks.

CRA'NNY, S. [cran, cren, Sax.] a chink, cleft, or a small narrow hole.

CRA'PE, S. [crepe, low Lat.] a light transparent manufacture, like gauze, made of raw silk gummed and twisted in the mill, much used in mourning.

CRA'PULOUS, Adj. [crapulosus, Lat.] drunk; sick or disordered in the head by excessive drinking.

To CRASH, V. N. [schranssen, Belg.] to make a loud noise. Actively, to break or bruise by means of force. Figuratively, to drink, applied to liquor. "I grip you come and crash a cup of wine." Shak. Warburton reads crush; Sir Thomas Hanmer observes, that crash is the right word, and signifies to be merry; the substantive crash being still used in some countries for a merry bout; but if crash according to Hanmer signifies by itself to be merry, what must be done with the remainder part of the sentence? This difficulty has induced Johnson to propose crack as the true reading; to crack a bottle, being a common phrase. But as in merry hours it is common to make a crash by every one of the company's clashing the glasses together, there seems no necessity of altering the reading, as it is very expressive of the noise made by such a circumstance.

CRA'SH, S. a loud, sudden, mixed sound, occasioned by several things being dashed together.

CRA'SSITUDE, S. [crassitudo, Lat.] that state of a fluid, which enables it to support solid things; grossness.

CRASTINA'TION, S. [craftino, Lat.] the delaying a thing to another time.

CRA'VAT, S. a piece of cloth worn round the neck; a neckcloth.

To CRA'VE, [crafian, Sax.] to ask a thing earnestly. Figuratively, to ask or with eagerly for, without being satisfied. To require as necessary; to claim. Used with for before the thing required. "Once one may crave for love." Shak.

CRA'VEN, S. a cock void of courage. Figuratively, a coward.

To CRA'VEN, V. A. To render a person a coward, or affect with fear or cowardice.

To CRAU'NCH, V. A. to crush in the mouth or between the teeth.

CRAW, S. [craw, Dan.] the crop or first stomach of birds.

CRA'WFISH, S. [sometimes written crayfish, from ecrevisse, Fr.] in natural History, a small fresh-water fish in the form of a lobster. They shed their shells every year; and in order to supply the want of this natural armour, they moisten their bodies with a liquor which hardens by degrees, and becomes a shell. At the time of their moulting, two stones are found included in bags, one on each side of their stomachs; improperly termed crab's eyes by apothecaries: as these stones decrease in proportion to the perfection of the new shell, and disappear when it is perfectly formed, they are supposed to contain the liquor, which they employ to repair their shells.

To CRA'WL, V. A. [kriclen, Belg.] to move slowly along the ground, like a worm. Figuratively, to move slowly, occasioned by weakness. To move in an abject posture, hated and despised by all; alluding to the serpent at the fall, which was condemned to crawl with his belly on the ground, by way of punishment.

CRA'YFISH, S. See CRAWFISH.

CRA'YON, [Fr.] any colour formed into a kind of pencil with which pictures are drawn. Figuratively, any design formed with crayons.

To CRA'ZE, V. A. [ecraser, Fr.] to break. Figuratively, to crush; to disorder the senses or brain of a person; to make him mad.

CRA'ZEDNESS, S. the state of a thing broken; weakness, madness, insanity.

CRA'ZINESS, S. the state of being mad; weakness, owing to brokenness.

CRA'ZY, Adj. [ecrasé, Fr.] broken. Figuratively, weak, decrepit, feeble, disordered in mind.

To CREAK, V. N. [corrupted from crack] to make a harsh, shrill noise, like that of a rusty thing.

CREAM, S. [creme, Fr.] the thick substance rising on the surface of milk when

it has stood some time. Figuratively, the best or most valuable part of a thing.

To CREAM, V. N. to rise in cream. Figuratively, to resemble cream. "Whose visages do cream and mantle." Shak. Actively, to skim off the cream of milk. Figuratively, to collect the flower or quintessence of a thing.

CREAM-FACED, Adj. pale, pale with fear.

CREA'MY, Adj. abounding with, or partaking of the nature of cream.

CREASE, S. [crea, Lat.] a mark made in a thing by folding it.

To CREASE, V. A. to make a mark by folding or doubling a thing.

To CREA'TE, V. A. [creatum, Lat.] to form out of nothing. Figuratively, to produce. To occasion. To confer an honour. "I create you knights." In Law, to give a thing new qualities.

CREA'TION, S. the act of giving existence to a thing which had no pre-existent matter. Figuratively, the act of conferring titles. "The creation of a knight or peer." The things created, the world.

CREA'TIVE, Adj. having the power to form or produce out of nothing.

CREA'TOR, S. [Lat.] the being that forms or bestows existence, or forms without any pre-existent matter.

CREA'TURE, S. a being which owes its existence to something else. A created being.

CRE'DENCE, S. [Norm. Fr. credens, Lat.] belief, credit, the act of the mind whereby it places confidence in a person's claim or assent. Figuratively, that notion a person to belief or credit. "Letters of credence."

CREDE'NDA, S. [Lat.] things or articles necessary to be believed; those articles which are merely the objects of faith.

CRE'DENT, Adj. [credens, Lat.] credulous; believing; claiming credit; not to be disputed. "My authority bears a credent bulk." Shak.

CREDE'NTIAL, S. [credens, Lat.] that which deserves belief and credit. That which warrants a person's assuming any authority or office.

CREDIBI'LITY, S. the quality or evidence which renders a thing fit to be believed or assented to; probability.

CRE'DIBLE, Adj. credibilis, [Lat.] worthy of credit or belief.

CRE'DIBLY, Adv. in such a manner as to claim or deserve belief.

CRE'DIT, S. [Fr. from credo, Lat. to believe or affirm to] belief of a thing. Figuratively, honour, esteem, testimony, reputation. The faith reposed in the government or private persons by lending money at interest. If we consider how the public credit of this nation has been supported unshaken, during

during the late war, and the shock or entire destruction of it in France, we must naturally conclude that a marine war is rather to the advantage than disadvantage of these kingdoms, the proper exertion of our natural strength, the surest means of humbling our enemies, and the best step that can be taken either for our security, or aggrandizing the state. In Commerce, it signifies something sold upon trust, and the *crosts* of a person's account, that on which his payments are registered.

To CREDIT, V. A. [*credo*, Lat.] to believe what a person says. Figuratively, to reflect honour on a person. To confide in. To let a person have goods on trust. In Commerce, to enter an article on the *credit* side of an account.

CRE'DITABLE, Adj. deserving confidence, or esteem. In Commerce, that which may procure trust. Honourable, estimable, reputable.

CRE'DITABLY, Adv. in such a manner as to preserve one's reputation.

CRE'DITOR, S. [Lat.] one who lets another have goods or any thing on trust. One to whom a debt is due.

CREDU'LITY, S. (*credulité*, Fr.) belief without evidence. Too great easiness in believing.

CRE'DULOUS, Adj. [*credulus*, Lat.] assenting to any thing as true, without examining into its truth.

CRE'DULOUSNESS, S. the quality of believing or assenting to things too easily or without examination.

CREE'D, S. (from the word *credo*, the first word in Latin) a brief summary of the principle articles of a person's faith; used in a scriptural as well as political sense.

To CRE'EK, V. A. [*kraic*, Belg.] to make a harsh noise.

CRE'EK, S. [*crecca*, Sax. *kreke*, Belg.] in Geography, part of the sea which runs into the land, a port, or bay. A narrow turning or winding.

CRE'EKY, Adj. having many creeks and windings.

To CRE'EP, V. N. [*Preter creps*; *creopan*, Sax.] to move with the belly to the ground, like reptiles, or animals without legs, such as worms and serpents. Figuratively, to grow along the ground, applied to vegetables. To move slowly, through feebleness. Used with *along*, to proceed in a low manner, without any flights or soaring, applied to writings; to proceed without venturing into dangers. To steal out or into a place unperceived and unheard. To behave with abjectness; to fawn.

CRE'EPER, S. a plant which runs along the ground. An iron used on a kitchen grate. A kind of patten worn by women in the country.

CREE'PINGLY, Adv. slowly, like a reptile.

CRE'MOR, S. [Lat.] a milky substance, a fluid like cream. "Reduced into a chyle, or *cremor*." Ray.

CRE'NATED, Adj. [from *crena*, Lat.] in Botany, notched, jagged, or, in *Miller*'s phrase, sawed on the edges.

To CRE'PITATE, V. N. [*crepito*, Lat.] to make a crackling noise.

CREPITA'TION, S. a kind of small crackling noise.

CREPU'SCULOUS, Adj. glimmering, of a middle state between light and darkness. "A crepusculous obscurity." Glanv.

CRE'SCENT, Adj. [*crescens*, Lat.] growing, increasing, in a state of increase.

CRE'SCENT, S. the moon in her increasing state. In Heraldry, a bearing in the form of a half moon.

CRES'CIVE, Adj. increasing, growing, improving. "Crescive in his faculty." Shak.

CRE'SS, S. [plural *cresses*, from *cresse*, Lat.] an herb, used for sallet, the garden *cress*, and the water *cress* are the most known.

CRE'ST, S. [*creste*, Fr. *crista*, Lat.] the plume of feathers on the top of helmets. The comb of a cock. In Heraldry, that part of the armoury over the crest or helmet next to the mantle, which contains the ornament. Any natural tuft on the head. Figuratively, pride, spirit, or courage.

CRE'STED, Adj. (*cristatus*, Lat.) adorned with a plume, crest; or having a tuft on the head.

CREST-FA'LLEN, Adj. dispirited; cowed; dejected; owing to some sudden accidents, or fear.

CRE'STLESS, Adj. not honoured with coat-armoury; not of a genteel or noble family.

CRETA'CEOUS, Adj. [*creta*, Lat.] abounding with qualities of chalk.

CRE'VICE, S. [*crevasse*, Fr.] a narrow opening generally applied to walls or wainscots.

CRE'W, S. [*cawb*, Sax. *terw*, Perf.] formerly an assembly, or company met together. "A noble *crew* of lords and ladies." Fairy Queen. At present applied to a ship's company; or to signify a company of low, wicked, contemptible persons.

CRE'W, the Preter of CROW.

CRE'WEL, S. [*kluwel*, Belg.] fine worsted, or yarn twisted.

CRI'B, S. [*cryblic*, Sax. *kryblic*, Dan.] the rack in a stable, wherein hay is placed for cattle. A manger. Figuratively, the stall of an ox. A small house or habitation. The cards which each party lay out for the benefit of the dealer, at the game of cribbage.

CRI'BBAGE, S. a well-known game at cards, wherein the players endeavour to make pairs,

pairs, fequents, pairs royals, and one and thirty in playing, and to hold in their hands as many fifteens, pairs, flushes, and fequences as they can.

CRICK, S. [*crice*, Ital.] the noise made by a door with rufty hinges. A pain and ftiffness in the neck.

CRICKET, S. [*krekel*, from *kreken*, Belg.] an infect frequenting fire-places, remarkable for a continual chirping or creaking noife. A game which is played at with a bat and ball, from *cryce*, Sax. a ftake. A low feat or ftool, from *kirbben*, Teut. to creep.

CRIER, S. one who proclaims things that are loft, or to be fold.

CRIME, S. [Fr. *crimen*, Lat.] a voluntary breach of any known law. An offence. Guilt.

CRIMELESS, Adj. free from blame; innocent.

CRIMINAL, Adj. [from *criminis*, genitive of *crimen*, Lat.] contrary to law. Figuratively, faulty, worthy of blame. Guilty; fubject to punifhment for the violation of a law. In Law, opposed to civil. "A *criminal* profecution."

CRIMINAL, S. one accused of a breach of a known law. A perfon who has wilfully acted contrary to law.

CRIMINALLY, Adv. in a manner which implies guilt. In a manner which deferves blame or punifhment.

CRIMINATION, S. [*criminatio*, Lat.] the accusing a perfon of guilt, or the breach of fome law.

CRIMINOUS, Adj. [*criminofus*, Lat.] chargeable with a wilful breach of any known law.

CRIMINOUSNESS, S. wickedness, or a great degree of guilt.

CRIMP, Adj. eafily broken, crumbling; eafily reduceable to powder.

To CRIMPLE, V. A. to draw together in wrinkles. "Crimpled up."

CRIMSON, S. [*cramofin*, Fr.] a deep red colour. In poetical language, ufed for any degree of a red. A blufh. "The virgin *crimfon* of modefty." *Shak*.

To CRIMSON, V. A. to colour with a crimfon.

CRIM-TARTARS, are a people of Afia, fo called, becaufe they originally came from Crimea, who rove from place to place in fearch of paftures, their houfes being drawn on carts. There are great numbers of them about Aftrachan, which place they flock to in the winter time; but they are not permitted to enter the city; for this reafon they erect huts up and down in the open fields, which are made either of bull rufhes or reeds, being about 12 feet in diameter, of a round form, and with a hole at the top to let out the fmoke. Their fuel is turf or cow-dung, and, when the weather is very cold, they cover the hut with a coarfe cloth, and fometimes they pafs

feveral days without ftirring out. They are generally of fmall ftature, with large faces, little eyes, and of an olive complexion. The men are generally fo wrinkled in their faces, that they look like old women. Their common food is fifh dried in the fun, which ferves them inftead of bread, and they eat the flefh of horfes, as well as camels. Their drink is water and milk, efpecially mares milk, which they carry about in nafty leathern bags. Their garments are of coarfe grey cloth, with a loofe mantle, made of a black fheep's fkin, with a cap of the fame. The women are cloathed in white linen, with which they likewife they drefs their heads, hanging a great many Mofcovian pence about them, and there is likewife a hole left to ftick feathers in. As for their religion, they are a fort of Mahometans, but do not coop up their women like the Turks.

CRINCUM, S. [a cant word, perhaps from *krinkeln*, Belg.] a cramp; or whimfy.

CRINGE, S. a low bow; fawning; fervility.

To CRINGE, V. A. [*kriechen*, Teut. to crawl on the ground] to form into wrinkles. Neuterly, to behave in a fervilely, complaifant manner. To fawn.

CRINIGEROUS, Adj. [*criniger*] hairy.

To CRINKLE, V. N. [*krinckelen*, Belg.] to meander, to go in and out. To wrinkle. Actively, to draw a thing into wrinkles; or make a thing uneven.

CRINKLE, S. a wrinkle.

CRINNOSE, Adj. hairy.

CRINOSITY, S. hairynefs.

CRIPPLE, S. [*cryppel*, Sax.] one who has not the proper ufe of his limbs, particularly his legs.

To CRIPPLE, V. A. to make lame or deprive of the ufe of limbs.

CRIPPLENESS, S. the ftate of a perfon who has not the ufe of his limbs.

CRISIS, S. [*κρισις*, Gr. judgment] in Medicine, a change in a diforder, which either indicates a patient's death or recovery. A period of time, wherein an undertaking is arrived at its greateft height. Any particular or critical period of time.

CRISP, Adj. [*crifpus*, Lat.] curled. Indented, winding. "Leave your *crifp* channels.' *Shak*. Dry; brittle. "The inftrument is made more *crifp*." *Bac.*

To CRISP, V. A. [*crifpo*, Lat.] to curl; to twift. To run in and out, to wind. "The *crifped* brooks." *Par. Loft.* To make a thing eafy to be broken by drying it.

CRISPNESS, S. eafinefs to be broken, occafioned by drynefs. In Cookery, brittlenefs formed by a brifk fire.

CRISPY, Adj. curled, brown, and brittle.

CRITERION, S. [*κριτηριον*, Gr. from *κρινω*, Gr. to judge] a mark or ftandard by which

which the properties of a thing may be measured and judged.

CRITIC, S. [κριτικος, Gr. from κρινω, Gr. to judge] a person qualified to point out the perfection or defects of any of the productions in the arts or sciences, or to distinguish the beauties or defects of an author. Figuratively, a censurer, or person addicted to finding fault.

CRITIC, Adj. belonging or relating to criticism.

CRITIC, S. [critique, Fr.] a comment or criticism on the works of an author, whereln both taste and learning are used as guides. A criticism.

To CRITIC, V. N. to play the critic, to write remarks on the works of an author.

CRITICAL, Adj able to point out the beauties and defects of any author. Nice, exact, accurate; according to the rules of criticism. "He wrote a critical dissertation." Captious; censorious. In Medicine and Politics, that in which some crisis happens. "Critical times." "In so critical a juncture." Swift.

CRITICALLY, Adv. in a critical manner, so as to distinguish beauties or defects; exactly; curiously.

To CRITICISE, V. N. to distinguish beauties and defects of any author. Figuratively, to find fault with, used with on or upon. "To criticise on his expences." Locke. Actively, to censure or blame.

CRITICISM, S. the art of judging of literary productions. An observation made by a critic.

To CROAK, V. N. [cræcettan, Sax. crocare, Ital.] to make a hoarse noise like a frog, or raven. Figuratively, to covet or crave.

CROAK, S. the noise like a frog, raven, or crow.

CROCEOUS, Adj. [croceus, Lat.] resembling saffron, yellow.

CROCK, S. [krull, Belg. cruc, Fr.] a large cup or earthen vessel. Figuratively, the soot on the outside of a boiling pot.

CROCKERY, S. [from kruick, Belg.] earthen-ware in general.

CROCODILE, S. [crocodilus, Lat. from κροκη, Gr. saffron, and δειλω, Gr. fearing] In Natural History, an amphibious animal, resembling a lizard, covered with very hard scales, scarce vulnerable, unless under the belly, having four short legs, of incredible swiftness, but cannot easily turn itself. Its sight is very piercing on land, but very dim in water. Its colour is of a dark brown, speckled with blackish spots. Its eggs, which are about the size of those of a goose, are laid by the female to the number of 90 or 60, and covered with sand, on the water side, where they are hatched by the sun. The prodigious fecundity of this creature, so dreadful both to the human race, and to the inhabitants of the water, is counter-acted by providence, in giving the male an unnatural instinct, whereby he devours his offspring as soon as hatched. In Rhetoric, the word is applied to a sophistical and captious kind of argument, contrived to seduce and ensnare the unwary.

CROCODILINE, Adj. [crocodilinus, Lat.] captious, ensnaring, hypocritical.

CROFT, S. [...] a field, or close near or adjoining to a house. "I'th' hilly croft that brow this bottom glade." Milt.

CROISADE, CROISADO, S. [croisade, Fr. from croix, Fr. a cross] an holy war, or expedition against Infidels and heretics, applied to those formerly carried on by the Christian powers against the Turks, for the recovery of Palestine.

CRONY, S. [from χρονος, Fr. time] an old and very intimate acquaintance, friend, or confidant.

CROOK, S. [croc, Fr. crycce, Sax.] any thing bent. A sheep-hook, or shepherd's hook. A meander.

To CROOK, V. A. [kroken, Belg.] to bend, so as to resemble a hook. Figuratively, to pervert or wrest.

CROOKED, Adj. [crochu, Fr.] bent, formed into an angle or hook. Winding. Perverse, bad.

CROOKEDLY, Adv. untowardly, perversely, so as to be bent.

CROOKEDNESS, S. the bending of a body, whereby it deviates from a strait or perpendicular line. Figuratively, a deformity of the body, from any of its limbs being distorted. Perversity of mind or temper.

CROP, S. [crop, Sax.] the craw of birds, wherein their food is prepared for digestion.

CROP, S. [croppa, Sax. an ear of corn] the highest part or end of a thing. The quantity of corn collected in a harvest. The product of a field. Any thing cut off.

To CROP, V. A. to cut or lop off the top or ends of a thing; to shorten or consume in eating. "My goats crop the flow'ry thyme." Dryd. Neuterly, to yield or produce a harvest.

CROPSICK, Adj. sick by excessive eating or drinking.

CROSIER, S. [crosier, Fr.] the pastoral staff of a bishop.

CROSLET, S. [croiselet, Fr.] a small or little cross. "An unblemish'd di'mond croslet." Gay.

CROSS, S. [croix, Fr. cruce, Ital.] an instrument on which malefactors were executed among the Romans; as this punishment was inflicted only on the most abject persons, our Saviour's dying in this manner much heighten his sufferings, and when duly reflected on, throw light on the expressions of its ignominy, often occurring in Scripture. Cross is also the ensign of the Christian religion. The sign made by the priest on the

forehead of a person when baptized. Figuratively, any thing which is contrary to a person's wishes, and is a trial of his patience. Money, so called because marked on the reverse with a cross.

CROSS, Adj. opposed to a person's wishes. Perverse. Peevish, displeased about trifles. Reciprocal, on each side, interchanging. "A cross match."

CROSS, Prep. intersecting from one side to another. In Riding, having one leg on each side of a horse. "Cross the horse."

To CROSS, V. A. to lay one body or line so as to form angles with another. To sign with a cross. In Commerce, to cancel an article, by drawing two black lines over each other, from opposite corners. To go over a river, road, &c. To oppose the designs of another. To contradict. Neuterly, to lie on one another, so as to form angles. To be inconsistent with, joined to with.

CROSS-BOW, S. an engine made of a bow fixed across a piece of wood, used in shooting deer, &c. it will carry a bullet: and do execution at a considerable distance.

CROSS-GRAINED, Adj. the grain of the branch shooting forward, and crossing that of the trunk. Figuratively, peevish, perverse, troublesome.

CROSSLY, Adv. athwart, oppositely, contrary, untowardly.

CROSS ROW, S. the alphabet; so called from a cross's being put at the beginning of it.

CROSS-WAY, S. a small path intersecting a main road or way.

CROTCH, S. [croc, Fr.] a hook. "Some called it his fork, and some his crotch." Bar.

CROTCHET, S. [crochet, Fr.] in Music, one of the notes and marks of time, it is equal to half a minim or double quaver. In Building, a support, or piece of wood fitted into another to sustain it. Figuratively, a fancy, odd conceit, device, or whim.

To CROUCH, V. N. [croucher, Fr. crooked] to stoop low, applied to the posture of beasts. Figuratively, to stoop to a person in a fawning and servile manner.

CROUP, S. [croupe, Fr.] the rump of a fowl. The buttocks of a horse.

CROW, S. [crawe, Sax. kraye, Belg.] a black bird feeding on carrion. To pluck a crow, is to contend or dispute with a person. A strong iron bar used as a lever, to lift up the ends of great heavy timber, force open doors, &c. also the noise made by a cock.

To CROW, V. N. [preter, I crew, crowed, or have crowed, from crawan, Sax.] to make a loud shrill noise like a cock. Figuratively, to boast, bully, or puff.

CROWD, S. [cruth, Sax.] a great number of people close together. Figuratively, the mob or lower sort of people. A fiddle, from croud, Brit.

To CROWD, V. A. to fill a place with

people. To force a great many things into the same place. To press close together. In the marine, joined to sail, to spread all the sails wide upon the yards for the sake of expedition. Neuterly, to go in great multitudes. To thrust among many others, used with in.

CROWDER, S. a word seldom used.

CROWN, S. [couronne, Fr. kroon, Belg.] an ornament of state worn on the head by monarchs. Figuratively, a garland of flowers, &c. worn on the head; a reward for some meritorious deed; royalty; a kingdom; the top of any thing, but particularly the head. "The snowy crowns of the bare mountains." Dryd. that part of a hat which covers the head; a piece of money, worth five shillings; honour, ornament, completion.

To CROWN, V. A. to place a crown on the head to dignify, to reward, to perfect, to complete.

CROWN-OFFICE, S. an office under the king's bench.

CROWN-WORKS, S. in fortification, an out-work running into the field, in order to cover the other works of a place, &c. It consists of two demi-bastions at the extremes, and an entire bastion in the middle with curtains.

CRUCIAL, Adj. [from crucis, Lat.] resembling or in form of a cross.

To CRUCIATE, V. A. [crucianus, Lat.] to torture or torment.

CRUCIBLE, S. [crucibulum, low Lat.] a little vessel used by refiners, chemists, and others, to melt metals, &c. in.

CRUCIFIER, S. one who fixes another to a cross; one who crucifies.

CRUCIFIX, S. [crucifixus, Lat.] a cross whereon the crucifixion of Jesus Christ is represented.

CRUCIFIXION, S. the act of nailing to a cross, or crucifying.

To CRUCIFY, V. A. [crucifigo] to fasten a person on a cross; to execute a person on the cross.

CRUDE, Adj. [crudus, Lat.] raw, not dressed; unaltered by any process or preparation; unfinished; not brought to perfection; not properly examined by the mind; imperfect, unpolished, inadequate, unrefined.

CRUDELY, Adv. without any preparation; without consideration; grossly.

CRUDENESS, S. unripeness, imperfection, indigestion.

CRUDITY, S. rawness, unripeness, indigestion.

CRUDY, Adj. curdled, congealed, raw, chill. "Crudy vapours." Shak.

CRUEL, Adj. [cruel, Lat.] void of mercy, or pity, and delighted in the sufferings of others. Figuratively, implacable inveterate, severe.

CRUELLY, Adv. in an inhuman manner,

her, wherein the tortures of others are beheld with delight and joy.

CRU'ELNESS, S. the exercise of cruelty or barbarity towards another.

CRU'ELTY, S. a savage disposition; delighting in the sufferings of another.

CRUENTATE, Adj. [*cruentatus*, Lat.] smeared with blood. " The *cruentate* cloth." *Glanville.*

CRU'ET, S. [*kruicke*, Belg.] a phial for vinegar, oil, or mustard.

CRU'ISE, S. [*croise*, Fr. *kruis*, Belg.] a voyage made up and down a coast to guard it from any attack.

To CRU'ISE, V. N. to sail to and fro about a coast without any certain destination.

CRU'ISER, S. a ship that sails to and fro in quest of an enemy's ships.

CRUM, CRUMB, S. [*cruma*, Sax. *krume*, Belg.] the soft part of bread, opposed to the crust. Figuratively, a small particle, or bit.

To CRU'MBLE, V. N. [*kruymelen*, Belg. *krummeln*, Teut.] to break into small pieces. Neuterly, to fall into small pieces, applied to dry bodies, whose particles separate of themselves.

CRUM'MY, Adj. resembling the crum of bread; soft, plump, or fleshy. " A *crummy* dame."

CRUMPLING, S. a small degenerate kind of apple.

CRU'PPER, S. [from *croupe*, Fr.] that part of the furniture of a horse that reaches from the saddle to the tail.

To CRUSH, V. A. [*escraser*, Fr.] to break to pieces; by squeezing; to press with force. Figuratively, to depress, subdue, or destroy by force. Neuterly, to thicken, to condense, by a nearer approach of the particles, and lessening the pores of the body.

CRUSH, S. the destruction of a thing by means of force; by squeezing; collision; destruction.

CRU'ST, S. [*crusta*, Lat.] the hard external surface of a body; the case which contains the materials of a pye or pudding; the hard part of bread; a piece of the outer or hard surface of a loaf.

To CRU'ST, V. A. to cover with a hard case; to have its external surface hardened.

CRUSTA'CEOUS, Adj. being covered with a shell, applied to fish. " Lobsters, crabs, and others of the *crustaceous* kinds." *Woodw.*

CRUSTA'CEOUSNESS, S. the quality of having shells.

CRU'STILY, Adv. morosely, peevishly.

CRU'STINESS, S. the hardest part of bread; peevishness, moroseness.

CRU'STY, Adj. having a hard surface. Figuratively, not easily prevailed on, morose.

CRUTCH, S. [*cruce*, Sax. *cruce*, Fr.] a

support placed under the arm-pits, and used by some persons to walk with.

To CRY, V. N. [*crier*, Fr.] to speak with loudness. To speak to, with great sorrow; used with *to* or *on*. To proclaim; to exclaim, or speak loudly against; to speak with a mournful tone, attended with tears; to make a squalling, to weep or shed tears. In hunting, to yelp. Joined to *out*, to scream, or make a shriek. To complain loudly. To blame or censure, used with *of*, *against*, or *at*. To be in labour. " Is she *crying out?*" *Shak.* Actively, to give notice that any thing that is lost or to be sold. Joined to *down*, to depreciate or under-value; to forbid; to overbear. " I'll to the king—and quite *cry down*—this Ipswich fellow's impudence." *Shak.* Joined to *up*, to praise, or increase the value of a thing by applause. To raise the price of a thing by proclamation.

CRY, S. [*cri*, Fr.] lamentation, shriek, scream, clamour, or outcry; a proclamation; the manner in which the hawkers proclaim what commodity they sell. " The *cries* of London." Figuratively, the favour of the multitude; acclamation. " The *cry* went once *to* thee." *Shak.* The method of utterance, of animals to express their wants, &c. In hunting, the yelping of dogs.

CRY'PTIC, CRY'PTICAL, Adj. [*kruptos*, Gr.] dark, obstruse, secret, hidden.

CRY'PTICALLY, Adv. in a dark, hidden, private manner. Used by Boyle by a mistake, for *critically*. " Without *cryptically* distinguishing it."

CRYPTO'GRAPHY, S. [from *kruptos*, and *grapho*, Gr.] the art of writing in secret characters.

CRY'STAL, S. [*crystallos*, Gr. Ice] In natural history, a hard, transparent, colourless stone composed of simple plates, giving fire with steel, supposed by some to be formed of dew, congulated by ahre. Island *crystal*, is a genuine spar, of an extreme pure, clear, and fine texture, seldom blemished with flaws or spots. It has the remarkable property of a double refraction, for when laid over a black line, drawn on paper, it shows two lines of the same colour and thickness, and running parallel to each other at a certain distance. This phenomenon is solved by Mr. Benjamin Martin, in his experimental lectures. *Crystal* glass, is that which is carried to a degree of perfection beyond the common glass. In chemistry, applied to expressly salts, or other matters, congealed in the manner of a *crystal*.

CRY'STAL, Adj. consisting of *crystal*; bright, clear, shining, transparent. " *Crystal* streams." *Dryd.*

CRY'STALLINE, Adj. [*crystallinus*, Lat.] consisting of crystal, bright, clear, transparent. *Crystalline* humour, in anatomy, the second humour of the eye, lying behind the uvea.

M r   It

It is conves on both fides, and is covered with a fine coat called the uranea.

CRYSTALLIZA'TION, S. in chemistry, a combination of saline particles in the form of a cryftal, varioufly modified according to the nature of the falts. A mass formed by congelation or concretion.

To CRYSTALLIZE, V. A. to form into a mass refembling cryftals; to coagulate.

CUB, S. [from cube, Lat.] the young of a bear or fox; fometimes used for the off-fpring of a human creature, by way of re-proach.

To CUB, V. A. to bring forth, applied to a fox or bear. Figuratively, to be deli-vered, applied to a woman in contempt or reproach.

CUBA, an ifland of North America, at the entrance of the gulf of Mexico, about 700 miles in length, and 87 in breadth. It was difcovered by Chriftopher Columbus, in 1492. The Spaniards are entirely mafters of it, they have rooted out the ancient inhabitants. The foil is not extremely fertile, but there are paftures fufficient to feed a great number of beeves, fheep, and hogs, which were origi-nally brought thither. There are feveral forts of mines in the mountains, and forefts full of game. The produce is fugar-canes, ginger, caffia, wild cinnamon, and very good tobacco, called by the Spaniards Cigarror. The hills run through the middle of the ifland from eaft to weft, but, near the coaft, the land is generally plain. Here are a great many rivulets, which run down from the hills to the north and fouth, but they have a very fhort courfe. The air is pretty tem-perate and wholefome, and here are cedar-trees fo large, that canoes made of them will carry 50 men. Between St. Jago and St. Salvadore there is a valley full of round ftones, which, upon occafion, might ferve for great guns; Havannah is the capital town, and is feated on the weftern fide of the ifle, next Florida. The galleons that return annually to Spain rendezvous at Ha-vannah. This ifland is about 120 miles S. of Florida, 50 W. of Hifpaniola, and 75 N. of Jamaica.

CU'DATURE, S. the finding or difcover-ing the folid contents of a body.

CUBE, S. [kubos, Gr. a die] in geometry, a folid body, confifting of fix equal square fides. In arithmetic, a number arifing from the multiplication of a fquare number by its root.

CU'BIC, or CUBICAL, Adj. belonging or relating to a cube.

CU'BICALNESS, S. the ftate of being cubical.

CU'BICULARY, Adj. [cubicularius, Lat.] fitted for lying down. "Changed their cu-bicuary beds into difcubitory." Brown.

CU'BIFORM, Adj. in the form of a cube.

CU'BIT, S. [cubitus, Lat. an elbow] meafure in ufe among the ancients, which was the diftance from the elbow to the ex-tremity of the middle finger.

CU'BITAL, Adj. containing the meafure of a cubit.

CU'CKING-STOOL, S. [from cuquin, Fr. and ftool] a chair for plunging women into the water, as a punifhment for fcolding.

CU'CKOLD, S. [cocu, Fr.] one whofe wife has violated the marriage bed.

To CU'CKOLD, V. A. to lay with ano-ther man's wife; to lay with another man tho' married.

CU'CKOLDLY, Adv. like a cuckold. Fi-guratively, mean, bafe, fneaking.

CU'CKOLDOM, S. the ftate or condition of a cuckold.

CU'CKOO, S. [cuccus, Brit. cucu, Fr.] in natural hiftory, a bird, which appears in the fpring, which feeks the eggs of other birds, and lays her own to be hatched in their ftead; hence it was ufual to give the hufband a fign of the approach of an adul-terer by crying cuckoo, hence in procefs of time it was ufual to call the perfon whofe bed was defiled, a cuckold.

CU'CULLATE, CU'CULLATED, Adj. [cucullatus, Lat.] hooded. Refembling a hood.

CU'CUMBER, [pronounced cowcumber, from concumbre, Fr.] in Botany, hath male and female flowers, at a diftance, on the fame plant, with a bell-fhaped empalement of one leaf, terminated with five briftles. The flowers are bell-fhaped, with one petal, cut into five oval rough fegments. The male flowers have three fhort ftamina; the female flowers have none, but have three fmall pointed filaments without fummits. The germen is fituated under the flower, fupports a fhort cylindrical ftyle, and be-comes an oblong flefhy fruit, with three cells including many oval feeds. It is rang-ed by Linnæus in the 10th feft. of his 21ft clafs; and by Tournefort in the 7th fect. of his firft. The fpecies are three.

CUD, S. [cad, Sax.] the infide of the throat. The food kept by a cow in the firft ftomach, which is chewed a fecond time.

CU'DDEN, CU'DDY, S. a clown, a ftupid, aukward, ruftic fellow.

To CU'DDLE, V. A. to lye clofe; to fquat, to hug, to embrace clofely.

CU'DGEL, S. [kudfe, Belg.] a ftick to ftrike with.

To CU'DGEL, V. A. to beat with a ftick. To think deeply or intenfely on a thing. "Cudgel thy brains no more." Shak.

CUE, S. [queue, Fr. a tail] the tail, or end. A hint. "Give them their cue to at-tend." Swift. The part which a perfon is to play in his turn. "Were it my cue to fight."

fight." *Shakesp.* Humour, temper, disposition. I am not in the proper *cir.*

CUFF, S. [*coffa*, Ital.] a box or stroke given with the fist.

CUFF, S. [*coiffe*, Fr.] a part of the sleeve which is turned back again from the wrist.

CUIRASS, S. [*cuiraffe*, Fr.] a part of defensive armour made of iron covering the body from the neck to the girdle.

CU'LINARY, S. [*culina*, Lat.] belonging to the kitchen; belonging or used in cookery.

To CULL, V. A. [*cueillir*, Fr.] to pick, choose or select from a great many.

CULLER, S. one who picks, selects, or chooses a thing from a great many others.

CU'LLY, S. [*cogline*, Ital.] a man deceived, imposed upon, or seduced by sharpers, or prostitutes.

To CU'LLY, V. A. to deceive, seduce, or impose upon.

CULMI'FEROUS, Adj. [*culmus*, Lat.] in botany, applied to such plants as have a smooth, jointed stalk, usually hollow; and have their seeds contained in chaffy husks; such as wheat, barley, oats, &c.

To CU'LMINATE, V. N. [*culmen*, Lat. the top] in Astronomy is to be at its greatest altitude; to be in its meridian.

CULMINA'TION, S. in Astronomy, the transit of a star over the meridian.

CULPABI'LITY, S. the quality which subjects a person or thing to blame.

CU'LPABLE, Adj. [*culpabilis*, Lat.] deserving blame, blameable.

CU'LPABLENESS, S. that which renders a person deserving of blame.

CU'LPABLY, Adv. so as to deserve blame.

CU'LPRIT, S. a malefactor or criminal. "Then first the *culprit* answered." *Dryd.* A person guilty of any offence.

CU'LTER, S. [Lat.] the iron of a plough which cuts the ground perpendicular to the plough-share; commonly spelt *coulter.*

To CU'LTIVATE, V. A. [*cultiver*, Fr.] to promote the fertility of the earth by manuring it, or other methods of husbandry. Figuratively, to improve by education and study.

CULTIVA'TION, S. the act of improving land by husbandry. Figuratively, the improvement of the mind by education. Improvement in any particular science.

CU'LTURE, S. [*cultura*, Lat.] the act of cultivating the ground. Figuratively, improvement by education and study. Improvement in any branch of learning. The eradicating or rooting out any vice from the mind.

To CU'LTURE, V. A. [from the noun] to cultivate; to manure, till, or improve soil by other methods of husbandry. Used by Thomson, without other authority.

CU'LVER, S. [*culfre*, Sax.] a pigeon. "Born on liquid wing, the *culver* shoots." *Tickell.*

CU'LVERIN, S. [*colevorine*, Fr.] a slender piece of ordnance or artillery.

To CU'MBER, V. A. [*kummeren*, Belg.] to hinder by its weight. To put a person to difficulty in managing a thing, by its weight, or length. Figuratively, to load with something useless. To disturb, distress, or involve in difficulties.

CUMBERLAND, a county of England, 75 miles in length, and 27 in breadth, and is bounded on the N. by Scotland, and part of Northumberland, on the W. by the Irish sea, on the S. by Lancashire, and on the E. by Westmorland, Durham, and Northumberland. It contains 14300 houses, 88920 inhabitants, 1 city, 14 market-towns, 58 parishes, and sends 6 members to parliament. The air is sharp and cold, and the land for the most part hilly. It yields plenty of fish, flesh, and fowls, with abundance of large salmon. The principal mountains are, Skiddaw, which is very high, from whence run a ridge of mountains, called the Fells, to the most northern part of the county; it is watered by several rivers, besides lakes and meres; and part of the Picts wall runs through this county. In this county, near Keswick, are mines of black lead, which, if not the only ones in the world, are certainly the best. Besides which, there are mines of coal, copper, and lapis calaminaris. Carlisle is the principal town.

CU'MBERSOME, Adj. occasioning great trouble. Burthensome, perplexing. Unwieldy.

CU'MBROUS, Adj. troublesome, vexatious, burthensome, heavy, disagreeable.

To CU'MULATE, V. A. [*cumulatum*, supine of *cumulo*, Lat.] to add one thing to another; to heap together.

CUMULA'TION, S. the act of heaping things on one another.

CUNCTA'TION, S. [*cunctatio*, Lat.] the act of deferring the doing of a thing to another time. Sometimes delay, in a good sense. "Celerity should always be contempered with *cunctation*." *Brown.*

CU'NEAL, Adj. [from *cuneus*, Lat.] relating to, resembling or having the shape of a wedge.

CU'NEATED, Part. [*cuneus*, Lat.] in the form of a wedge.

CUN'NING, Adj. [from *cunnan*, Sax.] learned, knowing, wise. Performed with skill; curious. "Thou *cunning'st* pattern of excelling nature." *Shakesp.* Figuratively, sly; designing; crafty; artful. *Cunning* man, is vulgarly used for a conjurer.

CUN'NING, S. [*cunninge*, Sax.] artifice; deceit; superior talents of mind, employed in deceiving others. Art, skill, knowledge, penetration.

B r 2   CUN'-

CUN'NINGLY, Adv. in a fly, crafty manner, including the idea of deceiving another.

CUN'NINGNESS, S. craftiness, flyness. The quality of carrying on a defign againft another, without his difcovery, till he feels the effects of it.

CUP, S. [cuppe, Sax.] a fmall veffel to drink in. Figuratively, the liquor contained in a cup. In the plural cups, an entertainment of drinking.

To CUP, V. A. to bleed a perfon by fixing a cupping-glafs to the place.

CUP'BOARD, S. a place fitted with fhelves and a door in which victuals, &c. are placed.

To CUP'BOARD, S to put or place in a cupboard. To hoard. "Still cupboarding the viand." Shakefp.

CUP'OLA, S. [Ital.] In Architecture, the round of the top of the dome of a church, refembling a cup inverted; called alfo a lanthorn.

CUP'PER, S. one who applies a cupping glafs, and cues.

CUP'PING, S. the applying a cupping-glafs for the difcharge of blood, &c. by the fkin.

CUP'PING-GLASS, S. a glafs veffel, which having its air rarified, gives room for that contained in the part to which it is applied, to expand itfelf, and bring with it fuch humours as it is involved in, which are afterwards difcharged by a fcarifier, which by means of a fpring enter the fkin at the fame time.

CUR, S. [korre, Belg.] a degenerate, worthlefs kind of dog. Ufed alfo as a term of reproach for a man.

CU'RABLE, Adj. that which may be healed or cured.

CU'RABLENESS, S. the poffibility of being healed.

CU'RACY, S. the employment of a clergyman, who does the duty of another for a certain falary.

CU'RATE, S. a clergyman who does the duties of another for a certain falary. A parifh prieft.

CU'RATIVE, Adj. relating to a cure. Able to recover from a diforder, oppofed to prefervative. "Both prefervative and curative." Arbuth.

CU'RATOR, S. [Lat.] a perfon who has the cure and fuperintendance of a thing, or perfon.

CURB, S. [courber, Fr. to bend] an iron chain faftened to the upper part of the branches of a bridle, ufed to manage a hard mouthed horfe. Figuratively, a reftraint put on the inclinations of a perfon. A hard and callous tumour, running along the infide of a horfe's hoof, or that part of the hoof which is oppofite to the leg of the lame fide.

To CURB, V. A. to manage a horfe by means of a curb. Figuratively, to check, or reftrain the paffions.

CURD, S [kruden, Belg.] the thickening, coagulating, or cluttering of any liquor, generally applied to that of milk, occafioned by mixing runnet with it.

To CUR'DLE, V. N. to grow into clots; to grow thick. Actively, to make a thing grow thick, clot, or coagulate. Figuratively, ufed for the chill or fenfation of cold arifing from a ftagnation of blood caufed by fear.

CUR'DY, Adj. coagulated; clotted; thick.

CURE, S. [cura, Lat.] a remedy; the recovering from a difeafe. The employment of a curate.

To CURE, V. A. [curo, Lat.] to heal a wound; to recover from a difeafe. In Cookery, to preferve from corrupting by falting. Figuratively, to remedy any diforder of the mind, to reform from vice.

CU'RELESS, Adj. without remedy; not to be cured.

CU'RER, S. a healer, or phyfician; one who cures.

CUR'FEW, S. [couvre-feu, Fr. cover the fire] an evening bell, on the found of which every man was obliged to extinguifh his fire and candle, in the time of William the Conqueror. Figuratively, any bell which tolls conftantly in the night time. A cover for a fire.

CURI'OSITY, S. a propenfity to enquire after new objects, and to delight in viewing them. Figuratively, an act of curiofity, a nice experiment. A rarity.

CU'RIOUS, Adj. [curiofus, Lat.] difpofed to enquire into novelties. Attentive to, or diligent. "Curious of antiquities." Dryd. Accurate, without impropriety. "Men were not curious what fyllables or particles of fpeech they ufed." Shakefp. Exact; nice; artful; elegant; neat; compofed with great care. Rigid, fevere, ftrict. "Curious I cannot be with you." Shak.

CU'RIOUSLY, Adj. in an inquifitive, accurate, or elegant manner. Captioufly.

CURL, S. a ringlet of hair formed into a kind of ring. Figuratively, a wave, or waving line.

To CURL, V. A. [gyrian, Sax.] to place the hair in circles. To writhe, or twift round. To drefs with curls. Neuterly, to form itfelf into ringlets, or circular lines. To twift.

CURMU'DGEON, S. [a corrupt pronunciation and fpelling of coeur méchant, Fr. a bad heart] one who is void of generofity; a niggardly or avaritious perfon. A mifer.

CURMU'DGEONLY, Adv. avaritioufly, covetoufly. After the manner of a curmudgeon.

CUR'RANT, S. in Botany, the tree hath prickles; the flower have five petals expanded in the form of a rofe, the germen arifes from the center of the flower, becomes a glo-

a globular fruit, and are white, red, or black, produced in bunches. Likewise a small dried grape. See CORINTH.

CU'RRENCY, S. circulation; passing and acknowledged as legal, applied to money or bills. General reception. Figuratively, fluency of speech, easiness of utterance. Constant flow, uninterrupted course.

CU'RRENT, Adj. [*currens*, Lat.] passing, circulating from hand to hand, legal, applied to money. Generally received, applied to opinions. Popular, fashionable. Passible, or to be admitted. " No excuse *current*." *Shak.* What is now passing, " the *current* expences."

CUR'RENT, S. a running stream. In Navigation, a progressive motion of the water of the sea.

CUR'RENTLY, Adv. in a constant motion. Without opposition; generally.

CU'RRIER, S. [*currier*, Ital. *coriarius*, Lat.] one who dresses leather.

CUR'RISH, Adj. like a cur; snappish, quarrelsome, snarling.

To CU'RRY, V. A. [*conroyer*, Fr.] to dress leather, &c. To rub a horse with a comb, to smooth his hide, promote circulation. Figuratively, to tickle, or flatter, joined to *with*. " I would *curry with* master Shallow." *Shak.* To *curry favour with*, is to strive to gain the esteem of another by trivial services.

CU'RRYCOMB, S. an iron instrument set with iron teeth or wires, used to dress a horse.

To CU'RSE, V. A. [*cursian*, Sax.] to wish a person ill; to desire destruction. To afflict, or torment. " To be *cursed* with such a wife."

CU'RSE, S. the action of wishing or praying for any tremendous evil to another. The act of devoting to torment. Affliction, misery.

CU'RSED, Part. under a curse. Figuratively, hated, detestable. Unholy, impious, affected by a curse. Vexatious, troublesome. Sometimes used only to express the superlative degree, as " *Cursed* dirty," *cursed* proud."

CU'RSEDLY, Adv. miserably; shamefully, prodigiously, abominably.

CU'RSITOR, S. [Lat.] an officer belonging to the court of Chancery, who makes out original writs. There are 24, having each particular shires allotted them, for which they make such writs as are required.

CU'RSORILY, Adv. in a hasty inattentive manner.

CURSO'RINESS, S. haste, want of attention.

CU'RSORY, Adj. [*corsorius*, Lat.] hasty; quick; careless; inattentive.

CU'RST, Adj. [*boosid*, Belg.] froward; snarling; mischievous.

To CU'RTAIL, V. A. [*kortom*, Belg. to

cut. *Accortare*, Ital. *curto*, Lat. Johnson, who perhaps did not know the Dutch derivation, imagines that the antient word *curtal*, which he acknowledges to be the most proper, being commonly applied to dogs, who had their *tails* cut, and were thence called *curtail dogs*, was vulgarly conceived to mean *to cut the tail*, and was thence [spelt *curtail*] to cut off; to shorten by cutting. Figuratively, to retrench, applied to expences. Used with *of* before the thing shortened or cut off.

CU'RTAIN, S. [*curtine*, Fr. *cortina*, Ital. Span. and Lat.] a cloth hung before a window, or round a bed, and running on an iron rod, by which means it is spread, or contracted, made use of to exclude the light, or air, or to conceal any thing. To *draw* a *curtain*, is to spread it so before a thing that it cannot be seen; but when it is spread before, to *draw*, is used for to contract it, so as an object may be seen, which was before hid by it; this is more properly to undraw. In fortification, that part of a wall or rampart which lies between two bastions. A *curtain lecture*, is a reproof given by a wife to her husband in bed.

To CU'RTAIN, V. A. to furnish with curtains.

CURTA'TION, S. [*curtatum*, Lat.] in Astronomy, a little part cut off from the line of a planet's distance from the sun.

CUR'VATED, Adj. [*curvatus*, Lat.] bent, crooked.

CUR'VATION, S. the act of bending or crooking.

CUR'VE, Adj. [*curvus*, Lat.] crooked, bent, formed from a straight surface to an angular one.

CUR'VE, S. any thing bent. A bending. In Geometry, a line whose points extend different ways, and may be cut by a right line in more points than one.

To CUR'VE, S. to bend, to crook, to fold.

To CUR'VET, V. N. [*corvettare*, Ital.] to bound, leap or jump; to frisk, to grow wanton.

To CUR'VET, S. [see CORVET] in the manage, a leap, or bound. A frolic, or a prank.

CURVILI'NEAR, Adj. [from *curvus*, Lat. and *linea*, Lat.] consisting of crooked lines.

CUR'VITY, S. crookedness.

CU'SHION, S. [*kussen*, Belg. *cuffin*, Fr.] a case of silk, &c. stuffed placed on the seat of a chair to render the seat easy.

CU'SHIONED, Adj. supported by or seated on a cushion.

CU'STARD, S. [*cuffard*, Brit.] a kind of pastry made with milk, eggs, and sugar, which are thickened into a mass either by baking or boiling.

CU'STODY, S. [*custodia*, Lat.] confinement in prison; restraint. Figuratively, the

the charge or keeping of a perfon. Defence, prefervation, fecurity.

CU'STOM, S. [*couſtume*, Fr.] habitual practice; faſhion; an eſtabliſhed manner; a great run of trade. In Law, a right or law not written, which being eſtabliſhed by long uſe, and the conſent of our anceſtors, has been and is daily practiſ'd. A tax paid to the government on goods imported or exported. *Cuſtom-houſe*, is the place where thoſe taxes are paid.

CU'STOMABLE, Adj. commonly practiſed.

CU'STOMABLY, Adv. according to the common practice.

CU'STOMARILY, Adv. commonly, generally, frequently.

CU'STOMARINESS, S. frequency of repetition, commonneſs.

CU'STOMARY, Adj. agreeable to the practice of a majority; habitual; uſual.

CU'STOMED, Adj. uſual, common, frequently practiſed.

CU'STOMER, S. one who purchaſes any thing of a tradeſman. A common woman "I marry her! what, a *cuſt mer!*" *Shak.* This ſenſe is now obſolete.

To CUT, V. A. (preter and participle paſſive *cut*, from *couteau*, Fr. a knife) to enter or divide with a ſharp edged inſtrument. Figuratively, to hew; to carve; to wound. In Gaming, to ſeparate a pack of cards, by taking off ſome of them from the others; to interſect; to *cut down*, to fell, or hew. Figuratively, to excel or ſurpaſs. "He *cut down* the fineſt orator." *Addiſ.* To *cut off*, to ſeparate from the other parts by a ſharp inſtrument. Figuratively, to deſtroy, to put to an untimely death. To *cut out*, to ſhape, to form, to contrive, to fit, to debar, to excel. To *cut ſhort*, is hinder from proceeding by a ſudden interruption, to deprive, deſtroy, or abridge of an uſual allowance. To *cut up*, to carve or divide a joint, or foul properly. Neuterly, to make its way by dividing, or forcing a paſſage through all obſtructions. To perform the operation, for extracting the ſtone. To interfere; "a horſe that *cuts.*" To *cut a feather*, is applied to a well-bowed ſhip, which preſſes the water ſo ſwiftly as to make it foam and ſwell; to *cut a ſail*, is to unfurl and let it fall down.

CUT, Part. prepared, fit, or proper for uſe.

CUT, S. the effect of a ſharp inſtrument. A channel made by art. A ſmall piece, or ſhred. A *ſhort cut*, a ſhort way, by which ſome winding is cut off. A picture taken from a copper-plate. That part of a pack of cards divided from the reſt. Faſhion, or ſhape of cloaths or dreſs.

CUTA'NEOUS, Adj. [from *cutis*, Lat.] relating to the ſkin.

CU'TICLE, S. [*cuticula*, Lat.] the outermoſt covering of the body, commonly called the ſearf-ſkin, which ariſes on the application of a

blifter plaſter. When examined through a microſcope, it ſeems made up of ſeveral lays of exceeding ſmall ſcales, covering one another; according to *Leeuwenhoek*, each of theſe ſcales has 500 excretory ducts, and a grain of ſand will cover 250 ſcales and 125:000 pores, through which we perſpire. Figuratively, a thin ſkin formed on the ſurface of any liquor.

CUTI'CULAR, Adj. belonging to the ſkin.

CUTLASS, S. [*couſeloſ*, Fr. ſometimes written *cutlaſe*] a broad cutting ſword.

CU'TLER, S. [from *cuteau*, Fr. a knife] one who makes and ſells knives, &c.

CUT-PURSE, S. a thief, a robber, a pick-pocket.

CU'TTER, S. a perſon, or inſtrument, which cuts any thing; a nimble veſſel; the fore teeth. An officer in the exchequer, who provides wood for the tallies, cuts the ſum paid upon them, and caſts them into the court to be written upon.

CUT-THROAT, S. a murderer.

CUT-THROAT, Adj. cruel, barbarous, inhuman.

CU'TTING, S. a ſhread or piece ſeparated by a ſharp inſtrument.

CY'CLOD, S. [*kuklos*, Gr. a circle, and *eidos*, Gr. a form or ſhape] a geometrical curve formed by the line which a nail, in the circumference of a wheel, makes in the air, while the wheel revolves in a ſight line.

CYCLO'IDAL, Adj. relating to a cycloid.

CYCLOPE'DIA, S. [from *kuklos*, Gr. a circle, and *paideia*, Gr. ſcience] a circle of knowledge; a general courſe of ſciences.

CY'GNET, S. [*cygnus*, Lat.] a young ſwan.

CY'LINDER, S. [*kulindros*, Gr.] in Geometry, a round ſolid, having its baſes circular, in the form of a rolling ſtone uſed by gardeners.

CYLINDRIC, CYLINDRICAL, Adj. partaking of the form of a cylinder.

CY'MBAL, S. [*cymbalum*, Lat.] a muſical inſtrument among the ancients, ſuppoſed to be made of braſs, and in the form of a kettle-drum.

CUNA'NTHROPY, S. [from *kuon*, Gr. a dog, and *anthropos*, Gr. a man] the ſpecies of madneſs contracted by the bite of a mad dog.

CY'NIC, CY'NICAL, Adj. [*kunikos*, Gr.] ſatirical, ſnarling; brutal, partaking of the qualities of a cynic philoſopher, who was remarkable for his rigorous reprehenſion of vice.

CY'NIC, S. a philoſopher, who had an utter contempt of every thing, except morality. A ſect founded by Diogenes.

CY'ON, S. Lee CION.

CY'PRESS, S. [*cypreſſus*, Lat. *cyprès*, Fr.] in Botany, bath male and female flowers, at a di-

a distance, on the same plant, the male formed into oval katkins without petals, or stamina. The wood of this tree is of so lasting a nature, that the gates of St. Peter's church at Rome, which were made of it, lasted 600 years, without any sensible decay. Figuratively used for mourning.

CE'ST, S. [*kuste*, Gr.] In Surgery, a bag containing morbid matter.

CY'STIC, Adj. In Surgery, contained or included in a bag.

CYSTO'TOMY, S. [from *kuste* and *temno*, Gr. to cut] the act of opening encysted tumours, to let out morbid matter.

CZ'AR, S. the title of the emperor of Russia.

CZA'RINA, S. [from *czar*] the title of the empress of Russia.

D.

D, The fourth letter in the English alphabet, and the third consonant. It has the same shape in the Roman, Saxon, and our alphabet, and seems formed from the Δ Delta of the Greeks; It is pronounced by placing the top of the tongue to the fore part of the palate, and then separating them by a gentle breathing, the lips being open at the same time. As a numeral it stands for 500. As an abbreviature, D stands for doctor, D. D. doctor in divinity, D. C. *da capo*, [Ital. from the head or beginning] in Music, implies that the beginning of a tune is to be played over again.

To DAB, V. A. [*dauber*, Fr.] to touch gently, generally applied to something soft, or moist.

DAB, S. a small lump, generally applied to something moist. A blow, with something moist or soft. In low language, a person expert in any thing, but not used in writing. In Natural History, a small flat fish. A *dabwash*, is a small wash of cloaths, to answer a particular emergence, till the stated period of washing returns.

To DA'BBLE, V. A. [*dabbelen*, Belg.] to smear or dab with something wet. Neuterly, to play in the water. Figuratively, to do any thing superficially.

DA'BBLER, S. one that dabbles in water. Figuratively, one who performs a thing superficially; one who never goes to the bottom of an affair.

DA'CE, S. [*darceau*, Fr.] a small river fish, something less than a roach.

DA'CTYL, S. [*dactylus*, Lat.] a foot in Latin and Greek poetry, consisting of one long and two short syllables.

DAD, DA'DDY, S. [*tad*, Brit. *atto*, Goth. דד, *dad*, Heb.] a father.

DÆ'DAL, Adj. [*dædalus*, Lat.] various, variegated, skilfull. "The *dædal* hand of

nature" *Phillips*. Johnson observes that this is not the true sense of the word, and should not be imitated: Those who know the table of Dædalus, are the best judges.

DA'FFODIL, DAFFODI'LLY, DAFFO-DOWNDI'LLY, S. In Botany, the Narcissus. The flowers are included in an oblong spatha, or sheath, which tears open, and then withers.

To DA'FT, V. A. to toss aside, with slighting and contempt; to postpone.

To DA'G, V. A. [*dag, dag*, Sax.] to bemire the lower parts of a gown or other garment.

DA'GGER, S. [*dague*, Fr.] a short sword. In Printing, the obelus, used as a mark of reference, of this form. †.

To DA'GGLE, V. A. [from *dag*,] to wet, or daub the bottom of the cloaths, in the dirt, dew, or wet. Neuterly, to hang in the mire or dirt.

DA'ILY, Adj. [*dag 'lic*, Sax.] happening every day. Adverbially, every day. Figuratively, constantly, frequently, often.

DA'INTILY, Adv. curiously, elegantly, deliciously, pleasantly.

DA'INTINESS, S. delicacy, elegance, nicety, squeamishness; or, the not being easily pleased.

DA'INTY, Adj. [derived by Skinner from *dain* old Fr. for delicate, which Johnson cannot find; perhaps from *dainte*, Gr. an entertainment] pleasing to the taste and dearly purchased; delicate, squeamish, scrupulous, elegant, well formed, affected. "Your *dainty* speakers." *Prior*.

DA'INTY, S. some curious food of exquisite taste.

DA'IRY, S. the making several kinds of food from milk. Pasturage; a place where butter or cheese are made.

DA'IRY-MAID, S. a woman servant, who manages the dairy, and makes butter or cheese.

DAISY, S. [*dæges eage* Chauc, *dais*, Fr.] In Botany, the *bellis*, It hath a radiated discous flower, composed of many hermaphrodite flowers in the disk, and female flowers forming the border, or rays, which are included in a common emplacement.

DA'LE, S. [*dal, del*, Belg.] a hollow place between hills; a vale, a vally.

DA'LLIANCE, S. [from *dally*] acts of fondness between lovers. Figuratively, the caresses of a married couple. Delay, or deferring. "You use this *dalliance* to excuse — your breach of promise." *Shak.*

DA'LLIER, S. a trifler. Also a person who uses acts of fondness.

To DA'LLY, V. N. [*dollen*, Belg.] to trifle; to amuse one's self idly; to exchange caresses of fondness. To sport, to frolic. To delay. "Wherein he *dallied* with them." *Wisd.* xii. 26. Actively, to put off.

DAM,

DA'M. [from *dam*] the mother, generally applied to beasts.

DAM, S. [*dam*, Belg.] a mole, a bank, &c. to confine waters.

To DAM, V. A. [*davonan*, Fr.] to confine water by banks, moles, or other obstructions. Figuratively, to damp, obstruct, or interrupt. "The more thou *damm'st* it up, the more it burns." *Shak.*

DA'MAGE, S. [*damage*, Fr.] mischief, hurt, detriment, loss, generally applied to that hurt, hindrance, and detriment which a person receives in his estate. Hence in Law, the giving of damages to a plaintiff, is the allowing him so much as may be supposed to compensate for his loss or hindrance of business during a prosecution.

To DA'MAGE, V. A. to spoil, hurt or injure any thing. To affect a person with loss, to impair.

DA'MAGEABLE, Adj. that which may be damaged or spoiled by time. Mischievous, hurtful.

DA'MASCENE, S. [*damascenus*, Lat.] a small round black plumb, of a rough and astringent taste; it is pronounced *damson*.

DA'MASK, S. [*damasquin*, Fr.] a manufacture of linnen or silk woven with raised flowers. Likewise a very fine steel used for sword and cutlass blades, and of a very fine temper. Figuratively, a red colour, alluding to the colour of the damask rose.

To DA'MASK, V. A. to weave in raised figures. To variegate, diversify or embellish. "*Damask'ng* the ground with flowers." *Fenn.*

DA'MASK-ROSE, in Botany, the flowers are of a soft, pale red, not very double, of an agreeable odour, and the tops are long and smooth. See ROSE.

DA'ME, S. [Fr. *Dame*, Ital.] originally applied to a person of a noble birth, as it is at present used in law; but commonly used now for a farmer's wife, or one of the lower sort. Used in poetry for a person of rank.

To DAMN, V. A. [*damno*, Lat. *damner*, Fr.] to devote or curse to eternal torments. To explode or render any person or performance unpopular, by hissing, &c.

DA'MNABLE, Adj. deserving eternal punishment. Used in a ludicrous sense, for pernicious or odious.

DA'MNABLY, Adv. in such a manner as to incur eternal punishments. Indecently used for odiously, hatefully, detestably; prodigiously.

DAMNA'TION, S. a state of exclusion from divine mercy.

DA'MNATOR, Adj. [*damnatorius*, Lat.] containing the sentence to everlasting punishment.

DA'MNED, Part. hateful; detestable; abominable; deplorable.

DAMNI'FIC, Adj. procuring loss, mischievous, hurtful.

To DA'MNIFY, V. A. [*damnifico*, Lat.] to occasion loss. To spoil, hurt, or impair.

DA'MP, Adj. [*dampe*, Belg.] moist; wettish. Figuratively, dejected; full of sorrow, on account of some unexpected calamity.

DA'MP, S. a fog, or mist. A moist vapour. Figuratively, dejection or sorrow.

To DA'MP, V. A. to wet or moisten. To chill; or lessen heat by water. Figuratively, to lessen any quality. To smother, check, or depress.

DA'MPISHNESS, S. tendency to wetness, or moisture.

DA'MPNESS, S. a cold, chilly moisture.

DA'MPY, Adj. moist or wet with mist, fogs, or other vapours. Figuratively, dejected; sorrowful. "The lords did spread *dampy* thoughts." *Hayw.*

DA'MSEL, S. [*damoiselle*, Fr.] originally used for an attendant of the higher rank; but at present for a young country lass.

DA'MSON, See DAMASCENE.

To DA'NCE, V. N. [*danser*, Fr.] to move in a graceful attitude, agreeable to an air sung, or play'd. To *dance attendance* is to wait in a suppliant manner on a person. To *dance after*, to go frequently in order to see a person.

DA'NCE, S. [Fr. *dans*, ID.] an agreeable motion of the body and feet, adjusted by art, to the tone of a musical instrument.

DA'NCER, S. one who dances.

DANCING-MASTER, S. one who teaches the art of dancing.

To DA'NDLE, V. A. [*dandeien*, Belg.] to keep a child in motion, to quiet. Figuratively, to treat with too much fondness; to use like a child or infant.

DA'NDLER, S. a person that plays with or fondles a child.

DA'NGER, S. [pronounced *dainger*, *danger*, Fr.] hazard, risque, a condition which is liable to mischief.

To DA'NGER, V. A. to expose to loss, or calamity.

DA'NGERLESS, Adj. out of a possibility of meeting with any accident.

DA'NGEROUS, Adj. exposed to accidents, injury, loss, or harm.

DA'NGEROUSNESS, S. a condition which exposes to accidents.

To DA'NGLE, V. N. to hang loose, so as to be easily put in motion by the wind, &c. Figuratively, to hang as a dependant upon another.

DA'NGLER, S. one who frequents the company of women purely to pass time.

DANK, Adj. [*rantre*, Teut. half dry] moist, wettish.

DANUBE, the largest and most considerable river in Europe; which rises in the Black Forest, near Zunberg; and running N. E. through Suabia, passes by Ulm, the capital of that country; then running E. through
                      Bavaria

Bavaria and Austria, passes by Ratisbon, Passau, Ens, and Vienna. It then enters Hungary, and runs S. E. from Presburg to Buda, and so on to Belgrade; after which it divides Bulgaria from Wallachia, and Moldavia, discharging itself by several channels into the Black Sea, through the province of Bessarabia. Towards the mouth, it was called the Ister by the ancients; and it is now said, that four of the mouths are choaked up with sand, and that there are only two now remaining. It begins to be navigable for boats at Ulm, and receives several large rivers as it passes along. It is so deep between Buda and Belgrade, that the Turks and Christians have had men of war upon it; and yet it is not navigable to the Black Sea, on account of the cataracts.

DAN'KISH, Adj. somewhat moistish, wet.

DAPPER, Adj. [dapper, Belg.] small of stature, and full of life, spirit, and vivacity.

DAPPLE, Adj. marked or variegated with different colours.

To DAPPLE, V. A. to streak, variegate, or diversify with a different colour.

To DA'RE, V. N. (preter. I durst, or have dared, from dearran, dyrran, Sax.) to undertake a thing without being discouraged by danger. Actively, to challenge a person to fight.

DA'RE, S. a provocation; a challenge; a defiance.

DA'REFUL, Adj. courageous, without fear. "We might have met them dareful; beard to beard." Shak.

DA'RING, Adj. bold; adventurous; courageous; taking an affair notwithstanding the dangers attending it. Attempting a thing without regarding the laws.

DA'RINGLY, Adv. boldly, courageously, outrageously, impudently.

DA'RINGNESS, S. boldness, impudence.

DARK, Adj. [deorc, Sax.] without light. Dull, applied to colours. Not to be seen through. Figuratively, not easy to be understood; obscure. Ignorant, gloomy, applied to the temper.

DARK, S. want of light, by which things become invisible. Obscurity; want of knowledge.

To DA'RKEN, V. A. [adeorcian, Sax.] to deprive of light. Figuratively, to cloud or perplex. Neuterly, to grow dark.

DA'RKLY, Adj. void of light. Obscurely.

DA'RKNESS, S. a state wherein light is absent and objects become invisible. Opakeness. Figuratively, obscurity; the internal regions; wickedness.

DA'RKSOME, Adj. gloomy; obscure; almost without light.

DARLING, S. [deorling, Sax.] a person greatly careffed. A favourite.

No. VIII.

To DA'RN, V. A. to mend holes in stockings, &c. by cross stitches.

To DARRA'IGN, V. A. to prepare for fight; to set in battle array. "Darrain your battle, for they are at hand." Shak.

DART, S. [dard, Fr.] a small lance, thrown by the hand.

To DART, V. A. to cast or throw a dart. To wound at a distance. To emit, or call; to fly.

To DA'SH, V. A. [caster, Fr. to sprinkle] to break by throwing with violence. To besprinkle; to wet by beating the water with a stick, &c. To mix with another liquor. To form at once or without study, used without. To obliterate, or cancel a writing by drawing a stroke over it with a pen. To make a person ashamed or confounded. Neuterly, to fly in waves or sparkles over the surface of a vessel or bank.

DASH, S. the stroke occasioned by flinging one thing against another. A stroke made with a pen. A blow. A mixture of another liquor.

DA'STARD, S. [adestrigan, Sax.] a coward; a person infamously timid and fearful.

To DA'STARD, V. A. to terrify. "And dastards manly souls with hope and fear." Dryd.

To DA'STARDIZE, V. A. to intimidate, or render cowardly.

DA'STARDY, S. fear, cowardice.

DA'TE, S. [datte, Fr.] the day in which a writing is signed, or an event happens. Continuance. The fruit of the palm tree.

To DA'TE, V. A. to minute down the time in which any thing is performed.

DA'TELESS, Adj. without any fixed term, date, or period.

DA'TIVE, S. [datif, Fr. dativus, Lat.] the case of a noun which signifies the person to whom any thing is given or due. In Law, such executors as are appointed by a judge's decree.

To DAU'B, V. A. [dauber, Fr.] to smear, to spoil. Figuratively, to paint coarsely. To cover with something gaudy. To flatter grossly, to play the hypocrite. "I cannot daub it further." Shak.

DAU'BER, S. a person who soils or smears a thing. Figuratively, a coarse, indifferent painter.

DAU'BRY, S. something which bespeaks craftiness; artifice. "Spells and such daubry." Shak. Not in use.

DA'VENTRY, or DAI'NTRY, a town of Northamptonshire, with a market on Wednesdays and five fairs, on easter Monday, for horses and horned cattle; on June 6, for hogs, and all sorts of goods; on August 6, for horned cattle; on October 2, for cattle, cheese, and onions; and on October 27, called rood-fair, chiefly for sheep. It is seated on the side of a hill, and is a pretty bounded

some

some town on the great road to Chester and Carlisle; and the market is well supplied with horses, cattle, sheep, corn, and provisions. It is 11 m. W. of Northampton, 20 S. E. of Coventry, and 73 N. W. of London. Lon. 16. 20. lat. 52. 12.

DAU'GHTER, S. [daubtar, Goth. dabter, Sax.] the female offspring of a man and woman. Figuratively, any female. A female who confesses to a priest.

To DAUNT, V. A. [dompter, Fr. domito, Lat.] to discourage, to affect with fear.

DAU'NTLESS, Adj. without fear, brave.

DAU'NTLESSNESS, S. a condition void of fear.

DAW, S. [taf, dof, Bav.] a small bird of a black and white colour.

To DAWK, V. A. In Carpentry, to cut a hollow in a work.

To DAWN, V. N. [dagian, Sax.] to grow light. Figuratively, to afford an obscure light to the understanding. To give some indication of approaching splendor.

DA'WN, S. the first appearance of light, after night, a beginning.

DA'Y, S. [dag, Sax.] that space of time wherein it is light; but a natural or civil day is that space of time wherein the earth performs one rotation on its axis, so as in different parts shall successively enjoy the light of the sun; this consists of a period of 24 hours. In Scripture, some particular period or remarkable incident in a person's life.

DA'Y-BED, S. a bed used in the day-time, for idleness and luxury. " Having come from a day bed." Shak.

DA'Y-LABOUR, S. a portion of labour, claimed or exacted of a person every day.

DA'Y-LABOURER, S. one who is hired to work by the day.

DA'YS'PRING, S. the dawn; the day-break. " With day-spring born." Milt.

DA'Y-STAR, S. the morning-star. " So sinks the day-star, in the ocean bed." Milt.

To DAZE, V. A. [dwos, Sax.] to overpower with too much light or refulgence.

DA'ZIED, Adj. adorned with daisies " The prettiest dazied spot we can." Shak.

To DA'ZZLE, V. A. to over-power the eyes with too great a degree of light or splendor. To lose the use of sight for a time, by too much light, or reading. " Thy sight is young — and you shall read when mine begins to dazzle." Shak.

DE'ACON, S. a lower degree of clergy, rather a state of probation for one year, after which a person is ordained priest.

DE'AD, Adj. [Sax. dead, Belg. dod] deprived of life, used with of before the cause of death. Figuratively, without sense or motion; hence a deep sleep is called a dead sleep. Unactive. Dull, applied to colours. To lie dead. Useless. Unaffecting; void of ardour.

" How cold and dead does a prayer appear." Addif. Tasteless, insipid, or vapid, applied to liquors. Without any force or influence; dull. " A dead fire." Without any capacity for growing; withered. " A dead bough or plant." Not to be influenced or seduced by: used with to. " We being dead to sin." 1 Peter II. 24. In Scripture, generally applied to signify those whose consciences are so seared by an habitual course of sin, as to be insensible to the calls of grace.

To DE'AD, DE'ADEN, V. A. to deprive of any quality or sensation. Figuratively, to make liquors vapid or tasteless. Neuterly, to lose any force or quality.

DEAD-LIFT, S. a pressing call, or exigence. A last resource. " To help itself at a dead-lift." Hud.

DE'ADLY, Adj. murtherous. Mortal, inveterate, not satisfied with any thing less than the death of another. " Deadly enemies to the Turks." Knolles.

DE'ADLY, Adv. resembling death. " Look-ed deadly pale." Shak. Mortally, so as to deprive of life. Sometimes used in familiar discourse or implying very much, deadly hungry; exceedingly. " Though deadly weary." Orrery.

DE'ADNESS, S. want of motion. Languor or faintness. Vapidness, loss of spirit.

DE'AF, Adj. [deaf, Belg.] not having the sense of hearing. Figuratively, regardless, inattentive.

To DE'AF, DE'AFEN, V. A. to deprive of the sense of hearing.

DEA'FLY, Adv. [deaflic, Sax.] without any sense of sounds, without hearing.

DEA'FNESS, S. the state of a person whose hearing is entirely lost, or greatly impaired. Figuratively, inattention, disregard.

DE'AL, S. [dal, Sax.] a part, share, or portion. The practice of distributing cards to those who are engaged in any game.

To DE'AL, V. A. [delan, Sax.] to distribute to different persons. To scatter promiscuously. Neuterly, to transact business. To act; joined with by. To deal in; to sell, to be conversant in; to practise. To behave towards.

DE'AL, a sea-port town in Kent, which though pretty large has no market, nor fair. It is seated near the sea, and is a member of Sandwich, governed by a mayor and jurats. It has a church, a chapel, and about 1000 houses, which are mostly low and built with bricks; these form three long but narrow streets. The inhabitants amount to about 4500; but as no manufacture is carried on here, the trades-people chiefly depend on the sea-faring men who resort thither. This place is defended by a castle built by Henry VIII. and near it are two others. Between this place and Goodwin Sands are the Downs, where the ships usually ride at going out or com-

coming home. It is 7 miles S. by E. of Sandwich, 7 N. by E. of Dover, and 75 E. by S. of London. Lon. 19. 5. Lat. 51. 16.

DEALBA'TION, the act of rendering things white, which were no so before. "It receives a manifold *dealbation*." *Brown*.

DEA'LER, S. one who trades. One who practises any thing. One who distributes cards.

DEALING, S. practice, behaviour, treatment. Business.

DE'AN, S. [*doyen*, Fr.] a person in collegiate churches who is president of the chapter.

DE'ANERY, S. the office, revenue, or residence of a dean.

DE'ANSHIP, S. the office of a dean.

DE'AR, Adj. [*deore*, *dyre*, Sax.] an object of great affection; beloved. Valuable; of high price, scarce, not plentiful. "A *dear* season." used by Shak. for *dere*, of *dear*, Sax. wild, fierce, ferocious, or inveterate. "Would I had met my *dearest* foe." *Shak*.

DE'AR, S. a word of fondness, implying that the person is valued as much as the most costly purchase.

DE'AR-BOUGHT, Adj. bought at too high a price. "*Dear-bought* with so much woe." *Milt*.

DE'ARLING, S. [*deorling*, Sax.] a person caressed and esteemed with great affection.

DE'ARLY, Adv. with great affection; at too great a price.

To DEARN, V. A. [*dyrnan*, Sax. to hide] to mend holes. See DARN.

DE'ARNESS, S. fondness; warmth of affection. Scarcity; costliness.

DE'ARTH, S. scarcity. Want. Need. Famine. Barrenness.

DE'ATH, S. [pronounced *deth*, from *death*, Sax.] the departure of the soul from the body. Loss of motion, and all the functions of animal life. The state of the dead. Murder. The cause of death. "The feather'd *death*." *Dryd*. In Divinity, a state of insensibility, so as not to be seduced by allurements of any kind, used with *unto*. "A *death* unto sin." *Church Catech*. "The gates of *death*." *Psal*. ix. 13. are the grave.

DE'ATH-BED, S. the bed whereon a person dies.

DE'ATHFULL, Adj. mortal, fatal, destructive.

DE'ATHLESS, Adj. not subject, or liable to death; immortal.

DE'ATHLIKE, Adj. [*deathlic*, Sax.] resembling death.

DE'ATH'S-DOOR, S. [*tanas alaw*, Gr.] a near approach to death. On the verge of dying.

DE'ATH-WATCH, S. in Natural History, a small insect, making a noise like the beating of a watch, described by Dr. Derham in the Philosophical Transactions. It very

much resembles a louse both in shape and colour; but is more nimble; is common in every house in the warm months; but in the cold season hides itself in dry dusty places. It is hatched by the warmth of the spring, and at its first leaving its egg, is perfectly like a cheese-mite, but so exceeding small, as scarce to be discerned without a microscope. In this state it continues two months, after which it grows gradually to its more perfect state. Their ticking noise is a wooing act, or a kind of courtship, and happens commonly in July, or the beginning of August. But they do not beat alike every year, sometimes beginning it sooner, sometimes later, sometimes for a longer and sometimes for a shorter time. It feeds on dust of powdered horn, fruits, &c. Some have imagined this to have been a house-spider; it being customary for them when they first come into a place, to make a noise or be stir on a wainscot, to which if any other of the same species answers, they settle there, but on the contrary, go farther in quest of company. A person may hold converse with this creature by imitating its sound, who will answer as regularly with its noise, as a human creature can in discourse with his voice.

To DEBA'RK, V. A. [*débarquer*, Fr.] to come out of a ship to shore.

To DEBA'R, V. A. to hinder a person from the enjoyment of a thing.

To DEBA'SE, V. A. to reduce to a lower value. To adulterate by the addition of something less valuable. To spoil, or render less perfect.

DEBA'SEMENT, S. the act of debasing, or degrading a thing by the mixture of something worthless.

DEBA'SER, S. the person who lessens the value of a thing by some mixture. One who adulterates or debases.

DEBA'TABLE, Adj. that which may be disputed, or debated.

DEBA'TE, S. [*debat*, Fr. *dibatto*, Ital.] a dispute or controversy. Figuratively, a quarrel or contest.

To DEBA'TE, V. A. [*debattre*, Fr.] to controvert; to produce arguments; to support any side of a question; to deliberate.

DEBA'TEFUL, Adv. fond of dispute or contradiction; quarrelsome.

DEBA'TEMENT, S. contest, dispute, contradiction, or opposition of opinions. "Without *debatement* further." *Shak*.

DEBA'TER, S. a disputant, or one fond of engaging in disputes.

To DEBAU'CH, V. A. [*débaucher*, Fr.] to seduce a person; to corrupt a person's morals; to corrupt by intemperance.

DEBAU'CH, S. Intemperance in meat or drink. Lewdness.

DEBAU'CHEE, S. [*débauché*, Fr.] a person given to intemperance or lewdness.

DEBAUCHMENT, S. the act of corrupting the morals of persons.

To DEBEL, DEBELLATE, V. A. [debello, Lat.] to conquer or subdue by force of arms. " The extirpating or debellating of giants." Bacon.

DEBENTURE, S. [from debeo, Lat.] a writ, memorandum, or note by which a debt is claimed.

DEBILE, Adj. [debilis, Lat.] weak, feeble, faint through loss of strength or spirit. " Failed some debile wretch." Shak.

To DEBILITATE, V. A. [debilitatum, Lat.] to deprive of strength; to weaken.

DEBILITATION, S. the act of depriving a person of strength.

DEBILITY, S. loss of strength; weakness; want of strength; infirmity.

DEBONAIR, Adj. [debonnair, Fr.] lively, affable, civil, well-bred, elegant, polite.

DEBONAIRLY, Adj. elegantly, genteelly, civilly.

DEBT, S. [debitum, Lat. dette, Fr.] that which one person owes to another. Figuratively, that which it is a person's duty, or which he is under a necessity to do or suffer.

DEBTED, Part. owing, indebted; placed on the debtor side of an account.

DEBTOR, S. [debitor, Lat.] he that owes another money, or goods; that side of an account which contains what a person has had on trust.

DECADE, S. [dus, Gr.] a number consisting of ten.

DECADENCY, S. [decadence, Fr.] decay.

DECAGON, S. [from dus, Gr. ten, and gonia, Gr. a corner] in Geometry, a figure having ten sides.

DECALOGUE, S. [decalogos, Gr.] the ten commandments, given by God to Moses, now placed in the 20th chapter of Exodus.

To DECAMP, V. N. [decamper, Fr.] to shift a camp; to remove from one place to another.

DECAMPMENT, S. the act of moving from one place to another.

To DECANT, V. A. [decanter, Fr. decanto, Lat.] to pour liquor off gently.

DECANTATION, S. [Fr.] the act of pouring liquor off the lees.

DECANTER, S. a bottle of white or transparent glass, used to contain liquors in.

To DECAY, V. N. [dechoir, Fr.] to lose of its value, substance, or perfection; to be insensibly impaired; to consume gradually.

DECAY, S. a gradual loss of substance, value, or perfection. The effects of consumption or decline. Declension from prosperity.

DECEASE, S. [decessus, Lat.] death; departure from life; loss of life.

To DECEASE, V. N. [decessum, Lat.] to die.

DECEIT, S. [deceptio, Lat.] falshood; a

fraud; cheat; artifice; stratagem. In Law, every subtile, wily shift or devise, used to deceive, defraud, or impose on another.

DECEITFUL, Adj. full of fraud or artifice; not to be confided in, not sincere.

DECEITFUL, Adj. in a fraudulent, insincere manner.

DECEITFULNESS, S. the quality of imposing on a person to injure him.

DECEIVABLE, Adj. exposed to fraud or imposture; capable of leading a person into an error.

DECEIVABLENESS, S. the possibility of being imposed upon by false representations.

To DECEIVE, V. A. [decevoir, Fr.] to impose on a person's credulity by false appearances; to lead into an error or mistake. Figuratively, to disappoint, to misrepresent.

DECEIVER, S. one who imposes on the credulity of another.

DECEMBER, S. [from decem, Lat. ten] the twelfth month of the year, according to the modern computation of time; but formerly the tenth, as its name imports, the year then began in March.

DECEMPEDAL, Adj. [decempedalis, Lat.] measuring ten feet.

DECENCE, DECENCY, [decence, Fr.] a method of address or action becoming a person's sex, character, or rank. Figuratively, modesty. " Want of decency is want of sense." Roscom.

DECENNIAL, Adj. [decennium, Lat.] continuing, enduring the space of ten years.

DECENT, Part. [decens] becoming; fit, suitable, or proper. Neat.

DECENTLY, Adv. properly. Consistent with character, or the rules of good-breeding. Figuratively, modestly. With immodesty.

DECEPTIBILITY, S. [from deceptio, Lat.] liableness to be imposed on. " I be deceptibility of our decayed nature." Glanv.

DECEPTIBLE, Adj. liable to be deceived, or imposed on.

DECEPTION, S. [deceptio, Lat.] the act of imposing on a person, or leading him into an error; the state of a person imposed on, or in a mistake; a cheat; fraud; mistake, fallacy, or misrepresentation.

DECEPTIOUS, Adj. apt to impose upon, apt to deceive.

DECEPTORY, Adj. containing the means of leading a person into a mistake.

DECESSION, S. [decessio, Lat.] a departure.

To DECHARM, V. A. [decharmer, Fr.] to counteract a charm. " He was suddenly cured by decharming the witchcraft." Harvey.

To DECIDE, V. A. [decido, Lat.] to put an end to a dispute, or event.

DECIDER, S. the person who decides or determines a quarrel, or cause.

DECIDUOUS, Adj. [deciduus] in botany, soon withering, not lasting the whole year.

DE-

DECIDUOUSNESS, S. aptness to fall. In Botany, the quality of withering every year.

DECIMAL, Adj. [decimus, Lat. the tenth] numbered, or increasing by tens. Decimal arithmetic, is that which computes by decimal fractions.

To DECIMATE, V. A. [decimatum, Lat.] to tithe; to take the tenth part.

DECIMATION, S. the act of tithing; a selection of every tenth soldier by lot, for punishment, in a general mutiny.

To DECIPHER, V. A. [dechiffrer, Fr.] to explain something written in ciphers. Figuratively, to describe, to unfold, to discover, to unravel. "To decipher a perplexed affair."

DECIPHERER, S. one who explains any thing written in ciphers; an explainer.

DECISION, S. the determination of a dispute or difference; the result of an event.

DECISIVE, Adj. having the power of determining, or settling a difference.

DECISIVELY, Adv. conclusively, so as to put an end to a dispute.

DECISIVENESS, S. the power of determining or settling any difference.

DECISORY, Adj. able to determine, or fix beyond dispute.

To DECK, V. A. [decken, Belg.] to dress by way of ornament. "To deck with clouds th' uncolour'd sky." Par. Lost. To adorn or embellish with dress.

DECK, S. [decke, Dan.] the floor of a ship.

DECKER, S. one who adorns or dresses; one who covers a table.

To DECLAIM, V. A. [declamer, Fr.] to speak in a florid manner, like a rhetorician. To speak much against a thing; to run a thing down.

DECLAIMER, S. one who makes a florid speech in order to move the passions; an orator, or one who depreciates a person or thing.

DECLAMATION, S. [declamatio, Lat.] a florid discourse addressed to the passions. Figuratively, an ostentatious display of oratory.

DECLAMATOR, S. [Lat.] one who speaks or inveighs against a thing, or person. An orator. "This generous declamator." Tatler, No. 56.

DECLAMATORY, Adj. [declamatoire, Fr.] appealing to the passions; merely rhetorical flourish, oritorical.

DECLARATION, S. [Fr.] the discovery of a thing by words. Explanation. Affirmation. In Law, the laying out an action in any suit.

DECLARATIVE, Adj. explaining; making proclamation; express.

DECLARATORILY, Adv. in the form of a declaration; in a decretory form, expressly; opposed to promissively.

DECLARATORY, Adj. expressive; affirmative.

To DECLARE, V. A. [declaro, Lat.] to explain, or render free from obscurity. To manifest. To publish, or proclaim.

DECLAREMENT, S. discovery; manifestation. "A declarement of very different parts." Brown.

DECLARER, S. one who publishes, proclaims or makes any thing known.

DECLENSION, S. [declinaison, Fr. declinatio, Lat.] a gradual decrease from a greater degree to a less. Descent, declination, or declivity. "The declension from the land from that place to the sea." Burnet. In Grammar, the variation of the last syllable of a noun, whilst it continues to signify the same thing.

DECLINABLE, Adj. having a variety of endings according to the different relations it stands for.

DECLINATION, S. [declinatio, Lat.] descent; a change to a less perfect state. Decay. The act of bending down. "A declination of the head." An oblique direction. Variation from a fixed point; such as that of the needle from the north. In Astronomy, the distance of the sun, or a star from the equator. In Grammar, the inflexion, or declining a noun.

DECLINATOR, DECLINATORY, S. an instrument used in dialling to determine the declination, reclination, and inclination of planes.

To DECLINE, V. N. [decline, Lat. decliner, Fr.] to lean downwards. Figuratively, to go astray. To shun, refuse, or avoid to do a thing. To be impaired, to decay. To elude the force of an argument. To mention the different terminations of a declinable word.

DECLINE, S. decay, owing to age, time, or disease.

DECLIVITY, S. [declivis, Lat.] the gradual descent of an eminence, or hill.

DECLIVOUS, Adj. [declivis, Lat.] gradually descending from an eminence.

To DECOCT, V. A. [decoctum, Lat.] to prepare for use by boiling. In Pharmacy, to boil in water, so as to draw out its virtue. To boil till it grows thick, or strong.

DECOCTIBLE, Adj. that which may be boiled, or decocted.

DECOCTION, S. [decoction, Lat.] the act of boiling any thing to extract its virtues. Figuratively, the strained liquor, after it is boiled in water.

DECOCTURE, S. a preparation formed from boiling ingredients in water.

DECOLLATION, S. [decollatio, Lat.] the act of beheading. Figuratively, destruction. "He by decollation of all hope, annihilated his mercy." Brown.

DECOMPOSITE, Adj. [decompositus, Lat.] compounded a second time.

DECOM-

DECOMPOSITION, S. the act of compounding things, that have been compounded before.

To DECOMPOUND, V. A. [decompono, Lat.] to compound a second time. To form by a second composition.

DECOMPOUND, Adj. composed of words or things, as already compounded. Compounded a second time.

DECORAMENT, S. [from decus, Lat.] an embellishment or ornament. At Oxford, used for vinegar, mustard, salt, pepper, and other sauces, and the vessels which they are contained in.

To DECORATE, V. A. [decoratum, Lat.] to set off, adorn, or embellish with ornaments.

DECORATION, S. an ornament, an embellishment.

DECORATOR, S. one who adorns, decorates, or embellishes.

DECOROUS, Adj. [decorus, Lat.] suitable, agreeable, becoming. "It is not so decorous, in respect of God, that he should immediately do all the meanest and triflingest things himself." Ray.

To DECORTICATE, V. A. [decortico, Lat.] to strip off the bark or husk. To peel.

DECORTICATION, S. the act of stripping a thing of its bark or husk.

DECORUM, S. [Lat.] a behaviour suitable to the character of a person, considering likewise of a due observance of the established rules of politeness.

To DECOY, V. A. [koy, Belg. a cage] to lure or intice into a cage, or snare. Figuratively, to seduce.

DECOY, S. a place calculated to draw wild fowl into snares. Figuratively, allurements, temptation, a snare, alluding to the methods used by decoy-ducks to draw others of their species into a snare. "The devil could never have had such numbers, had he not used some as decoys to ensnare others." Government of the Tongue. A decoy-duck, is one that is trained to allure or draw others into a snare.

To DECREASE, V. N. [decresco, Lat. decroistre, Fr.] to become less either in length, weight, force, or bulk. To diminish. To make less.

DECREASE, S. the state of growing less; decay; the change made in the face of the moon from its full, till it return to its full again.

To DECREE, V. N. [decretum, Lat. decree, Fr.] to establish by law. To resolve. Actively, in dispose of a thing by law. To give judgment.

DECREE, S. [decret, Fr. decretum, Lat.] a law. The determination of a suit. A decision. In Canon Law, an ordinance established by the pope.

DECREMENT, S. [decrementum, Lat.]

the state of being reduced, or becoming less. The quantity lost by decay, or decrease.

DECREPIT, Adj. [decrepitus, Lat.] wasted, worn out, emaciated and enfeebled by age.

To DECREPITATE, V. A. [decrepo, Lat.] to calcine salts on the fire, till they cease to crackle.

DECREPITATION, S. the crackling noise made by salt, when over a fire in a crucible.

DECREPITNESS, DECREPITURE, S. the weakness and feebleness attending old age.

DECRESCENT, Part. [decrescens, Lat.] becoming less. Decaying.

DECRETAL, Adj. [decretum Lat.] relating to a decree.

DECRETAL, S. a letter of the Pope, by which some point in the ecclesiastical law is solved. A book of decrees or laws. A collection of the Pope's decrees.

DECRETORY, Adj. judicial, final; decisive.

DECRIAL, the endeavouring to lessen the esteem of any thing. Censure; condemnation.

To DECRY, V. A. [decrier, Fr.] to censure, blame, inveigh, or exclaim against a thing.

DECUMBENCE, DECUMBENCY, S. [decumbens, decumbo, Lat.] the act or posture of lying down. "The ancient manner of decumbency." Brown.

DECUMBITURE, S. the time a person takes to his bed in a disease.

DECUPLE, Adj. [decuplus, Lat.] tenfold, repeated, or continued ten times.

DECURSION, S. [decursio, Lat.] the act of flowing down. "The decursion of waters."

DECURTATION, S. The act of shortening.

To DECUSSATE, V. A. [decussatum, Lat.] to intersect, to cross at right angles.

DECUSSATION, S. the state of being crossed at right angles. The point in which two lines cross each other.

DEDENTITION, S. [from de and dentitio, Lat.] loss, or shedding of the teeth. "Dedentition or falling of teeth." Brown.

To DEDICATE, V. A. [dedicatum Lat.] to devote or appropriate for divine uses. Figuratively, to appropriate peculiarly to a purpose. To inscribe to a patron. "Dedicated to lord Chatham."

DEDICATE, Adj. [dedicatus, Lat.] devoted to a particular use.

DEDICATION, S. The act of consecrating some place or thing to divine uses. The address of an author to his patron, generally prefixed to his work.

DEDICATOR, S. one who ascribes or inscribes a work to a patron,

DEDI.

DE'DICATORY, Adj. belonging to, or in the style of a dedication.

DEDI'TION, S. [_deditio_, Lat.] a surrendering to an enemy.

To DEDU'CE, V. A. [_deduco_, Lat.] to describe in a continual or connected series. To infer from certain propositions.

DEDUCEMENT, S. that which is understood or inferred from any premises.

DEDU'CIBLE, Adj. to be inferred or known from principles laid down.

DEDU'CIVE, inferring or concluding from principles already laid down.

To DEDU'CT, V. A. [_deductum_, Lat.] to subtract, or take from.

DEDU'CTION, S. a consequence or inference drawn. That which is subtracted, or taken away from any sum, number, quantity, &c.

DEDU'CTIVE, Adj. that which may be deduced or inferred.

DEDU'CTIVELY, Adv. by way of inference, or consequence.

DEED, S. [_deed_, Sax. _daed_, Belg.] an action, or thing done. An exploit. Written evidence of any legal act. Fact, reality, opposed to fiction, preceded by every. " So now in very deed I might behold." _Lev._

DEE'DLESS, Adj. unactive, idle; without doing any thing.

To DEEM, V. N. [Part. _deemed_, from _deman_, Sax.] to judge; to think; to imagine; to suppose; To determine on due consideration.

DEEM, S. [from the verb.] judgment, decision, sentence. " What wicked _deem_ is this?" _Shal._

DEEP, Adj. [_deop, deope_, Sax.] applied to situation, low, opposed to high. Below the surface, or measured from the surface downwards. Figuratively, piercing far. Far from the entrance. " _Deep_ ambush'd in her silent den." _Dryd._ Not to be discovered at first sight; not obvious. " The sense lies _deep_." _Locke._ Sagacious, penetrating, profound, learned. " A _deep_ mathematician." _Arbuf._ Dark, applied to colours. Excessive. " _Deep_ ditties." Grave, applied to sounds.

DEEP, S. [_deope_, Belg.] the sea. " _Deep_ night," the stillest part thereof; midnight.

To DEE'PEN, V. A. to sink a great way below the surface. Applied to colours; to make a shade darker. To add to the dolefulness of a sound. " _Deepen_ the murmurs of the falling floods." _Pope._

DEE'PLY, Adv. far below the surface. With great study and application. Sorrowfully, profoundly, when used with words expressing grief. Nearly black, applied to colour. Excessively, vastly, highly; " He had _deeply_ offended both." _Bac._

DEE'PNESS, S. distance measured from the surface downwards.

DEER, S. [_deor_, Sax.] in natural History, a class of animals, the males of which

nare their heads adorned with branching horns; when killed, their flesh is called venison, there are various species.

To DEFA'CE, V. A. [_defacer_, F.] to destroy; to annihilate; to ruin; to disfigure.

DEFA'CEMENT, S. the act of defacing or disfiguring. " The image of God is purity, and the _defacement_, sin." _Tate._

DEFA'CER, S. one who destroys, or defaces.

To DEFA'LCATE, S. [_defalquer_, Fr.] to cut, or lop off. To take away or abridge a person's salary. Generally applied to money affairs.

DEFALCA'TION, S. diminution; abridgment; or deduction.

DEFAMA'TION, S. the uttering of reproachful language with an intent to lessen another person's character.

DEFA'MATORY, Adj. tending to lessen the character of another. Tending to make a person infamous.

To DEFA'ME, V. A. [from _de_ and _fama_, Lat.] to utter words with an intent to lessen a man's reputation, or render him infamous.

DEFA'ME, S. disgrace. Infamy.

DEFA'MER, S. one who asserts things injurious to the reputation of another. One who speaks against a thing or person.

DEFAU'LT, S. [_defaute_, Fr.] omission. Neglect. Fault. Defect. Want. In Law, absence from court at the time, or on the day appointed.

To DEFAU'LT, V. A. to fail; to forfeit, by breaking a contract.

DEFEA'SANCE, S. [_defaisance_, Fr.] the act of rendering a contract void. In Law, a condition annexed to an act, which when performed by the contracting party, the act is made void. The writing in which a _defeasance_ is contained. A defeat, or conquest. " After his loss _defeasance_." _F. Queen._

DEFEA'SIBLE, Adj. [_defaire_, Fr.] that which may be annulled, abrogated, or made void.

DEFEA'T, S. the overthrow of an army or navy. An act of destruction; deprivation; murther. " Upon whose life a damn'd defeat was made." _Shak._ This last, sense is seldom used.

To DEFEA'T, V. A. to beat or overcome an army; to frustrate, to disappoint.

To DEFE'CATE, V. A. [_defecatum_, Lat.] to clear liquors from dregs. Figuratively, to clear or brighten truth from any thing which renders it obscure. To purify; to brighten.

DEFE'CATE, Adj. [_defecatus_, Lat.] cleared, or purifying.

DEFECA'TION, S. the act of clearing or purifying.

DEFE'CT, S. [_defectus_, Lat.] imperfection; failing; want; a mistake or error; a fault.

To

To DEFE'CT, V. N. [*defectum*, Lat.] to be deficient; to fall short off. "The enquiries of moſt deſiſted by the way." Brown.

DEFECTIBILITY, S. a ſtate of failing; deficiency; imperfection.

DEFECTIBLE, Adj. imperfect; deficient; wanting.

DEFECTION, S. [*defectio*, Lat.] with failure; imperfection. A falling away; rebellion.

DEFECTIVE, Adj. [*defectivus*, Lat.] not adequate or ſuitable to the purpoſe for which it is deſigned; imperfect; inadequate to the rules, or ſtandard for perfecting any work; faulty, blameable. *Defective* nouns, or verbs in grammar, are thoſe without caſes, numbers, perſons, tenſes, or moods.

DEFECTIVENESS, S. the ſtate of being deficient in ſomething. A ſtate of imperfection.

DEFENCE, S. [*defenſe*, Fr. *defenſio*, Lat.] the method uſed to defend a perſon. Figuratively, guard, protection, ſecurity, reſiſtance, vindication, or juſtification. In Fortification, any thing which ſerves to ſecure the ſoldiers or the place. Formerly, a prohibition, from *defenſe*, Fr. "Severe *defences* may be made againſt wearing any linen." Temple.

DEFENCELESS, Adj. without any defence. Figuratively, unarmed, impotent, weak, unable to reſiſt.

To DEFEND, V. A. [*defendo*, Lat.] to guard, to protect, to ſupport, to ſecure, to forbid. "His taſte of that *defended* fruit." Par. Loſt. To vindicate, or juſtify.

DEFENDABLE, Adv. that which may be maintained or defended againſt attacks; that which may be vindicated or juſtified.

DEFENDANT, Adj. that which may defend or protect againſt the attack of an enemy.

DEFENDANT, S. he that endeavours to keep off an enemy. In Law, the perſon who is proſecuted or ſued, or defends a ſuit.

DEFENDER, S. one who protects or defends againſt an enemy. Figuratively, one who anſwers the objections raiſed againſt doctrine. In Law, one who eſpouſes the cauſe of one perſon againſt another, in a court of juſtice.

DEFENSATIVE, S. that which is made uſe of as a ſecurity or defence; guard.

DEFENSIBLE, Adj. that which may be defended. Figuratively, that which may be juſtified or vindicated.

DEFENSIVE, Adj. [*defenſif*, Fr.] proper for defence, oppoſed to *offenſive*. In a ſtate, poſture, or condition, proper to ward off the blows of an enemy.

DEFENSIVE, S. means to ſecure from danger. Figuratively, a ſafe-guard; a ſtate of defence.

DEFENSIVELY, Adv. ſo as to guard againſt the attacks of an enemy.

To DEFER, V. N. [*differo*, Lat.] to put off, to delay; to pay a regard, or reſpect to another's opinion, ſeldom uſed in the verb. Actively, to withold or delay the giving or performance of a thing expected; to refer or leave to the judgment of another. "The commiſſioners *deferred* the matter to the earl of Northumberland." Bac.

DEFERENCE, S. [Fr.] regard, reſpect, reverence, complaiſance, ſubmiſſion.

DEFIANCE, S. [*defi*, Fr.] a challenge upon a perſon to make good an accuſation. Figuratively, a daring contemptuous challenge.

DEFICIENCE, DEFICIENCY, S. [*deficiens*, Lat.] the want of ſomething; an imperfection, failure, or defect.

DEFICIENT, Adj. [*deficiens*, Lat.] imperfect, defective.

DEFFER, S. a challenger; a contemner; one who dares or defies a perſon to make good a charge.

To DEFILE, V. A. to render a thing unclean, or impure. Figuratively, to pollute, or render either legally, or ritually impure; to commit any ſin againſt the purity of the marriage bed, or the chaſtity of a virgin; to be guilty of any crime, that ſhall ſully our character.

To DEFILE, V. N. [*defiler*, Fr.] to march or divide in files; applied to an army.

DEFILE, S. [*defile*, Fr.] a narrow paſs, or paſſage, where only a few men can march a-breaſt.

DEFILEMENT, S. that which renders a thing foul or polluted. Figuratively, that which corrupts the virtue of a perſon.

DEFILER, S. one who pollutes the chaſtity of another; one who acts inconſiſtent with purity or chaſtity.

DEFINABLE, Adj. that which may be defined, or aſcertained.

To DEFINE, V. A. [*define*, Fr.] to explain a thing or word by the particular enumeration of its properties. In Law, to aſcertain the property of a thing.

DEFINER, S. one who explains the nature of a thing, by enumerating and particulariſing all its properties.

DEFINITION, S. [Fr. *definitio*, Lat.] an enumeration of all the ſimple ideas of words, in order to diſtinguiſh, aſcertain, or explain its nature. A *nominal* definition is that which explains the ſignification of a word; a *real* definition, is an enumeration of the principal attributes of a thing.

DEFINITIVE, Adj. [*definitivus*, Lat.] expreſs, poſitive, concluſive, deciſive, free from any ambiguity or uncertainty.

DEFINITIVELY, Adv. in a poſitive, expreſs, deciſive, concluſive manner.

DEFLAGRATION, S. [*deflagratio*, Lat.] in Chemiſtry, the ſetting fire to a thing, which will burn till it is totally conſumed.

To DEFLECT, V. N. [*deflecto*, Lat.] to turn aſide from its true courſe; to bend from a ſtraight line.

DE-

DEFLECTION, S. [from deflecto, Lat.] the act of deviating from its proper course or direction.

DEFLE'XURE, S. [from deflecto, Lat.] a bending or inclining downwards; the state of a thing turned aside, or from its right direction.

DEFLORA'TION, S. [Fr. defloratio, Lat.] the act of violating the chastity of a virgin.

To DEFLOUR, V. A. [deflorer, Fr.] to violate or pollute a virgin by acts of immodesty. Figuratively, to destroy the beauty or excellence of a thing.

DEFLOU'RER, S. a ravisher; or one who violates the chastity or honour of a virgin.

DEFLU'XION, S. [defluxio, Lat.] the act of flowing or falling down.

DEFLY, Adv. nimbly; elegantly. " They daunein defly." Spenf.

DEFOEDA'TION, S. [defoedus, Lat.] the act of rendering foul or filthy. The corrupting of the sense of an author. '' The defoedation of so many parts by a bad printer," Brahy.

To DEFO'RM, V. A. [deformo, Lat.] to disfigure, or injure the beauty or shape of any thing. To render unseemly and disagreeable.

DEFORMA'TION, S. [deformatio, Lat.] the act of distorting or spoiling the shape of a thing, or making it ugly. The state of a thing which has been deprived of its beauty.

DEFO'RMEDLY, Adv. in an ugly illshaped manner.

DEFO'RMITY, S. [deformitas, Lat.] the state of a thing which has lost its beauty, or other quality, which rendered it pleasing to the sight. Figuratively, any irregularity. Dishonour; disgrace.

To DEFRAU'D, V. A. [defraudo, Lat.] to deprive a person of his property by some fraud, or trick; used with of before the thing lost by the cheat.

DEFRAU'DER, S. one who deprives another by some trick, or false appearance.

To DEFRA'Y, V. A. [defrayer, Fr.] to pay or repay the expences a person has been at on our account.

DEFRA'YER, S. one who pays or discharges an expence.

DEFRA'YMENT, S. the payment of expences.

DEFTLY, Adv. in a neat, sprightly or skilful manner. " Deftly tune the reed." Gay.

DEFU'NCT, Adj. [defunctus, Lat.] dead; expired, deceased.

DEFUNCT, S. a person who is dead.

DEFUNCTION, S. death, or decease.

To DEFY, V. A. [defier, Fr.] to challenge or dare a person to fight. To treat with disdain and contempt.

No. IX.

DEFY, S. [defi, Fr.] a provocation, or challenge. " At this the challenger with fierce defy." Shakesp.

DEFY'ER, S. a person who challenges another to fight. Figuratively, one who treats a person disdainfully.

DEGE'NERACY, S. [degeneratio, Lat.] the acting unworthy of one's ancestors. Figuratively, the quitting a life of godliness for one of impiety. Meanness, whereby a person loses all sense or thought of the dignity of his nature.

To DEGE'NERATE, V. N. [degenero, Lat.] to act inconsistent with the virtues of one's ancestors. To sink from a noble to a mean or base state. To grow wild, base, or lose its perfection, applied to vegetables.

DEGE'NERATE, Adj. [degener, Lat.] beneath the character of the merits and virtue of one's ancestors. Unworthy, corrupted; having lost its virtue or value.

DEGE'NERATENESS, S. corruption, depravity.

DEGENERA'TION, S. a deviation from the virtues of one's ancestors. A sinking from a state of excellence, to an inferior one. Figuratively, the thing which has changed the properties of its kind.

DEGE'NEROUS, Adj. [degener, Lat.] depraved, sunk from the virtue of one's ancestors. Base, mean, unworthy.

DEGE'NEROUSLY, Adv. in a degenerate, base, or unworthy manner.

DEGRADA'TION, S. [Fr.] the depriving a man of any office or dignity. Figuratively, depravation, or placing in a lower and meaner state.

To DEGRA'DE, V. A. [degrader, Fr.] to deprive a person of any post or dignity. Figuratively, to lessen or diminish the excellence or value of a thing.

DEGRE'E, S. [degré, Fr. from gradus, Lat] station, quality, rank, condition, or dignity. Measure, proportion, or quantity. In Geometry, the 360th part of the circumference of a circle. The space of one degree, has been variously determined by different persons, in different times, but that of the French missionaries is the most exact. In Chemistry, a greater or less increments of heat. In Canon Law, an interval in kinship, from whence nearness of blood are computed. The different orders or classes of the angelic bodies. In the university, a dignity conferred on persons of a certain standing, and have performed the exercises required by the statutes.

By DEGRE'ES, Adv. gradually; by little and little imperceptibly.

To DEHO'RT, V. A. [dehortor, Lat.] to dissuade a person not to do something.

DEHORTA'TION, S. a dissuasion. Argument, counsel, or advice, used to keep a person from doing any action.

T t   DEHORTA-

DEHORTATORY, Adj. belonging or relating to dissuasion.

DEHORTER, S. one who uses arguments to dissuade a person from any thing.

DEICIDE, S. (from *deus*, Lat. and *cædo*, Lat.) the crime of murdering a Deity, applied peculiarly to the death of our blessed Saviour.

To DEJECT, V. A. (*dejectum*, Lat.) to render sorrowful, or melancholy. Figuratively, to affect a person's countenance by grief.

DEJECTED, Part. (*dejectus*, Lat.) cast down; mournful, melancholy.

DEJECTEDLY, Adv. in a dull, sorrowful, grievous, or mournful manner.

DEJECTEDNESS, S. the state of a person who is cast down, and dejected.

DEJECTION, S. a lowness of spirits occasioned by some loss, disappointment, or approaching calamity. Loss or an impaired state. "*Dejection* of appetite." *Arbuth.* The going to stool. "To provoke *dejection*." *Ray.*

DEIFICATION, S. the act of worshiping a person as a God.

DEIFORM, Adj. (from *deus*, Lat. and *forma*, Lat.) of a God like form.

To DEIFY, V. A. (*deifier*, Fr.) to make a God. To rank among the deities or gods. Figuratively, to praise too much. To enrol in a great degree of adulation.

To DEIGN, V. N. (pronounced *dain*, from *daigner*, Fr.) to condescend, to vouchsafe to submit. Actively, to grant a favour, to permit. "We *deign* him burial of his men." *Shak.*

DEIGNING, S. a condescension, permission, compliance.

DEIPAROUS, Adj. (from *deus*, Lat. a god, and *pario*, Lat. to bring forth) the bringing forth a god; an epithet applied to the blessed Virgin, the mother of our Saviour.

DEISM, S. (*deisme*, Fr.) the opinion of those, who own the belief of a God, but deny his having ever given a revelation.

DEIST, S. (*deiste*, Fr.) one who believes the existence of God, but disbelieves all revelation in general.

DEISTICAL, Adj. the opinion of one who denies all revealed religion.

DEITY, S. (*deité*, Fr.) divinity. The nature and essence of God. An idol, a heathen god.

DELATION, S. the act of carrying, or conveying. "The *delation* of sounds." *Bacon.* An accusation, charge, or information.

DELATOR, S. (Lat.) an accuser, or informer.

To DELAY, V. A. (*delayer*, Fr.) to defer, or put off. To keep a person in suspense. Figuratively, to hinder. Neuterly, to stop; to hinder.

DELAY, S. the act of deferring or putting off; a stay; a stop.

DELAYER, S. one who defers or postpones a thing; a putter off.

DELECTABLE, Adj. (*delectabilis*, Lat.) affording or conveying pleasure either to the sight, ear, taste, or mind.

DELECTABLENESS, S. pleasantness, agreeableness.

DELECTABLY, Adv. in such a manner as to afford pleasure, delight, or satisfaction.

DELECTATION, S. (*delectatio*, Lat.) pleasure; delight.

DELEGATE, V. A. (*delegatum*, supine of *delego*, Lat.) to send away. To send in the character of an embassador. To intrust; or give a person authority to exercise a power; to communicate authority. In Law, to appoint judges to determine a particular cause.

DELEGATE, S. (*delegatus*, Lat.) any person authorized to act for another. The *court of Delegates*, is that court wherein all causes of appeal by way of devolution from either of the arch-bishops, are decided.

DELEGATE, Adj. (*deputatus*, Lat.) deputed; or authorized to act for another.

DELEGATION, S. (*delegatio*, Lat.) the act of sending away; the assignment of a debt. In Law, an extraordinary commission given a judge to take cognisance of some cause, which would not otherwise come before him.

DELETERIOUS, Adj. (*deleterius*, Lat. ... Gr.) noxious, hurtful, deadly, fatal; applied to such things as are of a poisonous or pernicious nature.

DELETERY, Adj. (*deleterius*, Lat.) hurtful, destructive; deadly; poisonous. "Well stored with *deletery* med'cines." *Hud.*

DELETION, S. (*deletio*, Lat.) destruction. "If there be a total *deletion* of every person." *Hale.*

DELF, DELFE, (*delfan*, Sax. to dig) a mine, a quarry, or large cavity made by digging. "The *delf* would be overflown." *Ray.* A *delf* of coal is that which lies in veins under ground. In Heraldry, one of the abatements in honour, being a square in the middle of an escutcheon, and is used to denote cowardice. Glazed earthen ware, poorly imitating china.

DELIBATION, S. (*delibatio*, Lat.) taste; a smack. Figuratively, an essay, a trial.

To DELIBERATE, V. N. (*delibero*, Lat.) to think on, to consider, to hesitate.

DELIBERATE, Part. (*deliberatus*, Lat.) circumspect; discreet; wary; considerate. Figuratively, slow, tedious.

DELIBERATELY, Adv. circumspectly, warily, discreetly.

DELIBERATENESS, S. circumspection. Coolness; caution, consideration.

DELIBER-

DELIBERA'TION, S. [deliberatio, Lat.] the act of considering or weighing things before the making a choice.

DELI'BERATIVE, Adj. [deliberativus, Lat.] relating to consideration; or premeditation.

DE'LICACY, S. [delicatesse, Fr. of delicia, Lat.] daintiness. Any thing which affects the senses with great pleasure. Elegant softness of form. Nicety, or accuracy, neatness. Politeness. Tenderness of constitution. A disposition that cannot bear any excess.

DE'LICATE, Adj. [delicat, Fr.] fine, opposed to coarse. Beautiful or pleasing and delightful to the eye. Pleasant to the taste. Dainty in the choice of food. Chaste, seclof, polite. Soft, effeminate, or unfit for labour. Pure; free; serene, clear. "The air is delicate." Shakesp.

DE'LICATELY, Adv. beautifully. Finely, opposed to coarsely. Daintily; luxuriously. "Eat not delicately or nicely." Taylor. Choicely; politely; effeminately.

DE'LICATENESS, S. softness; effeminacy.

DE'LICATES, S. niceties, rarities, delicious food.

DELI'CIOUS, Adj. [delicieux, Fr.] giving or conveying exquisite pleasure to the senses or the mind.

DELI'CIOUSLY, Adv. in an elegant, luxurious or rapturous manner.

DELI'CIOUSNESS, S. the quality of affording or conveying exquisite pleasure to the senses.

DELIGA'TION, S. [deligatio, Lat.] the combining the several parts of a thing together by binding.

DELI'GHT, S. [delice, Span. delice, Fr.] that which affords pleasure to the mind or the senses.

To DELI'GHT, V. A. [delecto, Lat. delecter, Ital.] to take pleasure in the enjoyment of a thing. To satisfy; to repeat any action with pleasure, to communicate pleasure; used with in. Neuterly, to be pleased, satisfied or contented.

DELI'GHTFUL, Adj. that which affords or conveys pleasure to the senses or mind.

DELI'GHTFULLY, Adv. in such a manner, as to afford pleasure, satisfaction, and delight.

DELI'GHTFULNESS, S. pleasure, satisfaction, gratification, joy. The quality of communicating pleasure.

DELI'GHTSOME, Adj. affording great delight or pleasure.

DELI'GHTSOMELY, Adv. in such a manner as to afford great delight or pleasure.

To DELI'NEATE, V. A. [delineare, Lat.] to draw the first sketch; to design. To paint the resemblance of a thing. Figuratively, to describe accurately.

DELINEA'TION, S. the first draught or design of a thing. Figuratively, a description.

DELI'NQUENCY, S. [delinquentis, Lat.] a failure. An omission. A thing done wilfully against any known law.

DELI'NQUENT, S. [delinquens, Lat.] one who has been guilty of some crime or fault. An offender. A criminal.

To DELI'QUATE, V. N. [deliquesco, Lat.]. to melt. To dissolve. To be dissolved.

DELIQUA'TION, S. [deliquatio, Lat.] the act of melting or dissolving. Figuratively, a solution, or the state of a thing dissolved.

DELI'QUIUM, S. [Lat.] in Chymistry, the act of distilling by fire.

DELI'RIOUS, Adj. [delirius, Lat.] insane; light-headed; raving from the violence of some disorder. Figuratively, doting.

DELI'RIUM, S. [Lat.] a kind of phrensy or madness, caused often in fevers, by the too impetuous a motion of the blood.

To DELI'VER, V. A. [delivrer, Fr.] to give or present a thing which was given for that purpose by another. To call off. To deliver from, to free from any danger. To pronounce, to relate, to repeat. To bring into the world, used with of. Actively, to surrender, to put into a person's hands, or leave to his discretion. To deliver over, used with down or over, to transmit any transaction by means of writing. Joined to up, to surrender.

DELI'VERANCE, S. [delivrance, Fr.] the act of giving or surrendering a thing. The act of freeing a person from captivity, or distress. The manner of pronouncing or speaking. The act of producing or bringing children into the world.

DELI'VERER, S. one who gives a thing into the hands of another. One who frees another from danger or captivity. One who pronounces or relates a thing.

DELI'VERY, S. the act of surrendering a thing to another. A release from bondage or distress. Speech, pronunciation. The bringing a former child from the womb.

DE'LL, S. [dal, Belg. see DELF] a pit, valley, or any hollow made in the ground. "Bushy dell in this wild wood." Par. Lost.

DEL'PH, S. [from delf] a glazed kind of earthen ware.

DELU'DABLE, Adj. liable to be deceived, deluded, or drawn aside.

To DELU'DE, V. A. [deludo, Lat.] to beguile; to deceive; seduce or impose on. Figuratively, to disappoint.

DELU'DER, S. one who deceives, imposes on, beguiles, seduces, or deludes.

To DELVE, V. A. [delvan, Belg.] to dig or open the ground. Figuratively, to

        T t 2   found

found one's opinion, to fathom, to get to the bottom of an affair. " I cannot delve him to the root." *Shak.*

DE'LVER, S. a digger, or one who opens the ground with a spade, &c.

DE'LUGE, S. [Fr. from *diluvium*, Lat.] a flood, or inundation of water covering the earth. Figuratively, the overflowing of a river. Any sudden, unforeseen, and irresistible calamity. Any corruption, or depravation, which spreads rapidly.

To DE'LUGE, V. A. to drown or cover with water. To overflow with water. Figuratively, to overwhelm with any calamity.

DELU'SION, S. [*delusio*, Lat.] the act of deluding, or imposing on a person. Figuratively, a false appearance or illusion.

DELU'SIVE, Adj. [*delusus*, Lat.] having the power to deceive, impose on, or delude.

DELU'SORY, Adj. [from *delusus*, Lat.] apt to deceive.

DEMAGOGUE, S. [from *demos*, Gr. and *ago*, Gr.] the ringleader of a faction or tumult.

DEMA'ND, S. [*demande*, Fr.] the asking of a thing with authority. Sometimes implying a necessity of granting in the person applied to. Enquiry after in order to buy. " The demand, for these my papers entreats daily." *Spect.* In Law, the asking or claiming what is due.

To DEMA'ND, V. A. [*demander*, Fr.] to claim ; to ask for with authority ; to ask.

DEMA'NDABLE, Adj. that which may be claimed or demanded as a due.

DEMA'NDANT, S. in Law, the person who is plaintiff in a real action.

DEMA'NDER, S. one who claims or asks with authority. Figuratively, a dun or one who asks or demands a debt.

To DEME'AN, [*demener*, Fr.] to behave. To lessen, or undervalue. To do any thing below one's character or rank in life.

DEME'ANOUR, S. [*demener*, Fr.] behaviour, carriage, conduct.

DEME'ANS, S. [plural] in Law, an estate which a man possesses in his own right.

DEME'RIT, S. [*demerite*, Fr.] the want of merit. Used formerly, instead of merit or desert. " My demerits may speak unbecoming." *Shak.*

To DEME'RIT, V. A. [*demeriter*, Fr.] to act contrary to one's duty, and thereby deserve blame.

DEME'RSION, S. [*demersio*, Lat.] the plunging under the water, or drowning. In Chemistry, the putting any thing into a dissolving liquid.

DEMI-CULVERIN, S. In Gunnery, is from four inches to four and three quarters bore, from ten feet, to ten feet and one third long, and from two thousand to three thousand pound weight.

DEMI-GOD, S. one who was mortal by birth from one of his parents, but had a deity for the other ; and was raised to cohabit with the deities on account of his exploits.

DEMI'SE, S. [*demis*, Fr.] death, decease. Used chiefly in law writings.

To DEMI'SE, V. A. [*demis demisi*, Fr.] bequeath or dispose of by will. " My executors shall not have power to demise my lands." *Swift.*

To DEMI'T, V. A. [*demitto*, Lat.] to depress, to hang or bend down ; to let fall. " They presently demit and let fall the same." *Brown.*

DEMO'CRACY, S. [*dēmokratia*, Gr.] form of government wherein the supreme power or authority is lodged in the people.

DEMOCRA'TICAL, Adj. belonging to that government wherein the supreme power is lodged in the people.

To DEMO'LISH, V. A. [*demolir*, Fr.] to pull down, raze or destroy. Figuratively, to destroy reputation, or fame by remarks or criticism. " I expected the fabric of my book would, long since, have been demolished." *Tillot.*

DEMO'LISHER, S. one who destroys, demolishes, or pulls down.

DEMOLI'TION, S. the act of demolishing, or destroying ; destruction.

DE'MON, S. [*daemon*, Lat.] a spirit. An evil spirit.

DEMO'NIAC, DEMONI'ACAL, Adj. devillish. Possessed or produced by the devil, or some evil spirit.

DEMO'NIAC, S. one possessed by the devil or some evil spirit.

DEMO'NIAN, Adj. [from *daemon*] devillish ; belonging or relating to the devil. " Demonian spirits." *Par. Lost.*

DEMONO'LOGY, S. [from *daemon*, Gr. and *logos*] a discourse on the nature and practices of evil spirits.

DEMON'STRABLE, Adj. [*demonstrabilis*, Lat.] that which may be proved beyond a contradiction.

To DEMON'STRATE, V. A. [*demonstro*, Lat.] to prove in such a manner as to convince the most prejudiced ; to prove by incontestible evidence.

DEMONSTRA'TION, S. [Fr. *demonstratio*, Lat.] a clear and invincible proof of the truth of a proposition. The shewing the agreement or disagreement of two ideas, by the intervention of one or more proofs which have a constant, immutable and visible connection one with another. Figuratively, indubitable evidence or proof.

DEMON'STRATIVE, Adj. [*demonstrativus*, Lat.] applied to such proofs as cannot be denied.

DEMON'STRATIVELY, Adv. evidently. Figuratively, clearly, plainly, certainly.

DEMON-

DEMONSTRATOR, S. one who proves by demonstration, one who explains a thing. A lecturer. "Demonstrator of anatomy."

DEMULCENT, Part. [demulcens, Lat.] in Phyfic, softening, mollifying.

To DEMUR, V. N. [demeurer, Fr.] to delay a procefs in Law. To make; to hefitate; to doubt; to deliberate; to fufpend ones judgment.—To doubt.

DEMUR, S. doubt. Hefitation. Sufpenfe of judgment.

DEMURE, Adj. [des mœurs, Fr.] behaving in a fober, precife, or modeft manner. Affectedly. Grave, or modeft.

To DEMURE, V. N. [from the noun] to look precifely; to behave with affected modefty. "Your wife Octavia with her modeft eyes drawing upon me." Shak.

DEMURELY, Adv. in an affected, fober, precife, or modeft manner.

DEMURENESS, S. affected modefty, fobriety or gravity. Precifenefs.

DEMURRAGE, S. [demeurer, Fr.] in Commerce, an allowance made by merchants and mafters of fhips, for their ftay in a port beyond the time appointed.

DEMURRER, S. in Law, a kind of proof made in an action, for a court to take time to confider of fome different point.

DEMY, S. [demi, Fr. of dimidium, Lat.] a larger fized paper, the fame as that on which this dictionary is printed.

DEN, S. [den, Sax. denne, Belg.] a cavern or hollow place under ground. The cave of a wild beaft.

DENAY, S. denial, refufal. "My love can give no place, bids no denay." Shak.

DENBIGHSHIRE, a county of N. Wales, thirty-nine miles in length, and fifteen in breadth, is bounded on the E. by Flintfhire and Shropfhire, on the W. by Caernarvonfhire, on the S. by Merionethfhire, and on the N. by the Irifh fea. It contains fix thoufand four hundred houfes, thirty-eight thoufand four hundred inhabitants, fiftyfeven parifhes, and four market-towns. It has fome good paftures, and feeds a great number of horned cattle, fheep, and goats. The air is good, but fharp, and the foil hilly, intermixed with fruitful valleys. Among the hills there are ftones called Druid-ftones, and fmall pillars, with infcriptions, which no one hitherto has been able to read.

DENDROLOGY, S. [from dendron, Gr. and logos, Gr.] a Natural Hiftory of trees.

DENHAM, Sir John.—This elegant writer was the only Son of Sir John Denham, Knight, of little Horfley, who was, at the time of our Author's Birth, which happened in 1615, Lord Chief Baron of the Exchequer in Ireland, and one of the Lords Juftices of that Kingdom; In confequence of which our Author was born in Dublin, but was brought over from thence at two years old, on the promotion of his Father to the Bank of a Baron of the Exchequer in England.

His grammatical Learning he received in London, and in Michaelmas Term 1631, was removed from thence to Oxford, where he was enter'd a Gentleman Commoner of Trinity College; but inftead of fhewing any early Dawnings of that Genius which afterwards fhone forth in him, he appear'd a flow dreaming young Man, and one whofe darling Paffion was Gaming.—Here he continued for three Years, when, having pafs'd his Examinations, and taken a Degree at Bachelor of Arts, he came to London, and entered himfelf at Lincoln's-Inn, where he applied pretty clofely to the Study of the Law.—Yet his darling Vice was ftill predominant, and he frequently found himfelf ftripped to his laft Shilling, by which he fo greatly difpleas'd his Father, that he was obliged, in Appearance at leaft, to reform, for fear of being abfolutely abandoned by him.—On his Death, however, being no longer reftrained by parental Authority, he again gave Way to it, and being a Dupe to Sharpers, foon fquander'd away feveral thoufand Pounds.

In the latter end of 1641, however, to the Aftonifhment of every one, his Genius broke forth in a full blaze of Meridian brightnefs, in that juftly celebrated and admir'd Tragedy the Sophy, and foon after fhone out again in his Poem of Cooper's Hill.—In the fame year he was prick'd for High Sheriff for the County of Surry, and made governor of Farnham Caftle, for the King.—But being poffefs'd of no great Share of military Knowledge, he prefently quitted that Poft, and retired to his majefty at Oxford.

And now the grand rebellion being broke out in its full Force, he fhewed the warmeft Attachment to the Royal Family, and in the courfe of their unhappy affairs, became of fignal fervice to them.—In the year 1647, when the King had been delivered into the hands of the Army, he undertook, on the behalf of the queen mother, to gain accefs to his Majefty, which he found means to do by the Affiftance of Hugh Peters.—On this occafion the King converfed with him in an unreferved manner, with regard to his affairs, and entrufting him with nine cyphers, commanded him to ftay privately in London, in order to receive all his letters to and from his correfpondents, all which were conftantly decypher'd and undecypher'd by Mr. Cowley, at that time with the Queen mother in France. This truft he performed with great punctuality and fafety for fome time, till at length Mr. Cowley's head being known, this affair was difcovered, and Mr. Denham obliged to make his efcape to France.—In 1648 he was fent ambaffador, together with lord Crofts, to Poland, where he fucceeded fo well as to bring back ten thoufand pounds for the King.

invied

ferved there on his Majefty's Scottish fubjects.

About 1652 he return'd to England, and refided about a year at the Earl of Pembroke's at Wilton, having quite exhaufted his own fortune, by his paffion for gaming, and the expences he had been at during the civil war. —It does not clearly appear what became of him between that time and the reftoration, though it is moft probable he went over again to France, and refided there till King Charles II's return from St. Germain's to Jerfey, when he was immediately appointed, without any follicitation, furveyor general of all his Majefty's buildings, and at the coronation of that Monarch made knight of the Bath.

On fome difcontent arifing from a fecond marriage, he for a little Time loft his fenfes, but on his recovery, continued in great efteem at court for his poetical abilities, efpecially with the king, who was fond of poetry, and during his exile us'd frequently to give Mr. Denham arguments to write on.

This ingenious gentleman died at an office he had built for himfelf near Whitehall, March 10, 1668, Ætatis 55, and was buried in Weftminfter Abbey, leaving behind him among the feveral works wherby his poetical fame ftands eftablifhed, only one dramatic one, viz.

The Sophy, a tragedy.

As a poet we need only refer to the teftimonials of many writers, particularly Dryden and Pope, in his favour.—As to his moral character, he has had no vice imputed to him but that of gaming, and although authors have been filent as to his Virtues, yet if we may judge from his works, he was a good-natur'd man and an eafy companion; and from his actions it appears that he was one of ftrict honour and integrity, and in the day of danger and tumult of unfhaken loyalty to the fuffering intereft of his fovereign.

DENIABLE, Adj. that which may be refufed to be granted, or believed.

DENIAL, S. [from deny] refufal. The perfifting in one's innocence. Abjuration, or renouncing.

DENIER, S. one who refufes to grant a favour or affent to a truth. One who will not acknowledge.

DENIGRATION, S. [denigratio, Lat.] the act of blackening.

DENIZATION, S. [from deniza] the act of enfranchifing a ftranger, by which means he enjoys the fame privileges as a natural fubject, fuch as the power of purchafing lands, &c.

DENIZEN, DENISON, S. [denofchyr, Brit.] in Law, an alien enfranchifed or made free; and thereby enabled to purchafe and poffefs lands, to hold any office or dignity, &c.

To DENIZEN, V. A. to enfranchife, to

make free. Figuratively, to proteft, encourage, or defend. " Falfhood is denizen'd." *Drum.*

DENMARK, a kingdom of Europe, bounded on the E. by the Baltick fea, on the W. and N. by the ocean, and on the S. by Germany. The country is generally flat, and the foil a barren fand. The air is rendered foggy by the neighbourhood of the feas and the lakes, of which it is full. Denmark, properly fo called, confifts of Jutland and the iflands of Zeeland, and Funen, with the little ifles about them; but the king of Denmark's dominions contain the kingdom of Norway, the duchies of Holftein, Oldenburgh, and Delmenhorft. There is no confiderable river, and the winter continues feven or eight months. In the fummer the heat is very confiderable, and the days are long. The commodities are corn, pulfe, but chiefly horfes, and large beeves. The kingdom of Denmark was formerly elective, but fince 1660 it was rendered hereditary, even to the daughters, partly by confent, and partly by force; at which time the nobility loft moft of their privileges, by the weaknefs of their prefent king, who has been prevailed upon by the queen dowager to imprifon the queen confort, and other fteps equally ridiculous, it is imagined the ftate of Denmark is now at the eve of a revolution. They have very few laws, and thofe are fo plain that they have little need of lawyers, for caufes are foon tried. They allow but of one apothecary in a town, except at Copenhagen, where there are two. Their fhops are vifited by the phyficians once a-week, and all the perifhed drugs are deftroyed. The inhabitants are proteftants fince the year 1522, when they embraced the confeffion of Augfburg. The forces which the king of Denmark has ufually on foot are near 40,000, but moft of them are in the pay of other princes. The revenues are computed at 500,000 L a-year, which arife from the crown lands and duties. The produce of Norway confifts in pitch, tar, fifh, oil, and deal boards. Copenhagen is the capital town. Len. from 25. 25. to 30. 30. lat. from 54. 0. to 57. 30.

To DENOMINATE, V. A. [denominatus, Lat.] to name, to give a name or appellation to.

DENOMINATION, S. [denominatio, Lat.] a name given to a thing arifing from fome peculiar quality belonging to it.

DENOMINATIVE, Adj. that which gives or obtains a diftinct or peculiar name or appellation.

DENOMINATOR, S. that which gives a particular name or appellation to a thing. In Fractions, the number below the line, fhewing the number of parts, which any integer is fuppofed to be divided into.

DENO-

DENOTA'TION, S. [denotatio, Lat.] the act of ascertaining that a particular thing belongs to a particular person.

To DENO'TE, V. A. [denoto, Lat.] to point out; to mark; to be a sign of; to imply, or signify. "A quick pulse denotes a fever."

To DENOUNCE, V. A. [denoncer, Fr.] to declare or threaten by proclamation. Figuratively. In Law, to pass sentence.

DENOU'NCEMENT, S. the act of proclaiming any threat, or sentence.

DENOU'NCER, S. one who declares some menace, or impending sentence, or punishment.

DENSE, Adj. [densus, Lat.] close, compact, thick, containing much in a small compass. Having few or very small pores.

DE'NSITY, S. [densitas, Lat.] a property of bodies arising from the closeness of their particles, and the smallness of their pores. Thickness; solidity; compactness.

DENT, S. [Fr.] a notch, defect made by breaking a piece out of the edge of a thing. A mark made in the surface of a thing.

DE'NTAL, Adj. [dentalis, Lat.] belonging to the teeth. In Natural History, a small shell-fish.

DENTE'LLATED, Adj. In Botany, notched, jagged, formed like the teeth of a saw on the edges; named savoid by Miller.

DENTI'CULATED, Part. [denticulatus, Lat.] set with small jagged teeth.

DENTICULA'TION, S. [denticulatus, Lat.] In Natural History, set with small teeth, notched, or jagged.

DE'NTIFRICE, S. [from dens, Lat. and frico, Lat.] in Medicine, a powder to cleanse or fasten the teeth.

DENTI'TION, S. [dentitio, Lat.] the act, or time of breeding teeth.

DENUDA'TION, S. the act of stripping naked. The act of freeing or divesting one's self from incumbrances.

To DENU'DE, V. A. [denudo, Lat.] to make naked. Figuratively, to divest a thing of its natural covering. "Denude a vine-branch of its leaves." Ray. Seldom used, unless by technical writers.

DENUNCIA'TION, S. [denonciation, Lat.] the act of publishing any menace; or threatening any punishment.

DENU'NCIATOR, S. [from denuncio, Lat.] the person who threats.

To DENY, V. A. [denier, Fr. denego, Lat.] to contradict an accusation, opposed to confess. To refuse a thing requested. To disown. To renounce. To disregard. Used in Scripture with the personal pronouns, to forego all prejudices, and advantages, that nothing may obstruct the work of grace, or hinder our growth in piety.

To DEOBSTRUCT, V. A. [deobstruo, Lat.] to clear from impediments; to free a passage.

DEOBSTRUENT, S. [deobstruens, Lat.] a medicine which, by its dissolving viscidities, opens the pores or passages of the human body.

DE'ODAND, S. [deodandum, Lat.] In Law, a thing devoted or forfeited to God for the pacifying his wrath, in case of a Christian's coming to a violent end, without the fault of a reasonable creature; thus, if a horse should strike its keeper and kill him, the horse is to be a deodand, i. e. forfeited, sold, and the money given to the poor.

To DEO'PPILATE, V. A. [from deoppilo, Lat.] to clear a passage from obstructions.

To DEPAINT, V. A. [depeint, Fr.] to form the resemblance of a thing by painting. To describe.

To DEPA'RT, V. N. [depart from departir, Fr.] to go away from a place. Figuratively, to cease from practising a thing. To revolt; to quit; to leave, or apostatize; joined to away from. To perish; to be lost; used with away. To die. Actively, to quit, or leave a person or place.

DEPA'RT, S. [depart, Fr.] the act of going away. Figuratively, death. "Tidings were brought me of your loss and his depart." Among refiners, a method of separating gold from silver, silver from copper, copper from iron, iron from calaminaris, and calaminaris from fixed nitre by means of aqua fortis. The silver and gold are at first incorporated together in a crucible by means of fire, then cast into cold water; afterwards the particles thus produced are put into a stone vessel with aqua fortis over a fire for an hour, after which the gold will be found precipitated in a calx, to the bottom of the vessel, and the silver will be imbibed by the aqua fortis; this silver may again be precipitated in the same manner, by adding water to the aqua fortis in which the gold was precipitated, and adding a piece of copper, which will be dissolved in the same manner as the silver was, and the silver will then be found precipitated in the same manner as the gold was at the first experiment.

DEPA'RTER, S. a refiner, one who purifies metals by aqua fortis, &c. one who departs.

DEPA'RTMENT, S. [departement, Fr.] a peculiar province, lot, or employment.

DEPA'RTURE, S. [from depart] the act of going from a person or place. Death; the act of forsaking, or quitting.

To DEPA'STURE, V. A. [departus from depascor, Lat.] to graze, to eat up. "Removing to fresh land, as they have depastured the former." Spenser.

To DEPAU'PERATE, V. A. [depauperatum] to make poor, or barren; to impoverish liquors.

To

To DEPE'ND, V. N. [*dependeo*, Lat.] to hang. To proceed from. To be subject to the will of another. To be supported by another. To be in suspense, or undetermined. To *depend upon*; to confide in, rely on.

DEPE'NDANCE, S. [Fr.] something hanging from another. Relation, or connexion of one thing to another. The state of being subject to, or at the disposal of another. Figuratively, the things or persons which are subject to, and at the disposal of another. Reliance, trust, confidence.

DEPE'NDANT, Adj. [Fr.] subject to, or in the disposal of another.

DEPE'NDANT, S. [Fr.] one who is subject to, at the disposal of, or maintained by another.

DEPE'NDENCE, DEPE'NDENCY, S. [this word with many others of the same ending, are indifferently written, with *ance* or *ence*, *ancy* or *ency*] one who is subject to the will of another. That which is subordinate to, or appendant to another. Connexion or a series, having a mutual relation to each other. Figuratively, trust, reliance, confidence.

DEPE'NDENT, Adj. [*dependens*, Lat. this, and other words of the same ending, are written either *ant* or *ent*] hanging down.

DEPE'NDENT, S. indebted to another for protection, safety, or support.

DEPE'NDER, S. a person who confides in another.

To DEPI'CT, V. A. [*depictum*, Lat.] to paint the likeness of any thing. Figuratively, to convey the idea of a person or thing by an accurate or elegant description thereof.

DEPI'LOUS, Adj. [fee DEPILATORY] without hair or fur. " Corticated and *depilous*." *Brown.*

DEPLE'TION, S. [*depletus* of *depleo*, Lat.] in Physic, the act of emptying. " *Depletion* of the vessels gives room to the fluid to expand itself." *Arbuth.*

DEPLO'RABLE, Adj. [*deploro*, Lat.] that which causes or produces sorrow. Figuratively, used to increase the signification of a word, implying sometimes *very great*, despicable or contemptible. " *Deplorable* nonsense." " I have a most *deplorable* head."

DEPLO'RABLENESS, S. the state of being an object of grief, or wretchedness.

DEPLO'RABLY, Adv. lamentably, miserably; sorrowfully.

DEPLO'RATE, Adj. [*deploratus*, Lat.] wretched, occasioning sorrow; lamentable. " The case or thing is then swift *deplorate*, when reward goes over to the wrong side." *L'Estrange.*

To DEPLO'RE, V. A. [*deploro*, Lat.] to lament, or mourn for any calamity, or misfortune.

DEPLO'RER, S. one who laments, or grieves.

DEPLUMA'TION, S. [*deplumatio*, Lat.] the act of plucking off feathers.

DEPO'NENT, S. [*deponens*, Lat.] one who gives evidence or testimony in a court of justice; an evidence, or witness. In Grammar, those verbs which have an active signification, though they have no active voice.

To DEPO'PULATE, V. N. [*depopulatus*, Lat.] to unpeople ; to lay waste a country, to make desolate.

DEPOPULA'TION, S. the act of rendering a country waste, desolate, or uninhabited.

DEPOPULA'TOR, S. one who destroys the inhabitants of a country. A destroyer.

To DEPO'RT, V. A. [*deporter*, Fr.] to carry, or behave, " *deport himself* in the most graceful manner."

DEPO'RT, S. demeanour; behaviour. Carriage. See DEPORTMENT.

DEPO'RTMENT, S. [*deportment*, Fr.] conduct, demeanour; behaviour, carriage.

To DEPO'SE, V. A. [*depositum*, Lat.] to lay down, used with *upon*. To deprive a person of a post, or dignity. To give testimony on oath in a court of justice.

DEPO'SITARY, S. [*depositaire*, Fr.] one who is intrusted with the care of a thing.

To DEPO'SITE, V. A. [*depositum*, Lat.] to lay up. To give as a pledge or security. To place at interest.

DEPO'SITE, S. [*depositum*, Lat.] any thing committed to the care or charge of another, generally applied to things of value. A pledge, a pawn, or security. The state of a thing pledged. " And have now put in *deposite*." *Bacon.*

DEPOSI'TION, S. the act of giving testimony in a court on oath. The act of dethroning a prince.

DEPO'SITORY, S. the place where things which are intrusted with a person, are laid up.

DEPRAVA'TION, S. [*depravatio*, Lat.] the act of spoiling, corrupting or rendering a thing less perfect, or valuable. The state of a thing which hath lost any good quality or virtue. Figuratively, defamation whereby the esteem of a person or thing is destroyed. " Without a theme for *depravation*." *Shak.*

To DEPRA'VE, V. A. [*depravo*, Lat.] to corrupt, to spoil, to seduce from goodness ; to adulterate.

DEPRA'VEMENT, S. that which renders a thing vicious or bad.

DEPRA'VER, S. one who corrupts or makes bad.

DEPRA'VITY, S. corruption ; a change from good to bad, or from virtue to vice.

To DE'PRECATE, V. N. [*deprecatus*, of *deprecor*, Lat.] to pray for the averting some punishment : to ask pardon for a crime.

To

To requeſt with importunity and humility. Actively, to pray for mercy, or to avert puniſhment.

DEPRECA'TION, S. [*deprecatio*] a begging pardon, or prayer for the averting ſome imminent puniſhment.

DEPRECATIVE, DE'PRECATORY, Adj. uſed as an apology; excuſe, or means of averting ſome miſchief.

DEPRECA'TOR, S. [Lat.] one who ſues or intercedes for another. An interceſſor. One who apologizes for another, in order to excuſe him from puniſhment.

To DEPRE'CIATE, V. A. [*de* and *pretium*, Lat. a price] to ſpeak meanly of a thing. To under-value, to under-rate.

To DEPREDATE, V. A. [*deprædatus*, Lat.] to rob, plunder, or pillage. To ſeize. To conſume, or deſtroy. " Leſs ſubject to be conſumed and depredated by the ſpirits." *Bac.*

DEPREDA'TION, S. [*depredatio*] the act of ſpoiling, robbing, or ſeizing on as plunder. Waſte, deſtruction.

DEPREDA'TOR, S. [*deprædator*, Lat.] a robber, a ſpoiler. A devourer, a deſtroyer, or conſumer.

DEPREHEN'SIBLE, Adj. [from *deprehenſus*, Lat.] that which may be detected, apprehended, diſcovered, or underſtood.

DEPREHEN'SION, S. [*deprehenſio*, Lat.] detection ; a diſcovery.

To DEPRESS, V. A. [*depreſſum*, Lat.] to preſs down, to look downwards. " Raiſing, or depreſſing the eyes or otherwiſe moving it." *Newt. Opt.* To abaſe, or deject, applied to the mind.

DEPRESSION, S. [*depreſſio*, Lat.] the act of preſſing down. The ſinking in of a ſurface. Figuratively, degradation, abaſement, or humbling. Depreſſion, in Algebra, applied to equations, is the bringing them to their loweſt terms by diviſion. In Aſtronomy, the diſtance of a ſtar from the horizon, meaſured from the horizon downwards. In Geography, the depreſſion of the pole, is the travelling ſo much from the pole, nearer to the horizon. Depreſſion of the ſenſible horizon, is its ſinking ſo much below the real horizontal plane, owing either to the variation of the atmoſphere, or the different ſituation of an obſerver's eye, above the ſurface of the ſea.

DEPRES'SOR, S. [Lat.] one that preſſes down ; an oppreſſor.

DEPRI'VATION, S. [from *de* and *privo*, Lat.] the act of taking away a quality or exiſtence of a thing. In Law, the depoſing or taking away the preferment of a clergyman for ſome crime.

To DEPRI'VE, V. A. [from *de* and *privo*, Lat.] to take away that which is enjoyed by another. In Law, to ſtrip a clergyman out of a benefice.

DEP'TH, S. [See DEEP, *dept*, Belg.] the meaſure of a thing, from the ſurface downwards. Quantity of water, oppoſed to a ſhoal,

No. LCX

The ſea, the abyſs. Figuratively, the middle of a ſeaſon, or night. " The depth of winter." Profoundneſs, difficulty, obſcurity, applied to learning.

To DEP'THEN, V. A. [*depten*, Belg.] to make deep.

DEPUL'SION, S. [*depulſio*, Lat.] the act of beating, or driving away.

DEPUL'SORY, [*depulſorius*, Lat.] thruſting or driving away.

To DE'PURATE, V. A. [*depurer*, Fr.] to purify, to cleanſe from any impurities.

DE'PURATE, Adj. [from the verb] cleanſed from dregs or foulneſs. Figuratively, pure, not tainted, or corrupted.

DEPURA'TION, S. [*depuratio*, Lat.] the act of extracting the impure or foul parts of any thing. In Surgery, the cleanſing a wound.

To DEPU'RE, V. A. [*depurer*, Fr.] to cleanſe from drops, or filth. To purge or cleanſe from any noxious qualities.

DEPUTA'TION, S. [Fr.] the ſending ſome perſons ſelected out of a body, to treat of matters in their behalf or name. The commiſſion of treating in behalf of others.

To DE'PUTE, V. A. [*deputer*, Fr.] to ſend with a ſpecial commiſſion ; to ſelect one or more perſons to negotiate a public or private affair.

DE'PUTY, S. [*deputé*, Fr.] one that is commiſſioned or deputed to tranſact an affair for another. A vice-gerent. Any one who tranſacts buſineſs for another. An officer of a ward, choſen by the alderman, from the body of common council of that ward, to tranſact buſineſs relating to it in his abſence. In Law, any perſon who exerciſes an office in right of another.

To DERA'CINATE, V. A. [*deraciner*] to pluck up by the roots ; to aboliſh or extirpate. " The cunſer ruſts—which ſhould deracinate ſavagery." *Shak.*

DERA'Y, V. A. [*desrayer*, *desrayer*, Fr.] a confuſion, tumult, diſorder, merriment.

DERELIC'TION, S. [*derelictio*, Lat.] the utter forſaking a perſon.

DERBY, the county town of Derbyſhire, with 3 markets, on Wedneſdays, Fridays, and Saturdays, and 8 fairs, on February 2d, which is a meeting, for cheeſe ; on Wedneſday in the Lent-aſſize-week for horſes, now almoſt neglected ; Friday in Eaſter-week for horned cattle ; firſt Friday in May, Friday in Whitſun week, and July 25 for horned cattle : September 27 for cheeſe ; firſt Friday before Michaelmas for horned cattle. It is ſeated on the river Derwent, over which there is a handſome ſtone bridge, and a ſmall brook runs through the town, under ſeveral bridges. It is a large, populous, and well frequented place, containing five pariſh churches, whereof All-Saints is the chief, whoſe tower-ſteeple is as high as moſt in the nation. The ſhire-hall is a ſtone building, where the aſſizes are kept. It has the title of an earldom, and ſends

U 2

fends two members to parliament. In 1734 there was a mill erected here, of a great length, by Sir Thomas Lombe, for the manufacturing of filk, the model of which he brought from Italy. It is governed by a mayor, 9 aldermen, and other officers, but is a place of no great trade, except in corn. The rebels came as far as this town in 1745, and then returned back into Scotland. It is 36 miles N. of Coventry, 24 N. W. of Leicester, and 122 N. W. by N. of London. The town is well paved, and adorned with many handsome buildings. Lon. 16. 10. lit. 52. 57.

DERBYSHIRE, an English county, 54 miles in length, and 34 in breadth, is bounded on the E. by Nottinghamshire, on the S. by Leicestershire, on the W. by Staffordshire, and on the N. by Yorkshire. It contains 22,140 houses, 126,900 inhabitants, 106 parishes, and 11 market towns. The air in general is pretty good and temperate, except among the mountains of the Peak, where it is sharp and cold. The N. and W. parts are hilly and stony, but in the S. there is some very rich land. The produce is lead, iron, coals, and mill-stones, besides what is common to other counties. The Peak country is taken notice of for several caves, and holes, commonly called the Wonders of the Peak, of which notice will be taken in their proper place. The principal rivers are, the Trent, the Dove, and the Derwent. In some place they have a manufactory of knit stockings.

DERHAM, [William] a most excellent Christian philosopher and divine, was born at Stowton near Worcester in 1657. In 1675 he was entered at trinity college Oxon, where his tutor was the learned Dr. Wilkes, father of the late lord chief justice of the common pleas. In 1678-9 he took his bachelor's degree, by which time he had so distinguished himself by his learning, and other eminent qualifications, that Dr. R. Bathurst, then president of trinity college, earnestly recommended him to Dr. Seth Ward, bishop of Salisbury, by whose interest he was, when he entered into holy orders in 1682, made chaplain to the lady Dowager Grey of Warke: In 1689 he was presented by Mrs. Jane Bray, to the rectory of Upminster in Essex, worth 200l. per ann. and not more than 15 miles from London. His proximity to the metropolis was subservient to the highest purposes of a scholar and a divine, and his retirement was employed in studying both the volumes of his creator, the scriptures, and the book of nature. As a natural historian, no person ever made a greater figure; but as his studies in this branch had always the honour of God, the promotion of religion, and the good of mankind for their guide, he richly deserved all the honours which they prepared for him, and the notice taken of him by the Royal Society, the archbishop of Canterbury, his late majesty, and the university of Oxford, who presented

him with his doctor's degree, were rather so many evidences of his merit, than marks of honour. While true, masculine and rational piety, unspotted reputation, or extensive learning, have any advocates, this gentleman's name must be held in veneration. As his private life was no less beneficial than his writings, as he was not only the teacher, but the example of his parishioners; and as he was not only a physician to their souls, but their bodies likewise, he deserves no less praise as a man, than as an author; and as an author his Physico Theology, Astro Theology, and curious pieces in the Philosophical Transactions, will show, that he is, in that character, inferior to none.

To DERIDE, V. A. to laugh at, mock, ridicule, or turn to scorn.

DERIDER, S. one who makes a mock, or ridicules a thing or person.

DERISION, S. the act of ridiculing, mocking, or deriding. The object of ridicule.

DERISIVE, Adj. ridiculing, mocking.

DERISORY, Adj. [derisorius, Lat.] mocking, ridiculing.

DERIVABLE, Adj. that which may be communicated from one to another.

DERIVATION, S. [derivatio, Lat.] the draining water from its course. In Grammar, the tracing a word from its original. In genealogy, descent. Figuratively, the tracing any thing from its source.

DERIVATIVE, Adj. [derivativus, Lat.] derived from another.

DERIVATIVE, S. the thing or word which is derived or taken from another.

DERIVATIVELY, Adv. after a derivative manner, from another, not originally.

To DERIVE, V. A. [deriver, Fr. derivo, Lat.] to let out water, or turn its course. Figuratively, to divide or separate. To trace from its original or source. To communicate as a cause to an effect. To descend to a person, or to communicate by descent of blood. In Grammar, to trace a word from its origin; to proceed, or descend from.

DERIVER, S. one who partakes of, or derives a thing by descent, pedigree, or communication.

To DEROGATE, V. A. [derogatus, suspice of derogo, Lat.] to act contrary or inconsistent with the dignity of a family; to degenerate; to undervalue, or lessen the esteem of a thing.

DEROGATE, Adj. [derogatus, Lat.] degenerated, depraved, lessened in value or fertility. "And from her derogate body." Shak.

DEROGATION, S. [derogatio, Lat.] an act done contrary to law, by which means its force and value is lessened. The act of disparaging a thing. Used with to, and sometimes, though not so properly, with from.

DEROGATIVE, Adj. lessening the value of a person or thing.

DERO-

DERO'GATORILY, Adv. in such a manner as to lessen the value of a thing, or the reputation of a person.

DERO'GATORY, Adj. [derogatorius, Lat.] that which lessens the value of a thing.

DER'VIS, or **DER'VISE**, S. [from صوفی Perſ.] a kind of monks among the Turks, who profess extreme poverty, and lead a very austere life.

DESC'ANT, S. [accented on both the first and last syllables, by Shakespeare, in different parts of his works, and by Milton, on the first syllable, from discanto, Ital.] a song or tune composed in parts. Figuratively, a discourse or treatiſe. In Mufic, the art of composing several parts.

To DESC'ANT, V. N [from the noun] to fing in parts. In Mufic, to compose in descant. Figuratively, to criticise minutely and find fault with the actions of another; to censure.

To DESCEND, V. A. [descendre, Fr. descendo, Lat.] to come or go to a lower place. To go gradually downwards; to fink; to invade an enemy's country; to proceed to the next heir; to change a difcourfe from a general view, to a more minute and particular one. Actively, to walk or roll downwards.

DESCEN'DANT, S. [Fr. descendens, Lat.] the offspring or posterity of a person.

DESCEN'DENT, Part. [descendens, Lat. It is the general custom to write the substantive as if derived from the French, and the participle as if derived from the Latin] moving from a higher to a lower situation; finking; proceeding, as from an ancestor, or from a cause. In Astronomy, it is divided into right or oblique. Right descension is a point or arch of the equator, which descends with a ſtar, or fign, in a right sphere. Oblique descension, is that which descends in an oblique sphere.

DESCENT, S. [descente, Fr. descensus, Lat.] the act of passing to a lower place; a slope or sloping situation. " The heads and sources of rivers flow upon a descent." Woodw. Invasion on an enemy's country; birth, extraction. Lineal descent, is that which is conveyed down in a right line from the grand-father to the father, from the father to the fons; &c. Collateral descent, is that which springs out of the fide of the line or blood, as from a man to his brother, nephew, &c.

To DESCRI'BE, V. A. [describo, Lat.] In Painting, to form or paint the resemblance of a thing. In Logic, to convey an idea of a thing. In Geometry, to draw or make a figure. Figuratively, to delineate, or convey fome notion of a thing by words.

DESCRI'BER, S. a person who relates a matter of fact; a battle, &c.

DESCRI'ER, S. [from descry] one who fees, discovers, or descries a thing at a distance.

DESCRI'PTION, S. [descriptio, Lat.] the act of conveying the idea of a person or thing. In Logic, a collection of this most remarkable properties of a thing; the qualities expressed in representing a thing.

To DESCR'Y, V. A. [descrier, Fr.] in its primary sense it implied the giving notice, by calling out, on the sudden discovery or fight of a thing or person. In its secondary sense, the other being obsolete, it implies, to reconnoitre, to examine or view at a distance; to discover, or discern.

DESCR'Y, S. discovery, or the thing discovered.

To DESECRATE, V. A. [desecratum, from desecro, Lat.] to convert a thing to an use different from that to which it was originally consecrated.

DESECRA'TION, S. the converting of a thing consecrated, to some common use.

DE'SERT, S. [desertum, Lat.] a waste uninhabited place; a solitude; a place at some distance from any city.

DE'SERT, Adj. [desertum, Lat.] wild, waste, uncultivated, uninhabited, solitary.

To DESERT, V. A. [deserter, Fr.] to quit, to leave, to forsake; to abandon a person who has a reliance on one. To run away from an army or company, applied to soldiers.

DESE'RT, S. [dessert, Fr.] the last course of an entertainment; confiding in fruits or sweetmeats. Also, the fruits or sweetmeats of which compose the last course.

DESE'RT, S. the behaviour, conduct, or actions of a person considered. A claim to praise or reward. Excellence, or virtue. Degree of merit.

DESE'RTER, S. [deserteur, Lat.] one who leaves or abandons a person. One who abandons, quits or leaves his post, or the army or navy to which he belongs.

DESERTA'TION, S. the act of abandoning a person, cause, post, or place in an army. In Divinity, a persuasion, that a person is abandoned by divine grace or mercy.

DESE'RTLESS, Adj. without merit; without those qualifications which render a person a proper object of approbation and reward.

To DESE'RVE, V. A. [deservir, Fr.] to be an object of reward or punishment, on account of one's actions. To be a proper object of reward.

DESE'RVEDLY, Adj. according to a person's merits, whether good or ill.

DESE'RVER, S. a man who is an object either of approbation and reward. This and other words of the fame derivation, are most properly used in a good sense, or that which implies merit.

DESHABI'LLE, S. [Fr.] an undress. Not dressed in a proper manner for receiving company. " He is in dishabille."

DESIC'CANT, Part. [desiccans, Lat.] In Medicine, such applications as dry up the humours.

To DE'SICCATE, V. A. [desiccatum, Lat.] to dry up.

DESICCA'TION, S. the act of drying up.

DE-

DESICCATIVE, Adj. that which has the power of drying up moisture.

To DESIGN, V. A. [deſſaer, Fr. deſigno, Lat.] to purpose or intend to mean. To keep for a particular purpose, uſed with for. To intend or ſet apart to a certain uſe or end. To plan, project, or contrive. To ſketch the plan of a work, or the out-lines of a picture.

DESIGN, S. an intention, purpoſe, meaning. A plan. A ſcheme, formed for the prejudice of another. The plan of a painting, poem, books, building, &c.

DESIGNABLE, Adj. that which can be deſcribed, or expreſſed.

DESIGNATION, S. [deſignatio, Lat.] appointment, direction, import or ſignification. Intention.

DESIGNEDLY, Adv. purpoſely. In a manner agreeable to the intention, not accidentally.

DESIGNER, S. one who contrives ſome thing ill. A perſon who invents a draught, or original, in painting.

DESIGNING, Part. contriving, or meditating, ſomething amiſs, or prejudicial.

DESIGNLESS, Adj. without intending; without meaning; without any bad intention.

DESIGNMENT, S. an intended expedition againſt an enemy. A plot. The ſketch of a work.

DESIRABLE, Adj. an object of deſire, delight or longing.

To DESIRE, V. A. [deſirer, Fr.] to wiſh for ſome abſent good. To appear in longing, or covet a thing. "A deſiring look," Dryd. To aſk to entreat.

DESIROUS, Adj. full of longing; wiſhing; cov...

DESIROUSLY, Adv. in ſuch a manner as to covet, to ... ... poſſeſſed.

To DESIST, V. N. [deſiſto, Lat.] to ceaſe from a thing which is begun. To ſtop, uſed with ...

DESISTANCE, S. the act of ſtoping or c...

DESISIVE, Adj. [deſitus of deſino, Lat.] ending or concluſive.

DESK, S. [diſch, Belg.] a ſloping board or table, uſed by writers or readers.

DESOLATE, Adj. [deſolatus, Lat.] uninhabited, laid waſte. Solitary.

To DESOLATE, V. A. [deſolatus, Lat.] to deprive of inhabitants; to lay waſte; to make ſolitary.

DESOLATELY, Adv. in an unfrequented deſolate manner.

DESOLATION, S. the act of making a place a waſte, or uninhabited. Figuratively, melancholy or grief. A place waſted and forſaken. "How is Babylon become a deſolation?" Jer. i. 23.

DESPAIR, S. [deſeſpoir, Fr.] loſs of hope. That which deprives a perſon of hope. A Paſſion excited by imagining that the object or ſubject of deſire is not to be attained. In Divinity, loſs of confidence or reliance on the divine mercy.

To DESPAIR, V. N. [deſpero, Lat. deſeſperer, Fr.] to give a thing over as unattainable. To ceaſe to hope, uſed with of.

DESPAIRER, S. one who is without hope, or who ceaſes to hope.

DESPAIRFUL, Adj. without hope; deep in diſpair. "That ſweet but ſour deſpairful care." Spenſ.

DESPAIRINGLY, Adv. in ſuch a manner as to be without hope.

DESPATCH, S. quickneſs or expedition in performing. Figuratively, conduct, management. "You ſhall put—this night's great buſineſs into my diſpatch." Shak. A meſſage or meſſenger ſent in haſte; an expreſs, "diſpatches were ſent away."

DESPERATE, Adj. [deſperatus, Lat.] without hope, without any regard to ſafety, ariſing from deſpair. Figuratively, not to be retrieved or ſurmounted. Mad, furious with deſpair. Sometimes uſed for perſons habituated to ſomething bad. "Mere deſperate ſins." Pope. Violent, applied to things. "Deſperate remedies."

DESPERATELY, Adv. in a manner of a perſon grown furious by deſpair. Madly, in a very great degree.

DESPERATENESS, S. madneſs, fury, rage.

DESPERATION, S. a ſtate void of all manner of hope.

DESPICABLE, Adj. [deſpicabilis, Lat.] deſerving contempt, mean, baſe, and vile, applied both to perſons and things.

DESPICABLENESS, S. the quality which renders a thing or perſon contemptible.

DESPICABLY, Adv. in a mean, ſordid, vile, contemptible, or baſe manner.

DESPICABLE, Adj. deſerving of contempt on account of its worthleſsneſs, applied both to perſons or things. "The moſt deſpicable thing in the world." Arbuth.

To DESPISE, V. A. [deſpiſer, and Fr. deſpicio, Lat.] to ſcorn or contemn, with ſome degree of diſdain, on account of its worthleſsneſs, meanneſs. To diſregard.

DESPISER, S. one who regards a thing with ſcorn or contempt.

DESPITE, S. [deſpite, Fr. diſpetto, Ital.] malice, anger, defiance. "In diſpite of heat by day." Blackm. An act of malice, or reſentment; ſomething done to counteract the deſigns of another, through malice, revenge, or reſentment.

To DESPITE, V. N. to counter-act or fruſtrate the deſigns of another, through a principle of malice or reſentment.

DESPITEFUL, Adj. full of malice or ſpleen, acting contrary to the deſigns of another, purely to make him unhappy. Malignant.

DES.

DESPITEFULNESS, S. malice, or an endeavour to make a person miserable through malice, and resentment.

To DESPOIL, V. A. [despoiller, Fr.] to deprive a person of what he possesses by some act of violence. Figuratively, to deprive a person of some post, employment, or honour. Used with of, before the thing taken away.

DESPOILATION, S. the act of depriving a person of something he possesses.

To DESPOND, V. A. [despondeo, Lat.] to become melancholy, through a persuasion that something to be done is impossible. In Divinity to despair of the divine mercy.

DESPONDENCY, S. the state of a person who imagines a thing desired to be done is impossible.

DESPONDENT, Adj. [despondens, Lat.] without any hopes of attaining what is ardently desired.

DESPOT, S. [despotes, Gr.] a despotic, absolute, unconstroulable prince.

DESPOTIC, DESPOTICAL, Adj. of unlimited absolute power.

DESPOTICALNESS, S. the quality of exercising authority, without any restraint.

DESPOTISM, S. [despotisme, Fr.] absolute power, applied to those governments, wherein the power of the prince is absolute, unlimited or arbitrary.

To DESPUMATE, V. A. [despumatum, Lat.] to skim the froth off.

DESSERT, S. [desert, Fr.] the last course of an entertainment, consisting of fruits and sweetmeats. See also DESERT.

To DESTINATE, V. A. [destinatum, Lat.] to design for any particular purpose or end. "Birds are destinated to fly." Ray

DESTINATION, S. the purpose or ultimate end for which any thing is designed.

To DESTINE, V. A. [destino, Lat.] to doom; to appoint to any end or purpose. To devote, or doom to punishment or misery. To fix or determine unalterably.

DESTINY, S. [destinie, Fr.] in mythology, fate or the power who determines the lot of mortals. The order of second causes fixed by some unalterable decree. Doom; fortune.

DESTITUTE, Adj. [destitutus, Lat.] deprived of; in want of; forsaken by.

DESTITUTION, S. [from destitute] want; defect; deprivation; deficiency.

To DESTROY, V. A. [destruire, Fr. destruo, Lat.] to demolish. To kill. To make desolate. To ruin, to put an end to, reduced to nothing, or deprive a thing of its present qualities.

DESTROYER, S. one who lays a town waste. One who deprives of life. One who defaces a thing.

DESTRUCTIBLE, Adj. [destructum, Lat.] possible or liable to be destroyed, defaced or demolished.

DESTRUCTIBILITY, S. possibility of being destroyed.

DESTRUCTION, S. [destructio, Lat.] the act of ruining, destroying, or demolishing. Murder. The state of a thing ruined, demolished, or destroyed. In Divinity, a state wherein a person is cut off from all hopes of divine mercy, sometimes termed eternal death, or a state of eternal torment.

DESTRUCTIVE, S. [destructivus, low Lat.] that which demolishes, destroys or lays waste. Used with to.

DESTRUCTIVELY, Adv. so as to destroy, demolish, or ruin both persons and things.

DESTRUCTIVENESS, S. the quality which destroys, ruins, or demolishes.

DESTRUCTOR, S. a consumer, a demolisher, a destroyer.

DESULTORY, DESULTORIOUS, Adj. [desultorius, Lat.] unfixed; unsettled; removing from one thing or idea to another, as it were by leaps without any connection or method.

To DETACH, V. A. [detacher, Fr.] to separate something, which was joined before. To send out or draw off a part of a body of forces.

DETACHED, Part. drawn off, separated from, disengaged. In Painting, well detached, is applied to such figures which appear free, and not intangled, having a good relievo.

DETACHMENT, S. a body of troops from the main army.

To DETAIL, V. A. [detailler, Fr.] to relate a fact minutely and circumstantially.

DETAIL, S. an account containing all the minute circumstances of an affair.

To DETAIN, V. A. [detenir, Fr. detineo, Lat.] to keep or reserve that which is due to another. To hinder a person from departing. To keep a person in custody or confinement.

DETAINDER, S. In Law, a writ for detaining a person in custody.

DETAINER, S. he that withholds another person's right. He that hinders the departure of a person or thing.

To DETECT, V. A. [detectus, Lat.] to discover, find out, or surprise a person in the commission or after the commission of a crime. To lay open the artifices or sophistry of a person.

DETECTOR, S. a discoverer of some criminal or hider. One who exposes the sophistry of an author.

DETECTION, S. the discovery of a criminal, crime, fault, or error. The discovery of something concealed.

DETENTION, S. the withholding what is due to another. Confinement, restraint or imprisonment.

To DETER, V. A. [deterreo, Lat.] to discourage a person from doing a thing either by menaces, or by laying before him the consequences that may attend it.

DETER-

DETER'MENT, S. that which difcourages. The caufe or obstacle which binders or difcourages.

To DETER'GE, V. A. [*detergo*, Lat.] to cleanfe a fore from its pus or matter. To clenfe the body by purges.

DETER'GENT, Adj. [*detergens*, Lat.] having the power of cleanfing.

DETER'MINABLE, Adj. [from *determine*] that which may be afcertained, determined, or defired.

To DETER'MINATE, V. N. [*determiner*, Fr.] to limit; to fettle; to fix; to determine; to eftablifh.

DETER'MINATE, S. [*determinatus*, Lat.] limited; determined; fettled; eftablifhed; decifive.

DETER'MINATELY, Adv. refolutely fixed; firmly refolved or eftablifhed.

DETER'MINATION, S. abfolute direction to a certain point or end. A refolution formed after mature deliberation. The decifion of fome contefted point.

DETER'MINATIVE, Adj. having the power to direct to a particular end. That which reftrains the fignification of a word.

DETERMIN'ATOR, S. one who determines, afcertains, fettles, or decides a controverfy.

To DETER'MINE, V. A. [*determiner*, Fr. *determino*, Lat.] to fettle a point in debate. To conclude; to decide; to reftrain within limits. To afcertain the fenfe of an expreffion, or ufe a word invariably to fignify the fame thing. To fix. To direct to a certain point; to influence the choice; to refolve. To decide. To put an end to. "Till ficknefs has *determin'd* me." *Shak*. Neuterly, to conclude; to end.

DETER'SION, S. [from *deterfum*, Lat.] In Surgery, the act of cleanfing a wound.

DETER'SIVE, Adj. [*deterfif*, Fr.] having the power of cleanfing.

DETER'SIVE, S. In Medicine, that which cleanfes a wound, or cleanfes the body.

To DETEST, V. A. [*deteftor*, Fr. *detestor*, Lat.] to hate a thing with fome vehemence, to abhor.

DETE'STABLE, Adj. [Fr.] that which is hated and abhorred with great vehemence.

DETE'STABLY, Adv. In fuch a manner as to deferve the greateft loathing, averfion or hatred.

DETESTA'TION, S. [Fr.] the act of abhorring, difliking or hating.

DETE'STOR, S. one who has a very great hatred, averfion, or deteftation.

To DETHRONE, V. A. [*detroner*, Fr.] to depofe a prince, to deprive of royalty.

DETI'NUE, S. [*detenue*, Fr.] a writ lying againft a perfon, who refufes to deliver a thing up, which was given him to keep for another.

DETONA'TION, S. [*detonatus*, Lat.] In Chemiftry, the operation of expelling the impure, volatile and fulphureous parts from antimony.

To DETO'NIZE, V. A. [*detono*, Lat.] In Chemiftry, to calcine with detonation.

To DETO'RT, V. A. [*detortus*, Lat.] to wreft a word from its original meaning or defign. " *Detorted* text of fcripture to fedition. *Dryd*.

To DETRACT, V. A. [*detractum*, Lat.] to leffen the reputation of another by flander and calumny. To leffen the value of a thing. To under-value. Ufed with *from*.

DETRA'CTER, S. one who leffens the reputation of another, or the value of a thing, by fpeaking ill of them.

DETRA'CTION, S. [Fr. *detractio*, Lat.] the leffening the reputation of another, by fpeaking flanderoufly of him.

DETRA'CTORY, Adj. leffening the value of a thing, or reputation of a perfon. Ufed with *from*, and fometimes, but not fo properly, with *to*.

DETRIMENT, S. [*detrimentum*, Lat.] that which caufes lofs, difadvantage, injury or damage

DETRIMEN'TAL, Adj. caufing harm, mifchief, lofs, damage or injury.

To DETRUDE, V. A. [*detrudo*, Lat.] to thruft down. To thruft into a lower place. " *Detruded* to the root." *Thomp*.

DETRU'SION, S. the act of forcing a thing downwards.

DEVASTA'TION, S. [from *devaftatum*, Lat.] the act of deftroying, laying wafte, demolifhing, or unpeopling towns.

DEUCE, S. [*deux*, Fr. *two*, Gr.] In Gaming a card that has two marks, or a die with two fpots. Satan, the devil. See DEUSE.

To DEVE'LOP, V. A. [*developper*, Fr.] to take off any covering, which conceals a thing. To lay open, and difcover any ftratagem.

To DEVEST, V. A. [*devefter*, Fr.] to make a perfon naked. Figuratively, to deprive of any advantage, or good. To free from any thing bad.

To DEVIATE, V. N. [of *de*, Lat. and *via*] to leave the right way or road. Figuratively, to err, to go aftray. In Divinity, to act contrary to the rules prefcribed by the divine commandments. Ufed with *from*.

DEVIA'TION, S. the act of quitting or departing from the right way. Figuratively, the acting contrary to fome eftablifhed rule. Sin. Offence. A wandering or going aftray.

DEVICE, S. [*devife*, Fr. *divifa*, Ital.] a contrivance, ftratagem, project, fcheme or plan. In Heraldry, or Painting, an emblem which has fome refemblance, to a perfon's name. The reprefentation of fome natural body, with a motto or fentence; applied in a figurative fenfe to the advantage of fome perfon.

DEVIL, S. [*deofol*, *diabal*, Sax. *diafvol*, Brit. *diable*, Fr. *diable*, Span. *diabolo*, Ital. *diabolus*, Gr.] In its primary fignification a calum-

calumniator; but peculiarly applied to signify Satan, or the fallen angel, who was the tempter, and seducer of mankind. Figuratively, a wicked person.

DEV'ILISH, Adj. [*deoflise*, Sax.] partaking of the wicked qualities of the *devil*. Figuratively, holding commerce with the *devil*. Vulgarly used to express the superlative degree. "*Devilish* hot." "*Devilish* fine." *Devilish* clever."

DEVIL'ISHLY, Adv. In a wicked or mischievous manner. Suitable to the wickedness of the *devil*. Diabolically.

DEVI'OUS, Adj. [*devius*, Lat.] out of the common track, or path. Wandering, erring, or going astray.

To DEVISE, V. A. [*deviser*, Fr.] to invent, contrive, or plan; implying a great deal of art. Neuterly to form schemes. In Law, to bequeath or leave by will.

DEVISE, S. [all Fr. a will] in Law, the act of bequeathing by will. Contrivance, scheme.

DEVISER, S. one who projects, contrives, or bequeaths by will.

DEVISES, a town in Wiltshire, with a market on Thursdays, and six fairs, on February 13 for cattle, and Holy Thursday for cattle, horses, and sheep, on June 13 for horses, on July 5 for wool, on October 2 for sheep, and on October 20 for sheep and hogs. It is seated on a hill which lies in a bottom, and formerly was a place of great note. It is at present pretty large, and sends two members to parliament. It is twenty-four miles N. W. of Salisbury, and eighty-nine W. of London. Lon. 15, 29. lat. 51, 25.

DEVOID, Adj. [*vuide*, Fr.] empty, vacant, destitute, void.

DEVOIR, S. [Fr.] In its primary sense, a duty. At present used to signify some act of ceremony or respect due to a person on account of rank, office, or relation.

To DEVOLVE, V. A. [*devolvo*, Lat.] to roll to a lower place. "The matter which *devolves* from the hills." To remove from one to another. Used with *into* or *upon*. "They *devolved* their whole authority into the hands of the council." *Addif.* Neuterly, to descend to order of succession. Used with *to*.

DEVOLU'TION, S. [*devolutio*, Lat.] the rolling of a thing to a lower place. Succession from one person or order to another.

DEVONSHIRE, an English county, seventy-three miles in length, and fifty-three in breadth, bounded by the Irish Sea on the N. Somersetshire and Dorsetshire on the E. the English channel on the S. and Cornwall on the W. with the title of a duchy. It contains fifty-six thousand, three hundred and ten houses, three hundred thirty-seven thousand, eight hundred and forty inhabitants, three hundred ninety-four parishes, and

thirty-eight market-towns. The air is pretty temperate in the valleys, but sharp and cold on the hills. It has mines of tin, copper, and other metals. The sea-coasts abound in herrings, pilchards, and other salt-water fish. The hills are barren, but the lower grounds are fruitful, when manured. Besides the common productions, it is noted for cyder and perry. The chief rivers are, the Ex, the Towridge, the Tame, and the Taw.

DEVORA'TION, S. [*devoratus*, Lat.] the act of devouring.

To DEVOTE, V. A. [*devoveo*, Lat.] to dedicate, or set apart to any particular purpose. To abandon or addict to evil, or destruction.

DEVOTEE, S. [*devot*, Fr.] one extravagantly, enthusiastically, or erroneously religious. A bigot.

DEVOTION, S. [Fr. of *devotio*, Lat.] a religious and fervent exercise of some public act of religion, or a disposition of the mind properly affected with such exercises. Properly prayer. A fervent affection for a person. Disposal; used with *at*. "At his majesty's *devotion*." Clarend.

DEVO'TIONAL, Adj. relating to divine worship. Pious. Zealous.

DEVO'TIONALIST, S. one who is superstitiously, and enthusiastically religious.

To DEVOUR, V. A. [*devorer*, Fr.] to eat up eagerly, or ravenously. Figuratively, to destroy with rapidity. To swallow up.

DEVO'URER, S. one that consumes or eats up eagerly or ravenously.

DEVO'UT, Adj. [*devot*, Fr. *devotus*, Lat.] pious, religious, fervent. Full of zeal, or expressive of ardent piety. "With eyes *devout*." Par. Lost.

DEVOU'TLY, Adv. in a pious, fervent, zealous manner.

DEUSE, S. the devil, satan, used in a ludicrous language. "Well the *deuse* take me." Cong.

DEUTERONOMY, S. [*δευτερος*, Gr. the second, and *νομος*, Gr. law] the last book of the five books written by Moses. The Jewish rabbins on this account stile it מִשְׁנֶה, *Mishneh*, or the repetition. It is generally named אֵלֶּה הַדְּבָרִים, *Elleb-Hadderharim*, which is one of the first words in the Hebrew. It was written, all but the last chapter, by Moses, in the 120th year of his age, the last chapter being supposed by some to have been added by Joshua immediately after Moses's death; but some suppose it to have been written by Ezra.

DEW, S. [*deaw*, Sax. a light, thin, insensible mist, or rain, raised from the earth after the sun has descended below the horizon, by the heat it has communicated to the earth during the day; which mist meeting with the cold in the atmosphere, is condensed and precipitated on the earth again. The quantity of dew falling or evaporated through-

out the year, is ingeniously calculated by the Rev. Dr. Hales, in his *Vegetable Statics*, and the great benefit this meteor is to all the vegetable creation, and its sufficiency to answer all the purposes it is designed for by the great architect of the world, may from thence be inferred with all that force, which can strike a reasonable mind with conviction, or elevate a devout disposition to rapture.

To DEW, V. A. to moisten as with dew.

DEW-BERRY, S. in Natural History. supposed by Sir Thomas Hanmer to be the same as the raspberry. " Feed him with a-pricots and dewberries."

DEW-WORM, S. in Natural History, a worm found in dew, called also the lob-worm.

DEWY, Adj. resembling dew; moist with dew.

DEXTER, Adj. [Lat.] in Heraldry, the right side.

DEXTERITY, S. [dexteritas, Lat.] readi-ness, activity, applied to the use of the limbs. Quickness of contrivance, readiness or fertility of invention, applied to the mind.

DEXTEROUS, Adj. [dexter, Lat.] ex-pert, active, or quick at any manual exercise or trade which consists in the use of the limbs; subtle, full of expedients, skilful in ma-nagement; fertile in invention.

DEXTEROUSLY, Adv. expertly, readi-ly, skilfully.

DEXTRAL, Adj. [dexter, Lat.] on the right side.

DIABETES, S. [diaσaiτω, Gr.] the dis-charge of any liquor through the urinary passages, without any or little alteration, at-tended with insatiable thirst.

DIABOLIC, DIABOLICAL, [from dia-bolus, Lat.] impious, partaking of the quali-ties of the devil; extremely wicked.

DIACOUSTICS, S. [from δια, and ακουω, Gr.] in Philosophy, the doctrine of refracted sounds as they pass through diffe-rent mediums.

DIADEM, S. [diadema, Lat.] formerly a bandage of silk encompassing the heads of kings, and tied behind. It was sometimes enriched with pearls, and sometimes with the leaves of some ever-greens. In Heraldry, certain circles, or rims inclosing the crowns of princes, and to bear the globes, crosses or flower de luces for their crests.

DIADEMED, Part. adorned with wear-ing a diadem; crowned.

DIAGNOSTIC, S. [δια, and γνωσις, Gr.] in Medicine, a sign by which the pre-sent state, nature and cause of a disease may be known or discovered.

DIAGONAL, Adj. [from διαγωνιος, Gr.] drawn across from one corner or angle to ano-ther.

DIAGONAL, S. a right line drawn a-

cross a figure, from one angle or corner to another.

DIAGONALLY, Adv. in a cross direc-tion from one corner to another.

DIAGRAM, S. [διαγραμμα, Gr.] in Geometry, a scheme drawn for explaining any figure or its properties.

DIAL, S. [from dies, Lat. a day] a plate marked with two sets of figures, used to shew the time of the day by clocks, or by the shadow of the sun.

DIALECT, S. [διαλεκτος, Gr.] the pecu-liar manner of speaking, in any language by the inhabitants in different parts of the coun-try. Figuratively, stile, manner of expres-sion; language.

DIALECTICAL, Adj. belonging or re-lating to logic.

DIALECTIC, S. [διαλεκτικη, Gr.] the art of reasoning, or logic.

DIALLING, S. the art of describing lines on any given plane, that the sun's shadow, or its rays, if transmitted through a hole, shall touch any given line at any given hour.

DIALIST, S. a person who constructs or makes dials.

DIALOGIST, S. one who is introduced as a speaker in a dialogue.

DIALOGUE, S. [διαλογος, Gr.] a con-ference, or debate on any subject.

To DIALOGUE, V. A. to hold conver-sation or conference with. To discourse.

DIAMETER, S. [δια and μετρον, Gr.] the line which passes through the centre of a circle or any other figure, and divides it into two equal parts.

DIAMETRAL, Adj. relating to a dia-meter.

DIAMETRALLY, Adv. agreeable to the direction of a diameter.

DIAMETRICAL, Adj. DIAMETRI-CALLY, Adv. now used instead of DIA-METRAL, which see.

DIAMOND, S. [generally pronounced dimond, from diamans, Fr.] the most va-luable and hardest of all the gems, when pure, perfectly clear, and pellucid, and dis-tinguished by its vivid splendour and the brightness of its reflections from all other substances. Its hue is various, but the larger ones are extremely rare. The dia-mond bears the force of the strongest fires, ex-cept the concentrated solar rays, without hurt. The East Indies and Brazils, furnish us with this species of precious stones.

DIAPASON, S. in Music, an interval, including an octave; the first and most per-fect of the concords.

DIAPER, S. [diapre, Fr.] a kind of lin-nen cloth, woven in figures.

To DIAPER, V. A. to variegate, diver-sify, or flower.

DIAPHANIC, Adj. transparent.

DIAPHANOUS, Adj. [from δια, Gr. and φανω,

pare, tranſparent. That which may be ſeen through.

DIAPHORESIS, S. [διαφορησις, Gr.] In Medicine, a diſcharge made through the ſkin, whether ſenſible or inſenſible.

DIAPHORETIC, Adj. [διαφορητικος, Gr.] In Medicine, that which cauſes a ſweat or diſcharge through the ſkin.

DIAPHRAGM, S. [from διαφραγμα, Gr.] In Anatomy, a nervous muſcle, vulgarly called the midriff, and by anatomiſts, ſeptum tranſverſalis, or croſs wall, from its dividing the breaſt or thorax from the abdomen. It is contracted, when we draw our breath inward in order to extend the dimenſions of the breaſt, but relaxed, and in its natural ſtate, when we breathe. The actions of coughing, ſneezing, yawning, laughing, and hiccough depend on this muſcle.

DIARRHOEA, S. [διαρροια, Gr.] In Medicine, a profuſe evacuation of liquid excrements by ſtool.

DIARRHOETIC, Adj. in medicine, promoting a looſeneſs. Purging.

DIARY, S. [diarum, Lat.] an account of the daily tranſactions of a perſon; a journal.

DIBBLE, S. [from dipped, Belg.] a ſmall ſpade, or pointed inſtrument, uſed by gardners.

DICE, S. the plural of DIE.

DICER, S. one who is fond of playing at dice; a gameſter.

DICH, corrupted from dit or do it. "Much good dich thy good heart." Shak.

DICHOTOMY, S. [διχη, and τομη, Gr.] in Logic, the diviſion of ideas into pairs. In Aſtronomy, the phaſis of the appearance of the moon wherein ſhe ſhews but half her diſk.

DICKENS, an adverbial exclamation, uſed with what, and implying wonder, or in the ſame ſenſe of wonder. "What a dickens does he mean?" Cong. Seldom uſed.

To DICTATE, V. N. [dictatum, Lat.] to command another; to ſpeak with authority. To deliver a ſpeech in words, which is to be committed to writing.

DICTATE, S. [dictatum, Lat.] a rule or maxim delivered by ſome perſon of power or authority.

DICTATION, S. the act of preſcribing, or giving orders.

DICTATOR, S. [Lat.] a Roman magiſtrate inveſted with conſular and ſovereign power. Figuratively, one who by his authority directs and regulates the conduct of others.

DICTATORIAL, Adj. after the manner of a dictator; imperious, authoritative.

DICTATORSHIP, S. the office of a dictator. Imperiouſneſs.

No. IX.

DICTATURE, S. [dictatura, Lat.] the office of a dictator.

DICTION, S. [from dictio, Lat.] the peculiar manner in which an author expreſſes himſelf.

DICTIONARY, S. [dictionarium, Lat.] a book containing the words of any language ranged in their alphabetical order, with explanations of their meaning, or definitions: how little thoſe books which go by this name in the Engliſh language may deſerve it, may eaſily be perceived by conſidering that few or none claim any other merit but ſcraping together as many ſynonimes as they can, and leaving the reader to pick out the meaning from the rubbiſh that is collected.

DID, the Preter of do.

DIDACTIC, DIDACTICAL, Adj. [διδακτικος, Gr.] containing or conſiſting of precepts, or rules.

DIDST, the ſecond perſon of the preter tenſe of DO.

To DIE, V. A. [deagan, Sax.] to tinge, or colour a thing.

DIE, S. [deag, Sax.] a colour given to a thing; a ſtain.

To DIE, V. N. [dradian, Sax.] to loſe life; to looſe all the animal functions, and have the ſoul ſeparated from the body. To periſh by violence, or any diſeaſe. To be puniſhed with death. Figuratively, to be ſtill, periſh, or be entirely laid aſide. "Thoſe thoughts which ſhould have died." Shak. To faint, or loſe its vital functions. "His heart died within him," 1 Sam. To languiſh, or be overcome with pleaſure or tenderneſs. "To ſounds of heavenly harp ſhe dies away." Pope. To vaniſh or ſleep away. To wither, applied to vegetables. To grow ſpiritleſs, taſteleſs, or vapid, applied to liquors. In Divinity, to periſh everlaſtingly, by loſing communication with God, the fountain and author of true life.

DIE, S. [plural dice, from dé, Fr.] a ſmall cube, marked on each of its ſides with dots, from one to ſix, uſed by gameſters to play with. Figuratively, hazard, or chance.

DIE, S. plural dies. The ſtamp uſed in coining, the mold in which medals, &c. are caſt.

DIER, S. one who follows the trade of colouring ſilks, ſtuff, or cloths.

DIET, S. [δίαιτα, Gr.] food; proviſions for ſatisfying hunger. A regular courſe of food or regimen.

To DIET, V. A. to eat according to the rules of medical writers. To give food to. To board, or furniſh with victuals.

DIET, S. [an appointed day] an aſſembly of the ſtates, or circles of the empire to deliberate on ſome public or important affair.

DIETER, S. one who preſcribes rules for eating, or takes his food by medical rules.

X 2   DIETE-

DIETE'TIC, DIETE'TICAL, Adj. [διαιτητικος, Gr.] belonging or relating to food.

To DI'FFER, V. N. [differo, Lat.] to have properties or figure, not the same as those of another. To oppose in opinion. To be of another opinion.

DI'FFERENCE, S. [differentia, Lat.] the state of being distinct or opposite some other thing. A dispute, debate, or controversy; that which distinguishes one thing from another. In Arithmetic, the remainder after one quantity is taken from another. In Heraldry, something added to or altered in a coat, whereby the younger families are distinguished from the elder. Difference in Logic, is an essential attribute of some species not found in the genus, being the idea that defines the species.

DI'FFERENT, Adj. [Fr. differens, Lat.] distinct, opposed to the same. Of contrary qualities. Unlike.

DIFFE'RENTIAL, Adj. In Geometry, an infinitely small quantity, so small as to be less than any assignable one. Differential method, is that of finding an infinite small quantity, which, taken an infinite number of times, is equal to a given quantity.

DI'FFERENTLY, S. in a different manner.

DI'FFERINGLY, Adv. In a various or different manner.

DI'FFICIL, Adj. [difficile, Fr. difficilis, Lat.] not easy to be understood or learnt, hard, difficult. "Latin was not more difficil." Lit-Lib. Scrupulous, not easily to be persuaded.

DI'FFICULT, Adj. [difficile, Fr.] hard to be done, performed or understood. Troublesome, peevish, morose.

DI'FFICULTLY, Adv. hardly with much labour, or perseverance.

DI'FFICULTY, S. [difficulté, Fr. difficultas, Lat.] that which requires labour, care, and attention. Figuratively, distress. Perplexity or uneasiness.

To DI'FFIDE, V. N. [diffido, Lat.] to distrust, to have no confidence in; used with in.

DI'FFIDENCE, S. [diffidentia, Lat.] want of trust, confidence, resolution, or courage.

DI'FFIDENT, Part. [diffidens, Lat.] wanting in confidence, distrustful, suspicious, timorous, modest.

DI'FFLUENT, Part. [diffluens, Lat.] flowing or falling away.

DI'FFORM, Adj. [from de and forma, Lat.] not of the same form, irregular; having parts of different structures; as a difform flower, is that which has leaves unlike each other.

DIFFRA'NCHISEMENT, S. [from di and franchise, Fr.] the act of taking away the charter of a city.

To DIFFU'SE, V. A. [from diffusum, Lat.] to pour or spread a liquid on a plain surface. Figuratively, to spread, scatter, disperse.

DIFFU'SE. Adj. [diffusus, Lat.] scattered or spread. Applied to stile, copious, verbose.

DIFFU'SED, Part. [from diffuse] used by Shakespear to signify something in disorder, wild, or not composed. "Swearing and stern looks, diffused attire." Hen. V.

DIFFU'SEDLY, Adv. In a copious, liberal, spreading, and excessive manner.

DIFFU'SEDNESS, S. the state of being spread or scattered abroad. Copiousness of stile.

DIFFU'SELY, Adv. widely, extensively, copiously.

DIFFU'SION, S. the being spread abroad. Copiousness, exuberance.

DIFFU'SIVE, Adj. spread abroad. Extended.

DIFFU'SIVELY, Adv. widely; extensively, copiously.

DIFFU'SIVENESS, S. extension; diffusion. The being spread abroad. Applied to stile, copiousness.

To DIG, V. N. [Preter and Particip. Passive dug, or digged, die, Sax.] to open the earth by a spade. Figuratively, to pierce with a pointed instrument, &c. "Still for the growing liver digg'd his breast." Dryd. To discover, or acquire by digging, used with out or from. Actively, to work with a spade, or making holes therewith in the ground. To throw up, or uncover that which is buried under the earth; used with up.

DIGE'ST, S. [digesta, Lat.] a collection of the civil law, ranged under proper titles; a system of any law digested.

To DIGE'ST, V. A. [digestum, supine of digero, Lat.] to range methodically into different classes. To concoct food in the stomach so as to fit it for the supply of the animal excretions. To reduce to any plan, or scheme. In Surgery, to ripen a humour, or prepare it for evacuation. Neutrally, to suppurate, or produce matter like a wound.

DIGE'STER, S. one whose food easily turns into chyle. That which dissolves food.

DIGE'STIBLE, Adj. that which is capable of being dissolved or converted into chyle in the stomach.

DIGE'STION, S. that change which the food undergoes in the stomach, to render it fit to supply the continual loss sustained by perspiration, the natural emissions or excesse. In Chemistry, the preparation of plants by putting them with some proper fluid into a vessel, and heating them gradually with the same degree of fire or heat as that of an animal body. The act of maturing things to a certain pitch. In Surgery, a disposition, in abscesses, to ripen and come to suppuration; likewise maturation, or that change

change where some morbid matter is so altered as to become less violent, hurtful and dangerous.

DIGE'STIVE, Adj. having the power to alter, or turn the food into chyle. Capable of dissolving by its heat. Reducing to method.

DI'GGER, S. one that penetrates or opens the ground with a spade.

To DI'GHT, V. A. [dihtan, Sax.] to dress, embellish or adorn.

DI'GIT, S. [digitus, Lat. a finger] three fourths of an inch. In Astronomy, the 12th part of the diameter of the sun and moon. In Arithmetic, any number expressed by a single figure.

DIGITA'TED, Adj. [from digitus, Lat.] branched out into divisions, like fingers.

DI'GNIFIED, Adj. enjoying some honourable post, or preferment, more particularly applied to the clergy.

DIGNIFICA'TION, S. the act of conferring or bestowing honour.

To DI'GNIFY, V. A. [dignus, Lat. worthy, and facio to make] to advance, or exalt to some place which demands honour and reverence, chiefly applied to the clergy. To honour.

DI'GNITARY, S. [from dignitas, Lat.] a clergyman advanced to some office, which demands respect and reverence.

DI'GNITY, S. [dignitas, Lat.] rank. Preferment or post which requires reverence. Applied to the look, grandeur, or a majestic appearance. Among the clergy, a promotion or preferment to which any jurisdiction is annexed. Maxims, general principles. "The sciences concluding from dignities and principles known by themselves." Brown. In Astrology, applied to a planet which is in any sign.

To DIGRE'SS, V. N. [digressus, of digredior, Lat.] to turn out of the road, or path. Figuratively, to depart from the main scope of an argument. To wander. To err; to deviate.

DIGRE'SSION, S. [digressio, Lat.] a passage that has not the least connection with the main scope of a discourse. Deviation, wandering.

DI'KE, S. [dic or dire, Sax.] a channel to receive water. A mount to keep waters from overflowing.

To DILA'CERATE, V. A. [dilaceratum, supine of dilacero] to tear; to read.

DILACERA'TION, S. [from dilaceratio, Lat.] the act of tearing or reading in two.

DILAPIDA'TION, S. [dilapidatio, Lat.] in Law, is where an incumbent, on a church benefice, suffers the parsonage-house, or the out-houses, to fall down, or be in decay for want of necessary reparation. It is also applied to the pulling down any buildings belonging to any spiritual living, or suffering

any wilful waste upon the inheritance of the church.

DILATABI'LITY, S. [from dilatable] the quality of admitting of extension.

DILA'TABLE, Adj. [from dilate] that which may be stretched or extended.

DILATA'TION, S. [from dilatatio, Lat.] the act of extending into a greater space. The state of a thing whose parts are stretched, or extended.

To DILA'TE, V. A. [dilato, Lat.] to extend, spread out, or stretch. Figuratively, to relate a thing at large, or with all its particular circumstances. Neuterly, to grow wider; to widen; to speak largely or copiously.

DILA'TOR, S. that which widens or extends any passage. "The dilators of the nose." Arbuth.

DILATORINESS, S. the quality of deferring or delaying a thing through sloth.

DI'LATORY, Adj. [dilatoire, Fr.] putting off, or deferring a thing from time to time through sloth.

DILE'CTION, S. [dilectio, Lat.] the act of loving. "So free is Christ's dilection." Boyle.

DILE'MMA, S [λημμα, Gr.] In Logic, an argument consisting of several propositions, so disposed, that grant which you will, you will be pressed by the conclusion. Figuratively, a difficult choice.

DI'LIGENCE, S. [diligentia, Lat.] assiduity; constant endeavour; unremitted labour, or practice.

DI'LIGENTLY, Adv. with constant labour, caution care and assiduity.

DILU'CID, Adj. [dilucidus, Lat.] clear, plain and transparent, opposed to opaque. Clear, plain, obvious, easy to be understood, opposed to abstruse.

To DILU'CIDATE, V. A. [from dilucidatus, Lat.] to make a proposition, clear and easy to be understood. To explain.

DILUCIDA'TION, S. [from dilucidatio, Lat.] the making a sentence easy to be understood. An explanation.

DI'LUENT, Adj. [diluens, Lat.] having the power of thinning or attenuating.

DI'LUENT, S. [diluens, Lat.] that which renders another fluid thin.

To DILU'TE, V. A. [diluo, Lat.] to weaken or thin a liquor by mixing another with it. To make weak, applied to colours. "If the red and blue colours were more dilute and weak." News. Opt. To drink often, in order to quench thirst, and promote perspiration.

DILU'TER, S. that which renders a body more liquid; that which dilutes.

DILU'TION, S. [dilutio, Lat.] the act of rendering a liquid more thin, by adding some other.

X x 2   DILU-

DILU'VIAN, Adj. [from diluvium, Lat.] relating to, or resembling the deluge.

DIM, Adj. [dim, dam, Sax.] having something which obstructs the sight. Figuratively, deprived of its splendour. Grown dark. Dull of apprehension.

To DIM, V. A. to darken, or obstruct the fight. Figuratively, to make less bright; to darken.

DIMENSION, S. [dimensio, Lat.] space. The three dimensions are length, breadth, and thickness or depth. In Algebra, the values of the unknown quantities of equations.

DIMENSIONLESS, Adj. without any dimensions; not occupying any place like body. Of no certain bulk.

DIMENSIVE, that which marks out the boundaries, limits, or out-lines.

To DIMINISH, V. A. [diminuo, Lat.] to make a thing less, to reduce. Figuratively, to impair, lessen; to degrade " improperly they translate there to diminish." Per Esq. To take any thing from that to which it belongs. To erase from a writing; to falter or decline practising some part of a law. Neuterly, to grow less, to be impaired.

DIMINISHINGLY, Adv. so as to lessen the character and reputation of another. " Speak diminishingly of any one that was at feast." Locke.

DIMINUTION, S. [diminutio, Lat.] the act of rendering a thing less. The state of growing less either in bulk or weight. Figuratively, loss. Diffeded. " Diminution of me." A. Charles.

DIMINUTIVE, Adj. [diminutivus, Lat.] small of size, or dimensions.

DIMINUTIVE, S. in Grammar, a word used to express smallness, or littleness. Thus mannikin in English, signifies littleness among the antients as well as moderns, these words are used to convey the idea of great affection, and applied both to persons and things, which are very dear, or very much revered. A thing of small value. " Miss Dimble is down—for puny'll diminutive, but down" Miss.

DIMINUTIVELY, Adv. in a small diminutive manner.

DIMITY, S. [dimitum or dimiton, Fr.] a fort of cotton fluid, resembling fustian.

DIMLY, Adv. [dimic, Sax.] in a dull, obscure manner. Without a clear perception, either of the fight or understanding. Deprived of its light, or brightness.

DIMNESS, S. [dimnes, Sax. dimme, and dimn, Isl.] want of a clear fight. Want of apprehension.

DIMPLE, S. [from dint, a hole, dith, a little hole, hence dimple, by eveckt; pronuncigtion, a small hollow on the surface of the face.

To DIMPLE, V. N. to appear with little hollows, dents, or inequalities of surface.

DIMPLED, Part. having dimples.

DIMPLY, Adv. full of dimples, or little dents.

DIN, S. [dyn, Isl.] a loud noise. A violent found. An uproar, or shout.

To DIN, V. A. [dynan, Sax. dyn, Isl.] to stun with frequent uproar, noise and clamour.

To DINE, V. N. [diner, Fr.] to eat one's second meal about the middle of the day. Actively, to give or bellow a dinner.

To DING, V. A. [from dingen, Teut.] to dash with violence. Neuterly, to bluster, bounce, or become insolent.

DINING-ROOM, S. the principal, or most elegant apartment of a house, wherein entertainments are made, usually applied to the room on the first floor.

DINNER, S. [diner, Fr.] the meal which is eaten about the middle of the day.

DINT, S. [dynt, Sax. a stroke; a blow or stroke. Figuratively, the mark made by a blow. See DENT. Violence, strength, force, power. " By dint of arms" Addif.

To DINT, V. A. [from the noun] to mark or print any part of a surface inwards by a blow or pressure.

DIOCESAN, S. [erected on the second syllable; likewise, from Diocese] a bishop, considered in the relation he stands in to his inferior clergy.

DIOCESE, S. [dioecesis, of dioxeas, Gr.] the circuit or extent of every bishop's jurisdiction.

DIOPTRICK, DIOPTRICAL, Adj. [from dioptras] affording a medium for the light, or assisting the fight in the view of distant objects.

DIOPTRICS, S. the science of refractive vision, which contains the different refractions of light, in its passage through different mediums; as air, water, glass, &c.

To DIP, V. A. [partidp. dipped; or dipt, from dippan, Sax.] to put or dive into any liquor. To moisten, or wet. Figuratively, to engage as a party or principal in any affair. To mortgage, or pledge or security. " To dip his estate." Neuterly, to sink, or plunge into any liquor. Figuratively, to pierce, or force a passage below the surface of a solid body. " The vulture dipping in' Prometheus' side." Garth. To take a curfory or flight view, to read a page or two in a book. Upon dipping in the first volume." Pope. To glich upon by chance, or without deliberation.

DIPPER, S. one who dips in the water. Figuratively, one that takes a superficial view of an author.

DIPHTHONG, S. [diphthongos, Gr.] the joining two vowels together, so as to form one found.

DIPLO-

DIPLO'MA, S. [διπλωμα, Gr.] a writing, conferring some privilege, degree, or title.

DI'RE, Adj. [dirus, Lat.] dreadful, horrible.

DIRE'CT, Adj. [directus, Lat.] strait, oppofed to crooked. Not oblique. In Aftronomy, appearing to the eye to move progreffively through the zodiac, oppofed to retrograde. In Pedigree or Genealogy, from grandfather to grandfon, &c. See DESCENT, oppofed to collateral. Plain; open in fpeech, expreß, oppofed to crafty, ambiguous, or evafive.

To DIRE'CT, V. A. [directum, Lat.] to lead or go in a ftrait line. To aim at as a mark. To regulate, or adjuft, applied to conduct. To prefcribe meafures. To order. To direct a letter is, to write the perfon's name and abode on the outfide, to whom it is to be carried. To direct a perfon, is to inform him what way he is to go to reach a certain place.

DIRE'CTION, S. [directio, Lat.] tendency, or aim. Order, command. The fuperfcription of a letter. An information given to a perfon to find out a place or perfon.

DIRE'CTIVE, Adj. having the power of directing, or informing.

DIRE'CTLY, Adv. In a ftrait line; immediately, prefently, foon, without delay, applied to time. Without circumlocution or evafions.

DIRE'CTNESS, S. the quality of proceeding in a ftrait line. The neareft way.

DIRE'CTOR, S. [Lat.] one who prefides in an affembly or public company, as, "a director of the bank." One who is inftructed with the guidance, or management of any defign. One who regulates the conduct of another; an inftructor.

DIRE'CTORY, S. that which guides or directs.

DI'REFUL, Adj. [ufed commonly in Poetry, though cenfured as not confiftent with analogy, becaufe compounded of dire an adjective; and full, other nouns having full (ubjoined; being fubftantives) full of terror. Very terrible, or terrifying. Difmal.

DIRGE, S. [dyrke, Teut.] a mournful fong fung at the funeral of fome perfon; and the name of the fervice ufed for dead perfons in the Romifh church.

DI'RK, S. a kind of dagger ufed among the Highlanders of Scotland.

To DI'RKE, V. A. to deftroy, or fpoil. "And dirks the beauties of my bloffoms." Spenf.

DI'RT, S. [drut, Belg.] mud; foil, or filth, found in ftreets or highways. Any thing which foils a thing.

To DI'RT, V. A. to daub with filth, mud, or duft. To foil, or bedawb.

DI'RTILY, Adv. fo as to daub or foil. Figuratively, difhoneftly, meanly.

DI'RTINESS, S. filthinefs, foulnefs. Difhoneftly, meannefs, bafenefs.

DI'RTY, Adj. foul, daubed. Figuratively, difhoneft, mean, bafe.

To DI'RTY, V. A. to foil, fmear, or daub.

DIRU'PTION, S. the act of burfting, or breaking afunder.

DISABI'LITY, S. [from difable] the want of fufficient power, or abilities, to accomplifh any defign, or to underftand any propofition or doctrine.

To DISA'BLE, V. A. to deprive of power. To weaken. To impair, or diminifh. "I have difabled mine eftate." Shak. To render inactive, or unfit. To rob of power, influence, efficacy, ufefulnefs, or pleafure. "Worfe than age difable your delights." Dryd. To render a perfon unfit for an office.

To DISABU'SE, V. A. to free a perfon from fome miftake. To undeceive.

DISACCOMMODA'TION, S. the ftate of being unfit, or unprepared.

DISADVA'NTAGE, S. the want or diminution of fame, credit, honour, or any thing defirable, or neceffary to give a perfon a preheminence. Lofs; injury.

To DISADVA'NTAGE, V. A. to weaken the credit, intereft, ufefulnefs or influence of a perfon or thing.

DISADVANTAGEABLE, Adj. contrary to profit; producing lofs, prejudice, damage, or detriment. "Hafty felling is commonly as difadvantageable as intereft." Bacon.

DISADVANTA'GEOUS, Adj. contrary to intereft or profit; convenience; unfavourable.

DISADVANTA'GEOUSLY, Adv. fo as to be inconfiftent with intereft or profit. In a manner not favourable.

DISADVANTA'GEOUSNESS, S. oppofition to profit, convenience or advantage.

DISADVE'NTUROUS, Adj. unhappy; unfuccefsful, unprofperous. "My doleful difadventurous death." Fairy Q.

To DISAFFE'CT, V. A. to alienate or turn afide the affections of a perfon.

DISAFFE'CTED, Part. alienated; having loft all affection for a perfon; generally applied to thofe who ufe enamies to government.

DISAFFE'CTEDLY, Adv. in a difloyal difaffected manner.

DISAFFE'CTEDNESS, S. the quality of being no well-wifher to government.

DISAFFE'CTION, S. want of zeal for the government, or a reigning prince.

To DISAGRE'E, V. N. to differ with refpect to qualities or opinion. To be in a ftate of oppofition. Ufed with from or with.

DISAGREE'ABLE, Adj. contrary to. Unpleafing to the tafte, fight, hearing, or other fenfes.

DISA-

DISAGREE'ABLENESS, S. unsuitable-
ness; unpleasantness; offensiveness.

DISAGREE'MENT, S. difference of
qualities. Contrariety of sentiments. Contention, strife, quarrel.

To DISALLO'W, V. A. to deny the
authority of a person. To censure, or refuse
countenancing a thing. Neuterly, to refuse
permission; to deny.

DISALLO'WABLE, Adj. not to be suffered, permitted, owned, or allowed.

DISALLO'WANCE, S. the refusal of
permission, leave, or countenance.

To DISA'NIMATE, V. A. to kill, flay,
or deprive of life. To discourage, or dishearten. "It disanimates his enemies."
Bacon.

DISANIMA'TION, S. the loss of life;
death; decease.

To DISANNU'L, V. A. (ungrammatical,
although supported by very great authorities)
to annul, to deprive of authority; to abolish,
to disallow, to forbid. "They gave him
power of disannulling the laws." Bacon.

DISANNU'LMENT, S. the act of abolishing or rendering void.

To DISAPPE'AR, V. N. to be lost to
view, or out of sight. To vanish.

To DISAPPOINT, V. A. to hinder
from enjoying or receiving what was expected. To frustrate an expectation. Used
with of.

DISAPPOINTMENT, S. the not receiving or enjoying a thing expected.

DISAPPROBA'TION, S. an act of dislike, arising from something disagreeable to a
person's taste, choice, or judgment.

To DISAPPROVE, V. A. [disapprove,
Fr.] to dislike; to shew that a thing does
not deserve our love or esteem.

To DISA'RM, V. A. [desarmer, Fr.] to
take away arms from a person; used with
before the arms. "Disarmed of their great
magazine."

To DISARRA'Y, V. A. to undress, strip,
or spoil of a person's clothes.

DISARRA'Y, S. disorder, confusion;
undress.

DISA'STER, S. [desastre, Fr.] the blast,
stroke, or influence of an unlucky planet.
Misfortune, sorrow, or some accident occasioned by its being unexpected and un-
contrived.

To DISA'STER, V. A. to blast any project by the influence of some unfavourable
star. To afflict by some unexpected misfortune.

DISA'STROUS, Adj. unlucky; unfortunate; calamitous; afflicted by some sudden
and unexpected misfortune; gloomy, or threatening misfortune.

DISA'STROUSLY, Adv. in an unlucky,
unfortunate, sorrowful, or afflicting manner.

DISA'STROUSNESS, S. misfortune; un-

luckiness, or the quality of rendering any
happy, in supposed, through the influence of
some malignant planet.

To DISAVOU'CH, V. A. to refuse, deny,
or disown.

To DISAVO'W, V. A. to disown; to
deny the knowledge of a thing; to refuse
concurring in a design; to set aside, decline,
or shun. "Expressly to disavow all evasions." Addis.

DISAVO'WAL, S. denial; disowning;
abhorrence; refusal.

DISAVO'WMENT, S. denial, refusal.

To DISAU'THORIZE, V. A. to lessen
or weaken the credit of a thing, or render it
suspicious.

To DISBA'ND, V. A. to dismiss from an
army. "To disband soldiers." Figuratively, to discharge from service. To free from
restraint, or the power of restriction, whereby fluids are kept within their present limits
or boundaries. "A quantity of water sufficient for such a deluge; when the business
was done, was disbanded again and annihilated." Woodw. Neuterly, to quit the
service of the army, to break up or separate.

To DISBA'RK, V. A. [debarquer, Fr.]
to bring to land; to put on shore from some
vessel.

DISBELIE'F, S. refusal of giving assent
or credit to a thing which is proposed to be
believed.

To DISBELIE'VE, V. A. to refuse assenting to a thing proposed as true. To deny the
truth of a doctrine.

DISBELIE'VER, S. (pronounced disbe-
leever) one who refuses to assent to the truth
of a thing. One who refuses to believe a
truth or doctrine. Generally applied to those
persons who, notwithstanding the demonstra-
tions made of the being of, and attributes of
God, and the evidences of the truth of Christianity, still withhold their assent. An infidel.

To DISBE'NCH, V. A. to drive or remove from a seat by force. "I have my
words disbench'd you not." Shak.

To DISBRA'NCH, V. A. to separate a
branch from a tree; to disjoin or separate.
"She that herself will sliver and disbranch
from her material sap." Shak.

To DISBU'RDEN, V. A. to free from
any troublesome weight or load. To clear
from any encumbrance or impediment. To
communicate one's afflictions to another, and
thereby lessen their pressure. "Disburden
all thy cares on me." Addis.

To DISBU'RSE, V. A. [debourser, Fr.] to
spend, pay, or lay out money.

DISBU'RSEMENT, S. [deboursement, Fr.]
the spending, paying, or laying out money.

DISBU'RSER, S. one that lays out, ex-
pends, or pays money.

To DISCA'RD, V. A. in its primary
sense,

fenfe, to lay fuch cards out as are of no ufe.
To difcharge from any fervice or employment. To refufe any further acquaintance.

DISCA'RNATE, Adj. (from *dis* and
caro, Lat.) ftripped of firfh. "A load of
broken and *difcarnate* bones." *Glan.*

To DISCE'RN, V. A. [*difcerno*, Lat.]
to defcry, difcover, perceive, or diftinguifh.
To make a difference or diftinction between
things.

DISCE'RNER, S. a difcoverer; a de-
fcrier. A judge, one capable of diftinguifhing the differences of things.

DISCE'RNIBLE, Adj. that which may be
feen or difcovered. Diftinguifhable; apparent.

DISCE'RNIBLY, Adv. fo as to be diftinguifhed, perceived, or difcerned.

DISCE'RNING, Part. being capable of
making a diftinction between things, or perceiving thofe qualities in which they differ.
Judicious, fenfible.

DISCE'RNINGLY, Adv. with difcretion,
or prudence; judicioufly.

DISCE'RNMENT, S. judgment, penetration, fagacity, or the power of diftinguifhing the qualities in which things differ from
each other.

DISCE'RPTION, S. the act of pulling a
thing in pieces. The act of breaking or
tearing a thing.

To DISCHA'RGE, V. A. [*decharger*,
Fr.] to free from any load, incumbrance,
or employment, ufed with *of*. To turn
away from a fervice, or poft. To fhoot off a
gun. To pay a debt. To free from an
obligation, ufed with *of* or *from*. "If one
man's fruit could difcharge another *of* his
duty." L'Eftr. To clear from an accufation, or charge. To execute an office. To
take away, or deftroy a colour, or quality
"Whofe ill quality may, perhaps, be *difcharged*." Bacon. To difband an army,
or difmifs from attendance. Neuterly, to
clear up, or vanifh. "The cloud, if it were
oily, would not *difcharge*." Bacon.

DISCHA'RGE, S. vent, explofion. Difmiffion from an office, or paft payment of a
debt. Performance of a duty. Exemption,
or acquittance. Difmiffion from confinement.

DISCHA'RGER, S. one who performs or
difcharges a duty; makes a payment; dif-
miffes a fervant; frees from attendance or
confinement, or fires a gun, piftol, &c.

To DISCI'ND, V. A. [*difcindo*, Lat.] to
divide or feparate. "So foft that we could
difcind them between our fingers." Boyle.

DISCI'PLE, S. [*difcipulus*, Lat.] a fcholar, or learner, or one who attends the lectures, and profeffes the tenets of another.

To DISCI'PLE, V. A. to teach, or inftruct; to join as a follower or fcholar.

DISCI'PLINABLE, Adj. [*difciplinabilis*,

Lat.] capable of inftruction or improvement;
deferving punifhment for not attending to the
inftructions of a tutor.

DISCIPLINA'RIAN, Adj. belonging to,
or relating to difcipline.

DISCIPLINA'RIAN, S. one who rules
or teaches with great rigour. A differter;
fo called from their fuppofed clamour againft
the church, for want of rigidnefs in its difcipline.

DISCIPLINE, S. [*difciplina*, Lat.] inftruction, education, tuition, or the method
taken to infufe virtuous habits. Figuratively, method of government. Military government, or regulations. A ftate of fubjection, or obedience. Any thing taught.
A doctrine, art, or fcience. Punifhment,
correction, or chaftifement.

To DISCIPLINE, V. A. to communicate the rudiments of learning to others.
To inftruct; to regulate; to punifh, correct,
or chaftife for neglect of inftruction. To
reform, or advance in inftruction. "*Dif-
cipli'd*—from fhadowy types to truth."
Milton.

To DISCLA'IM, V. A. to difown having any knowledge of, or acquaintance with.
To renounce.

DISCLA'IMER, S. one who difowns,
denies, or renounces.

To DISCLO'SE, V. A. [*difcludo*, Lat.]
to reveal or difcover a thing which has been
hid. To hatch, from *culover*, Fr. "The
heat of the fun *difclofeth* them." Bacon.
To reveal what fhould be, or is hid, or
fecret.

DISCLO'SER, S. one who difcovers a
thing, or reveals fome fecret.

DISCLO'SURE, S. the act of making a
thing feen, which was hidden from fight.
The revealing a fecret.

DISCOLO'RATION, S. the act of
changing the colour of a thing, or ftaining,
ufed in a bad fenfe. A ftain, or change of
colour for the worfe.

To DISCO'LOUR, V. A. to fpoil or deftroy the colour of a thing. To ftain, or
daub.

To DISCO'MFIT, V. A. [*defconfire*, Fr.]
to overcome, beat, or conquer.

DISCO'MFIT, S. a defeat, a rout, or
victory over an enemy.

DISCO'MFITURE, S. overthrow; defeat; rout; ruin.

DISCO'MFORT, S. a great degree of
uneafinefs, melancholy, defpair, diftrefs.

To DISCO'MFORT, V. A. to grieve, afflict, fadden, diftrefs, or deprive of comfort.

DISCO'MFORTABLE, Adj. refufing
comfort or confolation. That which occa-
fions fadnefs, melancholy, or diftrefs.

To DISCOMME'ND, V. A. to blame,
difapprove, reprove, or cenfure.

DISCOMME'NDABLE, Adj. deferving
blame, cenfure, or reproach.

DISCOM-

DISCOMMENDATION, S. blame, censure, reproach, disapprobation. "Without *discommendation*, a person might become an accuser." *Ayliffe.*

DISCOMMENDER, S. one who blames, censures, or reproaches.

To DISCOMMODE, V. A. to put to an inconvenience; to confuse. To rumple or disorder dress.

DISCOMMODIOUS, Adj. inconvenient, displeasing, troublesome.

To DISCOMPOSE, [*decomposer*, Fr.] to put into disorder. To ruffle, applied to the temper. To rumple cloaths. To vex, fret, or disorder. To displace, or discard. "He never put down or *discomposed* a counsellor." *Bacon.*

To DISCONCERT, V. A. to unsettle, disorder, or discompose. To frustrate a design.

DISCONFORMITY, S. want of agreement, inconsistency, opposition.

DISCONGRUITY, S. disagreement, difference, inconsistency, opposition.

DISCONSOLATE, Adj. without hope or comfort; melancholy, or grieved on account of some severe affliction.

DISCONSOLATELY, Adv. in a hopeless, or comfortless manner.

DISCONSOLATENESS, S. the state of a person under severe affliction.

DISCONTENT, S. want of content; uneasiness; dissatisfaction.

DISCONTENT, Adj. uneasy, or dissatisfied with one's present condition.

DISCONTENTED, Part. uneasy, dissatisfied with one's present condition; malevolent, unhappy.

DISCONTENTEDNESS, S. uneasiness; the not being pleased or satisfied; the not approving, unhappiness, malevolence.

DISCONTENTMENT, S. the state of being dissatisfied, uneasy, or unhappy.

DISCONTINUANCE, S. want of union or adhesion; cessation, intermission, interruption, or stop, applied to action.

DISCONTINUATION, S. the breaking the continuity, or union; separation of the parts of a thing.

To DISCONTINUE, V. N. [*discontinuer*, Fr.] to break off; to separate; to put an end to an established privilege or custom; to leave off; to cease, to interrupt.

DISCONTINUITY, S. want of cohesion; breaking off union; separation.

DISCONVENIENCE, S. incongruity, disagreement, inconsistency. "In these disconvenience of nature, deliberation hath no place at all." *Hakewill.*

DISCORD, S. [*discordia*, Lat.] a state wherein persons, together they are christians, mutually endeavour to hurt each other, and are both to all the tender sentiments of humanity. A disposition wherein persons mutually oppose the interest of each other. Disagreement. Figuratively, difference, contrariety, or opposition of qualities. In Music, the relation of two sounds which are in themselves disagreeable, whether applied in succession or consequence. If two simple notes when sounded together, make a mixture, or compound sound which is disagreeable to the ear, it is a discord. *Consonant discords*, are such as have nothing very disagreeable in themselves, have a good effect in music only by their opposition, as they heighten that pleasure we receive from music by increasing its variety.

To DISCORD, V. N. [*discordo*, Lat.] to disagree, to produce a disagreeable sound when joined together.

DISCORDANCE, DISCORDANCY, S. disagreement, opposition, inconsistency, want of harmony.

DISCORDANT, Adj. [*discordans*, Lat.] inconsistent, disagreeing, or at variance; opposite, contrary, not conformable.

DISCORDANTLY, Adj. so as to be at variance, or inconsistent with itself. Not harmonizing, or agreeing with each other, applied to sounds. Peevishly. Angrily.

To DISCOVER, V. A. [*decouvrir*, Fr.] to make a thing seen by uncovering it; to make known; to find out something; to disclose, or reveal something which is secret.

DISCOVERABLE, Adj. that which may be found out or discovered; apparent, obvious.

DISCOVERER, S. one who finds out a thing, place, or position not known before; a scout, or one sent to make discoveries in an army, a spy. "Send *discoverers*—to know the numbers of our enemies." *Shak.*

DISCOVERY, S. the act of finding out, discovering, or revealing any thing secret.

To DISCOUNSEL, V. A. to dissuade, to turn aside from any vice or persuasion.

DISCOUNT, S. a sum allowed a person for payment, before any bill or debt becomes due, which is generally as much as the interest would amount to for the space the bill has to run.

To DISCOUNT, V. A. to give a person cash for a bill beforedue, deducting interest for the time which it has to run. To abate a certain sum for prompt payment, on the purchase of any article.

To DISCOUNTENANCE, V. A. to discourage by coolness or indifference. To shew one's disapprobation of any measure, by indifference, or by taking methods that may defeat it; to abash, confound, or put to shame.

DISCOUNTENANCE, S. coldness or indifference of behaviour; disregard.

DISCOUNTENANCER, S. one who discourages by cold treatment, indifference, or an unfavourable aspect.

To DISCOURAGE, V. A. to dishearten, or deter from any attempt; used with *from*

and improperly with *to*. " *Disparage* them to stay with you." *Temple.*

DISCOU'RAGER, S. one who deters, checks, or frightens a person from an attempt.

DISCOU'RAGEMENT, S. the act of deterring a person from any attempt, by representing the dangers attending it. Any impediment or difficulty which renders a person unwilling to undertake a design.

DISCOU'RSE, S. [the *a* is dropped and the *o* pronounced long, like *that* in *port*; from *discours*, Fr. of *dycursus*, Lat.] in Logic, an act or operation of the mind, whereby it proceeds from premises to consequences. Conversation, wherein persons mutually convey their ideas or sentiments to each other; speech; a treatise or dissertation. " Plutarch, in his *discourse* upon garrulity." *Pope.*

To DISCOU'RSE, V. N. to converse or talk with another. To reason, or proceed from propositions to their consequences. Actively, to treat of, or make a thing the subject of conversation.

DISCOU'RSER, S. a speaker, talker, or writer on any subject.

DISCU'RSIVE, Adj. passing, or advancing from a known thing to an unknown; partaking of the nature of talk, dialogue, or conversation.

DISCOU'RTEOUS, Adj. void of civility, politeness, or complaisance.

DISCOU'RTESY, S. rudeness, disrespect, or incivility.

DISCOU'RTEOUSLY, Adv. uncivilly, or rudely.

DISCRE'DIT, S. [*discredere*, Fr.] disgrace, ignominy, infamy, or that which involves a person in shame or infamy. The imputation of a fault, which lessens the fame and esteem of a person.

To DISCRE'DIT, V. A. to destroy or lessen the reputation of a thing or person. To render a thing suspicious which is believed to be true.

DISCRE'ET, Adj. [*discretus*, Lat.] able to distinguish between things and their consequences. Prudent, cautious. Modest, not forward for fear of the consequences of lasciviousness.

DISCRE'ETLY, Adv. prudently, cautiously, modestly, moderately.

DISCRE'ETNESS, S. a conduct guided by deliberation, prudence, and discretion.

DISCRE'TE, Adj. [*discretus*, Lat.] applied to quantity, separate, distinct. Applied to propositions, such as contain truths or sentiments set in contrast to each.

DISCRE'TION, S. [*discretio*, Lat.] prudent behaviour. Figuratively, an unlimited power, or one which is to be limited by no conditions. " He surrenders at *discretion*."

DISCRE'TIONARY, S. without any other restraint or guide, than a person's own discretion.

DISCRI'MINABLE, [*discrimen*, Lat.] distinguishable by some external or outward marks.

No. IX.

To DISCRI'MINATE, V. A. [*discrimino*, Lat.] to distinguish, or mark so as to shew a difference. To separate as different.

DISCRI'MINATENESS, S. distinction, difference, separation.

DISCRI'MINATION, S. [*discriminatio*, Lat.] the state of a thing distinguished for peculiar uses; distinction; the notes or marks which distinguish things from each other.

DISCRI'MINATIVE, Adj. that which constitutes the difference between things.

DISCU'BITORY, Adj. [*discubitorius*, Lat.] fitted for lying down. " Changed their curbicularly beds to *discubitory*." *Brown.*

DISCU'MBENCY, S. [*discumbens*, Lat.] the posture of lying along at meals, after the Roman manner. " The Greeks and Romans used the custom of *discumbency* at meals." *Brown.*

To DISCU'MBER, V. A. to disengage from any thing which hinders a person from a free use of his limbs. " The limbs *discumbered* from the clinging vest." *Pope.*

DISCU'RSIVE, Adj. [*discursif*, Fr.] in perpetual motion, hurry, or agitation. In Logic, proceeding from things known to things unknown.

To DISCU'SS, V. A. [*discussum*, Lat.] to examine, or explain a difficulty by meditation or debate.

DISCU'SSER, S. one who examines and determines a point, or explains a difficulty.

DISCU'SSION, S. the explaining a difficulty. The examining into some knotty point. In surgery, the dispersion of any humour or swelling.

DISCU'SSIVE, Adj. having the power to remove or disperse any humor.

DISCU'TIENT, S. [*discutiens*, Lat.] in Physic, a medicine which opens the pores, and disperses humors, by insensible perspiration, or otherwise.

To DISDA'IN, V. A. [*dedeigner*, Fr.] to reject with scorn and contempt; to refuse or decline with abhorrence and detestation.

DISDA'IN, S. contempt, abhorrence, scorn, or contemptuous anger.

DISDA'INFUL, Adj. abounding with indignation, haughtily, scornful, contemptuous.

DISDA'INFULLY, Adv. in a contemptuous, haughty manner.

DISDA'INFULNESS, S. contempt or scorn, including haughtiness and pride.

DISE'ASE, S. the state of a living body, wherein it is prevented from the use and exercise of any of its functions, attended with a sensation of uneasiness. In Botany, that state of a plant, rendered incapable of answering the several purposes for which it was formed.

To DISE'ASE, V. A. to affect the body, unable to exercise its functions. To affect with pain.

To DISEMBA'RK, V. A. to carry from a ship or vessel to land. To go to land, or on shore from a ship.

To DISEMBITTER, V. A. to free from bitterness or pain. To sweeten.

DISEMBO'DIED, Adj. stripped, deprived, or divested of body.

To DISEMBO'GUE, V. A. [disemboucher, old Fr.] to discharge at its mouth into the sea, applied to rivers. Neuterly, to flow. Among mariners, to go out of a river into the main ocean, applied to a ship.

DISEMBO'WELLED, Part. taken from the bowels.

To DISEMBRO'IL, V. A [debrouiller, Fr.] to free from confusion, disorder, perplexity, or quarrels.

To DISENA'BLE, V. A. to deprive of power, to weaken, or incapacitate.

To DISENCHA'NT, V. A. to free from the power of any spell, charm, enchantment, or infatuation.

To DISENCUM'BER, V. A. to free from any thing which oppresses a person with a sensation of burthensomeness or uneasiness. To free from any hindrance, obstruction, or incumbrance.

DISENCU'MBRANCE, S. freedom from hindrance, perplexity, or uneasiness.

To DISENGA'GE, V. A. to separate from any thing. To separate from any thing which is an encumbrance. To clear from impediments or obstructions. To withdraw, or divert the mind from any thing. Neuterly, to set ourselves free from. "We may disengage from the world by degrees." Collier. Used with from.

DISENGA'GED, Adj. at leisure, unoccupied, not fixed to any particular object.

DISENGA'GEMENT, S. freedom from any obligation, attendance, or leisure.

To DISENTA'NGLE, V. A. to set free from an obstacle, perplexity, or impediment.

To DISENTHRA'L, V. A. to free from any slavery or bondage; to set free, deliver, or release. "Thereby disenthral themselves." South.

To DISENTHRO'NE, V. A. to depose, or drive from the throne.

To DISENTRA'NCE, V. A. to free from a trance or swoon.

DISESTE'EM, S. want of esteem; a slight; loss of credit or esteem.

To DISESTE'EM, V. A. to regard slightingly; to consider or regard with less esteem, but not to rise to contempt.

DISFA'VOUR, S. want of countenance, or such a concurrence as may render a design successful. A state wherein a person merits with no encouragement or assistance. Want of beauty, or symmetry of features.

To DISFA'VOUR, V. A. to discountenance, to discourage, to withdraw kindness from a person.

DISFIGURA'TION, S. the act of spoiling or destroying the form of a thing or person. The state of a thing whose natural form and beauty is spoiled. Figuratively, deformity.

To DISFI'GURE, V. A. to change any thing to a worse form. To render a thing less beautiful.

DISFI'GUREMENT, S. change from beauty to ugliness, or from a pleasing agreeable form to one which is less so.

To DISFO'REST, V. A. to reduce ground from the state of a forest, to that of common ground.

To DISFRA'NCHISE, V. A. to deprive of its charter, privileges or immunities; to deprive a person of his freedom as a citizen.

DISFRA'NCHISEMENT, S. the act of depriving a person or place of freedom, privileges or immunities.

To DISFUR'NISH, V. A. to take away goods or furniture; to strip, spoil, or plunder. To deprive. "He durst not disfurnish that country either of so great a commander." Knolles.

To DISGO'RGE, V. A. [degorger, Fr.] to vomit or discharge by the mouth. To discharge, eject, or pour out with violence.

DISGRA'CE, S. [Fr.] shame, infamy, disesteem; a state wherein a person or thing has lost those qualities which rendered it worthy of respect. The state of a person out of favour.

To DISGRA'CE, V. A. to deprive of honour, esteem, or dignity.

DISGRA'CEFUL, Adj. full of dishonour, infamy, or shame.

DISGRA'CEFULLY, Adv. so as must subject a person to infamy, dishonour, shame, or reproach.

DISGRA'CER, S. one who exposes another to infamy, shame, dishonour, and reproach.

DISGRA'CIOUS, Adj. unfavourable, offensive, or disagreeable. "Disgracious in the city's eye." Shak.

To DISGUI'SE, V. A. [disguiser, Fr.] to conceal a person by means of some strange dress. Figuratively, to dissemble, or conceal by a false appearance. To disfigure a thing. To intoxicate by drinking.

DISGUI'SE, S. a dress made use of to conceal a person. A false appearance made use of to conceal some design.

DISGUI'SEMENT, S. any dress, habit, or artifice used to make a person appear different from what he does generally, or naturally.

DISGUI'SER, S. one who alters the appearance of a person or thing. One who masks or conceals his real designs.

DISGU'ST, S. an aversion, distaste, displeasure, arising from some disagreeable action, or behaviour.

To DISGU'ST, V. A. [degouter, Fr.] to raise an aversion, or nauseousness in the stomach by a disagreeable taste. To raise an aversion, by some disagreeable, or offensive action, used with at or from. To raise an aversion, or make a person avoid through aver-

aversion; used with *from*. " What *disgusts* me *from* having to do with answer-jobbers." *Swift.*

DISGU'STFUL, Adj. producing aversion or dislike.

DI'SH, S. [*dife*, Sax.] a broad shallow vessel with a rim, either of silver, pewter, china, &c. used for holding joints, or other victuals at a table, and differing from a plate in size. Figuratively, the meat placed in a *dish*.

To DI'SH, V. A. to serve meat up elegantly, or place it in a *dish*. To *dish out*, to adorn, deck, or set off.

DISHABI'LLE, S. [Fr.] an undress; a loose and negligent morning dress.

DISHABI'LLE, Adj. loosely, carelessly, and negligently dress'd.

To DISHA'BIT, V. A. to displace or uncover a thing. " From their fixed beds of lime had been *dishabited*." *Shak.*

To DISHEA'RTEN, V. A. to deprive of courage; to terrify; to make a person imagine a thing to be impracticable.

DISHERI'SON, S. the act of debarring or hindering a person from an inheritance.

To DISHE'RIT, V. A. to debar or cut off from an inheritance.

To DISHEVE'L, V. A. [*decheveler*, Fr.] to spread hair in a loose, negligent, careless, and disorderly manner.

DISHO'NEST, Adj. fraudulent, or inconsistent with justice. Reproachful, or shameful.

DISHO'NESTLY, Adv. so as to be inconsistent with honour, honesty, or justice.

DISHO'NESTY, S. want of probity. The act of doing any thing to defraud another. Injustice. Unchasteness, or lewdness. " If you suspect me in any *dishonesty*," *Shak.*

DISHO'NOUR, S. that which affects a person with disgrace. Figuratively, reproach, loss of reputation.

To DISHO'NOUR, V. A. to bring to shame or disgrace. To blast or injure the character of a person. To violate a person's chastity. To treat with indignity, or contempt.

DISHO'NOURABLE, Adj. void of respect, reverence, or esteem. Shameful; reproachful; disreputable.

DISHO'NOURER, S. one who treats another with indignity, or violates the chastity of a female.

To DISINCA'RCERATE, V. A. to free from imprisonment. Figuratively, to release, or free from confinement. " Open the surface of the earth for to *disincarcerate* the same reserve bodies." *Harvey.*

DISI'NCLINATION, S. want of affection, or bias. Want of propensity, less than aversion.

To DISINCLI'NE, V. A. to lessen or abate one's affections for a thing or person.

DISINGENU'ITY, S. unfairness; low and mean artifice; cunning.

DISINGE'NUOUS, Adj. not openly and frankly. Meanly, sly, cunning, subtle.

DISINGE'NUOUSLY, Adv. in an unfair, sly, or subtile manner.

To DISINHE'RIT, V. A. to cut off or deprive of an inheritance.

DISINTERE'STED, Adj. [from *dis* and *interesse*, Fr.] without any regard to private interest; without any bias on account of a person's own emolument, or advantage. Impartial.

DISI'NTEREST, S. that which is contrary to a person's interest or interest. A disadvantage or loss. Disregard of profit or private advantage.

DISINTERE'STED, Adj. not influenced by any selfish views of private lucre, or advantage.

To DISJOI'N, V. A. [*disjoindre*, Fr.] to separate things which are united. To part, or sever.

To DISJOI'NT, V. A. [pronounced *disjint*, with the i long] to put out of joint. To separate things at the joint. To carve or cut into pieces. To make loose-herent. To marr or destroy the connection of words, or sentences. " Her words *disjointed*." *Smith.* Neuterly, to fall in pieces.

DISJOI'NT, Part. divided. " Thanks —one slate to be *disjoint*." *Shak.*

DISJU'NCTION, S. [*disjunctio*, Lat.] separation; division. " The *disjunction* of the body and the soul." *South.*

DISJU'NCTIVE, Adj. [*disjunctivus*, Lat.] disuniting; unfit for union. In grammar, applied to such particles as denote a separation, or contrast. In Logic, applied to such propositions whose parts are opposed to each other by disjunctive particles.

DISJU'NCTIVELY, Adj. in a separate manner, distinctly; separately.

DI'SK, S. [*dijc*, Sax. *discus*, Lat.] in astronomy, the body of the sun or planets, divided by astronomers into 12 parts. In optics, the magnitude of the glass of a telescope, or the width of its aperture. In botany, the middle part of radiated flowers.

DISKI'NDNESS, S. want of kindness, affection, charity, or benevolence. An act whereby a person receives detriment, and is supposed to be derived from ill-will.

DISLI'KE, S. want of approbation, affection, or esteem.

To DISLI'KE, V. A. to disapprove. To look on as improper, or faulty. To hate. To shew disgust, or disesteem.

To DISLI'KEN, V. A. to change the appearance of a thing from what it was before.

To DI'SLOCATE, V. A. [from *dis* and *locatus*, Lat.] to put, or force out of its proper place. To disjoint.

DISLOCA'TION, S. [from *disloco*] the putting

putting things out of their proper places. In furgery, a joint put out, or the forcing a bone from its focket. A luxation.

To DISLO'DGE, V. A. to remove from a place by force. To drive an enemy from a poſt. To remove an army to other quarters. Neuterly, to decamp. "He resolved—with all his legions to diſlodge." Par. Loſt.

DISLO'YAL, Adj. [deſloyal, Fr.] falſe, or diſobedient to a ſovereign. "The lady is diſloyal." Shak. Diſhoneſt. "A falſe diſloyal knave." Shak.

DISLO'YALLY, Adj. In a faithleſs, diſobedient, diſloyal manner.

DISLO'YALTY, S. want of fidelity to a ſovereign. "Want of fidelity or conſtancy in love." "Such ſeeming truths of hero's diſloyalty, that jealouſy ſhall be called aſſurance." Shak.

DI'SMAL, Adj. [duys-mael, Belg.] horrible; melancholy; gloomy; ſorrowful.

DISMA'LLY, Adv. ſo as to excite horror, ſorrow, or melancholy.

DI'SMALNESS, S. the quality which excites horror, melancholy, grief, or ſorrow.

To DISMA'NTLE, V. A. to ſtrip a perſon of any dreſs or ornament. To unfold, or deſtroy. To deſtroy the out-works. To deſtroy any thing external. "His noſe diſmantled." Dryden.

To DISMA'SK, V. A. to pull off a maſk; to uncover. "Fair ladies m ſk'd, are roſes in the bud—are roſes blown diſmaſk'd." Shak.

To DISMA'Y, V. A. [deſmayer, Span.] to diſcourage, intimidate, or diſhearten with fear.

DISMA'Y, S. [deſmayo, Span.] loſs of courage, occaſioned by ſome frightful object; fear.

To DISME'MBER, V. A. to divide or ſeparate one member from another. To cut or tear to pieces.

To DISMI'SS, V. A. [diſmiſſus, Lat.] to ſend away. To diſcharge. To permit leave to depart. Uſed with from before the thing or perſon quitted.

DISMI'SSION, S. [dimiſſio, Lat.] the act of ſending away. A diſcharge from an office. Deprivation, or the being turned out of any office.

To DISMO'RTGAGE, V. A. to redeem from a mortgage, by paying the money lent on any lands or eſtate. "He diſmortgaged the crown demeſnes." Howel.

To DISMO'UNT, V. A. [demonter, Fr.] to throw by force from an horſe. To diſlodge, or force cannon from their carriages. Neuterly, to alight from an horſe. To deſcend from any eminence.

DISNA'TURED, Part. unnatural; not having the natural affections of humanity. "Athwart diſnatur'd torment." Shak.

DISOBE'DIENCE, S. the acting contrary to the commands of a ſuperior.

DISOBE'DIENT, Part. guilty of acting contrary to the laws, or the commands of a maſter, or ſuperior.

To DISOBE'Y, V. A. to act contrary to the commands of a ſuperior. To break, or tranſgreſs the laws.

DISOBLIGA'TION, S. an act which alienates the affections of a perſon, or friend. An act which occaſions diſlike.

To DISOBLI'GE, V. A. to do ſomething which offends another; to diſpleaſe, generally uſed as a ſofter expreſſion for diſlike.

DISOBLI'GING, Part. unpleaſing; offenſive; unkind.

DISOBLI'GINGLY, Adv. in ſuch a manner as to diſpleaſe, or offend.

DISO'RBE, Part. [from dis and orb] caſt from its proper orbit, wherein it performs its revolutions.

DISO'RDER, S. [deſordre, Fr.] want of method, or regularity. Tumult, or confuſion. Breach, or violation of laws. The ſtate of an animal body, wherein the regular exerciſe of its functions is interrupted; diſeaſe; diſcompoſure of mind.

To DISO'RDER, V. A. to throw into confuſion, or irregularity. To ruffle, or confuſe. To affect with ſome ſlight diſeaſe. To diſcompoſe, or render unfit to exerciſe its faculties, applied to the mind.

DISO'RDERED, Part. indiſpoſed with a ſlight diſeaſe, applied to the body. Confuſed, tumultuous, or rebellious, applied to ſtates. Rumpled, applied to a perſon's dreſs.

DISO'RDERLY, Adv. inconſiſtent with law, or virtue. In an irregular, or tumultuous manner, applied to the motion of the animal ſpirits. In a manner wanting method, applied to the placing, or diſtribution of things.

DISO'RDINATE, S. irregular; inconſiſtent with the rules of virtue. "Theſe not diſordinate." Milton.

To DISPA'RAGE, V. A. [from diſpar, Lat.] to match with what is not equal. To diſgrace, by joining a thing of ſuperior excellence, with one below it. To diſgrace, by compariſon with ſomething of leſs value. To treat with contempt and diſhonour. To expoſe, to blame, cenſure, leſſen, or reproach.

DISPA'RAGEMENT, S. diſgrace, or diſhonour, ariſing from comparing a thing with ſomething of inferior excellence and dignity. In law, the marrying an heir with a perſon of an inferior, or mean degree. Diſgrace, diſhonour, or reproach. Uſed with to, before the perſon or thing injured.

DISPARA'GER, S. one who treats another with indignity, and endeavours to leſſen the value of a thing by comparing it with ſomething of leſs value.

DISPA'RITY, S. [diſpar, Lat.] oppoſition of qualities. Difference in degree. Unlikeneſs, or diſſimilitude.

1

To

To DISPA'RT, V. A. [departer, Fr. dispertire, Lat.] to divide into two. To separate; to burst; to rend.

DISPA'RT, S. the mark set on the muzzle ring of a piece of ordnance.

DISPA'SSION, S. coolness; freedom from the passions or affections of the mind.

DISPA'SSIONATE, Adj. free from anger, or other passions. Calm, cool, serene, and temperate.

To DISPATCH, V. A. to send a person or thing away hastily; to murder; to perform business quickly.

DISPA'TCH, S. quickness, expedition, a message, an express.

To DISPE'L, V. A. [dispello, Lat.] to disperse; to clear away any obstruction by dissipating it.

DISPEN'SARY, S. the place where medicines are sold and physician's bills are made up. A book containing receipts for making medicines.

DISPENSA'TION, S. [dispensatio, Lat.] the economy observed by divine Providence in the general distribution of rewards and punishments to all mankind. A permission to do something contrary to the laws, or a suspension of their force for a certain time.

DISPEN'SATORY, S. a book containing receipts by which medicines are made.

To DISPE'NSE, V. A. [dispenser, Fr.] to distribute, or give among several persons. To make up a receipt or medicine, in physic. To dispense with. To excuse from a duty. To render an equivalent. To make compensation. "Can'st thou dispense with heaven for such an oath." Shak.

DISPE'NSE, S. excuse; dispensation. "Indulgences, dispenses, pardons, bulls." Par. Lost.

DISPE'NSER, S. one who distributes, gives, or bestows.

To DISPE'OPLE, V. A. to deprive a country of its inhabitants.

To DISPE'RSE, V. A. [dispersus, Lat.] to scatter; to drive to different parts; to separate a body of men.

DISPER'SEDLY, Adv. in a separate manner; separately.

DISPE'RSER, S. one who distributes or spreads abroad; one who makes public by communicating to many.

DISPE'RSION, S. [dispersio, Lat.] the act of scattering, distributing, or spreading. The state of persons which are divided or separated from each other.

To DISPI'RIT, V. A. to strike with fear; to discourage, to exhaust the spirits.

DISPI'RITEDNESS, S. want of alacrity, courage, vigour, or vivacity.

To DISPLA'CE, V. A. to put out of a place. To remove from one place to another. To supersede, remove, or abolish in order to introduce some other person or thing in the room. To put an end to disorder. "You have displaced the mirth." Shak.

DISPLA'CENCY, S. [displicentia, Lat.] behaviour which occasions displeasure, or disgust.

DISPLANTA'TION, S. the removal of a plant. The driving people out of a plantation or settlement. "The Assyrians, whose displantation Senacherib vaunted of."

To DISPLA'Y, V. A. [desplier, desployer, Fr.] to spread abroad or wide. To explain a thing minutely. To set ostentatiously to view. To set off to the best advantage. In Carving, to cut up a crane, &c.

DISPLAY, S. the act of exhibiting a thing to view; to discover its excellencies.

DISPLA'YED, Part. in Heraldry, applied to a bird in an erect posture, with its wings expanded.

To DISPLE'ASE, V. A. to offend. To raise the ill-will of a person. To disgust, or raise an aversion, applied to the senses.

DISPLE'ASINGNESS, S. the quality of creating dislike, or being disagreeable.

DISPLE'ASURE, S. a disagreeable sensation; uneasiness, or pain. Anger. A state of disgrace, wherein a person has lost the favour of another.

To DISPLE'ASURE, V. A. to be guilty of some action which may give offence. "The way of pleasuring or displeasuring." Bacon.

DISPO'RT, S. play, sport, pastime, diversion, fun, mirth.

To DISPO'RT, V. A. to amuse, or divert. "Hunting this way to disport himself." Shak. Neuterly, to play, toy, or wanton, beautifully applied to inanimate things. "Where light disports in ever mingling dyes." Pope.

DISPO'SAL, S. the act of regulating any thing. Distribution, dispensation. The right of bestowing. Management; government.

To DISPO'SE, V. A. [disposer, Fr.] to apply to any use. To bestow, give, or grant, to lay out money. To adapt; fit or form for any purpose. To give a light; to influence the mind. To regulate or adjust; used with of. To apply to any purpose; to transfer to any other person. To employ; to place in any condition. To sell; to get rid of. Neuterly, to bargain or make terms. "She had disposed with Cæsar." Shak.

DISPO'SER, S. one who has the management of any affair. He that gives, bestows, or regulates. A director. One who distributes or acts without controul.

DISPOSI'TION, S. [dispositio, Lat.] a regular arrangement, distribution of things. Natural fitness, or tendency. Propensity, or temper of the mind. Affections of kindness or ill will. "The dispositions of each people towards the other." Swift.

DISPO'SITOR, S. in Astrology, the supposed

posed lord of the sign in which the planet is, and the ruler of its influence.

To DISPOSSE'SS, V. A. to turn a person out of a place. Generally used with *of*, before the thing taken away. "To *dispossess* the pirate *of* his own gotten kingdom." *Knolles.* Formerly used with *from*. "And quite *dispossess*—concord and law of nature *from* the earth." *Par. Loft.*

DISPO'SURE, S. the power of bestowing or ordering in a manner most agreeable to one's self. State, or posture. "They remained in a kind of warlike *disposure.*" *Wotton.*

DISPRA'ISE, S. blame. Censure. Reproach. Abuse.

To DISPRA'ISE, V. N. to blame, to find fault with; to censure; to abuse.

DISPRA'ISER, S. one who blames, censures, or finds fault.

DISPRA'ISINGLY, Adv. with blame, reproach, or censure.

To DISPRE'AD, V. A. to spread abroad; to spread, or scatter different ways.

DISPRO'OF, S. confutation; or the proving a thing to be false.

DISPRO'FIT, S. loss; damage; that by which a person receives loss.

DISPROPORTION, S. the disagreement or inequality between things.

To DISPROPO'RTION, V. A. to join things which disagree with each other.

DISPROPO'RTIONABLE, Adj. disagreeing in quantity or quality. Not well suited or proportioned.

DISPROPO'RTIONABLENESS, S. the want of agreement, with respect to quantity, &c., or quality.

DISPROPO'RTIONAL, Adj. unsuitable or disagreeing in quantity, quality, or value.

DISPROPO'RTIONATE, Adj. disagreeing in quantity, or value. Wanting symmetry.

DISPROPO'RTIONATELY, Adv. wanting symmetry; or disagreeing in quantity or value with something else.

To DISPRO'VE, V. A. to confute an assertion. To shew a thing or practice to be inconsistent with truth.

DISPRO'VER, S. one who confutes, or proves a thing to be false, or erroneous.

DISPU'TABLE, Adj. that which may admit of arguments on both sides. Liable to dispute. Lawful to be contested.

DI'SPUTANT, S. [*disputans*, Lat.] one who argues against, or opposes the opinions, or doctrines of another.

DISPUTATION, S. [*disputatio*, Lat.] the art of opposing the sentiments of others. Controversy, or argument in opposition to the sentiments of another.

DISPUTA'TIOUS, Adj. fond of opposing the opinions of others; given to debate, or cavilling.

DISPUTATIVE, Adj. fond of opposing the opinions of others. Fond of controversy or cavilling.

To DISPU'TE, V. N. [*dispute*, Lat.] to oppose the sentiments of another. To argue against any received opinion. To contend for a thing either by words or actions. To oppose, or question. To discuss a question. "*Dispute* it like a man." *Shak.*

DISPU'TE, S. the act of opposing the opinion of another. Controversy.

DISPU'TELESS, Adj. without controversy. Undisputed.

DISPU'TER, S. one engaged, or delighting in controversy.

DISQUALIFICA'TION, S. that which renders a person unfit for the discharge of an employ, or the keeping an office.

To DISQUA'LIFY, V. A. to make unfit. To disable. To exempt, or disable, from any right, claim, or practice, by law.

DISQUI'ET, S. uneasiness; restlessness; want of ease of mind. Anxiety.

DISQUI'ET, Adj. uneasy, restless, or disturbed in mind.

To DISQUI'ET, V. A. to disturb the mind. To fret; to vex. To make uneasy, or restless.

DISQUI'ETER, S. a disturber; or one who vexes and frets another.

DISQUI'ETLY, Adv. anxiously; in such a manner as to make uneasy.

DISQUI'ETUDE, S. care; uneasiness; or disturbance of mind. Anxiety. Want of tranquillity.

DISQUISI'TION, S. [*disquisitio*, Lat.] an act of the mind, whereby it examines into a subject, in order to understand its importance. A strict search, scrutiny, or examination of a thing or matter.

DISREGA'RD, S. slight notice; contempt; neglect; disesteem; indifference.

To DISREGA'RD, V. A. to take no notice of; to slight; to neglect; to contemn; to be indifferent about.

DISREGA'RDFUL, Adj. negligent; contemptuous; indifferent.

DISREGA'RDFULLY, Adj. in a negligent, contemptuous, indifferent, or slighting manner.

DISRE'LISH, S. a bad taste; disgust, or dislike.

To DISRE'LISH, V. A. to make a thing nauseous. To affect the taste, with a disagreeable sensation. To dislike.

DISREPUTA'TION, S. disgrace; disesteem; or that which will lessen a person's character.

DISREPU'TE, S. disgrace; an ill character; loss of reputation. Reproach.

DISRESPE'CT, S. incivility; want of esteem; a behaviour, which approaches to rudeness and argues want of reverence.

DISRESPE'CTFUL, Adj. uncivil; without esteem; unmannerly; impolite.

DIS-

DISRESPE'CTFULLY, Adv. in an uncivil, indecent, irreverent, or unmannerly
manner.

To DISRO'BE, V. A. to undress. To lay
aside, to divest, applied to the mind. " Who
will be perfuaded to difrobe himfelf at once of
all his old opinions." Locke.

DISRU'PTION, S. the act of breaking or
burfting afunder. A breach, or rent.

DISSATISFA'CTION, S. the ftate of a
perfon who is not contented, but wants fomething to compleat his wifh or happinefs. Difcontent. Figuratively, want of fome quality
to caufe pleafure.

DISSA'TISFA'CTORY, Adj. that which
is not able to produce content, or fatisfaction.

To DISSA'TISFY, V. A. to be difcontent. To difpleafe. To be deficient in
fome quality requifite to pleafe or content.

To DISSE'CT, V. A. [diffecum] in Anatomy, to divide the parts of an animal body
with a knife, in order to confider each of
them apart. Figuratively, to divide, and examine any fubject minutely.

DISSE'CTION, S. in Anatomy, the act
of cutting or dividing the feveral parts of an
animal body afunder, to examine into their
nature and refpective ufes. To divide the feveral parts of a plant, leaf, or any piece of
work, in order to examine into the mutual
connection of their feveral parts.

DISSEI'ZOR, S. one who deprives or dif-
poffeffes another of his right.

To DISSE'MBLE, V. A. [diffimulo, Lat.]
to hide under a falfe appearance. To pretend that to be, which is not. To play the
hypocrite.

DISSE'MBLER, S. one who conceals his
real defigns, temper, under a falfe and fpecious appearance. An hypocrite.

DISSE'MBLINGLY, Adv. in an hypocritical manner, fo as to conceal one's real
fentiments under a falfe and fpecious appearance.

To DISSE'MINATE, V. A. [diffeminatum]
to featter feed; to fow. Figuratively, to
fpread abroad a report.

DISSEMINA'TION, S. [diffeminatio, Lat.]
the act of fowing. The act of propagating
a report, &c.

DISSE'MINATOR, S. he that fows.
One who fpreads or propagates a report, or
doctrine.

DISSE'NSION, S. [diffenfio, Lat.] difference or difagreement in opinion, or politics.
A breach of union. Contention; or warm
oppofition.

DISSE'NSIOUS, Adj. difpofed to ftrife;
quarrelfome. Factious, turbulent.

To DISSE'NT, V. N. [diffentio, Lat.] to
difagree. To think differently. To be of a
contrary nature; to differ.

DISSE'NT, S. difagreement, difference
of opinion.

DISSENTA'NEOUS, Adj. difagreeable;
inconfiftent.

DISSE'NTER, S. one who difagrees to
an opinion; one who feparates himfelf from
the communion of the church of England.

DISSERTA'TION, S. [differtatio, Lat.]
a fet difcourfe or treatife.

To DISSE'RVE, V. A. to act contrary
to the interefts and advantage of a perfon or
caufe. To do injury or damage to. To
hurt.

DISSE'RVICE, S. harm; hurt; injury;
prejudice, or an ill-turn.

DISSE'RVICEABLE, Adj. difadvantage-
ous. Injurious. Hurtful.

To DISSE'VER, V. A. to break, divide,
or part in two. To feparate; to divide.

DISSILE'NCE, S. [diffiliens, Lat.] the
act of ftarting afunder; burfting in two.

DISSILI'TION, S. the act of ftarting
afunder; or burfting after being united.
" The diffilum of that air was great."
Boyle.

DISSI'MILAR, Adj. [diffimilis, Lat.]
differing in quality or fhape. Unlike; of a
different kind, nature, or degree.

DISSIMILA'RITY, S. unlikedinefs in
quality, temper, bulk or difpofition.

DISSIMI'LITUDE, S. difference of form
or quality. Want of refemblance.

DISSIMULA'TION, S. [diffimulatio, Lat.]
the act of putting on a falfe or feigned appearance, to conceal one's intention, or difpofition.

To DISSIPATE, V. A. [diffipatus, Lat.]
to feparate any collection, and difperfe the
parts. To divide the attention between a
diverfity of objects. To fcatter or fquander
wealth, or fpend a fortune.

DISSIPA'TION, S. [Fr. diffipatio, Lat.]
the act of feparating. The ftate of the parts
of a body feparated. Figuratively, inattention; attention divided among a variety of
objects, and incapable to fix properly on any.

To DISSO'CIATE, V. A. [diffociatum,
Lat.] to feparate things or perfons which are
united.

DISSO'LVABLE, Adj. that which is capable of having its parts feparated, by moisture, or fome fluid; " Not diffolvable by
the moifture of the tongue." Newt. Opt.
Diffoluble is more frequently ufed.

DISSO'LUBLE, Adj. [diffolubilis, Lat.]
capable of having its parts feparated or diffolved by moifture or heat.

DISSOLUBI'LITY, S. the poffibility of
being diffolved or liquified by moifture or
heat.

To DISSO'LVE, V. A. [diffolvo, Lat.]
To melt, or liquify with moifture or heat.
To deftroy. To feparate, to break the ties
of any thing. To part perfons who are
united by any bonds. To clear up a doubt
or difficulty. " To diffolve doubts." Dan.
v. 16. To break or deftroy the force of an
inchant-

Inchantment. To be overcome, or over-powered with something pleasing. To consume or fall into pieces. To melt with pleasure; to break up or discharge an assembly.

DISSO'LVENT, Adj. [*dissolvens*, Lat.] having the power of separating, melting or dissolving.

DISSO'LVENT, S. that which has the power of separating the parts of any thing.

DISSO'LVER, S. that which has the power of melting, or liquifying.

DISSO'LVIBLE, Adj. [commonly written *dissolvable*, but less properly] liable to have its parts separated by heat or moisture. Liable to perish by the separation of its parts.

DI'SSOLUTE, S. [*dissolutus*, Lat.] dissolved in. Loose, wanton; abandoned, or unrestrained by the rules of morality, or religion.

DI'SSOLUTELY, Adv. in such a manner as is inconsistent with virtue. In debauchery, and wantonness.

DI'SSOLUTENESS, S. looseness of manners. A conduct regulated by no restraint. Wantonness; debauchery. Wickedness.

DISSOLU'TION, S. the act of liquifying and melting by heat or moisture. The destruction of any thing by the separation of its parts. Death, or the separation of the body and soul. The act of breaking up an assembly. "The *dissolution* of the house." Licentiousness; more commonly stiled dissoluteness. "An universal *dissolution* of manners began to prevail." *Atterb.*

DISSO'NANCE, S. [Fr. *dissonance*, Lat.] a mixture of unharmonious sounds. Discord.

DISSO'NANT, Adj. [*dissonans*, Lat.] sounding harsh and disagreeable to the ear. Figuratively, inconsistent; disagreeing; "What can be more *dissonant from* reason." *Hestren*, "Any thing *dissonant to* truth" *Smith*. Generally, used with *to*, though sometimes with *from*.

To DISSUA'DE, V. A. [*dissuadeo*, Lat.] to make use of arguments to hinder a person from doing what he intends. To represent a thing as improper, disadvantageous or wrong.

DISSUA'DER, S. one who endeavours to dissuade or divert a person from a design.

DISSUA'SION, S. an argument made use of to divert a person, from closing in with any design, including the idea of a previous intention or resolution of doing it.

DISSUA'SIVE, Adj. tending to divert or turn aside from any purpose.

DISSUA'SIVE, S. a motive or argument made use of to dissuade or prevail on a person to decline any design.

DISSY'LLABLE, S. [*dissyllable*, *dissyllabe*, Gr.] in Grammar, a word consisting of two syllables.

DI'STAFF, S. [*distaef*, Sax.] the staff on the extremity of which the tow or hemp is fastened for spinning. Figuratively, a woman, a female. "A *distaff* in the throne." *Dryd.*

To DISDAI'N, V. A. to mark with a different colour; to spoil the colour of a thing. To blot; to mark with infamy; pollute, or defile.

DISTA'NCE, S. [Fr. *distance*, Lat.] the space between any two objects, applied to place or situation. A space marked in a horse-course. The space between a thing present, and one that is past or future, applied to time. A modest or respectful behaviour, without too much familiarity. Reserve; coolness, opposed to the close caresses and familiar nearness between friends.

To DI'STANCE, V. A. to remove from the view; or further from a person. To leave behind at a race, the length of a distance-post. Figuratively, to surpass or excell a person.

DI'STANT, Adj. [Fr. *distant*, Lat.] far from, or at a distance. Apart, separate, asunder. Removed from the present instant, applied to time past, or future. Reserved, opposed to familiar, applied to behaviour or affection. Not obvious, or bearing a remote sense, applied to words, and opposed to *primary*.

To DISTA'STE, V. A. to occasion a disagreeable or nauseous taste. Figuratively, to dislike. To offend, or displease. To make a person angry; in ver. "Diseased, *distasted*, and distracted souls."

DISTA'STEFUL, Adj. affecting the palate, a nauseous sensation. That which gives offence, or is unpleasing. "*Distasteful* looks." *Shak.*

DISTE'MPER, S. a disproportionate, or inadequate mixture of ingredients. In Medicine, some disorder of the animal machine, generally applied to a slight indisposition. A disorder of the mind, arising from the predominance of any passion or appetite. Want of due balance between contraries. Ill-humour. Tumultuous disorder, applied to states.

To DISTE'MPER, V. A. to affect with some disease. To disorder. To fill the mind with perturbation. To render rebellious, or disaffected.

DISTE'MPERATE, Adj. immoderate. "The *distemperate* heat." *Raleigh.*

DISTE'MPERATURE, S. excess of heat, cold, or other qualities. Violent commotions. Perturbation of mind. Confusion. Mixture of contrary qualities.

To DISTE'ND, V. A. [*distendo*, Lat.] to stretch by filling. To stretch out, or extend in breadth.

DISTE'NT, S. the space through which any thing is stretched; breadth. "*Distended* one fourteenth part longer; which addition of

of *diftens* will add much to their beauty."
Wotten.

DISTE'NTION, S. [*diftentis*, Lat.] the act of stretching out, or in breath. Breadth. The act of separating one thing from another. "Your legs do labour more in elevation than in *diftraston*." *Wotten*.

DI'STICH, S. [*diftichon*] a couplet; a couple of lines; a poem of only two verses. A theme or subject treated of in two lines.

To DISTI'L, V. N. [*diftillo*, Lat.] to fall by drops. To drop or fall gently, applied to fluids. To use a still. Actively, to let fall in drops. To extract the virtues of ingredients by a still.

DISTILLA'TION, S. [*diftillatio*, Lat.] the act of separating the oily, watery, or spirituous parts of ingredients, inclosed in a still, by means of fire. The act of distending in drops. That which diftends in drops from a still.

DISTI'LLER, S. one who makes and sells distilled liquors.

DISTI'LLERY, S. the business, trade, or employment of a distiller.

DISTI'NCT, Adj. [*diftinctus*, Lat.] different in number and kind; separate, apart, asunder, opposed to *conjoined*. Uncomixed. Easy to be distinguished from any other.

DISTI'NCTION, S. [Fr. *diftinction*, Lat.] a note or mark which shews the difference between objects. A note or mark of superiority. That by which one thing differs from another. Difference made between persons of various ages, sexes, or ranks. Division into different parts. The notation, or shewing the difference between things which are in some respects like one another. Discernment. Judgment. High rank, or dignity.

DISTI'NCTIVE, Adj. having the power to distinguish, manifest, or perceive the difference between things. Judicious.

DISTI'NCTIVELY, Adv. in right order. Without confusion, clearly.

DISTI'NCTLY, Adv. without confusion. Plainly, clearly.

DISTI'NCTNESS, S. an accurate observation of the difference between things. A separation of things either externally, or in the mind, which renders their difference from each other manifest.

To DISTI'NGUISH, V. A. [*diftinguo*, Lat.] to note or mark the difference between things. To separate from others by some mark of honour. To know from another by some mark of difference. To perceive; to discern critically. To conciliate a difference. To make known or to make eminent. Neuterly, to make known, or shew the point or particular in which things differ from each other.

DISTI'NGUISHABLE, Adj. that which may be separated or easily known or distinguished from another. Worthy of note, or regard.

DISTI'NGUISHED, Adj. eminent. Easily to be seen from others, on account of some remarkable excellence.

DISTI'NGUISHER, S. one who observes and notes the difference of things. A judicious observer.

To DISTO'RT, V. A. [*diftortus*, Lat.] to twist; to deform. To put out of its natural state. "*Diftort* the underftanding." *Tillotf*. To wreft an expression from its true meaning, to one which makes for one's own opinion.

DISTO'RTION, S. [*diftortio*, Lat.] in Medicine, a contraction of one side of the mouth, by a convulsion of the muscles of one side of the face. An irregular motion by which any of the parts of animal bodies are rendered deformal. The wrefting an expression or a word from its true and intended meaning, in order to favour some particular sentiment.

To DISTRA'CT, [participle passive *diftracted*, from *diftractus*, Lat.] to pull a thing different ways at the same time. To separate; to part. "*Diftract* your army." *Shak*. To fill and attract the mind with variety of different views or confiderations. To make a person mad or insane. "Fetch my poor *diftracted* husband home." *Shak*.

DISTRA'CTEDLY, Adv. crazily, after the manner of a madman.

DISTRA'CTEDNESS, S. the state of a person who is mad, or crazy.

DISTRA'CTION, S. [*diftractio*, Lat.] separation; division. Confusion. A state in which the attention is called to different and sometimes contrary objects. Perturbation of mind. Madness. Disturbance, tumult, applied to government. Difference of sentiments.

To DISTRA'IN, V. A. [*deftraindre*, Fr.] in Law, to seize the property of another for debt. To make a seizure.

DISTRA'INER, S. he that seizes or distrains for debt.

DISTRA'INT, S. in Law, the act of seizing, or that which is seized for debt.

DISTRA'UGHT, S. Old Participle of *diftract*. "*Diftraught* of his wits." *Camden*.

DISTRE'SS, S [*diftresse*, Fr.] in Law, any thing seized or distrained. The act of making a seizure. Figuratively, any calamity or toil. The condition of a person who has not the necessaries to supply the demands of nature.

To DISTRE'SS, V. A. in Law, to seize for rent unpaid; to harrass, or ruin.

DISTRE'SSFUL, Adj. miserable; wretched; deprived of the comforts and conveniences of life.

To DISTRI'BUTE, V. A. [*diftributum*, Lat.] to divide amongst several persons. To give to several.

DISTRI'BUTER, S. one who gives, bestows, or distributes.

DISTRIBU'TION, S. the act of bestowing sharing or dividing. The act of giving charity. The thing given in alms. In Logic, the distinction of an universal whole in to several kinds of species.

DISTRIBUTIVE, Adj. employed in assigning portions to others. Distributive justice is that which allots each man the reward, punishment or claim due to him. That which distinguishes a general term into its various species.

DISTRIBUTIVELY, Adv. singly; particularly. In Logic, in a manner which expresses singly all the particulars included in a general term.

DISTRICT, S. [districtus, Lat.] the circuit or territory within which a person's jurisdiction, power, or authority is confined. A region, or country.

To DISTRUST, V. A. to suspect; to want confidence in a person. To be diffident.

DISTRUST, S. loss of credit. Suspicion of a person's fidelity, or ability. Diffidence.

DISTRUSTFUL, Adj. suspicious, diffident of the fidelity of another. Modest, timorous.

DISTRUSTFULLY, Adv. suspiciously, or diffidently.

DISTRUSTFULNESS, S. the state of being suspicious of another. Want of confidence.

To DISTURB, V. A. [disturbo, Lat.] to perplex, disquiet or make uneasy. To confound To interrupt or hinder the continuation of any action. To divert, or turn aside from a particular or destined end, used with from. "Disturb—their inmost councils from their destined aim." Par. Lost.

DISTURBANCE, S. interruption, confusion, or disorder of mind. Tumult, uproar, noise, or violation of the peace.

DISTURBER, S. one who breaks the peace, or causes tumults, one who affects the mind of another with confusion, trouble, anxiety and uneasiness.

To DISVA'LUE, V. A. to undervalue to set a low price on a thing; to esteem below its worth or value. "Her reputation was disvalued" Shakesp.

To DISVE'LOP, V. A. [developer, Fr.] to unfold.

DISUNION, S. the separation or disjunction of the parts of a body, or persons who formed an alliance. Figuratively, breach of concord, or disagreement between friends.

To DISUNITE, V. A. to part, or divide. To separate or part friends.

To DISUNITE, V. A. to part, or divide. To separate or part friends.

DISUNITY, S. the state of separation. "Disunity is the natural property of matter." Ala.

DISUSAGE, S. the leaving off or discon-

inuing a practice or custom by degrees.

DISUSE, S. the breaking off, or discontinuing a custom, or practice.

To DISUSE, V. A. to cease to make use of, or practice.

To DISVOUCH, V. A. to destroy credit by contrary proofs. To confute, or contradict. "Every letter he hath writ hath disvouched another." Shak.

DISWITTED, Part. deprived of one's wits; mad. "As she had been diswitted." Drayton. Not in use.

DITCH, S. [dic, dul, Erse.] a trench made to separate and defend grounds and to carry off superfluous water. In Fortification, a trench formed by digging between the scarp and counterscarp of a fort, and is either dry, or filled with water. Any long, narrow cavity formed in the ground for holding water; hence a narrow river is, in contempt, called a ditch. This word is used in composition, as a term of contempt, as any thing worthless, or deserving to be thrown into a ditch, hence a ditch-dog in Shakespear.

To DITCH, V. A. to form a long trench in the ground for the boundary of land, or to receive water to make a ditch.

DITTIED, Part. sung; set to music. "Smooth dittied song." Milton.

DITTY, S. [dicht, Belg. dittum, Lat.] a poem or song set to music.

DIVAN, S. [Arab.] a council chamber, wherein justice is administered among the Eastern nations. A council of Eastern princes. Figuratively, any council assembled. "The consult of the dire divan." Pope.

To DIVARICATE, V. A. [divaricatus, Lat.] to part into two. Neuterly, to become parted into two.

DIVARICATION, S. a dividing of a thing into two. Figuratively, difference of opinions.

To DIVE, V. N. [dauppan, Goth.] to go under water and remain there some time. Figuratively, to make strict enquiry or examination into another person's designs or business. To go to the bottom of any question, science or doctrine To conceal or hide from the sight or observation of another. "Dive thoughts within my breast." Shak. Actively, to explore by diving. "The Castle bravely div'd the gulph of fame" Denham.

DIVER, S. one who goes voluntarily under water. One who is hired to go under water in quest of things lost by shipwreck, &c. Figuratively, one who makes himself master of any branch of science; one who dives or goes to the bottom of an affair. "A diver into causes." Wotton.

To DIVERGE, V. N. [diverge, Lat.] to recede farther from each other.

DIVERGENT, Particip. [divergens, Lat.] in Geometry, applied to those lines which con-

constantly recede from each other. In Optics, applied to those rays which separate
and continually depart from one another.

DI'VERS, Adj. [diversus, Lat.] sundry;
several; more than one. Seldom used, only
in Law and Commercial Affairs.

DIVERSE, S. [diversus, Lat.] different
in form or nature. Various. In different
directions.

DIVERSIFICA'TION, S. the act of
changing forms or qualities. Variation. A
mixture. Change, or alteration. "A di-
versification at the will." Ibid.

To DIVE'RSIFY, V. A. [diversifier, Fr.]
to make different. To vary. To mark
with variety of colours. To variegate.

DIVE'RSION, S. [from divers] the act
of turning or diverting a thing aside from its
course. The cause by which a thing is
turned from its proper course. Something
which unbends the mind; something lighter
or more pleasing than amusement, and less
forcible than pleasure; sport, pastime. The
public exhibitions of plays, operas, &c.
In war, the act of drawing off an enemy
from some design, by an attack made or pretended to be made at some other place.

DIVE'RSITY, S. [diversite, Fr. diversitas,
Lat.] difference from each other. Variety.
Distinct being, difference of existence, opposed to identity. Variegation, or a composition of different colours. "Blushing in
bright diversities of day." Pope.

DIVE'RSLY, Adv. In different ways,
methods, manners, or directions. "O'er
life's vast ocean diversely we sail." Pope.

To DIVE'RT, V. A. [diverto, Lat.] to
turn aside from any direction. In War, to
draw forces to a different part. To seduce,
from a rule of conduct. "How simple was
that crude apple that diverted Eve." Par.
Reg. To please by any thing which affords
pleasure. See DIVERSION. To subvert,
or destroy. "Frights,—divert and crack,
rend and deracinate,—the unity and married
calm of states." Shak. The last is an uncommon and improper application of this
word.

DIVERTER, S. any thing that unbends
the mind and diverts.

To DIVERTISE, V. A. [divertiser, Fr.]
to please, amuse, or divert. "Let orators
instruct, let them divertise." Dryd.

DIVE'RTISEMENT, S. [divertissement,
Fr.] diversion. or that which affords sports
"How food so ever men are of bad divertise
ment." Government of the Tongue.

DIVE'RTIVE, Adj. having the power to
divert, unbend and recreate the mind.

To DIVE'ST, V. A. [this is the most
common spelling, though devester, Fr. from
whence it is derived, shews it is more properly written with an E, in the first syllable. To take off a person's cloaths. To
make naked. To strip.

DIVE'STURE, S. the act of putting off.
"The vesture of mortality." Exra.

DIVI'DABLE, Adj. separate; distinct;
not joined. That which may be divided.
"Dividable shores." Shak

To DIVI'DE, V. A. [divido, Lat.] to separate a thing into parts. To stand between
things as a partition. To part one person
from another. To separate friends by discord. To give or distribute among several
persons. Neuterly, to part, or break friendship.

DIVI'DEND, S [dividendus, Lat.] a share;
a part allotted. In Commerce, the portion
of interest given by a public company. In
Arithmetic, the number given to be parted,
separated or divided.

DIVI'DER, S. that which separates. One
who distributes to others. A particular kind
of compasses.

DIVI'DUAL, Adj. [dividuus, Lat.] divided; shared with or communicated to several
others. "Her reign—with thousand lesser
lights dividual holds." Par. L.fl.

DIVINA'TION, S. [divinatio, Lat.] the
act of foretelling future events; prognosti-
cation.

DIVI'NE, Adj. [fr. of divinus, Lat.]
partaking of the nature of God. Figuratively, excellent, extraordinary, seemingly
beyond the nature of mankind. Presaging;
foreseeing: or prognosticating. His heart,
divine of something ill." P. r. L.fl. This
last sense is uncommon.

DIVI'NE, S. a minister of the gospel.
A clergyman, or one peculiarly dedicated to
the service of the church.

To DIVI'NE, V. A. [diviner, Fr.] to
foretell future events, &c. To foresee, foreknow, or presage. To conjecture, or guess.

DIVI'NELY, Adv. In a divine manner.
By the operation of God. In a supreme or
superlative degree.

DIVI'NER, S. one who professes to fore-
tel or discover future events. A guesser.
"He must be a notable diviner of thoughts."
Brown.

DI'VING, the art or act of descending
under water to considerable depths, and a-
biding there a competent time; the uses of
which are particularly in fishing for pearls,
corals, sponges, wrecks of ships, &c. There
have been various engines contrived to render the business of diving safe and easy; the
great point is to furnish the diver with fresh
air, without which he must either make but
a short stay, or perish. Those who dive for
sponges in the Mediterranean, carry down
sponges sipped in oil in their mouths. But
considering the small quantity of air that can
be contained in the pores of a sponge, and
how much that little will be contracted by
the

the pressure of the incumbent air, such a supply cannot subsist a diver long, since a gallon of air is not fit for respiration above a minute. Dr. Halley assures us, a naked diver cannot subsist above two minutes under water, with or without a sponge; besides, if the depth be considerable, the pressure of the water makes the eyes blood-shot, and frequently occasions a spitting of blood.

DIVI'NITY, S. [*divinité*, F. *divinitas*, Lat.] a partaking of the nature of God; Godhead. " Fancy that they feel—*divinity* within them." Figuratively, God, the supreme Being, the creator and preserver of all things. A false deity or idol. " Beastly *divinities*." *Par. Loft.* Celestial or heavenly being. " These subservient *divinities*." *Cheyne.* The science conversant about God, heavenly things, and the duties we owe to him. Something miraculous, or supernatural. " They say there is *divinity* in odd numbers." *Shak.*

DIVI'SIBLE, Adj. [*divisibilis*, Lat.] capable of being actually, or mentally divided into part.

DIVISIBILITY, S [*divisibilité*, Fr.] the quality of admitting division.

DIVI'SIBLENESS, S. the quality of being divided.

DIVI'SION, S. [*divisio*, Lat.] the act of separating. The state of a thing, whose parts are divided. That by which any thing is kept separate, or divided. The part which is separated by dividing. Discord, or difference which occasions a separation between friends. In Music, the dividing the interval of an octave into a number of lesser intervals. A distinction. " I will put a *division* between my people and thy people." *Exod.* viii. 23. In Arithmetic, that rule whereby we find how often a less quantity is contained in a greater. In Logic, the separating a general term into its parts.

DIVI'SOR, S. [Lat.] in Arithmetic, that number by which the dividend is divided.

DIVO'RCE, S. [Fr. *divortium*, Lat.] the legal separation of people that are married together, whereby the marriage contract is rendered null and void. Forcible separation, or division of things intimately united. Divorces are now become so very common, and so easily obtained, that people of fashion no longer look upon the matrimonial tie as binding for life; but as a temporary knot dissoluble at pleasure, and at a very small expence, by the mutual agreement of both parties, which may be done without any difficulty. If the woman will admit the charge of infidelity against her to be true, whether it is really so or not. And as such a charge is no longer disgraceful, from its happening so frequently, any lady will submit to get rid of a troublesome husband.

To DIVO'RCE, V. A. to separate a husband and wife from each other. To annul the marriage contract. Figuratively, to force

asunder by violence. To take away by force. " Nothing but death shall e'er *divorce* my dignities." *Shak.*

DIVO'RCEMENT, S. the abrogating or setting aside the marriage contract.

DIURE'TIC, Adj. [from *δια* and *ουρεω*, Gr.] having the power to provoke urine, or force a person to make water frequently.

DIU'RNAL, Adj. [*diurnus*, Lat.] relating to the day. Constituting the day. Performed in a day.

DIU'RNALLY, Adv. daily, or every day.

DIUTU'RNITY, S. [*diuturnitas*, Lat.] length of time. " Of such *diuturnity*." *Brown.*

To DIVU'LGE, V. A. [*divulgo*, Lat.] to publish; to make known. To proclaim. " The just man, and *divulges* him through heaven—to all his angels." *Par. Loft.*

DIVU'LGER, S. a publisher; one that reveals a secret.

To DI'ZEN, V. A. to dress; to set off with ornaments or cloaths. " For sure I had *dizen'd* you out like a queen." *Swift.*

DI'ZZINESS, S. [from *dizzy*] giddiness, lightness, or swimming in the head.

DI'ZZY, Adj. [*dig, diſig*, Sax.] giddy, having a swimming in the head. Figuratively, causing giddiness. Thoughtless.

To DI'ZZY, V. A. to make giddy. " Not the dreadful spout—shall *dizzy* with more clamour Neptune's ear." *Shak.*

To DO, V. A. [Preter *did*, Part. Pass. *done*, from *don*, Sax.] to perform, act, or practice. To execute or discharge. To cause. To have recourse to, used as sudden and passionate question. " What will you *do* in the end." *Jer.* v. 31. To perform for the benefit of another, to assist, joined with *for*. To exert or put forth. " *Do* thy diligence to come." 2 *Tim.* iv. 9. To have business, to have concerns, or connections, to deal, joined to *with*. To gain a point, or have influence on. " It is much that a jest with a sad brow will *do* with a soldier." *Shak. What to do with*, signifies to bestow, to employ, to dispose of, or what use to make of. " They would not know *what to do with themselves*." *Tillotson* " He knows not *what to do with* his money." Neuterly, to act or behave, joined to *with*, to dispatch or conclude a thing undertaken, to quit a subject. " I have *done with* Chaucer, when I have answered some objections." *Dryd.* To fare, to be conditioned with respect to health or sickness. " Good woman, how *do'st* thou." *Shak.* To be able to succeed. " We shall *do without* him." *Addiſ.* Formerly used as an auxiliary verb, to denote the present and preter tenses of other verbs, but by moderns looked on as mere expletives. " I *do* love her." *Shak.* Sometimes, however, it is used to save the repetition of another verb. " I shall *come*, but if I *do* not, go away."

Some-

Sometimes it is used as a word of peremptory and positive command. "At help me, do." "I did love him, but scorn him now."

DO'CILE, Adj. [docilis, Lat.] teachable; easily taught; tractable. Used with to, before the thing taught. "Soon docile to the secret arts of ill." Locke.

DO'CIBLE, Adj. [docibilis, Lat.] submitting to instructions. Easy to be taught. Tractable, governable.

DO'CILITY, S. [docilité, Fr.] aptness to receive instruction. Readiness to be taught.

DOCK, S. [docce, Sax.] in botany, lapathum, or rumex. The essence of the water-dock has of late been introduced into the Materia Medica, and very much cried up for its virtues by Dr. Hill; but has not as yet recommended itself equally to the countenance of regular practitioners, notwithstanding the known abilities of the Doctor, and the great character he has given it in the public papers, and in an essay wrote on purpose to display its virtues.

DOCK, S. the stump part of a horse's tail. A place where water is let in or out at pleasure, wherein ships are built, repaired, or laid up; from dugum, Gr.

To DOCK, V. A. to cut a tail off, or short. Figuratively, to cut any thing short. To lay a ship in a dock. In law, to cut off an entail.

DO'CKET, S. a direction or title tied or fastened to goods. A summary or abridgment of a larger writing.

DO'CTOR, S. [Lat.] one so well versed in any science as to be able to teach it to others. One who has taken the highest degree in music, law, physic, or divinity.

DOCTO'RAL, Adj. [doctoralis, Lat.] belonging or relating to a doctor's degree.

DO'CTRINAL, Adj. [from doctrina, Lat.] belonging to, or containing doctrine.

DO'CTRINALLY, Adv. positively; in the form of precepts or instructions.

DO'CTRINE, S. [doctrina, Lat.] the principles of any sect, or matter. The thesis or maxims delivered in a discourse. Any thing taught.

DO'CUMENT, S. [documentum, Lat.] an instruction, admonition, precept, or direction. Vouchers, or original writings produced in support of any charge, or accusation; this last sense is very lately adopted.

DODE'CAGON, S. [from dodeka, Gr. and gonia, Gr.] a figure having twelve sides.

To DO'DGE, V. A. to use craft, evasions, or shifts. To shift from your place as another approaches. Figuratively, to play fast and loose. To shuffle, shift, or baffle.

DOD'KEN, S. [doytken, Belg.] a little doit, a contemptuous word for a piece of the lowest coin or money. "I would not buy them for a dodkin." Lilly's Gram. construed.

DOE, S. a she-deer; the female of a buck.

DO'ER, S. [from to do] one who does, or performs any thing. One who practises. "Be ye doers of the word." Jam. i. 22.

To DOFF, V. A. [from do off; to put off cloaths, or any covering. "All do disfire "lion's usual skin." Howe. Now obsolete, unless among country folks.

DOG, S. [dogghe, Belg.] a domestic animal, the species of which are remarkably various; the larger sort are used as guards, and the less for sports. In astronomy, the name of a constellation, called likewise Sirius or Canicula. When added to the name of other animals, it signifies a male of the species, as a dog-fox. Added to another word, it signifies something worthless, as a dog-rose. Come to the dog, implies ruined or destroyed.

To DOG, V. A. to hunt or pursue like a hound; to dog.

DOG'BANE, or DOG'S-BANE, S. [called likewise apocynum. Lat. and exstinct, Gr.] It is ranged by Linnæus in the second division of his 6th, and is divided into eleven species.

DOG'BRIAR, S. in Botany, the briar which bears the hip.

DOG'CHEAP, Adj. extremely cheap; as cheap as dogs-meat.

DOG'DAYS, S. the days on which the dog-star rises and sets with the sun; on account of the great heat of that season supposed to be very unwholsome.

DOG'FISH, S. in Natural History, a salt-water fish, remarkable, according to Oppian, for receiving its young into her belly on any storm or danger, which are said to come out again after the fright is over. If we consider a similar custom of the opossum, which is known to be a matter of fact, we may look on this suggestion as something less romantic.

DUGE, S. [Ven. of dux, Lat.] the title of the supreme magistrate of Venice and Genoa.

DOG'FLY, S. a voracious, biting fly.

DOG'GED, Adj. sullen, sour, morose. Not easily pleased, or moved by pleasantry. Ill humoured.

DOG'GEDLY, Adv. in a sour, morose, sullen, or ill humoured manner.

DOG'GEDNESS, S. a disposition of mind not to be moved to pleasantry by any objects of mirth, or pleased by offices of kindness and civility. Sullenness; moroseness; ill-nature.

DOG'GER, S. a small ship, or fishing vessel, built after the Dutch fashion.

DOG'GEREL, S. [see DOG] in poetry, applied to such compositions as have neither accuracy, rhimes, harmony, dignity of expression, fertility of invention, or elevation of sentiment. Burlesque.

DO'GMA,

DO'GMA, S. [Lat.] an established principle, rule, axiom, or maxim.

DOGMA'TIC, DOGMA'TICAL, Adj. positive; strongly attached to any opinion. Authoritative, or imperious in forcing one's opinions, or notions.

DOGMA'TICALLY, Adv. In a positively, imperiously, peremptorily manner.

DO'GMATIST, S. one who advances his opinions as infallible, and supports them with great obstinacy.

To DO'GMATIZE, V. A. to advance any opinion positively, and endeavour to propagate it magisterially, or imperiously.

DOGMATI'ZER, S. one who advances opinions with an air of insolent confidence, and demands assent to them in a magisterial and imperious manner.

DIVGSLEEP, S. a pretended, affected, or dissembled sleep.

DO'GSTAR, S. the star which rises and sets with the sun during the dog-days.

DO'G-TEETH, S. in anatomy, the four teeth, two in each jaw, which are situated between the incisors and the grinders; they end in a sharp point, are admirably adapted for dividing flesh, especially such as requires tugging, being fixed very deep in the sockets, and thereby enabled to resist such violence as would pull out the incisors or fore-teeth. From their resembling the teeth in the same situation in a dog's mouth they derive their name, and are also called the eye-teeth.

DO'G-TROT, S. a gentle, easy trot, resembling that of a dog. "Rode—a dog-trot through the bawling crowd." Hud.h.

DO'INGS, S. any thing performed. Performances, exploits, behaviour, conduct, bustle, tumult, merriment. A word seldom used by elegant writers.

DO'IT, S. [doyt, Belg. doreft, Frie] a small piece of money current in Holland. Figuratively, a thing of trifling value.

DO'LE, s. [dal, dæl, al dælen, Sax.] the act of dividing into shares. In law, a portion or share. Portion or condition. Grief, sorrow, misery, calamity. "In equal scale weighing delight and dole." Shak.

To DO'LE, V. A. [dælan, Sax.] to divide in shares. To deal out, or distribute.

DO'LEFUL, Adj. dismal, sorrowful, melancholy, afflicted with, and causing grief.

DO'LEFULLY, Adv. in such a manner as to show, produce, or cause sorrow.

DO'LESOME, Adj. full of grief, sorrowful, applied to persons. Gloomy, dull, or affecting with melancholy.

DO'LESOMELY, Adv. in such a manner as to affect a person with, or to express deep sorrow or grief.

DO'LESOMENESS, S. the quality of affecting a person with extreme sorrow, grief, or melancholy.

DO'LL, S. a contraction of Dorothy, and applied to a wooden image, clothed, used by children as a play thing.

DO'LLAR, S. [daler, Teut.] a silver coin used in Germany, nearly of the value of a French crown.

DO'LORIFIC, Adj [dolorificus, Lat.] that which causes or produces grief or pain.

DO'LOROUS, Adj [dolor, Lat.] mournful or sorrowful; affecting with grief or pain.

DO'LOUR, S. [dolor, Lat.] grief or sorrow. "Th' abundant dolour of the heart." Shak. Pain or pang. "The dolours of death." Bac. Lamentation or complaint, occasioned by any object causing pain, or affecting with sorrow.

DOL'PHIN, S. [delphinus, Lat. δελφιν, Gr.] the name of a large sea-fish, which mariners suppose to prognosticate storms or calms by their appearance. In Astronomy, a constellation of the north hemisphere, consisting of 18 stars. In History, the title of the French king's eldest son, from dauphin, Fr.

DO'LT, S. [doll, Teut.] a fool, one of dull apprehension, a blockhead.

DO'LTISH, Adj. stupid, foolish.

DOMA'IN, S. [domaine, Fr.] land possessed by one as a proprietor, heir, governor, or master.

DO'ME, S. [dome, Fr. domus, Lat.] a house, or building, generally applied to a building set apart for divine service. In Architecture, a roof of a spherical form resembling the hell of a great clock, raised over the middle of a building, called also a Cupola.

To DOME'STICATE, V. A. to withdraw from the public and make private, or a constant dweller at home. A word for which we are obliged to the fertile invention of the author of Clarissa, but what authority he may have for coining, let those determine, who are masters of style and language.

DOMES'TIC, DOMES'TICAL, Adj. [domesticus, Lat.] belonging to a house, or the management of a family; fit to inhabit a house, opposed to wild; applied to wars, intestine or civil.

DOMES'TIC, S. a servant or attendant who lives in the same house with the master.

To DO'MINATE, V. A. [dominatus, Lat.] to prevail over others. "The dominating humour makes the dream." Dryd. We use PREDOMINATE at present.

DOMINA'TION, S. [dominatio, Lat.] exercise of power; government. Tyranny, or too great a stretch of power.

DOMINA'TOR, S. [Lat.] the presiding superior, or predominating power or influence. "Jupiter and Mars, are dominators, for this north west part of the world." Camb.

To DOMINE'ER, V. N. [dominor, Lat.]

to exert authority in an infolent and tyrannical manner.

DOMI'NICAL, Adj. noting the lord's
day or Sunday. The dominical letter, in
Chronology, is that which denotes the Sunday in Almanacs, &c. throughout the year.
Of these letters there are consequently feven, beginning with the first letter of the alphabet, and as in leap year, there is an in-
tercalary day, there are then two, the first of
which denotes every Sunday till the inter-
calary day, and the second all the Sundays
which follow after it.

DOMI'NION, S. [dominium, Lat.] the
exercise of authority. The territory fubject
to a person or prince. Predominancy, pre
ference.

DON, S. [Span. of dominus, Lat.] the
Spanish title for a gentleman.

To DON, V. A. [from do on] to put on.
" Should I don this robe." Shak. Not used
unless in country places at a distance from the
metropolis.

DO'NARY, S. [donarium, Sax.] a thing
given or bequeathed for sacred uses.

DONATION, S. [donatio, Lat.] the act
of giving any thing voluntarily. The grant
by which a thing is given; title to a thing
given.

DON'ATIVE, S. [donatif, Fr.] a gift,
or some considerable present. In Law,
a benefice given and collated by the
patron, without either presentation to the
ordinary, institution by the ordinary, or in-
duction by his orders.

DONCASTER, a town in the West-Riding of Yorkshire, with a market on Saturdays, and two fairs, on April 4, and August
5, for cattle, and pedlars ware. It had its
name from the river Don, on which it is
seated, and a castle now in ruins. It is a
large, well-built corporation-town, and has
good manufactures in stockings, knit-waist-
coats and gloves, and the market is good for
cattle, corn, and provisions. It is 37 miles
S. of York, and 155 N. by W. of London.
Lon. 16. 35. lat. 53. 37.

DO'NE, participle of DO.

DO'NE, an interjection made use of by the
party, who accepts of a wager, and implies
let it be done.

DONOR, S. [from dono, Lat.] one who
gives or grants a thing to another.

• To DOOM, V. A. [deman, Sax.] to judge;
to pass sentence against. To condemn. To
be freed, by some irresistible influence.

DOOM, S. [dom, Sax.] the sentence of
a judge. The great judgment at the last day.
The state to which a person is destined. Fate.
" Both felt their doom." Pope.

DOOMSDAY, S. [domesday] the day of
judgment. " As it were doomsday." Shak.
The day in which a person is condemned.
Doomsday Book, a book of the survey of En-

gland, made by William the Conqueror, still
used to determine the questions whether tenures are of ancient demesne, or not.

DOOR, S. [from dura, or dore, Sax. deor,
Goth.] a vacant space left in a building or
house, through which persons enter or go
out. Figuratively, a house, passage, avenue,
inlet, or any means by which a thing may
make its approach or entrance. " Shuts the
door against all temptations." Next door to
implies approaching to, bordering on, or next
route to; " Next door to a tumult."L'Estrange
Out of doors, is sometimes used for a thing abolished, laid aside, exploded or sent away. At
the door; implies something near, impendent
or imminent. " Death is at the door." At
the door of a person signifies something that
may be imputed to a person, seeming to allude the custom of dropping children at the
doors of the supposed parents. " The fault
lies wholly at my door." Dryd.

DO'QUET, S. in Law, a paper containing a warrant.

DORCHESTER, the capital town of Dorsetshire, with a market on Saturdays, and four
fairs, on February 12, for cattle and sheep,
on Trinity Monday, and July 5, for cattle,
sheep, and lambs; and on August 5, for cattle, sheep, wool, and leather. It in a town
of great antiquity, and was much larger than
it is at present, the ruins of the walls being
still to be seen in some places. It is pleasantly seated on the river Frome, on a Roman
road. The houses are well-built, and it has
three handsome streets. It sends two members to parliament, is the place where the affizes are held, and gives title to a marquis.
It is governed by a mayor, 12 aldermen,
a recorder and 24 common council-men.
It has 3 churches, and about 600 houses.
The streets are broad and paved, and a fine
terrace-walk, planted with trees, almost surrounds the town. This place was formerly a
city. At about half a mile's distance, stands
Maiden-castle, with intrenchments 40 feet
deep, thrown up round it in the time of the
Romans. It is 8 miles N. of Weymouth and
124 W. by S. of London. Lon. 15. 0. lat.
15. 40.

DO'RMANT, Adj. [Fr.] sleeping; in a
sleeping posture. Secret, or private, opposed to public. " There were other " dormant musters of soldiers." Bacon. Cancel-
led. " Leaning, opposed to strait or perpendicular. " Old dormant windows must confess—her beams." Clevel.

DO'RMITORY, S. [dormitorium, Lat.] a
place furnished for sleeping in. In old records, a burial place.

DO'RMOUSE, S. [mus dormiens, Lat.] a
mouse, which sleeps a great part of the winter.

DORSETSHIRE, S. a county of Eng-
land, 52 miles in length, and 20 in breadth.

It

It is bounded on the N. by Wiltshire and Somersetshire, on the S. by the English channel, on the W. by Devonshire, and on the E. by Hampshire. It contains 21,040 houses, 131,640 inhabitants, 248 parishes, and 22 market-towns, nine of which sends members to parliament. It produces all the commodities common to other countries; besides which, it has both linen and woollen manufactures. The air is good, but sharp on the hills, and on the sea-coast it is mild and pleasant. The soil is sandy, except in some rich meadows, plains, and valleys. There are many hills, which feed great numbers of sheep; and on the sea-coasts there is plenty of fish. The principal rivers are the Stour, the Frome, and the Piddle.

DORATURE, S. [dortoir, Lat.] a chamber to sleep in; a bed-chamber. "He led us to a gallery like a dorture." Bacon.

DOSE, S. [δοσις, Gr.] as much of any medicine as it is proper to take at one time. Figuratively, as much of any thing as falls to a person's lot. "Married his punctual dose of wives." Hudib. As much of any liquor as a person can bear; sometimes used for that quantity which intoxicates. "I have had my dose."

DOT, S. [supposed to be a corruption of jot, by Johnson] a small point or spot made with a pen, to mark any thing, &c.

To DOT, V. A. to make round spots or points in writing.

DOTAGE, S. weakness of understanding. Excessive fondness for any person or thing, generally applied to persons greatly advanced in years.

DOTAL, Adj. [dotalis, Lat.] relating to, or making part of a marriage portion.

DOTARD, S. a person whose strength and understanding are impaired by age.

To DOTE, V. N. [doten, Belg.] to have one's understanding impaired by age, or passion. Actively, to regard with excessive fondness, used with upon.

DOTER, S. one whose understanding is impaired by years; one who loves with excessive fondness.

DOTINGLY, Adv. with an excess of love or fondness.

DOUBLE, Adj. [Fr. double, Erse] two things of the same sort, answering each other. Twice as much, applied to quantity. The same number repeated. Having twice the effect, power, or influence. Deceitful, acting two parts, "acted a double part."

To DOUBLE, V. N. to encrease to twice the quantity, number, value, weight, or strength. To turn back, to wind in running. Actively, among sailors, to pass round a cape or promontary; to pass. Figuratively, to play tricks; to use slight or evasions. To fold. To repeat the same word. To encrease by addition.

DOUBLE, S. twice the quantity, number, value, weight, or quality. In Hunting, a turning back or winding made by game, in order to put the hounds at fault.

DOUBLE-DEALING, S. one who is so deceitful as to act two parts at the same time.

DOUBLE-DEALER, S. artifice; dissimulation. The acting two different parts, by pretending friendship, and at the same time pretending to be a friend with his enemy Low, insidious, cunning.

DOUBLENESS, S. the state of a thing repeated twice, the state of a thing folded.

DOUBLE-TONGUED, Adj. giving contrary or opposite accounts of the same thing. Deceitful.

DOUBLET, S. an under garment, so called from its affording double the heat or warmth of another.

DOUBLY, Adv. in a twofold manner. In twice the quantity, to twice the degree, twice as much.

To DOUBT, V. N. [from douter, Fr. dubito, Lat.] to question, to be unable to determine, to be in a state of uncertainty To question or be apprehensive of some future event. Used with of, in all the foregoing senses. "Whereof he doubted not," Knolles. To fear, to suspect, to hesitate, to desist. "Stand at the door of life and doubt to enter the year." Actively, to look on as wanting proof or authority. To question a person's right or claim. To fear; to suspect. To distrust.

DOUBT, S. uncertainty. Suspence. A state of the mind wherein it remains undetermined to act or judge on account of the equality of proofs or motives on each side of a question. Figuratively, a question, or some point undetermined and unsettled. A scruple. Perplexity. Uncertainty of condition. Suspicion. Apprehension of ill. A difficulty.

DOUBTER, S. one who is in an uncertain state of mind, on account of the equality of proofs on opposite sides of a question.

DOUBTFUL, Adj. full of uncertainty or doubt. Not settled in opinion. Ambiguous, or not clear. Not determined. Not secure. Suspicious. Timorous. "With doubtful feet and wavering resolution." Milt.

DOUBTFULLY, Adv. with uncertainty and irresolution. With ambiguity, or want of clearness, applied to the meaning and signification of words.

DOUBTFULNESS, S. a state of the mind, wherein it is unable to determine certainly. Uncertainty. That which may admit of various and contrary senses.

DOUBTINGLY, Adv. in such a manner as to be uncertain. In such a manner as to be fearful, or apprehensive of some future ill.

DOUBT;

DOUBTLESS, Adj. without any fear or apprehension. Without doubt. Certainly.

DOUCEURS, [plural, Fr.] flattering and engaging careſſes in order to inſinuate one's ſelf into another's good opinion. This word is adapted by ſome moderns, and as it ſeems rather an intruder than a native, ſhould be expelled the community. In the ſingular, a bribe.

DOVE, S. [duua, Sax. duif, Belg.] a wild pigeon, uſually applied to the female of the ſpecies.

DOVE-COT, S. a ſmall building in which pigeons or doves are kept; a pigeon-houſe.

DOVE-TAIL, S. In Carpentry, a manner of joining timber, by letting one piece into another, in the form of a wedge reverſed, or a dove's tail. This is reckoned one of the ſtrongeſt kinds of joinings.

DOVER, S. a ſea-port town in the county of Kent, with two markets, on Wedneſdays and Saturdays, and one fair, on November 22, for wearing apparel and haberdaſhery ware. It is ſtrong both by nature and art, being ſituated between high cliffs, and defended by a ſtrong caſtle built on a high hill E. from the town. It was repaired in 1756; and there are barracks for 3000 men. The town was once walled round, and had ten gates; but there only now remains three, and theſe much out of repair. It is one of the cinque ports, and a corporation, conſiſting of a mayor, and 12 jurats. It ſends two members to parliament, and is the ſtation of the packet boats, that, in time of peace, paſs between Dover and Calais, from which it is diſtant only 21 miles. It was once of much larger extent, and had ſeven churches, which are now reduced to two in the town, and one in the caſtle. It conſiſts of four long narrow ſtreets, and ſeveral croſs-ſtreets, or alleys. The houſes, which are about 500, are low, ſome built with brick, and others with flint-ſtone. The inhabitants, who amount to about 5600, are chiefly ſupported by the ſhipping, and by ſhip-building, rope-making, and a ſmall manufactury of ſacking. From hence, in fine weather, there is a proſpect of the coaſt of France. It is 15 miles S. E. of Canterbury, and 71 S. E. by E. of London. Lon. 19. 0. lat. 51. 6.

DOUGH, S. [pronounced do, from dah, Sax.] the paſte made for bread or pies, before it is baked. My tale is dough, a phraſe uſed to ſignify that a deſign has miſcarried, or has never come to maturity. "Aſs cake is dough, but I'll in among the reſt." Shak.

DOUGH-BAKED, Adj. unfiniſhed; ſoft or effeminate. "In dough bak'd men, ſome harmleſsneſs we ſee." Donne.

DOUGHTY, Adj. [pronounced dowty, from dohty, Sax.] brave, noble, illuſtrious. Obſtinately brave; ſtiff; generally uſed by moderns to convey ſome ironical idea of ſtrength and courage.

No. X.

DOUGHY, Adj. not baked; not ſufficiently baked. Figuratively, ſoft, not confirmed by years or education, in the love of virtue. "Whoſe villainous faſhion would have made all the unbaked and doughy youth of a nation of his colour. Shak.

To DOUSE, V. A. [houſe, Gr.] to plunge over head in the water. To give a perſon a blow or box on the ear. To fall ſuddenly into the water.

DOUSE, S. a blow or box on the ear.

DOWAGER, S. [douairie, Fr.] a widow who has a jointure. A title given to the widows of kings, princes, or other nobility.

DOWDY, S. an awkward, ill-dreſſed, ſluttiſh and clowniſh woman.

DOWER, DOWERY, S. [douaire, Fr. dos, Lat.] the fortune which a woman brings her huſband at marriage. That which a widow poſſeſſes as her right or jointure. In eaſtern nations, and among the antients, the preſents the bride-groom was accuſtomed to make to the bride's father. An endowment, or gift.

DOWERED, Part. portioned, jointured.

DOWERLESS, Adj. without a portion, or jointure.

DOWLASS, S. a coarſe kind of linen cloth.

DOWN, S. [from dun, Iſl.] ſoft feathers, generally applied to thoſe which grow on the breaſts of fowls. Figuratively, that which ſoftens or alleviates any uneaſy or diſagreeable ſenſation. Soft wool, or tender hair. "Scarce had the down to ſhade his cheeks begun." Dryd.

DOWN, S. [dun dune, Sax.] a large open plain or valley. In the plural, uſed for a road near the coaſt of Deal in Kent. A hill or riſing ground; this ſenſe, though the ſame as the Saxon, from whence the word is derived, is very unuſual, or uncommon.

DOWN, Part. to a lower ſituation; along a deſcent, from a riſing ground to the plain on which it ſtands. Towards the mouth, applied to a river. "Conveyed down the river."

DOWN, Adv. on the ground, to a lower ſituation; tending to the ground or towards the centre. Below the horizon, applied to the ſituation of the ſun, moon, &c. "The moon is down." Shak. Uſed with boil, ſo as to exhauſt all its ſtrength, or ſo as to boil to pieces. D'iſgrace, or loſs of reputation. "A man who has written himſelf down." Addiſ. Up and down, every where, or without any confinement to place. "Let them wander up and down for meat." Pſal. liv. 15. To go down, to be digeſted, to be eaten freely, or received. "Bread alone will go down." Locke.

DOWN, Interject. to fling a perſon on the

the ground, or make him fall. To destroy a building." "Down with them all." *Shak.*

DOWNFALL, S. ruin, calamity, disgrace, or change from a state of dignity and affluence, to one of indigence, misery, and disgrace.

DOWNLOOKED, Adj. with the eyes cast towards the ground.

DOWNRIGHT, Adv. strait down, in a perpendicular line. In plain terms, without any dissimulation, flattery, or ceremony. Completely, without any delay or stop. "She fell downright into a fit." *Hist. of John Bull.*

DOWNRIGHT, Adj. plain, open, without disguise, or dissimulation; without circumlocution, artless, without ceremony, honestly.

DOWNSITTING, S. the act of going to rest, alluding to the eastern custom of lying on the ground. Rest, repose. "Thou knowest my downsitting." *Psal. cxxxix. 2.*

DOWNWARD, DOWNWARDS, Adv. [dun ward, Sax.] towards the center, or to a lower situation. In a course of succession, applied to descent or genealogy.

DOWNWARD, Adj. moving from a higher to a lower situation; declining, bending, or sloping towards the ground. Depressed, melancholy, dejected. "The lowest of my downward thoughts." *Sidney.* Seldom used in the last sense.

DOWNY, Adj. covered with soft, short feathers, or with a nap. Made of soft feathers or down. Soft, tender, soothing. "Shake off this downy sleep." *Shak.*

DOXOLOGY, S. [from *doxa*, Gr. and *logos*,] a short sentence including praise and thanksgiving to God; such as "Glory be the Father, and to the Son, and to the Holy Ghost." This was called the greater doxology, and received its latter name from its beginning with the word *Gloria* in Greek, which signifies *glory*. Supposed by some to be instituted by the catholics of Antioch in the year 350, and by others to have been first used in 341.

DOXY, S. [from *docken*, Belg.] a strumpet, a prostitute.

To DOZE, V. N. [*dwæs*, Sax. *does*, Brig.] to slumber, to be half asleep. Actively, to stupify, or make dull and heavy.

DOZEN, S. twelve things or persons.

DOZINESS, S. sleepiness, drowsiness, heaviness; a strong propensity to sleep.

DOZY, Adj. inclined to sleep; drowsy, heavy, sluggish.

DRAB, S. [*drabble*, Sax.] a common prostitute; an unchaste woman.

DRACHM, S. [pronounced *dram*] the 16th part of an ounce avoirdupoise weight. Among apothecaries, the 8th part of an ounce, weighing either three scruples or 60 grains.

DRAFF, S. [from *draf*, Sax.] any thing thrown away, sweepings, refuse, offals, chaff,

or dregs. "Lately come from swine-keeping, and from eating draff and husks." *Shak.* "Younger brothers, but the draff of nature." *Dryd.*

To DRAG, V. A. [*dragon*, Sax.] to pull along the ground by force or violence. To draw along contemptuously, and as unworthy any notice. Neuterly, to hang so low as to trail, and grate upon the ground, applied to a door, which is hung badly on the hinges, and sweeps upon the floor with its bottom edge in opening and shutting.

DRAG, S. [*drag-net*, Sax.] a net which is drawn along the bottom of the water. An instrument with hooks, used to catch hold of things under water.

To DRAGGLE, V. A. to make dirty by trailing along the ground.

DRAGON, S. [Fr. *dragon*, Ital. *draco*, Lat.] a serpent, whether real or imaginary, supposed to be furnished with wings, and to grow to an enormous size. Figuratively, one of a violent temper. In Scripture, hieroglyphically applied to signify the serpent or the devil.

DRAGON-FLY, S. In Natural History, a bluish flying insect with a narrow and long body, with two pair of wings, and a sting at the tail.

DRAGON-LIKE, Adj. resembling a dragon in disposition. Fiery, furious. "He fights dragon like." *Shak.*

DRAGOON, S. [*dragon*, Teut.] a soldier, who serves both on foot and horseback.

To DRAGOON, V. A. to deliver up to the mercy of soldiers. To compel a person to embrace or quit an opinion by force of arms.

To DRAIN, V. A. [*trainer*, Fr.] to draw off fluids gradually. To empty a vessel by gradually drawing off its contents. To exhaust, by setting in such a posture as the fluid must necessarily run out.

DRAIN, S. a channel through which waters are exhausted or drawn. A water-course. A sluice; a ditch.

DRAKE, S. [*dravd*, Belg.] the male of a duck. A small piece of cannon.

DRAKE, (Sir FRANCIS) the son of Edmund Drake, a sailor, and born near Tavistock in 1545, and educated at the expence and under the care of sir John Hawkins, his kinsman. He was one of the most distinguished naval heroes in the reign of queen Elizabeth. To recite all his great and serviceable actions, would require a volume. Thus much we must add, that he was a man, who might be said to have a head so cunning, a heart to undertake, and a hand ready to execute whatever promised glory to himself, and good to his country. The most distinguishing action of his life, his voyage round the globe, gives us such a signal instance of courage, intrepidity, sagacity, and discretion, as scarce seem to have met in one man before him.

him. And if we confider him as the great author of our navigation to the Weft and Eaft-Indies, as one who fhewed it practicable to act againft the Spaniards, both by fea and land; as the introducer of tobacco into this kingdom; as the promoter of the cheft at Chatham, for the relief of feamen wounded in the fervice of their country, and of his raifing the reputation of the Englifh failors fo high, that they were fought after and employed by all nations of the world, we may look on him as the remote caufe of our grandeur, and the extenfivenefs of our commerce. As fome account of his perfon and character may not be unacceptable, we add, that his ftature was low, but well fet, his cheft open and broad, his head very round, his hair of a fine brown, his beard full and comely, his eyes large and clear, his complexion fair, and his countenance frefh, chearful and engaging. As navigation had been his whole ftudy, fo he knew it thoroughly, and was a perfect mafter of every fcience, efpecially aftronomy, which could render him complete in the nautic art. Though he did not polifh his fpeech by ftudy, yet it was ftrong, nervous, concife, and though not diffufe, eloquent, and captivating: and to conclude his character with the words of Fuller, "He was a religious man towards God, and his houfes, where he came chafte in his life, juft in his dealings, true of his word, and merciful to thofe, which were under him, hating nothing fo much as idlenefs." Such was the character of this great man! See Campbell's Lives of the Admirals.

DRA'M, S. [*drachm* or *drachma*, Lat.] the eighth part of an ounce, applied to weight. Figuratively, a fmall quantity. "No dram of judgment." *Dryd.* Such a quantity of fpirituous liquors, as is ufually drank at once. Spirituous liquors. "From the ftrong fate of drams if thou get free." *Pope.*

To DRA'M, V. A. to drink, or accuftom one's felf to drink fpirituous liquors.

DRA'MA, S. [*drama*, Gr.] in Poetry, a piece or poem compofed for the ftage, in which fome action is reprefented. The deficiency of the Englifh in this fpecies of compofition is difplayed with great oftentation by French critics, who notwithftanding can have no other boaft of fuperiority, but their fervility to rules; the noble ftrokes, which the magic hand of a Shakefpear has fnatched beyond any of their favourite authors, and the knowledge he difplays of human nature, muft notwithftanding all their outcries, claim their aftonifhment; to enter into a minute criticifm on the excellencies of this fingle author, would require too much room; but the curious may meet with abundant fatisfaction in the critical works of our own writers.

DRAMA'TIC, DRAMA'TICAL, Adj. reprefented by action, or on the ftage.

DRAMA'TICALLY, Adv. after the manner of a poem acted on the ftage.

DRA'MATIST, S. the author of a dramatic piece.

DRA'NK, S. the preter of *drink*.

DRA'PER, S. one who deals in either linnen or woollen cloth.

DRA'PERY, S. the art of making cloth. Cloth made either of linnen or woollen. "Served the lord with drapery ware." *Hift. of John Bull.*" In Painting and Sculpture, the reprefentation of the garments or clothing of figures

DRA'STIC, Adj. [*drafticus*, Gr. *from draw*, Gr. to act or work] powerful, forcible, vigorous, efficacious. In Medicine, a remedy which works foon.

DRA'UGHT, S. [from *draw*, *draught*, Belg.] the act of drinking. A quantity of liquor drank at once. That which is fit or proper for a perfon to drink. The act on of moving, or dragging carriages. "Oxen for all forts of draught." *Temple.* The quality of being moved by pulling. A reprefentation by painting a fketch. A picture. In Fifhing, the act of catching a fifh by a drag-net. In War, forces drawn off from the main army. The depth which a fhip or veffel finks into the water. In Commerce, a bill drawn by one perfon on another for money. Draughts is a game played on a chequered table with round pieces of box and ebony.

To DRA'W, V. A. [preter, *drew*; Part. paff. *drawn*, *dragen*, Sax.] to pull from one place to another. To attract, to draw towards itfelf. To breathe, or inhale, applied to air. To take from a cafk or veffel. "To drain or empty, applied to liquors. fometimes ufed with *off*. To pull out of the fcabbard, to unfheath. To take bread out of an oven. To open or feparate from each other. To unclofe if clofe before, but to clofe together if open, applied to curtains. To lengthen or protract, applied to literary compofitions. In Painting, to reprefent the likenefs of any perfon or thing. To imply, to infer. To compofe, to form in writing. To draw a brief. In Cookery, to take out the guts of poultry. To draw in, to wreft or force any expreffion to favour a particular caufe, applied towards argument. To entice, to feduce, to prevail on by fondnefs. To draw off, to entrast by diftillation; to exhauft, to abftract, to withdraw or turn afide or divert, applied to the mind. To deduce as a confequence or inference. To expofe, joined to hatred or envy. "This would draw on him the hatred of all good men." To unfheath a fword in order to ftab a perfon. "He drew on or upon him in a full company." In Commerce, to addrefs a bill for a fum of money to a perfon. To draw over, to perfuade a perfon to revolt, or change his fentiments or party. To draw out, to lengthen the fpace of time or place a thing would otherwife occupy; to protract. In military affairs, to detach or feparate from the main body; to

prepare for action. To *draw up*, to form in writing, to compose. Neuterly, to move by force, applied to the manner in which beasts move any carriage. To influence, attract, or act upon as a weight or force. To contract or shrink. "*Draw* into less room." *Bacon*. Joined to an adverb or adjective, implying approach, to advance or move towards. To take a card out of a pack. To describe in words or colours. To make a free discharge matter. To *draw back*, to retreat or retire. To *draw off*, to decline an engagement, or make a retreat. To *draw on*, to come nearer, to advance or approach, applied to time, or the existence of some event.

DRAW, S. the act of drawing; the lot taken or drawn.

DRAWBACK, S. money paid back or abated for ready money. Figuratively, a deduction of the value or qualities of a thing. In Commerce, certain duties either of the customs or excise, allowed upon the exportation of some of our own manufactures, or on certain foreign merchandizes that have paid a duty on importation.

DRAWBRIDGE, S. a bridge moving on hinges, and by means of chains, lifted up or let down at pleasure.

DRAWER, S. one employed in fetching water. In taverns, one who draws liquors. One who forms the resemblance of a person, with a pen, pencil or brush. Applied to things, that which has the power of attracting towards itself. In Surgery, that which discharges humours. A box which slides in a groove or case. In the plural, that part of dress which covers the thighs and posteriors.

DRAWING, S. the act of taking the likeness of a thing or person. A picture or sketch.

DRAWING-ROOM, S. a room for company to retire after an entertainment. A room for the reception of company at court.

DRAWN, Part. pass. from DRAW.

To DRAWL, V. N. to pronounce one's words with a slow drawling disagreeable whine.

DRAY, S. a low cart, used by brewers to convey their beer.

DREAD, S. [from *dred*, Sax.] terror or fear, the sensation occasioned by the sight of some terrible object. Awful or venerable.

To DREAD, V. N. [*dradan*, Sax.] to fear to an excessive degree.

DREADFUL, Adj. causing excessive fear. Frightful, terrible.

DREADFULLY, Adv. in such a manner as to cause fear, terror, or dread.

DREADFULNESS, S. that quality which causes excessive fear or terror.

DREADLESS, Adj. void of fear. Undaunted, bold.

DREAM, S. [pronounced *dreme*, from

dream, Belg.] the images which are represented to the mind during sleep. Figuratively, a chimera, a groundless fancy, or conceit.

To DREAM, V. N. to have ideas in the mind, while the outward senses are stopped during sleep. To think, to fancy without reasons.

DREAMER, S. one who perceives things during sleep. A person fond of conceits. A fanciful man; a man lost in wild imaginations.

DREAR, Adj. [*dreorig*, Sax.] affecting with sorrow, grief, or melancholy. Mournful.

DREARY, Adj. [*dreorig*, Sax.] full of sorrow or mournful. Gloomy, dismal, or afflicting with melancholy.

DREDGE, S. a thick, strong net, generally used for catching oysters, and is a species of a drag-net.

To DREDGE, V. A. to fish with a *dredge*. In Cookery, to strew flour over meat while it is roasting.

DREDGER, S. one who fishes with a *dredge*. A box with holes at the top used for strewing flour on meat when it is roasting.

DREGGINESS, S. fullness of lees, *dregs*, or foulness, abounding with a ropy substance, or sediment.

DREGGISH, Adj. abounding with lees, dregs, or sediment.

DREGGY, Adj. muddy, foul, full of sediment.

DREGS, S. [from *dreste*, Sax.] the lees or foul part of any liquor. Figuratively, the refuse, sweeping, or worthless part of any thing.

To DRENCH, V. A. [*drincan*, Sax.] to soak, to plunge all over in some liquor. To wash. To steep. To moisten. To administer physic by force or violence.

DRENCH, S. a draught, or swill. A potion or drink for a sick horse. Physic, which must be given by force. " Their counsels are more like a *drench* that must be poured down." *K. Charles*. A channel of water.

DRENCHER, S. a person who dips, steeps, or soaks any thing. One who administers physic by violence.

To DRESS, V. A. [*dresser*, Fr.] to adorn, deck, or set out with cloaths. In Surgery, to apply a plaister or other remedy to a wound. To curry or rub, applied to horses. To keep free from weeds, to adjust, or keep regular, applied to gardening. To prepare for any purpose. To trim, applied to lamps. To prepare victuals fit for eating. To comb out, or adorn the hair or periwig.

DRESS, S. that which a person wears to cover his body. Cloaths, or splendid attire.

DRESSER, S. one who is employed in dressing a person. A long kind of a table

in

In a kitchen. One employed in keeping a garden or plantation in order. A gardener. "The *dresser* of his vineyard." *Lutc.*

DRESSING, S. in Surgery, the plaister, or other remedy, applied to a sore.

DREST, participle of DRESS.

To DRIB, V. A. [from *dribble*] to steal, to cut off, or take a part of the gains of a person. "He who drives their bargains, *dribs* a pin." *Dryd.*

DRIBBLE, V. N. [from *drip* or *dripen*, Sax.] to fall in drops. To let fall from one's mouth. Actively, to throw down, or scatter in drops. "*Dribble* all the way up stairs." *Swift.*

DRIBLET, S. a small, or trifling sum of money.

DRIFT, S. the force which impells or drives. A stratum, layer, or covering of any matter blown together by the wind. Tendency, or particular design. The scope or tenor of a discourse, or argument.

To DRILL, V. A. [*drillen*, Belg.] to make a hole with an augur, gimlet, or drill. To bore. Figuratively, to draw step by step, used with *on.* "To *drill* him on from one lewdness to another." To range in battle array "The foes appear'd drawn up and *drill'd.*" *Hudib.* To drain, or make its passage through small holes or interstices. "*Drill* through the sandy stratum every way,—the waters with the sandy stratum rise." *Thomson.*

DRILL, [from the verb] an instrument used to bore holes.

To DRINK, V. N. to swallow liquors. Figuratively, to swallow liquors to excess. To *drink to*, to salute in drinking. Figuratively, to suck up or absorb. To receive by an inlet, applied to the eyes to see; applied to the ears, to hear. To make a person drunk.

DRINK, S. liquor to be swallowed. Any kind of liquor.

DRINKABLE, Adj. that which is fit to be drank.

DRINKER, S. one who is fond of swallowing large quantities of liquors.

To DRIP, V. N. [*drippen*, Belg.] to let fall in drops, applied to the fat which falls from meat, while roasting.

DRIP, S. that which drops, or falls in drops.

DRIPPING, S. the fat which drops or falls from meat while roasting.

To DRIVE, V. A. [preter. *drove*, part. pass. *driven* or *drove*, *driven*, Goth.] to force along by some violent impulse or pressure. To send to any place, by force. To force, or break by force, joined to *asunder.* To convey animals, or force them to walk from one place to another. To force or compel. To enforce or push home a proof or argument. To *drive trade*, to carry it on. To *drive out*, to expel or force from a place.

To rush with violence. To conduct a carriage. To *drive at*, to intend, to endeavour to accomplish, to have a tendency to.

To DRIVEL, V. N. [a corruption from DRIBBLE] to let the spittle, or slaver fall out of one's mouth.

DRIVEL, S. slaver, spittle, or mollara from the mouth.

DRIVELLER, S. a fool or idiot.

DRIVELLING, Part. doting; weak, foolish. "This *drivelling* love is like a great natural." *Shak.*

DRIVEN, Part. of DRIVE.

DRIVER, S. that which communicates motion by force. One who conveys beasts from one place to another. One who guides the cattle which draw any carriage.

To DRIZZLE, V. A. [*drijsen*, Teut.] to shed in small drops like dew. To let fall in small, slow drops.

DRIZZLY, Adj. descending in small, slow drops. Resembling a mist, dew, or moist vapour.

To DROIL, V. N. to work sluggishly and lowly; to plod. "The *drilling* peasant." *Govern. of the Tongue.*

DROLE, Adj. [*drôle*, Fr.] comical; queer, exciting laughter.

DROLE, S. [*drôler*, Fr.] a person who endeavours to raise mirth by antic gestures, or comical jests. A merry-andrew, buffoon, or jack pudding. A comical farce.

To DROLE, V. N. to jest, or play the merry andrew, or buffoon.

DROLLERY, S. jests, ridicule; or an endeavour to excite mirth, or laughter

DROMEDARY, S. [*dromedaris*, Fr. *dromedare*, Ital.] in Natural History, a sort of camel reported to travel 100 miles a day. It is smaller, slenderer and nimbler than the common camel; it is about seven feet and a half high, from the ground to the top of its head.

DRONE, S. the male bee, which hatches the young, makes no honey, has no sting, and is driven from the hive, when the hatching time is over. Figuratively, an inactive, or sluggish person.

To DRONE, V. N. to live an inactive, useless life. "A long restive race of *droning* kings." *Dryd.*

DRONISH, Adj. like a drone, sluggish, useless.

To DROOP, V. A. [*drues*, Belg.] to languish or hang down the head with sorrow. To grow faint, or dispirited. To sink; to lean downwards. To decline, or wear away. "Till day *droops.*" *Par. Lost.*

DROP, S. [*droppa*, Sax.] a small particle of water or other fluid. The roundness of a *drop* of any fluid is by Sir Isaac Newton attributed to the greater attraction between the primary particles of the drop, than that between the particles of the drop and those of the circumambient air. As much liquor

as falls at once, when there is not a continued stream. A diamond hanging from the ear, so called from its resembling the form of a drop of any fluid in its descent. In Physic, any spirituous medicine to be taken in drops.

To DROP, V. A. [droppan, Sax.] to pour in small particles. To let a thing fall from the hand, to utter slightly, without caution. 4 drop in, to visit a perfon cafually, or without intending out with that defign. To intermit ceafe, or decline. To deliver or relate following or affociating with. To lose in its progrefs. To bedrop or speckle. " Their wav'd coats dropp'd with gold." Milt. Neaterly, to fall in feparate particles. To let drops fall, to fall from a higher fituation. To fall without violence. To fall fuddenly, to die. To let drop, to pafs over without mentioning; to bury in oblivion or filence.

DROPLET, S. a fmall drop. " Thofe droplets which—forming good-nature fall." Shak.

DROPSIED, Part. affected, or afflicted with a dropfy.

DROPSY, S. [from hydropifie, Fr. hydrops, Fr. Ital.] in Phyfic, a preternatural collection of aqueous ferum, or water in any part of the body, which greatly diftends the velfels, is attended with a weaknefs of digeftion, and a continual thirft.

DROSS, S. the wafte, fcum, or fediment of any metal. The ruft of a metal. Figuratively, the moft worthlefs parts of any thing.

DROSSINESS, S. the fcum, impurity of metals. Foulnefs; ruft.

DROSSY, Adj. full of impurities, or confifts fo. Figuratively, as worthlefs as drofs.

DROVE, S. a number of cattle collected together, under the guidance of one or more perfons. Any collection of animals. Figuratively, a great multitude.

DROVER, S. one who conducts or drives oxen or fheep to market.

DROUGHT, S. [drugothe, Belg.] dry weather, want of rain. Thirft.

DROUGHTINESS, S. the ftate of a fluid or foil which is in want of rain. The ftate of a perfon afflicted with thirft.

DROUGHTY, Adj. wanting rain, parched with heat or thirft. Thirfty.

To DROWN, V. A. [drync?, Sax. to drink] to plunge and fuffocate under water. To overflow, or cover with water. Figuratively, to fubmerge, plunge in, or overwhelm with any thing. To die, or be fuffocated under the water.

To DROWSE, V. A. [drofen, Belg.] to be ftrongly inclined to fleep. " My drowfy ftates." Shak. Neuterly, to become heavy with fleep, to flumber. To look heavy, oppofed to chearful.

DROWSILY, Adv. in fuch a manner as fpeaks a propenfity to fleep. Heavily; fluggifhly.

DROWSINESS, S. a ftrong propenfity to fleep. Slothfulnefs.

DROWSY, Adj. inclined to fleep. Figuratively, caufing fleep. Dull or ftupid, " like drowfy reafoning." Atterb.

To DRUB, V. A. [drubes, Dan.] to beat with a ftick. To thump, or cudgel. A word of contempt. " I fhould have been drubbed." Locke.

DRUB, S. a thump, knock, or blow. A found beating with a ftick.

To DRUDGE, V. A. [drevan, Sax.] to work hard at fervile employments. To flave.

DRUDGE, S. one employed in mean and fatiguing labour. A flave.

DRUDGER, S. a mean hard labourer. A box with holes on the top, from whence flower is fcattered upon meat while roafting. See DREDGE.

DRUDGERY, S. low; mean; fervile labour.

DRUDGINGLY, Adj. in a laborious, fatiguing, fervile, and toilfome manner.

DRUG, S. [drogue, Fr. drow, Perf.] an ingredient ufed in phyfic or dying. Figuratively, any thing of a fmall value, this fenfe may probably be owing to a corruption of drag. A drudge. " Such as may the paffive drugs freely command." Shak.

DRUGGET, S. a fort of thin ftuff, fometimes all wool, fometimes half wool, half thread, and fometimes corded.

DRUGGIST, S. [drogiste, Belg.] one who fells phyfical ingredients or medicines, differing from an apothecary becaufe felling by wholefale, not prefcribing for diforders of vifiting patients, or not making up phyficians receipts; though it muft be confeffed that the trade have at prefent intrenched on all thefe branches, and excepting the vifiting of patients, taking away all diftinction between the two profeffions.

DRUID, S. [deru, oaks, and bud, incantation] the priefts of religion amongft the Britons, Celtic Gauls, and Germans. They were in Britain the firft and moft diftinguifhed order in the ifland, felected out of the beft families, and the honours of their birth, added to thofe of their function, procured them the higheft veneration. They were verfed in aftronomy, geometry, natural philofophy, politics and geography; had the adminiftration of all facred things, were the interpreters of the gods, and fupreme judges in all caufes, whether ecclefiaftic or civil. From their determination was no appeal, and whoever refufed to acquiefce in their decifions was reckoned impious, and excommunicated. They were generally governed by a fingle perfon, called an arch-druid, who prefided in all their affemblies. Once a year they tird

to retire or rather affemble in a wood in the center of the ifland, at which time they ufed to receive applications from all parts, and hear caufes. Their peculiar opinions, are not well afcertained by writers, though it is agreed by all that they held the immortality of the foul, and its tranfmigration; that nothing could appeafe the gods more powerfully than human facrifices, and that there was one fupreme deity who prefided over all others, named *Truth*, whence we may eafily trace the Welfh *Drew*, or the French *Dieu* God, whence they feem more probably derived than from *Deus*, Lat. as fupofed by fome etymologifts. The Druids committed none of their principles to writing, but tranfmitted them to pofterity by oral tradition; for which purpofe they were reduced to verfe, and were learnt by their difciples. The great veneration to which this fect of men were held by the antients, and the many attempts made by learned critics to trace their origin, and difcover their principles, muft fet them in an advantageous light. Yet with all their fplendor are joined great defects; their acknowledgment of a plurality of gods, and their afferting the neceffity of human facrifices, muft detract very much from their character, and confirm us in this principle, that the hiftory of all nations, fhews the expediency of a divine revelation, and that thofe countries on which the fun of righteoufnefs has not rifen with healing in his wings, however famous for their intellectual abilities, or literary talents, have rather groped their way, than feen their path, with refpect to religious doctrines.

DRU'M, S. [*tromme*, Dan. *dromme*, Erfe.] a warlike inftrument, bent in a cylindrical form, covered at each end with vellum or perchment, which ftretches by means of braces running from one extremity to the other; and made to found by beating one of the ends with fticks. *Kettle-Drum*, is that whofe body is made of brafs or copper in the form of a kettle. The drum of the ear, is a fmall membrane in the inner part of that organ, which is fo ftretched as to convey the fenfation of found, by the vibration.

To DRU'M, V. N. to beat on a drum with a ftick.

DRU'M-MAJOR, S. the chief or principal drummer of a regiment.

DRU'MMER, S. one who beats or founds a drum.

DRUNK, Adj. [from *drink*] intoxicated by immoderate drinking. Figuratively, foak'd, beautifully applied to inanimate things. " I will make mine arrows *drunk* with blood." *Deut.* xxix, 6

DRU'NKARD, S. one given to exceffive ufe of ftrong liquors.

DRU'NKEN, Part. [from *drink*] intoxicated with liquor. Given to habitual drunkennefs: in intoxication.

DRU'NKENLY, Adv. after the manner of one intoxicated.

DRU'NKENNESS, S. in Medicine, a preternatural compreffion of the brain, cauſed by the fumes, or fpirituous parts of liquors, whereby perfons uſe fince every thing tranſmund; to thoſe motions alfo, an erect, reſtlefs of underſtanding, a voice fauttering and fierce articulate; an incapacity to walk, and all the figns of a temporary madnefs.

DRY, Adj. [*drige*, Sax. *droog*, Belg.] hard, or without wet. Without rain, applied to the feafons. Thirft. Figuratively, chilling or immoderately defirous of, applied to the affections. " So *dry* he was for fway." *Shak.* Jejune, barren, plain, void of ornament, or any embellifhment to make it pleafe; applied to ftyle or literary productions. Severe.

" Hard *dry* baſtings uſed to prove
" The reddeſt remedies of love." *Hudib.*

To DRY, V. A. to free from moifture, or wet. To wipe away moifture. To fcorch or affect with thirft. To drain, or drink up. " *Dry'd* an unmeafurable bowl." Neuterly, to grow free from, or be drained of moifture.

DRYDEN, [JOHN, Efq.] was the fon of Erafmus Dryden, Efq; of Tichmarfh, and grandfon of Sir Erafmus Dryden of Conoulbury, both in Northamptonfhire, and was born fome time in the year 1631, at Oldwincle, or Aldwinkle near Oundle, in the faid country, a village, which, as he himfelf informs us, belonged to the earl of Exeter, and which was alfo famous for giving birth to the celebrated Dr. Thomas Fuller, the hiftorian.

He received the rudiments of his grammar learning at Weftminfter fchool, under the learned Dr. Bufby, and from thence was removed in 1650 to Cambridge, being elected fcholar of Trinity College, of which he appears by his Latin verfes in the *Epicedamia Cantabrigienf.* 4to. 1662. to have been afterwards a fellow.—Yet in his earlier days, he gave no very extraordinary indications of genius, for, even the year before he quitted the univerfity, he wrote a poem on the death of lord Haftings, which was by no means a prefage of that amazing perfection in poetical powers which he afterwards poffeffed.—His firft play, viz. *The Wild Gallants*, did not appear till he was not much lefs than forty years of age, and then met with fuch indifferent fuccefs, that had not neceffity afterwards compelled him to purfue the arduous tafk, the Englifh ftage had perhaps never been favoured with fome of its brighteft ornaments.

But to proceed more regularly.—On the death of Oliver Cromwell he wrote fome heroic ftanzas to his memory; but on the reftoration; being defirous of ingratiating himfelf with the new court, he wrote, firft, a poem

poem entitled *Aftraea redux*, and afterwards a panegyrick to the king on his coronation. —In 1662, he addressed a poem to the lord chancellor Hyde, presented on New-Year's day; and in the same year a satire on the Dutch—In 1668 appeared his *Annus Mirabilis*, which was an historical poem in celebration of the duke of York's victory over the Dutch. —These pieces at length obtained him the favour of the crown, and Sir William D'Avenant dying the same year, Mr. Dryden was appointed to succeed him as poet-laureat.— About this time also his inclination for writing for the stage seems first to have shewn itself, for besides his concern with Sir William D'Avenant in the alteration of Shakespeare's *Tempest*, which was the last work that gentleman was engaged in, Mr. Dryden, in 1669, produced his *Wild Gallant*, a comedy.—This, as I have before observed, met with very indifferent success; yet the author, not being discouraged by its failure, soon after gave the public his *Indian Emperor*, which finding a more favourable reception, encouraged him to proceed, and that with such rapidity that, in the key to the Duke of Buckingham's *Rehearsal*, he is recorded to have engaged himself by contract for the writing of four plays a year; and indeed, in the years 1679 and 1680, he appears to have fulfilled that contract.—To this unhappy necessity that our author lay under, are to be attributed all those irregularities, those bombastic flights, and sometimes even puerile exuberances, which he has been so severely criticized on for, and which in the unavoidable hurry in which he wrote, it was impossible he should find time to revise, either for the lopping away or correcting.

In 1679 there came out, *An Essay on Satire*, said to be written jointly by Mr. Dryden and the earl of Mulgrave, containing some very severe reflections on the earl of Rochester and the dutchess of Portsmouth, and in 1681 Mr. Dryden published his *Absalom* and *Achitophel*, in which the well-known character of *Zimri*, drawn for the duke of Buckingham, is certainly severe enough to repay all the ridicule thrown on him by that nobleman in the character of *Bayes*.—Their sentiment shewn by the different peers was very different; lord Rochester, who was a coward as well as a man of the most depraved morals, basely hired three ruffians to cudgel Dryden in a coffee-house; but the duke of Buckingham, as we are told, in a more open manner, took that task on himself, and at the same time presented him with a purse containing no very trifling sum of money, telling him that he gave him the beating as a punishment for his impudence, but bestowed the gold on him as a reward for his wit.

Soon after the accession of King James II. our author changed his religion for that of the church of Rome, and wrote two pieces in

vindication of the Romish tenets, viz. *A Defence of the Papers*, written by the late king of blessed memory, found in his strong box, and the celebrated poem, afterwards answered by lord Halifax, entitled the *Hind* and the *Panther*.—By this extraordinary step, he not only engaged himself in controversy, and incurred much censure and ridicule from his cotemporary wits, but, on the completion of the revolution, being, on account of his newly-chosen religion, disqualified from bearing any office under the government, he was stripped of the laurel to which he had been appointed, which to his still greater mortification was bestowed on Richard Flecknoe, a man to whom he had the most settled aversion.—This circumstance occasioned his writing the very severe poem, called *Mac Flecknoe*.

Mr. Dryden's circumstances had never been affluent, but now being deprived of this little support, he found himself reduced to the necessity of writing for meer bread.—We consequently find him from this period engaged in works of labour as well as genius, viz. in translating works of others; and to this necessity perhaps our nation stands indebted for some of the best translations extant.—In the year he lost the laurel he published the *Life of St. Francis Xavier*, from the French. In 1693, came out a translation of *Juvenal* and *Persius*, in the first of which he had a considerable hand, and of the latter the entire execution.—In 1695 was published his prose version of Fresnoy's *Art of Painting*, and the year 1697 gave the world that translation of Virgil's works entire, which still does, and perhaps ever will, stand foremost among the attempts made on that author.—The Petite pieces of this eminent writer, such as Prologues, Epilogues, Epitaphs, Elegies, Songs, &c. are too numerous to specify here, and too much dispersed to direct the reader to.—The greatest part of them however are to be found in a Collection of Miscellanies, in 6x Vol. 12mo.—His last work is what is called his *Fables*, which consist of many of the most interesting stories in Homer, Ovid, Boccace and Chaucer, translated or modernized in the most elegant and poetical manner, together with some original pieces, among which is that amazing Ode on St. Cecilia's Day, which, tho' written in the very decline of its author's life, and at a period when old age and distress conspired as it were to damp his poetic ardor, and clip the wings of fancy, yet possesses so much of both, as would be sufficient to have rendered him immortal, had he never written a single line besides.

Dryden married the lady Elizabeth Howard, sister to the earl of Berkshire, who survived him eight years, though for the last four of them she was a lunatic, having been deprived of her senses by a nervous fever. By this lady he had three sons, who all survived him. Their names were Charles, John

John and Henry. Of the last of these I can trace no particulars. The second some little account will be given of in the succeeding article, and with respect to the eldest there is a circumstance related by Charles Wilson, esq; in his life of Congreve, which seems so well attested, and in itself of so very extraordinary a nature, that I cannot avoid admitting it to a place here. The event is as follows.

'Dryden, with all his understanding, was weak enough to be fond of judicial astrology, and used to calculate the nativity of his children. When his lady was in labour with his son Charles, he being told it was decent to withdraw, laid his watch on the table, begging one of the ladies then present, in a most solemn manner, to take exact notice of the very minute the child was born, which she did, and acquainted him with it. About a week after, when his lady was pretty well recovered, Mr. Dryden took occasion to tell her that he had been calculating the child's nativity, and observed, with grief, that he was born in an evil hour, for Jupiter, Venus, and the Sun, were all under the Earth, and the Lord of his ascendant afflicted with a hateful square of Mars and Saturn. If he lives to arrive at the eighth year, says he, " he will go near to die a violent death on his very birth day, but if he should escape, as I see but small hopes, he will in the twenty-third year be under the very same evil direction, and if he should escape that also, the thirty-third or thirty-fourth year is, I fear."—Here he was interrupted by the immoderate grief of his lady, who could no longer hear calamity prophesied to befall her son. The time at last came, and August was the inauspicious month in which young Dryden was to enter into the eighth year of his age. The court being in progress, and Mr. Dryden at leisure, he was invited to the country-seat of the earl of Berkshire, his brother-in-law, to keep the long vacation with him in Charlton, in Wilts; his lady was invited to her uncle Mordaunt's, to pass the remainder of the summer. When they came to divide the children, lady Elizabeth would have him take John, and suffer her to take Charles; but Mr. Dryden was too absolute, and they parted in anger; he took Charles with him, and she was obliged to be content with John. When the fatal day came, the anxiety of the lady's spirits occasioned such an effervescence of blood, as threw her into so violent a fever, that her life was despaired of, till a letter came from Mr. Dryden, reproving her for her womanish credulity, and assuring her that her child was well, which recovered her spirits, and in six weeks after she received an eclaircissement of the whole affair. Mr. Dryden, either through fear of being reckoned superstitious, or thinking it a science beneath his study, was extremely cautious of

letting any one know that he was a dealer in astrology; therefore could not excuse his absence, on his son's anniversary, from a general hunting match, lord Berkshire had made, to which all the adjacent gentlemen were invited. When he went out, he took care to set the boy a double exercise in the Latin tongue, which he taught his children himself, with a strict charge not to stir out of the room till his return; well knowing the task he had set him would take up longer time. Charles was performing his duty, in obedience to his father, but as ill fate would have it, the stag made towards the house; and the noise alarming the servants, they hasted out to see the sport. One of them took young Dryden by the hand, and led him out to see it also, when, just as they came to the gate, the stag being at bay with the dogs, made a bold push, and leaped over the court wall, which was very low, and very old; and the dogs following, threw down part of the wall ten yards in length, under which Charles Dryden lay buried. He was immediately dug out, and after six weeks languishing in a dangerous way he recovered; so far Dryden's prediction was fulfilled: In the twenty third year of his age, Charles fell from the top of an old tower belonging to the Vatican at Rome, occasioned by a swimming in his head; with which he was seized, the heat of the day being excessive. He again recovered, but was ever after in a languishing sickly state. In the thirty-third year of his age, being returned to England, he was unhappily drowned at Windsor. He had with another gentleman swum twice over the Thames; but returning a third time, it was supposed he was taken with the cramp, because he called out for help, though too late. Thus the father's calculation proved but too prophetical.

At last, after a long life, harassed with the most laborious of all fatigues, viz. that of the mind, and continually made anxious by distress and difficulty, our author departed this life on the first of May 1701, and was interred in Westminster-Abbey. On the 19th of April he had been very bad with the gout and erisipelas in one leg; but he was then somewhat recovered, and designed to go abroad; on the Friday following he eat a partridge for his supper, and going to take a turn in the little garden behind his house in Gerard-Street, he was seized with a violent pain under the ball of the great toe of his right foot; that, unable to stand, he cried out for help, and was carried in by his servants, who, upon sending for surgeons, they found a small black spot in the place affected; he submitted to their present applications, and when gone called his son Charles to him, using these words. " I know this black spot is a mortification: I know also, that it will seize my head, and that they will attempt to cut off my leg: but I command

you my son, by your filial duty, that you do not suffer me to be dismembered:" As he foretold, the event proved, and his son was too dutiful to disobey his father's commands.

On the Wednesday morning following, he breathed his last, under the most excruciating pains in the sixty-ninth year of his age.

The day after Mr. Dryden's death, the dean of Westminster sent word to Mr. Dryden's widow, that he would make a present of the ground, and all other able expenses for the funeral: The lord Halifax likewise sent to the lady Elizabeth, and to Mr. Charles Dryden, offering to defray the expences of our poet's funeral, and afterwards to bestow five-hundred pounds on a monument in the abbey; which generous offer was accepted. Accordingly, on Sunday following, the company being assembled, the corpse was put into a velvet hearse, attended by eighteen mourning coaches. When they were just ready to move, lord Jefferys, son of lord chancellor Jefferys, a name dedicated to infamy, with some of his rakish companions riding by, asked whose funeral it was; and being told it was Mr. Dryden's, he protested he should not be buried in that private manner, that he would himself, with the lady Elizabeth's leave, have the honour of the interment, and would bestow a thousand pounds on a monument in the Abbey for him. This put a stop to their procession; and the lord Jefferys, with several of the gentlemen, who had alighted from their coaches, went up stairs to the lady, who was sick in bed. His lordship repeated the purport of what he had said below; but the lady Elizabeth refusing her consent, he fell on his knees, vowing never to rise till his request was granted. The lady under a sudden surprise fainted away, and lord Jefferys pretending to have obtained her consent, ordered the body to be carried to Mr. Russel's, an undertaker in Cheapside, and to be left there till farther orders. In the mean time the abbey was lighted up, the ground opened, the choir attending, and the bishop waiting for some hours to no purpose for the corpse. The next day Mr. Charles Dryden waited on my lord Halifax, and the bishop, and endeavoured to excuse his mother, by relating the truth. Three days after the undertaker having received no orders, waited on the lord Jefferys; who pretended it was a drunken frolic, that he remembered nothing of the matter, and he might do what he pleased with the body. Upon this, the undertaker waited on the lady Elizabeth, who desired a day's respite, which was granted. Mr. Charles Dryden immediately wrote to the lord Jefferys, who returned for answer, that he knew nothing of the matter, and would be troubled no more about it. Mr. Dryden hereupon applied again to the lord Halifax,

and the bishop of Rochester, who absolutely refused to do any thing in the affair.

In this distress, Dr. Garth, who had been Mr. Dryden's intimate friend, sent for the corpse to the College of Physicians, and proposed a subscription; which succeeding about three weeks after Mr. Dryden's decease, Dr. Garth pronounced a fine Latin oration over the body, which was conveyed from the college, attended by a numerous train of coaches to Westminster-Abbey, but in very great disorder. At last the corpse arrived at the Abbey, which was all unlighted. No organ played, no anthem sung; only two of the singing boys preceding the corpse, who sung an ode of Horace, with each a small candle in their hand. When the funeral was over, Mr. Charles Dryden sent a challenge to lord Jefferys, who refusing to answer it, he sent several others, and went often himself; but could neither get a letter delivered, nor admittance to speak to him, that finding his lordship refused to answer him like a gentleman, he resolved to watch an opportunity, and have him to fight, though with all the rules of honour; but which his lordship hearing, quitted the town, and Mr. Charles never had an opportunity to meet him, though he sought it to his death, with the utmost application.

Mr. Dryden had no monument erected to him for several years; to which Mr. Pope alludes in his epitaph intended for Mr. Rowe, in this line.

" *Beneath a rude and nameless stone he lies.*"

In a note upon which we are informed, that the tomb of Mr. Dryden was erected upon this hint, by Sheffield duke of Buckingham, to which was originally intended this epitaph.

"*This Sheffield raised.*"—*The sacred dust below,*
Was Dryden once; the rest who does not know.

Which was since changed into the plain inscription now upon it, viz.

J. DRYDEN,
Natus Aug. 9, 1631.
Mortuus Maii 1, 1701.

Johannes Sheffield, dux Buckinghamiensis fecit.

Mr. Dryden's character has been very differently drawn by different hands, some of which have exalted it to the highest degree of commendation, and others debased it to the severest censure. The latter, however, we must charge to that strong spirit of party which prevailed during great part of Dryden's time, and ought therefore to be taken with great allowances. Were we indeed to form a judgment of the author from some of his dramatic writings, we should perhaps be apt to conclude him a man of a most licentious morals, many of his comedies containing a great share of loofeness, even extending to obscenity; but if we consider that, as the poet tells us,

Thefs.

3

"*These who live to please, must please to live.*"
If we then look back to the scandalous licence of the age he lived in, the indigence which at times he underwent, and the necessity he consequently lay under of complying with the public taste however depraved, we shall surely not refuse our pardon to the compelled writer, nor our credit to those of his contemporaries, who were intimately acquainted with him, and who have assured us there was nothing remarkably vicious in his personal character.

From some parts of his history he appears unsteady, and to have too readily temporized with the several revolutions in church and state. This however might in some measure have been owing to that natural timidity and diffidence in his disposition, which almost all the writers seem to agree in his possessing. Congreve, whose authority cannot be suspected, has given us such an account of him, as makes him appear no less amiable in his private character as a man, than he was illustrious in his public one as a poet. In the former light, according to that gentleman, he was humane, compassionate, forgiving, and sincerely friendly. Of an extensive reading, a tenacious memory, and a ready communication. Gentle in the correction of the writings of others, and patient under the reprehension of his own deficiencies. Easy of access himself, but slow and diffident in his advances to others; and of all men the most modest and the most easy to be diffcountenanced in his approaches, either to his superiors or his equals. As to his writings, he is perhaps the happiest in the harmony of his numbers of any poet who ever lived either before or since his time, not even Mr. Pope himself excepted. His imagination is ever warm, his images noble, his descriptions beautiful, his sentiments just and becoming. In his prose he is poetical without bombast, concise without pedantry, and clear without prolixity.

I shall, however, close my account of this celebrated author with the words of Mr. Congreve, who has borne the following strong testimonial to his poetical merit.

"I may venture (says that gentleman) to say in general terms, that no man has written in our language, so much, and so variously manners so well. Another thing, I may say, was very peculiar to him, which is, that his parts did not decline with his years, but that he was an improved writer to the last, even to near seventy years of age; improving even in fire and imagination as well as in judgment; witness his ode on St. Cæcilia's-Day, and his fables, his latest performance. He was equally excellent in verse and prose. His prose had all the clearness imaginable, without deviating to the language or diction of poetry. In his poems, his diction is, whenever his subject

requires it, so sublime, and so truly poetical, that its essence, like that of pure gold, cannot be destroyed.—Take his verses, and divell them of their rhimes, disjoint them of their numbers, transpose their expressions, make what arrangement or disposition you please in his words; yet shall there eternally be poetry, and some thing which will be found incapable of being reduced to absolute prose.—What he has done in any one species or distinct kind of writing, would have been sufficient to have acquired him a very great name.—If he had written nothing but his prefaces, or nothing but his songs and his prologues, each of them would have entitled him to the preference and distinction of excelling in its kind.

DRY'LY, Adv. without moisture. Figuratively, in a cold, or indifferent manner, with great reserve.

DRY'NESS, S. want of moisture, rain, or juice.

DRY'-NURSE, S. one that brings up a child without sucking. Sometimes used contemptuously of a person who takes care of another.

To DRY'-NURSE, V. A. to bring up an infant without the breast.

To DUB, V. A. [*dubban to robe*, Sax.] to create a man a knight. To confer any title, honour, or dignity.

DUBLIN, the capital town or city of Ireland, in the county of the same name, and province of Leinster. It is a rich, handsome, and populous place, with an archbishop's see, a parliament, and an university; the courts of justice are held much alike, it being the residence of the Viceroy or Lord-Lieutenant. The compass of the walls is not great; but it has four large suburbs, the principal of which is Oxmantown or Ormonby, to the N. of the river Liffey, and is joined to the city by a bridge. The number of houses in 1753, was 12,827. The cathedral church called St. Patrick's, lies in the S. suburb, and is very ancient and handsome; besides which there are about twelve more. The college, or university, is in the E. suburb, and was founded by Q. Elizabeth in 1591, and contains about 600 students. It is seated in view of the sea on one side, and a fine country on the other, and would have had a commodious and secure harbour, if the mouth had not been so choaked up, that vessels of burthen cannot come to the town. It is seated on the river Liffey, 60 miles W. of Holyhead, in Wales, and 330 N. W. of London. Lon. 11. 10. Lat. 53 14.

DUBIOSITY, S. a thing which is doubtful. "Men often swallow falsities for truths, *dubibsities* for certainties." *Brown.*

DUBIOUS, Adj. [*dubius*, Lat.] not fully proved,

proved, or that which has equal probability on either side.

DU'BIOUSLY, Adv. so as to admit of different senses.

DU'BIOUSNESS, S. uncertainty. Want of sufficient proof.

DU'BITABLE, Adj that which may be questioned or doubted.

DUBITA'TION, S. [dubitatio, Lat.] the act of doubting.

DU'CAL, Adj [from duke] belonging or relating to a duke.

DU'CAT, S. a foreign coin, current on the Continent, when of silver valued at four shillings and six pence, and when of gold at nine shillings and six pence.

DU'CK, S. [ducken, to dip] a water fowl, both wild and tame; as they grope for their food, with their bills out of sight, the wise contrivance of the supreme architect cannot be too much admired, who has furnished their bills with nerves, which come from their eyes, whereby they are enabled to reject what is unfit for food, even though it should lie so hid in mud, as not be discernable to their eyes. Figuratively, used as a word of great fondness and endearment. "My dainty duck." Shak. But this sense may, perhaps, be a corruption of duke. A sudden bending down of the head. A stone thrown so obliquely on the water, as to rebound several times.

To DU'CK, V. N. to dive under water. To bow low.

DUCKING-STOOL, S. a chair in which women are plunged under water for scold ing.

DU'CKLING, S. a young duck.

DU'CT, S. [ductus, Lat.] guidance or direction. In Anatomy, any canal or tube, in an animal body, through which the humours are conveyed.

DU'CTILE, S. [ductilis, Lat.] easy to be bent, or drawn out in length. Complying, or yielding, applied to the mind.

DU'CTILENESS, S. the quality of being bent or drawn out in length.

DUCTI'LITY, S. a property of certain bodies, whereby they become capable of being press'd, beaten, or drawn out to a great length without breaking. Tractableness, compliance.

DU'DGEON, S [dolch, Belg. dugen, dagyn, Teut.] a small dagger. Quarrel, ill-will, malice or commotion.

DUE, that which a person has a right to demand. That which a person ought to pay, or which a thing might lay claim to. "A due sense of the vanity of earthly expectations." Atterb. Applied to time, punctual, exact to a period appointed.

DU'E, Adv. among sailors, directly, exactly, without turning aside. "Due East, Due West."

DU'E, S. that which belongs to, or may

be claimed by a person. Right. Just title. In the plural, custom, tribute, taxes.

DU'EL, S. [duellum, Lat.] a combat between two persons.

To DU'EL, V. N. to fight in single combat.

DU'ELLER, S. one who engages another in a duel or single combat.

DU'ELIST, S. one who engages another in a duel or single combat.

DUE'NNA, S. [Span.] an old woman, kept as a domestic in Spain, to take care of the conduct of a young lady.

DU'G, [dryft, Dalm. dogliy, Boh.] a pap, nipple or teat, generally applied to that of a beast.

DU'G, the Preter of dig.

DU'KE, S. [duc, Fr. duca, Ital. dux. Lat.] in some foreign countries a sovereign prince. Among us it is the next title of honour below the prince. At first it was a name of office, not of honour, and given to those who were appointed to guard the frontier. In England none enjoyed this title till Edward III. created Edward his son duke of Cornwall. From that time many others have been created, whose titles are hereditary, and conferred by patent; their eldest sons are, by courtesy of England, stiled marquises, and their youngest, lords, with the addition of their christian names.

DU'KEDOM, S. the dominion of a duke.

DU'LCET, Adj [dulcis, Lat.] sweet to the taste. Harmonious and agreeable to the ear.

DULCIFICA'TION, S. in Pharmacy, the act of rendering any thing, which is acid, sweet, by mixing it with sugar.

To DU'LCIFY, V. A. [dulcifier, Fr.] to sweeten, to free from salts, sourness, or acrimony

DU'LCIMER, S. [dulcimello, Ital.] a musical instrument, strung with wires, played on with iron or brass pins.

To DU'LCORATE, V. A. [dulcis, Lat. sweet] to sweeten. To make less sour, or acrimonious.

DULCORA'TION, S. the act of sweetening.

DULL, S. [dwl, Brit. dole, Sax.] slow of apprehension. Blunt, applied to the edge of any instrument. Slow, applied to motion. Gross, dry, exhausting the spirits, or giving the mind no pleasure in the composition, applied to works of learning. "Dictionary writing is dull work." Not bright, or wanting vigour. "The looking glass is dull." "The fire is dull." Drowsy, sleepy.

To DU'LL, V. A. to blunt the edge of a thing. To sully brightness. To make a person sad or melancholy. To damp vigour.

DU'LLY, Adv. stupidly, foolishly. In a slow, sluggish manner.

DU'LNESS, S. weakness of understanding; slow-

flowness of apprehension; drowsiness, slug-
ishness. Dimness or want of lustre, blunt-
ness, or want of edge.

DU'LY, Adv. properly, fitly, regularly,
punctually. " Duly sent his family and wife."
Pope.

DU'MB, Adj. unable to speak. Deprived
of speech. Refusing to speak.

DU'MBLY, Adv. mutely; silently.

DU'MBNESS, S. incapacity of speaking.
Silence.

To DU'MFOUND, V. A. to confuse or
confound a person so as to render him unable to speak.

DUMP, S. [*dom*, Belg.] sullen and silent
sorrow; melancholy. A piece of leaden
coin or medal, with which children amuse
themselves.

DUMPISH, Adj. sad; silently, sorrowful; melancholy.

DU'MPLING, S. a kind of small and
coarse pudding boiled without bag or case.

DUN, Adj. [Sax. of *dun*, Brit.] a colour
partaking of a mixture of brown and black;
gloomy.

To DUN, V. A. [*dunan*, Sax. *dunar*, Ir.]
to demand a debt with vehemence.

DUN, S. one who demands a debt with
clamour, and importunity.

DUNCE, S. [*dun*, Belg.] one who has no
capacity for receiving instruction.

DUNG, S. [*ding*, Sax. *dung*, Teut.] the
excrement of animals used in manure.

To DUNG, V. A. to manure, improve,
or fatten with dung.

DUNGEON, S. [Fr.] a close prison, generally applied to a dark or subterraneous
one.

DUNG-HILL, S. a heap of dung. Figuratively, any mean abode. A situation of
meanness. A cock of spurious and degenerate kind, not fit for fighting, opposed to a
game cork.

DUNGHILL, Adj. sprung from the
dunghill; mean; base; or worthless.

DUNGY, Adj. abounding in dung.

DUNNER, S. a person employed in collecting debts.

DUNSTABLE, S. a town of Bedfordshire,
with a market on Wednesdays, and four fairs,
on Ash-Wednesday, May 21, August 12,
and November 12, for cattle. It is seated on
a hill, on a dry chalky ground, where no
springs are to be found, but there is a large
pond in the middle of the town, which serves
the inhabitants for common use. It has 4
streets, which regard the four corners of the
world, and is full of good inns, standing on
the road from London to Chester. The
church is the remainder of a priory, and opposite to it is a farm house, which was once a
royal palace. It is 17 miles S. of Bedford,
and 34 N. W. of London. Lon. 17. 5. lat.
51. 40.

DUODE'CIMO, S. [*duodecim*, Lat. twelve]

a thing divided into twelve parts. A book
is said to be in *duodecimo*, when twelve of its
leaves make a sheet of paper.

DUPE, S. one who is imposed on, on account of his credulity.

To DUPE, V. A. to cheat a person of too
great credulity.

DU'ILE, Adj. [*duplex*, Lat.] double.

To DU'PLICATE, V. A. [*duplicatus*,
Lat.] to double; to increase by the repetition of the same number. To fold together.

DUPLICATE, Adj. in Arithmetic, the
ratio or proportion of squares.

DU'PLICATE, S. the exact copy or
counter part of a letter, book, or deed. A
thing of the same kind as another.

DUPLICA'TION, S. the act of doubling;
the act of folding together.

DUPLI'CITY, S. [*duplicitas*, Lat.] doubleness; the division of things or ideas into
pairs. Deceit, or double-dealing.

DURABI'LITY, S. [*durabilis*, Lat.] the
power of bearing the injuries of time and
weather without being destroyed. The property of lasting a long while.

DU'RABLE, Adj. [*dur-bilis*, Lat.] not
easily destroyed. Lasting, permanent.

DU'RABLENESS, S. the property of
continuing in the same state, and resisting the
injuries of time without alteration.

DU'RABLY, Adv. in a lasting manner.

DU'RANCE, S. [*duresse*, low Fr.] the
state of a person confined. Confinement;
imprisonment; duration. " Of how short
durance was this new-made state." *Dryd.*

DURA'TION, S. [*duratio*, Lat.] distance
or length, applied to time; the idea of
which is acquired from considering the flee-
ing and perpetual parts of succession. Power
of continuing long without change.

To DURE, V. N. [*duro*, Lat.] to last; to
continue some time unaltered. " Most pleasing whilst they *dure*." *Raleigh.*

DU'RELESS, Adj. without continuance.
Short, transitory.

DU'RESSE, S. imprisonment; confinement.

DURHAM, S. the capital town or city,
of the bishoprick of Durham, with a market
on Saturdays, and three fairs, on March, 5,
which continues three days; the first day for
horned cattle, the second for sheep and hogs,
and the third for horses; those on Whit-
Tuesday and September 15 are for the same.
It is a bishop's see, and pleasantly and commodiously seated on an easy ascent, and almost surrounded by the river Weare, over
which there are two large stone-bridges. It
is surrounded by a wall, and has a castle,
now made use of for the bishop's palace, seated on the highest part of the hill. It is a
handsome and compact place, containing 6
parish-churches, besides its cathedral, but
the suburbs are straggling. It is well inhabited,

bited, and supplied with commodities of all forts, and is beautified with handsome buildings, both public and private, of which the most remarkable is the cathedral, which is somewhat like Westminster-abbey. Adjoining to this are the houses of the dean and prebends. It sends two members to parliament. It is 14 miles S. of Newcastle, 51. N. of York, and 262 N. by W. of London. Lon 16. 23. lat. 54. 50.

DURHAM, S. a county in England, commonly called the bishoprick of Durham, 35 miles in length, and 34 in breadth. It is bounded on the E. by the German ocean, on the S. by the river Teese, which divides it from Yorkshire, on the W. by Cumberland and Westmoreland, and on the N. by Northumberland. It contains 15.980 houses, 95,580 inhabitants, 113 parishes, and 9 market-towns. The air is good but cold upon the hills that lie on the N. and W. sides, which are very thinly inhabited, they being generally barren. The eastern part is a good country, and pretty fruitful. The particular commodities are coal, iron, and lead; and the principal rivers are the Teese, the Weare, the Tame, and the Tyne. It sends but two members to parliament, besides those for Durham.

DURING, Part. for the time any thing lasts or continues.

DURITY, S. [durité, Fr. durus, Lat.] hardness, or quality of a body.

DURST, preter of DARE.

DUSK, Adj. [duster, Teut.] approaching to darkness. Blackish, or of a dark colour.

DUSKISH, Adj. inclining to darkness; dark coloured.

DUSKISHLY, Adv. darkly; so as to afford but little light.

DUSKY, Adj. tending to darkness Tending to blackness, gloomy, sad, melancholy.

DUST, S. [dowst,] earth or other matter reduced to small particles. Figuratively, the state to which bodies are reduced after being long buried.

DUSTY, Adj. filled, clouded, or spread with dust.

DUTCHESS, S. [ducbesse, Fr.] the lady of a duke.

DUTCHY, S. a territory which gives title to a duke. Ducthy-Court, is that wherein all matters pertaining to the dutchy of Lancaster are decided.

DUTEOUS, Adj. obedient, obsequious, or complying.

DUTIFUL, Adj. obedient; performing the offices due to parents, &c. Respectful; reverential.

DUTIFULLY, Adv. in an obedient, respectful manner.

DUTIFULNESS, S. obedience. Performance of the offices which flow from our relations as children or subjects. Reverence, Respect.

DUTY, S. actions which flow from the relations we stand in to God or Man. That which a man is bound to perform by any natural or legal obligation. Everything which is required to be done or forborne by religion or morality. That which a person's station, rank, condition, or employment obliges him to perform. In Commerce, a tax or custom.

DWARF, S. [dwerg, Sax.] a man below the common size. In Gardening, a low fruit tree. Any animal or plant shorter than those of the same species. "A dwarfisher, A dwarf's foot."

To DWARF, V. A. in Botany, to make little.

DWARFISH, Adj. below the natural or common size. Small, very short.

DWARFISHNESS, S. shortness of stature. Extreme littleness, smallness.

To DWELL, V. N. [preter, dwelt, dwelo, old Teut.] to inhabit, or live in a place. Figuratively, to continue in a state or condition. To fix the eyes immoveably upon an object. "Such was the face on which I dwelt with joy." Pope. To treat of copiously, or to continue long in handling or displaying any topic or subject.

DWELLER, S. one who resides in a place. An inhabitant.

DWELLING, S. habitation, residence or abode.

To DWINDLE, V. N. [dwinen, Sax.] to decrease, consume, or grow shorter or less by degrees.

DYE, S. See DIE.

DYER, S. a person who gives a colour to stuffs &c.

DYING, Part. [of die] expiring. Giving a new colour.

DYNASTY, S. [dunasteia, Gr.] in History, a succession of kings. Government. Sovereignty.

DYSCRASY, S. [duskrasia] an ill temperament or habit of body.

DYSENTRY, S. [dysenteria, Fr.] in Medicine, a looseness wherein very flu humours are discharged by stool, attended or accompanied with blood.

DYSPEPSY, S. [duspepsia, Gr.] a bad or difficult digestion.

DYSPHONY, S. [dus, Gr. and phone, Gr.] a difficulty in speaking or uttering.

DYSPNOEA, S. [duspnoia, Gr.] a difficulty or hardness of breathing.

DYSURY, S. [Gr. from dus, and ouron, Gr.] difficulty in discharging urine, or making water.

E

E.

E, The fifth letter, and second vowel of the English alphabet. The form of the capital E certainly is borrowed by us from the Romans, who had it from the Greeks, who had the character from the Phenicians, who had the same character from the Hebrews. Our small e is the same as that of the Saxons, who seem to have formed it from their capital e, which is not angular, like the Roman, but roundish, and with a strait stroke projecting from the middle, as that of the Goths was likewise. It has two sounds, long and short. The long sound is generally signified by its being followed by an e final, as scene; the short is like that in pen. It is the most frequent vowel of any in the English language. Anciently almost every word ended with it, but even then it was not pronounced at the end of a word, so as to form a distinct syllable. The use of it at present is only to lengthen the sound of the preceding vowel, as in mete the e is short, but in mete it is long. When a word ending in an e final is formed into an active participle, the e is dropped; thus when formed into an active participle, is written have, having, not haveing. Before an e it is pronounced long, as in mean, which is pronounced mene, the sound of the a being dropped, excepting in great, &c. where it serves to lengthen the sound of the a, it being pronounced graat or grate, though formerly it seems to have been sounded according to the analogy observed in other nouns, where a is followed by e, as is evident from its being anciently written greet. " He seemeth a great wonder." Trevisa. In Music, it denotes the tones e, mi, la. In the calender it is the fifth dominical letter. On the compass it marks the East point; as E. S. E. i. e. East South E.

EACH, Pron. [elc, alc, Sax.] either of two. Every one of any number. The correspondent word is other. " Fright'ning each other." Addis. Before other it denotes one, as in the quotation, which signifies brightening one another; or one of the two brightening the other.

EAGER, Adj. [eager, Sax.] earnest, ardent, vehement in desire; longing. Impetuous. Quick, busy, easily put on action. Sharp or sour, applied to the taste. Keen or severe, applied to the sensation caused by cold. Brittle, inflexible, or not malleable, used of metals by artificers. " Gold will sometimes be so eager." Locke.

EAGERLY, Adv. with great ardour of desire; impatiently, sharply, quickly.

EAGERNESS, S. warmth of desire, impetuosity. An extreme impatience for the enjoyment of something which appears highly desirable.

EAGLE, S. [aigle, Fr.] a bird of prey, which builds on the top of mountains, and is reckoned to be the king of the feathered race. It is used in heraldry, spread, to represent a prince of the Roman empire.

EAGLE-SPEED, S. prodigious swiftness, like that of an eagle. " With eagle-speed the ears the sky." Pope. Perhaps coined by the author quoted.

EAGLET, S. a young eagle.

EALDERMAN, S. [ealderman, Sax.] the name of a Saxon magistrate, the same as our alderman.

EAR, S. [eare, Sax. eor, Belg.] the organ of hearing. The admirable construction of this part to answer the ends for which it is designed, would require too much room to be properly displayed; but the writers in comparative anatomy, will afford abundant satisfaction on this subject. In Music, a kind of peculiar and internal taste where we are able to judge of the harmony of sounds. Used with about, it signifies the whole head or person. " The city beaten down about their ears." Knolles. Up to the ears, all over or entirely, " Up to the ears in love." L'Estr. To listen to with attention, joined to give, or lend. In Botany, a long string of flowers or seeds. " An ear of corn." Figuratively, a prominency from any larger body whereby it is held. To fall together by the ears, signifies to quarrel, or fight. To set together by the ears, to promote strife.

To EAR, V. A. [erian, Sax.] to shoot, or branch into ears.

EARED, Part. having ears, or handles. Having ears or ripe corn.

EARL, S. [eorl, Sax. eorla, Dan.] a title of the third rank among the nobility. William the Conqueror was the first that made their title hereditary; in the time of Henry I. they were created with an addition of the name of the place to their own christian names. At first they were created only by the delivery of their charter; king John added the girding of a sword, at his coronation; afterwards were added a cap with a golden coronet with rays, and a robe of state.

EARL-MARSHAL, S. an officer who has the care and management of military ceremonies; this title is hereditary in the Duke of Norfolk.

EARLDOM, S. the jurisdiction of an Earl, or county or place from whence he receives his title.

EARLINESS, S. the being soon; or the priority of an action. Earliness in the morning, is the act of rising soon, compared to the rising of the sun. Earliness of growth, is the act of growing up soon. Earliness of coming, is quickness.

EARLESS, Adj. without ears; not having ears. " Earless on high stood unabash'd at Defoe." Pope.

EARLY,

EA'RLY, Adv. soon, betimes. In youth, or infancy.

To EA'RN, S. [earnian, Sax.] to gain as the reward of labour. To deserve; to obtain.

EAR'NEST, S. [pronounced both earnst and earst, of earnest, Sax.] ardent, warm, importunate, intent, fixed.

EAR'NEST, S. seriousness. A serious affair. A reality. Pledge; handsel. Something given by way of security and obligation. A token of something future. Money given to bind a bargain.

EAR'NESTLY, Adv. warmly; affectionately; zealously; eagerly; importunately.

EAR'NESTNESS, S. eagerness, vehemence, warmth. A vigorous endeavour to accomplish, or obtain a thing. Solemnity; seriousness. Solicitude.

EAR'-RING, S. jewels set in a ring, and worn in the ear. A ring worn in the ear.

EA'R-SHOT, S. that distance within which any thing may be heard. "Stand you out of ear-shot." Dryd.

EA'RSH, a plowed field. "Fires oft are good on barren earsh made." May.

EARTH', S. [eorth, Sax. aerd, Teut.] in Natural Philosophy, one of the four peripatetic elements, a simple, dry, and cold substance, and an ingredient in the composition of all natural bodies. In Chymistry, the fourth of the chymical elements; supposed to be the basis or substratum of all bodies. In Natural History, a fossil or terrestrial matter, whereof our globe consists, which is rather dissoluble by fire, water, or air, is not transparent, and generally contains some degree of oil, or fatty substance. The terraqueous globe. This world. Figuratively, the inhabitants of the earth.

To EARTH', V. A. [eardian, Sax.] to conceal under ground. To cover with earth.

EARTH'-BORN, Adj. sprung from the earth. Figuratively, meanly descended.

EARTH'EN, Adj. made, or consisting of earth, or clay.

EARTH'LING, S. an inhabitant of the earth, or one whose thoughts are seldom elevated above the earth. "To earthlings, the footstool of God,—seemeth magnificent." Drummond.

EARTH'LY, Adj. belonging to the earth; this present state of existence, opposed to that in the heavenly mansions. Gross. Corporeal.

EARTH'QUAKE, S. a tremor or shaking of the earth, supposed to be occasioned by the explosion of some subterraneous combustible matters.

EARTH'Y, Adj. consisting of, or inhabiting the earth. Gross.

EAR'-WAX, S. the excrementitious or viscous substance with which the ear is filled; designed by its viscousness to hinder insects

from entering, and by the bitterness and offensiveness of its taste, to drive them back again.

EAR'WIG, S. [from ear and wiga, Sax.] a sheath-wing'd insect, of a long body, having several legs, a fork at its tail, and of a dirty blackish colour, in gardens very prejudicial to fruit-trees and flowers.

EASE, S. [aise, Fr.] a freedom from care or disturbance; freedom from pain; body. Rest, in order to recover from fatigue. Freedom from obstruction, impediment, or difficulty. An elegant negligence, or freedom, applied to literary matters.

To EA'SE, V. A. to free from pain. To release from labour. To free from any thing which causes a disagreeable sensation.

EASE'MENT, S. exemption from any cost or expence. Indulgence. In law, a service which one neighbour has of another by charter or prescription, without profit; as a way through his ground, a sink, &c.

EASILY, Adv. without difficulty, labour, or impediment.

EA'SINESS, S. a freedom from difficulty. The quality of being soon persuaded to a thing. Compliance, without opposition. Credulity, without suspicion, or examination. Without the appearance of formality, an elegant negligence, applied to works of learning. Freedom from disturbance, pain.

EA'ST, S. [east, Sax.] the quarter from whence the sun rises when he enters the equinoctial points of aries or libra. The nations that are situated towards the point from whence the sun rises.

EA'STER, S. [eoster, Sax. ofter, Belg.] the time of the year when christians celebrate the resurrection of Christ from the grave.

EA'STERN, Adj. situated, or tending towards the east.

EA'STWARD, Adv. [eastward, Sax.] towards the east, or that point of the compass where the sun rises.

EA'SY, Adj. [from aise, see, Goth.] to be performed without fatigue or trouble. Free from disturbance. Believing without enquiry or opposition. Credulous. Free from bodily pain, or any disagreeable sensation. Ready, opposed to reluctant. Without any apparent labour, art, or formality.

To EA'T, V. A. [preter ate, or eat, participle eat, or eaten, from etan, or itan, Goth.] to consume by the mouth. Figuratively, to corrode, or destroy, applied to rust, &c. To retire, or away a thing. "I'll not eat my words." Neuterly, to take food.

EA'TABLE, Adj. fit, or proper food.

EA'TER, S. one who chews and swallows any food. That which corrodes.

EA'VES, S. [efese, Sax.] the edges of a roof hanging over a house.

To EA'VES-DROP, V. A. to catch what drops from the eaves. Figuratively, to listen under the windows of a house to discover secrets.

EA'VES-

EA'VES-DROPPER, S. one who listens to discover the secrets of a family; a tale-bearer.

EB'B, S. [*ebe-ffod*, Sax. *ebbe*, Dan.] the flowing retreat of water towards the sea. A shrinking of water in a river by the turn of its tide. Figuratively, decay, decline, waste.

To EBB, V. N. to flow back towards the sea. Figuratively, to decline; to decay; to waste; to be in an exhausted condition.

EBEN, EB'ON, EB'ONY, S. [*ebenum*, Lat.] in natural history, a kind of wood brought from the Indies, of a black colour, exceedingly hard and heavy.

EBO'N, EB'ONY, S. see EBEN.

EBO'N, Adj. made, or consisting of ebony. " Night in her *ebon* car." *Young*.

EBRI'ETY, S. [*ebrietas*, Lat.] intoxication; drunkenness.

EBRI'OSITY, S. [*ebriositas*, Lat.] habitual drunkenness.

EBULLI'TION, S. [*ebullio*, Lat.] the act of boiling up with heat. Figuratively, an intestine motion of the particles of the body. The commotion, struggle, fermentation occasioned by the mingling together any alcalinate and acid liquor.

ECCE'NTRIC, ECCE'NTRICAL, Adj. [*eccentricus*, Lat.] deviating from a center. Figuratively, not answering the design. " Eccentric to the ends of his master." *Brown*. Irregular; not consistent with any rule.

ECCE'NTRICITY, S. the departing from its center. Excursion from an employment, or proper sphere of action; an improper situation. " The duke at his return from his eccentricity, for so I account favourites abroad." *Wotton*.

ECCLESIA'STIC, ECCLESIA'STICAL, Adj. [*ecclesiasticus*, Lat.] relating to the service of the church, sometimes opposed to civil.

ECCLESIA'STIC, S. one devoted to the service of the church. A clergyman.

ECHINA'TE, ECHINA'TED, Part. [from *echinus*, Lat.] bristled, or prickled like a hedge-hog.

ECC'HO, S. [*ηχω*, Gr.] a sound reflected from a solid body, and returned or repeated to the ear. The place where the repetition of a sound is produced.

To ECC'HO, V. N. to resound, to be sounded back.

ECLAIRCI'SSEMENT, S. [Fr.] the act of elucidating, clearing up, or explaining.

ECLA'T, [Fr.] splendor, lustre, or glory.

ELE'GMA, S. [from *εκ* and *λειχω*, Gr.] a medicine of the consistence of a syrup, intended to heal or ease the lungs in coughs, &c.

ECLI'PSE, S. [*εκλειψις*, Gr. of *εκλειπω*] a darkening of one of the luminous bodies, NO. X.

by the interposition of some opake body. The sun is eclipsed by the moon's intervening between the earth and the sun. An eclipse of the moon is when the atmosphere of the earth, being between the sun and moon, hinders the light of the sun from being reflected by the moon; if the light of the sun is kept off from the whole body of the moon, it is a *total* eclipse, if from a part only, it is a partial one. A state of darkness, ignorance, or want of knowledge, applied to the mind or understanding.

To ECLI'PSE, V. A. to darken any luminary. To drown a lesser by superior light. To cloud; to obscure. Figuratively, to disgrace; to excell. " Her husband was *eclipsed* in Ireland." *Clarend*.

ECLI'PTIC, S. [Gr.] in astronomy, a line on the surface of the sphere of the world which the sun describes in its annual revolution. In geography, a great circle of the globe cutting the equator under an angle of 23 deg. 29 min. It is supposed to be divided in 12 parts, each of which are mark'd with one of the 12 signs, and contains the space of a month.

EC'LOGUE, S. [from *αιγες*, Gr. a goat, *λογος*, a discourse, because supposed to be held by goat-herds, and applied to such by Theocritus, the inventor of this species of poetry] a pastoral poem, whose scenes are confined to rural life, and whose personages are chiefly shepherds.

ECO'NOMY, S. [*οικος*, Gr. a house, and *νομος*, Gr. It is generally written according to its derivation *oeconomy*; but as *oe* is no English diphthong, it is introduced in this place, especially as there are great authorities to support this spelling] the management or government of a family. Figuratively, frugality in expence. The method used in governing or ruling. The disposition or arrangement of the parts of any work. " This *economy* must be observed in the minutest parts of an Epic poem." *Dryd*.

ECONO'MIC, ECONO'MICAL, Adj. belonging to the regulation or management of a family. Frugal.

EC'STACY, S. [*εκστασις*, Gr.] any sudden passion of the mind, by which the thoughts are for a time absorbed. Excessive joy or rapture.

ECSTA'SIED, Adj. enraptured; elevated or absorbed by some violent passion or emotion of the mind.

EXTA'TIC, EXTA'TICAL, Adj. enraptured, or elevated to an extacy. In the highest degree of joy.

EC'TYPE, S. [*εκτυπον*, Gr.] a copy or resemblance. " The complex ideas of substances are *ectypes*, copies, but not perfect ones." *Locke*.

E'CURIE, S. [Fr. from *equus*, Lat.] a covered place for horses.

EDDY, S. [from *ed*, Sax. and *a*, Sax.] which

3 C

water which is bent and returns back. Figuratively, a whirlpool, a circular motion, a whirlwind. *Eddy* water, among mariners, implies dead water.

E'DDY, Adj. whirling; moving circularly. " " Chaff with *eddy* winds is whirled round." *Dryd.*

EDEMATOS°, S. [ωδημα, Gr.] swelling; full of humours.

EDGE, S. [*ecge*, Sax. ⁊c, Gr.] the sharp, or thin side of any cutting instrument. The extremity, border, or outside of a thing. Joined to *give*, sharpness; a proper disposition for action, applied to the mind. *To set teeth* on *edge*, is to cause a tingling pain in teeth.

To E'DGE, V. A. to sharpen an instrument. To border. To exasperate. To excite. To put in such a position as to make way. To go close upon a wind, and sail slow.

E'DGED, Part. sharp.

E'DGING, S. something added to the extremities by way of ornament. A narrow lace.

E'DGELESS, Adj. without an edge; not fit to cut with; blunt.

E'DGEWISE, Adv. passing with the edge in a particular direction.

E'DIBLE, Adj. [*edo*, Lat.] fit, or proper to be eaten; fit for food.

E'DICT, S. [*edictum*, Lat.] a law, or proclamation.

EDIFICA'TION, S. [*ædes*, Lat. and *facio*] improvement; advancement in religion, the original word signifies the building a structure, and is beautifully applied to the improvements made in knowledge or religion, which begin low like the foundation of a house, and increase upwards, till we are carried nearer to the exalted beings in heaven.

E'DIFICE, S. [*ædificium*, Lat.] a building, or house, generally applied to some pompous building.

E'DIFIER, S. one who improves or instructs another.

To E'DIFY, V. A. [*ædifico*, Lat.] to build. To improve. To instruct, or teach.

E'DILE, S. [*ædilis*, Lat.] the title of an officer among the Romans, who resembled the city marshal in London, or a surveyor; he had the charge of taking care of all public edifices, and to see that no damage should be occasioned from want of repairing private ones; like our quesitmen, he had the inspection of weights and measures; like our justice of the peace, had the power of prohibiting unlawful games, and was judge in all cases relating to the selling or exchanging of estates.

EDINBURGH, the capital city of Scotland, where, for some ages before the union, the kings of Scotland had their usual residence at Holy rood-house. It consists principally of one street, with lanes, or wynds running

from it, which rises gradually from Holy-rood-house to the Canongate-head, which is a suburb, and from thence to the castle, which is the highest part of the city. The principal street, besides this, is called the Cowgate, and is on the S. side of the other; from this several lanes run up the hill, towards the university and Herriot's hospital. From the castle to the palace is usually reckoned a Scotch mile in length, but in breadth it is no where above half a mile. The houses are built of stone, and are, in the high-street, 6 or 7 stories high, each storey being a distinct house; and near the parliament-close they are 14 stories high, or upwards, but then they are built on the side of a hill, and on the other side they are of the common height. It has a lake on the N. side, and every where else is surrounded by a strong wall. The castle is very strong, both by art and nature, and was kept by the king's forces in the last rebellion, though the city itself was taken. The harbour of this city is at Leith, a pretty large town, to which there is a fine walk from Edinburgh. It is seated in the most plentiful part of this kingdom, and water is conveyed to it by leaden pipes, from excellent springs. The other remarkable buildings are, the parliament-house, with a large court called the Parliament-close, in the middle of which is the statue of king Charles II. On the W. side of it is the council-house, and to the S. the sessions-house, where the supreme courts of judicature are held. The high-church, which was the cathedral, is now divided into four, which, with the rest, and the chapel in the castle, makes twelve in all. Herriot's hospital is a stately structure, designed for the education of 140 boys. The college is on the S. side, which has large precincts, enclosed with high walls, and divided into three courts; the public schools are large and commodious, and here are houses for the professors to live in. It was built by king James VI. and has a very good library. The common burying-place of the city is Gray-friar's church-yard, where there are abundance of fine monuments. The castle is seated at the W. end, and is inaccessible, except on the side next the city. The palace, called Holy-rood-house, was formerly an abbey, and is a handsome, convenient structure. This city is governed by a Lord Provost, four bailiffs, and a common-council. It is not so flourishing as it was before the union, because the great men are usually at London. It was the see of a bishop before episcopacy was abolished in 1688. It is 2 miles N. of Leith, 54 W. N. W. of Berwick upon Tweed, 391 N. N. W. of London, 72 N. of Carlisle, and 203 N. N. W. of York; but if, as Norwood says, it is 200 miles from London to York, than Edinburgh will be 360 from London. It sends two members to parliament, one for the city, and another

another for the fhire. Lam. 14. 35. Im. 55. 57.

EDI'TION, S. [editio, Lat.] the impreffion of a book.

EDI'TOR, S. one who prepares a manufcript for the prefs, and corrects the errors of the proof fheets.

To EDUCA'TE, V. A. [educatum, fupine of educo, Lat.] to give inftruction to a perfon during his minority, to improve his underftanding, and regulate his morals.

EDUCA'TION, S. the care taken of a young perfon to adorn his mind with learning and virtue.

To EDU'CE, V. A. [educo, Lat.] to bring out; to extract; to bring to light.

To EDUL'CORATE, V. A. [from dulcis, Lat.] to fweeten.

EDULCORA'TION, S. the fweetening a thing. In chemiftry, the act of freshening or cleanfing a thing from its falts.

To EE'K, V. A. [eacan, ecan, ican, Sax.] to make bigger by the addition of fomething elfe. To fupply any deficiency, ufually including the idea of bungling, or botching.

EE'L, S. [el, Sax. aal, Dan.] In natural hiftory, a fifh of the ferpentine kind, which is found lurking in mud.

EE'N, Adv. contracted from even, ufed in familiar difcourfe and poetry.

E'FF, S. fee EFT.

To EFFA'CE, V. A. [effacer, Fr.] to deftroy any painting. To blot out. To deftroy, or erafe all marks or traces of a thing from the mind.

EFFE'CT, S. [effectus, Lat.] a confequence. Reality, ufed with in. Advantage, avail, profit, or fervice. " Chrift is become of no effect." Gal. v. 4. Purport, intention, or meaning. " They fpake to her to that effect." 2 Chron. xxxiv. 27. In the plural, goods, furniture.

To EFFE'CT, V. A. [effectum, Lat.] to bring to pafs. To produce as a caufe. To complete.

EFFE'CTIBLE, Adj. that which may be produced, done, or completed.

EFFE'CTIVE, Adj. able to produce an effect. Active, proper for action. " The army confifted of ten thoufand effective men."

EFFE'CTIVELY, Adv. powerfully; really; entirely; completely.

EFFE'CTLESS, Adj. without effect; without producing any effect; ineffectual.

EFFE'CTOR, S. [Lat.] one who caufes, or produces any effect. " Pay worfhip to that infinite Being, who was the effecter of it." Derham.

EFFE'CTUAL, Adj. [effectuel, Fr.] producing the end or defign for which it is propofed, or intended.

EFFE'CTUALLY, Adv. fo as to produce

the end for which it is applied, or intended.

To EFFE'CTUATE, V. A. [effectuer, Fr.] to bring to pafs; to complete; to accomplifh.

EFFE'MINACY, S. [from effeminate] the acting, or affecting too much delicacy, like a woman; foftnefs, or want of thofe qualities which diftinguifh and become a man. Figuratively, wantonnefs; lafcivioufnefs.

EFFE'MINATE, Adj. [effeminatus, Lat.] void of the qualities which adorn the male fex; acting or behaving like a woman; voluptuous, or luxurious; at prefent ufed as a word of reproach, but formerly in a good fenfe, alluding to the attractive foftnefs which adorns the fair fex. " Gentle, kind, effeminate remorfe." Shak.

To EFFE'MINATE, V. A. [effemino, Lat.] to make womanifh, or deprive of the hardnefs and other qualities which diftinguifh and adorn the male fex.

EFFEMINA'TION, S. the quality or caufe of rendering a perfon womanifh, or depriving him of hardnefs, ftrength, courage, and thofe qualities which diftinguifh and adorn the male fex.

To EFFERVE'SCE, V. N. [effervefco, Lat.] to grow warm, or produce by fermentation.

EFFERVE'SCENCE, S. [effervefco, Lat.] a light ebullition of the particles of a liquor, caufed by the firft action of heat.

EFFICA'CIOUS, Adj. [efficax, Lat.] producing the effect or end intended.

EFFICA'CIOUSLY, Adv. fo as to produce the effect intended.

E'FFICACY, S. power of producing the end or effect intended, or propofed.

EFFI'CIENCE, EFFI'CIENCY, S. [efficiens, Lat.] the act of producing effects or change. Agency.

EFFI'CIENT, S. [efficiens, Lat.] a caufe; one that makes or caufes things to be what they are.

EFFI'CIENT, Adj. [efficiens, Lat.] having the power to produce; productive.

E'FFIGY, S [effigies, Lat.] the refemblance of any thing drawn, painted, or carved; an idea.

EFFLORE'SCENT, Adj. [efflorefcentia, Lat.] fhooting out in the fhape of flowers. In Medicine, appearing in pimples on the fkin.

EFFLU'VIA, EFFLU'VIUM, S. [Lat.] the fmall particles continually emitted by a body, which, though they do not fenfibly decreafe the body from whence they proceed, have a perceptible effect on the fenfes. Smell, odour, ftink.

E'FFLUX, S. [effluxus, Lat.] the act of flowing out. Effufion; fpreading; an emanation.

To EFFLU'X, V. A. [effluxum, Lat.] to flow from; to move in fucceffion. " Some old

odd centuries of years are *effaxed* since the creation." *Beyle.*

EFFLUXION, S. [*effluxum*, Lat.] that which flows out. The act of flowing out.

To EFFO'RCE, V. A. [*efforcer*, Lat.] to break through, or make a passage by violence. Not in use.

To EFFO'RM, [*efformo*, Lat.] to make, or mould in any shape. To fashion. "Efforming us after thy own image." *Taylor.*

EFFORMA'TION, S. the act of producing, or giving form to. "The production and *efformation* of the universe." *Ray.*

EFFO'RT, S. [Fr.] a struggle; a laborious or vehement exertion.

EFFRA'IABLE, Adj. [*effroiable*, Fr.] able to procure, or causing terror; dreadful. "A proportionable efficient of their *effroiable* nature." *Howry.*

EFFRO'NTERY, S. [*effronterie*, Fr.] an immodest and undaunted boldness, including the idea of impudence.

EFFU'LGENCE, S. [*effulgens*, Lat.] brightness, splendor, or a glorious degree of light.

EFFU'LGENT, Adj. [*effulgens*, Lat.] shining with a superlative degree of light.

To EFFU'SE, V. A. [*fusus*, Lat.] to pour out; to spill; to shed.

EFFU'SION, S. [*effusio*, Lat.] the act of pouring out. Shedding. The act of pronouncing fluently. Profusion. Figuratively, the thing poured out. "Purge me with the blood of my Redeemer, and I shall be clean; wash me with that precious *effusion*, and I sha'l be whiter than snow." *K. Charles.*

EFFU'SIVE, Adj. pouring out; spilling.

EFT, S. [see EFF, *efte*, Sax.] a small kind of animal resembling the lizard or crocodile, found in watery places.

EGG, S. [*eg*, Sax. *eg*, Dan.] a part formed in the females of certain animals, which, under a spherical shell, encloses the young of the same species. The shell and the skin keep the yolk and two whites together; the chicken is formed out of, and nourished by the white alone, till it be grown large. The yolk serves for its nourishment after birth, and when it is hatched remains, and is received in its belly, and being reserved as in a store-house, is by the appendicula or ductus intestinalis, conveyed into the guts, and serves the creature instead of milk, till able to peck, which is not at its first exclusion. At each end of the egg is a treadle, or quantity of included air, which makes the yolk hang up, and by that means keeps the same part of it uppermost, for the position of the egg be what it will. On the surface, Derham supposes this the cicatricula, or sperm lies, and must give us no disadvantageous idea of the wisdom of Providence in this piece of mechanism. It may be asked likewise, if it does not appear from the shape of the

egg, which is the best calculated for defending the animalcule within it from external injuries; from its position in the egg, with its head opposite to that end, which is most easily forced; from the porosity of the shell, which may render the conveyance of air to the little prisoner not difficult, or not at all improbable for the purpose of breathing? But we must desist, lest we should be too prolix for the nature of our plan. Figuratively, the spawn, sperm, or seed of any animal.

To EG'G, V. A. [*eggian*, Sax. *eggia*, Run.] to incite. To instigate. To stir up.

E'GOTISM, S. [*egotisme*, Fr. from *ego*, Lat. I] a fault committed by too frequent and ostentatious an use of the pronoun I. Too frequent mention of a person's self. "The most violent *egotism* I have met with." *Spect.* No. 562.

E'GO'IST, S. [*egoiste*, Fr. from *ego*, Lat. I.] a person who mentions himself too frequently and ostentatiously.

To E'GOTIZE, V. A. to mention one's self too frequently.

EGRE'GIOUS, Adj. [*egregius*, Lat.] somewhat above the ordinary run. Remarkable; extraordinary, used either in a good or a bad sense.

EGRE'GIOUSLY, Adv. better or worse than ordinary. Uncommonly, prodigiously, extremely.

E'GRESS, S. [*egressus*, Lat.] passage, or liberty to go out of a place. Departure.

EGRE'SSION, S. [*egressio*, Lat.] the act of coming out. Departure.

EGRE'TTE, S. [Fr.] an ornament worn by ladies on the forehead, or front part of their hair.

E'GYPT, a celebrated and considerable country of Africa, about 550 miles in length, and 125 in breadth, where broadest. It is bounded on the N. by the Mediterranean sea, on the S. by Nubia, on the E. by the Red Sea and the isthmus of Suez, and on the W. by the kingdom and desert of Barca. The broadest part is from Alexandria to Damietta, and from thence it gradually grows narrower and narrower, till it approaches Nubia, where it is enclosed between two chains of mountains, having the Nile and a plain between them, not above half a day's journey over. These mountains run on each side of the Nile very far to the N. insomuch that, on the side of the desert, they are continued to the Mediterranean sea, but, on the E. side, they do not reach as far as Cairo. These mountains, from the cataracts of the Nile to Saidi, are not above as or 15 miles distant from the banks of that river, but there they begin to be more open, leaving large and beautiful plains, which are retrained by the waters of the Nile; then they begin to come nearer each other, as far as the pyramids of Chico. Hence it appears, that this kingdom,

so famous in history for its power, and the number of its people, has not an extent proportionable to the description the ancients have given of it. Egypt is divided into the Upper, the Middle, and the Lower, which last comprehends the Delta, which reaches from Alexandria to Damietta, and as far as Cairo; the Middle runs no farther S. than Benefuuf; and the Upper, called formerly Thebaid, ascends as far as Nubia, and the kingdom of Sennar. With regard to the complexion of the Egyptians, it is tawney, and, the farther S. the more dark, infomuch, that those on the confines of Nubia are almost black. They are most of them very indolent and cowardly, and the richer sort do nothing all day but drink coffee, smoke tobacco, and sleep; besides this, they are extremely ignorant, proud, haughty, and ridiculously vain. Egypt lies between 47 and 53 degrees of longitude, and between 21 and 31 of latitude. With regard to the weather in Egypt, the summer is most incommodious on account of the excessive heats, which bring on various distempers; but then the winter, autumn, and spring, are blest with so good an air, that Egypt, during those seasons, is a delightful country. It rains very seldom in Egypt, but that want is happily supplied by the regular inundation of the Nile, as is now known to almost every one. When the waters retire, all the ground is covered with mud, and then they only harrow their corn into it, without further trouble, and in the following March they have usually a plentiful harvest. Their rice-fields are supplied with water from their canals and reservoirs, because rice never thrives unless in watery grounds. There is no place in the world better furnished with corn, flesh, fish, sugar, fruits, and all forts of garden-stuff; and in Lower Egypt they have oranges, lemons, figs, dates, almonds, cassia, and plantains, in great plenty. The fands are so fubtile here, that they insinuate themselves into the closets, chests, and cabinets, which, together with the hot winds, are probably the cause of fore eyes being so very common here. The pyramids are taken notice of by all travellers into Egypt, and the largest of them takes up 10 acres of ground, and is, as well as the rest, built upon a rock; the external part is chiefly built of large square stones, of unequal sizes, and the height of it is about 700 feet; but travellers differ in this respect. The caverns, out of which they get the embalmed dead bodies, is another curiosity much taken notice of; they are found in coffins set upright in the niches of the walls, and have continued there 4000 years, at least. Many of these have been brought into England, and were formerly of great use in medicine; but they are now generally neglected. The crocodiles were formerly taken great notice of,

but are now to be seen in many other places, insomuch that there is scarce a tailor but what can describe them. Likewise, the sea and river horses were thought to be only found in Egypt, but it is now known that they are all over the southern parts of Africa. The principal city is Cairo.

To EJA'CULATE, V. A. [ejaculatus, Lat.] to dart or shoot out; to breathe a short occasional prayer.

EJACULA'TION, S. the act of throwing or darting out. Figuratively, an occasional, sudden, extemporary prayer.

EJA'CULATORY, Adj. suddenly darted out, expressed in unconnected sentences.

To EJE'CT, V. A. [ejectum, Lat.] to throw, cast, or dart out. Figuratively, to expel. To drive away with hatred. To exclude, fling away, or reject.

EJE'CTION, S. [ejectio, Lat.] the act of expelling, turning out, or driving from a place or possession.

EJE'CMENT, S. In Law, a writ by which any inhabitant of a house, or tenant of an estate, who owes arrears of rent, and has not sufficient on the premises to make a distress, is commanded and obliged to depart.

EI'GHT, Adj. [eahta, Sax.] a number consisting of twice four, or seven and one.

EI'GHTH, Adj. [see eahteotha, Sax.] a word expressing the order in which a thing stands from the first, and is next beyond the seventh.

EI'GHTEEN, Adj. a number consisting of twice nine added together.

EI'GHTEENTH, Adj. the order of a thing which is removed the distance of seventeen from the first.

EI'GHTY, S. a number consisting of eight times ten, or four times twenty, added together.

EI'THER, Pron. [ægther, Sax.] one or other of two persons. Both, or each. " Seven times the sun has either topic viewed." Dryd.

EJULA'TION, S. [ejulatio, Lat.] an outcry of afflicting grief.

E'KE, Conjunct. [eac, Sax.] likewise, also. " That this is eke the throne of love." Prior. Obsolete, except in Poetry.

To E'KE, V. A. [eacan] to increase; protract, lengthen, or spin out.

To ELA'BORATE, V. A. [elaboratus, Lat.] to produce with trouble, difficulty and labour. " They in full joy elaborate a sigh." Young.

ELA'BORATE, Adj. [elaboratus, Lat.] finished with great elegance, labour, and diligence.

ELA'BORATELY, Adj. so as to bespeak elegance, owing to labour and diligence.

To ELA'NCE, V. N. [elancer, Fr.] to dart, or throw out,

To

To ELA'PSE, V. N. [*elapsus*, of *elabor*, Lat.] to let flip; or to suffer to pass without notice, generally applied to time.

ELASTIC, ELA'STICAL, Adj. [from Gr.] having the property of returning to its own form or shape, after having lost it by some external force. Springy.

ELASTI'CITY, S. a property in bodies, by which they return forcibly, and of their own accord, to the same form they were of before compression.

ELA'TE, Adj. [*elatus*, from *effero*, Lat.] flushed, puffed up, or haughty with success.

To ELA'TE, V. A. to puff up, praise, or prosperity. To exalt or heighten; an unusual sense. " Truth divinely breaking on his mind—*elates* his being." *Thomson.*

ELA'TION, S. haughtiness, occasioned by success.

EL'BOW, S. the joint of the arm next below the shoulder. Figuratively, any bending or angle. *To be at a person's elbow*, is to be near or close to him.

To EL'BOW, V. A. to push with the elbow. To struggle for room. To incroach upon. To form in angles.

EL'BOW ROOM, S. room to stretch out the elbows. Figuratively, freedom from restraint, or confinement. " Now my soul hath *elbow room*." *Shak.*

EL'DER, Adj. [*eld, ellor*, Sax.] one who exceeds or surpasses another in years.

EL'DERS, S. [plural, *ealder*, Sax.] those who are born before others. Ancestors. Among the Jews, the rulers of the people, similar to the word *senator* among the Romans, which implied persons chosen for their greater age and experience.

EL'DER, S. [*ellorn*, Sax. *bulder*, Teut.] It is ranged by Linnæus in the 3d sect. of his 5th class. The species are five. The bark, flowers, leaves and berries are made use of in physic. The inner bark is by some esteemed good for dropsies; the leaves are outwardly used for the piles and inflammations, and form an ointment. The flowers are inwardly used to expel wind, and when made into an ointment, used outwardly as a cooler; the berries are esteemed cordial, and useful in hysteric disorders, are frequently put into gargarisms for sore mouths and throats, and used by housewives in making a wine which goes by this name.

EL'DERLY, Adj. [*old*]; the marks of old age. Advanced in years.

EL'DERSHIP, S. claim founded on seniority, or being born before another.

EL'DEST, Adj. exceeding or surpassing others in years; born before others.

ELECAM'PANE, S. in Botany, it hath a radiated compound flower, with an imbricated empalement, composed of loose spreading leaves. It is placed by Linnæus in the 3d sect. of his 19th class. The roots are used in medicine, and accounted carminative, sudorific and alexipharmic, and are of great service in shortness of breath, coughs, asthmas, and infectious distempers.

To ELE'CT, V. A. [*electum*, supine of *eligo*, Lat.] to choose a person. To take in preference of others. In Divinity, applied by some divines, to signify choice made of some persons by the Deity as objects of his peculiar favour and mercy.

ELE'CT, Adj. [*electus*, Lat.] chosen; taken by preference from other things. Chosen to supply an office, but not yet actually in possession. " The lord-mayor *elect*." In Divinity, persons of superior virtues and piety to others, and on that account selected or chosen by the Deity, as objects of his favour and mercy.

ELE'CTION, S. [*electio*, Lat.] the act of choosing. Choice. Figuratively, the power of choosing. The privilege of electing a person to discharge an employ. The ceremony or method of a public choosing of a person to discharge an employ.

ELE'CTIVE, Adj. conferred by election, free choice, or votes.

ELE'CTOR, S. a person who has a vote in the choice of an office. A prince who has a voice in the choice of the emperor of Germany. " The king of England is *elector* of Hanover."

ELE'CTORAL, Adj. having the title, dignity and privilege of an elector, belonging to an elector.

ELE'CTORATE, S. the territory, dominion or government of an elector.

ELE'CTRE, S. [*electrum*, Lat.] amber; which, when excited by friction, having the quality of attracting bodies, gives name to that species of attraction called *electricity*; and the bodies thus attracting are for the same reason named *electrical*.

ELE'CTRIC, ELE'CTRICAL, Adj. [see ELE'CTRE] able to attract by friction. Produced by an *electric* body.

ELECTRI'CITY, S. a property in some bodies, whereby they will attract others, when excited by attrition or friction. The great improvements made in this branch of natural philosophy within these late years, has opened to the mind a large field of knowledge before concealed, has introduced a new foundation for the systematical philosopher to build on, and enabled the student to make some discoveries, which are of no small service to mankind; by finding the analogy between electricity and lightning, methods have been invented to secure us from the effects of that dreadful phenomenon; the increase of vegetation has been found to be greatly augmented by several experiments, whereby plants have been electrified, but its services in medicine, in such cases as have been too obstinate for our present class of remedies to remove, are highly worthy of notice. The ingenious inventor of the patent

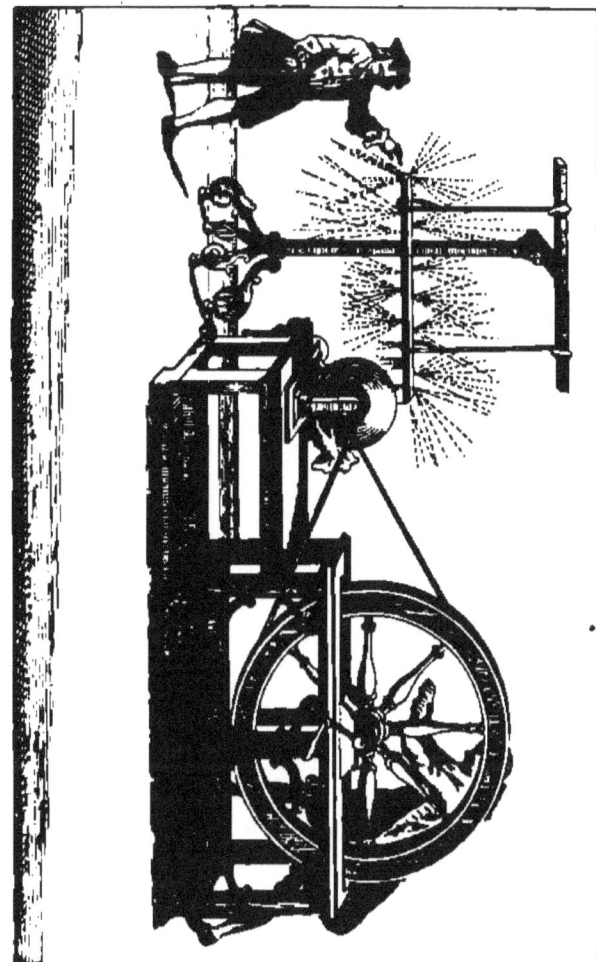

Positive Electricity.

teni globes has diftinguifhed himſelf in this branch above all others that I know of. The deaf have recovered their hearing by his means; the blind received their fight; thoſe that have been deprived of ſpeech have been reſtored to the uſe of their tongues by his affiſtance; the paralytic has likewiſe by means of him been able to walk, and make uſe of his limbs. But as experiments of this kind, if not properly conducted have no effect, I ſhall preſent the public with the following directions for that purpoſe: 1ſt. After having fully charged the phial, if the patient's malady conſiſts in that only of a ſingle joint, the end of the chain from the phial is to be put on one end of the joint, and the end of the wire through the top of the phial, to be applied to the other end, by which means the circle, which the electrical power will always make, will not be able to affect any other part of the body, the patient will be freed from the tortures which an ignorant practitioner would put him to, and the ſhock given to the part affected will have by much a greater efficacy. To be more particular; adly. If a perſon, by the ſtoppage of any blood-veſſel, has loſt the uſe of one leg from his knee downward, let the patient ſet his lame foot on the chain, while the operator touches the affected knee with the top of the wire; thus will the afflicted part only be within the electrical atmoſphere, and if the electric matter, either by the ſhock it gives, or in its paſſage, ſhall remove the obſtruction, open the paſſages, or promote the circulation of the blood, the cure will be effected. Experience has confirmed that ten or a dozen ſhocks at a time once a day, for ſome ſmall continuance, are ſufficient for this purpoſe. 3dly. If a perſon, by a paralytic diſorder, be ſuddenly deprived of the uſe of one ſide of his body, let him be held upright, ſo as to bear the weight of his body upon the chain lying on the floor with his lame foot, then let the operator touch his ſhoulder in the ſame manner as the knee in the former inſtance, and repeat the ſhock ſeveral times; and if experience will be a proper foundation for confidence, it is not doubted but the patient will receive benefit from the operation.

To ELE'CTRIFY, V. A. to communicate the electric virtue.

To ELECTRI'SE, V. A. to communicate the electrical power.

ELE'CTUARY, S. [electarium, corrupted to electuarium] a form of medicine made of conſerves, powders, ſyrups, or honey, in the conſiſtence of the latter.

ELEEMOSY'NARY, Adj. [eleemoſynarius] living on alms, depending on charity; obliged to for a favour; dependant. "That the cauſe ſhould be an eleemoſynary for its ſubſiſtence to its effects." Glanv.

ELE'GANCE, ELE'GANCY, S. [elegantia, Lat.] a ſymmetry of parts, and entire,

with is rather the Idea of neatneſs than beauty.

ELE'GANT, Adj. [elegans, Lat.] pleaſing, grand, neat, nice.

ELE'GANTLY, Adv. in ſuch a manner as to pleaſe by neatneſs, exactneſs, and magnificence.

ELE'GIAC, Adj. [elegiacus, Lat.] uſed in elegies. Mournful, ſorrowful, diſmal.

ELE'GY, S. [elegus, Lat.] a poem on ſome mournful ſubject. A poem on any ſubject in a ſimple, plaintive ſtile. A funeral ſong.

ELEMENT, in Phyſiology, a term uſed by philoſophers to denote the original component parts of bodies, or thoſe into which they are ultimately reſolvable.

The elements of Ariſtotle were four, earth, water, air, and fire.

The Carteſians admit only three elements; the firſt a materia ſubtilis, or fine duſt; the ſecond, a coarſer, but round kind; and the third, a ſtill more irregular and hooked kind of particles.

Concerning the true elements of nature, the incomparable Sir Iſaac Newton thus explains himſelf in his optics: "It ſeems probable to me that God in the beginning formed matter in ſolid maſſy, hard, impenetrable moveable, particles, of ſuch figns and figures, and with ſuch other properties, and in ſuch proportion to ſpace, as moſt conduced to the end for which he formed them; and that theſe particles, being ſolid, are incomparably harder than any porous bodies compounded of them; even ſo very hard, as never to wear or break in pieces, no ordinary power being able to divide what God himſelf made one in the firſt creation. While the particles continue entire they may compoſe bodies of one and the ſame nature and texture in all ages; but ſhould they wear away, or break in pieces, the nature of things depending on them, would be changed. Water and earth compoſed of old worn particles, and fragments of particles, would not be of the ſame nature and texture, now, with water and earth compoſed of entire particles in the beginning; and therefore, that nature may be laſting, the changes of corporeal things are to be placed only in the various ſeparations and new aſſociations and motions of theſe permanent particles; compounded bodies being apt to break, not in the midſt of ſolid particles, but where thoſe particles are laid together, and only touch in a few points."

The chemical elements or principles to which all bodies may be ultimately reduced, are theſe five: 1. Water, or phlegm, which in the chemical analyſis of them, riſes firſt in form of vapour. 2. Air, which eſcapes unſeen in great quantities from all bodies, ſo as to conſtitute half the ſubſtance of ſome of them. 3. Oil, which riſes after, and appears ſwimming on the ſurface of the water.

4. Salt

4. Salt, which is either volatile, or rises in the still, as that of animal substances; or fixed as that of vegetables, which is obtained by reducing them to ashes, making a lixivium or ley of these, and afterwards evaporating the moisture; by which means the common salt shoots into crystals. 5. Earth, or what is called *caput mortuum*, being what remains of the ashes after the salt is extracted. This is the last element of all bodies, which can be no farther altered by any art whatsoever. See WATER, AIR, &c.

To E'LEMENT, V. A. to compound of elements. "In those said to be *elemented* bodies. To constitute, or make as a first principle. "The thing which *elemented* it." *Donne.*

ELEMENTAL, Adj. composed of, or produced by the elements. Produced by some first principle.

ELEMENTARY, Adj. uncompounded; simple; without mixture.

E'LEPHANT, S. (*elephas*, Lat.) In Natural history, the largest of all the quadrupede animals. It is furnished with a trunk, a long cartilaginous tube, hanging between its teeth, with which it feeds itself, or assaults its enemy. It has two large tusks, one standing out on each side of its trunk, some of which are as large as a man's thigh, and a fathom in length. It feeds purely on vegetables, and is an enemy to flesh. Its nature is so gentle, that any animal may approach it without fear, and so dangerous when provoked, that none can escape its fury.

ELEPHA'NTINE, Adj. (*elephantinus*, Lat.) pertaining, belonging, or partaking of the qualities of an elephant.

To E'LEVATE, V. A. (*elevatus*, of *elevo*, Lat.) to raise aloft, or on high. To exalt or dignify. To raise the mind with great and sublime ideas. To elate or make proud.

E'LEVATE, Part. raised or lifted on high.

ELEVATION, S. (*elevatio*, Lat.) the act of raising. Exaltation, dignity or preferment. The raising the thoughts to contemplation. In Astronomy and Geography, the height of any object above the horizon. In Architecture, a draught of the principal side of a building, called its upright. In Gunnery, the angle which the chase of a piece of ordnance makes with the plane of the horizon.

ELEVA'TOR, S. (Lat.) a raiser or lifter up. In Anatomy, applied to those muscles, which raise or lift up the parts they belong to.

E'LEVE, S. (Fr. from *allevo*, Ital.) a scholar brought up under any master. A pupil.

ELE'VEN, Adj. one more than ten.

ELE'VENTH, Adj. an ordinal expressing the next beyond the tenth.

E'LF, S. (plural *elves*, from *alf*) a wandering spirit, a fairy; an evil spirit or devil.

To E'LF, V. A. to entangle hair, so as it is impossible to untangle it. Supposed by the vulgar to be the work of fairies in the night, whence all hair matted and entangled, is called *elf-locks*. "Elf all my hair in knots." *Shak.*

To ELI'CIT, V. A. (*elicitum*) to find out, or discover by dint of labour and art.

To ELI'DE, V. A. (*elido*, Lat.) to cut or divide into pieces, or separate parts. "When the force and strength of the argument is elided." *Hooker.*

ELIGIBI'LITY, S. worthiness or property of being chosen.

E'LLIGIBLE, Adj. (*eligibilis*, Lat.) fit or worthy of choice; preferable; possessing all those excellencies, which are sufficient to set it above others, and recommend it, on account of that preference, as an object of choice.

ELI'SION, S. (*elisio*, Lat.) In Grammar, the cutting of a vowel or syllable in a word, as in "th' eagle," where e is cut off, because coming before a vowel, this is called a synalæpha, frequently practised in English poetry, and always observed in Latin verse. A division, cutting, dividing, attenuating, or a separation of parts. "An elision of the air, whereby they mean a cutting, or dividing, or else an attenuating of the air." *Bacon.*

ELIXA'TION, S. (....... Lat.) boiling or stewing. Digestion.

ELI'XIR, S. (*elixir*, Arab.) a medicine made by strong infusion. The extract, or quintessence of any thing. Any cordial or invigorating fluid or substance. Among the Alchymists used for the philosophers stone, or liquor by which they pretend to transmute other metals into gold.

E'LK, S. (*elk*, Sax. *alce*, Lat.) a large and stately animal of the stag kind, but has a shorter and slenderer neck.

E'LL, S. (*eln*, Sax. *elne*, or *elle*, Belg.) a long measure containing 40 inches, 16 nails or five quarters of a yard.

ELLI'PSIS, ELLE'PSIS, S. (ελλειψις, Gr.) In Grammar, or Rhetoric, a figure by which something left out in a sentence, is to be supplied by the reader or hearer. In Geometry, a regular continued curve line, including a space which is longer than broad; frequently called *oval.*

ELLI'PTIC, or ELLI'PTICAL, Adj. having the form of an ellipsis; oval.

E'LM, S. (Sax. *elm-tree*, Dan. *alm*, Belg.) Linnæus ranges it in the 2d sect. of his 5th class. The wood of this tree is of singular use where it may be either wet or dry to an extreme; and in foreign countries is used as a support for vines; to which

our poets frequently allude, " Thou art an *elm* my husband ; I a vine." *Shak.*

ELOCU'TION, S. [*elocutio*, Lat.] the power of expressing one's ideas with fluency and grace. Eloquence. The power of expression, or diction. Its chief beauty consists in the use of figures or figurative expression in the periods, sentences, and the style of a discourse.

ELO'GY, S. [*eloge*, Fr.] praise, commendation, or panegyric.

To ELON'GATE, V. A. [*longus*, Lat.] to stretch, to lengthen. To go further off from a thing or place.

ELONGA'TION, S. the act of stretching or lengthening. The state of a thing stretched. In Astronomy, the digression of a planet from the sun, with respect to an eye placed on our earth.

To ELO'PE, V. N. [*hlopan*, Belg.] to run away, to break loose, or escape. In Law, to quit a husband.

ELOPEMENT, S. withdrawing from just restraint, or power. In Law, the voluntary departure of a wife from a husband.

ELOQUENCE, S. [*eloquentia*, Lat.] the art of speaking elegantly and so as to move the affections. The power of speaking fluently : a flowery and elegant style or diction, adopted to move the passions.

ELOQUENT, Adj. [*eloquens*, Lat.] having the power of speaking with elegance, fluency, and to affect the passions.

ELSE, Pron. [*elles*, Sax.] other, one besides.

ELSE, Adv. otherwise ; besides.

ELSEWHERE, Adv. in some other place or situation.

To ELUCIDATE, V. A. [*elucidatus*, Lat.] to cast light upon a subject. To explain, to make clear.

ELUCIDA'TION, S. the act of rendering a difficult subject plain ; an explanation, or clearing up.

ELUCIDA'TOR, S. one who explains. A commentator.

To ELU'DE, V. A. [*eludo*, Lat.] to escape by stratagem or artifice. To mock or disappoint the expectation by an unexpected escape.

ELUDIBLE, Adj. possible to escape by artifice. Possible to be defeated or eluded.

ELVES, S. the plural of ELF.

ELVISH, Adj. belonging to the elves or fairies.

ELU'SION, S. [*elusio*, Lat.] a concealed artifice. A fraud.

ELU'SIVE, Adj. using artifices or tricks to escape, or avoid.

ELU'SORY, Adv. fraudulent. Tending to deceive in order to escape notice, examination, punishment, or mischief.

To ELUTE, V. A. [*elutus*, supine of *eluo*, Lat.] to wash out, or to wash off. " *Eluted* by the blood." *Arbuth.*

ELY, a town or city of Cambridgeshire, with a bishop's fee, and a market on saturdays. The fairs are on Ascension day, for horses ; on Thursday in the week that St. Luke's day falls in, that is, October 18, for horses, cheese, and hops. It is seated on an island of the same name, in a fenny country, on the banks of the river Ouse, which renders it very unhealthy. The Bishop here has the same power as in a county-palatine, for he appoints a judge, holds the assizes, goal-delivery, and quarter-sessions of the peace, for the liberty ; and yet it is but an indifferent place, though the cathedral is a stately structure, which has a lanthorn of curious architecture ; and has also one church. The city consists of only about 600 good houses, and has but one good street, well paved, the rest being not paved, and very dirty. The assizes are held here every twelve months. The river is navigable from Lynn, and the town carries on a pretty good trade ; it is 17 miles N. of Cambridge, 30 S. of King's-Lynn, and 69 N. by E. of London. Lon. 17. 50. lat. 52. 24.

ELY'SIAN, Adj. [*elysius*, Lat.] pertaining to elysium. Pleasant, delicious, soothing, delightful.

ELY'SIUM, S. in the ancient mythology, a place furnished with pleasant fields, &c. and supposed to be the receptacle for the souls of the departed.

To EMA'CIATE, V. A. [*emaclatus*, from *macies*, Lat.] to make a thing waste, or grow lean. Neuterly, to grow lean, or waste away.

EMACIA'TION, S. [*emaciatus*, Lat.] the act of making lean. The state of a person wasted away, or in a consumption.

EMANENT, Adj. [*emanens*, Lat.] issuing, proceeding, or flowing from something else.

EMANA'TION, S. [*emanatio*, Lat.] the act of proceeding or flowing from something else. That which flows from substance, like effluvia.

EMA'NATIVE, Adj. [*emanatus*, Lat.] issuing, proceeding, or flowing from.

To EMA'NCIPATE, V. A. [*emancipatum*, Lat.] To set free from slavery. To restore to liberty.

EMANCIPA'TION, S. the act of setting free, or deliverance from slavery.

To EMA'SCULATE, V. A. [*emasculatum*, Lat.] to deprive of that property which distinguishes the male from the female. To castrate, or geld. To render soft, effeminate, or womanish. To deprive by unmanly softness.

EMASCULA'TION, S. the act of castrating. Effeminacy.

To EMBA'LM, V. A. [*embaumer*, Fr.] to impregnate dead bodies with gums and spices to prevent their putrefying.

EMBA'LNER, S. one who preserves by embalming the body of the dead.

EMBA'LMING, S. the practice of preparing the bodies of the dead with drugs, to prevent putrefaction.

EMBARKA'TION, S. the act of going on board ship.

EMBA'RGO, S. [embargo, Span.] a prohibition laid upon vessels by a sovereign, whereby they are prevented from going out or entering into a port for a certain time.

To EMBA'RK, V. A. [embarquer, Fr.] to put on board a ship. To engage in an affair. To go on shipboard.

To EMBA'RRASS, V. A. [embarrasser, Fr.] to perplex, or confound.

EMBA'RRASSMENT, S. perplexity, trouble, or confusion, arising from some difficult affair.

EMBA'SSADOR, EMBASSA'DOUR, See AMBASSADOUR.

EM'DASSAGE, EM'BASSY, S. a mission of a person from one prince to another, in order to treat of affairs relating to their respective states. Figuratively, any solemn message. An errand or message.

To EM'BATTLE, V. A. to range in battle array.

To EMBA'Y, V. A. to inclose in a bay or por.

To EMBE'LLISH, V. A. [embellir, Fr.] to adorn ; to beautify ; to grace or set off with ornaments

EMBEE'LLISHMENT, S. ornament, any thing which gives a grace to the person or mind.

EM'BERS, S. wood or coals half burnt, that are not extinguished. Ashes which retain fire.

EM'DER-WEEK, S. [Skinner derives it from embers, because it was a season for fasting, when it was usual to scatter ashes on the head] the time set apart by the church for public ordinations, at the four seasons of the year ; wherein some ember day falls, viz. the Wednesday, Friday, and Saturday, after the first Sunday in Lent ; the feast of Pentecost ; September the 14th, and December 13.

To EMBE'ZZLE, V. A. to convert to one's own use what is intrusted by another. Figuratively, to waste ; to consume ; to squander.

EMBE'ZZLEMENT, S. the act of making use of what is intrusted by another. Figuratively, the thing thus made use of.

To EMBLAZE, V. A. [blasonner, Fr.] to to adorn with ornaments. In Heraldry, to blazon, or paint a coat.

To EMBLA'ZON, V. A. [blasonner, Fr.] to adorn with bearings in Heraldry. To deck in gaudy colours ; to display ostentatiously.

EM'BLEM, S. [emblema, Gr.] a thing inserted in another ; an hieroglyphical or emblematical device or picture.

To EM'BLEM, V. A. to represent in hieroglyphicks, or by some picture. " The primitive light of elements does fitly emblem that of opinions." Glanv.

EMBLEMA'TIC, EMBLEMA'TICAL, Adj. conveying some truth or moral under an hieroglypical or pictural description.

EMBLEMA'TICALLY, Adv. in a figurative or allegorical manner.

EMBLEMA'TISTS, S. writers, inventors, or makers of emblems.

EM'BOLUS, S. the moveable part of a pump, or syringe, named likewise the piston, and by some the sucker.

To EMBO'SS, V. A. to form into knobs or protuberances. Figuratively, to adorn with embroidery, or other raised work. In Carving, to form in relievo, or so as the figures shall stand out from the ground which supports them.

EMBO'SSMENT, S. any thing jutting, projecting, or standing out. In Carving, figures which stand out and swell to the sight.

To EMBO'TTLE, V. A. to inclose in a bottle. " Some firmest fruit embottled." Philips.

To EMBO'WEL, V. A. to take out the bowels or entrails of a creature.

To EMBRA'CE, V. A. [embrasser, Fr. from em in and bras the arms) to clasp fondly in the arms. Figuratively, to seise on eagerly, and accept willingly. " You embrace th' occasion." Shak. To cachete, inclose, or contain. To admit, to receive or assent to as truth, applied to the mind. " What is there be may not embrate for truth." Locke. To receive or submit to. " Embrace the face of that dark hour." Shak.

EMBRA'CE, S. a fond clasp, squeeze, or hug.

EMBRA'CEMENT, S. the act of encircling a person with one's arms. Figuratively, the state of a thing encompassed by another. Conjugal caresses and endearments.

EMBRA'CER, S. one who clasps another fondly in his arms.

EMBRA'SURE, S. [Fr.] In Fortification, the hole through which cannon are pointed either in casemates, batteries, or in the parapets of walls

To EM'BROCATE, V. A. [embryo, Gr.] to rub any diseased part with medical liquors.

EMBROCA'TION, S. the act of rubbing any diseased part with medical liquor. The lotion with which it is rubbed.

To EMBROI'DER, S. [broder, Fr.] to border with ornaments. To adorn silk, velvet, &c. with ornaments, wrought with a needle.

EMBROI'DERER, S. one who works a thing with ornaments of raised needlework.

EMBROI'DERY, S. the enriching with figures

figures wrought with the needle. Figures raised on a ground with a needle.

To EMBROIL, V. A. [*brouiller*, Fr.] to fet perfons at variance; to excite quarrels. To involve in confusion and trouble.

EM'BRYO, EM'BRYON, S. [*embryon*, Gr.] the firſt rudiments of an animal. In Botany, the grain of a plant. Figuratively, the ſtate of any thing not finiſhed or come to maturity.

EMEN'DABLE, Adj. [from *emendo*, Lat.] that which may be made better.

EMENDA'TION, S. [*emendatus*, Lat.] the act of making a thing better by alteration, change or correction.

EMENDA'TOR, S. [Lat.] one who improves, or renders a thing better. A corrector.

EM'ERALD, S. [*ſmaragdus*, Lat.] In natural Hiſtory, the moſt beautiful of all the claſs of coloured gems, when perfect. It is found ſometimes in the roundiſh or pebble form, ſometimes in the columnar or cryſtaline one; the pebble emeralds, however, are the moſt valued; there are multitudes found of the ſize of a large pin's head, for one of any tolerable bigneſs; though now and then there occurs ſtones of the ſize of a horſe-bean, and even up to that of a walnut, tho' this laſt very rare. The pebble emeralds are found looſe in the earth of mountains, and in the beds of rivers; the cryſtalliform ones are uſually met with adhering to a white, opaque, cryſtalline matter, though ſometimes to pieces of jaſper or of the praſius, a coarſer and ſofter gem of the ſame colour, only with ſome tinge of a yellowiſh caſt, and called the root of the emerald. The pebble emeralds are, in their natural ſtate, bright and tranſparent, though leſs gloſſy than the columnar ones; both are always of a perfect and pure green. It has this green in all the different ſhades, from very dark to extremely pale, and is probable ſometimes colourleſs, though the Engliſh jewellers call it white ſapphire.

The ſmaragus of the ancients, properly ſo called, was evidently the ſame with our emerald; though they comprehended alſo under this name every gem, or even ſtone of any conſiderable beauty, and of a green colour.

To EMER'GE, V. N. [*emergo*, Lat.] to riſe out of any thing, with which it is covered. To iſſue, or proceed. To riſe from obſcurity, diſtreſs, or ignorance.

EMER'GENCE, EMER'GENCY, S. the act of riſing from any thing which covers or depreſſes. The riſing from a ſtate of obſcurity. Any preſſing neceſſity, a ſudden occaſion.

EMER'GENT, Part. [*emergens*, Lat.] riſing from that which covers, conceals, or depreſſes. Proceeding or iſſuing from, uſed with from. Sudden, or preſſing, joined to

occaſion. In Chronology, the *emergent* year, is that from which time is reckoned.

EMER'SION, S. [*emerſus*, Lat.] in Phyſics, the riſing of any ſolid above the ſurface of a fluid into which it is violently thruſt.

EM'ERY, S. [*emeril*, Fr. *ſmyris*, Lat.] in Natural Hiſtory, an iron ore, of a duſky, browniſh red on the ſurface, but when broken, of a fine, bright iron-grey, with ſome tinge of redneſs, and ſpangled all over with ſhining ſpecks; found in Guernſey, Tuſcany, and Germany, prepared by being ground in mills, uſed in cleaning and poliſhing ſteel, grinding an edge to tools, and by lapidaries to cut their ſtones with.

EMET'IC, S. [*emu*, Gr.] a medicine which excites vomiting.

EMET'IC, EMET'ICAL, Adj. having the quality of provoking vomits.

EMET'ICALLY, Adv. ſo as to provoke vomiting.

To EM'IGRATE, V. N. [*emigratus*, Lat.] to remove from one place to another.

EMIGRA'TION, S. change of dwelling from one place to another. Removal from one place to another.

EM'INENCE, EM'INENCY, S. [*eminentia*, Lat.] loftineſs; the ſummit, or higheſt part of a thing. A part riſing higher than the reſt. Figuratively, exaltation; preferment; fame; A ſupreme, or ſuperior degree. A title of dignity peculiar to cardinals.

EM'INENT, Part. [*eminens*, Lat.] high, lofty, applied to ſituation. Figuratively, exalted, preferred, or conſpicuous on account of rank, or merit.

EM'INENTLY, Adv. conſpicuouſly; deſerving notice. In a high degree.

EM'ISSARY, S. [*miſſarius*, low Lat.] a perſon ſent out on private meſſages; a ſpy. In Anatomy, that which emits, or ſends out, the ſame as *excretory*.

EMIS'SION, S. [*emiſſio*, Lat.] the act of ſending out; vent. The act of ejecting, throwing, or drawing a fluid from within outwards. The expulſion of the ſeed.

To EMIT', V. A. [*emitto*, Lat] to drive outwards; to dart; to ſend forth.

EM'MET, S. [*emette*, Sax.] ſee ANT.

EMOL'LIENT, Part. [*emolliens*, Lat.] ſoftening, or rendering ſoft and pliable.

EMOL'LIENTS, S. in Medicine, ſuch remedies as ſheath the acrimony of humour, and ſoften and ſupple the ſolids.

EMOLLI'TION, S. [*emollitio*, Lat.] the act of ſoftening, or ſuppling. The ſtate of a thing rendered. "Bathing and anointing give a relaxation or *emollition*." Bacon.

EMOL'UMENT, S. [*emolumentum*, Lat.] profit, gain, or advantage.

EMO'TION, S. [Fr.] a violent ſtruggle. A ſtrong ſenſation, or paſſion, excited either by a pleaſing, or a diſagreeable object.

To EMPA'LE, V. A. [*empaler*, Fr.] to fortify,

fortify, inclose, or defend. To put to death by driving a pale or stick through the body of a person.

EMPA'LEMENT, S. In Botany, the cup or outmost part of a flower, which incompasses the petals.

EMPA'NNEL, S. [from *panne*, Fr. a skin or parchment] the entering the names of a jury in a parchment by a sheriff.

To EMPA'NNEL, V. A. to summon a person to serve on a jury.

EMPA'RLANCE, S. [from *parler*, Fr.] in Law, a motion for a day of respite, to consider of the refute of a cause. The conference of a jury in a cause.

To EMPA'SSION, V. A. to move or excite the passions vehemently. " The tempter all empassioned, thus began." *Par. Loft.*

EMPE'RESS, S. See EMPRESS, for which it was formerly written.

EMPEROR, S. *empereur*, Fr. *imperator*, Lat.] an absolute monarch, or supreme governor or commander of an empire.

EMPE'RY, S. [*imperium*, Lat. *empire*, Fr.] the command of an emperor. Empire.

EMPHASIS, S. [Gr.] in Rhetorick, a force, stress, or energy in expression, action, or gesture. In Grammar, a stress of the voice placed on any particular word or syllable.

EMPHA'TICK, EMPHA'TICAL, Adj. forcible, strong, striking, energetic.

EMPHA'TICALLY, Adv. strongly, forcibly; full of energy. Spoken with a great stress of voice.

EMPIRE, S. [from *imperium*, Lat.] the territory under the command of an emperor. Imperial power, sovereign authority or command.

EMPIRICK, S. [*empeiria*, Gr.] one whose skill in Medicine depends purely on practice and experiment; without understanding the nature, cause, and effects of diseases. A quack.

EMPIRICK, EMPIRICAL, Adj. dealing, or versed in experiments. " Empiric alchymist." *Par. Loft.* Belonging or relating to a quack.

EMPIRICALLY, Adv. after the manner of a quack, or one who is not regularly bred to physick, but owes all his knowledge to experience, without being able to account for the operation of medicines on the human fabrick, or the nature and effect of diseases.

EMPIRICISM, S dependence on experience, without knowledge. Quackery.

EMPLA'STER, S. [*emplastrum*, Lat.] in Surgery, a medicine of a stiff, gluinous consistence, spread on paper, linen, or leather, and applied externally.

To EMPLA'STER, V. A. to cover with a plaster. " The sores emplastered with tar." *Dryd.*

EMPLA'STICK, Adj. vicious, glutinous; fit for a plaster.

To EMPLE'AD, V. A. In Law, to indict, accuse, or prefer a charge against, used with *of* before the crime.

To EMPLO'Y, V. A. [*employer*, Fr.] to set a person about a thing. To intrust with the management of an affair. To fill up time with study or business.

EMPLO'Y, S. the object which engages the mind. A person's trade, business. A public office.

EMPLO'YABLE, Adj. capable of being used or employed; fit to be applied or used.

EMPLO'YER, S. one who employs or sets a person about any undertaking.

EMPLOYMENT, S. business; the object of industry. A person's trade, office, or post.

To EMPO'ISON, V. A. [from *empoisonner*, Fr.] to destroy by poison, or venom. To taint with poison. Figuratively, to deprave the principles of a person by bad advice.

EMPO'ISONER, S. one who destroys another by poison, an ill-adviser.

EMPO'ISONMENT, S. the practice of destroying by poison.

EMPO'RIAM, S. [*emporion*, Gr.] a place of merchandise; a great city or sea-port town which carries on a foreign trade.

To EMPO'VERISH, V. A. [*pauvre*, Fr. poor] to make poor, unfertile or barren.

EMPO'VERISHER, S. the cause of poverty; the lessening riches, or fertility.

To EMPO'WER, V. A. to give a person authority to transact business, or carry on any undertaking. To give natural power or force. To enable or give strength sufficient for the performance of an undertaking or design.

EMPRESS, S. [contracted from *emperess*] the wife of an emperor. A female who governs an empire.

EMPRI'SE, S. [Fr.] an undertaking attended with hazard and danger. " Ambushed we lie, and wait the bold *emprise*." *Par. Loft.*

EMPTIER, S. one who makes any place or thing void, one who empties.

EMPTINESS, S. want of body, applied to space. Without having any thing in it. The state of a thing which has nothing in it. Figuratively, want of judgment or understanding.

EMPTION, S. [*emptio*, Lat.] the act of buying or purchasing; a purchase.

EMPTY, Adv. [*æmtig*] having nothing in it. Not possessing, furnished with. Devoid. " In civility thou seem'st so *empty*." *Shak.* Unsatisfactory. Void of judgment or understanding. Void of substance, solidity, or real existence. " Empty dreams." *Dryd.*

To EMPTY, V. A. to exhaust, drink up, or pour out what is contained in a vessel.

To EMPU'RPLE, V. A. to render of a

purple colour. "_Empurpl'd_ with celestial roses." _Par. Lost._

To EMPU'ZZLE, V. A. to perplex and confound

EMPY'REAL, Adj. [_εμπυρος_, Gr.] formed of ether, or pure and celestial fire; pertaining to the highest region of heaven.

EMPYRE'AN, EMPYRE'UM, S. [from εν, Gr. εν, Gr.] the highest heaven, wherein the pure element of fire or ether is supposed to exist.

To E'MULATE, V. A. [_æmulor_, Lat.] to rival. To imitate with an endeavour to excell or surpass. Figuratively, to copy, to resemble.

EMULA'TION, S. [_æmulatio_, Lat.] a noble jealousy whereby persons endeavour to surpass each other in virtue and excellence. An endeavour to surpass another in interest or riches, joined with contest, or envy.

EM'ULATIVE, Adj. inclined to contest superiority with another.

EMULA'TOR, S. [Lat.] one who endeavours to equal or surpass another, a rival.

EMU'LGENT, Part. [_emulgens_, Lat.] milking out. Used substantially, in Anatomy, applied to those arteries which bring the blood to the kidnies.

EM'ULOUS, Adj. [_æmulus_, Lat.] rivalling; contending for superiority in fame, riches, or virtue. Factious, contentious. "Made _emulous_ millions amongst the gods themselves."

EM'ULOUSLY, Adv. in the manner of a rival, or competitor. With a desire of surpassing or excelling another.

EMU'LSION, S. [_emulsio_, Lat.] a soft liquid medicine nearly of the colour and consistence of milk.

To ENA'BLE, V. A. to make able, or capable of the performance of a thing.

To ENA'CT, V. A. to do, act, or perform. "_Enacted_ wonders with his sword." _Shak._ To make a law; to decree; to establish by law. "It is _enacted_."

ENA'CTOR, S. one who forms decrees; one who establishes laws. One who acts or does any thing.
"The violence of either grief or joy,
Their own _enactors_ with themselves destroy."
The last sense is obsolete.   [_Shak._

ENA'LLAGE, S. [from παλλαγη, Gr. to change] in Rhetoric, a figure, wherein the order of words in a sentence is inverted.

ENA'MEL, S. a kind of mezalline colour; consisting of the finest crystal glass, made of the best Kali, from Alicant, and sand vitrified together; to which are added tin and lead in equal quantities, calcined by a reverberatory fire; besides other metallic, or mineral substances, intended to give them the colour required. Any thing painted with enamel.

To ENA'MEL, V. A. to paint with enamel,

or enamel. To lay colours upon a body so, as to adorn and vary it. "Go diffest trees appeared with gay _enamell'd_ colours mixt." _Par. Lost._ This use of the word is very elegant, and conveys such an idea of the beautiful polish, as well as the vivid colour of the fruit, that we are at a loss which to admire most, the elegance, or the propriety of the expression. Neuterly, to practice the use of enamel; to make use of enamel.

ENA'MELLER, S. one who paints or colours in enamel.

ENA'MELLING, S. the act of applying enamel of various colours on metals, &c. either after the method of painting, or by the lamp.

To ENA'MOUR, V. A. [from _en_, Fr. and _amour_, Fr.] to raise the affections or love of a person. To make a person fond; used with _of_, before the person or thing beloved.

To ENCA'GE, V. A. to shut up, or imprison, or confine in a cage.

To ENCA'MP, V. N. to pitch tents for a time, applied to an army. Actively; to form a regular camp.

ENCA'MPMENT, S. the act of encamping.

To ENCHA'FE, V. A. [_echauffer_, Fr.] to make warm with passion or rage. To provoke, or make angry; beautifully applied to inanimate things. "Then _enchafed_ blood." _Shak._

To ENCHA'IN, V. A. [_enchainer_, Fr.] to fasten with a chain. To confine. "While here I was _enchain'd_—no glimpse of godlike liberty remain'd." _Dryd._

To ENCHA'NT, V. A. [_enchanter_, Fr.] to influence by magic or sorcery. To lure exquisite delight.

ENCHA'NTER, S. one who practises magic or other spells supposed to have an irresistible power over others. One who delights irresistibly.

ENCHA'NTINGLY, Adv. delightfully; in such a manner, as to attract love irresistibly.

ENCHA'NTMENT, S. magical charms or spells, supposed to operate irresistibly both on the person and mind of another. That which has an irresistible influence, or can impart exquisite delight.

ENCHA'NTRESS, S. a woman who exercises magic, or spells. Figuratively, a woman whose beauty is irresistible.

To ENCHA'SE, V. A. [_enchasser_, Fr.] to set jewels in gold, &c. Figuratively, to adorn by being added. "King Henry's diadem—_enchas'd_, with all the honours of the world." _Shak._

To ENCI'RCLE, V. A. [from _circle_] to surround or encompass.

To ENCLO'SE, V. A. [_enclos_, Fr.] to surround ground by a fence. To surround or encompass.

ENCLO'SER,

ENCLO'SER, S. one who encloses. Any thing in which another is included.

ENCLO'SURE, S. the act of encompassing within a fence. The approbation of things which have been common. The space contained within any fence. Ground inclosed.

ENCO'MIAST, S. [εγκωμιαϛης, Gr.] one who commends, or bestows praise on another.

ENCOMIA'STIC, ENCOMIA'STICAL, Adj. containing praise or panegyric.

ENCO'MIUM, S. [εγκωμιον, Gr.] an advantageous representation of another's excellencies. Praise. A panegyric.

To ENCO'MPASS, V. A. [pronounced encumpass] to surround on all sides. To shut in. To go round any thing. "Lord Anson encompassed the world."

ENCO'RE, Adv. [Fr. pronounced awngcore] again; over again; once more. A word used at public shews to testify approbation, and to desire the person to repeat the part which gives so much satisfaction.

ENCOU'NTER, S. [rencontre, Fr.] a combat, or fight between two persons only. Figuratively, a battle, or attack. Eager and warm conversation relating either to love or anger. "In the instant of our encounter, after we had spoke the prologue of our comedy." Shak. Crowd, or accidental meeting. "To shun the encounter of the vulgar crowd." Address, or salutation. "The loose encounters of lascivious men." Occasion, casual incident. "It is necessary that the same spirit appear in all sort of encounters." Pope. Johnson observes, that this last sense is scarcely English.

To ENCOU'NTER, V. A. to meet face to face. To attack an enemy. To meet with mutual or reciprocal kindness. "They encounter thee with their hearts thanks." Shak. To meet with proof or evidence, to encompass on all sides with proofs. "We are encountered with clear evidences." Tillotf. To raise a kind of contradiction or opposition between the testimony of two evidences. "Jurors are not bound to believe two witnesses, if the probability of the fact does reasonably encounter them." To oppose, or engage with. To meet by accident or chance. "I am most fortunate thus to encounter you." Shak. Neuterly, to rush together, to join battle; to engage; to fight.

ENCOU'NTERER, S. an enemy or antagonist. An adversary or opponent.

To ENCOU'RAGE, V. A. [from encourager, Fr.] to animate, or exhort to a practice, used with the reciprocal pronouns themselves, &c. To countenance, to supply with authority or confidence. "This the judicious Hooker encourages to say." Locke.

ENCOU'RAGEMENT, S. an incitement to any action. Figuratively, favour, countenance, support, approbation.

ENCOU'RAGER, S. one who incites or encourages a person to do a thing.

To ENCRO'ACH, V. N. [accrocher, Fr.] to invade the property of another. To advance by stealth to that which a person has no right to. To come upon or seize the territories of another.

ENCRO'ACHER, S. one who gradually seizes, or advances upon the possessions of another.

ENCRO'ACHMENT, S. in Law, an unlawful trespass upon a man's grounds. Extortion, or the insisting upon the payment of more than is due.

To ENCU'MBER, V. A. [encombrer, Fr.] to load, hinder, or clog by any weight. Figuratively, to embarrass and distract the mind. To load with difficulties by debts. "His estate is encumbered."

ENCU'MBRANCE, S. an useless addition and burthen. A burthen or debt upon an estate.

ENCYCLOPE'DIA, ENCYCLOPE'DY, S. [εγκυκλοπαιδεια, G.] the circle of the sciences; applied by the Greeks to the seven liberal arts, and all the sciences.

ENCY'STED, Adj. [κυϛις, Gr.] inclosed in a bag.

E'ND, S. [San. ende, Belg.] the extremity of any thing extended in length. The last period of time. The conclusion, or last part. "At the wit's end." The furthest limits, or stretch of the understanding. A final determination, conclusion of a debate. Death. The cause of a person's death. Design, purpose, intention, or aim.

To E'ND, V. A. to perfect, or finish. To destroy, or put to death. To cease. To conclude. To terminate. To complete.

To ENDA'MAGE, V. A. to prejudice. To affect with loss. To spoil, or do harm.

To ENDA'NGER, V. A. to expose to danger, risque, hazard, or injury.

To ENDE'AR, V. A. to make dear, esteemed, or beloved.

ENDE'ARMENT, S. any thing which creates, or causes love.

ENDE'AVOUR, S. an attempt or trial to perform any thing.

To ENDE'AVOUR, V. A. to exert power. To make an attempt. To try.

ENDE'AVOURER, S. one who exerts his power. One who attempts or tries to do a thing.

ENDE'CAGON, S. [ενδεκα, Gr.] a figure with eleven sides.

ENDE'MIAL, ENDE'MIC, ENDE'MICAL, Adj. [εν, and δημος, Gr.] peculiar to a country. Applied to a disease peculiar to any certain country.

To ENDE'NIZE, V. A. to make free. Figuratively, to naturalize, or adopt the expressions or words of another language. "Partly

"Partly by enfranchifing and endenizing flrange words." *Camden.*

To ENDI'CT, or ENDI'TE, V. A. [*enditer*, Fr.] to charge any man with a crime, by a written accufation, before a court of juftice. To draw up, compofe, write, or relate.

ENDI'VE, S. [Fr. *intybum*, Lat.] in Botany, a fpecies of fuccory.

ENDLESS, Adj. [*endeleas*, Sax.] without end. Without bounds, applied to fpace. Without ceafing. Continual, or eternal.

ENDLESSLY, Adv. without ceafing, applied to action. Continually, applied to time. Without limits or bounds, applied to fpace.

ENDLESSNESS, S. want of bounds, or limits.

ENDLONG, Adj. with the end foremoft. In a ftraight line.

ENDMOST, Adj. further off, or at the furtheft end.

To ENDO'RSE, V. A. [*endoffer*, Fr. *dorfum*, Lat.] in Commerce, to write one's name on the back of a bill of exchange, or promiffory note, in order to pay it away, negotiate it. To cover on the back. "Elephants endors'd with tow'rs—of archers." *Par. Reg.*

ENDORSEMENT, S. in Commerce, the act of writing one's name on the back of a bill of exchange, or promiffory note. A ratification. "The endorfement of fupreme delight—by a friend and with his blood." *Herbert.*

To ENDO'W, V. A. [*enduouvier*, Fr. *indoto*, Lat.] to give a portion. To affign any eftate or fum to the fupport of any charity, or any alms-houfe. "Die and endow an alms-houfe, or a cat." *Pope.* To enrich or adorn with any natural excellence or virtue.

ENDOWMENT, S. wealth devoted to any particular ufe. The fetting apart a fum of money for the perpetual fupport of a vicar, or alms-houfe. The gifts of nature.

To ENDU'E, V. A. [*induo*, Lat.] to fupply or furnifh with virtues, or excellencies. "Endue them with thy holy fpirit." *Common Prayer.* To give as a portion or dowry.

ENDU'RANCE, S. continuance; laftingnefs. Patience, or the act of fupporting troubles without complaint.

To ENDU'RE, V. A. [*endurer*, Fr. *duro*, Lat.] to fuffer, undergo, or bear. To laft, remain, or continue. To bear patiently.

ENDU'RER, S. one that hath ftrength and patience to fupport any fatigue or hardfhip.

ENDWISE, Adv. on end. Upright, or perpendicularly.

E'NEMY, S. [*enemi*, Fr. *nemico*, Ital.] one who is of an oppofite fide in war. One who oppofes the welfare of another. One

who has a ftrong diflike to a perfon. The foe of mankind, the devil.

ENERGE'TIC, Adj. [*energetikos*, Gr.] acting fo as to perform or produce. Actively, operative, or working. "A being eternally energetic." *Grew.*

E'NERGY, S. [*energeia*, Gr.] power in the abftract. Power, force, or efficacy. Action. Force of expreffion, applied to language.

To ENERVATE, V. A. [*enervatus*, Lat.] to weaken. To render effeminate.

ENERVA'TION, S. the act of weakening, or making effeminate. Effeminacy.

To ENE'RVE, V. A. [*enervo*, Lat.] to weaken; to leffen ftrength; to render effeminate. "Such object hath the pow'r to foft'n and tame fevereft temper—Enerve, and with voluptuous hope diffolve." *Paradife Regain'd.*

To ENFE'EBLE, V. A. to make feeble; to weaken or deprive of ftrength.

To ENFE'OF, V. A [*feoffamentum*, low Lat.] in Law, to inveft with any title or poffeffion.

ENFEOFMENT, S. in Law, the act whereby a perfon is invefted with any dignity or poffeffion. The inftrument or deed by which one is invefted.

ENFILA'DE, S. [Fr.] a feries of things difpofed as it were in a ftraight line; hence in Architecture, an effilade of doors, windows, or buildings, is fuch a dillribution that they may all be feen in a direct line. In War, applied to thofe trenches, &c. which are ranged in a right line, and may be fwept or fcoured by the cannon lengthwife.

To ENFILA'DE, V. A. to pierce or fweep in a right line. "The avenues were enfiladed by the Spanifh cannon." *Expedition to Carthage.*

To ENFO'RCE, V. A. [*enforcer*, Fr.] to ftrengthen. To fling with ftrength, or violence. "As ftones—enfir'd from the old Affyrian flings." *Shak.* To animate. To incite. To urge. To compel to do a thing. To prefs with a charge or accufation. "If he evade us there, enforce him with his envy to the people." *Shak.* Neuterly, to prove, or fhew beyond contradiction.

ENFO'RCE, S. power. Exertion of ftrength. "A pretty enterprize of fmall enforce." *Milton's Agon.*

ENFO'RCEDLY, Adv. by violence, force, or compulfion.

ENFO'RCEMENT, S. [from *enforce*] violence; compulfion. An evidence, proof, or confirmation. A motive of conviction. A preffing occafion.

ENFO'RCER, S. one who caufes, or produces any thing by force, or violence.

To ENFRA'NCHISE, V. A. to admit to the privileges of a freeman. To free from flavery. To free from cuftody. To naturalize

rather a foreign word. "These words have been *enfranchised* among us." *Watts.*

ENFRANCHISEMENT, S. the act of incorporating a person into any body politic. A release from slavery.

To ENGAGE, V. A. [*engager*, Fr.] to give as a security for a debt. To stake, or hazard. "*Engag'd* their lives for them." *Lock.* To embark, or take part in an affair. To employ one's self in an attempt. To unite by some attraction or amiable quality. "This humanity and good nature *engages* every body to him." *Spect.* No. 106. To encounter, to fight. Neuterly, to be obliged by promise or appointment. To embark in any business.

ENGAGEMENT, S. the act of giving security. An obligation by promise or contract. Employment of the attention. Fight, conflict, or battle. A strong motive or inducement.

To ENGOAL, V. A. [pronounced *enjoil*, Fr.] to imprison. Figuratively, to lay under constraint, to confine, or deprive of liberty. "Within my mouth you have *engoaled* my tongue." *Shak.*

To ENGENDER, V. A. [*engendrer*, Fr.] to beget between different sexes. To form, or produce. To cause, to cause. To bring forth. "Vice *engenders* shame." *Prior.*

ENGINE, S. [*engin*, Fr. *ingens*, Ital.] an instrument consisting of a complication of mechanic powers, such as wheels, screws, levers, &c. united and conspiring together to effect the same end. A military machine. An instrument for casting water to great heights, in order to extinguish fires. Figuratively, any means used to bring a thing to pass, and applied generally in an ill sense. An agent for another.

ENGINEER, S. [*ingenieur*, Fr. *ingegniero*, Ital.] one who invents, makes, or works at engines. An officer in an army, who inspects the works, attacks, defences, &c.

ENGINERY, S. the art of conducting or managing artillery. Artillery, or ordnance.

To ENGIRD, V. A. to surround, or encompass.

ENGLAND, a considerable country of Europe, and the principal part of the Island of Great Britain, surrounded on all sides by the sea, except where Scotland lies, to the N. It is 400 measured miles in length, from Berwick upon Tweed to Chichester; and 370 in breadth, from Dover in Kent to Seian in Cornwall. But in other places it varies greatly, particularly in the breadth; for it grows narrower (but not gradually) from the southern coast to the town of Berwick: therefore it would be worth while, for a more particular account of it, to consult a good map. It is happily situated with regard to trade, there being many good towns and

harbours on the sea coast, which are particularly taken notice of in their proper places. The air is generally very good and wholesome, except in the hundreds of Essex and Kent, the fens in Lincolnshire and Cambridgeshire, and some other low marshes near the sea. The winters indeed are sometimes rainy and foggy, and the weather is subject to great variations, which, however, does not much impair the health of the inhabitants who are accustomed thereto, for they generally live as long as in any other countries, and we have frequent instances of people who have lived to a very great age; particularly Henry Jenkins, a Yorkshire man, who was 168 years old when he died; and Thomas Parr, of Shropshire, who was 152, and might have lived longer, if he had not been sent for up to court as a curiosity. The frequent rains, though they may sometimes damage the hay and corn, have yet their peculiar advantages; for upon that account they have generally good pastures throughout the year. There are thunder, storms, hurricanes, and earthquakes, as in other countries, but they are, in general, less violent, and do less damage. The principal rivers are the Thames, the Severn, the Trent, the Ouse; besides a great number of others, which will be taken notice of in their proper places. England is a level and open country; for, what hills there are, of any note, are chiefly towards the north; for this reason, it is extremely proper for the diversion of hunting. There are some remarkable forests, as Windsor Forest, the Forest of Dean, and the New Forest; which last was made by William the Conqueror, who demolished several towns and villages, and thirty-six parish-churches, in order to make it. The soil is different in different parts, but in general very fruitful. There are indeed many heaths, downs, and barren places, which, however, generally produce grass enough to feed flocks of sheep; besides, it is thought, that the care and diligence of good husbandmen might turn many of them to great advantage. It produces all sorts of fruits, trees, and herbs which are proper to the climate: it must be acknowledged there are no vines that are so fit to produce good wine, as in warmer countries; but then there are variety enough which yield good grapes that are made use of as other fruits. However, there are great quantities of cyder, perry, mead, and several kinds of made wines; but the principal drink of the generality is beer, or ale. The English wool is famous all over the world, as well as the manufactures made therefrom; particularly broad-cloth, which is not to be equalled in any other country. There might also be excellent linen manufactures, if it was worth while; but as they are come to a great perfection in all kinds of linen in Scotland and Ireland, where they can be made cheaper,

Tracing Vaulouis Engine

we are now chiefly supplied from thence: what linen we have made amongst us, is generally the coarser sort, known by the name of dowlass. Here are all sorts of materials for building; and there are excellent stone-quarries in several parts. The firing is pit-coal, wood, and turf, which last is used where coals are dear; but in most counties there is plenty of pit-coal. It is generally said that there might be found coal-mines on Black-Heath; but they are not permitted to be opened, because the ships which bring coals from Newcastle to London, are a nursery for seamen. No country in the world is better provided with horses of all sorts, and for every use; and particularly with regard to race-horses, they are seldom equalled by those of other countries. There are dogs of every kind, except wolf-dogs, which, since the wolves were destroyed in England, have been generally neglected; however, the race of these animals is still maintained in Ireland. But there is one sort that is not to be equalled in any part of the world, which is the bull-dog; for these will not only attack the fiercest bull, but any kind of wild beast; nor can any thing, when they have once fastened upon the animal, oblige them to let go their hold. But, what is more strange, when any of them is transported beyond sea, they lose their courage; and the same is said of English cocks. With regard to minerals, there are mines of iron, tin, lead, copper, and in some places silver, besides others of less note. As for the curiosities, they will be mentioned in their proper places, when the counties in particular are treated of. As for the manners, customs, and abilities of the inhabitants, nothing need be said, because they fall under every one's own observations; nor yet of the government, religion, and laws, of which very few can be ignorant. Lat. from 49. 50. to 55. 45.

EN'GLISH, Adj. [Englisc, Sax.] belonging or relating to England. Substantively, the language spoken by the people of England. The natives of England.

To ENGO'RGE, V. A. [gorge, Fr.] to swallow, devour, or gorge. Neuterly, to feed with eagerness or gluttony. " Greedily she engorg'd without restraint." *P. r. Lost.*

To ENGRA'FT, V. A. [greffer, Fr.] in Gardening, to take a shoot from one tree and insert it into another, so as both shall unite and grow together.

ENGRA'FTING, S. in Gardening, the act of taking a shoot from one tree and inserting into the stock of another.

To ENGRA'IN, V. A. to dye deep; to dye in the grain.

To ENGRA'VE, V. A. [engraver, Fr.] to cut copper, iron, &c. so as to represent figures thereon. Figuratively, to make a deep or lasting impression on the mind.

ENGRA'VER, S. one who cuts figures on metals, &c. One who engraves.

ENGRA'VING, S. the art of cutting metals and precious stones, in order to represent figures or other ornaments thereon.

To ENGRO'SS, V. A. [grossir, Fr.] to enlarge the bulk of a thing. " Pillars, by channelling, be seemingly engross'd to the sight." *Warton.* To seize upon the whole of any thing. To buy up any commodity in order to sell it again at an advanced price. In Law, to copy writings in a large hand.

ENGRO'SSER, S. one who purchases large quantities of any commodity in order to sell it at an advanced price. One who seizes the whole of any thing to himself.

ENGRO'SSMENT, S. an exorbitant acquisition. The act of encroaching upon the whole of any thing.

To ENHA'NCE, V. A. [hausser, Fr. innuo, Ital.] to raise the price of a thing. To heighten the esteem of any quality. " Contribute to enhance our pleasure." *Atterb.* " Contribute to enhance their guilt." *Atterb.*

ENHA'NCEMENT, S. increase of esteem, of value, of price, or of degree.

ENI'GMA, S. [ænigma, Lat. ænigma, Gr.] a proposition delivered in obscure terms, in order to puzzle or exercise the wit, or invention.

ENIGMA'TICAL, S. of the nature of an enigma; obscure, darkly, ambiguously. Obscurely or imperfectly conceived.

ENIGMA'TICALLY, Adv. in the manner of an enigma. Different from the obvious sense of the words.

To ENJOI'N, V. A. [enjoindre, Fr.] to order, to charge; it implies something more than direct, and less than command.

ENJOI'NER, S. a person who directs, or gives a strict charge.

To ENJOY', V. A. [jouir, rejouir, Fr.] to feel a flow of joy. To obtain possession of. To gladden, to delight. Neuterly, to be in fruition, or possession. To live happily, and comfortably.

ENJOY'ER, S. one who has a thing in his possession. One who receives joy, or satisfaction from the possessing a thing.

ENJOY'MENT, S. joy or pleasure arising from possession or fruition. Possession.

To ENKI'NDLE, V. A. to set on fire. To inflame. To rouse or inflame the passions. To incite to any act or wish. " That might yet enkindle you unto the crown." *Shak.* The last sense is not in use.

To ENLA'RGE, V. A. [elargir, Fr.] to make greater in quantity, dimensions, quality or appearance. Figuratively, to magnify. To extend the capacity of the mind. To be very minute in a description of a thing. To free from confinement. Neuterly, to expatiate on a subject.

ENLA'RGMENT, S. increase of dimension, quality, bulk, or degree. Release. A magnifying description. A minute, and copious discourse on any topic.

ENLA'RGER, S. one who increases. One who magnifies in discourse.

To ENL'IGHT, V. A. to communicate light, information, or knowledge. "Wit —enlights the present, and shall warm the last." Pope.

To ENLI'GHTEN, V. A. to supply with light. Figuratively, to supply with knowledge, or information. To cheer, or gladden.

To ENLI'NK, V. A. to join, or connect like the links of a chain. "Enlinks to waste and desolation." Shak.

To ENLI'VEN, V. A. to make alive. To inspire with new vigour; to animate. To make sprightly or gay.

ENLI'VENER, S. that which gives motion, or communicates spirit, gaiety or vigour.

EN'MITY, S. [inimicitia, Lat.] a disposition of mind which excites a person to oppose the welfare of another. Contrariety of interests. A state of irreconcilable opposition. Malice.

ENNE'AGON, S. [from ennea, Gk and gwnia,] a figure with nine angles.

To ENNO'BLE, V. A. [ennoblir, Fr.] to raise a person from a commoner to be a peer. Figuratively, to communicate worth, to dignify. To raise, exalt, or elevate. To make famous, or remarkable. "Ennobled some of the coasts thereof by shipwrecks." Bacon.

ENNO'BLEMENT, S. the act of rising to the degree of a peer. Elevation, exaltation, dignity, state.

ENOR'MITY, S. [from enormis, Lat.] a departure from any rule or standard. An irregularity, a corruption. In the plural, used for the greatest of crimes.

ENOR'MOUS, [enormis, Lat.] irregular; without restraint. "Wild above rule or art, enormous bliss!" Par. Lost. Disordered, in a state of anarchy or confusion, applied to government. Exceedingly wicked. Exceeding the common bulk, applied to size.

ENOR'MOUSLY, Adv. prodigiously, exceedingly; beyond measure.

ENOR'MOUSNESS, S. excess of guilt or villainy.

ENOU'GH, Adj. [pronounced enuff, from genoh, getig, Sax. ganoh, Goth. genowg, Belg. genoeg, Teut.] Johnson acknowledges it to be difficult to determine whether it be an adjective or an adverb; yet imagines that when joined to a substantive it is the former, that enow is its plural, and that in other cases it is an adverb, unless when it follows the verb have, when he thinks it is properly a substantive; but as the word satis in Latin, which has the same signification, is acknow-

ledged by all grammarians an adjective, this conjecture seems too refined, and when applied to that word would equally prove it to be both an adverb, adjective and substantive; which every one must acknowledge an absurdity; however, that we may not seem singular, we have followed that author's distinctions, though we cannot acquiesce in their propriety) sufficient; that which will answer any purpose or design. "I know enough for their herds." Locke. It should be observed that though other adjectives are placed in English before their substantives, yet this always follows it, as in the sentence quoted, room enough, not enough room.

ENOU'GH, S. that which will answer a person's expectations or wishes. Used with for. A quantity answerable to any design, used with to.

ENOU'GH, Adv. so as to give content or satisfaction. When used after an adjective it denotes that a thing is not perfectly so, and is used to express great indifference or slight. "The girl was well enough." i. e. Not so well as might be expected. Sometimes it denotes such a degree of any quality as is rather culpable than excusable. "I am ready enough to quarrel." i. e. more ready than I should be. Steel.

ENO'W, Adj. sufficient number. See ENOUGH, Adj.

To ENRA'GE, V. A. [enrager, Fr.] to put a person in a violent passion or rage.

To ENRA'NK, V. A. to place in order.

To ENRA'PT, V. A. to transport to a great degree of joy, ecstasy, or enthusiasm. "Nor hath he been so caught in those studies, as to neglect the polite arts." Mort. Scrib. Johnson supposes this an erroneous spelling, instead of enwrapt, i. e. involved; yet I must acknowledge, I see no reason for the supposition, as it is no impropriety to say that a person may be so excessively delighted or enraptured with one branch of study, as to neglect all others.

To ENRA'PTURE, V. A. to transport to the highest degree of delight.

To ENRA'VISH, V. A. to affect with the most exalted degree of joy, or extasy. "At sight thereof so much enravish'd." Shak.

To ENRI'CH, V. A. to give or bestow riches. Figuratively, to make fat or fruitful, applied to ground. To adorn the mind with knowledge. "Enrich his own understanding." Raleigh.

ENRI'CHMENT, S. an increase of wealth. Improvement, applied to soil, books, or the mind.

To ENRI'PEN, V. A. to make ripe, or mature. "The summer — how it enripen'd the year." Donne.

To ENRO'BE, V. A. to dress, to adorn, or to embellish with dress.

Tv

To ENRO'LL, V. A. [*enroller*, Fr.] to enter in a lift, or roll. To record.

ENRO'LLER, S. a person who writes or enters another's name in a lift.

ENRO'LMENT, S. a record. The act of registering.

To ENRO'OT, V. A. to fix by the root. Figuratively, to fasten, or implant deeply.

To ENSCHE'DULE, V. A. [pronounced *enscedule*] to insert in a schedule.

To ENSE'AR, V. A. to rub, or stop bleeding with a red hot iron. To cauter (w. " *Ensear* thy fertile and conceptious womb." *Shak.*

To ENSHRI'NE, V. A. to preserve in a religious, sacred or hallowed place.

ENSI'GN, S. [*ensigne*, Fr. *insigne*, Lat.] the flag or standard of a regiment. A signal. A mark, or distinction and authority. An officer among the foot who carries the flag, or ensign.

ENSI'GN-BEARER, S. one who carries the flag.

To ENSLA'VE, V. A. to deprive of liberty or freedom.

ENSLA'VEMENT, S. the state of a slave. Figuratively, a state of mean obedience to the violence of any passion.

ENSLA'VER, S. one who deprives of liberty.

To ENSUE, V. A. [*ensuivre*, Fr.] to follow; to pursue. Neuterly, to follow as a consequence. To succeed in a train of events, or course of time.

ENSURA'NCE, S. security from loss or accidents obtained by payment of a certain sum of money. A sum of money paid to be secured from loss or accidents.—See INSUR-ANCE.

To ENSU'RE, V. A. [*sure, assurer*, Fr.] to secure or make certain for a time. To secure from loss, on condition of receiving a certain sum in advance. — See INSUR-ANCE.

ENSU'RER, S. a person who indemnifies another from any loss or hazard, in consideration of a sum of money paid to him.

ENTA'BLATURE, ENTA'BLEMENT, S. [Fr.] in architecture, that part of an order of a column, which is over the capital.

ENTA'IL, [*taillé*, Fr. *foedum taliatum*, low Lat.] in law, a fee estate entailed, i. e. limited to certain conditions, at the will of the granter, or donor.

To ENTA'IL, V. A. in law, to settle the descent of an estate, so that it cannot be bequeathed at pleasure. To fix unalienably on any person or thing.

To ENTA'ME, V. A. to tame; to conquer, or subdue. " *Entame* my spirits to your worship." *Shak.*

To ENTA'NGLE, V. A. [from *tang*, Sax.] to ensnare, or involve in something which is not easily got clear from, as briars, and as a net. To twist in such a perplexed

manner, as cannot be easily unravelled. Figuratively, to perplex or confuse. To distract with a variety of affairs.

ENTA'NGLEMENT, S. that which involves a thing in intricacies. The confused state of thread, which requires great patience to unravel and undo. An obscurity, or difficulty.

ENTA'NGLER, V. A. one that ensnares, or involves in difficulties.

To ENTER, V. A. [*entrer*, Fr. *intro*, Lat.] to go into any place. To deliver the first rudiments of any art or science to a person. In Commerce, to set down any article in a book. To give notice at the customhouse, and pay the duties for the import or export of any commodity. Neuterly, to come in. " To *enter* into." To discover, or penetrate by the application of the mind. To begin, or engage in, used with *on* or *upon*. To be initiated in a science, or art; to have a taste of a thing.

ENTERING, S. an avenue by which a person may enter a place. The motion by which a person enters a place.

ENTERO'LOGY, S. [*enteron*, and *logos*, Gr.] a treatise on the bowels.

ENTERPRISE, S. [Fr.] an undertaking attended with some hazard and danger.

To ENTERPRISE, V. A. to attempt; to undertake, or try to perform, to hazard.

ENTERPRISER, S. one who undertakes or engages in important and hazardous designs.

To ENTERTA'IN, V. A. [*entretenir*, Fr.] to treat. To receive hospitably. To retain a person as a servant. To conceive, applied to the mind. To please, amuse, or give pleasure. To attempt; or admit as a truth. " I *entertain* that opinion."

ENTERTA'INMENT, S. a treat or feast. Hospitable reception. Reception, admission, or assent, applied to opinion. Amusement, or diversion. A farce, or pantomime.

To ENTHRO'NE, V. A. to place on a throne. Figuratively, to invest with the authority of a king.

ENTHU'SIASM, S. [*enthousiasmos*, Gr.] a strong persuasion that a person is inspired in an extraordinary manner, by immediate impulses and operations of the Holy Ghost. An extraordinary elevation of the soul, which warms the imagination, and enables it to conceive and express things both exalted and amazing.

ENTHU'SIAST, S. one who vainly imagines he is inspired by God. One of a warm imagination, or violent passions. One of an elevated fancy.

ENTHUSIA'STIC, ENTHUSIA'STI-CAL, Adj. vainly persuaded of receiving extraordinary communications from the Deity. Violent in any cause. Of elevated fancy.

E 2   To

To ENTI'CE, V. A. to feduce, allure or draw to fomething bad.

ENTI'CEMENT, S. the practice of drawing or alluring a perfon to do ill. The alluring means by which a perfon is drawn to commit fomething wrong.

ENTI'CER, S. one that allures or entices to ill.

ENTI'CINGLY, Adv. in fuch a manner as to charm, entice or allure. " fings moft enticingly." Addif.

ENTI'RE, Adj. (entier, Fr. integer, Lat.) whole; undivided. Complete. Full, or containing every thing requifite. Firm, fixed, folid. " Entire and fure the monarch's rule muft prove." Prior. Unmixt, unadulterated, applied primarily to liquors, and figuratively to happinefs.

ENTI'RELY, Adv. wholly; without exception, completely.

ENTI'RENESS, S. the ftate of a thing having parts.

To ENTI'TLE, V. A. (entituler, Fr.) to grace with a title of honour. To call by a particular name. To give a claim or right. To fuperfcribe.

ENTI'TY, S. (entitas, low Lat.) the being or exiftence of any thinking thing. A collection of qualities which conftitute the nature of a thing.

To ENTO'MB, V. A. to place or fhut up in a tomb.

EN'TRAILS, S. (has no fingular, entrailles, Fr. πτρα, Gr.) the inteftines, guts, or inward parts of an animal. Figuratively, the inmoft parts of any thing.

EN'TRANCE, S. (entrent, Fr.) the avenue by which a perfon may enter any place. Figuratively, the power, or act of going in. The beginning, or firft rudiments of a fcience or art. Beginning, applied to time.

To ENTRA'NCE, V. A. (of tranfe, Fr.) to reduce to fuch a ftate that the foul feems to be abfent from the body. To exalt to fuch a pitch of extafy, as to be infenfible to external objects. Neuterly, to be in the higheft pitch of extafy, fo as to be loft to furrounding objects.

To ENTRA'P, V. A. (entraper, Fr.) to catch in a trap, or fnare. Figuratively, to betray. To take advantage of. " To entrap thee in thy words." Ecclef. viii. 11.

To ENTRE'AT, V. A. (from traiter, Fr.) to afk or requeft with humility and earneftnefs. To treat. To entertain, divert, or amufe. " I muft entreat the time alone." Shak. To make a petition or requeft for a perfon in an humble manner. " Entreat for him." Shak.

ENTRE'ATY, S. a requeft for fome favour in an humble manner.

EN'TREMETS, S. (Fr. from entre and mettre) in Cookery, fmall plates that are placed between the chief and large difhes.

EN'TRY, S. (entrée, Fr.) the paffage by which a perfon goes into or out of a houfe. The act of going in. In Commerce, the act of writing an article in a book; double entry, is the entering an article on different fides in different accounts. A public procefsion to a place.

To ENVE'LOP, V. A. (enveloper, Fr.) to inwrap; to inclofe in a covering. Figuratively, to furround, or conceal.

ENVELOPE, S. (Fr.) a wrapper. A cover; an outward cafe for a letter, &c. " No letter with an invelope." Swift.

To ENVE'NOM, V. A. to mix with poifon; to make poifonous. Figuratively, to make odious.

ENVI'ER, S. one who is affected with grief at the fuccefs of another.

EN'VIOUS, Adj. affected with grief at the excellence or profperity of another.

EN'VIOUSLY, Adv. fo as to fhew difpleafure on account of the happinefs or excellence of another.

To ENVI'RON, V. A. (environner, Fr.) to furround; to encompafs. Figuratively, to hem in. To inclofe; to inveft.

ENVI'RONS, S. (Fr.) the neighbourhood, or places fituated round about, near any town or city.

To ENU'MERATE, V. A. (enumero, Lat.) to reckon up or count over. To relate minutely, all the circumftances of a thing.

ENUMERA'TION, S. (enumeratio, Lat.) the act of numbering or counting. A minute detail.

ENUNCIA'TION, S. (enunciatio, Lat.) a declaration, proclamation, or public atteftation.

ENU'NCIATIVE, Adj. declarative, expreffing either affirmatively or negatively.

EN'VOY, S. (Fr. of envoyer, Fr. to fend) a public minifter fent from one prince to another. A meffenger.

To EN'VY, V. A. (envie, invideo, Lat.) to grieve at the excellence, or profperity of another. To hate another for excellence, profperity or happinefs. To grudge, to impart with reluctance, or to withhold malicioufly.

EN'VY, S. (from the verb) pain arifing in the mind, from obferving the profperity of thofe efpecially with whom a perfon has had a rivalfhip; it is likewife extended to thofe perfons who refufe to be guided by our perfuafions, this being likewife a rivalfhip for fuperiority of judgment, and gives rife to fuch malicious criticifms as fhall tend to perfuade the world of our own fuperiority, or to weaken the efteemed fuperiority of our opponent. Anger and difpleafure at feeing another poffeffed of any good we want.

EPA'CT, S. (epacte, Gr.) in Chronology, a number, whereby is noted the excefs of the common folar, above the lunar year, and

and thereby may be found out the age of the moon every year.

EPAU'LEMENT, EPAU'LMENT, S. [from *epaule*, Fr. shoulder] in Fortification, a sidework of earth hastily thrown up, of bags filled with sand, or of gabions, fascines, &c. with earth to cover the men or cannon.

EPHE'MERA, S. [Gr. of *up*, and *ημερα*, Gr. a day] a fever which terminates in one day. In Natural History, an insect which lives but a single day. In Botany, such flowers as open and expand themselves at sun-rise, and shut and wither at sun-setting.

EPHEMERAL, Adj. lasting only one day. "An *ephemeral* fit of applause." *Watt.* Not in use.

EPHEMERIC, Adj. See EPHEMERAL.

EPHE'MERIS, S. [*εφημερις*, Gr.] a journal of a person's daily transactions. In Astronomy, a table calculated to shew the places of the planets at noon.

EPHE'MERON, S. [see EPHEMERA] in Natural History, an animal whose life is confined to the space of five hours, i.e. within the hours of six in the evening, and eleven at night; when becomes a fly it needs no food; in the beginning of its life in that state, it sheds its coat, and by that means becoming alert and light, it spends the rest of its short span in frisking over the waters, and at the same time the female drops her eggs on the waters, and the male his spawn on them to impregnate them. The eggs are spread about by the waters, descend to the bottom by their own gravity, and are hatched by the warmth of the sun, into little worms, which make themselves cases in the clay, and feed on the same substance without any need of parental care. In order to enable them to dig their cells, the Wise Creator hath furnished them with two fore legs, somewhat like those of moles, or the gryllotalpa, to which he has added two toothy cheeks, somewhat like the sheers of lobsters, which enables them to bore the clay with ease. That though their life is short, it is supplied with every thing to render it convenient, and when we behold the joy with which they frisk upon the waters, we may conclude that it abounds with all the pleasures which can be crowded into so narrow a span of existence.

EPHESUS, an ancient and celebrated town of Turkey in Asia, and in Natolia, and in that part of it which was anciently called Ionia. It is now called Ajasaluoc; and there is no other city in the world that has so many remains of its ancient splendour. There is nothing to be seen about it but heaps of marble, overturned walls, columns, chapters, and pieces of statues, heaped upon one another. The fortress, which is upon an eminence, seems to be a work of the Greek empire. The eastern gate has three Basso-Relievos, taken from some ancient monuments; and that in the middle was constructed by the Romans. The most remarkable structure of all, was, the Temple of Diana, which the ancient Christians had turned into a church; but it is now so entirely ruined, that it is no easy matter to find out the ground-plot: however, there are some ruins of the walls, and of five or six marble columns, all of a piece, 40 feet in length, and 7 in diameter. It was counted one of the seven wonders of the world. It is seated near a gulph of the same name, and has still a good harbour, 40 miles S. of Smyrna. Lon. 48. 8. lat. 37. 58.

EPHOD, S. [?, Heb.] an ornament, or kind of girdle, worn by the Jewish priests when they attended at the temple.

EPIC, Adj. [*epicus*, Lat. from *επος*, Gr. to speak] narrative, in opposition to *dramatic*. An *epic* poem, is an heroic poem, invented with art to form the manners, by instructions disguised under the allegory of an important action, in a probable, and entertaining manner.

EPICURE, S. [*epicurus*, Lat.] Figuratively, a person abandoned wholly to luxury.

EPICURE'AN, S. [*epicurus*, Lat.] a disciple of Epicurus, who held that pleasure was the chief good of man; that the deities had no regard for, and never interposed in the affairs of mankind; that the world was made by chance, or a fortuitous concourse of atoms, and some other absurdities, which though not openly professed by the other sects of philosophers, might be deduced from their principles. The word is used at present, for an indolent, effeminate, and voluptuous person, who only consults his private and particular pleasure, without concerning himself with any thing serious.

EPICURE'AN, Adj. luxurious in eating or drinking; contributing to luxury. "*Epicurean* cooks." *Shak.*

EPICURISM, S. [see EPICUREAN] the doctrine of Epicurus. Figuratively, luxury in eating. Voluptuousness; sensual enjoyments.

EPICYCLOID, S. [*επι*, Gr. *κυκλος*, Gr.] in Geometry, a curve generated by the revolution of a point of the circumference of a circle along the convex or concave part of another circle.

EPIDEMIC, EPIDE'MICAL, Adj. [from *επι*, Gr. and *δημος*] that which affects a great number of people at the same time; applied to diseases, and particularly the plague.

EPIGRAM, S. [*epigramma*, Lat. of *επιγραμμα*, Gr.] in Poetry, a short poem, susceptible of all kinds of subjects, and ending with a lively, just and unexpected thought, point, or sting.

EPIGRAMMA'TIC, EPIGRAMMA'TICAL, Adj. [*epigrammaticus*, Lat.] having the nature or properties of an epigram,

EPI-

EPIGRA'MMATIST, S. one who writes or makes epigrams.

EPI'LEPSY, S. [from επιλαμβανω, Gr.] In Medicine, a convulsion either of the whole body or some of its parts, attended with a loss of sense and understanding. The English call it the falling sickness, because persons generally fall down when afflicted with it.

EPILE'PTIC, Adj. affected with an epilepsy. Convulsed.

E'PILOGUE, S. [epilogus, Lat.] a poem pronounced after a play.

EPI'PHANY, S. [επιφανεια, Gr.] a church festival, celebrated on the 12th day after Christmas, in commemoration of our Saviour's being manifested to the Gentile world, by the appearance of a miraculous blazing star, which directed the Magi to the place where he was born.

EPI'PHORA, S. [Gr.] in Medicine, a defluxion of rheum into the eyes.

EPI'SCOPACY, S. [episcopatus, Lat.] the government of the church by bishops.

EPI'SCOPAL, Adj. [episcopalis, Lat.] belonging to a bishop.

EPI'SCOPATE, S. [episcopatus, Lat.] the dignity or government of a bishop. A bishopric.

E'PISODE, S. [επεισοδιον, Gr.] In poetry, a separate incident, story, or action, which a poet invents, and connects with his principal action, that his work may abound with a greater diversity of events; though, in a more limited sense, all the particular incidents whereof the action or narration is compounded, are called episodes.

The episode, in its original, was only something rehearsed between the parts of the chorus, or ancient tragedy, for the diversion of the audience. Episodes serve to promote the action, to illustrate, embellish, and adorn it, and carry it to its proper period. Episodes are either absolutely necessary, or very requisite. All episodes are incidents, though all incidents are not episodes; because some incidents are not adventitious to the action, but make up the very form and series of it. Examples will clear up this distinction: the storm in the first Æneid of Virgil, driving the fleet on the coast of Carthage, is an incident, not an episode, because the hero himself and the whole body of his forces are concerned in it; and so it is a direct, and not a collateral part of the main action. The adventures of Nisus and Euryalus, in the ninth Æneid, are episodes, not incidents, i. e. not direct parts of the main action.

It is particularly by the art of episodes, that the great variety of matter which adorns a poem is brought into the principal action: but though the episodes are a kind of digression from the subject, yet they ought to have a natural relation to the principal action, never be far-fetched, and must be handled with judgment, to avoid confusion and bur-

dening the subject with too much action. Without this restriction, the episode is no longer probable, and there appears an air of affectation which becomes ridiculous.

EPISO'DIC, EPISO'DICAL, Adj. partaking of the nature of an episode. Swelled with unnecessary incidents, or episodes which are unconnected with the principal action.

EPI'STLE, S. [epistola, Lat.] a letter; moderns use only the word letter.

EPI'STOLARY, Adj. relating, or transacted by letters.

E'PITAPH, S. [from επι, and ταφος, Gr.] a poem or inscription on a tomb, or grave-stone.

EPITHALA'MIUM, S. [from επι, and θαλαμος, Gr.] a complimental poem wrote on the marriage of a person.

E'PITHEM, S. [επιθεμα, Gr.] in Pharmacy, a kind of fomentation applied externally to the regions of the heart, liver, &c. to strengthen and comfort them.

E'PITHET, S. [επιθετον, Gr.] an adjective denoting the quality of the word to which it was joined; those of Milton and Shakespear, are very judicious and bold. A title or surname. A phrase or expression. "Sister love! a good epithet! I do suffer love indeed, for I love thee against my will." Shak.

E'PITOME, S. [Gr. from επιτεμνω, Gr.] an abridgment, or reduction of the substance of a book.

To EPITOMI'SE, V. A. to abridge. To reduce the substance of a book into a narrower compass. To cut short, or curtail. "We have epitomised many particular words." Spect. No. 135. Johnson thinks the last sense to be improper, though it be a literal translation of the Greek, from whence this word is derived.

EPITOMI'SER, EPI'TOMIST, S. one who abridges, or epitomises a work.

E'POCH, E'POCHA, S. [εποχη, Gr.] in Chronology, a fixed point or period from whence the succeeding years are numbered.

E'PODE, S. [επωδος, Gr.] in lyric poetry, the third or last part of the ode; the ancient lyric poem being divided into strophe, antistrophe, and epode.

E'QUABLE, Adj. [equabilis, Lat.] even; alike; consistent with itself, in the same proportion; uniform with respect to form, motion, or temperature.

E'QUABLY, Adv. uniformly; consistently; in the same proportion.

E'QUAL, Adj. [equalis, Lat.] like another in bulk, excellence, or any other quality. Fit, proper, or adequate to any purpose. Even, uniform; unruffled by passion. In proportion. Impartial, neutral, favouring both parties alike. Indifferent.

E'QUAL, S. a thing or person neither inferior nor superior to another. One of the same age.

To

To E'QUAL, V. A. to make one thing or person resemble another. Neuterly, to resemble. to be equal. To answer. "Equall'd all her love." Dryd.

To EQUALISE, V. A. to make even, To be equal to. "To equalise and fix a thing bigger than it is." Digby.

EQUA'LITY, S. likeness. The same degree of quality.

E'QUALLY, Adv. in the same degree with any other, Alike. Impartially. "Equally determine." Shak. The laft fenfe not in ufe.

EQUA'NGULAR, Adj. [from æquus. Lat. and angulus, Lat.] that has equal angles.

EQUANI'MITY, S. [æquanimitas, Lat.] a ftate of mind which is neither elated with fuccefs, nor depreffed with loffes. Evennefs of mind.

EQUANI'MOUS, Adj. [æquanimis, Lat.] even; neither elated nor dejected.

EQUA'TION, S. [æquatio, Lat. of æquo, Lat.] the act of making one thing equal to another. In Algebra, an expreffion of the fame quantity in two diffimilar but equal terms; 2 3 × = 4 + 3 i. e. twice 3, is equal to 4 added to 2. In Aftronomy, the reducing the apparent unequal motion of the heavenly bodies to equable or mean time.

EQUA'TOR, S. [æquator, Lat.] a great circle of the terreftrial fphere, called the equinoctial on the celeftial, whofe poles are the poles of the world. It divides the globe into two equal parts, called the northern and fouthern hemifpheres; paffes through the E. and W. points of the horizon, and at the meridian is raifed above the horizon, as many degrees as the complement of the latitude of any given place. Whenever the fun comes to this circle, the days and nights are equal all round the globe.

EQUATO'RIAL, Adj. belonging to the equator.

EQUE'STRIAN, Adj. [equeftris, Lat.] appearing on horfeback. Skilled in horfemanfhip.

EQUERRY, S [ecurie, Fr. from equus, Lat.] a mafter of the horfe.

EQUIDI'STANT, Adj. [from æquus, Lat. and diftans, Lat.] at an equal diftance.

EQUIFOR'MITY, S. [æquus, Lat. and forma, Lat.] equality, or uniformity.

EQUILA'TERAL, Adj. [æquus, Lat. and latus, Lat.] having its fides equal.

To EQUIPO'NDRATE, V. A. [from æquus, Lat. and libratus] to balance equally.

EQUILIBRA'TION, S. equipoife. The act of balancing equally.

EQUILI'BRIUM, S. [Lat.] equipoife. Equality of weight, Equality of evidence.

EQUINO'CTIAL, Adj. [from æquus, Lat. equal, and nox, Lat. night] a great circle on the celeftial globe, to which, when the fun comes, the days and nights are equal all round the globe.

EQUINO'CTIAL, [Adj. from æquinox] pertaining to the equinox; happening about the time of the equinoxes.

E'QUINOX, S. [æquus, Lat. equal, and nox, Lat. night] In Aftronomy, the time when the fun enters the equinoctial points Aries or Libra, the former being the 31ft of March, is called the vernal equinox, and the latter on the 23d of September, the autumnal equinox. Figuratively, an equal meafure. "'Tis to his virtue a juft equinox." Shak.

To EQUIP, V. A. [equipper, Fr.] to furnifh a horfeman with riding furniture. Figuratively, to furnifh, accoutre, or drefs out.

E'QUIPAGE, S. [Fr.] furniture for a horfe. A carriage. "Harnefs'd at hand—celeftial equipage!" Par. Loft. A fet of China. "Tea equipage." Attendants or retinue. Furniture, accoutrements.

EQUIPE'NDENCY, S. [æquus, Lat. and pendeo, Lat.] freedom from any bias.

EQUIPMENT, S. the act of accoutering. The accoutrement or equipage.

EQUIPOISE, S. [from æquus, Lat. and poids, Fr.] equality of weight; equality of force. That ftate of a balance, when neither fcale will defcend.

EQUIPO'NDERANCE, EQUIPO'NDERANCY, S. [æquus, Lat. and ponderous, Lat.] equality of weight.

EQUIPO'NDRANT, Adj. [æquus, Lat. and ponderans, Lat.] being of equal weight.

EQUITABLE, Adj. [equitable, Fr.] juft; impartial; mitigating, or foftening the rigour of a law, fo as to be confiftent with juftice.

EQUITABLY, Adv. confiftent with juftice and mercy.

EQUITY, S. [equité, Fr. æquitas, Lat.] juftice, or right; temperand and mitigated by a confideration of particular circumftances. A correction or abatement of the feverity of fome law. A temperament, which, without being unjuft, abates the rigour of the law. Impartiality.

EQUIVALENCE; EQUIVALENCY, S. [æquus, Lat. and valeo, Lat.] equality of power, ftrength, or worth.

EQUIVALENT, Adj. [from æquus, and valeo, Lat.] equal in value, force, importance, weight in meaning.

EQUIVALENT, S. a thing of the fame weight, power, dignity, or value.

EQUIVOCAL, Adj. [æquivocus, Lat.] having different fenfes or meanings Uncertain, doubtful. Equivocal generation, is the opinion of the production or plants without feed, or animals without parents; called by fome fpontaneous generation. The opinion is univerfally exploded.

EQUIVOCAL, S. a word of doubtful meaning. "Shall two or three wretched equivocals have the force to corrupt us?" *Dennis.*

EQUIVOCALLY, Adv. in a doubtful sense, applied to words. By spontaneous or irregular birth.

To EQUIVOCATE, V. A. *æquivocor,* Lat.] to use words of a doubtful meaning. To quibble.

EQUIVOCATION, S. [*æquivocatio,* Lat.] the using a term, which has a double signification in order to impose on; used in a bad sense. The using a word or phrase, which has two different significations; the one common, and obvious; the other more unusual and remote; the latter of which being understood by the speaker, and the former by the hearers, makes them conceive something different from each other. Of this kind is the word *sleepeth,* applied by Christ to Lazarus, *John* xi. which was understood in its literal signification by the disciples, but meant to imply death by Christ. This kind of equivocation, being no more than a figurative expression is allowed by moral divines to be lawful.

EQUIVOCATOR, S. one who uses terms or words in doubtful or double meaning.

E'RA, S. [*æra,* Lat.] an account of time reckoned from any particular period.

To ERADICATE, V. A. [*eradicatus,* Lat.] to pluck up by the root. Figuratively, to extirpate, or destroy.

ERADICATION, S. the act of pulling up by the roots. Extirpation, total destruction.

ERADICATIVE, Adj. [*eradicatus,* Lat.] that which cures radically; that which drives entirely away.

To E'RASE, V. A. [*raser,* Fr. *erasus,* Lat.] to blot or scratch out any thing written. To expunge.

ERASEMENT, S. entire destruction and demolition. Applied to writings, an entire blotting, expunging, or scratching out.

ERE, Adv. [*ær,* Sax. *ær,* Goth. *er,* Belg.] prior to before, sooner than. "Ere yet the pine descended to the seas." *Dryd.*

To ERECT, V. A. [*erectus,* of *erigo,* Lat.] to raise or place perpendicular to the horizon; la Geometry, to erect a perpendicular, is to raise a right line upon another, so as they may form right angles. Figuratively, to build, applied to houses. To establish a new, to found, applied to government, or societies.

ERECT, Adj. [*erectus,* Lat.] upright, or not leaning. Lifted upwards.

ERECTION, S. [*erectio,* Lat. Vitruv.] the act of raising, or the state of a thing raised. The act of building houses. Establishment, settlement, or founding, applied to society. Elevation or exaltation of sentiments and ideas, applied to the mind.

ERECTNESS, S. uprightness of posture; form, or figure.

ERINGO, [*eryngium,* Lat.] in Botany, called likewise the sea holly. Linnæus ranges it in the 2d sect. of his fifth class.

ERMINE, S. [*armins,* Lat. from Armenia, the place whence it is brought] in Natural History, an animal found in close countries, which nearly resembles the weasel in shape; having a white pile and the tip of its tail black, and furnishing a choice and valuable fur. In Heraldry, a white field or fur interspersed with black spots.

ERMINED, Adj. richly attired, clothed in ermine. "In ermin'd pride." *Pope.*

EROSION, S. [*erosio,* Lat.] the act of eating away, or corroding. The state of being eaten away or corroded.

To ERR, V. A. [*erro,* Lat. *errer,* Fr.] to wander. To stray, or miss the right way. "We have erred and strayed from thy ways like lost sheep." *Com. Prayer.* Figuratively, to commit an error, mistake or fault.

ERRAND, S. [*ærend,* Sax.] a message; something to be done or said by a person sent to another.

ERRABLE, Adj. [from *err*] liable to error, liable to mistake.

ERRABLENESS, S. liableness to error or mistake.

ERRANT, Adj. [Fr. *errans,* Lat.] wandering; roving, rambling; applied to an order of knights celebrated in romances, who went about in search of adventures. Vile; abandoned; entire or finished. "An errant fool." *Johnson.*

ERRANTRY, S. the condition of a wanderer. The profession of a knight-errant.

ERRATA, S. [plural of *erratum,* Lat.] the faults of the printer; inserted generally in the beginning of a book.

ERRATIC, Adj. [*erraticus,* Lat.] irregular; changeable.

ERRONEOUS, Adj. [from *erroneus,* Lat.] wandering. Irregular, or leaving the right road. Mistaken, faulty, false.

ERRONEOUSLY, Adv. in such a manner as to err, or mistake.

ERROR, S. [*error,* Fr. *error,* Lat.] a mistake. An act which implies the taking a thing to be what it is not. A blunder. A roving excursion, a wandering. "Driven by the winds and errors of the sea." *Dryden.* A writ of error, is that which is brought to have a new trial, or to reverse a false judgment.

ERST, Adj. [*ræst,* Teut. *ærist,* Sax.] at first. "Seem'd erst so lavish and profuse." *Milton.* Formerly; till now. Used at present in poetry, but disused in prose.

ERUBESCENT, Adj. [*erubescens,* Lat.] growing red; somewhat red; inclining to red; reddish; blushing.

ERUDITION, S. [*eruditio,* Lat.] learning

ing, or knowledge acquired from reading, or ſtudy.

FERUGINOUS, Adj. [_ferruginulus_, Lat.] partaking of the qualities of copper.

ERUPTION, S. [_eruptio_, Lat.] the act of burſting from any confinement. A burſt of combuſtible matter or gunpowder. A ſudden excurſion of an enemy. A violent exclamation. A breaking out of puſtules or pimples on the ſkin.

ERUPTIVE, Adj. burſting from an incloſure or confinement. "The ſudden planre--appears far ſouth _eruptive_ through the cloud." _Thompſon._ Having puſtules or pimples.

ERYSIPELAS, S. [_nuʒtoʒʒac_, Gr.] In Medicine, a diſorder, generated by hot ſerum in the blood, the ſuperficies of the ſkin with a ſhining pale red, generally called St. Anthony's fire.

ESCALADE, S. [Fr.] a furious attack of a wall or fort, by means of ſcaling ladders.

ESCALOP, S. [_eſcalpe_, Fr.] a fiſh whoſe ſhell is ſomewhat of the cockle kind, but rather flatter and conſiderably longer, and larger, and is irregularly indented.

To ESCALOP, V. A. In Cookery, to ſtew in the ſhell of a eicalop fiſh. To cut or form the edge of a thing in waves, like thoſe of an eicalop ſhell See SCALLOP, which is the more common, but the leaſt proper way of ſpelling.

To ESCAPE, V. A. [_eſchapper_, Fr.] to avoid or fly from any inconvenience. To paſs unobſerved. Neuterly, to get free from danger.

ESCAPE, S. Flight from danger, or confinement. Subterfuge or evaſion. A miſtake owing to a perſon's want of care or attention. In Law, an evaſion from ſome lawful reſtraint, confinement.

ESCARGATOIRE, S. [Fr.] a ſquare place boarded in and fixed with a vaſt quantity of large ſnails, which in ſome foreign countries are eſteemed excellent food, when well dreſſed. "At the Capuchins I ſaw _eſcargatoire_." _Addiſ._

ESCHALOT, S. [Fr. pronounced _ſhallot_] a plant having a tunicated bulbous root, like that of an onion. They give an excellent reliſh to moſt ſauces.

ESCHEAT, S. [_eſcheir_, Fr.] In Law, any lands, &c. that fall to a lord of the manor by forfeiture, or the death of his tenant without heir general or eſpecial. The place in which the king or other lord has eſcheats of his tenants.

To ESCHEAT, V. A. In Law, to fall to the king or lord of the manor by forfeiture or for want of heirs.

ESCHEATOR, S. in Law, an officer that takes notice of the eſcheats of the king and certifies them to the Exchequer.

To ESCHEW, V. A. (pronounced _eſchew_ from _eſchewir_, old Fr.) to fly, avoid,

ſhun or decline. "Univerſally in practice the one and _eſchews_ the other." _Atterb._ Almoſt obſolete.

ESCORT, S. [Fr.] a company of ſoldiers, or fleet of ſhips of war, attending whom to keep them from being taken by the enemy.

To ESCORT, V. A. [_eſcorter_, Fr.] to guard or convoy by ſea or land, with an armed force.

ESCRITOIR, S. [Fr.] a kind of bureau, or cheſt of drawers, the top of which is furniſhed with a deſk for writing.

ESCULENT, Adj. [_eſculentus_, Lat.] eatable; in Botany, applied to ſuch plants or roots as may be eaten.

ESCULENT, S. ſomething proper or fit for food. "When the fruit is _eſculent_." _Bacon._

ESCUTCHEON, S. (from _ſcutum_, Lat.) in Heraldry, the ſhield or coat wherein the bearing or arms of any perſon is painted. It is of a ſquare figure excepting the bottom, the angles of which are a little rounded, and the middle of the lowermoſt line waved and ending in a point. "Till within a few hundred years the eſcutcheons of the Engliſh and French were triangular; thoſe of the Spaniards are ſtill quite round, without any point at the bottom, and thoſe of the Italians oval. Anciently they were couched or inclined, and were not placed erect or upright till crowns were ſet over them for creſts. An _eſcutcheon of pretence_ is a ſmall one which a man, who has married an heireſs, may bear with her arms over his own; and the ſurviving iſſue may bear both arms quarterly.

ESCURIAL, a famous village of Spain, in New-Caſtile, where Philip II. built a famous monaſtery in 1563, in memory of the victory gained over the French near St. Quintin; it is called by the Spaniards the eighth wonder of the world. It conſiſts of a royal palace, a church, cloiſters, a college, a library, the ſhops of different artiſts, apartments for a great number of people, beautiful walks, large allies, an extenſive park, and great gardens, adorned with a vaſt number of fountains. It is built in a dry, barren country, ſurrounded with rugged mountains, and where nothing grows, but what is cultivated with extraordinary care. It is built with grey ſtones, which were found in the neighbourhood, and is the principal reaſon of its being erected on ſo diſagreeable a ſpot. They worked at this ſtructure twenty-two years, and it coſt 6,000,000 of crowns; ſome ſay the expence was 20,000,000, but then they muſt mean French livres. It is a long ſquare of 580 feet, and four ſtories high; they reckon 800 pillars, 11,000 ſquare windows, and 14000 gates. The moſt remarkable part is the vaulted chapel, wherein is a magnificent ſepulchre, called the Pantheon, becauſe it is built in imitation of that church at Rome; it is the burying-place

place of all the kings and queens of Spain, and is thought by some to be the most curious piece of architecture in the world. The fathers, which belong to the monastery, are 200 in number, and have an income of 40,000 ducats a-year, which is sufficient to maintain them in great plenty. The church is built after the model of St. Peter's at Rome. It was taken by the allies in 1706, and is seated on the river Guadara, 15 miles N W. of Madrid, and 25 S. of Segovia. Lon 14. 0. Lat. 40. 3t.

ESPALIER, S. [espalier, Fr. spalliera, Ital.] in Gardening, rows of trees planted round a garden, and trained up flat to a close hedge, for the defence of tender plants, or the security of fruit trees against violence and injury of wind and weather; generally applied to hedges of fruit-trees which are trained up regularly to a lattice work of wood, formed of ash poles, or square long timbers of fir, &c. The trees chiefly planted for espaliers, are apples, and pears.

ESPECIAL, Adj. [specialis, Lat.] principal, chief; eminently serviceable, instrumental.

ESPECIALLY, Adv. in an extraordinary manner; principally; chiefly; above all others; particularly

ESPLANADE, S. [Fr.] in Fortification, the empty space between the glacis of a citadel, and the first houses of a town.

ESPOUSALS, S. [epous, Fr. sponsalia, Lat.] the act of affiancing a man and woman to each other; the ceremony of betrothing. Figuratively, a wedding.

ESPOUSAL, Adj. belonging to the ceremony of betrothing. "Espousal sheets." Bacon.

To ESPOUSE, V. A. [espouser Fr.] to contract a marriage, to betroth, used with to To marry. To defend or maintain an opinion, cause, party, or person.

To ESPY, V. A. [espier, Fr.] to see at a distance. To discover a thing intended to be concealed. To see unexpectedly. To discover. Neuterly, to watch; to take notice; to look about.

ESQUIRE, S. [pronounced squire, esquire, Fr.] the arm-or-bearer, or attendant upon a knight. A title of dignity next to that of knight Every knight was anciently served by two of them, who carried his helmet and buckler, holding lands of him in escuage. At first the name was a name of office only. This title is now given to all the sons of noblemen and their heirs male for ever; the four esquires of the king's body; the eldest sons of baronets, and of the knights of the Bath, and their heirs in the right line; to those who serve the king in any respectable employment. The chief of some families enjoy this title by prescription, those that bear any superior office in the commonwealth, as high sheriff of any county, justice of the

peace, barristers, and those who bear a commission.

To ESSAY, V. A. [essayer, Fr.] to attempt, try, strive, or endeavour. To try the purity of metals. "The standard of our Mint being now settled, the methods of essaying suitable to it, &c." Locke. This latter sense is now spelt, ASSAY.

ESSAY, S. [pronounced indifferently on either syllable] an attempt, endeavour, or trial A loose sally of the mind, a piece wherein the thoughts are set down as they occur without any regard to method.

ESSENCE, S. [Fr. essentia, Lat.] In Logic, the very nature of any being That which constitutes the nature of a thing. Figuratively, being, or a person which has existence. "Heavenly essence." Par. Lost. In Chemistry, the virtues extracted from any simple, reduced to a narrow compass. A perfume, or odour. "Nor let th' imprison'd essences exhale." Pope.

To ESSENCE, V. A. to scent with any essence or perfume. "The husband rally'd—at essenced fop." Spect. N°. 182.

ESSENTIAL, Adj. [essentiel, Fr. of essentialis, Lat.] necessary to the existence of a thing. Important in the highest degree. Containing all the best, refined and most elaborated parts material.

ESSENTIAL, S. being or essence. "Reduce—to nothing this essential." Par. Lost. Nature; a chief or principal point.

ESSENTIALLY, Adv. [essentialiter, low Lat.] naturally, or by the constitution of nature, materially.

ESSEX, S. an English county, 44 miles in length, and 42 in breadth, bounded on the S by the river Thames, on the W. by Hertfordshire and Middlesex, on the N. by Cambridge and Suffolk, and on the E. by the sea. It contains 34,300 houses, 208,000 inhabitants, 415 parishes, and 27 market-towns; the productions are corn, fish, fowls, cloth, stuffs, hops, oysters, and saffron, which last is the best in the world. The rivers, besides the Thames, are, the Stour, the Lee, the Cohn, the Chelmer, the Crouch, and the Roden. The air in the inland parts is healthy, but in the marshes, near the sea, it produces agues, particularly in the hundreds. It sends 8 members to parliament, that is, 6 for Colchester, Harwich, and Maldan, and 2 for the county. The county-town is Chelmsford; but Colchester is the largest, and most famous.

ESSOIGN, or ESSOIEN, S. [essoin, Fr. an excuse] in law an excuse allowed for the absence of a person who is summoned to appear in a court of justice. The person who is excused.

To ESTABLISH, V. A. [etablir, Fr.] to settle firmly; to fix unalterably. To make firm, or ratify a law. To found, build, or place in such a manner, as not to be

be fubject to fall or move. "He hath
founded it upon the feas, and *established* it
upon the floods." Pfal. xxiv. 12. To make
a fettlement of an eftate on a perfon. To
entail. "We will *establish* our eftate —upon our eldeft Malcolm." Shak.

ESTA'BLISHMENT, S. [*establissement*,
Fr.] a confirmation, or ratification. A fettled form of management. A foundation,
fundamental principle, or fettled law. Income, fallary or penfion. "By gradually
leffening your *eſtabliſhment*." Gulliv. Trav.

ESTA'TE, S. [*eſtate*, Fr.] condition, circumftance, or rank of life. Fortune, generally applied to a perfon's poffeffions in
land. Rank or quality.

To ESTEEM, V. A. [*estimer*, Fr *æſtimo*,
Lat.] to fet a value on a thing. To prize;
to value; to regard; to refpect, or account.

ESTEE'M, S. the act of refpect paid to a
perfon. The value, refpect, or reputation
of a perfon or thing.

E'STIMABLE, Adj. [Fr.] valuable, to
be purchafed at a high price. Worthy of
honour, refpect, or efteem.

ESTIMABLENESS, S. that quality
which renders a thing worthy of efteem.

To E'STIMATE, V. A. [*æſtimatus* or
æſtimo, Lat.] to rate; to fix the value of a
thing; to judge of a thing. To calculate or
compute.

E'STIMATE, S. a calculation or computation. Value. Valuation. A judgment
formed from comparing things.

ESTIMA'TION, S. the affigning the
proper proportion of a thing. A calculation
or computation. Judgment, or opinion
formed on comparing. That degree of refpect
paid to a perfon from confidering their
merits.

E'STIMATIVE, Adj. having the power
of making a comparifon or calculation.

ESTIMA'TOR, S. a perfon, who from
confidering the nature of things, eftimates
their worth, preference, value, or importance.

To ESTRA'NGE, V. A. [*estranger*, Fr.]
to withdraw; to alienate, or divert a thing
from its original ufe. To change from kindnefs to indifference, applied to the affections.
To withdraw, or withho'd. "We muſt
endeavour to *eſtrange* our belief." Glanv.
Ufed with from.

ESTRA'NGEMENT, S. difufe. Removal, the act of confulting a thing with
indifference, which was once an object of ardent affection.

E'STUARY, S. [*eſtuarium*, Lat.] an arm
of the fea; the mouth of a lake or river,
communicating with the fea. A frith.

'ETC, a contraction of *et cetera*. Lat. fm-
plying, and fo on; and the like; and the
reſt; and fo forth.

To E'TCH, V. A. [*etizen*, Teut.] to engrave on copper with aqua fortis.

E'TCH, S. in hufbandry, a crop taken

off ground which is fallow. "When they
fow their etch crops." Mortim.

ETE'RNAL, Adj. [Fr. *æternus*, Lat.]
without beginning or end. Without beginning. Without ceafing to be; endlefs, immortal. Figuratively, perpetual, conſtant,
without interruption. "Fires *eternal* in thy
temples fhine." Dryd. That which has been
and always will be the fame. "*Eternal*
truths." Dryd.

ETE'RNAL, S. [*eternel*, Fr.] one of the
appellations of God, implying his exiftence
before all time. "The *Eternal* to prevent
fuch horrid fray." Par. Loft.

ETE'RNALIST, S. one who holds that
the world was not created, but exifted from
all eternity.

To ETE'RNALISE, V. A. to make eternal, immortal, or endlefs.

ETE'RNALLY, Adv. without beginning
or end. From eternity to eternity. Perpetually, conftantly. "Where writers gain
eternally refide." Addif.

ETE'RNITY, S. [*eternité*, Fr. *æternitas*,
Lat.] duration without beginning or end;
duration without beginning. It what the
fchoolmen call *eternity a parte ante*, and duration without end, what they imply by *æter-
nity a parte poſt*.

To ETE'RNIZE, V. A. [*eterniſer*, Fr.]
to render perpetual, or endlefs. To render
immortal.

E'THER, S. [*æther*, Lat. of *aither*, Gr.]
a thin fubtle matter, much finer than air,
which commences from the limits of our at-
mofphere, and poffeffes the whole heavenly
fpace.

ETHE'REAL, Adj. formed of ether.
Figuratively, heavenly.

ETHE'REOUS, Adj. [*æthereus*, Lat.]
formed of ether. Heavenly. "Of this
ethereous mould." Par. Loft.

E'THICAL, Adj. [*ethikos*, Gr.] moral;
treating on morality.

E'THICALLY, Adj. after the manner
of ethics, or moral philofophy.

E'THIC, Adj. [*ethikos*, Gr.] moral; containing precepts of morality.

E'THICS, S. [*ethica*, Gr.] that part of
philofophy which treats of our duty as members of fociety, or as men. Morality.

ETH'NIC, Adj. [*ethnikos*, Gr.] heathen,
pagan, not enlightened with the knowledge
of the true God.

E'THNICS, S. heathens, idolaters.

ETHOLO'GICAL, Adj. [from *ethos*, Gr.]
treating of morality.

E'TNA-MOUNT, the name of a volca-
no, now called Gibel by the inhabitants.
It is one of the moſt celebrated mountains in
Europe, and the higheſt in Sicily, feated in
the Val-di-Demona, 10 miles W. of Catania.
It is well cultivated all round the foot, and
is covered with vines on the S. fide; but on
the N. there is nothing but large foreſts.

3 F 2   As

As for the top, it is always covered with fnow, and yet it never ceafes to fmoke, and often fends forth flame. The embers, which are thrown out in fmall quantities ferve for manure to the adjacent lands, but a large torrent does a great deal of mifchief. There are new openings made, from time to time, with fuch a great noife, that the inhabitants are put into terrible frights. The greateft eruptions known of late, happened in the year 1536, 1544, 1566, 1579, 1669, and 1693; which laft was very terrible, and was attended with an earthquake which overturned the town of Catania, in a moment, and buried 18000 perfons in its ruins. This mountain is 63 miles in circumference at the foot.

ETYMOLO'GICAL, Adj. [from *etymo logy*] relating to the derivation of words.

ETYMO'LOGIST, S. one who fearches out the original, explains, or fhews the derivation of words.

ETYMOLOGY, S. [of *etymologia*, Lat. from *etymos*, and *logos*, Gr.] that part of grammar which treats of the derivation of words, and thereby arrives at their primary fignification. The derivation of a word; the analyfis of words.

E'TYMON, S. [Gr.] the original word from whence another is derived.

EVA'CUANT, S. [*evacuans*, Lat.] in medicine, a remedy to expel or carry off any ill prefent or redundant humours, by the proper outlets, or emunctories.

To EVA'CUATE, V. A. [*evacuo*, of *evacuo*, Lat.] to clear a thing of its contents. To throw out as noxious and offenfive. To avoid by ftool, or through any of the excretory paffages. To make void or annul. "It would not evacuate a marriage." *Bacon*. To quit, or withdraw from a place. "He never effectually evacuated Palestine." *South*.

EVACUA'TION, S. [*evacuatio*, Lat.] a difcharge, emiffion or difcharge. Abolition or annulling. The quitting of a country. A difcharge procured by medicines.

To EVA'DE, V. A. [*evado*, Lat.] to efcape, elude or avoid an artifice or ftratagem. To decline by fubterfuge. To efcape or elude by fophiftry. To efcape as imperceptible; to reconquer; he, or as too great or too much to be laid hold on, feized or withftand. Neuterly, to make an efcape, to flip away. To efcape by fubtilty, ftratagem, or fophiftry.

EVAGA'TION, S. [*evagatio*, Lat.] the wandering, or going aftray or out of line.

EVANE'SCENT, adj. [*evanescens*, Lat.] vanifhing; paffing fo as not to be perceived; vyinifhing.

EVANGE'LICAL, Adj. [*evangelique*, Fr. *evangelicus*, Lat.] agreeable to the gospel. According to the doctrines of Chriftianity as fet forth in the gospel.

EVANGELIST, S. [*euaggelistes*, Gr.] a writer of the gospel. One who propagates Chriftianity.

To EVANGELIZE, V. A. [*euangelizo*, Lat. *euaggelizo*, Gr.] to inftruct in the doctrines contained in the gospel. To convert to Chriftianity.

EVA'NID, Adj. [*evanidus*, Lat.] faint, weak, vanifhing or growing imperceptible.

EVA'PORABLE, Adj. [*evaporer*, Fr.] that which may be difperfed in fumes or vapours.

To EVA'PORATE, V. A. [*evaporo*, Lat.] to exhale or diffipate moifture in fumes, fteam and vapours. Neuterly, to fly away in vapours and fumes; to wafte infenfibly like a volatile fpirit.

EVAPORA'TION, S. [Fr. *evaporatio*, Lat.] the act of flying away in fumes and vapours. In Philofophy, the act of wafting the moifture of a body, or of diffipating it in fumes and vapours. In Pharmacy, an operation by which the aqueous and volatile parts are diffolved by fire in fteam, fo as to leave the remaining part ftronger and of a higher confiftence. Figuratively, a vent, or dich avenue.

EVA'SION, S. [Fr. *evasio*, [*m*. of *evado*, Lat.] a ftratagem, artifice or fophiftry, made ufe of as an excufe.

EVA'SIVE, Adj. practifing artifices, fophiftry, or ftratagems, to avoid coming to the point.

EVA'SIVELY, Adj. fo as to be guilty of foolifhly, quibbles, tricks, fubterfuges, or artifice in order to avoid a difficulty. A word of reproach.

EU'CHARIST, S. [from *eu*, and *xaris*] the act of giving thanks; applied by divines to fignify the thankful remembrance of the death of Chrift in the bleffed facrament, or Lord's fupper.

EUCHARI'STICAL, Adj. containing acts of thankfgiving. Relating to the Lord's fupper.

EVE, EVEN, S. [*aefen*, Sax.] the latter part of the day; the interval between broad light and darkness. The vigil, or fast to be obferved the day before a holiday. In this fenfe eve is only ufed; in the other, even or eve indifferently.

EVELYN, (JOHN) a learned writer of the 17th century; defcended from a very ancient and honourable family which flourifhed originally at a place called Evelyn, in the county of Salop. This name, originally written Avelian, or Ivelin, fignifies a liberd or hazel. He was born October 31, 1620, at Wotton in Surrey, a place which owed its little praife to his ancestors, who were all of them fond of planting. He was educated at the free fchool of Lewes in Suffex, from whence he was removed to Oxford, where he was entered in 1637, a gentleman commoner; having profecuted his ftudies here in logic and philofophy, he removed

4   to

to the Middle-Temple, London, where he continued till 1644, and then by leave obtained from under king Charles III's own hand, left England in quest of improvements abroad. The accuracy wherewith he examined every thing curious in architecture, in painting, antiquities, and natural philosophy, is scarcely conceivable to any but those who have perused his works, and his readers are always struck with satisfaction. When he returned home the noble fund of knowledge he had laid in abroad was disseminated for the benefit of his countrymen; but his life was not only that of a scholar, but likewise that of a politician; and he was not only an admirer of nature, but likewise a lover of his king and country; the prudent step he took to justify the character of Charles II. from the virulence of calumny, and the advances he made to colonel Morley, to render his restoration easy, are sufficient confirmations of his loyalty. The arduous employments he was engaged in during the reigns of Charles II. and his brother, and the manner in which he acquitted himself in the discharge of them, shewed that he wanted not abilities for public employs. And if we consider the high character he bore among the fellows of the Royal Society, the utility of all his treatises, which tended not only to the embellishing, but likewise the security of his country; we must even in these days own ourselves indebted to his pen. No man ever cultivated botany, all the branches of natural philosophy, the designing arts, architecture, engraving, painting, gardening and antiquities, with more assiduity, and with more success. The university of Oxford is indebted to his mediation for the Arundelian marbles, the learned editor of Cambden for the additions to the county of Surrey, and Mr. Houghton for great embellishments to his treatise on husbandry. He was not only master of several languages, but likewise a great improver of them. Though learned, he was humble, and ready to communicate his stores to any person. As he lived an ornament to our nation, so he died an example to all that succeed him; and as he spent a life of 86 years in the service of his Creator, so he took care that his death should not be without instruction, as appears from the inscription on his tombstone, which informs us, " That living in an age of extraordinary events and revolutions, he had learned from thence this truth, which he desired might be communicated to posterity — That all is vanity which is not honest, and that there is no solid Mazim but in real piety.

E'VEN, Adj. [efen, even, Sax. even, Belg.] smooth, not rugged; level. Not odd, expressive of being divided into equal parts, equal with another, or not exceeding, applied to number, and with us and to, &c. Calm, applied to the passions. Of the same height, used comparatively, and followed by with.

To E'VEN, V. A. to make the heighth of two things, or the quantity of two numbers the same. To make level, applied to surface, joined to with. Neuterly, to become even.

E'VEN, Adv. [contracted in Poetry to e'en, or e'e] equal to. Even though, notwithstanding. When used as an heightening phrase, it implies a tacit comparison, which gives great force to the words immediately following. In common discourse, pronounced e'en, and used as a word of concession. " I shall e'en let it pass." Collier.

EVEN-HA'NDED, Adj. impartial, unbiassed, alluding to a balance whose scales hang even, when nothing is in either of them. " Even-handed justice." Shak.

E'VENING, S. [æfen, Sax. avend, Belg.] the close of the day; or that part which is somewhat light after sunset.

E'VENLY, Adv. equally; in the same manner; with the same force; uniformly. Levelly, applied to surface; without inclining to either side, parallel to the horizon, applied to posture or situation. In an impartial manner; or without favouring one person more than another. Without elation, or dejection, with equanimity, applied to the state of the mind. " He bore his virtues so evenly." Shak.

E'VENNESS, S. the being free from ruggedness; smoothness; levelness. That which is neither up one side or the other. Impartiality, freedom from bias. Calmness.

EVE'NT, S. [eventus, Lat.] an incident, action, any thing which happens. The result. The conclusion, or upshot.

EVE'NTFUL, Adj. full of incidents, or events.

EVE'NTUAL, Adj. happening, succeeding in consequence. Consequentially.

EVE'NTUALLY, Adv. in the event, result, or consequence. " Hermione was but intentionally, not eventually disobedient to you." Boyle.

E'VER, Adv. [æfre, Sax.] at any time, if ever. Before, or any time before, joined with then, at, or any comparative adverb. Always; for ever. At all times past, and to all time to come. To all eternity, when repeated it implies a stronger affirmation that the time or duration of a thing shall never end, " ever and ever." Followed by some, it implies frequently, or successively. " Ever and anon a silver ewer stole down." Dryd. Ever a, from ever ich, or every, implies any. " Better than I love e'er a scurvy young boy." Shak.

EVER-GREEN, Adj. green throughout the year.

EVER-GREEN, S. a plant which retains

tains its leaves and green colour through all the seasons.

EVERLASTING. Adj. enduring for ever. Immortal.

EVERLASTING. S. eternity, eternal duration, whether past or future. Likewise a cold woollen stuff, which receives its name from its supposed strength, or lasting, a property called.

EVERLASTINGLY. Adv. eternally; for ever. Without end.

EVERLASTINGNESS. S. eternity. A boundless or infinite duration.

EVERLIVING. Adj. having life without end. Immortal.

EVERMORE. Adv. always, according to Johnson, is an expletive accidentally added; but as in Greek, negatives added to negatives only increase their force; to more, which is a comparative adjective, being added to ever, is intended to increase its force, and to them a greater impossibility of ending, or a stronger affirmation of eternal duration] always; incessantly; eternally.

EVER-PLEASING. Adj. always giving or affording pleasure.

To EVERT. V. A. [everto, Lat.] to destroy or overthrow.

EVERY. Adj. [æfer, eulc, Sax.] each individual, each article. Every-where, in all places.

EVESDROPPER. S. one who gets under a window, to hearken and discover the secrets of a family.

To EVICT. V. A. [evictus, Lat.] in Law, to cast out of a possession, or to dispossess by due course of law; used with out, or from. To prove, or evince. "Its necessity evicted." Chapm.

EVICTION. S. dispossession by a sentence at law. Proof, evidence.

EVIDENCE. S. [Fr.] undoubted certainty. Testimony, proof. A person who is summoned to give testimony.

To EVIDENCE. V. A. to prove. To discover or testify.

EVIDENT. Adj. plain with respect to proof. Proved beyond doubt. Notorious.

EVIDENTLY. Adv. so as to appear plain, indubitable and clear.

EVIL. Adj. [yfel, yfel, Sax.] having bad qualities of any kind. Wicked, malicious, applied to morals. Figuratively, calamitous or miserable, applied to condition or circumstances. Mischievous, destructive; infernal "An evil spirit."

EVIL. S. natural evil, is that defect which arises from natural causes, without our own consent or knowledge. Moral evil is that inconvenience which arises from natural causes, by our own consent or choice. When applied to acting contrary to the revealed laws of the Deity, it is termed wickedness, or sin; applied to acting contrary to the laws of government, a crime; and applied

to acting contrary to the meer rule of fitness, a fault. Applied to the inconveniencies resulting from want of wealth or friends, it is termed calamity, or misery, but when to want of health, it is called a distemper, or disease; on the whole, evil is what is apt to produce or increase any pain, or diminish any pleasure in us; or else to procure us any inconvenience, or deprive us of any good.

EVIL. Adv. [contracted commonly into ill] in a manner inconsistent with virtue and innocence.

To EVINCE. V. A. [evinco, Lat.] to prove, make evident, or convince.

EVINCIBLE. Adj. capable of being proved, or made evident.

EVINCIBLY. Adv. so as to force assent or convince on.

EVITABLE. Adj. [evitabilis, Lat.] that which may be surmounted, or avoided.

To EVITATE. V. A. [evitatus, Lat. of evito to avoid, shun, or escape.

EULOGY. S [from eu, Gr. and λογος] a praise, commemoration, or panegyric. A discourse in praise of a person.

EUNUCH. S. [from eun, Gr. and ευη] one who has been castrated. Figuratively, a chief officer of the houshold of an eastern monarch, such persons only being suffered to attend.

To EUNUCHATE. V. A. to castrate, or make an eunuch.

EVOCATION. S. [evocatio, Lat.] the act of calling out. "An evocation, of the dead from hell." Pope. Used with from.

To EVOLVE. V. A. [evolvo, Lat.] to unroll; to unfold, or disentangle. Neuterly, to open or disclose itself.

EVOLVENT. S. [evolvens, Lat] in Geometry, a curve, which results from the evolution of a curve.

EVOLUTION. S. [evolutus, Lat.] the act of unrolling, or unfolding. In Geometry, the opening or unfolding of a curve or circle. In Algebra, the extraction of roots from any given power. The divers figures, turns, and motions made by a body of soldiers, either in ranging themselves in form of battle, or in changing their form; whether by way of exercise, or during an engagement.

EUPHONY. S. [from eu, Gr. and φωνη] in Grammar, an easiness, smoothness, and elegancy of pronunciation. An agreeable found. A figure, whereby we omit a harsher letter or substitute a smoother in its place for the sake of pronunciation.

EUPHRASY. S [euphrasia, Lat.] In Botany, the herb called eyebright from its supposed virtue in clearing the sight; it grows naturally in commons and fields, always among grass, heath, and furs, &c. "Purged with euphrasy and rue.—the visual nerve." Par. Lost.

EUROPE, called by the people of Asia, Frankistan, is one of the three general parts

parts of our continent, and one of the four of the habitable world. It is bounded on the N. by the frozen, or icy sea, on the S. by the Mediterranean, on the W. by the western, and northern ocean, and on the E. by Asia. It lies between 8 and 90 degrees of longitude, and between 35 and 72 degrees of latitude, though it does not fill up all that space. From cape St. Vincent to the mouth of the river Oby, it is near 3600 miles in length; and from cape Matapam, in the Morea, to the N. cape in Lapland, it is about 2100 miles in breadth. It is much less than either Asia or Africa; but then it surpasses them in many things, and it is entirely within the temperate zone, except a small part of Norway and Muscovy; so that there is neither the excessive heat, nor the insupportable cold, that are to be met with in the other parts of the continent. It does not abound in gold and silver mines, much less in precious stones; nor does it produce sugar and spices; nor yet does it nourish jackals, hyaenas, lynxes, leopards, tygers, lions, rhinoceroses, elephants, dromedaries, camels, or crocodiles; but it produces corn, wine, fruits, sheep, oxen, horses, and all other necessaries of life. Besides, it is much more populous, and better cultivated than either Asia or Africa. It is fuller of villages, towns and cities, and the buildings are more strong, more elegant and commodious, generally speaking, than in the two former. The inhabitants are all whites, and for the most part, much better made than the Africans, and even the Asiatics. With regard to arts and sciences, there is no manner of comparison; nor yet in trade, navigation, and war. They are more civilised, prudent, sociable and generous; and consequently are neither savage nor cruel, unless spurred on by the mistaken principles of religion. Whereas in Asia and Africa, there are people who make robbery a profession, and live by pillaging merchants and others. With respect to the division of Europe, it contains, Norway, Sweden, Denmark, Great-Britain and Ireland, Muscovy, France, Germany, Poland, Spain, Portugal, Hungary, Switzerland, and Turky in Europe, besides several small islands, in the Mediterranean and elsewhere. There are three empires; namely, of Germany, Muscovy, and Turk, which last is commonly called the Grand Seignior. The pope is an ecclesiastical prince, and yet has several territories under his dominion. The kings are those of great Britain and Ireland, France, Spain, Portugal, Poland, Prussia, Denmark, Sweden, Sardinia, Hungary, and of the two Sicilies. Besides there is an archduke of Austria, and a great duke of Tuscany. There are four considerable republics; namely, Venice, the State of Holland, the Swiss Cantons, and the republic of Geneva. There are four less, viz. of Geneva, Lucca, San Marino, and

Ragusa. The languages are, the Latin, of which the Italian, French, and Spanish, are dialects; the Teutonic, from which proceeds those of Germany, Flanders, Holland, Sweden, Denmark, and England; the Sclavonian, which reigns (though in disguise) in Poland, Muscovy, Bohemia, and a great part of Turky in Europe; the Celtic, of which there are dialects in Wales, the Highlands of Scotland, Ireland, Britagne in France, and Lapland. Besides these are the Greek, and several others. The principal rivers are the Danube, and the Rhyne in Germany; the Wolga and Dwina, in the Russian empire; the Loire in France; and the Severn and Thames, in England. The chief lakes are those of Constance in Germany; of Geneva, and Guarda, in Italy; the Weser, in Sweden; and of Ladoga and Onega, in Russia. The chief mountains are the Pyreneans, in Spain; the Alps in Italy; the Dofrin hills in Sweden; the Crapach hills in Hungary; and some of the mountains in Wales. The religions of Europe, are the Jewish, and the Christian, as also the Mahometan.

EUROPE'AN, Adj. (of *Europe*, *Europaeus*, Lat. some accent it on the second syllable, but the authority of all the great poets are against them) belonging to, or a native of Europe.

EU'RUS, S. [Lat.] the east wind.

EUTHANA'SIA, EUTHANASY, S. [Gr. from εὖ Gr. and θάνατος] an easy pleasant death. " The kindred wish of my friends is *euthanasia*." *Arbuth.*

EVUL'SION, S. (*evulsio*, Lat.) the act of plucking off. " The *evulsion*, or biting off any parts." *Brown.*

EWE, S. [*ewu*, Sax.] a female sheep.

EW'ER, S. [from *eau*, Fr. water, supposed by Dr. T. H. Skinner, and Johnson, to have been formerly written *ew*] a bason, or vessel in which water is put for washing the hands. Obsolete, unless in poetry.

To EXAC'ERBATE, V. A. (*exacerbatus*, of *exacerbo*, Lat.) to make rougher, to exasperate, or heighten any disagreeable quality.

EXACT', Adj. (Fr. *exactus*, Lat.) methodical, applied to the manner of transacting business. Accurate in reckoning. Honest, punctual, and strictly conforming to the rule of right.

To EXAC'T, V. A. (*exactus* of *exigo*, Lat.) to demand with rigour and authority. To demand as due. To enjoin, or insist upon. Neuterly, to be guilty of extortion. Used with *upon* before the person who is the object of extortion.

EXAC'TER, S. one that claims more than his due; or demands his due, with outrage and rigour. One who obliges a person to perform a duty by authority. One who is rigid in his demands or orders.

EXAC'TION, S. the act of making a demand with authority. Extortion. A toll;

a heavy tax. " Pay an unreasonable *exation* at every ferry." *Addi.*

EXA'CTLY, Adv. accurately; perfectly. With great nicety.

EXA'CTNESS, S. a conduct regulated with the greatest strictness according to some rule.

To EXA'GGERATE, V. A. [*exaggero*, *exaggeratus*, Lat. of *ex* *gero*.] to heighten by description. To represent things to be worse or better than they really are.

EXAGGERA'TION, S. the act of heaping together. " The *exaggeration* of sand." *Hale.* A representation, wherein the good, or ill qualities of a thing or person are heightened.

To EXA'GITATE, V. A. [*exagitatus*, Lat. of *exagito*, Lat.] to put in motion. " The warm air of the blood *exagitates* the blood." *Arbuth.* To reproach, to inveigh against. " I had rather lament than *exagitate*." *Healer.*

To EXA'LT, V. A. [*exalter*, Fr. from *altus*, Lat.] to lift upwards. To place on high. Figuratively, to prefer, or raise to power, wealth, or dignity. To elate with joy. To magnify with praise. To raise or make louder, applied to the voice. In Chemistry, to sublime, refine or heighten the qualities of a thing by fire. To raise or elevate the ideas or expressions of a composition. In Scripture, followed by *against*, to oppose, or set one's self in opposition. " Against whom thou hast *exalted* thy voice." 2 Kings xix. 22.

EXALTA'TION, S. the act of placing on high. Preferment, advancement, applied to power, wealth or dignity. A state of grandeur or dignity.

EXA'MEN, S. [Lat.] an exact search or enquiry, to discover the truth or falsehood of a thing.

EXAMINA'TION, S. [*examinatio*, Lat.] a search into the truth of any fact. An accurate, exact, nice, and scrupulous enquiry, after truth.

EXAMINA'TOR, S. [Lat.] an examiner; one that searches into the reality of any truth or fact.

To EXA'MINE, V. A. [*examino*, Fr. *examin*, Lat.] to try. To ask a criminal or witness questions on a trial, either to search into the truth of his evidence, or that of the fact which he is summoned to confirm or destroy. To make enquiry into; to try by experiment.

EXA'MINER, S. one who searches into the veracity of an evidence, by proposing such questions as shall be suitable to that purpose. In Chancery, applied to those, whose office it is to examine the evidences on oath produced on both sides, upon such interrogatories or questions as the parties to the suit exhibit for that purpose. Applied in the custom-house to the officer of a person, whose business is to

re-examine accounts brought in. One who searches, or makes enquiry into the nature, truth, or reality of things with care and diligence.

EXA'MPLE, S. [*exemple*, Fr. *exemplum*, Lat.] any thing proposed to be imitated. A precedent. A rule of conduct sought of the imitation of others. A person fit to be a pattern for others to imitate. A person punished in order to deter them from being guilty of the same crimes. An instance, or something produced as an illustration or confirmation of what has been asserted.

EXA'NIMATE, Adj. [*exanimatus*, Lat.] deprived of life. Figuratively, spiritless, dejected. " Exanimate by love." *Thomp.*

EXANIMA'TION, S. death; loss of life.

EXANTHE'MATOUS, Adj. in Medicine, pustulous, eruptive; efflorescent; discolouring, or forming pustules on the skin.

EXARTICULA'TION, S. [from *ex* and *articulus*, Lat. a joint] dislocation, or the putting a bone out of joint.

To EXA'SPERATE, V. A. [*exasperatus*, Lat. of *exaspero*, Lat.] to provoke a person to anger. To aggravate a difference.

EXASPERA'TION, S. great provocation. A provocation which excites to violent anger or rage.

To EXAUCTORATE, V. A. [*exauctoratus*, of *exauctoro*, Lat.] to dismiss or discharge from an employment. To turn out or deprive of a benefice. " Deposition, degradation, or *exauctoration*, is nothing else but the removing a person from some dignity or order in the church." *Ayliffe.*

To EXCAVATE, V. A. [*excavatus*, Lat. of *excavo*, Lat.] to hollow, or make hollow.

EXCAVA'TION, S. the act of scooping out. A hollow, or cavity.

To EXCEE'D, V. A. [*exceder*, Fr. *excedo*, Lat.] to go beyond any limit, measure, or standard. To excell, or surpass. Neuterly, to go too far; to be guilty of excess. To go beyond any limits, or number.

EXCEE'DING, Part. surpassing, excelling, or going beyond. Sometimes used adverbially, for a very great or remarkable degree. " Exceeding handsome."

EXCEE'DINGLY, Adv. to a very great degree.

To EXCE'L, V. A. [*exceller*, Fr. *excello*, Lat.] to surpass, or have good qualities to a greater or higher degree than another.

EXCELLENCE, EXCELLENCY, S. [*excellence*, Fr. *excellentia*, Lat.] the state of abounding in any good quality. The possessing any good quality to a greater degree than another. That in which one person has the advantage of, or surpasses another. Purity, goodness. A title of honour usually given

given to generals, ambassadors, and governors.

EX'CELLENT, Adj. [Fr. *excellent*, Lat.] possessed of great talents or virtues. Eminent, good, virtuous.

EX'CELLENTLY, Adv. extremely well. To an eminent or remarkable degree.

To EXCEPT, V. A. [*excepter*, Fr.] to leave out. Neuterly, to object to. "Which our author could not *except against*." Lacke.

EXCEPT, Prep. [though marked here, and generally taken as a preposition or conjunction, Johnson asserts that this word is indubitably a participle passive, which, like most others, had two terminations, being written both *except* and *excepted*; thus, "All *except* one, is all, one being excepted." But adds our author, with greater shew of probability, the word may be, according to the Teutonic idiom, a verb of the imperative mood, and then, "All *except* one, will signify, all but one, which I would have you, or which you must *except*"] Excluding, not including, "God and his Son *except* none he feared." Par. Loft. Unless, "Except we know it." Tillof.

EXCEPTING, Part. [this word is marked as a preposition by Johnson, but our reasons for not following him may be seen in the word *except*] not including.

EXCEPTION, S. [*exception*, Fr.] exclusion; used properly with *from*, before the rule or law to which the exception refers; but by some great authors used with *to*. "An *exception to* some." Addif. "In *exception to* all general rules." Pope. The thing mentioned in an *exception*. An objection, or cavil, used with *against* or *to*. A dislike, or offence, when following take. "He first took *exception* at this badge." Shak.

EXCE'PTIONABLE, Adj. liable to objection, or exception.

EXCE'PTIOUS, Adj. fond of making objections. Peevish.

EXCE'PTIVE, Adj. including an exception, or objection.

EXCE'PTOR, S. one who makes exceptions.

EXCE'SS, S [*excès*, Fr. *excessus*, Lat.] that which exceeds the bounds of moderation. Applied to passion, a height or violence beyond the bounds of reason. The transgressing the bounds of reason, wisdom, or prudence. Intemperance, or too great an indulgence in meat or drink. That quantity or number in which things surpass, or are more than others.

EXCE'SSIVE, Adj. [*excessif*, *excessive*, Fr.] beyond, or exceeding any limits. Vehement, or beyond the just bounds or measures prescribed by reason, applied to the affections of the mind, or the practice of virtue.

EXCE'SSIVELY, Adv. in a great or immoderate degree.

No. XI.

To EXCHA'NGE, V. A. [*changer*, Fr.] to give one thing for another. To give and take reciprocally, used with *for* before the thing changed, and *with* before the person consenting to the change.

EXCHA'NGE, S. the act of giving one thing for another. In Commerce, the doing of the actual and momentary value of money between different countries. The thing given or received in lieu of another. The place, or spot where merchants meet to negotiate their affairs. A bill of exchange, is that which is drawn by a person at a distance, for such a sum as is equivalent to a sum paid or estimated here, this article is of so great importance both to the mercantile world, and the kingdom in general, that an exact knowledge of it may bring immense riches to the one, and turn the balance of trade in favour of the latter.

EXCHE'QUER, S [*escheqnier*, Norm. Fr.] the court to which all the revenues of the crown are brought.

EXCI'SE, S. [*accijs*, Belg. *excisum*, Lat.] a tax laid by the government on commodities for supporting and answering the exigencies of the state. If this tax were levied only on the luxuries of life, or laid on such things in time of war, that it must necessarily cease in time of peace, it would be of little disservice to the price of labour, and increase of commerce, the two essentials of his island, besides shewing an uncommon skill and penetration in this or any future administration.

To EXCI'SE, V. A. to levy a tax.

EXCI'SEMAN, S. an officer employed in the inspection of goods which are exciseable, and in collecting the excise.

EXCI'SION, S. [*excisio*, Lat.] the act of cutting off, or entirely destroying.

EXCITA'TION, S [Fr. from *excitatus*, Lat.] the act of putting into motion. The act of rousing.

To EXCI'TE, V. A. [*exciter*, Fr. *excito*, Lat.] to rouse from a state of inactivity, to action; or from a state of dejection and despair, to one of courage and vigour. To put into motion; to awaken; to rouse.

EXCI'TEMENT, S. the motion by which a person is excited, or roused from a state of indolent inactivity.

EXCI'TER, S one who stirs up to action. The cause by which any thing is put into motion.

To EXCLAI'M, V. N. [*exclamo*, Lat.] to cry out with vehemence. To speak against, decry, or reproach with outrage; used with *against*.

EXCLA'IM, S. an outcry, clamour, or lamentable elevation of voice. "Gloster's blood doth more solicit me than examine." Shak. Not in use.

EXCLA'IMER, S. a person that makes use of frequent exclamations. One that runs

     U   down

down and rolls against a person or thing. "I must tell the passionate exclaimer." *Attert.*

EXCLAMA'TION, S. [Fr. of *exclamatio*, Lat.] a vehement outcry. A calling reproach of a person or thing. An emphatical utterance. A figure in rhetoric, wherein by raising the voice, and using an interjection, either expressed or understood, we testify an uncommon warmth and passion of the mind. In Grammar, a point placed after an exclamation, marked thus!

EXCLAMATORY, Adj. consisting of exclamation.

To EXCLU'DE, V. A. [*excludo*, Lat.] to shut out. To debar of any privilege. To except to any doctrine. To deny a person a right or enjoyment in any grant.

EXCLU'SION, S. [Fr.] the act of shutting out, or denying admission. Rejection. An exception.

EXCLU'SIVE, Adj. [*exclusif*, *exclusive*, Fr. from *exclusus*, Lat.] having the power to deny entrance, or admission. Debarring from the enjoyment of a right, privilege, or grant. Excepting.

EXCLU'SIVELY, Adv. without being admitted to enjoy a privilege, or right with another. Without comprehending or including.

To EXCO'GITATE, V. A. [*excogito*, Lat.] to find out by thought, or intense thinking. To invent. "Exc gitated by the heathen." *Blair.*

To EXCOMMU'NICATE, V. A. [*excommunico*, low Lat.] to exclude a person from having any fellowship with a visible church, and particularly from partaking of the Sacrament of the Lord's Supper.

EXCOMMUNICA'TION, S. [Fr.] an ecclesiastical censure, whereby a person is deprived the privileges of a church, or from communicating at the blessed Sacrament. This is founded on the natural right all societies have of excluding such members as violate their laws, and consequently sap their very essentials. It is invested in the bishop of the diocese to which the person to be excommunicated belongs, and is divided into major, i. e. greater, or minor, i. e. less. The major is that whereby a person is cut off from all society with other Christians, becomes an outlaw, is disabled from defending his rights, by bringing an action in a court of justice, &c. The lesser excommunication only excludes a person from partaking of the Sacrament of the Lord's supper. The few instances, if not the total abuse of the power of excommunication in the established church of late years, is an amiable instance of the benevolence of its rulers, and should not only raise admiration and praise, but likewise conversion and amendment.

To EXCO'RIATE, V. A. [of *ex* Lat. and *corium.*] to flay or strip off the skin.

EXCORIA'TION, S. loss of skin; the act of flaying or stripping off the skin. Figuratively, plunder, pillage, or oppression of the poor.

EXCORTICA'TION, S. [from *ex* and *cortex*, Lat.] in botany, the pulling off the bark of trees.

EX'CREMENT, S. [Fr. of *excrementum*, Lat.] that which is discharged at the natural passage of the body.

EXCREME'NTAL, Adj. that which is of the nature of excrement.

EXCRE'SCENCE, EXCRE'SCENCY, S. [*excrescens*, Lat.] a superfluous part growing out of another, contrary to the common production of nature. In Surgery, superfluous, and luxuriant flesh.

EXCRE'SCENT, Adj. [Fr. *excrescens*, Lat.] superfluously or growing out of a thing.

EXCRE'TION, S. [*excretio*, Lat.] in Medicine, the act of separating excrements and excrementitious humours from the aliments or blood, and expelling them from the body.

EXCRE'TIVE, Adj. [*excretivus*, Lat.] having the power of separating or ejecting excrementitious humours from the body.

To EXCRU'CIATE, V. A. [*excrucio*, of *crucio*, Lat.] to torture or torment.

To EXCU'LPATE, V. A. [from *ex* and *culpatus*, Lat.] to clear from any accusation, or charge.

EXCULPA'TION, S. vindication of one charged with fault. An endeavour to vindicate a person.

EXCU'RSION, S. [Fr. *excursio*, Lat. of *excurso*, Lat.] a ramble. An expedition into distant parts. A progress beyond the common limits. A digression.

EXCU'RSIVE, rambling; wandering; straying.

EXCU'SABLE, Adj. [Fr.] that for which any apology may be admitted.

To EXCU'SE, V. A. [*excuser*, Fr. *excuso*, Lat.] to lessen guilt by assigning some reasons which may render the commission of a fault less blameable. To remit a debt or a duty. To pass by without blame; or by permitting an apology to be made. To make an apology, defence or vindication, in order to wipe off any aspersion.

EXCU'SE, S. an apology or plea. A reason alleged to justify some accusation or guilt. The act of passing by a fault without blame or notice.

EXCU'SELESS, Adj. without any motive or reason to expect excuse.

EXCU'SER, S. one who pleads for, or one who forgives another.

EXCU'SSION, S. [*excussio*, Lat.] the act of seizing. "It upon an estate there be not goods to satisfy." *Ayliffe.*

EX'ECRABLE, Adj. [Fr.] detestable, abominable, extremely wicked, very bad.

EXECRA-

EX'ECRABLY, Adv. detestably. Figuratively, abominably; hatefully.

To EX'ECRATE, V. A. [execratus of execror, Lat.] to curse, to detest, to despise, to abominate.

EXECRA'TION, S. a curse; an imprecation or wishing some evil to befal a person.

To EX'ECUTE, V. A. [executer, Fr. executus, Lat.] to perform a commission or duty. To put any thing planned, in practice. To put to death according to law. Figuratively, to kill. "Whom with my bare fists I would execute." Shak.

EXECU'TION, S. the performance of a thing, Action. In Law, the last act in cause of debt, wherein power is given to the plaintiff of the defender's goods and body. Death inflicted by law. Death; slaughter. In Music, the manner of singing or performing a song. Effect.

EXECU'TIONER, S. he that inflicts punishment on an offender. That by which any thing is performed.

EXECU'TIVE, Adj. having the quality of executing. Active, or putting into execution, opposed to deliberative or legislative.

EXECU'TER, S. he that performs or executes a design. A person who inflicts the punishment sentenced by the law. "Deliver over to executers." Shak.

EXECU'TOR, S. a person who is nominated by the will of a testator, to perform the articles contained in his will.

EXECU'TORSHIP, S. the office of a person appointed executor.

EXECU'TRIX, S. a woman intrusted with the performance of a testator's will.

EXEGE'TICAL, Adj. [exegetes, Gr.] explaining. By way of explanation.

EXE'MPLAR, S. [Lat.] a model, pattern or original to be imitated, or copied.

EXE'MPLARILY, Adv. so as to deserve imitation. So as to warn or deter others, applied to punishment.

EXE'MPLARINESS, S. the state of being proposed as a pattern worthy of imitation.

EXE'MPLARY, Adj. worthy of being proposed as a pattern for the imitation of others. Such as may give warning to others. Remarkable.

To EXE'MPLIFY, V. A. to illustrate or explain. In law, to copy or transcribe.

To EXE'MPT, V. A. [exemptus, Lat.] brought off; to free from any obligation, tax or duty. To privilege.

EXE'MPT, Adj. freed from service, office, obligation, duty or tax. Not liable to. Cut off from. "Exempt from ancient gentry." Shak. The last sense is obsolete.

EXE'MPTION, S. [from ex and emptio, Lat.] freedom from any service, obligation, or tax.

To EXEN'TERATE, V. A. [exenteratus, Lat. of exentero] to take out the entrails or bowels of an animal. "Any that exenterate or dissects them." Brown. Seldom used.

EXE'QUIAL, Adj. [from exequiæ, Lat.] belonging to a funeral.

EXE'QUIES S. [it has no singular, from exequiæ, Lat. Johnson observes that exequies is often used in its stead, but not so properly, and if we attend to the ideas which the Romans seem to have assured to the word expriam his opinion is not at all improbable] funeral rites or ceremonies. "The tragical end of the two brothers, whose exequies." Dryd.

EXER'CENT, Adj. [exercent, Lat.] practising; following any trade, employment, or vocation.

EX'ERCISE, S. [exercise, Fr. exercitium, Lat.] a motion of the limbs or action of the body, considered as conducive and necessary to health. An action by which the body is formed to gracefulness and strength. Any practice by which a person is rendered skilful in the performance of a duty or discipline.

To EX'ERCISE, V. A. [exercise of exerceo, Fr. exerceo, Lat.] to use such action of the body as is necessary to keep the fluids in motion and preserve health. To train or teach a person by frequent practice. To task, employ, or keep busy. To practice. "To exercise dominion over them." Adam. xx. 25. Neuterly, to use such action as is conducive to health. To practice the different evolutions of an army.

EXER'CISER, S. one who acts, performs or practices.

EXERCITA'TION, S. [Fr. of exercitatio, Lat.] exercise; practice; repetition.

To EXE'RT, V. A. [exertus of exero, Lat.] to use with force, vehemence or vigour. To put forth or perform.

EXER'TION, S. the bringing into action, including the idea of force, vehemence, or strength.

EXE'TER, a town, or city, of Devonshire, with two markets, on Wednesdays and Fridays, and four fairs, viz. on Ash-Wednesday, Whit-Monday, August 1, and December 6, for horses, horned cattle, and commodities of all sorts. It is commodiously seated on the top of an easy ascent on the eastern bank of the river Ex, from whence it took its name, and over which there is a handsome stone-bridge. It is a mile and a half in circumference about the walls and ditches; and, with its suburbs, contains sixteen parish-churches, and four chapels of ease, besides the cathedral, it being a bishop's see. It suffered greatly in the civil wars; and its river is choaked up with sand, so that at present they are obliged to load and unload their goods at Topsham, about three miles distant. It has the title of an earldom,

dom, and is still in a flourishing condition, driving a good trade. Here are several streets well-paved, and a large manufactury of serges, druggets, long-ells, duroys, and saguthys. It is governed by a mayor, recorder, twenty-four aldermen, &c. and finds two members to parliament. It is seventy-eight miles S. : of Bristol, thirty-nine N. N. E. of Dartmouth, forty nine S. S. E. of Barnstaple, forty four N. E. of Plymouth, eighty-eight W. S. W. of Salisbury, and 173 W. by N. of London. Lon. 13. 35. lat. 50. 44.

To EXFO'LIATE, V. A. [of *ex* and *folium*, Lat.] in Surgery, to scale a bone.

EXFOLIAT'N, S. the act of scaling a bone, the state or condition of a bone which breaks off in scales.

EXFO'LIATIVE, Adj. that which has the power of scaling or producing exfoliation.

EXHA'LABLE, Adj. that which may be raised or dispersed in fumes or exhalations.

EXHALA'TION, S. [*exhalatio*, Lat.] a fume, consisting of dry, subtle corpuscules or effluvia, loosened from hard terrestrial bodies, either by the heat of the sun, agitation of the air, or some other cause, ascending by the laws of hydrostatics, to a certain height in the atmosphere, where they mix with other vapours and form clouds, &c. The act of exhaling, or emitting or sending forth effluvia.

To EXHA'LE, V. A. [*exhalo*, Lat.] to draw forth or emit effluvia. Figuratively, but improperly used to exhaust, dry up or disperse any moisture.

To EXHAU'ST, V. A. [*exhaustus*, Lat.] to drain any fluid. To draw out till nothing remains.

EXHAUS'TLESS, Adj. not to be emptied, drained, drawn dry, inexhaustible.

To EXHI'BIT, V. A. [*exhibitus*, Lat.] to offer or expose to view. To propose in a public manner. When applied to a charge or accusation, used with *against* before the person accused. To shew publickly or display.

EXHI'BITER, S. he that publickly offers any thing as a charge or accusation. He that exposes any curiosity to public view.

EXHIBITION, S. [Fr. *exhibitio*, Lat.] the act of displaying or rendering visible and sensible. The act of exposing to public view. In Law, the bringing an accusation against a person in a public court. Allowance, salary, or pension. " Driven to live in exile on a small exhibition." *Swift.* General y applied to those small pensions or allowances given by the companies of London to scholars towards their support at the universities.

EXHIBITIVE, Adj. containing a representation or display.

To EXHI'LARA E, V. A. [*exhilararo*, Lat.] to chear, comfort or inspire with gaiety or mirth.

EXHILARA'TION, S. the act of inspiring with chearfulness. The state of one inspired with joy or pleasure.

To EXHO'RT, V. A. [*exhortor*, Fr. of *e* and *hortor*, Lat.] to chide, request, or call upon a person to perform, or remind him of his duty. " We beseech and exhort you by the Lord Jesus." 2 *Thess.* iv. 1.

EXHOR ATION, S. [Fr. *exhortatio*, Lat.] the motives which can induce a person to perform any duty. The act of laying those motives before a person.

EXHO'RTER, S. one who endeavours to persuade a person to perform any duty.

EXICCA'TION, S. the act of consuming or drying up moisture. " An universal drought or exiccation of the earth." *Bacon.*

EXICCATIVE, Adj. of a drying quality, having the power to dry or consume moisture.

EXIGENCE, EXIGENCY, S. [*exigens*, Lat.] a want, necessity or distress which demands immediate assistance. Any pressing want, or sudden occasion.

EXIGEN T, S. [*exigens*, Lat.] a pressing business, or what requires immediate assistance and relief. Figuratively, death or the end of life, an unusual sense. Thes eyes wax dim as drawing on their *exigents*." *Shak.* In Law, a writ sued when the defendant is not to be found.

EXIGUITY, S. [*exiguitas*, Lat.] smallness, littleness.

EXIGUOUS, Adj. [*exiguus*, Lat. *exigu*, Fr.] small, minute.

EXILE, S. [*exil*, *exilé*, Fr.] a person driven from his country, and forbid to return.

To EXILE, V. A. to expel a person from a country. Figuratively, to expel or banish any bad or good quality from the mind." " His brutal manners from his breast exil'd." *Dryd.*

EXI'TMENT, S. the state of a person driven or banished his country.

To EXI'ST, V. N. [*exister*, Fr. of *existo*, Lat.] to be; to have actual existence.

EXISTENCE, EXISTENCY, S. [*existentia*, Lat.] that whereby a thing has an actual being. The state of being.

EXI'STENT, Adj. [*existant*, Fr. *existens*, Lat.] in being; in actual existence.

EXISTIMA'TION, S. [*existimatio*, Lat.] opinion, esteem, reputation.

EXIT, S. [of *exeo*, Lat. to go out] in dramatic writings, a word set solemnly that a person is gone off the stage. Figuratively, a departure from life; death. A passage out of any place. The way or avenue by which a person may go out of a place.

EXI-

EXI'TIAL EXI'TIOUS, Adj. [*exitialis*, Lat., that which kills; destructive, fatal or mortal. " *Exitial* fevers." *Harvey*

EXO'DUS, EXO'DY, S. [εξ, Gr. and *οδος*,] the second book of the old Testament written by Moses, so called by the Septuagint translators, because it contains the departure of the Israelites from Egypt: It also comprehends the history of Moses's birth, education, and flight; the oppressions of the Israelites in Egypt, Moses's return from Midian, his commission to Pharaoh, the plagues he wrought in Egypt; the departure of the Jews, their passage through the Red-Sea and the Wilderness, the manner of giving the law, the erection of the tabernacle and celebration of the second passover, and contains the transactions of 145 years, beginning from the death of Joseph in the 1586th year of the world, and 1691, before Christ.

To EXO'NERATE, V. A. *exoneratus*, of *exonero*, Lat.] to unload; to disburthen; to free from any thing which is troublesome.

EXONERA'TION. S. the act of disburthening, or getting rid of a thing which oppresses.

EXO'RABLE, Adj. [Fr. of *exorabilis*, Lat.] to be moved by solicitation, prayer or entreaty.

EXORBITANCE, EXO'RBITANCY, S. [*exorbitans*, Fr.] the act of going out of the common track. A gross deviation from the rules of virtue. Boundless depravity.

EXO'RBITANT, Adj. [Fr. of *ex* and *ordino*, Lat.] leaving any rule prescribed. Not comprehended in any law. " Causes *exorbitant*, and such as their laws had not provided for." *Hooker* Enormous; immoderate; excessive; beyond bounds, extravagant. " So endless and *exorbitant* are the desires of men " *Swift*.

To EXO'RBITATE, V. N. [from *ex* and *orbita*, Lat.] to leave any track or path prescribed.

To EXO'RCISE, V. A. [εξορκιζω, Gr.] to adjure or to drive away evil spirits by using some holy name. To free a person from the influence of evil spirits.

EXORCISER, S. a person who professes to drive away evil spirits by religious ceremonies.

EXORCISM, S. [εξορκισμος, Gr.] the form of adjuration, or religious ceremonies used to free a person from the pretended influence of evil spirits.

EXO'RCIST, S. [εξορκιστης, Gr.] one who by adjurations, prayers, or religious acts drives away evil spirits. An enchanter or conjurer, but very improperly. " Is there no *exorcist*?—beguiles the truer office of mine eyes?" *Shak.*

EXO'RDIUM, S. [Lat.] in oratory, the beginning of a speech, wherein the audience is prepared to attend what follows.

EXO'TIC, Adj. [εξωτικος, Gr.] foreign; from a foreign country.

EXO'TIC, S. a foreign plant, or a plant growing abroad.

To EXPA'ND, V. A. [*expando*, Lat.] to spread, or lay open. Figuratively, to dilate; to spread out every way; to diffuse.

EXPA'NSE, S. [*expansum*, Lat.] a body widely extended, and smooth on its surface. A surface. Extent considered abstractedly, or without any relation to the body extended.

EXPANSIBI'LITY, S. capableness of being expanded, or stretched out.

EXPA'NSIBLE, Adj. capable to be stretched or expanded.

EXPA'NSION, S. distance or space abstractedly considered. In metaphysics, the idea of lasting and persevering distance, all the parts whereof exist together. In physics, the act of dilating, stretching, or spreading out a thing, whereby its dimension is increased. Figuratively. The act of spreading out a thing folded or doubled up. Extent, or space to which any thing is spread.

EXPA'NSIVE, Adj. having the power to spread or expand to a large space.

To EXPA'TIATE, V. A. [*expatiatus*, Lat. of *expatior*, Lat.] to rove, or range without regard to prescribed limits. To treat of in a copious manner used with *on*. To let loose; to revel without controul. " Afford art ample field of matter wherein to expatiate itself." *Dryd.*

To E'XPECT, V. A. [*expecto*, Lat.] to look out after; to have an apprehension or expectation of future good and evil. To wait, or stay for a person's coming. Neuterly, to stay in a place till a person or thing comes. To wait.

EXPECTANCE, EXPECTANCY, S. [*expectant*, Fr.] the state of a person who waits for something. Something waited for. Hopes; or that which people had formed vast hopes from. " The *expectancy* and rose of the fair state." *Shak.*

EXPE'CTANT, Adj. [Fr.] waiting in expectation of the arrival of any person, time, or thing, or of succeeding another. " The *expectant* heir." *Swift.*

EXPE'CTANT, S. [Fr. *expectant*, Lat.] a person who waits for the arrival of a person, or thing.

EXPECTA'TION, S. [Fr. *expectatio*, Lat.] the state of a person, who waits for the arrival of any person, period, or thing. Dependence on the promises and favours of another for future good. " Wait thou only upon God, for all my *expectation* is from him." *Psal* lxii. 5. The object which people form great hopes of. The Messiah. " Why our great *expectation* should be called — the seed of woman." *Par. Lost.*

EXPE'CTER, S. one who waits for, or has hopes of preferment in a state. One who waits for the arrival of a person or thing.

To

To EXPEC'TORATE, V. A. [from *ex*, Lat. and *pituo*, *pituitis*, Lat.] to void phlegm, or other matter from the lungs, by coughing, hawking, or spitting.

EXPECTORA'TION, S. the act of discharging matter from the breast. The freeing the breast from phlegm, or any vifcid matter.

EXPEC'TORATIVE, Adj. having the quality to promote the cleanfing the breaft or lungs of phlegm, or other vifcid matter.

EXPE'DIENCE, EXPE'DIENCY, S. [*expedient*, Fr.] the fitnefs or propriety of a means to the attainment of an end. An expedition, adventure, or attempt. " Forwarding the dear *expedience*." *Shak* Hulle. " Eight tall fhips—are making hither with all due *expedience*." *Shak*. The two laft fenfes feem peculiar to the author quoted, and fhould not be imitated.

EXPE'DIENT, Adj. [Fr.] proper to attain any particular end. Hafty or quick. " His marches are *expedient* to this town." *Shak*.

EXPE'DIENT, S. [Fr.] a means proper to promote any end. A fhift or fcheme, to ward off any calamity or diftrefs.

EXPE'DIENTLY, Adj. in a manner proper to attain an end. Quickly. " Do this *expediently*." *obex*. The laft fenfe is ufed for *expeditiofly*; and fhould not be imitated.

To EXPE'DITE, V. A. [*expedito*, Lat.] to free from any obftruction. To haften or quicken. To difpatch.

EXPE'DITELY, Adv. with quicknefs, nimblenefs, readinefs, or hafte.

EXPEDI'TION, S. [Fr.] quicknefs, applied to time or motion. A march or voyage to attack an enemy.

To EXPE'L, V. A. [*expello*, Lat.] to drive out, or make a perfon to quit a place or habitation by force. To ejeft or throw out.

To EXPE'ND, V. A. [*expendo*, Lat.] to lay out, difburfe, or fpend money.

EXPE'NSE, S. [*expenfum*, Lat.] coft, charge, money laid out, or expended.

EXPE'NSELESS, Adj. without coft, charge, or expence.

EXPE'NSIVE, Adj. prodigal, extravagant; coftly. Liberal, generous, giving money freely. In a good fenfe. " This re quires an active, *expenfive*, and indefatigable genius." *Spratt*.

EXPE'NSIVELY, Adv. prodigally, extravagantly.

EXPE'NSIVENESS, S. profufenefs, dearnefs, extravagance.

EXPE'RIENCE, S. [Fr. *experientia*, Lat.] practice; frequent trial. Knowledge gained by obfervation on the occurrences of life.

To EXPE'RIENCE, V. A. to try, or practife.

EXPE'RIENCED, Part. fkilful or wife, from experience.

EXPERI'MENT, S. [*experimentum*, Fr. *experimentum*, Lat.] trial of any thing. A trial made of the rufult of certain application and motion of bodies, in order to difcover the true caufe of the phenomenon occafioned thereby.

EXPERIME'NTAL, Adj. [Fr.] pertaining to, or founded on experiments. Known by trial and experiment. *Experimental* philofophy is that which deduces the laws of nature, the properties and powers of bodies and their actions on each other, by fenfible experiments and trials made with that view. The advantage modern philofophy has over the ancient is chiefly owing to this method; and when we recollect that it was lord Bacon who paved the way by recommending this practice, we may affume to ourfelves no fmall pride on that account.

EXPERIME'NTALLY, Adv. by experience; by trial.

EXPE'RT, Adv. [Fr. *expertus*, Lat.] fkilful in any particular art, or bufinefs. Dexterous.

EXPE'RTLY, Adv. in fuch a manner as difcovers fkill or knowledge.

EXPE'RTNESS, S. fkill or knowlege in any affair.

EX'PIABLE, Adj. capable of being atoned, by fuffering or punifhment.

To EX'PIATE, V. A. [*expio*, Fr. *expiatus*, Lat.] to make atonement for fins by fuffering the punifhment due to them.

EXPIA'TION, S. [*expiatio*, Lat.] any fuffering endured, or facrifice offered to avert the punifhment due to fin, and to render the Deity propitious to the offender.

EX'PIATORY, Adj. endued with the power to avert the divine wrath from punifhing fins.

EXPIRA'TION, S. [*expiratus*, of *expiro*, Lat.] that act by which the breath is forced out of the lungs. The laft gafp, or breath. Vapour, breath, or the matter expired. The end of any period of time.

To EXPI'RE, V. A. [*expiro*, Fr. *expiro*, Lat.] to breathe out, to fend out fumes, vapours, or exhalations. To clofe, to conclude. Neuterly, to force breath outwards. To die, or breathe one's laft. To perifh. To fly out with a blaft. To conclude, finifh, or terminate.

To EXPLA'IN, V. A. [*explano*, Lat.] to clear up any difficulty. To illuftrate.

EXPLA'INABLE, Adj. that which may be rendered more eafy or plain.

EXPLA'INER, S. one who clears up any difficulty, or illuftrates a thing.

EXPLANA'TION, S. the act of interpreting, or rendering a thing more eafy to be underftood. An illuftration or comment whereby a paffage is rendered more eafy to be underftood.

EXPLA-

EXPLA'NATORY, Adj. containing an illustration, or explanation.

EXPLETIVE, S. [expletivum, Lat.] a word used merely to fill up a vacancy, or make up the number of feet in a verse.

EXPLICABLE, Adj. that which may be explained, illustrated, or rendered intelligible.

To EXPLICATE, V. A. [explico, Lat.] of explico, Lat.] to unfold. "They explicate their leaves." Bloom. To explain or render easy to be understood.

EXPLICA'TION, S. [Fr.] the act of opening, or unfolding. Figuratively, the act of making any difficult passage easy to be understood. The sense given by an explainer. An interpretation.

EXPLICATIVE, Adj. having a tendency to explain, or render a thing clear and easy.

EXPLICATOR, S. one who expounds, or explains any difficulty.

EXPLICIT, Adj. [explicite, Fr. explicitus, Lat.] unfolded. Figuratively, plain, easy, obvious clear.

EXPLICITLY, Adv. plainly; directly; clearly; not by implication or inference.

To EXPLODE, V. A. [explodo, Lat.] to drive out with contempt and disgrace. Figuratively, to reject with scorn.

EXPLODER, S. one who shews contempt. One who rejects an opinion with scorn.

EXPLOIT, S. [Fr.] a successfull design, a successful and remarkable action in war.

To EXPLOIT, V. A. [exploiter, Fr.] to perform or atchieve. "He exploited great matters." Carew.

EXPLORATORY, Adj. searching; examining.

To EXPLORE, V. A. [explore, Lat.] to make trial of; to discover by examination; to search or try in order to make discoveries.

EXPLOSION, S. [explosio, Lat.] the act of driving out any thing with noise and violence. The noise made by the firing of gunpowder.

EXPLOSIVE, Adj. driving out with noise and violence.

EXPONENT, S. [exponens, Lat.] In Arithmetic, the number which expresses how often a given power is to be divided by its root ere it be brought to unity; thus the exponent of a square number is 2, of a cube 3. The exponent of a ratio is the quotient arising from the division of the antecedent by the consequent; thus the ratio of 3 to 2 is 1½, and the ratio of 2 to 3 is ⅔. If the consequent be unity, the antecedent itself is the exponent; and, therefore the exponent of a ratio is to unity, as the antecedent is to the consequent.

EXPONENTIAL, Adj. In Geometry, applied to curves which partake of the na-

ture of algebraic curves, as consisting of a finite number of terms.

To EXPORT, V. A. to send goods to foreign countries for sale.

EXPORT, S. a commodity sent to foreign parts.

EXPORTATION, S. the act or practice of sending goods to foreign markets for sale. It is necessary for the subsistence of a commercial nation, that its exports should be greater than its imports.

EXPORTER, S. one who sends commodities to foreign countries.

To EXPOSE, V. A. [exposer, Fr.] to lay open or subject to censure, examination, punishment or danger.

EXPOSITION, S. [expositio, Lat.] the situation in which a thing is placed. An interpretation, comment, or treatise to explain the sense of a writer.

EXPOSITOR, S. [Lat.] an explainer, a commentator.

To EXPOSTULATE, V. N. [expostulo, Lat.] to debate, or argue with a person by way of complaint.

EXPOSTULATION, S. the act of reasoning, arguing, or representing a thing to another by way of complaint.

EXPOSTULATOR, S. a person who argues or expostulates with another.

EXPOSURE, S. the act of laying open to public view. The state of being liable to blame, punishment, ridicule or danger. A situation in which a thing lays open or is exposed to the sun and air.

To EXPOUND, V. A. [expono, Lat.] to interpret, illustrate, or explain any difficult passage.

EXPOUNDER, S. on who explains, or expounds.

To EXPRESS V. A. [expressus, of exprimo, Lat.] to represent in words, or by poetry, sculpture, or painting. To utter, applied either to language. To declare one's sentiments, used with the reciprocal pronouns, himself, &c.

EXPRESS, Adj. copied or bearing a near resemblance, applied to drawing, sculpture, and poetry. In direct terms, applied to languages. Clear, not ambiguous.

EXPRESS, S. [exprés, Fr. a messenger sent with expedition to deliver a particular message. A message, a declaration in direct terms.

EXPRESSIBLE, Adj. that which may be uttered, or communicated.

EXPRESSION, S. [Fr.] the act of communicating ideas by language. The particular form, manner, or style used to convey one's thoughts, applied to painting. In painting a natural representation of the subject, or of the several objects intended to the picture, whereby the human body and its parts have the action suitable to it, the passions

bits the feveral paffions proper to the figures, and proper obfervation is had of the motions they imprefs on the other external parts.

EXPRE'SSIVE, Adj. having the power of uttering or reprefenting ; ufed with *of* before the thing uttered.

EXPRE'SSIVELY, Adv. clearly, diftinctly.

EXPRE'SSIVENESS, S. the power of conveying ideas to the mind.

EXPRE'SSLY, Adj. in direct terms ; plainly ; pofitively ; clearly.

EXPRE'SSURE, S. [from *expreffus*, Lat.] expreffion. " More divine than breath or, pro can give *expreffure* to." *Shak.* The form, or likenefs defcribed. " The *expreffure* of his eye, &c." *Shak.* Mark or impreffion. " The *expreffion* that it bears." *Shak.*

To **EXPROBRATE**, V. A. [*exprobrans*, Lat.] to reproach ; to upbraid.

To **EXPROPRIATE**, V. A. [from *ex* and *proprius*, Lat.] to alienate ; to make a thing no longer one's own. " When you have refigned, or rather configned, your *expropriated* will to God." *Boyle*.

To **EXPULSE**, V. A. [*expulfus*, Lat ; to drive or force out. " Pelens was *expulfed* from his kingdom." *Notes on the Ouff.* Not to be imitated, *expel* is the word.

EXPU'LSION, S. the act of driving out ; the ftate of a perfon driven out.

EXPU'LSIVE, Adj. having the power of driving out.

To **EXPUNCE**, V. A. [*expurgo*, Lat.] to blot out ; to efface, or annihilate.

EXPURGA'TION, S. [*expurgatio* Lat.] the act of purging or cleanfing. Figuratively, purification from bad mixtures, or from error.

EXPU'RGATORY, Adj. employed in clearing away what is noxious, erroneous, or amifs. The *expurgatory* index of Romanifts is employed in effacing or abolition of fuch paffages in authors as are oppofite to popery.

EXQ'UISITE, Adj. [*exquifitus*, Lat.] fo excellent as to fhow great exactnefs and labour in the production. Superlative. " With *exquifite* malice." *K. Charles.*

EXQ'UISITELY, Adv. perfectly ; accurately ; completely ; fuperlatively.

EXQ'UISITENESS, S. nicety, perfection, accuracy.

EXSUDA'TION, S. [*exfudatio*, of *exfudo*, Lat.] the act of perfpiring or difcharging by fweat.

To **EXSUDE**, V. A. [*exfudo*, Lat.] to perfpire or difcharge by fweat. To diftil, or exhale.

EXSUFFLA'TION, S. [from *ex* and *fufflatus*, Lat.] a blaft blown upwards or from underneath. " Fly upwards, up a kind of *exfufflation*." *Bacon.*

EXTANCY, S. [from *ex* and *fto*, Lat.] the ftate of rifing above, projecting beyond

other parts of a furface. " The order of the little *extancies* " *Boyle.*

EXTANT, Adj. [*extans*, Lat.] ftanding out or above the other parts of the furface. " That part of the teeth which is *extant* above the gum." *Ray.* Public, ftill to be had or met with ; applied to books.

EXTATIC, EXTATICAL, Adj. tending to fomething without. Rapturous or elevating to the higheft degree of blifs and tranfport.

EXTE'MPORAL, Adj. [*extemporalis*, Lat.] fudden, unpremeditated.

EXTE'MPORALLY, Adv. quickly ; without ftudy or preparation.

EXTEMPORA'NEOUS, Adj. [*extemporaneus*, Lat.] occafional ; fudden ; without preparation, or premeditation.

EXTE'MPORARY, Adj. [*extemporarius*, Lat.] fudden, quick ; without ftudy, preparation, or premeditation.

EX TE'MPORE, Adv. fuddenly, without previous thought, or ftudy. Sometimes ufed as an adjective. " A long *extempore* differtation." *Spect.* No. 247. Johnfon cenfures this as improper, though produced by the pen of *Addifon*.

To **EXTE'MPORIZE**, V. A. to fpeak without ftudy or premeditation.

To **EXTE'ND**, V. A. [*extendo*, Lat.] to ftretch out ; to fpread ; to enlarge the furface of a thing ; to exercife ; to communicate or impart. In Law, to feize.

EXTE'NDIBLE, Adj. capable of being extended, made wider, or longer.

EXTENSIBI'LITY, S. the quality of being made wider or longer.

EXTE'NSIBLE, Adj. capable of being ftretched wider or longer. Capable of comprehending more ideas.

EXTE'NSIBLENESS, S. the quality of being ftretched wider or longer.

EXTE'NSION, S. [*extenfio*, Lat.] the act of increafing or extending the length or breadth of a thing. The ftate of a thing extended. In Phyfics, the diftance between the extremes of a thing.

EXTE'NSIVE, Adj. wide ; large ; capacious.

EXTE'NSIVELY, widely, largely.

EXTE'NSIVENESS, S. largenefs ; widenefs ; diffufivenefs. A quality by which a thing can occupy a certain portion of fpace, or that quality of the mind by which it is enabled to comprehend a particular doctrine, or number of ideas.

EXTE'NT, S. [*extentus*, Lat.] the diftance between the extremities of a thing. The fpace filled by a body. Communication, diftribution. In Law, an execution, or feizure of goods.

To **EXTE'NUATE**, V. A. [*extenuatus*, Lat.] to make fmall, narrow, or flender ; applied to quantity ; to leffen ; to make lean.

EXTE-

EXTENUATION, S. [extenuatus, Lat.] the act of representing things less ill than they are. Mitigation or alleviation. A leanness of flesh, or decay of the body, in Medicine.

EXTE'RIOR, Adj. [Lat. exterior, Fr.] outward; external; not essential.

EXTE'RIORLY, Adv. outwardly; externally.

To EXTE'RMINATE, V. A. [extermino, of extermino, Lat.] to root out; to destroy utterly.

EXTERMINA'TION, S. [extermino, Lat.] total destruction, or rooting out.

EXTERMINA'TOR, S. [Lat.] the person who lays waste or destroys a country.

EXTE'RNAL, Adj. outward. Outward appearance.

EXTE'RNALLY, Adv. outwardly.

EXTILA'TION, S. [from ex and stillo, Lat.] the act of falling in drops. "Exillation of purifying juices." Derb. Distillation.

To EXTI'MULATE, V. A. [extimulatus, Lat.] to prick or incite.

EXTIMULA'TION, S. pungency; or the power of exciting motion or sensation.

EXTINCT', Adj. [extinctus, Lat.] quenched, applied to fire. At a stop or end, without any survivors, applied to succession. Abolished, applied to law.

EXTINC'TION, S. [extinctio, Lat.] the act of quenching, applied to fire. The state of a thing quenched. Utter destruction. Suppression, abolition.

To EXTI'NGUISH, V. A. [extinguo, Lat.] quench, applied to fire. Figuratively, to suppress, applied to the passions. To cloud, eclipse or obscure. "Her natural graces that extinguished art." Shak.

EXTI'NGUISHABLE, Adj. that may be quenched, suppressed or destroyed.

EXTI'NGUISHER, S. a hollow cone which is put on a candle to extinguish it.

EXTI'NGUISHMENT, S. the act of suppressing or destroying. Abolition, applied to laws. The act of taking away all the descendants of a family.

To EXTI'RPATE, V. A. [extirpatus, Lat. of extirpo, Lat.] to root out, abolish, or destroy utterly.

EXTIRPA'TION, S. [Fr. extirpatio, Lat.] the act of rooting out, abolishing, or destroying.

EXTIRPA'TOR, S. [Lat.] a destroyer.

To EXTO'L, V. A. [extollo, Lat.] to commend or praise; to magnify.

EXTO'LLER, S. one who praises or extols.

EXTO'RSIVELY, Adj. violently.

To EXTO'RT, V. A. [extortus, Lat.] to draw by force. To gain or acquire by violent means. To wrest an expression from its obvious meaning. To gain by violence and oppression. Neuterly, to practise oppression and violence.

No. XL.

EXTO'RTER, S. one who makes use of oppression, violent or indirect means to acquire a thing.

EXTOR'TION, S. [extorsion, Fr.] the act of acquiring by force or oppression. The violence made use of to gain a thing.

EXTOR'TIONER, S. one who grows rich by violence, or extortion.

To EXTRACT', V. A. [extractum, Lat.] to draw, derive, or take one thing from another. To draw by chemistry. To abridge or transcribe any passage from a book. Used with far.

EX'TRACT, S. [extractus, Lat.] In Pharmacy, the purest and finest part of any substance, separated by dissolution or digestion of a proper menstruum. In Literature, an abridgment or a transcript of a book.

EXTRACT', Part. drawn out. Separated or taken from.

EXTRAC'TION, S. [extractio, Lat.] In Chemistry and Pharmacy, an operation whereby essences, tinctures, &c. are drawn from natural bodies. In Genealogy, the stock or family from which a person is descended. In Arithmetic, extraction of roots is the method of finding the roots of given numbers.

EXTRAC'TOR, S. a person or instrument by which any thing is taken out or extracted.

EXTRAJUDI'CIAL, Adj. [from extra, Lat. and judicium, Lat.] out of the regular course of proceeding in law.

EXTRAJUDI'CIALLY, Adv. in a manner different from the common course of procedure at law.

EXTRAMUNDA'NE, Adj. [from extra, Lat. and mundus, Lat.] beyond the bounds of this world or system.

EXTRA'NEOUS, Adj. [extraneus, Lat.] not intrinsic or essential to a thing; foreign.

EXTRAO'RDINARILY, Adv. uncommonly; eminently; curiously; remarkably.

EXTRAOR'DINARY, Adj. [from extra and ordinarius, Lat.] different from, or out of the common course. Something more or better than common.

EXTRAPARO'CHIAL, Adj. [extra, Lat. and parochia, Lat.] not included, comprehended, or belonging to any parish.

EXTRAPROVI'NCIAL, Adj. [from extra, Lat. and provincia, Lat.] not within the same province.

EXTRAVA'GANCE, EXTRAVA'GANCY, S. [extravagance, Fr. extra and vagans, Lat.] an excursion beyond prescribed bounds. Irregularity; wildness. An immoderate heat or violence, applied to the passions. An unnatural swelling or bombast, applied to style. Waste or superfluous expence.

EXTRAVA'GANT, Adj. [Fr. extravagant, Lat.] wandering beyond the prescribed bounds. "The extravagant and erring spirit."

3 H

Spirit." *Shak.* Roving beyond the bounds of moderation; immoderate. Irregular, not reduced to rule. Prodigal, or profusely expensive. Not comprehended in a rule. " Twenty constitutions of Pope John XXII. are called *extravagants.*" *Ayliffe.*

EXTRAVA'GANTLY, Adv. contrary to all rule. In an immoderate degree. Profusely expensive.

EXTRAVA'SATED, Adj. (*extravaser,* Fr.) forced out of the vessels.

EXTRAVASA'TION, S. the act of forcing out of his proper vessels.

EXTRA'UGHT, Part. (an obsolete participle from *extract*) extracted, or descended. " Knowing whence thou art *extraught.*" *Shak.*

EXTRE'ME, Adj. (Fr. of *extreme,* Lat. the adding of to it, which is a superlative termination borrowed from the Saxons, is a great corruption, because its sense is superlative without h) greatest, applied to degree. Utmost, or furthermost applied to situation or time. Last, or that which has nothing beyond it. Most pressing, applied to danger. *Extreme unction* is one of the sacraments of the Romish church, is administered to people dangerously ill, and consists in anointing them with holy oil, &c.

EXTRE'ME, S. the highest degree of any thing.

EXTRE'MELY, Adv. in the utmost or highest degree. Very much or greatly, in familiar language.

EXTRE'MITY, S. (*extremité,* Fr.) the utmost parts. Those points which are most opposite to each other. The remotest or farthest part of a country. The utmost degree of violence, distress, poverty, or calamity.

To EXTRICATE, V. A. (*extricatum,* Lat.) to free a person from any perplexity, difficulty or danger.

EXTRICA'TION, S. the act of freeing from perplexity or difficulty.

EXTRI'NSIC, Adj. (*extrinsecus,* Lat.) outward, external.

EXTRI'NSICAL, Adj. (*extrinsecus,* Lat.) external; outward; from without.

To EXTRU'DE, V. A. (*extrudo,* Lat.) to thrust out; to drive away by violence.

EXTRU'SION, S. (*extrusus,* Lat.) the act of thrusting or driving out, or away. " An *extrusion* and elevation of others." *Burn.*

EXTU'BERANCE, S. (from *ex* and *tuber,* Lat.) a knob or part above the rest of a surface.

EXU'BERANCE, S. (Fr. *exuberantia,* Lat.) overgrowth. Superfluous shoots. Luxuriance.

EXU'BERANT, Adj. (*exuberans,* Lat.) growing with superfluous shoots. Luxuriant. Superabundantly plentiful.

EXU'BERANTLY, Adv. abundantly even to the highest or a superfluous degree, luxuriantly.

To EXU'BERATE, V. A. (*exubero,* or *exuberas,* Lat.) to abound in the greatest or highest degree. " That vast confluence and immensity that *exuberates* in God." *Boyle.*

EXUDA'TION, S. (*exudatio,* see EXU'DATION) the act of emitting moisture, in sweat or perspiration. The manner issuing from any body in the form of sweat.

To EXU'LCERATE, V. A. (*exulceratus,* Lat.) to make sore with an ulcer; to afflict, enrage, or corrode.

EXULCERA'TION, S. the act of producing ulcers. The act of inflaming or enraging, applied to the mind.

To EXU'LT, V. N. (*exulto,* Lat.) to be affected with a high degree of joy.

EXULTA'TION, S. (*exultatio,* Lat.) joy; rapturous delight.

EXU'LTANCE, S. a transport of joy, gladness, or delight.

EXUNDA'TION, S. (*exundatio,* Lat.) an overflowing. Figuratively, a great abundance. " The *exundation* and overflowing of his transcendent and infinite goodness." *Ray.*

EXU'PERANCE, (*exuperantia,* Lat.) a surplus, or greater quantity.

EYE, S. (formerly *eyne* in the plural, at present *eyes,* *eage,* Goth. *eag,* Sax.) the organ of sight. If we were to examine into the structure, form, construction, and other particulars relating to this organ, we shall find abundant cause of adoration. Sight, or evidence conveyed by the sight. The countenance. Aspect; regard. Notice; attention. Opinion formed by observation. The place from whence any thing can be seen. View. " In *eye* of every exercise." *Shak.* Any thing formed like an *eye.* In Architecture, any round window made in a pediment; hence, *Bullock's eye,* is a sky-light in a roof; applied to a *dome,* it signifies an aperture at the top. In Agriculture or Gardening, a little bud or shoot, inserted into a tree by way of a graft; or a gem or bud. " The *eye* of a needle." Any hole or aperture. In Printing, the thickness of the types, or the graving in relievo at the top of the letter, otherwise called its face; thus the *eye* of the e is the aperture or bow, at the top of the letter, which distinguishes it from the e. The power of perception or discerning, applied to the understanding.

To EYE, V. A. to watch; to observe; to keep in view.

EYE-BALL, S. (*eag-apple,* Sax.) the apple of the eye.

EYE-BROW, S. (*eag-brow,* Sax.) the hairy arch over the eye, intended by providence to defend it from any injury.

EYE-DROP, S. a tear. " With gentle *eye-drops.*" *Shak.*

EYE'LESS, Adj. without eyes; blind; unable to see. " That *eyeless* face." *Pope.*

EYE'LET, S. (*œillet,* Fr.) a hole through
S   which

which light may enter. A small hole, usually termed an eyelet-hole.

EYE'-LID, S. the membrane, or skin, which closes or covers the eye.

EYE'-SERVANT, S. a servant who works only while he is watched.

EYE'-SERVICE, S. service performed only while the master is present to observe.

EYE'SHOT, S. the look, or glance of an eye. " I have preserved many a young man from the eye-shot." Spect. No. 284.

EYE'-SIGHT, S. the sight of the eye.

EYE'-SORE, S. something offensive or disagreeable to the sight.

EYE'STRING, S. the tendon by which the eye is held to its proper place.

EYE'-WITNESS, S. a person who gives testimony to facts which he has seen himself.

EYRE, S. [Fr. ier, Lat.] in Law, the court of justices itinerants.

EY'RY, S. [ey, Teut.] the place where birds of prey generally build their nests, or hatch their young.

F.

F, The sixth letter of the English alphabet, and the fourth consonant. It is found or formed by the compression of the whole lips, and a forcible breath. Its form is the same in the Roman and Saxon alphabets as in ours. In medicinal prescriptions it stands for far, or let it be made. In Music, the fourth note of the gamut; and when standing at the beginning of the line, the bass cleff. On monumental inscriptions, is signifies Filius, or son.

FA, in Music, the fourth note in the scale or gamut.

FA'BLE, S. [Fr. fabula, Lat.] a feigned tale or story invented to enforce some useful precept. A fiction. A vitious or foolish story, or fiction. A series of events which compose a moral, epic, or dramatic poem. In common discourse, a lie, or falshood.

To FA'BLE, V. N. to feign, or write fictions. To tell, or relate falshoods. To lye. Actively, to deliver in fables and falshoods.

FA'BLED, Part. mentioned, or celebrated in fables.

FA'BLER, S. a writer of feigned stories or fictions. A softer term to express a person guilty of lying, or uttering falshoods.

FA'BRIC, see FABRICK.

To FA'BRICATE V. A. [fabricatus, of fabrico, Lat.] to build, or construct. To forge, or devise falsely.

FABRICA'TION, S. [fabricatio, Lat.] the act of building; construction.

FA'BRICK, S. [should be written fabrica, of fabrico, Lat.] a building. Any thing composed of different parts. The texture of a silk, cloth, or stuff.

To FA'BRICK, V. A. [more properly written fabric, of fabrico, Lat.] to build, form or construct.

FA'BULIST, S. [fabuliste, Fr.] a writer, composer, or inventer of fables.

FABULO'SITY, S. [fabulositas, Lat.] the quality of dealing in falshood, or telling lies, or falshoods.

FA'BULOUS, Adj. [fabulosus, Lat.] dealing in fables, fiction, falshood or lies.

FA'BULOUSLY, Adj. in a feigned, false, or fabulous manner.

FA'CE, S. [Fr. face, Lat.] the countenance. The surface of a thing. The front, or forepart of a thing. Appearance, look, or countenance. Presence, or sight. Confidence, boldness. " Ignorance, and face alone." Hudib. " To make face," a distortion of the features; a grimace.

To FA'CE, V. N. to assume a false appearance, or act the hypocrite, to face about, to turn the face a different way; to come in front. Actively, to meet in front, to march against an enemy, or danger with boldness. To face down, to deny or oppose, or put to silence by mere impudence. " He faced men down that he stood Gül." Prior. To stand opposite to. To cover the external part. " Faced with marble." Addis.

FACE'TIOUS, Adj. [facetieux, facetieuse, Fr.] witily gay, merry, humorous.

FACE'TIOUSLY, S. diveringly cheerfully, jocosely.

FA'CILE, Adj. [Fr. of facilis, Lat.] to be attained or performed with ease. " Will render the work facile and delightful." Evelyn. Easily surmounted. " The facile gates of hell." Par. Lost. Easy of access, opposed to haughtiness or austerity. Easily persuaded. " Adam and his facile consort Eve." Par. Lost.

To FACI'LITATE, V. A. [faciliter, Fr.] to make easy, or to clear from impediments.

FACI'LITY, S. [facilitas, Lat.] easiness to be performed. Freedom from difficulty. Readiness in performing. Easiness to be persuaded, credulity. Easiness of access; condescension; or compliance.

FA'CING, Part. opposite to, over against.

FA'CING, S. an ornamental covering put upon the external part of a thing.

FACI'NOROUS, Adj. [facinorosus, Lat.] wicked; vicious; detestably bad.

FACT, S. [factum, Lat.] a thing done. A reality, opposed to a mere supposition. A truth. An action.

FA'CTION, S. [Fr. factio, Lat.] a tumult, discord, confusion or distraction.

FA'CTIONARY, S. a party man, or one of a faction. " Always factionary of the party." Shak.

FA'CTIOUS, Adj. [factieux, Fr.] given to faction, or dissentions; vehement in support of any faction or party.

FA'CTIOUSLY, Adv. In a tumultuous manner, or forming parties in a government.

FA'CTIOUSNESS, S. Inclination to public dissension

FACTI'TIOUS, Adj. [factitius, Lat.] made by art, counterfeited, not natural.

FA'CTOR, S. [Lat. facteur, Fr.] an agent; one who transacts business for another.

FA'CTORY, S. a house, place, or district inhabited by traders in a foreign country. Several traders associated in a place.

FA'CTO'TUM, S. [Lat. do it all] a servant employed in all kinds of business.

FA'CULTY, S. [facultas, Lat.] the power of doing any thing. The powers of the mind, whether imagination, memory, or reason. In Physic, a power of performing any action, whether natural, vital, or animal. A knack, skill, art, or dexterity gained by habit. A quality or disposition. Power, or authority. "Hath born his faculties so meekly." Shak. Privilege, or right to do any thing. "Almost every faculty or favour shall be granted." Hooker. The profession of any science, in London peculiarly applied to physicians. "The gentlemen of the faculty."

To FA'DDLE, V. N. to trifle, toy, or play.

To FA'DE, V. N. [fade, Fr. insipid] to decline; to grow weak, or languish. To alter to a weaker or paler colour. To wither, applied to plants, or other vegetables. To die away, vanish, or wear out gradually. Actively, to wear away; to reduce to a languid state; to lessen the brightness of a colour, or gradually diminish strength.

To FA'DGE, V. N. [gefegen, Sax. fegen, Teut.] to suit, or fit. To have one part agree, or consistent with another. "How will this fadge?" Shak. To agree; to live in concord. "When they thriv'd they never fodg'd." Hudib. This word is never used but in ludicrous compositions.

To FA'G, V. N. [fatigo, Lat.] to make weary or tired. "Till the Italians began to fag." Mackenzie. Actively, to beat.

FA'GOT, S. [Fr. faggotto, Ital.] a bundle of sticks, or brushwood bound together for fuel, or any other purpose. A pretended soldier entered in a muster roll only to make up the number.

To FA'GOT, V. A. to tie up, bind, or bundle together.

To FA'IL, V. N. [faillir, Fr. falan, Brit.] to grow deficient; to become unequal to the demand or use. To be extinct. To cease, or be lost. To languish through fatigue. To decay. To miss producing his effect. To miss, or not succeed in an attempt. To disappoint a person's expectations. To be deficient in keeping an appointment, or in performing a duty.

FAIL, S. a miscarriage; miss. Omission; neglect, or non-performance. Deficience; want. Death. "How grounded his ble title to the crown, upon ony fail?" Shak.

FAI'LING, S. a deficience, imperfection, or slight fault. A defect.

FAI'LURE, S. deficience, or cessation. An omission, or slip, applied to duty. A slight fault. A bankruptcy.]

FA'IN, Adj. [fægn, Sax. of fægen,] in its primary sense, glad, joyful. "My lips would be fain when I sing unto thee." Psal. lxxii. To be forced or compelled. "Castillo was fain to make trenchers at Basil." Lord.

FA'IN, Adv. gladly; joyfully; desirously; willingly. "Would fain have a law enacted." Swift.

To FA'INT, V. N. [faner, Fr.] to fade or waste away. To grow languid, to swoon, or fall into a fit. To sink down through dejection. Actively, to deject, depress; to make a person languid. "It faints me." Shak.

FAINT, Adj. [faon, Fr.] void of strength, or spirit; pale, dead; applied to colour. Slow, not loud, applied to sound. Cowardly; timorous.

FA'INTING, S. a fit, a swoon, wherein a person is senseless, and appears almost lifeless for a short time.

FA'INTLING, Adj. timorous. "Such a fainting silly creature." Hist. of J. Bull.

FA'INTLY, Adv. feebly, languidly. Deadly, applied to colour. Without force, applied on description. Not loud, or scarcely audible, applied to sound. Timorously, or without courage.

FA'INTNESS, S. languor, fear. Want of vigour. Want of force, applied to description. Want of loudness, applied to sound. Timorousness. Dejection.

FAIR, Adj. [fægr, Sax. fagr, Goth.] beautiful; handsome; of a white, or fair complexion. Clean, pure, applied to water. Serene, or not cloudy, applied to the weather. "To stand fair." A probability of succeeding, or gaining a person's favour. Equal, just, or honest in affairs, applied to morals. Gentle; mild; opposed to violent, when joined with mean. Commodious, easy. "Wilkes stood a fair chance to be sheriff"

FAIR, Adv. gently, without violence, joined to softly. "To speak fair." In a civil and complaisant manner. Happiness, or success, joined with happen, or befal. "Now fair befal thee." Shak. On good terms, free from strife, or contention, after keep. "If he intends to keep fair with the world," Collier.

FAIR, S. a beauty; a beautiful woman. A woman. "One of the fair." Honesty, or honest dealing. "Fair and square, Nic keeps folks together." Hist. of J. Bull.

FAIR, S. [fure, Fr. forum, Lat.] a public

the place, where traders resort to dispose of their wares, and where diversions are usually exhibited at such times.

FAI'RING, S. something purchased for a present at a fair.

FAI'RLY, Adv. honestly, or without fraud or deceit; applied to the manner of action. Candidly. Without blots or blurs; applied to writings. Completely; entirely; perfectly. " All this they fairly overcame." *Spenser.*

FAI'RNESS, S. beauty, elegance of form or figure. Honesty, or freedom from fraud or deceit.

FAI'R-SPOKEN, Adj. using civil or complaisant expressions.

FAI'RY, S. (*farhth, Sax. fee, Fr.*) a kind of tabled, or imaginary being, supposed to appear in a diminutive form, dance in meadows, and to reward cleanliness. An enchantress. " To this great fairy I'll commend thine acts." *Shak.* A *fairy* ring, is a round circle in a field wherein the grass grows higher than in any other part near it, supposed by the vulgar to be caused by the fairies dancing; but may be accounted for from the effects of lightning.

FAI'RY, Adj. belonging or relating to fairies.

FAI'TH, S. (*fede, Ital. fides, Lat. foi, Fr.*) an assent to the truth of a thing barely on account of the credit or authority of the person who delivers it; this principle of assent and assurance is so great, that it leaves no manner of room for doubt or hesitation. An assent to any proposition, on the credit of the proposer, as coming from God in some extraordinary way of communication. Figuratively, belief of the truths of revealed religion. The system of revealed truth, held by Christians. Trust or confidence in God. Trust in the honesty, honour, or veracity of another. Fidelity, strict adherence to a promise. Sincerity. "A promise given."

FAI'THFUL, Adj. firm in adhering to the truth of revealed religion. True to any obligation, promise, or contract; honest or upright.

FAI'THFULLY, Adv. with firm belief in the truth of revealed religion, and reliance on the promises of God. With strict adherence to duty, loyalty, and the discharge of any obligation or promise. Honestly, or without fraud. Fervently, earnestly, confidently. " I should not urge it half so faithfully." *Shak.* The last sense is not much used.

FAI'THFULNESS, S. honesty; uprightness; truth or veracity. Firm adherence to duty as a subject.

FAI'THLESS, Adj. not believing in the revealed truths of religion. Without trust or confidence in the assurances of another. Perfidious; disloyal; dishonest.

FAI'THLESSNESS, S. treachery; perfidy; dishonesty. In Divinity, unbelief of the truths of revealed religion.

FALCA'TED, Adj. (*falcatus, Lat.*) hooked; bent like a scythe; applied by astronomers to the appearance of the moon while moving from the conjunction to the opposition.

FALCA'TION, S. (*falcatus, Lat.*) crookedness; in a form resembling a scythe.

FA'LCHION, S. (*fauchon, Fr.*) a short crooked sword or cymeter.

FA'LCON, S. (pronounced fawkon of faucon, Fr.) a bird of prey of the hawk kind, superior to all others for courage, docility, gentleness and nobleness of nature. This title or name is applied only to the female, the male being called a tassel, or tiercelet.

FA'LCONER, S. (from fauconier, Fr.) one who breeds, tames and tutors birds of prey.

FA'LCONRY, S. the art of teaching birds of prey to pursue and take game.

FA'LDSTOOL, S. a stool placed at the outside of the altar whereon the kings of England kneel at their coronation.

To FA'LL, V. N. (preter, *I fell* or *have fallen*, or *fain*, Part. Pass *fallen*, of *falla*, Isl. *feallan*, Sax.) to descend by accident to a lower place. To change an erect posture to a prone one, used with *down* " To fall off." To drop, or be no longer fastened. To move down any descent. To die, to be degraded from a high station to a low one. To come into a state of weakness, terror, or distress, used with *under*. To decrease, or diminish in value, weight, or quantity, used with *from*, or *under*. To decline from a state of violence to one of rest and calmness. To enter into any state of the body or mind. " Fell asleep." *Shak.* " Fell into such a rage." *Knolles.* " She fell in labour." To sink below a thing in a comparison, used with *short*. To languish or grow faint; to fall away, to grow lean, or decrease in bulk. To decline gradually; to fade, or languish. Used to fall hard, to fail performing a promise. To recede; yield, or give way. To fall in, to concur, coincide, or make one in a party. To comply, or yield to joined to off, to separate or break from. To fall on, to begin to do a thing eagerly; to assault, or make an attack. Used with over to, to change sides or parties. To fall out, to quarrel; to happen. To fall in, to begin, to set with eagerness; to apply one's self to. Used with under, to be subject to; to be the object of; to be ranged, or reckoned with. Actively, to drop, or let a thing slip; to sink or depress. To diminish in value, to lessen the price of a commodity. So yean, or bring forth, applied to sheep. " Fall partycoloured lambs." *Shak.*

FA'LL, S. (*fall, Isl.*) the act of descending or dropping by accident from on high. The act of tumbling prostrate upon the ground. The violence suffered from dropping from a high-

high-place. Figuratively, death. Ruin. Loss of greatness; or derivation from a state of grandeur, populousness, power, riches, prosperity and popularity, to one of dishonour, meanness, poverty, calamity, distress and disgrace. Decrease of price or value. Lessening of sound, or cadence, applied to Music. A cascade or descent of water from a high place. The outlet of a current into any other water. Autumn. In Divinity, the state of our first parents, wherein on account of eating the forbidden tree, they lost the happiness of living in Paradise, and as Milton expresses it, " brought death into the world and all our woe."

FALLA'CIOUS, Adj. [*fallacieux*, Fr.] producing mistakes; full of sophistry, applied only to things, writings or propositions, never to persons. Raising false expectations; deceitful. " That *fallacious* fruit." *Par. Lost.*

FALLA'CIOUSLY, Adv. so as to deceive by false appearances, or sophistry.

FALLA'CY, S. [*fallace*, Fr. *fallacia*, Lat.] an argument made use of to lead a person into an error or mistake. A sophism.

FALLIBI'LITY, S. [from *fallo*, Lat.] possibility of being deceived, or imposed upon.

FA'LLIBLE, Adj. [*fallo*, Lat.] liable to error, imposition, or mistake.

FA'LLOW, Adj. [*fealuw*, Sax. *vaalouw*, Belg.] a pale red, or yellow, applied to colours. Unsowed; or left to rest or lie idle after certain years of tillage. Plowed but not sowed. Figuratively, unplowed; uncultivated, applied to ground. Unoccupied, or neglected. " Let the crease lie *fallow*." *Shak.*

FA'LLOW, S. [*fealge*, *feald*, Sax.] ground plowed in order for a second plowing; or land untilled and suffered to rest after bearing for a certain time.

To FA'LLOW, V. N. to plow in order to a second plowing, or to lie fallow.

FA'LLOWNESS, S. the act of letting ground rest before it be stocked or sowed again. Figuratively, barrenness.

FALMOUTH, a sea-port town of Cornwall, with a market on Thursdays, and two fairs, on July 27, and October 10, for horses, oxen, sheep, cloth, and a few hops. It is now large to what it was formerly; for, about 180 years ago, there were not more than two or three houses; but it is now governed by a mayor, four aldermen, and a town-clerk, and gives title to a viscount. It is a place of good trade, and is resorted to by ships; and the inhabitants also have ships of their own. The harbour is so large, that one hundred sail may fairly ride at anchor at a time; and those of the greatest burthen may come up to the key. The entrance into it is well defended by Pendennis-castle,

and two forts: The town has one church, and about three hundred houses; is chiefly consists of one paved street, which is pretty broad, and about three quarters of a mile in length. It is ten miles S. of Truro, and 268 W. by N. of London. Lon. 12. 5. Lat. 50. 15.

FALSE, Adj. [*falfus*, Lat.] representing a thing to be what it is not. Fictitious, or counterfeit, opposed to natural or real. Treacherous, or unjust, opposed to faithful, or honest; hypocritical or feigned, opposed to real.

FALSEHEA'RTED, Adj. treacherous, hypocritical, unfaithful.

FA'LSEHOOD, S. the representing a thing to be different from what it is or what we think it to be. Want of faithfulness, or honesty. A lie.

FA'LSELY, Adj. contrary to truth. Erroneously, perfidiously.

FA'LSENESS, S. contrariety to truth, dishonesty, perfidy.

FALSIFICA'TION, S. the act of altering words so as to make them signify something contrary the opinion of the author. Contradiction, or confutation. " To preserve his story from detection of *falfisication*." *Notes on the Odyss.*

FA'LSIFIER, S. one who alters the sense of an author. One who counterfeits, or makes a thing appear to be what it is not. A liar.

To FA'LSIFY, V. A. [*falsifier*, Fr.] to counterfeit; or forge. To alter the sense of a book or author. Figuratively, to confute, or prove false. To violate by treachery. " *Falsifying* the most important trust." *Decay of Piety.* To render improper for the purpose intended; to pierce through; from *falfer*, Ital. " His ample shield is *falfified*." *Dryd.* Though Dryden has by a long note on this term endeavoured to naturalize this word; yet no other author seems to have adopted it. Neuterly, to lie, or tell an untruth.

FA'LSITY, S. [*falfitas*, Lat.] the representing a thing to be different from what it is. A falsehood, or lie. Figuratively, an error; a principle, or position inconsistent with, or contrary to the nature of things.

To FA'LTER, V. N. [*falter*, of *falta*, Span.] to hesitate, or stammer in speaking. To fail in any act of the body or mind. Actively, to sift or cleanse.

FA'LTERINGLY, Adj. with hesitation and stammering. With languor, feebleness, debility, or weakness, applied to the body or mind.

FAME, S. [*fama*, Lat. *φημη*, Gr.] honourable report, honour, glory. Figuratively, rumour, or report.

FA'MED, Part. spoken of with honour and esteem.

A'ME-

FA'MELESS, Adj. not known for any production of the understanding, invention or action; of no repute.

FAMI'LIAR, Aj. (*familiaris*, Lat.) belonging to a family. Affable, or easy in conversation, opposed to formal. Without ceremony, with the freedom of persons long and intimately acquainted. Accustomed; common; frequent. Too free. "A poor man found a priest *familiar* with his wife." *Camden*.

FAMI'LIAR, S. one long and intimately acquainted with another. "A noble gentleman, and my *familiar*." *Shak*. A demon.

FAMILIA'RITY, S. an easiness and freedom of access and discourse. Figuratively, habit.

To FAMILIARIZE, V. A. (*familiarifer*, Fr.) to wear away the impressions of awe, ceremony, or distant respect, occasioned by novelty. To bring down from a state of distant superiority to that of a friendly familiarity.

FAMI'LIAR, Adv. with a freedom of access and discourse observed between persons long acquainted. Without ceremony or formality.

FAMI'LLE, *en famille*, Fr. (pronounced *awng famerel*) in a family manner; without restraint or formality. "Who at their dinners, *en famille*." *Swift*.

FA'MILY, S. those who live in the same house; or descend from the same progenitor. A class, tribe, or species. "There be two families of things." *Bacon*. The last sense is seldom used.

FA'MINE, S. (Fr. from *fames*, Lat.) scarcity of food. Distress for want of necessary food. There never was so dreadful a prospect of a famine before our eyes as at present, from the extravagant high price of all kinds of provisions. Insomuch, that those who were a few years ago able to live comfortably upon their incomes, are obliged to abridge themselves of the common necessaries of life, and the families of the mechanic and labourer are literally starving. Strange that legislation will not remove this grievance! But, when we consider, how many thousand lives were lost, at Patna, and other parts of the East-Indies, in order to make a few individuals immensely rich, we cannot wonder that an able ———— m ————y should be inattentive to the cries and miseries of the poor!

To FA'MISH, V. A. (*fames*, Lat. *famis*, old Fr.) to kill with hunger. To kill with want of something necessary to support life. "*Famish* him of breath, if not of bread." *Par. Lost*. Figuratively, to die, or be in great distress for want of food.

FA'MISHMENT, S. the pain of hunger; extreme distress for want of necessary food. "To suffer thirst and *famishment*." *Hakew*.

FA'MOUS, Adj. (*fameux*, Fr. *famous*, Lat.) celebrated for remarkable virtue, great exploits, useful inventions, or ingenious compositions. Sometimes though improperly applied to bad as well as good actions." "A *famous* highwayman."

FA'MOUSLY, Adv. spoken of with esteem for something extraordinary.

FAN, S. (*vannus*, Lat.) a thin film, piece of paper, taffety or other light stuff, cut semicircularly, plaited and mounted on several little sticks of wood, ivory, tortoiseshell, &c. which are joined together by a rivet at the other end, and used by the ladies to defend their complexions from the sun, to raise wind and cool themselves, &c. Any thing by which the air is moved; wings. "Stretch his feathered *fans*." *Dryd*. An instrument, by which chaff is winnowed from the corn. An instrument to blow up or raise a fire, flame or passion. "A *fan* to inflame that love." *Hooker*.

To FAN, V. A. to cool by the motion of a fan. To raise a fire. "*Fans* the poet's fire." *Pope*. To separate, or winnow.

FANA'TIC, S. a person who has wild notions in religion; an enthusiast. A person who pretends to immediate revelation, or inspiration.

FANA'TICISM, S. religious madness. The entertaining odd, wild, or enthusiastic notions in religion.

FAN'CIFUL, Adj. entertaining odd and whimsical notions; changing or taking up an opinion, without knowing why.

FAN'CIFULLY, Adv. in a manner inconsistent with the sober dictates of reason; changing upon slight grounds; whimsically.

FAN'CIFULNESS, S. the habit of following the wild notions of the fancy or imagination; whim.

FAN'CY, S. (*phantasia* from *phainesthai*, *phainō*, Gr.) a power or faculty of the mind, which forms objects, persons, representations, and other ideas which have no existence without us. The imagination. An opinion formed barely by the imagination, without the interposition of reason. An idea, image or conception of the mind. A liking, inclination, or fondness; humour, whim or caprice.

To FAN'CY, V. A. to conceive or form an idea in the mind, or imagination. "Whom I *fancy*, but can ne'er express." *Dryd*. To like, or grow fond of. "*Fancied* her so strongly." *Raleigh*.

FANCY'MONGER, S. one who is moved purely by the heat and sallies of the imagination.

To FANG, V. A. (*fangen*, Sax. *vangen*, Belg.) to seize; to gripe; to bite. "Destruction *fang* mankind." *Shak*.

FANG, S. the long tusks of a boar. The nails or claws of a bird or beast.

FA'NGLE, S. (*fangen*, Sax.) a silly attempt, a frivolous scheme. At present it is

seldom used, unless joined with the word new.

FANGLED, Part. gaudy; ridiculously; or oftentatiously showy. " In this *fangled* world." *Shak.*

FA'NGLESS, Adj. without fangs, claws, or teeth. " Like a *fangless* bear." *Shak.*

FA'NNER, S. one who makes use of a fan.

FANTASI'D, Part. troubled with odd imaginations, whims, or fancies.

FANTA'STIC, FANTA'SICAL, [*fantastique,* Fr.] Imaginary; irrational; not really exiftent, or refembling phantoms, fuppofed to affume fenfible bodies only to become perceptible. Capricious, governed by whim and fancy. Conceited, or fetting too much on one's own opinion, and thereby becoming ridiculously affected.

FANTA'STICALLY, Adv. In a manner which can exift only in imagination. Capriciously.

FANTASTICALNESS, FANTA'STICK-NESS, S. the quality of being guided by the firft fallies of imagination or fancy, without confulting reafon. Whimficalnefs. Capriciousnefs.

FAR, Adv. [*feor,* Sax. of *farr,* Sax.] to a great diftance. Almoft. Nearly. In a great meafure. " The day was *far* fpent." *Judges.* Greatly, and in comparifon. Much, or to a certain point. To a great height of complement or praife. " You fpeak him *far.*" *Shak.*

FAR', Adj. diftant from any place; Ufed with off. both as an adverb and as an adjective. *From far* is an elliptical expreffion for from a *far* or remote place. " The Lord fhall bring a nation againft thee *from afar.*" *Deut.* xxviii. 49.

To FARCE, V. A. [*farcir,* Fr. *farcio,* Lat.] to ftuff with different ingredients. Figuratively, to fwell out by pompous additions. " The *farced* title." *Shak.*

FARCE, S. [*farce,* Fr. to mock] a dramatic entertainment of the comic kind, feldom exceeding two acts, but confined to the eftablifhed laws of the drama. Figuratively, any incident, or circumftance which is rather diverting and ridiculous.

FARCICAL, Adj. belonging to a farce, ridiculous or comical.

FA'RCY, S. [*farcin,* Fr. *farcino,* Ital.] a difeafe in horfes or oxen, which vitiates their mafs of blood, appears in hard puftules, or running ulcers; in knots or ftrings along the veins, and is both a fpecies of, and as contagious as the leprofy.

FAR'DEL, S. [*fardello,* Ital. *fardeau,* Fr.] a bundle, weight, or burthen. " Who would *fardels* bear." *Shak.*

To FA'RE, V. N. [*faran,* Sax. *fare,* Fr.] to go. To walk, go or move from one place to another. " So can he *farre.*" *Per. Lyf.* To be in any ftate or condition,

either good, bad or indifferent. To live, applied to the manner of eating. " The rich man *fared* fumptuoufly." *Luke* xvi. 19.

FA'RE, S. the price paid for a paffage in any carriage, boat, &c. Food or provifion for eating.

FA'REWELL, Adv. a compliment ufed at parting, whereby we wifh the perfon well; whom we take leave of. Sometimes ufed merely to imply feparation or abfence, without including the idea of kindnefs. " Farewell, a long farewell to all my greatnefs." *Shak.*

FA'REWELL, S. leave; the act of parting. Sometimes ufed as an adjective, for fomething in which leave is taken. " In farewell papers." *Spect.* No. 445.

FARINA'CEOUS, Adj. [*farina,* Lat.] mealy; refembling meal. " The farinaceous or mealy feeds." *Arbuthn.*

FAR'M, S. [*ferme,* Fr. *feorm,* Sax.] ground occupied in tillage or pafturage. The ftate of lands let out at a certain annual fum. A certain fum of money paid a government for the right to its cuftoms, &c.

To FAR'M, V. A. (from the noun) to let or hire land of another for tillage. To cultivate land. To rent the cuftoms, taxes, &c.

FAR'MER, S. one who cultivates land. One who rents the taxes of a ftate.

FAR'MING, S. the art of cultivating land and breeding cattle.

FAR'MOST, Adj. [fuperlative of *far*] at the greateft diftance from a thing or place mentioned or implied.

FAR'NESS, S. the quality of being remote, or at a diftance. " Farnefs from timely fuccour." *Carew.* Followed by from.

FARNHAM, a town in Surry, with a market on Thurfdays, and three fairs, viz. on Holy-Thurfday, and June 24, for horfes, cattle, fheep, and hogs; and on November 2, for horfes and cattle. It is feated on the river Wye, and is a pretty good town, with a caftle feated on an eminence, where the bifhops of Winchefter ufually have refided; but is now much decayed. The houfes are handfome, and the ftreets well paved; and the market is large for wheat, oats, and barley. It is 12 miles W. of Guilford, 38 E. N. E. of Southampton, and 42 W. S. W. of London. Lon: 10. 45. lat. 51. 16.

FARQUHAR, Mr. George. This gentleman was defcended from a family of no inconfiderable rank in the North of Ireland, his father being a clergyman, and, according to fome, dean of Armagh. Our author was born at Londonderry in 1678, where he received the rudiments of erudition, and from whence, as foon as he was properly qualified, he was fent to the univerfity of Dublin, in 1694. He had given very early teftimony of a promifing genius, and difcovered even

at ten years of age a strong inclination for the service of the muses. By the progress he made in his studies at the university, he acquired a considerable reputation, but does not appear to have taken any degree there, for the natural blithiness and volatility of his disposition soon rendered him weary of an academic life. The public entertainments of the town more forcibly attracted his attention, but among them all none seemed to fix so strong a claim on his regards as the theatre, of which he soon found himself a propensity for being not only a spectator but a performer. His intimacy with the celebrated Mr. Wilks might probably strengthen that inclination in him, and when that gentleman engaged himself to Mr. Ashbury, the manager of the Dublin theatre, Mr. Farquhar was soon introduced on the stage through his means. In this situation he continued no longer than part of one season, nor made any very considerable figure. For though his person was sufficiently in his favour, and that he was possessed of the requisites of a strong retentive memory, a just manner of speaking, and an easy and elegant deportment, yet his natural diffidence and timidity, or what is usually termed the stage-terror, which he was never able to overcome, added to a thin insufficiency of voice, were strong bars, in the way of his succefs, more especially in tragedy.——However, notwithstanding these disadvantages, it is not improbable, as from his amiable private behaviour he was much esteemed, and had never met with the least repulse from the audience in any of his performances, that he might have continued much longer on the stage, but for an accident which determined him to quit it on a sudden; for being to play the part of Guyomar in Dryden's Indian Emperor, who kills Vasquez, one of the Spanish Generals, Mr. Farquhar, by some mistake, took a real sword instead of a foil on the stage with him, and in the engagement wounded his brother tragedian, who acted Vasquez, in so dangerous a manner, that although it did not prove mortal, he was a long time before he recovered it; and the consideration of the fatal consequences that might have ensued, wrought so strongly on our author's humane disposition, that he took up a resolution never to go on the stage again, or submit himself to the possibility of such another mistake. Thus did Mr. Farquhar quit the stage, at a period of life when few have even attempted to go on it, for at this juncture he could not have been much more than seventeen years of age, since some time afterwards, when Mr. Wilks, being engaged again to Drury-Lane theatre, left Dublin, Mr. Farquhar accompanied him to London; and this event happened no later than in the year 1696, at which time he was but eighteen. Here his abilities and agreeable address met with considerabl-

encouragement, and in particular recommended him to the patronage of the earl of Orrery, who gave him a lieutenant's commission in his own regiment, then in Ireland, which he held several years, and in his military capacity constantly behaved without reproach, giving on many occasions proofs of great bravery and conduct.

But these were not all the perfections which appeared in Mr. Farquhar; and Mr. Wilks, who well knew his humour and abilities, and was convinced that he would make a much more conspicuous figure as a dramatic writer than as a theatrical performer, never ceased his solicitations on that head, till he had prevailed on him to undertake a comedy, which he compleated and brought on the stage in 1698. This was his Love and a Bottle, a comedy, which, though written by its author when under twenty years of age, yet contain such a variety of incidents and characters, and such a sprightliness of dialogue, as must convince us, that even then he had a very considerable knowledge of the world, and a very clear judgment of the manners of mankind; and the success of it, even notwithstanding that Mr. Wilks, the town's great favourite in comedy, had no part in it, was equal to it's desert. Whether this play made it's appearance before or after he received his commission, does not seem very clear, but it is evident that his military avocations did not check his dramatic talents, but on the contrary rather improved them, since in many of his plays, more especially in his Recruiting Officer, he has admirably availed himself of the observations of life and character, which the army was able so amply to supply him with. And with such an easy pleasantry, and yet so severe a critical justice, has he rallied the foibles, follies and vices even of those characters that he might have been supposed the most partial to, that it has been observed, if he had not been himself an Irishman and an officer, it wou'd have been almost impossible for him to have avoided the resentments which would probably have fallen on him for the liberty he has taken in some of his pieces with the characters of some of the gentlemen of the army, as well as with those of a neighbouring kingdom. The success of his first play establish'd his reputation, and encouraged him to proceed, and the winter season of the jubilee year 1700. gave the public his favourite play of the Constant Couple, In which the gay airy humour thrown into the character of Sir Harry Wildair, were so well suited to Mr. Wilks's talents, that they gave him such an opportunity of exertion, as greatly heightened his reputation with the public, and in great measure repaid those acts of friendship which he had ever bestowed on Mr. Farquhar. This piece was played fifty-three nights in the first season, and has justly continued in high esteem

era fince. The following year produced a fequel to it; which, though much the moft indifferent of all his plays, yet met with tolerable fuccefs, and indeed with much better than the comedy of the *Inconftant*, which he gave to the public two years afterwards, viz. in 1703, and which vaftly excelled it in point of intrinfic merit. But the failure of the laft-mentioned piece was entirely owing to the inundation of foreign entertainments of mufic, finging, dancing, &c. which at that time broke in upon the Englifh ftage in a torrent, feemed with a magical infatuation at once to take poffeffion of British tafte, and occafioned a total neglect of the more valuable and intrinfic productions of our own countrymen. This little difcouragement, however, did not put a ftop to our author's ardour for the entertainment of the public, fince we find him ftill writing till almoft the hour of his death; his *Beaux Stratagem* having been written during his laft illnefs, and his death happening during the run of it. Notwithftanding the feveral difappointments and vexations which this gentleman met with during his fhort ftay in this tranfitory world, nothing feems to have been able to overcome the realinefs of his genius or the eafy goodnature of his difpofition; for he began and finifhed his well-known comedy of the *Beaux Stratagem* in about fix weeks, during his laft illnefs, notwithftanding that he, for great part of the time, was extremely fenfible of the approaches or death, and even foretold what actually happened, viz. that he fhould die before the run of it was over. Nay, fo calm and manly a manner did he treat the expectation of that fatal event, as even to be able to exercife his wonted pleafantry on the very fubject. For while his play was in rehearfal, his friend Mr. Wilks, who frequently vifited him during his illnefs, obferving to him that Mrs. Oldfield thought he had dealt too freely with the character of Mrs. Sullen, in giving her to Archer, without fuch a proper divorce as might be a fecurity for her honour, —" Oh," replied the author, with his accuftomed vivacity, " I will, if fhe pleafes, give that immediately, by getting a real divorce, marrying her myfelf, and giving her my bond that fhe fhall be a real widow in lefs than a fortnight." But nothing can give a more perfect idea of that difpofition I have hinted at in him, than the very heroic but expreffive billet which Mr. Wilks found after his death among his papers directed to himfelf, and which, as a curiofity in it's kind, I cannot refrain from giving to my readers; it was as follows,

Dear Bob,

" I have not any thing to leave thee to " perpetuate my memory, but two helplefs " girls; look upon them fometimes, and

" think of him that was, to the laft mo- " ment of his life, thine

George Farquhar."

nor would it be doing juftice to Mr. Wilks's memory not to obferve in this place, that he paid the moft punctual regard to the requeft of his dying friend, by fhewing thofe every act of regard, and when they became fit to be put out into the world, procured a benefit for each of them for that purpofe.

FARRA'GINOUS, Adj. (*farrago, farraginis,* Lat.) compofed of different things or perfons. Huddled. Mixed.

FARRA'GO, S. [Lat.] a mixed mafs; a medley.

FAR'RIER, S. [*ferrier,* Fr. from *ferre,* Fr. iron,] one who makes and fixes fhoes on horfes. One who profeffes to cure the difeafes of horfes.

To FAR'RIER, V. N. to practife phyfic on horfes.

FAR'ROW, S. [*farr,* Sax. *fearh.* Sax.] a litter of pigs.

To FARROW, V. N. to produce or bring forth pigs, applied to fwine.

FART, S. [*fert,* Sax. *vert,* Belg. *furz,* Teut.] wind let loofe behind.

To FART, V. N. to break wind behind.

FAR'THER, Adj. [this is erroneoufly taken to be the comparative degree of *far,* which would analogically make only *farer,* the ancient fpelling might poffibly be *forth, further,* from *further,* or *farther,* the *e* and *o* being frequently changed for each other in moft languages] at a greater diftance, applied to fituation. Longer. One more, or a ftronger, applied to arguments. Adverbially; at, or to a great diftance. Moreover; again; befides.

FAR'THERMORE, Adv. [more properly *furthermore*] moreover; befides, over and above. " Farthermore, the knaves, body, &c. Raleigh.

To FAR'THER, V. A. to promote, advance, countenance, or encourage. More properly fpelt, *further.*

FARTHEST, Adj. [from *far* or *forth* and *eft,* a Sax. termination for the fuperlative degree] moft diftant; at or to the greateft diftance.

FARTHING, S. [*feorthling,* Sax. from *feortha,* Sax.] the fmalleft Englifh coin, being the fourth part of a penny.

FAR'THINGALE, S. [*vertugalle,* Fr. *verdugal,* Span. *degarde,* Belg.] a hoop, or petticoat ufed to make the others ftand out, by means of circles of whalebone, or cane.

FAS'CES, S. [Lat.] axes tied up to a bundle with rods or ftaves, and borne before the Roman magiftrates, as an enfign of authority.

FASCIA'TION, S. in Surgery, a bandage, or the act and manner of binding parts.

To

To FA'SCINATE, V. A. [fascinatus, Lat.] to bewitch, or influence by enchantment, witchcraft, or spells.

FASCINA'TION, S. [fascinatio, Lat.] the act of bewitching or enchanting.

FASCI'NE, S. [Fr. pronounced fasseen] in Fortification, fagots, or small branches of trees, bound up in bundles, which are mixed with earth, and serve to fill up trenches, to screen the men, make parapets of trenches, &c.

FA'SCINOUS, S. [fascinum, Lat.] occasioned, or operating by witchcraft, spells, or enchantment.

FA'SHION, S. [façon, Fr. fattion, Ital.] the form, make, mode, or cut of any thing. Custom, or the form which is most commonly made use of. Men of fashion, implies rank, state, dignity.

To FA'SHION, V. A. [façonner, Fr.] to make or mould into a particular form or shape. To fit, or adapt. To make according to the mode.

FA'SHIONABLE, Adj. established by custom, fashion, or mode. According to the general taste. Observant of the mode.

FA'SHIONABLENESS, S. conformity to the reigning taste or mode.

FA'SHIONABLY, Adj. in a manner conformable to the reigning taste, or mode.

FA'SHIONIST, S. a person who follows the mode to dress to a degree of affectation. A fop.

To FAST, V. A. [fastan, Sax. fasta, Goth. wassan, Belg.] to abstain from eating or drinking. To mortify the body by abstaining from food, on a religious account.

FAST, S. [from the verb] a space of time, wherein a person takes little or no food. An abstinence from food on account of religion.

FAST, Adj. [fest, Sax. vest, Belg.] firm, or not in danger of falling or of being moved. Fixed. Deep or sound, applied to sleep. Closed or shut close, applied to a door, or the eyelids, &c. With a quick motion.

FAST, Adv. firmly; immoveably; swiftly; frequently.

To FA'STEN, V. A. to make firm. To cement, tie, or link together. To affix. To settle or make a thing stick without falling off. To lay on with force and strength; to impose. Neuterly, to stick or adhere. Used with on.

FA'STENER, S. a person or thing that makes firm, ties or binds, so as a thing will not move or fall off.

FA'STER, S. one who fasts or abstains from food.

FASTI'DIOUS, Adj. [fastidiosus, Lat.] disdainful; nice; squeamish.

FASTI'DIOUSLY, Adv. in a disdainful or squeamish manner.

FA'STNESS, S. [fastnesse, fastnisse,

Sax.] firmness, or firm adherence. A strong hold; a fortress. Closeness or compactness, applied to stile. "Being far from all loose grossness to such firm fastness in Latin, as in Demosthenes." Ascham.

FAT, Adj. [fet, Sax. fet, Teut.] full fed, fleshy, plump, or covered with an oily substance. Gross, dull. "Fat minds." Dryd. Figuratively, wealthy, rich, or sufficient to enable a person to live on luxuries or such things as may make him fat. "A fat benefice." Ayliffe.

FAT, S. [from the Adjective in Anatomy, a white oily and sulphureous part of the blood, to be found immediately under the skin, in all parts of the body except the forehead, eyelids, lips, under-part of the ear, scrotum, &c. It is divided into two sorts, 1st. that which we have already described, which is stiled by anatomists pinguedo; the other is whiter, harder, more brittle, and less easy to liquefy than the former, and is found in the cavities of the abdomen, omentum, &c. Both kinds serve as a natural balsam to preserve the body, and by mixing with and enveloping or sheathing the salts with which the blood abounds, keep them from corroding those parts through which they pass.

FAT, S. [fat, fatte, Sax.] a vessel in which any thing is put to ferment or soak. It is generally written and pronounced vat, but improperly if derived from the Saxon, as most of our monosyllables are.

To FAT, V. A. to make fat, plump or fleshy by feeding. Neuterly, to grow plump, fleshy or fat.

FA'TAL, Adj. [Fr. fatalis, Lat.] causing inevitable destruction. Caused by fate, destiny or necessity.

FA'TALISM, S. the doctrine or opinion that the occurrencies of life are established by an unalterable necessity. "Some persons have secured our author of fatalism." Waterland.

FA'TALIST, S. one who believes that all things happen by invincible necessity.

FATA'LITY, S. [fatalité] a pre-determined order or series of things and events. A decree of fate. An invincible influence or bias. A tendency to danger, destruction or death; Mortality. "The most unalterable fatality." Brown.

FA'TALLY, Adv. mortally; so as to occasion death. By the decree of fate.

FA'TE, S. an inevitable necessity depending on some fixed, or superior cause. The decree of God, whereby he has inevitably ordained what shall or shall not come to pass. The Stoical fate is a natural and invariable succession of all things from eternity, indissolubly linked together. Physical fate is an order and series of natural causes appropriated to their effects. Astrological fate is a necessary series or order of events, supposed to flow from the influence and position of the

3 I 2   heavenly

heavenly bodies. Figuratively, a necessary or predetermined event. Death; destruction. The cause of death.

FA'TED, adj. decreed by fate. Invested with any quality by fate. Having the power of fatal determination. "Thy fated sky." *Shak.*

FA'THER, S. [the *a* pronounced broad, from *fader*, Sax. *fader*, Dan.] one who has contributed to the generation of one of his own kind. Figuratively, the first ancestor; a title generally given to a person in years. An inventor, "Jubal was the *father* of all such as handle the harp." *Gen.* iv. 21. A title given to the ecclesiastical writers of the first centuries. One who deals with, and acts towards another with the kindness and affection of a parent. The title of a popish confessor, particularly that of a jesuit. The appellation of one of the persons in the blessed and adorable Trinity; likewise called our Father, on account of giving us being, of protecting us with a fatherly kindness, and of adopting us as coheirs with Christ in the system of redemption; alluding to these benefits we stile him in our prayers. "Our Father which art in heaven." *Matt.* vi.

FA'THER-IN-LAW, S. a husband, or wife's father.

To FA'THER, V. A. to adopt a person for one's son or daughter. To adopt or pretend to be the author of a thing. To ascribe a person or thing to another as his offspring or production.

FA'THERHOOD, S. the state of a parent or father.

FA'THERLESS, Adj. [*faderlies*, Sax.] without a father.

FA'THERLINESS, S. the tenderness and affection of a father.

FA'THERLY, Adj. [*faderlic*, Sax.] with the affection and tenderness of a father.

FA'THOM, S. [*fædm*, *færbm*, Sax.] a long measure containing six feet, or two yards, being taken from the space a man can reach with both his arms extended. At sea there are three kinds of fathoms, estimated according to the different bulks of vessels; 1st, that of men of war contain six feet. 2dly, the middling, or that of merchant ships five and a half feet. 3dly, the small fathom, used in fly-boats or fishing vessels, and is only five feet. Figuratively, depth of penetration; comprehensiveness, or extent of understanding. "Another of his *fathom* they have none." *Shak.*

To FA'THOM, V. A. to sound or find the depth of water at sea or in a river. Figuratively, to reach or comprehend. To penetrate, found; or go to the bottom of a subject or design.

FA'THOMLESS, Adj. having no bottom, or which is so deep as not to be measured. That which cannot be encompassed

with both arms extended. "Buckle in a waist most *fathomless.*" *Shak.* Not to be comprehended.

To FA'TIGATE, V. A: [*fatigatum*, Lat. of *fatigo*, Lat.] to exhaust, to make faint, languid or weary with excess of labour. "Requickened what in flesh was *fatigate.*" *Shak.*

FATI'GUE, S. [Fr. from *fatigo*, Lat.] languor, faintness. Figuratively, the cause of weariness.

FATI'GUE, V. A. to tire, exhaust, or make faint and languid with labour.

FA'TLING, S. a young beast or animal fattened for slaughter.

FA'TNER, S. that which makes fat. "The encomium of *fatner* of the earth." *Mort. Scribl.*

FA'TNESS, S. the quality of being fleshy, plump, or fat. Grease. Slimeness; fertility. That which causes or produces plenty. "The clouds drop *fatness.*" *Psalm.*

To FA'TTEN, V. A. to make fat by feeding. To make fruitful, applied to ground. To feed grossly. To increase. Neuterly, to grow fat or fleshy; to be pampered.

FA'TUOUS, Adj. [[*fatuus*, Lat.] stupid; foolish, applied to the understanding. Illusory, deceitful, alluding to the meteor called jack-a-lanthorn, which often lures the ignorant and unwary into dangers. "Hence *fatuous* fires and meteors take their birth." *Denh.*

FATUI'TY, S. [*fatuité*, Fr.] foolishness; a low degree of madness or frenzy.

FA'TTY, Adj. abounding in fat; oily; greasy.

FAU'CET, S. [*fausset*, Fr.] a wooden pipe, forced into a barrell to give passage to the liquor, and stopped with a peg or spigot.

FAVI'LLOUS, Adj. [*favilla*, Lat.] consisting of ashes. "The *favillous*, particles." *Brown.*

FAULT, S. [*faut*, *faute*, Fr. *feht*, Spm.] a slight defect or crime. A deviation from, or transgression of a rule in some trifling circumstance. A defect; blame; absence; want; from the French, *faute d'un autre.* "For *fault* of a better." *Shak.* This fault is not in use. Perplexed; embarrassed; alluding to the hunting phrase. "The hounds are at *fault.*" i. e. Have lost scent, and cannot find out the game again.

FAU'LTILY, Adv. blameably; wrongly. Improperly, or defectively.

FAU'LTINESS, S. the quality of transgressing a law in some slight particular.

FAU'LTLESS, Adj. without defect; perfect; blameless.

FAU'LTY, Adj. blameable, or to be found fault with in a slight degree. Defective. "A *faulty* helmet." *Brown.*

To FA'VOUR, V. A. [*favere*, Lat.] to support, encourage, promote, or advance an under-

undertaking. To resemble in features. "The gentleman *savoured* his matter." *Spect.* To assist, support, or encourage a person.

FA'VOUR, S. [*favour*, Fr. *favor*, Lat.] countenance, support or encouragement. Defence, or vindication. "In *favour* of which they are here alledged." *Rogers.* A kindness granted. Leave, permission, or pardon. "With your *favour*," *Dryd.* The object of favour or kindness. "His chief delight and *favour* art." *Par. Loft.* A ribband formed into a rose, and worn as a cockade. Features of the face. Look, or aspect. "A youth of fine *favour* and shape," *Bac.*

FA'VOURABLE, Adj. kind; affectionate; conducive to; tender. None can have the *favourable* thought." *Dryd.* Convenient; suited to a particular design. "*Favourable* for the making of levies." *Clarend.*

FA'VOURABLENESS, S. kindness shewed in pardoning a perfon's defects, and in encouraging his undertakings.

FA'VOURABLY, Adv. kindly, tenderly, or affectionately.

FA'VOURED, Part. regarded with kindness. "Oft with some *favour'd* traveller they ftray." *Pope.* Featured ; but always joined either with *well* or *ill.* "All *ill-favour-ed.*" *F. Queen.*

FA'VOURER, S. one who encourages or countenances.

FA'VOURITE, S. [from *favori*, *favorite*, Fr. *favorito*, Ital.] one regarded with particular kindness, and distinguished from others by the familiarities or kindnesses shewn him.

FA'VOURITE, Adj. esteemed, or beloved above others. "A *favourite* child.

FA'WN, S. [*faon*, Fr. from *fan*, old Fr.] a young deer.

To FA'WN, V. A. [*faang*, Ifl. the bofom; it being ufual to hug a child amidst parental endearments to that place,] to make use of infinuating and alluring geftures, applied to a dog. Figuratively, to endeavour to gain a perfon's favour, by fervile compliances. To bring forth a *fawn*, in its primary fignification.

FA'WNER, S. one who endeavours to gain favour by fervile compliances.

FA'WNINGLY, Adv. in a cringing fawning, and fervile manner.

FE'ALTY, S. [*feaulté*, Fr. of *feal*, Fr. a fubject] duty due from a fubject to a king; duty to a fuperior.

FEA'R, S. [*faran*, *afaran*, Sax. *vaer*, Belg. *faith*, Erfe] an uneafinefs of mind arifing from the thought of future evil that may befal us. Dejection, or dread at the prefence of any perfon or thing, who is able or may be inclined to hurt us. Figuratively, the caufes, or the object of fear. Something made ufe of to fcare deer or birds by its noife. "He who fleeth from the *noife* of the *fear* fhall fall into the pit." *Ifa.* xxiv. 18.

To FEA'R, V. A. [*faran*, Sax.] to ap-

prehend evil from. To affect with an apprehenfion of mifchief or evil. "Seeing it up to *fear*, the birds of prey." *Shak.* Neutrally to be affected with dread from the apprehenfion of future evil.

FEA'RFUL, Adj. timorous, afraid. Ufed with *of* before the object of terror. Awful, commanding reverence. "Glorious in holinefs, *fearful* in praifes." *Exod.* xv. 11. Terrible; frightful; affecting with an apprehenfion of future evil, or *fear*.

FEA'RFULLY, Adv. in a manner which fhews or caufes *fear*.

FEA'RFULNESS, S. an habitual dread or *fear*. Timorousnefs. An apprehenfion of having done, or doing any thing which is amifs, or may expose to blame or punifhment.

FEA'RLESS, Adj. free from *fear*. Not hindered from action by the apprehenfion of either mifchief or evil. Not regarding danger.

FEASIBI'LITY, S. [from *faifible*] a thing that is practicable. The poffibility of a thing being done.

FEA'SIBLE, Adj. [*faifible*, Fr.] practicable, fuch as may be done.

FEA'SIBLY, Adv. foas to be practicable, or poffible.

FEA'ST, S. [*fefte*, Fr. *fiftum*, Lat.] a fumptuous entertainment for a number of perfons. An anniverfary day of rejoicing. Something nice, or delicious.

To FEA'ST, V. N. to eat fumptuoufly; to live on coftly and delicious food. To gratify.

FEA'STFUL, Adj. feftival, or rejoicing, "On *feaftful* days." *Milton.* Luxurious, riotous.

FEA'T, S. [*fait*, Fr.] a thing done ; an act or exploit. A trick. An odd or extraordinary motion or exertion of the limbs. "All *feats* of activity." *Bacon.*

FEA'THER, S. [pronounced *fether*, with *e* fhort, from *fether*, Sax.] the covering of birds, and thereby which they are enabled to fly. Whoever confiders the commodioufnefs of this drefs for the inhabitants of the air, either for keeping them warm or dry, for enabling their flight, by the manner in which they are difpofed all over their bodies, and feveral other particulars refpecting their conftruction &c. muft acknowledge that they proclaim the wifdom of an omnifcient maker. Figuratively, kind, nature, or fpecies. "I am not of that *feather.*" *Shak.* An ornament. A mere empty title. A mere play thing, or fomething fit only to divert. "A wit's *feather.*" *Pope.*

To FEA'THER, V. A. to drefs in, or fit with feathers. To tread, applied to a cock. To enrich, to adorn. "To *feather* himfelf." *Sax.* To *feather* one's eft, is to grow rich, to fcrape riches together ; alluding to a bird's collecting feathers for lining its neft.

FEA-

FEA'THERED, Adj. cloathed or carrying feathers.

FEA'THERLESS, Adj. without feathers.

FEA'TLY, Adv. in a neat, skillful, curious, or dexterous manner.

FEA'TURE, S. [faiture, old Fr.] the make of the face, or any lineament of it.

To FEA'TURE, V. A. to resemble in countenance. To favour. Figuratively, to reflect the likeness of a person. " A glass that featured them." Shak.

To FEAZE, V. A. to untwist the end of a rope, and reduce it again to flax.

FE'BRIFUGE, S. [Fr. febris, Lat. and fugo, Lat.] in Medicine, a remedy to cure a fever.

FE'BRIFUGE, Adj. having the power of curing a fever.

FE'BRUARY, S. [so called from februa, the name of a feast held by the Romans in behalf of the manes of the deceased. Februus, Lat. is the name for Pluto] the name of the second month in the year.

FE'CULENCE, FECULENCY, S. [fæculentia, Lat.] foulness, applied to liquors. Figuratively, dregs; sediments.

FE'CULENT, Adj. foul, not clear, applied to liquors.

FECUND, S. [fœcundus, Lat.] fruitful; abounding in children. " The less fecund or fruitful of children they be." Graunt.

FECUNDA'TION, S. [fœcundatio, Lat.] the act of making fruitful. " As a medicine of fœcundation." Brown.

FECU'NDITY, S. the quality of producing our bringing forth in great abundance. The power of producing or bringing forth.

FED, the preter and participle passive of FEED.

FE'DERAL, Adj. [from fœdus, Lat.] relating to a contract.

FEE, S. [feo, feo, feoh, Sax. faihu, Goth.] in law, lands and tenements held in perpetual right. A property. A reward, or money given to a physician or lawyer. A perquisite due or given to a person in an office.

FEE-FARM, S. in law, lands holden by a man and his heirs for ever.

FEE-SIMPLE, S. in law, that whereof we are seised to us and our heirs for ever.

FEE-TAIL, S. in law, is when lands are given to a man, and the heirs of his body; so that if he have children by a third venter, and not of the first, they shall inherit.

To FEE, V. A. to pay a counsellor or physician. To bribe. To keep in hire or pay.

FEE'BLE, Adj. [faible, Fr.] wanting strength, weak.

To FEE'BLE, V. A. to weaken, or deprive of strength. " Shall that victorious hand be feebled here ?" Shak.

FEE'BLENESS, S. want of strength and vigour.

FEE'BLY, Adv. in a weak, feeble, manner.

To FEED, V. A. [Preter. & Part. pass, fed; fodian, Goth.] to supply with food. Figuratively to supply. To graze, or consume by feeding cattle. " Feed your mowing lands." Tomsuild, cherish, or keep alive. To entertain; or keep pleasantly employed. " The alteration of scenes feeds and relieves the eye." Bac. Neuterly, to take food, generally applied to irrational animals. To turn cattle to pasture, or to graze. To live upon, to prey upon; used with on or upon.

FEE'DER, S. one who supplies with food. One that eats. Figuratively, a nourisher, supporter, or encourager. " A feeder of my riots." Shak.

To FEE'L, V. N. [Preter. & Part. Pass. felt; felan, Sax.] to perceive by the touch. Figuratively, to grope after; to search for by the touch. To have a quick sensibility of good or evil which happens to others. Actively, to perceive by touching. Figuratively, to have the sense of pain or pleasure. To be affected by. To know, or be acquainted with. " He felt himself." To try, found, or discover. " He hath writ this, to feel my affection to your honour." Shak.

FEE'L, S. the sense of feeling, the touch.

FEE'LER, S. one who can distinguish by the touch, one who feels.

FEE'LING, S. the sense whereby we get the ideas of hard, soft, dry, wet, smooth, rough, hot, cold, &c. It is both the grossest, and the most extensive of all the senses; it is that which includes all the rest. Figuratively, perception, sensibility, tenderness.

FEE'LINGLY, Adv. in such a manner, as if sensible of feeling any thing one's felt. So as to affect others deeply.

FEET, S. the plural of FOOT.

FEE'TLESS, Adj. without feet; having no feet.

To FEI'GN, V. A. [feindre, Fr.] to invent; to pretend a thing which is not. To counterfeit or put on the appearance of a thing. " Feigns a laugh." Pope. To relate fictitiously; to fable.

FEI'GNEDLY, Adv. in a fictitious, counterfeit, or fabulous manner.

FEI'GNER, S. an inventor. The author of a fable, falshood or fiction.

FEI'NT, Part. [feint, Fr.] invented. Opposed to true, or real. " Any feint appearance." Locke.

FEINT, S. [feint, Fr.] a mere show; a false appearance or attempt; a disguise. In Fencing, a false offer made at one part to draw a person off from his guard, when the design is to make a real pass at another. In Rhetoric, a figure wherein the speaker touches

touches on a subject, while he pretends to pass it by. In Music, a semitone.

To FELI'CITATE, V. A. [*felicitans*, Lat.] to make happy. " To fill and felicitate his spirits." *Watts.* To congratulate; to wish a person joy, or rejoice with a person on account of his having met with success, preferment, or some remarkable good occurrence.

FELICITA'TION, S. [Fr.] the act of wishing joy.

FELI'CITY, S. [*felicité*, Fr. *felicitas*, Lat.] a state wherein a person is easy without pain, and joyful without any dash or mixture of sorrow.

FELL', Adj. [*fell*, Sax.] void of mercy, cruel; barbarous; savage.

To FELL', V. A. [*fell*, Isl. and *feallan*, Sax.] to knock down. To hew or cut down.

FELL', Preter of FALL.

FELL'ER, S. one who hews or cuts down timber, &c.

FELL'MONGER, S. [from *fel*, Sax.] one that deals in pelfry or skins.

FELL'OE, S. [*felge*, Dan. and Teut.] the pieces of wood which make the circumference of a wheel. Sometimes wrote *felly* or *felly*.

FELL'OW, S. a companion. One united in the same undertaking. An equal. One thing suited to another, or one of a pair. " The *fellow* to my shoe." One like to, or resembling another. Sometimes used in familiar discourse for a man or person. " A valiant *fellow*." *Shak.* Sometimes used in contempt, to convey the idea of a low or despicable person. A member of a society. A member of a college, who partakes in its government and revenues.

To FELL'OW, V. A. to suit or match. To pair or produce one thing resembling another in size, colour, &c.

FELL'OW-COMMONER, S. one who has the right of common with another. In Cambridge, a commoner of the higher order, who eats his commons with the fellows of the college.

FELL'OW-FEELING, S. sympathy; or the being affected with the sufferings of another. A combination in order to cheat. " Your milkwoman and your nursery maid have a *fellow-feeling*." *Hist. of J. Bull.*

FELL'OW-LABOURER, S. one who labours to promote the same end or design. " My *fellow-labourers*." *Dryd.*

FELL'OWSHIP, S. company; society. Association; a confederacy or union of two or more persons by some contract, bond, or obligation. A partnership or joint interest. Equality. Fondness for feasting or entertainments of drinking, used with *good*. An establishment at a university. In Arithmetic, a rule by which the stock of any company is divided in proportion to the several sums each partner brought in.

FE'LLY, S. See FELLOE.

FE'LO *de se*, S. [law Lat.] in Law, one who wilfully and deliberately kills himself.

FEL'ON, [Fr. *felo*, law Lat. *felonia*, Teut. *feolian*, Sax. to be deficient] a person guilty of some crime, which will subject him to death by the law. A whitlow.

FEL'ON, Adj. [*felle*, Sax.] cruel; barbarous; savage. " His *felon* hate." *Pope.*

FELO'NIOUS, Adj. relating to a felon; figuratively, wicked; barbarous.

FELO'NIOUSLY, Adv. after the manner of a felon.

FEL'ONY, S. [*felonie*, Fr. *felonia*, Lat.] any crime which subjects a man to the punishment of death by the law.

FE'LT, the Preter. of FEEL.

FELT, S. [Sax.] a kind of stuff, or cloth, either of wool alone, or of castors, camels, conies hair, and lambs wool, wrought and fulled with lees and size, and afterwards shaped into the form of a hat upon a block. A hide or skin of animals; from *fel*, Sax. " See that the *felt* be loose." *Mort.*

To FE'LT, V. A. to make cloth or stuff only by fulling, without weaving or crossing. " The same wool one man *felts* into a hat." *Hale.*

FELU'CCA, S. [*felow*, Fr. *feilow*, Arab.] a small six-oared vessel, much used in the Mediterranean.

FE'MALE, S. [*femelle*, Fr.] that sex which bears, produces, or brings forth young.

FE'MALE, Adj. belonging to that sex which conceives or bears offspring.

FE'ME covert, S. [Fr.] in Law, a married woman.

FE'ME sole, S. [Fr.] in Law, a single, or unmarried woman. A *feme sole merchant*, is a woman in London who carries on a trade without her husband, and is therefore charged without him. *Cup. of Lond.*

FE'MININE, Adj. [*femininus*, Lat.] of that sex which conceives and bears young. Figuratively, soft, delicate. Like a woman, womanish. " Not a man of war, but altogether *feminine*." *Raleigh.* In Grammar, that gender which denotes a word to belong to a female.

FE'MININE, S. a female. " Masculine without *feminine*." *Par. Lost.*

FEN, S. [*fen*, *fenne*, Sax.] a wet, moist, or boggy place on land overflowed with water, so as not to be solid enough to support the weight of a person; or else having some eminencies of dry land interspersed with rivulets, or pieces of water.

FE'NCE, S. [a contraction of *defence*] any thing made use of to guard from danger. " There is no *fence* against inundations." L'*Estrange.* An inclosure, hedge, or paling.

To FE'NCE, V. A. to inclose in a hedge or paling. To defend or guard. Neuterly, to practise the art of fencing. To guard against

against; to use such methods as to hinder the progress of any vice or evil.

FEN'CELESS, Adj. open, or without any inclosure or fence.

FEN'CER, S. a person who fences. One who teaches fencing or the art of using the sword.

FEN'CIBLE, Adj. capable of defence.

FEN'CING, S. the art of defence, or of using the sword. This is in so great repute in the East, that none but princes are allowed to reach it; but in Kouraigar's time, the nobility of France, looked upon a skill in this science, in the same manner as the Romans did on a perfection in dancing, i. e. as a very great disgrace. Fencing, likewise signifies the hedge or pales used to inclose ground.

To FEN'D, V. A. [from defend] to keep off. "To fend the bitter cold." Dryden. Neuterly, to dispute; or shift off a charge. "Able to fend and prove with them." Locke. Amongst the sailors, the same as defend; thus, to fend the boat, is to keep it from dashing to pieces, or driving against rocks.

FEN'DER, S. a plate of iron or brass laid before a fire to prevent the coals that fall, from rolling upon the floor. Among mariners, any thing laid or hung on the side of a ship to keep off violence.

FEN'NEL, S. [finel, finol, fenshel, Teut. fenoüil, Fr.] in Botany, an umbellated flower. Linnæus, somewhat improperly, has joined it with the ox thorn, which belongs to the second sect of his fifth class. The leaves, seeds, and roots of the common sort are used in medicine; the root one of the five opening roots, the seed one of the four carminative seeds, and the leaves made use of in distilling a simple water.

FEN'NY, Adj. [from fen] soft, applied to ground; marshy; moorish. Inhabiting, or dwelling in a marsh. "A fenny snake." Shak.

FE'ODAL, Adj. [feodal, Fr.] held from another.

FE'ODARY, S. [from fodum, law Lat.] one who holds his estate under a superior lord.

To FE'OFF, V. A. [fief, fuffer, Fr. feofo, law Lat.] to put in possession. To give a right of possession.

FEOFFE', S. [feoffum, law Lat. fuffé, Fr.] a person put in possession.

FEOF'FER, S. one who gives possession in fee simple.

FEOF'FMENT, S. [feoffamentum, law Lat.] in Law, a grant of lands to another in fee, that is to him and his heirs for ever.

FE'RITY, S. [feritas, Lat.] barbarity; cruelty; wildness. "The most abject and stupid ferity." Woodw. Now in use.

To FER'MENT, V. A. [fermenter, Fr. fermento, Lat.] to exalt, or rarify by put-

ting the particles into an intestine commotion. Neuterly, to have its parts put into intestine commotion.

FER'MENT, S. [Fr. fermentum, Lat.] that which causes an intestine motion in a fluid. Figuratively, the intestine motion of the particles applied to fluids. A commotion or tumult.

FERMEN'TABLE, Adj. capable of having its parts fermented.

FERMENTA'TION, S. [Fr. fermentatio, Lat.] intestine motion of the small insensible particles of a thing.

FERMENTA'TIVE, Adj. causing an intestine commotion.

FERN, S. [fearn, Sax.] in Botany, a plant growing on clumps of trees in woods, and on the banks of ditches.

FERNANDES, JUAN, a little uninhabited island of the S. Sea, reckoned to be in S. America, and province of Chili. It seems to sailors to be a very mountainous place at a distance, and extremely rugged and irregular, but, when they come near it, they are agreeably deceived, for it is covered with woods, every where interspersed with the finest valleys, clothed with a most beautiful verdure, and watered with numerous streams and cascades, there being no valley of any extent but what is watered with a rill. It is visited by all the English ships that pass through the S. Sea, and is of excellent use for recovering the sailors who are sick of the scurvy, for the refreshments it produces soon restore them to their health and vigour. It is the only commodious place in those seas where the British cruisers can refresh and recover their men, after their passage round Cape Horn, where they may remain some time without alarming the Spanish coast. This island lies in lat. S. 43, 40, and is 330 miles from the continent of Chili. Its greatest length is between 15 and 16 miles, and its greatest breadth not quite 6. The only safe anchoring is on the N. side of this island, in Cumberland-bay. The soil on the northern part is very loose, and shallow, so that trees soon perish for want of root. They are most of them of the aromatic kind, and there are none fit for timber, except the myrtles. Here are also pimento and cabbage-trees, and a great number of plants, of various kinds, which are unknown in these parts, except water-cresses, purslain, and wild sorrel, besides a vast number of turnips, and Sicilian raddishes, formerly sown here. Here were a great number of goats, but the Spaniards have diminished them by putting large dogs on shore, who have destroyed all those they could come at. There are a great number of seals about the island, and another amphibious creature, called a Sea-lion; they bear some resemblance to a seal, though much larger, for they are from 12 to 20 feet in length, and from 8 to 15 in circum-

ference,

ference. Their skins are covered with short hair, of a light dun colour, but their tails and ears, which serve them for feet and shoe-s, are almost black. The fatters feed upon both of these, eating the one veal, and the other veal. Besides, there are very large cod, crawfish, groupers, large breams, maids, silver-fish, congers of a peculiar kind, and, above all, a black fish which is very delicious, called by some a chimney-sweeper, and in shape somewhat resembles a carp. Admiral Anson landed here in 1741, and Alexander Selkirk, a Scotchman, lived here four years and four months alone, till he was taken in by an English ship which passed that way.

FER'NEY, Adj. overgrown or abounding with fern.

FERO'CIOUS, Adj. [ferox, Fr. ferus, Lat.] wild, untamed, savage, brutal; " Each ferocious feature." *Pope*.

FERO'CITY, S. [ferocité, Fr. ferocitas, Lat.] fierceness or savageness of disposition.

FER'RET, S. [fured, Brit. furet, Fr.] a small animal with red eyes, and a long snout, used to catch rabbets, or rats. A kind of narrow ribband made of silk, with a mixture of thread or cotton.

To FER'RET, V. A. to hunt or drive out of a lurking place. " The arch-bishop had ferreted him out of all his holds." *Heylin*. Used with out before the hiding place.

FER'RETER, S. one who hunts another, and discovers him in his hiding places.

FER'RIAGE, S. the sum of money paid for passage at a ferry.

FER'RULE, S. [from ferrum, Lat.] an iron or brass cap, put round or at the end of a cane, &c. to hinder it from wearing.

To FER'RY, V. A. [faran, Sax. fero, Ital.] to row a boat, or vessel across the river; used with over. Neuterly, to cross a river in a boat.

FER'RY, S. a boat in which persons cross the water. Figuratively, the place where boats ply. The common passage for a boat across a river.

FER'RY-MAN, S. one who keeps a ferry; or rows a boat across the water.

FER'TILE, Adj. [Fr. fertilis, Lat.] producing a great quantity. Fruitful; with of before the thing produced.

To FER'TILITATE, V. A. to make fruitful, or fertile.

FERTI'LITY, S. [fertilité, Fr. fertilitas, Lat.] the quality of producing in great plenty or abundance. Fruitfulness.

To FER'TILIZE, V. A. [fertiliser, Fr.] to make fruitful, or fertile.

FER'VENCY, S. [ferveur, Fr. fervens, Lat.] eagerness, warmth of application. Zeal, or warmth of devotion, Ardency.

FER'VENT, Adj. [Fr. fervens, Lat.] hot, vehement, or warm. Ardent, warm, zealous.

No. XI.

FER'VENTLY, Adv. eagerly, vehemently; earnestly, zealously.

FER'VID, Adj. [fervidus, Lat.] hot, or ardent, zealous; vehement, fervent.

FERVI'DITY, S. heat opposed to cold; warmth of temper.

FER'VIDNESS, S. the quality of being warm of temper, earnest or zealous in devotion.

FE'RULA, S. [Lat. ferula, Fr. from ferio, Lat.] in Botany, fennel-giant. Likewise an instrument made use of by schoolmasters, to slap the hands of their scholars with by way of punishment.

To FE'RULE, V. A. to strike with a ferula.

FER'VOUR, S. [ferveur, Fr. fervor, Lat.] heat, eagerness, warmth, or heat of temper; ardour, or zeal in devotion.

FESSE, S. [fascia, Lat. a band or girdle] in Heraldry, one of the nine honourable ordinaries, representing a band or belt, dividing the escutcheon horizontally in the middle, and separating the chief from the point.

To FESTER, V. N. [fester, Sax.] to rankle, to grow inflamed or angry.

FES'TIVAL, Adj. [festivus, Lat.] belonging to feasts, or public entertainments. " Festival entertainments." *Art*.

FES'TIVAL, S. a time of public or general feasting. A day of religious or public joy.

FES'TIVE, Adj. [festivus, Lat.] gay; joyous, merry.

FESTI'VITY, S. [festivitas, Lat.] a feast, or time of public rejoicing. Gaiety; joyfulness. A temper or behaviour suitable to a feast.

FES'TOON, S. [feston, Fr.] in Architecture, an ornament of carved work in the form of a garland of flowers twisted together thickest at middle, and suspended at the ends.

To FETCH, V. A. [Preter fetched, fetean, Sax.] to go, in order to bring something to a person. To drive, applied to family descent. To bring to any state, by some powerful means. To perform with suddenness and violence. To take, or make an exertion. " To fetch a turn about the garden." *Shak*. To reach, arrive at, to come up to, or equal in motion. To equal in value. " Silver in the coin, will never fetch so much as silver in bullion." *Locke*.

FETCH, S. a stratagem, a trick, or artifice.

FETCHER, S. one who makes use of tricks or artifice. One who goes for a thing from a distant place.

FE'TID, Adj. [fœtidus, Lat.] stinking; having a strong and disagreeable smell.

FE'TIDNESS, S. the quality of having a stinking and offensive smell.

FET'LOCK, S. in Farriery, a tuft of hair

y K   grows

growing behind the pastern joint ; horses of
low size have it not.

FET'TER, S. [*fetter*, Sax.] chains put
on prisoners feet to prevent their escape. Figuratively, any restraint or confinement.

To FET'TER, V. A. to put chains or
shackles on the legs. To bind; to deprive
of freedom.

FE'TUS, S. [*fœtus*, Lat.] any animal in
embrio, or in the womb.

FEUD, S. [*feahd*, Sax.] quarrel; opposition ; war ; enmity.

FEUDS, S. [plural ; *feodum*, Lat.] in
Law, lands that are hereditary. " Lands
were originally held at will, and then called
munera, or grants ; afterwards they were held
for life, and then termed *beneficia*, henceforth ;
after which they were made hereditary in families, and then called *feuds*." ; Salt. xvi. 5.

FEU'DAL, Adj. [*feudalis*, low Lat.] pertaining to fees or tenures, by which lands
are held of a superior lord.

FEU'DATORY, S. [*feudataire*, Fr.] one
who holds from a superior.

FE'VER, S. [*fevre*, *fievre*, Dan. and
Teut. *febris*, Fr. *febris*, Lat] a disease in
which the body is violently heated, and the
pulse quickened ; or in which heat and cold
prevail by turns ; the last is termed an intermittent fever.

FE'VERISH, Adj. troubled slightly with
a fever. Figuratively, inconstant, alluding
to the alternate sensation of heat and cold in
intermittent fevers. " We toss and turn a-
bout our *feverish* will. *Dryd.*

FE'VEROUS, Adj. [*fiévreux*, *fiévreuse*,
Fr.] troubled with a fever. Having a tendency to produce fevers. " A *feverous* disposition of the year." *Bacon.*

FE'VERSHAM, S. a town of Kent, with
two fairs, on February 25 and August 21,
for linen, woollen-drapery, and toys. It
is seated on a creek of the river Medway, and
is well frequented by small vessels ; it is
large, well built, and inhabited by tradesr-
men and innkeepers. It is opposite to the isle
of Sheppy, and a member of the town and
port of Dover. It is governed by a mayor,
12 aldermen, 24 jurats, and a peace-officers.
It has one large church built with stone,
newly repaired, and contains about 1100
houses, built with brick. The streets are wide
and paved, and the town contains about 8000
inhabitants. It has a large corn-market
every Thursday, but no particular manufacture is carried on here. It is nine miles W.
of Canterbury, and 48 E. by S of London
Lon. 18. 13. lat. 51. 20.

FEW', Adj. [*feo*, *feawe*, Sax. *faer*, Brit.
not many, applied most properly to number ;
but by Londoners sometimes applied to
quantity ; as " a *few* broth," i. e. a small
quantity of broth. Sometimes elliptical use
with *in* ; as, " The firm resolve there in *few*

distress." *Pope.* The term *words* is understood.

FEW'EL, or FU'EL, S. [*feu*, Fr. fire]
materials for a fire.

To FEW'EL, V. A. to keep up a fire
with fuel. " *Fuels* the infernal flame."
Cowley.

FEW'NESS, S. smallness, applied to number.

FIB', S. [a corruption of *fable*, Lat.] an
untruth, a falsehood.

To FIB', V. N. to tell lies, falsehoods, or
untruths.

FIB'BER, S. one that speaks falsehoods.

FI'BRE, S. [Fr. *fibra*, Lat.] a small
thread or string. In Physics, a long fine
part or thread whereof natural bodies consist.
In Anatomy, a long slender thread, which
forms the various solid parts of an animal
body.

FI'BRIL, S. [*fibrilla*, Fr. *fibrilla*, Lat.]
a small fibre.

FI'BROUS, Adj. [*fibreux*, Fr.] consisting or abounding with small threads or
fibres.

FICK'LE, Adj. [*feol*, Sax.] inconstant.
Not fixed ; liable to change. " *Fickle* their
state." *For Lose.*

FICK'LENESS, S. a disposition of mind
liable to frequent change. A state of incon-
stancy, applied to the mind.

FIC'TION, S. [Fr. *fictio*, Lat.] the act
of forming a fable or story. The thing
feigned. A falsehood. A work of imagination.

FIC'TIOUS, Adj. [*fictus*, Lat. of *fingo*,
Lat.] imaginary. " *Fictious* circles" *Prior.*
A word coined by the author quoted ; but
frequently made use of, though *fictitious* is
the word.

FIC-TI'TIOUS, Adj. [*fictitius*, Lat.]
counterfeit. Made in order to resemble or
pass for something else. Imaginary, not
real.

FICTI'TIOUSLY, Adv. in a false counterfeit or chimerical manner.

FID'DLE, S. [*fithele*, Sax. *fidel*, Teut.]
in music, a stringed instrument. See
VIOLIN.

To FID'DLE, V. A. [*fidlen*, Teut.] to
play on a violin or fiddle. Figuratively,
to trifle, to spend a great deal of time on
trifles.

FID'DLE-FADDLE, S. [see FADDLE]
trifling or trifles. " Abundance of *fiddle-
faddle* of that nature." *Spell.* No. 299.

FID'DLE-FADDLE, Adj. trifling ; making a bustle about nothing. " A troublesome, *fiddle-faddle* old woman." *Hist. of J.
Bull.*

FID'DLER, S. [*fithelere*, Sax. *fidler*,
Belg.] one who plays on the fiddle or
violin.

·FIDDLE-

FIDD'LESTICK, S. the bow furnished with hair with which the musician plays on the fiddle.

FIDEL'ITY, S. [*fidelité*, Fr. *fidelitas*, Lat.] honesty, veracity or truth in testimony; firmness in adherence or in loyalty. Faithfulness.

To FID'GE or FIDGET, V. N. [a cant word if not from *fyco*, Sax. to be anxious through ill-will, or *fyd*, id. to be driven about by the wind] to move nimbly but uncouthly, or awkwardly. "You wriggle, fidge, and make a rant." *Swift.*

FIDU'CIAL, Adj. [*fiducia*, Lat.] confident; without any degree of doubt. That which may be depended on.

FIDU'CIARY, S. [*fiduciarius*, Lat.] one that has any thing in trust. In divinity, one who places so much confidence in faith, as to look on good works as unnecessary to his salvation.

FI'EF, S. [Fr.] in law, a possession held by some tenure of a superior.

FI'ELD, S. [pronounced *feeld*, *feld*, Sax.] ground not inhabited or built on. A space of ground which is cultivated. The open country, opposed to quarters. Figuratively, the ground where a battle is fought. A wide extent or expanse. "Where *fields* of light and liquid æther flow." *Dryd.* Compass; or a subject which will afford an opportunity for a person to display his abilities. "A large *field* to expatiate in." *Spect.* In painting or heraldry, the ground on which figures or bearings are drawn.

FIELD-FARE, S. [from *feld*, Sax. and *faren*, Sax.] a bird of passage, generally supposed to come from the Northern countries.

FIELDING, HENRY, Esq; this well-known and justly celebrated writer of our own time, was born at Sharpham-Park in Somersetshire, April 22, 1707. His father, Edmund Fielding, Esq; who was a younger son of the earl of Denbigh, was in the army, and towards the close of king George I's reign, or the accession of George II. was promoted to the rank of a lieutenant-general. His mother was daughter to judge Gould, and aunt to the present Sir Henry Gould. This lady, besides our author, who seems to have been her first born, had another son and four daughters, one of the latter being the celebrated Miss Fielding, author of David Simple, the countess of Delvio, the Cry, and many other very ingenious pieces. And, in consequence of his father's second marriage, Mr. Fielding had six half brothers, all of whom are dead, excepting the present Sir John Fielding, now in the commission of the peace for the counties of Middlesex, Surry, Essex, and the liberties of Westminster. Our author received the first rudiments of his education at home, under the care of the Rev. Mr. Oliver, for whom

he seems to have had no very great regard, as he is said to have designed a portrait of his character in the very humorous yet detestable one of parson Trulliber, in his Joseph Andrews. When taken from under this gentleman's charge, he was removed to Eton school, where he had an opportunity of cultivating a very early intimacy and friendship with several, who afterwards became the first persons in the kingdom, such as lord Littleton, Mr. Fox, Mr. Pitt, Sir Charles Hanbury Williams, &c. who ever through life retained a warm regard for him. But these were not the only advantages he reaped at that great seminary of education; for by an assiduous application to study and the possession of strong and peculiar talents, he became, before he left that school, uncommonly versed in the Greek authors, and a perfect master of the Latin classics. Thus accomplished, at about eighteen years of age he left Eton, and went to Leyden, where he studied under the most celebrated civilians for about two years, at the expiration of which time, the remittances from England not coming so regularly as at first, he was obliged to return to London. In short, general Fielding's family being very greatly increased by his second marriage, as may be seen from what we have said above, it became impossible for him to make such appointments for the eldest son, as he could have wished; the utmost that he could afford to allow him being no more than two hundred pounds a year, with which slender income, a strong constitution, a lively imagination, and a disposition naturally but little formed for œconomy, he found himself his own master, in a place where the temptations to every expensive pleasure are so numerous, and the means of gratifying them so easily obtainable. From this unfortunately pleasing situation sprung the source of every misfortune or uneasiness that Mr. Fielding afterwards felt through life. He very soon found that his finances were by no means adequate to the frequent draughts made on him from the consequences of the brisk career of dissipation which he had launched into; yet, as disagreeable impressions never continued long upon his mind, but only on the contrary roused him to struggle through his difficulties with the greater spirit and magnanimity, he flattered himself that he should find his resources in his wit and invention, and accordingly commenced a writer for the stage in the year 1727, at which time he had not more than attained the completion of his twentieth year. His first attempt in the drama was a piece called Love in several Masques, which, though it immediately succeeded the long and crowded run of the Provoked Husband, met with a favourable reception, as did likewise his second play, which came out in the following year, and was

was ratified, The Temple Beau. He did not however meet with equal success in all his dramatic works, for he has even printed in the title page of one of his farces, as it was damned at the theatre royal in Drury-Lane; and he himself informs us, in the general preface to his miscellanies, that for the Wedding-Day, though acted six nights, his profits from the house did not exceed fifty pounds. Nor did a much better fate attend on some of his earlier productions, so that, though it was his lot always to write from necessity, he would probably, notwithstanding his writings, have laboured continually under this necessity, had not the severity of the public and the malice of his enemies met with a noble alleviation from the patronage of several persons of distinguished rank and character, particularly the late dukes of Richmond and Roxburgh, John duke of Argyle, the present lord Lyttelton, &c. the last-named of which noblemen not only by his friendship softened the rigour of our author's misfortunes while he lived, but also by his generous ardour has vindicated his character and done justice to his memory after death. About six or seven years after Mr. Fielding's commencing a writer for the stage, he fell in love with and married one Miss Craddock, a young lady from Salisbury, possessed of a very great share of beauty, and a fortune of about fifteen hundred pounds, and about the same time his mother dying, an estate at Sanwer in Dorsetshire, of somewhat better than two hundred pounds per annum came into his possession.—With this fortune, which, had it been conducted with prudence and economy, might have secured to him a state of independence for life, and with the helps it might have derived from the productions of a genius unincumbered with anxieties and perplexities, might have even afforded him an affluent income; with this, I say, and a wife whom he was fond of to distraction, and for whose sake he had taken up a resolution of biding adieu to all the follies and intemperances to which he had addicted himself in that short but very rapid career of a town life which he had run, he determined to retire to his country seat, and there reside entirely.

But here, in spite of this prudent resolution, one folly only took place of another, and family pride now brought on him all the inconveniences in one place, that youthful dissipation and libertinism had done in another. The income he possessed, though sufficient for ease and even some degree of elegance, yet was in no degree adequate to the support of either luxury or splendour. Yet, fond of figure and magnificence, he incumbered himself with a large retinue of servants, and his natural turn leading him to a fondness for the delights of society and convivial mirth, he threw wide open the gates of hospitality, and suffered his whole patrimony to be devoured up by hounds, horses and entertainments. In short, in less than three years, from the mere passion of being esteemed a man of great fortune, he reduced himself to the displeasing situation of having no fortune at all; and through an ambition of maintaining an open house for the reception of every one else, he soon found himself without a habitation which he could call his own. In a word, by a desire, as Shakespeare expresses it,

—*of shewing a more sweltry port*

Than his faint means would grant continuance, he was, in the course of a very short period, brought back to the same unfortunate situation which he had before experienced; but with this aggravation to it, that he could now have none of those resources in future to look forward to, which he had thus indifferently lavished. He had undermined his own supports, and had now nothing but his own abilities to depend on for the recovery of what he had so wantonly thrown from him, an easy competence. Not discouraged, however, he determined to exert his best abilities, betook himself closely to the study of the law, and after the customary time of probation at the Temple, was called to the bar, and made no inconsiderable figure in Westminster-Hall. To the practice of the law Mr. Fielding now applied himself with great assiduity both in the courts here and on the circuits, so long as his health permitted him, and it is probable would have risen to a considerable degree of eminence in it, had not the intemperances of his early parts of life put a check, by their consequences, to the progress of his success. In short, though but a young man, he began now to be molested with such violent attacks from the gout, as rendered it impossible for him to be so constant at the bar as the laboriousness of his profession required, and would only permit him to pursue the law by snatches, at such intervals as were free from indisposition. However, under these united severities of pain and want, he still found resources in his genius and abilities.—He was concerned in a political periodical paper, called the Champion, which owed its principal support to his pen; a pen which seems never to have lain idle, since it was perpetually producing, almost as it were extempore, a play, a farce, a pamphlet, or a news-paper, but whose full exertion of power seemed reserved for a kind of writing different from, and indeed, superior to them all; nor will it perhaps be necessary in proof of this more than to mention his celebrated novels of Joseph Andrews and Tom Jones, which are too well known, and too justly admired to leave us any room for expatiating on their merits.—Precarious, however, as this means of subsistence unavoidably must be, it was scarcely possible he should be enabled

bled by it to recover his shattered fortunes, and was therefore at length obliged to accept of the office of an acting magistrate in the commission of the peace, for the county of Middlesex, in which station he continued till pretty near the time of his death;—an office however which seldom fails of being hateful to the populous, and of course liable to many infamous and unjust imputations, particularly that of venality; a charge which the ill-natured world, not unacquainted with Mr. Fielding's want of œconomy and passion for expence, were but too ready to cast upon him.—Yet from this charge Mr. Murphy, in the life of this author, prefixed to a late edition of his works, has taken great pains to exculpate him, as has likewise Mr. Fielding himself, in his Voyage to Lisbon, which was not only his last work, but may with some degree of propriety be considered as the last words of a dying man; that voyage having been undertaken only as a dernier resort in one last desperate effort for the preservation of life, and the restoring a constitution broken with chagrin, distress, vexation and public business, for his strength was at that time entirely exhausted, and in about two months after his arrival at Lisbon, he yielded his last breath, in the forty-eighth year of his age, and of our Lord 1754.

As to Mr. Fielding's character, as a man it may in a great measure be deduced from the incidents I have above related of his life, but cannot perhaps be with more candour set forth than by his Biographer, Mr. Murphy in the work I before made mention of, and with some of whose words therefore, I shall close this article.

"It will be, says that gentleman, an humane and generous office to set down in the account of slander and defamation, a great part of that abuse which was discharged against him by his enemies in his life-time; deducing however from the whole this useful lesson, *that quick and warm passions should be early restrained, and that dissipation and extravagant pleasures are the most dangerous palliatives that can be found for disappointments and vexations in the first stages of life.*—We have seen, adds he, how Mr. Fielding very soon squandered away his small patrimony, which, with œconomy, might have procured him independence;—we have seen how he ruined into the bargain, a constitution, which in its original texture seemed formed to last much longer.—When illness and indigence were once let in upon him, he no longer remained the master of his own actions; and that nice delicacy of conduct which alone constitutes and preserves a character, was occasionally obliged to give way—When he was not under the immediate urgency of want, those who were intimate with him are ready to aver, that he had a mind greatly superior to any thing mean or little; when his finances were exhausted, he

was not the most elegant in his choice of the means to redress himself, and he would instantly exhibit a farce or a puppet-shew, in the Hay-market theatre, which was wholly inconsistent with the profession he had embarked in—Both his intimates are witness how much his pride suffered when he was forced into measures of this kind.—No man having a juster sense of propriety, or more honourable ideas of the imployment of an author and a scholar."

FIE'LD-MARSHAL, S. the governor or commander of an army in the field.

FIE'LD-OFFICER, S. an officer whose command extends to a whole regiment; such as the colonel, lieutenant-colonel, and major.

FIE'LD-PIECE, S. in Gunnery, small cannon used in battles, but not in sieges.

FIEND, S. [*fynd*, Sax. *fiend*, Belg.] the devil. Any infernal being.

FIERCE, Adj. [*fier*, Fr. *ferus*, Lat. φυη, Gr.] wild, furious. Violent; outrageous, "Fierce winds." *James* ii. 1. Terrible, or causing terror. "Fierce look."

FIE'RCELY, Adv. in a furious or outrageous manner.

FIE'RCENESS, S. wildness. Boldness. Eagerness after slaughter. Quickness to attack. Outrageousness. Violence with respect to passion.

FIE'RI-FACIAS, S. in Law, a writ, by which the sheriff is commanded to levy the debt and damages on the defendants goods and chattels.

FI'ERY, Adj. consisting of hot particles. Burning with passion. Heated with fire. "The sword which is made fiery." *Hooker.*

FIFE, S. [*fifre*, Ital.] a shrill pipe, blown in the same manner as a German flute, used to accompany the drum.

FIFTE'EN, Adj. [from *five* and *ten*, *fiftyne*, Sax.] a number consisting of five and ten.

FIFTE'ENTH, Adj. [*fiftoothe*, *fiftynthe*, Sax.] that which follows next to the fourteenth.

FIFTH, Adj. [*fifth, fifta, fiftha*, Sax.] the ordinal of five; that which is next to the fourth.

FI'FTHLY, Adv. in the fifth place.

FI'FTIETH, Adj. [*fiftuguthe*, Sax.] the next in order after forty-nine.

FI'FTY, Adj. [*fiftig*, Sax.] a number consisting of five times ten.

FIG, S. [*figue*, Fr. *figo*, Span. *ficus*, Lat.] the name of a sweet fruit. Linnæus ranges it in the third sect of his twenty-third class.

To FIGHT, V. A. [*preter.* and *part.* pass. *fought*, *fyhtan*, Sax.] to contend with another. To endeavour by blows, or other forcible means, to get the better of an enemy; used both of war and single combat. To contend; it has *with* before the persons opposed.

FIGHT, S. [*fyght*, Sax.] a violent struggle

gle for conquest between enemies, whether armies or single persons.

FI'GHTER, S. a person engaged in combat. One fond of fighting.

FI'GHTING, Part. fit for battle. "As host of *fighting* men." *Chron.* The place where a battle is fought. "In *fighting* fields." *Pope.*

FI'GMENT, S. [*figmentum*, Lat.] a fabulous story. A fable. A mere fiction.

FI'GURABLE, Adj. [from *figura*, Lat.] capable of being moulded in a certain form.

FI'GURAL, Adj. represented by delineation. "The *figural* resemblances of several regions." *Brown.*

FI'GURATE, Adj. [*figuratus*, Lat.] of a certain and determinate form. Resembling any thing of a determinate form.

FI'GURATIVE, Adj. [*figuratif*, Fr.] in Divinity, serving as a type, to represent something else. In Rhetoric, changed from the literal meaning to one more remote. Full of rhetorical figures or embellishments, applied to stile.

FI'GURATIVELY, Adv. by a figure; in a sense different from the literal meaning.

FI'GURE, S. [Fr. of *figura*, Lat.] the form of any thing, shape, person, or external form. "To make a *figure*," some distinguished or eminent appearance. A statue. Any thing represented by drawing or painting. A character denoting a number, as 1, 2, 3, &c. In Astrology, the diagram of the aspects of the astronomical houses. In Divinity, some hieroglyphical or typical representation. In Rhetoric, any mode of speaking, by which words are used in a sense different from their literal meaning. In Dancing, the making the figure of eight in going round a couple; the different turns and windings in any dance.

To FI'GURE, V. A. [*figurer*, Fr. *figuro*, Lat.] to form or mould into any particular shape. To form a resemblance. To represent by type, or hieroglyphics. To form an idea of a thing in the mind. To foreshew by some sign or token. "The heaven *figures* some event." *Shak.* To use in a figurative and figurative sense.

FILA'CEOUS, Adj. [*filum*, Lat.] a thread] composed of threads. "It is the stalk that maketh the *filaceous* matter." *Bacon.*

FI'LAMENT, S. [Fr. *filamentum*, Lat.] a fine slender thread. The same as Fibre.

FIL'BERT, S. [derived by Junius and Skinner from *full beard*, or *full of beards*, on account of its long beard, or husk; but Johnson thinks it more probable that it took its name, as well as some other vegetables, from *Filbert*, or *Filibert*, the person's name who first introduced it into these parts, or cultivated it] a fine large hazel-nut with a thin shell, and a long bearded husk.

To FILCH, V. A. [*filouz*, Teu.] to take away the property of another privately; generally applied to taking away trifles.

FIL'CHER, S. one who privately defrauds or robs another.

FI'LE, S. [Fr. *filum*, Lat.] a thread, or series. "Let me remove the *file* of my relation." *Watts.* A line or wire on which papers or letters are strung to keep them. A roll, or catalogue. A line of soldiers ranged behind one another.

FI'LE, S. [*fiol*, Sax. *wîre*, Belg.] an instrument of iron used to smooth iron or steel by rubbing.

To FI'LE, V. A. [*filum*, Lat.] to string upon a thread, or wire. In Law, to *file* a bill, is to offer it for the judge's notice. To cut or wear away any roughness with a *file*. To defile, pollute, or sully. "For Banquo's issue have I *fil'd* my mind." *Shak.* Nevertheless, to march like soldiers in a line one after another.

FI'LE-CUTTER, S. a maker of *files*.

FI'LER, S. one who uses a *file*.

FI'LIAL, Adj. [Fr. of *filius*, Lat.] having the affection of a son; standing in the relation of a son.

FILIA'TION, S. [of *filius*, Lat.] the relation of a son to a father.

FI'LINGS, S. the particles worn off by the rubbing of a *file* on iron, &c.

To FILL, V. A. [*fyllan*, *fullan*, Sax.] to pour till a thing can contain no more. To store abundantly. To satisfy, or content the appetite, wish or desires. To *fill out*, to pour liquor out of one vessel till it *fills* another; to swell or extend by means of something contained. To *fill up*, to employ. To occupy any space; to employ a vacant time. To grow full. To glut, or satiate. To be incapable of containing any more.

FILL, S. as much as a thing can contain. As much as may satisfy, or content. The place between the shaft of a carriage. "The mule being put to the *fill* of a cart." *Mortim.* This last sense seems to arise from erroneously using *fill* instead of *thill*.

FIL'LET, S. [*filet*, Fr. *filum*, Lat.] a band to tie round the head or any other part. The fleshy part of the thigh, applied to a joint of veal. In Cookery, any meat rolled together. In Architecture, a little member which appears in ornaments and mouldings.

To FIL'LET, V. A. to bind with a *fillet*. In Architecture, to adorn with an astragal, or listell.

To FIL'LIP, V. A. to strike with the nail by a sudden jerk of the finger.

FIL'LIP, S. a blow given with the nail by a jerk of the finger, from being bent so as to meet with the thumb, to a strait position.

FIL'LY, S. [*filly*, Brit. *file*, Fr. *filla*, Lat.]

Lat.] a young horse or mare. A young mare, opposed to a colt or young horse.

FIL'M, S. [Sax.] a thin skin, membrane, or pellicle.

To FIL'M, V. A. to cover with a skin. " It will but skin and *film* the ulcerous place." Shak.

FIL'MY, Adj. consisting of membranes, skins, or pellicles.

To FIL'TER, V. A. [*filtre*, low Lat.] to clarify, or purify liquors. To strain through paper, flannel, cloth, &c.

FIL'TER, S. [*filtrum*, Lat.] a twist of thread, one end of which is dipped in some fluid to be cleared, and the other hanging down on the outside of the vessel, the liquor by that means dripping from it. Figuratively, a strainer.

FILTH, S. [Sax. of *ful*, Sax.] dirt, or any thing which fouls. Any thing which pollutes the body or the soul.

FIL'THILY, Adv. in such a manner as to render a thing nasty, or to pollute the mind, and excite offence and loathing in another.

FIL'THINESS, S. dirtiness; any thing soiled or daubed. Corruption; pollution; a state of mind arising from being conversant in things which are opposite to decorum, decency, or elegance.

FIL'THY, Adj. foul, nasty, or dirty. Gross or polluted.

To FIL'TRATE, V. A. to strain liquor through a cloth, &c. to clear it from dregs.

FILTRATION, S. the art of making liquor fine and clear by straining; the common method used by apothecaries is to strain the liquor through paper, which, by the smallness of its pores, admits only the finer parts through, and keeps the grosser behind.

FIN, S. [*fin*, Sax. *finna*, Teut.] a part of a fish made somewhat like a feather, serving to keep the fish upright.

FI'NABLE, Adj. that which admits a fine.

FI'NAL, Adj. [Fr. *finalis*, Lat.] last; at the end. Conclusive; decisive; complete. " The *final* conquest of Ireland." Davies.

FI'NALLY, Adv. lastly; to conclude; perfectly; decisively; completely.

FI'NANCE, S. [Fr.] the amount of the taxes of a government, or income of a private person.

FI'NANCER, or FINANCIER, S. [Fr.] one who collects or farms the taxes; one who projects new taxes.

FI'NARY, S. [from *fine*] in iron-works, the second forge at the iron-mills.

FINCH, S. [*Fine*, Sax.] a small singing-bird of which there are three species, viz. the gold-finch, chaf-finch, and bull-finch.

To FI'ND, V. A. [Preter. I *have found*, Part. Pret *found finden*, Sax.] to discover any thing lost, mislaid, or out of sight before. To attain the knowledge of a thing

by study. To observe, remark, or meet with. To *find* guilty, to affirm the truth of an accusation. Joined to *bill*, to approve of. Joined to *self*, &c. to be, with respect to health. To *find out*, to solve a difficulty; to discover something hidden; to invent; to search for or select from several others of the same species.

FI'NDER, S. a person who discovers something lost or mislaid.

FI'NE, Adj. [*fanne*, Fr. *fin*, Belg. and Erse] made of very slender threads, applied to linens or cloth, not coarse. Refined, or pure from dross, applied to metals. Clear and free from sediments, applied to liquors. Artful, or dexterous. Elegant, applied to silk, or expression. Handsome and majestic. Accomplished; perfect, or complete, applied to any improvement, or acquisition of the mind. Showy; splendid, applied to dress. Ironically used as an expression of something rather deserving contempt than approbation. " My husband has the gout, and I have a *fine* time of it."

FI'NE, S. [*fin*, Brit.] in Law, an agreement made before justices, and entered upon record, to secure the title a person has in his estate against all others, or to cut off intails. A sum paid for the income of lands. A certain sum paid to excuse a person from duty. A sum of money, or forfeit paid as a punishment for an offence committed.

IN FINE Adv. [*en fin*, Fr. of *finis*, Lat.] to conclude; in conclusion; in short.

To FI'NE, V. A. [from *fine*, adj.] to refine, or purify from dross, applied to metals. To make less coarse. " It *fines* the grass." Mortim. To clear from sediments or foulness, applied to liquors. To make a person pay money as a punishment. To pay money to be excused from serving an office.

To FI'NEDRAW, V. A. to sew up a rent in such a manner, as the seam shall not be visible.

FI'NEDRAWER, S. a person who professes finedrawing.

FI'NELY, Adv. with a thin edge or point. Splendidly; richly, applied to dress; in very small particles, applied to powder. Wretchedly; in such a manner as to deserve contempt; used ironically, " I am *finely* trick'd."

FINENESS, S. elegance of sentiment and expression, applied to the productions of the understanding. Show, splendor, or gaiety, applied to dress. Subtilty, ingenuity, " The *fineness* of their souls." Shak. Freedom from dross, or impure mixtures, applied both to metals and liquors.

FI'NERY, S. gaiety, or splendor of dress.

FINE'SSE, S. [Fr.] a sly, artful stratagem, a trick.

FI'NER, S. one that cleans or purifies.

FI'NER,

FINER, Adj. the comparative degree of fine.

FINFOOTED, Adj. having a skin growing between the toes; applied to the feet of water fowl.

FINGER, S. [*finger*, Sax. Dan. and Teut. of *fangen*, Sax.] one of the five members at the extreme part of the hand, by which we catch and hold any thing. A measure of two barley corns in length. Figuratively, the hand.

To **FINGER**, V. A. to touch slightly. Figuratively, to take by stealth. In Music, to touch or sound an instrument.

FINICAL, Adj. nice; foppish; affected.

FINICALLY, Adv. foppishly, affectedly.

FINICALNESS, S. too great an affectation of niceness and elegance, applied both to dress and behaviour.

To **FINISH**, V. A. [*finir*, Fr. *finio*, Lat.] to cease from working. To accomplish, or complete an undertaking. To polish or bring to perfection. To put an end to.

FINISHER, S. a performer; an accomplisher. One who puts an end to an undertaking. One who gives a work its greatest charms and excellencies. Among watchmakers, one who puts all the parts of the work or the movements together.

FINITE, Adj. [*finitus*, Lat.] that which is limited. That which may be rendered greater, more numerous, or more perfect. That which may receive an addition to any of its qualities.

FINITELY, Adv. within certain bounds, limits or degrees.

FINITENESS, S. the quality of being limited, or confined within certain bounds and degrees.

FINLESS, Adj. having no fins.

FINNED, Adj. having fins. Having broad edges.

FINLIKE, Adj. resembling fins. "Our finlike oars." Doyd.

FINNY, Adj. furnished with fins.

FINTOED, Adj. having a skin growing between the toes.

FIR, S. [*fyre*, Belg. *fyrr* Dan.] in Latin, the *Abies*. The tree which produces deal boards.

FIRE, S. [*fyr*, Sax, *feur*, Teut. *feu*, Fr.] among moderns, the effect of a rapid internal motion of the particles of a body, by which their cohesion is destroyed, or in other words, whatever heats, warms, liquefies or burns. Figuratively, a conflagration, or burning, whereby houses are destroyed. Flame, lustre or brightness. "Stars, hide your fires." Shak. Heat of temper or passion. Liveliness of imagination; vigour of mind; susceptibility of anger. The passion of love. In medicine, an eruption attended with a sensation of heat, or such an inflam-

mation; hence St. Anthony's fire. To set on fire; is to kindle, or wrap in flames. In war, the discharge of fire-arms.

FIRE, is a general name, by which men form to understand a certain sensation, or complex notion, of light, heat, burning, melting, &c. The power of fire is so great, its effects so extensive, and the manner of its acting so wonderful, that some of the wisest nations of old, reverenced and worshipped it as the supreme deity. Some of the chymists also, after they had discovered its surprising operations, suspected it to be an uncreated being; and, indeed, the most famous of them have acknowledged it as the source of all their knowledge; and hence have professed themselves philosophers by fire, nor thought they could be honoured with a nobler title. Now amongst all the wonderful properties of fire, there is none more extraordinary than this, that though it is the principal cause of almost all the sensible effects that continually fall under our observation, yet it is itself of so infinitely a subtle nature, that it eludes the most sagacious enquirers, nor ever comes within the cognisance of our senses; and hence others have been led to be of opinion, that it ought to be looked upon as spirit rather than body. Fire is generally divided into three kinds of species, viz. celestial, subterraneous, and culinary. By celestial fire is principally understood that of the sun, without regard to that of the fixed stars, though this, perhaps, may be of the same nature. By subterraneous fire we understand that which manifests itself in fiery eruptions of the earth, volcanoes, or burning mountains; or by any other effects it produces in mines, or the more central parts of the earth. By culinary fire we mean that employed in all chymical operations, and the common occasions of life. The sun's heat appears to be the actuating principle, or general instrument of all the operations in the animal, vegetable, atmospherical, marine, and mineral kingdoms. Fire, considered in itself seems to exist, in the greatest purity and perfection in the celestial regions; at least, we are insensible of any considerable smoke it yields; for the rays of light come to us from the sun, unmixed with any of that gross, feculent, or terrestrial matter, found in culinary and subterranean fires: but, allowing for this difference, the effects of the solar fire appear the same as those of culinary fire. If we examine the effects of subterraneous fires, we shall find them the same with those produced by culinary fire. Thus burnt coals, cinders, and melted minerals, are thrown up by Vesuvius and other burning mountains. Warm nephritic exhalations, natural hot springs, steams, vapours, smoke, &c. are found in several parts of the globe, rising nearly in the same manner as if they were produced by the heat of a furnace.

Whence

Whence it appears, the subterraneous fires are of the same nature with the culinary. All the physical knowledge we can have of a subject, must arise from attending to its properties and effects; but these properties and effects can never be discovered without the help of experiments; which, in philosophical enquiries, are the only interpreters betwixt the senses and the reason; whence all those notions of fire should be rejected as precarious and unsound, that are taken from the direct testimony of the senses, or the naked reason unassisted by experiments. In this enquiry, therefore, the mind should particularly be kept unprepossessed, and, before it pronounces, wait for full information. As men generally affix to the word fire, a complex idea of burning, light, heat, melting, &c. this idea should be analysed, in order to see what parts are essential, and what precarious or arbitrary. We frequently find the effects of fire produced, where no visible fire appeared. Thus the fingers are easily burnt by an iron heated below the degree of ignition, or so as to be no ways visibly red-hot or fiery; whence it follows, that the eye is no judge of fire. So likewise the touch gives us no positive notice of any degree of fire below the natural heat of the body, or any so great as to destroy the organ. Again, the effects of fire are often produced without any manifest signs of burning, melting, &c. as in evaporations, &c. If this method of exclusion and rejection were pursued to its due length, we should, perhaps, find no criterion, infallible mark, or characteristic of fire in general, but that of a particular motion struggling among the minute parts of bodies, and tending to throw them off at the surface. If this should prove the case, then such a motion will be the form and essence of fire, and which, being present, makes fire also present; and, when absent, makes fire also absent; whence to produce, and produce this motion in bodies, will be one and the same thing. The great and fundamental difference in respect to the nature of fire is, whether it be originally such, formed thus by the Creator himself at the beginning of things, or whether it be mechanically producible from other bodies, by inducing some alterations in the particulars thereof. The former opinion is maintained by Homberg, Boerhaave, the younger Lemery, and s'Gravesande; the latter is chiefly supported by the English philosophers, lord Bacon, Mr. Boyle, and sir Isaac Newton. Bacon, in the treatise De Forma Calidi, deduces, from a great number of particulars, that heat in bodies is no other than motion, so and so circumstanced; so that, to produce heat in a body, nothing is required but to excite a certain motion in the parts thereof. Boyle seconds him in an express treatise of the mechanical origin of heat and cold, and maintains

the same doctrine with new observations and experiments.

To FI'RE, V. A. to destroy by fire. To drive away, used with some adverb of place or motion. " Fire or hence." Shak. Neuterly, to burn, to take fire. Figuratively, to be inflamed with anger or passion. In War, to discharge any fire-arm.

FIRE-ARMS, S. those which are charged or loaded with powder and ball.

FIRE'-BALL, S. a ball filled with combustibles, bursting where it is thrown, and used in war. A grenado.

FI'REBRAND, S. a piece of wood kindled. Figuratively, a public incendiary.

FI'RE-LOCK, S. that part of a gun which holds the prime, &c. Figuratively, a gun.

FIRE-MAN, S. one who is employed by the insurance companies, in extinguishing burning houses. Figuratively, a person given to anger, or easily inflamed with passion. " Drank a bottle with one of these firemen." Tatler, No. 61.

FI'RE-PAN, S. [fyre-panne, Sax.] a pan of metal used in holding fire. A shovel. That part of a gun which holds the prime.

FIR'ESHIP, S. [fyrdscip, Sax.] a ship filled with combustibles, and let drive among the fleet of an enemy to set it on fire.

FI'RESHOVEL, S. [fyrescofl, Sax.] an instrument with which coals are thrown on fires. See FIRE-PAN.

FI'RESIDE, S. the hearth, chimney, or place near a grate. Figuratively, a family.

FI'RESTONE, S. in Natural History, the pyrites, a fossil compounded of vitriol, sulphur, and earth. That used in medicine is of a greenish colour, of a shapeless form, found in our clay-pits, and produces the green vitriol.

FI'REWORK, S. a preparation of gunpowder, and other inflammable substances, used on public rejoicings.

FI'RING, S. combustibles or burning. The act of discharging fire-arms.

FIR'KIN, S. [feorthan, Sax.] the fourth part of a barrel. The firkin of ale, soap and butter, contains eight gallons, and that of beer nine gallons.

FIR'M, Adj. [firmus, Lat.] strong, not easily pierced, or moved. Hard. Steadfast, fixed, or unshaken, steady.

FIRMAMENT, S. [Fr. firmamentum] the sky; the heavens.

FIRMAMEN'TAL, Adj. celestial, heavenly, or belonging to the sky. " Firmamental waters." Dryd.

FIR'MLY, Adv. in such a manner as not to be moved, shaken, or penetrated easily. Steadily; without doubt, applied to opinion.

FIR'MNESS, S. a state of body wherein the parts cohere so strongly, that they cannot easily be penetrated. A state of mind free from doubt or change.

FIRST, Adj. [firrſt, Sax. fyrſt, Rom.] that which is before all others in time or order. That which is nobleſt, in Dignity. That which exceeds all others.

FIRST, Adv. in the firſt place.

FIRST-FRUITS, S. that which is fooneſt ripe in the ſeaſon. The firſt profits; or firſt year's income of a benefice.

FIRSTLING, S. the firſt produce of animals, Figuratively, the firſt thing done. " The firſtlings of my hand." Shak.

FISCAL. S. [ſiſcal, Lat.] a public revenue; Exchequer. " The ordinary fiſcal and receipts." Bacon.

FISH, S. [fiſſies, plural, but fiſh is generally uſed in converſation, fiſh, Sax.] an animal inhabiting the water.

To FISH, V. N. to be employed in catching fiſh. Figuratively, to endeavour to diſcover any ſecret by ſubtlety. Actively, to ſearch the waters in queſt of fiſh.

FISHER, S. [fiſcere, Sax. fiſcher, Teut.] a perſon who is employed in catching fiſh.

FISHERMAN, S. one who lives by catching fiſh.

FISHERY, S. the action of catching fiſh. The place where fiſh abound.

FISH-HOOK, S. a bearded hook uſed in catching fiſh.

To FISHIFY, V. A. [of fiſh and fie, Lat.] to turn to or become fiſh. " O fleſh, fleſh, how art thou fiſhified." Shak.

FISHMEAL, S. a meal conſiſting of fiſh. Figuratively, abſtemious or low diet. " Many fiſhmeals." Shak.

FISHY, Adj. having the qualities of or reſembling fiſh. Taſting like fiſh.

FISSILE, Adj. [fiſſilis, Adj.] that which may be cleft.

FISSILITY, S. the quality of being fit to be cloven.

FISSURE, S. [Fr. fiſſure, Lat.] a cleft, a narrow chaſm.

To FISSURE, V. A. to cleave, or make a cleft. " The ſkull may be fiſſured." Wiſem.

FIST, S. [fyſt, Sax. of fuſtis, Lat.] the hand clenched, in order to give a blow, or hold a thing faſt.

To FIST, V. A. to ſtrike or hold with the hand clenched. " Fiſting each others throat." Shak.

FISTICUFFS, S. battle or blows with the fiſt.

FISTULA, S. [Lat.] in Surgery, a deep, winding, callous, cavernous ulcer, generally yielding a ſharp and virulent matter. Fiſtula in ano, is a fiſtula formed in the fundament, fiſtula lachrymalis, a diſorder of the canals leading from the eye to the noſe, which obſtructs the natural progreſs of the tears, and in its laſt ſtage diſcharges matter, ſometimes from an orifice broken through the ſkin between the noſe and corner of the eye. The cure of this diſorder may be ſeen in the third volume of the Medical Eſſays of the ſociety of Edinburgh, Sect. xv. p. 279.

FISTULAR, Adj. in Surgery, having the nature of a fiſtula. In Botany, reſembling a pipe, applied to the leaves of plants which are hollow within.

FISTULOUS, Adj. having the nature of a fiſtula; compoſed of a collection of pipes.

FIT, S. [from fyht, Sax. Vit, Belg.] in Medicine, an acceſs or paroxyſm of a diſorder. Any ſhort return after ceſſation or intermiſſion. Any violent affection of the mind. The hyſterics in women; the convulſions in children; the epilepſy in men, or that ſtate wherein all the animal functions ſeem on a ſudden ſuſpended.

FIT, Adj. [vitten, Belg.] proper, ſuitable. Right.

To FIT, Adj. [vitten, Flem.] to make one thing ſuit another; to match. To furniſh with a thing proper for the uſe to which it is deſigned, or proper for the ſhape of the perſon who is to wear it. To adapt. To ſuit. To ſir out; to furniſh with neceſſaries for a deſign, and undertaking; to equip. To fir up, to furniſh; to make proper for the reception of a perſon. Neuterly, to be decent, proper, or advantageous.

FITFUL, Adj. ſubject to fits, or faintings. " After life's fitful fever." Shak.

FITLY, Adv. in a fit or proper manner. Reaſonably.

FITNESS, S. a relative term, implying the propriety of a means to an end. Reaſonableneſs.

FIVE, Adj. [fif, Sax. fimf, Goth.] a number conſiſting of two and three added together.

FIVES, S. a kind of play conſiſting of ſtriking a ball againſt a wall. In Farriery, a diſeaſe in horſes.

To FIX, V. A. [fixer, Fr. figo, Lat.] to faſten a thing. To eſtabliſh without changing. To direct without variation; to look at with attention, or without moving the eyes to any other object. " Them eyes fixt to the ſolid earth." Shak. To make any thing of a volatile nature capable of bearing fire without evaporating, or the hammer without breaking or flying. To pierce. " A bow of ſteel ſhall fix his trembling thighs." Sandys. This ſenſe is a latiniſm! Neuterly, to ſettle the opinion, determine the reſolution; or chooſe as the object of our thoughts and enquiries, uſed with on. To reſt, to ceaſe from wandering. To loſe its volatility, ſo as to be able to bear the hammer. " The quickſilver will fix and run no more." Bacon.

FIXATION, S. the act of fixing the mind without wavering; reſolution. " Your fixation in matters of religion." K. Charles. In chimiſtry, the act of reducing a volatile and fluid ſubſtance to a hard one, ſo that it may bear fire without evaporating, or hammering without flying.

FIXEDLY,

FIX'EDLY, Adv. certainly ; firmly ; inveterably.

FIX'ED. Part. not moving; firm, fteady.

FLIX'ITY, S. a ftrong cohefion of parts, oppofed to volatibility.

FIX'TURE, S. (a corruption of *fixure*) things which are fixed to the premifes, and fometimes advertifed to be fold to the perfon who fhall take a houfe of another.

FIX'URE, S. a pofition. " The *fixure* of her eye hath motion in it." *Shak.* A ftrong preffure. Flammed.

FLAB'BY, Adj. [*flappe*, Ital. *flacba*, Fr. *flaxo*, Ital. from *flaccidus*, Lat.] wanting firmnefs ; eafily fhaking and yielding to the touch; wanting ftiffnefs.

FLAC'CID, Adj. [*flaccidus*, Lat.] weak ; wanting ftiffnefs.

FLACCI'DITY, S. want of ftiffnefs, or tenfion.

To FLAG', V. N. [*flaggeren*, Belg. *flac-care*, Ital.] to hang down limber. Figuratively, to grow faint, fpiritlefs or dejected by too great a fatigue, or fome difmal occurrence. To loofe vigour, or grow feeble. Actively, to let fall, or fuffer to droop. " *Flag* their wings." *Pr*i*or.* To lay, or pave with broad ftones.

FLAG', S. [from the verb, *flagg*, Id.] a water plant, with a broad black leaf. The colours or enfigns of a fhip, or regiment. A fpecies of broad ftone ufed for pavements.

FLA'GELET, S. [*flagtolet*, Fr.] a kind of fmall flute with fix holes or ftops.

FLAGELLA'TION, S. [*flagellatum*, Lat.] the act of whipping or ftriking with a fcourge. By Painters applied to the fcourging of our Lord and Saviour before his crucifixion. " A painting of the *flagellation*." " The *flagellation* of, &c.

FLAG'GINESS, S. the ftate of a thing which hangs for want of ftiffnefs.

FLAG'GY, Adj. weak ; limber ; not ftiff ; weak of tafte ; infipid.

FLAGI'TIOUS, Adj. [*flagitious*, Lat.] committed with deliberation, exceffively wicked and villainous

FLAGI'TIOUSNESS, S. obftinate and wilful villainy, vice or wickednefs.

FLAG-OFFICER, S. the commander of a fquadron.

FLAG'GON, S. [*flaccd*, Belr. *flax*, Sax. *ληχως*, Gr.] a large drinking pot with a narrow mouth.

FLA'GRANCY, S. [*flagrantia*, Lat.] a burning, flaming, glittering, or heat. Ardor of affliction. Notoriety of a crime or wickednefs.

FLA'GRANT, Adj. [Fr. of *flagrans*, Lat.] ardent ; hot, or vehement, applied to the defires, or affections of the mind. Glowing, flufhed ; applied to colour. Red ; inflamed, or appearing red. " The bradles lafh, ftill *flagrant* on their back." *Prior.* Notorious, applied to crimes.

FLA'IL, S. [Fr. *legel*, Teut. *vleghel*, Belg.] an inftrument to beat corn out of the ear.

FLA'KE, S. [*fiocco*, Ital. *floccus*, Lat.] any thing which appears loofely held together. Any thing which breaks in thin pieces ; a layer or ftratum.

To FLA'KE, V. A. to form in flakes, or thin pieces.

FLA'KY, Adj. breaking in fmall pieces like fcales ; formed of fmall pieces eafily feparated or loofely joined together. Lying in layers or ftratus.

FLAM, S. [*llama*, Bob.] a lie,' an untruth, or falfe report. A mere deceit or pretext. A fham ; a pretext.

To FLAM, V. A. (from the noun] to deceive with a fabulous or feigned ftory ; to put off with an idle tale, or mere idle pretext. " God is not to be *flamm'd* with lies." *South.*

FLA'ME, S. [*flamme*, Fr. Lat.] a fume or vapour, heated fo as to emit light, or fhine. Figuratively, fire; brightnefs of imagination or fancy. Ardour of warmth of temper. The paffion of love. The object of affection.

To FLAME, V. N. to burn fo as to emit a fhining light. Figuratively, to fhine like flame.

FLAMMABI'LITY, S. the quality of being able to be fet on flame.

FLAM'MEOUS, Adj. [*flammeus*, Lat.] confifting of, or refembling flame.

FLA'MY, Adj. burning fo as to emit flames. Inflamed.

FLANDERS, a province of the Netherlands, which may be divided into Dutch Flanders, Auftrian Flanders, and French Flanders. It is bounded by the German ocean and the United Provinces on the N. by the province of Brabant on the E. by Hainhalt and Artois on the S. and by another part of Artois and the German ocean on the W. being about 60 miles in length, and 50 in breadth. It is a flat level country, which is very fertile in grain and paftures, and the air is good. They reckon it contains near 30 walled towns, befides thofe that are open, 1158 villages, 48 abbeys, and a great number or priories, colleges, and monafteries. The men are heavy, but labourious and lovers of good cheer ; and the women are reckoned to be very handfome. They are Papifts in all parts, except that which belongs to the Dutch. The produce is fine linen, lace and tapiftry.

FLANK, S. [*flanc*, Fr.] that part of an animal where the ribs are wanting, and below the loins. The fide of an army or fleet, In Fortification, that part of a baftion which reaches from the curtain to the face, and defends the oppofite face.

To FLANK, V. A. to attack the fide of a battalion or fleet. To be on the fide.

FLANEL, S. [*gwalanen*, Brit. *lanella*, Lat.

3 L 2   Lat.

Lat, from *lana*, Lat. wool] a kind of loose woollen stuff, very warm, composed of a woof and warp, woven on a loom, after the manner of bays &c.

FLAP, S. (*lappa*, Sax. *flable*, low Sax.] any thing which hangs down broad and loose. The meaning of any thing broad and loose. A blow given with the palm of the hand, &c.

To FLAP, V. A. to strike with the palm of the hand, or something broad which hangs loose. Neuterly, to ply the wings up and down with a noise. To fall or hang down with a broad surface.

To FLARE, V. A (*fledren*, *flerd.ren*, Teut. Johnson imagines it is a corruption of *glare*) to glitter with ostentatious show. To glitter with a transient, or short-lived lustre. To glister. "When the sun begins to fling his *flaring* beams." *Milton*. To be overpowered with light. "*Flaring* in sunshine." *Prior*. To *flare* in one's face, is to stare at a person with boldness and impudence. Neuterly, to waste away lavishly, applied to the consuming of a candle.

FLASH, S. [*eus*, Gr.] a sudden, quick, blaze, or flash of light. Figuratively, a sudden blaze, or burst of wit, whose pleasure is of a short duration. A short transient state. Water driven by force or violence.

To FLASH, V. N. to glitter with a quick and transient light. To burst out into any irregularity, or violence, "He *flashes* into one gross crime or other." *Shak*. To break out into a burst of wit, merriment, or a bright thought. "They *flash* out sometimes into an irregular greatness of thought." *Felton*. Actively, to dash out large quantities from the surface, applied to water.

FLASHILY, Adv. in an ostentatious or showy manner. With the show or appearance rather than the real power of wit or solidity of thought.

FLASHY, Adj empty; vain; ostentatious; showy without reality or subsistence. Insipid; unfavoury; watery; without force or spirit; from *flaccidus*, Lat. "Distilled books are like distilled waters, *flashy* things." *Bacon*.

FLASK, S. [*flaxa*, Sax. *flask* Dan. *flasco*, Ital.] a thin bottle with a long neck, generally covered with wicker. A small horn to carry gunpowder in. The bed in the carriage of a piece of ordnance. A narrow and deep wicker basket, used by gardeners to put their sieves in. In Heraldry, an ordinary formed by an arched line, beginning at the corners of the chief and ending at the base of the escutcheons, but usually drawn double.

FLASKET, S. a wicker basket, wherein cloaths are generally put. A vessel in which victuals are served up.

FLAT, Adj. [*fatus*, Ill. *plat*, Fr.] horizontal, even, or level. "The houses are *flat* roofed." *Addif*. Smooth, Level with the ground. "Lays cities *flat*." *Par*.

Reg. Prostrate, or lying along on the ground *after lay*. "Lying *flat*." *Spenf*. Thin and broad, or more broad than thick. "A *flat* fish." Insipid, or unsavoury, applied to taste. Dull, without spirit, applied to writings. Tasteless. "All earthly satisfactions most grow *flat* and unsavoury." *Atterb*. Downright; plain. "A *flat* contradiction." Not shrill, acute, or sharp, applied to sound.

FLAT, S. a level, smooth and extended plane. A shallow, strand, or place where the water is not deep enough for ships. The broad part of a weapon. A surface without relief, or projection. In Architecture, a small ornament over the door of a house, to cover and shield a person from the rain. In Music, a particular mark implying that the note which it stands against, is to be played or sung half a note or tone lower.

To FLAT, V. A. to make smooth and level. To make tasteless, or vapid, applied to liquor. To deprive of its vigour, spirit, or pleasure. Neuterly, to grow smooth or flat. To obstruct or deprive of ardour, spirit, or zeal.

FLATLY, Adv. horizontally. Smoothly, applied to surface. Without spirit; dully applied to thoughts or language. Plainly; in a blunt, downright manner or without equivocation or disguise; from *flatte*, prefer of *flat*. Ill. to explain.

FLATNESS, S. evenness, levelness, applied to situation. Smoothness, applied to surface. Deadness, applied to liquors or foods. Dejection, or languor, applied to the mind. Want of force, vigour or spirit. Dulness, applied to sentiments or writings. Not shrill, or acute, applied to sound.

To FLATTEN, V. A. to make smooth or flat. To beat level with the ground. To make tasteless, or spiritless. Neuterly, to grow even or level, applied to surface. To grow dull, tasteless, and void of charms. "Satisfactions that *flatten* in the very tasting." *L'Efran*.

FLATTER, Adj. the comparative degree of *flat*.

FLATTER, S. the person, or thing by which any unequal surface is made plain and level.

To FLATTER, V. A. [*flater*, Fr.] to compliment with false or undue praise. To please or sooth. To excite false hopes and expectations. "*Flattering* gales." *Milt*.

FLATTERER, S. one who endeavours to gain the favour of another by recommending all he does and says, by praising him for virtues he has not, and by servile compliances with his humours.

FLATTERY, S. servile and fawning behaviour, attended with servile compliments, and compliances.

FLATTISH, Adj. somewhat level, smooth, or broad.

                        FLATU-

FLA'TULENCE, FLA'TULENCY, S. [from *flatulent*] fulnefs of wind. A fwelling occafioned by wind lodged in the interftimes. Emptinefs, Vanity, airinefs; want of folidity, applied to fentiments, or opinions, " The natural *flatulence* of that airy fcheme." *Glanv.*

FLA'TULENT, Adj. [*flatulentus*, Lat.] fwelling with air; windy. Empty; vain; tumid or fwelling without fubftance. " Thefe *flatulent* writers.

FLATUO'SITY, S. [*flatuofité*, Fr. from *flatus*, Lat.] windinefs. A fwelling occafioned by an expanfion of air included in any part of the body.

FLA'TUOUS, Adj. abounding with wind. Windy.

FLA'TUS, S [Lat.] in Medicine, wind gathered in any part of the body, generally caufed by indigeftion.

To FLAUNT, V. A. to make an oftentatious or vain fhow in drefs. Figuratively, to behave with pride and arrogance. " One *flaunts* in rags, one flutters in brocade." *Pope.*

FLAUNT, S. any thing loofe, fhowy or gaudy.

FLA'VOUR, S. a relifh, or an agreeable fenfation on the organs of tafte. Figuratively, fweetnefs, or an agreeable odour, applied to the fmell.

FLA'VOUROUS, Adj. agreeable to the tafte. Fragrant, or pleafing to the fmell.

FLAW, S. [*flah*, Sax. *floro*, Belg. *flaw*, Brit. *plaw*, Cr.] a crack, breach, fault or defect. A blaft of wind, from *fh*, Lat. to blow. " The winter's *flaw*." *Shak.*

To FLAW, V. A. to crack. Figuratively, to break, or violate. " France hath *flaw'd* the league." *Shak.* The laft fenfe is abfolete.

FLAW'T, Adj. full of cracks, flaws, breaches or defects.

FLAX, S. [*flaex*, *flex*, Sax. *vlas*, Belg. *flachs*, Teut.] in Botany, *linum*, Lat. and *lin*, Fr. Linnæus ranges it in the fifth fect of his fifth clafs. There are fourteen fpecies. As the improvement of the linen manufactory depends very much on the raifing of flax, it is to be hoped that all the true patriots of this country will turn their thoughts that way, in order to bring it to its utmoft perfections, and if we may judge from what has appeared for a few years backward, it is not doubted, but Ireland and Scotland will in the end abundantly vindicate and recommend any rewards or encouragement given them with this view. This word is ufed for the fibre of the plant of which thread is made, when fit for fpinning.

FLAX-DRESSER, S. one who prepares flax for the fpinner.

FLAX'EN, Adj. made of flax. Refembling flax in colour.

To FLAY, V. A. [*fleo*, preter *flea*, infinitive *ed flaa*, Ifl.] to take off the pellicle, membrane or fkin of any thing.

FLA'YER, S. one who ftrips off the fkin.

FLEA, S. [*flrah*, *fleah*, *flea*, Sax.] in Natural Hiftory, a fmall red infect remarkable for its nimblenefs, which fucks the blood of large animals. They bring forth eggs or nits, which they depofit on animals proper to nourifh their young when hatched; from the eggs proceed white worms of a fhining pearl colour, which feed on the fcurfy fubftance of the cuticle, or downy matter gathered in the piles of clothes. In a fortnight they come to a tolerable fize, are fprightly and active, and, if at any time difturbed, roll themfelves into the form of a ball. After this they creep after the manner of worms, but with a very fwift motion; and in this ftage they hide themfelves as much as poffible, fpin a filken thread out of their mouths, with which they weave themfelves a fmall round bag, or cafe, white within, and always dirty and fouled with duft without; in this tomb they retire for a fortnight, during which time they abfolutely ceafe from motion, but at the expiration of that time burft forth a perfect flea, leaving the exuviæ in the bag. While the animalcule remains in the bag, it is milk-white till the fecond day before its eruption, when it becomes coloured, grows hard, and is fo ftrong, that upon its firft delivery from its voluntary fepulchre, it fprings nimbly away.

To FLEA, V. A. to cleanfe from fleas.

FLEA'-BITE, FLEA'-BITING, S. the red marks or wounds, caufed by a flea in fucking the blood of human creatures. Figuratively, a fmall, infignificant or trifling hurt.

FLE'ABITTEN, Adj. ftung or bitten by fleas. White, fpeckled with dark reddifh fpots, applied to the colour of a horfe. Figuratively, mean, or worthlefs. " Flea-bitten fynod." *Cleavel.*

FLE'AM, S. [*vulnus*, Belg. *flamme*, Fr.] a fmall inftrument of fteel, compofed of two or three moveable lancets, ufed in bleeding cattle.

To FLECK, V. A. [*flecker*, Ifl. *fleck*, Teut.] to fpot; to mark. " Fleckd in her face." *Dryd.*

To FLECKER, V. A. [fee FLECK] to ftreak, or mark with different colours. " The grey ey'd morn fmiles on the frowning night — And darknefs *flecker'd*, &c. *Shak.*

FLED, the Preter and Participle of *flee*, to run away; not properly ufed for that of *fly*, to make ufe of wings. *Johnfon.*

FLED'GED, Adj. [*flidderen*, Belg.] fullfeathered; able to fly.

To FLEDGE, V. A. [*flack*, *fackwerken*, Teut.] to furnifh with wings or feathers.

To

To FLEE', V. N. [Pret. and Part. *fled*. Johnson observes that this word is improperly written *fly*, because *fly* is *of fl open*, Sax. is to move with wings, and *flee of fleon*, Sax. to run away. Yet with due deference let it be observed, that when *fly* is used to imply running away, it is owing neither to any confusion or impropriety, but is derived from *fly*, *lh.* which signifies the same) to run away from danger; to endeavour to avoid danger by flight.

FLEE'CE, S. [*fleos*, *flyse*, *frofe*, Sax. *vellus*, Lat.] the wooly covering shorn off the bodies of sheep. As much wool as is shorn off one sheep. Figuratively, 'a sum carried, painted, and used for a sign.

To FLEE'CE, V. A. to sheer the wool off a sheep. Figuratively, to strip or plunder. "To *fleece* the people." Addif.

FLEE'CED, Adj. having fleeces. "The rich *fleeced* flock." Fairy Q. Stripped or plundered.

To FLEE'R, V. N. [*flard*, Isl.] to ridicule. To mock. To deride with insolence. To leer; to make use of a deceitful grin of civility, used with at.

FLEE'R, S. mockery, ridicule.

FLEE'T, S. [*flota*, Sax. *fuota*, Ital.] a number of ships or vessels going in company.

FLEE'T, Adj. [*flotus*, Ill.] swift, nimble, applied to pace, or motion.

To FLEE'T, V. N. [*flo*, Ill. *fleain*, Sax.] to fly swiftly; to vanish. To be transitory. "*fleeting* joys." Par. Lost. Actively, to skim the water. To live merrily. "*Fleet* the time carelesly." Shak. To skim milk, or take off the cream.

FLEE'TLY, Adv. swiftly; nimbly; quickly.

FLEE'TNESS, S. swiftness, nimbleness.

FLESH, S. [*flæc*, *flæsc*, *flesc*, Sax.] in Anatomy, a fibrous part of an animal body, soft, bloody, and serving as a covering to the bones. The body. The muscles, or soft part of an animal body. Animal food, opposed to vegetable. The soft part of beasts or birds, opposed to that of fishes. Animal nature. Figuratively, carnality, or sensual appetites. A carnal state. A near relation. The outward or literal sense, or first appearance. "So judge after the *flesh*." John xviii. 15. A person given up to sensual enjoyments. "*Flesh* and blood cannot enter into the kingdom of heaven." John iv. That part of an animal or fruit which may be eaten.

FLESH-HOOK, S. a hook to take meat out of a pot.

FLESH'LESS, Adj. without flesh.

FLESH'LINESS, S. [*fleshlineffe*, *fleshlineffe*, Sax.] carnal or sensual passions and appetites. Carnality.

FLESH'LY, Adj. [*fleshlic*, Sax.] corpo-

real. Carnal, lascivious, opposed to *spiritual*. Animal, opposed to *vegetable*.

FLESH'MEAT, S. [*fleshmeat*, Sax.] the flesh of animals used for food.

FLESH'Y, Adj. plump; full of flesh; fat.

FLET'CHER, S. [*flechi*, Fr.] one who makes bows and arrows.

FLEW', the Pret. of FLY.

FLEW', S. the large chaps of a deep mouthed hound. A chimney belonging to coppers, or land heats.

FLEXIBI'LITY, S. the quality of submitting to be bent. Easiness of being persuaded.

FLEX'IBLE, Adj. [Fr. *flexibilis*, Lat.] easy to be bent; pliant. Obsequious; easily complying with. Ductile or manageable. "The tender and *flexible* years of his life." Locke. To be suited to any purpose. "*Flexible* to their purpose." Rogers. Easy to be persuaded, or managed.

FLEX'IBLENESS, S. easiness to be bent. Compliance. Tractableness. Easiness to be moved by persuasion.

FLEX'ILE, Adj. [*flexilis*, Lat.] pliant, or easy to be bent.

FLEX'ION, S. [*flexio*, Lat.] the act of bending. A double; a bending; the state of a thing bent.

FLEX'UOUS, Adj. [*flexuosus*, Lat.] winding; full of meanders. Bending; crooked; variable; unsteady; irregular. "The *flexuous* burning of flames." Bacon.

FLEX'URE, S. [*flexura*, Lat.] the form in which any thing is bent. The act of bending. The part bent; a joint. Obsequious or servile fawning or cringing. "Will it give place to *flexure*?" Shak.

To FLICK'ER, V. N. [*flickeren*, Belg.] to flutter. To move the wings up and down with a quick motion. "*flickering* on her nest." Dryd.

FLI'ER, S. a person who runs away from danger. That part of a machine which equalises, regulates, and continues the motion of the rest. "The *flier* of a jack."

FLIGHT, S. [*flyght*, Sax. *flught*, old Fr.] the act of running away to avoid danger. The act of moving with wings. A flock of birds moving in the air together. The birds produced in the same season. The space past in flying. Figuratively, the soaring of imagination. A soaring excursion. The power of flying. Fancy.

FLI'GHTY, Adj. fleeting. Swift in motion. Wild or fanciful; whimsical.

FLIM'SEY, Adj. weak; feeble; without strength, or stiffness, applied to manufactures. Mean; spiritless; without force, applied to literary productions. "A vast extent of *flimsy* lines." Pope

To FLINCH, V. N. to shrink from any suffering, pain, or danger. To fail.

FLINCHER,

FLIN'CHER, S. he who shrinks, flinches, or falls.

To FLING, V. A. [Pret and Part. *flung* Johnson gives us *flang* as the Participle Paſſive beſides, but it is now obſo'ete] to caſt from the hand. To dart, or throw with violence. To drive with violence. To drive by force. To move forcibly. To eject, or caſt away as uſeleſs or hurtful. "I chance thee *fling* away ambition." *Shak.* To caſt, or charge with reproach. "Fling but th' appearance of diſhonour on it." *Addiſ.* To force into a worſe condition. To *fling down*, to throw upon the ground with force; to demoliſh, or deſtroy. To *fling off*, in Hunting; to baffle in a chace; to deliver of a prey by ſuperior fwiftneſs. "Fling off by any falſe ſteps or doubles." *Addiſ.* To diſmount; or tumble from a horſe's back. Neuterly, to flounce; to wince; to fly into violent and irregular motions through paſſion. To *fling out*; to grow unruly or outrageous, alluding to a horſe's throwing out its legs. "When angry Duncan's horſes—turn'd wild in nature, broke their ſtalls, *flung out*." *Shak.*

FLING, S. the act of throwing; the diſtance to which any thing is thrown. A gibe; a ſneer of contempt.

FLING'ER, S. one who throws. One who caſts a contemptuous ſneer.

FLINT, S. [*flint*, Sax. *flint*, Flem. &c. Fr.] a ſemi-pellucid ſtone, of a ſimilar ſubſtance, of a blackiſh grey, free from veins, naturally inveſted with a whitiſh cruſt; ſometimes ſmooth and equal, but more frequently rough; remarkably hard; uſed for ſtriking fire with ſteel, and in glaſs-making. Figuratively, any thing impenetrable, or obdurate. "The flint and hardneſs of my fault." *Shak.*

FLINT, the capital town of Flintſhire, in N. Wales. It has no market, but has four fairs, viz. on February 15, June 24, Auguſt 10, and November 30, for cattle. It is commodiouſly ſeated on the river Dee, and is but a ſmall place, though it ſends one member to parliament. It was formerly noted for its caſtle, where Richard II. took ſhelter on his arrival from Ireland; but having quitted it, he was taken priſoner by the duke of Lancaſter. The caſtle now is in a ruinous condition; the aſſizes are ſtill held in the town. It is 12 miles S. W. of Cheſter, 5 N. E. of Holywell, and 201 N. W. of London. Lon. 14, 23. Lat. 53 10.

FLINT'SHIRE, a county of N. Wales, 29 miles in length, and 18 in breadth; and is bounded on the N. by the ſea, on the N. E. by an arm of the ſea, on the S. by Denbighſhire, and on the S. W. by the ſame county. It contains about 5400 houſes, 33,400 inhabitants, 28 pariſhes, and a market town, which is St. Aſaph, for the capital has no market. It is full of hills, intermixed with a few valleys, which are very fruit-

ful; and the inhabitants are long-lived. The rivers are the Wheler, the Tagidog, the Severn, and the Dee. It ſends 2 members to parliament; one for the town, and the other for the county.

FLINT'Y, Adj. made of or abounding in flints or ſtones. Hard, obdurate, not to be penetrated, or moved by prayers, or entreaties "Flinty Tartar's boſom." *Shak.*

FLIP, S. [a cant word] a drink uſed among ſailors, made of ſpirits, beer, and ſugar.

FLIP'PANT, Adj. [from *flap*] nimble; quick, applied to the tongue. "A woman's tongue—ſo wonderfully voluble and *flippant*, *Addiſ.* Pert; talkative.

FLIP'PANTLY, Adv. in a pert, talkative, impertinent, or fluent manner. Always applied to ſpeech.

To FLIRT, V. A. to throw any thing with a jerk. "The ſcavenger—*flirts* from his cart the mud." *Swift.* To move with quickneſs. "Flirt your fan." *Dorſet.* To be irregular, unſteady and fluttering.

FLIR'T, S. a quick, ſudden, elaſtic motion; a jerk. A ſudden trick. "To play at the hedge, a flirt." *Johnſ.* A pert girl, a young gadding laſs.

FLIRTA'TION, S. a quick ſprightly motion; or the appearance of a flirt.

To FLIT, V. N. [*flit*, Iſl. *flytt*, Ill.] to fly away. To remove or migrate. "Flit out of one body into ſome other." *Hooker.* To flutter on the wing. "To flit in air." *Pope.* To be tranſient, unſteady, or unſtable.

FLITCH, S. [*flicce*, Sax. *flicko*, Fr. *flim*, Teut.] the ſide of a hog, ſalted and cured.

FLITTING, [*flit*, Sax.] a reproachful accuſation. An offence, or fault. "Thou relleſt my flittings." *Pſalm.* lvi.

To FLOAT, V. N. [*flueter*, Fr.] to ſwim on the water. To move eaſily in the air, applied to the flight of birds. "Float in air." *Dryd.* To ſwim in, or appear unfought in, the mind, applied to ideas. Actively, to cover with waters.

FLO'AT, S. the act of flowing, oppoſed to the ebb, or reflux of the tide. Any thing contrived ſo as to ſwim on the water. The cork, or quil by which the bite of a fiſh is diſcovered. A cant word for a level. "Banks are meaſured by the float or floor." *Mortim.*

FLOCK, S. [*floce*, Sax.] a company of birds, ſheep, or cattle. Figuratively, a multitude of men. "The heathen that fled out by flocks." *Maccab.* xlv. 14. A lock of wool, from *floccus*, Lat.

To FLOCK, V. N. to gather together in crowds.

To FLOG, V. A. [*flagrum*, Lat.] to whip with a rod.

FLOOD, S. [*flod*, Ill. *flod*, Sax.] a body of water; a ſea or river. An inundation, or overflowing of water. A flow, or that of tide. To

To FLO'OD, V. A. [see the noun] to cover or overflow with waters.

FLOODGATE, S. a gate by which any water-course is stopped.

FLOOK, S. [flog, Ten. plough, Belg.] the bearded part of an anchor which fixes in the ground.

FLOOR, S. [flor, flore, Sax.] that part of a house or room on which a person treads. A story; flight, or order of rooms.

To FLOOR, V. A. to cover the bottom of a room with planks.

FLOORING, S. the matter with which the bottom of a room is laid. The bottom.

To FLOP, V. A. to clap the wings with a noise. To let down the flap of a hat.

FLORET, S. [fleurette, Fr.] in Botany, an imperfect flower, or one that has not petals, spices, stamina and style.

FLORID, Adj. [floridus, Lat.] productive of or covered with flowers. Bright, or lively, applied to colour; flushed with red, applied to the complexion. Embellished with rhetorical figures, applied to stile.

FLORIDITY, S. freshness or redness of colour. "A floridity in the face" Floy.

FLORIDNESS, S. freshness, or redness of colour. A rhetorical embellishment, applied to stile, or language.

FLORIFEROUS, Adj. [florifer, Lat.] producing flowers.

FLORIST, S. [fleuriste, Fr.] a person skilled in the nature and culture of flowers.

To FLOUNCE, V. N. [plonsen, Belg.] to move, struggle, or dash in the water or mire. To move with violence and outrage. "Six flouncing Flanders mares." Prior. To move with passion or anger. "You neither fume, nor fret, nor flounce." Swift. Actively, to adorn or embellish with flounces, applied to dress.

FLOUNCE, S. any thing sowed or fixed on a garment by way of ornament or embellishment, and hanging loose. "A muslin flounce." Pope.

FLOUNDER, S. [flynder, Dan.] a small flat fish, of the plaise species kind, living either in fresh or salt water. The best baits are red worms, wasps and gentles.

To FLOUNDER, V. N. to struggle with violent and irregular motions.

FLOUR, S. the fine white powder of wheat.

To FLOURISH, V. N. [fleurir, Fr. floreo, or floresco, Lat.] to bloom, or be in bloom. Figuratively, to be in the vigour without feeding. To be in a prosperous state. To make use of rhetorical figures. In Music to play an overture. Actively, to adorn with blossoms. In music work, to embellish with flowers. In fencing, to move a weapon in circles or quick vibrations. To adorn with rhetorical figures, or embellishments of stile. In Penmanship, to make ornaments of loose or join-

ed strokes wantonly united, and forming something pleasing to the eye. To adorn; embellish; to grace or set off.

FLOURISH, S. any embellishment. Figuratively, beauty. An ostentatious display of wit. In Penmanship, ornaments formed by lines curiously and wantonly interwoven.

FLOURISHER, S. a busy bustler. One who prospers.

To FLOUT, V. A. [fleyten, Belg. flouten, Fris.] to mock, deride, or insult. Neuterly, to behave with contempt; to sneer.

FLOUT, S. a mock; a jeer; a contemptuous insult.

FLOUTER, S. one who derides, mocks, insults, or jeers another.

To FLOW, V. N. [flowan, Sax.] to run or spread, applied to water. To move, or be in motion. To rise, or swell, applied to the tide. To melt, applied to the effect of heat; on metals, wax, &c. To proceed from, as an effect; to be owing to, used with from. To abound or be crowded, followed by with. To be full of liquor, applied to drinking vessels. "Flowing cups." Shak. To hang loose, low, and waving. "A flowing mantle." Martin. Actively, to cover with water. "A stream at hand to flow the ground." Spell. No 425. To be free from harshness. "A flowing period." To write smoothly or speak eloquently. "A flow of words."

FLOW, S. the rise or swell of water. A sudden plenty or abundance. "A flow of spirits." Pope.

FLOWER, S. [flour, Fr. flor, Ital.] that part of a plant which contains the parts necessary for the propagation of the species. The male flowers are those which have no germen, stile, or fruit. Female flowers are such as contain the germen, style, and are called fruitful flowers. Hermaphrodite flowers, are such as contain both the male and female parts. Figuratively, an ornament or embellishment. The prime, bloom, or flourishing part of life. The most valuable part of any thing.

To FLOWER, V. N. [fleurir, Fr.] to put forth flowers or blossoms. To bloom, or be in blossom. Figuratively, to be in the prime of age. To flourish, or be in a prosperous state. To froth, ferment, or mantle, applied to liquor. To come from the surface, like cream, used with off. "These few observations, which have flower'd off." Milk. To adorn with the resemblance of flowers.

FLOWERET, S. [a diminutive of flower, fleurette. See FLORET] a small imperfect flower.

FLOWER, Adj. abounding, adorned with, or full of flowers.

FLOWINGLY, Adv. with readiness, quickness, or volubility. With abundance.

FLOWN, Part. [of fly or flee] gone away; departed either by running away or being

flying. Puffed up; fwelled, or elated. "Flown with infolence." *Par. Loft.*

FLUC'TUANT, Part. [*fluctuans*, Lat.] wavering; uncertain; doubting; unfteady.

To FLUCTUATE, V. N. [*fluctuas*, of *fluctuo*, Lat.] to roll to and fro. To float backwards and forwards. Figuratively, to hefitate between two contrary opinions. To be irrefolute, undetermined, or in doubt. To be in an uncertain ftate, or fubject to changes and viciffitudes.

FLUCTUA'TION, S. [Fr. *fluctuatio*, Lat.] the motion of waves or water backwards and forwards. Figuratively, a ftate of fufpenfe, irrefolution, uncertainty, or indetermination, applied to the mind.

FLUE, S. [*fig.* 1ft] a fmall pipe or chimney. Soft down, or fur, eafily wafted by the wind.

FLU'ENCY, S. the quality of flowing, or continuing in motion. Smoothnefs of ftile, or numbers. Copioufnefs, or volubility of fpeech. Affluence; an old and obfolete fenfe.

FLU'ENT, Adj. [*fluens*, Lat.] liquid; flowing; in motion. Ready; copious, applied to fpeech.

FLU'ENT, S. a ftream; or running water. "To cut the outrageous fluent." *Philips.*

FLU'ID, Adj. [*fluidus*, Lat.] having the parts eafily feparable; flowing like water or any liquid.

FLU'ID, S. In Medicine, any animal juice. A liquor, whofe parts yield to the fmalleft force impreffed, and by yielding are eafily moved among each other.

FLU'DITY, S. [*fluidité*, Fr.] a quality of a body, whereby the parts are fo difpofed as to flide over each other, and give way to the leaft preffure.

FLU'IDNESS, S. that quality in bodies oppofite to firmnefs, by which they yield to the leaft preffure.

FLU'MMERY, S. a kind of food made of oatmeal and water. Figuratively, mere pretence; flattery.

FLU'NG, [Particip. and Preter. of *fling*] thrown, or caft.

FLU'OR, S. [Lat.] a fluid ftate. "Which keep liquors in a *fluor*." *Newt.*

FLU'RRY, S. a guft; an hafty, fudden blaft, or ftorm of wind. "A *flurry* from the north." *Gulliv. Trav.* Hurry; a violent emotion.

To FLUSH, V. N. [*fluo*, Belg.] to flow with violence. To come in hafte. To produce a reddifh colour in the face, by a fudden flux of blood. Actively, to colour or redden. To elate, or elevate. "Flufhed with great victories." *Atter.* The laft fenfe feems to be derived from the verb *fluf.*

FLU'SH, Adj. frefh; full of vigour. "Flufh as May." *Shak.* Affluent; abounding; full of money.

No. XII.

FLU'SH, S: an afflux; a fudden impulfe; a violent flow. In Gaming, a number of cards of the fame fort.

To FLUSTER, V. A. to make hot with drinking. To make half drunk.

FLU'TE, S. [*flute*, Fr. *flauto*, Span. *fiuto*, Ital.] a wind inftrument, divided into the common and German flute; the common flute is played by putting one end into the mouth and breathing into it; the notes and tones are formed and changed by ftopping and opening the holes, fix in number, placed along the front, and one behind the neck. The German flute, the moft mellow of the two, and moft refembling the human voice, is not put into the mouth, but founded by a hole, a little diftant from the upper end; the end itfelf being ftopped with a tompion or plug, It has fix holes befides that of the mouth, and the keyhole, or pinch note. In Architecture, perpendicular channels or cavities cut along the fhaft of a column.

To FLU'TE, V. A. to cut channels in columns or pilafters.

FLU'TED, Adj. having channels or hollows.

To FLUTTER, V. N. [*flotteran*, Sax. *flotter*, Fr.] to move the wings with a quick motion. To take fhort flights with great agitation, or motion of the wings. Figuratively, to move about with great fhow and buftle, but with no confequence. To be in agitation. To move irregularly. To be in a ftate of uncertainty. To beat quick and irregularly; to palpitate, applied to the heart. Actively, to drive in diforder, like a flock of birds fuddenly roufed. To hurry the mind, or put it into confufion, or violent commotion. To put into confufion, or to diforder the pofition of things. To move with a quick vibration, or a trembling motion, applied to the playing of a fan.

FLUTTER, S. vibration; or a quick and irregular motion. Confufion; diforder.

FLUX, S. [Fr. *fluxus*, Lat.] the act of flowing. The ftate of paffing away, and giving place to others. In Medicine, an extraordinary evacuation of fome humour or matter. A difeafe in which the bowels are excoriated and bleed, called a bloody flux. That which is evacuated by animals. In hydrography, a regular periodical motion of the fea, happening twice in twenty-four hours, whereby the water is raifed. Figuratively, a concourfe, or confluence. "The flux of company." *Shak.* The ftate of being melted.

FLUX, Adj. [*fluxus*, Lat. of *fluo*, Lat.] inconftant; not durable; flowing; fucceffive.

To FLUX, V. A. to melt. To f_livate; to evacuate by fpitting.

FLUXIVITY, S. poffibility of being melted. "Fluidity, or at leaft *fluxility*." *Boyle.*

3 M   FLUXION,

FLUX'ION, S. [Fr. *fluxio*, Lat.] the act of flowing; the matter that flows. In Medicine, a sudden collection of morbid matter. The velocity by which a flowing quantity is increased by its generating motion. In arithmetic, the method of finding an infinitely small quantity, which, being taken an infinite number of times, becomes equal to a given quantity.

To FLY, V. N. [*fleon*, *fleow* or *fled*; past, *fled* or *flown*; *flowen*, Sax. "To fly, Johnson observes, is properly to use wings, and gives *flew* and *flown*. To *flee*, it to escape, or go away, from *fleon* Sax. and makes *fled*. They are now confounded:" but, with submission, if the word *fly* be derived from *fly*, (D. which signifies to escape, then the using the English word in that sense, is owing to no confusion of words; and the similitude between that word and *fly*, in the D. language, which signifies to use wings, may be the reason why fly is in English used both for the act of using wings, and that of escaping danger by running away) to move through the air by means of wings. To ascend in the air. " As the sparks fly upwards." *Job. v.* To perform a journey with great expedition. To hurl. " Your bottle *flies*." *Swift.* To break, or shiver. To *fly on*, to dart upon; to attack, or spring with violence; to fall on suddenly. To *fly in the face* of a person, is to insult him. " Neglect him, or fly in his face." *Swift.* To *fly out*, to burst suddenly into any heat or passion; to break out from any restraint; to start violently from any direction. To let *fly*, to discharge a gun or other fire-arms. To be light and unencumbered. To vanish or fade, applied to colour. To run away, or attempt to escape any danger. Actively, to avoid; to shun. To decline. To refuse association or acquaintance with. To attack, by a hawk or bird of prey. " With her fly — other ravening fowl." *Bacon.*

FLY', S. [*flie*, *fleoge*, *fleege*, Sax.] a small winged insect, of different species. That part of a machine, which, when put into motion, continues it with great swiftness.

To FLY'BLOW, V. A. to taint with flies; to fill with maggots.

FLY'BOAT, S. a kind of light vessel for failing.

FLY'ER, S. a person who runs away from battle, or evil events, to escape danger by flight. One that cuts its passage through the air by means of wings. That part of a jack which moves round on a pivot horizontally. In architecture, stairs made of an oblong square figure, whose fore and back sides are parallel to each other, as likewise their ends.

To FLY'FISH, V. N. to angle with a fly for a trout.

FOAL, S. [*fola*, Sax.] the offspring or young of a mare, or other beast of burthen. At present use is made for a young horse, and

for a young mare; but formerly the latter was used for the young of either sex.

To FOAL, V. A. to bring forth young, applied to a mare or ass.

FOA'M, S. [*fam*, Sax.] the white spirit or saliva, which appears in the mouth of a high-mettled horse. The white substance which gathers on the top of liquors. See FROTH.

To FOA'M, V. N. to have the mouth covered with frothy spittle. To froth; to gather foam. To be in a rage; to be in violent emotions of passion, alluding to a high-mettled horse, who foams at the mouth when checked. " He *foameth*."

FOA'MY, Adj. covered with froth; or foam.

FOB', S. [*fuppe*, *fupfacke*, Teut.] a small breeches pocket, wherein the watch is usually carried.

To FOB', V. A. [*fuppen*, Teut.] to cheat; to trick; to defraud. " Find myself *fobbed* in it." *Shak.* To *fob off*, to shift; or put off by some trick, or artifice. " The rascal *fobbed* me off with only wine." *Addis.*

FO'CAL, Adj. [from *focus*] belonging or relating to a *focus*.

FO'CIL, S. [*focile*, Fr. *focilis*, Lat.] In anatomy, the greater or less bone between the knee and ankle, or between the elbow and wrist.

FO'CUS, S. [Lat.] In optics, the point where the rays meet and cross the axis after refraction by a glass. The points from which rays diverge, or to which they converge. Applied to an ellipse, a point upwards each end of the longer axis, whence two right lines, being drawn to any point in the circumference, shall be, together, equal to the axis itself.

FOD'DER, S. [*fodr*, *fother*, *futhur*, Sax.] dry food stored up for cattle in winter.

To FOD'DER, V. A. [*foder*, Dan.] to supply with dry food.

FOD'DERER, S. one who supplies cattle with dry food.

FOE, S. [*feh*, Sax. *fac*, Scot.] an enemy. An adversary; an opponent, applied to opinions. " A foe to receive doctrines." *Watts.*

FOE'MAN, S. an enemy in war. " What valiant *foemen*." *Shak.*

FOE'TUS, S. [Lat. pronounced *fœtus*] a child in the womb, when it is perfectly formed.

FOG', S. [Dan. a storm] a low cloud consisting of gross watery vapours near the surface of the earth.

FOG'GILY, Adv. like a fog. Cloudily; darkly.

FOG'GINESS, S. the state of being dark or misty by a low cloud, consisting of watery vapours.

FOG'GY, Adj. full of dark, cloudy and moist vapours. Figuratively, dull, or stupid.

FOIL,

FOH, Interject. [*ſub*, Sax. *va*, Lat.] an interjection used to express abhorrence, or offence. "*Feb!* one may smell in such a will most rank." *Shak.* Commonly made use of when offended by a very offensive ſmell.

FOIBLE, S. [Fr.] a weak or blind ſide. A natural infirmity or failing. A weakneſs.

To FOIL, V. A. [*affoler*, old Fr.] to get the better of an enemy.

FOIL, S. a defeat, or miſcarriage. An advantage gained over an enemy. Something of another colour, uſed by jewellers to augment the luſtre, or heighten the colour of a ſtone, or a diamond. A blunt ſword uſed in fencing. Something indifferent uſed to diſplay the excellence of ſomething elſe to advantage.

FOILER, S. one who has gained an advantage.

To FOIN, V. A. [*poindre*, Fr.] to puſh or make a lunge with a weapon.

FOIN, S. a thruſt or puſh with a weapon.

To FOIST, V. A. [*fauſſer*, Fr.] to inſert ſomething that was not in an original. To interpolate: Uſed with in.

FOLD, S. [*falod*, *folde*, Sax.] the ground where ſheep are confined. The place, or ſtable where ſheep are houſed. "Time drives the flocks from field to *fold.*" *Raleigh.* Figuratively, a flock of ſheep. A boundary or limit. "Nor leave their ſeats, and paſs the dreadful *fold.*" *Creech.* A double; one part turned over upon another. The plait of a garment, from *fl'd*, or *ſoul'd*, Sax.

To FOLD, V. A. to pen ſheep in a fold. To double; to plait. Figuratively, to incloſe; to include; to ſhut; to embrace with the arms claſped round a perſon. Neuterly, to cloſe over another of the ſame kind. To join with another of the ſame kind.

FOLIACEOUS, Adj. [*foliaceus*, Lat.] conſiſting of thin plates, or leaves.

FOLIAGE, S. [*fruillage*, Fr. from *folium*, Lat.] an aſſemblage of flowers, branches, or leaves.

To FOLIATE, V. A. [*foliatus*, Lat.] to beat gold into thin plates, or leaves. "Gold *foliated.*" *Newt. Optic.*

FOLIATING, S. applied to looking-glaſſes, is the ſpreading a compoſition to the back of the glaſs, that will reflect images. The compoſition is called *foil*, and made of quickſilver, &c.

FOLIATION, S. [*foliatio*, of *folium*, Lat.] the act of beating into leaves. In botany, a collection of thoſe tranſitory coloured leaves called petals, which conſtitute the compaſs or body of a flower; of great uſe in the generation and preſervation of the young fruit or ſeed.

FOLIO, S. [Ital. of *in folio*, Lat.] a large book, whoſe pages are formed by a

ſheet of paper only once doubled. In cometer, a page or leaf.

FOLK, S. [pronounced with the *o* long, like that in *proſe*, *folk*, Sax.] people. Nations, multitudes, or mankind in general.

FOLKSTONE, S. a town of Kent, with a market on Thurſdays, and one fair, on June 28, for pedlars ware. It was once a flouriſhing town of large extent, containing five pariſh-churches, which are now reduced to one ſmall church, and three meeting houſes. It is a member of the port of Dover, and is governed by a mayor, and 12 jurats. It contains about 350 houſes, moſtly built with brick, and diſpoſed into three narrow paved ſtreets. The inhabitants are chiefly employed in fiſhing. Near it is Sangate-caſtle. It is ſeated on the ſea-coaſt, 8 miles S. W. of Dover, 17 S. E. of Canterbury, and 69 E. by S. of London, Lon. 13. 55. lat. 51. 8.

To FOLLOW, V. A. [*folgian*, Sax. *folgen*, Teut.] to go after a perſon. To purſue. To attend on as a ſervant. To ſucceed or happen after, in order of time. To proceed from as a conſequence, or effect. To imitate, or copy. To obey; to obſerve, to aſſent, or give credit to. "All who do not "*follow* real tradition." *Tillots.* To attend to; to be buſied with. "He *follows* the trade of a goldſmith." Neuterly, to come after another. To ſucceed or be after another in time. To proceed from as an effect or conſequence. To continue or purſue any endeavour, uſed with on. "It we *follow* on to know the Lord." *Hoſea.*

FOLLOWER, S. one who goes after another. Figuratively, a dependant; attendant; aſſociate; companion; or imitator.

FOLLY, S. [*foladd*, Brit. *folie*, Fr. *follis*, Ital.] weakneſs or want of underſtanding: Not uſed in the plural of this ſenſe. Figuratively, an act of negligence, or paſſion unbecoming the great dictates of cool and unbiaſſed reflection: In this ſenſe it has a plural.

To FOMENT, V. A. [*fomenter*, Lat.] to cheriſh with heat. To bathe with warm lotions. Figuratively, to encourage; to cheriſh.

FOMENTATION, S. [Fr.] in medicine, the applying hot flannels to any part dipped in medicated decoctions. The liquor or decoction made from boiling medicinal ingredients.

FOMENTOR, S. an encourager or ſupporter, one who foments or bathes.

FOND, S. Adj. [*fondiari*, Sax. *fun*, Scot. *foeliſh*.] fooliſh; ſilly; weak; indiſcreet. "'Tis *fond* to wail inevitable ſtrokes." *Shak.* Trifling. Fooliſhly or indiſcretely tender, and indulgent. Loving to an exceſs. Pleaſed in too great a degree. Taking too much delight in a thing.

To FOND, V. A. to treat with an indiſcrete

3 M 2   crea

ever excess of love, or tenderness. "I'll fond it as the frow and child of love." *Dryd.* Neuterly, to be fond of ; to doat on ; to love to excels. "I, poor moniter, *feed* as much on him." *Shak.*

To FON'DLE, V. A. the same as *fond*, which see.

FON'DLING, S. a person used with too much indulgence, or regarded with an excess of affection.

FON'DLY, Adv. foolishly ; indiscreetly ; imprudently ; injudiciously. With an excess of tenderness or indulgence.

FOND'NESS, S. foolishness ; folly ; want of judgment. " *Fondness* it were for any, being free — to covet letters." *Spens.* An excess of love, or tenderness.

FONT, S. [*fonte*, Fr. *fons*, Lat.] a vessel generally of marble in which the water used in baptism is contained.

FOOD, [*fodor*, Sax. *fode*, Ifl.] whatever is swallowed to repair the wants of nature. Figuratively, any thing which encourages or cherishes. "The *food* of thy abused father's wrath." *Shak.*

FOOD'FUL, Adj fruitful ; fertile. "The *foodful* earth." *Dryd.*

FOOL, S. [*fol*, Brit. and Arm. *fol*, Fr.] one who has not the proper use of reason. Figuratively, one who counterfeits folly ; a buffoon, or jester. "Call my *fool* hither." *Shak.* In scripture, an idolater, a very wicked person. "The *fool* hath said in his heart there is no God." *Psal.* xlv. 1. In common conversation, used as a word of great contempt. *To play the fool*, is to trifle, or play pranks like an hired jester, merely to divert or make sport, or to act like a person void of common understanding. *To make a fool of a person*, is, to raise his expectations and disappoint them. "To break promise with him, and *make a fool of him*." *Shak.*

To FOOL, V. N. to trifle ; to toy ; to idle. Neuterly, to impose on. To raise a person's expectations, and afterwards disappoint them. To deceive. To cheat, used with *out of*. "To *fool* him *out of* his money."

FOOL'ERY, S. folly. An act of tonly ; a trifling practice. An act of indiscretion. "It is mere *foolery* to multiply distinct particulars." *Harris.* An object of folly ; a thing which induces folly.

FOOL'HARDINESS, S. daring and indifferent courage.

FOOL'HARDY, Adj. bold, without discretion, or prudence.

FOOL'TRAP, S. a snare to catch the ignorant in. "Beus, at the first, were *fooltraps*." *Dryd.*

FOOL'ISH, Adj. entirely or naturally void of understanding. Figuratively, wanting prudence, indiscreet. Ridiculous, unreasonable. In scripture, foreign, idolatrous, or wicked.

FOOL'ISHLY, Adv. weakly ; without

understanding ; indiscreetly. In scripture, idolatrously ; wickedly.

FOOT, S. [Plural *feet*, *fater*, Ifl. *fu*, *fet*, *fotur*, Goth.) that part of an animal whereon it stands or walks. In Anatomy, the extremity of the leg, consisting of the *tarsus*, or *space* of the ankle from the body of the foot, the *metatarsus*, or body of the foot, and the toes ; the wisdom which shines forth in the construction in this part of the human machine, would require so copious a description, that our narrow bounds will not permit us the pleasure of indulging ourselves in it. Figuratively, that part with which any thing is supported, in the same manner as the foot supports the body of an animal. The lower part, or base. " *Foot* of the hill." On foot, walking, opposed to riding. Condition ; state. "On the same *foot* with our fellow subjects." *Swift.* A plan ; scheme, or settlement. "Upon the *foot* of our constitution." *Swift.* To *set on foot* ; is to give rise to. "If such a tradition were, at any time, *set on foot* " *Tillot.* In Poetry, a certain number of long and short syllables constituting a distinct part of a verse. A measure of twelve inches.

To FOOT, V. A. to spurn, or kick with the foot. In Dancing, to make a noise with the foot, imitating the tune played by the music. To knit a *foot* to a stocking.

FOOT'BALL, S. a ball made of leather, and filled with wind by means of a bladder included in the inside ; also the game played with it.

FOOT'ED, having a foot, or something to contain the foot, applied to stockings, or hose.

FOOT'HOLD, S. space or room enough to tread on securely. "So little *foothold*." *L'Estrange.*

FOOT'ING, S. ground or substance for the foot or any thing to rest on. "The unsteadfast *footing* of a spear." *Shak.* Foundation ; basis ; support ; place. "Tread ; walk ; or the sound of a person's foot. "I hear the *footing* of a man." *Shak.* In Dancing a particular manner of moving the feet, so as to echo the sound of the tune. Steps ; track ; road. Figuratively, entrance ; beginning. "No useful arts have yet found *footing* here." *Dryd.* State ; condition. "On what *footing* is Denmark with England?"

FOOT'MAN, S. a menial servant in livery. One who walks or runs.

FOOT'PACE, S. in Building, part of a pair of stairs, whereon, after four or five steps, you arrive to a broad place ; where you may take two or three paces, before you ascend another flip. A pace no faster than walking.

FOOT'PATH, S. a narrow way ; which will admit only foot passengers.

FOOT'STEP, S. an impression made by the

the foot in treading. Figuratively, any trace, mark, token, sign, or example.

FOOT-STOOL, S. a stool whereon a person puts his feet when sitting.

FOP, S. [a word, by Johnson, supposed to be formed by chance, and without etymology] a person of weak understanding, and affecting delicacy too much both in dress and behaviour.

FOPPERY, S. impertinence, ignorance, or folly. "Let not the sound of shallow foppery enter my house." Shak. Affectation in dress, and importance. Foolery.

FOPPISH, Adj. foolish; idle; vain. Gayly. Attended with too great an affectation of ceremony in behaviour.

FOPPISHLY, Adv. vainly ostentatiously, like a coxcomb.

FOPPISHNESS, S. showy, gaudy, and affected vanity.

FOPLING, S. an imitator of a fop. A petty fop.

FOR, Prep. [for, Sax. faar, or faure, Goth.] on account of. "That which we for our unworthiness, are unworthy to crave." Hooker. Instead of; in the character, or likeness of. "Embrace for truth." Locke. "Lay for dead." Dryd. "He refused not to die for those that killed him." Boyle. Conducive, promoting, or tending to. "It is for the general good." Tillots. Towards a certain place. "We sailed directly for Jamaica." With approbation. "Shadow will serve for summer." Shak. In confirmation, applied to proofs. "There is a natural, immutable, and eternal reason for that which we call virtue." Tillots. Noting possibility, power. "For a holy person to be humble is as hard as for a prince to submit, &c." Taylor. Left, by way of prevention, or for fear. "And, for the time shall not seem tedious." Shak. Against, as a remedy for. "Good for the gout." Garros. In exchange; instead, or in the place of. Through a certain space of time. In search, or quest of. In favour of; on the side of. "Aristotle is for particular justice." Denh. Fit; becoming. "Is it for you to ravage sea and land?" Dryd. Followed by all, it implies notwithstanding. Considering, or in proportion to.

FOR, Conj. because. "Yet for that the work men are most ready." Spenser. For as much as, implies since, or because. "For as much as it is a fundamental law." Bac. For why; because for this reason that.

FORAGE, S. [fourage, Teut. foragium, low Lat.] search of provisions. Provisions sought abroad. Provisions of any kind.

To FORAGE, V. N. to wander or rove at a distance. To wander in search of provisions, or litter. To ravage or feed on spoil. Actively, to plunder, strip, or spoil.

FORAMINOUS, Adj. [foramin, Lat.] full of holes, or pores. Porous.

To FORBEAR, V. A. preter. I forbore; or I bore forbore; forbaran, Sax.; to cease. To pause, or delay. To decline; to omit, or abstain from. To endure with patience. "By long forbearance is a prince persuaded." Prov. xxv. 15. Actively, to decline; to shun, or avoid the presence of a person or thing. To abstain from any action. To spare; to endure provocation, without any sign of anger or resentment. "Forbearing one another in love." Eph. iv. 2.

FORBEARANCE, S. the act of abstaining from any crime or fault. The act of enduring offences without complaint, resentment or anger.

To FORBID, V. A. [preter. forbade, compound preter. I have forbidden, part. forbidden,] to command a person not to perform a thing. To bid a person not to enter. "Have I not forbid her my house." Shak. To oppose or hinder. "A blaze of glory that forbid the fight." Dryd. To curse or devote to endless misery. "He shall live a man forbid." Shak. The last sense is obsolete. Neuterly, to utter a prohibition; "Now the good gods forbid!" Shak.

FORBIDDANCE, S. a prohibition; or command to desist.

FORBIDDENLY, Adv. in such a manner as is prohibited; unlawfully. "You have touched his queen forbiddenly." Shak.

FORBIDDER, S. one who commands a person not to do a thing.

FORBIDDING, Part. raising abhorrence, aversion, awe, distaste.

FORCE, S. [Fr. force, Ital.] power; vigour. Violence. Validity. An armament; warlike preparations; used generally in the plural. Virtue, or efficacy. In Law, an offence, by which violence is used either to persons or things. Destiny; necessity; irresistible power, or fatal compulsion; emphasis on a sentence.

To FORCE, V. A. [forcer, Fr.] to compel a person to do a thing contrary to his will. To overpower by strength. To drive by violence or strength, used with from or out. To draw or push by main strength. To get from by violence; used with from. In War, to take or enter a city by violence; to storm. To ravish; to lay with a woman by violence. To man; to strengthen with soldiers. "The passages be already forced." Raleigh. To force out, to extort a thing which should be concealed.

FORCED, Part. obliged or compelled to do a thing. Wrested; unnatural; applied to the use of words. "Forced conceits." Addis.

FORCEDLY, Adv. violently; compulsively; constrainedly; unnaturally.

FORCELESS, Adj. without strength, force or violence.

FORCEPS, S. [Lat.] in Surgery, an instrument used to extract any thing out of wounds.

FORCER,

FOR'CER, S. that which drives, compels, constrains or forces. In Mechanics, the embolus of a pump working by passion or force.

FO'RCIBLE, Adj. strong; powerful, opposed to weak; violent; active, or efficacious. Caused by strength, force, violence, or compulsion. "The abdication—the advantage on the other side looked upon it to have been forcible," Swift. Valid; binding in law; obligatory.

FO'RCIBLENESS, S. the quality of efficacy; any end by force.

FO'RCIBLY, Adv. strongly; powerfully; by irresistible power, strength or force.

FOR'CIPATED, Adj. [from forceps, Lat.] formed like a pair of pincers. "Hold it with their forcipated mouth." Derham.

FORD, S. [Sax. from faran, to pass, for, Isl.] a shallow part of a river, which may be passed without swimming. Sometimes it signifies any stream, current or river. "Permit my ghost to pass the Stygian ford." Dryd.

To FORD, V. A. to pass a river without swimming.

FO'RDABLE, Adj. that which is passable on foot.

FORE, Adj. [Sax.] that part which comes first when a body moves. "Greater pressing on the fore than hind part." Cheyne.

FORE, Adv. that part which appears first to those that meet it. "A slight spar deck fore and aft." Raleigh.

To FO'REARM, V. A. to provide with weapons for an attack or resistance, before either happen.

To FO'REBODE, V. N. [forebidan, Sax.] to predict or foretell. To presage; or have a secret sense impressed of something future, generally applied to some future calamity.

FO'REBODER, S. a prognosticator; soothsayer; foreteller, a presager.

To FO'RECAST, V. A. to plan. To contrive. To foresee or provide against. "In forecast consequences." L'Estrange.

FO'RECAST, S. contrivance. A scheme; a plan. Provision against any accident or emergence. Foresight.

FO'RECASTER, S. one who foresees and provides against future events.

FO'RECASTLE, S. the part of a ship, where the foremast stands, and is divided from the rest of the floor by a bulk head.

FO'RECITED, Part. quoted or cited before.

To FO'RECLOSE, V. A. to shut up; to prevent; to put a stop to. In Law, to foreclose a mortgage, is to cut off the power of the equity of redemption.

To FO'REDOOM, V. A. to predestinate; to predict.

FO'REEND, S. the foremost part; the first part, applied to time.

FO'REFATHER, S. an ancestor.

To FOREFE'ND, V. A. to forbid; to avert; to deprecate. "Heav'n forefend!" Shak. To provide for; to secure beforehand.

FO'REFOOT, S. [plural, forefeet] the foot of a beast which is nearest the head; in contempt, a hand. "Give me thy fist, thy forefoot to me give." Shak. In Sea Language, applied to a vessel which falls, or lies across another's way.

To FORE'GO, V. A. to quit, resign, or let go. To go before; to be past.

FO'REGROUND, S. that part of the ground of a picture, which appears to be before the figures.

FO'REHAND, S. that part of a horse which is before a rider.

FO'REHANDED, Adj. early; timely. Formed in the foreparts. "A substantial, true bred beast, bravely forehanded." Dryd.

FO'REHEAD, S. the part of the face from the eyebrows to the hair of the head. Figuratively, impudence; confidence; undaunted assurance. "I fain would know to what branch—they can have the forehead to reply." Swift.

FO'REIGN, Adj. [forain, Fr. foreus, Span.] of another country. Alien; removed; not allied. Opposite; irreconcilable with; used with to, but more properly from. "A language foreign to my heart." Addis. "Not foreign from some people's thoughts," Swift. Excluded, or not admitted to one's acquaintance or company. "Keep him a foreign man still." Shak. A foreign plea in Law, is that which is out of a proper court of justice, or not triable in the country wherein it is made; this is more properly called a foreign answer, or foreign matter.

FO'REIGNER, one who is born in another country. The produce of another country; exotics.

FO'REIGNNESS, S. remoteness; strangeness. Having no relation to something. "Let not the foreignness of the subject." Locke.

To FOREJU'DGE, V. A. to judge beforehand. To be prepossessed or prejudiced for or against.

To FOREKNO'W, V. A. to have knowledge of a thing before it happens; to predict; to presage, to foresee.

FOREKNOW'LEDGE, S. knowledge of a thing before hand.

FO'RELAND, S. In Navigation, a point of land jutting into the sea. A promontory.

To FORELA'Y, V. A. to lay wait for. "An ambush'd thief forelays a traveller." Dryd.

FO'RELOCK, S. a lock of hair which grows on the forepart of the head. In a ship, a little flat wedge, like a piece of iron used at the ends of bolts, to keep them from starting.

FO'REMAN, S. the chief or principal person

person in any assembly, or among any work-men.

FOREMAST, S. in a ship, a round large piece of timber, found in the forepart, on which is borne the foresail.

FOREMENTIONED, Part. mentioned or quoted before.

FOREMOST, Adj. first. Chief, principal, or before others in dignity.

FORENAMED, Par. See FOREMENTIONED, named or mentioned before.

FORENOON, the first part of the day, measured from the dawn to 12 o'clock at noon.

To FOREORDAIN, V. A. to determine or fix an event before it happens or exists.

FOREPART, S. the first part, applied to time. " The *forepart* of the day" *Raleigh*. That part which is first when a thing or person moves along.

FOREPAST, Part. that which has past before a certain period. " Of all *forepast* sins." *Howe*.

FORERANK, S. the first rank ; front or beginning." " Within the *forerank* of our articles." *Shak*. Not in use.

To FORERUN, V. A. to precede, or go before as an earnest or token of something which is to follow ; To introduce as a messenger or harbinger. " Pity still *forerun* approaching love." *Dryd*. To have the start of.

FORERUNNER, S. an harbinger, or messenger. A sign or omen foreshewing or presaging the approach of some future event.

To FORESEE, V. A. to see or have knowledge of something which is to happen.

To FORESHORTEN, V. A. to shorten figures, in order to shew those behind them.

To FORESHOW, V. A. [Preter, I have *foreshown*, Part. *foreshown*] to discover or give notice of a thing before it happens. To represent a thing before it exists. " What is the law but the gospel *foreshowed*." *Hooker*. The participle in the quotation is out of use.

FORESIGHT, S. the act of perceiving a thing before it happens. The act of providing against any future event or calamity.

FORESKIN, S. the prepuce.

To FORESLOW, V. A. to delay, impede, or obstruct. " The Nereids though they rais'd no storm—*foreslow'd* her passage." *Dryd*. To neglect or omit. " No coldness *foreslowing*, but wisdom in chusing." *Bac*.

To FORESPEAK, V. A. [from *fore* and *speak*] to foretel, or show before it happens. " No ominous *forespeaking* to lie in names." *Camden*. To forebid, from *for*, &c. negative, and *speak* i. e. to speak against, or unsay. " Thou hast *forespoke* my being in these wars." *Shak*.

FOREST, S. [*forest*, Brit. *forest*, Fr.] a large uncultivated track of ground over-

grown with trees. In Law, a certain territory of woods, grounds, and fruitful pastures, privileged for wild beasts, fowls of the *forest*, chase, and warren to rest and abide in, in the safe protection of the king for his pleasure ; bounded with irremoveable marks, and replenished with beasts of venery or chase, and with great coverts of vert for their succour and abode ; for the preservation of which place, vert and venison, there are certain particular laws.

FOREST, Adj. of or belonging to a forest. *Forest* cloth, a peculiar kind of broad cloth made in Yorkshire, nor so wide as that made in the western counties, nor of so good a fabric.

FORESTAFF, S. an instrument used at sea for taking the altitudes of heavenly bodies ; so called because the observer, in using it, turns his face towards the object.

To FORESTALL, V. A. [*forestallan*, Sax.] to anticipate ; to take up before-hand. " What need a man *forestall* his date of grief." *Milt*. To hinder a person from doing a thing by doing it before him. " I will not *forestall* your judgment of the rest." To buy commodities before another in order to enhance their price.

FORESTALLER, S. one who intercepts customers as they go to market. One who buys up great quantities of provisions or commodities, only to raise their price.

FORESTER, S. [*forestier*, Fr.] one who inhabits a forest.

To FORETASTE, V. A. to have an antetaste of ; to have a strong idea and earnest of a thing before it exists. To anticipate. To taste before another, or before a determinate time. " *Foretasted* fruit." *Milt*.

To FORETELL, V. A. [Preter and Participle, *foretold*] to prophecy ; to give notice of a thing before it happens. To foretoken, or predict.

FORETELLER, S. one who predicts, or gives notice of things before they happen.

To FORETHINK, V. A. [Preter and Part. *forethought*] to have an idea of a thing in the mind before it happens. To plan, or contrive before-hand.

FORETHOUGHT, S. anticipation, or foresight. A provident care against some future event. A sedate consideration of the consequences which will follow some future event, with proper preparations either to obviate, or render them tolerable.

To FOREWARN, V. A. to give proper notice, and caution a person from doing a thing beforehand.

FORFEIT, S. [*forfeit*, Br. *forfait*, Fr.] something by way of punishment for a crime, or a breach of contract. A person liable to punishment, or one who is condemned to death for a crime. " Your brother is a *forfeit* of the law." *Shak*.

To FORFEIT, V. A. to lose a privilege

oz

or advantage enjoyed before, or pay a sum of money as a punishment for some crime, or breach of condition or contract.

FORFEIT, Particip. liable to be seized, or lost, either on account of the commission of a crime ; or the breach of a contract.

FORFEITABLE, Adj. liable to be lost for crimes ; non-performance of certain conditions.

FORFEITURE, S. [forfeiture, Fr.] the act of losing or paying on account of some omission or crime. The thing paid forfeited or lost as a punishment. A fine.

FORGAVE, Preter. of forgive.

FORGE, S. [Fr. forge, Ital.] the furnace where iron is properly tempered, or beaten into any particular form. In common discourse, forge is used for large work, and smithy for small ; but this distinction is not preserved in books. Figuratively, any place where a thing is formed, made, or contrived.

To FORGE, V. A. [forger, Fr.] to form or beat by the hammer. To make by any means. To counterfeit, or falsify.

FORGER, S. one who makes or forms by beating. One who counterfeits.

FORGERY, S. the crime of counterfeiting with intent to defraud or impose upon. The act of fabrication. Smith's work made by forging.

To FORGET, V. A. [Preter. forgot, Part. forgot, or forgotten, forgotten, Belg.] to lose the remembrance of. Figuratively, to neglect, or take no more thought of, than of a thing entirely forgotten. " Can a woman forget her sucking child." Isai. xlix. 5.

FORGETFUL, Adj. not retaining anything in the memory. Causing forgetfulness. Negligent ; neglectful ; careless.

FORGETFULNESS, S. the habit of losing the remembrance of a thing. Negligence, or neglect.

FORGETTER, S. one who ceases to remember a thing. Figuratively, one who is careless or negligent.

To FORGIVE, V. A. [forgifan, Sax.] to pardon a crime, or a criminal. To forego, or not to insist upon a right. " Forgave him the debt." Matth. xviii. 27.

FORGIVENESS, S. [forgifnesse, Sax.] the act of passing by the offence of a person without anger or punishment. Willingness to pardon. Remission of a fine, or the giving a person a debt which he owes.

FORGIVER, S. one who forgives his right to a debt, mitigates or lessens a fine, or passes by an offence without punishment or anger.

FORK, S. [forch, Brit. furcha, Fr. furca, Lat.] an instrument made with iron prongs, sharp at the point, and used to stick into and take up meat and other things with ; when it has a very long handle and three prongs, it is called a trident. The point or

forked part of an arrow. The prong, or point of a fork.

To FORK, V. N. to shoot into blades, prongs, or divisions like those of corn.

FORKED, Adj. formed with parts resembling the prongs of a fork.

FORKEDLY, Adv. in the form of a fork ; awkwardly.

FORKY, Adj. pointed like the prongs of a fork, or the head of an arrow. " Their forky tongue and pointless sting." Pope.

FORLORN, Adj. [forloren, Sax.] destitute ; deprived of ; forsaken ; wretched. Lost ; desperate. Small ; in a ludicrous sense. " So forlorn, that his dimensions to any thick sight were invincible." Shak. Forlorn hope, those soldiers who are sent on any desperate enterprize, or make the first onset in a battle ; being, as the term imports, destitute of all hopes, and in some measure doomed to perish.

FORLORN, S. a lost, forsaken, friendless, or helpless person. " To live in Scotland a forlorn." Shak.

FORM, S. [forme, Fr. forma, Lat.] the external appearance, shape, or model. Figuratively, beauty. " He hath no form." Isai. liii. 2. Regularity ; method ; order, applied to placing things, or the arrangement of the parts of a discourse. External appearance, or mere show. Any stated method or established practice. A long seat or bench. In schools, a class, or division of scholars. In Hunting, the seat or bed of a hare. That which gives effect to a thing. In Physic, that which denotes the manner of being peculiar to each body, or constitutes it such a particular body and distinguishes it from every other. In Printing, a certain number of pages contained in an iron square or chase. In the mechanic arts, a kind of mould whereon a thing is fashioned or modelled.

FORMA pauperis, [Lat. after the manner of a poor man] in Law, is applied when a person has cause of suit, but is not able to pay the charges. In which case, he makes oath that he is not worth five pounds, his debts being paid, and bringing a certificate from some lawyer, that his cause is a just one, the judge admits him to sue in forma pauperis, i. e. without paying fees to the counsellor, attorney, clerk, or the stamp-duty. This custom has its beginning from stat. 11. Hen. VII. c. 12. The professors of the law, at present, discourage as much as possible, this mode of proceeding at law, which is not the least to be wondered at ; for how can it be imagined that a counsel, who will endeavour to mislead a jury, and pervert justice, because he has received a small sum for that purpose from his client, will ever condescend to plead a poor man's cause, merely because he is poor, and has only justice and equity on his side ?

FORMAL,

FOR'MAL, Adj. [*formel*, Fr. *formalis*, Lat.] applied to dress or behaviour, ceremonious; solemn; precise; exact to affectation. Done according to certain rules or methods; regular; methodical. Merely external; having the appearance only, not the power, essence or substance. Having the power of making a thing to be what it is; constituent; essential. Retaining its original and proper or former shape. " Till I have said the approval means I have to make of him a *formal* man again." *Shak.*

FOR'MALIST, S. [*formaliste*, Fr.] one who practises external ceremonies. One who prefers appearance to reality.

FORMA'LITY, S. ceremonious exactness to excess; essence, or quality, by which any thing is what it is. In Law, the rules prescribed, or customs observed in carrying on any cause. Solemn order, habit, or dress.

To FOR'MALIZE, [*formaliser*, Fr.] to form, make, or model. To affect formality; to be fond of ceremony.

FOR'MALLY, Adv. according to established rules. In a precise manner; with too great affectation of ceremony. In outward appearance. Adequately; essentially; really.

FORMA'TION, S. [Fr. *formatio*, Lat.] the act of forming, or producing a thing. The manner in which a thing is made.

FOR'MATIVE, Adj. [*formatus*, Lat. of *formo*,] having the power to make or form. " By any *formative* power residing in the soil." *Bentley.*

FOR'MER, S. [from *form*] one who forms a thing. A maker. " The *former* of our bodies." *Ray.*

FOR'MER, Adj. [*forme*, Sax. *fremist*,] Goth. first. Hence *former* and *formest*, commonly written *foremost*, as if derived of *fore*, Sax. before and *most*, a superlative adjective. *Foremost*, according to Johnson, " is only applied to place, rank, or degree, and *former* to time; for when we say the last rank of a procession is like the *former*, we respect time rather than place, and mean that which we saw before, rather than that which had preceded in place." Yet with deference to so celebrated a writer, I am of opinion, that in that first instance alledged, we mean rather that which is passed by, or has a place beyond us, rather than the time in which it passed; before in time. Mentioned before; another; past. " This was the custom in *former times*."

FOR'MERLY, Adv. in times past.

FOR'MIDABLE, Adj. [Fr. *formidabilis*, Lat.] terrible; dreadful. Occasioning great fear. To be feared.

FOR'MIDABLENESS, S. the quality of exciting terror or fear.

FOR'MIDABLY, Adv. so as to excite fear.

FOR'MLESS, Adj. shapeless; without any regular form.

FOR'MULARY, S. [*formulaire*, Fr.] a book containing the prescribed rules of performing any thing.

FOR'MULE, S. [Fr. *formula*, Lat.] a set rule, form, or model.

To FOR'NICATE, V. A. [*fornix*, Lat.] to commit lewd actions.

FORNICA'TION, S. [Fr. *fornicatio*, Lat.] the act of incontinency between unmarried persons. *Simple fornication*, is that which is committed with a common prostitute, and supposed by some casuists to be the lowest degree of this crime. In Scripture, *fornication* is used for idolatry, the compact between God and the Jews, with respect to the theocracy, being considered in the light of a marriage contract.

FORNICA'TOR, S. a single man who is guilty of incontinency with an unmarried woman.

FORNICA'TRESS, S. a single woman guilty of incontinence with an unmarried man.

To FORSA'KE, V. A. [Preter *forsook*, Part. Pass. *forsook* or *forsaken*, *forsacan*; Part.] to leave in resentment, neglect, or dislike. To break off friendship or commerce with. To leave or go away from. To desert; or withdraw any kind offices or assistance from a person.

FORSA'KER, S. one who quits or deserts.

FORSOO'TH, Adv. [*forsoth*, Sax.] in truth: Surely, certainly. Used at present only in a ludicrous and contemptuous sense. Formerly it was used as a word of honour, it being probable that an inferior being called, used to answer, yes, *forsooth*. which in time losing its meaning, was used as a compellation, and, as the Courrier says, instead of the French word *Madam* to a lady, and from *obedience* it appears likewise to have been used instead of *Sir*, when speaking to a man.

To FORSWEA'R, [Preter *forswore*, Part. *forsworn*,] to renounce, quit, or deny upon oath. Neuterly, to swear falsely.

FORSWEA'RER, S. one who swears falsely.

FORT, S. [Fr. *fort*, Lat.] a small castle or fortress; or a work encompassed with a moat, rampart, and parapet, to secure some high ground, or passage.

FO'RTED, Adj. strengthened, or guarded by forts. " A *forted* residence." *Shak.*

FORTH, Adv. [*forth*, Sax.] forward; onward, or in advance, applied to time. Before another; or in advance, applied to place. Abroad or out of doors, joined with the verbs *came* or *go*. Out of, or beyond the boundaries of a place. Washed his father's fortunes *forth* of France." *Shak.*

FORTHCOMING, Adj. ready to appear or come forth. " See that he be forthcoming." Shak.

FORTHWITH, Adv. immediately; without delay; now.

FORTIETH, Adv. [georteogotha, Sax.] that which is next after the thirty-ninth.

FORTIFICATION, S. [Fr.] a place strengthened with ramparts, &c. in order to defend it from the attacks of an enemy.

FORTIFIER, S. one who erects works to defend a place. Figuratively, one who supports, countenances, or upholds.

To FORTIFY, V. A. [fortifier, Fr.] to strengthen a place against attacks by fortifications. Figuratively, to confirm, encourage, or invigorate. To fix from altering; to confirm in a resolution.

FORTILAGE, S. a little fort or blockhouse. " In all narrow passages—there should be some little fortilage." Spenser.

FORTITUDE, S. [Fr. fortitudo, Lat.] the act of undertaking hazardous or dangerous enterprizes with calmness and serenity, and pursuing virtuous designs unshaken by menaces or temptations. Bodily strength, or force. " His own arm's fortitude." Shak.

FORTNIGHT, S. [contracted form fourteen nights. Thus the northern nations counted their time by nights; we have not only the assertions of Cæsar and Tacitus to confirm; but it seems to have been derived to them from the Jews, and is a traditionary confirmation of the Mosaic account of the creation, wherein the nights are placed first in the order of time, thus: " The evening and morning were the first day."] The space of two weeks.

FORTRESS, S. [fortresse, Fr.] a strong hold; a general name for all fortified places.

FORTUITOUS, Adj. [fortuit, Fr. fortuitus, Lat.] happening without any rational cause. Accidental; Casual.

FORTUITOUSLY, Adv. by chance; without the design or operation of any intelligent cause.

FORTUITOUSNESS, S. the quality of having no apparent cause, or being produced without design.

FORTUNATE, Adj. [fortunatus, Lat.] lucky; happy; successful; applied both to persons and things.

FORTUNATELY, Adv. successfully; so as to attain one's end, or the object of one's wishes.

FORTUNE, S. [fortuna, Lat.] chance; a power or deity supposed to distribute the lots of mankind only according to caprice or humour. The good or ill which befals is a person. The chance of obtaining a support or livelihood. Estate; or possessions. The money which a man or woman brings with them on marriages. The fu-

ture events, whether good or bad, which may happen to a person.

To FORTUNE, V. N. to happen; to fall out; to come to pass by chance, or without the interposition of any rational or natural cause. To predict a future event, accented on the second syllable. " Fortun'd the dying notes of Rome." Dryd. Juv.

FORTUNED, Adj. happening successfully; successful. Foretold.

FORTUNE-HUNTER, S. a man who seeks after persons of great positions to enrich himself by marrying one.

FORTUNETELLER, S. one who pretends to foretell future events.

FORTY, Adj. [feowertig, Sax.] a number consisting of four times ten.

FORUM, S. [Lat.] a public place at Rome, where lawyers and orators made their speeches in matters of property, or in criminal causes. Any public place. Among casuists, a jurisdiction; thus, in foro legis, is in the eye of the law; in foro conscientiæ, in the eye of God, or our own conscience.

FORWARD, Adv. [forweard, Sax.] towards a place; straight before a person.

FORWARD, Adj. warm; anxious willing or ready to do a thing. Premature; or ripe too soon. Presumptuous; confident; not having the reserve or modesty suitable to a person's years. " A forward girl." In the fore part, opposed to behind. " Take the instant by the forward top." Shak. Quick; hasty. Almost finished; far advanced.

To FORWARD, V. A. to promote a design; to accelerate, hasten, or advance in growth, improvement, &c. To encourage, or patronize an undertaking.

FORWARDLY, Adv. eagerly; hastily; rashly; In a hurry, rashly.

FORWARDNESS, S. eagerness or readiness to do a thing; readiness to learn; early ripeness. Confidence, rudeness.

FORWARDS, Adv. straight before. In a straight line or motion from a person's face.

FOSSE, S. [fn, Brit. fofs, Fr. fossa, Lat.] in Fortification, a ditch or moat. In Anatomy, a kind of cavity in a bone, which has no passage or perforation through it; when the passage is narrow, it is called a sinus.

FOSSET, S. See FAUCET.

FOSSEWAY, S. one of the great Roman highways in England; so called, according to Camden, because ditches on both sides, from fossa, Lat. a ditch.

FOSSIL, Adj. [fossile, Fr. fossilis, Lat.] dug out of the earth.

FOSSIL, S. a body formed under the surface of the earth.

To FOSTER, V. A. [fostrian, Sax.] to nourish, to cherish with food; to nurse or bring up a young child. Figuratively, to pamper, encourage, or train up. To cherish,

rith, or forward. "Ye *fostering* breezes." *Thom.*

FOSTERAGE, S. the employ of nursing of bringing up a young child. "The charge and *fosterage* of this child." *Raleigh.*

FOSTER-BROTHER, S. [*foster brother*, Sax.] one bred up by the same woman

FOSTER-DAME, S. a woman who brings up another person's child.

FOSTERER, S. one who brings up a child instead of its parents. One who nourishes or cherishes.

FOSTER-MOTHER, S. [*foster moder*, Sax.] a woman who brings up the child of another.

FOSTER-NURSE, S. [an improper compound, because *foster* and *nurse* convey the same idea] a nurse, or one who feeds or brings up a child for another. "Our *foster-nurse* of nature is repose." *Shak.*

FOSTER-SON, S. a boy nursed from his infancy, by a person not his parent.

FOUL, Adj. [*ful*, Sax. *faul*, Teut.] dirty, filthy, not fair, or clean, impure; polluted. Using indelicate, or obscene expressions. "With *foul* mouth." *Shak.* Not lawful, or honest. Hateful, ugly, loathsome. "The *foul* witch." *Shak.* Disgraceful, shameful. "Overthrow and *foul* defeat." *Par. Lost.* Full of gross and bad humours, applied to the habit of the body. Cloudy, or tempestuous, applied to weather. Muddy, thick, applied to liquors, "To fall *foul.*" Rough force, or unseasonable violence. Among seamen, entangled; as "a rope is *foul* of an anchor." Overgrown with moss or other impurities, which hinder a ship's way; applied to a ship bottom. To make *foul* water, applied to a ship whose keel approaches so near to the bottom of a river, as to raise mud from thence, and disturb or thicken the water thereby.

To FOUL, V. A. to daub; to bemire, or soil.

FOULFACED, Adj. having a dirty or ill-looking countenance.

FOULLY, Adv. filthily, nastily; dirty or soiled in such a manner, as to raise loathing. In an unfair or dishonest manner.

FOULNESS, S. the quality which excites an idea of dirtiness. Pollution. Hatefulness. Ugliness. Deformity. Dishonesty.

FOUND, preter and participle passive of *find.*

To FOUND, V. A. [*fonder*, Fr. *fundo*, Lat.] to lay the foundation of any building. To establish or erect. To give birth to. "He *founded* an art." To fix firm. "*Founded* as the rock." *Shak.* To set apart a sum of money as a fund for maintaining an hospital, &c.

To FOUND, V. N. [*fondre*, Fr. *fundo*, Lat.] to form by melting and pouring into moulds. To cast metals into any particular form or shape.

FOUNDATION, S. [*fondation*, Fr.] be lower parts which support the rest of a house or building. The act of laying the basis of any thing. The original, or rise. A revenue settled and established for any purpose. An establishment or settlement.

FOUNDER, S. a builder; one who erects an edifice. One who endows, or establishes a revenue for the support of any hospital, college, &c. One who gives rise or origin to any art or manufacture. One who forms figures of melted metal by pouring it into moulds

To FOUNDER, V. A. [*fondre*, Fr.] to cause such a soreness in a horse's feet that he is not able to set them on the ground without pain.

To FOUNDER, V. N. [*fond*, Fr.] among mariners, to sink to the bottom. Figuratively, to fall. "All his tricks *founder.*" *Shak.*

FOUNDERY, S. [*fonderi*, Fr.] a place where melted metal is cast into various forms or shapes.

FOUNDLING, S. a drone child; a child exposed by its parents. The hospital for orphans of this class, projected by Thomas Coram, supported by voluntary contributions of nobility, and several large gifts of parliament is an institution, that might be rendered both a support and an ornament to this kingdom. Its utility was very visible from this consideration, that whilst open, there scarce was one person tried for the murder of a bastard child; but when shut up, the very first sessions afterwards was opened with a trial of a woman who was hanged for this crime; and the very next day the public papers was foiled with an advertisement of another infant found murdered. "Strange that so useful a charity should be so much neglected!"

FOUNDRESS, S. a woman who builds, or endows any thing.

FOUNT, FOUNTAIN, S. [*font*, Sax. *fons*, Lat.] a place were the waters of a river first break out of the earth. A small bason of springing water. A jet which has an artificial spout of water. Figuratively, an original, first cause, or first principle.

FOUR, Adj. twice two.

FOURBE, S. [Fr. pronounced *fourbe*] a cheat; a bite. "Thou art an impostor and a *fourbe.*" *Drab.*

FOURFOLD, Adj. [*fowerfeald*, Sax.] a thing repeated four times.

FOURSCORE, Adj. four times twenty.

FOURSQUARE, Adj. having four sides equal; perfectly square.

FOURTEEN, Adj. [*feowertyne*, Sax.] twice seven.

FOURTEENTH, Adj. [*feowerteotha*, Sax.] the fourth in order after the tenth.

FOURTH, Adj. [*feortha*, Sax.] the first after the third.

FOURTHLY, Adv. in the fourth place.

FOWL, S. [fu°, Scot. fugel, Sax. a bird In conversation, applied to the larger sort of edible birds, to distinguish them from the smaller, which are called birds; but in books the term is applied to all the feathered race. Among poultry a cock or hen.

To FOWL, V. A. [fugelan, Sax.] to shoot birds or game.

FOWLER, S. [fuglere, Sax.] a person who shoots birds.

FOWLING-PIECE, S. a light, small gun, with a pretty long barrel, used for shooting birds, wild fowl, and other game.

FOX, S. [Sax. and Ml.] a tourtoriid animal, with a large bushy tail, sharp ears, of a rank smell, remarkable for its artifices; runs very swiftly, and preying upon fowl and small animals. Figuratively, a sly, cunning, crafty or subtle person.

To FOX, V. A. to cheat, deceive, or trick

FOXSHIP, S. the character and qualities of a fox. Cunning or mischievous craftiness. Intrigue. "Hast thou fox-ship to banish him." Shak.

FRACTION, S. [Fr. fractio, Lat.] the act of violating any obligation, or treaty. A rent in a piece of cloth, &c. In arithmetic, a part of an integer or whole number. A proper or simple fraction is that which expresses less than an integer or whole number, and has its numerator less than its denominator, as ⅓. An improper fraction, is that which expresses more than an unit, or whole thing, and has its numerator greater than its denominator as 5⁄2. A compound fraction may be more or less than an integer, or whole thing, and is always expressed by two or more quantities with the word of between them; as ¾ of ⅖ of ⅗ of ⅞ of 1⁄10.

FRACTIONAL, Adj. belonging or relating to a fraction.

FRACTIOUS, Adj. [Lat.] peevish; quarrelsome; pettish.

FRACTIOUSNESS, S. peevishness, the being uneasy at trifles.

FRACTURE, S. [fractura, Lat.] a dissolution, or breaking of the parts of a solid body from each other. In Surgery, the breaking or separation of a bone by some accidental violence. When the bone is broken across, it is called a transverse fracture; when in one part only a simple fracture; when in two or more places, a compound fracture; and when broken lengthwise, a fissure.

To FRACTURE, V. A. to break a bone.

FRAGILE, Adj. [Fr. fragilis, Lat.] brittle. Figuratively, weak; uncertain; easily destroyed. "Fragile arms" Par. Reg.

FRAGILITY, S. easiness of being broken. Weakness; or the quality of being easily destroyed. Frailty; or liableness to a fault. "In this lower age of fragility." Hooker.

FRAGMENT, S. [fragmentum, Lat.] a broken piece, or part.

FRAGRANCE, FRAGRANCY, S. [fragrantia, Lat.] sweetness of smell. A pleasant and agreeable scent; odour.

FRAGRANT, Adj. [fragrans, Lat.] odorous; smelling sweet.

FRAGRANTLY, Adv. with a sweet smell.

FRAIL, Adj. [fragilis, Lat.] weak; subject to faults or foibles; easily destroyed. Liable to error. Weak of resolution.

FRAILNESS, S. weakness, or liableness to decay. Liableness to error or fault.

FRAILTY, S. [frailties, plural] weakness of resolution; infirmity; liableness to decay, applied to the body. Liableness to do amiss, applied to the mind. A fault proceeding from the weakness and infirmity of our reason.

FRAICHEUR, S. [Fr.] freshness; refreshing coolness. "To taste the fraicheur of the purer air." Dryden Joined very politely says that this word was forcibly innoval d by Dryden.

FRAISE, S. [Fr.] a pancake with bacon in it.

To FRAME, V. A. [fremman, Sax. to form things so, that they may match each other. To regulate; to adjust; to form to any rule. To plan. To invent; in a bad sense. "To frame a story."

FRAME, S. the supports of a chair. Any thing made so, as to inclose, admit, or hold together something else. Order; regularity; method and disposition of parts. "Still a repairing, ever out of frame." Shak. Shape. Contrivance. Projection. Scheme.

FRAMER, S. a maker; a contriver; a planner.

FRANCE, a large country of Europe, bounded on the N. by the Netherlands, on the E. by Germany, Switzerland, Savoy, and the Alps, on the S. by the Mediterranean-Sea, and the Pyrenees, and on the W. by the ocean. It is about 600 miles in length, and 560 in breadth, and the air is pure, healthy, and temperate. It is so happily seated in the middle of the temperate zone, that some make it equal to Italy, with regard to the delightfulness of the landscapes, and the fertility of the soil; however, it is certainly much more healthful. The politeness of the inhabitants is well known, but most think them too ceremonious. The soil produces corn, wine, oil, and flax, in great abundance, and they have very large manufactures of linen, woolen, silk, and lace. They have a foreign trade to Spain, Italy, Turkey, and to the E. and W. Indies, which is prodigiously increased, though the

late war has given a great check to it. They themselves reckon that the number of the inhabitants is 20,000,000. This kingdom contains 11 universities, 18 archbishopricks, 12 parliaments, 12 boards of accounts, 11 courts of aids, 2 courts, and 30 mints for coining money, and a supreme council, besides the grand council, and 31 governors. The king has the title of most christian, and is an absolute prince, to whom his subjects are extremely devoted, though he rules them never so severely. In general they are men of bright parts, and have so high an opinion of themselves, that they look upon other nations with contempt; however they are of a very restless disposition, and are engaged in war more than any other country in Europe, for which reason they are generally poor, though they might certainly be very rich, if they could let their neighbours live in quiet, without attempting continually to enlarge their dominions. They are such ill observers of treaties of peace, that a French faith is now become a proverb; for they are bound by no ties, and never fail beginning a war, when they think it is for their advantage. The king's revenue is large, his army very numerous, and he has 10,000 men always about his person. The principal provinces are, Alsace, Argoumois, Anjou, Aunis, Auvergne, Beaujolois, Bearne, Berry, Bigorre, Bourbonnois, Burgundy, the Franche Comté, Bresse, Bretagne, Brie, Bugey, Comb etat, Champagne, Dauphiny, Flanders, Franche Comté, Guienne, Hainault, the Isle of France, Languedoc, Limosin, Lionnois, Maine, Marche, Navarre, Nivernois, Normandy, Orleannois, Perche, Perigord, Picardy, Poitou, Provence, Quercy, Rouergue, Roussillon, Saintonge, Touraine, Vivarais, and Lorrain; all these provinces are divided into districts, which have their particular names. This kingdom is watered by a great number of rivers, of which the four principal are, the Loire, the Seine, the Rhone, and the Garonne, or Gironde. The parliaments have little or no share in the government, and their only business is to pass the arrets or laws which the king is pleased to send them; however, they first always pay a blind obedience to the king, for we have instances of their making a noble stand, and that but a few years since. In civil causes these parliaments are still the last resort, providing the court does not interpose. That of Paris is the most considerable, where the king often comes in person to see the royal acts recorded. It consists of the dukes and peers of France, besides the ordinary members, who purchase their places; and they only take cognizance of causes belonging to the crown. The revenues of the crown arise from the taille or land-tax, and the aids which proceed from the customs and

duties on all merchandise, except salt, for the tax upon that commodity is called the Gabelles; besides these there are other taxes, as the capitation or poll-tax, the tenths of all estates, offices, and employments; besides the fifteenth penny, from which neither the nobility or clergy are exempted. Add to these the tenths, and free gifts of the clergy, who are allowed to tax themselves; and lastly, the crown-rents, fines, and forfeitures, which bring in a considerable sum. All these are said to amount to 15,000,000 sterling a year. But the king has other resources and ways of raising money, whenever necessity obliges him. The army, in time of peace, is said to consist of 200,000 men, and in time of war 4,00,000; among which are many Swiss, Germans, Scotch, Irish, Swedes and Danes. There is no religion allowed in France but the Roman Catholick ever since the revocation of the edict of Nantz, in 1685, though they are not so devoted to the pope as other nations of that communion, nor have they any inquisition among them.

FRAN'CHISE, S. [Fr.] exemption from any burthensome duty. A privilege, or immunity. A district, or the extent of jurisdiction.

To FRANCHISE, V. A. to make free.

FRAN'GIBLE, Adj. brittle; easily broken.

FRANK, Adj. [franc, Fr.] liberal; generous, free. Open, unreserved. Without restraint or conditions.

FRANK, S. a case of a letter signed by a member of parliament, and thereby intitled to go free or without paying postage.

To FRANK, V. N. to shut up in a sty. Figuratively, to confine or imprison. "My son George Stanley is frank'd up in hold." Shak. in Commerce, to exempt letters from paying postage, a privilege given every peer or member of parliament, who writes the superscription and figns it with his own name.

FRANK'INCENSE, S. a dry, resinous, inflammable substance, of a pale yellowish or white colour, a strong but not offensive smell, a bitter, acrid, and resinous taste; used in disorders of the breast, and in diarrhœas, or dysenteries.

FRANK'LY, Adv. generously; freely. Openly, ingenuously.

FRANK'NESS, S. plainness; openness of speech. Liberality; or bounteousness.

FRANK'PLEDGE, S. a pledge for a freeman.

FRAN'TIC, Adj. [corrupted from phrenetic, of φρενιτικος, Gr.] mad; deprived of understanding. Figuratively, transported by an outrageous passion.

FRAN'TICLY, or FRAN'TICKLY, Adv. madly; like one who is mad.

FRAN'TICNESS, or FRAN'TICKNESS, S. madness. outrageousness of passion.

         FRA

FRATE'RNAL, Adj. [fraternel, Fr. of fraternus, Lat.] brotherly; pertaining to brothers.

FRATE'RNALLY, Adv. brotherly; like brothers.

FRATE'RNITY, S. [fraternitas, Lat.] the state, religion, or quality of a brother. A body of men united, or incorporated. Men of the same class or character. "With what respect knaves and fools will speak of their fraternity." South.

FRA'TRICIDE, S. [fratricidium, Lat.] the murder of a brother.

FRAU'D, S. [fraude, Fr. from, fraudis, Lat.] the practice of deceit, in order to deprive another of his property. The act of imposing on a person by artful appearances. A stratagem, artifice, or trick.

FRAU'DFUL, Adj. treacherous; deceitful; trickish; subtle. "He full of fraudful arts." Dryd.

FRAU'DFULLY, Adv. in an indirect, and dishonest manner.

FRAU'DULENCE, FRAU'DULENCY, S. [fraudulentia, Lat.] deceitfulness; proneness to artifice and villainy.

FRAU'DULENT, Adj. [fraudulentus, Lat.] full of artifice. Dishonest. Indirect. Treacherous.

FRAU'DULENTLY, Adv. in a deceitful and dishonest manner.

FRAUGHT, Part. of freight, now written freight. "A vessel richly fraught." Shak.

To FRAU'GHT, V. A. to freight, load, or crowd.

FRAY, S. [formerly written affray, of effrayer, Fr.] a battle; a broil; a fight; a duel; a quarrel.

To FRAY, V. A. [effrayer, Fr.] to fright or terrify. To wear out by rubbing.

FRE'AK, S. [frac, Sax.] a whimsical change; a whim or a capricious prank.

To FREAK, V. A. [faccus, Isl. a spot, corrupted into freak] to spot, or mark with various colours. "Freakd with many a mingled hue." Thomps. Perhaps freaked may be owing to an error of the press instead of streaked, it being no uncommon thing for a caseman to use the straight f instead of an f, and as an ſ may chance to be in the cell of the long ſ, the mistake is easily accounted for.

FRE'AKISHLY, Adv. wantonly, humorously, capriciously, whimsically.

FRE'AKISHNESS, S. capriciousness, or a boyish wantonness of behaviour.

FRE'CKEL, S. [freyne, Dan. freckne, Isl.] a spot raised in the skin by the heat of the sun's rays. Any small spot.

FRE'CKLED, Adj. having spots on the skin; spotted.

FRE'CKLY, Adj. having spots on the skin, occasioned by the heat of the sun.

FRE'E, Adj. [freoh, free, Sax.] at liberty,

under no constraint or necessity. Open; ingenuous; expressing one's sentiments without reserve, applied to speech. Generous, or liberal, applied to the giving money. Not gained by importunity; voluntary. "His free offers." Bac. Guiltless; innocent. "Make mad the guilty, and appall the free." Shak. Exempt; invested with privileges; possessing any thing without vassalage; admitted to the privileges of a corporation. A freeman. Without charge. Hence a freeschool, i. e. a school where children are taught without expence or charge to their parents. The utility of these wise institutions is now universally acknowledged.

To FREE, V. A. to set at liberty, or deliver from slavery, captivity, imprisonment, danger, or the tyranny of passion. To exempt. "Freed from sin." Rom. vi. 7. Used with from.

FREEBOOTER, S. a robber, a pillager, a plunderer.

FREEBOOTING, S. robbery; plundering.

FRE'EBORN, Adj. born under a free government.

FRE'ECOST, S. freedom from expence. Exemption from charges.

FREE'DOM, S. an exemption from slavery, imprisonment, or restraint. Independance; a state wherein a person has a power of acting as he pleases. The privilege of a corporation; franchise. The state of being without any particular evil or inconvenience. Ease or facility, applied to motion, or speaking.

FREEHEA'RTED, Adj. liberal; generous. Unconstrained; voluntary. "Love must freehearted be and voluntary." Decay.

FREE'HOLD, S. a free estate which a man holdeth in fee, or fee-tail, or for term of life.

FREEHOLDER, S. one who has or enjoys a freehold.

FREE'LY, Adv. at liberty; without restraint, dependance, reserve or necessity. Liberally, opposed to niggardly.

FREE'MAN, S. one who is a member of a community or corporation, and entitled to its privileges.

FREE'NESS, S. the quality of being void of constraint, or impediment. Openness of behaviour, opposed to reservedness. Generosity, or liberality, applied to giving.

FREE'SCHOOL, S. a school wherein children are taught without expence to their relations.

FREE'SPOKEN, Adj. accustomed to speak without hesitation or reserve.

FREETHI'NKER, S. one who is not biassed by any prejudices; a term improperly assumed by persons who deny Revelation, and are no friends to religion.

FREEWILL, S. the power of directing our own actions, without bias, constraint, or
any

any neceffitating force. Voluntarinefs.

FREEWOMAN, S. a woman born under a free government.

To FREEZE, V. N. [Preter *froze, frize,* 1ſ.] to be of that degree of cold by which waters grow hard. Actively, to harden by cold. To kill with excefs of cold. To chill by loſs of power or motion.

To FREIGHT, V. A. [Preter *freighted, frachten,* Teut. *fretter,* Fr.] to put a cargo on board a ſhip. To load as the burthen within a veſſel.

FREIGHT, S. [*fracht,* Teut, *fret,* Fr.] any thing with which a ſhip is loaded. The money paid for the carriage of goods in a veſſel.

FRENCH, Adj. [*frans,* Fr. *franco,* Ital.] belonging to France. Uſed elliptically for the language ſpoken by the inhabitants of France. " He ſpeaks *french.*" i. e. the french language. *French chalk,* in Natural Hiſtory, is an indurated clay, extremely denſe, of a ſmooth, gloffy ſurface, and unctuous to the touch; of a greyiſh wite colour, variegated with a duſky green, and ſomewhat approaching to the confiſtence of a ſtone.

To FRENCHIFY, V. A. to infect with the airs of a Frenchman; generally uſed in a contemptuous ſenſe, and including the idea of affected ceremoniouſneſs.

FRENZY, S. [*φρενσις,* Gr.] madneſs; the loſs of reaſon attended with raving. Figuratively, any outrageous paſſion reſembling madneſs.

FREQUENCE, S. [Fr. *frequentia,* Lat.] a concourſe, crowd, or aſſembly.

FREQUENCY, S. [*frequentia,* Lat.] the condition of a thing often done or ſeen. Repetition.

FREQUENT, Adj. [Fr. *frequens,* Lat.] often done, ſeen, occurring, or common.

To FREQUENT, V. A. [*frequento,* Lat.] to viſit frequently, often. To be often in any place.

FREQUENTABLE, Adj. converſible, or fit for company. " Made him more *frequentable,* and leſs dangerous." *Sidney.*

FREQUENTER, S. one who reſorts often or frequently to a place.

FREQUENTLY, Adv. often; commonly; ſeveral times; more than once or twice.

FRESCO, S. [Ital.] coolneſs; ſhade; duſkineſs; reſembling the morning or evening. In Painting, a picture painted with water colours, on a wall laid with mortar not dry.

FRESH, Adj. [*fraiche,* Fr.] cool, not four, or vapid, applied to liquors. Lately made; not ſalt. Florid; not faded; vigorous; ruddy of countenance; briſk, ſtrong, violent, applied to a gale of wind. Sweet, not ſtinking.

To FRESHEN, V. A. to recover a thing

grown ſtale. To chaniſh or revive. Neuterly, to blow ſtrongly, applied to the wind. " A *freſhening* breeze." *Pope.* To free from its ſalts.

FRESHET, S. a pool of freſh water. " Sea or ſhore—*freſhet,* or purling brook." *Par. Loſt.*

FRESHLY, Adv. coaly; newly; appearing a ſecond time in its former ſtate. With a healthy or ruddy countenance.

FRESHNESS, S. newneſs; unabated vigour; ſpirit or briſkneſs, applied to liquors. Freedom from decay or injury by time, oppoſed to ſtaleneſs. Freedom from fatigue. Coolneſs, applied to the weather. Ruddineſs, applied to the colour of the countenance. Freedom from ſaltneſs.

FRESHWATER, Adj. raw; unſkilled. A low term borrowed from mariners, who call thoſe that firſt come to ſea, freſh-water ſailors, i. e. ſuch as are unacquainted with the toils and dangers, which they are to encounter at ſea.

FRET, S. [of *fretum,* Sax. *fretum,* Lat.] a ſtrait of the ſea, where the water is generally rough. Any fermentation, or agitation of liquors from ſome internal principle. In Muſic, a ſtop, or ſtring tied round the finger board of ſome inſtruments, to regulate the vibrations of the ſtrings and give the proper diſtance that each note ſhould be ſtruck at. Anxiety of mind; peeviſhneſs or commotion of the temper cauſed by ſome offence or diſlike. In Architecture, work riſing in relief, uſed for ornamenting ceilings and inlaying knots, flowers, &c. the timber-work of a roof, laid acroſs.

To FRET, V. A. to wear by rubbing againſt. To move violently. To corrode or eat away. To form into raiſed work or relievo. To vex or make angry. Neuterly, to be grieved or uneaſy on account of ſome offence. To be worn away by rubbing; to be corroded or eaten away. To ferment, or be upon the turn, applied to liquors, growing four by the exceſſive heat of the weather.

FRETFUL, Adj. eaſily made uneaſy, peeviſh.

FRETFULLY, Adv. in a peeviſh manner; like one offended with trifles.

FRETFULNESS, S. the being grieved at ſlight offences. Peeviſhneſs.

FRIABILITY, S. a capacity of being reduced to a powder.

FRIABLE, Adj. [Fr. *friabilis,* Lat.] eaſily reduced to powder.

FRIAR, S. (a corruption of *frere,* Fr. brother) a brother of ſome regular order, a religious in the Roman Catholic countries.

FRIAR-LIKE, Adj. monaſtic; reſembling a friar; unſkilled in the world.

FRIARY, S. a monaſtry, or convent of friars.

FRIARY, Adj. like a friar; worn by a friar.

FRIA-

FRI'BBLE, or FRIBBLER, S. one who professes ecstatic raptures for a woman, but dreads her consent. One who affects effeminacy.

FRICASSE'E, S. a dish consisting of meat cut into small pieces and fried.

FRICA'TION, S. [fricatio, Lat.] the act of rubbing one thing against another.

FRI'CTION, S. [Fr. frictio, Lat.] the act of rubbing things together. The resistance caused in machines, by the rubbing of one part against another. In Medicine, the rubbing any part by the flesh-brush, cloaths, or hand.

FRI'DAY, S. [frigedag, Sax.] the sixth day of the week.

FRIEND, S. [of friend, freand, frynd, Sax.] one joined to another in mutual benevolence and intimacy. An attendant, or companion. A favourer, or encourager, used with to. Sometimes used only as a familiar compellation. "Friend how camest thou hither." Matt. xxii. 12.

To FRIEND, V. A. to show favour. To countenance, encourage, assist, or support.

FRIE'NDLESS, Adj. [freandleafe, Sax.] having no friends. Without hopes, assistance, or countenance. Friendless man, among the Saxons, signified an outlaw, because a person in such a condition was generally denied all help from his friends.

FRIE'NDLINESS, S. the exertion of generosity or benevolence, or performance of kind offices.

FRIE'NDLY, Adj. kind; disposed to do acts of kindness. Figuratively, disposed to union, or easily uniting. "Like friendly colours." Pope. Salutary, or contributing to health. "To life so friendly." Milton.

FRIE'NDLY, Adv. in a kind, affectionate, and benevolent manner; with the appearance of friends; with good nature; like friends.

FRIE'NDSHIP, S. the state of minds united together by mutual benevolence. A state of mind wherein a person looks on another as a second self, does him all possible good offices without expecting a return, and endeavours to promote his welfare and interest as much as his own. Figuratively, the highest degree of intimacy. Favour, or personal kindness. Partiality. Conformity, correspondence, or aptness to unite. "Those colours that have a friendship with each other." Dryd.

FRIEZE, S. [drap de frieze, Fr.] a coarse warm cloth. In Architecture, a large flat member, which separates the architrave from the cornice; from fraise, Fr.

FRI'GATE, S. [frigate, Fr. fregate, Ital.] a small ship which carries less than 50 guns. Figuratively, any small vessel.

To FRI'GHT, V. A. [frihtan, Sax.] to disturb, or daunt with fear. To raise apprehension of danger. Fear,

To FRI'GHTEN, V. A. to shock with an apprehension of danger.

FRI'GHTFUL, Adj. causing fear; exciting terror; disturbing, or making uneasy with an apprehension of danger. Used by some as a cant word for something extremely disagreeable.

FRI'GHTFULLY, Adv. in such a manner as to disturb with an apprehension of danger. Disagreeably, opposed to beautifully; a cant word used chiefly by the ladies.

FRI'GHTFULNESS, S. the quality or power of daunting with an apprehension of danger.

FRI'GID, Adj. [frigidus, Lat.] cold or without warmth; used in the sciences. Figuratively wanting zeal, or warmth of affection. Dull, or wanting both force, warmth of imagination, figures of speech, and other embellishments, applied to stile. Impotent; or without vigour or warmth of body.

FRIGI'DITY, S. [frigiditas, Lat.] coldness; dullness, or want of imagination which renders a stile agreeable, applied to writings. Want of vigour. Coldness of affection or constitution.

FRI'GIDLY, Adv. in a cold, indifferent, or unaffecting manner.

FRILL, S. a narrow border of lace, &c. sowed on the neck of a woman's shirt, or on a man's shirt.

FRINGE, S. [frange, Fr. freggio, Ital.] an ornament of threads of gold, silver, worsted, &c. fastened at one end by weaving, but hanging down loose at the other.

To FRINGE, V. A. to adorn with fringes.

FRI'PPERY, S. [friperie, Fr. frippania, Ital.] the place where second hand cloaths or goods are sold. Old cloaths; cast dresses; tattered rags, or other lumber, gawdy apparel of little value.

FRISK, V. N. [frisque, Fr.] to leap, or skip about. To dance in a wanton, brisk, frolicksome, gay manner.

FRISK, S. a frolic. A fit of wanton gaiety, or liveliness.

FRI'SKER, S. a wanton, frolicksome person.

FRI'SKINESS, S. gaiety; liveliness wantonness.

FRITH, S. [freoth, Brit.] a strait of the sea. A net.

FRITIL'LARY, S. [fritillaire, Fr.] in botany, the name of a plant. In natural history, the name of a moth, which feeds on the plant of the same name.

FRI'TTER, S. [friture, Fr.] a small kind of pancake, a fragment, remnant, or small piece.

To FRI'TTER, V. A. to cut meat into small pieces. To break into small pieces.

FRI'VOLOUS, Adj. [frivole, Lat.] trifling; of no importance or consequence.

— FRIVO-

FRIVOLOUSNESS, S. want of weight or confequence.

FRIVOLOUSLY, Adv. without weight or importance; triflingly.

To FRIZZLE, V. A. [*frifer*, Fr.] to turn hair in fhort and fmall rings. "With frizzl'd hair." Par. Loft.

FRO, Adv. [*fra*, Sax.] ufed only with and in oppofition to the word to, and implying backward. To and fro, is forwards and backwards.

FROCK, S. [*froc*, Fr.] a coat. An untrimmed coat for men. A clofe fort of gown worn by children.

FROG, S. [*froxca*, Sax.] a fmall animal with four feet, living both by land and water, breeding in marfhes; placed by naturalifts among the mixed animals as partaking of the nature of a beaft and fifh; the young is called a tadpole, and at firft refembles a fifh with a large head. The hollow part of a horfe's hoof.

FROISE, S. [*fraiffe*, Fr.] a kind of pancake with bacon fried in it.

FROLIC, Adj. [*vrolick*, Belg.] gay; full of levity.

FROLIC, S. a fally of galety and levity, purely to caufe diverfion.

To FROLIC, V. N. to divert one's felf with follies of galety. To play merry and diverting pranks.

FROLICKSOME, Adj. full of wild and wanton galety.

FROLICKSOMENESS, S. wanton galety. Pranks. Sallies of humour.

FROM, Prep. [*from*, Goth. Sax.] away, ufed with a word fignifying depriving. Out of, noting place. Motion, or tranfmiffion. Succeffion, ufed with to. Out of, applied to abftraction, or vocation. Whence, noting place. Noting a principle or foundation, applied to argument. Becaufe of, applied to the reafon or motive of an act or effect. Separation, applied to abfence, diftance, or deliverance. Since, applied to time. Contrary or foreign, applied to relation. "From the purpofe." Shak. Removal or motion. "Thrice from the ground he leaped." Dryd. It is frequently joined by an ellipfes with adverbs, as, from above, i. e. from the part above; from below, &c.

FRONT, S. [*front*, Fr.] the forehead. Figuratively, the face. Countenance or look, generally joined with an adjective implying diflike. The part or place oppofite to the face; the fore part. The van of an army. The moft confpicuous part.

To FRONT, V. A. to be oppofite or face to face. To cover the fore part of a building with any materials. "The houfe was fronted with ftone." Neuterly, to ftand foremoft, or in front.

FRONTIER, S. [*frontiere*, Fr.] the common limits or bound aries of a country, by which it is feparated from another.

No. XLII.

FRONTIER, Adj. bordering; adjacent. "The frontier grounds." Addif.

FRONTISPIECE, S. [*frontifpiece*, Fr.] that part of a building, &c. which directly meets the eye. A picture fronting the title page of a book.

FRONTLESS, Adj. without blufhes, fhame, or diffidence; confident.

FROST, S. [*froft*, Sax.] an exceffive cold ftate of the weather, or that ftate of the air whereby fluids are converted into ice. That laft effect of, or congivation of water by cold. The appearance of plants and trees, when the dew is become ice by the excefs of cold.

FROSTBITTEN, Adj. nipped, withered, or deftroyed by froft.

FROSTILY, Adv. after the manner of froft. With exceffive cold. Figuratively, with indifference, or coldnefs.

FROSTINESS, S. the quality of appearing like froft. Cold or freezing cold.

FROSTWORK, S. work in which the matter is laid on lightly, and in inequalities like the dew which is frozen on vegetables.

FROSTY, Adj. having the power of freezing. Exceffive cold. Figuratively, indifferent. "A frofty fpirited rogue." Shak. Hoary; grey beaded. "The frofty head." Shak.

FROTH, adj. [*frer*, Dan.] the white bubbles on the top of fermenting liquor. Figuratively, an empty difplay of wit.

To FROTH, V. N. to make liquors appear with a whitifh head or furface.

FROTHILY, Adv. having a white head; applied to liquors. Figuratively, in an empty, vain, trifling, and infignificant manner.

FROTHY, Adj. full of foam. Soft. "Their bodies are fo folid—you need not fear bathing fhould make them frothy." Bacon. Vain, oftentatious.

FROUSY, Adj. dim; mufty; of a nafty, ftinking, or difagreeable fcent.

FROWARD, Adj. [*fromweard*, Sax.] peevifh; fretful; angry; morofe; perverfe.

FROWARD, Adv. peevifh; perverfe.

To FROWN, V. A. [*froigner*, or *froncer*, Fr.] to exprefs difpleafure or uneafinefs by contracting the forehead into wrinkles. To lower ftern.

FROWN, S. a look when a perfon contracts his forehead into wrinkles, in token of difpleafure or difguft.

FROWNINGLY, Adv. in a ftern manner.

FRUCTIFEROUS, Adj. [*fructifer*, Lat.] bearing fruit.

To FRUCTIFY, V. A. [*fructifier*, Fr.] to make fruitful. Neuterly, to bear fruit.

FRUCTIFICATION, S. the act of making away barrennefs; the power of producing fruit.

FRUCTUOUS, Adj. [*fructueux*, Fr.] making

3 O

making fruitful or fertile; enabling to produce.

FRU'GAL, Adj. [Fr. *frugalis*, Lat.] thrifty; not spending prodigally. Not lavish.

FRU'GALLY, Adv. in a sparing, frugal, or parsimonious manner.

FRUGA'LITY, S. [*frugalitas*, Lat.] the virtue of keeping due bounds in expences, and steering between avarice or prodigality. Good husbandry, Parsimony

FRUIT, S. [pronounced *frute* of *fruit*, Fr.] the produce of a tree or plant. A consequence or an effect. "The fruit of the spirit." Ex. v. 9. The off-spring or young of an animal. An advantage or disadvantage from any undertaking. "The fruit of my actions."

FRU'ITAGE, S. [Fr.] fruits or products of different vegetables.

FRUI'TBEARING, Adj. having the quality of bearing fruit, opposed to barren.

FRUI'TERER, S. [*fruitier*, Fr.] one who buys and sells fruit.

FRU'ITERY, S. [*fruiterie*] fruit taken collectively. A place where fruit is kept.

FRU'ITFUL, Adj. producing large quantities of fruit. Fertile. Loaded with fruit. Bearing children, applied to womens bearing young, applied to animals. Abounding in any thing.

FRU'ITFULLY, Adv. in such a manner as to produce or bear fruit. Plenteously; abundantly.

FRU'ITFULNESS, S. fertility; the act or quality of producing in abundance. The quality of bearing off-spring, applied to animals. Luxuriance, applied to writings. "The remedy of fruitfulness is easy." Ecc. 7. 1. &c.

FRU'ITGROVE, S. a shade, or close plantation of fruit-trees. "To tend the fruit-grove." Pope.

FRUI'TION, S. [*fruitus* of *fruor*, Lat.] the act of enjoying, or possessing.

FRU'ITLESS, Adj. barren, or not bearing fruit, or children. Figuratively, vain; unprofitable; idle.

FRU'ITLESSLY, Adv. without acquiring any advantage: in an unprofitable manner.

FRUIT-TREE, S. a tree which bears fruit.

FRU'MENTY, [pronounced, commonly, *furmity*, of *frumentum*, Lat. corn] a kind of pottage made of wheat and raisins boiled in milk.

To FRUSH, V. A. [*froisser*, Fr.] to crush, or break in pieces by violent blows. "I like thy arms out. – I'll frush it." Shak. Not in use.

To FRUSTRATE, V. A. [*frustratus*, Lat.] to defeat; to render a design of no effect. To make null or void. To annull. "To frustrate the end of it." Smith.

FRUSTRATE, Part. [*frustratus*, Lat.] vain; ineffectual. Null; defeated; void.

FRUSTRA'TION, S. disappointment. Defeat. "Smites their most retired policies with frustration." South.

FRU'STRUM, S. [Lat.] in mathematics, a piece cut off from a regular figure.

FRY, S. [*frey*, Fr.] young fish just produced from the spawn. Figuratively, a swarm of young animals; a multitude of young people; a word of contempt.

To FRY, V. A. [*frire*, Brit. *fim*, Fr. *frige*, Lat.] to dress meat in a pan over a fire. Neuterly, to be dressed in a pan over the fire. To contain meat which is dressing over a fire. Figuratively, to be troubled with excess of heat. To be agitated like the fat in a frying pan when over the fire.

FRY, S. a dish of meat fried.

To FUDDLE, V. A. to intoxicate with liquors. To deprive a person of the right use of his faculties by drink. Neuterly, to drink to excess.

FUEL, S. [*feu*, Fr.] combustibles fit for kindling and supporting a fire.

To FUEL, V. A. to supply with combustibles, or such substances as are fit for supporting a fire. To store with firing.

FUGA'CITY, S. [*fugax*, Lat.] volatility. The quality of evaporating. Uncertainty. Instability.

FU'GITIVE, Adj. [*fugitivus*, Lat.] one who deserts his station or duty. One who shelters himself in a foreign country.

FU'GITIVENESS, S. volatility; the quality of evaporating. Instability; uncertainty.

To FULFIL, V. A. to accomplish, answer or confirm any prophecy. To answer any purpose. To perform exactly, or to accomplish what is prescribed by any law. To answer or gratify any desire.

FULFRAUGHT, Adj. plentifully stored; opulent; no ways defective.

FU'LGENCY, S. [*fulgens*, Lat.] splendour, glitter.

FU'LGENT, Adj. [*fulgens*, Lat.] shining; dazzling; glittering; excessively bright.

FU'LGID, Adj. [*fulgidus*, Lat.] shining; glittering; dazzling.

FULGI'DITY, S. a dazzling glitter.

FULI'GINOUS, Adj. [*fuligineux*, Fr.] sooty; smoky.

FULL, Adj. [Sax. and Teut.] not capable of containing more. Abounding in any quality. Advanced in years, applied to age. Plump or fat, applied to size. "A gentleman of a full body." Wiseman. Satisfied, fitted or glutted. "I am full of the burnt offerings." Isai. I. 11. Continually talking of, and much affected with. "Every one is full of the miseries done by cold baths." Locke. That which fills the stomach; large and plentiful. "a full meal." Complete,

Complete, or wanting nothing to compleatit. The whole matter is very expressive. applied to the sense of words. Strong. Having every part of its surface illuminated, applied to the moon, "a full moon." Noting completion, or the perfection of a sentence "A full stop." Placed so as to be seen in front. "A full face." Addif.

FULL, S. freedom from defect - The highest state or degree. "At full of tide." Shak. The state of being fated, or able to contain no more, applied both to eating and drinking. Applied to the moon, the time when every part of her surface is illuminated.

FULL, Adv. entirely; without any abatement or difference. "They are full as scrupulous." Dryd. With all a person's force; or with the whole effort. "The dispassion closing full in men." Dryd. Directly. It is placed before adverbs and adjectives to increase their signification, and generally carries the signification of entirely. When used in composition it denotes that a thing is come to its highest state or perfection.

FULL-BOTTOMED, Adj. having a Large, or broad bottom.

FULLFED, Part. fated; not able to eat any longer: Applied by naturalists to express that state of an insect when it is arrived at its full growth, and is going into its aurelian state, wherein it eats no food.

To FULL, V. A. [fullo, Lat.] to cleanse cloth from.

FULLER, S. one who cleanses and dresses cloth. Fuller's-earth, is a marl of a close texture, extremely soft and unctuous to the touch, when dry, of a greyish brown colour, with somewhat of a greenish cast in it. That of England exceeds any yet discovered in goodness, and is prohibited to be exported by act of parliament.

FULLY, Adv. without any empty space. Completely; to satisfaction. Without more to be desired.

FULMINANT, Part. [Fr. of fulminans, Lat.] thundering; making a noise resembling that of thunder.

To FULMINATE, V. N. [fulminatus, Lat. of fulmen, Lat. fulminor, Fr.] to thunder. To make a loud noise like thunder. Figuratively, to denounce threatenings, or issue out ecclesiastical censures.

FULMINATION, S. [Fr. fulminatio, Lat.] the act of thundering. The act of denouncing threats. "The fulminations from the vatican." Ayliffe.

FULMINATORY, Adj. [from fulminatori, Lat.] thundering; denouncing threats and censures. Affecting with horror.

FULNESS, S. the state of leaving no part empty. The state of abounding in any quality, whether good or bad. Completeness. Perfection. Freedom from defect. Repletion. Plenty; or a state of affluence,

Largeness, or extent. Force; vigour; compleat effect.

FULSOME, Adj. [from full, Sax.] nauseous; offensive either to the sight, taste, or smell. Tending to obscenity; odious.

FULSOMELY, Adv. nauseously; rankly; obscenely; so as to excite loathing and detestation.

FULSOMNESS, S. nauseousness, applied to the objects of sight, or smell. Figuratively, obscenity.

To FUMBLE, V. N. [fummelen, Belg.] to attempt any thing in an aukward or clumsy manner. Figuratively, to hesitate, or strain the wit for an excuse, to get rid of a perplexity. To play childishly. Actively, to handle, or perform with aukwardness.

FUMBLER, S. one who does a thing aukwardly or clumsily.

FUMBLINGLY, Adv. In an aukward clumsy manner.

FUME, S. [fumée, Fr. fumus, Lat.] smoke. Vapour, or any volatile substance. An exhalation. An idle conceit; a chimera.

To FUME, V. N. [fumo, Lat.] to smoke. "The golden altar fum'd." Par. Lost. To pass over in vapours. Figuratively, to be in a rage. Actively, to smoke or dry in smoke. To perfume or scent. "She fum'd the temples with ad'rous flame." Dryd. To disperse in smoke or vapours.

To FUMIGATE, V. A. [from fumus, Lat. smoke] to smoke, scent, or perfume by vapours. To cleanse from contagion by smoking.

FUMIGATION, S. [Fr. fumigatio, Lat.] scent raised by fire. The act of smoking any part in medicated fumes.

FUMINGLY, Adv. angrily; in a rage; in a fret.

FUMOUS, FUMY, Adj. [fumeux, Fr.] producing or emitting fumes, smoke, or vapours.

FUN, S. sport, mirth, merriment, or joy.

FUNCTION, S. [functio, Lat.] discharge or performance. An employment, office, or trade. Power; faculty; the office of any particular part or member of the body.

FUND, S. [fond, Fr. fundus, Lat. a bag] stock, or capital. That by which any expense is supported. The public security given to those who lend money to supply the exigences of the state.

FUNDAMENT, S. [fundamentum, Lat.] that part of the body whereon a person sits.

FUNDAMENTAL, Adj. [fundamentalis, Lat.] that on which the rest is built; essential; that which cannot be given without the destruction of a whole system; important.

FUNDAMENTAL, S. a leading, essential

tial or necessary proposition, which is the groundwork, foundation, and support of all the others in a system.

FUNDAMENTALLY, Adv. essentially; originally; necessarily.

FU'NERAL, [*funerailles*, Fr.] the procession made in carrying a corpse or dead body to the grave. The ceremony used at interring or putting a person into the grave.

FU'NERAL, Adj. [*funereus*, Lat.] suiting a funeral. Dark, or dismal, applied to colour.

FUNGO'SITY, S. [of *fungus*, Lat.] sponginess. Porosity.

FU'NGOUS, Adj. [*fungosus*, Lat.] excrescent; spongy; porous; wanting firmness, or texture.

FU'NGUS, S. [Lat.] a mushroom; or any excrescence growing on trees. In Surgery, an excrescence of flesh on the lips or wounds.

To FU'NK, V. A. to stifle or smother with smoke. A low word.

FU'NNEL, S. [in *fundibulum*, Lat.] an inverted hollow cone with a pipe, through which liquors are poured into bottles, &c. Any pipe or passage. "Two large funnels—to let in the light and air."

FUR, S. [*fourrure*, Fr.] skin with soft hair, generally used for lining garments. The soft hair of beasts, in moisture exhaled to such a degree, that the remainder grows thick and sticks on the part. The sediments or liquors adhering to the vessel.

To FUR, V. A. to line or cover with fur. To cover with sediments.

FURA'CITY, S. [*furax*, *furacis*, Lat.] an inclination or disposition to theft.

FUR'BELOW, S. [*falbala*, Fr.] an ornament of ruffled or plaited silk, &c. sewn on womens gowns and other garments.

To FUR'BELOW, V. A. to adorn with borders of silk, linen, &c. sewn on in plaits.

To FUR'BISH, V. A. [*fourbir*, Fr. *forbire*, Ital.] to burnish, polish, or make bright.

FUR'BISHER, S. [*fourbisseur*, Fr.] one who polishes, or burnishes.

FU'RIOUS, Adj. [*furieux*, Fr.] mad. Raging; violently transported by passion.

FU'RIOUSLY, Adv. madly; violently; ragingly.

FU'RIOUSNESS, S. fierceness; violence. Raging.

To FURL, V. A. [*fesler*, Fr.] to contract; or roll close to the yard, applied to sails.

FUR'LONG, S. [*furlang*, Sax.] a measure containing 220 yards or 1/8 of a mile.

FUR'LOUGH, S. [*verlove*, Belg.] a permission given by a superior officer to an inferior, or a certain soldier to be absent for a limited time.

FUR'NACE, S. [*fournais*, Lat.] a place built like an oven, sometimes applied to a vessel of iron or copper to melt ores, metals, &c. in.

To FUR'NACE, V. A. to throw out like heat, or sparks from a furnace. "He furnaces—the thick sighs from him." Shak.

To FUR'NISH, V. A. [*fournir*, Fr.] to supply with what is wanting. To give for use. To fit up with things that are wanted. To equip or fit out for any undertaking. To adorn; to embellish; as a piece of ornamental furniture.

FUR'NISHER, S. one who supplies, furnishes, or fits out.

FUR'NITURE, S. [*fourniture*, Fr.] any goods, accessories, or materials, proper to render a house, place, or thing convenient, and fit for the purpose it is designed. An appendage; equipage; embellishment.

FUR'RIER, S. one who deals in furs.

FUR'ROW, S. [*furh*, Sax.] a small trench made by the plough. A narrow channel made in a field for conveying water. The marks or wrinkles made in the face by age; a wrinkle.

To FUR'ROW, V. A. to plough or cut into narrow channels or hollows.

FUR'RY, Adj. covered with fur; consisting of fur. Covered with the sediments of any liquor.

FUR'THER, Adj. at a greater distance. Beyond, or greater than this. "What further need have we of witnesses." Matt. xxvi. 65. See FARTHER.

FUR'THER, Adv. [See FARTHER] to a greater distance.

To FUR'THER, V. A. [*fyrthrian*, Sax.] to promote, advance, or countenance.

FUR'THERANCE, S. the act of promoting or countenancing any design.

FUR'THERMORE, Adv. moreover. More than what has been said; besides.

FU'RY, S. [*fureur*, Fr. *furor*, Lat.] raging, owing to a loss of reason. Figuratively, a violent emotion of passion. Enthusiasm; or the effect of sudden inspiration. One of the internal deities. Hence applied to a turbulent woman.

FUR'ZE, S. [*firs*, Sax.] a plant which grows wild on heaths and commons.

FUR'ZY, Adj. overgrown with furze.

To FUSE, V. A. [*fusum*, Lat.] to melt or liquefy by heat. Neuterly, to be melted, or to be capable of being liquefied by heat.

FUSE'E, S. [*fuseau*, Fr.] the spindle round which the chain of a clock or watch is wound. In a bomb, a wooden pipe filled with wildfire, by which the whole powder or composition in the shell takes fire. A firelock, or small neat musket.

FU'SIBLE, Adj. capable of being melted or liquefied.

FU.

FUSIBILITY, S. a capacity of being melted by fire.

FUSIL, Adj. [*fusile*, Fr. *fusilis*, Lat.] capable of being melted by fire. Running, or liquefied by heat. " Turn into a *fusil* sea." *Paps.*

FUSIL, S. [Fr. pronounced *fusee*] a firelock or small neat musquet. In Heraldry, a bearing, resembling a spindle.

FUSILIER, S. a soldier armed with a small musquet.

FUSION, S. [*fusio*, Lat.] the act of melting; the state of being melted.

FUSS, S. [*fus*, Sax. ready] a bustle through too much officiousness. A tumult. A low word.

FUST, S. a strong offensive smell, like that of a mouldy barrel, from *fusti*, Fr.

To FUST, V. N. to grow mouldy; to smell like a mouldy vessel.

FUSTIAN, S. [*futaine*, Fr.] a kind of cotton stuff. In Criticism, a high swelling and turgid stile, made up of big and pompous expressions, but conveying only mean, low, and contemptible ideas. Bombast.

FUSTIAN, Adj. made of fustian. Swelling; ridiculously pompous, applied to stile.

FUSTIC, S. a wood imported from the Antilles, used for dying, and is one of the ingredients made use of in blacks.

FUSTINESS, S. stink; the scent of a mouldy cask.

FUSTY, Adj. stinking; mouldy.

FUTILE, Adj. [Fr. of *futilis*, Lat.] talking much. Trifling; insignificant; worthless; of no weight or importance.

FUTILITY, S. [*futilité*, Fr.] the fault of talking too much. Triflingness. Want of weight. Want of solidity. Want of importance.

FUTURE, Adj. [*futur*, Fr. *futurus*, Lat.] that which shall or will be; that which has never yet existed but is approaching.

FUTURE, S. time to come; that which will happen hereafter. In Grammar, a tense by which we express a thing neither present nor past, but one which is to come.

FUTURITION, S. the state of a thing which is to exist after a certain period is past. " In respect of its *futurition*." *Smith.*

FUTURITY, S. that which may come after a certain period of time. The state of being to happen after a certain future time.

FUZZBALL, S. a kind of *fungus*, which, when touched or pressed, bursts to pieces, and scatters dust.

FY, Interject. [Fr. See FAH] a word used to express blame, censure, and disapprobation; or that a person has done, or intends to do something amiss, and unworthy a man of honour and honesty.

G.

G, the seventh letter of the English alphabet, and the fifth consonant. Its form is borrowed from that of the Romans, who likewise formed it from the gamma of the Greeks, as may be easily perceived from consulting the manuscripts in that language, and by considering the form of the Gothic and Saxon capitals; the Greeks likewise are supposed to have borrowed the form of the gamma, r, from the J, ghimel, of the Hebrews, which being turned the contrary way will easily show that this conjecture has some little degree of probability. The letter G is of the mute kind, and cannot be sounded with a vowel; it has two sounds, one of which is called hard, this sound it retains before a, o, u, l. The other sound, which is termed soft, resembles the sound of the J, and is commonly, though not always, found before e or i, as in *gem* and *gill*. Before n at the end of a word it is not sounded, but serves only to lengthen the vowel, which comes before it, according to the French, from whence these words are derived, as *condign*, *sign*, which are pronounced *condine*, *sine*. It is often silent before h in the middle of words, as in *sight*.

GABARDINE, S. [*gavardina*, Ital.] a coarse frock, or mean dress. " To creep under his *gabardine*." *Shak.*

To GABBLE, V. N. [*gabbare*, Ital. *gabberen*, Belg.] to make a loud and inarticulate noise. To prate loudly without meaning.

GABBLE, S. an inarticulate noise. Loud talk without meaning.

GABBLER, S. a prater, or talkative person.

GABEL, S. [*gabelle*, Fr.] among the French, a duty or tax upon salt. Any tax, or excise.

GABION, S. [Fr.] a wicker basket filled with earth; used in batteries to screen the engineers; and for a parapet on lines where the ground is too hard to be digged.

GABLE, S. [*geval*, Brh. *gobbl*, Fr.] the sloping roof of a building. The *gable* end, is the upright triangular end of a house from the eaves to the top of the roof.

GAD, S. [*gad*, Sax.] a wedge or ingot of steel. " Flemish steel is brought—some in bars and some in *gads*." *Mitson.* Used by Shakespeare for a style, *goad*, or pointed piece of steel to write with, from *gad*, Sax. a *goad*. " With a *gad* of steel will write these words."

To GAD, V. N. [*gadew*, Brit.] to ramble about without any necessary call, or business.

GADDER, S. one who rambles about without any business.

GAD-

GADDING, Part. rambling about without any business.

GADDINGLY, Adv. in a roving manner.

GADFLY, S. a large stinging fly.

GAFFER, S. [gossipe, Sax.] a term of familiarity to an old country fellow. "Gaffer Treadwell to'd us by the bye." Gay.

GAFFELS, S. [gafs'ocas, Sax.] artificial spurs of steel, put on a cock's legs, in room of his natural ones. A contrivance made of steel to bend cross bows with.

To GAG, V. N [geghi, Belg.] to force something in the mouth that may keep the jaws distended, and prevent a person's speaking.

GAG, S. something put into the mouth to hinder a person from speaking.

GAGE, S. [Fr.] something given or deposited as a security; a pledge.

To GA'GE, V. A. [gager, Fr.] to wager. To give as a pledge or security. To measure the contents of any vessel. In this sense it is more properly written gauge.

To GAO'GLE, V. N. [gag, Belg.] to make a noise resembling that of a goose, or like one who is gagged.

GAIETY, S. See GAYETY.

GAILY, Adj. with cheerful sprightliness. Splendidly; pompously; with great show, applied to dress.

GAIN, S. [Fr.] profit or advantage. Interest, lucre, or more lucrative and mercenary views. After make, a selfish, designing, or unlawful advantage. Overplus in the balance of an account, or more than a thing cost, opposed to loss.

To GAIN, V. A. [gagner, Fr.] to obtain as a profit. To receive above what it emit. To have the overplus on a comparison. To attain, obtain, or acquire. To obtain an increase or addition to any thing allotted. To win. To draw over to any interest or party. To reach or attain in walking or travelling. To gain o'er, to draw from an opposite interest or party. Neutrally, to encroach. Figuratively, to gain upon, to obtain an advantage over; to get round; to prevail against; to obtain an influence over a person. To grow rich. To have an advantage; to be advanced with respect to riches and affluence.

GAIN'ER, S. one who receives a profit or advantage from a thing.

GAIN'FUL, Adj. profitable; advantageous. Lucrative; productive of money or profit.

GAIN'FULLY, Adv. in a profitable manner.

GAIN'GIVING, S. the act of giving again or giving against; a compound of the same nature as gainsaying. "Such a kind of gaingiving, as would trouble a woman." Shak. Hamlet.

GAIN'LESS, Adj. unprofitable; producing no profit.

To GAIN'SAY, V. A. [geanjecçan, Sax.] to contradict, to deny. "Gainsaying so gainsay what he did." Shak.

GAINSAY'ER, S. an opponent, adversary, or one who opposes the opinions of another.

GAI'RISH, Adj. [geariou, Sax. to dress fine, according to Johnson; but I must confess I cannot find that word in any Saxon author; perhaps it may be derived from garsome, Sax. expence; gaudy; showy; fine. "Hide me from day's gairish eye." Milt. Excessively gay, or flighty, applied to the mind. "Makes the mind look and garish." Swift.

GAI'RISHNESS, S. finery, gaudiness, applied to dress. Extravagant joy or gaiety. "Let your hope be without vanity, or garishness of spirit." Taylor.

GAIT, S. [scot, ger, Belg.] the manner or air of walking. A way. "Address thy gait unto her." Shak.

GA'LAXY, S. [galaxia, Fr. pohala, Gr.] the milky way; or that part of the sky which appears with a stream of light, supposed to be occasioned by a profusion of stars.

GA'LBANUM, S. [Lat. and Sax.] a substance of a middle nature between a gum and a resin, being inflammable like the latter, and soluble in water like the former. It is the produce of an umbelliferous plant, frequent in Persia. Its virtues are considerable in asthmas, coughs, and hysteric complaints.

GA'LE, S. [galbur, Teut.] a current of air, or a gentle blast of wind.

GA'LEATED, Adj. [galeatus, Lat.] covered with an helmet. "A galeated coiffure." Woodw. In Botany, applied to such plants as bear a flower resembling a helmet.

GA'LIOT, S. [galliote, Fr.] a small galley, or a brigantine.

GALL, S. [geale, Sax.] a yellow juice, secreted from the blood, in the glands of the liver, and lodged in the gall bladder. The vulgar opinion of its bitterness is an error, Dr. Harvey, asserting that nothing can taste sweeter. Figuratively, any thing extremely bitter. Rancour, or malignity, applied to the temper of the mind. A sore or hurt occasioned by fretting or rubbing off the skin. In natural history, excrescencies produced on various trees, by being wounded by an insect of the fly kind; often which the lacerated vessels form a tumour or woody case, about the hole, which is called a gall nut; and is used in making ink, in dying and dressing leather, and in medicine.

To GALL, V. A. [galer, Fr.] to make sore by rubbing off the skin. Figuratively, to impair; or wear away. "My sheep being polled with my expence." Shak. To vex; to fret; to tease. "Nothing but it pleaseth the latter, it it galleth them." Hooker. To harass;

harrafs; to diſturb, to miſchief. "We uſed to *gall* them with our bows." *Addiſ.* Neuterly, to fret; to be uneaſy. "*Galling* at this gentleman." *Shak.*

GAL'LANT, Adj. [*galante*, Ital.] gay; ſhowy, or magnificent. Brave, high ſpirited; courageous, inclined to courtſhip.

GAL'LANT, S. a gay, ſprightly, and courageous perſon. One who courts a woman. A perſon who keeps company with a proſtitute; or one who ſtrives to debauch a perſon. In all ſenſes but the firſt it is accented on the laſt ſyllable.

GAL'LANTLY, Adv. in a gay, ſprightly, ſhowy, or ſplendid manner. Bravely, courageouſly.

GAL'LANTRY, S. [*galanterie*, Fr.] ſplendour, grandeur, or oſtentatious finery, applied to dreſs. Bravery, nobleneſs; generoſity, applied to the mind. Courtſhip; elegant and refined addreſs to women. Vicious love.

GAL'LEON, S. [pronounced *gallon*] a large ſhip with four or five decks. Now applied to thoſe ſhips which the Spaniards employ between Mexico and Peru.

GAL'LERY, S. [*galleria*, Ital.] a little walk in a houſe above ſtairs, having as a common paſſage to ſeveral rooms placed in a row. Likewiſe a covered place in a houſe, uſually placed in the wings of a building. Sometimes embelliſhed with pictures, and ſerving to walk in. The ſeats in a playhouſe above the boxes. In fortification, a covered walk or paſſage made acroſs the ditch of a town beſieged, with timbers faſtened on the ground and planked over. The *gallery* of a mine, is the branch, or that narrow paſſage under ground, which leads to a mine carrying on under any work deſigned to be blown up.

GAL'LEY, S. [plural, *gallies*, *galeas*, Ital.] a low built veſſel going both with oars and ſails, having two maſts and two Latin or ſquare ſails. It is uſually from twenty to twenty-two fathoms long, three broad, and one deep. Figuratively uſed to imply a ſtate of extreme miſery, alluding to the condition of the ſlaves by whom theſe veſſels are navigated.

GAL'LEY SLA'VE, a perſon condemned to row in the gallies.

GAL'LIARDISE, S. [Fr.] merriment; exceſſive gaiety. "The mirth and *galliardiſe* of company." *Brown.*

GAL'LICISM, S. [*gallicifme*, Fr. of *gallicus*, Lat. French] a manner of expreſſion peculiar to the French language. Johnſon gives us, "He *figured* in controverſy; he *held* this conduct; he *told* the ſame language that others had *held* before, from the pages of Bolinbroke." But there is ſcarce a ſingle tranſlation from that language, ſcarce an account of a battle in a gazette, or a common news-paper, which do not afford us me-

lancholy proofs of an univerſal conſpiracy to corrupt our language, by adopting phraſes, which, inſtead of being an ornament to the ſtile of thoſe that uſe them, is a flagrant proof of their ignorance and want of true taſte.

GAL'LIGASKINS, S. a large, open, or trunk hoſe. A pair of breeches. "My *galligaſkins*, &c." *Philips.*

GALLIMA'TIA, S. [*galimatihas*, Fr.] a dark perplexed diſcourſe, wherein words and things are ſo huddled together, as to make a confuſed and unintelligible jargon. Non-ſcale.

GALLIMAUFRY, S. [*galimafrè*, Fr.] in its primary ſenſe, a hoch poch, haſh, or ragou of ſeveral ſorts of broken meat. Figuratively, any inconſiſtent and ridiculous medley. A woman, who has few perſonal charms. "He loves the *gallimaufry* friend." *Shak.* The laſt ſenſe is peculiar to the author.

GAL'LIPOT, S. a pot made of clay glazed, commonly uſed to put medicines in.

GAL'LON, S. [*galo*, or *galle*, low Lat.] a liquid meaſure, containing four quarts; that for wine contains two hundred thirty-one cubic inches, that for ale or beer two hundred thirty-two, and that for grain two hundred ſeventy-two.

To GAL'LOP, V. N. [*galoper*, Fr.] to move forwards very quick, the two foreſeet being raiſed almoſt at the ſame time, and when they are juſt going to touch the ground again, the two hind feet are lifted up in the ſame manner. To move on horſeback by reaches and leaps. Figuratively, to move very faſt.

GAL'LOP, S. the ſwifteſt natural pace of a horſe.

GAL'LOPER, S. a horſe that gallops. A perſon who rides faſt, or makes a horſe gallop.

GAL'LOWAY, S. a horſe, not more than fourteen hands high.

To GAL'LOW, V. A. to terrify; to make afraid; to fright, generally applied to fear, occaſioned by ſome horrible noiſe.

GAL'LOWS, S. a frame of wood, a beam laid over with a beam or ſupporters, on which criminals are hanged. A part of a printing-preſs. Figuratively, a perſon that deſerves to be hanged. "Cupid hath been five thouſand years a boy—ay, and a ſhrewd unhappy *gallows* too." *Shak.*

GAMBA'DO, S. [*gamba*, Ital.] a ſort of leather boot fixed to a ſaddle, inſtead of ſtirrups, to put the legs in and preſerve them clean.

GAMBIA, S. a great river of Africa, in Negroland, which running from E. to W. falls into the Atlantic Ocean. Some of the Engliſh factors affirm, that it is navigable for ſloops above 600 miles. However, it is certain, that if veſſels were ſent up it ſoon after the

the rainy feafon, when the channel is full of water, they might go a great deal farther, and make new difcoveries. The Englifh have a large factory on James-Ifland, which lies 30 miles up the river, and almoft in the middle of it, 1 mile from the neareft fhore. This ifland is about a mile in circumference, and there is a fort built, mounted with cannon, with a fmall garrifon to defend it. Befides this, there are fmall factories at feveral places, a great way up the river; and they trade with the natives for gold, elephants-teeth, bees-wax, and flaves. They had found out a way to purchafe gum-fenega; but fince the taking of Senegal, the gum-trade is entirely in poffeffion of the Englifh, and it is greatly hoped care will be taken to preferve it. There are feveral countries and people about this river. It overflows annually like the Nile, at the fame time, and for the fame reafons, namely, the heavy and conftant rains, that fall at the fame time of the year up the country.

GAM'BLER, S. one who draws in the unwary to game, in order to cheat them of their property.

GAMBOGE, S. [gamboid, the place whence it comes] a concreted vegetable juice, partly of a gummy, and partly of a refinous nature; heavy, of a bright yellow colour, and fcarce any fmell, brought from Cambaja, or Cambogia in the Eaft Indies, whence it derives its name. It was not known in Europe till 1609, but being found, when introduced into medicine, to be a very rough purge, it was difufed in prefcriptions defigned for mankind, and prefcribed only for horfes, and from thence being ufed as a paint, it ftill retains its credit.

To GAMBOL, V. N. [gambiller, Fr.] to dance, fkip, frifk, tumble or play frifk-tive tricks with the legs through excefs of joy. Figuratively, to leap or ftart.

GAMBOL, S. a fkip, hop; or leap. Figuratively, a trick or merry prank.

GAME, S. [gamen, Sax. games, Ifl.] fport. A jeft, oppofite to earneft. After made ridicule, or infulting mirth. A fingle match at play. Advantage in play. Field fports, applied to the chafe. Animals purfued in the field. Solemn fhows, diverfions, or contefts exhibited as fpectacles to the people in Greece and Rome. "Entering the Olympic Game." Denh. figuratively, a fcheme or plan. "This feem to be the prefent game of that crown." Temple.

To GAME, V. N. [gamenian, Sax.] to play at any diverfion. To play extravagantly, or for large fums.

GAME-COCK, S. a peculiar fpecies of cocks bred for fighting.

GAME-KEEPER, S. a perfon who looks after game, and prevents it from being deftroyed.

GAME-NUT, S. a gingerbread-nut made

very hot with ginger, and ufed by frolickfome people to deceive others

GAME'SOME, S. [frolickfome; merry] full of fport and mirth; gay.

GAME'SOMENESS, S. fportivenefs. Wantonnefs. A gay difpofition of mind, exerting itfelf in merry and wanton pranks.

GAME'SOMELY, Adv. in a pleafant, merry, fportive gay manner.

GAME'STER, S. one who plays to excefs, or one who plays with a defign to cheat; ufed in a bad fenfe. One who is engaged in play, or underftands a game; ufed in a good fenfe. A merry or frolickfome perfon. "You're a merry gamefter—my lord Sandy." Shak. A proftitute. "She's impudent—and was a common gamefter to the camp." Shak. The two laft fenfes are obfolete.

GAMING, S. [gaming, Sax.] the act of gaming; an immoderate love of play for large fums.

GAM'MON, S. [gambone, Ital.] the buttock or thigh of an hog; the lower end of a flitch of bacon. A term made ufe of in the play of backgammon.

GAMUT, S. [gama, Ital.] a fcale by which we are taught mufic or to found the mufical notes.

GAN'DER, S. [gandra, Sax.] a large water fowl, the male of the goofe.

To GANG, V. N. [gangon, Sax.] to go, to walk. "Your running bouts gang with their breafts open." Arbuth. Seldom ufed in the fouth of England, unlefs in a ludicrous manner.

GANGES, a large and celebrated river of Afia. In India it has its fource in the mountains, which border on little Thibet, in 86 degrees of longitude, and 35.43 of latitude. It croffes feveral kingdoms, running from N. to S. and falls into the bay of Bengal, by feveral mouths. The waters are loweft in April and May, and higheft before the end of September. It overflows yearly like the Nile; and renders the kingdom of Bengal as fruitful as that of the Delta in Egypt. The people in thefe parts have the water of this river in high veneration; and it is vifited annually by a prodigious number of pilgrims from all parts of India. The Englifh have feveral fettlements on this river. The greateft happinefs that many of the Indians wifh for is to die in this river.

GANG, S. a company going together on fome exploit; ufed of a fhip's crew; or a company of robbers: generally implying contempt and abhorrence, unlefs in the firft fenfe.

GANG'LION, S. [gayglion, Gr.] in Surgery, a hard moveable tumour, formed commonly, near the tendons or ligaments of the mufcles, and proceeding from a fall or ftroke.

GAN'GRENE, S. [gangrene, low Lat.] in Surgery, a diforder in any flefhy part of the

the body tending to a mortification, the flesh is soon turning black and spreading itself to the adjacent parts. It arises from a stoppage or interruption of the circulatory motion of the blood, from such things as render the fluids so acrid as to destroy the vessels, from those things which produce a mortification of the extremities, as old age, &c. and from poisons of an extraordinary kind.

To GAN'GRENE, V. N. [*gangrener*, Fr.] to tend towards a mortification. Actively, to affect with a deadish corruption, tending towards a mortification.

GAN'GRENOUS, Adj. of the nature of a gangrene. Producing, or tending to a mortification.

GANG'WAY, S. [See GANG] In a ship, the several passages from one part of it to another.

GANTELOPE, GANT'LET, S. a military punishment, wherein the offender is stripped naked to the waist, and obliged to run through a lane of soldiers, with green switches, who give him a blow as he passes.

GAOL, S. [pronounced jail, *geol*, Brit.] a place of confinement or imprisonment for debtors or criminals.

GAOL'ER, S. [*geolier*, Fr.] a keeper of a prison.

GAP, S. an opening in a broken fence. A breach, passage, avenue, open way, hole, a interstice, or interval. An opening of the mouth during the pronunciation of two vowels immediately succeeding each other. To *stop a gap*, used figuratively, implies to escape by means of some mean shift or stratagem, alluding to the mending of hedges with dead bushes, till the quicksets grow. " In finding ways and means and *stopping gaps*." Swift.

To GAPE, V. N. of *gape*, [H.] to open the mouth wide. To yawn. Figuratively, to covet, crave, or desire earnestly, with *for after*, or *at*. To open in holes or breaches; applied to wounds, whose lips are distant from each other, like those of the mouth when wide open. To behold with ignorant wonder and wish the mouth open, used with *at*. To stare at with irreverence, ridicule, or malice, used with *upon*. " They *gaped upon* me with their mouths." Job xvi. 10.

GAPER, S. one who opens his mouth. One who stares with his mouth open through ignorant admiration. Figuratively, one who longs or craves.

GARB', S. [*garbe*, Fr. of *garbo*, Ital.] dress; a habit or dress. External appearance.

GARBAGE, S. [*garbeor*, Span.] the bowels, which in beasts is thrown away. The entrails.

To GARBLE, V. A. [*garbellen*, Ital.] to sift; to separate the good from the bad. To cleanse from dross, filth, dirt or foreign mixtures.

GARBLER, S. one who separates one

thing from another. One who picks out the dirt, &c. from any commodity. Applied to an officer in the city of London, who is empowered to enter into any shop or warehouse to view, search, and cleanse drugs from any impure mixture.

GARD', S. [*garde*, Fr.] wardship, care, custody; the charge of a person. Figuratively, an orphan left to the care of a person.

GAR'DEN, S. [*gardd*, Brit, *garde*, Goth.] a piece of ground cultivated with care, planted with herbs, flowers or fruits, or laid out so as to entertain the eye, and please with beautiful walks. When used in composition it has the signification of an adjective, and implies, belonging to a garden. " A *garden* wall."

GAR'DENER, S. [*jardinier*, Fr.] one who has the care of a garden.

GARDENING, S. the act of cultivating a garden.

GAR'GARISM, S. [*gargarisme*, Fr.] a liquid medicine to wash the mouth with.

To GARGARIZE, V. A. [*gargariser*, Fr.] to wash, or cleanse the mouth with a liquid medicine.

To GARGLE, V. A. [*gargouiller*, Fr. *gorgoliar*, Ital.] to wash the throat with some liquor without swallowing it. Figuratively, to warble; to trill, to modulate in the throat. " *Gargle* in their throat a song." *Waller*. " *Gargl'd* in a conduit's throat." *Tickell*.

GAR'GLE, S. a liquor with which the mouth or throat is washed, without swallowing it.

GAR'GOL, S. [*gargas*, Sax.] a distemper to hogs.

GAR'LAND, S. [*garland*, Fr. *ghirlanda*, Ital.] a wreath of flowers, worn on the head. Likewise a milk-maid's pail adorned with flowers, and plate, which is carried about the streets in London, at the beginning of May. In a ship, the collar of a rope round about the head of a main-mast, to keep the shrouds from galling.

GAR'LIC, or GAR'LICK, S. [*garleac*, or *garlec*, Sax.] In Botany, the *allium*; its flowers are included in one common spatha; and are composed of six oblong erect petals, and six awl shaped stamina. The species are nineteen.

GARLIC-EATER, S. a stinking or mean fellow. " The breath of *garlic-eaters*." Shak.

GAR'MENT, S. [*garniment*, old Fr.] something to cover the body. Clothes; dress.

To GAR'NER, V. A. to store; to keep as in a storehouse. " There, where I have *garner'd* up my heart." Shak.

GAR'NET, S. [*gurnet*, H.] a gem of a middle degree of hardness between the sapphire and common crystal; found in various sizes, having its surfaces neither so smooth nor polished as the ruby; the Bohemian is

red with a slight cast of flame colour; and the Syrian red with a slight cast of purple. In ships, the tackle by which goods are loaded or unloaded.

To GAR'NISH, V. A. [from *garnir*, Fr.] In Cookery, to embellish or set off a dish with flowers, or other ornaments.

GAR'NISH, S. ornament. Embellishment. Things placed to ornament the brim of a dish. A fee or treat paid by a prisoner on his entrance in a gaol.

GAR'NISHMENT, S. an ornament, or something added to make a thing seem beautiful or agreeable to the eye.

GAR'NITURE, S. furniture; embellishment.

GAR'RET, S. [*garite*, Fr.] a room on the highest floor of a house. Rotten wood. "The part of rotten wood, in some places white; and in some red, they call the white and red *garret*." *Bac.*

GARRETTEER, S. one who lives in a garret.

GARRICK, [DAVID, Esq;] It would surely be needless here to mention, that the gentleman just named is at this time a living writer, were it not for the sake of future theatrical chronology, which may at some period hereafter have occasion for such information. He was born in the city of Hereford, in the year 1717, his father bearing a captain's commission in the army, which rank he maintained for several years; and at the time of his death was possessed of a majority, which that event however prevented him from ever enjoying. Our author received the first rudiments of his education at the *free-school of Litchfield*, which he afterwards compleated at Rochester, under the celebrated Mr. Colson, since mathematical professor at Cambridge. On the 19th of March 1736, he was entered of the honourable society of Lincoln's Inn, being intended for the law. But whether he found the study of the law too heavy, saturnine, and barren of amusement for his more active and lively disposition, or that a genius like his could not continue circumscribed within the limits of any profession but that to which it was more peculiarly adapted, and like the magnetic needle pointed directly to its proper center, or perhaps both, it is certain that he did not long pursue the municipal laws; for in the year 1740-1, he quitted it entirely for the stage, and made his first appearance at the theatre in Goodman's Fields, then under the management of Mr. Henry Giffard. The character he first represented was that of king Richard III. in which, like the sun bursting from behind an obscure cloud, he displayed, in the very earliest dawn, a somewhat more than meridian brightness. In short, his excellence dazzled and astonished every one, and the seeing a young man, in no more than his twenty-fourth year, and a novice to the stage, reaching at one single step to that height of perfection, which maturity of years and long practical experience had not been able to bestow on the then capital performers of the English stage, was a phenomenon which could not but become the object of universal speculation, and as universal admiration. The rumour of this bright star appearing in the east flew with the rapidity of lightning through the town, and drew all the theatrical [illegible] thither to pay their devotions to this new-born sun of genius; the theatres towards the court-end of the town were deserted, persons of all ranks flocking to Goodman's-Fields, where Mr. Garrick continued to act till the close of the season, when having very advantageous terms offered him for his performing in Dublin during some part of the summer, he went over thither, where he found the same just homage paid to his merit, which he had received from his own countrymen. To the service of the latter, however, he esteemed himself more immediately bound; and therefore, in the ensuing winter, engaged himself to Mr. Fleetwood, then manager of Drury-lane play-house, in which theatre he continued till the year 1745, in the winter of which he again went over to Ireland, and continued there through the whole of that season, being joint manager with Mr. Sheridan in the direction and profits of the Theatre-royal in Smock-alley. From thence he returned to England, and was engaged for the season of 1746 with the late Mr. Rich, patentee of Covent-garden. This, however, was his last performance as an hired actor; for in the close of that season, Mr. Fleetwood's patent for the management of Drury-lane being expired, and that gentleman having no inclination further to pursue a design by which, from his want of acquaintance with the proper conducting it, or some other reasons, he had already considerably impaired his fortune, Mr. Garrick, in conjunction with Mr. Lacy, purchased the property of that theatre, together with the renovation of the patent, and, in the winter of 1747, opened it with the best part of Mr. Fleetwood's former company, and the great additional strength of Mr. Barry, Mrs. Pritchard and Mrs. Cibber from Covent-garden.

In this station Mr. Garrick has continued ever since; and both by his conduct as a manager, and his unequall'd merit as an actor, has from year to year added to the entertainment of the public; which he has ever, with an indefatigable assiduity, consulted. Nor has the public been by any means ungrateful in its returns for that assiduity; but has, on the contrary, by the warm and deserved encouragement which it has given him, raised him to that state of ease and affluence, in which it must surely be the wish of every honest heart

to

to fee superior excellence of any kind ex-
aled.

Mr. Garrick in his person is low, yet well
ſhaped and neatly proportioned; and, having
added the qualifications of dancing and
fencing to that natural quickneſs of manner
which no art can beſtow, but which are great
another name conduce to many wiſh, even from
infancy, his deportment is conſtantly eaſy …
natural and engaging; his complexion is …
dark, and the features of his face, which are
pleaſingly regular, are animated by a full
black eye, brilliant and penetrating; his …
voice is clear, melodious and commanding;
and, although it wants not perhaps the ſtrong
overbearing powers of Mr. Moſſop's, or the
mellow ſweetneſs of Mrs. Barry's, yet it appears to have a much greater compaſs of variety than either; and from Mr. Garrick's
judicious manner of conducting it, enjoys
that articulation and piercing diſtinctneſs,
which renders it equally intelligible, even to
the moſt diſtant parts of an audience. In the
gentle whiſpers of murmuring love, the half-
ſmothered accents of ſoft paſſion, or the
profeſſed and ſometimes awkward conceal-
ments of invalide ſpeech in comedy, as in the
rants of rage, the darings of deſpair, or all
the open violence of tragical exclamation.

As to his particular ſorts or ſuperior caſt in
acting, it would be perhaps as difficult to determine it, as it would be minutely to deſcribe
his ſeveral excellencies in the very different
caſts in which he at different times thinks
proper to appear.—Particular ſuperiority is
ſwallowed up in his univerſality, and ſhould
it even be contended, that there have been
performers equal to him in their own reſpec-
tive forms of playing, yet even their partizans
would acknowledge, there never exiſted any
one performer that came near his excellence.
In ſo great a variety of parts.—Tragedy, comedy and farce, the lover and the hero, the
jealous huſband, who ſuſpects his wife's virtue
without cauſe, and the thoughtleſs lively
rake, who attacks it without deſign, are all
alike open to his imitation, and all alike do
honour to his execution. Every paſſion of
the human breaſt ſeems ſubjected to his
powers of expreſſion; nay, even time itſelf
appears to ſtand ſtill or advance as he would
have it.—Rage and ridicule, doubt and deſpair, tranſport and tenderneſs, compaſſion
and contempt, love, jealouſy, fury, fire and
ſimplicity, all take in turn poſſeſſion of his
features, while each of them in turn appears
to be the ſole poſſeſſor of thoſe features. One
night old age ſits on his countenance, all the
wrinkles that had ſtamp'd there were indelible;
the next the gaiety and bloom of youth ſeems
to ſpread his face, and ſmooth even thoſe
marks which time and muſcular confirmation
may have really made there. Of theſe truths
no one can be ignorant, who has ever ſeen

him in the ſeveral characters of Lear or Hamlet, Richard, Douglas, Romeo, or Lothario;
… Ranger, Bayes, Drugger, Kitely, Brute,
or Benedict. In ſhort, Nature, the miſtreſs
from whom alone this great performer has
borrowed all his leſſons, being ſo herſelf in-
exhauſtible, and her variation not to be numbered, is it by no means ſurpriſing, that this,
… darling ſon, ſhould find an unlimited
ſcope for ſtudies and diverſity in his manner
of copying from her various productions;
and, as if ſhe had from his cradle marked him
out for her trueſt repreſentative, ſo has beſtowed on him ſuch powers of expreſſion in
the working of his face, as no performer ever
yet poſſeſſed; not only for the diſplay of a
ſingle paſſion, but alſo for the combination
of thoſe various conflicts with which the human breaſt at times is fraught; ſo that in his
countenance, even when his lips are ſilent,
his meaning ſtands pourtrayed in characters
too legible for any to miſtake it.

His ſuperiority to all others in one branch
of excellence, however, muſt not make us
overlook the rank he is entitled to hold in another; nor our remembrance of his being the firſt actor living, induce us to forget
that he is far from being the laſt writer.—
Notwithſtanding the numberleſs and laboriou-
ous avocations attending on his profeſſion as
an actor, and his ſtation as a manager, yet ſtill
his active genius has been perpetually burſting
forth in various little productions, both in the
dramatic and poetical way, where we muſt not
too late make us regret his want of time for
the purſuance of more extenſive and important works.

GARRISON, S. [garriſon, Fr. ger. Six.
a ſpear] ſoldiers placed in a fortified town or
caſtle. A fortified place ſtored with ſoldiers.
The ſtate of perſons placed in a town or
caſtle to defend it.

To GARRISON, V. A. to ſtore a place
with ſoldiers for the defence of it.

GARRULOUS, Adj. [garrulus, Lat.]
talkative; prattling; fond of talking. "Old
age—garrulous recounts the feats of youth."
Thomſon.

GARTER, S. [jartier, Fr.] a ſtring or
ribband with which the ſtockings are tied up.
The mark of an order of knights inſtituted
by Edward III. In 1352, who wore a garter
on the left leg, ſet with precious ſtones, and
embroidered with this motto, Loni ſoit qui
mal y penſe. It is the higheſt order of
knighthood in England, and the knights
wear a blue ribband.

GARTER, S. ſometimes called garter
principal king at arms; an officer who attends the knights of the garter at their aſ-
ſemblies, marſhals the ſolemnities at the funerals of the higheſt nobility, carries the
garter to kings and princes beyond ſea, is allowed a mantle, badge, a houſe in Windſor
caſtle.

cattle, pestacs, and fees from the sovereign and neighbour. In husbandry, the moiety, half, of a head.

To GARTER, V. A. to bind or tye up the stocking with a garter.

GASCONADE, S. a boast, or vaunt of something improbable, and almost impossible.

To GASCONADE, V. N. to boast, brag, or vaunt.

To GASH, V. A. [hacher, Fr.] to cut deep, so as to cause a gash, wound.

GASH, S. a deep and wide wound.

To GASP, V. N. to open the mouth wide to catch or draw breath. To force out breath with difficulty. "With short fobs he gasps away his breath." Dryd. Figuratively, to long for. "Gasp after liberty." Spect. No. 193, "This beautiful metaphor which so strongly marks out the dying struggle and wishes of a person in captivity. Johnson gensures, "as improper, as nature never expresses desire by gasping." But let the gentleman ask the question of those who are gasping for breath, for his information.

GASP, S. the act of opening the mouth wide for want of breath. The convulsive struggle for breath in the agonies of death.

GASTRIC, Adj. [from γαστηρ,] belonging to, or situated in the belly.

GASTROCNEMIUS, S. in Anatomy, the name given to the two muscles which compose the up or calf of the leg.

GAT, the Preter of GET.

GATE, S. [gate, Sax.] a large door of a city, castle, palace, &c. a frame of timber on hinges to open a passage. Figuratively, a way, avenue, or introduction. "Opening a gate to a long war." Knolles.

GATE-VEIN, S. in Anatomy, the vena porta, a name given to one of the larger veins which communicate with the heart. "He could not endure to have trade sick, nor any obstruction in the gate-vein, which dispersed that blood." Bac.

GATEWAY, S. a passage through the gates of inclosed ground.

To GATHER, [gatherian, Sax.] to collect many things into one place. To pick up, to glean; sometimes used with up. To pluck a vegetable from the tree or plant. Used with together, to assemble. To heap up, or accumulate. To collect or take, used with from. "To collect charitable contributions". To bring into one body, or interest; used with in. To collect or deduce reasoning or inference. "Gathering his flowing robe." Pope. "To gain, used with ground. "The gathers ground upon her." Dryd. To run cloth in very small folds, in needlework. To deduce, to collect logically, or by inference. To gather breath, is to pause from any fatiguing employ, which puts a person out of breath, in order to recover both breath and strength; and proverbially, for having

a person in any calling power to have a mind for recovering strength, generally applied to an army defeated, or retired. Neuterly, to thicken, or grow thick, by being condensed; applied to the clouds before a shower. "To grow larger by the addition of fresh matter." To assemble; applied to a discharge. To suppurate, in general, or break into a sore, applied to an inflammation.

GATHERER, S. one who collects or gathers.

GATHERING, S. [in Anatomy,] something that gathers from festering; applied to the risible conformation.

GAVE, V. [from gave, Fr.] an over-ment; a relief; a joy.

GAUTRY, S. finery; a showy dress. Ostentation, bravery of dress.

GAUDILY, S. but in a showy manner, or with ostentation dress; expensive of finery.

GAUDINESS, S. an appearance of splendour from finery without any real value.

GAUDY, Adj. striking the sight with some splendid appearance, tho' showy; silly, the idea of something of trifling value.

GAVE, the Preter of GIVE.

GAVEL-KIND, S. [gafol-kind, Sax.] in Law, a custom whereby the lands of a father are, at his death, equally divided among his sons; to the exclusion of those relations, or those of a brother are equally divided among the brothers, if he died without issue. Davies calls it a which poffessed and, according to Powel, it is still in date in Kent and divers places of England.

To GAUGE, V. A. [pronounced gage, from jauge, Fr.] to find how many gallons a vessel contains by means of a staff or rod. Figuratively, to proportion the size of one thing to another.

GAUGE, S. [pronounced gage] a standard by which any thing is measured, &c.

GAUGER, S. one who measures how much is contained in a cask.

GAUGING, S. the art of measuring how much liquor is contained in a cask, &c.

GAUNTLET, S. [gantelet, Fr.] an iron glove used for defence, thrown on the ground in challenge.

GAVOT, S. [gavotte, Fr.] in Music, a dance, brisk, lively air, composed to common time.

GAUZE, S. a kind of very thin transparent silk or linen.

GAY, Adv. [Fr.] brisk, nimble, cheerful, or merry, applied to the disposition of a person. Fine, or showy, applied to dress.

GAY, (Mr. John.) This gentleman was descended from an ancient family in Devonshire, was born at Exeter, and received his education at the free-school of Barnstaple, in that county, under the care of Mr. William Rayner. He was bred a mercer in London, and having a small fortune, independent of business.

business, and considering the attendance occasion as a degradation of those talents which
he found himself possessed of, he quitted that
occupation, and applied himself to other
views, and to the indulgence of his inclination for the muses. In what year Mr. Gay
was born does not appear. From the accounts
of any of his biographers, but in 1712
we find him secretary, or rather domestic
steward, to the dutchess of Monmouth, in
which station he continued till the beginning
of the year 1714, at which time he accompanied the earl of Clarendon to Hanover, whi-
ther that nobleman was dispatched by Q. Anne.

In the latter end of the same year, in consequence of the queen's death, he returned to England, where he lived in the highest estimation
and intimacy of friendship with many persons
of the first distinction both in rank and abilities. He was even particularly taken notice
of by queen Caroline, then princess of Wales,
to whom he had the honour of reading in manuscript his tragedy of the Captives, and in
1726 dedicated his fables, by permission, to
the duke of Cumberland. From this countenance shewn to him, and a numberless promises made him of preferment, it was reasonable to suppose, that he would have been
genteelly provided for in some office suitable
to his inclination and abilities. Instead of
which, in 1727, he was offered the place of
gentleman usher to one of the youngest prin-
cesses; an office which, as he looked on it as
rather an indignity to a man, whose talents
might have been much better employed, he
thought proper to refuse, and some pretty
warm remonstrances were made on the occasion by his sincere friends and zealous patrons
the duke and dutchess of Queensberry, which
terminated in those two noble personages
withdrawing from court in disgust.

Mr. Gay's dependencies on the promises of
the great, and the disappointments he met
with, he has figuratively described in his fable of the "Hare with many friends."
However, the very extraordinary success he
met with from public encouragement made
an ample amends, both with respect to satisfaction and emolument, for those private disappointments. For, in the season of 1727-8,
appeared his Beggar's Opera, the vast success
of which was not only unprecedented, but
almost incredible. It had an uninterrupted
run in London of sixty-three nights in the
first season, and was renewed in the ensuing
one with equal approbation. It spread into
all the great towns of England; was played
in many places to the thirtieth and fortieth
time, and at Bath and Bristol fifty; made its
progress into Wales, Scotland and Ireland,
in which last place it was acted for twenty-
four successive nights, and last of all it was
performed at Minorca. Nor was the fame
of it confined to the reading and represent-

ing alone, for the ladies and drawing-
rooms of those with the theatre and related in this
respect, the ladies carried about the favourite
songs of it, engraven on their fan mounts,
and screens and other pieces of furniture,
were decorated with the same. Miss Fenton,
who acted Polly, though till then perfectly
obscure, became all at once the idol of the
town; her pictures were engraven and sold in
great numbers; her life written; books of
letters and verses to her published; and
pamphlets made of even her very sayings
and jests; nay, she herself attained the
highest rank a female subject can acquire.
In short, the satire of this piece was so
striking, so apparent and so perfectly adapted to the taste of all degrees of people,
that it even for that season overthrew the
Italian opera, that Dagon of the nobility and
gentry, which had so long seduced them to
idolatry, and which Dennis, by the labours
and censures of a whole life, and many other
writers, by the force of reason and reflection,
had in vain endeavoured to drive from the
throne of public taste. Yet the Herculean
exploit did this little piece at once bring to
its completion, and for some time recalled
the devotion of the town from an admiration
of mere sound and shew, to the admiration
of, and relish for, true satire and sound understanding.

The profits of this piece was so very great,
both to the author and Mr. Rich, the manager, that it gave rise to a quibble, which became frequent in the mouths of many, viz.
"That it had made Rich Gay, and Gay
rich;" and I have heard it asserted, that the
author's own advantages from it were not
less than two thousand pounds. In consequence of this success, Mr. Gay was induced
to write a second part to it, which he entitled
Polly. But the disgust subsisting between
him and the court, together with the misre-
presentations made of him, as having been
the author of some disaffected libels and seditious pamphlets, a charge which, however,
he warmly disavows in his preface to this
opera; a prohibition and suppression of it
was sent from the lord chamberlain, at the
very time when every thing was in readiness
for the rehearsal of it. This disappointment,
however, was far from being a loss to the
author, for, as it was afterwards considered,
even by his very best friends, to be in every
respect infinitely inferior to the first part, it
is more than probable, that it might have
failed of that great success in the representation which Mr. Gay might promise himself
from it, whereas, the profits arising from the
publication of it afterwards in quarto, in consequence of a very large subscription, which
this appearance of persecution, added to the
author's great personal interest procured for
him, were at least adequate to what could have
accrued

extraced to him from a moderate sum, had it been represented. This was the last dramatic piece of Mr. Gay's that made its appearance during his life; his opera of Achilles, and the comedy of the distress'd wife, being both brought on the stage after his death.

As a man, he appears to have been morally amiable. His disposition was sweet and affable, his temper generous, and his conversation agreeable and entertaining. He had indeed one foible, too frequently incident to men of great literary abilities, and which subjected him at times to inconveniencies, which otherwise he needed not to have experienced, viz. an excess of indolence, without any knowledge of œconomy; so that, though his emoluments were, at some periods of his life, very considerable, he was at others greatly strait-ened in his circumstances; nor could he prevail on himself to follow the advice of his friend Dean Swift, whom we find in many of his letters endeavouring to persuade him to the purchasing of an annuity, as a resource for the exigencies that might attend on old age. Mr. Gay chose rather to throw himself on patronage, than to secure to himself an independent competency by the means pointed out to him; so that, after having undergone many vicissitudes of fortune, and being for some time chiefly supported by the liberality of the duke and duchess of Queensberry, he died at their house in Burlington-gardens, in December 1732. He was interred in Westminster-abbey, and a monument erected to his memory, at the expence of his afore-mentioned noble benefactors, with an inscription, repetitive of their regards, and his own deserts, and an epitaph in verse by Mr. Pope, but as both of them are still in existence, and free of access to every one, it would be improper to repeat either of them in this place.

GA'YETY, S. a chearful, sprightly and joyous disposition of mind. Pleasures, which are proper to youth, used in the plural Finery, or splendid dress which attracts the eye by the brightness of its colour and the richness of its ornaments.

GA'YLY, Adv. merrily, chearfully, applied to the mind. Fine, or showy, applied to apparel.

GA'YNESS, S. finery, applied to dress. Chearfulness and mirth; the mind.

To GAZE, V. A [gesan, Sax.] to look at a thing with earnestness.

GAZE, S. a fixed and earnest look. The object of intent admiration, or gazing. "Made of mine enemies the scorn and gaze." Milton.

GA'ZER, S. a person who looks at a thing with great earnestness.

GA'ZEFUL, Adj. looking intensly and earnestly.

GA'ZEHOUND, S. a hound which purs sues by sight, not by scent. "Or if thou gaze the pine-hand?" Tickel.

GAZE'TTE, S. a paper of news, published by authority. His majesty appointed a genuine writer at a very considerable salary.

GAZETTEE'R, S. a writer or publisher of news. A paper which contains articles of news both foreign and domestic. As this paper was formerly employed to support and defend the measures of a current administration it is used by the contrary party as a term of reproach and contempt. "No Gazetteer more innocent than I." Pope.

GA'ZING-STOCK, S. an object of public notice and contempt.

GAZON, S. in fortification, pieces of fresh earth covered with grass, used to line parapets, and the traverses of galleries.

GEAR, S. (the g is pronounced hard, geapan, Sax.) houshold furniture; dress or cloaths. The traces by which oxen or horses draw. Stuff. "She's a good wench for this gear." In Scotland, applied to goods, estate, or riches. "He has good enough."

GECK, S. a bubble, or person easily cheated or imposed on. "To become the geck and scorn o'th' other's villainy." Shak.

GEESE, S. the plural of goose.

GE'LABLE, Adj. (from gelu, Lat.) what may be thickened into a jelly.

GE'LATINE, GELA'TINOUS, Adj. (gelatine, beau.) formed into a jelly; full of viscus. "That pellucid gelatinous substance." Woodw.

To GELD, V. A [Preter and Part. pass. gelded or gelt, gyldan, Teut.] to castrate, cut or deprive of the power of generation. Figuratively, to diminish or deprive of any essential part. "Gelding the opposed continent." Shak. To cut out of a book any passage that is immodest, or liable to objection. "Gelds is so sickly in some plural." Dryd. Castrate is the term now used in the last sense.

GE'LDER, S. one who castrates or gelds.

GE'LDING, S. an horse or any animal that is emasculated.

GE'LID, Adj. (gelidus, Lat.) extremely cold. "The deep cold and gelid cavern." Thomson.

GELI'DITY, S. extreme coldness.

GE'LIDNESS, S. extreme coldness.

GE'LLY, S. (gelatine, Lat.) any thick, viscous, or glutinous substance.

GELT, Preter and Part. Pass. of GELD.

GEM, S. (gemma, Lat.) a jewel, or precious stone. In botany, the first bud.

To GEM, V. A. (from the noun) to put forth the first buds. Actively, to adorn as with jewels or buds.

GEMILLI'PAROUS, Adj. (from gemellus, Lat.) bearing twins.

To

To GE'MINATE, V. [from geminus, Lat.] to double.

GEMINA'TION, S. [geminatio, Lat.] a repetition of a word or sentence.

GE'MINI, S. [Lat.] in astronomy, the twins, the third constellation in the Zodiac, containing eighty-nine stars marked on the globes by the hieroglyphic of two kids, because as this time the sheep generally bring forth their young in pairs, in the place of the Egyptian hieroglyphic, the Greeks have substituted the twin-brothers Castor and Pollux, but without any propriety.

GEM'MARY, Adj. [of gemma, Lat.] belonging to jewels, or precious stones. "The principal and gemmary affection—its translucency." Brown.

GEM'MEOUS, Adj. [gemmeus, Lat.] having the nature of gems; resembling gems. "In the gemmeous matter itself." Woodw.

GE'NDER, S. [this is pronounced soft, gentre, Fr. genus, Lat.] a sort. "One party of barbers' shops. A sex. In grammar, a name given to nouns according to the different sexes they signify.

To GE'NDER, V. A. [engendrer, Fr.] to beget. To produce. Neuterly, to copulate; to breed.

GENEALO'GICAL, Adj. pertaining to the descent of families, or the history of the successions, in houses.

GENEA'LOGY, S. [of genos, Gr. and logos,] an account of the several descendants in a family. A series of succession of progenitors; a pedigree.

GE'NERABLE, Adj. [genero, Lat.] that which may be produced or begotten.

GE'NERAL, Adj. [Fr. generalis, Lat.] comprehending many species or individuals. Not restrained in its signification, applied to words. A general idea, is that which is considered as separate from time or place, and so capable of representing more individuals than one, or any particular being conformable to it. Public; comprising the whole; common; usual. Not directed to a single object. Extensive, or comprehending a great many, but not universal. Applied to the officers of an army, those whose office and authority extends over a body of several regiments of horse and foot. This word is likewise used in composition to imply chief, one in greater authority than any other of the same kind, or one who is a check upon, or a person to which others of the same class are accountable, thus, the major-general is one who receives all the collections of the inferior collections.

GE'NERAL, S. the whole; the main. The public, or interest of the whole; in opposite sense. One who commands an army. A particular march or beat of the drum.

GENERALIS'SIMO, S. [Ital. generalissime, Fr.] a supreme and absolute commander in the field.

GENERA'LITY, Adj. [generalité, Fr.] the quality of including several species. The main body, bulk, or greater part.

GE'NERALLY, Adv. in such a manner as to include all without exception. Commonly, or frequently. In the main, or without descending to particulars. "Generally speaking." Addis.

GE'NERALNESS, S. wide extent or comprehension. Frequency; commonness.

GE'NERANT, S. [generans, Lat.] the power producing, or begetting. "The generating, or active principle." Ray.

To GE'NERATE, V. A. [genero, Lat.] to beget, or propagate. Figuratively, to cause or produce.

GENERA'TION, S. [Fr.] the act of begetting. A family, race, or offspring. A single succession, or gradation in the scale of descent. "So generations in their course decay." Pope. Figuratively, an age.

GE'NERATIVE, Adj. [generatif, Fr.] having the power of propagation. Prolific.

GENERA'TOR, S. the power which begets, or produces.

GENE'RIC, GENE'RICAL, Adj. [generique, Fr.] that which comprehends the genus, or distinguishes one genus from another.

GENERO'SITY, S. [generosité, Fr. generositas, Lat.] the quality of giving or bestowing money freely, of overlooking faults without censure, of pardoning crimes with good nature, and considering the disagreement of other persons opinions with charitable allowances. In common discourse this word is applied mostly to readiness in spending and bestowing money.

GE'NEROUS, Adj. [genereux, Fr. generosus, Lat.] of good birth and ancestry. Open of heart; liberal. In Physic, strong, or vigorous. "This generous wine." Boyle.

GE'NEROUSNESS, S. the quality of spending and bestowing freely, and of making allowance for the diversity of opinions in others, with good nature.

GE'NESIS, S. [genesis, Gr.] the first book of the Old Testament, so called by the Greeks, because it contains the history of the generation of all things. It comprehends the account of the creation, the origins of all nations, the history of the first patriarchs, taken in the space of 2363 years, and was written by Moses. The Jews are told it contains the beginning of this book and that of Ezekiel, till they are 30 years of age. The noble and majestic simplicity in which the grandest occurrences are reported, the manner in which the creation of the world is described, so much superior to all the accounts we have in heathen authors, refer us to some higher origin for its superiority, than any those sages could boast of, and if consi-

4

dered

dered in its due extent, will naturally lead us to conclude that none but the CREATOR of the world could so minutely, so wisely have described the manner in which it was called into being.

GENETHLI'ACAL, Adj. [γενεθλιακὸς, Gr.] In Astrology, belonging to a person's birth or nativity.

GENE'THLIACS, S. the science of calculating nativities, or foretelling future events from the configuration or predominancy of stars at a person's birth.

GENE'VA, S. [genevre, Fr. a juniper berry] a spirituous liquor, distilled from juniper berries. According to Dr. Hill, the common fort is drawn from the turpentine, mixed with the coarsest spirits.

GENE'VA, an ancient, large, and populous town, capital of a republic of the same name, near the confines of France and Switzerland. It is very ancient, and was well known in the time of the Romans. Julius Cæsar made use of it as a bulwark against the Helvetians. It is well built, rich, and strongly fortified. Here are always a great number of strangers, who are travelling from France to Italy, or from Italy to France. It is divided by the river Rhone into two unequal parts, and which also forms an isle, full of fine houses, and here is an ancient structure, called the tower of Cæsar. The largest part is built on a hill, which descends by a gentle declivity, and lies to the S. of the river; the other part communicates with the island by two large wooden bridges. St. Peter's church is a vast structure, built in the Gothick taste, and has three towers, the least of which is covered with tin plates. The arsenal is well furnished, and there is a strong garrison. The college, where there is a magnificent library, is well worth observation. In general it is a very agreeable place, and there is nothing omitted to render it delightful. The principal riches of the inhabitants proceed from their manufactures, of which they have a great number; but the most considerable are, watches, clocks, and gold and silver lace. The revenues of the republick arise from the duty on merchandizes which are carried out of the city, and from a prodigious quantity of corn which the magistrates buy, and fell to the inhabitants. The sovereignty of this republick is lodged in the assembly of the citizens and burghers, but there are several bodies of the magistracy, who have each their proper province, and whose heads are chosen by the people. The great council consists of two persons, from among whom there are 25 counsellors chosen, of which 4 are syndics, who are heads of the republick, and chosen every year. They are jealous of their liberties, and are in alliance with the cantons of Bern, Zurich, and Soleure. It was formerly a free imperial city, and a bishop's see, but the bishop was expelled

when they embraced Calvinism, in 1553. They will not allow playing at cards, or drinking at publick houses; but they exercise their militia, play at bowls, and use other exercises on a sunday. It is 30 miles N. E. of Lyons, 65 S. of Besançon, 40 N. E. of Chambery, and 135 N. by W. of Turin. Lon. 23. 30. lat. 46. 23.

GE'NIAL, Adj. [genialis, Lat.] that which contributes or conduces to propagation. "The genial bed." Par. Lost. That which cherishes, supports life, or causes chearfulness. "So much I find my genial spirits droop." Milt. Natural, or native.

GE'NIALLY, Adv. by genius; naturally. "Some men are genially disposed to some opinion." Glanville. Gayly; chearfully. The first sense is seldom used.

GE'NIO, S. [Ital. of genius, Lat.] a person of a particular turn of mind. The disposition of the mind. "Some genio's are not capable of pure affection." Tatler, No. 53.

GE'NITALS, S. [genitalis, Lat.] the parts contributing to generation.

GE'NITING, S. an early apple gathered in June.

GE'NITIVE, Adj. [genitif, Fr. genitivus, Lat.] In Grammar, a case, which signifies the possessor, author, or relation of one thing to another. In the English language it is the only case we have; and is formed by adding an s to the termination of the nominative, in which we imitate the Saxon in their first, third, and fourth declensions, who formed it by adding es to the termination of the nominative. Hence it appears that the promiscuous use of an apostrophe before the s of the genitive is improper, and should never obtain place but when some letter is left out, thus it is used in man's, because derived from mannes, Sax. wherein the n is left out, but it is omitted in wife's, because the original genitive is the same, and nothing left out. If a word end in s, another s is added to express the genitive singular, as St. James's; but to apostrophize the genitive plural seems for the reason assigned to be highly improper. When three substantives come together, the genitive is formed by adding s to the second, because the first substantive is considered as an adjective, or making a compound word with the second; thus we write, the King of England's fleet, nor but we may find two or three of these genitives following each other, as Peter's wife's passion; the reason of this difference seems to be the omission of the particle of, and Peter's and wife's being considered as separate words, for was of added, the sentence would run like the former; as the passion of Peter's Wife. In English, like the Hebrew and Saxon, the genitive is always put before the word which it is joined to, or that which governs it. Thus we say man's nature, and the

the Simone *Guides Swane*, the Son of God, or God's Son. The particle *of*, sometimes used to express the genitive transition from another language, is only a preposition, and the word joined with it not properly in English called the genitive case, because case is an alteration of the end of the noun, and where *of* is used, the noun suffers no alteration, as, "the *son of Mary*."

GE'NIUS, S. [Lat. *gnius*, Fr.] a supposed protecting, or ruling power. A person endowed with faculties superior to others. A perfection of understanding. Nature or disposition.

GENOA, a town of Italy, and capital of a republick of the same name. It is very ancient and large, being about 6 miles in circumference, built like an amphitheatre, and is full of magnificent structures, such as churches and palaces, and particularly those of the doge and of Doria, whence it has the name of Genoa the Proud. It is very populous, and one of the most trading places in Italy. They reckon there is 90,000 inhabitants; of which 30,000 families are employed in making velvets, silks, and the like. It is an archbishop's see, has an academy, a good harbour, and lofty walls, fortified in such places where they are most likely to be attacked. There is a large aqueduct, which supplies a great number of fountains with water. In all parts of the city. The houses are well-built, and are 5 or 6 stories high; and here are 57 churches, 17 convents and a large hospitals. The government is aristocratic, because none but the nobility can have any share in it; these are of two sorts, the old and the new, from whence there are 80 persons chosen, who make the great council, in which their sovereignty resides. Besides these, there is a senate, composed of the doge and 12 senators, who have the common administration of affairs. The doge continues in his office but two years. The harbour is very considerable, and to preserve it they have built a mole of 360 paces in length, and 25 in breadth; they have raised it 15 feet above the level of the water, that it may the better shelter the ships, and break the force of the waves. Upon this mole there is a tower, with 360 steps to go up to the top, where in the night time they place a great number of lanthorns. The harbour may be shut up with a chain, which will hinder the going out or coming in of the vessels. It was bombarded by the French in 1684, and submitted to the Florentines in 1746, but a citizen being abused by an Austrian officer, the inhabitants rose and murdered part of the soldiers, and drove away the rest. It was besieged afterwards by the Austrians; but the French coming to the assistance of the town, they were obliged to raise the siege, in July 1747. The ordinary revenue of this republick is

1,200,000 L. a year, and there is a bank, which is partly supported by publick duties. They generally keep two or three years provision of corn, wine, and oil, in their magazines, which they sell to the people in scarce times. It is 70 miles S. of Milan, 62 S. E. of Turin, 85 S. W. of Parma, 112 N. W. of Florence, and 225 N. W. of Rome. Lon. 26, 32. Lat. 44. 25.

GENTEE'L. Adj. [*gentil*, Fr.] polite, or elegant in behaviour or address. Graceful in mien.

GENTE'ELY, Adv. politely; elegantly, gracefully; handsomely.

GENTE'ELNESS, S. elegance; gracefulness or politeness. Qualities becoming a person of rank.

GENTIAN, S. [*gentiane*, Fr.] In Botany, fellwort, or bad money. It is ranged by Linnæus in the second sect. of his fifth class, and by Tournefort in the third sect. of his first. The species are twelve. The root, used in medicine, is brought from Germany.

GENTILESSE, S. [Fr.] complaisance; the ceremony and address of polite behaviour; civility. "Her complaisance and *gentilesse*." *Hud.*

GEN'TILISM, S. [*gentesme*, Fr.] heathenism; the worship of the heathens; idolatry.

GENTILE, S. [*gentilis*, Lat.] one who worships idols. Used adjectively, for belonging to idolatry.

GENTILI'TIOUS, Adj. [*gentilitium*, Lat.] belonging to a particular nation. "An unsavoury odour is *gentilitious* unto the Jews." *Brown.* Hereditary; entailed on a family.

GENTILI'TY, S. [*gentilité*, Fr.] good extraction; dignity of birth. The class of those who are well born. Paganism, heathenism, or the practice of idolatry.

GEN'TLE, Adj. [*gentil*, Lat.] of an ancient and good family. Mild; tame; not easily provoked, soothing or pacifying. "This sense first *gentle* made in use." *Dryd.*

GEN'TLE, S. a gentleman. "*Gentles*, methinks you frown." *Shak.* A kind of worm used for a bait in fishing.

GEN'TLEFOLK, S. persons distinguished by their birth from the lower class.

GEN'TLEMAN, S. [*gentil homme*, Fr. *gentilhuomo*, Ital.] a person of good family, one above the vulgar. Used as a term of deference and complaisance, when speaking of a person. The servant who waits upon a person out of livery. Used as a word to denote great extraction, or wealth, be the rank what it will. "The king is a noble *gentleman*." *Shak.* A person who to a good birth, and different fortune, has joined the qualifications of polite address, and virtuous conduct.

GENTLEMANLIKE, GEN'TLEMANLY, Adv. becoming a man of birth, breeding and fortune. Polite, affable and generous.

GEN'TLENESS, S. dignity of birth, or rank. Softness, mildness, sweetness, or freedom from violence, applied to disposition. Kindness, benevolence. "The gentleness of all the gods go with thee." *Shak.*

GENTLEWOMAN, S. a woman of birth, or one superior to the vulgar. A woman who waits upon a person of high rank. Used likewise as a term of compliment, or of irony.

GEN'TLY, Adv. softly, or without violence. Slowly, or without haste; kindly, or without severity.

GEN'TRY, S. birth. A rank of persons between the nobility and the vulgar. A term of civility, or irony.

GENUFLEXION, S. [Fr. of *genu*, Lat. and *flecto*, Lat.] the bending the knee. Worship, or adoration expressed by bending the knee. " All the rights of adoration, *genuflexion*" *Stillingfl.*

GENUINE, Adj. [*genuinus*, Lat.] pure, or without mixture; natural, true, or real.

GENU'INELY, Adv. without adulteration, or any safe mixture, naturally.

GENU'INENESS, S. freedom from any adulteration. Purity, or the natural state of a thing.

GE'NUS, S. [Lat.] in Logic, a class of beings, or one common nature agreeing to and comprehending under it many species, or several other common natures; thus *animal*, is a *genus*, because it agrees to, and comprehends under it, the several species of men, horses, whales, lions, &c. Logicians distinguish it into *summum* and *subalternum*. The *genus summum*, is that which holds the uppermost place in the class of predicaments, and may be divided into several species, each of which may be confidered as a *genus* with respect to those below it; this *genus* therefore can never be a species. But the *genus subalternum* may, because when considered with respect to the species below it, it is a *genus*; but when considered with respect to the *summum genus*, it is then a species; thus *bird*, when compared with the word animal is a species, but when with a crow, &c. it is a *genus*. In Botany, a system or assemblage of several plants agreeing in some one or more common characters, in respect to certain parts, whereby they are distinguished from all other plants. The system of Linnæus, wherein all plants are classed according to their generative parts, the number of stamina in their flowers, &c. is the best as well as the most universally followed.

GEOCENTRIC, Adj. [from *ya*, Gr. and *κεντρον*] in Aftronomy, having the same center with the earth. The *geocentric latitude* of a planet, is its latitude seen from the earth. The *geocentric place* of a planet, is its place in the ecliptic, as seen from the earth.

GEODÆ'SIA, S. [*geodæsie*, Fr.] that part of practical geometry, which teaches to

measure surfaces.

GEODÆ'TICAL, Adj. relating to the art of meafuring surfaces.

GEO'GRAPHER, S. [of *ya*, Gr. the earth, and *γραφω*, Gr. to describe] one who can describe the earth, and is skilled in making maps, the use of the globes, and the situations and extent of the several countries in the world.

GEOGRA'PHICAL, Adj [*geographique*, Fr.] belonging or relating to geography.

GEOGRA'PHICALLY, Adv. according to the rules of geography.

GEO'GRAPHY, S. [*geographie*, Fr. of *ya*, Gr. the earth, and *γραφω*, Gr. to describe] the knowledge of the circles of the earthly globe, and the situation of the various countries on its surface. In a more extensive sense, it takes in a knowledge of the seas also; and in its largest sense a knowledge of the various customs, habits, and governments of the different nations; the figures, magnitude, motion, and the different strata and product of its soil; the various animals of different countries; their climates, seasons, heat, weather, &c.

GEO'LOGY, S. [from *ya*, Gr. and *λογος*, Gr. knowledge of the nature and state of the earth.

GEO'MANCY, S. [from *ya*, Gr. the earth and *μαντεια*, Gr. soothfaying or foretelling] the art of foretelling future events, by casting little pebbles on the ground; by means of clefts or chinks made in the earth, or by means of a number of dots made at random, and considering the various lines and figures they prefent.

GEO'MANCER, one who pretends to tell future events by means of *geomancy*.

GEO'MANTIC, Adj. belonging to geomancy.

GEO'METER, S. [*geometre*, Fr.] one skilled in geometry.

GEOME'TRAL, Adj. [Fr.] pertaining to geometry.

GEOME'TRIC GEOME'TRICAL, Adj. [*geometrique*, Fr. *γεωμετρικος*, Gr.] belonging to, prescribed, laid down by, or disposed according to, the principles or rules of geometry.

GEOME'TRICALLY, Adv. according to the principles or rules of geometry.

To GEO'METRIZE, V. N. [*γεωμετρεω*, Gr.] to perform according to the principles of geometry.

GEO'METRY, S. [*geometrie*, Fr. of *ya*, Gr. earth, and *μετρεω*, Gr. measure] in its primary sense, the art of measuring the earth or any distances thereon; at present used for the science of quantity, extension, or magnitude considered in themselves, and without any regard to matter. It is divided into speculative and practical; speculative geometry is that which considers the properties of continued quantity abstractedly,

and is again divided into elementary, which
is employed in confidering right lines, plane
furfaces, and folids generated therefrom;
and fublime or lighter geometry, which is
employed in the confideration of curve lines,
conic fections, and bodies formed therefrom.
Practical geometry is that which applies the
theorems of fpeculative geometry to practice.
This fcience, very probably, had its rife in
Egypt, where the inundations of the Nile rendered it neceffary to diftinguish lands by confidering their figures; to be able to meafure their refpective quantities; to know how
to plot them, and lay them out again in their
juft dimenfions and fituations, &c.

GEORGE, S. [pronounced *Jorge*, *Geor-
gius*, Lat.] the figure of S. George on horfeback, worn by the knights of the garter as
an enfign of their order. Ufed with *brown*,
a fmall penny loaf of houfhold bread; a
word commonly ufed in the colleges at Oxford, &c. but obfolete in London.

GEORGE, St. a fort and town of Afia,
in the peninfula on this fide the Ganges, and
on the coaft of Coromandel, belonging to
the Englifh; it is otherwife called Ma-
drafs, and by the natives Chili-petam.
It fronts the fea, and has a falt-water river
on its backfide, which hinders the frefh water
fprings from coming near the town, fo that
they have no good water within a mile of
them. In the rainy feafon it is incommoded by inundations, and from April to
September it is fo fcorching hot, that if the
fea-breezes did not cool the air, there would
be no living there. There are two towns,
one of which is called the white town,
which is walled round, and has feveral
bulwarks and baftions to defend it; It
is 400 paces long, and 150 broad, and is
divided into regular ftreets. Here are two
churches, one for the proteftants, and
the other for the papifts; as alfo a good
hofpital, a town-hall, and a prifon for
debtors. They are a corporation, and have
a mayor and aldermen, with other proper officers. The black town is inhabited by the
Gentows, Mahometans, Portuguefe, and
Armenian Chriftians, and each religion have
their temples and churches. This, as well as
the white town, is ruled by the Englifh governor, and his council. The diamond
mines are but a week's journey from this
place, which renders them pretty plentiful,
but there are no large ones fince that
great diamond was procured by governor
Pitt. This colony produces very little of its
own growth or manufacture for foreign markets, and the trade is in the hands of the Ar-
menians and Gentows. The chief things
the Englifh deal in befides diamonds are
calicoes, chints, muflins, and the like.
This colony may confift of 80,000 inhabitants, in the towns and villages, and there
are generally 4 or 500 Europeans; their rice

is brought by fea from Ganghim and Oriza,
their wheat from Surat and Bengal, and
their fire-wood from the iflands of Diu, infomuch that no enemy with a fuperior force
at fea, may eafily diftrefs them. The houfes of the white town are built with brick,
and have lofty rooms, and flat roofs; but
the black town confifts chiefly of thatched
cottages. The military power is lodged in
the governor and council, who are alfo the
laft refort in civil caufes. The company
have two chaplains who officiate by turns,
and have each 100l. a year, befides the advantages of trade. They never attempt to
make profelytes, but leave that to the po-
pifh miffionaries. The falaries of the company's writers are very fmall, but, if they
have any fortune of their own, they make
it up by trade, which muft generally be the
cafe, for they commonly grow rich. It is
63 miles north of Pondicherry. Lon. 98. 8
lat. 13. 15.

GEOR'GIC, S. [*georgique*, Fr.] fome
part of the fcience of hufbandry, fet off with
all the beauties and embellifhments of poetry;
the beft Greek poem of this kind is that of
Hefiod's, but Virgil has excelled him by far
in Latin, and Philips, our countryman,
feems in fome meafure to difpute the palm
with him in his Cyder.

GER'MAN, S. [*german*, Fr. *germanus*,
Lat.] one approaching to a brother in near-
nefs of blood; generally applied to the children of brothers and fifters, who are called
coufins germans.

GER'MANY, a large country, lying in
the middle of Europe, bounded on the E. by
Hungary and Poland, on the N. by the Baltick Sea and Denmark, on the W. by the
Netherlands, France and Switzerland, and on
the S. by the Alps, Italy, and Switzerland;
being about 640 miles in length, and 500 in
breadth. The air is temperate and wholefome, but more inclinable to cold than
heat, efpecially by the fea-fide. The foil is
very proper for corn and paftures, and, in
fome places, efpecially along the Rhine, it
produces large quantities of wine, known by
the name of Rhenifh. As to the difpofition of the people in general, they are robuft,
brave, good foldiers, free, laborious, inured
to labour, dextrous in manufactures, and
fruitful in inventions. The nobility in Germany is the pureft in Europe, and they will
fooner choofe the daughter of a nobleman,
without a fortune, than that of the richeft
citizen. One reafon of this is, that
there is no obtaining rich benefices, fuch
as canonicates, abbeys, bifhopricks, and
archbifhopricks, without a full proof of
their nobility, as thefe are almoft fo
many independent fovereignties. Germany
is the moft fingular country in the world, for
it contains a great many princes, as well fe-
cular as ecclefiaftic, who are abfolute in their
own

own dominions, and independent of each othe. There are a great number of free towns which are so many little republics, governed by their own laws, and only animated by a head, who is elective, and has the title of emperor, who, properly speaking, has but little authority, except in the dominions belonging to him before he was chosen. Upon this account they generally choose one who has territories of his own, and who is able to keep up his dignity. For this reason the emperors have been so often chosen out of the house of Austria. The election of the emperor formerly was made by the German princes, as well ecclesiastick as secular, but by the famous constitution of the golden bull, the electors were restrained to seven; that is three ecclesiasticks, which are, the archbishops of Treves, Cologne, and Mentz, and four seculars, namely the king of Bohemia, the count palatine of the Rhine, the duke of Saxony, and the marquis of Brandenburgh. But in 1648 they were obliged, by the treaty of Munster, to constitute an eighth electorate, in favour of the son of Frederic V. count palatine of the Rhine, who had been deprived of his dominions and marks in 1622, and put to the ban of the empire because he had been proclaimed king of Bohemia, and his title conferred on the duke of Bavaria. Lastly, in 1692, the emperor Leopold created another electorate in favour of Ernest of Brunswick, duke of Hanover, whose son George became king of England in 1714. Each elector bears the title of one of the principal offices of the empire; the elector of Mentz is high chancellor of Germany, and director of the archives of the empire; that of Treves or Triers, has the title of chancellor of the Gauls, and that of Cologne, that of Italy; the duke of Bavaria is grand master of Bavaria, and carries the golden apple; the elector of Saxony is grand esquire, and bears the sword; that of Brandenburgh is grand chamberlain, and carries the sceptre; the Palatine is grand treasurer. When the empire is vacant or the emperor absent, and there is no king of the Romans, the electors Palatine and of Saxony are viceroys, or regents of the empire, though the duke of Bavaria disputes the right of the former. When the emperor would be certain of a successor, he endeavours to prevail with the electors to choose a king of the Romans, and then he will become emperor after the other's death. The emperor assumes the title of always August, of Cæsar, and of sacred majesty. Although he is chief of the empire, he does not govern alone, but the supreme authority resides in the general assemblies, called Diets, which he only has a right of appointing, and to which he may send commissioners to preside in his room. These assemblies are composed of three bodies, or colleges; the first

of which is that of the electors, the second that of the princes, and the third that of the imperial towns. The electors and princes send their deputies, as well as the imperial towns. When that of the electors and that of the princes disagree, that of the towns cannot decide the difference; but they are obliged to give their consent when they are of the same opinion. These assemblies have the power of making peace or war, of settling general impositions, and of regulating all the important affairs of the empire. But their deliberations have not the force of a law till the emperor gives his consent; who also gives the investiture of fiefs, and disposes of those which have devolved to the empire for want of successors, or confiscations.

GE'RME, S. [Fr. *germe*, Lat.] a sprout, or shoot. That part which grows and spreads. "Mure out of the *germe* or treadle of the egg." *Brown.* In Botany, that part of a flower or plant which contains the seed.

GER'MEN, S. [*germen*, Lat.] a young sprout, or shoot. A sprouting seed.

To GER'MINATE, V. N. [*germinatus*, Lat.] to sprout, bud, shoot, or grow.

GERMINA'TION, S. [Fr.] the act of sprouting. Growth.

GE'RUND, S. [*gerundium*, Lat.] in the Latin grammar, a verbal noun ending in *di*, *do*, or *dum*, and governing cases like a verb.

GESTA'TION, S. [*gestatio*, Lat.] the act of bearing the young in the womb.

To GESTI'CULATE, V. N. [*gesticulatus*, Lat. *gesticuler*, Fr.] to make odd or antic postures.

GESTICULA'TION, S. [Fr. *gesticulatio*, Lat.] the forming odd and antic postures. An odd posture.

GE'STURE, S. [*geste*, Fr. *gestus*, Lat.] the postures or attitudes expressive or suitable to a person's sentiments. Any movement or motion of the body.

To GE'STURE, V. N. to accompany one's speech with proper action, attitude, or motion of the body.

To GET, V. A. to procure, or acquire. To attain by success, to win. To possess. To beget. In acquiring to gain. To earn by labour and pains. Used with *from*, to learn. "*Get ly heart* the more command and useful words." *Watts.* To procure or cause a thing to be. To prevail on or persuade. "The king could not get him to engage." *Spell.* To get out, to discover a person's secrets. To wheedle, or coax a person out of his property. "After having gotten of you every thing you can spare." *Guard. No.* 197. To move from or to a place, when followed by *out* or *on.* To rise, or quit one's bed, *to get up.* To remove or separate by force, art, or pains, used with *off.* Neuterly, to depart from a place, or arrive at any

any state or posture by degrees, with some kind of labour, effort, or difficulty. To toil; to come by accident, used with *among*. "Two or three men are *got among* them." *Taylor.* To force or find a passage, *to get in.* To move, or remove to a certain place, used with adverbs of place, or motion. To ascend, used with *up, to get up.* To have recourse to, used with *into.* "Lying is so cheap a cover for any miscarriage—a child can scarce be kept from *getting into* it." *Locke.* To become by any act what one was not before. "Bathes and *gets* drunk." *Dryd.* To get off, to escape from any danger. Used with *over*, to surmount, or conquer; to extricate one's self from any obstacle or impediment.

GET'TER, S. one that procures, obtains, or begets.

GET'TING, S. the act of acquiring or obtaining. In commerce gain or profit.

GEW'GAW, S. [*gwageaw*, Brit.] a showy, empty trifle; a bauble, or plaything.

GEW'GAW, Adj. showy and gaudy, but of no value. "See the poor *gewgaw* happiness of Feliciana." *Law.*

GHAST'FUL, Adj. [of *gast*, Sax. and *full*, Sax.] dreary; dismal, or melancholy, applied to the mind or to place. Appearing dismal, melancholy, or like a ghost, applied to the person.

GHAST'LINESS, S. horror, or melancholy impressing on the countenance. Dismal paleness.

GHAST'LY, Adj. like a ghost, with horror and dread. Dreadful; horrible; shocking. "Mangled with *ghastly* wounds." *Milt.*

GHER'KIN, S. [*gurcke*, Teut.] a pickled cucumber. *Skinner.*

GHOST, S. [*gast*, Sax. a soul, spectre or spirit] the soul. A spirit or spectre, seen after the death of a person. When joined with *Holy*, it implies the third person of the Holy Trinity; otherwise termed the *Spirit.* "And he *gave up the* Ghost." *Matt.* lii. 26. "Furnish on *halycon* Ghost." ver. 11. "The *Leigam* Ghost." *Matt.* xxviii. 18. Saxon transl. To this agrees the Gothic version. "*Ab* *mih weihama.*" To give up the ghost, is to expire; to die; or to yield our soul into the hands of him that gave it.

GHOST'LINESS, S. spirituality; the quality of relating to the spirit.

GHOST'LY, Adj. spiritual, relating to the soul; opposed to carnal or secular.

GI'ANT, S. [*geant*, Fr. *gigas*, Sax.] a person of uncommon stature.

GI'ANTESS, S. a woman taller than the rest of her sex naturally are.

GI'ANTLIKE, GI'ANTLY, Adj. resembling a giant. Figuratively, any thing of enormous bulk.

To GIB'BER, V. N. [from *jabber*, ac-

cording to Johnson *gabberen*, Belg. *gabb* Run. *sport.*] to speak in an unintelligible manner.

GIB'BERISH, S. [derived by Skinner from *gaber*, Fr. to cheat, imagined by others to be corrupted from *jabber*. Johnson, as it was formerly written *gebrish*, supposes it to be derived from or allude to the chymical cant of *Gheber* and his followers. Those who do not approve of these conjectures, may remember, that *gabb*, Run. implies sport, and may have given rise to this word] cant; the private language of rogues, gypsies, &c. words derived from no language, and having no meaning.

GIB'BET, S. [Fr. *gibbet*, Ital.] a gallows; or a cross post whereon malefactors are executed, or hung in chains.

To GIB'BET, V. A. to hang on a gibbet.

GIB'BIER, S. [Fr.] game or wild fowl. "The fowl and *gibbier* are too free." *Addis.*

GIBBOS'ITY, S. [*gibbosité*, Fr.] the quality of rising in a protuberance. A prominence. Convexity. "The *gibbosity* of the interjacent water." *Ray.*

GIB'BOUS, S. [*gibbus*, Lat.] convex; rising in knobs. Crookbacked.

GIB'CAT, S. [See GIBB] an old worn-out cat. "I am as melancholy as a *gib-cat.*" *Shak.*

To GIBE, V. N. [*gaber*, old Fr.] to sneer. Actively, to deride; to mock; to treat with scorn.

GIBE, S. a taunt; sneer; or expression of contempt.

GI'BER, S. a sneerer; a derider.

GI'BINGLY, Adv. in a ridiculing, or sneering manner.

GIB'LET, S. [*giblet*, Sax.] the offal parts of a duck or goose, consisting of the head or neck, part of the wings, gizzard, heart, liver, &c.

GIBRALTER, S. a strong town of Spain, in Andalusia, near a mountain of the same name, formerly called Calpe, and supposed to be one of Hercules's pillars, and which he looked upon to be the end of the world. Tarick, a general of the Moors, built a fortress here, which he called Gibel-Tarick, that is to say, Mount Tarick. Since that time a town has here been built at the foot of this rock, which is very well fortified; it can only be approached by a very narrow passage between the mountain and the sea, across which the Spaniards have drawn a line, and fortified it, to prevent the garrison from having a communication with the country. It was formerly thought to be impregnable, but, in 1704, it was taken by the confederate fleet, commanded by Sir George Rook. The French and Spaniards attempted to retake it the same year, and 4 or 500 of them crept up the rock which re-

vers

was the town, in the night-time, but were drove down headlong the next morning. In 1727, the Spaniards besieged it again, and they attempted to blow up the rock, which they found impregnable, and were at length obliged to raise the siege. Those that have courage enough to climb to the top of the rock, will find a plain on the top, from whence they may have a prospect of the sea on the side the strait, and the kingdoms of Barbary, Fez, and Morocco, besides Seville, and Grenada in Spain. The garrison here are cooped up in a very narrow compass, and have no provisions but what are brought from Barbary and England. The strait here is about 24 miles in length, and 15 in breadth, and there is always a strong current run through it from the Ocean to the Mediterranean. It was ceded to England by the treaties of Utrecht and Seville. It is 15 miles N of Ceuta, 45 S. E. of Cadiz, and 80 S. of Seville. Lon. 12. 20. lat 36 o.

GIDDILY, Adv. with a swimming in the head. Figuratively, without steadiness. Rashly.

GIDDY, Adj. [gidi, Sax.] having a swimming in the head, whereby external things seem to turn round. Figuratively, a swift whirling motion, which may cause giddiness. Changeable, inconstant, unsteady; that which causes giddiness either by its circular motion, or its excessive height. Heedless, rash, or wanting caution. Tottering. Elated too much with success or praise.

GIDDY-BRAINED, Adj. careless; thoughtless; rash; imprudent.

GIDDY-HEADED, Adj. without thought, caution, or steadiness.

GIFT, S. [Sax. gift, Isl. gafa, Run.] something bestowed on, or given to another. The act of giving. When applied to the deity, an offering, or oblation. In a bad sense, a bribe; or present made use of to corrupt a judge, &c. Any peculiar talent and faculty, so called because given, or implanted in our nature, not acquired by art. "He who has the gift of ridicule." Spect. No. 291.

GIFTED, Adj. given or bestowed. "With my heaven gifted strength." Mid. Samson. Endowed with extraordinary powers. Possessed with a vain imagination of being inspired, used ironically. "Two of their gifted brotherhood." Dryd.

GIG, S. a small top made of horn, which is kept spinning by whipping. A small fiddle.

GIGANTIC, S. [gigant, Lat.] resembling a giant: Of uncommon or an enormous size.

To **GIGGLE**, V. N. to laugh heartily at trifles.

GIGGLER, S. one who bursts into laughter at the smallest trifle.

To **GILD**, V. A. [preter gilded, or gilt, of gyldan, Sax.] to wash over, or cover with leaf-gold. Figuratively, to cover with any thing of a yellow colour; to adorn with sunshine, or lustre. To brighten. To gild over, to recommend a thing, or hide its defects by some additional ornament; alluding to the method of apothecaries who cover their pills with gold leaf, in order to render them more pleasing to the eye.

GILDER, S. one who covers the surface of a thing with gold. A coin valued from one shilling and sixpence to two shillings.

GILDING, S. gold laid on any surface, by way of ornament. The act of covering with gold.

GILL, S. [gil, Isl. gula, Lat.] the apertures on each side of the head of fish, which they breath through, instead of their mouths. The red flap which hangs down from the beak of a fowl. A liquid measure containing the fourth part of a pint; from gille, low Lat. A woman or female companion, from Gillian, the old English way of writing Julian, or Juliana. "Each Jack with his Gill." Ben. Johnson. In Botany, the plant called ground-ivy. Likewise ale wherein ground-ivy has been steeped, is called Gill-ale. It may not be improper to remark, that the g in Gills of a fish is sounded hard, as Guills; and in Gill, a measure, it is sounded soft as Jill.

GILLY-FLOWER, S. [corrupted from July flower, so called from the month it blows in] in Botany, the Dianthus; under which genus are included, pinks, carnations, and the sweet-william; but the term is vulgarly applied to that species called the clove July-flower.

GILT, S. [from gild] gold laid on any surface. Figuratively, show, or splendour. "When thou wast in thy gilt and thy perfume." Shak.

GILT, Part. of gild.

GILT, Adj. [gilt, Sax.] neat; spruce; well dressed.

GIMCRACK, or **GIMCRANK**, S. a slight piece of mechanism, more curious than useful, or valuable.

GIMLET, S. [the g is pronounced hard, of giblet, Fr. signifying the same] a borer with a kind of screw at the end.

GIMMER, S. a movement; a part of a machine. Machinery.

GIMP, S. a kind of silk twist; or open lace.

GIN, S. [contracted from engine] a trap or snare. A pump. A distilled liquor drawn from juniper-berries, &c.

GINGER, S. [gengere, common, gingiber, Sax. zingiber, Lat.] an aromatic root, of a yellow

a yellow colour, a very hot and pungent taſte, uſed in cookery, as a ſpice, by apothecaries as a medicine, and brought from Calecut in the Eaſt-Indies. In botany, it is ſtiled by Linnæus, the *amomum*. Though placed by Linnæus in his firſt claſs; yet is more properly belongs to his ſecond, as the flowers have two ſtamina, one of which is joined to the upper ſegment of the flower; but ſoon loſing its ſummit appears to be only a ſegment. The ſpecies are three.

GIN'GERBREAD, S. a kind of bread made of flower and treacle, and mixed with ginger, and aromatic ſeeds.

GIN'GERLY, Adv. [*gingre*, Sax. younger] in a ſoft, tender, cautious, and ſlow manner, for fear of breaking or hurting on account of the weakneſs of its form, or the ſeenneſs of its make. "What is't that you —took up ſo gingerly." *Shak.*

GIN'GERNESS, S. caution, tenderneſs, niceneſs.

To GIN'GLE, V. N. [formed from the ſound] to have a ſharp noiſe. Actively, to ſhake any pieces of metal together, ſo as to make them ſound. Figuratively, to make a diſagreeable found by words ending the ſame ſyllables, applied to ſtile.

GIN'GLE, S. the ſound made by ſeveral pieces of metal ſhook together. Figuratively, the ſound made by ſeveral periods ending with the ſame ſyllables.

GIN'NET, S. [*genet*, Fr.] a nag; a mule, or degenerated breed.

GIN'SENG, S. [Chin. the figure of a man, ſo called from the ſhape of its root] a root, lately brought from China, into Europe, of a browniſh colour on the outſide, and ſomewhat yellowiſh within, ſo pure and fine, that it ſeems almoſt tranſparent; its taſte is acrid, ſpicy, and ſomewhat bitter, its ſmell agreeable, aromatic, but not very ſtrong. It is valued ſo highly by the Chineſe, that they ſell it for three times its weight in ſilver: Europeans eſteem it a good medicine in vertigoes, convulſions, and nervous complaints, and recommend it as one of the beſt reſtoratives known. Its doſe is from ten to twenty grains in powder, and from one drachm to two to a pint, in infuſion.

GIP'SY, S. [corrupted from Egyptian, for when they firſt appeared in Europe, they declared, and perhaps truly, according to Johnſon, they were driven from Egypt by the Turks, who adds, they are now mingled with all nations] a vagabond, of a dark complexion, who pretend to tell future events. Figuratively, uſed to imply a perſon of a dark complexion.

To GIRD, V. A. [preter. *girded*, or *girt*; part. paſſ. *girt*, of *gird*, or *gyrdan*, Sax.] to faſten by binding round. Figuratively, to inveſt, or cloath. To reproach in an unuſual ſenſe. "He will not ſpare to gird the god." *Shak.* To incloſe, incircle.

"The Nyſean iſle —girt with the river Triton." *Par. R.* Neuterly, uſed with at, to reproach, to caſt a reproach, or break a ſcornful jeſt on a perſon. "Men of all ſorts take a private gird at me." *Shak.*

GIRD, S. a twitch, or pang. "Many fearful girds and twinges, which the atheiſt feels." *Tillotf.*

GIR'DER, S. in Architecture, the largeſt piece of timber in a floor.

GIR'DLE, S. [*girdl, gyrdl*, Sax.] any bandage drawn round the waiſt, and tied or buckled. Figuratively, an incloſure or circumference. "Within the girdle of theſe walls." *Shak.* The equator, a great circle ſurrounding the world like a girdle. "Under the girdle of the world." *Bacon.*

To GIR'DLE, V. A. to encompaſs and ſurround. "The gentle babes girding one another — within their innocent alabaſter arms." *Shak.* To incloſe, ſhut in, or inviron.

GIR'L, S. [as this word is pronounced by Londoners *gal*, it ſeems to point out its origin to be that of *gagl*, Ill. a worthleſs woman; the Saxon has *gagsterwoffe*, for wantonneſs, the characteriſtic ſoible of a girl, and *girlen*, or *gyrlen*, clothed or dreſſed; which alludes to another foible, not leſs remarkable in young women. Dr. Hickes derives it from *kerlinne*, Ill. a woman, but as moſt of the derivations of this word are only conjectures, we have offered the former ones as ſuch, and doubt not but we ſhall be indulged the ſame liberty as our predeceſſors] a young female, or woman; applied to one who is playful, giddy, and thoughtleſs, not arrived to years of diſcretion, or not acting with a proper degree of reſerve.

GIR'LISH, Adj. like a girl. Wanton, playful, or giddy.

GIR'LISHLY, Adj. in a wanton, playful, thoughtleſs manner, applied to females.

GIRT, Part. Paſſ. of GIRD.

To GIRT, V. A. to gird; to ſurround. "The radiant line that girts the globe." *Tickel.*

GIRT, S. a band which goes round a horſe's belly, and faſtens the ſaddle, &c. In Surgery, a circular bandage.

GIR'TH, S. [from *gead*] the band by which the ſaddle is faſtened upon a horſe. The circumference of a perſon's waiſt.

To GIRTH, V. A. to put on, or bind with a girth.

To GIVE, V. A. [preter. *gave*, participle paſſive, *given*, from *giſan*, Sax.] to beſtow, or confer on another. To tranſmit, or impart to another by hand, ſpeech, or writing. To aſſign; to put into a perſon's poſſeſſion; to conſign. Uſed with *for*, to exchange one thing for another. Uſed with *ear*, to liſten, hearken, or attend to what a perſon ſays. "Where he gave no ear." *Bac.* To expoſe without reſtraint. "Give

10

to the wanton winds their flowing hair." *Dryd.* To grant; to permit as a favour. "I'm *given* me once again to behold my friend." *Rowe.* To give way, to yield without resistance, or denial. To enable, and chiefly in Poetry. "Give the flowers to blow." To show, alluding to the product of an arithmetical calculation, which is expressed by this word "This instance gives the impossibility of an eternal existence in any thing essentially alterable" *Hale.* "Divided by the number—*gives* 414 mm." *Arbuthn.* To offer. "To *give* no offence." *Barnet.* Used with *to*, to addict, apply, or habituate. "*Give* to pleasure." *Bacon.* Followed by *for*, to abandon, resign or yield up. "Virtue *given for* lost." *Mill.* When *for* is understood it implies to suppose, to conclude, or give over. "A'l *gave* you lost." *Garth.* To *give away*, to make over, or transfer to another. Sometimes used to express a prodigal transferring of property, without receiving an equivalent. To *give back*, to restore, or return. Used with *over*, to quit, leave, or cease from an action or practice; but when followed by *to*, or *unto*, to be strongly addicted, attached or habituated to. "Had grown themselves over unto all manner of vice." *Grew.* To *give out*, to proclaim; publish; or utter. To spread a false report or rumour. To *give up*, to resign, quit, yield, abandon, or deliver. Neuterly, to rush forwards, to attack or make an assault, used with *at* or *upon*, in imitation of *donner*, Fr. to charge an enemy, which Johnson says is not to be adopted. "The enemy *give us* with fury." *Dryden.* To grow moist; to melt; to thaw; and figuratively, to relent. To *give in*, to comply with; to assent to; to yield to; to adopt or embrace. Used with *off*, to cease, or forbear an action. To *give out*, to cease from a contest, to yield. Used with *way*, or *place*, to yield, to make room.

GIV'ER, S. one who bestows a thing.

GIZ'ZARD, S. [*gesier*, Fr. *gigeria*, Lat. It is pronounced *gizzern* in Lincolnshire, and written so by Dr. More] a strong musculous stomach in birds, wherein their meat by means of stones which they swallow, is ground in pieces, as if on a mill. This contrivance of the Divine architect in animals that have no teeth to comminute their food before they swallow, deserves our admiration and praise. Figuratively used for the stomach in human creatures, whence *to grumble in the gizzard*, is applied to those who are dissatisfied, discontented, or cannot digest something they are required to comply with.

GLACIATION, S. [*glacies*, Lat. ice, *glacer*, Fr.] the act of turning into ice. Ice.

GLA'CIS, S. [Fr.] in Fortification, a sloping bank, usually applied to that which reacheth from the parapet of the covered way

to the counterscarp or level on the side of the field.

GLAD, Adj. [*glæd*, *glad*, Sax.] cheerful; gay; rejoicing at some good which has happened either to ourselves or others. Used generally with *of*, and sometimes with *at* or *with*, before the cause of joy, expressing or occasioning gladness. "Hark! a *glad* voice the lonely desert cheers." *Pope.* Figuratively, used for any thing which appears fertile, or showy. "The solitary place shall be *glad* for them." *Isi.* xxxv.

To GLAD, V. A. [*glad*, Ill.] to make a person joyful; to excite a sensation of pleasure; to cheer.

To GLAD'DEN, V. A. to cheer; to affect with a sensation of pleasure or delight.

GLADE, S. [*glad*, Dan.] a lawn or opening in a wood.

GLADIA'TOR, S. [Lat. *gladeaur*, Fr.] a person who used to fight in the publick shows at Rome. Figuratively, a prize fighter, or sword player.

GLAD'LY, Adv. in a joyful or chearful manner. In such a manner as would communicate pleasure or delight.

GLAD'NESS, S. a sensation of joy or delight.

GLAD'SOME, Adj. delighted, pleased; causing joy; having the appearance of gaiety.

GLAD'SOMELY, Adv. with some sensation of delight.

GLAD'SOMENESS, S. gaiety. A sensation of joy.

GLAIRE, S. [*glaire*, *glæ*,] the white of an egg. Also a kind of halbert.

To GLAIRE, V. A. [*glaiver*, Fr.] to varnish with the white of an egg.

GLAMORGANSHIRE, a county of S. Wales, 27 miles in length, 25 in breadth, and is bounded on the N. by Brecknockshire; on the S. by the Severn sea; on the E. by Monmouthshire; and on the W. by Carmarthenshire. It contains about 9840 houses, 67830 inhabitants, 118 parishes, and 9 market towns. It has 25 castles, and 3 monasteries; but they are now mostly demolished. It sends two members to parliament, one for the county, and one for Cardiff. The air is very sharp on the mountains, which are covered with snow; but very mild and temperate near the sea. The N. part is full of steep, high, barren mountains; but the S. is more plain, rich, and fertile, and feeds abundance of cattle and sheep; hence they supply Bristol with many firkins of good butter; and it has likewise several coalpits. The chief town is Cardiff.

GLANCE, S. [*glantz*, Belg.] a sudden shoot of light or splendor. A strike or dart of light. Figuratively, a snatch of sight; a quick view.

To GLANCE, V. A. [*glantzen*, Teut.]

to shoot a sudden ray of light. Figuratively, to hint at a person's faults by some oblique hints. Actively, to move quickly. To take a quick, or transient view. "*Glancing* so *gay* of pity on his losses*," *Knot.*

GLANC'INGLY, Adv. In an oblique, transient manner.

GLAND, S. [Fr. *glans*, *glandit*, Lat.] in Anatomy, a soft spongy substance, which serves to separate a particular humour from the blood. A conglobate, and a conglomerate gland, are the two species into which they are divided.

GLAN'DERS, S. In Farriery, a running of corrupt matter from an horse's nose.

GLANDI'FEROUS, Adj. [of *glans*, Lat. and *fero*, Lat.] bearing acorns, or fruit like acorns.

GLAN'DULE, S. [Fr. *glandule*, Lat.] in Anatomy, a small gland.

GLANDU'LOSITY, S. a collection of glands.

GLAN'DULOUS, Adj. [*glanduleux*, Fr.] pertaining to, or having the nature of, the glands.

To GLARE', V. N. [*glaren*, Belg.] to shine so bright as to dazzle the eyes. Figuratively, to look sharp, or with piercing eyes. Also to shine with ostentation, or with a lustre too much laboured, applied to writings. Actively, to shoot such a splendour as the eye cannot bear; to flash. "Every eye—glar'd lightening." *Milt.*

GLARE', S. a dazzling lustre. A fierce piercing look. "A lion now he stalks with fiery glare." *Par. Loft.*

GLAR'ING, Part. [of *glare*] flagrant; enormous; applied to crimes.

GLASS, S. [*glas*, Sax. *glas*, Belg.] an artificial substance made by mixing fixed salts, flint, and sand together, with a vehement fire; transparent to the sight, ductile when hot, but not malleable. A glass vessel of any kind; particularly a cup, with a foot, to drink out of; hence figuratively, it is used for that quantity of liquor, which such a vessel contains. A glass to view ones face in. A perspective. A glass made use of for measuring time, by means of sand which runs through a small aperture, and called an hour-glass. Used adjectively, for any thing made of glass.

To GLASS', V. A. to see as in a glass. To glaze.

GLASS'-GAZING, Adj. finical; or often contemplating himself in a looking-glass. "A—glass-gazing, super-serviceable, finical rogue." *Shak.*

GLASS'-HOUSE, S. a house where glass is manufactured.

GLAS'SY, Adj. partaking of the nature of glass; resembling glass.

GLASTENBURY, S. [*glastenburig*, Sax. from *burig*, Sax. a town, and *glasta*, glass, which latter name it derives from its situa-

No XIII.

tion in *Glasta-ey*, Sax. called *Inis N'itrra*, Brit. or Glassy Island] a town in Somersetshire, almost encompassed with rivers, famous for a monastry, deriving its origin from Joseph of Arithmathea, supposed to have been here; the walnut-tree, which never budded before the feast of St. Barnabas; the hawthorn-tree blooming on Christmas day; the burial place of king Arthur, which was discovered by means of the songs of the antient bards in the reign of Hen. II. the pyramids near the church, one of which is said to have been twenty-six feet high; and the mineral spring, said to have been discovered by means of a dream, which happened to a poor man, whose condition stood in need of its salutary streams. It is distant 109 computed, and 121 measured miles from London.

GLAS'TENBURY-THORN, S. in Botany, a variety of the common hawthorn, from which it differs in flowering twice a year; because, in mild seasons, it often flowers in November and December, and again at the usual time with the common sort.

To GLAZE, V. A. [accidently veiled from *glass*] to furnish windows with glass. To cover with a substance resembling glass. To cover with something shining. "Sorrow's eye glaz'd with blinding tears." *Shak.*

GLA'ZIER, S. one whose trade it is to make glass windows.

GLEAM', S. [pronounced *gleem*, *leme*, Sax.] a transient shoot of splendor; lustre; brightness.

To GLEAM', V. N. to shine with sudden and transient flashes.

GLEA'MY, Adj. flashing; darting sudden flashes of light.

To GLEAN', V. A. [pronounced *gleen*] to collect what is scattered and left by those who carry in a harvest. To gather any thing thinly scattered. To collect from different authors.

GLEAN', S. a collection made by slow degrees. "The *gleam* of yellow thyme defend his thighs." *Dryd.*

GLEAN'ER, S. one who gathers or picks up after the reapers. Figuratively, one who collects from a variety of authors.

GLEAN'ING, S. the act of picking up corn scattered and left by the husbandmen; the act of gathering any thing slowly. The act of collecting from different authors.

GLEBE', S. [*gleba*, Lat.] a clod; turf; soil; land. In Law, church land, or land possessed as part of an ecclesiastical benefice.

GLE'BOUS, Adj. abounding in clods.

GLE'BY, Adj. abounding in clods. Figuratively, fertile. "Diffus'd o'er virtue's gleby land." *Prior.*

GLEE', S. [*gli*, Sax.] joy or mirth; cheerfulness.

GLEE'FUL, Adj. full of joy; gay; cheerful; merry.

J R

To GLEEN', V. N. [perhaps either derived from, or a corruption of gleam] to shine with heat, or polish. "Hard gleaning armour." Prior.

GLEET. S. [written gleet, by Skinner, and derived from glidan, Belg. or glidan, Sax. to run slowly, or glide] the flowing or dripping of a humour from any wound. Usually applied to a flux or dripping of thin humour from the urethra.

To GLEET. V. N. to drop slowly, or flow with a thin humour. Figuratively, to run slowly. "Gleet down the rocky cavern." Cleyne.

GLEETY, Adj. resembling a gleet. Thin and serous.

GLEW, S. [glew, Brit.] a viscid, tenacious matter, used as a cement to join things together.

GLIB, Adj. [glib, Isl.] smooth; slippery; voluble, applied to speech. "Hear, on the clergy how glib his tongue ran." Swift.

GLIB'LY, Adv. [from glib, the adjective] smoothly; without any obstacle or impediment. "Slide glibly into detraction." Gov. of the Tongue.

GLIB'NESS, S. smoothness; slipperiness. Such smoothness of surface that any thing will slip off, if there be the least inclination. Volubility, applied to the tongue.

To GLIDE, V. N. [glidan, Sax.] to flow, or pass gently, smoothly, or without any tumult.

GLIDE, S. a falling motion. The act of passing smoothly.

To GLIM'MER, V. N. [glimmer, Dan.] to shine faintly, or feebly.

GLIM'MER, S. a faint or dim light.

GLIM'MERING, S. an imperfect view. "Got a glimmering who they were." Watson. A faint resemblance. A trace.

GLIMPSE, S. [glimmer, Dan.] a weak, faint, imperfect light. A sudden flashing light. "Light at the lightning glimpse they ran." Par. Lost. A transient lustre. A short fleeting enjoyment. "That I should know glimpse of delight." Prior. A faint resemblance, or likeness.

To GLISTEN, V. N. [glisigena, Sax.] to shine with lustre, brightness, or splendor.

GLISTER, S. See CLYSTER, which is the most proper spelling.

To GLIT'TER, V. N. [glitenan, Sax.] to shine with lustre. To gleam. To appear pompous.

GLIT'TER, S. lustre; splendour; brightness.

GLIT'TERINGLY, Adv. with a sparkling lustre.

To GLOAT', V. N. to look sideways at a person. To cast a stolen glance.

GLOBATED, Adj. in the shape of a globe.

GLOBE', S. [Fr. globus, Lat.] a round body having every part of its surface equally distant from the center. The earth. A sphere in which the various regions of the earth, seas, &c. are depicted in their proper forms, magnitudes, &c. and situations.

GLOBOSE, Adj. [globosus, Lat.] round or spherical.

GLOBOSITY, S. roundness.

GLOBOUS, Adj. [globosus, Lat.] round. "Large globous irons fly, of dreadful hiss." Philips.

GLOBULAR, Adj. [globulus, Lat. globul, Brit.] round; in the form of a globe, spherical.

GLOBULE, S. [globulus, Lat.] a small particle of matter of a round or spherical form.

GLOBULOUS, Adj. spherical; round.

To GLOMERATE, V. A. [glomerous, Lat.] to gather several parts or particles into a round body or sphere.

GLOMERATION, S. [glomeratio, Lat.] the act of forming several parts into a round ball or sphere. Something formed into a ball.

GLOMEROUS, Adj. [glomerosus, Lat.] gathered into a ball or sphere.

GLOOM', S. [glomung, Sax.] an imperfect, faint light; dulness.

To GLOOM', V. N. to shine obscurely. To be cloudy. Figuratively, to be melancholy, or sullen.

GLOO'MINESS, S. Duskiness. Darkishness, like that of twilight. Dismalness. Figuratively, want of chearfulness. Sullenness. Cloudiness of aspect. Sadness.

GLOO'MILY, Adv. dimly; Figuratively, sullenly. "How gloomily he look'd." Dryd.

GLOO'MY, Adj. obscure; imperfectly lightened. Dismal for want of light. Dark or blackish, applied to the complexion. Sullen; melancholy; sad, applied to the mind and look.

GLO'RIED, Adj. illustrious; honoured; dignified.

GLORIFICA'TION, S. [Fr.] the act of giving glory, attributing honour and praise. The act of exalting a person to the highest degree of dignity. A state of the highest dignity.

To GLO'RIFY, V. A. [glorifier, Fr.] To pay honour or praise in worship. To extol; honour, or praise. To exalt to a state of dignity, or glory.

GLO'RIOUS, Adj. [gloriosus, Lat.] haughty; proud; ostentatious. Figuratively, adorned with glory. Exalted to a state of dignity. Noble; illustrious.

GLO'RIOUSLY, Adv. illustriously; nobly; excellently.

GLO'RY, S. [gloire, Fr. gloria, Lat.] praise or honour. In Scripture, a state of felicity prepared for the righteous in heaven. Honour; praise; fame; renown. "Glory

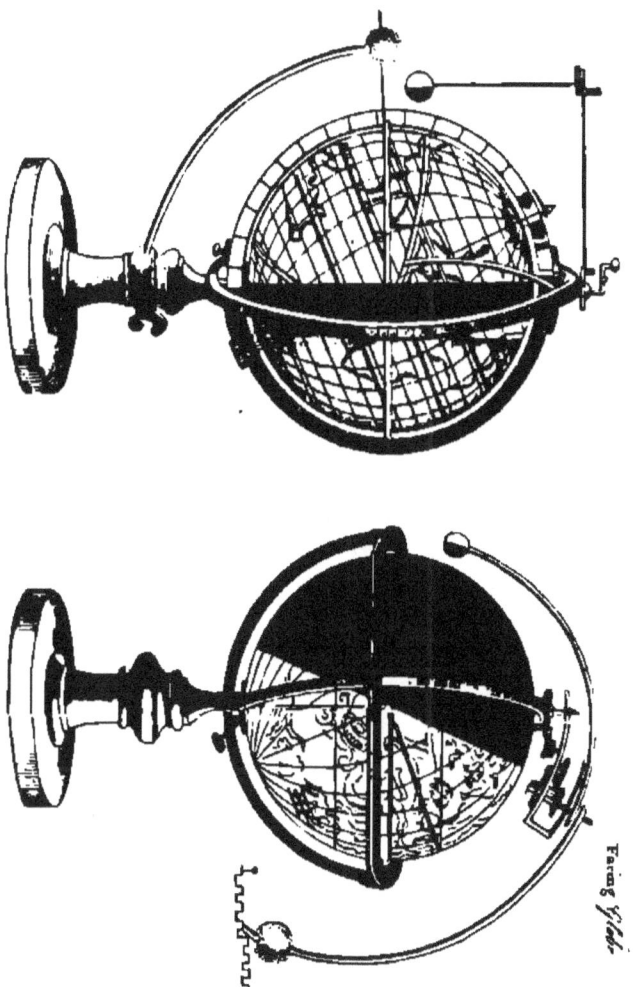

is like a circle in the water." *Shak.* A flame of splendour, dignity, and magnificence. "Solomon in all his *glory.*" *Mat.* vi. 29. Lustre, or brightness. In painting, a circle of rays surrounding the head of a person. Used with some pride; boasting, or arrogance. " By the *same glory* of men they entered into the world. *Wisd.* xix. 14.

To GLO'RY, V. N. to boast; to be proud of; to vaunt.

GLOSS, S. [Fr. *gloss*, Sax *glessa*, Gr.] an explanation of the sense or an author. Figuratively, a specious explanation of the words of an author to serve a particular purpose. A superficial lustre appearing on the surface; any smooth or polished body.

To GLOSS, V. N. [*gloss*, Fr.] to comment, on the sense of an author. Actively, to explain by a comment or note. To palliate by some specious reason or interpretation. " You have the art to *gloss* the foolishest cause." *Philips.* To make a thing shine. To embellish with superficial shew; used with *over.* " *Gloss'd* over only with a Giant-like shew." *Dryd.*

GLOSSARY, S. [*glossaire*, Fr.] a dictionary explaining obscure, provincial, and obsolete words.

GLOSSER, S. [*glossarius*, low Lat.] one who comments on and explains the writings of an author. A polisher.

GLOSSINESS, S. [*glossy*, Sax.] the shining lustre on the surface of a thing.

GLOSSY, Adj. having a shining and polished surface.

GLOVE, S. a covering worn upon the hands.

To GLOVE, V. A. to cover with a glove. " Must *glove* this hand." *Shak.*

GLOVER, S. one who makes and sells gloves.

GLOUCESTER, the capital town, or city, of Gloucestershire, with two markets, on Wednesdays and Saturdays, and four fairs, on April 5, for large quantities of cheese; on July 5, September 28, and November 28, for cattle and horses. It is seated on the E. side of the river Severne, where, by two several streams, it makes the isle of Alney. It is a large and well inhabited place, containing 12 churches, of which 6 only are in use, besides the cathedral of St. Peter, which is a handsome structure. It is remarkable for its large cloister, and whispering gallery. It is a city and county of itself, and is governed by a mayor, 12 aldermen, and common-council, who are never fewer than 28, nor above 39, a town-clerk, and a sword-bearer; the mayor is recorder of the city. The houses amount to some thousands, and the streets are broad and paved. It contains 5 hospitals and a free schools, and was fortified with a wall, which king Charles II. after the restoration ordered to be demolished. It

sends two members to parliament, and had the title of a dutchy. The eminent persons that were buried here were Lucius the first Christian king, Robert duke of Normandy, ledest son of William the Conqueror, and the unfortunate Edward II. Great quantities of pins are made here. It is 36 miles N. N. E. of Bristol, and 101 W. by N. of London. Lon. 2. 16 W. lat. 51. 50 E.

GLOUCESTERSHIRE, a county of England, 65 miles in length, and 32 in breadth; bounded on the W. by Herefordshire and Monmouthshire; on the N. by Worcestershire; on the E. by Warwickshire and Oxfordshire; and on the S. by Wiltshire and Somersetshire. It contains 26760 houses, 102,960 inhabitants, 280 parishes, and 27 market-towns. It sends only 8 members to parliament, 6 for three towns, and 2 for the county. The air is generally good, and the soil extremely fruitful. Cotswold hills are noted for feeding many flocks of sheep; and the rich vale of Evesham is remarkable for producing excellent wheat. The forest of Dean lies westward of the Severn, and was once full of oak-trees; but the iron-mines have consumed the greatest part. The rivers of most note are, the Isis, the Cherne, the Colne, the Lathe, the Windrush, the Evenlode, the Leden, the Avon, the Swilliate, the Caron, and the Stour.

To GLOUT, V. N. [of uncertain etymology] to pout; to look sullen. " *Glout-by* with full eyesight." *Garth.* A low word; still in use in Scotland, though obsolete in the southern part of this island.

To GLOW, V. N. [*glowan*, Sax.] to be heated without flame. To burn with vehement heat. To feel a heat in any part of the body. " Did not his temples *glow.*" *Addis.* To feel a warmth of passion, arising from the ardour of the mind. " The inward *glowings* of a heart in love." *Addis.* Figuratively, to rage or burn, applied to the manner in which any passion operates. Actively, to make hot so as to shine, or appear heated. " To *glow* the delicate cheeks." *Shak.*

GLOW, S. a shining heat. Vehemence or ardour. Brightness, or ruddiness.

GLOW-WORM, S. [from *glowe,* Sax.] a small creeping insect, which appears luminous in the dark.

GLOZE, S. flattery; soothing words. Insinuation. " Now to plain dealing; lay these *glozes* by." *Shak.*

GLUE, S. [*glue,* Brit.] a viscous substance to join bodies together. See GLEW.

To GLUE, V. A. [*gluer,* Fr.] to join together by a viscous cement. To hold together. Figuratively, to make a thing join; to unite as it were with glue. " Sink us down to sense, and *glue* us to those inferior things." *Tillots.* Used with *to.*

GLUM',

3 R 2

GLUM, Adj. sullen; affectedly grave. " Some when they hear a story look glum." *Guardian.*

To GLUT, V. A. [*glutir*, Brit. *englautir*, Fr.] to swallow or devour with little chewing. To cloy. To sate, or disgust. " Enough to *glut* the hearers." *Bac.* To feast or delight to satiety. " With death's excess *glut* the grave." *Milt.* To bring in large quantities; to overfill. " *Glutting* the market." *Arbuth.*

GLUT, S. that which is gorged in a ravenous manner. Plenty, or a quantity which occasions loathing and satiety. More than enough. Any thing which fills or stops up a passage by its excessive quantity.

GLUTINOUS, Adj. [*glutinous*, Fr.] resembling glue; viscous; Tenacious.

GLUTINOUSNESS, S. the quality of being viscid, or of sticking to those bodies which it touches. The quality of joining or cementing bodies by viscidity.

GLUTTON, S. [*glouton*, Fr. *glutio*, Lat.] one who eats to excess. Figuratively, one eager of any thing to excess. In Natural History, the name of a bird in the West-Indies.

To GLUTTONIZE, V. N. to eat to excess.

GLUTTONOUS, Adj. given to excess in eating.

GLUTTONOUSLY, Adv. after the manner of a glutton.

GLUTTONY, S. [*gloutonie*, Fr.] excess in eating.

GLUY, Adj. sticking; viscous; tenacious.

To GNASH, V. A. [*knatschen*, Belg. *gnasten*, Teut.] to strike, or clash together, applied to the teeth. To grind or strike the teeth together with a repeated, quick, or convulsive motion, either on account of rage, or from a sensation of excessive cold or agony.

GNAT, S. [*gnæt*, Sax.] a small winged insect, or fly, of which there are at least forty distinct species. The first thing remarkable in the generation of this insect is its vast spawn, being above an inch and half a quarter diameter, made to float on the water, and tied to some stick or other fixed thing by means of a small stem or stalk. This spawn is the receptacle for their eggs; which when hatched by the sun or warmth of the season into small maggots, descend to the bottom, and by means of some of the gelatine matter of the spawn, stick to stones, &c. where they make themselves little cases or cells, which they creep into and out of, till arrived to a more mature nympha state, and then swim about to seek for what food they have occasion; at this time they become red worms about half an inch long. Thus far this insect is an instance of the divine Providence; but if we proceed we shall find more

illustrious traces of the divine œconomy. In its vermicular state it is a red maggot, as we have just mentioned, and hath a mouth and other parts accommodated to food: in its aurelia state it has no such parts, because it subsists without food; but in its mature, gnat state, its mouth is furnished with a curious well made spear to wound and suck out the blood of other animals. Any thing remarkably, or proverbially small. " The blind guides, who strain at a *gnat*." *Matth.* xxiii. 14.

To GNAW, V. A. [*gnagan*, *gnafan*, Sax.] to bite and tear off by means of the teeth. To eat or chew. To fret, waste, or corrode, applied to the action of corrosive liquors. Neuterly, to bite, or tear in pieces with the teeth.

GNAWER, S. one who tears in pieces with the teeth.

GNOMON, S. [Gr. *γνωμων*] the hand, or index of a dial.

GNOMONICS, S. [*γνωμονικη*, Gr.] dialling. Or a science which teaches the doctrine of shadows for the construction of all sorts of sun dials.

To GO, V. N. [Preter. I *went*, I have *gone*, Participle *gone*, from *gan*, or *gangan*, Sax.] to walk. To move slowly. " Run to him, then had staid so long that going will not serve the turn." *Shak.* Used with *forth*, in Scripture, to walk in solemn procession. To proceed from one to another. " The jest goes round." *Dryd.* To depart, or move to a place. To move or pass in any manner; to go over, to peruse, or read through; to proceed in any operation of the mind. To pursue, used with *after*. To quit or change an opinion; to act contrary to a promise, or break a contract, to go *from*. To have recourse to, or to prosecute; joined with *low*. To go to *law*. To any send, or be near, undertaking a thing. " I was going to say." *Lock.* To let go, to give a person his liberty; to free from confinement or custody. To go *near*, to tend towards an act. Used with *for*, to pass, to be received for. " She goes *for* a woman." *Sidney.* To toll, applied to a bell. " The bell *goeth* for him." *Bac.* To move or to be in a state of motion, applied to machines, &c. " Clocks will go." *Otway.* To be regulated by any method; to proceed upon principles; to observe as a rule; used with *by*, or *upon.* To go *beyond*, to exceed in any quality. To go *further*, to extend in meaning, applied to words. Used with *about*, to attempt, or endeavour. To go *against*, to be offensive, applied to taste. To go *aside*, to err, or quit a rule of conduct. Used with *between*, to interpose, to mediate, or endeavour to reconcile. To go *by*, to pass unnoticed; to go *down*; to be swallowed; to be received with some difficulty, applied to opinion. Used with *in and out*, in Scripture, to be at liberty.

" He

" He shall go in and out." *John* x. 9. To die, used with *off*, to depart from a post, to run away or disappear, in order to escape some punishment. To *go to*, to proceed : Used with *over*, to revolt, or change ones party ; to pass upon a river or bridge. To *go out*. To be extinguished, applied to flame, or fire. Used with *through*, to perform thoroughly. To *go against the hair*, or *against the grain*, is a proverbial expression to express something extremely repugnant, or disagreeable.

GOA, a large and strong town of Asia, in the peninsula on this side the Ganges, and on the Malabar coast. It was taken by the Portuguese in 1508, and is the chief town of all the settlements which the Europeans have in India. It stands in an island about twelve miles in length, and six in breadth, and the city is built on the north side of it, having the conveniency of a fine salt-water river, capable of receiving ships of the greatest burthen, where they lie within a mile of the town. The banks of the river are beautified with a great number of handsome structures, such as churches, castles, and gentlemen's houses. The air within the town is unwholesome, for which reason it is not so well inhabited now as it formerly was. The viceroy's palace is a noble building, and stands at a small distance from the river, over one of the gates of the city, which leads to a spacious street, terminated by a beautiful church. This city contains a great number of handsome churches, convents, and cloisters, with a stately large hospital, all well endowed, and kept in good repair. The market place takes up an acre of ground ; and, in the shops about it may be had the produce of Europe, China, Bengal, and other countries of less note. Every church has a set of bells, some of which are continually ringing. Their religion is the Roman catholick ; and they have a severe inquisition. There are a great many Indian converts ; but they generally retain some of their old customs, particularly they cannot be brought to eat beef. However, there are many Gentoes in the city who are tolerated, because they are more industrious than the Christians, and better artists. The clergy are very numerous, and illiterate ; and the churches are finely embellished, and have great numbers of images. Their houses are large, and make a fine shew ; but within they are poorly furnished. The inhabitants are contented with greens, fruits, and roots, which, with a little bread, rice, and fish, is their principal diet, though they have hogs and fowls in plenty. However, they are very much addicted to women, and are generally weak, lean, and feeble. Our author, Capt. Hamilton, stood on a hill near the city, and counted above eighty churches, convents, and monasteries ; and he was told, that there were a-

bout 30,000 priests and monks. The body of St. Francis Xavier is buried in St. Paul's church, and at they pretend performs great many miracles. It is remarkable, that none of the churches, except one, have glass-windows ; for they make use of clear oyster-shells instead of glass, and all their fine houses have the same. Goa itself has few manufactures or productions, their best trade being in arrack, which they distill from toddy, which is the sap of the cocoa nut tree. The river's mouth is defended by several forts and batteries, well planted with large cannon, on both sides ; and there are several other forts in different places. It is 250 miles N. by W. of Cochin. Lon. 91. 35. lat. 15. 31.

GO'CART, S. a machine going upon casters, in which children are inclosed before they are able to walk.

GO'AD, S. [*gaad*, Sax.] a stick armed with a sharp point at the end, with which oxen, &c. are driven.

To GO'AD, V. A. to prick with a goad. Figuratively, to incite, or stimulate.

GOAL', S. a starting post. Figuratively, the design, or final purpose of any undertaking.

CO'AR, S. [pronounced *gore* from *gore*, Brit.] an edging sowed on cloth to strengthen it. The warm blood of any creature.

GO'AT, S. [*gat*, *ga*, Sax.] an horned animal, with coarse shag hair, which divides the hoof, is of a middle nature between a deer and sheep, remarkable for lasciviousness, and a rank smell when old. Figuratively, a rank, or lascivious person.

GOAT-CHAFFER, S. an insect resembling a beetle.

GOAT-HERD, S. [from *gat*, Sax. and *byrd*, Sax.] one who keeps goats.

GO'ATISH, Adj. resembling a goat, either in rankness or in lust.

GOB', S. [*gobe*, Fr.] a small quantity, generally applied to something glutinous, viscous or flabby.

GO'BBET, S. a mouthful.

To GO'BBLE, V. A. [*gober*, old Fr.] to swallow hastily, or ravenously.

GO'BBLER, S. one that devours hastily and without chewing.

GO'BETWEEN, S. a mediator ; or one who is sent backwards and forwards with messages between two parties.

GO'BLET, S. [*gobelet*, Fr.] a bowl or cup, that contains a large draught.

GO'BLIN, S. an evil spirit ; a spectre ; an elf, or fairy. " Go charge my goblins that they grind their joints." *Shak.*

GOD, S. [*God*, Sax. *God*, Isl. and Dan. *Gott*, *gudt*, Goth. *Gord*, Belg. *Gott*, Teut. of *Gad*, Sax. the adj. implying good ; the amiable and generous idea which our ancestors had of the divine being, may be seen from the denominating him from his attribute of good.

goodness; and the lesson this remark teaches us, is that which only can render our species amiable, and keep up his dignity] the self-existent infinitely perfect being, who created and preserves all things that have existence. The object of adoration and worship. Any person or thing which a person adores or esteems.

To GOD', V. A. to deify, or worship. Figuratively, to confer the greatest honours. " Lov'd me above the measure of a father, nay, godded me." *Shak.*

GOD'CHILD, S. an infant for whom one is a sponsor in baptism.

GOD'DAUGHTER, S. a female infant for whom a person is sponsor in baptism.

GOD'DESS, S. a female deity or divinity.

GOD'DESS-LIKE, Adj. beautiful resembling a goddess.

GOD'FATHER, S. [*godfæder*, Sax.] a man that is sponsor for a child at baptism.

GOD'HEAD, S. the condition, or nature of a god. Figuratively, " Nymphs and native goddeds yet unknown." *Dryd.*

GOD'LESS, Adj. without sense of acting. Atheistical; irreligious.

GOD'LIKE, Adj. divine; resembling God. Superlatively good.

GOD'LINESS, S. duty towards God. A general observation of all the duties flowing from our relations to, or prescribed by, God.

GOD'LY, Adj. having a proper sense of our duty to God. Pious, righteous.

GOD'LY, Adv. in a pious, religious and righteous manner.

GOD'MOTHER, S. a woman that is sponsor for a child in baptism.

GOD'SHIP, S. the office or character of a god. Figuratively, a deity. " O'er hills and dales their godships came." *Prior.*

GOD'SON, S. [*godsune*, Sax.] a male child whom a person has been sponsor to in baptism.

GOD'WARD, Adj. with respect to God. " Such trust have we through Christ godward." *a Cor.*

GO'ER, S. one that moves or runs. One that has a good pace, applied to a horse. One that keeps time, or is regular in its motions, applied to a watch or clock.

To GO'GGLE, V. N. to look asquint.

GOG'GLE-EYED, Adj. [*scêl-eye*, Sax.] not looking strait; or with the balls of the eye turned contrary ways.

GO'ING, S. the act of moving from one place to another. Pregnancy, applied to women. Departure, used with *from*, either expressed or understood.

GOLD', S. [Sax. and Teut. *gold*, Brit.] the heaviest, most dense, most ductile, and most fixed of all bodies; not to be injured by air or fire; its colour is of a shining and radiating yellow, which differs according to its purity. Figuratively, money, or any

thing very valuable, or very desirous.

GOLDBEATER, S. one who hammers gold into thin leaves, which are used by gilders. It is amazing to consider the fineness to which gold may be beaten; an ounce may be thus hammered into 1600 leaves, each three inches square, in which state it occupies more than 159,092 times its former space; twenty-five leaves of the smallest books weigh only five or six grains, and the same number of the largest only nine or ten grains. Goldbeater's skin is the latstinum rectum of an ox or bullock, well scoured and prepared, which is laid by goldbeaters between the leaves of the metal while they beat it.

GOLDEN, Adj. consisting of gold. Gilt. Figuratively, shining; bright: Splendid. Of the colour of gold. Happy; resembling the first age or state of innocence. Golden number, in chronology, is that which shews what year of the moon's cycle any particular year is. Golden rule, in Arithmetic, called also the Rule of three, by that by which a fourth number is sought, which is proportional to any three numbers given; the excellence and extent of this rule in most arithmetical operations, is the reason of its obtaining this title.

GOLDENLY, Adv. in a pompous commendable or splendid manner. " Report speaks goldenly of his profit." *Shak.*

GOLDEN-ROD, S. in Botany, called the *verge dora* in French, and *solidago* in Latin. Linnæus places it in the second sect of his 19th class, and Tournefort in the first sect of his 14th. There are thirty three species.

GOLDFINCH, S. [*goldfinc*, Sax.] a singing bird, having a reddish circle bordered with a yellow or golden colour on each side of its head. The Staffordshire people term it a *proud taylor*.

GOLDFINDER, S. one who finds gold; a name ludicrously given to a person that empties privies or jakes.

GOLDSMITH, S. [*goldsmið*, Dan.] one who makes and sells golden wares; as they were formerly, till banking became a separate business, the persons with whom merchants and traders lodged their cash; we find the word used, not only in banker's hands, but likewise in books, to denote a banker. " The goldsmith or scrivener, who takes all your fortune." *Swift.*

GONDOLA, S. [Ital. *gondola*, Fr.] a flat boat, very long, and very narrow, rowed by pushing forwards, and used upon the canals at Venice.

GONE, [Præter of go] advanced or proceeded in. Figuratively, lost or undone. " He must know 'tis none of your daughter — we are your elk." *Shak.* Used with *by*, past, applied to motion or change of place. Lost; departed; consumed; at an end. " The

"The hope of their gains was gone." *Atts.* xxi. 10. Dead. "A dog loses all figns of life; but carried into air, &c. recovers, if not quite gone." *Addif.*

GONORRHOE'A, S. [from γονη, Gr. and ρεω, Gr.] in medicine, an involuntary dripping of feed or other humour, occafioned by fome ftrain or venereal hurt.

GOOD, Adj. [comparative *better*, fuperlative *beft*; from *god* the feminine, of *goder*, Ifl.] requifite, fit and proper for the end. Wholefome. "Good to eat." *Prior.* Pleafant or agreeable to the tafte. "Eat thou honey becaufe it is good." *Prov.* xxiv. 13. Complete; full; great. "A good third of its people." *Addif.* "I have got a good deal." Sound; confiftent with reafon, applied to arguments. Valid. After *make*, confirmed, valid, eftablifhed, proved. "Make god your accufation." *South.* Ufed with *as* before and after it, no better than. "And him as good as dead." *Heб.* xl. No worfe. "As good as his word." *L'Eftran.* Good at; fkilful, or ready; dexterous. "But you are good at a retreat." *Dryd.* Happy, or profperous. "Good morrow, Portia." *Advif.* Joined to *name*, character; reputation. "Good name in man or woman—is the immediate jewel of their fouls." *Shak.* Cheerful; gay; inclined to acts of benevolence and kindnefs. *Good breeding*, elegant, decent, delicate, polite, confiftent with the character of gentlemen. "Patterns of wit and good breeding." *Swift.* In commerce, a good man, one who is rich, or able to difcharge all his engagements and obligations. Virtuous, or endowed with all moral qualities or virtues. *Good to*, kind, or benevolent. "The men were very good to us." 1 *Sam.* xxv. 15. Joined with *fellow*, fociable; free; fond of elegant feafts or drink. "Though he did not draw the good fellows to him by eating." *Clarend.* Ties, good, early, joined to *make*, to perform what is promifed or expected; to keep or maintain. "Make good their retreat." *Clarend.*

GOOD, S. It is divided into phyfical and moral; *Phyfical good*, tends naturally to promote our happinefs, benefit, advantage or health. *Moral good*, is that which is chofen agreeable to the laws of reafon or God, and has a tendency to promote both our own happinefs and that of others. Figuratively, profperity. "The gods are fund of the ftate." *Ben Jonfon.* Ufed after *had*, with *as*, it feems a fubftantive, but has rather an adverbial fenfe, and is ufed improperly for *will*. "He had as good leave his veffel to the waves." *South.*

GOOD, Adv. equal, thus *as good* implies no worfe.

GOOD, Interject. well; right.

GOOD-CONDITIONED, Adj. without any ill qualities; laudable, applied to matter, in Surgery... In commerce, without

any injury, or damage. Lufty, or plump, applied to perfons.

GOODLINESS, S. beauty; grace; elegance.

GOODLY, Adj. beautiful; graceful; fine; fplendid. Bulky; fwelling. Happy; defirable. "We have many goodly days to fee." *Shak.*

GOODMAN, S. a flight appellation of civility, fometimes ufed ironically, and fometimes applied in the country dialect in the fame fenfe as gaffer. "Here your goodman deliver." *Shak.*

GOODNESS, the fitnefs or propriety of a thing. Perfection. Kindnefs, or benevolence, applied to actions.

GOOD-NOW, Interj. prithee. "Goodnow fit down and tell me." *Shak.* Sometimes ufed to exprefs wonder. "Good-now, good-now, how your devotions jump with mine!" *Dryd.*

GOODS, S. the furniture of a houfe. Wares bought and fold in trade; commodities in a fhip.

GOODY, S [godig, Sax.] a low term of civility ufed to perfons of the female fex.

GOOSE, S. [plural, geefe of gis, Sax.] a large water fowl, proverbially noted for foolifhnefs. A taylor's preffing iron.

GOOSEBERRY, S. [fuppofed to be derived from gofe and berry, becaufe eaten with geefe as fauce; in Botany, named groffularia in Lat. and groffeiur, Fr. Linnæus places it in the firft fect. of his fifth clafs, and Tournefort in the fifth fect. of his twenty-firft. The fpecies are five.

GORBELLY, S. a large portuberant belly.

GORBELLIED, Adj. lufty; fat; large; having a large and fwelling belly. "Hang ye, gorbellied knaves." *Shak.*

GORE, S. [Sax. gor, Brit.] blood; congealed blood.

To GORE, V. A. to pierce with a weapon, or the horns of an animal, fo as to make a wound. Among femftreffes, to widen any thing, by fowing in a piece of cloth.

GORGE, S. In Falconry, the uppermoft bag, ftomach, or crop of a hawk. Figuratively, the throat, or fwallow. That which is gorged or fwallowed.

To GORGE, V. N. [gorger, Fr.] to fill up to the throat. To glut or fatiate, followed by *with*. To fwallow. "The fifh has gorged the hook."

GORGED, Adj. In Heraldry, ufed when a crown or coronet is borne round the neck of fome fowl; or when the neck of a bird is of a different colour from the reft.

GORGEOUS, S. [gorgias, old Fr.] fine; fplendid; glittering in various colours; pompous; generally applied to drefs.

GORGEOUSLY, Adv. in a fplendid, pompous, fhowy manner.

GOR'-

GO'RGEOUSNESS, S. splendor; lustre; magnificence; pomposity.

GO'RGET, S. the piece of armour which is worn round the thrust.

GO'RMAND, S. [*gourmand*, Brit.] a person who eats to excess.

To GO'RMANDIZE, V. N. to eat to excess.

GO'RMANDIZER, S. one who eats to excess.

GO'RY, Adj. covered with congealed blood. Bloody; murtherous. " A *gory* emulation 'twixt us twain." *Shak.*

GO'SLING, S. [of *gos*, Sax.] a young goose.

GO'SPEL, S. [*gospel* implies rather good news, than the history of God, as some imagine, as may be evident from considering that *godspiel*, (S. *gospel*, Brit. and *evangy*, Saxe, bear the same signification, not to mention that it is confirmed by all translations of the New Testament; whether in Syriac, Persic, Æthiopic, Coptic, Russian, Bohemian, Teutonic, Danish, &c. &c.] the title of books containing the history of the transactions of our blessed Lord and Saviour from his birth to his ascension. Figuratively, applied to signify the Christian dispensation, and an infallible standard of truth.

GO'SSIP, S. [from *godsibe*, Sax.] a person who is the sponsor for a child at baptism. Figuratively, one who runs about tattling and prating.

To GO'SSIP, V. N. to chat; to prate; to spend time in frivolous discourse. ..

GOT, Preter, and participle of GET.

GOTTEN, participle passive of GET.

To GO'VERN, V. A. [*gouverner*, Fr.] to rule over as a superior. Figuratively, to direct, influence, manage, or restrain. In Grammar, to require. "I Amo *govern* an accusative case." In Navigation, to pilot, or to direct a ship's motions. Neuterly, to keep superiority or authority over others. Figuratively, to command over others. To behave with haughtiness and tyranny.

GO'VERNABLE, Adj. obedient to command, rule, and authority.

GO'VERNANCE, S. the act of exercising authority over others. Government. The authority of a guardian. " Under the surly Gloster's *governance*." *Shak.*

GO'VERNANTE, S. [Fr.] a woman who has the care of young ladies. See GOVERNESS.

GO'VERNESS, S. [*gouvernesse*, old Fr.] a female invested with authority to rule. " The moon, the *governess* of floods." *Shak.* A woman who has the care of instructing young ladies. The teacher or mistress of a lady's boarding school.

GO'VERNMENT, S. [*gouvernement*, Fr.] an establishment, or administration of public affairs. The authority exercised by magistrates over their subjects, or by one person

over another. Regularity of behaviour; dominion over the passions; command, or use of one's limbs or faculties. " Each part deprived of supple *government*." *Shak.* In Grammar, the particular construction any word in a sentence requires.

GO'VERNOR, S. [*gouverneur*, Fr.] one who has the supreme direction of a thing or person. One invested with supreme authority in a state. One who presides over, or rules in, any place by warrant or commission from the supreme magistrate. One who has the care of young gentlemen.

GOU'GE, S. [Fr.] a chissel with a round edge.

GOUG'EE, S. [Fr.] in Surgery, a remedy used in venereal complaints to keep the passage open for the urine.

GO'UARD, S. [*gouardes*, Fr.] a plant which creeps along the earth like the cucumber, and produces a yellow fruit of the size and colour of an orange.

GOU'T, S. [*goutte*, Fr.] in Medicine, a painful kind of disease principally affecting the joins, seated in their ligaments, the tendons of the muscles subservient to their motions, and the membranes surrounding the bones. When seated in the joints it is called *arthritis*; when in the feet *podagra*, and when in the hands, *chiragra*. A drop. " *Gouts* of blood." *Shak.*

GOU'T, S. [pronounced *goo*, Fr. *gustus*, Lat.] a taste; relish; or flavour. " A *gout* for the like studies." *Watts*. Johnson censures this phrase as affected earn.

GOU'TY, Adj. affected with the gout. Relating to the gout. Figuratively, swelled or shaped like one that has the gout.

GOWN, S. [*gwn*, Brit. *gonna*, Ital.] a long loose upper garment, worn by men. A woman's upper garment. The long, loose, habit worn by those matriculated at universities; by the ministers of the established church; or the livery and other persons belonging to a corporation. Figuratively, peace, or the dress of peace. " He Mars deposed and *gowns* to arms made yield." *Dryd.*

GOW'NED, Adj. wearing a gown.

GOW'NMAN, S. one matriculated at an university. A student; a clergyman; a lawyer, &c.

To GRA'BBLE, V. N. to grope; to search.

GRACE, S. [Fr. *gratia*, Lat.] favour, or kindness. Virtue, or the effect of the divine influence. Pardon. A kindness; a privilege, or favour conferred. Elegant behaviour, or the air and appearance wherewith any thing is done. Beauty, an embellishment; ornament; flower; or perfection. " By their hands, the *grace* of kings must die." *Shak.* A physical virtue, or power. " Mickle is the powerful *grace* that lies in plants." *Shak.* The title of a duke. A short prayer said at meals, expressive of gratitude

titude in the divine providence for supplying our necessities. One of the heathen deities, supposed to bestow beauty.

To GRA'CE, V. A. to adorn, embellish, set off, or recommend. To confer an honour on a person; to dignify or raise by an act of favour. "Grac'd by a nod." *Dryd.* To favour, or honour. "Nor grac'd with kind adieu." *Dryd.*

GRA'CED, Adj. beautiful; graceful. "The properest and best grac'd men that ever I saw." *Shocp.* Virtuous; regular; chaste; consistent with dignity and decorum. "More like a tavern or a brothel—than a grac'd palace." *Shak.*

GRA'CEFULLY, Adv. elegantly; majestically.

GRA'CEFULNESS, S. elegance. Dignity joined with beauty.

GRA'CELESS, Adj. without any virtue, either religious, or moral. Without a sense of duty to, or any influence arising from the favour of, God. Wicked or impious.

GRA'CES, S. [seldom used in the plural] joined with good, favour or esteem.

GRA'CIOUS, Adj. [gracieux, Fr.] merciful; benevolent; kind; favourable; or bestowing favours. Acceptable; received with pleasure. Virtuous or good, "Their life not being gracious." *Shak.* Excellent, graceful, or becoming.

GRA'CIOUSLY, Adv. with kind condescension. In a favourable manner.

GRA'CIOUSNESS S. kind condescension. A favourable manner.

GRADA'TION, S. [Fr. of gradus, Lat.] a regular progress or advance from one degree to another, or step by step. An arrangement of proofs rising out of, and increasing the strength of those which precede.

GRA'DUAL, Adj. [graduel, Fr.] proceeding by degrees. Advancing step by step, or from one stage to another.

GRA'DUAL, S. [gradus] a flight of steps. "Before the gradual prostrate they ador'd." *Dryd.*

GRADU'ALITY, S. a regular progression, or advancing by degrees. "The graduality of opacity." *Brown.*

GRA'DUALLY, Adv. by degrees. In regular progression; by steps.

To GRA'DUATE, V. A. [of gradus, Lat.] to dignify with a degree in an university. To mark with degrees, in measuring. "He graduates his thermometers." *Derham.* In Chemistry, to raise to a higher place or value in the scale of metals. To heighten or improve.

GRA'FF, or GRAFT, S. [greffe, Fr.] in Gardening, the shoot of a tree inserted in, and becoming one with another tree.

To GRAFT, V. A. [greffer, Fr.] to take a shoot from one tree, and insert it into another, that both may unite closely, and become one

No. XIII.

tree. To insert into a place, or body, to which it did not originally belong. Figuratively, to join or unite one thing so as to receive support from another. Used with in or upon, "Graft my love immortal on thy fame." *Pope.* Among sempstresses, &c. to mend, by joining a piece, in a particular manner, to a garment.

GRA'IN, S. [grawn, Brit. graine, Fr. granum, Lat.] a single seed of corn or fruit. Figuratively, corn. Any minute particle. Any thing proverbially small. Joined with allowance; some small indulgence, which implies a remission of rigour or severity. "He whose very best actions must be seen with some grains of allowance." *Addis.* A weight used in physic, twenty of which make one scruple; in troy weight, twenty-four make a penny weight. The direction in which the fibres of wood, leather, &c. grow. In Dying, a method of communicating colours, so as to make them more lasting than in the common way, this is done by dying the commodities before they are wrought in the loom, &c. Figuratively, a colour. "Sky-tinctur'd grain," *Par. Los.* The form of the surface, with regard to smoothness, roughness, or the size of the constituent fibres, or particles of a body. "Bringing its roughness to a very fine grain." *Newt. Opt.* Temper; disposition; inclination. "Though much against the grain forced to retire." *Dryd.*

GRA'INED, Adj. rough, or weatherbeaten. "Then now this grained face of mine be hid." *Shak.*

GRAIN'S, S. [it has no singular in this sense] the bulks of malt after beer has been made.

GRA'INY, Adj. full of corn or seeds.

GRAMINI'VOROUS, Adj. [of gramen, and voro, Lat.] eating, or living upon grass. "The graminivorous kind." *Sharp.*

GRA'MMAR, S [grammaire, Fr.] the art which teaches the rules for speaking, or writing any language properly. Figuratively, an expression agreeable to the rules of grammar. A book which delivers rules for speaking or writing a language with propriety. *Grammar-school,* is a place where the classics are taught.

GRAMMA'RIAN, S. [grammairien, Fr.] one who is skilful in, the rules of grammar.

GRAMMA'TICAL, Adj. [Fr. of grammaticus, Lat.] belonging or relating to grammar. Consistent with the propriety of any language.

GRAMMA'TICALLY, Adv. agreeable to the rules of grammar.

GRAMATICA'STER, S. [Lat.] a mere verbal critic, or low grammarian. A word of reproach and contempt.

GRA'MPLE, S. [grampie, Fr. grandis, Ital.] a crab-fish.

GRAM-

GRA'MPUS, S. a large fish something of the whale kind.

GRANA'DO, S. a hollow ball or shell, of iron, brass, glass, or potter's earth, filled with gunpowder, and fitted with a fuse to give it fire. There are two forts, that which is thrown by a mortar, and called a bomb; but that which is thrown by the hand more properly bears this name, and is commonly called a hand grenado.

GRA'NARY, S. [granarium, Lat.] a storehouse for corn.

GRA'NATE, S. [from granum, Lat.] a kind of marble so called from it refembling grains in its variegations; more properly spelt Granite. A precious stone of a high red colour, so called from the refemblance it bears to that of a kernel of a pomegranate, is is vulgarly named a garnet. The oriental are by far the best.

GRA'ND, Adj. [Fr. grand; Lat.] great, illustrious, powerful, applied to place or dignity. Splendid or magnificent, applied to appearance. Noble, sublime, or lofty, applied to sentiments or style.

GRA'NDAM, or GRANDA'ME, S. a term of consanguinity, denoting the father's or mother's mother. Figuratively, an old decrepit woman. "To the grandame hag." Dryd.

GRAND CHILD, S. the son or daughter of a person's son or daughter.

GRA'ND-DAUGHTER, S. the daughter of a son or daughter.

GRANDE'E, S. [grand, Fr. grandis, Lat.] a person of rank, dignity, or power.

GRA'NDEUR, S. [Fr.] splendor, pomp, or magnificence, applied to rank and external appearance. Elevation or sublimity, applied to sentiment or language.

GRA'ND-FATHER, S. the father of a person's father or mother.

GRA'NDSIRE, S. a grandfather. In Poetry, any ancestor. In the pedigree of a horse, the horse that begot the dam or horse from whence that which is mentioned proceeded.

GRA'NDSON, S. the son of a person's son or daughter.

GRANGE, S. [Fr.] a farm. A barn, or threshing floor. A farm house.

GRA'NITE, S. [grani, Fr. of granum, Lat. because representing small grains or particles] a stone or marble composed of separate and very large concretions, rudely compacted together, of great hardness, giving fire when struck with steel; fermenting with acids, and imperfectly calcinable in a great fire.

GRANI'VOROUS, Adj. [granum, Lat. and voro, Lat.] living upon grain. "Granivorous birds." Arbut.

GRA'NNAM, S. grandmother. A low word, used only in burlesque.

To GRANT, V. A. [of garantir, Fr.] to admit or allow a thing not proved. To bestow something which cannot be claimed.

GRANT, S. the act of giving a thing which cannot be claimed as a right. The thing granted. A conceffion, or admiffion of something in a difpute.

GRA'NTABLE, Adj. that which may be yielded to another, though it cannot be claim it.

GRANTE'E, S. In Law, the person to whom a grant is made.

GRANTHAM, a town of Lincolnshire, with a market on Saturdays, and five fairs on the fifth Monday in Lent, for horned cattle, horfes, and sheep; on Holy Thursday, for sheep and horfes; on July 10, October 16, and December 17, for horned cattle and horfes. It is seated on a bottom on the river Witham, and is a noted place, with a good free school, and a handsome church, famous for its high spire, which seems to lean on one fide. It is a corporation, sends two members to parliament, and has the title of an earldom. It is 21 miles N. by W. of Stamford, 14 N. by E. of Newark, and 104 N. by W. from London. Lon. 16. 55 lat. 52. 50.

GRA'NTOR, S. the person that grants any thing to another.

GRA'NULARY, Adj. [from granule] small and compact, refembling a small grain.

To GRA'NULATE, V. N. [granuler, Fr.] to be formed into small particles. Actively, to break into small maffes or grains. To raife in inequalities. "Granulated into a multitude of glandules." Ray.

GRANULA'TION, S. [Fr.] the act of forming into small maffes like grains.

GRA'NULE, S. a particle. A small compact particle refembling a feed or grain.

GRA'NULOUS, Adj. full of little grains or feeds.

GRAPE, S. [grappe, Fr. grappillo, Ital. druppo, Belg.] a fingle berry of the vine, which grows in clusters.

GRA'PHICAL, Adj. [from graphe, Gr.] appearing as if written. Well deferibed or delineated. "The letters will grow more large and graphical." Bacon.

GRA'PHICALLY, Adv. well deferibed; deferibed minutely.

GRA'PNEL, S. [grapin, Fr.] a small anchor belonging to a little veffel.

To GRA'PPLE, V. N. [grappen, grappelen, Sax.] to lay fast hold on a person like wreftlers. To engage in close fight. Actively, to faften, unite, or join infeparably. "Grapple you to the heart and love of us." Shak. To feize, or lay fast hold of.

GRA'PPLE, S. a close combat or engagement. An iron instrument to fasten one ship to another.

GRA'SIER, S. See GRAZIER.

To

To GRA'SP, V. A. [grafpare, Ital.] to hold fast in the hand with the fingers shut. Figuratively, to seize, or catch at. Neuterly, to catch, or endeavour to seize. To struggle, strive, or grapple; perhaps a corruption instead of gripe. " As one that grasps and tugg'd for life." Shak. To gripe; to encroach. " Who grasps and gripes till he can hold no more." Dryd.

GRA'SP, S. the gripe or seizure of the hand. The act of holding a thing fast in the hand with the fingers shut or doubled over it. Figuratively, possession, or hold. " The whole space that's in the tyrant's grasp." Sink. The power or opportunity of seizing. " Had it within their grasp." Shread.

GRA'SPER, S. one who seizes or grasps.

GRA'SS, S. [græs, Goth.] the common herbage of the fields, on which cattle feed, of which there are several species. All flesh is grass; though by some taken to be expressive of its frail and transient state; may be applied in its literal sense, as appears from Barbaut's Academ. Lect. Vol. I.

To GRA'SS, V. N. to produce grass.

GRA'SSHO PER, S. a small insect, found among the summer grass, named from its hopping, for which it is remarkably formed by nature with brawny thighs, long, slender and strong legs, &c. Though our poets translate the cicada of the Latins, and the cicala of the Italians by this word, yet it is an impropriety, because not only Latin and his best authors, but likewise Homer represents them as having a shrill musical note, which can by no means be applied to our grasshopper. In Scripture, it is used as a proverbial expression to denote something very small.

GRA'SSINESS, S. the state of abounding in grass.

GRA'SSPLAT, S. a piece of ground in a garden, &c. covered with grass.

GRA'SSY, Adj. covered with, or abounding in grass.

GRA'TE, S. [crates, Lat.] a partition made with iron bars, &c. placed at the windows of prisons, or cloisters. An immoveable receptacle with iron bars, fixed in kitchens, in which fires are made.

To GRA'TE, V. A. [gratter, Fr.] to wear off the particles from any thing by rubbing it on a rough body. To offend by any thing harsh or vexatious. To offend the ear by a harsh and disagreeable sound. Neuterly, to rub hard, so as to offend or hurt. To offend either by oppression or importunity.

GRA'TEFUL, Adj. [gratus, Lat.] having a due sense of benefits conferred, and being ready both to acknowledge and return them. Pleasing; agreeable; delightful; delicious.

GRA'TEFULLY, Adv. in a manner

willing to acknowledge and repay a proper sense of the obligation arising from a favour or benefit received. In a pleasing or agreeable manner.

GRA'TEFULNESS, S. gratitude. The quality of being agreeable, or affording delight or pleasure.

GRA'TER, S. [grattoir, Fr.] a kind of instrument made of tin punched in holes, with which soft things are rubbed to powder.

GRATIFICA'TION, S. [Fr. gratificatio, Lat.] the act of pleasing. The act of answering the cravings of the sensual appetites. Pleasure. Delight. A reward, or recompence. The last sense is censured by Johnson as low; let others judge whether he has reason for so doing.

To GRA'TIFY, V. A. [gratifier, Fr.] to indulge; to please by compliance. To do a thing in order to please or delight. To requite, or reward. " I'll gratify you for your trouble."

GRA'TINGLY, Adv. harshly; offensively; in such a manner as to offend the ears with an harsh and disagreeable sound.

GRA'TIS, Adv. [Lat.] for nothing. Without receiving any thing in return.

GRA'TITUDE, S. a virtue, consisting in a due sense of a benefit received, together with a readiness to return the same.

GRATU'ITOUS, Adj. [gratuitus, Lat. gratuit, Fr.] voluntary. Asserted without proof. " This gratuitous declination of atoms." Ray.

GRATU'ITOUSLY, Adv. without claim or merit. Without proof.

GRATU'ITY, S. [gratuité, Fr.] a free gift; a present; an acknowledgement; a compensation.

To GRA'TULATE, V. A. [gratulator, Lat.] to congratulate. To complement with expressions of joy on account of success, of some good in possession, or escape from some danger.

GRATULA'TION, S. [gratulatio, Lat.] salutations made by expressing joy. Compliments expressing joy on account of success, the possession of some good, preferment, or escape from danger. An expression of joy. " The earth — gave signs of gratulation." Par. Lost.

GRA'TULATORY, Adj. expressing joy for the success of another. Congratulatory.

GRA'VE, S. [graf, Sax. graft] a hole dug in the ground wherein a dead body is to be buried.

To GRA'VE, V. A. [preter graved, participle pass. graven, of grafen, Sax.] to copy pictures or writings with a sharp pointed instrument, on wood, copper, or pewter, in order to be printed on paper. To carve, or form any image or statue by means of a chissel. " What profiteth the graven image   that

that the maker thereof hath *graven* it."
Heb. ii. 11. To inter, entomb, or bury.
To clean, caula, or fcrape the bottom of a
fhip, from *krauwen*, Belg. to fcrape. Neuterly, to write or form letters on a hard
fubftance by means of a fharp pointed inftrument.

GRA'VE, Adj. [Fr. *gravis*, Lat.] folemn;
ferious. Of a mixtell, plain colour. Not
fharp or acute, applied to found. Credible;
not fighty, applied to writing or ftile. " The
grave of their writers." *Grew.*

GRA'VEL, S. [*gravele*, Fr. *gravelle*,
Ital.] a kind of earth ufed for walks in
gardens, the finer part of which is yellow,
and appears like a large printed fand. In
Phyfic, a difeafe in the kidneys or bladder,
occafioned by a gritty collection of matter
therein, whereby the due fecretion and ex-
cretion of the urine is impeded, from gra-
vels. Fr. When this fubftance forms a hard
mafs, it is called the ftone.

To GRA'VEL, V. A. to pave, or cover
with gravel. Figuratively, to puzzle, put to
a ftand, or embarrafs a perfon with fome
difficulty he cannot folve. In Farriery, to
hurt the foot of a horfe, by fmall ftones, or
gravel, which gets in between the fhoe and
hoof.

GRA'VELESS, S. without a grave or
tomb.

GRA'VELLY, Adj. [*graveleux*, Fr.] confifting of gravel.

GRA'VELY, Adv. in a folemn, or ferious
manner; oppofed to levity or mirth. Without gaudinefs or fhow, applied to drefs or
fike.

GRA'VENESS, S. ferioufnefs. Solemnity. A behaviour free from levity, or the
fudden fourth of mirth, and regulated by wifdom and fobriety.

GRA'VER, S. [*graveur*, Fr.] an engraver. The fharp pointed inftrument ufed
by an engraver.

GRA'VESEND, a town of Kent, with
two markets, on Wednefdays and Saturdays,
and two fairs, on April 17, and November
25, for horfes and all other goods, cloaths,
and toys. It is feated on the banks of the
Thames, and is a place of great refort, becaufe it is the common landing place for feamen and ftrangers in their paffages to London, there being tilt boats ready to carry
them every tide. It is well ftocked with
houfes of entertainment; and here is a block-
houfe over againft Tilbury fort. A great
part of it was burnt down with the church in
1727, which has been fince rebuilt as
one of the fifty new churches, and the
houfes are much handfomer than before
It is commonly called the corporation of
Gravefend and Milton, thefe two places being
united under the government of a mayor, 12
aldermen, 24 common council, a town-clerk,

&c. This parifh, with that of Milton, confifts of about 700 houfes, moftly fmall, and
built with bricks; the ftreets are alfo narrow,
but paved with flints. The chief employment of the labouring people is fpinning of
hemp, to make nets for fifhing, and ropes.
It is alfo famous for gardening, the beft afpa-
ragus being produced here of any in the
kingdom.

GRAVI'DITY, S. [*graviditas*, Lat.] the
ftate of being with child. " The figns of
gravidity." *Arbuth.*

GRA'VING, S. any piece engraved.
Carved work.

To GRA'VITATE, V. N. [from *gravis*,
Lat.] to tend to the center.

GRAVITA'TION, S. the act of tending
to the center.

GRA'VITY, S. [*gravitas*, Lat.] weight;
heavinefs. The power by which bodies naturally tend to the center. *Abfolute gravity*,
is that property which is in all bodies, in
proportion to their quantity of matter without any regard to their bulks; or the whole
force by which any body tends downwards.
Relative gravity, is the excefs of gravity in
one body above that of another of equal
bulk, and is always as the quantity of matter
under thofe dimenfions. *Gravity*, applied to
the nature of actions, denotes their nature,
or quality; but when applied to crimes, their
atrocioufnefs. Applied to the countenance,
or behaviour; ferioufnefs, folemnity, or
majefty.

GRA'VY, S. the juice which runs from
meat when not too much done.

GRAY, Adj. [*gray*, Sax. *grav*, Dan.
graew, Belg.] white with a mixture of
black. White or hoary with age; blue with
a mixture of black, refembling the colour
of afhes. Applied to the light of the clofing
or opening day, dark.

GRA'Y-BEARD, S. figuratively, an old
man; ufed in contempt. " Aterud to tell
gray-beards the truth." *Shak.*

GRA'YNESS, S. the quality of being
gray.

To GRAZE, V. N. [*grafan*, Sax.] to
feed on grafs. To produce grafs. Figuratively, to move or devour. " The fire perpetually *grazed*." *Fac.* To brufh in paffing,
to touch lightly; generally applied to a bullet. " Lice to lie bullet's *grazing*." *Shak.*
To eat grafs. " Lambs with wolves fhall
graze the verdant mead." *Pope.*

GRA'ZIER, S. one who feeds or breeds
cattle for food.

GREASE, S. [*graiffe*, Fr.] the foft part
of the fat of animals.

To GREASE, V. A. to fmear, or anoint
with greafe. Figuratively, to bribe or corrupt with prefents. " The *greas'd* advocate."
Dryd.

GREA'SINESS, S. fatnefs.

GREA'SY,

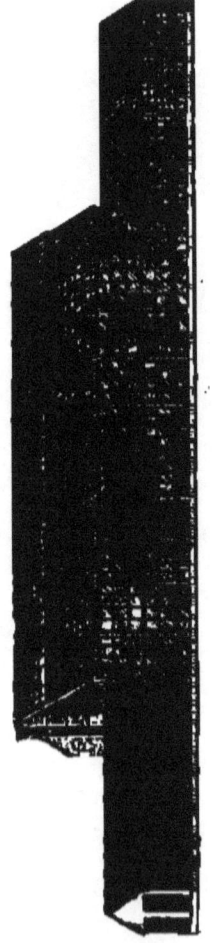

Shed

Ground Plan.

Shed

GRE'ASY, Adj. oily; fat, (potted; corpulent.

GREAT, Adj. [great, Sax. groot, Belg.] Having any quality in a high degree. Long, applied to time, or duration. Chief or principal. "The great seal." Shak. High in rank. Illustrious, or eminent. "Great in might." Jer. n. h. Majestic, or grand in aspect o mein, "She walks serenely great." Waller. Haughty, swelling, or proud. Great with, familiar, intimately acquainted. "Those that are great with them." Bac. Teeming, or with child. with matter; difficult; hard; grievous. "It is no great matter to live lovingly with good-natured, and meek persons,". Taylor. In pedigree, it is added in every step of ascending consanguinity beyond a father or grandfather, and in every step of descending consanguinity beyond a grandson: Thus a great grandson is the son of a person's grandson. A great grandfather, the father of a person's grandfather.

GREAT-BELLIED, Adj. pregnant. "Great-bellied women." Shak.

To GRE'ATEN, V. N. to enlarge; to make great, powerful or rich. "After they sought to greaten themselves in Italy." Raleigh.

GRE'ATLY, Adv. In a great degree, very much. Nobly; In an illustrious manner. "Thou greatly didst expire Dryd. Courageously, bravely "Great'y turn their backs against the foe." Addisf. An ironical expression.

GRE'ATNESS, S. largeness, applied to quantity, size, or number. Excess, arising from a comparative view of things. An high degree of any quality. High place or dignity; large extent, or influence, applied to power or empire. A consciousness of superior birth or rank. "'Tis not of pride or greatness he cometh not on board." Bac. Magnanimity, nobleness, or a state wherein a person is above doing or thinking of low and mean things. "Greatness of mind and nobleness." Par. Lost. Grandeur; state; magnificence; largeness, applied to size. Greatness with Timon- brings all Embalming before your thought." Pope.

GRE'CISM, S. [græcismus, Lat.] a construction, or idiom, peculiar to the Greek language.

GREE'DILY, Adv. In an eager, hasty, or ravenous manner.

GREE'DINESS, S. [grædignesse, Sax.] ravenousness. Figuratively, eagerness of appetite or desire.

GREE'DY, Adj. [grædig, Sax.] ravenous; hungry; lacked with a violent desire of food. Figuratively, eager; vehemently desirous; generally taken in a bad sense, for the effects of an insatiably covetous disposition of mind.

GREEN, Adj. [grene, Sax.] having colour resembling grass. Figuratively, flourishing; fresh, undecayed New, or lately made. "A green wound." Having its juice, opposed to dry, and applied to wood. Not well roasted; half raw, applied to meat. "We say the meat is green, when half roasted." Watts. Unripe; immature; young; alluding to fruits being green when in their first state, before they are ripe. "Green geese." Martim.

GREEN, S. the colour of grass. In Optics, it is one of the original or primary rays of light; but in dying is caused by compounding blue and yellow, &c. As this colour refreshes the sight, the goodness of providence is manifested in causing it to be reflected from the surface of vegetables, preferably to any other. Figuratively, a plain covered with grass. In Cookery, used in the plural for those plants which are eaten boiled, and are of this colour.

To GREEN, V. A. to make a green colour. "Green'd all the year." Turf.

GREEN'CLOTH, S. a board held in the counting-house of the king's houshold, for taking cognisance of all matters of government and justice within the king's court royal; and for correcting all the servants that offend.

GREEN'FINCH, S. [grønfinc, Teut.] a bird so called from its colour.

GREE'NGAGE, S. a species of plum, of a green colour.

GREEN'HOUSE, S. a house or place in which exotics or tender plants are kept from the inclemencies of our climate, and furnished with such a degree of heat as is proper to make them grow.

GREE'NISH, Adj. somewhat green.

GREE'NLY, Adj. with a greenish colour. Figuratively, newly; freshly; immaturely. Pale, or wan. "I cannot look greenly." Shak.

GREE'NNESS, S. the quality of being green, applied to vegetables. Figuratively, a state of immaturity, or unripeness. Freshness; full of vigour; before it has suffered any decay. Newness.

GREE'NSICKNESS, S. in Medicine, a disorder incident to virgins, so called from the paleness of countenance with which it is attended.

GREE'NSWARD, or GREE'NSWORD, Adj. the turf on which grass grows.

GREEN'WICH, a town in Kent, five miles E. of London, noted for its magnificent hospital for decayed seamen, its delightful park, and its astronomical observatory. The hospital is thought to be the finest structure of this kind in the world; and its noble hall is finely painted by Sir James Thornhill. It was formerly noted for its palace, where

where Queen Elizabeth was born; but that was pulled down, and what is so called now serves for apartments for the governor of the hospital, and the ranger of the park. The king's yachts generally lye at this place.

GREENWOOD, S. wood considered as it appears when the leaves are out; used sometimes as a single word. "To the greenwood shade he took his way." *Dryd.*

To GREET, V. A. [*gretan, gretan, Sax.*] To salute in kindness or respect. To congratulate. To wish health. To send or pay compliments at a distance. To exert, like those that go to pay their compliments or congratulations. "Our eyes, unhappy, never greeted one," *I'ope.* Neuterly, to meet and salute.

GREETER, S. one that salutes or pays his compliments to another.

GREETING, S. salutation, or compliment. A distant compliment paid to a person, wishing his welfare.

GREGARIOUS, Adj. [*gregarius, Lat.*] assembling in flocks or herds.

GRENADE, S. See GRANADO. This seems the most proper spelling.

GRENADIER, S. [*grenadier, Fr.*] a tall soldier, armed with a firelock fusil, and a pouch full of granadoes, from whence the name is derived.

GREW, Preter. of *Grow.*

GREY, Adj. See GRAY.

GREYHOUND, S. a tall fleet hound.

To GRIDE, V. N. [*gridare, Ital.*] to cut or make way by cutting. "The griding sword." *Par. Lost.* A word elegant, but not in use. *Johnson.*

GRIDIRON, S. [from grind, it's grate and iron] a frame or grate of iron bars placed parallel to each other, used to dress victuals over a fire.

GRIEF, S. [pronounced *greef*, from *grief, Brit.*] sorrow; a grievance, oppression or injury, of *grief, Fr.* "For redress of all these griefs." *Shak. Prin.*

GRIEVANCE, S. that which makes a person uneasy. A state of uneasiness.

To GRIEVE, V. A. [pronounced *greeve, grever, Fr.*] to afflict; to hurt. To make a person uneasy by some unkind action. Neuterly, to be sorrowful on account of the loss of something in which a person delighted.

GRIEVINGLY, Adj. sorrowfully.

GRIEVOUS, Adj. [*grievus, Lat.*] afflictive. Causing sorrow. Expressing great uneasiness. "Grievous complaints." *Clar.* Great, or atrocious, applied to crimes. "It was a grievous crime." *Shak.* Used adverbially to express a great degree. "He was grievous sick." *Mat. i.e.* dangerously.

GRIEVOUSLY, Adv. with great offence, deformity, or ill will, vexed with care. "How grievously the matter was taken." *Knolles.* Prodigiously, or so as to occasion

great unkindness. "Grievously vexed." *Luther.*

GRIEVOUSNESS, S. sorrow; pain; oppression or wretchedness. "The grievousness of war." *Isai. xxi. 15.*

GRIFFIN, S. [it should rather be written *griffon*, or *gryfon*; as it is derived from *gryps*,] a fabled animal, said to be generated between a lion and an eagle.

GRIG, S. in its primitive sense, applied to any thing below the natural size. A very small species of eels. Figuratively, a merry, active and brisk person.

To GRILL, V. N. [*griller, Fr.*] to broil meat on a gridiron.

GRIM, Adj. [*grimma, Sax. grimur, Isl.*] having a fierce or sullen countenance. Hideous; frightful; ugly. "Grim visag'd war has smooth'd his wrinkled front." *Shak.*

GRIMACE, S. [Fr. See GRIM] a distortion of the countenance. An air of affectation. "Vice in a vizard, to avoid grimace—allows all freedom." *Gran.*

GRIMY, S. [from *grim*] dirt that is ingrained and not easily to be washed off.

To GRIME, V. A. to dirt so as it cannot be easily washed off.

GRIMLY, Adv. in a terrible, hideous, horrible, fierce, stern, or sullen manner.

GRIMNESS, S. a look which proceeds from the sullenness or fierceness of a person's disposition.

To GRIN, V. N. [*grinnian, Sax.*] to place the teeth together and withdraw the lips, used both as a sign of mirth and pain.

GRIN, S. the act of shewing the teeth, used as an effect of mirth, or anguish.

GRIN, S. [*Sax.*] a trap, or snare. "The grin shall take him by the heel." *Job xviii. 9.*

To GRIND, V. A. [preter and participle pass. *ground*, *grindan*, Sax.] to reduce to powder by attrition or rubbing. To sharpen or smooth by rubbing on something hard. To rub one against another. Figuratively, to harrass or oppress by extortion. "To grind the poor." To sharpen an instrument on a round stone, which is turned about the while. Neuterly, to perform the act of grinding. To move a mill. To set the teeth close and move them so as to make a noise. To be moved as in the act of grinding, or eating. "Sundry ferns sets o'er my grinding jaws." *Rowe.*

GRINDER, S. one who grinds. The instrument of grinding. The broad back teeth, made flat and broad at top, somewhat uneven and rugged, that by means of their knobs and little cavities, they may the better retain; grind and mix the aliment. In many the teeth in general are called by this name.

GRINDLESTONE, or GRINDSTONE, S. the stone whereon edged tools are sharpened.

GRINER, S. one who grins.

GRIN,

GRINNINGLY, Adv. In a grinning manner.

To GRIPE, V. A. [gripan, Goth. gripan, Sax.] to fqueeze in the hand with the fingers clofed over it. To catch eagerly; to feize. To clutch, or clofe. To pinch, prefs, or fqueeze. Neuterly, to pinch the belly; to give the cholic, or loufenefs.

GRIPE, S. [fee the verb] a grafp of the hand or paw. A fqueeze, or preffure. Figuratively, oppreffion, or extortion. Affliction, or pinching diftrefs. In the plural, the belly-ach; the cholic.

GRIPER, S. an oppreffor. An ufurer; An extortioner.

GRIPINGLY, Adv. attended with a pain in the belly; ufurioufly.

GRISKIN, S. [gryfyn, Ir.] the back bone of a hog.

GRISLY, Adj. [griflic, Sax.] dreadful; horrid; caufing fear or an apprehenfion of danger.

GRIST, S. [faz. from grindan, Sax.] corn to be ground. Figuratively, a fupply of provifion. To bring grift to the mill, is a figurative and proverbial expreffion for producing profit or advantage.

GRISTLE, S. [Sax. grifle, Sax.] in Anatomy, a cartilage, very elaftic, tough, and next in hardnefs to a bone.

GRISTLY, Adj. cartilaginous; having the nature or properties of a griftle.

GRIT, S. [grite, Sax.] bran, or the courfe part of meal. Oats boiled and coarfely ground. Sand; a particle of fand.

GRITTINESS, S. fandinefs. The quality of abounding in grit.

GRITTY, Adj. full of fandy particles.

GRIZZLE, S. [grifaille, Fr.] a colour formed of a mixture of white and black; gray.

GRIZZLED, Adj. confifting of black and white hairs; gray.

To GROAN, V. N. [granian, Sax.] to breathe with a hoarfe or dull noife when a perfon is in pain or agony.

GROAN, S. [gran, Brit.] a deep figh, attended with a hoarfe noife, made by perfons in pain. Figuratively, any hoarfe found.

GROAT, S. [pronounced grot, grut, Belg.] a filver coin, in value four-pence. Groats in the plural, fignifies oats with the hulls taken off.

GROCER, S. [it fhould be written groffer from grofs, a large quantity; a grocer originally being one who dealt by wholefale, or bought up large quantities, as appears from ftat. 37. Edward II. cap. 5. or from groffa, Lat. a fig. which their prefent ftate feems to confirm) one who buys and fells rum, fugars, plumbs, &c.

GROCERY, S. the wares or goods fold by a grocer.

GROGRAM, GROGRAN, GRO-

GRAN, S. a fort of ftuff, all filk, woven with a large woof.

GROIN, S. [generally pronounced grin. The etymology uncertain] that part of the body between the belly and the thigh.

GROOM, S. [grom, Belg.] one who looks after horfes. A man newly married. "By this the brides are waked, their grooms are drefs'd." Dryd.

GROOVE, S. a hollow in a mine. "Work in a groove, or mine-pit." Boyle. A channel or hollow cut in wood.

To GROOVE, V. A. to cut hollow, or in grooves.

To GROPE, V. N. [grapan, grapian, Sax.] to feel one's way om in cafe of darknefs. Figuratively, to be in the dark, or to have an imperfect idea of a thing. To feel after a thing where a perfon cannot fee. "A boy was groping for eels." L'Eftrange. Actively, to fearch after in the dark by feeling. To feel without being able to fee. Ufed with for.

GROPER, S. one who fearches after a thing in the dark.

GROSS, Adj. [grois, Fr. groffo, Ital.] large, thick, or bulky, applied to fize. Blunderful, very erroneous, courfe; applied to fentiments Clumfy, or inelegant, applied to fhape. Thick, applied to the confiftence of any fluid. Stupid, or dull, applied to the underftanding. Courfe, or rough, oppofed to delicate. Impure; foul, applied to the humours of the body.

GROSS, S. the bulk, the whole confifting of a collection of various parts. The major part or body. The chief part, or main mafs. A number confifting of twelve dozen.

GROSSLY, Adv. in large or courfe particles. Without any fubtlety, or delicacy. Flagrantly: "Grofsly mifreprefented." Swift.

GROSSNESS, S. courfenefs, or largenefs of parts. Rankuefs; over great corpulence, or fatnefs. Want of delicacy, or refinement, applied to fentiments, or expreffions.

GROT, S. [grotte, Fr. grotta, Ital.] a cave, or cavern.

GROTESQUE, Adj. [Fr. grottefco, Ital.] diftorted in figure; unnatural. Wildly formed.

GROTTO, S. [grotte, Fr. grotta, Ital.] a cavern or cave made or formed for coolnefs or pleafure. Ufed fometimes, as by the Italians, from whom it is derived, for a dark or horrid cavern.

GROVE, S. [graf, Sax.] a walk formed by trees, whofe branches meet.

To GROVEL, V. N. [grufle, M. fl. on the face: Johnfon imagines it may have been gradually formed from a corruption of ground-fall, perhaps he means ground-fell] in lie proftrate, or creep along with one's belly

on the ground. Figuratively, to have low, or abject notions.

GROU'ND, S. [ground, Sax.] the earth, as opposed to air or water. Figuratively, land; a country; a farm, estate, or possession. The floor of a place. The dregs or lees at the bottom of liquors. In Painting, the first layer of colours, on which the figures are painted and described; applied in this sense to silks. The first hint, trace, or that which gave rise to an invention. The first principles, applied to knowledge or science. The fundamental cause; the true reason, or original principle of a person's conduct or opinions. The space occupied by an army, as they fight, advance or retreat.

To GROU'ND, V. A. to be upon the ground. To settle in the first principles or rudiments of knowledge.

GROUND, S. the preter of GRIND.

GROU'ND-ASH, S. a tree so called because its shoots grow near the ground.

GROUNDIVY, S. a plant likewise named alehoof, or tunhoof.

GROU'NDLESS, Adj. without any foundation or reason.

GROU'NDLESSLY, Adv. unjustly. Without reason, cause, or foundation.

GROU'NDLESSNESS, S. want of cause or foundation.

GROU'NDLING, S. [from ground Sax. and ling, Sax.] a fish, which keeps at the bottom of the water. Figuratively, a person of mean, grovelling, or vulgar thoughts. With due deference to Sir Thomas Hanmer, this word seems by Shakespeare applied to those of the audience, who sit in the lowest part or the pit of a theatre. " To split the ears of the groundlings." Hamlet.

GROUND-PLAT, S. the ground on which any building is placed. The ichnography of a building.

GROU'ND-RENT, S. rent paid for the ground on which a house is built.

GROU'NDSELL, S. the timepost of a door; or the timber or raised pavement of a house next the door.

GROU'NDSEL, S. [groundswylg, Sax.] in Botany, the senecio, Lin. and somera, Fr. It is placed in the second sect. of Linnæus's 19th class. The species are seventeen.

GROU'NDWORK, S. in Painting, that colour on which all the figures are drawn. A foundation of a building. Figuratively, the first part of an undertaking. The first means of a science. The true cause or reason.

GROUP, S. [pronounced groop, groupee, Fr.] in Painting, and Sculpture, an assemblage of two or more figures of men, &c. in Architecture, applied to any number of columns, exceeding two, standing on the same pedestal. Figuratively, a crowd; a clutter; a huddle; a number thronged together.

To GROUP, V. A. in Painting, to introduce several figures into one piece.

GROU'SE, S. a kind of fowl named a heathcock.

GROUT, S. [grut, grut, Sax.] coarse meal or pollard.

To GROW, V. N. [preter grew part. pass. grown, growen, Sax.] to increase, applied to vegetation. To be produced by vegetation. To increase in stature. To arrive progressively from infancy to manhood. To shoot in any particular form. To improve or make a progress. To come, arrive, or advance to any state by degrees. To proceed or arise, as from a cause. Used with together, to stick or adhere closely together. To accrue, or become due, applied to the interest due on money lent. Applied to the sea, by mariners, to swell or roll. " When the sea is never so little grown." Raleigh.

GROW'ER, S. that which vegetates, or increases.

To GROWL, V. N. [grolen, Teut.] to snarl, or murmur, applied to the noise made by an angry dog. Figuratively, to murmur, or grumble, with discontent or rage.

GROWN, part. pass. [of grow] increased by growth; covered or filled by the growth of any thing. Arrived at full growth or stature.

GROWTH, S. vegetable life; increase by vegetation. The thing produced. Increase in number, bulk, stature or improvement.

To GRUB, V. A. [graban, Pret.] to extirpate by digging up the soil. To pull up by the roots. To dirt one's cloaths or flesh. Neuterly, to appear in a mean, nasty, or dirty manner. In Cooking, to cut off the feathers under the wings.

GRUB, S. in Natural History, a small worm. In Medicine, a white unctuous pimple, arising on the face, chiefly on the size of the nose.

GRU'BSTREET, S. the name of a street near Moor-fields in London, once remarkable for the residence of hireling authors. Used as an adjective to signify mean, low, and dull, applied to compositions. " Grub-street Essays."

To GRU'DGE, V. A. to view the advantages of another with discontent and uneasiness. To give or take unwillingly. Neuterly, to murmur or repine. To be unwilling, reluctant, or envious.

GRU'DGE, S. an old quarrel. Figuratively, ill-will; resentment. Unwillingness to benefit; envy; odium; or envious resentment. " Those to whom you have with grudge preferred me," Ben Jonson. Remorse of conscience.

GRU'DGING, S. the act of envying a person, or of giving with great reluctance.

GRU'EL, S. [gruau, gruelle, Fr.] a kind of spoon meat made of oatmeal boiled in water. Any kind of mixture made by boiling ingredients in water. " Gruel made of

of grain, broth, malt drink not much lop-
ged, &c." *Arbuthnot.*

GRUFF, Adj. S. [*gruf*, Belg.] four,
furly, morose.

GRU'FFLY, Adv. furly, morosely.

GRU'FFNESS, S. harshness, or furliness,
moroseness.

GRU'M, Adj. [contracted from *grumble*]
furly or morose.

To GRU'MBLE, V. N. [*grommelen*, *grom-
mer*, Belg.] to murmur. "To growl or snarl.
Grumbling o'er his prey."

GRU'MBLER, S. one that murmurs. A
discontented person.

GRU'MBLING, S. a murmuring, a snarling.

GRU'ME, S. [*grumeau*, Fr. *grumus*,
Lat.] a thick viscid consistence of a fluid,
like that of the white of an egg.

GRU'MLY, Adv. in a morose or furly
manner.

GRU'MOUS, Adj. thick, or clotted.

GRU'NSEL, [usually spelt *groundsel*, from
grund, Sax.] the lower part, floor, or threshold
of a building. "On the *grunsel* edge—
where he fell flat." *Par. Lost.*

To GRUNT, or GRUNTLE, V. A
[*grvo*, Brit.) to make a hoarse noise, applied
to a hog.

GRUNT, S. [See the verb] the noise
made by a hog.

GRU'NTER, S. one that grunts.

GUA'ICUM, S. [*guaiac*, Ind.] a medicinal wood, called also lignum vitæ, the
bark and wood is used in physick as an ar-
tenuant; in the Indies it is used in the venereal difeafe, but is not efficacious in these
climates. The rosin is improperly called
gum guaiacum, and is of greater service in either case, than the wood or bark.

GUARANTE'E, S. [*garant*, Fr.] a
power who undertakes to fee the conditions
of any league performed.

To GUA'RANTY, V. A. to undertake
to fee the articles of any treaty performed.

To GUA'RD, V. A. (pronounced *gard*,
as well as in its derivatives, *garder*, Fr.;
to watch in order to fecure from furprize, or fudden danger. To protect or defend. To anticipate, or fecure against objections. To adorn, or bind the extremities
of a cloth with fills, laces, or other ornamental borders, "In a long motley robe,
guarded with yellow." *Shak.*

GUARD, S. (of *garde*, Fr.] one or more
perfons employed to watch in order to defend
from danger or prevent a furprize. The duty done by fouldiers to prevent a furprize. A
ftate of caution or vigilance. A limitation
A border, ornamental hem or lace at the extremities of a garment. Part of the hilt of a
fword. In Fencing, an action or posture
proper to defend the body from the efforts of
an antagonist. *Guards*, in the plural, is par-

No. XIII.

ticularly applied to those troops which are
kept to guard the king

GUA'RDER, S. one who protects, defends, guards, or watches.

GUA'RDIAN, S. [*gardien*, Fr.] a perfon who has the care of an orphan. One
to whom the care of any thing is committed;
fometimes named *warden*. *Guardian* of the
fpiritualities, is one to whom the fpiritual jurifdiction of any diocese is committed during the vacancy of the fee.

GUA'RDIAN, Adj. performing the office of a kind protector and defender. The
doctrine of guardian angels, drawn from the
famous text; "Their *angels* ftand before
the face of my father," has many advocates,
and as it is no bad illustration of the divine
benevolence and providence, and at the
fame time enforces the dignity of the human
fpecies, it may ferve fome nobler pur-
pofes.

GUA'RDLESS, Adj. without defence.
Without any aid or fupport.

GUA'RDSHIP, S. care, protection; or
the ftate of a perfon under guardians. A
king's fhip, that guards the coaft.

GUBERNA'TION, S. government or
fuperintendency. "This extenfive *guberna-
tion.*" *Watts*

GUDGEON, S. [*goujon*, Fr.] a fmall fifh
found in brooks and rivers, and eafily caught;
Whence it is ufed figuratively for a perfon
eafily cheated or impofed upon: "To draw
you in like fo many *gudgeons*, to fwallow his
falfe arguments." *Swift*. Something to be
caught or received to a man's own difadvantage; alluding to gudgeons being a common
bait for pike.

GUERNSEY, or GARNSEY, an ifland
on the coaft of Normandy, in the Englifh
channel, and fubject to Great Britain. It is
naturally ftrong, being furrounded with high
rocks, and is well fituated for trade in time
of peace; likewife, in time of war, it lies
well to annoy the French with their priva-
teers. It is about ten miles in length, as
much in breadth, and contains ten parifhes.
The natives fpeak French, it having been a
part of Normandy, and is ftill governed by
Norman laws.

To GUESS, V. A. [*ghiffen*, Belg.] to
conjecture; to fuppofe, to imagine.

GUESS, S. a conjecture; a judgment
without any pofitive or certain grounds.

GUE'SSER, S. a conjecturer. One who
judges without certain knowledge.

GUE'SSINGLY, Adv. forming a true
judgment; cafually; uncertainly.

GUEST, S. [*guaftai*, Brit. *goft*, *gift*, Sax.]
one entertained in the houfe of another. A
ftranger.

To GUG'GLE, V. N. [*gorgolare*, Ital.]
To found like water running out of a narrow
mouthed bottle.

3 T

GUI'DAGE, S. the reward or money given to a guide.

GUI'DANCE, S. direction; government exercised in regulating a person's actions; regulation, according to rules, in order to prevent him from falling into danger.

To GUI'DE, V. A. [guider, Fr.] to govern, direct, instruct, regulate, or superintend a person.

GUI'DE, S. [Fr.] one who directs another in his way. One who directs or regulates the conduct of another by his counsel. A director.

GUI'DELESS, Adj. without a guide, or a person to shew one the way.

GUI'DER, S. a director, guide, or regulator.

GUI'LD, S. [sometimes pronounced like gild, and sometimes like gilde. of gild, Sax. gilde, Belg.] a society, corporation, or company united together. Hence Guildhall; a place or hall belonging to a corporation, wherein affairs relating to the corporation in their united capacity are transacted.

GUI'LE, S. [pronounced gile, with the g hard, gile, Pers.] low cunning or craft. Deceit.

GUI'LEFUL, Adj. full of deceit; wily; fraudulent. Treacherous; imputing or over-reaching.

GUI'LELESS, Adj. without any intention to deceive, cheat, or impose upon a person.

GUI'LT, S. [gilt, Sax.] a crime; a consciousness of having done amiss or having done a crime one is accused of. Figuratively, a crime, or offence. "Close pent up guilt—rive your concealing continents" Shak.

GUI'LTILY, Adv. criminally.

GUI'LTINESS, S. the state of being guilty of a crime.

GUI'LTLESS, S. free from consciousness of having done a crime. Innocent. Free from sin, or punishment. "The Lord will not hold him guiltless that taketh his name in vain." Exod. xx. 7.

GUI'LTLESSLY, Adv. innocently.

GUI'LTY, Adj [giltig, Sax.] having committed a crime. Wicked, or corrupt. "All the turmoil of a guilty world." Thomson.

GUINEA, S [so called from Guinea in Africa, from whence the gold was brought, of which they were at first formed] a gold coin current in England. At first it was valued at twenty shillings; but gold growing scarce it was advanced to twenty-one shillings and six pence, but is now funk to twenty-one shillings.

GUINEA, S. a large country of Africa, of which little is known except the coasts, for which reason it is so called, the coast of Guiney. It is divided into the lower and upper. This last comprehends the Malaguen-coast, the Tooth-coast, the Gold-coast, Whidav, Great Ardra, and Benin. The lower part is commonly called Congo. It is very unhealthy for Europeans, though the Negroes live a considerable time. The water is so bad, that it is common for worms to breed between the skin and the flesh, of above an ell long, and of a white silver colour. Most imagine, that this disorder is peculiar to the country; but bad waters do the same in other parts of the world, particularly to the E. of the Caspian Sea, in Asia. The inhabitants in general go almost naked, and there seems to be very little religion or honesty among them. The men take as many wives as they please; and the women are as incontinent as in any part of the world. The commodities purchased there are, gum-senega, at Senegal; grain, upon the Grain-Coast; elephants-teeth, upon the Tooth-Coast; the greatest plenty of gold, upon the Gold-Coast; and all, in general, furnish slaves, more or less: and indeed some of all these commodities are to be had in all parts of it. The English, Dutch, French, Danes, and other nations, have factories upon this coast; and purchase slaves, and other commodities, for the benefit of their employers. The inhabitants of the coast generally buy, steal, or take captive, men and women from the inland parts, to sell for slaves; yet in many places, they make no scruple of selling one another; and even the kings themselves, if their wives displease them, will sell them to the Europeans. There are abundance of little states, whose heads, or chiefs, the sailors have dignified with the name of kings; however, there are very few that deserve that title. When they are at war with each other, as they often are, the people that are taken, on both sides are sold for slaves; and it is not uncommon for the nearest of kin to sell each other, when they have power so to do. Though they come on board the ships naked, they seldom fail of stealing something or other, though never so well watched, they are such dexterous thieves. Some make Guiney to extend from Cape Blanco, in 20 degrees of N. latitude, to Angola in 10 degrees of S. while others include Guiney within the bounds of the coast above mentioned; but this is a distinction of very little consequence. The French pretend, that some sailors from Dieppe first discovered this country in 1364; but this seems to be a fable: however, it is certain that the Portuguese found it out in the beginning of the fifteenth century, and began a settlement here.

GUINEA HEN, S. a small Indian hen.

GUINEA-PEPPER, S. in Botany, the poivre d' Inde ou de Guinée, Fr. capsicum, Lat. the emplacement is of one leaf, divided into five parts, and erect. It is ranged in the first sect. of Linnæus's 5th class, and in the 7th sect. of Tournefort's 2d. The species are 10.

GUISE,

GUI'SE, S. [Fr. guife, Ital. grwofe, Teut.] manner; appearance; behaviour. "By their guife wife men they feem." Par. Loft. Cuftom, or practice. "It never was our guife ---to flight the poor." Pope. External appearance; drefs or habit.

GUITA'R, S. [gkitarra, S. guitarre, Fr.] In Mufic, a ftringed inftrument with a neck like a violin, an oval body, played on with the fingers.

GU'LES, S. [zxaulrs, Fr. תָל, Heb.] In Heraldry, red. In the arms of noblemen it is called ruby, in thofe of fovereign princes Mars, and in engraving is fignified by ftraight ftrokes from the top of the efcutcheon to the bottom.

GU'LF, S. [golfe, Fr. golfo, Ital.] an arm, or part of the ocean running up into the land. Figuratively, an abyfs. "Follow thine enemy in a fiery gulf." Shak. Any thing infatiable.

GU'LFY, Adj. full of eddies, gulfs, or whirlpools.

To GU'LL, S. [poluffa, Sclav.] to trick; to cheat; to deceive or defraud by artifice.

GU'LL, S. a fea bird. A cheat, or trick. A ftupid animal; a perfon eafily impofed upon.

GU'LLER, S. a cheat or impofter. A defrauder.

GU'LLERY, S. artifice ufed to trick or impofe on a perfon.

GU'LLET, S. [goulet, Fr. gula, Lat.] the throat, paffage, or pipe through which the food paffes into the body.

To GU'LLY, V. N. to run with a fmall noife, applied to water.

GU'LLY-HOLE, S. See GULLY, the hole where gutters empty themfelves into the common fewer.

To GU'LP, V. N. [golpro, Belg.] to fwallow eagerly; to drink down with one fwallow.

GU'LP, S. as much liquor as can be drank at one fwallow.

GU'M, S. [gummi, Lat.] a vegetable juice cumming through the pores of certain plants, and there hardening into a fticking mafs, more vifcid and lefs friable than refins, and diffolving in water. In Anatomy, the hard fiefhy fubftance of the mouth in which the teeth grow; generally ufed in the plural, from gima, Sax.

GU'MMINESS, S. the ftate of a thing abounding with gum.

GUMMO'SITY, S. the nature of gum; vifcidity; gumminefs.

GUM'MY, Adj. confifting of gum; of the nature of gum. Sticky.

GUN', S. [gun, 10.] a weapon which forcibly difcharges a ball, fhot, or other offenfive matter, through a cylindrical barrel by means of gunpowder. Great guns are ge-

nerally called cannon, and ordnance. Small guns are fuch as are portable, and include mufquets, mufquetoons, carbines, blunderbuffes, fowling pieces, &c. Gunners, in the plural, are officers employed in looking after, and managing the ordnance mounted on lines, batteries, or forts.

GU'NNELL, S. See GUNWALE.

GU'NNER, S. a perfon who manages, and has the charge of the artillery of a fhip, &c.

GU'NNERY, S. the fcience or art of fhooting with guns, and mortars, including the knowledge of the force and effects of gunpowder, the dimenfions of pieces; the method of elevating, raifing a piece fo as to hit any given object; of computing its range, &c.

GU'NPO'WDER, S. a compofition of falt-petre, folphur, and charcoal, which takes fire eafily, and, when fired, expands with great vehemence and noife, by means of its elaftic force. Bartholdus Schwartz, is by fome fuppofed to have invented it in 1380, but it appears that Roger Bacon, our countryman, knew of it 150 years before Schwartz was born, fince he mentions it in exprefs terms in his treatife De nullitate magia, publifhed at Oxford, in 1216. "You may raife thunder and lightning at pleafure, fays he, by only taking fulphur, nitre, and charcoal, which fingly, have no effect; but, mixed together and confined into a clofe place, caufe an exploſion greater than that of a clap of thunder."

GU'N-SHOT, S. the diftance to which a ball can be fhot out of a gun.

GU'N-SMITH, S. one who makes and fells guns.

GUN-STOCK, S. the wood to which the barrel of a gun is fixed.

GUNWALE, S. [of gun and woalden, Sax.] a piece of timber reaching on either fide of the fhip, from the half deck to the forecaftle, wherein they put the ftanchions, which fupport the wafte tree.

GU'RGE, S. [gurges, Lat.] a whirlpool; a gulf.

GU'RGION, S. the coarfer part of meal fifted from the bran.

To GU'SH, V. N. [guffden, Belg.] to flow out in a large quantity, and with violence.

GU'SH, S. a fudden and large flowing of water, or any other fluid. Any thing poured out with a fudden eruption.

GU'SSET, S. [gouffet, Fr.] any thing fewed on cloath to ftrengthen it; by femftreffes, peculiarly applied to the triangular pieces of cloth at the neck, under the arms, and at the openings of the flaps of a fhirt, &c.

GU'ST, S. [guftus, Lat. gouft, Fr.] the fenfe of tafting. The height of fenfual enjoyment.

Joyment, Love, or liking. Turn of fancy; peculiar taste or genius. Pleasure, caprice, or whim. " Destroy all creatures for thy sport or gust." *Pope*. A sudden violent blast of wind, from *gustus*, lil. " As doth a sail, fill'd with a fretting gust." *Shak*. A sudden burst of passion. " A weak distemper'd soul that swells—with sudden gust of passion." *Addis*.

GU'STABLE, Adj. fit to be tasted; to be tasted; the object of taste; pleasant to the taste.

GUSTA'TION, S. [*gustatio*, Lat.] the act of tasting. " The nerves of *gustation*." *Browe*.

GU'STFUL, Adj. pleasing to the taste. Figuratively, that which communicates pleasure to the mind, or that which is most agreeable to the mind or senses.

GU'STO, S. [Ital.] the relish, flavour, or taste which a thing causes. The power by which any thing excites a sensation in the palate. Liking, or prejudice, applied to the mind.

GU'STY, Adj. windy, stormy. " The gusty wind." *Thomson*.

GUT, S. [*kuttel*, Belg.] in the plural, the entrails. Figuratively, the stomach or receptacle of food. Gluttony. The inside of any thing, particularly a clock or watch.

To GUT, V. A. to take out the entrails of an animal. Figuratively, to plunder or rob any thing of its contents.

GUTTA SE'RENA, S. [Lat. a clear drop] a disease of the eyes, being an entire loss of sight, without any apparent fault or disorder of the part, excepting that the pupil looks somewhat larger and blacker than before.

GUTTATED, Adj. [*gutta*, Lat.] besprinkled with drops.

GUTTER, S. [*gouttier*, Fr.] a narrow passage for water.

To GUTTER, V. A. to cut or wear into small channels, hollows, or furrows.

To GUTTLE, V. N. to feed luxuriously, or intemperately. Actively, to swallow, or eat in a ravenous manner.

GUTTLER, S. a greedy or intemperate eater.

GUTTULOUS, Adj. [*guttula*, Lat.] in the form of a small drop. " Figured in its *guttulous* descent." *Browe*.

GUTTURAL, Adj. [*gutturalis*, Lat.] pronounced in the throat; belonging or appertaining to the throat.

GUTTY, or GUTTE, Adj. [*gutta*, Lat. a drop] in Heraldry, marked with drops. " Gutty of sable," that is marked with black drops.

GUY, S. the rope by which any thing is lifted into a ship. *Skinner*.

To GUZZLE, V. N. [from *gut* or *guzz*, whence *gorzle*, *guzzle*] to feed immoderately; to swallow any liquor greedily. Actively, to swallow with excessive pleasure.

GUZZLER, S. an immoderate drinker, sometimes applied to an eater.

GYBE, S. To GYBE, V. N. See GIBE, or To GIBE.

GYMNA'SIUM, S. [Lat. *gymnasium*, Gr.] a place suited to perform public exercises. Figuratively, a school.

GYMNA'STIC, Adj. [*gymnasticos*, Gr.] something relating or belonging to bodily exercise, such as wrestling, &c.

GYMNIC, Adj. [*gymnique*, Fr. *gymnica*, Gr.] practising or using such exercises as relate to the body. " Gymnic artists." *Milt*.

GYRA'TION, S. [*gyratio*, Lat.] the act of turning any thing about in a circle. " Moved round in a circle with *gyration*." *Newt. Opt*.

GYRE, S. [*gyrus*, Lat.] a circle or orbit described by any thing in motion. " He spins in giddy *gyres*." *Dryd*. Not in use.

GYVES, S. [*geoga*, Brit.] fetters consisting of two links. " I thought *gyves* and the mill had tamed thee." *Milt. Sam*.

To GYVE, V. A. to fetter or shakle; to confine; to ensnare. " I will gyve thee in thine own courtship." *Shak*.

THE END OF VOLUME I.

www.ingramcontent.com/pod-product-compliance
Lightning Source LLC
Chambersburg PA
CBHW021940110726
47901CB00003B/913